FOUND IN TRANSLATION

Born in Sligo, Ireland, Frank Wynne has been a literary translator for twenty years. His authors include Michel Houellebecq, Patrick Modiano and Virginie Despentes. He lived for many years in Central and South America, and has translated a number of Hispanic authors, including Tomás González, Andrés Caicedo and Javier Cercas. In the course of his career, he has won the IMPAC Prize (2002), the *Independent* Foreign Fiction Prize (2005), and has twice been awarded both the Scott Moncrieff Prize and the Premio Valle-Inclán. He has spent time as translator in residence at Lancaster University, City University, and the Villa Gillet, Lyon.

FOUND IN TRANSLATION

SELECTED BY
FRANK WYNNE

HEAD
of ZEUS

An Apollo Book

9 7 5 3 1 2 4 6 8

A catalogue record for this book is available from the British Library.

ISBN (HB) 9781786695291
ISBN (E) 9781786695284

Typeset by Adrian McLaughlin

Printed and bound in Germany by CPI Books GmbH

Head of Zeus Ltd
First Floor East
5–8 Hardwick Street
London ECIR 4RG
WWW.HEADOFZEUS.COM

In memory of David Miller

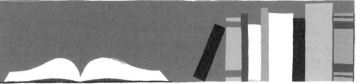

CONTENTS

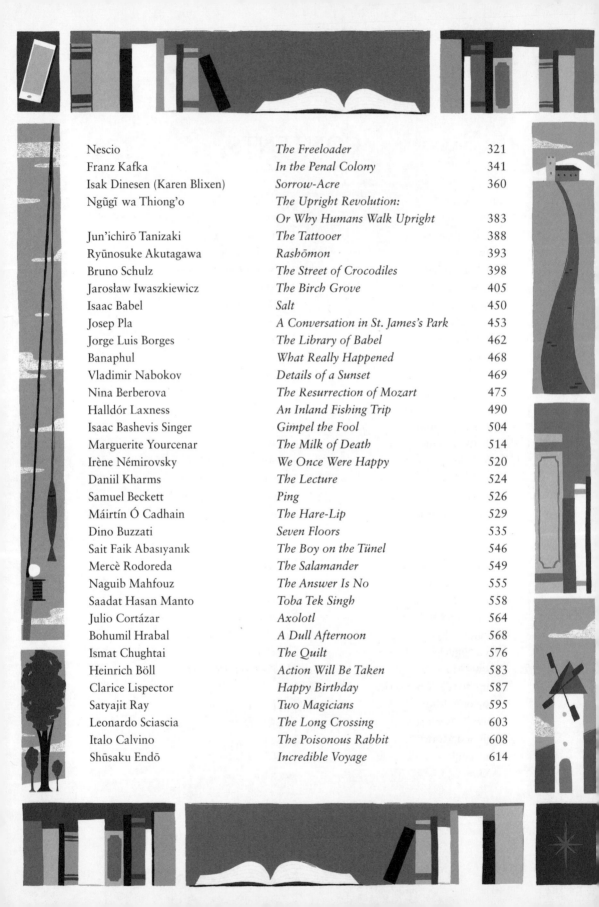

INTRODUCTION

I have a memory of the first short story that made an impression on me that is so vivid, so visceral that the hair on the back of my neck still prickles thirty years later. I would have been fourteen, perhaps fifteen, when I read it, sitting in Miss Collins' French class, in Sligo Grammar School. She had told us to read "En mer" by Guy de Maupassant, a brief story, no more than five pages long, whose sparse, plain language was just within the grasp of our rudimentary French. It is the simple story of an accident aboard a fishing trawler manned by two brothers. On their return to port, the net is almost lost in a heavy squall and the younger brother's arm is trapped between the ropes and the gunwale. To save the arm would mean cutting the rope and losing the valuable net. The elder brother instead drops anchor and, eventually, the fishermen manage to free the arm, now shattered and horribly mangled. Gangrene quickly sets in. I can still remember sitting at my desk, reading the sentence where the younger brother ". . . began to cut his own arm. He cut carefully, painstakingly, slicing through the last tendons with a blade as sharp as a razor; soon there was nothing but a stump." I apologise for this spoiler, but an even greater emotional shock awaits the reader in the final sentences.

This was the story that first offered me a glimpse of the unique power of the short story. Maupassant's tone is detached and unemotional, something that makes the horror all the more devastating. I began to devour short stories wherever I could find them – I remember the profoundly unsettling feeling of reading Ian McEwan's stories in *First Love, Last Rites*, and my first encounters with John Cheever and Flannery O'Connor. Long before I was fortunate enough to stumble into a career as a translator – or had an inkling of what such a peculiar shapeshifter might be – translators introduced me to other masters of the genre: to Chekhov and Pushkin, Borges and Calvino.

I discovered that a short story has the matchless ability to capture a mood or a moment, to halt time, to suspend the commonplace and imbue everyday objects with startling power. A short story can conjure a whole world in a handful of pages, it can be poignant, tragic, funny or surreal, it can leave a reader tearful, terrified or inexplicably serene, it can be as fleeting and unfinished as lives glimpsed from a moving train or as forensically precise as an autopsy report. In the words of the great American writer, Walter Mosley: "A good short story asks a question that can't be answered in simple terms. And even if we come up with some understanding, years later, while glancing out of a window, the story still has the potential to return, to alter right there in our mind and change everything."

Although every language, as it emerges, develops an oral tradition of storytelling intended to entertain or edify – countless anecdotes, parables and fables that range from the Book of Job to the folk tales told by Scheherazade to Sultan Shahriyar – the short story as we know today is the most recent literary genre. It begins to flourish in the nineteenth century – almost three hundred years after the novel – spurred by the rise of literacy in industrialised countries and the appearance of magazines and periodicals eager to publish shorter fictions. As William Boyd succinctly puts it: "The short story arrived fully fledged in the middle of the 19th century and by its end, in the shape of Anton Chekhov, had reached its apotheosis."

Even taking this narrow definition of a short story, the task of selecting one hundred from the countless stories translated from any language, from any country is – to say the least – a daunting task. So, when I was asked to edit this anthology I was both preposterously excited and utterly terrified. Obviously, it is impossible to read *every story*; how then do you decide when you have read enough? Since an introduction is usually the last part of a book to be written, I now know the answer: you will *never* have read enough.

From the outset, I decided that I wanted to cast my net as widely as possible, to offer a glimpse of as many countries and cultures, as many languages as would fit between these covers and simultaneously to try to chart a course from the seventeenth century to short masterpieces of the twenty-first century. The usual suspects are here – the Russians, the French and the Germans who (with the British and the Americans) dominated the short story form for almost a century – but there are also stories from countries as varied as Guinea and Vietnam, and stories translated from Azerbaijani and Gikuyu. There are a dozen writers in these pages who have won the Nobel Prize for Literature and others who are all but unknown outside their homelands.

These, then, are the writers. But with the exception of those few authors who have translated their own work (Isak Dinesen, Ngũgĩ wa Thiong'o), the words you are reading are those of translators. If, as Susan Sontag says, translation is "the circulatory system of the world's literatures", then translators are the beating heart that makes it possible for stories to flow beyond borders and across oceans. Their task is as simple as it may seem impossible: to quote Günter Grass, "Translation is that which transforms everything so that nothing changes." It is not a matter of finding equivalent words (since there is never an exact equivalence), but of weighing the weight and heft of words while striving to preserve the cadence and the rhythm of a sentence, to reinvent a pun, to produce a voice that lives on the page. Like a pianist transforming a written score into a performance of the *Goldberg Variations*, or an actor taking a play and becoming Hedda Gabler, a translator must interpret and perform, while hewing as closely as possible to the shape of the original. It is a process that is thrilling and frustrating, often challenging and always rewarding. The debt we owe to translators often goes unacknowledged; we talk about having read Tolstoy or Proust when actually we have read Constance Garnett or C.K. Scott Moncrieff. We talk about the style of García Marquez or Murakami, but the style we so admire owes much to Edith Grossman or Jay Rubin. All literature is a continuum, an intertwining of voices and languages, of dialects, and it is impossible to imagine the evolution of the English novel without the availability of translations. As Milan Kundera says: ". . . it was to Rabelais that Laurence Sterne was reacting, it was Sterne who set off Diderot, it was from Cervantes that Fielding drew constant

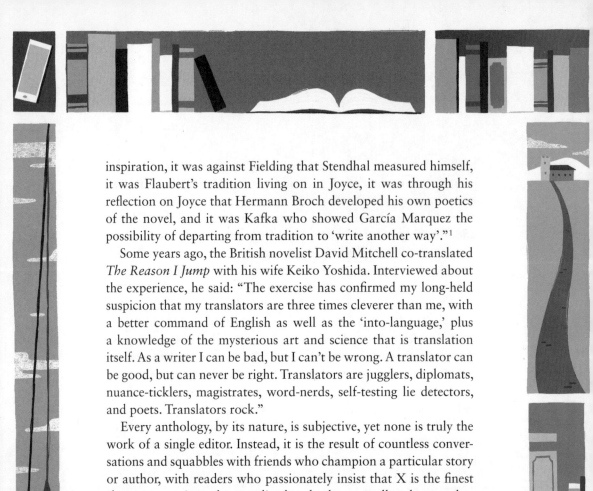

inspiration, it was against Fielding that Stendhal measured himself, it was Flaubert's tradition living on in Joyce, it was through his reflection on Joyce that Hermann Broch developed his own poetics of the novel, and it was Kafka who showed García Marquez the possibility of departing from tradition to 'write another way'."[1]

Some years ago, the British novelist David Mitchell co-translated *The Reason I Jump* with his wife Keiko Yoshida. Interviewed about the experience, he said: "The exercise has confirmed my long-held suspicion that my translators are three times cleverer than me, with a better command of English as well as the 'into-language,' plus a knowledge of the mysterious art and science that is translation itself. As a writer I can be bad, but I can't be wrong. A translator can be good, but can never be right. Translators are jugglers, diplomats, nuance-ticklers, magistrates, word-nerds, self-testing lie detectors, and poets. Translators rock."

Every anthology, by its nature, is subjective, yet none is truly the work of a single editor. Instead, it is the result of countless conversations and squabbles with friends who champion a particular story or author, with readers who passionately insist that X is the finest short story writer who ever lived and others equally adamant that X is meretricious and wildly overrated. It is impossible to overstate the debt I owe to the editors, readers, writers, and especially to the fellow translators who have guided me. In reading the stories recommended to me, I rediscovered the thrill of finding voices that are new to me, and the ineffable pleasure of rediscovering authors (often in new translations). Editing an anthology, I have discovered, is a microcosm of a reading life; it is a journey filled with startling finds and occasional disappointments. An anthology is a miniature library of stories that one particular editor feels everyone needs to read. But just as space on bookshelves is limited, so too are the pages of any collection. The final choice presented is inescapably personal and, like the lists of *100 Greatest Novels of All Time* beloved of Sunday

1 From *The Curtain* translated by Linda Asher

supplements that immediately trigger family feuds, Facebook rants and disbelieving wails, every anthology is bound to frustrate and infuriate by some of its choices.

I have never much liked the word "anthology"; to my ear, it has a textbook ring of authority at odds with the curious cabinet of wonders that make up any collection. But I have always loved the old English term "rattle-bag" (famously a title used by Seamus Heaney and Ted Hughes); it has the clank and clatter of things found, scavenged, unearthed and retrieved, all jostling between the covers, clamouring for attention. But however modest its intentions, every collection aspires to the ideal described by Robert Graves:

> *A well chosen anthology is a complete dispensary of medicine for the more common mental disorders, and may be used as much for prevention as cure.*

FRANK WYNNE, 2018

"A short story is the ultimate close-up
magic trick – a couple of thousand words
to take you around the universe or
break your heart."

—NEIL GAIMAN

THE GLASS GRADUATE

Miguel de Cervantes

Translated from the Spanish by C. A. Jones

Miguel de Cervantes Saavedra (1547 (assumed)–1616) is widely regarded as the greatest writer in the Spanish language, and the greatest novelist of all time. His major work, *Don Quixote*, is considered the first modern novel, a classic of Western literature, and is regarded among the best works of fiction ever written. His influence on the Spanish language has been so great that the language is often called la lengua de Cervantes ("the language of Cervantes"). *Don Quixote* has been translated into more languages than any other book except the Bible. All the existing portraits of Cervantes were based on a brief description of himself in one of his own novels. A boat on which Cervantes was sailing was captured by Algerian pirates and he was imprisoned in Algiers for five years. After four unsuccessful escape attempts, he was eventually bailed out by his parents, who clubbed together with a religious order to raise a handsome ransom for his return. Cervantes was an inveterate dueller: the first written record of his activities is a warrant for his arrest in 1569 issued after he wounded his opponent. In fact, his third and final stint in prison was occasioned by the death of a man following a duel. Cervantes was shot three times, twice in the chest and once in the arm, with a harquebus – a forerunner of the musket – during the Battle of Lepanto in 1571.

Two gentlemen students were walking along the banks of the Tormes, when they found, asleep beneath a tree, a lad of some eleven years of age, in peasant dress. They sent a servant to wake him, and when he awoke, they asked him where he came from and what he was doing asleep in that deserted place. The lad replied that he had forgotten the name of his birthplace, and that he was going to the city of Salamanca to look for a master who, in exchange for his services, would give him the opportunity to study. They asked him if he could read, to which he said that he could, and write as well.

'So that it is not poor memory', said one of the gentlemen, 'that has made you forget the name of your country.'

'Whatever the reason,' answered the lad, 'no one shall know the name of my country or my parents until I can bring honour to them both.'

'And in what way do you propose to honour them?' asked the other gentleman.

'By the fame I win through my studies,' replied the boy, 'because I have heard that even bishops start off as men.'

This reply made the two gentlemen decide to accept him into their service, and take him along with them, so they did, giving him a chance to study according to the customary way with servants in that university. The lad said he was called Thomas Rodaja, whereby his masters inferred, from his name and dress, that he must be the son of some poor peasant. A few days later they dressed him in black, and after a few weeks Thomas showed signs of such extraordinary talent, serving his masters so faithfully, punctually and diligently that, although he never failed in any way to pursue his studies, he seemed to be solely occupied in serving them; and since a servant who gives good service gets treated well, Thomas Rodaja became his masters' companion, and no longer their servant. Eventually, in the course of the eight years he was with them, he became so famous in the university by reason of his keen intelligence and remarkable talents, that he won the esteem and affection of people of every kind. His principal study was law, but he was even more outstanding in the humanities; and he possessed such an astoundingly good memory, illuminated with such good judgement, that he became famous alike for both qualities.

The time came at last when his masters completed their studies and went off to their home, which was in one of the finest cities in Andalusia. They took Thomas off with them, and he stayed with them for a few days, but as he was anxious to return to his studies and to Salamanca, whose charms make everyone who has enjoyed the pleasure of living there determine to go back, he asked his masters' leave to return. They, being kind and generous, gave him leave, setting him up with the means to support himself for three years.

He thanked them, said good-bye, and left Málaga – for this was where his masters lived. As he was coming down the Zambra hill, on the road to Antequera, he met a nobleman on horseback, in splendid travelling clothes, with two servants also on horseback. He joined him and found out that they were going the same way; they shared lodgings, chatted about various things, and Thomas soon gave signs of his unusual talent and the gentleman of his magnificent and courtly bearing. He said that he was an infantry captain in the King's Guard, and that his ensign was recruiting in the Salamanca area. He praised the soldier's life, and gave him a vivid picture of the beauty of the city of Naples, the delights of Palermo, the prosperity of Milan, the banquets in Lombardy, and the splendid food in the inns. He gave a delightful and exact account of the way they shouted, 'Here, landlord', 'This way, you rogue', 'Let's have the maccatella, the polastri and the macaroni'. He praised to the skies the soldier's free life and the easy ways of Italy; but he said nothing to him about the cold of sentry duty, the danger of attacks, the horror of battles, the hunger of sieges, the destruction of mines, and other things of this kind, which some consider to be the extra burdens of a soldier's life, when in fact they are the main part of it. In short, he told him so many things and in such an attractive way, that our Thomas's judgement began to waver, and his will to be set on that way of life, where death is always so near at hand.

The captain, whose name was Don Diego de Valdivia, delighted with Thomas's good bearing, talent and free and easy manner, begged him to go with him to Italy, if he was interested in seeing it. He offered him his table and even a commission as ensign, a post which the present holder was about to give up. Thomas didn't need much pressing to take up the offer, and quickly persuaded himself that it would be a good thing to see Italy and Flanders and various other lands and countries. After all, travel makes men wise, and at the most he would spend three or four years which, considering his youth, would not be enough to prevent his returning to his studies. And thinking that everything would turn out as he wished, he told the captain that he was happy to go off with him to Italy, but only on condition that he need not take any commission or enlist as a soldier, for he did not want to be obliged to follow the flag. The captain told him that enlisting would not make any difference except that it would have the advantage of enabling him to enjoy the allowances and payments the company might receive, because he would give him leave whenever he requested it. But Thomas replied, 'That would be going against my conscience and against yours, captain; and so I would rather go as a free agent than be under an obligation.'

'Such a scrupulous conscience', said Don Diego, 'is more becoming to a monk than a soldier; but in any case, we shall go together.'

They got to Antequera that night and, by spending long periods on the road, in a few days they reached the place where the company was duly assembled. It was about to set out again for Cartagena, intending, with four other companies, to put up at such places as they should come across. Thomas took due note of the authority of the commissaries, the bad temper of some of the captains, the importunity of the billeting officers, the keenness of the paymasters, the complaints of the townspeople, the trading of passes, the insolence of the recruits, the quarrels of the tavern-keepers, the vast amount of excess baggage, and finally the way one more or less had to do all those things which he saw and disliked so much.

Thomas was now got up in all the finery of a soldier, having thrown aside his student garb, and was dressed to kill, as they say. He got rid of all his books with the exception of a copy of the Hours of our Lady, and a Garcilaso without commentary, which he carried in his pockets. They got to Cartagena more quickly than he would have wished, because life in lodgings is easy and has plenty of variety, and every day one comes across new and pleasing things. At Cartagena they embarked on four galleys going to Naples, and Thomas Rodaja was struck by the strange life that goes on in those floating houses, where most of the time one is pestered by the bedbugs, robbed by the galley slaves, annoyed by the sailors, gnawed by the mice and worn out by the heavy seas. He was terrified by the great squalls and storms, especially in the Gulf of Lyons, where they had two, one of which drove them as far as Corsica, while the other brought them back to Toulon in France. In short, deprived of sleep, soaked to the skin and hollow-eyed, they reached the beautiful city of Genoa. Disembarking in its sheltered harbour, they visited a church, and then the captain with all his companions came to an inn, where they forgot all about the storms of the past in the merry-making of the present.

There they became acquainted with the smooth Trebbiano, the full-bodied Montefiascone, the strong Asprino, the generous Greek wines Candia and Soma, the great Five Vineyards, the sweet and gentle Vernaccia and the rough Centola, the lowly Roman wines never being allowed a place among these lordly creatures. And when mine host had gone through all these different wines, he volunteered to bring in, without recourse to trickery or sleight of hand, the genuine Madrigal, Coca, Alaejos and Cuidad Real (which deserves to be called Imperial rather than

Royal) which is sacred to the god of laughter; he offered Esquivias, Alanis, Cazalla, Guadalcanal and Membrilla, not forgetting Ribadavia and Descargamaría. In short, our host named and offered them more wines than Bacchus himself can have had in his vaults.

Our good Thomas was also fascinated by the fair hair of the girls of Genoa, the elegance and noble bearing of the men and the remarkable beauty of the city, whose houses are set on its hills like diamonds in gold. The next day all the companies which were to go to Piedmont disembarked; but Thomas did not want to go on this journey, but to go overland from there to Rome and Naples, which he did. He resolved to come back via the great city of Venice, through Loretto to Milan and then to Piedmont, where Don Diego de Valdivia said he would meet him, if they hadn't already been carried off to Flanders, as rumour said they might.

Thomas took his leave of the captain a couple of days later, and within five days reached Florence, having first seen Lucca, a small but very well-appointed city in which Spaniards are better received and entertained than in other parts of Italy. He was delighted with Florence, both because of its splendid situation and its cleanness, magnificent buildings, cool river and quiet streets. He was there for four days, and then set off for Rome, the queen of cities and mistress of the world. He visited its shrines, worshipped its relics and marvelled at its great size; and just as one realizes the greatness and ferocity of the lion by its claws, so he came to realize the greatness of Rome by its marble ruins, its statues, damaged or intact, its broken archways and ruined baths, its magnificent porticos and great amphitheatres, and by its famous and sacred river, which always fills its banks with water and blesses them with the countless relics of the bodies of martyrs which have been buried there; by its bridges, whose arches are like eyes looking at each other, and by its streets whose names alone make them superior to those of every other city in the world: the Via Appia, the Via Flaminia, the Via Julia, and others like them. But he was no less amazed by the way its hills were laid out within the boundaries of the city: the Caelian, the Quirinal and the Vatican, with the other four, whose names testify to the greatness and majesty of Rome. He was also impressed by the pomp of the College of Cardinals, the majesty of the Supreme Pontiff, the mass and variety of peoples and nations. He saw and took careful note of it all. And when he had gone the rounds of the Seven Churches, and made his confession to a penitentiary, and kissed His Holiness's feet, he decided to go off to Naples, loaded with Agnuses and beads. As it was unsettled weather, which made it dangerous to leave or enter Rome overland, he went off to Naples by sea, where he added to the delight of seeing Rome that of seeing Naples, a city which in his opinion, and in that of everyone who has seen it, is the best in Europe and even in the world.

From there he went off to Sicily, and saw Palermo, and then Messina. He was favourably impressed by the situation and beauty of Palermo, by the port of Messina, and by the abundance of the whole island, which is justly and truthfully called the granary of Italy. He went back to Naples and to Rome, and from there he went to Our Lady of Loretto, in whose holy shrine he did not see any walls at all, because they were all covered with crutches, shrouds, chains, shackles, manacles, switches of hair, wax busts, paintings and altar pieces, which gave testimony to the innumerable favours received by so many from God's hand through the intercession of His divine mother, to whose holy image He chose to give power and authority by many miracles, as a reward for the reverence which is shown to her by those who have adorned the walls of her house with these signs of devotion. He saw the very room and spot which witnessed the most exalted and important charge ever witnessed, though not comprehended, by the heavens, the angels, and all the dwellers of eternity.

From there, embarking at Ancona, he went to Venice, a city which if Columbus had never lived would be unmatched by any in the world. Thanks be to heaven and to the great Hernando Cortés, who conquered the great city of Mexico, whereby this great city of Venice came to have something of a rival. These two famous cities are alike in that their streets are all water; the European one is the wonder of the old world; the American one, the marvel of the new. Its richness seemed to him to know no limits, and the way it was governed seemed a model of prudence, its situation impregnable, its prosperity vast, its surroundings delightful. In short, the whole and all the parts deserve the reputation they have in every part of the globe, and to which its famous arsenal, which is the place where the galleys, together with countless other craft, are made, adds even further fame.

The delights and pastimes our traveller found in Venice were nearly as dangerous as those of Calypso, for they almost made him forget his original intention. But after he had been there a month, he came back by way of Ferrara, Parma and Piacenza to Milan, that Vulcan's forge and envy of the kingdom of France; a city of which it is said that they only have to think of something for it to be done. The size of the city and its great church and the marvellous abundance of everything necessary for human life are truly magnificent. From there he went off to Asti, and got there just a day before the regiment was leaving for Flanders. He was very well received by his friend the captain, and in his company went over to Flanders, and to Antwerp, a city no less worthy of admiration than those he had seen in Italy. He saw Ghent and Brussels, and he saw that the whole country was preparing to take up arms to go out on campaign the following summer. Having fulfilled the desire which prompted him to see what he had seen, he decided to go back to Spain and to complete his studies at Salamanca. It was no sooner said than done, to the great sorrow of his comrade, who begged him, as they parted, to let him know how he got on with his journey, how he was and what happened to him. He promised to do as he asked, and returned to Spain through France, without seeing Paris, since there was fighting going on there. He finally reached Salamanca, where he was warmly welcomed by his friends, and with the help they gave him he continued his studies until he finally graduated as a licenciate in Law.

It so happened that at that time there came to the city a certain lively lady who was up to all the tricks. Everybody rushed into the trap and fell for the decoy, and not one of the lads failed to pay her a call. They told Thomas that this lady said she had been in Italy and Flanders, and just to see if he knew her, he went to call on her. The result of this visit was that as soon as she saw Thomas she fell in love with him. He, not realizing it, would not have gone to her house unless he had been marched off to it by someone else. In the end she declared her love for him and offered him all she had. As he was more devoted to his books than to anything else, he did not respond at all to the lady's fancy, and she, seeing herself scorned, and, as she thought, hated, and realizing that she could not conquer the rock of Thomas's will by ordinary means, decided to look for other methods which seemed to her more effective and capable of achieving what she wanted. So, taking the advice of a Moorish woman, she gave Thomas one of those things they call love potions, hidden in a Toledo quince, thinking that by this means she would force his will to love her, as if there were herbs, charms or words in the world powerful enough to force free will. Those who give these aphrodisiac drinks or foods are called 'poisoners': because all they do is to poison those who take them, as experience has shown on many and varied occasions.

Thomas ate the quince to such ill effect that straight away he began to shake in his feet and hands as if he had epilepsy, and lost consciousness for many hours, after which he came to in a stupefied condition. He declared in a confused and stammering way that a quince he had eaten had done for him, and gave the name of the person who had given it to him. When the Officers of the Law learned of the affair, they went in search of the culprit; but she, seeing what had happened, had made herself scarce and was never seen again.

Thomas was in bed for six months, during which time he became completely dried up, and was nothing but skin and bones, as they say. Moreover, his senses seemed completely at sixes and sevens; and although they gave him all the treatment they could, they only managed to cure his bodily complaints, but not his mind. He got better but remained possessed by the strangest madness anybody had ever seen. The poor wretch imagined that he was all made of glass, and under this delusion, when someone came up to him, he would scream out in the most frightening manner, and using the most convincing arguments would beg them not to come near him, or they would break him; for really and truly he was not like other men, being made of glass from head to foot.

In order to relieve him of this strange delusion, many people, taking no notice of his shouts and pleas, went up to him and embraced him, telling him to look and he would see that in fact he was not getting broken. But all that happened as a result of this was that the poor wretch would throw himself on the ground shouting for all he was worth, and would then fall into a faint, from which he did not recover for several hours; and when he did come to he would start begging people not to come near him again. He told them to speak to him from a distance and ask him what they wanted, because being a man of glass and not of flesh, he would answer them all so much the more intelligently; for glass being a fine and delicate material, the mind could work through it more promptly and effectively than through an ordinary, solid, earthly body. Some wanted to experiment to see if what he said was true, and so they asked him many difficult things, to which he answered straight away, and very astutely too. It amazed the most learned men in the university and the professors of medicine and philosophy to see how in a person afflicted by such an extraordinary madness as to make him think he was made of glass there should be such a fund of knowledge that he could answer every question correctly and intelligently.

Thomas asked them to give him some sort of case in which he could place the fragile vessel of his body, so that if he wore any close-fitting clothes he would not break; and so they gave him a robe made of drab stuff and a very loose-fitting shirt, which he put on very carefully and tied with a cotton cord. He was not at all willing to put shoes on, and the arrangement he had for getting himself fed without people coming near him was to put on the end of a stick a basket, in which they would put whatever fruit was in season. He did not want meat or fish; he drank only from a fountain or a river, and then with his hands; when he went about the streets he went in the middle of them, looking up at the roofs, in fear lest some tile should fall on him and break him; in summer he slept in the country in the open, and in winter he would go into an inn, and bury himself up to the neck in the straw-loft, saying that that was the safest and most suitable bed for a man of glass. When it thundered, he would shake like a leaf and go off into the country, and would never go into the town until the storm was over. His friends kept him shut up for a long time; but seeing that his affliction showed no sign of being cured, they decided to do what he asked, which was to let him go free; and so they left him and he went about the city, arousing amazement and pity in all who knew him.

Then the boys flocked round him, but he would stop them with his staff, and beg them to speak to him from a distance, so that he did not break; for as he was a man of glass, he was very fragile. Boys, being the most mischievous creatures in the world, in spite of his pleas and shouts began to throw rags at him and even stones, to see if he really was made of glass as he said; but he shouted so much and made such a fuss that the men scolded and punished the children to stop them throwing things at him. But one day when they worried him a lot, he turned to them and said,

'What do you want, you wretched boys, who keep pestering me like flies, who are as dirty as bedbugs and as impudent as fleas? Do you think I'm Mount Testaccio in Rome, to hurl all these pots and tiles at me?'

When they heard him tell them all off they always followed him in crowds, and the boys thought it would be a much better game to listen to him than to throw things at him. On one occasion, when he was going through the old-clothes market in Salamanca, a woman who kept one of the stalls said to him,

'I'm sorry in my heart for you, Licenciate; but what can I do, for I can't shed any tears?'

He turned to her and very deliberately said to her,

'Filiae Hierusalem, plorate super vos et super filios vestros.'

The woman's husband realized what a subtle answer it was and said to him,

'Brother Glass,' for that is what he said he was called, 'you are more of a rogue than a fool.'

'I don't care a bit,' he answered, 'as long as I'm not stupid.'

One day when he was going past the brothel he saw at the door several of the inmates, and declared that they were the baggage of Satan's army, lodging in the inn of hell. Someone asked him what advice or comfort he would give to a friend of his who was very sad because his wife had gone off with someone else. To which he replied,

'Tell him to thank God for having allowed his enemy to be taken away from his house.'

'Then shouldn't he go and look for her?' said the other.

'Not on your life,' replied Glass, 'because if he found her he would be finding a true and everlasting testimony to his dishonour.'

'Since that is the case,' said the same man, 'what shall I do to live at peace with my wife?'

He replied, 'Give her what she needs; let her rule over everyone in the house; but don't allow her to rule over you.'

A boy said to him, 'Licenciate Glass, I want to leave my father because he's always beating me.'

To which he replied, 'Bear in mind, my boy, that the beatings that fathers give their children bring honour to them, and those which the executioner gives are the ones that cause offence.'

As he was standing at a church door, he saw one of those peasants who are always boasting of being old Christians go in, and behind him came another man who did not enjoy as good a reputation as the first. The licenciate shouted to the peasant,

'Domingo, wait for old Sabbath to pass.'

He used to say that schoolmasters were lucky, because they were always dealing with angels, and that they would be supremely happy if the little angels weren't so saucy. Someone else asked him what he thought of bawds. He answered that he had never known any who lived in seclusion, but only those who were neighbours.

The news of his madness and of his answers and clever sayings spread all through Castile, and when it came to the ears of a certain prince or gentleman of the court, he wanted to send for him. So he commissioned a nobleman who was a friend of his and who was in Salamanca to send him to him. When the gentlemen bumped into him one day, he said to him,

'Licenciate Glass, you know there is a great man at Court who wants to see you and has sent for you.'

To which he replied, 'Please offer my excuses to this gentleman, for I'm no good for palaces, because I'm bashful and don't know how to flatter.'

All the same, the gentleman sent him to court, and in order to get him there they used the following device: they put him into a wicker basket of the kind they use for carrying glass, filling in the spaces with stones, and putting some pieces of glass in the straw, so that he would get the impression that they were carrying him like a glass vessel. He got to Valladolid at night, and they unpacked him in the house of the gentleman who had sent for him, and who welcomed him with the words,

'You are very welcome, Licenciate Glass. How was the journey? How are you?'

To which he replied, 'There's no road so bad that it does not come to an end, except the one that leads to the gallows. As far as my health is concerned, I'm neither one thing nor the other, for my pulse and my brain are at odds.'

Another day, when he had seen a lot of falcons and hawks and other fowling birds on perches, he said that falconry was a fine thing for princes and great nobles; but that they should bear in mind that in this sport pleasure outweighed profit two-thousand-fold. Hunting hares he said was very pleasant, and especially when one was hunting with borrowed greyhounds.

The nobleman liked his brand of madness, and let him go out in the city, under the protection of a man to take care that the children did not harm him. In a week he was known to them and the whole court, and at every step, in every street and on every corner he would reply to all the questions they put to him. Among them was one from a student who asked whether he was a poet, since there seemed no limit to his gifts.

He replied, 'Until now, I have been neither so stupid nor so fortunate.'

'I don't understand what you mean by stupid and fortunate,' said the student.

And Glass replied, 'I haven't been so stupid as to be a bad poet, nor so fortunate as to be a good one.'

Another student asked him what he thought of poets. He replied that poetry he esteemed highly; but poets not at all. They went on to ask him why he said that. He answered that of the infinite number of poets in existence, the good ones were so few that they hardly counted, and so being unworthy of consideration, he did not hold them in any esteem; but that he admired and revered the art of poetry, because it contained within it all the other sciences put together. It makes use of all of them, and they all adorn it, so that it gives lustre and fame to their wonderful works, and brings great profit, delight and wonder to all the world. He added,

'I am well aware of the esteem in which a good poet should be held, because I remember those verses of Ovid which say:

Cura deum fuerunt olim regumque poetae.
Praemiaque antiqui magna tulere chori.
Sanctaque majestas, et erat venerabile nomen
Vatibus, et largae saepe dabantur opes.

And I am not unaware either of the great worth of poets, for Plato calls them interpreters of the gods, and Ovid says of them: "Est Deus in nobis, agitanti calescimus illo." And he also says: "At sacri vates, et divum cura vocamur." This is what they say of good poets; as for the bad ones, the mere windbags, what is there to say except that they are the most idiotic and arrogant creatures in the world?'

And he went on, 'What a thing it is to see one of these poets, when he wants to recite a sonnet to those of his circle, wheedling them with such words as, "Pray listen to a little sonnet which I composed last night for a certain occasion. Although it's of no value, I think it's quite nice in a way." And with that, he purses his lips, raises his eyebrows, and hunting about in his pocket, pulls out from the mass of grubby, torn papers, among which there are another thousand or so sonnets, the one he wants to recite, and finally pronounces it in mellifluous and sugary tones. And if by any chance his listeners, out of malice or not knowing any better, don't praise it, he says, "Either you haven't understood the sonnet, or I haven't recited it properly; so I'd better say it again, and you'd better listen to it more carefully, for there's no doubt at all that the sonnet is worth it." And then he starts to recite it all over again, with new gestures and new pauses. And have you seen the way they tear each other to pieces? You should see how these modern young puppies bark at the hoary old mastiffs. Not to mention those who snipe at some of those illustrious and worthy persons in whom the true light of poetry shines, and who find it a comfort and recreation among their many serious occupations, who show the divine nature of their genius and the nobility of their thoughts, in spite of those meddlesome ignoramuses who pass judgement on what they do not know, and hate what they cannot understand; and those who only want praise for the stupid folk who sit beneath canopies, and the ignorant who cling to the seats of the mighty.'

On another occasion they asked him why it was that poets in general were poor. He replied that it was because they chose to be, for it was in their power to be rich, if they knew how to take advantage of the opportunity which they had at their disposal all the time; namely their ladies, who were all extremely rich, for their hair was gold, their brow burnished silver, their eyes green emeralds, their teeth ivory, their lips coral and their throats clear crystal, while their tears were liquid pearls. Moreover, where their feet trod, however hard and barren the earth, it would immediately bring forth jasmine and roses; and their breath was of amber, musk and civet; all these things being signs and proof of their great wealth. These and other things he said about bad poets; but he always spoke well of the good ones and praised them to the skies.

One day he saw on the pavement outside San Francisco church some badly painted figures, and this gave rise to the remark that good painters imitated nature, but bad ones vomited it up. One day he went up to a book shop, with the greatest caution lest he should break, and said to the bookseller,

'I should be very happy about this trade of yours if it were not for one drawback it has.'

The bookseller asked him to tell him what it was.

He replied, 'The fuss they make when they buy the privilege of a book, and the tricks they play on its author if by any chance he prints it at his own expense. Instead of fifteen hundred, they print three thousand books, and when the author thinks they are selling his, they're dispatching other people's.'

It happened that the same day there passed through the square six men who had been flogged, and when the crier said, 'The first one, for thieving,' Glass shouted to those who were standing in front of him,

'Keep out of the way, brothers, lest the list start with the name of one of you.'

And when the crier got to the point where he said, 'The last . . . ,' he commented, 'That must be the one who goes bail for the children.'

A boy said to him, 'Brother Glass, tomorrow they're going to whip a bawd.'

He replied, 'If you told me they were going to whip a pimp, I'd assume they were going to whip a coachman.'

One of those men who carry sedan chairs said to him, 'Haven't you anything to say about us, Licenciate?'

'No,' answered Glass, 'except that any one of you knows more sins than a confessor; but with this difference: that when the confessor knows them he keeps them secret, whereas you publish them in every inn.'

A mule-boy heard this (for all sorts of people used to come and listen to him all the time), and said to him,

'There's little or nothing to be said about us, Mr Flask, because we are honest folk, needful to the state.'

To which Glass replied,

'The master's honour is a sign of the servant's; and so you must look whom you serve, and then you'll see what honour you have. You boys are the scum of the earth. Once, when I was not made of glass, I went on a journey on a hired mule on which I counted a hundred and twenty-one marks, all big ones and harmful to humans. All mule-boys are scoundrels and thieves, not to say crooks: if their masters (which is the name they give to the people they take on their mules) are easily duped, they play more tricks on them than they've had in this city for years; if they are foreigners they rob them; if they're students they curse them; if they're monks, they hurl blasphemy at them; and if they're soldiers, they're afraid of them. These boys, like sailors and carters and muleteers, have a way of life which is unique and peculiar to them. The carter spends most of his life in the space of a yard and a half, for it can't be much farther from the yoke of his mules to the front of the cart; he sings half his time, and curses the rest, and spends a lot more time saying "stand back there"; and if by any chance he has to get a wheel out of a ditch, he'd rather use two curses than three mules. Sailors are barbarous, ill-mannered folk who know no other language than that which is used on board ship; when it is calm they are industrious, and when storms come they are lazy; in bad weather there are lots to command and few to obey. Their god is their chest and their mess, and their favourite pastime is to watch the passengers being sick. Muleteers are people who have abjured sheets and become wedded to pack-saddles; they are so industrious and so quick that in order not to lose a fare they will lose their soul; their favourite music is the sound of the mortar; their sauce is hunger; their morning praises consist in getting up to feed the animals; and as for masses, they never go near them.'

As he was saying this, he was at the door of an apothecary's shop, and turning to the owner, he said to him,

'You'd have a healthy trade if only you weren't so hard on your lamps.'

'In what way am I hard on my lamps?' asked the chemist.

Glass replied, 'Because whenever you're short of oil you make it up with what's in the lamp nearest to hand; and there's something else in your profession which is enough to ruin the reputation of the most reliable doctor in the world.'

Asked what he meant, he replied that there were chemists who, so as not to say that they were out of what the doctor prescribed, put in substitutes for what they hadn't got, which they thought had the same properties and quality, when this was not in fact the case; and so the medicine which had been wrongly made up had the opposite effect to that of the proper prescribed one. Then someone asked him what he thought about doctors, and this is what he said:

'Honora medicum propter necessitatem, etenim creavit eum Altissimus. A Deo enim est omnis medela, et a rege accipiet donationem. Disciplina medici exaltabit caput illius, et in conspectu magnatum collaudabitur. Altissimus de terra creavit medicinam, et vir prudens non abhorrebit illam. This is what Ecclesiasticus says about medicine and about good doctors; and of the bad ones you might say exactly the opposite, because there are no people more harmful to the State than they. The judge can distort or delay justice, the lawyer uphold an unjust cause for his own interest, the merchant can filch our property; in short, all those with whom we have to deal can do us some harm; but not one of them can take away our lives without fear of punishment; only doctors can and do kill us quietly without fear of trouble, without unsheathing any sword more powerful than a "prescription". And there's no way of uncovering their crimes, because they put them under ground straight away. I remember that when I was a man of flesh and not of glass, as I am now, a patient dismissed one of those doctors of the second class and went to another for treatment; and the first, a few days later, happened to go to the apothecary's where the second had his prescriptions made up. He asked the chemist how the patient whom he had left was getting on, and whether the other doctor had prescribed any sort of purge for him. The chemist replied that he had a prescription for a purge which the patient was to take the following day. He asked him to show it to him, and he saw that at the bottom of it was written: "Sumat diluculo", and so he said, "Everything in this purge seems all right to me, except for this 'diluculo', because it's too humid."'

Because of all these things which he said about all the various professions, people ran after him, without doing him any harm, but without giving him any peace; all the same, he couldn't have defended himself against the boys if his guardian hadn't protected him. Someone asked him what he should do in order not to be envious. He replied, 'Sleep; for as long as you sleep you'll be the equal of the person you envy.'

Someone else asked him how he would set about getting away with a commission for which he'd been trying for two years. And he said to him, 'Ride off and watch out for the person who's got it, and go with him until he goes out of the city, and that's how you'll get away with it.'

On one occasion a court judge happened to pass by the place where he was, on his way to a criminal case, with two constables and a crowd of people. Glass asked who he was, and when they told him, he said,

'I'll bet that judge has enough vipers in his bosom, pistols in his belt and lightning in his hands to destroy everything within his jurisdiction. I remember that I had a friend who was working on a criminal charge and who gave a sentence which was far in excess of the crime. I asked him why he had given such a cruel sentence and committed such a manifest injustice. He replied that he intended to grant the appeal, and by this means he was leaving the field open to the members of the Council to show their mercy by moderating and reducing to its proper proportions the harsh sentence he had passed. I replied that it would have been better to have given a sentence which would save them this trouble, for in this way they would consider him to be an upright and just judge.'

In the circle which, as I've said, always crowded round to listen to him was an acquaintance of his dressed as a lawyer, whom someone addressed as 'Licenciate'; and as Glass knew that the man they called licenciate hadn't even qualified for his first degree he said to him,

'Take care, my friend, that the friars who devote themselves to ransoming prisoners don't get hold of your degree, or they'll take it off you as vagrant's property.'

To which the friend replied, 'Let's behave properly to each other, Mr Glass, for you know that I'm a man of lofty and profound learning.'

Glass replied, 'I know very well that you're a Tantalus as far as learning is concerned, for it eludes you by reason of its loftiness and you can't reach it because of its profundity.'

Once when he was near a tailor's shop, he saw the tailor standing with his hands together, and said to him, 'Doubtless, master, you are on the way to salvation.'

'How do you arrive at that conclusion?' asked the tailor.

'How do I arrive at that conclusion?' answered Glass. 'I arrive at it by seeing that since you have nothing to do, you won't have any reason to tell lies.' And he added, 'Woe to the tailor who does not lie and who sews on a holiday; it's a marvellous thing that of all the members of that trade you'll hardly find one who'll make a suit fit, for there are so many sinners who make them.'

Of cobblers he said that never, in their way of thinking, did they make a bad shoe; because if the shoe was too narrow and tight for the person for whom they were making it, they told him that that was how it should be, for elegant people wore their shoes close-fitting, and that if they wore them for a couple of hours they'd be broader than sandals; and if they were too broad, they said that was how they should be, for the sake of the gout.

A bright boy, who was a clerk in a provincial office, and who pestered him a good deal with questions and requests, and brought him news of what was going on in the city (for he would discourse on and give an answer to everything), said to him on one occasion, 'Glass, last night a money-changer who was condemned to be hanged died in prison.'

To which he replied, 'He did well to hurry up and die before the executioner got his hands on him.'

On the pavement outside San Francisco church there was a group of Genoese, and as he walked by, one of them called him and said to him,

'Come here, Mr Glass, and tell us a tale.'

He answered, 'I'd rather not, lest you give me the bill for it in Genoa.'

On one occasion he bumped into a shopkeeper who was going along with a daughter of hers, who was very ugly, but covered in trinkets and finery and pearls, and he said to the mother, 'You've done very well to cover her with stones, to make her fit for walking.'

About pastry-cooks he said that they had been playing a double game for many years without paying any penalty, because they had charged fourpence for cakes worth twopence; eightpence for those worth four and half a real for those worth eight, just as they took it into their heads.

Of puppeteers he said thousands of bad things: he said they were vagrants, who treated divine things without due respect, because they made a mockery of worship with the figures they put on in their shows, and sometimes they would stuff in a sack all or nearly all the figures in the Old and New Testaments and then sit on the sack to eat and drink in the eating-houses and taverns. In short, he said he was amazed that the powers that be didn't put an end to their shows or banish them from the realm.

One day an actor happened to pass, dressed like a prince, and when he saw him, he said, 'I remember seeing this fellow come out of the theatre with his face covered with flour and wearing a sheepskin inside out, and yet, off stage, he's always swearing by his noble blood.'

'He must be a nobleman,' answered one of the spectators, 'because there are many actors who are very well born and of noble blood.'

'That may be true,' replied Glass, 'but the last people you need in a farce are people who are nobly born; they need to be good-looking, elegant and well spoken. I can say this for them too: they earn their bread by the sweat of their brow with intolerable hard work, always learning things by heart. They're perpetual gipsies wandering from village to village and from inn to inn, losing sleep in order to give pleasure to others, because their own profit lies in the satisfaction they give to the public. They have this in their favour too: they deceive no one by their trade, for they are always showing their merchandise in public, for all to see and judge. The work of theatrical managers is incredible, and the worry they have remarkable, for they have to earn a great deal in order to avoid having so many debts at the end of the year that they have to go bankrupt. Yet they are necessary to the State, in the same way as woods, groves, restful landscapes, and all those things which provide honest recreation.'

He said that in the opinion of a friend of his anyone who paid court to an actress was the slave of a whole mass of ladies at the same time – a queen, a nymph, a goddess, a kitchenmaid, a shepherdess – and very often it also fell to his lot to serve a page and a lackey too; for all these roles and many more are normally played by actresses.

Someone asked him who had been the happiest person in the world. His answer was, 'Nemo'; because 'Nemo novit patrem; nemo sine crimine vivit; nemo sua sorte contentus; nemo ascendit in coelum.'

Of fencers he said on one occasion that they were masters of a science or art which was of no use to them when they needed it, and that they were somewhat presumptuous, since they wanted to reduce to mathematical demonstrations, which are infallible, the movements and the angry intentions of their opponents.

He was particularly hostile to those who dyed their beards; and once when he came upon two men quarrelling, the one who was Portuguese said to the Castilian, grasping his beard, which had been heavily dyed,

'By this beard I name . . .'

Glass retorted,

'Hey man, don't say "I name", but rather "I stain".'

Another man had a beard that was a mixture of various colours, as a result of unskilful dyeing; and Glass told him that he had a beard like a speckled dung-heap. To another man, whose beard was half black and half white because he hadn't bothered about it, and the natural colour was growing out, he said that he should not wrangle or quarrel with anyone, because he ran the risk of being told that he was lying by half his beard.

On one occasion he told how a bright and intelligent girl, in order to satisfy her parents' wishes, consented to marry a white-haired old man, who the night before the wedding went, not to the river Jordan, as the old women say, but to the phial of silver nitrate, with which he touched his beard up to such effect that when he went to bed it was like snow and when he got up like pitch. When the time came to plight their troth, the girl looked at him with his beard all dyed, and she asked her parents to give her the same husband that they had shown her; for she wanted no other. They told her that the man she was looking at was the same as the one they had shown to her and given her as a husband. She replied that he was not, and brought as evidence that the man her parents had given her was a venerable white-haired man, and as this one had no white hair, it wasn't the same one, and she was withdrawing on the ground that she had been tricked. She stuck to this, the man with the dyed beard was put to shame and the engagement was broken off.

Glass had the same antipathy towards duennas as he had towards those who dyed their hair; he talked endlessly of their permafoy, the shrouds of their head-dresses, all their affected ways, their scruples, and their extraordinary meanness;

he was annoyed by the way they complained about their stomachs and about their dizziness in the head, the way they had of speaking, which had more frills than their headdresses and their useless affectations.

Someone said to him, 'Why is it, Licenciate, that I've heard you speak ill of many professions and you've never said a bad word about notaries, when there is so much to be said?'

He replied, 'Although made of glass, I am not so fragile as to allow myself to be carried along by the crowd, which is usually wrong. It seems to me that notaries are what grammar is to backbiters and "la, la, la" to singers; because just as you cannot get at other branches of knowledge except by way of grammar, and just as the musician hums the tune over before he sings, so backbiters first show their tendency to slander by speaking ill of notaries and constables and other officers of the law, when the notary's profession is one without which the truth would be suppressed, abused and brought into disgrace. And so Ecclesiasticus says: "In manu Dei potestas hominis est, et super faciem scribae imponet honorem." The notary is a public figure, and the judge's profession cannot be carried out properly without his. Notaries must be freemen, not slaves, nor sons of slaves; legitimate, and not bastards, or born of inferior race. They swear to keep secrets, to be true to their word and not to make statements for payment; that neither friendship, nor enmity, profit nor injury, will prevent them from performing their duty with a good Christian conscience. If this profession requires so many good qualities, why should one think that from the more than twenty thousand notaries in Spain the devil should reap the reward, as if they were shoots of his vine? I have no wish to believe it, nor is it right that anyone should believe it; because the long and the short of it is that they are the most necessary people in a well-ordered state, and if they have made off with too many dues, they have also done many things which were not their due, and between these two extremes one could find a happy mean which could make them take care what they're about.'

On the subject of constables he said that it was not surprising that they should have some enemies, since their profession was either to make arrests, or to remove property from houses, or to keep people in their houses under custody and eat at their expense. He condemned the negligence and ignorance of attorneys and solicitors. As with doctors who get their fee, whether the patient gets better or not, so it is with attorneys and solicitors, whether or not the cause they are pleading is successful.

Someone asked him which was the best country. He replied that it was the one which gave prompt rewards.

The other replied, 'That's not what I'm asking, but which is the better place: Valladolid or Madrid?'

And he answered, 'Madrid, for the highest and lowest; Valladolid for the parts in the middle.'

'I don't understand,' said the questioner.

And he replied, 'In Madrid, the top and the bottom; in Valladolid the part between.'

Glass heard one man telling another that as soon as he got to Valladolid, his wife had fallen very ill, because the place didn't agree with her. To this Glass said, 'It would be better if it had finished her off, if she's inclined to be jealous.'

About musicians and those who ran messages he said that they were limited in hopes and fortunes, because the messengers reached the end of theirs when they could go on horseback, and the others when they became musicians at the court.

Of ladies known as courtesans, he said that all or most of them were more courtly than they were sanitary.

One day when he was in a church he saw an old man being brought to be buried, a child to be baptized, and a woman to be married, all at the same time; and he made the comment that churches were battle fields, where the old meet their end, the young win the day and the women triumph.

On one occasion a wasp stung him on the neck, and he did not dare to shake it off, for fear of being broken: but all the same he complained. Someone asked him how he felt the wasp, if his body was made of glass. He answered that the wasp must be a backbiter, and that the tongues and mouths of backbiters were enough to penetrate bodies of bronze, let alone glass.

As a very fat monk happened to pass one of the bystanders said, 'The father is so weak he can't move.'

Glass said impatiently, 'Let no one forget what the Holy Spirit says: "Nolite tangere christos meos".' And getting more impatient, he bade them consider that of the many saints canonized or included in the ranks of the blessed by the Church in recent years, no one had been called Captain So-and-So, or Secretary Such-and-Such, or the Count, Marquess or Duke of such-and-such a place, but Friar James, Friar Jacinto, Friar Raymond; in other words, they were all friars and monks, because the religious orders are heaven's garden, whose fruits are placed on God's table. He said that the tongues of backbiters were like the feathers of the eagle, which rub away and spoil those of all the other birds which come near them.

He said some extraordinary things about keepers of gaming-houses and about gamblers: that the former were a public menace, because once they had extracted the winnings from those who were in luck, they wanted them to lose and the cards to pass on, so that their opponents should win and they should collect their pile too. He had a lot to say about the patience of the gambler, who spent the whole night playing and losing, and although angry as a fiend, so that his opponent did not leave with his winnings, didn't say a word and suffered like a martyr of the devil. He also had great things to say about the conscientiousness of some honourable gamblers who would not think of allowing their house to be used for any other games but pool and piquet: and by this means, slowly but surely, without fear of scandal, would find themselves at the end of the month with more winnings than those who played wilder games like reparolo and basset.

In short, he said so many things, that if it hadn't been for such sure signs of his madness as his cries when anyone touched him, or came up to him, and for his dress, his frugality, his way of drinking, his unwillingness to sleep anywhere but out of doors in summer and in straw lofts in the winter, as we've said, no one would have believed that he wasn't one of the sanest men in the world.

He suffered from this illness for some two years, and then a monk of the Jeromite order, who had a special gift for making deaf mutes hear and speak after a fashion, and for curing madness, out of charity took it upon himself to cure Glass. He managed to restore him to health, and to his previous good sense, intelligence and way of life. And as soon as he saw that he was sane, he dressed him up as a lawyer and sent him back to court, where, showing as many signs of sanity as he had previously shown indications of madness, he could practise his profession and make himself famous by it. This he did, and calling himself Licenciate Rueda, and not Rodaja, he went back to the court. As soon as he got there, he was recognized by the children; but as they saw him dressed so differently from the way he usually went about they didn't dare to hoot at him or ask him questions; but they followed him, and said to each other,

'Isn't this the madman Glass? Of course it is. He looks sane now. But he might still be just as mad when he's wearing good clothes as when he wore bad ones. Let's ask him something, and we'll find out the truth of the matter.'

All this the licenciate heard, but he kept silent, and was more bewildered and confused than when he was out of his mind.

The children passed on the word to the men, and before the licenciate reached the courtyard of the Consejos he was being followed by more than two hundred people of all kinds. With this following, which was bigger than that of a professor, he reached the courtyard, where all the people there gathered round him. Seeing himself surrounded by such a crowd he spoke up as follows:

'Gentlemen, I am Licenciate Glass; but not the man I used to be: now I am Licenciate Rueda. Events and misfortunes which happen in the world by heaven's design put me out of my mind, and God's mercies have now restored me to it. Bearing in mind the things they say I said when I was mad you can get an idea of what I shall say and do when I am sane. I am a Law graduate from Salamanca, where I was a poor student, and where I came out with a second; from this you can infer that I won my degree more by merit than as a result of influence. I have come here to this great sea of the capital to practise as a lawyer and to earn my living; but if you don't leave me alone, I shall merely sweat away and die at the end of it. For heaven's sake don't follow me to the point of persecution, and make me lose when I am sane the living I made when I was mad. What you used to ask me in the squares, ask me now at home, and you will see that the man who gave you good answers extempore, as they say, will give you better answers when he's thought them out.'

They all listened to him and some of them left him. He went back to his lodgings, with almost as many people as he had taken with him.

He went out the next day, and the same thing happened; he delivered another sermon, and it was no use. He lost a great deal and earned nothing; and seeing himself about to die of hunger, he decided to leave the court and go back to Flanders, where he thought he would avail himself of the strength of his arm, since he could get no advantage from that of his mind. And putting his decision into effect, he said, as he left the court,

'Oh court, you who build up the hopes of bold office-seekers, and cut short those of them who are virtuous and bashful; who keep shameful rogues in prosperity and starve modest and discreet men to death.'

This said, he went off to Flanders, where, accompanied by his good friend Captain Valdivia, he added eternal fame by deeds of arms to that which he had begun to acquire by his learning, leaving behind him after his death a reputation as a prudent and most valiant soldier.

THE TIGER GUEST

Pu Songling

Translated from the Chinese by Herbert A. Giles

> **Pu Songling** (1640–1715) was born to a poor merchant family from
> Zichuan during the Qing Dynasty. Despite being a gifted child, and
> despite lifelong efforts, academic success eluded him and he failed to pass
> the Imperial Examinations required to advance socially. Pu spent much
> of his life as a rural schoolteacher and private tutor. His best known
> work is *Strange Stories from a Chinese Studio*, a collection of more than
> 400 supernatural tales which were to revive the classical story form in
> Chinese. Sadly, he did not live to know fame, he died in obscurity –
> his fame spread as his stories were published almost half a century after
> his death.

A young man named Kung, a native of Min-chou, on his way to the examination at Hsi-ngan, rested awhile in an inn, and ordered some wine to
drink. Just then a very tall and noble-looking stranger walked in, and,
seating himself by the side of Kung, entered into conversation with him. Kung
offered him a cup of wine, which the stranger did not refuse; saying, at the same
time, that his name was Miao. But he was a rough, coarse fellow; and Kung,
therefore, when the wine was finished, did not call for any more. Miao then rose,
and observing that Kung did not appreciate a man of his capacity, went out into
the market to buy some, returning shortly with a huge bowl full. Kung declined
the proffered wine; but Miao, seizing his arm to persuade him, gripped it so
painfully that Kung was forced to drink a few more cups, Miao himself swilling
away as hard as he could go out of a soup-plate. "I am not good at entertaining
people," cried Miao, at length; "pray go on or stop just as you please." Kung
accordingly put together his things and went off; but he had not gone more than
a few miles when his horse was taken ill, and lay down in the road. While he was
waiting there with all his heavy baggage, revolving in his mind what he should do,
up came Mr. Miao; who, when he heard what was the matter, took off his coat
and handed it to the servant, and lifting up the horse, carried it off on his back to
the nearest inn, which was about six or seven miles distant. Arriving there he put
the animal in the stable, and before long Kung and his servants arrived too. Kung
was much astonished at Mr. Miao's feat; and, believing him to be superhuman,
began to treat him with the utmost deference, ordering both wine and food to
be procured for their refreshment. "My appetite," remarked Miao, "is one that
you could not easily satisfy. Let us stick to wine." So they finished another stoup

together, and then Miao got up and took his leave, saying, "It will be some time before your horse is well; I cannot wait for you." He then went away.

After the examination several friends of Kung's invited him to join them in a picnic to the Flowery Hill; and just as they were all feasting and laughing together, lo! Mr. Miao walked up. In one hand he held a large flagon, and in the other a ham, both of which he laid down on the ground before them. "Hearing," said he, "that you gentlemen were coming here, I have tacked myself on to you, like a fly to a horse's tail." Kung and his friends then rose and received him with the usual ceremonies, after which they all sat down promiscuously. By-and-by, when the wine had gone round pretty freely, some one proposed capping verses; whereupon Miao cried out, "Oh, we're very jolly drinking like this; what's the use of making oneself uncomfortable?" The others, however, would not listen to him, and agreed that as a forfeit a huge goblet of wine should be drunk by any defaulter. "Let us rather make death the penalty," said Miao; to which they replied, laughing, that such a punishment was a trifle too severe; and then Miao retorted that if it was not to be death, even a rough fellow like himself might be able to join. A Mr. Chin, who was sitting at the top of the line, then began:—

"From the hill-top high, wide extends the gaze—"

upon which Miao immediately carried on with

"Redly gleams the sword o'er the shattered vase."

The next gentleman thought for a long time, during which Miao was helping himself to wine; and by-and-by they had all capped the verse, but so wretchedly that Miao called out, "Oh, come! if we aren't to be fined for these, we had better abstain from making any more." As none of them would agree to this, Miao could stand it no longer, and roared like a dragon till the hills and valleys echoed again. He then went down on his hands and knees, and jumped about like a lion, which utterly confused the poets, and put an end to their lucubrations. The wine had now been round a good many times, and being half tipsy each began to repeat to the other the verses he had handed in at the recent examination, all at the same time indulging in any amount of mutual flattery. This so disgusted Miao that he drew Kung aside to have a game at "guess-fingers;" but as they went on droning away all the same, he at length cried out, "Do stop your rubbish, fit only for your own wives, and not for general company." The others were much abashed at this, and so angry were they at Miao's rudeness that they went on repeating all the louder. Miao then threw himself on the ground in a passion, and with a roar changed into a tiger, immediately springing upon the company, and killing them all except Kung and Mr. Chin. He then ran off roaring loudly. Now this Mr. Chin succeeded in taking his master's degree; and three years afterwards, happening to revisit the Flowery Hill, he beheld a Mr. Chi, one of those very gentlemen who had previously been killed by the tiger. In great alarm he was making off, when Chi seized his bridle and would not let him proceed. So he got down from his horse, and inquired what was the matter; to which Chi replied, "I am now the slave of Miao, and have to endure bitter toil for him. He must kill some one else before I can be set free. Three days hence a man, arrayed in the robes and cap of a scholar, should be eaten by the tiger at the foot of the Ts'ang-lung Hill. Do you on that day take some gentleman thither, and thus help your old friend." Chin was too frightened to say much, but promising that he would do so, rode away home. He then began to consider the matter over with himself, and, regarding it as a plot, he determined to break his engagement, and let his friend remain the tiger's devil. He chanced, however, to repeat the story to a Mr. Chiang who was a relative of his, and one of the local scholars; and as this gentleman had a grudge against another scholar, named Yu, who had come out equal with him at the examination, he made up his mind to destroy him. So he invited Yu to accompany him on that day to the place in question, mentioning that he himself should appear in undress only. Yu could not make out the reason for this; but when he reached the spot there he found all kinds of wine and food ready for his entertainment. Now that very day the Prefect had come to the hill; and being a friend of the Chiang family, and hearing that Chiang was below, sent for him to come up. Chiang did not dare to appear before him in undress, and borrowed Yu's clothes and hat; but he had no sooner got them on than out rushed the tiger and carried him away in its mouth.

THE SANDMAN

E. T. A. Hoffmann

Translated from the German by John Oxenford

E.T.A. Hoffmann (1776–1822) worked as a government official in the Prussian judiciary for much of his life, known for his ability to draw scurrilous caricatures, he is remembered as the author of gothic tales, a composer, critic, and illustrator whose influence marked the German Romantic movement of the nineteenth century, but also writers further afield like Balzac and Edgar Allan Poe. Hoffmann's tales are perhaps now more famous from the many operas, ballets and musical works they inspired – from Offenbach's *The Tales of Hoffmann* to Tchaikovsky's ballet *The Nutcracker* and Delibes' *Coppélia*.

NATHANIEL TO LOTHAIRE

Certainly you must all be uneasy that I have not written for so long—so very long. My mother, I am sure, is angry, and Clara will believe that I am passing my time in dissipation, entirely forgetful of the fair angel-image that is so deeply imprinted in my heart and mind. Such, however, is not the case. Daily and hourly I think of you all, and in my sweet dreams the kindly form of my lovely Clara passes before me, and smiles upon me with her bright eyes as she was wont when I appeared among you. Alas, how could I write to you in the distracted mood which has hitherto disturbed my every thought! Something horrible has crossed my path of life. Dark forebodings of a cruel, threatening, fate spread themselves over me like dark clouds, which no friendly sunbeam can penetrate. Now will I tell you what has befallen me. I must do so, that I plainly see—but if I only think of it, it will laugh out of me like mad. Ah, my dear Lothaire, how shall I begin it? How shall I make you in any way sensible that that which occurred to me a few days ago could really have such a fatal effect on my life? If you were here you could see for yourself, but now you will certainly take me for a crazy ghost-seer. In a word, the horrible thing which happened to me, and the painful impression of which I in vain endeavour to escape, is nothing more than this; that some days ago, namely on the 30th of October, at twelve o'clock at noon, a barometer-dealer came into my room and offered me his wares. I bought nothing, and threatened to throw him down stairs, upon which he took himself off of his own accord.

You suspect that only relations of the most peculiar kind, and exerting the greatest influence over my life can give any import to this occurrence, nay, that the person of that unlucky dealer must have a hostile effect upon me. So it is, indeed.

I collect myself with all my might, that patiently and quietly I may tell you so much of my early youth as will bring all plainly and clearly in bright images before your active mind. As I am about to begin I fancy that I hear you laughing and Clara saying: "Childish stories indeed!" Laugh at me I beseech you, laugh with all your heart. But, heavens, my hair stands on end, and it seems as if I am asking you to laugh at me, in mad despair, as Franz Moor asked Daniel. But to my story.

Excepting at dinner time I and my brothers and sisters saw my father very little during the day. He was, perhaps, busily engaged at his ordinary occupation. After supper, which, according to the old custom was served up at seven o'clock, we all went with my mother into my father's work-room, and seated ourselves at the round table. My father smoked tobacco and drank a large glass of beer. Often he told us a number of wonderful stories, and grew so warm over them that his pipe continually went out. I had to light it again, with burning paper, which I thought great sport. Often, too, he would give us picture-books, and sit in his arm-chair silent and thoughtful, puffing out such thick clouds of smoke that we all seemed to be swimming in the clouds. On such evenings as these my mother was very melancholy, and immediately the clock struck nine, she would say: "Now children, to bed—to bed! The Sandman is coming, I can see." And certainly on all these occasions I heard something with a heavy, slow step go bouncing up the stairs. That I thought must be the Sandman. Once that dull noise and footstep were particularly fearful, and I asked my mother, while she took us away: "Eh, mamma, who is this naughty Sandman, who always drives us away from papa? What does he look like?" "There is no Sandman, dear child," replied my mother. "When I say the Sandman comes, I only mean that you are sleepy and cannot keep your eyes open,—just as if sand had been sprinkled into them." This answer of my mother's did not satisfy me—nay, in my childish mind the thought soon matured itself that she only denied the existence of the Sandman to hinder us from being terrified at him. Certainly I always heard him coming up the stairs. Full of curiosity to hear more of this Sandman, and his particular connection with children, I at last asked the old woman who tended my youngest sister what sort of man he was. "Eh, Natty," said she, "do you not know that yet? He is a wicked man, who comes to children when they will not go to bed, and throws a handful of sand into their eyes, so that they start out bleeding from their heads. These eyes he puts in a bag and carries them to the half-moon to feed his own children, who sit in the nest up yonder, and have crooked beaks like owls with which they may pick up the eyes of the naughty human children."

A most frightful image of the cruel Sandman was horribly depicted in my mind, and when in the evening I heard the noise on the stairs, I trembled with agony and alarm. My mother could get nothing out of me, but the cry of "The Sandman, the Sandman!" which was stuttered forth through my tears. I then ran into the bedroom, where the frightful apparition of the Sandman terrified me during the whole night. I had already grown old enough to perceive that the nurse's tale about the Sandman and the nest of children in the half-moon could not be quite true, but, nevertheless, this Sandman remained a fearful spectre, and I was seized with the utmost horror, when I heard him not only come up the stairs, but violently force open my father's room-door and enter. Sometimes he stayed away for a long period, but oftener his visits were in close succession.

This lasted for years, and I could not accustom myself to the terrible goblin; the image of the dreadful Sandman did not become more faint. His intercourse with my father began more and more to occupy my fancy. An unconquerable fear prevented me from asking my father about it, but if I—I myself could penetrate the mystery, and behold the wondrous Sandman—that was the wish which grew upon me with years. The Sandman had brought me into the path of the marvellous and wonderful, which so readily finds a domicile in the mind of a child. Nothing was to me more delightful than to read or hear horrible stories of goblins, witches, pigmies, &c.; but above them all stood the Sandman, whom, in the oddest and most frightful shapes, I was always drawing with chalk or charcoal on the tables, cupboards, and walls. When I was ten years old, my mother removed me from the children's room into a little chamber, situated in a corridor near my father's room. Still, as before, we were obliged speedily to take our departure as soon as, on the stroke of nine, the unknown was heard in the house. I could hear in my little chamber how he entered my father's room, and then it soon appeared to me that a thin vapor of a singular odor diffused itself about the house. Stronger and stronger with my curiosity grew my resolution to form in some manner the Sandman's acquaintance. Often I sneaked from my room to the corridor, when my mother had passed, but never could I discover any thing, for the Sandman had always gone in at the door when I reached the place where I might have seen him. At last, urged by an irresistible impulse, I resolved to hide myself in my father's room and await the appearance of the Sandman.

By the silence of my father, and the melancholy of my mother, I perceived one evening that the Sandman was coming. I, therefore, feigned great weariness, left the room before nine o'clock, and hid myself in a corner close to the door. The house-door creaked, and the heavy, slow, groaning step went through the passage and towards the stairs. My mother passed me with the rest of the children. Softly—very softly, I opened the door of my father's room. He sat as usually, stiff and silent, with his back turned to the door. He did not perceive me, and I swiftly darted into the room and behind the curtain, drawn before an open press, which stood close to the door, and in which my father's clothes were hanging. The steps sounded nearer and nearer—there was a strange coughing and scraping and murmuring without. My heart trembled with anxiety and expectation. A sharp step close—very close to the door,—a smart stroke on the latch, and the door was open with a rattling noise. Screwing up my courage with all my might, I cautiously peeped out. The Sandman was standing before my father in the middle of the room, the light of the candles shone full upon his face. The Sandman, the fearful Sandman, was the old advocate Coppelius, who had often dined with us.

But the most hideous form could not have inspired me with deeper horror than this very Coppelius. Imagine a large broad-shouldered man, with a head disproportionately big, a face the colour of yellow ochre, a pair of gray bushy eyebrows, from beneath which a pair of green cat's eyes sparkled with the most penetrating lustre, and with a large nose curved over his upper lip. His wry mouth was often twisted into a malicious laugh, when a couple of dark red spots appeared upon his cheeks, and a strange hissing sound was heard through his compressed teeth. Coppelius always appeared in an ashen-gray coat, cut in old-fashioned style, with waistcoat and breeches of the same colour, while his stockings were black, and his shoes adorned with buckles set with precious stones. The little wig scarcely reached further than the crown of his head, the curls stood high above his large red ears, and a broad hair-bag projected stiffly from his neck, so that the silver buckle which fastened his folded cravat might be plainly seen. The whole figure was hideous and repulsive, but most disgusting to us children were his coarse brown hairy fists; indeed, we did not like to eat what he had touched with them. This he had remarked, and it was his delight, under some pretext or other, to touch a piece of cake, or some nice fruit, that our kind mother might privately have put in our plate, in order that we, with tears in our eyes, might, from disgust and abhorrence, no longer be able to enjoy the treat intended for us. He acted in the same manner on holidays, when my father gave us a little glass of sweet wine. Then would he swiftly draw his fist over it, or perhaps he would even raise the glass to his blue lips, and laugh most devilishly, when we could only express our indignation by soft sobs. He always called us the little beasts, we dared not utter a sound when he was present, and we heartily cursed the ugly, unkind man, who deliberately marred our slightest pleasures. My mother seemed to hate the repulsive Coppelius as much as we did, since as soon as he showed himself her liveliness, her free and cheerful mind was changed into a gloomy solemnity. My father conducted himself towards him, as though he was a superior being, whose bad manners were to be tolerated, and who was to be kept in good humour at any rate. He need only give the slightest hint, and the favourite dishes were cooked, and the choicest wines served.

When I now saw this Coppelius, the frightful and terrific thought took possession of my soul, that indeed no one but he could be the Sandman. But the Sandman was no longer that bugbear of a nurse's tale, who provided the owl's nest in the half-moon with children's eyes,—no, he was a hideous spectral monster, who, wherever he appeared, brought with him grief, want, and destruction—temporal and eternal.

I was rivetted to the spot as if enchanted. At the risk of being discovered, and as I plainly foresaw, of being severely punished, I remained with my head peeping through the curtain. My father received Coppelius with solemnity. "Now to our work!" cried the latter with a harsh, grating voice, as he flung off his coat. My father silently and gloomily drew off his night-gown, and both attired themselves in long black frocks. Whence they took these, I did not see. My father opened the door of what I had always thought to be a cupboard, but I now saw that it was no cupboard, but rather a black hollow, in which there was a little hearth. Coppelius entered, and a blue flame began to crackle up on the hearth. All sorts of strange utensils lay around. Heavens!—As my old father now stooped down to the fire, he looked quite another man. A frightful convulsive pain seemed to have distorted his mild reverend features into a hideous repulsive diabolical countenance. He looked like Coppelius: the latter was brandishing red hot tongs, and with them taking shining masses busily out of the thick smoke, which he afterwards hammered. It seemed to me, as if I saw human faces around without any eyes—but with deep holes instead. "Eyes here, eyes!" said Coppelius in a dull roaring voice. Overcome by the wildest terror, I shrieked out, and fell from my hiding place upon the floor. Coppelius seized me, and showing his teeth, bleated out, "Ah—little wretch,—little wretch!"—then dragging me up, he flung me on the hearth, where the fire began to singe my hair. "Now we have eyes enough—a pretty pair of child's eyes." Thus whispered Coppelius and taking out of the flame some red-hot grains with his fists, he was about to sprinkle them in my eyes. My father upon this raised his hands in supplication, and cried: "Master, master, leave my Nathaniel his eyes!" Coppelius uttered a yelling laugh, and said: "Well let the lad have his eyes and cry his share in the world, but we will examine the mechanism of his hands and feet." And then he seized me so forcibly that my joints cracked, and screwed off my hands and feet, and then put them on again, one here and the other there. "Every thing is not right here!—As good as it was— the old one has understood it!" So did Coppelius say, in a hissing, lisping tone, but all around me became black and dark, a sudden cramp darted through my bones and nerves—and I lost all feeling. A gentle warm breath passed over my face; I woke as out of a sleep of death. My mother had been stooping over me. "Is the Sandman yet there?" I stammered. "No, no, my dear child, he has gone away long ago,—he will not hurt you!"—So said my mother, and she kissed and embraced her recovered darling.

Why should I weary you, my dear Lothaire! Why should I be so diffuse with details, when I have so much more to tell. Suffice it to say, that I had been discovered while watching, and ill-used by Coppelius. Agony and terror had brought on delirium and fever, of which I lay sick for several weeks. "Is the Sandman still there?" That was my first sensible word and the sign of my amendment—my recovery. I can now only tell you, the most frightful moment in my juvenile years. Then you will be convinced that it is no fault of my eyes, that all to me seems colourless, but that a dark fatality has actually suspended over my life a gloomy veil of clouds, which I shall perhaps only tear away in death.

Coppelius was no more to be seen; it was said he had left the town.

About a year might have elapsed, when, according to the old custom, we sat at the round table. My father was very cheerful, and told much that was entertaining, about his travels in his youth; when, as the clock struck nine, we heard the house-door creak on the hinges, and slow steps, heavy as iron, groaned through the passage and up the stairs. "That is Coppelius," said my mother, turning pale. "Yes!—that is Coppelius!" repeated my father, with a faint broken voice. The tears started from my mother's eyes. "But father—father!" she cried, "must it be so?" "He comes to me for the last time, I promise you," was the answer. "Only go now—go with the children—go—go to bed. Good night!"

I felt as if I were pressed into cold, heavy stone,—my breath was stopped. My mother caught me by the arm as I stood immoveable. "Come, come, Nathaniel!" I allowed myself to be led, and entered my chamber! "Be quiet—be quiet—go to bed—go to sleep!" cried my mother after me; but tormented by restlessness, and an inward anguish perfectly indescribable, I could not close my eyes. The hateful, abominable Coppelius stood before me with fiery eyes, and laughed at me maliciously. It was in vain that I endeavoured to get rid of his image. About midnight there was a frightful noise, like the firing of a gun. The whole house resounded. There was a rattling and a rustling by my door, and the house-door was closed with a violent sound. "That is Coppelius!" I cried, and I sprang out of bed in terror. There was then a shriek as if of acute inconsolable grief. I darted into my father's room; the door was open, a suffocating smoke rolled towards me, and the servant girl cried: "Ah, my master, my master!" On the floor of the smoking hearth lay my father dead, with his face burned and blackened, and hideously distorted,—my sisters were shrieking and moaning around him,—and my mother had fainted. "Coppelius!—cursed Satan, thou hast slain my father!" I cried, and lost my senses. When, two days afterwards, my father was laid in his coffin, his features were again as mild and gentle as they had been in his life. My soul was comforted by the thought that his pact with the devilish Coppelius could not have plunged him into eternal perdition.

The explosion had awakened the neighbours, the occurrence had become the common talk, and had reached the ears of the magistracy, who wished to make Coppelius answerable. He had, however, vanished from the spot, without leaving a trace.

If I tell you, my dear friend, that the barometer-dealer was the accursed Coppelius himself, you will not blame me for regarding a phenomenon so unpropitious as boding some heavy calamity. He was dressed differently, but the figure and features of Coppelius are too deeply imprinted in my mind, for an error in this respect to be possible. Besides, Coppelius has not even altered his name. As I hear he gives himself out as a Piedmontese optician, and calls himself Giuseppe Coppola.

I am determined to cope with him, and to avenge my father's death, be the issue what it may.

Tell my mother nothing of the hideous monster's appearance. Remember me to my dear sweet Clara, to whom I will write in a calmer mood.—Farewell.

CLARA TO NATHANIEL

It is true that you have not written to me for a long time, but nevertheless I believe that I am still in your mind and thoughts. For assuredly you were thinking of me most intently, when designing to send your last letter to my brother Lothaire, you directed it to me, instead of him. I joyfully opened the letter, and did not perceive my error till I came to the words: "Ah, my dear Lothaire." Now, by rights I should have read no farther, but should have handed over the letter to my brother. Although you have often in your childish teasing mood, charged me with having such a quiet, womanish, steady disposition, that like the lady, even if the house were about to fall in, I should smooth down a wrong fold in the window curtain before I ran away, I can hardly tell you how your letter shocked me. I could scarcely breathe,—my eyes became dizzy. Ah, my dear Nathaniel, how could such a horrible event have crossed your life? To be parted from you, never to see you again,—the thought darted through my breast like a burning dagger. I read and read. Your description of the repulsive Coppelius is terrific. For the first time I learned, how your good old father died a shocking violent death. My brother Lothaire, to whom I gave up the letter as his property, sought to calm me, but in vain. The fatal barometer-maker, Giuseppe Coppola followed me at every step, and I am almost ashamed to confess that he disturbed my healthy and generally peaceful sleep with all sorts of horrible visions. Yet soon,—even the next day, I was quite changed again. Do not be offended, dearest one, if Lothaire tells you, that in spite of your strange misgiving, that Coppelius will in some manner injure you, I am in the same cheerful unembarrassed frame of mind as ever.

I will honestly confess to you that, according to my opinion, all the terrible things of which you speak, merely occurred in your own mind, and that the actual external world had little to do with them. Old Coppelius may have been repulsive enough, but his hatred of children was what really caused the abhorrence of your children towards him.

In your childish mind the frightful sandman in the nurse's tale was naturally associated with old Coppelius, who, even if you had not believed in the sandman, would still have been a spectral monster, especially dangerous to children. The awful nightly occupation with your father, was no more than this, that both secretly made alchemical experiments, and with these your mother was constantly dissatisfied, since besides a great deal of money being uselessly wasted, your father's mind being filled with a fallacious desire after higher wisdom was alienated from his family—as they say, is always the case with such experimentalists. Your father no doubt, by some act of carelessness, occasioned his own death, of which Coppelius was completely guiltless. Would you believe it, that I yesterday asked our neighbour, the clever apothecary, whether such a sudden and fatal explosion was possible in such chemical experiments? "Certainly," he replied, and in his way told me at great length and very circumstantially how such an event might take place, uttering a number of strange-sounding names, which I am unable to recollect. Now, I know you will be angry with your Clara; you will say that her cold disposition is impenetrable to every ray of the mysterious, which often embraces man with invisible arms, that she only sees the varigated surface of the world, and has the delight of a silly child, at some gold-glittering fruit, which contains within it a deadly poison.

Ah! my dear Nathaniel! Do you not then believe that even in free, cheerful, careless minds, here may dwell the suspicion of some dread power, which endeavours to destroy us in our own selves? Forgive me, if I, a silly girl, presume in any manner to indicate, what I really think of such an internal struggle; I shall not find out the right words after all, and you will laugh at me, not because my thoughts are foolish, but because I set about so clumsily to express them.

If there is a dark power, which with such enmity and treachery lays a thread within us, by which it holds us fast, and draws us along a path of peril and destruction, which we should not otherwise have trod; if, I say, there is such a power, it must form itself within us, or from ourselves; indeed, become identical with ourselves, for it is only in this condition that we can believe in it, and grant it the room which it requires, to accomplish its secret work. Now, if we have a mind, which is sufficiently firm, sufficiently strengthened by cheerful life, always to recognise this strange hostile operation as such, and calmly to follow the path which belongs to our inclination and calling, then will the dark power fail in its attempt to gain a power, that shall be a reflection of ourselves. Lothaire adds that it is certain, that the dark physical power, if of our own accord, we have yielded ourselves up to it, often draws within us some strange form, which the external world has thrown in our way, so that we ourselves kindle the spirit, which, as we in our strange delusion believe, speaks to us in that form. It is the phantom of our own selves, the close relationship with which, and its deep operation on our mind casts us into hell, or transports us into heaven. You see, dear Nathaniel, that I and my brother Lothaire have freely given our opinion on the subject of dark powers, which subject, now I find I have not been able to write down the chief part without trouble, appears to me somewhat deep. Lothaire's last words I do not quite comprehend. I can only suspect what he means, and yet I feel as if it were all very true. I beg of you, get the ugly advocate, Coppelius, and the barometer-seller, Giuseppe Coppola, quite out of your head. Be convinced that these strange fears have no power over you, and that it is only a belief in their hostile influence that can make them hostile in reality. If the great excitement of your mind did not speak from every line of your letter, if your situation did not give me the deepest pain, I could joke about the Sandman-Advocate, and the barometer-seller, Coppelius. Be cheerful, I have determined to appear before you as your guardian-spirit, and if the ugly Coppelius takes it in his head to annoy you in your dreams, to scare him away with loud peals of laughter. I am not a bit afraid of him nor of his disgusting hands; he shall neither spoil my sweetmeats as an advocate, nor my eyes as a sandman. Ever yours, my dear Nathaniel.

NATHANIEL TO LOTHAIRE

I am very sorry that in consequence of the error occasioned by my wandering state of mind, Clara broke open the letter intended for you, and read it. She has written me a very profound philosophical epistle, in which she proves, at great length, that Coppelius and Coppola only exist in my own mind, and are phantoms of myself, which will be dissipated directly I recognise them as such. Indeed, one could not believe that the mind which often peers out of those bright, smiling, childish eyes, like a sweet charming dream, could define with such intelligence, in such a professor-like manner. She appeals to you—you, it seems have been talking about me. I suppose you read her logical lectures, that she may learn to divide and sift everything acutely. Pray leave it off. Besides it is quite certain that the barometer-dealer, Guiseppe Coppola, is not the advocate Coppelius. I attend the lectures of the professor of physics, who has lately arrived. His name is the same as that of the famous natural philosopher, Spalanzani, and he is of Italian origin. He has known Coppola for years, and moreover it is clear from his accent that he is really a Piedmontese. Coppelius was a German, but I think no honest one. Calmed I am not, and though you and Clara may consider me a gloomy visionary, I cannot get rid of the impression, which the accursed face of Coppelius makes upon me. I am glad that Coppola has left the town, as Spalanzani says. This professor is a strange fellow—a little round man, with high cheek-bones, sharp nose, pouting lips, and little piercing eyes. Yet you will get a better notion of him than by this description, if you look at the portrait of Cagliostro, designed by Chodowiecki, in one of the Berlin annuals, Spalanzani looks like that exactly. I lately went up the stairs, and perceived that the curtain, which was generally drawn completely over a glass door, left a little opening on one side. I know not what curiosity impelled me to look through, a tall and very slender lady most symmetrically formed, and most splendidly attired, sat in the room by a little table on which she had laid her arms, her hands being folded together. She sat opposite to the door, so that I could completely see her angelic countenance. She did not appear to see me, and indeed there was something fixed about her eyes as if, I might almost say, she had no power of sight. It seemed to me that she was sleeping with her eyes open. I felt very uncomfortable, and therefore I slunk away into the auditorium, which was close at hand. Afterwards I learned that the form I had seen was that of Spalanzani's daughter Olympia, whom he kept confined in a very strange and improper manner, so that no one could approach her. After all, there may be something the matter with her; she is silly perhaps, or something of the kind. But why should I write you all this? I could have conveyed it better and more circumstantially by word of mouth. Know that I shall see you in a fortnight. I must again behold my dear; sweet, angelic Clara. The ill-humour will then be dispersed, which, I must confess, has endeavoured to get the mastery over me, since that fatal, sensible letter. Therefore I do not write to her to-day. A thousand greetings, &c.

Nothing more strange and chimerical can be imagined than that which occurred to my poor friend, the young student Nathaniel, and which I, gracious reader, have undertaken to tell you. Have you, kind reader, ever known a something that has completely filled your heart, thoughts, and senses, so as to exclude everything else? There was in you a fermentation and a boiling, and your blood inflamed to the hottest glow bounded through your veins, and gave a higher colour to your cheeks. Your glance was so strange, as if you wished to perceive, in empty space, forms which to no other eyes are visible, and your speech flowed away into dark sighs. Then your friends asked you: "What is it, revered one?" "What is the matter, dear one." And now you wished to express the internal picture with all its glowing tints, with all its light and shade, and laboured hard to find words only to begin. You thought that in the very first word you ought to crowd together all the wonderful, noble, horrible, comical, frightful, that had happened, so that it might strike all the hearers at once like an electric shock. But every word, everything that is in the form of speech, appeared to you colourless, cold and dead. You hunt and hunt, and stutter and stammer, and the sober questions of your friends dart like icy breezes upon your internal fire until it is ready to go out; whereas if, like a bold painter, you had first with a few daring strokes drawn an outline of the internal picture, you might with small trouble have laid on the colours brighter and brighter, and the living throng of various forms would have carried your friends along with it, and they, like you, would have seen themselves in the picture that had proceeded from your mind. Now I must confess to you, kind reader, that no one has really asked me for the history of the young Nathaniel, but you know well enough that I belong to the queer race of authors, who, if they have any thing in their mind, such as I have just described, feel as if every one who comes near them, and indeed perhaps the whole world besides, is asking them: "What is it then—tell it, my dear friend?" Thus was I forcibly compelled to tell you of the momentous life of Nathaniel. The singularity and marvellousness of the story filled my entire soul, but for that very reason and because, my reader, I had to make you equally inclined to endure oddity, which is no small matter, I tormented myself to begin the history of Nathaniel in a manner as inspiring, original and striking as possible. "Once upon a time," the beautiful beginning of every tale, was too tame. "In the little provincial town of S——

lived"—was somewhat better, as it at least prepared for the climax. Or should I dart at once *in medias res*, with "'Go to the devil', cried the student Nathaniel with rage and horror in his wild looks, when the barometer-seller, Guiseppe Coppola?"—I had indeed already written this down, when I fancied that in the wild looks of the student Nathaniel, I could detect something ludicrous, whereas the story is not comical at all. No form of language suggested itself to my mind, which even in the slightest degree seemed to reflect the colouring of the internal picture. I resolved that I would not begin it at all. So take, gentle reader, the three letters, which friend Lothaire was good enough to give me, as the sketch of the picture which I shall endeavour to colour more and more as I proceed in my narrative. Perhaps, like a good portrait-painter, I may succeed in catching many a form in such a manner, that you will find it is a likeness without having the original, and feel as if you had often seen the person with your own corporeal eyes. Perchance, dear reader, you will then believe that nothing is stranger and madder than actual life, and that this is all that the poet can conceive, as it were in the dull reflection of a dimly polished mirror.

In order that that which it is necessary in the first place to know, may be made clearer, we must add to these letters the circumstance, that shortly after the death of Nathaniel's father, Clara and Lothaire, the children of a distant relative, who had likewise died, and left them orphans, were taken by Nathaniel's mother to her own home. Clara and Nathaniel formed a strong attachment for each other, and no one in the world having any objection to make, they were betrothed, when Nathaniel left the place to pursue his studies in G——. He is, according to the date of his last letter, hearing the lectures of the celebrated professor of physics, Spalanzani.

Now I could proceed in my story with confidence, but at this moment Clara's image stands so plainly before me, that I cannot look another way, as indeed was always the case when she gazed at me, with one of her lively smiles. Clara could not by any means be reckoned beautiful; that was the opinion of all who are competent judges of beauty, by their calling. Nevertheless, the architects praised the exact symmetry of her frame, and the painters considered her neck, shoulders, and bosom almost too chastely formed, but then they all fell in love with her wondrous Magdalen-hair, and above everything prated about battonisch colouring. One of them, a most fantastical fellow, singularly compared Clara's eyes to a lake by Ruysdael, in which the pure azure of a cloudless sky, the wood and flowery field, the whole cheerful life of the rich landscape are reflected. Poets and composers went still further. "What is a lake—what is a mirror!" said they, "can we look upon the girl without wondrous, heavenly songs and tunes flashing towards us from her glances, and penetrating our inmost soul, so that all there is awakened and stirred. If even then we sing nothing that is really sensible, there is not much in us, and that we can feelingly read in the delicate smile which plays on Clara's lips, when we presume to tinkle something before her, which is to pass for a song, although it is only a confused jumble of tones." So it was. Clara had the vivid fancy of a cheerful, unembarrassed child, a deep, tender, feminine disposition, an acute, clever understanding. The misty dreams had but a bad chance with her, since, though she did not talk,—as indeed talking would have been altogether repugnant to her tacit nature, her bright glance and her firm ironical smile would say to them: "Good friends, how can you imagine that I shall take your fleeting shadowy images for real forms with life and motion?" On this account Clara was censured by many as cold, unfeeling and prosaic; while others, who conceived life in its clear depth, greatly loved the feeling, acute, childlike girl, but none so much as Nathaniel, whose perception in art and science was clear and strong. Clara was attached to her lover with all her soul, and when he parted from her, the first cloud passed over her life. With what transport did she rush into his arms when, as he had promised in his last letter to Lothaire, he had actually returned to his native town and entered his mother's room. Nathaniel's expectations were completely fulfilled; for directly he saw Clara he thought neither of the Advocate Coppelius, nor of her "sensible" letter. All gloomy forebodings had gone.

However, Nathaniel was quite right, when he wrote to his friend Lothaire that the form of the repulsive barometer-seller, Coppola, had had a most hostile effect on his life. All felt, even in the first days, that Nathaniel had undergone a thorough change in his whole temperament. He sank into a gloomy reverie, and conducted himself in a strange manner, that had never been known in him before. Everything, his whole life, had become to him a dream and a foreboding, and he was always saying that every man, although he might think himself free, only served for the cruel sport of dark powers. These he said it was vain to resist, and man must patiently resign himself to his fate. He went even so far as to say, that it is foolish to think that we do anything in art and science according to our own self-acting will, for the inspiration which alone enables us to produce anything, does not proceed from within ourselves, but is the effect of a higher principle without.

To the clear-headed Clara this mysticism was in the highest degree repugnant, but contradiction appeared to be useless. Only when Nathaniel proved that Coppelius was the evil principle, which had seized him at the moment when he was listening behind the curtain, and that this repugnant principle would in some horrible manner disturb the happiness of their life, Clara grew very serious, and said: "Yes, Nathaniel, you are right. Coppelius is an evil, hostile principle; he can produce terrible effects, like a diabolical power that has come invisibly into life; but only then, when you will not banish him from your mind and thoughts. So long as you believe in him he really exists, and exerts his influence; only your belief is his power."

Nathaniel, quite indignant that Clara established the demon's existence only in his own mind, would then come out with all the mystical doctrine of devils and fearful powers. But Clara would break off peevishly, by introducing some indifferent matter, to the no small annoyance of Nathaniel. He thought that such deep secrets were closed to cold, unsusceptible minds, without being clearly aware that he reckoned Clara among these subordinate natures, and therefore he constantly endeavoured to initiate her into the mysteries. In the morning, when Clara was getting breakfast ready, he stood by her, and read out of all sorts of mystical books, till she cried: "But, dear Nathaniel, suppose I blame you as the evil principle, that has a hostile effect upon my coffee? For if to please you, I leave everything standing still, and look in your eyes, while you read, my coffee will run into the fire, and none of you will get any breakfast."

Nathaniel closed the book at once, and hurried indignantly to his chamber.

Once he had a remarkable forte for graceful, lively tales, which he wrote down, and to which Clara listened with the greatest delight; now, his creations were gloomy, incomprehensible, formless, so that although Clara, out of compassion, did not say so, he plainly felt how little she was interested. Nothing was more insupportable to Clara than tediousness; in her looks and in her words a mental drowsiness, not to be conquered, was expressed. Nathaniel's productions were, indeed, very tedious. His indignation at Clara's cold, prosaic disposition, constantly increased, and Clara could not overcome her dislike of Nathaniel's dark, gloomy, tedious mysticism, so that they became more and more estranged from each other in mind, without perceiving it. The form of the ugly Coppelius, as Nathaniel himself was forced to confess, grew more dim in his fancy, and it often cost him trouble to colour with sufficient liveliness in his pictures, when he appeared as a ghastly bugbear of fate. At last it struck him that he would make the gloomy foreboding, that Coppelius would destroy his happiness in love, the subject of a poem. He represented himself and Clara as united by true love; but occasionally it seemed as though a black hand darted into their life, and tore away some newly-springing joy. At last, while they were standing at the altar, the hideous Coppelius appeared, and touched Clara's lively eyes. They flashed into Nathaniel's heart, like bleeding sparks, scorching and burning, when Coppelius caught him, and flung him into a flaming, fiery circle, which flew round with the swiftness of the stream, and carried him along with it, amid its roaring. The roar is like that of the hurricane, when it fiercely lashes the foaming waves, which, like black giants with white heads, rise up for the furious combat. But through the wild tumult he hears Clara's voice: "Can you not, then, see me? Coppelius has deceived you. Those, indeed, were not my eyes, which so burned in your breast— they were glowing drops of your own heart's blood. I have my eyes still—only look at them!" Nathaniel reflects: "That is Clara, and I am hers for ever!" Then it seems to him as though thought forcibly entered the fiery circle, which stands still, while the noise dully ceases in the dark abyss. Nathaniel looks into Clara's eyes, but it is only death that, with Clara's eyes, kindly looks on him.

While Nathaniel composed this poem he was very calm and collected; he polished and improved every line, and having subjected himself to the fetters of metre, he did not rest till all was correct and melodious. When at last he had finished and read the poem aloud to himself, a wild horror seized him, and he cried out: "Whose horrible voice is that?" Soon, however, the whole appeared to him a very successful work, and he felt that it must inflame Clara's cold temperament, although he did not clearly consider for what Clara was to be excited, nor what purpose it would answer to torment her with the frightful images which threatened a horrible destiny, destructive to their love. Both of them—that is to say Nathaniel and Clara—were sitting in their mother's little garden, Clara very cheerful, because Nathaniel, during the three days in which he had been writing his poem, had not teased her with his dreams and his forebodings. Even Nathaniel spoke lively and joyfully about pleasant matters, as he used to do formerly, so that Clara said: "Now for the first time I have you again! Do you not see that we have driven away the ugly Coppelius?" Then it first struck Nathaniel that he had in his pocket the poem, which he had intended to read. He at once drew the sheets out and began, while Clara, expecting something tedious as usual, resigned herself and began quietly to knit. But as the dark cloud rose ever blacker and blacker, she let the stocking fall and looked full into his face. He was carried along unceasingly by his poem, an internal fire deeply reddened his cheeks, tears flowed from his eyes. At last when he had concluded, he groaned in a state of utter exhaustion, and catching Clara's hand, sighed forth, as if melted into the most inconsolable grief: "Oh Clara!—Clara!" Clara pressed him gently to her bosom, and said softly, but very solemnly and sincerely: "Nathaniel, dearest Nathaniel, do throw that mad, senseless, insane stuff into the fire!" Upon this Nathaniel sprang up enraged, and thrusting Clara from him, cried: "Thou inanimate, accursed automaton!" He ran off; Clara, deeply offended, shed bitter tears, and sobbed aloud: "Ah, he has never loved me, for he does not understand me." Lothaire entered the arbour; Clara was obliged to tell him all that had occurred. He loved his sister with all his soul, and every word of her complaint fell like a spark of fire into his heart, so that the indignation which he had long harboured against the visionary Nathaniel, now broke out into the wildest rage. He ran to Nathaniel and reproached him for his senseless conduct towards his beloved sister in hard words, which the infuriated Nathaniel retorted in the same style. The appellation of "fantastical, mad fool," was answered by that of "miserable common-place fellow." A duel was inevitable. They agreed on the following morning, according to the academical custom of the place, to fight with sharp rapiers behind the garden. Silently and gloomily they slunk about. Clara had overheard the violent dispute, and seeing the fencing-master bring the rapiers at dawn, guessed what was to occur. Having reached the place of combat, Lothaire and Nathaniel had in gloomy silence flung off their coats, and with the fierce desire of fighting in their flaming eyes, were about to fall upon one another, when Clara rushed through the garden door. Sobbing, she cried aloud, "Ye wild cruel men! Strike me down before you attack each other, for how shall I live longer in the world if my lover murders my brother, or my brother murders my lover." Lothaire lowered his weapon, and looked in silence on the ground; but in Nathaniel's heart, amid the most poignant sorrow, revived all the love for the beautiful Clara, which he had felt in the best days of his happy youth. The weapon fell from his hand, he threw himself at Clara's feet. "Can you ever forgive me, my only—my beloved Clara? Can you forgive me, my dear brother, Lothaire?"

Lothaire was touched by the deep contrition of his friend; all three embraced in reconciliation amid a thousand tears, and vowed eternal love and fidelity.

Nathaniel felt as though a heavy burden, which pressed him to the ground, had been rolled away, as though by resisting the dark power, which held him fast, he had saved his whole being, which had been threatened with annihilation. Three happy days he passed with his dear friends, and then went to G——, where he intended to stay a year, and then to return to his native town for ever.

All that referred to Coppelius was kept a secret from the mother, for it was well known that she could not think of him without terror, as she, as well as Nathaniel, accused him of causing her husband's death.

How surprised was Nathaniel, when proceeding to his lodging, he saw that the whole house was burned down, and that only the bare walls stood up amid the ashes. However, notwithstanding the fire had broken out in the laboratory of the apothecary who lived on the ground-floor, and had therefore consumed the house from bottom to top, some bold active friends had succeeded in entering

Nathaniel's room in the upper story, in time to save the books, manuscripts, and instruments. They carried all safe and sound into another house, where they took a room, which Nathaniel entered at once. He did not think it at all remarkable that he lodged opposite Professor Spalanzani; neither did it appear singular when he perceived that his window looked straight into the room where Olympia often sat alone, so that he could plainly recognise her figure, although the features of her face were indistinct and confused. At last it struck him, that Olympia often remained for hours in this attitude, in which he had once seen her through the glass-door, sitting at a little table without any occupation, and that she plainly enough looked over at him with an unvarying glance. He was forced to confess that he had never seen a more lovely form, but with Clara in his heart, the stiff Olympia was perfectly indifferent to him. Occasionally, to be sure, he gave a transient look over his compendium, at the beautiful statue, but that was all. He was just writing to Clara, when he heard a light tap at the door; it paused at his words, and the repulsive face of Coppola peeped in. Nathaniel's heart trembled within him, but remembering what Spalanzani had told him about the countryman, Coppola, and also the sacred promises he had made to Clara with respect to the Sandman Coppelius, he felt ashamed of his childish fear, and collecting himself with all his might, said as softly and civily as possible: "I do not want a barometer, my good friend; pray, go." Upon this, Coppola advanced a good way into the room, and said in a hoarse voice, while his wide mouth distorted itself into a hideous laugh, and his little eyes under their long gray lashes sparkled forth piercingly: "Eh, eh—no barometer—no barometer? I have besides pretty eyes—pretty eyes!"—"Madman!" cried Nathaniel with horror, "how can you have eyes?—Eyes?" But Coppola had already put his barometer aside, and plunged his hand into his wide coat-pocket, whence he drew lunettes and spectacles, which he placed upon the table "There—there—spectacles on the nose, those are my eyes—pretty eyes!" And so saying he drew out more and more spectacles so, that the whole table began to glisten and sparkle in the most extra-ordinary manner. A thousand eyes glanced, and quivered convulsively, and stared at Nathaniel; yet he could not look away from the table, and Coppola kept still laying down more and more spectacles, while flaming glances were intermingled more and more wildly, and shot their blood-red rays into Nathaniel's breast. Overcome with horror, he shrieked out: "Hold, hold, frightful man!" He seized fast by the arm Coppola, who was searching his pockets to bring out still more spectacles, although the whole table was already covered. Coppola had greatly extricated himself with a hoarse repulsive laugh, and with the words: "Ah, nothing for you—but here are pretty glasses;" he had collected all the spectacles, put them up, and from the breast-pocket of his coat had drawn forth a number of telescopes large and small. As soon as the spectacles were removed Nathaniel felt quite easy, and thinking of Clara, perceived that the hideous phantom was but the creature of his own mind, and that Coppola was an honest optician, and could by no means be the accursed double of Coppelius. Moreover, in all the glasses which Coppola now placed on the table, there was nothing remarkable, or at least nothing so ghost-like as the spectacles, and to make matters right Nathaniel resolved to buy something of Coppola. He took up a little and very neatly worked pocket-telescope, and looked through the window to try it. Never in his life had he met a glass which brought the objects so sharply, plainly, and clearly before his eyes. Involuntarily he looked into Spalanzani's room; Olympia was sitting as usual before the little table, with her arms laid upon it, and her hands folded. For the first time could he see the wondrous beauty in the form of her face;—only the eyes seemed to him singularly stiff and dead. Nevertheless, as he looked more sharply through the glass, it seemed to him as if moist morn-beams were rising in the eyes of Olympia. It was as if the power of seeing was kindled for the first time; the glances flashed with constantly increasing liveliness. As if spell-bound, Nathaniel reclined against the window, meditating on the charming Olympia. A hemming and scraping aroused him as if from a dream. Coppola was standing behind him: "Tre zecchini—three ducats!" Nathaniel, who had quite forgotten the optician, quickly paid him what he asked. "Is it not so? A pretty glass—a pretty glass?" asked Coppola, in his hoarse, repulsive voice, and with his malicious smile. "Yes—yes," replied Nathaniel, peevishly; "good bye, friend." Coppola left the room, not without casting many strange glances at Nathaniel. He heard him laugh loudly on the stairs. "Ah," thought Nathaniel, "he is laughing at me because no doubt, I have paid him too much for this little glass." While he softly uttered these words, it seemed as if a deep deadly sigh was sounding fearfully through the room, and his breath was stopped by inward anguish. He perceived, however, that it was himself that had sighed. "Clara," he said to himself, "is right in taking me for a senseless dreamer, but it is pure madness—nay, more than madness, that the stupid thought, that I have paid Coppola too much for the glass, pains me even so strangely. I cannot see the cause." He now sat down to finish his letter to Clara; but a glance through the window convinced him that Olympia was still sitting there, and he instantly sprang out, as if impelled by an irresistible power, seized Coppola's glass, and could not tear himself from the seductive view of Olympia, till his friend and brother Sigismund, called him to go to Professor Spalanzani's lecture. The curtain was drawn close before the fatal room, and he could neither perceive Olympia now nor during the two following days, although he scarcely ever left the window, and constantly looked through Coppola's glass. On the third day the windows were completely covered. Quite in despair, and impelled by a burning wish, he ran out of the town-gate. Olympia's form floated before him in the air, stepped forth from the bushes, and peeped at him with large beaming eyes from the clear brook. Clara's image had completely vanished from his mind; he thought of nothing but Olympia, and complained aloud and in a murmuring tone: "Ah, thou noble, sublime star of my love, hast thou only risen upon me, to vanish immediately, and leave me in dark hopeless night?"

When he was retiring to his lodging, he perceived that there was a great bustle in Spalanzani's house. The doors were wide open, all sorts of utensils were being carried in, the windows of the first floor were being taken out, maid servants were going about sweeping and dusting with great hair-brooms, and carpenters and upholsterers were knocking and hammering within. Nathaniel remained standing in the street in a state of perfect wonder, when Sigismund came up to him, laughing, and said: "Now, what do you say to our old Spalanzani?" Nathaniel assured him that he could say nothing because he knew nothing about the professor, but on the contrary perceived with astonishment the mad proceedings in a house otherwise so quiet and gloomy. He then learnt from Sigismund that

Spalanzani intended to give a grand festival on the following day,—a concert and ball—and that half the university was invited. It was generally reported that Spalanzani, who had so long kept his daughter most painfully from every human eye, would now let her appear for the first time.

Nathaniel found a card of invitation, and with heart beating highly went at the appointed hour to the professor's, where the coaches were already rolling, and the lights were shining in the decorated saloons. The company was numerous and brilliant. Olympia appeared dressed with great richness and taste. Her beautifully turned face, her figure called for admiration. The somewhat strange bend of her back inwards, the wasp-like thinness of her waist, seemed to be produced by too tight lacing. In her step and deportment there was something measured and stiff, which struck many as unpleasant, but it was ascribed to the constraint produced by the company. The concert began, Olympia played the piano with great dexterity, and executed a bravura, with a voice, like the sound of a glass bell, clear, and almost cutting. Nathaniel was quite enraptured; he stood in the hindermost row, and could not perfectly recognise Olympia's features in the dazzling light. He, therefore, quite unperceived, took out Coppola's glass, and looked towards the fair Olympia. Ah! then he saw, with what a longing glance she looked towards him, how every tone first resolved itself plainly in the glance of love, which penetrated, in its glowing career, his inmost soul. The artistical roulades seemed to Nathaniel the exultation of a mind illuminated with love, and when, at last, after the cadence, the long trill sounded shrilly through the saloon, he felt as if grasped by glowing arms; he could no longer restrain himself, but with mingled pain and rapture shouted out, "Olympia!" All looked at him, and many laughed. The organist of the cathedral made a more gloomy face than usual, and simply said: "Well, well." The concert had finished, the ball began. "To dance with her—with her!" That was the aim of all Nathaniel's wishes, of all his efforts; but how to gain courage to ask her, the queen of the festival? Nevertheless—he himself did not know how it happened—no sooner had the dancing begun, than he was standing close to Olympia, who had not yet been asked to dance, and, scarcely able to stammer out a few words, had seized her hand. The hand of Olympia was as cold as ice; he felt a horrible deadly frost thrilling through him. He looked into her eye—that was beaming full of love and desire, and at the same time it seemed as though the pulse began to beat, and the stream of life to glow in the cold hand. And in the soul of Nathaniel the joy of love rose still higher; he clasped the beautiful Olympia, and with her flew through the dance. He thought that his dancing was usually correct as to time, but the peculiar rhythmical steadiness with which Olympia moved, and which often put him completely out, soon showed him, that his time was very defective. However, he would dance with no other lady, and would have liked to murder any one who approached Olympia for the purpose of asking her. But this only happened twice, and to his astonishment Olympia remained seated after every dance, when he lost no time in making her rise again. Had he been able to see any other object besides the fair Olympia, all sorts of unfortunate quarrels would have been inevitable, for the half-soft, scarcely-suppressed laughter, which arose among the young people in every corner, was manifestly directed to Olympia, whom they pursued with very curious glances—one could not tell why. Heated by the dance, and by the wine, of which he had freely partaken, Nathaniel had laid aside all his ordinary reserve. He sat by Olympia, with her hand in his, and, highly inflamed and inspired, told his passion, in words which no one understood—neither himself nor Olympia. Yet, perhaps, she did; for she looked immoveably in his face, and sighed several times, "Ah, ah!" Upon this, Nathaniel said, "Oh, thou splendid, heavenly lady! Thou ray from the promised land of love—thou deep soul, in which all my being is reflected!" with much more stuff of the like kind; but Olympia merely went on sighing, "Ah—ah!" Professor Spalanzani occasionally passed the happy pair, and smiled on them, with a look of singular satisfaction. To Nathaniel, although he felt in quite another region, it seemed all at once as though Professor Spalanzani was growing considerably darker; he looked around, and, to his no small horror, perceived that the two last candles in the empty saloon had burned down to their sockets, and were just going out. Music and dancing had ceased long ago. "Separation—separation!" he cried, wildly, and in despair; he kissed Olympia's hand, he bent towards her mouth, when his glowing lips were met by lips cold as ice! Just as when he touched Olympia's cold hand, he felt himself overcome by horror; the legend of the dead bride darted suddenly through his mind, but Olympia pressed him fast, and her lips seemed to recover to life at his kiss. Professor Spalanzani strode through the empty hall, his steps caused a hollow echo, and his figure, round which a flickering shadow played, had a fearful, spectral appearance. "Dost thou love me, dost love me, Olympia? Only this word!—Dost thou love me?" So whispered Nathaniel; but Olympia, as she rose, only sighed, "Ah—ah!" "Yes, my gracious, my beautiful star of love," said Nathaniel, "thou hast risen upon me, and thou wilt shine, ever illuminating my inmost soul." "Ah—ah!" replied Olympia, going. Nathaniel followed her; they both stood before the professor.

"You have had a very animated conversation with my daughter," said he, smiling; "so, dear Herr Nathaniel, if you have any taste for talking with a silly girl, your visits shall be welcome."

Nathaniel departed, with a whole heaven beaming in his bosom. The next day Spalanzani's festival was the subject of conversation. Notwithstanding the professor had done every thing to appear splendid, the wags had all sorts of incongruities and oddities to talk about, and were particularly hard upon the dumb, stiff Olympia, to whom, in spite of her beautiful exterior, they ascribed absolute stupidity, and were pleased to find therein the cause why Spalanzani kept her so long concealed. Nathaniel did not hear this without increased rage; but, nevertheless, he held his peace, for, thought he, "Is it worth while to convince these fellows that it is their own stupidity that prevents them from recognising Olympia's deep, noble mind?"

One day Sigismund said to him: "Be kind enough, brother, to tell me how it was possible for a sensible fellow like you to fall in love with that wax face, that wooden doll up there?"

Nathaniel was about to fly out in a passion, but he quickly recollected himself, and retorted: "Tell me, Sigismund, how it is that Olympia's heavenly charms could escape your glance, which generally perceives every thing so clearly—your active senses? But, for that very reason, Heaven be thanked, I have not you for my rival; otherwise, one of us must have fallen a bleeding corpse!"

Sigismund plainly perceived his friend's condition, so he skilfully gave the conversation a turn, and added, after observing that in love-affairs there was no disputing about the object: "Nevertheless it is strange, that many of us think much the same about Olympia. To us—pray do not take it ill, brother,—she appears singularly stiff and soulless. Her shape is symmetrical—so is her face— that is true! She might pass for beautiful, if her glance were not so utterly without a ray of life—without the power of seeing. Her pace is strangely measured, every movement seems to depend on some wound-up clockwork. Her playing—her singing has the unpleasantly correct and spiritless measure of a singing machine, and the same may be said of her dancing. To us, this Olympia has been quite unpleasant; we wished to have nothing to do with her; it seems as if she acts like a living being, and yet has some strange peculiarity of her own." Nathaniel did not completely yield to the bitter feeling, which was coming over him at these words of Sigismund; he mastered his indignation, and merely said, with great earnestness, "Well may Olympia appear awful to you, cold prosaic man. Only to the poetical mind does the similarly organised develop itself. To me alone was her glance of love revealed, beaming through mind and thought; only in the love of Olympia do I find myself again. It may not suit you, that she does not indulge in idle chit-chat like other shallow minds. She utters few words, it is true, but these few words appear as genuine hieroglyphics of the inner world, full of love and deep knowledge of the spiritual life in contemplation of the eternal yonder. But you have no sense for all this, and my words are wasted on you." "God preserve you, brother," said Sigismund very mildly, almost sorrowfully; "but it seems to me, that you are in an evil way. You may depend upon me, if all—no, no, I will not say any thing further." All of a sudden it seemed to Nathaniel as if the cold prosaic Sigismund meant very well towards him, and, therefore, he shook the proffered hand very heartily.

Nathaniel had totally forgotten, that there was in the world a Clara, whom he had once loved;—his mother—Lothaire—all had vanished from his memory; he lived only for Olympia, with whom he sat for hours every day, uttering strange fantastical stuff about his love, about the sympathy that glowed to life, about the affinity of souls, to all of which Olympia listened with great devotion. From the very bottom of his desk, he drew out all that he had ever written. Poems, fantasies, visions, romances, tales—this stock was daily increased with all sorts of extravagant sonnets, stanzas, and canzone, and he read all to Olympia for hours in succession without fatigue. Never had he known such an admirable listener. She neither embroidered nor knitted, she never looked out of the window, she fed no favourite bird, she played neither with lap-dog nor pet cat, she did not twist a slip of paper nor any thing else in her hand, she was not obliged to suppress a yawn by a gentle forced cough. In short, she sat for hours, looking straight into her lover's eyes, without stirring, and her glance became more and more lively and animated. Only when Nathaniel rose at last, and kissed her hand and also her lips, she said "Ah, ah!" adding "good night, dearest!" "Oh deep, noble mind!" cried Nathaniel in his own room, "by thee, by thee, dear one, am I fully comprehended." He trembled with inward transport, when he considered the wonderful accordance that was revealed more and more every day in his own mind, and that of Olympia, for it seemed to him as if Olympia had spoken concerning him and his poetical talent out of the depths of his own mind;—as if the voice had actually sounded from within himself. That must indeed have been the case, for Olympia never uttered any words whatever beyond those which have been already mentioned. Even when Nathaniel, in clear and sober moments, as for instance, when he had just woke in the morning, remembered Olympia's utter passivity, and her paucity and scarcity of words, he said: "Words, words! The glance of her heavenly eye speaks more than any language here below. Can a child of heaven adapt herself to the narrow circle which a miserable earthly necessity has drawn?" Professor Spalanzani appeared highly delighted at the intimacy of his daughter with Nathaniel. To the latter he gave the most unequivocal signs of approbation, and when Nathaniel ventured at last to hint at a union with Olympia, he smiled with his white face, and thought "he would leave his daughter a free choice in the matter." Encouraged by these words, and with burning passion in his heart, Nathaniel resolved to implore Olympia on the very next day, that she would say directly, in plain words, that which her kind glance had told him long ago; namely, that she loved him. He sought the ring which his mother had given him at parting, that he might give it to Olympia as a symbol of his devotion, of his life which budded forth and bloomed with her alone. Clara's letters and Lothaire's came into his hands during the search; but he flung them aside indifferently, found the ring, put it up and hastened over to Olympia. Already on the steps, in the hall he heard a strange noise, which seemed to proceed from Spalanzani's room. There was a stamping, a clattering, a pushing, a hurling against the door, intermingled with curses and imprecations. "Let go, let go, rascal!—scoundrel! Body and soul ventured in it? Ha, ha, ha! that I never will consent to—I, I made the eyes, I the clockwork—stupid blockhead with your clockwork—accursed dog of a bungling watch-maker—off with you—Satan—stop, pipe-maker—infernal beast—hold—begone—let go!" These words were uttered by the voices of Spalanzani, and the hideous Coppelius, who was thus raging and clamoring. Nathaniel rushed in, overcome by the most inexpressible anguish. The professor held a female figure fast by the shoulders, the Italian Coppola grasped it by the feet, and thus they were tugging and pulling, this way and that, contending for the possession of it, with the utmost fury. Nathaniel started back with horror, when in the figure he recognised Olympia. Boiling with the wildest indignation, he was about to rescue his beloved from these infuriated men, but at that moment, Coppola, turning himself with the force of a giant, wrenched the figure from the professor's hand, and then with the figure itself gave him a tremendous blow, which made him reel and fall backwards over the table, where vials, retorts, bottles, and glass cylinders were standing. All these were dashed to a thousand shivers. Now Coppola flung the figure across his shoulders, and, with frightful, yelling laughter, dashed down the stairs, so that the feet of the figure, which dangled in the ugliest manner, rattled with a wooden sound on every step. Nathaniel stood paralysed; he had seen but too plainly that Olympia's waxen, deadly pale countenance had no eyes, but black holes instead—she was, indeed, a lifeless doll. Spalanzani was writhing on the floor; the pieces of glass had cut his head, heart, and arms, and the blood was spirting up, as from so many fountains. But he soon collected all his strength. "After him—after him—why do you pause? Coppelius, Coppelius, has robbed me of my best automaton—a work of twenty years—body and soul set upon it—the clock-work—the speech—the walk, mine; the eyes stolen from you. The infernal rascal—after him; fetch Olympia—there you have the eyes!"

And now Nathaniel saw how a pair of eyes, which lay upon the ground, were staring at him; these Spalanzani caught up, with the unwounded hand, and flung against his heart. At this, madness seized him with its burning claws, and clutched into his soul, tearing to pieces all his thoughts and senses. "Ho—ho—ho—a circle of fire! of fire!—turn thyself round, circle! merrily, merrily, ho, thou wooden doll—turn thyself, pretty doll!" With these words he flew at the professor and pressed in his throat. He would have strangled him, had not the noise attracted many people, who rushed in, forced open Nathaniel's grasp, and thus saved the professor, whose wounds were bound immediately. Sigismund, strong as he was, was not able to master the mad Nathaniel, who with frightful voice kept crying out: "Turn thyself, wooden doll!" and struck around him with clenched fists. At last the combined force of many succeeded in overcoming him, in flinging him to the ground, and binding him. His words were merged into a hideous roar, like that of a brute, and raging in this insane condition he was taken to the mad-house.

Before, gentle reader, I proceed to tell thee what more befel the unfortunate Nathaniel, I can tell thee, in case thou takest an interest in the skilful optician and automaton-maker, Spalanzani, that he was completely healed of his wounds. He was, however, obliged to leave the university, because Nathaniel's story had created a sensation, and it was universally deemed an unpardonable imposition to smuggle wooden dolls instead of living persons into respectable tea-parties—for such Olympia had visited with success. The lawyers called it a most subtle deception, and the more culpable, inasmuch as he had planned it so artfully against the public, that not a single soul—a few cunning students excepted—had detected it, although all now wished to play the acute, and referred to various facts, which appeared to them suspicious. Nothing very clever was revealed in this way. For instance, could it strike any one as so very suspicious, that Olympia, according to the expression of an elegant tea-ite, had, contrary to all usage, sneezed oftener than she had yawned? "The former," remarked this elegant person, "was the self-winding-up of the concealed clockwork, which had, moreover, creaked audibly"—and so on. The professor of poetry and eloquence took a pinch of snuff, clapped first the lid of his box, cleared his throat, and said, solemnly, "Ladies and gentlemen, do you not perceive how the whole affair lies? It is all an allegory—a continued metaphor—you understand me—*Sapienti sat.*" But many were not satisfied with this; the story of the automaton had struck deep root into their souls, and, in fact, an abominable mistrust against human figures in general, began to creep in. Many lovers, to be quite convinced that they were not enamoured of wooden dolls, would request their mistress to sing and dance a little out of time, to embroider and knit, and play with their lap-dogs, while listening to reading, &c.; and, above all, not to listen merely, but also sometimes to talk, in such a manner as presupposed actual thought and feeling. With many did the bond of love become firmer, and more chaining, while others, on the contrary, slipped gently out of the noose. "One cannot really answer for this," said some. At tea-parties, yawning prevailed to an incredible extent, and there was no sneezing at all, that all suspicion might be avoided. Spalanzani, as already stated, was obliged to decamp, to escape the criminal prosecution for fraudulently introducing an automaton into human society. Coppola had vanished also.

Nathaniel awakened as from a heavy, frightful dream; he opened his eyes, and felt an indescribable sensation of pleasure streaming through him, with soft heavenly warmth. He was in bed in his own room, in his father's house, Clara was stooping over him, and Lothaire and his mother were standing near. "At last, at last, oh beloved Nathaniel, hast thou recovered from thy serious illness—now thou art again mine!" So spoke Clara, from the very depth of her soul, and clasped Nathaniel in her arms. But with mingled sorrow and delight did the brightly glowing tears fall from his eyes, and he deeply groaned forth: "My own—my own Clara!" Sigismund, who had faithfully remained with his friend in the hour of trouble, now entered. Nathaniel stretched out his hand to him. "And thou, faithful brother, hast not deserted me?" Every trace of Nathaniel's madness had vanished, and he soon gained strength amid the care of his mother, his beloved, and his friends. Good fortune also had visited the house, for an old penurious uncle, of whom nothing had been expected, had died, and had left the mother, besides considerable property, an estate in a pleasant spot near the town. Thither Nathaniel, with his Clara, whom he now thought of marrying, his mother, and Lothaire, desired to go. Nathaniel had now grown milder and more docile than he had ever been, and he now understood, for the first time, the heavenly purity and the greatness of Clara's mind. No one, by the slightest hint, reminded him of the past. Only, when Sigismund took leave of him, Nathaniel said: "Heavens, brother, I was in an evil way, but a good angel led me betimes to the path of light! Ah, that was Clara!" Sigismund did not let him carry the discourse further for fear that deeply wounding recollections might burst forth bright and flaming. It was about this time that the four happy persons thought of going to the estate. They were crossing, at noon, the streets of the city, where they had made several purchases, and the high steeple of the town-house already cast its gigantic shadow over the market-place. "Oh," said Clara, "let us ascend it once more, and look at the distant mountains!" No sooner said than done. Nathaniel and Clara both ascended the steps, the mother returned home with the servant, and Lothaire, not inclined to clamber up so many steps, chose to remain below. The two lovers stood arm in arm in the highest gallery of the tower, and looked down upon the misty forests, behind which the blue mountains were rising like a gigantic city.

"Look there at that curious little gray bush, which actually seems as if it were striding towards us," said Clara. Nathaniel mechanically put his hand into his breast pocket—he found Coppola's telescope, and he looked on one side. Clara was before the glass. There was a convulsive movement in his pulse and veins,—pale as death, he stared at Clara, but soon streams of fire flashed and glared from his rolling eyes, and he roared frightfully, like a hunted beast. Then he sprang high into the air, and, in the intervals of a horrible laughter, shrieked out, in a piercing tone, "Wooden doll—turn thyself!" Seizing Clara with immense force he wished to hurl her down, but with the energy of a desperate death-struggle she clutched the railings. Lothaire heard the raging of the madman—he heard Clara's shriek of agony—fearful forebodings darted through his mind, he ran up, the door of the second flight was fastened, and the shrieks of Clara became louder and louder.

Frantic with rage and anxiety, he dashed against the door, which, at last, burst open. Clara's voice became fainter and fainter. "Help—help—save me!"—with these words the voice seemed to die in the air. "She is gone—murdered by the madman!" cried Lothaire. The door of the gallery was also closed, but despair gave him a giant's strength, and he burst it from the hinges. Heavens—Clara, grasped by the mad Nathaniel, was hanging in the air over the gallery,—only with one hand she still held one of the iron railings. Quick as lightning Lothaire caught his sister, drew her in, and, at the same moment, struck the madman in the face with his clenched fist, so that he reeled and let go his prey.

Lothaire ran down with his fainting sister in his arms. She was saved. Nathaniel went raging about the gallery and bounded high in the air, crying, "Fire circle turn thyself—turn thyself!" The people collected at the sound of the wild shriek, and among them, prominent by his gigantic stature, was the advocate Coppelius, who had just come to the town, and was proceeding straight to the market-place. Some wished to ascend and secure the madman, but Coppelius laughed, saying, "Ha, ha,—only wait—he will soon come down of his own accord," and looked up like the rest. Nathaniel suddenly stood still as if petrified; he stooped down, perceived Coppelius, and yelling out, "Ah, pretty eyes—pretty eyes!"—he sprang over the railing.

When Nathaniel lay on the stone pavement, with his head shattered, Coppelius had disappeared in the crowd.

Many years afterwards it is said that Clara was seen in a remote spot, sitting hand in hand with a kind-looking man before the door of a country house, while two lively boys played before her. From this it may be inferred that she at last found that quiet domestic happiness which suited her serene and cheerful mind, and which the morbid Nathaniel would never have given her.

THE SHOT

Alexander Pushkin

Translated from the Russian by T. Keane

Alexander Sergeyevich Pushkin (1799–1837) was a Russian poet, play-wright, and novelist of the Romantic era who is considered by many to be the greatest Russian poet and the founder of modern Russian literature. Pushkin was fatally wounded in a duel with his brother-in-law, Georges-Charles de Heeckeren d'Anthès, also known as Dantes-Gekkern, a French officer serving with the Chevalier Guard Regiment who attempted to seduce the poet's wife, Natalia Pushkina. *Onegin* is a work of such complexity that, while only about a hundred pages long, translator Vladimir Nabokov needed two full volumes of material to fully render its meaning in English. Pushkin's matrilineal great grandfather was a black African page brought over to Russia as a slave. A man of honour, Pushkin is believed to have fought as many as twenty-nine duels.

I

We were stationed in the little town of N--. The life of an officer in the army is well known. In the morning, drill and the riding-school; dinner with the Colonel or at a Jewish restaurant; in the evening, punch and cards. In N--- there was not one open house, not a single marriageable girl. We used to meet in each other's rooms, where, except our uniforms, we never saw anything.

One civilian only was admitted into our society. He was about thirty-five years of age, and therefore we looked upon him as an old fellow. His experience gave him great advantage over us, and his habitual taciturnity, stern disposition, and caustic tongue produced a deep impression upon our young minds. Some mystery surrounded his existence; he had the appearance of a Russian, although his name was a foreign one. He had formerly served in the Hussars, and with distinction. Nobody knew the cause that had induced him to retire from the service and settle in a wretched little village, where he lived poorly and, at the same time, extravagantly. He always went on foot, and constantly wore a shabby black overcoat, but the officers of our regiment were ever welcome at his table. His dinners, it is true, never consisted of more than two or three dishes, prepared by a retired soldier, but the champagne flowed like water. Nobody knew what his circumstances were, or what his income was, and nobody dared to question him about them. He had a collection of books, consisting chiefly of works on military matters and a few novels. He willingly lent them to us to read, and never asked for them back; on the other hand, he never returned to the owner the books that were lent to him. His principal amusement was shooting with a pistol. The walls of his room were riddled with bullets, and were as full of holes as a honeycomb. A rich collection of pistols was the only luxury in the humble cottage where he lived. The skill which he had acquired with his favorite weapon was simply incredible: and if he had offered to shoot a pear off somebody's forage-cap, not a man in our regiment would have hesitated to place the object upon his head.

Our conversation often turned upon duels. Silvio—so I will call him—never joined in it. When asked if he had ever fought, he dryly replied that he had; but he entered into no particulars, and it was evident that such questions were not to his liking. We came to the conclusion that he had upon his conscience the memory of some unhappy victim of his terrible skill. Moreover, it never entered into the head of any of us to suspect him of anything like cowardice. There are persons whose mere look is sufficient to repel such a suspicion. But an unexpected incident occurred which astounded us all.

One day, about ten of our officers dined with Silvio. They drank as usual, that is to say, a great deal. After dinner we asked our host to hold the bank for a game at faro. For a long time he refused, for he hardly ever played, but at last he ordered cards to be brought, placed half a hundred ducats upon the table, and sat down to deal. We took our places round him, and the play began. It was Silvio's custom to preserve a complete silence when playing. He never disputed, and never entered into explanations. If the punter made a mistake in calculating, he immediately paid him the difference or noted down the surplus. We were acquainted with this habit of his, and we always allowed him to have his own way; but among us on this occasion was an officer who had only recently been transferred to our regiment. During the course of the game, this officer absently scored one point too many. Silvio took the chalk and noted down the correct account according to his usual custom. The officer, thinking that he had made a mistake, began to enter into explanations. Silvio continued dealing in silence. The officer, losing patience, took the brush and rubbed out what he considered was wrong. Silvio took the chalk and corrected the score again. The officer, heated with wine, play, and the laughter of his comrades, considered himself grossly insulted, and in his rage he seized a brass candlestick from the table, and hurled it at Silvio, who barely succeeded in avoiding the missile. We were filled with consternation. Silvio rose, white with rage, and with gleaming eyes, said:

"My dear sir, have the goodness to withdraw, and thank God that this has happened in my house."

None of us entertained the slightest doubt as to what the result would be, and we already looked upon our new comrade as a dead man. The officer withdrew, saying that he was ready to answer for his offence in whatever way the banker liked. The play went on for a few minutes longer, but feeling that our host was no longer interested in the game, we withdrew one after the other, and repaired to our respective quarters, after having exchanged a few words upon the probability of there soon being a vacancy in the regiment.

The next day, at the riding-school, we were already asking each other if the poor lieutenant was still alive, when he himself appeared among us. We put the same question to him, and he replied that he had not yet heard from Silvio. This astonished us. We went to Silvio's house and found him in the courtyard shooting bullet after bullet into an ace pasted upon the gate. He received us as usual, but did not utter a word about the event of the previous evening. Three days passed, and the lieutenant was still alive. We asked each other in astonishment: "Can it be possible that Silvio is not going to fight?"

Silvio did not fight. He was satisfied with a very lame explanation, and became reconciled to his assailant.

This lowered him very much in the opinion of all our young fellows. Want of courage is the last thing to be pardoned by young men, who usually look upon bravery as the chief of all human virtues, and the excuse for every possible fault. But, by degrees, everything became forgotten, and Silvio regained his former influence.

I alone could not approach him on the old footing. Being endowed by nature with a romantic imagination, I had become attached more than all the others to the man whose life was an enigma, and who seemed to me the hero of some mysterious drama. He was fond of me; at least, with me alone did he drop his customary sarcastic tone, and converse on different subjects in a simple and unusually agreeable manner. But after this unlucky evening, the thought that his honor had been tarnished, and that the stain had been allowed to remain upon it in accordance with his own wish, was ever present in my mind, and prevented me treating him as before. I was ashamed to look at him. Silvio was too intelligent and experienced not to observe this and guess the cause of it. This seemed to vex him; at least I observed once or twice a desire on his part to enter into an explanation with me, but I avoided such opportunities, and Silvio gave up the attempt. From that time forward I saw him only in the presence of my comrades, and our confidential conversations came to an end.

The inhabitants of the capital, with minds occupied by so many matters of business and pleasure, have no idea of the many sensations so familiar to the inhabitants of villages and small towns, as, for instance, awaiting the arrival of the post. On Tuesdays and Fridays our regimental bureau used to be filled with officers: some expecting money, some letters, and others newspapers. The packets were usually opened on the spot, items of news were communicated from one to another, and the bureau used to present a very animated picture. Silvio used to have his letters addressed to our regiment, and he was generally there to receive them.

One day he received a letter, the seal of which he broke with a look of great impatience. As he read the contents, his eyes sparkled. The officers, each occupied with his own letters, did not observe anything.

"Gentlemen," said Silvio, "circumstances demand my immediate departure; I leave to-night. I hope that you will not refuse to dine with me for the last time. I shall expect you, too," he added, turning towards me. "I shall expect you without fail."

With these words he hastily departed, and we, after agreeing to meet at Silvio's, dispersed to our various quarters.

I arrived at Silvio's house at the appointed time, and found nearly the whole regiment there. All his things were already packed; nothing remained but the bare, bullet-riddled walls. We sat down to table. Our host was in an excellent humor, and his gayety was quickly communicated to the rest. Corks popped every moment, glasses foamed incessantly, and, with the utmost warmth, we wished our departing friend a pleasant journey and every happiness. When we rose from the table it was already late in the evening. After having wished everybody good-bye, Silvio took me by the hand and detained me just at the moment when I was preparing to depart.

"I want to speak to you," he said in a low voice.

I stopped behind.

The guests had departed, and we two were left alone. Sitting down opposite each other, we silently lit our pipes. Silvio seemed greatly troubled; not a trace remained of his former convulsive gayety. The intense pallor of his face, his sparkling eyes, and the thick smoke issuing from his mouth, gave him a truly diabolical appearance. Several minutes elapsed, and then Silvio broke the silence.

"Perhaps we shall never see each other again," said he; "before we part, I should like to have an explanation with you. You may have observed that I care very little for the opinion of other people, but I like you, and I feel that it would be painful to me to leave you with a wrong impression upon your mind."

He paused, and began to knock the ashes out of his pipe. I sat gazing silently at the ground.

"You thought it strange," he continued, "that I did not demand satisfaction from that drunken idiot R---. You will admit, however, that having the choice of weapons, his life was in my hands, while my own was in no great danger. I could ascribe my forbearance to generosity alone, but I will not tell a lie. If I could have chastised R--- without the least risk to my own life, I should never have pardoned him."

I looked at Silvio with astonishment. Such a confession completely astounded me. Silvio continued:

"Exactly so: I have no right to expose myself to death. Six years ago I received a slap in the face, and my enemy still lives."

My curiosity was greatly excited.

"Did you not fight with him?" I asked. "Circumstances probably separated you."

"I did fight with him," replied Silvio; "and here is a souvenir of our duel."

Silvio rose and took from a cardboard box a red cap with a gold tassel and embroidery (what the French call a bonnet de police); he put it on—a bullet had passed through it about an inch above the forehead.

"You know," continued Silvio, "that I served in one of the Hussar regiments. My character is well known to you: I am accustomed to taking the lead. From my youth this has been my passion. In our time dissoluteness was the fashion, and I was the most outrageous man in the army. We used to boast of our drunkenness; I beat in a drinking bout the famous Bourtsoff [Footnote: A cavalry officer, notorious for his drunken escapades], of whom Denis Davidoff [Footnote: A military poet who flourished in the reign of Alexander I] has sung. Duels in our regiment were constantly taking place, and in all of them I was either second or principal. My comrades adored me, while the regimental commanders, who were constantly being changed, looked upon me as a necessary evil.

"I was calmly enjoying my reputation, when a young man belonging to a wealthy and distinguished family—I will not mention his name—joined our regiment. Never in my life have I met with such a fortunate fellow! Imagine to yourself youth, wit, beauty, unbounded gayety, the most reckless bravery, a famous name, untold wealth—imagine all these, and you can form some idea of the effect that he would be sure to produce among us. My supremacy was shaken. Dazzled by my reputation, he began to seek my friendship, but I received him coldly, and without the least regret he held aloof from me. I took a hatred to him. His success in the regiment and in the society of ladies brought me to the verge of despair. I began to seek a quarrel with him; to my epigrams he replied with epigrams which always seemed to me more spontaneous and more cutting than mine, and which were decidedly more amusing, for he joked while I fumed. At last, at a ball given by a Polish landed proprietor, seeing him the object of the attention of all the ladies, and especially of the mistress of the house, with whom I was upon very good terms, I whispered some grossly insulting remark in his ear. He flamed up and gave me a slap in the face. We grasped our swords; the ladies fainted; we were separated; and that same night we set out to fight.

"The dawn was just breaking. I was standing at the appointed place with my three seconds. With inexplicable impatience I awaited my opponent. The spring sun rose, and it was already growing hot. I saw him coming in the distance. He was walking on foot, accompanied by one second. We advanced to meet him. He approached, holding his cap filled with black cherries. The seconds measured twelve paces for us. I had to fire first, but my agitation was so great, that I could not depend upon the steadiness of my hand; and in order to give myself time to become calm, I ceded to him the first shot. My adversary would not agree to this. It was decided that we should cast lots. The first number fell to him, the constant favorite of fortune. He took aim, and his bullet went through my cap. It was now my turn. His life at last was in my hands; I looked at him eagerly, endeavoring to detect if only the faintest shadow of uneasiness. But he stood in front of my pistol, picking out the ripest cherries from his cap and spitting out the stones, which flew almost as far as my feet. His indifference annoyed me beyond measure. 'What is the use,' thought I, 'of depriving him of life, when he attaches no value whatever to it?' A malicious thought flashed through my mind. I lowered my pistol.

"'You don't seem to be ready for death just at present,' I said to him: 'you wish to have your breakfast; I do not wish to hinder you.'

"'You are not hindering me in the least,' replied he. 'Have the goodness to fire, or just as you please—the shot remains yours; I shall always be ready at your service.'

"I turned to the seconds, informing them that I had no intention of firing that day, and with that the duel came to an end.

"I resigned my commission and retired to this little place. Since then not a day has passed that I have not thought of revenge. And now my hour has arrived."

Silvio took from his pocket the letter that he had received that morning, and gave it to me to read. Some one (it seemed to be his business agent) wrote to him from Moscow, that a CERTAIN PERSON was going to be married to a young and beautiful girl.

"You can guess," said Silvio, "who the certain person is. I am going to Moscow. We shall see if he will look death in the face with as much indifference now, when he is on the eve of being married, as he did once with his cherries!"

With these words, Silvio rose, threw his cap upon the floor, and began pacing up and down the room like a tiger in his cage. I had listened to him in silence; strange conflicting feelings agitated me.

The servant entered and announced that the horses were ready. Silvio grasped my hand tightly, and we embraced each other. He seated himself in his telega, in which lay two trunks, one containing his pistols, the other his effects. We said good-bye once more, and the horses galloped off.

II

Several years passed, and family circumstances compelled me to settle in the poor little village of M---. Occupied with agricultural pursuits, I ceased not to sigh in secret for my former noisy and careless life. The most difficult thing of all was having to accustom myself to passing the spring and winter evenings in perfect solitude. Until the hour for dinner I managed to pass away the time somehow or other, talking with the bailiff, riding about to inspect the work, or going round to look at the new buildings; but as soon as it began to get dark, I positively did not know what to do with myself. The few books that I had found in the cupboards and storerooms I already knew by heart. All the stories that my housekeeper Kirilovna could remember I had heard over and over again. The songs of the peasant women made me feel depressed. I tried drinking spirits, but it made my head ache; and moreover, I confess I was afraid of becoming a drunkard from mere chagrin, that is to say, the saddest kind of drunkard, of which I had seen many examples in our district.

I had no near neighbors, except two or three topers, whose conversation consisted for the most part of hiccups and sighs. Solitude was preferable to their society. At last I decided to go to bed as early as possible, and to dine as late as possible; in this way I shortened the evening and lengthened out the day, and I found that the plan answered very well.

Four versts from my house was a rich estate belonging to the Countess B---; but nobody lived there except the steward. The Countess had only visited her estate once, in the first year of her married life, and then she had remained there no longer than a month. But in the second spring of my hermitical life a report was circulated that the Countess, with her husband, was coming to spend the summer on her estate. The report turned out to be true, for they arrived at the beginning of June.

The arrival of a rich neighbor is an important event in the lives of country people. The landed proprietors and the people of their households talk about it for two months beforehand and for three years afterwards. As for me, I must confess that the news of the arrival of a young and beautiful neighbor affected me strongly. I burned with impatience to see her, and the first Sunday after her arrival I set out after dinner for the village of A---, to pay my respects to the Countess and her husband, as their nearest neighbor and most humble servant. A lackey conducted me into the Count's study, and then went to announce me. The spacious apartment was furnished with every possible luxury. Around the walls were cases filled with books and surmounted by bronze busts; over the marble mantelpiece was a large mirror; on the floor was a green cloth covered with carpets. Unaccustomed to luxury in my own poor corner, and not having seen the wealth of other people for a long time, I awaited the appearance of the Count with some little trepidation, as a suppliant from the provinces awaits the arrival of the minister. The door opened, and a handsome-looking man, of about thirty-two years of age, entered the room. The Count approached me with a frank and friendly air; I endeavored to be self-possessed and began to introduce myself, but he anticipated me. We sat down. His conversation, which was easy and agreeable, soon dissipated my awkward bashfulness; and I was already beginning to recover my usual composure, when the Countess suddenly entered, and I became more confused than ever. She was indeed beautiful. The Count presented me. I wished to appear at ease, but the more I tried to assume an air of unconstraint, the more awkward I felt. They, in order to give me time to recover myself and to become accustomed to my new acquaintances, began to talk to each other, treating me as a good neighbor, and without ceremony. Meanwhile, I walked about the room, examining the books and pictures. I am no judge of pictures, but one of them attracted my attention. It represented some view in Switzerland, but it was not the painting that struck me, but the circumstance that the canvas was shot through by two bullets, one planted just above the other.

"A good shot that!" said I, turning to the Count.

"Yes," replied he, "a very remarkable shot. . . . Do you shoot well?" he continued.

"Tolerably," replied I, rejoicing that the conversation had turned at last upon a subject that was familiar to me. "At thirty paces I can manage to hit a card without fail,—I mean, of course, with a pistol that I am used to."

"Really?" said the Countess, with a look of the greatest interest. "And you, my dear, could you hit a card at thirty paces?"

"Some day," replied the Count, "we will try. In my time I did not shoot badly, but it is now four years since I touched a pistol."

"Oh!" I observed, "in that case, I don't mind laying a wager that Your Excellency will not hit the card at twenty paces; the pistol demands practice every day. I know that from experience. In our regiment I was reckoned one of the best shots. It once happened that I did not touch a pistol for a whole month, as I had sent mine to be mended; and would you believe it, Your Excellency, the first time I began to shoot again, I missed a bottle four times in succession at twenty paces. Our captain, a witty and amusing fellow, happened to be standing by, and he said to me: 'It is evident, my friend, that your hand will not lift itself against the bottle.' No, Your Excellency, you must not neglect to practise, or your hand will soon lose its cunning. The best shot that I ever met used to shoot at least three times every day before dinner. It was as much his custom to do this as it was to drink his daily glass of brandy."

The Count and Countess seemed pleased that I had begun to talk.

"And what sort of a shot was he?" asked the Count.

"Well, it was this way with him, Your Excellency: if he saw a fly settle on the wall—you smile, Countess, but, before Heaven, it is the truth—if he saw a fly, he would call out: 'Kouzka, my pistol!' Kouzka would bring him a loaded pistol— bang! and the fly would be crushed against the wall."

"Wonderful!" said the Count. "And what was his name?"

"Silvio, Your Excellency."

"Silvio!" exclaimed the Count, starting up. "Did you know Silvio?"

"How could I help knowing him, Your Excellency: we were intimate friends; he was received in our regiment like a brother officer, but it is now five years since I had any tidings of him. Then Your Excellency also knew him?"

"Oh, yes, I knew him very well. Did he ever tell you of one very strange incident in his life?"

"Does Your Excellency refer to the slap in the face that he received from some blackguard at a ball?"

"Did he tell you the name of this blackguard?"

"No, Your Excellency, he never mentioned his name, . . . Ah! Your Excellency!" I continued, guessing the truth: "pardon me . . . I did not know . . . could it really have been you?"

"Yes, I myself," replied the Count, with a look of extraordinary agitation; "and that bullet-pierced picture is a memento of our last meeting."

"Ah, my dear," said the Countess, "for Heaven's sake, do not speak about that; it would be too terrible for me to listen to."

"No," replied the Count: "I will relate everything. He knows how I insulted his friend, and it is only right that he should know how Silvio revenged himself."

The Count pushed a chair towards me, and with the liveliest interest I listened to the following story:

"Five years ago I got married. The first month—the honeymoon—I spent here, in this village. To this house I am indebted for the happiest moments of my life, as well as for one of its most painful recollections.

"One evening we went out together for a ride on horseback. My wife's horse became restive; she grew frightened, gave the reins to me, and returned home on foot. I rode on before. In the courtyard I saw a travelling carriage, and I was told that in my study sat waiting for me a man, who would not give his name, but who merely said that he had business with me. I entered the room and saw in the darkness a man, covered with dust and wearing a beard of several days' growth. He was standing there, near the fireplace. I approached him, trying to remember his features.

"'You do not recognize me, Count?' said he, in a quivering voice.

"'Silvio!' I cried, and I confess that I felt as if my hair had suddenly stood on end.

"'Exactly,' continued he. 'There is a shot due to me, and I have come to discharge my pistol. Are you ready?'

"His pistol protruded from a side pocket. I measured twelve paces and took my stand there in that corner, begging him to fire quickly, before my wife arrived. He hesitated, and asked for a light. Candles were brought in. I closed the doors, gave orders that nobody was to enter, and again begged him to fire. He drew out his pistol and took aim. . . . I counted the seconds. . . . I thought of her. . . . A terrible minute passed! Silvio lowered his hand.

"'I regret,' said he, 'that the pistol is not loaded with cherry-stones . . . the bullet is heavy. It seems to me that this is not a duel, but a murder. I am not accustomed to taking aim at unarmed men. Let us begin all over again; we will cast lots as to who shall fire first.'

"My head went round. . . . I think I raised some objection. . . . At last we loaded another pistol, and rolled up two pieces of paper. He placed these latter in his cap—the same through which I had once sent a bullet—and again I drew the first number.

"'You are devilish lucky, Count,' said he, with a smile that I shall never forget.

"I don't know what was the matter with me, or how it was that he managed to make me do it . . . but I fired and hit that picture."

The Count pointed with his finger to the perforated picture; his face glowed like fire; the Countess was whiter than her own handkerchief; and I could not restrain an exclamation.

"I fired," continued the Count, "and, thank Heaven, missed my aim. Then Silvio . . . at that moment he was really terrible . . . Silvio raised his hand to take aim at me. Suddenly the door opens, Masha rushes into the room, and with a loud shriek throws herself upon my neck. Her presence restored to me all my courage.

"'My dear,' said I to her, 'don't you see that we are joking? How frightened you are! Go and drink a glass of water and then come back to us; I will introduce you to an old friend and comrade.'

"Masha still doubted.

"'Tell me, is my husband speaking the truth?' said she, turning to the terrible Silvio: 'is it true that you are only joking?'

"'He is always joking, Countess,' replied Silvio: 'once he gave me a slap in the face in a joke; on another occasion he sent a bullet through my cap in a joke; and just now, when he fired at me and missed me, it was all in a joke. And now I feel inclined for a joke.'

"With these words he raised his pistol to take aim at me—right before her! Masha threw herself at his feet.

"'Rise, Masha; are you not ashamed!' I cried in a rage: 'and you, sir, will you cease to make fun of a poor woman? Will you fire or not?'

"'I will not,' replied Silvio: 'I am satisfied. I have seen your confusion, your alarm. I forced you to fire at me. That is sufficient. You will remember me. I leave you to your conscience.'

"Then he turned to go, but pausing in the doorway, and looking at the picture that my shot had passed through, he fired at it almost without taking aim, and disappeared. My wife had fainted away; the servants did not venture to stop him, the mere look of him filled them with terror. He went out upon the steps, called his coachman, and drove off before I could recover myself."

The Count was silent. In this way I learned the end of the story, whose beginning had once made such a deep impression upon me. The hero of it I never saw again. It is said that Silvio commanded a detachment of Hetairists during the revolt under Alexander Ipsilanti, and that he was killed in the battle of Skoulana.

THE SEVERED HAND

Wilhelm Hauff

Translated from the German by C. A. Feiling

> **Wilhelm Hauff** (1802–1827) was an extraordinarily prolific writer and poet, given that he died at the age of twenty-five, Hauff was considered among the most promising German writers of his generation. He was much inspired by the novels of Sir Walter Scott, whose work clearly influenced Hauff's historical novel of sixteenth-century Württemberg, *Lichtenstein*. He is well known in his home country for a series of fairy tales, which have had a lasting popularity.

I was born at Constantinople, where my father was a dragoman to the Sublime Porte, and carried on besides, a tolerably lucrative trade in perfumes and silks. He gave me a good education, partly instructing me himself, and partly engaging a priest of our religion for that purpose. He originally intended me for his own business, but as I displayed greater talents than he expected, he determined, by the advice of his friends, to make me a physician, being of opinion that a physician, if he has learned more than the common charlatans, could make his fortune in Constantinople. Our house was frequented by many Franks, one of whom urged my father to let me go to the city of Paris, in his native country, where people might study such things gratis and in the best manner, saying, he would take me with him for nothing when he returned thither.

My father, who in his youth had also travelled, agreed, and the Frank told me to be ready in three months. I was delighted beyond measure at the prospect of seeing foreign lands, and could scarcely await the time when we should embark. Having at length concluded all his business, the Frank prepared for his voyage, and on the evening previous to our departure my father took me to his lodgings. Here I saw beautiful dresses and arms lying on the table; but what most attracted my eyes was a large heap of gold, as I had never before seen so much together. My father embraced me, saying, "Behold, my son, I have provided these clothes for your voyage; those arms are yours, and they are the same your grandfather gave me when I went forth to foreign countries. I know you can wield them, but never use them excepting in self-defence, and then fight bravely. My fortune is not large; but see, I have divided it into three parts, of which one is yours, one shall be for my support and wants, but the third shall be sacred property, and devoted to the purpose of saving you in the hour of need." Thus spoke my aged father, and tears trembled in his eyes, perhaps from a certain presentiment, for I never saw him again.

Our voyage was prosperous; we soon reached the land of the Franks, and in six days' journey, after landing, we came to the great city of Paris. Here my Frankish friend hired a room and advised me to use proper discretion in laying out my money, which in all was two thousand thalers. I lived for three years in this city, and learned what every skilful physician ought to know; but I should not speak the truth were I to say that I liked the place, for the manners and customs of this people did not suit me. Moreover, I had but few friends, though these were indeed noble young men.

The desire of seeing my native country, at length, became strong; and having all this time heard nothing of my father, I seized a favourable opportunity to return home.

This opportunity was afforded me by an embassy from the land of the Franks to the Sublime Porte. I engaged myself as surgeon in the suite of the ambassador, and was fortunate enough to return to Constantinople. There I found my father's house closed, and the neighbours were astonished when they saw me, and told me that my father had died two months since. The priest who had instructed me in my youth brought me the keys of the now desolate house, which I entered alone and forsaken. I found every thing as my father had left it, only the money he had promised to bequeath me was not there. I inquired of the priest about it, who, with a bow, told me that my father had died as a holy man, since he had bequeathed all his money to the church.

The latter circumstance has ever since been inexplicable to me. Yet what could I do? I had no witnesses against the priest, and could not but consider myself fortunate that he had not also claimed as a legacy the house and goods of my father. This was the first calamity that befell me, but from that time misfortunes succeeded each other. My reputation as a physician spread but slowly, because I was ashamed to play the quack, and I wanted everywhere the recommendation of my father, who would have introduced me to the wealthiest and noblest persons, who now no longer thought of poor Zaleukos. Neither could I find customers for my father's goods, for all had gone elsewhere after his death, and new ones come but slowly. Once sadly reflecting on my situation it occurred to me that I had often seen in France men of my native land, who travelled through the country, exposing their goods in the market-places of the towns; I remembered that they easily found customers because they came from a foreign country, and that by such traffic one might profit a hundred-fold. My resolution was soon taken. I sold my father's house, gave part of the money I received for it to a tried friend to keep for me, and with the rest I purchased such things as are seldom seen in the west—viz: shawls, silks, ointments, and perfumes. Having engaged a berth in a ship, I thus set out on my second voyage to France. As soon as I had turned my back on the castles of the Dardanelles it seemed as if fortune would again smile on me. Our passage was short and prosperous.

I travelled through large and small towns, and found everywhere ready purchasers of my goods. My friend in Constantinople supplied me constantly with fresh goods, and I daily became more wealthy.

When at length I thought I had saved enough to risk a greater enterprise, I went to Italy. But I must here mention that I derived no small additional profit from the healing art. Whenever I entered a town, I announced, by bills, that a Greek physician had arrived, who had already cured many; and truly my balsams and medicines brought me in many a zechino. I now reached the city of Florence, in Italy, where I purposed remaining for some time, as I liked it much, and wished to recover from the fatigues of my travels. I hired a shop in the quarter called Santa Croce, and in an inn not far from thence two beautiful rooms which led to a balcony. Having made these arrangements, I had my bills placarded about, announcing myself as a physician and merchant. I had no sooner opened my shop than I had crowds of customers, and though my prices were rather high, I sold more than others, because I was civil and obliging to my customers. When I had thus pleasantly spent four days in Florence, I was one evening about closing my shop, and only had to examine my stock of boxes of ointments, as was my custom, when I found in a small jar a piece of paper which I did not recollect to have put there. On opening it I discovered that it was an invitation for me to appear that night at twelve o'clock precisely on the bridge called Ponte Vecchio. I conjectured a long time who it could possibly be that invited me thither, but, not knowing a soul in Florence, I thought some one wished, perhaps, to take me secretly to some sick person, which was not uncommon, and I therefore determined to go. However, I took the precaution to buckle on the sword my father had given me.

When it was near midnight I set out on my way, and soon arrived at the Ponte Vecchio. I found the bridge forsaken and lonely, and determined to await the person who had appointed to meet me.

It was a cold night, the moon shone brightly, and I looked down on the waves of the Arno, glistening in the moonlight. The church clocks now struck the midnight hour, I looked up and saw before me a tall man, enveloped in a red cloak, a corner of which he had drawn over his face.

At first, I was rather terrified, at his suddenly appearing behind me, but soon recovered myself, and said, "If you have summoned me hither, say what is your command." The Red Cloak turned round, and slowly said, "Follow me." I felt somewhat uneasy at the thought of following the stranger alone; so I stood still, saying, "Nay, sir, please first to tell me whither. Moreover, you might let me have a peep at your face, that I may see whether you intend any good with me." But the Red Cloak did not seem to mind my words, "If you will not follow, Zaleukos, stop where you are," he said, and then went on. Now my anger was roused, and I cried, "Think you a man like me, will submit to be tantalized by any fool, and to wait for nothing in a cold night like this?" In three leaps I overtook him, seized him by the cloak, and cried still louder, while grasping my sword with the other hand. But the cloak alone remained in my hand, and the stranger vanished round the next corner. My rage gradually subsided, but still I held the cloak, and this I expected would give me a clue to this singular adventure. I wrapped it round me, and walked home. When I was about a hundred paces from my house, some one passed close by me, and whispered to me in French, "Be on your guard, Count, there is nothing to be done to night." But before I could look round, this somebody had passed, and I only saw his shadow glide along the houses. That those words were addressed to the owner of the cloak and not to me was pretty evident, but this threw no light on the affair. The following morning, I considered what I should do. At first I intended to have the cloak cried, as if I had found it: on reflection, however, I thought the owner might send another person for it, and that I might still have no clue to the discovery. While thus considering, I looked at the cloak more narrowly; It was of heavy Genoese reddish purple velvet, edged with Astracan fur, and richly embroidered with gold. The sight of this splendid cloak suggested an idea to me, which I resolved to execute. I carried it to my shop, and exposed it for sale, but set upon it so high a price, that I felt sure I should not find a purchaser. My object in this was to look closely at every person who might ask the price; for I thought I could discover, among a thousand, the figure of the stranger, which after the loss of the cloak had shown itself to me distinctly, though but for a moment. Many came desirous of buying the cloak, the extraordinary beauty of which attracted every eye, but no one had the remotest resemblance to the stranger, and none would pay for it the high price of two-hundred zechinos. What struck me most was, that all whom I asked whether they had ever seen such a cloak in Florence before, replied in the negative, assuring me they had never seen such costly and tasteful work.

As evening approached, a young man came who had often been in my shop, and had also during the day made a handsome offer for it. He threw a purse of zechinos on the table, saying, "By Heavens, Zuleukos I must have your cloak, though it will beggar me!" At these words he counted down the gold. I was greatly embarrassed, having only exposed the cloak for sale in hopes of attracting the looks of its owner, and now comes a young madcap to pay the exorbitant price. But what could I do? I yielded; for the idea was pleasing of being so handsomely recompensed for my nocturnal adventure. The young man put on the cloak and went away; but returned at the door, as he took off a paper which was fastened to it, threw it to me, and said, "Here, Zaleukos is something which I think does not belong to the cloak." I took the paper carelessly, when behold! it contained these words:

"Bring the cloak to night at the usual hour to the Ponte Vecchio, and four hundred zechinos shall be yours." I was thunderstruck. Thus then I had trifled with my good luck, and utterly missed my aim; but I soon recovered, took the two-hundred zechinos, followed him, and said, "Take back your money, my friend, and leave me the cloak, I cannot possibly part with it." He thought at first I was joking, but when he perceived I was in earnest, he flew into a rage at my demand, called me a fool, and we at length came to blows. In the scuffle, I was fortunate enough to secure the cloak, and was about to run off with it, when the young man called the police to his assistance, and brought me before the magistrate. The latter was much surprised at the accusation, and awarded the cloak to my opponent. I now offered the young man twenty, fifty, eighty, nay, a hundred zechinos, if he would let me have it. My gold effected what my entreaties could not. He took my money, I went off triumphant with the cloak, and was obliged to submit to be called mad by all Florence. But I cared little for the opinion of the people, since I knew more than they, viz: that I still gained by my bargain.

I awaited the night with impatience. About the same time as before I went to the Ponte Vecchio, with the cloak under my arm. The figure approached me with the last stroke of the clock, and I could not be mistaken as to its identity. "Have you the cloak?" was the question. "I have, sir," I answered, "but it cost me a hundred zechinos." "I know it," he replied; "here are four hundred for it." With these words he stepped to the broad balustrade and counted down the gold, four hundred pieces, which sparkled beautifully in the moonlight; their glitter delighted my heart, which, alas! little imagined that this was its last joy. I put the money in my pocket, and was going to take a close survey of the kind unknown, but he had on a mask, through which his dark eyes flashed at me frightfully. "I thank you, sir, for your kindness," said I. "What else do you desire of me? for I must tell you beforehand that it must be nothing underhanded." "Unnecessary fear," he replied, as he wrapped the cloak round him. "I want your assistance as a physician, not, however, for one living, but for one who is dead."

"How can that be?" I exclaimed, astonished. He beckoned me to follow him, and related as follows: "I came here from foreign lands with my sister, and have lived with her at the house of a friend, where she died suddenly yesterday. Her relatives wish her to be buried to-morrow; and by an ancient custom in our family every member is to be buried in the vault of our ancestors, where many who died in foreign countries now repose embalmed. I wish to leave her body to our relations here, but must take to my father her head, at least, that he may see his daughter's face once more."

This custom of cutting off the head of beloved relatives seemed to me somewhat repulsive, but I did not venture to raise any objections, fearing to give offence to the stranger. I therefore told him that I well understood embalming the dead and begged him to take me to the deceased. At the same time I could not refrain from asking him why all this must be done so mysteriously, and in the night. To this he answered, that his relations, considering his intention as somewhat cruel, would prevent him if he attempted it during the daytime; but that if the head was once severed they would say little about it; that he, indeed, would have brought me the head himself had not a natural feeling deterred him from performing the operation.

In the meanwhile we arrived at a large, splendid mansion, which my companion pointed out as the end of our nocturnal walk. Passing the principal gate we entered the house by a small door, which he carefully fastened after him, and ascended, in the dark, a narrow winding staircase. This led to a faintly lighted corridor through which we came to an apartment, which was lighted by a lamp suspended from the ceiling.

In this apartment was a bed in which the corpse lay. The stranger averted his face and seemed anxious to hide his tears. Pointing to the bed, he ordered me to do my business well and expeditiously, and left the apartment.

I took my knives out of the case, which, as a doctor, I always carried, and approached the bed. Only the head of the corpse was visible; it was so beautiful that, involuntarily, I felt compassion in my inmost heart; the dark hair hung in long tresses over the pale face, and the eyes were closed. I commenced, according to the custom of surgeons when they amputate a limb, by making an incision in the skin. Then taking my sharpest knife I cut the throat with one stroke. Oh! horror! the dead opened her eyes, but closed them again immediately, and with one deep sigh now breathed forth her life. At the same time a stream of hot blood gushed over me from the wound. I was convinced that I only had killed the poor lady. That she was dead now I could no longer doubt, since such a wound was sure to be fatal. I stood for some minutes in fearful anxiety as to what I had done. Had the Red Cloak imposed on me, or had his sister only been apparently dead?

The latter seemed to me the more probable, but I dare not tell the brother of the dead that a less speedy cut would perhaps have aroused her without killing her. I was going, therefore, to sever the head entirely, when the dying lady once more groaned, stretched herself in painful convulsions, and then expired. Overcome by terror, I rushed shuddering from the apartment. It was dark in the corridor without, the lamp was extinguished, no trace of my companion was to be discovered, and I was obliged to grope my way along the wall at hazard in order to reach the winding staircase. I found it at length, and hurried down precipitately. There was no one visible below, the door was ajar, and when I reached the street I breathed more freely, having felt oppressed with horror in the house. Spurred on by terror, I hastened towards my lodging and buried myself in the pillows of my couch, to forget the atrocious deed I had perpetrated. But sleep fled from me, and the morning first summoned me to composure. It seemed to me probable that the man who had seduced me to the fearful act, as it now appeared to me, would not inform against me. I determined to go into my shop to business and assume, if possible, a cheerful air. But alas! a new circumstance which I observed only now, increased my anxiety; I missed my cap and belt, as well as the knives, and was uncertain whether I had left them in the apartment of the murdered lady, or had lost them in my flight. The former, unfortunately, seemed more probable, and the knives would therefore betray me as the murderer.

I opened my shop at the usual time, and my neighbour came in, as he usually did in the morning, being fond of a chat. "Well, neighbour," said he, "what do you think of this horrible occurrence which took place last night?" I pretended not to know any thing about it. "What! do you pretend not to know what is known all over the town? Not to know that the fairest flower in Florence, Bianca, the daughter of the governor, was murdered last night?" Ah me! I saw her even yesterday go in her carriage with her bridegroom, for it was only yesterday she was married. Every word spoken by my neighbour was a dagger in my heart. How often were these my tortures renewed, for each of my customers repeated the story, one painting it more frightfully than the other, though none could speak all the horrors I had myself witnessed. About noon an officer from the magistrate entered my shop, and requesting me to dismiss the customers, and, producing the things I missed, he said, "Senore Zaleukos, do you own these things?" I hesitated a moment whether I had not better disown them altogether, but seeing through the half-open door my landlord and several acquaintances, who might perhaps witness against me, I determined not to aggravate the affair by telling a falsehood, and so owned the things produced. The officer desired me to follow him, and led me to a large building, which I soon recognised as a prison. He showed me into an apartment to await further orders.

My situation was terrible as I reflected on it in my solitude; the thought of having committed murder, though unintentionally, constantly returned. Neither could I deny to myself that the glitter of gold had captivated my senses, or I could not so easily have been caught in the snare. Two hours after my arrest, I was led from my room up several staircases into a large hall. Twelve persons, mostly old men, were sitting at a round table, covered with black cloth. Along the walls stood benches occupied by the nobility of Florence. In the galleries above stood the spectators, densely crowded together. When I stepped to the table, a man, with a gloomy and melancholy expression of countenance, rose: it was the president of the tribunal. Addressing the assembly, he said, that as the father of the murdered, he could not pass judgment in this matter, and therefore, ceded his place to the senior of the senators. The latter was an aged man of at least ninety years. He was bent with age, and his temples were scantily covered with a few white hairs, but his eyes still burned with lustre, and his voice was strong and firm. He began by asking me whether I confessed the murder? I demanded to be heard, and fearlessly, and in a very audible voice, related what I had done, and what I knew. I observed that the president, during my statement, was alternately flushed and pale, and that when I concluded, he started up furiously, crying to me, "What, wretch! Do you wish to charge the crime you committed from avarice upon another?" The senator called him to order for his interruption, as he had voluntarily resigned his right of judgment, remarking, moreover, that it was by no means proved that I committed the crime from avarice, as, by his own deposition, nothing had been stolen from the murdered. Indeed, he went still further, declaring that the president must give an account of the life of his daughter, for that only could enable them to determine whether I had spoken the truth or not. He now dismissed the court for that day to consult, as he said, the papers of the deceased, which the president would deliver to him.

I was again led back to my prison where I spent a sorrowful day, still ardently hoping that some connexion between the dead lady and the Red Cloak might be discovered. Full of this hope I entered the judgment hall the following day. Several letters lay on the table, and the aged senator asked me whether they were written by me. I looked at them, and found they must be by the same hand as the two slips of paper I had received. This I stated to the senate, but they did not seem to regard it, and answered that I could, and must, have written both, the initial on both letters being evidently a Z, the initial letter of my name. The letters contained menaces to the deceased, and warnings against the marriage which she was about to contract.

The president appeared to have given singular information respecting my person, for they treated me on this day more suspiciously and severely. In justification of myself I appealed to my papers which must be found in my lodgings, but they told me that they had searched and found nothing. Thus, at the closing of the court, all my hopes vanished, and when, on the third day, I was again led into the hall, the sentence was read to me that I was convicted of premeditated murder and was to die. To this condition had I come! Forsaken by all that was dear on earth, far distant from my native country, I was, though innocent, to die by the axe in the flower of youth. As I was sitting in my lonely dungeon on the evening of this terrible day that had decided my fate, all my hopes having fled, and all my thoughts being seriously fixed on death, the door opened and a man entered, who looked silently at me for a long time.

"Do I thus find you again, Zaleukos?" said he.

The faint glimmer of my lamp prevented me from recognising him, but the sound of his voice awakened in me recollections of former days. It was Valetti, one of the few friends I had known in Paris while there pursuing my studies. He told me that he happened to come to Florence where his father lived much respected, that he had heard my history, and had come to see me once more, and to learn from me how I could have committed such a heavy crime. I told him the whole story. He seemed much astonished, and conjured me to tell him, my only friend, every thing, that I might not depart this life with a lie on my conscience. I swore to him with a most solemn oath that I had spoken the truth, and that no other guilt oppressed me, but that, being dazzled by the gold, I had not at once recognised the improbability of the stranger's story.

"You did not then know Bianca?" he asked.

I assured him I had never seen her. Valetti now related to me that a deep secret was connected with the deed, that the president had very much hastened my sentence, and that a report was circulated that I had long known Bianca, and now had murdered her out of revenge for her marrying another. I observed to him, that all this applied well to the Red Cloak, but that I could not prove his participation in the deed. Valetti embraced me, weeping, and promised to do all in his power to save my life at least. I had little hope, though I knew him to be a wise man and well conversant in the law, and that he would not fail to do his utmost to save me. For two long days I remained in suspense; at length he came and exclaimed, "I bring a consolation though a sad one. You will live to be free, but must lose one hand." Deeply affected, I thanked my friend for having saved my life. He told me the president had been inexorable as to granting a new investigation into the affair, but, that he might not appear unjust, he at length agreed that if they could find a similar case in the annals of Florence, my punishment should be according to that awarded in such a case. He, therefore, with his father had now read day and night in the archives, and had, at length, found a case similar to mine, the punishment for which was that the perpetrator should have his left hand cut off, his property confiscated, and that he himself should be banished for life. This was now my sentence, and I was to prepare for the painful moment which awaited me. I will spare you this terrible moment: in the open market-place I placed my hand on the block, and my own blood gushed over me.

When all was over, Valetti took me to his house until my recovery was completed, and then nobly provided me with money for my journey, for all I had earned with so much labour had been taken from me. From Florence I went to Sicily, and thence by the first ship to Constantinople. Here I hoped to find the sum of money I had left with my friend, and begged him to receive me into his house, but what was my astonishment when he inquired why I did not take possession of my own? He informed me that a stranger had purchased a house in my name in the quarter of the Greeks, and had told the neighbours that I was soon coming. I immediately repaired thither with my friend, and was joyfully welcomed by all my old acquaintance. An aged merchant gave me a letter that had been left by the purchaser of the house for me. Its contents were as follows:

"Zaleukos! Two hands shall be constantly ready to work for you that you may not feel the loss of the one. The house you now own with all in it is yours, and you will receive every year sufficient to make you rank among the wealthy of your countrymen. May you forgive him who is more wretched than yourself!"

I could guess who was the writer of these lines, and the merchant told me, on inquiry, that he took the stranger, who wore a red cloak, for a Frank. I now knew sufficient to convince me that the stranger was not devoid of generous feelings. I found all in my new house arranged admirably, and also a shop with goods more beautiful than I ever possessed. Ten years have now elapsed, and I have continued my commercial travels more from former habit than necessity, yet I have never again seen the country where I met such a misfortune. Ever since I have annually received a thousand gold pieces, but though I rejoice to know that that unfortunate man is generous, he cannot with his money relieve my soul from its grief, for the awful picture of the murdered Bianca will for ever be present with me.

IMMENSEE

Theodor W. Storm

Translated from the German by C. W. Bell

Theodor W. Storm (1817–1888). Born in Husum, Schleswig, a town he dismissed as "the grey town by the grey sea", Storm was one of the most important figures in nineteenth-century German poetic realism. He was forced to move to Potsdam, where he spent a decade while Schleswig was occupied by Denmark, but returned when the occupation ended in 1863. A year later, the death of his wife, Constanza, prompted him to write a searing cycle of poems, *Tiefe Schatten* (Deep Shadows) and thereafter he primarily wrote novellas, the best known of which are *Immensee* and *The Rider on the White Horse.*

THE OLD MAN

One afternoon in the late autumn a well-dressed old man was walking slowly down the street. He appeared to be returning home from a walk, for his buckle-shoes, which followed a fashion long since out of date, were covered with dust.

Under his arm he carried a long, gold-headed cane; his dark eyes, in which the whole of his long-lost youth seemed to have centred, and which contrasted strangely with his snow-white hair, gazed calmly on the sights around him or peered into the town below as it lay before him, bathed in the haze of sunset. He appeared to be almost a stranger, for of the passers-by only a few greeted him, although many a one involuntarily was compelled to gaze into those grave eyes.

At last he halted before a high, gabled house, cast one more glance out toward the town, and then passed into the hall. At the sound of the door-bell some one in the room within drew aside the green curtain from a small window that looked out on to the hall, and the face of an old woman was seen behind it. The man made a sign to her with his cane.

"No light yet!" he said in a slightly southern accent, and the housekeeper let the curtain fall again.

The old man now passed through the broad hall, through an inner hall, wherein against the walls stood huge oaken chests bearing porcelain vases; then through the door opposite he entered a small lobby, from which a narrow staircase led to the upper rooms at the back of the house. He climbed the stairs slowly, unlocked a door at the top, and landed in a room of medium size.

It was a comfortable, quiet retreat. One of the walls was lined with cupboards and bookcases; on the other hung pictures of men and places; on a table with a green cover lay a number of open books, and before the table stood a massive arm-chair with a red velvet cushion.

After the old man had placed his hat and stick in a corner, he sat down in the arm-chair and, folding his hands, seemed to be taking his rest after his walk. While he sat thus, it was growing gradually darker; and before long a moonbeam came streaming through the window-panes and upon the pictures on the wall; and as the bright band of light passed slowly onward the old man followed it involuntarily with his eyes.

Now it reached a little picture in a simple black frame. "Elisabeth!" said the old man softly; and as he uttered the word, time had changed: he was young again.

THE CHILDREN

Before very long the dainty form of a little maiden advanced toward him. Her name was Elisabeth, and she might have been five years old. He himself was twice that age. Round her neck she wore a red silk kerchief which was very becoming to her brown eyes.

"Reinhard!" she cried, "we have a holiday, a holiday! No school the whole day and none to-morrow either!"

Reinhard was carrying his slate under his arm, but he flung it behind the front door, and then both the children ran through the house into the garden and through the garden gate out into the meadow. The unexpected holiday came to them at a most happily opportune moment.

It was in the meadow that Reinhard, with Elisabeth's help, had built a house out of sods of grass. They meant to live in it during the summer evenings; but it still wanted a bench. He set to work at once; nails, hammer, and the necessary boards were already to hand.

While he was thus engaged, Elisabeth went along the dyke, gathering the ring-shaped seeds of the wild mallow in her apron, with the object of making herself chains and necklaces out of them; so that when Reinhard had at last finished his bench in spite of many a crookedly hammered nail, and came out into the sunlight again, she was already wandering far away at the other end of the meadow.

"Elisabeth!" he called, "Elisabeth!" and then she came, her hair streaming behind her.

"Come here," he said; "our house is finished now. Why, you have got quite hot! Come in, and let us sit on the new bench. I will tell you a story."

So they both went in and sat down on the new bench. Elisabeth took the little seed-rings out of her apron and strung them on long threads. Reinhard began his tale: "There were once upon a time three spinning-women . . ."[1]

"Oh!" said Elisabeth, "I know that off by heart; you really must not always tell me the same story."

Accordingly Reinhard had to give up the story of the three spinning-women and tell instead the story of the poor man who was cast into the den of lions.

"It was now night," he said, "black night, you know, and the lions were asleep.

---

1 The beginning of one of the best known of Grimm's fairy tales.

But every now and then they would yawn in their sleep and shoot out their red tongues. And then the man would shudder and think it was morning. All at once a bright light fell all about him, and when he looked up an angel was standing before him. The angel beckoned to him with his hand and then went straight into the rocks."

Elisabeth had been listening attentively. "An angel?" she said. "Had he wings then?"

"It is only a story," answered Reinhard; "there are no angels, you know."

"Oh, fie! Reinhard!" she said, staring him straight in the face.

He looked at her with a frown, and she asked him hesitatingly: "Well, why do they always say there are? Mother, and aunt, and at school as well?"

"I don't know," he answered.

"But tell me," said Elisabeth, "are there no lions either?"

"Lions? Are there lions? In India, yes. The heathen priests harness them to their carriages, and drive about the desert with them. When I'm big, I mean to go out there myself. It is thousands of times more beautiful in that country than it is here at home; there's no winter at all there. And you must come with me. Will you?"

"Yes," said Elisabeth; "but mother must come with us, and your mother as well."

"No," said Reinhard, "they will be too old then, and cannot come with us."

"But I mayn't go by myself."

"Oh, but you may right enough; you will then really be my wife, and the others will have no say in the matter."

"But mother will cry!"

"We shall come back again of course," said Reinhard impetuously. "Now just tell me straight out, will you go with me? If not, I will go all alone, and then I shall never come back again."

The little girl came very near to crying. "Please don't look so angry," said she; "I will go to India with you."

Reinhard seized both her hands with frantic glee, and rushed out with her into the meadow.

"To India, to India!" he sang, and swung her round and round, so that her little red kerchief was whirled from off her neck. Then he suddenly let her go and said solemnly:

"Nothing will come of it, I'm sure; you haven't the pluck."

"Elisabeth! Reinhard!" some one was now calling from the garden gate.

"Here we are!" the children answered, and raced home hand in hand.

IN THE WOODS

So the children lived together. She was often too quiet for him, and he was often too head-strong for her, but for all that they stuck to one another. They spent nearly all their leisure hours together: in winter in their mothers' tiny rooms, during the summer in wood and field.

Once when Elisabeth was scolded by the teacher in Reinhard's hearing, he angrily banged his slate upon the table in order to turn upon himself the master's wrath. This failed to attract attention.

But Reinhard paid no further attention to the geography lessons, and instead he composed a long poem, in which he compared himself to a young eagle, the schoolmaster to a grey crow, and Elisabeth to a white dove; the eagle vowed vengeance on the grey crow, as soon as his wings had grown.

Tears stood in the young poet's eyes: he felt very proud of himself. When he reached home he contrived to get hold of a little parchment-bound volume with a lot of blank pages in it; and on the first pages he elaborately wrote out his first poem.

Soon after this he went to another school. Here he made many new friendships among boys of his own age, but this did not interrupt his comings and goings with Elisabeth. Of the stories which he had formerly told her over and over again he now began to write down the ones which she had liked best, and in doing so the fancy often took him to weave in something of his own thoughts; yet, for some reason he could not understand, he could never manage it.

So he wrote them down exactly as he had heard them himself. Then he handed them over to Elisabeth, who kept them carefully in a drawer of her writing-desk, and now and again of an evening when he was present it afforded him agreeable satisfaction to hear her reading aloud to her mother these little tales out of the notebooks in which he had written them.

Seven years had gone by. Reinhard was to leave the town in order to proceed to his higher education. Elisabeth could not bring herself to think that there would now be a time to be passed entirely without Reinhard. She was delighted when he told her one day that he would continue to write out stories for her as before; he would send them to her in the letters to his mother, and then she would have to write back to him and tell him how she liked them.

The day of departure was approaching, but ere it came a good deal more poetry found its way into the parchment-bound volume. This was the one secret he kept from Elisabeth, although she herself had inspired the whole book and most of the songs, which gradually had filled up almost half of the blank pages.

It was the month of June, and Reinhard was to start on the following day. It was proposed to spend one more festive day together and therefore a picnic was arranged for a rather large party of friends in an adjacent forest.

It was an hour's drive along the road to the edge of the wood, and there the company took down the provision baskets from the carriages and walked the rest of the way. The road lay first of all through a pine grove, where it was cool and darksome, and the ground was all strewed with pine needles.

After half an hour's walk they passed out of the gloom of the pine trees into a bright fresh beech wood. Here everything was light and green; every here and there a sunbeam burst through the leafy branches, and high above their heads a squirrel was leaping from branch to branch.

The party came to a halt at a certain spot, over which the topmost branches of ancient beech trees interwove a transparent canopy of leaves. Elisabeth's mother opened one of the baskets, and an old gentleman constituted himself quarter-master.

"Round me, all of you young people," he cried, "and attend carefully to what

I have to say to you. For lunch each one of you will now get two dry rolls; the butter has been left behind at home. The extras every one must find for himself. There are plenty of strawberries in the wood—that is, for anyone who knows where to find them. Unless you are sharp, you'll have to eat dry bread; that's the way of the world all over. Do you understand what I say?"

"Yes, yes," cried the young folks.

"Yes, but look here," said the old gentleman, "I have not done yet. We old folks have done enough roaming about in our time, and therefore we will stay at home now, here, I mean, under these wide-spreading trees, and we'll peel the potatoes and make a fire and lay the table, and by twelve o'clock the eggs shall be boiled.

"In return for all this you will be owing us half of your strawberries, so that we may also be able to serve some dessert. So off you go now, east and west, and mind be honest."

The young folks cast many a roguish glance at one another.

"Wait," cried the old gentleman once again. "I suppose I need not tell you this, that whoever finds none need not produce any; but take particular note of this, that he will get nothing out of us old folks either. Now you have had enough good advice for to-day; and if you gather strawberries to match you will get on very well for the present at any rate."

The young people were of the same opinion, and pairing off in couples set out on their quest.

"Come along, Elisabeth," said Reinhard, "I know where there is a clump of strawberry bushes; you shan't eat dry bread."

Elisabeth tied the green ribbons of her straw hat together and hung it on her arm. "Come on, then," she said, "the basket is ready."

Off into the wood they went, on and on; on through moist shady glens, where everything was so peaceful, except for the cry of the falcon flying unseen in the heavens far above their heads; on again through the thick brushwood, so thick that Reinhard must needs go on ahead to make a track, here snapping off a branch, there bending aside a trailing vine. But ere long he heard Elisabeth behind him calling out his name. He turned round.

"Reinhard!" she called, "do wait for me! Reinhard!"

He could not see her, but at length he caught sight of her some way off struggling with the undergrowth, her dainty head just peeping out over the tops of the ferns. So back he went once more and brought her out from the tangled mass of briar and brake into an open space where blue butterflies fluttered among the solitary wood blossoms.

Reinhard brushed the damp hair away from her heated face, and would have tied the straw hat upon her head, but she refused; yet at his earnest request she consented after all.

"But where are your strawberries?" she asked at length, standing still and drawing a deep breath.

"They were here," he said, "but the toads have got here before us, or the martens, or perhaps the fairies."

"Yes," said Elisabeth, "the leaves are still here; but not a word about fairies in this place. Come along, I'm not a bit tired yet; let us look farther on."

In front of them ran a little brook, and on the far side the wood began again.

Reinhard raised Elisabeth in his arms and carried her over. After a while they emerged from the shady foliage and stood in a wide clearing.

"There must be strawberries here," said the girl, "it all smells so sweet."

They searched about the sunny spot, but they found none. "No," said Reinhard, "it is only the smell of the heather."

Everywhere was a confusion of raspberry-bushes and holly, and the air was filled with a strong smell of heather, patches of which alternated with the short grass over these open spaces.

"How lonely it is here!" said Elisabeth. "I wonder where the others are?"

Reinhard had never thought of getting back.

"Wait a bit," he said, holding his hand aloft; "where is the wind coming from?" But wind there was none.

"Listen!" said Elisabeth, "I think I heard them talking. Just give a call in that direction."

Reinhard hollowed his hand and shouted: "Come here!"

"Here!" was echoed back.

"They answered," cried Elisabeth clapping her hands.

"No, that was nothing; it was only the echo."

Elisabeth seized Reinhard's hand. "I'm frightened!" she said.

"Oh! no, you must not be frightened. It is lovely here. Sit down there in the shade among the long grass. Let us rest awhile: we'll find the others soon enough."

Elisabeth sat down under the overhanging branch of a beech and listened intently in every direction. Reinhard sat a few paces off on a tree stump, and gazed over at her in silence.

The sun was just above their heads, shining with the full glare of midday heat. Tiny, gold-flecked, steel-blue flies poised in the air with vibrating wings. Their ears caught a gentle humming and buzzing all round them, and far away in the wood were heard now and again the tap-tap of the woodpecker and the screech of other birds.

"Listen," said Elisabeth, "I hear a bell."

"Where?" asked Reinhard.

"Behind us. Do you hear it? It is striking twelve o'clock."

"Then the town lies behind us, and if we go straight through in this direction we are bound to fall in with the others."

So they started on their homeward way; they had given up looking for strawberries, for Elisabeth had become tired. And at last there rang out from among the trees the laughing voices of the picnic party; then they saw too a white cloth spread gleaming on the ground; it was the luncheon-table and on it were strawberries enough and to spare.

The old gentleman had a table-napkin tucked in his button-hole and was continuing his moral sermon to the young folks and vigorously carving a joint of roast meat.

"Here come the stragglers," cried the young people when they saw Reinhard and Elisabeth advancing among the trees.

"This way," shouted the old gentleman. "Empty your handkerchiefs, upside down, with your hats! Now show us what you have found."

"Only hunger and thirst," said Reinhard.

"If that's all," replied the old man, lifting up and showing them the bowl full of fruit, "you must keep what you've got. You remember the agreement: nothing here for lazybones to eat."

But in the end he was prevailed on to relent; the banquet proceeded, and a thrush in a juniper bush provided the music.

So the day passed. But Reinhard had, after all, found something, and though it was not strawberries yet it was something that had grown in the wood. When he got home this is what he wrote in his old parchment-bound volume:

> Out on the hill-side yonder
>   The wind to rest is laid;
> Under the drooping branches
>   There sits the little maid.
> She sits among the wild thyme,
>   She sits in the fragrant air;
> The blue flies hum around her,
>   Bright wings flash everywhere.
> And through the silent woodland
>   She peers with watchful eyen,
> While on her hazel ringlets
>   Sparkles the glad sunshine.
> And far, far off the cuckoo
>   Laughs out his song.
> I ween Hers are the bright, the golden
>   Eyes of the woodland queen.

So she was not only his little sweetheart, but was also the expression of all that was lovely and wonderful in his opening life.

BY THE ROADSIDE THE CHILD STOOD

The time is Christmas Eve. Before the close of the afternoon Reinhard and some other students were sitting together at an old oak table in the Ratskeller.[2]

The lamps on the wall were lighted, for down here in the basement it was already growing dark; but there was only a thin sprinkling of customers present, and the waiters were leaning idly up against the pillars let into the walls.

In a corner of the vaulted room sat a fiddler and a fine-featured gipsy-girl with a zither; their instruments lay in their laps, and they seemed to be looking about them with an air of indifference.

A champagne cork popped off at the table occupied by the students. "Drink, my gipsy darling!" cried a young man of aristocratic appearance, holding out to the girl a glass full of wine.

"I don't care about it," she said, without altering her position.

---

2 The basement of the *Rathaus* or Town Hall. This, in almost every German town of importance, has become a restaurant and place of refreshment.

"Well, then, give us a song," cried the young nobleman, and threw a silver coin into her lap. The girl slowly ran her fingers through her black hair while the fiddler whispered in her ear. But she threw back her head, and rested her chin on her zither.

"For him," she said, "I'm not going to play."

Reinhard leapt up with his glass in his hand and stood in front of her.

"What do you want?" she asked defiantly.

"To have a look at your eyes."

"What have my eyes to do with you?"

Reinhard's glance flashed down on her. "I know they are false."

She laid her cheek in the palm of her hand and gave him a searching look. Reinhard raised his glass to his mouth.

"Here's to your beautiful, wicked eyes!" he said, and drank.

She laughed and tossed her head.

"Give it here," she said, and fastening her black eyes on his, she slowly drank what was left in the glass. Then she struck a chord and sang in a deep, passionate voice:

> To-day, to-day thou think'st me
>   Fairest maid of all;
> To-morrow, ah! then beauty
>   Fadeth past recall.
> While the hour remaineth,
>   Thou art yet mine own;
> Then when death shall claim me,
>   I must die alone.

While the fiddler struck up an allegro finale, a new arrival joined the group.

"I went to call for you, Reinhard," he said. "You had already gone out, but Santa Claus had paid you a visit."

"Santa Claus?" said Reinhard. "Santa Claus never comes to me now."

"Oh, yes, he does! The whole of your room smelt of Christmas tree and ginger cakes."

Reinhard dropped the glass out of his hand and seized his cap.

"Well, what are you going to do now?" asked the girl.

"I'll be back in a minute."

She frowned. "Stay," she said gently, casting an amorous glance at him.

Reinhard hesitated. "I can't," he said.

She laughingly gave him a tap with the toe of her shoe and said: "Go away, then, you good-for-nothing; you are one as bad as the other, all good-for-nothings." And as she turned away from him, Reinhard went slowly up the steps of the Ratskeller.

Outside in the street deep twilight had set in; he felt the cool winter air blowing on his heated brow. From some window every here and there fell the bright gleam of a Christmas tree all lighted up, now and then was heard from within some room the sound of little pipes and tin trumpets mingled with the merry din of children's voices.

Crowds of beggar children were going from house to house or climbing up on to the railings of the front steps, trying to catch a glimpse through the window of a splendour that was denied to them. Sometimes too a door would suddenly be flung open, and scolding voices would drive a whole swarm of these little visitors away out into the dark street. In the vestibule of yet another house they were singing an old Christmas carol, and little girls' clear voices were heard among the rest.

But Reinhard heard not; he passed quickly by them all, out of one street into another. When he reached his lodging it had grown almost quite dark; he stumbled up the stairs and so gained his apartment.

A sweet fragrance greeted him; it reminded him of home; it was the smell of the parlour in his mother's house at Christmas time. With trembling hand he lit his lamp; and there lay a mighty parcel on the table. When he opened it, out fell the familiar ginger cakes. On some of them were the initial letters of his name written in sprinkles of sugar; no one but Elisabeth could have done that.

Next came to view a little parcel containing neatly embroidered linen, handkerchiefs and cuffs; and finally letters from his mother and Elisabeth. Reinhard opened Elisabeth's letter first, and this is what she wrote:

"The pretty sugared letters will no doubt tell you who helped with the cakes. The same person also embroidered the cuffs for you. We shall have a very quiet time at home this Christmas Eve. Mother always puts her spinning-wheel away in the corner as early as half-past nine. It is so very lonesome this winter now that you are not here.

"And now, too, the linnet you made me a present of died last Sunday.

It made me cry a good deal, though I am sure I looked after it well.

"It always used to sing of an afternoon when the sun shone on its cage. You remember how often mother would hang a piece of cloth over the cage in order to keep it quiet when it sang so lustily.

"Thus our room is now quieter than ever, except that your old friend Eric now drops in to see us occasionally. You told us once that he was just like his brown top-coat. I can't help thinking of it every time he comes in at the door, and it is really too funny; but don't tell mother, it might easily make her angry.

"Guess what I am giving your mother for a Christmas present! You can't guess? Well, it is myself! Eric is making a drawing of me in black chalk; I have had to give him three sittings, each time for a whole hour.

"I simply loathed the idea of a stranger getting to know my face so well. Nor did I wish it, but mother pressed me, and said it would very much please dear Frau Werner.

"But you are not keeping your word, Reinhard. You haven't sent me any stories. I have often complained to your mother about it, but she always says you now have more to do than to attend to such childish things. But I don't believe it; there's something else perhaps."

After this Reinhard read his mother's letter, and when he had read them both and slowly folded them up again and put them away, he was overcome with an irresistible feeling of home-sickness. For a long while he walked up and down his room, talking softly to himself, and then, under his breath, he murmured:

> I have err'd from the straight path,
> Bewildered I roam;

By the roadside the child stands
And beckons me home.

Then he went to his desk, took out some money, and stepped down into the street again. During all this while it had become quieter out there; the lights on the Christmas trees had burnt out, the processions of children had come to an end. The wind was sweeping through the deserted streets; old and young alike were sitting together at home in family parties; the second period of Christmas Eve celebrations had begun.

As Reinhard drew near the Ratskeller he heard from below the scraping of the fiddle and the singing of the zither girl. The restaurant door bell tinkled and a dark form staggered up the broad dimly-lighted stair.

Reinhard drew aside into the shadow of the houses and then passed swiftly by. After a while he reached the well-lighted shop of a jeweller, and after buying a little cross studded with red corals, he returned by the same way he had come.

Not far from his lodgings he caught sight of a little girl, dressed in miserable rags, standing before a tall door, in a vain attempt to open it.

"Shall I help you?" he said.

The child gave no answer, but let go the massive door-handle. Reinhard had soon opened the door.

"No," he said; "they might drive you out again. Come along with me, and I'll give you some Christmas cake."

He then closed the door again and gave his hand to the little girl, who walked along with him in silence to his lodgings.

On going out he had left the light burning.

"Here are some cakes for you," he said, pouring half of his whole stock into her apron, though he gave none that bore the sugar letters.

"Now, off you go home, and give your mother some of them too."

The child cast a shy look up at him; she seemed unaccustomed to such kindness and unable to say anything in reply. Reinhard opened the door, and lighted her way, and then the little thing like a bird flew downstairs with her cakes and out of the house.

Reinhard poked the fire in the stove, set the dusty ink-stand on the table, and then sat down and wrote and wrote letters the whole night long to his mother and Elisabeth.

The remainder of the Christmas cakes lay untouched by his side, but he had buttoned on Elisabeth's cuffs, and odd they looked on his shaggy coat of undyed wool. And there he was still sitting when the winter sun cast its light on the frosted window-panes, and showed him a pale, grave face reflected in the looking-glass.

HOME

When the Easter vacation came Reinhard journeyed home. On the morning after his arrival he went to see Elisabeth.

"How tall you've grown," he said, as the pretty, slender girl advanced with a smile to meet him. She blushed, but made no reply; he had taken her hand in his own in greeting, and she tried to draw it gently away. He looked at her doubtingly, for never had she done that before; but now it was as if some strange thing was coming between them.

The same feeling remained, too, after he had been at home for some time and came to see her constantly day after day. When they sat alone together there ensued pauses in the conversation which distressed him, and which he anxiously did his best to avoid. In order to have a definite occupation during the holidays, he began to give Elisabeth some instruction in botany, in which he himself had been keenly interested during the early months of his university career.

Elisabeth, who was wont to follow him in all things and was moreover very quick to learn, willingly entered into the proposal. So now several times in the week they made excursions into the fields or the moors, and if by midday they brought home their green field-box full of plants and flowers, Reinhard would come again later in the day and share with Elisabeth what they had collected in common.

With this same object in view, he entered the room one afternoon while Elisabeth was standing by the window and sticking some fresh chick-weed in a gilded birdcage which he had not seen in the place before. In the cage was a canary, which was flapping its wings and shrilly chirruping as it pecked at Elisabeth's fingers. Previously to this Reinhard's bird had hung in that spot.

"Has my poor linnet changed into a goldfinch after its death?" he asked jovially.

"Linnets are not accustomed to do any such thing," said Elizabeth's mother, who sat spinning in her arm-chair. "Your friend Eric sent it this noon from his estate as a present for Elisabeth."

"What estate?"

"Why, don't you know?"

"Know what?"

"That a month ago Eric took over his father's second estate by the Immensee."[3]

"But you have never said a word to me about it."

"Well," said the mother, "you haven't yet made a single word of inquiry after your friend. He is a very nice, sensible young man."

The mother went out of the room to make the coffee. Elisabeth had her back turned to Reinhard, and was still busy with the making of her little chick-weed bower.

"Please, just a little longer," she said, "I'll be done in a minute."

As Reinhard did not answer, contrary to his wont, she turned round and faced him. In his eyes there was a sudden expression of trouble which she had never observed before in them.

"What is the matter with you, Reinhard?" she said, drawing nearer to him.

"With me?" he said, his thoughts far away and his eyes resting dreamily on hers.

"You look so sad."

"Elisabeth," he said, "I cannot bear that yellow bird."

She looked at him in astonishment, without understanding his meaning.

"You are so strange," she said.

3 i.e. the 'Lake of the Bees'

He took both her hands in his, and she let him keep them there. Her mother came back into the room shortly after; and after they had drunk their coffee she sat down at her spinning-wheel, while Reinhard and Elisabeth went off into the next room to arrange their plants.

Stamens were counted, leaves and blossoms carefully opened out, and two specimens of each sort were laid to dry between the pages of a large folio volume.

All was calm and still this sunny afternoon; the only sounds to be heard were the hum of the mother's spinning-wheel in the next room, and now and then the subdued voice of Reinhard, as he named the orders of the families of the plants, and corrected Elisabeth's awkward pronunciation of the Latin names.

"I am still short of that lily of the valley which I didn't get last time," said she, after the whole collection had been classified and arranged.

Reinhard pulled a little white vellum volume from his pocket. "Here is a spray of the lily of the valley for you," he said, taking out a half-pressed bloom.

When Elisabeth saw the pages all covered with writing, she asked:

"Have you been writing stories again?"

"These aren't stories," he answered, handing her the book.

The contents were all poems, and the majority of them at most filled one page. Elisabeth turned over the leaves one after another; she appeared to be reading the titles only. "When she was scolded by the teacher." "When they lost their way in the woods." "An Easter story." "On her writing to me for the first time." Thus ran most of the titles.

Reinhard fixed his eyes on her with a searching look, and as she kept turning over the leaves he saw that a gentle blush arose and gradually mantled over the whole of her sweet face. He would fain have looked into her eyes, but Elisabeth did not look up, and finally laid the book down before him without a word.

"Don't give it back like that," he said.

She took a brown spray out of the tin case. "I will put your favourite flower inside," she said, giving back the book into his hands.

At length came the last day of the vacation and the morning of his departure. At her own request Elisabeth received permission from her mother to accompany her friend to the stage-coach, which had its station a few streets from their house.

When they passed out of the front door Reinhard gave her his arm, and thus he walked in silence side by side with the slender maiden. The nearer they came to their destination the more he felt as if he had something he must say to her before he bade her a long farewell, something on which all that was worthy and all that was sweet in his future life depended, and yet he could not formulate the saving word. In his anguish, he walked slower and slower.

"You'll be too late," she said; "it has already struck ten by St Mary's clock."

But he did not quicken his pace for all that. At last he stammered out:

"Elisabeth, you will not see me again for two whole years. Shall I be as dear to you as ever when I come back?"

She nodded, and looked affectionately into his face.

"I stood up for you too," she said, after a pause.

"Me? And against whom had you to stand up for me?"

"Against my mother. We were talking about you a long time yesterday evening after you left. She thought you were not so nice now as you once were."

Reinhard held his peace for a moment: then he took her hand in his, and looking gravely into her childish eyes, he said:

"I am still just as nice as I ever was; I would have you firmly believe that. Do you believe it, Elisabeth?"

"Yes," she said.

He freed her hand and quickly walked with her through the last street. The nearer he felt the time of parting approach, the happier became the look on his face; he went almost too quickly for her.

"What is the matter with you, Reinhard?" she asked.

"I have a secret, a beautiful secret," said Reinhard, looking at her with a light in his eyes. "When I come back again in two years' time, then you shall know it."

Meanwhile they had reached the stage-coach; they were only just in time. Once more Reinhard took her hand. "Farewell!" he said, "farewell, Elisabeth! Do not forget!"

She shook her head. "Farewell," she said. Reinhard climbed up into the coach and the horses started. As the coach rumbled round the corner of the street he saw her dear form once more as she slowly wended her way home.

A LETTER

Nearly two years later Reinhard was sitting by lamplight with his books and papers around him, expecting a friend with whom he used to study in common. Some one came upstairs. "Come in." It was the landlady. "A letter for you, Herr Werner," and she went away.

Reinhard had never written to Elisabeth since his visit home, and he had received no letter from her. Nor was this one from her; it was in his mother's handwriting.

Reinhard broke the seal and read, and ere long he came to this paragraph:

"At your time of life, my dear boy, nearly every year still brings its own peculiar experience; for youth is apt to turn everything to the best account. At home, too, things have changed very much, and all this will, I fear, cause you much pain at first, if my understanding of you is at all correct.

"Yesterday Eric was at last accepted by Elisabeth, after having twice proposed in vain during the last three months. She had never been able to make up her mind to it, but now in the end she has done so. To my mind she is still far too young. The wedding is to take place soon, and her mother means to go away with them."

IMMENSEE

Again years have passed. One warm afternoon in spring a young man, whose sunburnt face was the picture of health, was walking along a shady road through the wood leading down to the valley below.

His grave dark eyes looked intently into the distance, as though he was expecting to find every moment some change in the monotony of the road, a change however which seemed reluctant to come about. At length he saw a cart slowly coming up from below.

"Hullo! my friend," shouted the traveller to the farmer, who was walking by the side of the cart, "is this the right road to Immensee?"

"Yes, straight on," answered the man touching his slouch hat.

"Is it still far off?"

"You are close to the place, sir. In less time than it takes to smoke half a pipe of tobacco you'll be at the lake side, and the manor is hard by."

The farmer passed on while the other quickened his pace as he went along under the trees. After a quarter of an hour's walk the shade to the left of him suddenly came to an end; the road led along a steep slope from which the ancient oaks growing below hardly reared their topmost branches.

Away over their crests opened out a broad, sunny landscape. Far below lay the peaceful, dark-blue lake, almost entirely surrounded by green sun-lit woods, save where on one spot they divided and afforded an extensive view until it closed in the distant blue mountains.

Straight opposite, in the middle of all this forest verdure, there lay a patch of white, like driven snow. This was an expanse of blossoming fruit-trees, and out of them, up on the high lake shore, rose the manor-house, shining white, with tiles of red. A stork flew up from the chimney, and circled slowly above the waters.

"Immensee!" exclaimed the traveller.

It almost seemed as if he had now reached the end of his journey, for he stood motionless, looking out over the tops of the trees at his feet, and gazing at the farther shore, where the reflection of the manor-house floated, rocking gently, on the bosom of the water. Then he suddenly started on his way again.

His road now led almost steeply down the mountain-side, so that the trees that had once stood below him again gave him their shade, but at the same time cut off from him the view of the lake, which only now and then peeped out between the gaps in the branches.

Soon the way went gently upwards again, and to left and right the woods disappeared, yielding place to vine-clad hills stretching along the pathway; while on either side stood fruit-trees in blossom, filled with the hum of the bees as they busily pried into the blossoms. A tall man wearing a brown overcoat advanced to meet the traveller. When he had almost come up to him, he waved his cap and cried out in a loud voice:

"Welcome, welcome, brother Reinhard! Welcome to my Immensee estate!"

"God's greeting to you[4], Eric, and thank you for your welcome," replied the other.

By this time they had come up close to one another, and clasped hands.

"And is it really you?" said Eric, when he at last got a near sight of the grave face of his old school-fellow.

"It is I right enough, Eric, and I recognize you too; only you almost look cheerier than you ever did before."

At these words a glad smile made Eric's plain features all the more cheerful.

"Yes, brother Reinhard," he said, as he once more held out his hand to him,

---

4 This form of salutation is especially common in the south of Germany.

"but since those days, you see, I have won the great prize; but you know that well enough."

Then he rubbed his hands and cried cheerily: "This will be a surprise! You are the last person she expects to see."

"A surprise?" asked Reinhard. "For whom, pray?"

"Why, for Elisabeth."

"Elisabeth! You haven't told her a word about my visit?"

"Not a word, brother Reinhard; she has no thought of you, nor her mother either. I invited you entirely on the quiet, in order that the pleasure might be all the greater. You know I always had little quiet schemes of my own."

Reinhard turned thoughtful; he seemed to breathe more heavily the nearer they approached the house.

On the left side of the road the vineyards came to an end, and gave place to an extensive kitchen-garden, which reached almost as far as the lake-shore. The stork had meanwhile come to earth and was striding solemnly between the vegetable beds.

"Hullo!" cried Eric, clapping his hands together, "if that long-legged Egyptian isn't stealing my short pea-sticks again!"

The bird slowly rose and flew on to the roof of a new building, which ran along the end of the kitchen-garden, and whose walls were covered with the branches of the peach and apricot trees that were trained over them.

"That's the distillery," said Eric. "I built it only two years ago. My late father had the farm buildings rebuilt; the dwelling-house was built as far back as my grandfather's time. So we go ever forward a little bit at a time."

Talking thus they came to a wide, open space, enclosed at the sides by farm-buildings, and in the rear by the manor-house, the two wings of which were connected by a high garden wall. Behind this wall ran dark hedges of yew trees, while here and there syringa trees trailed their blossoming branches over into the courtyard.

Men with faces scorched by the sun and heated with toil were walking over the open space and gave a greeting to the two friends, while Eric called out to one or another of them some order or question about their day's work.

By this time they had reached the house. They entered a high, cool vestibule, at the far end of which they turned to the left into a somewhat darker passage.

Here Eric opened a door and they passed into a spacious room that opened into a garden. The heavy mass of leafage that covered the opposite windows filled this room at either end with a green twilight, while between the windows two lofty wide-open folding-doors let in the full glow of spring sunshine, and afforded a view into a garden, laid out with circular flower-beds and steep hedgerows and divided by a straight, broad path, along which the eye roamed out on to the lake and away over the woods growing on the opposite shore.

As the two friends entered, a breath of wind bore in upon them a perfect stream of fragrance.

On a terrace in front of the door leading to the garden sat a girlish figure dressed in white. She rose and came to meet the two friends as they entered, but half-way she stood stock-still as if rooted to the spot and stared at the stranger. With a smile he held out his hand to her.

"Reinhard!" she cried. "Reinhard! Oh! is it you? It is such a long time since we have seen each other."

"Yes, a long time," he said, and not a word more could he utter; for on hearing her voice he felt a keen, physical pain at his heart, and as he looked up to her, there she stood before him, the same slight, graceful figure to whom he had said farewell years ago in the town where he was born.

Eric had stood back by the door, with joy beaming from his eyes.

"Now, then, Elisabeth," he said, "isn't he really the very last person in the world you would have expected to see?"

Elisabeth looked at him with the eyes of a sister. "You are so kind, Eric," she said.

He took her slender hand caressingly in his. "And now that we have him," he said, "we shall not be in a hurry to let him go. He has been so long away abroad, we will try to make him feel at home again. Just see how foreign-looking he has become, and what a distinguished appearance he has!"

Elisabeth shyly scanned Reinhard's face. "The time that we have been separated is enough to account for that," she said.

At this moment in at the door came her mother, key-basket on arm.

"Herr Werner!" she cried, when she caught sight of Reinhard; "ah! you are as dearly welcome as you are unexpected."

And so the conversation went smoothly on with questions and answers. The ladies sat over their work, and while Reinhard enjoyed the refreshment that had been prepared for him, Eric had lighted his huge meerschaum pipe and sat smoking and conversing by his side.

Next day Reinhard had to go out with him to see the fields, the vineyards, the hop-garden, the distillery. It was all well appointed; the people who were working on the land or at the vats all had a healthy and contented look.

For dinner the family assembled in the room that opened into the garden, and the day was spent more or less in company just according to the leisure of the host and hostess. Only during the hours preceding the evening meal, as also during the early hours of the forenoon, did Reinhard stay working in his own room.

For some years past, whenever he could come across them, he had been collecting the rhymes and songs that form part of the life of the people, and now set about arranging his treasure, and wherever possible increasing it by means of fresh records from the immediate neighbourhood.

Elisabeth was at all times gentle and kind. Eric's constant attentions she received with an almost humble gratitude, and Reinhard thought at whiles that the gay, cheerful child of bygone days had given promise of a somewhat less sedate womanhood.

Ever since the second day of his visit he had been wont of an evening to take a walk along the shore of the lake. The road led along close under the garden. At the end of the latter, on a projecting mound, there was a bench under some tall birch trees. Elisabeth's mother had christened it the Evening Bench, because the spot faced westward, and was mostly used at that time of the day in order to enjoy a view of the sunset.

One evening Reinhard was returning from his walk along this road when he was overtaken by the rain. He sought shelter under one of the linden trees that grew by the water-side, but the heavy drops were soon pelting through the leaves.

Wet through as he was he resigned himself to his fate and slowly continued his homeward way.

It was almost dark; the rain fell faster and faster. As he drew near to the Evening Bench he fancied he could make out the figure of a woman dressed in white standing among the gleaming birch tree trunks. She stood motionless, and, as far as he could make out on approaching nearer, with her face turned in his direction, as if she was expecting some one.

He thought it was Elisabeth. But when he quickened his pace in order that he might catch up to her and then return together with her through the garden into the house, she turned slowly away and disappeared among the dark side-paths.

He could not understand it; he was almost angry with Elisabeth, and yet he doubted whether it had really been she. He was, however, shy of questioning her about it—nay, he even avoided going into the garden-room on his return to the house for fear he should happen to see Elisabeth enter through the garden-door.

BY MY MOTHER'S HARD DECREE

Some days later, as evening was already closing in, the family was, as usual at this time of the day, sitting all together in their garden-room. The doors stood wide open, and the sun had already sunk behind the woods on the far side of the lake.

Reinhard was invited to read some folk-songs which had been sent to him that afternoon by a friend who lived away in the country. He went up to his room and soon returned with a roll of papers which seemed to consist of detached neatly written pages.

So they all sat down to the table, Elisabeth beside Reinhard. "We shall read them at random," said the latter, "I have not yet looked through them myself."

Elisabeth unrolled the manuscript. "Here's some music," she said, "you must sing it, Reinhard."

To begin with he read some Tyrolese ditties[5] and as he read on he would now and then hum one or other of the lively melodies. A general feeling of cheeriness pervaded the little party.

"And who, pray, made all these pretty songs?" asked Elisabeth.

"Oh," said Eric, "you can tell that by listening to the rubbishy things—tailors' apprentices and barbers and such-like merry folk."

Reinhard said: "They are not made; they grow, they drop from the clouds, they float over the land like gossamer, hither and thither, and are sung in a thousand places at the same time.[6] We discover in these songs our very inmost activities and sufferings: it is as if we all had helped to write them."

He took up another sheet: "I stood on the mountain height . . ."[7]

---

5 Dialectal for *Schnitterhüpfen*, i.e. 'reapers' dances,' sung especially in the Tyrol and in Bavaria.

6 These fine cobwebs, produced by field-spiders, have always in the popular mind been connected with the gods. After the advent of Christianity they were connected with the Virgin Mary. The shroud in which she was wrapped after her death was believed to have been woven of the very finest thread, which during her ascent to Heaven frayed away from her body.

7 An ancient folk-song which treats of a beautiful but poor maiden, who, being unable to marry 'the young count,' retired to a convent.

"I know that one," cried Elisabeth; "begin it, do, Reinhard, and I will help you out."

So they sang that famous melody, which is so mysterious that one can hardly believe that it was ever conceived by the heart of man, Elisabeth with her slightly clouded contralta taking the second part to the young man's tenor.

The mother meanwhile sat busy with her needlework, while Eric listened attentively, with one hand clasped in the other. The song finished, Reinhard laid the sheet on one side in silence. Up from the lake-shore came through the evening calm the tinkle of the cattle bells; they were all listening without knowing why, and presently they heard a boy's clear voice singing:

> I stood on the mountain height
> And viewed the deep valley beneath. . . .

Reinhard smiled. "Do you hear that now? So it passes from mouth to mouth."

"It is often sung in these parts," said Elisabeth.

"Yes," said Eric, "it is Casper the herdsman; he is driving the heifers home."[8]

They listened a while longer until the tinkle of the bells died away behind the farm buildings. "These melodies are as old as the world," said Reinhard; "they slumber in the depths of the forest; God knows who discovered them."

He drew forth a fresh sheet.

It had now grown darker; a crimson evening glow lay like foam over the woods in the farther side of the lake. Reinhard unrolled the sheet, Elisabeth caught one side of it in her hand, and they both examined it together. Then Reinhard read:

> By my mother's hard decree
> Another's wife I needs must be;
> Him on whom my heart was set,
> Him, alas! I must forget;
> My heart protesting, but not free.
> Bitterly did I complain
> That my mother brought me pain.
> What mine honour might have been,
> That is turned to deadly sin.
> Can I ever hope again?
> For my pride what can I show,
> And my joy, save grief and woe?
> Oh! could I undo what's done,
> O'er the moor scorched by the sun
> Beggarwise I'd gladly go.

During the reading of this Reinhard had felt an imperceptible quivering of the paper; and when he came to an end Elisabeth gently pushed her chair back and passed silently out into the garden. Her mother followed her with a look. Eric made as if to go after, but the mother said:

8 *Starke* is the southern dialect word for *Färse*, 'young cow,' 'heifer.'

"Elisabeth has one or two little things to do outside," so he remained where he was.

But out of doors the evening brooded darker and darker over garden and lake. Moths whirred past the open doors through which the fragrance of flower and bush floated in increasingly; up from the water came the croak of the frogs, under the windows a nightingale commenced his song answered by another from within the depths of the garden; the moon appeared over the tree-tops.

Reinhard looked for a little while longer at the spot where Elisabeth's sweet form had been lost to sight in the thick-foliaged garden paths, and then he rolled up his manuscript, bade his friends good-night and passed through the house down to the water.

The woods stood silent and cast their dark shadow far out over the lake, while the centre was bathed in the haze of a pale moonlight. Now and then a gentle rustle trembled through the trees, though wind there was none; it was but the breath of summer night.

Reinhard continued along the shore. A stone's throw from the land he perceived a white water-lily. All at once he was seized with the desire to see it quite close, so he threw off his clothes and entered the water. It was quite shallow; sharp stones and water plants cut his feet, and yet he could not reach water deep enough for him to swim in.

Then suddenly he stepped out of his depth: the waters swirled above him; and it was some time before he rose to the surface again. He struck out with hands and feet and swam about in a circle until he had made quite sure from what point he had entered the water. And soon too he saw the lily again floating lonely among the large, gleaming leaves.

He swam slowly out, lifting every now and then his arms out of the water so that the drops trickled down and sparkled in the moonlight. Yet the distance between him and the flower showed no signs of diminishing, while the shore, as he glanced back at it, showed behind him in a hazy mist that ever deepened. But he refused to give up the venture and vigorously continued swimming in the same direction.

At length he had come so near the flower that he was able clearly to distinguish the silvery leaves in the moonlight; but at the same time he felt himself entangled in a net formed by the smooth stems of the water plants which swayed up from the bottom and wound themselves round his naked limbs.

The unfamiliar water was black all round about him, and behind him he heard the sound of a fish leaping. Suddenly such an uncanny feeling overpowered him in the midst of this strange element that with might and main he tore asunder the network of plants and swam back to land in breathless haste. And when from the shore he looked back upon the lake, there floated the lily on the bosom of the darkling water as far away and as lonely as before.

He dressed and slowly wended his way home. As he passed out of the garden into the room he discovered Eric and the mother busied with preparations for a short journey which had to be undertaken for business purposes on the morrow.

"Where ever have you been so late in the dark?" the mother called out to him.

"I?" he answered, "oh, I wanted to pay a call on the water-lily, but I failed."

"That's beyond the comprehension of any man," said Eric. "What on earth had you to do with the water-lily?"

"Oh, I used to be friends with the lily once," said Reinhard; "but that was long ago."

ELISABETH

The following afternoon Reinhard and Elisabeth went for a walk on the farther side of the lake, strolling at times through the woodland, at other times along the shore where it jutted out into the water. Elisabeth had received injunctions from Eric, during the absence of himself and her mother to show Reinhard the prettiest views in the immediate neighbourhood, particularly the view toward the farm itself from the other side of the lake. So now they proceeded from one point to another.

At last Elisabeth got tired and sat down in the shade of some overhanging branches. Reinhard stood opposite to her, leaning against a tree trunk; and as he heard the cuckoo calling farther back in the woods, it suddenly struck him that all this had happened once before. He looked at her and with an odd smile asked:

"Shall we look for strawberries?"

"It isn't strawberry time," she said.

"No, but it will soon be here."

Elisabeth shook her head in silence; then she rose and the two strolled on together. And as they wandered side by side, his eyes ever and again were bent toward her; for she walked gracefully and her step was light. He often unconsciously fell back a pace in order that he might feast his eyes on a full view of her.

So they came to an open space overgrown with heather where the view extended far over the country-side. Reinhard bent down and plucked a bloom from one of the little plants that grew at his feet. When he looked up again there was an expression of deep pain on his face.

"Do you know this flower?" he asked.

She gave him a questioning look. "It is an erica. I have often gathered them in the woods."

"I have an old book at home," he said; "I once used to write in it all sorts of songs and rhymes, but that is all over and done with long since. Between its leaves also there is an erica, but it is only a faded one. Do you know who gave it me?"

She nodded without saying a word; but she cast down her eyes and fixed them on the bloom which he held in his hand. For a long time they stood thus. When she raised her eyes on him again he saw that they were brimming over with tears.

"Elisabeth," he said, "behind yonder blue hills lies our youth. What has become of it?"

Nothing more was spoken. They walked dumbly by each other's side down to the lake. The air was sultry; to westward dark clouds were rising. "There's going to be a storm," said Elisabeth, hastening her steps. Reinhard nodded in silence, and together they rapidly sped along the shore till they reached their boat.

On the way across Elisabeth rested her hand on the gunwale of the boat. As he rowed Reinhard glanced along at her, but she gazed past him into the distance. And so his glance fell downward and rested on her hand, and the white hand betrayed to him what her lips had failed to reveal.

It revealed those fine traces of secret pain that so readily mark a woman's fair hands, when they lie at nights folded across an aching heart. And as Elisabeth felt his glance resting on her hand she let it slip gently over the gunwale into the water.

On arriving at the farm they fell in with a scissors grinder's cart standing in front of the manor-house. A man with black, loosely-flowing hair was busily plying his wheel and humming a gipsy melody between his teeth, while a dog that was harnessed to the cart lay panting hard by. On the threshold stood a girl dressed in rags, with features of faded beauty, and with outstretched hand she asked alms of Elisabeth.

Reinhard thrust his hand into his pocket, but Elisabeth was before him, and hastily emptied the entire contents of her purse into the beggar's open palm. Then she turned quickly away, and Reinhard heard her go sobbing up the stairs.

He would fain have detained her, but he changed his mind and remained at the foot of the stairs. The beggar girl was still standing at the doorway, motionless, and holding in her hand the money she had received.

"What more do you want?" asked Reinhard.

She gave a sudden start: "I want nothing more," she said; then, turning her head toward him and staring at him with wild eyes, she passed slowly out of the door. He uttered a name, but she heard him not; with drooping head, with arms folded over her breast, she walked down across the farmyard:

> Then when death shall claim me,
>   I must die alone.

An old song surged in Reinhard's ears, he gasped for breath; a little while only, and then he turned away and went up to his chamber.

He sat down to work, but his thoughts were far afield. After an hour's vain attempt he descended to the parlour. Nobody was in it, only cool, green twilight; on Elisabeth's work-table lay a red ribbon which she had worn round her neck during the afternoon. He took it up in his hand, but it hurt him, and he laid it down again.

He could find no rest. He walked down to the lake and untied the boat. He rowed over the water and trod once again all the paths which he and Elisabeth had paced together but a short hour ago. When he got back home it was dark. At the farm he met the coachman, who was about to turn the carriage horses out into the pasture; the travellers had just returned.

As he came into the entrance hall he heard Eric pacing up and down the garden-room. He did not go in to him; he stood still for a moment, and then softly climbed the stairs and so to his own room. Here he sat in the arm-chair by the window. He made himself believe that he was listening to the nightingale's throbbing music in the garden hedges below, but what he heard was the throbbing of his own heart. Downstairs in the house every one went to bed, the night-hours passed, but he paid no heed.

For hours he sat thus, till at last he rose and leaned out of the open window. The dew was dripping among the leaves, the nightingale had ceased to trill. By degrees the deep blue of the darksome sky was chased away by a faint yellow gleam that came from the east; a fresh wind rose and brushed Reinhard's heated brow; the early lark soared triumphant up into the sky.

Reinhard suddenly turned and stepped up to the table. He groped about for a pencil and when he had found one he sat down and wrote a few lines on a sheet of white paper. Having finished his writing he took up hat and stick, and leaving the paper behind him, carefully opened the door and descended to the vestibule.

The morning twilight yet brooded in every corner; the big house-cat stretched its limbs on the straw mat and arched its back against Reinhard's hand, which he unthinkingly held out to it. Outside in the garden the sparrows were already chirping their patter from among the branches, and giving notice to all that the night was now past.[9]

Then within the house he heard a door open on the upper floor; some one came downstairs, and on looking up he saw Elisabeth standing before him. She laid her hand upon his arm, her lips moved, but not a word did he hear.

Presently she said: "You will never come back. I know it; do not deny it; you will never come back."

"No, never," he said.

She let her hand fall from his arm and said no more. He crossed the hall to the door, then turned once more. She was standing motionless on the same spot and looking at him with lifeless eyes. He advanced one step and opened his arms toward her; then, with a violent effort, he turned away and so passed out of the door.

Outside the world lay bathed in morning light, the drops of pearly dew caught on the spiders' webs glistened in the first rays of the rising sun. He never looked back; he walked rapidly onward; behind him the peaceful farmstead gradually disappeared from view as out in front of him rose the great wide world.

THE OLD MAN

The moon had ceased to shine in through the window-panes, and it had grown quite dark; but the old man still sat in his arm-chair with folded hands and gazed before him into the emptiness of the room.

Gradually, the murky darkness around him dissolved away before his eyes and changed into a broad dark lake; one black wave after another went rolling on farther and farther, and on the last one, so far away as to be almost beyond the reach of the old man's vision, floated lonely among its broad leaves a white water-lily.

The door opened, and a bright glare of light filled the room.

"I am glad that you have come, Bridget," said the old man. "Set the lamp upon the table."

Then he drew his chair up to the table, took one of the open books and buried himself in studies to which he had once applied all the strength of his youth.

---

9 Literally, "sang out pompously, like priests." The word seems to have been coined by the author. The English 'patter' is derived from Pater noster, and seems an appropriate translation.

THE DOG

Ivan Turgenev

Translated from the Russian by Constance Garnett

Ivan Sergeyevich Turgenev (1818–1883) was a Russian novelist, short story writer and playwright. His first major publication, a short story collection entitled *A Sportsman's Sketches* (1852), was a milestone of Russian realism, and his novel *Fathers and Sons* (1862) is regarded as one of the major works of nineteenth-century fiction. When Turgenev was nineteen, while traveling on a steamboat in Germany, the boat caught fire and Turgenev reacted in a "cowardly manner", an accusation that dogged him for the rest of his life. While traveling together in Paris, Tolstoy wrote in his diary, "Turgenev is a bore." His rocky friendship with Tolstoy in 1861 wrought such animosity that Tolstoy challenged Turgenev to a duel.

"But if one admits the possibility of the supernatural, the possibility of its participation in real life, then allow me to ask what becomes of common sense?" Anton Stepanitch pronounced and he folded his arms over his stomach.

Anton Stepanitch had the grade of a civil councillor, served in some incomprehensible department and, speaking emphatically and stiffly in a bass voice, enjoyed universal respect. He had not long before, in the words of those who envied him, "had the Stanislav stuck on to him."

"That's perfectly true," observed Skvorevitch.

"No one will dispute that," added Kinarevitch.

"I am of the same opinion," the master of the house, Finoplentov, chimed in from the corner in falsetto.

"Well, I must confess, I cannot agree, for something supernatural has happened to me myself," said a bald, corpulent middle-aged gentleman of medium height, who had till then sat silent behind the stove. The eyes of all in the room turned to him with curiosity and surprise, and there was a silence.

The man was a Kaluga landowner of small means who had lately come to Petersburg. He had once served in the Hussars, had lost money at cards, had resigned his commission and had settled in the country. The recent economic reforms had reduced his income and he had come to the capital to look out for a suitable berth. He had no qualifications and no connections, but he confidently relied on the friendship of an old comrade who had suddenly, for no visible reason, become a person of importance, and whom he had once helped in thrashing a card sharper. Moreover, he reckoned on his luck—and it did not fail him: a few days after his arrival in town he received the post of superintendent of government warehouses, a profitable and even honourable position, which did not call for conspicuous abilities: the warehouses themselves had only a hypothetical existence and indeed it was not very precisely known with what they were to be filled—but they had been invented with a view to government economy.

Anton Stepanitch was the first to break the silence.

"What, my dear sir," he began, "do you seriously maintain that something supernatural has happened to you? I mean to say, something inconsistent with the laws of nature?"

"I do maintain it," replied the gentleman addressed as "My dear sir," whose name was Porfiry Kapitonitch.

"Inconsistent with the laws of nature!" Anton Stepanitch repeated angrily; apparently he liked the phrase.

"Just so . . . yes; it was precisely what you say."

"That's amazing! What do you think of it, gentlemen?" Anton Stepanitch tried to give his features an ironical expression, but without effect—or to speak more accurately, merely with the effect of suggesting that the dignified civil councillor had detected an unpleasant smell. "Might we trouble you, dear sir," he went on, addressing the Kaluga landowner, "to give us the details of so interesting an incident?"

"Certainly, why not?" answered the landowner and, moving in a free-and-easy way to the middle of the room, he spoke as follows:

"I have, gentlemen, as you are probably aware, or perhaps are not aware, a small estate in the Kozelsky district. In old days I used to get something out of it, though now, of course, I have nothing to look forward to but unpleasantness. But enough of politics. Well, in that district I have a little place: the usual kitchen garden, a little pond with carp in it, farm buildings of a sort and a little lodge for my own sinful person . . . I am a bachelor. Well, one day—some six years ago—I came home rather late; I had had a game of cards at a neighbour's and I was—I beg you to note—the least little bit elevated, as they say; I undressed, got into bed and put out the candle. And only fancy, gentlemen: as soon as I put out the candle there was something moving under my bed! I wondered whether it was a rat; no, it was not a rat: it moved about, scratched on the floor and scratched itself. . . . At last it flapped its ears!

"There was no mistake about it; it was a dog. But where could a dog have come from? I did not keep one; could some stray dog have run in, I wondered. I called my servant; Filka was his name. He came in with a candle.

"'How's this,' I said, 'Filka, my lad? Is that how you look after things? A dog has got under my bed?' 'What dog?' said he. 'How do I know,' said I, 'that's your business—to save your master from disturbance.' My Filka bent down, and began moving the candle under the bed. 'But there's no dog here,' said he. I bent down, too; there certainly was no dog there. What a queer thing!—I glanced at Filka and he was smiling. 'You stupid,' I said to him, 'why are you grinning. When you opened the door the dog must have whisked out into the passage. And you, gaping idiot, saw nothing because you are always asleep. You don't suppose I am drunk, do you?' He would have answered, but I sent him out, curled up and that night heard nothing more.

"But the next night—only fancy—the thing was repeated. As soon as I blew out the candle, he scratched himself and flapped his ears again. Again I called Filka; again he looked under the bed—again there was nothing! I sent him away, blew out the candle—and, damn it all, the dog was there again and it was a dog right enough: one could hear it breathing, biting its coat, looking for fleas. . . . It was so distinct —'Filka,' I said, 'come here without the candle!' He came in. 'Well, now,' I said, 'do you hear?' 'Yes,' he said. I could not see him, but I felt that the fellow was scared. 'What do you make of it?' said I. 'What do you bid me make of it, Porfiry Kapitonitch? It's sorcery!' 'You are a foolish fellow,' I said, 'hold your tongue with your sorcery. . . . ' And our voices quavered like a bird's and we were trembling in the dark as though we were in a fever. I lighted a candle, no dog, no sound, only us two, as white as chalk. So I kept a candle burning till morning and I assure you, gentlemen, you may believe me or you may not, but from that night for six weeks the same thing was repeated. In the end I actually got used to it and began putting out the candle, because I couldn't get to sleep in the light. 'Let him fidget,' I thought, 'he doesn't do me any harm.'"

"Well, I see you are not one of the chicken-hearted brigade," Anton Stepanitch interrupted in a half-contemptuous, half-condescending tone! "One can see the Hussar at once!"

"I shouldn't be afraid of you in any case," Porfiry Kapitonitch observed, and for an instant he really did look like a Hussar.

"But listen to the rest. A neighbour came to see me, the very one with whom I used to play cards. He dined with me on what luck provided and dropped some fifty roubles for his visit; night came on, it was time for him to be off. But I had my own idea. 'Stay the night with me,' I said, 'Vassily Vassilitch; tomorrow, please God, you will win it back.' Vassily Vassilitch considered and stayed. I had a bed put up for him in my room. . . . Well, we went to bed, smoked, chatted— about the fair sex for the most part, as is only suitable in bachelor company—we laughed, of course; I saw Vassily Vassilitch put out his candle and turn his back towards me: as much as to say: 'Good night.' I waited a little, then I, too, put out my candle. And, only fancy, I had hardly time to wonder what sort of trick would be played this time, when the sweet creature was moving again. And moving was not all; it came out from under the bed, walked across the room, tapped on the floor with its paws, shook its ears and all of a sudden pushed against the very chair that was close by Vassily Vassilitch's bed. 'Porfiry Kapitonitch,' said the latter, and in such an unconcerned voice, you know, 'I did not know you had a dog. What sort is it, a setter?' 'I haven't a dog,' I said, 'and never have had one!' 'You haven't? Why, what's this?' 'What's this?' said I, 'why, light the candle and then you will see for yourself.' 'Isn't it a dog?' 'No.' Vassily Vassilitch turned over in bed. 'But you are joking, dash it all.' 'No, I am not joking.' I heard him go strike, strike, with a match, while the creature persisted in scratching its ribs. The light flared up . . . and, hey presto! not a trace remained! Vassily Vassilitch looked at me and I looked at him. 'What trick is this?' he said. 'It's a trick,' I said, 'that, if you were to set Socrates himself on one side and Frederick the Great on the other, even they could not make it out.' And then I told him all about it. Didn't my Vassily Vassilitch jump out of bed! As though he had been scalded! He couldn't get into his boots. 'Horses,' he cried, 'horses!' I began trying to persuade him, but it was no use! He positively gasped! 'I won't stay,' he said, 'not a minute! You must be a man under a curse! Horses.' However, I prevailed upon him. Only his bed was dragged into another room and nightlights were lighted everywhere. At our tea in the morning he had regained his equanimity; he began to give me advice. 'You should try being away from home for a few days, Porfiry Kapitonitch,' he said, 'perhaps this abomination would leave you.' And I must tell you: my neighbour was a man of immense intellect. He managed his mother-in-law wonderfully: he fastened an I. O. U. upon her; he must have chosen a sentimental moment! She became as soft as silk, she gave him an authorisation for the management of all her estate—what more would you have? You know it is something to get the better of one's mother-in-law. Eh! You can judge for yourselves. However, he took leave of me in some displeasure; I'd stripped him of a hundred roubles again. He actually abused me. 'You are ungrateful.' he said, 'you have no feeling'; but how was I to blame? Well, be that as it may, I considered his advice. That very day I drove off to the town and put up at an inn, kept by an old man I knew, a Dissenter. He was a worthy old fellow, though a little morose from living in solitude, all his family were dead. But he disliked tobacco and had the greatest loathing for dogs; I believe he would have been torn to pieces rather than consent to let a dog into his room. 'For how can one?' he would say, 'the Queen of Heaven herself is graciously pleased to be on my wall there, and is an unclean dog to put his infidel nose there?' Of course, it was lack of education! However, to my thinking, whatever wisdom a man has he had better stick to that."

"I see you are a great philosopher," Anton Stepanitch interrupted a second time with the same sarcastic smile.

This time Porfiry Kapitonitch actually frowned.

"How much I know of philosophy I cannot tell," he observed, tugging grimly at his moustache, "but I would be glad to give you a lesson in it."

We all simply stared at Anton Stepanitch. Every one of us expected a haughty reply, or at least a glance like a flash of lightning. . . . But the civil councillor turned his contemptuous smile into one of indifference, then yawned, swung his foot and—that was all!

"Well, I stayed at that old fellow's," Porfiry Kapitonitch went on. "He gave me a little room, not one of the best, as we were old friends; his own was close by, the other side of the partition—and that was just what I wanted. The tortures I faced that night! A little room, a regular oven, stuffiness, flies, and such sticky ones; in the corner an extraordinarily big shrine with ancient ikons, with dingy setting in relief on them. It fairly reeked of oil and some other stuff, too; there were two featherbeds on the beds. If you moved the pillow a black beetle would run from under it. . . . I had drunk an incredible quantity of tea, feeling so dreary—it was simply dreadful! I got into bed; there was no possibility of sleeping—and, the other side of the partition, my host was sighing, clearing his throat, repeating his prayers. However, he subsided at last. I heard him begin to snore, but only faintly, in the old-fashioned polite way. I had put my candle out long ago, but the little lamp was burning before the ikons. . . . That prevented it, I suppose. So I got up softly with bare feet, climbed up to the lamp, and blew it out. . . . Nothing happened. 'Oho!' I thought, 'so it doesn't come off in other people's houses.'

"But I had no sooner got into bed than there was a commotion again. He was scraping on the floor and scratching himself and shaking his ears . . . the usual thing, in fact. Very good! I lay still and waited to see what would happen. I heard the old man wake up. 'Sir,' he said, 'hey, sir.' 'What is it?' 'Did you put out the lamp?' But without waiting for my answer, he burst out all at once. 'What's that? What's that, a dog? A dog! Ah, you vile heretic!' 'Wait a bit, old man, before you scold,' I said. 'You had better come here yourself. Things are happening,' I said, 'that may well make you wonder.' The old man stirred behind the partition and came in to me, with a candle, a very, very thin one, made of yellow wax; I was surprised when I looked at him! He looked bristling all over, with hairy ears and eyes as fierce as a weasel's; he had on a white woollen night cap, a beard to his waist, white too, and a waistcoat with copper buttons on it over his shirt and fur boots on his feet and he smelt of juniper. In this attire he approached the ikons, crossed himself three times with his two fingers crossed, lighted the lamp, crossed himself again and, turning to me, just grunted: 'Explain!' And thereupon, without delay, I told him all that had happened. The old man listened to my account and did not drop one word, simply shook his head. Then he sat down on my bed and still said nothing. He scratched his chest, the back of his head and so on and said nothing. 'Well,' I said, 'Fedul Ivanitch, what do you think? Is it some devil's sorcery or what?' The old man looked at me. 'What an idea! Devil's sorcery! A tobacco-smoker like you might well have that at home, but not here. Only think what holiness there is here! Sorcery, indeed!' 'And if it is not sorcery, what is it, then?' The old man was silent again; again he scratched himself and said at last, but in a muffled voice, for his moustache was all over his mouth: 'You go to the town of Belyov. There is no one who can help you but one man. And that man lives in Belyov. He is one of our people. If he is willing to help you, you are lucky; if he is not, nothing can be done.' 'And how am I to find this man?' I said. 'I can direct you about that,' he answered; 'but how can it be sorcery? It is an apparition, or rather an indication; but you cannot comprehend it, it is beyond your understanding. Lie down to sleep now with the blessing of our Lord Christ; I will burn incense and in the morning we will converse. Morning, you know, brings wisdom.'

"Well, we did converse in the morning, only I was almost stifled by that incense. And this was the counsel the old man gave me: that when I reached Belyov I should go into the market place and ask in the second shop on the right for one Prohoritch, and when I had found Prohoritch, put into his hand a writing and the writing consisted of a scrap of paper, on which stood the following words: 'In the name of the Father, the Son and the Holy Ghost. Amen. To Sergey Prohorovitch Pervushin. Trust this man. Feduly Ivanitch.' And below, 'Send the cabbages, for God's sake.'

"I thanked the old man and without further discussion ordered my carriage and drove to Belyov. For I reflected, that though I suffered no harm from my nocturnal visitor, yet it was uncanny and in fact not quite the thing for a nobleman and an officer—what do you think?"

"And did you really go to Belyov?" murmured Finoplentov.

"Straight to Belyov. I went into the market place and asked at the second shop on the right for Prohoritch. 'Is there such a person?' I asked. 'Yes,' they told me. 'And where does he live?' 'By the Oka, beyond the market gardens.' 'In whose house?' 'In his own.' I went to the Oka, found his house, though it was really not a house but simply a hovel. I saw a man wearing a blue patched coat and a ragged cap, well . . . he looked like a working-man, he was standing with his back to me, digging among his cabbages. I went up to him. 'Are you so and so?' I said. He turned round and, I tell you the truth, I have never seen such piercing eyes in my life. Yet the whole face was shrunk up like a little fist with a little wedge-shaped beard and sunken lips. He was an old man. 'I am so and so,' he said. 'What are you needing?' 'Why, this is what I am needing,' I said, and put the writing in his hand. He looked at me intently and said: 'Come indoors, I can't read without spectacles.'

"Well, I went with him into his hut—and a hut it certainly was: poor, bare, crooked; only just holding together. On the wall there was an ikon of old work-manship as black as a coal; only the whites of the eyes gleamed in the faces. He took some round spectacles in iron frames out of a little table, put them on his nose, read the writing and looked at me again through the spectacles. 'You have need of me?' 'I certainly have,' I answered. 'Well,' said he, 'if you have, tell it and we will listen.' And, only fancy, he sat down and took a checked handkerchief out of his pocket, and spread it out on his knee, and the handkerchief was full of holes, and he looked at me with as much dignity as though he were a senator or a minister, and he did not ask me to sit down. And what was still stranger, I felt all at once awe-stricken, so awe-stricken . . . my soul sank into my heels. He pierced me through with his eyes and that's the fact! I pulled myself together, however, and told him all my story. He was silent for a space, shrank into himself, chewed his lips and then questioned me just like a senator again, majestically, without haste. 'What is your name?' he asked. 'Your age? What were your parents? Are you single or married?' Then again he munched his lips, frowned, held up his finger and spoke: 'Bow down to the holy ikon, to the honourable Saints Zossima and Savvaty of Solovki.' I bowed down to the earth and did not get up in a hurry; I felt such awe for the man and such submission that I believe that whatever he had told me to do I should have done it on the spot! . . . I see you are grinning, gentlemen, but I was in no laughing mood then, I assure you. 'Get up, sir,' said he at last. 'I can help you. This is not sent you as a chastisement, but as a warning; it is for your protection; someone is praying for your welfare. Go to the market now and buy a young dog and keep it by you day and night. Your visions will leave you and, moreover, that dog will be of use to you.'

"I felt as though light dawned upon me, all at once; how those words delighted me. I bowed down to Prohoritch and would have gone away, when I bethought me that I could not go away without rewarding him. I got a three rouble note out of my pocket. But he thrust my hand away and said, 'Give it to our chapel, or to the poor; the service I have done you is not to be paid for.' I bowed down to him again almost to the ground, and set off straight for the market! And only fancy: as soon as I drew near the shops, lo and behold, a man in a frieze overcoat comes sauntering towards me carrying under his arm a two months' old setter puppy with a reddish brown coat, white lips and white forepaws. 'Stay,' I said to the man in the overcoat, 'what will you sell it for?' 'For two roubles.' 'Take three!' The man looked at me in amazement, thought the gentleman had gone out of his wits, but I flung the notes in his face, took the pup under my arm and made for my carriage! The coachman quickly had the horses harnessed and that evening I reached home. The puppy sat inside my coat all the way and did not stir; and

I kept calling him, 'Little Trésor! Little Trésor!' I gave him food and drink at once. I had some straw brought in, settled him and whisked into bed! I blew out the candle: it was dark. 'Well, now begin,' said I. There was silence. 'Begin,' said I, 'you so and so!' . . . Not a sound, as though to mock me. Well, I began to feel so set up that I fell to calling it all sorts of names. But still there was not a sound! I could only hear the puppy panting! 'Filka,' I cried, 'Filka! Come here, you stupid!' He came in. 'Do you hear the dog?' 'No, sir,' said he, 'I hear nothing,' and he laughed. 'And you won't hear it ever again,' said I. 'Here's half a rouble for vodka!' 'Let me kiss your hand,' said the foolish fellow, and he stooped down to me in the darkness. . . . It was a great relief, I must tell you."

"And was that how it all ended?" asked Anton Stepanitch, this time without irony.

"The apparitions ended certainly and I was not disturbed in any way, but wait a bit, the whole business was not over yet. My Trésor grew, he turned into a fine fellow. He was heavy, with flopping ears and overhanging lip and a thick tail; a regular sporting dog. And he was extremely attached to me, too. The shooting in our district is poor, however, as I had set up a dog, I got a gun, too. I took to sauntering round the neighbourhood with my Trésor: sometimes one would hit a hare (and didn't he go after that hare, upon my soul), sometimes a quail, or a duck. But the great thing was that Trésor was never a step away from me. Where I went, he went; I even took him to the bath with me, I did really! One lady actually tried to get me turned out of her drawing-room on account of Trésor, but I made such an uproar! The windows I broke! Well, one day . . . it was in summer . . . and I must tell you there was a drought at the time such as nobody remembered. The air was full of smoke or haze. There was a smell of burning, the sun was like a molten bullet, and as for the dust there was no getting it out of one's nose and throat. People walked with their mouths wide open like crows. I got weary of sitting at home in complete deshabille, with shutters closed; and luckily the heat was beginning to abate a little. . . . So I went off, gentlemen, to see a lady, a neighbour of mine. She lived about three-quarters of a mile away— and she certainly was a benevolent lady. She was still young and blooming and of most prepossessing appearance; but she was of rather uncertain temper. Though that is no harm in the fair sex; it even gives me pleasure. . . . Well, I reached her door, and I did feel that I had had a hot time of it getting there! Well, I thought, Nimfodora Semyonovna will regale me now with bilberry water and other cooling drinks—and I had already taken hold of the doorhandle when all at once there was the tramping of feet and shrieking, and shouting of boys from round the corner of a hut in the courtyard. . . . I looked round. Good heavens! A huge reddish beast was rushing straight towards me; at the first glance I did not recognise it as a dog: its jaws were open, its eyes were bloodshot, its coat was bristling. . . . I had not time to take breath before the monster bounded up the steps, stood upon its hind legs and made straight for my chest—it was a position! I was numb with terror and could not lift my arms. I was completely stupefied. . . . I could see nothing but the terrible white tusks just before my nose, the red tongue all covered with white foam. But at the same instant, another dark body was whisking before me like a ball—it was my darling Trésor defending me; and he hung like a leech on the brute's throat! The creature wheezed, grated its

teeth and staggered back. I instantly flung open the door and got into the hall. . . .
I stood hardly knowing what I was doing with my whole weight on the door, and
heard a desperate battle going on outside. I began shouting and calling for help;
everyone in the house was terribly upset. Nimfodora Semyonovna ran out with
her hair down, the voices in the yard grew louder—and all at once I heard: 'Hold
the gate, hold it, fasten it!' I opened the door—just a crack, and looked out: the
monster was no longer on the steps, the servants were rushing about the yard in
confusion waving their hands and picking up bits of wood from the ground; they
were quite crazy. 'To the village, it has run off to the village,' shrieked a peasant
woman in a cap of extraordinary size poking her head out of a dormer window.
I went out of the house.

"'Where is my Trésor?' I asked and at once I saw my saviour. He was coming
from the gate limping, covered with wounds and with blood. . . . 'What's the
meaning of it?' I asked the servants who were dashing about the yard as though
possessed. 'A mad dog!' they answered, 'the count's; it's been hanging about here
since yesterday.'

"We had a neighbour, a count, who bred very fierce foreign dogs. My knees
shook; I rushed to a looking-glass and looked to see whether I had been bitten.
No, thank God, there was nothing to be seen; only my countenance naturally
looked green; while Nimfodora Semyonovna was lying on the sofa and cackling
like a hen. Well, that one could quite understand, in the first place nerves, in the
second sensibility. She came to herself at last, though, and asked me whether I
were alive. I answered that I was and that Trésor had saved me. 'Ah,' she said,
'what a noble creature! and so the mad dog has strangled him?' 'No,' I said, 'it
has not strangled him, but has wounded him seriously.' 'Oh,' she said, 'in that
case he must be shot this minute!' 'Oh, no,' I said, 'I won't agree to that. I shall
try to cure him. . . . ' At that moment Trésor began scratching at the door. I was
about to go and open it for him. 'Oh,' she said, 'what are you doing, why, it will
bite us all.' 'Upon my word,' I said, 'the poison does not act so quickly.' 'Oh, how
can you?' she said. 'Why, you have taken leave of your senses!' 'Nimfotchka,' I
said, 'calm yourself, be reasonable. . . . ' But she suddenly cried, 'Go away at once
with your horrid dog.' 'I will go away,' said I. 'At once,' she said, 'this second! Get
along with you,' she said, 'you villain, and never dare to let me set eyes on you
again. You may go mad yourself!' 'Very good,' said I, 'only let me have a carriage
for I am afraid to go home on foot now.' 'Give him the carriage, the coach, the
chaise, what he likes, only let him be gone quickly. Oh, what eyes! Oh, what eyes
he has!' and with those words she whisked out of the room and gave a maid who
met her a slap in the face—and I heard her in hysterics again.

"And you may not believe me, gentlemen, but that very day I broke off all
acquaintance with Nimfodora Semyonovna; on mature consideration of everything, I am bound to add that for that circumstance, too, I shall owe a debt of
gratitude to my friend Trésor to the hour of my death.

"Well, I had the carriage brought round, put my Trésor in and drove home.
When I got home I looked him over and washed his wounds, and thought I would
take him next day as soon as it was light to the wise man in the Yefremovsky
district. And this wise man was an old peasant, a wonderful man: he would
whisper over some water—and some people made out that he dropped some

snake spittle into it—would give it as a draught, and the trouble would be gone completely. I thought, by the way, I would be bled myself at Yefremovsky: it's a good thing as a precaution against fright, only not from the arm, of course, but from the falcon."

"What place is that, the falcon?" Mr. Finoplentov asked with demure curiosity.

"Why, don't you know? It is here on the fist near the thumb, the spot on which one shakes the snuff from one's horn, just here. It's the best place for letting blood. For only consider, the blood from the arm comes from the vein, but here it is of no consequence. The doctors don't know that and don't understand it, how should they, the idle drones, the wretched Germans? It's the blacksmiths who go in for it. And aren't they skilful! They get a chisel, give it a tap with a hammer and it's done! . . . Well, while I was thinking it over, it got quite dark, it was time for bed. I went to bed and Trésor, of course, was close by me. But whether it was from the fight, from the stuffiness, from the fleas or from my thoughts, I could not get to sleep, do what I would! I can't describe the depression that came over me; I sipped water, opened the window and played the 'Kamarinsky' with Italian variations on the guitar. . . . No good! I felt I must get out of the room—and that was all about it! I made up my mind at last: I took my pillow, my quilt and my sheet and made my way across the garden to the hayloft; and settled myself there. And how pleasant I felt in there, gentlemen: it was a still, still night, only from time to time a breath of air like a woman's hand caressed one's cheek; it was so fresh; the hay smelt as sweet as tea; among the apple trees the grasshoppers were chirping; then all at once came the cry of the quail—and one felt that he, too, the rogue, was happy, sitting in the dew with his little lady. . . . And the sky was magnificent. . . . The stars were glowing, or a cloud would float by, white as cotton wool, scarcely moving. . . ."

At this point in the story Skvorevitch sneezed; Kinarevitch sneezed, too—he never failed in anything to follow his colleague's example. Anton Stepanitch looked approvingly at both of them.

"Well," Porfiry Kapitonitch went on, "well, so I lay there and again could not go to sleep. I fell to musing, and what I thought of most was the strangeness of it all: how correctly Prohoritch had explained it as a warning and I wondered why it was to me such marvels had happened. . . . I marvelled—particularly because I could make nothing of it—and Trésor kept whining, as he twisted round in the hay; his wounds hurt him. And I will tell you what else prevented me from sleeping—you won't believe it—the moon. It was just facing me, so big and round and yellow and flat, and it seemed to me that it was staring at me, it really did. And so insolently, so persistently. . . . I put out my tongue at it at last, I really did. What are you so inquisitive about? I thought. I turned away from it and it seemed to be creeping into my ear and shining on the back of my head, so that I felt caught in it as in rain; I opened my eyes and every blade of grass, every paltry being in the hay, the most flimsy spider's web—all were standing out as though they were chiselled! As though asking to be looked at! There was no help for it: I leaned my head on my hand and began gazing. And I couldn't help it: would you believe it: my eyes bulged out like a hare's; they opened so wide—as though they did not know what sleep was! It seemed as though I would devour it all with my eyes. The doors of the barn were wide open; I could see for four miles into the open country, distinctly and yet not, as it always is on a moonlight night. I gazed and gazed without blinking. . . . And all at once it seemed as though something were moving, far, far away . . . like a faint glimmer in the distance. A little time passed: again the shadow stirred—now a little nearer; then again nearer still. 'What can it be?' I wondered, 'a hare, no,' I thought, 'it is bigger than a hare and its action is not the same.' I looked, and again the shadow came in sight, and was moving across the grazing meadow (the meadow looked whitish in the moonlight) like a big blur; it was clear that it was a wild animal, a fox or a wolf. My heart seemed to stand still . . . though one might wonder why I was frightened. All sorts of wild creatures run about the fields at night. But curiosity was even stronger than fear. I sat up, I opened my eyes wide and I turned cold all over. I felt frozen, as though I had been thrust into the ice, up to my ears, and why? The Lord only knows! And I saw the shadow growing and growing, so it was running straight towards the barn. And I began to realise that it certainly was a wild beast, big, with a huge head. . . . He flew like a whirlwind, like a bullet. . . . Holy saints! what was it? He stopped all at once, as though he scented something. . . . Why it was . . . the same mad dog! It was . . . it was! Heavens! And I could not stir, I could not cry out. . . . It darted to the doors, with glittering eyes, howled and dashed through the hay straight at me!

"Out of the hay like a lion leapt my Trésor, here he was. They hung on to each other's jaws and rolled on the ground. What happened then I don't remember; all I remember is that I flew headlong between them into the garden, and home and into my bedroom and almost crept under the bed—why not make a clean breast of it? And what leaps, what bounds I took in the garden! The *première danseuse* dancing before the Emperor Napoleon on his nameday couldn't have kept pace with me. However, when I had recovered myself a little, I roused the whole household; I ordered them all to arm themselves, I myself took a sword and a revolver (I bought that revolver, I must own, soon after the emancipation, you know, in case anything should happen, but it turned out the man who sold it was such a rogue—it would be sure to miss fire twice out of every three shots). Well, I took all this and so we went, a regular horde of us with stakes and lanterns, to the barn. We approached and called—there was not a sound; at last we went into the barn. . . . And what did we see? My poor Trésor lay dead with his throat torn open, and of the other, the damned brute, not a trace to be seen!

"And then, gentlemen, I howled like a calf and I am not ashamed to say so; I stooped down to the friend who had saved my life twice over and kissed his head, again and again. And I stayed in that position until my old housekeeper, Praskovya (she, too, had run in at the uproar), brought me to my senses. 'How can you, Porfiry Kapitonitch,' she said, 'distress yourself so about a dog? And you will catch cold, too, God forbid.' (I was very lightly clad.) 'And if this dog has lost his life in saving you, it may be taken as a great blessing vouchsafed him!'

"Though I did not agree with Praskovya, I went home. And next day a soldier of the garrison shot the mad dog. And it must have been its destined end: it was the first time in his life that the soldier had fired a gun, though he had a medal for service in 1812. So this was the supernatural incident that happened to me."

The speaker ceased and began filling his pipe. We all looked at each other in amazement.

"Well, perhaps, you have led a very virtuous life," Mr. Finoplentov began, "so in recompense . . ."

But he broke off at that word, for he saw Porfiry Kapitonitch's cheeks grow round and flushed while his eyes screwed up—he was on the point of breaking into a guffaw.

"But if one admits the possibility of the supernatural, the possibility of its participation in everyday life, so to say," Anton Stepanitch began again, "then allow me to ask, what becomes of common sense?"

None of us found anything to say in reply and we remained in perplexity as before.

A SIMPLE HEART

Gustave Flaubert

Translator unknown

Gustave Flaubert (1821–1880). Arguably the most influential exponent of realism in literature, Flaubert, according to the critic James Woods, "changed literature forever". Born and educated in Rouen, he studied law in Paris but ill-health forced him to give up his studies. He spent several years travelling in the Mediterranean, the Middle East and North Africa. His first novel was published in 1849, but it was *Madame Bovary* published in 1856, that established him as a major writer. When first published in serial form, both Flaubert and his publisher were arraigned for immorality but later acquitted.

I

For half a century the housewives of Pont-l'Évêque had envied Madame Aubain her servant Félicité.

For a hundred francs a year, she cooked and did the housework, washed, ironed, mended, harnessed the horse, fattened the poultry, made the butter and remained faithful to her mistress—although the latter was by no means an agreeable person.

Madame Aubain had married a comely youth without any money, who died in the beginning of 1809, leaving her with two young children and a number of debts. She sold all her property excepting the farm of Toucques and the farm of Geffosses, the income of which barely amounted to 5,000 francs; then she left her house in Saint-Melaine, and moved into a less pretentious one which had belonged to her ancestors and stood back of the market-place. This house, with its slate-covered roof, was built between a passage-way and a narrow street that led to the river. The interior was so unevenly graded that it caused people to stumble. A narrow hall separated the kitchen from the parlour, where Madame Aubain sat all day in a straw armchair near the window. Eight mahogany chairs stood in a row against the white wainscoting. An old piano, standing beneath a barometer, was covered with a pyramid of old books and boxes. On either side of the yellow marble mantelpiece, in Louis XV style, stood a tapestry armchair. The clock represented a temple of Vesta; and the whole room smelled musty, as it was on a lower level than the garden.

On the first floor was Madame's bed-chamber, a large room papered in a flowered design and containing the portrait of Monsieur dressed in the costume of a dandy. It communicated with a smaller room, in which there were two little cribs, without any mattresses. Next, came the parlour (always closed), filled with furniture covered with sheets. Then a hall, which led to the study, where books and papers were piled on the shelves of a bookcase that enclosed three quarters of the big black desk. Two panels were entirely hidden under pen-and-ink sketches, Gouache landscapes and Audran engravings, relics of better times and vanished luxury. On the second floor, a garret-window lighted Félicité's room, which looked out upon the meadows.

She arose at daybreak, in order to attend mass, and she worked without interruption until night; then, when dinner was over, the dishes cleared away and the door securely locked, she would bury the log under the ashes and fall asleep in front of the hearth with a rosary in her hand. Nobody could bargain with greater obstinacy, and as for cleanliness, the lustre on her brass saucepans was the envy and despair of other servants. She was most economical, and when she ate she would gather up crumbs with the tip of her finger, so that nothing should be wasted of the loaf of bread weighing twelve pounds which was baked especially for her and lasted three weeks.

Summer and winter she wore a dimity kerchief fastened in the back with a pin, a cap which concealed her hair, a red skirt, grey stockings, and an apron with a bib like those worn by hospital nurses.

Her face was thin and her voice shrill. When she was twenty-five, she looked forty. After she had passed fifty, nobody could tell her age; erect and silent always, she resembled a wooden figure working automatically.

II

Like every other woman, she had had an affair of the heart. Her father, who was a mason, was killed by falling from a scaffolding. Then her mother died and her sisters went their different ways; a farmer took her in, and while she was quite small, let her keep cows in the fields. She was clad in miserable rags, beaten for the slightest offence and finally dismissed for a theft of thirty sous which she did not commit. She took service on another farm where she tended the poultry; and as she was well thought of by her master, her fellow-workers soon grew jealous.

One evening in August (she was then eighteen years old), they persuaded her to accompany them to the fair at Colleville. She was immediately dazzled by the noise, the lights in the trees, the brightness of the dresses, the laces and gold crosses, and the crowd of people all hopping at the same time. She was standing modestly at a distance, when presently a young man of well-to-do appearance, who had been leaning on the pole of a wagon and smoking his pipe, approached her, and asked her for a dance. He treated her to cider and cake, bought her a silk shawl, and then, thinking she had guessed his purpose, offered to see her home. When they came to the end of a field he threw her down brutally. But she grew frightened and screamed, and he walked off.

One evening, on the road leading to Beaumont, she came upon a wagon loaded with hay, and when she overtook it, she recognised Theodore. He greeted her calmly, and asked her to forget what had happened between them, as it "was all the fault of the drink."

She did not know what to reply and wished to run away.

Presently he began to speak of the harvest and of the notables of the village; his father had left Colleville and bought the farm of Les Écots, so that now they would be neighbours. "Ah!" she exclaimed. He then added that his parents were looking around for a wife for him, but that he, himself, was not so anxious and preferred to wait for a girl who suited him. She hung her head. He then asked her whether she had ever thought of marrying. She replied, smilingly, that it was wrong of him to make fun of her. "Oh! no, I am in earnest," he said, and put his left arm around her waist while they sauntered along. The air was soft, the stars were bright, and the huge load of hay oscillated in front of them, drawn by four horses whose ponderous hoofs raised clouds of dust. Without a word from their driver they turned to the right. He kissed her again and she went home. The following week, Theodore obtained meetings.

They met in yards, behind walls or under isolated trees. She was not ignorant, as girls of well-to-do families are—for the animals had instructed her;—but her reason and her instinct of honour kept her from falling. Her resistance exasperated Theodore's love and so in order to satisfy it (or perchance ingenuously), he offered to marry her. She would not believe him at first, so he made solemn promises. But, in a short time he mentioned a difficulty; the previous year, his parents had purchased a substitute for him; but any day he might be drafted and the prospect of serving in the army alarmed him greatly. To Félicité his cowardice appeared a proof of his love for her, and her devotion to him grew stronger. When she met him, he would torture her with his fears and his entreaties. At last, he announced that he was going to the prefect himself for information, and would let her know everything on the following Sunday, between eleven o'clock and midnight.

When the time grew near, she ran to meet her lover.

But instead of Theodore, one of his friends was at the meeting-place.

He informed her that she would never see her sweetheart again; for, in order to escape the conscription, he had married a rich old woman, Madame Lehoussais, of Toucques.

The poor girl's sorrow was frightful. She threw herself on the ground, she cried and called on the Lord, and wandered around desolately until sunrise. Then she went back to the farm, declared her intention of leaving, and at the end of the month, after she had received her wages, she packed all her belongings in a handkerchief and started for Pont-l'Évêque.

In front of the inn, she met a woman wearing widow's weeds, and upon questioning her, learned that she was looking for a cook. The girl did not know very much, but appeared so willing and so modest in her requirements, that Madame Aubain finally said:

"Very well, I will give you a trial."

And half an hour later Félicité was installed in her house.

At first she lived in a constant anxiety that was caused by "the style of the household" and the memory of "Monsieur," that hovered over everything. Paul and Virginia, the one aged seven, and the other barely four, seemed made of some precious material; she carried them pig-a-back, and was greatly mortified when Madame Aubain forbade her to kiss them every other minute.

But in spite of all this, she was happy. The comfort of her new surroundings had obliterated her sadness.

Every Thursday, friends of Madame Aubain dropped in for a game of cards, and it was Félicité's duty to prepare the table and heat the foot-warmers. They arrived at exactly eight o'clock and departed before eleven.

Every Monday morning, the dealer in second-hand goods, who lived under the alley-way, spread out his wares on the sidewalk. Then the city would be filled with a buzzing of voices in which the neighing of horses, the bleating of lambs, the grunting of pigs, could be distinguished, mingled with the sharp sound of wheels on the cobble-stones. About twelve o'clock, when the market was in full swing, there appeared at the front door a tall, middle-aged peasant, with a hooked nose and a cap on the back of his head; it was Robelin, the farmer of Geffosses. Shortly afterwards came Liebard, the farmer of Toucques, short, rotund and ruddy, wearing a grey jacket and spurred boots.

Both men brought their landlady either chickens or cheese. Félicité would invariably thwart their ruses and they held her in great respect.

At various times, Madame Aubain received a visit from the Marquis de Gremanville, one of her uncles, who was ruined and lived at Falaise on the remainder of his estates. He always came at dinner-time and brought an ugly poodle with him, whose paws soiled their furniture. In spite of his efforts to appear a man of breeding (he even went so far as to raise his hat every time he said "My deceased father"), his habits got the better of him, and he would fill his glass a little too often and relate broad stories. Félicité would show him out very politely and say: "You have had enough for this time, Monsieur de Gremanville! Hoping to see you again!" and would close the door.

She opened it gladly for Monsieur Bourais, a retired lawyer. His bald head and white cravat, the ruffling of his shirt, his flowing brown coat, the manner in which he took snuff, his whole person, in fact, produced in her the kind of awe which we feel when we see extraordinary persons. As he managed Madame's estates, he spent hours with her in Monsieur's study; he was in constant fear of being compromised, had a great regard for the magistracy and some pretensions to learning.

In order to facilitate the children's studies, he presented them with an engraved geography which represented various scenes of the world; cannibals with feather head-dresses, a gorilla kidnapping a young girl, Arabs in the desert, a whale being harpooned, etc.

Paul explained the pictures to Félicité. And, in fact, this was her only literary education.

The children's studies were under the direction of a poor devil employed at the town-hall, who sharpened his pocket-knife on his boots and was famous for his penmanship.

When the weather was fine, they went to Geffosses. The house was built in the centre of the sloping yard; and the sea looked like a grey spot in the distance. Félicité would take slices of cold meat from the lunch basket and they would sit down and eat in a room next to the dairy. This room was all that remained of a cottage that had been torn down. The dilapidated wallpaper trembled in the drafts. Madame Aubain, overwhelmed by recollections, would hang her head, while the children were afraid to open their mouths. Then, "Why don't you go and play?" their mother would say; and they would scamper off.

Paul would go to the old barn, catch birds, throw stones into the pond, or pound the trunks of the trees with a stick till they resounded like drums. Virginia would feed the rabbits and run to pick the wild flowers in the fields, and her flying legs would disclose her little embroidered pantalettes. One autumn evening, they struck out for home through the meadows. The new moon illumined part of the sky and a mist hovered like a veil over the sinuosities of the river. Oxen, lying in the pastures, gazed mildly at the passing persons. In the third field, however, several of them got up and surrounded them. "Don't be afraid," cried Félicité; and murmuring a sort of lament she passed her hand over the back of the nearest ox; he turned away and the others followed. But when they came to the next pasture, they heard frightful bellowing.

It was a bull which was hidden from them by the fog. He advanced towards the two women, and Madame Aubain prepared to flee for her life. "No, no! not so fast," warned Félicité. Still they hurried on, for they could hear the noisy breathing of the bull behind them. His hoofs pounded the grass like hammers, and presently he began to gallop! Félicité turned around and threw patches of grass in his eyes. He hung his head, shook his horns and bellowed with fury. Madame Aubain and the children, huddled at the end of the field, were trying to jump over the ditch. Félicité continued to back before the bull, blinding him with dirt, while she shouted to them to make haste.

Madame Aubain finally slid into the ditch, after shoving first Virginia and then Paul into it, and though she stumbled several times she managed, by dint of courage, to climb the other side of it.

The bull had driven Félicité up against a fence; the foam from his muzzle flew in her face and in another minute he would have disembowelled her. She had just time to slip between two bars and the huge animal, thwarted, paused.

For years, this occurrence was a topic of conversation in Pont-l'Évêque. But Félicité took no credit to herself, and probably never knew that she had been heroic.

Virginia occupied her thoughts solely, for the shock she had sustained gave her a nervous affection, and the physician, M. Poupart, prescribed the salt-water bathing at Trouville. In those days, Trouville was not greatly patronised. Madame Aubain gathered information, consulted Bourais, and made preparations as if they were going on an extended trip.

The baggage was sent the day before on Liebard's cart. On the following morning, he brought around two horses, one of which had a woman's saddle with a velveteen back to it, while on the crupper of the other was a rolled shawl that was to be used for a seat. Madame Aubain mounted the second horse, behind Liebard. Félicité took charge of the little girl, and Paul rode M. Lechaptois' donkey, which had been lent for the occasion on the condition that they should be careful of it.

The road was so bad that it took two hours to cover the eight miles. The two horses sank knee-deep into the mud and stumbled into ditches; sometimes they had to jump over them. In certain places, Liebard's mare stopped abruptly. He waited patiently till she started again, and talked of the people whose estates bordered the road, adding his own moral reflections to the outline of their histories. Thus, when they were passing through Toucques, and came to some windows draped with nasturtiums, he shrugged his shoulders and said: "There's a woman, Madame Lehoussais, who, instead of taking a young man—" Félicité could not catch what followed; the horses began to trot, the donkey to gallop, and they turned into a lane; then a gate swung open, two farm-hands appeared and they all dismounted at the very threshold of the farmhouse.

Mother Liebard, when she caught sight of her mistress, was lavish with joyful demonstrations. She got up a lunch which comprised a leg of mutton, tripe, sausages, a chicken fricassee, sweet cider, a fruit tart and some preserved prunes; then to all this the good woman added polite remarks about Madame, who appeared to be in better health, Mademoiselle, who had grown to be "superb," and Paul, who had become singularly sturdy; she spoke also of their deceased grandparents, whom the Liebards had known, for they had been in the service of the family for several generations.

Like its owners, the farm had an ancient appearance. The beams of the ceiling were mouldy, the walls black with smoke and the windows grey with dust. The oak sideboard was filled with all sorts of utensils, plates, pitchers, tin bowls, wolf-traps. The children laughed when they saw a huge syringe. There was not a tree in the yard that did not have mushrooms growing around its foot, or a bunch of mistletoe hanging in its branches. Several of the trees had been blown down, but they had started to grow in the middle and all were laden with quantities of apples. The thatched roofs, which were of unequal thickness, looked like brown velvet and could resist the fiercest gales. But the wagon-shed was fast crumbling to ruins. Madame Aubain said that she would attend to it, and then gave orders to have the horses saddled.

It took another thirty minutes to reach Trouville. The little caravan dismounted in order to pass Les Écores, a cliff that overhangs the bay, and a few minutes later, at the end of the dock, they entered the yard of the Golden Lamb, an inn kept by Mother David.

During the first few days, Virginia felt stronger, owing to the change of air and the action of the sea-baths. She took them in her little chemise, as she had no bathing suit, and afterwards her nurse dressed her in the cabin of a customs officer, which was used for that purpose by other bathers.

In the afternoon, they would take the donkey and go to the Roches-Noires, near Hennequeville. The path led at first through undulating grounds, and thence to a plateau, where pastures and tilled fields alternated. At the edge of the road, mingling with the brambles, grew holly bushes, and here and there stood large dead trees whose branches traced zigzags upon the blue sky.

Ordinarily, they rested in a field facing the ocean, with Deauville on their left, and Le Havre on their right. The sea glittered brightly in the sun and was as smooth as a mirror, and so calm that they could scarcely distinguish its murmur; sparrows chirped joyfully and the immense canopy of heaven spread over it all. Madame Aubain brought out her sewing, and Virginia amused herself by braiding reeds; Félicité wove lavender blossoms, while Paul was bored and wished to go home.

Sometimes they crossed the Toucques in a boat, and started to hunt for sea-shells. The outgoing tide exposed star-fish and sea-urchins, and the children tried to catch the flakes of foam which the wind blew away. The sleepy waves lapping the sand unfurled themselves along the shore that extended as far as the eye could see, but where land began, it was limited by the downs which separated it from the "Swamp," a large meadow shaped like a hippodrome. When they went home that way, Trouville, on the slope of a hill below, grew larger and larger as they advanced, and, with all its houses of unequal height, seemed to spread out before them in a sort of giddy confusion.

When the heat was too oppressive, they remained in their rooms. The dazzling sunlight cast bars of light between the shutters. Not a sound in the village, not a soul on the sidewalk. This silence intensified the tranquility of everything. In the distance, the hammers of some calkers pounded the hull of a ship, and the sultry breeze brought them an odour of tar.

The principal diversion consisted in watching the return of the fishing-smacks. As soon as they passed the beacons, they began to ply to windward. The sails were lowered to one third of the masts, and with their fore-sails swelled up like balloons they glided over the waves and anchored in the middle of the harbour. Then they crept up alongside of the dock and the sailors threw the quivering fish over the side of the boat; a line of carts was waiting for them, and women with white caps sprang forward to receive the baskets and embrace their men-folk.

One day, one of them spoke to Félicité, who, after a little while, returned to the house gleefully. She had found one of her sisters, and presently Nastasie Barette, wife of Leroux, made her appearance, holding an infant in her arms, another child by the hand, while on her left was a little cabin-boy with his hands in his pockets and his cap on his ear.

At the end of fifteen minutes, Madame Aubain bade her go.

They always hung around the kitchen, or approached Félicité when she and the children were out walking. The husband, however, did not show himself.

Félicité developed a great fondness for them; she bought them a stove, some shirts and a blanket; it was evident that they exploited her. Her foolishness annoyed Madame Aubain, who, moreover did not like the nephew's familiarity, for he called her son "thou";—and, as Virginia began to cough and the season was over, she decided to return to Pont-l'Évêque.

Monsieur Bourais assisted her in the choice of a college. The one at Caen was considered the best. So Paul was sent away and bravely said good-bye to them all, for he was glad to go to live in a house where he would have boy companions.

Madame Aubain resigned herself to the separation from her son because it was unavoidable. Virginia brooded less and less over it. Félicité regretted the noise he made, but soon a new occupation diverted her mind; beginning from Christmas, she accompanied the little girl to her catechism lesson every day.

III

After she had made a curtsey at the threshold, she would walk up the aisle between the double lines of chairs, open Madame Aubain's pew, sit down and look around.

Girls and boys, the former on the right, the latter on the left-hand side of the church, filled the stalls of the choir; the priest stood beside the reading-desk; on one stained window of the side-aisle the Holy Ghost hovered over the Virgin; on another one, Mary knelt before the Child Jesus, and behind the altar, a wooden group represented Saint Michael felling the dragon.

The priest first read a condensed lesson of sacred history. Félicité evoked Paradise, the Flood, the Tower of Babel, the blazing cities, the dying nations, the shattered idols; and out of this she developed a great respect for the Almighty and a great fear of His wrath. Then, when she had listened to the Passion, she wept. Why had they crucified Him who loved little children, nourished the people, made the blind see, and who, out of humility, had wished to be born among the poor, in a stable? The sowings, the harvests, the wine-presses, all those familiar things which the Scriptures mention, formed a part of her life; the word of God sanctified them; and she loved the lambs with increased tenderness for the sake of the Lamb of God, and the doves because of the Holy Ghost.

She found it hard, however, to think of the latter as a person, for was it not a bird, a flame, and sometimes only a breath? Perhaps it is its light that at night hovers over swamps, its breath that propels the clouds, its voice that renders church-bells harmonious. And Félicité worshipped devoutly, while enjoying the coolness and the stillness of the church.

As for the dogma, she could not understand it and did not even try. The priest discoursed, the children recited, and she went to sleep, only to awaken with a start when they were leaving the church and their wooden shoes clattered on the stone pavement.

In this way, she learned her catechism, her religious education having been neglected in her youth; and thenceforth she imitated all Virginia's religious practices, fasted when she did, and went to confession with her. At the Corpus-Christi Day they both decorated an altar.

She worried in advance over Virginia's first communion. She fussed about the shoes, the rosary, the book and the gloves. With what nervousness she helped the mother dress the child!

During the entire ceremony, she felt anguished. Monsieur Bourais hid part of the choir from view, but directly in front of her, the flock of maidens, wearing white wreaths over their lowered veils, formed a snow-white field, and she recognised her darling by the slenderness of her neck and her devout attitude. The bell tinkled. All the heads bent and there was a silence. Then, at the peals of the organ the singers and the worshippers struck up the 'Agnus Dei'; the boys' procession began; behind them came the girls. With clasped hands, they advanced step by step to the lighted altar, knelt at the first step, received one by one the Host, and returned to their seats in the same order. When Virginia's turn came, Félicité leaned forward to watch her, and through that imagination which springs from true affection, she at once became the child, whose face and dress became hers, whose heart beat in her bosom, and when Virginia opened her mouth and closed her lids, she did likewise and came very near fainting.

The following day, she presented herself early at the church so as to receive communion from the curé. She took it with the proper feeling, but did not experience the same delight as on the previous day.

Madame Aubain wished to make an accomplished girl of her daughter; and as Guyot could not teach English or music, she decided to send her to the Ursulines at Honfleur.

The child made no objection, but Félicité sighed and thought Madame was heartless. Then, she thought that perhaps her mistress was right, as these things were beyond her sphere. Finally, one day, an old fiacre stopped in front of the door and a nun stepped out. Félicité put Virginia's luggage on top of the carriage, gave the coachman some instructions, and smuggled six jars of jam, a dozen pears and a bunch of violets under the seat.

At the last minute, Virginia had a fit of sobbing; she embraced her mother again and again, while the latter kissed her on the forehead, and said: "Now, be brave, be brave!" The step was pulled up and the fiacre rumbled off.

Then Madame Aubain had a fainting spell, and that evening all her friends, including the two Lormeaus, Madame Lechaptois, the ladies Rochefeuille, Messieurs de Houppeville and Bourais, called on her and tendered their sympathy.

At first the separation proved very painful to her. But her daughter wrote to her three times a week and the other days she, herself, wrote to Virginia. Then she walked in the garden, read a little, and in this way managed to fill out the emptiness of the hours.

Each morning, out of habit, Félicité entered Virginia's room and gazed at the walls. She missed combing her hair, lacing her shoes, tucking her in her bed, and the bright face and little hand when they used to go out for a walk. In order to occupy herself she tried to make lace. But her clumsy fingers broke the threads; she had no heart for anything, lost her sleep and "wasted away," as she put it.

In order to have some distraction, she asked leave to receive the visits of her nephew Victor.

He would come on Sunday, after church, with ruddy cheeks and bared chest, bringing with him the scent of the country. She would set the table and they would sit down opposite each other, and eat their dinner; she ate as little as possible, herself, to avoid any extra expense, but would stuff him so with food that he would finally go to sleep. At the first stroke of vespers, she would wake him up, brush his trousers, tie his cravat and walk to church with him, leaning on his arm with maternal pride.

His parents always told him to get something out of her, either a package of brown sugar, or soap, or brandy, and sometimes even money. He brought her his clothes to mend, and she accepted the task gladly, because it meant another visit from him.

In August, his father took him on a coasting-vessel.

It was vacation time and the arrival of the children consoled Félicité. But Paul was capricious, and Virginia was growing too old to be thee-and-thou'd, a fact which seemed to produce a sort of embarrassment in their relations.

Victor went successively to Morlaix, to Dunkirk, and to Brighton; whenever he returned from a trip he would bring her a present. The first time it was a box of shells; the second, a coffee-cup; the third, a big doll of ginger-bread. He was growing handsome, had a good figure, a tiny moustache, kind eyes, and a little leather cap that sat jauntily on the back of his head. He amused his aunt by telling her stories mingled with nautical expressions.

One Monday, the 14th of July, 1819 (she never forgot the date), Victor announced that he had been engaged on a merchant-vessel and that in two days he would take the steamer at Honfleur and join his sailer, which was going to start from Le Havre very soon. Perhaps he might be away two years.

The prospect of his departure filled Félicité with despair, and in order to bid him farewell, on Wednesday night, after Madame's dinner, she put on her pattens and trudged the four miles that separated Pont-l'Évêque from Honfleur.

When she reached the Calvary, instead of turning to the right, she turned to the left and lost herself in coal-yards; she had to retrace her steps; some people she spoke to advised her to hasten. She walked helplessly around the harbour filled with vessels, and knocked against hawsers. Presently the ground sloped abruptly, lights flitted to and fro, and she thought all at once that she had gone mad when she saw some horses in the sky.

Others, on the edge of the dock, neighed at the sight of the ocean. A derrick pulled them up in the air, and dumped them into a boat, where passengers were bustling about among barrels of cider, baskets of cheese and bags of meal; chickens cackled, the captain swore and a cabin-boy rested on the railing, apparently indifferent to his surroundings. Félicité, who did not recognise him, kept shouting: "Victor!" He suddenly raised his eyes, but while she was preparing to rush up to him, they withdrew the gangplank.

The packet, towed by singing women, glided out of the harbour. Her hull squeaked and the heavy waves beat up against her sides. The sail had turned and nobody was visible;—and on the ocean, silvered by the light of the moon, the vessel formed a black spot that grew dimmer and dimmer, and finally disappeared.

When Félicité passed the Calvary again, she felt as if she must entrust that which was dearest to her to the Lord; and for a long while she prayed, with uplifted eyes and a face wet with tears. The city was sleeping; some customs officials were taking the air; and the water kept pouring through the holes of the dam with a deafening roar. The town clock struck two.

The parlour of the convent would not open until morning, and surely a delay would annoy Madame, so, in spite of her desire to see the other child, she went home. The maids of the inn were just arising when she reached Pont-l'Évêque.

So the poor boy would be on the ocean for months! His previous trips had not alarmed her. One can come back from England and Brittany; but America, the colonies, the islands, were all lost in an uncertain region at the very end of the world.

From that time on, Félicité thought solely of her nephew. On warm days she feared he would suffer from thirst, and when it stormed, she was afraid he would be struck by lightning. When she harkened to the wind that rattled in the chimney and dislodged the tiles on the roof, she imagined that he was being buffeted by the same storm, perched on top of a shattered mast, with his whole body bend backward and covered with sea-foam; or,—these were recollections of the engraved geography—he was being devoured by savages, or captured in a forest by apes, or dying on some lonely coast. She never mentioned her anxieties, however.

Madame Aubain worried about her daughter.

The sisters thought that Virginia was affectionate but delicate. The slightest emotion enervated her. She had to give up her piano lessons. Her mother insisted upon regular letters from the convent. One morning, when the postman failed to come, she grew impatient and began to pace to and fro, from her chair to the window. It was really extraordinary! No news since four days!

In order to console her mistress by her own example, Félicité said:

"Why, Madame, I haven't had any news since six months!—"

"From whom?—"

The servant replied gently:

"Why—from my nephew."

"Oh, yes, your nephew!" And shrugging her shoulders, Madame Aubain continued to pace the floor as if to say: "I did not think of it.—Besides, I do not care, a cabin-boy, a pauper!—but my daughter—what a difference! just think of it!—"

Félicité, although she had been reared roughly, was very indignant. Then she forgot about it.

It appeared quite natural to her that one should lose one's head about Virginia.

The two children were of equal importance; they were united in her heart and their fate was to be the same.

The chemist informed her that Victor's vessel had reached Havana. He had read the information in a newspaper.

Félicité imagined that Havana was a place where people did nothing but smoke, and that Victor walked around among negroes in a cloud of tobacco. Could a person, in case of need, return by land? How far was it from Pont-l'Évêque? In order to learn these things, she questioned Monsieur Bourais. He reached for his map and began some explanations concerning longitudes, and smiled with superiority at Félicité's bewilderment. At last, he took a pencil and pointed out an imperceptible black point in the scallops of an oval blotch, adding: "There it is." She bent over the map; the maze of coloured lines hurt her eyes without enlightening her; and when Bourais asked her what puzzled her, she requested him to show her the house Victor lived in. Bourais threw up his hands, sneezed, and then laughed uproariously; such ignorance delighted his soul; but Félicité failed to understand the cause of his mirth, she whose intelligence was so limited that she perhaps expected to see even the picture of her nephew!

It was two weeks later that Liebard came into the kitchen at market-time, and handed her a letter from her brother-in-law. As neither of them could read, she called upon her mistress.

Madame Aubain, who was counting the stitches of her knitting, laid her work down beside her, opened the letter, started, and in a low tone and with a searching look said: "They tell you of a—misfortune. Your nephew—"

He had died. The letter told nothing more.

Félicité dropped on a chair, leaned her head against the back, and closed her lids; presently they grew pink. Then, with drooping head, inert hands and staring eyes she repeated at intervals:

"Poor little chap! poor little chap!"

Liebard watched her and sighed. Madame Aubain was trembling.

She proposed to the girl to go to see her sister in Trouville.

With a single motion, Félicité replied that it was not necessary.

There was a silence. Old Liebard thought it about time for him to take leave.

Then Félicité uttered:

"They have no sympathy, they do not care!"

Her head fell forward again, and from time to time, mechanically, she toyed with the long knitting-needles on the work-table.

Some women passed through the yard with a basket of wet clothes.

When she saw them through the window, she suddenly remembered her own washing; as she had soaked it the day before, she must go and rinse it now. So she arose and left the room.

Her tub and her board were on the bank of the Toucques. She threw a heap of clothes on the ground, rolled up her sleeves and grasped her bat; and her loud pounding could be heard in the neighbouring gardens. The meadows were empty, the breeze wrinkled the stream, at the bottom of which were long grasses that looked like the hair of corpses floating in the water. She restrained her sorrow and was very brave until night; but, when she had gone to her own room, she gave way to it, burying her face in the pillow and pressing her two fists against her temples.

A long while afterward, she learned through Victor's captain, the circumstances which surrounded his death. At the hospital they had bled him too much, treating him for yellow fever. Four doctors held him at one time. He died almost instantly, and the chief surgeon had said:

"Here goes another one!"

His parents had always treated him barbarously; she preferred not to see them again, and they made no advances, either from forgetfulness or out of innate hardness.

Virginia was growing weaker.

A cough, continual fever, oppressive breathing and spots on her cheeks indicated some serious trouble. Monsieur Popart had advised a sojourn in Provence. Madame Aubain decided that they would go, and she would have had her daughter come home at once, had it not been for the climate of Pont-l'Évêque.

She made an arrangement with a livery-stable man who drove her over to the convent every Tuesday. In the garden there was a terrace, from which the view extends to the Seine. Virginia walked in it, leaning on her mother's arm and treading over the dead vine leaves. Sometimes the sun, shining through the clouds, made her blink her lids, when she gazed at the sails in the distance, and let her eyes roam over the horizon from the chateau of Tancarville to the lighthouses of Le Havre. Then they rested on the arbour. Her mother had bought a little cask of fine Malaga wine, and Virginia, laughing at the idea of becoming intoxicated, would drink a few drops of it, but never more.

Her strength returned. Autumn passed. Félicité began to reassure Madame Aubain. But, one evening, when she returned home after an errand, she met M. Boupart's coach in front of the door; M. Boupart himself was standing in the vestibule and Madame Aubain was tying the strings of her bonnet. "Give me my foot-warmer, my purse and my gloves; and be quick about it," she said.

Virginia had congestion of the lungs; perhaps it was desperate.

"Not yet," said the physician, and both got into the carriage, while the snow fell in thick flakes. It was almost night and very cold.

Félicité rushed to the church to light a candle. Then she ran after the coach which she overtook after an hour's chase, sprang up behind and held on to the straps. But suddenly a thought crossed her mind: "The yard had been left open; supposing that burglars got in!" And down she jumped.

The next morning, at daybreak, she called at the doctor's. He had been home, but had left again. Then she waited at the inn, thinking that strangers might bring her a letter. At last, at daylight she took the diligence for Lisieux.

The convent was at the end of a steep and narrow street. When she arrived almost at the middle of it, she heard strange noises, a funeral knell. "It must be for some one else," thought she; and she pulled the knocker violently.

After several minutes had elapsed, she heard footsteps, the door was half opened and a nun appeared. The good sister, with an air of compunction, told her that "she had just passed away." And at the same time the tolling of Saint-Leonard's increased.

Félicité reached the second floor. Already at the threshold, she caught sight of Virginia lying on her back, with clasped hands, her mouth open and her head thrown back, beneath a black crucifix inclined toward her, and stiff curtains which were less white than her face. Madame Aubain lay at the foot of the couch, clasping it with her arms and uttering groans of agony. The Mother Superior was standing on the right side of the bed. The three candles on the bureau made red blurs, and the windows were dimmed by the fog outside. The nuns carried Madame Aubain from the room.

For two nights, Félicité never left the corpse. She would repeat the same prayers, sprinkle holy water over the sheets, get up, come back to the bed and contemplate the body. At the end of the first vigil, she noticed that the face had taken on a yellow tinge, the lips grew blue, the nose grew pinched, the eyes were sunken. She kissed them several times and would not have been greatly astonished had Virginia opened them; to souls like this the supernatural is always quite simple. She washed her, wrapped her in a shroud, put her into the casket, laid a wreath of flowers on her head and arranged her curls. They were blond and of an extraordinary length for her age. Félicité cut off a big lock and put half of it into her bosom, resolving never to part with it.

The body was taken to Pont-l'Évêque, according to Madame Aubain's wishes; she followed the hearse in a closed carriage.

After the ceremony it took three quarters of an hour to reach the cemetery. Paul, sobbing, headed the procession; Monsieur Bourais followed, and then came the principal inhabitants of the town, the women covered with black capes, and Félicité. The memory of her nephew, and the thought that she had not been able to render him these honours, made her doubly unhappy, and she felt as if he were being buried with Virginia.

Madame Aubain's grief was uncontrollable. At first she rebelled against God, thinking that he was unjust to have taken away her child—she who had never done anything wrong, and whose conscience was so pure! But no! she ought to have taken her South. Other doctors would have saved her. She accused herself, prayed to be able to join her child, and cried in the midst of her dreams. Of the latter, one more especially haunted her. Her husband, dressed like a sailor, had come back from a long voyage, and with tears in his eyes told her that he had received the order to take Virginia away. Then they both consulted about a hiding-place.

Once she came in from the garden, all upset. A moment before (and she showed the place), the father and daughter had appeared to her, one after the other; they did nothing but look at her.

During several months she remained inert in her room. Félicité scolded her gently; she must keep up for her son and also for the other one, for "her memory."

"Her memory!" replied Madame Aubain, as if she were just awakening, "Oh! yes, yes, you do not forget her!" This was an allusion to the cemetery where she had been expressly forbidden to go.

But Félicité went there every day. At four o'clock exactly, she would go through the town, climb the hill, open the gate and arrive at Virginia's tomb. It was a small column of pink marble with a flat stone at its base, and it was surrounded by a little plot enclosed by chains. The flower-beds were bright with blossoms. Félicité watered their leaves, renewed the gravel, and knelt on the ground in order to till the earth properly. When Madame Aubain was able to visit the cemetery she felt very much relieved and consoled.

Years passed, all alike and marked by no other events than the return of the great church holidays: Easter, Assumption, All Saints' Day. Household happenings constituted the only data to which in later years they often referred. Thus, in 1825, workmen painted the vestibule; in 1827, a portion of the roof almost killed a man by falling into the yard. In the summer of 1828, it was Madame's turn to offer the hallowed bread; at that time, Bourais disappeared mysteriously; and the old acquaintances, Guyot, Liebard, Madame Lechaptois, Robelin, old Gremanville, paralysed since a long time, passed away one by one. One night, the driver of the mail in Pont-l'Évêque announced the Revolution of July. A few days afterward a new sub-prefect was nominated, the Baron de Larsonnière, ex-consul in America, who, besides his wife, had his sister-in-law and her three grown daughters with him. They were often seen on their lawn, dressed in loose blouses, and they had a parrot and a negro servant. Madame Aubain received a call, which she returned promptly. As soon as she caught sight of them, Félicité would run and notify her mistress. But only one thing was capable of arousing her: a letter from her son.

He could not follow any profession as he was absorbed in drinking. His mother paid his debts and he made fresh ones; and the sighs that she heaved while she knitted at the window reached the ears of Félicité who was spinning in the kitchen.

They walked in the garden together, always speaking of Virginia, and asking each other if such and such a thing would have pleased her, and what she would probably have said on this or that occasion.

All her little belongings were put away in a closet of the room which held the two little beds. But Madame Aubain looked them over as little as possible. One summer day, however, she resigned herself to the task and when she opened the closet the moths flew out.

Virginia's frocks were hung under a shelf where there were three dolls, some hoops, a doll's house, and a wash basin which she had used. Félicité and Madame Aubain also took out the skirts, the handkerchiefs, and the stockings and spread them on the beds, before putting them away again. The sun fell on the piteous things, disclosing their spots and the creases formed by the motions of the body. The atmosphere was warm and blue, and a blackbird trilled in the garden; everything seemed to live in happiness. They found a little hat of soft brown plush, but it was entirely moth-eaten. Félicité asked for it. Their eyes met and filled with tears; at last the mistress opened her arms and the servant threw herself against her breast and they hugged each other and giving vent to their grief in a kiss which equalised them for a moment.

It was the first time that this had ever happened, for Madame Aubain was not of an expansive nature. Félicité was as grateful for it as if it had been some favour, and thenceforth loved her with animal-like devotion and a religious veneration.

Her kind-heartedness developed. When she heard the drums of a marching regiment passing through the street, she would stand in the doorway with a jug of cider and give the soldiers a drink. She nursed cholera victims. She protected Polish refugees, and one of them even declared that he wished to marry her. But they quarrelled, for one morning when she returned from the Angelus she found him in the kitchen coolly eating a dish which he had prepared for himself during her absence.

After the Polish refugees, came Colmiche, an old man who was credited with having committed frightful misdeeds in '93. He lived near the river in the ruins of a pig-sty. The urchins peeped at him through the cracks in the walls and threw stones that fell on his miserable bed, where he lay gasping with catarrh, with long hair, inflamed eyelids, and a tumour as big as his head on one arm.

She got him some linen, tried to clean his hovel and dreamed of installing him in the bake-house without his being in Madame's way. When the cancer broke, she dressed it every day; sometimes she brought him some cake and placed him in the sun on a bundle of hay; and the poor old creature, trembling and drooling, would thank her in his broken voice, and put out his hands whenever she left him. Finally he died; and she had a mass said for the repose of his soul.

That day a great joy came to her: at dinner-time, Madame de Larsonnière's servant called with the parrot, the cage, and the perch and chain and lock. A note from the baroness told Madame Aubain that as her husband had been promoted to a prefecture, they were leaving that night, and she begged her to accept the bird as a remembrance and a token of her esteem.

Since a long time the parrot had been on Félicité's mind, because he came from America, which reminded her of Victor, and she had approached the negro on the subject.

Once even, she had said:

"How glad Madame would be to have him!"

The man had repeated this remark to his mistress who, not being able to keep the bird, took this means of getting rid of it.

IV

He was called Loulou. His body was green, his head blue, the tips of his wings were pink and his breast was golden.

But he had the tiresome tricks of biting his perch, pulling his feathers out, scattering refuse and spilling the water of his bath. Madame Aubain grew tired of him and gave him to Félicité for good.

She undertook his education, and soon he was able to repeat: "Pretty boy! Your servant, sir! I salute you, Marie!" His perch was placed near the door and several persons were astonished that he did not answer to the name of "Jacquot," for every parrot is called Jacquot. They called him a goose and a log, and these taunts were like so many dagger thrusts to Félicité. Strange stubbornness of the bird which would not talk when people watched him!

Nevertheless, he sought society; for on Sunday, when the ladies Rochefeuille, Monsieur de Houppeville and the new habitués, Onfroy, the chemist, Monsieur Varin and Captain Mathieu, dropped in for their game of cards, he struck the window-panes with his wings and made such a racket that it was impossible to talk.

Bourais' face must have appeared very funny to Loulou. As soon as he saw him he would begin to roar. His voice re-echoed in the yard, and the neighbours would come to the windows and begin to laugh, too; and in order that the parrot might not see him, Monsieur Bourais edged along the wall, pushed his hat over his eyes to hide his profile, and entered by the garden door, and the looks he gave the bird lacked affection. Loulou, having thrust his head into the butcher-boy's basket, received a slap, and from that time he always tried to nip his enemy. Fabu threatened to ring his neck, although he was not cruelly inclined, notwithstanding his big whiskers and tattooings. On the contrary, he rather liked the bird, and, out of devilry, tried to teach him oaths. Félicité, whom his manner alarmed, put Loulou in the kitchen, took off his chain and let him walk all over the house.

When he went downstairs, he rested his beak on the steps, lifted his right foot and then his left one; but his mistress feared that such feats would give him vertigo. He became ill and was unable to eat. There was a small growth under his tongue like those chickens are sometimes afflicted with. Félicité pulled it off with her nails and cured him. One day, Paul was imprudent enough to blow the smoke of his cigar in his face; another time, Madame Lormeau was teasing him with the tip of her umbrella and he swallowed the tip. Finally he got lost.

She had put him on the grass to cool him and went away only for a second; when she returned, she found no parrot! She hunted among the bushes, on the bank of the river, and on the roofs, without paying any attention to Madame Aubain who screamed at her: "Take care! you must be insane!" Then she searched every garden in Pont-l'Évêque and stopped the passers-by to inquire of them: "Haven't you perhaps seen my parrot?" To those who had never seen the parrot, she described him minutely. Suddenly she thought she saw something green fluttering behind the mills at the foot of the hill. But when she was at the top of the hill she could not see it. A hod-carrier told her that he had just seen the bird in Saint-Melaine, in Mother Simon's store. She rushed to the place. The people did not know what she was talking about. At last she came home, exhausted, with her slippers worn to shreds, and despair in her heart. She sat down on the bench near Madame and was telling of her search when presently a light weight dropped on her shoulder—Loulou! What the deuce had he been doing? Perhaps he had just taken a little walk around the town!

She did not easily forget her scare; in fact, she never got over it. In consequence of a cold, she caught a sore throat; and some time later she had an earache. Three years later she was stone deaf, and spoke in a very loud voice even in church. Although her sins might have been proclaimed throughout the diocese without any shame to herself, or ill effects to the community, the curé thought it advisable to receive her confession in the vestry-room.

Imaginary buzzings also added to her bewilderment. Her mistress often said to her: "My goodness, how stupid you are!" and she would answer: "Yes, Madame," and look for something.

The narrow circle of her ideas grew more restricted than it already was; the bellowing of the oxen, the chime of the bells no longer reached her intelligence. All things moved silently, like ghosts. Only one noise penetrated her ears; the parrot's voice.

As if to divert her mind, he reproduced for her the tick-tack of the spit in the kitchen, the shrill cry of the fish-vendors, the saw of the carpenter who had a shop opposite, and when the door-bell rang, he would imitate Madame Aubain: "Félicité! go to the front door."

They held conversations together, Loulou repeating the three phrases of his repertory over and over, Félicité replying by words that had no greater meaning, but in which she poured out her feelings. In her isolation, the parrot was almost a son, a love. He climbed upon her fingers, pecked at her lips, clung to her shawl, and when she rocked her head to and fro like a nurse, the big wings of her cap and the wings of the bird flapped in unison. When clouds gathered on the horizon and the thunder rumbled, Loulou would scream, perhaps because he remembered the storms in his native forests. The dripping of the rain would excite him to frenzy; he flapped around, struck the ceiling with his wings, upset everything, and would finally fly into the garden to play. Then he would come back into the room, light on one of the andirons, and hop around in order to get dry.

One morning during the terrible winter of 1837, when she had put him in front of the fire-place on account of the cold, she found him dead in his cage, hanging to the wire bars with his head down. He had probably died of congestion. But she believed that he had been poisoned, and although she had no proofs whatever, her suspicion rested on Fabu.

She wept so sorely that her mistress said: "Why don't you have him stuffed?"

She asked the advice of the chemist, who had always been kind to the bird.

He wrote to Le Havre for her. A certain man named Fellacher consented to do the work. But, as the mail-coach driver often lost parcels entrusted to him, Félicité resolved to take her pet to Honfleur herself.

Leafless apple-trees lined the edges of the road. The ditches were covered with ice. The dogs on the neighbouring farms barked; and Félicité, with her hands beneath her cape, her little black sabots and her basket, trotted along nimbly in the middle of the sidewalk. She crossed the forest, passed by the Haut-Chêne, and reached Saint-Gatien.

Behind her, in a cloud of dust and impelled by the steep incline, a mail-coach drawn by galloping horses advanced like a whirlwind. When he saw a woman in the middle of the road, who did not get out of the way, the driver stood up in his seat and shouted to her and so did the postilion, while the four horses, which he could not hold back, accelerated their pace; the two leaders were almost upon her; with a jerk of the reins he threw them to one side, but, furious at the incident, he lifted his big whip and lashed her from her head to her feet with such violence that she fell to the ground unconscious.

Her first thought, when she recovered her senses, was to open the basket. Loulou was unharmed. She felt a sting on her right cheek; when she took her hand away it was red, for the blood was flowing.

She sat down on a pile of stones, and sopped her cheek with her handkerchief; then she ate a crust of bread she had put in her basket, and consoled herself by looking at the bird.

Arriving at the top of Ecquemanville, she saw the lights of Honfleur shining in the distance like so many stars; further on, the ocean spread out in a confused mass. Then a weakness came over her; the misery of her childhood, the disappointment of her first love, the departure of her nephew, the death of Virginia; all these things came back to her at once, and, rising like a swelling tide in her throat, almost choked her.

Then she wished to speak to the captain of the vessel, and without stating what she was sending, she gave him some instructions.

Fellacher kept the parrot a long time. He always promised that it would be ready for the following week; after six months he announced the shipment of a case, and that was the end of it. Really, it seemed as if Loulou would never come back to his home. "They have stolen him," thought Félicité.

Finally he arrived, sitting bolt upright on a branch which could be screwed into a mahogany pedestal, with his foot in the air, his head on one side, and in his beak a nut which the naturalist, from love of the sumptuous, had gilded. She put him in her room.

This place, to which only a chosen few were admitted, looked like a chapel and a second-hand shop, so filled was it with devotional and heterogeneous things. The door could not be opened easily on account of the presence of a large ward-robe. Opposite the window that looked out into the garden, a bull's-eye opened on the yard; a table was placed by the cot and held a wash-basin, two combs, and a piece of blue soap in a broken saucer. On the walls were rosaries, medals, a number of Holy Virgins, and a holy-water basin made out of a coconut; on the bureau, which was covered with a napkin like an altar, stood the box of shells that Victor had given her; also a watering-can and a balloon, writing-books, the engraved geography and a pair of shoes; on the nail which held the mirror, hung Virginia's little plush hat! Félicité carried this sort of respect so far that she even kept one of Monsieur's old coats. All the things which Madame Aubain discarded, Félicité begged for her own room. Thus, she had artificial flowers on the edge of the bureau, and the picture of the Comte d'Artois in the recess of the window. By means of a board, Loulou was set on a portion of the chimney which advanced into the room. Every morning when she awoke, she saw him in the dim light of dawn and recalled bygone days and the smallest details of insignificant actions, without any sense of bitterness or grief.

As she was unable to communicate with people, she lived in a sort of somnam-bulistic torpor. The processions of Corpus-Christi Day seemed to wake her up. She visited the neighbours to beg for candlesticks and mats so as to adorn the temporary altars in the street.

In church, she always gazed at the Holy Ghost, and noticed that there was something about it that resembled a parrot. The likenesses appeared even more striking on a coloured picture by Espinal, representing the baptism of our Saviour. With his scarlet wings and emerald body, it was really the image of Loulou. Having bought the picture, she hung it near the one of the Comte d'Artois so that she could take them in at one glance.

They associated in her mind, the parrot becoming sanctified through the neighbourhood of the Holy Ghost, and the latter becoming more lifelike in her eyes, and more comprehensible. In all probability the Father had never chosen as messenger a dove, as the latter has no voice, but rather one of Loulou's ancestors. And Félicité said her prayers in front of the coloured picture, though from time to time she turned slightly towards the bird.

She desired very much to enter in the ranks of the "Daughters of the Virgin." But Madame Aubain dissuaded her from it.

A most important event occurred: Paul's marriage.

After being first a notary's clerk, then in business, then in the customs, and a tax collector, and having even applied for a position in the administration of woods and forests, he had at last, when he was thirty-six years old, by a divine inspiration, found his vocation: registrature! and he displayed such a high ability that an inspector had offered him his daughter and his influence.

Paul, who had become quite settled, brought his bride to visit his mother.

But she looked down upon the customs of Pont-l'Évêque, put on airs, and hurt Félicité's feelings. Madame Aubain felt relieved when she left.

The following week they learned of Monsieur Bourais' death in an inn. There were rumours of suicide, which were confirmed; doubts concerning his integrity arose. Madame Aubain looked over her accounts and soon discovered his numerous embezzlements; sales of wood which had been concealed from her, false receipts, etc. Furthermore, he had an illegitimate child, and entertained a friendship for "a person in Dozulé."

These base actions affected her very much. In March, 1853, she developed a pain in her chest; her tongue looked as if it were coated with smoke, and the leeches they applied did not relieve her oppression; and on the ninth evening she died, being just seventy-two years old.

People thought that she was younger, because her hair, which she wore in bands framing her pale face, was brown. Few friends regretted her loss, for her manner was so haughty that she did not attract them. Félicité mourned for her as servants seldom mourn for their masters. The fact that Madame should die before herself perplexed her mind and seemed contrary to the order of things, and absolutely monstrous and inadmissible. Ten days later (the time to journey from Besançon), the heirs arrived. Her daughter-in-law ransacked the drawers, kept some of the furniture, and sold the rest; then they went back to their own home.

Madame's armchair, foot-warmer, work-table, the eight chairs, everything was gone! The places occupied by the pictures formed yellow squares on the walls. They had taken the two little beds, and the wardrobe had been emptied of Virginia's belongings! Félicité went upstairs, overcome with grief.

The following day a sign was posted on the door; the chemist screamed in her ear that the house was for sale.

For a moment she tottered, and had to sit down.

What hurt her most was to give up her room,—so nice for poor Loulou! She looked at him in despair and implored the Holy Ghost, and it was this way that she contracted the idolatrous habit of saying her prayers kneeling in front of the bird. Sometimes the sun fell through the window on his glass eye, and lighted a spark in it which sent Félicité into ecstasy.

Her mistress had left her an income of three hundred and eighty francs. The garden supplied her with vegetables. As for clothes, she had enough to last her till the end of her days, and she economised on the light by going to bed at dusk.

She rarely went out, in order to avoid passing in front of the second-hand dealer's shop where there was some of the old furniture. Since her fainting spell, she dragged her leg, and as her strength was failing rapidly, old Mother Simon, who had lost her money in the grocery business, came every morning to chop the wood and pump the water.

Her eyesight grew dim. She did not open the shutters after that. Many years passed. But the house did not sell or rent. Fearing that she would be put out, Félicité did not ask for repairs. The laths of the roof were rotting away, and during one whole winter her bolster was wet. After Easter she spit blood.

Then Mother Simon went for a doctor. Félicité wished to know what her complaint was. But, being too deaf to hear, she caught only one word: "Pneumonia." She was familiar with it and gently answered:—"Ah! like Madame," thinking it quite natural that she should follow her mistress.

The time for the altars in the street drew near.

The first one was always erected at the foot of the hill, the second in front of the post-office, and the third in the middle of the street. This position occasioned some rivalry among the women and they finally decided upon Madame Aubain's yard.

Félicité's fever grew worse. She was sorry that she could not do anything for the altar. If she could, at least, have contributed something towards it! Then she thought of the parrot. Her neighbours objected that it would not be proper. But the curé gave his consent and she was so grateful for it that she begged him to accept after her death, her only treasure, Loulou. From Tuesday until Saturday, the day before the event, she coughed more frequently. In the evening her face was contracted, her lips stuck to her gums and she began to vomit; and on the following day, she felt so low that she called for a priest.

Three neighbours surrounded her when the dominie administered the Extreme Unction. Afterwards she said that she wished to speak to Fabu.

He arrived in his Sunday clothes, very ill at ease among the funereal surroundings.

"Forgive me," she said, making an effort to extend her arm, "I believed it was you who killed him!"

What did such accusations mean? Suspect a man like him of murder! And Fabu became excited and was about to make trouble.

"Don't you see she is not in her right mind?"

From time to time Félicité spoke to shadows. The women left her and Mother Simon sat down to breakfast.

A little later, she took Loulou and holding him up to Félicité:

"Say good-bye to him, now!" she commanded.

Although he was not a corpse, he was eaten up by worms; one of his wings was broken and the wadding was coming out of his body. But Félicité was blind now, and she took him and laid him against her cheek. Then Mother Simon removed him in order to set him on the altar.

V

The grass exhaled an odour of summer; flies buzzed in the air, the sun shone on the river and warmed the slated roof. Old Mother Simon had returned to Félicité and was peacefully falling asleep.

The ringing of bells woke her; the people were coming out of church. Félicité's delirium subsided. By thinking of the procession, she was able to see it as if she had taken part in it. All the school-children, the singers and the firemen walked on the sidewalks, while in the middle of the street came first the custodian of the church with his halberd, then the beadle with a large cross, the teacher in charge of the boys and a sister escorting the little girls; three of the smallest ones, with curly heads, threw rose leaves into the air; the deacon with outstretched arms conducted the music; and two incense-bearers turned with each step they took toward the Holy Sacrament, which was carried by M. le Curé, attired in his handsome chasuble and walking under a canopy of red velvet supported by four men. A crowd of people followed, jammed between the walls of the houses hung with white sheets; at last the procession arrived at the foot of the hill.

A cold sweat broke out on Félicité's forehead. Mother Simon wiped it away with a cloth, saying inwardly that some day she would have to go through the same thing herself.

The murmur of the crowd grew louder, was very distinct for a moment and then died away. A volley of musketry shook the window-panes. It was the postilions saluting the Sacrament. Félicité rolled her eyes, and said as loudly as she could:

"Is he all right?" meaning the parrot.

Her death agony began. A rattle that grew more and more rapid shook her body. Froth appeared at the corners of her mouth, and her whole frame trembled. In a little while could be heard the music of the bass horns, the clear voices of the children and the men's deeper notes. At intervals all was still, and their shoes sounded like a herd of cattle passing over the grass.

The clergy appeared in the yard. Mother Simon climbed on a chair to reach the bull's-eye, and in this manner could see the altar. It was covered with a lace cloth and draped with green wreaths. In the middle stood a little frame containing relics; at the corners were two little orange-trees, and all along the edge were silver candlesticks, porcelain vases containing sun-flowers, lilies, peonies, and tufts of hydrangeas. This mount of bright colours descended diagonally from the first floor to the carpet that covered the sidewalk. Rare objects arrested one's eye. A golden sugar-bowl was crowned with violets, earrings set with Alençon stones were displayed on green moss, and two Chinese screens with their bright land-scapes were near by. Loulou, hidden beneath roses, showed nothing but his blue head which looked like a piece of lapis-lazuli.

The singers, the canopy-bearers and the children lined up against the sides of the yard. Slowly the priest ascended the steps and placed his shining sun on the lace cloth. Everybody knelt. There was deep silence; and the censers slipping on their chains were swung high in the air. A blue vapour rose in Félicité's room. She opened her nostrils and inhaled with a mystic sensuousness; then she closed her lids. Her lips smiled. The beats of her heart grew fainter and fainter, and vaguer, like a fountain giving out, like an echo dying away;—and when she exhaled her last breath, she thought she saw in the half-opened heavens a gigantic parrot hovering above her head.

GOD SEES THE TRUTH, BUT WAITS

Leo Tolstoy

Translated from the Russian by Aylmer Maude

Count Lev Nikolayevich Tolstoy (1828–1910), usually referred to in English as Leo Tolstoy, was a Russian writer who is regarded as one of the greatest authors of all time. Born to an aristocratic Russian family in 1828, he is best known for the novels *War and Peace* (1869) and *Anna Karenina* (1877), often cited as pinnacles of realist fiction. Tolstoy died of pneumonia at the Astapavo train station, the same train station where, famously, his character Anna Karenina came to her end. Tolstoy proposed to his wife in code, taking a piece of chalk and scratching out dozens of intitals, which she was then asked to decipher – and which she did. The scene is recreated in Anna Karenina. He made his own shoes from thin strips of birch bark.

In the town of Vladimir lived a young merchant named Ivan Dmitrich Aksionov. He had two shops and a house of his own.

Aksionov was a handsome, fair-haired, curly-headed fellow, full of fun, and very fond of singing. When quite a young man he had been given to drink, and was riotous when he had had too much; but after he married he gave up drinking, except now and then.

One summer Aksionov was going to the Nizhny Fair, and as he bade good-bye to his family, his wife said to him, "Ivan Dmitrich, do not start to-day; I have had a bad dream about you."

Aksionov laughed, and said, "You are afraid that when I get to the fair I shall go on a spree."

His wife replied: "I do not know what I am afraid of; all I know is that I had a bad dream. I dreamt you returned from the town, and when you took off your cap I saw that your hair was quite grey."

Aksionov laughed. "That's a lucky sign," said he. "See if I don't sell out all my goods, and bring you some presents from the fair."

So he said good-bye to his family, and drove away.

When he had travelled half-way, he met a merchant whom he knew, and they put up at the same inn for the night. They had some tea together, and then went to bed in adjoining rooms.

It was not Aksionov's habit to sleep late, and, wishing to travel while it was still cool, he aroused his driver before dawn, and told him to put in the horses.

Then he made his way across to the landlord of the inn (who lived in a cottage at the back), paid his bill, and continued his journey.

When he had gone about twenty-five miles, he stopped for the horses to be fed. Aksionov rested awhile in the passage of the inn, then he stepped out into the porch, and, ordering a samovar to be heated, got out his guitar and began to play.

Suddenly a troika drove up with tinkling bells and an official alighted, followed by two soldiers. He came to Aksionov and began to question him, asking him who he was and whence he came. Aksionov answered him fully, and said, "Won't you have some tea with me?" But the official went on cross-questioning him and asking him. "Where did you spend last night? Were you alone, or with a fellow-merchant? Did you see the other merchant this morning? Why did you leave the inn before dawn?"

Aksionov wondered why he was asked all these questions, but he described all that had happened, and then added, "Why do you cross-question me as if I were a thief or a robber? I am travelling on business of my own, and there is no need to question me."

Then the official, calling the soldiers, said, "I am the police-officer of this district, and I question you because the merchant with whom you spent last night has been found with his throat cut. We must search your things."

They entered the house. The soldiers and the police-officer unstrapped Aksionov's luggage and searched it. Suddenly the officer drew a knife out of a bag, crying, "Whose knife is this?"

Aksionov looked, and seeing a blood-stained knife taken from his bag, he was frightened.

"How is it there is blood on this knife?"

Aksionov tried to answer, but could hardly utter a word, and only stammered: "I—don't know—not mine." Then the police-officer said: "This morning the merchant was found in bed with his throat cut. You are the only person who could have done it. The house was locked from inside, and no one else was there. Here is this blood-stained knife in your bag and your face and manner betray you! Tell me how you killed him, and how much money you stole?"

Aksionov swore he had not done it; that he had not seen the merchant after they had had tea together; that he had no money except eight thousand rubles of his own, and that the knife was not his. But his voice was broken, his face pale, and he trembled with fear as though he were guilty.

The police-officer ordered the soldiers to bind Aksionov and to put him in the cart. As they tied his feet together and flung him into the cart, Aksionov crossed himself and wept. His money and goods were taken from him, and he was sent to the nearest town and imprisoned there. Enquiries as to his character were made in Vladimir. The merchants and other inhabitants of that town said that in former days he used to drink and waste his time, but that he was a good man. Then the trial came on: he was charged with murdering a merchant from Ryazan, and robbing him of twenty thousand rubles.

His wife was in despair, and did not know what to believe. Her children were all quite small; one was a baby at her breast. Taking them all with her, she went to the town where her husband was in jail. At first she was not allowed to see him; but after much begging, she obtained permission from the officials, and was taken to him. When she saw her husband in prison-dress and in chains, shut up with thieves and criminals, she fell down, and did not come to her senses for a long time. Then she drew her children to her, and sat down near him. She told him of things at home, and asked about what had happened to him. He told her all, and she asked, "What can we do now?"

"We must petition the Czar not to let an innocent man perish."

His wife told him that she had sent a petition to the Czar, but it had not been accepted.

Aksionov did not reply, but only looked downcast.

Then his wife said, "It was not for nothing I dreamt your hair had turned grey. You remember? You should not have started that day." And passing her fingers through his hair, she said: "Vanya dearest, tell your wife the truth; was it not you who did it?"

"So you, too, suspect me!" said Aksionov, and, hiding his face in his hands, he began to weep. Then a soldier came to say that the wife and children must go away; and Aksionov said good-bye to his family for the last time.

When they were gone, Aksionov recalled what had been said, and when he remembered that his wife also had suspected him, he said to himself, "It seems that only God can know the truth; it is to Him alone we must appeal, and from Him alone expect mercy."

And Aksionov wrote no more petitions; gave up all hope, and only prayed to God.

Aksionov was condemned to be flogged and sent to the mines. So he was flogged with a knot, and when the wounds made by the knot were healed, he was driven to Siberia with other convicts.

For twenty-six years Aksionov lived as a convict in Siberia. His hair turned white as snow, and his beard grew long, thin, and grey. All his mirth went; he stooped; he walked slowly, spoke little, and never laughed, but he often prayed.

In prison Aksionov learnt to make boots, and earned a little money, with which he bought *The Lives of the Saints*. He read this book when there was light enough in the prison; and on Sundays in the prison-church he read the lessons and sang in the choir; for his voice was still good.

The prison authorities liked Aksionov for his meekness, and his fellow-prisoners respected him: they called him "Grandfather," and "The Saint." When they wanted to petition the prison authorities about anything, they always made Aksionov their spokesman, and when there were quarrels among the prisoners they came to him to put things right, and to judge the matter.

No news reached Aksionov from his home, and he did not even know if his wife and children were still alive.

One day a fresh gang of convicts came to the prison. In the evening the old prisoners collected round the new ones and asked them what towns or villages they came from, and what they were sentenced for. Among the rest Aksionov sat down near the newcomers, and listened with downcast air to what was said.

One of the new convicts, a tall, strong man of sixty, with a closely-cropped grey beard, was telling the others what he had been arrested for.

"Well, friends," he said, "I only took a horse that was tied to a sledge, and I was arrested and accused of stealing. I said I had only taken it to get home quicker, and had then let it go; besides, the driver was a personal friend of mine. So I said, 'It's all right.' 'No,' said they, 'you stole it.' But how or where I stole it they could not say. I once really did something wrong, and ought by rights to have come here long ago, but that time I was not found out. Now I have been sent here for nothing at all . . . Eh, but it's lies I'm telling you; I've been to Siberia before, but I did not stay long."

"Where are you from?" asked some one.

"From Vladimir. My family are of that town. My name is Makar, and they also call me Semyonich."

Aksionov raised his head and said: "Tell me, Semyonich, do you know anything of the merchants Aksionov of Vladimir? Are they still alive?"

"Know them? Of course I do. The Aksionovs are rich, though their father is in Siberia: a sinner like ourselves, it seems! As for you, Gran'dad, how did you come here?"

Aksionov did not like to speak of his misfortune. He only sighed, and said, "For my sins I have been in prison these twenty-six years."

"What sins?" asked Makar Semyonich.

But Aksionov only said, "Well, well—I must have deserved it!" He would have said no more, but his companions told the newcomers how Aksionov came to be in Siberia; how some one had killed a merchant, and had put the knife among Aksionov's things, and Aksionov had been unjustly condemned.

When Makar Semyonich heard this, he looked at Aksionov, slapped his own knee, and exclaimed, "Well, this is wonderful! Really wonderful! But how old you've grown, Gran'dad!"

The others asked him why he was so surprised, and where he had seen Aksionov before; but Makar Semyonich did not reply. He only said: "It's wonderful that we should meet here, lads!"

These words made Aksionov wonder whether this man knew who had killed the merchant; so he said, "Perhaps, Semyonich, you have heard of that affair, or maybe you've seen me before?"

"How could I help hearing? The world's full of rumours. But it's a long time ago, and I've forgotten what I heard."

"Perhaps you heard who killed the merchant?" asked Aksionov.

Makar Semyonich laughed, and replied: "It must have been him in whose bag the knife was found! If some one else hid the knife there, 'He's not a thief till he's caught,' as the saying is. How could any one put a knife into your bag while it was under your head? It would surely have woke you up."

When Aksionov heard these words, he felt sure this was the man who had killed the merchant. He rose and went away. All that night Aksionov lay awake. He felt terribly unhappy, and all sorts of images rose in his mind. There was the image of his wife as she was when he parted from her to go to the fair. He saw her as if she were present; her face and her eyes rose before him; he heard her speak and laugh. Then he saw his children, quite little, as they were at that time: one with a little cloak on, another at his mother's breast. And then he remembered himself as he used to be – young and merry. He remembered how he sat playing the guitar in the porch of the inn where he was arrested, and how free from care he had been. He saw, in his mind, the place where he was flogged, the executioner, and the people standing around; the chains, the convicts, all the twenty-six years of his prison life, and his premature old age. The thought of it all made him so wretched that he was ready to kill himself.

"And it's all that villain's doing!" thought Aksionov. And his anger was so great against Makar Semyonich that he longed for vengeance, even if he himself should perish for it. He kept repeating prayers all night, but could get no peace. During the day he did not go near Makar Semyonich, nor even look at him.

A fortnight passed in this way. Aksionov could not sleep at night, and was so miserable that he did not know what to do.

One night as he was walking about the prison he noticed some earth that came rolling out from under one of the shelves on which the prisoners slept. He stopped to see what it was. Suddenly Makar Semyonich crept out from under the shelf, and looked up at Aksionov with a frightened face. Aksionov tried to pass without looking at him, but Makar seized his hand and told him that he had dug a hole under the wall, getting rid of the earth by putting it into his high-boots, and emptying it out every day on the road when the prisoners were driven to their work.

"Just you keep quiet, old man, and you shall get out too. If you blab, they'll flog the life out of me, but I will kill you first."

Aksionov trembled with anger as he looked at his enemy. He drew his hand away, saying, "I have no wish to escape, and you have no need to kill me; you killed me long ago! As to telling of you—I may do so or not, as God shall direct."

Next day, when the convicts were led out to work, the convoy soldiers noticed that one or other of the prisoners emptied some earth out of his boots. The prison was searched and the tunnel found. The Governor came and questioned all the prisoners to find out who had dug the hole. They all denied any knowledge of it. Those who knew would not betray Makar Semyonich, knowing he would be flogged almost to death. At last the Governor turned to Aksionov whom he knew to be a just man, and said:

"You are a truthful old man; tell me, before God, who dug the hole?"

Makar Semyonich stood as if he were quite unconcerned, looking at the Governor and not so much as glancing at Aksionov. Aksionov's lips and hands trembled, and for a long time he could not utter a word. He thought, "Why should I screen him who ruined my life? Let him pay for what I have suffered. But if I tell, they will probably flog the life out of him, and maybe I suspect him wrongly. And, after all, what good would it be to me?"

"Well, old man," repeated the Governor, "tell me the truth: who has been digging under the wall?"

Aksionov glanced at Makar Semyonich, and said, "I cannot say, your honour. It is not God's will that I should tell! Do what you like with me; I am in your hands."

However much the Governor tried, Aksionov would say no more, and so the matter had to be left.

That night, when Aksionov was lying on his bed and just beginning to doze, some one came quietly and sat down on his bed. He peered through the darkness and recognised Makar.

"What more do you want of me?" asked Aksionov. "Why have you come here?"

Makar Semyonich was silent. So Aksionov sat up and said, "What do you want? Go away, or I will call the guard!"

Makar Semyonich bent close over Aksionov, and whispered, "Ivan Dmitrich, forgive me!"

"What for?" asked Aksionov.

"It was I who killed the merchant and hid the knife among your things. I meant to kill you too, but I heard a noise outside, so I hid the knife in your bag and escaped out of the window."

Aksionov was silent, and did not know what to say. Makar Semyonich slid off the bed-shelf and knelt upon the ground. "Ivan Dmitrich," said he, "forgive me! For the love of God, forgive me! I will confess that it was I who killed the merchant, and you will be released and can go to your home."

"It is easy for you to talk," said Aksionov, "but I have suffered for you these twenty-six years. Where could I go to now? . . . My wife is dead, and my children have forgotten me. I have nowhere to go . . ."

Makar Semyonich did not rise, but beat his head on the floor. "Ivan Dmitrich, forgive me!" he cried. "When they flogged me with the knot it was not so hard to bear as it is to see you now . . . yet you had pity on me, and did not tell. For Christ's sake forgive me, wretch that I am!" And he began to sob.

When Aksionov heard him sobbing he, too, began to weep. "God will forgive you!" said he. "Maybe I am a hundred times worse than you." And at these words his heart grew light, and the longing for home left him. He no longer had any desire to leave the prison, but only hoped for his last hour to come.

In spite of what Aksionov had said, Makar Semyonich confessed his guilt. But when the order for his release came, Aksionov was already dead.

THE TALL WOMAN

Pédro Antonio de Alarcón

Translated from the Spanish by Rollo Ogden

Pédro Antonio de Alarcón y Ariza (1833–1891) was a nineteenth-century Spanish novelist, best known as author of the novel *El Sombrero de Tres Picos* (*The Three-Cornered Hat*, 1874). He produced four other full-length novels, three travel books and many short stories and essays. He died in Madrid on July 20, 1891, after a prolonged illness. His play *El Hijo Pródigo* (*The Prodigal Son*) was so unpopular that it was booed and hissed off the stage in 1857. The failure so upset him that he enlisted as a volunteer in the Moroccan campaign of 1859–1860. A radical revolutionary, he led an insurrection in Granada against the clergy and army. Alarcón changed his political views as a result of a duel in which his life was spared – he became a conservative and a staunch defender of religion.

I

"How little we really know, my friends; how little we really know."

The speaker was Gabriel, a distinguished civil engineer of the mountain corps. He was seated under a pine tree, near a spring, on the crest of the Guadarrama. It was only about a league and a half distant from the palace of the Escurial, on the boundary line of the provinces of Madrid and Segovia. I know the place, spring, pine tree and all, but I have forgotten its name.

"Let us sit down," went on Gabriel, "as that is the correct thing to do, and as our programme calls for a rest here—here in this pleasant and classic spot, famous for the digestive properties of that spring, and for the many lambs here devoured by our noted teachers, Don Miguel Bosch, Don Máximo Laguna, Don Augustin Pascual, and other illustrious naturalists. Sit down, and I will tell you a strange and wonderful story in proof of my thesis, which is, though you call me an obscurantist for it, that supernatural events still occur on this terraqueous globe. I mean events which you cannot get into terms of reason, or science, or philosophy—as those 'words, words, words,' in Hamlet's phrase, are understood (or are not understood) to-day."

Gabriel was addressing his animated remarks to five persons of different ages. None of them was young, though only one was well along in years. Three of them were, like Gabriel, engineers, the fourth was a painter, and the fifth was a *littérateur* in a small way. In company with the speaker, who was the youngest, we had all ridden up on hired mules from the Real Sitio de San Lorenzo to spend the day botanizing among the beautiful pine groves of Pequerinos, chasing butterflies with gauze nets, catching rare beetles under the bark of the decayed pines, and eating a cold lunch out of a hamper which we had paid for on shares.

This took place in 1875. It was the height of the summer. I do not remember whether it was Saint James's day or Saint Louis's; I am inclined to think it was Saint Louis's. Whichever it was, we enjoyed a delicious coolness at that height, and the heart and brain, as well as the stomach, were there in much better working order than usual.

When the six friends were seated, Gabriel continued as follows:

"I do not think you will accuse me of being a visionary. Luckily or unluckily, I am, if you will allow me to say so, a man of the modern world. I have no super-stition about me, and am as much of a Positivist as the best of them, although I include among the positive data of nature all the mysterious faculties and feelings of the soul. Well, then, apropos of supernatural, or extra-natural, phenomena, listen to what I have seen and heard, although I was not the real hero of the very strange story I am going to relate, and then tell me what explanation of an earthly, physical, or natural sort, however you may name it, can be given of so wonderful an occurrence.

"The case was as follows. But wait! Pour me out a drop, for the skin-bottle must have got cooled off by this time in that bubbling, crystalline spring, located by Providence on this piny crest for the express purpose of cooling a botanist's wine."

II

"Well, gentlemen, I do not know whether you ever heard of an engineer of the roads corps named Telesforo X—; he died in 1860."

"No; I haven't."

"But I have."

"So have I. He was a young fellow from Andalusia, with a black moustache; he was to have married the Marquis of Moreda's daughter, but he died of jaun-dice."

"The very one," said Gabriel. "Well, then, my friend Telesforo, six months before his death, was still a most promising young man, as they say nowadays. He was good-looking, well-built, energetic, and had the glory of being the first one in his class to be promoted. He had already gained distinction in the practice of his profession through some fine pieces of work. Several different companies were competing for his services, and many marriageable women were also competing for him. But Telesforo, as you said, was faithful to poor Joaquina Moreda.

"As you know, it turned out that she died suddenly at the baths of Santa Agueda, at the end of the summer of 1859. I was in Pau when I received the sad news of her death, which affected me very much on account of my close friend-ship with Telesforo. With her I had spoken only once, in the house of her aunt, the wife of General Lopez, and I certainly thought her bluish pallor a symptom of bad health. But, however that may be, she had a distinguished manner and a great deal of grace, and was, besides, the only daughter of a title, and a title that carried some comfortable thousands with it; so I felt sure my good mathema-tician would be inconsolable. Consequently, as soon as I was back in Madrid, fifteen or twenty days after his loss, I went to see him very early one morning. He lived in elegant bachelor quarters in Lobo Street—I do not remember the number, but it was near the Carrera de San Jerónimo.

"The young engineer was very melancholy, although calm and apparently master of his grief. He was already at work, even at that hour, laboring with his assistants over some railroad plans or other. He was dressed in deep mourning.

"He greeted me with a long and close embrace, without so much as sighing. Then he gave some directions to his assistants about the work in hand, and afterwards led me to his private office at the farther end of the house. As we were on our way there he said, in a sorrowful tone and without glancing at me:

"'I am very glad you have come. Several times I have found myself wishing you were here. A very strange thing has happened to me. Only a friend such as you are can hear of it without thinking me either a fool or crazy. I want to get an opinion about it as calm and cool as science itself.

"'Sit down,' he went on when we had reached his office, 'and do not imagine that I am going to afflict you with a description of the sorrow I am suffering —a sorrow which will last as long as I live. Why should I? You can easily picture it to yourself, little as you know of trouble. And as for being comforted, I do not wish to be, either now, or later, or ever! What I am going to speak to you about, with the requisite deliberation, going back to the very beginning of the thing, is a horrible and mysterious occurrence, which was an infernal omen of my calamity, and which has distressed me in a frightful manner.'

"'Go on,' I replied, sitting down. The fact was, I almost repented having entered the house as I saw the expression of abject fear on my friend's face.

"'Listen, then,' said he, wiping the perspiration from his forehead."

III

"'I do not know whether it is due to some inborn fatality of imagination, or to having heard some story or other of the kind with which children are so rashly allowed to be frightened, but the fact is, that since my earliest years nothing has caused me so much horror and alarm as a woman alone, in the street, at a late hour of the night. The effect is the same whether I actually encounter her, or simply have an image of her in my mind.

"'You can testify that I was never a coward. I fought a duel once, when I had to, like any other man. Just after I had left the School of Engineers, my workmen in Despeñaperros revolted, and I fought them with stick and pistol until I made them submit. All my life long, in Jaén, in Madrid, and elsewhere, I have walked the streets at all hours, alone and unarmed, and if I have chanced to run upon suspicious-looking persons, thieves, or mere sneaking beggars, they have had to get out of my way or take to their heels. But if the person turned out to be a solitary woman, standing still or walking, and I was also alone, with no one in sight in any direction—then (laugh if you want to, but believe me) I would be all covered over with goose-flesh; vague fears would assail me; I would think about beings of the other world, about imaginary existences, and about all the super-stitious stories which would make me laugh under other circumstances. I would quicken my pace, or else turn back, and would not get over my fright in the least until safe in my own house.

"'Once there I would fall a-laughing, and would be ashamed of my crazy fears. The only comfort I had was that nobody knew anything about it. Then I would dispassionately remind myself that I did not believe in goblins, witches, or ghosts, and that I had no reason whatever to be afraid of that wretched woman driven from her home at such an hour by poverty, or some crime, or accident, to whom I might better have offered help, if she needed it, or given alms. Nevertheless, the pitiable scene would be gone over again as often as a similar thing occurred—and remember that I was twenty-four years old, that I had experienced a great many adventures by night, and yet that I had never had the slightest difficulty of any sort with such solitary women in the streets after midnight! But nothing of what I have so far told you ever came to have any importance, since that irrational fear always left me as soon as I reached home, or saw any one else in the street, and I would scarcely recall it a few minutes afterwards, any more than one would recall a stupid mistake which had no result of any consequence.

"'Things were going on so, when, nearly three years ago (unhappily, I have good reason for knowing the date, it was the night of November 15–16, 1857), I was coming home at three in the morning. As you remember, I was living then in that little house in Jardines Street, near Montera Street. I had just come, at that late hour, a bitter, cold wind blowing at the time, out of a sort of a gambling-house—I tell you this, although I know it will surprise you. You know that I am not a gambler. I went into the place, deceived by an alleged friend. But the fact was, that as people began to drop in about midnight, coming from receptions or the theatre, the play began to be very heavy, and one saw the gleam of gold in plenty. Then came bank-bills and notes of hand. Little by little I was carried away by the feverish and seductive passion, and lost all the money I had. I even went away missing a second sum, for which I had left my note behind me. In short, I ruined myself completely; and but for the legacy that came to me afterwards, together with the good jobs I have had, my situation would have been extremely critical and painful.

"'So I was going home, I say, at so late an hour that night, numb with the cold, hungry, ashamed, and disgusted as you can imagine, thinking about my sick old father more than about myself. I should have to write to him for money, and this would astonish as much as it would grieve him, since he thought me in very easy circumstances. Just before reaching my street, where it crosses Peligros Street, as I was walking in front of a newly-built house, I perceived something in its doorway. It was a tall, large woman, standing stiff and motionless, as if made of wood. She seemed to be about sixty years old. Her wild and malignant eyes, unshaded by eyelashes, were fixed on mine like two daggers. Her toothless mouth made a horrible grimace at me, meant to be a smile.

"'The very terror or delirium of fear which instantly overcame me gave me somehow a most acute perception, so that I could distinguish at a glance, in the two seconds it took me to pass by that repugnant vision, the slightest details of her face and dress. Let me see if I can put together my impressions in the way and form in which I received them, as they were engraved ineffaceably on my brain in the light of the street-lamp which shone luridly over that ghastly scene.

But I am exciting myself too much, though there is reason enough for it, as you will see further on. Don't be concerned, however, for the state of my mind. I am not yet crazy!

"'The first thing which struck me in that WOMAN, as I will call her, was her extreme height and the breadth of her bony shoulders. Then, the roundness and fixity of her dry, owl-eyes, the enormous size of her protruding nose, and the great dark cavern of her mouth. Finally, her dress, like that of a young woman of Avapies—the new little cotton handkerchief which she wore on her head, tied under her chin, and a diminutive fan which she carried open in her hand, and with which, in affected modesty, she was covering the middle of her waist.

"'Nothing could be at the same time more ridiculous and more awful, more laughable and more taunting, than that little fan in those huge hands. It seemed like a make-believe sceptre in the hands of such an old, hideous, and bony giantess! A like effect was produced by the showy percale handkerchief adorning her face by the side of that cut-water nose, hooked and masculine; for a moment I was led to believe (or I was very glad to) that it was a man in disguise.

"'But her cynical glance and harsh smile were of a hag, of a witch, an enchantress, a Fate, a—I know not what! There was something about her to justify fully the aversion and fright which I had been caused all my life long by women walking alone in the streets at night. One would have said that I had had a presentiment of that encounter from my cradle. One would have said that I was frightened by it instinctively, as every living being fears and divines, and scents and recognizes, its natural enemy before ever being injured by it, before ever having seen it, and solely on hearing its tread.

"'I did not dash away in a run when I saw my life's sphinx. I restrained my impulse to do so, less out of shame and manly pride than out of fear lest my very fright should reveal to her who I was, or should give her wings to follow me, to overtake me—I do not know what. Panic like that dreams of dangers which have neither form nor name.

"'My house was at the opposite end of the long and narrow street, in which I was alone, entirely alone with that mysterious phantom whom I thought able to annihilate me with a word. How should I ever get home? Oh, how anxiously I looked towards that distant Montera Street, broad and well lighted, where there are policemen to be found at all hours! I decided, finally, to get the better of my weakness; to dissemble and hide that wretched fear; not to hasten my pace, but to keep on advancing slowly, even at the cost of years of health or life, and in this way, little by little, to go on getting nearer to my house, exerting myself to the utmost not to fall fainting on the ground before I reached it.

"'I was walking along in this way—I must have taken about twenty steps after leaving behind me the doorway where the woman with the fan was hidden, when suddenly a horrible idea came to me—horrible, yet very natural nevertheless—the idea that I would look back to see if my enemy was following me. One thing or the other I thought, with the rapidity of a flash of lightning: either my alarm has some foundation or it is madness; if it has any foundation, this woman will have started after me, will be overtaking me, and there is no hope for me on earth. But if it is madness, a mere supposition, a panic fright like any other, I will convince myself of it in the present instance, and for every case that may occur hereafter, by seeing that that poor old woman has stayed in that doorway to protect herself from the cold, or to wait till the door is opened; and thereupon I can go on to my house in perfect tranquillity, and I shall have cured myself of a fancy that causes me great mortification.

"'This reasoning gone through with, I made an extraordinary effort and turned my head. Ah, Gabriel!—Gabriel! how fearful it was! The tall woman had followed me with silent tread, was right over me, almost touching me with her fan, almost leaning her head on my shoulder.

"'Why was she doing it?—why, my Gabriel? Was she a thief? Was she really a man in disguise? Was she some malicious old hag who had seen that I was afraid of her? Was she a spectre conjured up by my very cowardice? Was she a mocking phantasm of human self-deception?

"'I could never tell you all I thought in a single moment. If the truth must be told, I gave a scream and flew away like a child of four years who thinks he sees the Black Man. I did not stop running until I got out into Montera Street. Once there, my fear left me like magic. This in spite of the fact that that street also was deserted. Then I turned my head to look back to Jardines Street. I could see down its whole length. It was lighted well enough for me to see the tall woman, if she had drawn back in any direction, and, by Heaven! I could not see her, standing still, walking, or in any way! However, I was very careful not to go back into that street again. The wretch, I said to myself, has slunk into some other doorway. But she can't move without my seeing her.

"'Just then I saw a policeman coming up Caballero de Gracia Street, and I shouted to him without stirring from my place. I told him that there was a man dressed as a woman in Jardines Street. I directed him to go round by the way of Peligros and Aduana Streets, while I would remain where I was, and in that way the fellow, who was probably a thief or murderer, could not escape us. The policeman did as I said. He went through Aduana Street, and as soon as I saw his lantern coming along Jardines Street I also went up it resolutely.

"'We soon met at about the middle of the block, without either of us having encountered a soul, although we had examined door after door.

"'"He has got into some house," said the policeman.

"'"That must be so," I replied, opening my door with the fixed purpose of moving to some other street the next day.

"'A few moments later I was in my room; I always carried my latchkey, so as not to have to disturb my good José. Nevertheless, he was waiting for me that night. My misfortunes of the 15th and 16th of November were not yet ended.

"'"What has happened?" I asked him, in surprise.

"'"Major Falcón was here," he replied, with evident agitation, "waiting for you from eleven till half-past two, and he told me that, if you came home to sleep, you had better not undress, as he would be back at daybreak."

"'Those words left me trembling with grief and alarm, as if they had predicted my own death to me. I knew that my beloved father, at his home in Jean, had been suffering frequent and dangerous attacks of his chronic disease. I had written to my brothers that, if there should be a sudden and fatal termination of the sickness, they were to telegraph Major Falcón, who would inform me in some suitable way. I had not the slightest doubt, therefore, that my father had died.

"'I sat down in an arm-chair to wait for the morning and my friend, and, with them, the news of my great misfortune. God only knows what I suffered in those two cruel hours of waiting. All the while, three distinct ideas were inseparably joined in my mind; though they seemed unlike, they took pains, as it were, to keep in a dreadful group. They were: my losses at play, my meeting with the tall woman, and the death of my revered father.

"'Precisely at six Major Falcón came into my room, and looked at me in silence. I threw myself into his arms, weeping bitterly, and he exclaimed, caressing me:

"'"Yes, my dear fellow, weep, weep."'"

IV

"My friend Telesforo," Gabriel went on, after having drained another glass of wine, "also rested a moment when he reached this point, and then he proceeded as follows:

"'If my story ended here, perhaps you would not find anything extraordinary or supernatural in it. You would say to me the same thing that men of good judgment said to me at that time: that every one who has a lively imagination is subject to some impulse of fear or other; that mine came from belated, solitary women, and that the old creature of Jardines Street was only some homeless waif who was going to beg of me when I screamed and ran.

"'For my part, I tried to believe that it was so. I even came to believe it at the end of several months. Still, I would have given years of my life to be sure that I was not again to encounter the tall woman. But, to-day, I would give every drop of my blood to be able to meet her again.'

"'What for?'

"'To kill her on the spot.'

"'I do not understand you.'

"'You will understand me when I tell you that I did meet her again, three weeks ago, a few hours before I had the fatal news of my poor Joaquina's death.'

"'Tell me about it, tell me about it!'

"'There is little more to tell. It was five o'clock in the morning. It was not yet fully light, though the dawn was visible from the streets looking towards the east. The street-lamps had just been put out, and the policemen had withdrawn. As I was going through Prado Street, so as to get to the other end of Lobo Street, the dreadful woman crossed in front of me. She did not look at me, and I thought she had not seen me.

"'She wore the same dress and carried the same fan as three years before. My trepidation and alarm were greater than ever. I ran rapidly across Prado Street as soon as she had passed, although I did not take my eyes off her, so as to make sure that she did not look back, and, when I had reached the other end of Lobo Street, I panted as if I had just swum an impetuous stream. Then I pressed on with fresh speed towards home, filled now with gladness rather than fear, for I thought that the hateful witch had been conquered and shorn of her power, from the very fact that I had been so near her and yet that she had not seen me.

"'But soon, and when I had almost reached this house, a rush of fear swept over me, in the thought that the crafty old hag had seen and recognized me, that she had made a pretence of not knowing me so as to let me get into Lobo Street, where it was still rather dark, and where she might set upon me in safety, that she would follow me, that she was already over me.

"'Upon this, I looked around—and there she was! There at my shoulder, almost touching me with her clothes, gazing at me with her horrible little eyes, displaying the gloomy cavern of her mouth, fanning herself in a mocking manner, as if to make fun of my childish alarm.

"'I passed from dread to the most furious anger, to savage and desperate rage. I dashed at the heavy old creature. I flung her against the wall. I put my hand to her throat. I felt of her face, her breast, the straggling locks of her gray hair until I was thoroughly convinced that she was a human being—a woman.

"'Meanwhile she had uttered a howl which was hoarse and piercing at the same time. It seemed false and feigned to me, like the hypocritical expression of a fear which she did not really feel. Immediately afterwards she exclaimed, making believe cry, though she was not crying, but looking at me with her hyena eyes:

"'"Why have you picked a quarrel with me?"

"'This remark increased my fright and weakened my wrath.

"'"Then you remember," I cried, "that you have seen me somewhere else."

"'"I should say so, my dear," she replied, mockingly. "Saint Eugene's night, in Jardines Street, three years ago."

"'My very marrow was chilled.

"'"But who are you?" I asked, without letting go of her. "Why do you follow me? What business have you with me?"

"'"I am a poor weak woman," she answered, with a devilish leer. "You hate me, and you are afraid of me without any reason. If not, tell me, good sir, why you were so frightened the first time you saw me."

"'"Because I have loathed you ever since I was born. Because you are the evil spirit of my life."

"'"It seems, then, that you have known me for a long time. Well, look, my son, so have I known you."

"'"You have known me? How long?"

"'"Since before you were born! And when I saw you pass by me, three years ago, I said to myself, THAT'S THE ONE."

"'"But what am I to you? What are you to me?"

"'"The devil!" replied the hag, spitting full in my face, freeing herself from my grasp, and running away with amazing swiftness. She held her skirts higher than her knees, and her feet did not make the slightest noise as they touched the ground.

"'It was madness to try to catch her. Besides, people were already passing through the Carrera de San Jerónimo, and in Prado Street, too. It was broad daylight. The tall woman kept on running, or flying, as far as Huertas Street, which was now lighted up by the sun. There she stopped to look back at me. She waved her closed fan at me once or twice, threateningly, and then disappeared around a corner.

"'Wait a little longer, Gabriel. Do not yet pronounce judgment in this case, where my life and soul are concerned. Listen to me two minutes longer.

"'When I entered my house I met Major Falcón, who had just come to tell me that my Joaquina, my betrothed, all my hope and happiness and joy on earth, had died the day before in Santa Agueda. The unfortunate father had telegraphed Falcon to tell me—me, who should have divined it an hour before, when I met the evil spirit of my life! Don't you understand, now, that I must kill that born enemy of my happiness, that vile old hag, who is the living mockery of my destiny?

"'But why do I say kill? Is she a woman? Is she a human being? Why have I had a presentiment of her ever since I was born? Why did she recognize me when she first saw me? Why do I never see her except when some great calamity has befallen me? Is she Satan? Is she Death? Is she Life? Is she Antichrist? Who is she? What is she?'"

V

"I will spare you, my dear friends," continued Gabriel, "the arguments and remarks which I used to see if I could not calm Telesforo, for they are the same, precisely the same, which you are preparing now to advance to prove that there is nothing supernatural or superhuman in my story. You will even go further; you will say that my friend was half crazy; that he always was so; that, at least, he suffered from that moral disease which some call 'panic terror,' and others 'emotional insanity'; that, even granting the truth of what I have related about the tall woman, it must all be referred to chance coincidences of dates and events; and, finally, that the poor old creature could also have been crazy, or a thief, or a beggar, or a procuress—as the hero of my story said to himself in a lucid interval."

"A very proper supposition," exclaimed Gabriel's comrades; "that is just what we were going to say."

"Well, listen a few minutes longer, and you will see that I was mistaken at the time, as you are mistaken now. The one who unfortunately made no mistake was Telesforo. It is much easier to speak the word 'insanity' than to find an explanation for some things that happen on the earth."

"Speak, speak!"

"I am going to; and this time, as it is the last, I will pick up the thread of my story without first drinking a glass of wine."

VI

"A few days after that conversation with Telesforo I was sent to the province of Albacete in my capacity as engineer of the mountain corps. Not many weeks had passed before I learned, from a contractor for public works, that my unhappy friend had been attacked by a dreadful form of jaundice; it had turned him entirely green, and he reclined in an arm-chair without working or wishing to see anybody, weeping night and day in the most inconsolable and bitter grief. The doctors had given up hope of his getting well.

"This made me understand why he had not answered my letters. I had to resort to Major Falcón as a source of news of him, and all the while the reports kept getting more unfavorable and gloomy.

"After an absence of five months I returned to Madrid the same day that the telegraph brought the news of the battle of Tetuán. I remember it as if it were yesterday. That night I bought the indispensable *Correspondencia de España*, and the first thing I read in it was the notice of Telesforo's death. His friends were invited to the funeral the following morning.

"You will be sure that I was present. As we arrived at the San Luis cemetery, whither I rode in one of the carriages nearest the hearse, my attention was called to a peasant woman. She was old and very tall. She was laughing sacrilegiously as she saw them taking out the coffin. Then she placed herself in front of the pall-bearers in a triumphant attitude and pointed out to them with a very small fan the passage-way they were to take to reach the open and waiting grave.

"At the first glance I perceived, with amazement and alarm, that she was Telesforo's implacable enemy. She was just as he had described her to me—with her enormous nose, her devilish eyes, her awful mouth, her percale handkerchief, and that diminutive fan which seemed in her hands the sceptre of indecency and mockery.

"She immediately observed that I was looking at her, and fixed her gaze upon me in a peculiar manner, as if recognizing me, as if letting me know that she recognized me, as if acquainted with the fact that the dead man had told me about the scenes in Jardines Street and Lobo Street, as if defying me, as if declaring me the inheritor of the hate which she had cherished for my unfortunate friend.

"I confess that at the time my fright was greater than my wonder at those new COINCIDENCES and ACCIDENTS. It seemed evident to me that some supernatural relation, antecedent to earthly life, had existed between the mysterious old woman and Telesforo. But for the time being my sole concern was about my own life, my own soul, my own happiness—all of which would be exposed to the greatest peril if I should really inherit such a curse.

"The tall woman began to laugh. She pointed at me contemptuously with the fan, as if she had read my thoughts and were publicly exposing my cowardice. I had to lean on a friend's arm to keep myself from falling. Then she made a pitying or disdainful gesture, turned on her heels, and went into the cemetery. Her head was turned towards me. She fanned herself and nodded to me at the same time. She sidled along among the graves with an indescribable, infernal coquetry, until at last she disappeared for ever in that labyrinth of tombs.

"I say for ever, since fifteen years have passed and I have never seen her again. If she was a human being she must have died before this; if she was not, I rest in the conviction that she despised me too much to meddle with me.

"Now, then, bring on your theories! Give me your opinion about these strange events. Do you still regard them as entirely natural?"

THE FORTUNE TELLER

Joaquim Maria Machado de Assis

Translated from the Portuguese by Isaac Goldberg

Joaquim Maria Machado de Assis (1839–1908) is perhaps the most important and influential writer in Brazilian literature. Born in Rio de Janeiro, his father was a freed slave of mixed race and his mother from the Azores. As a child, he was frail and suffered from epilepsy. Though educated at a public school he was a poor pupil and, at seventeen, became apprentice to a printer. He began to write in his spare time and quickly began to publish poems and plays, and later short stories and novels. His prose style was considered innovative and experimental, often breaking with the nineteenth-century realist tradition. Among his most famous works are *Dom Casmurro* and *The Posthumous Memoirs of Bras Cubas*. A formidable autodidact, he went on to teach himself French, English, German and Greek. Though widely admired in Brazil, he did not gain a readership outside his homeland in his lifetime. In 1897 he founded and became the first President of the Brazilian Academy of Letters.

Hamlet observes to Horatio that there are more things in heaven and earth than are dreamt of in our philosophy. This was the selfsame explanation that was given by beautiful Rita to her lover, Camillo, on a certain Friday of November, 1869, when Camillo laughed at her for having gone, the previous evening, to consult a fortune-teller. The only difference is that she made her explanation in other words.

"Laugh, laugh. That's just like you men; you don't believe in anything. Well, let me tell you, I went there and she guessed the reason for my coming before I ever spoke a word. Scarcely had she begun to lay out the cards when she said to me: 'The lady likes a certain person . . .' I confessed that it was so, and then she continued to rearrange the cards in various combinations, finally telling me that I was afraid you would forget me, but that there were no grounds for my fear."

"She was wrong!" interrupted Camillo with a laugh.

"Don't say that, Camillo. If you only realized in what anguish I went there, all on account of you. You know. I've told you before. Don't laugh at me; don't poke fun at me . . ."

Camillo seized her hands and gazed into her eyes earnestly and long. He swore that he loved her ever so much, that her fears were childish; in any case, should she ever harbor a fear, the best fortune-teller to consult was he himself. Then he reproved her, saying that it was imprudent to visit such houses. Villela might learn of it, and then . . .

"Impossible! I was exceedingly careful when I entered the place."

"Where is the house?"

"Near here. On Guarda-Velha Street. Nobody was passing by at the time. Rest easy. I'm not a fool."

Camillo laughed again.

"Do you really believe in such things?" he asked.

It was at this point that she translated Hamlet into every-day speech, assuring her lover that there was many a true, mysterious thing in this world. If he was skeptical, let him have patience. One thing, however, was certain: the card reader had guessed everything. What more could he desire? The best proof was that at this moment she was at ease and content.

He was about to speak, but he restrained himself. He did not wish to destroy her illusions. He, too, when a child, and even later, had been superstitious, filled with an arsenal of beliefs which his mother had instilled, and which had disappeared by the time he reached twenty. The day on which he rid himself of all this parasitic vegetation, leaving behind only the trunk of religion, he wrapped his superstition and his religion (which had both been inculcated by his mother) in the same doubt, and soon arrived at a single, total negation. Camillo believed in nothing. Why? He could not have answered; he had not a solitary reason; he was content simply to deny everything. But I express myself ill, for to deny is in a sense to affirm, and he did not formulate his unbelief. Before the great mystery he simply shrugged his shoulders and went on.

The lovers parted in good spirits, he more happy than she. Rita was sure that she was loved; but Camillo was not only sure that she loved him, but saw how she trembled for him and even took risks, running to fortune-tellers. However much he had reproved her for this, he could not help feeling flattered by it. Their secret meeting-place was in the old Barbonos street at the home of a woman that came from Rita's province. Rita went off through Mangueiras Street, in the direction of Botafogo, where she resided; Camillo entered Guarda-Velha Street, keeping his eye open, as he passed, for the home of the card reader.

Villela, Camillo and Rita: three names, one adventure and no explanation of how it all began. Let us proceed to explain. The first two were friends since earliest childhood. Villela had entered the magistracy. Camillo found employment with the government, against the will of his father, who desired him to embrace the medical profession. But his father had died, and Camillo preferred to be nothing at all, until his mother had procured him a departmental position. At the beginning of the year 1869 Villela returned from the interior, where he had married a silly beauty; he abandoned the magistracy and came hither to open a lawyer's office. Camillo had secured a house for him near Botafogo and had welcomed him home.

"Is this the gentleman?" exclaimed Rita, offering Camillo her hand. "You can't imagine how highly my husband thinks of you. He was always talking about you."

Camillo and Villela looked at each other tenderly. They were true friends. Afterwards, Camillo confessed to himself that Villela's wife did not at all belie the enthusiastic letters her husband had written to him. Really, she was most prepossessing, lively in her movements, her eyes burning, her mouth plastic and piquantly inquiring. Rita was a trifle older than both the men: she was thirty,

Villela twenty-nine and Camillo twenty-six. The grave bearing of Villela gave him the appearance of being much older than his wife, while Camillo was but a child in moral and practical life . . . He possessed neither experience nor intuition.

The three became closely bound. Propinquity bred intimacy. Shortly afterwards Camillo's mother died, and in this catastrophe, for such it was, the other two showed themselves to be genuine friends of his. Villela took charge of the interment, of the church services and the settlement of the affairs of the deceased; Rita dispensed consolation, and none could do it better.

Just how this intimacy between Camillo and Rita grew to love he never knew. The truth is that he enjoyed passing the hours at her side; she was his spiritual nurse, almost a sister,—but most of all she was a woman, and beautiful. The aroma of femininity: this is what he yearned for in her, and about her, seeking to incorporate it into himself. They read the same books, they went together to the theatre or for walks. He taught her cards and chess, and they played of nights;— she badly,—he, to make himself agreeable, but little less badly. Thus much, as far as external things are concerned. And now came personal intimacies, the timorous eyes of Rita, that so often sought his own, consulting them before they questioned those of her own husband,—the touches of cold hands, and unwonted communion. On one of his birthdays he received from Villela a costly cane, and from Rita, a hastily pencilled, ordinary note expressing good wishes. It was then that he learned to read within his own heart; he could not tear his eyes away from the missive. Commonplace words, it is true; but there are sublime commonplaces,—or at least, delightful ones. The old chaise in which for the first time you rode with your beloved, snuggled together, is as good as the chariot of Apollo. Such is man, and such are the circumstances that surround him.

Camillo sincerely wished to flee the situation, but it was already beyond his power. Rita, like a serpent, was charming him, winding her coils about him; she was crushing his bones, darting her venomous fangs into his lips. He was helpless, overcome. Vexation, fear, remorse, desire,—all this he felt, in a strange confusion. But the battle was short and the victory deliriously intoxicating. Farewell, all scruple! The shoe now fitted snugly enough upon the foot, and there they were both, launched upon the high road, arm in arm, joyfully treading the grass and the gravel, without suffering anything more than lonesomeness when they were away from each other. As to Villela, his confidence in his wife and his esteem for his friend continued the same as before.

One day, however, Camillo received an anonymous letter, which called him immoral and perfidious, and warned him that his adventure was known to all. Camillo took fright, and, in order to ward off suspicion, began to make his visits to Villela's house more rare. The latter asked him the reason for his prolonged absence. Camillo answered that the cause was a youthful flirtation. Simplicity evolved into cunning. Camillo's absences became longer and longer, and then his visits ceased entirely. Into this course there may have entered a little self-respect,—the idea of diminishing his obligations to the husband in order to make his own actions appear less treacherous.

It was at this juncture that Rita, uncertain and in fear, ran to the fortune-teller to consult her upon the real reason for Camillo's actions. As we have seen, the card reader restored the wife's confidence and the young man reproved her for having done what she did. A few weeks passed. Camillo received two or three more anonymous letters, written with such passionate anger that they could not have been prompted by mere regard for virtue; surely they came from some violent rival of his. In this opinion Rita concurred, formulating, in ill-composed words of her own, this thought: virtue is indolent and niggardly, wasting neither time nor paper; only self-interest is alert and prodigal.

But this did not help to ease Camillo; he now feared lest the anonymous writer should inform Villela, in which case the catastrophe would follow fast and implacably. Rita agreed that this was possible.

"Very well," she said. "Give me the envelopes in which the letters came, so that I may compare the handwriting with that of the mail which comes to him. If any arrives with writing resembling the anonymous script, I'll keep it and tear it up . . ."

But no such letter appeared. A short time after this, however, Villela commenced to grow grave, speaking very little, as if something weighed upon his mind. Rita hurried to communicate the change to her lover, and they discussed the matter earnestly. Her opinion was that Camillo should renew his visits to their home, and sound her husband; it might be that Villela would confide to him some business worry. With this Camillo disagreed; to appear after so many months was to confirm the suspicions and denunciations of the anonymous letters. It was better to be very careful, to give each other up for several weeks. They arranged means for communicating with each other in case of necessity and separated, in tears.

On the following day Camillo received at his department this letter from Villela: "Come immediately to our house; I must talk to you without delay." It was past noon. Camillo left at once; as he reached the street it occurred to him that it would have been much more natural for Villela to have called him to his office; why to his house? All this betokened a very urgent matter; moreover, whether it was reality or illusion, it seemed to Camillo that the letter was written in a trembling hand. He sought to establish a connection between all these things and the news Rita had brought him the night before.

"Come immediately to our house; I must talk to you without delay," he repeated, his eyes staring at the note.

In his mind's eye he beheld the climax of a drama,—Rita cowed, weeping; Villela indignant, seizing his pen and dashing off the letter, certain that he, Camillo, would answer in person, and waiting to kill him as he entered. Camillo shuddered with terror; then he smiled weakly; in any event the idea of drawing back was repugnant to him. So he continued on his way. As he walked it occurred to him to step into his rooms; he might find there a message from Rita explaining everything. But he found nothing, nobody. He returned to the street, and the thought that they had been discovered grew every moment more convincing; yes, the author of the previous anonymous communications must have denounced him to the husband; perhaps by now Villela knew all. The very suspension of his calls without any apparent reason, with the flimsiest of pretexts, would confirm everything else.

Camillo walked hastily along, agitated, nervous. He did not read the letter again, but the words hovered persistently before his eyes; or else,—which was even worse—they seemed to be murmured into his ears by the voice of Villela himself. "Come immediately to our house; I must talk to you without delay." Spoken thus by the voice of the other they seemed pregnant with mystery and menace. Come immediately,—why? It was now nearly one o'clock. Camillo's agitation waxed greater with each passing moment. So clearly did he imagine what was about to take place that he began to believe it a reality, to see it before his very eyes. Yes, without a doubt, he was afraid. He even considered arming himself, thinking that if nothing should happen he would lose nothing by this useful precaution. But at once he rejected the idea, angry with himself, and hastened his step towards Carioca Square, there to take a tilbury. He arrived, entered and ordered the driver to be off at full speed.

"The sooner the better," he thought. "I can't stand this uncertainty."

But the very sound of the horse's clattering hoofs increased his agitation. Time was flying, and he would be face to face with danger soon enough. When they had come almost to the end of Guarda-Velha Street the tilbury had to come to a stop; the thoroughfare was blocked by a coach that had broken down. Camillo surveyed the obstruction and decided to wait. After five minutes had gone by, he noticed that there at his left, at the very foot of the tilbury, was the fortune teller's house,—the very same as Rita had once consulted. Never, as at this moment, had he so desired to believe in card-reading. He looked closer, saw that the windows were closed, while all the others on the street were opened, filled with folks curious to see what was the matter. It looked for all the world like the dwelling of indifferent Fate.

Camillo leaned back in his seat so as to shut all this from view. His excitement was intense, extraordinary, and from the deep, hidden recesses of his mind there began to emerge spectres of early childhood, old beliefs, banished superstitions. The coachman proposed another route; he shook his head and said that he would wait. He leaned forward to get a better look at the card-reader's house . . . Then he made a gesture of self-ridicule: it had entered his mind to consult the fortune-teller, who seemed to be hovering over him, far, far above, with vast, ash-colored wings; she disappeared, reappeared, and then her image was lost; then, in a few moments, the ash-colored wings stirred again, nearer, flying about him in narrowing circles . . . In the street men were shouting, dragging away the coach.

"There! Now! Push! That's it! Now!"

In a short while the obstruction was removed. Camillo closed his eyes, trying to think of other things; but the voice of Rita's husband whispered into his ears the words of the letter: "Come immediately . . ." And he could behold the anguish of the drama. He trembled. The house seemed to look right at him. His feet instinctively moved as if to leave the carriage and go in . . . Camillo found himself before a long, opaque veil . . . he thought rapidly of the inexplicability of so many things. The voice of his mother was repeating to him a host of extraordinary happenings; and the very sentence of the Prince of Denmark kept echoing within him:

> There are more things in heaven and earth, Horatio,
> Than are dreamt of in our philosophy.

What could he lose by it, if . . . ?

He jumped out to the pavement, just before the fortune-teller's door; he told the driver to wait for him, and hastened into the entry, ascending the stairs. There was little light, the stairs were worn away from the many feet that had sought them, the banister was smooth and sticky; but he saw and felt nothing. He stumbled up the stairs and knocked. Nobody appearing, he was about to go down; but it was too late now,—curiosity was whipping his blood and his heart beat with violent throbs; he turned back to the door, and knocked once, twice, three times. He beheld a woman; it was the card-reader. Camillo said that he had come to consult her, and she bade him enter. Thence they climbed to the attic by a staircase even worse than the first and buried in deeper gloom. At the top there was a garret, ill lighted by a small window. Old furniture, somber walls, and an air of poverty augmented, rather than destroyed, the prestige of the occupant.

The fortune-teller told him to be seated before the table, and she sat down on the opposite side with her back to the window, so that whatever little light came from without fell full upon Camillo's face. She opened a drawer and took out a pack of worn, filthy cards. While she rapidly shuffled them she peered at him closely, not so much with a direct gaze as from under her eyes. She was a woman of forty, Italian, thin and swarthy, with large, sharp, cunning eyes. She placed three cards upon the table, and said:

"Let us first see what has brought you here. The gentleman has just received a severe shock and is in great fear . . ."

Camillo, astonished, nodded affirmatively.

"And he wishes to know," she continued, "whether anything will happen to him or not . . ."

"To me and to her," he explained, excitedly.

The fortune-teller did not smile; she simply told him to wait. She took the cards hastily once more and shuffled them with her long tapering fingers whose nails were so long and unclean from neglect; she shuffled them well, once, twice, thrice; then she began to lay them out. Camillo's eyes were riveted upon her in anxious curiosity.

"The cards tell me . . ."

Camillo leaned forward to drink in her words one by one. Then she told him to fear nothing. Nothing would happen to him or to the other. He, the third, was aware of nought. Nevertheless, great caution was indispensable; envy and rivalry were at work. She spoke to him of the love that bound them, of Rita's beauty . . . Camillo was bewildered. The fortune-teller stopped talking, gathered the cards and locked them in the drawer.

"The lady has restored peace to my spirit," he said, offering her his hand across the table and pressing that of the card-reader.

She arose, laughing.

"Go," she said. "Go, *ragazzo innamorato* . . ."[1]

And arising, she touched his head with her index finger. Camillo shuddered, as if it were the hand of one of the original sybils, and he, too, arose. The fortune-teller went to the bureau, upon which lay a plate of raisins, took a cluster of them and commenced to eat them, showing two rows of teeth that were as white as her nails were black. Even in this common action the woman possessed an air all her own. Camillo, anxious to leave, was at a loss how much to pay; he did not know her fee.

1 Italian for "love-sick boy," "young lover," etc.

"Raisins cost money," he said, at length, taking out his pocket-book. "How much do you want to send for?"

"Ask your heart," she replied.

Camillo took out a note for ten milreis[2] and gave it to her. The eyes of the card-reader sparkled. Her usual fee was two milreis.

"I can see easily that the gentleman loves his lady very much . . . And well he may. For she loves the gentleman very deeply, too. Go, go in peace, with your mind at ease. And take care as you descend the staircase,—it's dark. Don't forget your hat . . ."

The fortune-teller had already placed the note in her pocket, and accompanied him down the stairs, chatting rather gaily. At the bottom of the first flight Camillo bid her good-bye and ran down the stairs that led to the street, while the card-reader, rejoicing in her large fee, turned back to the garret, humming a barcarolle. Camillo found the tilbury waiting for him; the street was now clear. He entered and the driver whipped his horse into a fast trot.

To Camillo everything had now changed for the better and his affairs assumed a brighter aspect; the sky was clear and the faces of the people he passed were all so merry. He even began to laugh at his fears, which he now saw were puerile; he recalled the language of Villela's letter and perceived at once that it was most friendly and familiar. How in the world had he ever been able to read any threat of danger into those words! He suddenly realized that they were urgent, however, and that he had done ill to delay so long; it might be some very serious business affair.

"Faster, faster!" he cried to the driver.

And he began to think of a plausible explanation of his delay; he even contemplated taking advantage of this incident to re-establish his former intimacy in Villela's household . . . Together with his plans there kept echoing in his soul the words of the fortune-teller. In truth, she had guessed the object of his visit, his own state of mind, and the existence of a third; why, then, wasn't it reasonable to suppose that she had guessed the rest correctly, too? For, the unknown present is the same as the future. And thus, slowly and persistently the young man's childhood superstitions attained the upper hand and mystery clutched him in its iron claws. At times he was ready to burst into laughter, and with a certain vexation he did laugh at himself. But the woman, the cards, her dry, reassuring words, and her good-bye—"Go, go, *ragazzo innamorato*," and finally, that farewell barcarolle, so lively and gracious,—such were the new elements which, together with the old, formed within him a new and abiding faith.

The truth is that his heart was happy and impatient, recalling the happy hours of the past and anticipating those yet to come. As he passed through Gloria Street Camillo gazed across the sea, far across where the waters and the heaven meet in endless embrace, and the sight gave him a sensation of the future,—long, long and infinite.

From here it was but a moment's drive to Villela's home. He stepped out, thrust the iron garden gate open and entered. The house was silent. He ran up the six stone steps and scarcely had he had time to knock when the door opened and Villela loomed before him.

2 In United States money ten Brazilian milreis are equivalent to about $5.50.

"Pardon my delay. It was impossible to come sooner. What is the matter?"

Villela made no reply. His features were distorted; he beckoned Camillo to step within. As he entered, Camillo could not repress a cry of horror:—there upon the sofa lay Rita, dead in a pool of blood. Villela seized the lover by the throat and, with two bullets, stretched him dead upon the floor.

IT SNOWS

Enrico Castelnuovo

Translated from the Italian by Edith Wharton

Enrico Castelnuovo (1839–1915) was born in Florence, and spent much of his life in Venice, where he moved with his mother as a child after his father abandoned the family. His family were unable to afford a classical education for him, so, despite his love of literature, he was educated at a technical school. From his twenties, he worked as a journalist, frequently travelling to Milan where he met prominent cultural figures of the time. In 1872, he left journalism to teach at what is now the Ca' Foscari University of Venice. He was a prolific writer, publishing almost several volumes of shorts stories and fourteen novels.

The thermometer marks barely one degree above freezing, the sky is covered with ominous white clouds, the air is harsh and piercing; what can induce Signor Odoardo, at nine o'clock on such a morning, to stand in his study window? It is true that Signor Odoardo is a vigorous man, in the prime of life, but it is never wise to tempt Providence by needlessly risking one's health. But stay—I begin to think that I have found a clue to his conduct. Opposite Signor Odoardo's window is the window of the Signora Evelina, and Signora Evelina has the same tastes as Signor Odoardo. She too is taking the air, leaning against the window-sill in her dressing-gown, her fair curls falling upon her forehead and tossed back every now and then by a pretty movement of her head. The street is so narrow that it is easy to talk across from one side to the other, but in such weather as this the only two windows that stand open are those of Signora Evelina and Signor Odoardo.

There is no denying the fact: Signora Evelina, who within the last few weeks has taken up her abode across the way, is a very fascinating little widow. Her hair is of spun gold, her skin of milk and roses, her little turned-up nose, though assuredly not Grecian, is much more attractive than if it were; she has the most dazzling teeth in the most kissable mouth; her eyes are transparent as a cloudless sky, and—well, she knows how to use them. Nor is this the sum total of her charms: look at the soft, graceful curves of her agile, well-proportioned figure; look at her little hands and feet! After all, one hardly wonder that Signor Odoardo runs the risk of catching his death of cold, instead of closing the window and warming himself at the stove which roars so cheerfully within. It is rather at Signora Evelina that I wonder; for, though Signor Odoardo is not an ill-looking man, he is close upon forty, while she is but twenty-four. So young, and already a widow—poor Signora Evelina! It is true that she has great strength of character;

but six months have elapsed since her husband's death, and she is resigned to it already, though the deceased left her barely enough to keep body and soul together. Happily Signora Evelina is not encumbered with a family; she is alone and independent, and with those eyes, that hair, that little upturned nose, she ought to have no difficulty in finding a second husband. In fact, there is no harm in admitting that Signora Evelina has contemplated the possibility of a second marriage, and that if the would-be bridegroom is not in his first youth—why, she is prepared to make the best of it. In this connection it is perhaps not uninstructive to note that Signor Odoardo is in comfortable circumstances, and is himself a widower. What a coincidence!

Well, then, why don't they marry—that being the customary denouement in such cases?

Why don't they marry? Well—Signor Odoardo is still undecided. If there had been any hope of a love-affair I fear that his indecision would have vanished long ago. *Errare humanum est.* But Signora Evelina is a woman of serious views; she is in search of a husband, not of a flirtation. Signora Evelina is a person of great determination; she knows how to turn other people's heads without letting her own be moved a jot. Signora Evelina is deep; deep enough, surely, to gain her point. If Signor Odoardo flutters about her much longer he will! singe his wings; things cannot go on in this; way. Signor Odoardo's visits are too frequent; and now, in addition, there are the conversations from the window. It is time for a decisive step to be taken, and Signor Odoardo is afraid that he may find himself taking the step before he is prepared to; this very day, perhaps, when he goes to call on the widow.

The door of Signor Odoardo's study is directly opposite the window in which he is standing, and the opening of this door is therefore made known to him by a violent draught.

As he turns a sweet voice says:

"Good-bye, papa dear; I'm going to school."

"Good-bye, Doretta," he answers, stooping to kiss a pretty little maid of eight or nine; and at the same instant Signora Evelina calls out from over the way:

"Good-morning, Doretta!"

Doretta, who had made a little grimace on discovering her papa in conversation with his pretty neighbor, makes another as she hears herself greeted, and mutters reluctantly, "Good-morning."

Then, with her little basket on her arm, she turns away slowly to join the maid-servant who is waiting for her in the hall.

"I am SO fond of that child," sighs Signora Evelina, with the sweetest inflexion in her voice, "but she doesn't like me at all!"

"What an absurd idea! . . . Doretta is a very self-willed child."

Thus Signor Odoardo; but in his heart of hearts he too is convinced that his little daughter has no fondness for Signora Evelina.

Meanwhile, the cold is growing more intense, and every now and then a flake of snow spins around upon the wind. Short of wishing to be frozen stiff, there is nothing for it but to shut the window.

"It snows," says Signora Evelina, glancing upward.

"Oh, it was sure to come."

"Well—I must go and look after my household. *Au revoir*—shall I see you later?"

"I hope to have the pleasure—"

"*Au revoir*, then."

Signora Evelina closes the window, nods and smiles once more through the pane, and disappears.

Signor Odoardo turns back to his study, and perceiving how cold it has grown, throws some wood on the fire, and, kneeling before the door of the stove, tries to blow the embers into a blaze. The flames leap up with a merry noise, sending bright flashes along the walls of the room.

Outside, the flakes continue to descend at intervals. Perhaps, after all, it is not going to be a snowstorm.

Signor Odoardo paces up and down the room, with bent head and hands thrust in his pockets. He is disturbed, profoundly disturbed. He feels that he has reached a crisis in his life; that in a few days, perhaps in a few hours, his future will be decided. Is he seriously in love with Signora Evelina? How long has he known her? Will she be sweet and good like THE OTHER? Will she know how to be a mother to Doretta?

There is a sound of steps in the hall; Signor Odoardo pauses in the middle of the room. The door re-opens, and Doretta rushes up to her father, her cheeks flushed, her hood falling over her forehead, her warm coat buttoned up to her chin, her hands thrust into her muff.

"It is snowing and the teacher has sent us home."

She tosses off her hood and coat and goes up to the stove.

"There is a good fire, but the room is cold," she exclaims.

As a matter of fact, the window having stood open for half an hour, the thermometer indicates but fifty degrees.

"Papa," Doretta goes on, "I want to stay with you all day long to-day."

"And suppose your poor daddy has affairs of his own to attend to?"

"No, no, you must give them up for to-day."

And Doretta, without waiting for an answer, runs to fetch her books, her doll, and her work. The books are spread out on the desk, the doll is comfortably seated on the sofa, and the work is laid out upon a low stool.

"Ah," she cries, with an air of importance, "what a mercy that there is no school to-day! I shall have time to go over my lesson. Oh, look how it snows!"

It snows indeed. First a white powder, fine but thick, and whirled in circles by the wind, beats with a dry metallic sound against the window-panes; then the wind drops, and the flakes, growing larger, descend silently, monotonously, incessantly. The snow covers the streets like a downy carpet, spreads itself like a sheet over the roofs, fills up the cracks in the walls, heaps itself upon the window-sills, envelops the iron window-bars, and hangs in festoons from the gutters and eaves.

Out of doors it must be as cold as ever, but the room is growing rapidly warmer, and Doretta, climbing on a chair, has the satisfaction of announcing that the mercury has risen eleven degrees.

"Yes, dear," her father replies, "and the clock is striking eleven too. Run and tell them to get breakfast ready."

Doretta runs off obediently, but reappears in a moment.

"Daddy, daddy, what do you suppose has happened? The dining-room stove won't draw, and the room is all full of smoke!"

"Then let us breakfast here, child."

This excellent suggestion is joy to the soul of Doretta, who hastens to carry the news to the kitchen, and then, in a series of journeys back and forth from the dining-room to the study, transports with her own hands the knives, forks, plates, tablecloth, and napkins, and, with the man-servant's aid, lays them out upon one of her papa's tables. How merry she is! How completely the cloud has vanished that darkened her brow a few hours earlier! And how well she acquits herself of her household duties!

Signor Odoardo, watching her with a sense of satisfaction, cannot resist exclaiming: "Bravo, Doretta!"

Doretta is undeniably the very image of her mother. She too was just such an excellent housekeeper, a model of order, of neatness, of propriety. And she was pretty, like Doretta, even though she did not possess the fair hair and captivating eyes of Signora Evelina.

The man-servant who brings in the breakfast is accompanied by a newcomer, the cat Melanio, who is always present at Doretta's meals. The cat Melanio is old; he has known Doretta ever since she was born, and he honors her with his protection. Every morning he mews at her door, as though to inquire if she has slept well; every evening he keeps her company until it is time for her to go to bed. Whenever she goes out he speeds her with a gentle purr; whenever he hears her come in he hurries to meet her and rubs himself against her legs. In the morning, and at the midday meal, when she takes it at home, he sits beside her chair and silently waits for the scraps from her plate. The cat Melanio, however, is not in the habit of visiting Signor Odoardo's study, and shows a certain surprise at finding himself there. Signor Odoardo, for his part, receives his new guest with some diffidence; but Doretta, intervening in Melanio's favor, undertakes to answer for his good conduct.

It is long since Doretta has eaten with so much appetite. When she has finished her breakfast, she clears the table as deftly and promptly as she had laid it, and in a few moments Signor Odoardo's study has resumed its wonted appearance. Only the cat Melanio remains, comfortably established by the stove, on the understanding that he is to be left there as long as he is not troublesome.

The continual coming and going has made the room grow colder. The mercury has dropped perceptibly, and Doretta, to make it rise again, empties nearly the whole wood-basket into the stove.

How it snows, how it snows! No longer in detached flakes, but as though an openwork white cloth were continuously unrolled before one's eyes. Signor Odoardo begins to think that it will be impossible for him to call on Signora Evelina. True, it is only a step, but he would sink into the snow up to his knees. After all, it is only twelve o'clock. It may stop snowing later. Doretta is struck by a luminous thought:

"What if I were to answer grandmamma's letter?"

In another moment Doretta is seated at her father's desk, in his arm-chair, two cushions raising her to the requisite height, her legs dangling into space, the pen suspended in her hand, and her eyes fixed upon a sheet of ruled paper, containing thus far but two words: Dear Grandmamma.

Signor Odoardo, leaning against the stove, watches his daughter with a smile.

It appears that at last Doretta has discovered a way of beginning her letter, for she re-plunges the pen into the inkstand, lowers her hand to the sheet of paper, wrinkles her forehead and sticks out her tongue.

After several minutes of assiduous toil she raises her head and asks:

"What shall I say to grandmamma about her invitation to go and spend a few weeks with her?"

"Tell her that you can't go now, but that she may expect you in the spring."

"With you, papa?"

"With me, yes," Signor Odoardo answers mechanically.

Yet if, in the meantime, he engages himself to Signora Evelina, this visit to his mother-in-law will become rather an awkward business.

"There—I've finished!" Doretta cries with an air of triumph.

But the cry is succeeded by another, half of anguish, half of rage.

"What's the matter now?"

"A blot!"

"Let me see? . . . You little goose, what HAVE you done? . . . You've ruined the letter now!"

Doretta, having endeavored to remove the ink-spot by licking it, has torn the paper.

"Oh, dear, I shall have to copy it out now," she says, in a mortified tone.

"You can copy it this evening. Bring it here, and let me look at it . . . Not bad,—not bad at all. A few letters to be added, and a few to be taken out; but, on the whole, for a chit of your size, it's fairly creditable. Good girl!"

Doretta rests upon her laurels, playing with her doll Nini. She dresses Nini in her best gown, and takes her to call on the cat, Melanio.

The cat, Melanio, who is dozing with half-open eyes, is somewhat bored by these attentions. Raising himself on his four paws, he arches his flexible body, and then rolls himself up into a ball, turning his back upon his visitor.

"Dear me, Melanio is not very polite to-day," says Doretta, escorting the doll back to the sofa. "But you mustn't be offended; he's very seldom impolite. I think it must be the weather; doesn't the weather make you sleepy too, Nini? . . . Come, let's take a nap; go by-bye, baby, go by-bye."

Nini sleeps. Her head rests upon a cushion, her little rag and horse-hair body is wrapped in a woollen coverlet, her lids are closed; for Nini raises or lowers her lids according to the position of her body.

Signor Odoardo looks at the clock and then glances out of the window. It is two o'clock and the snow is still falling.

Doretta is struck by another idea.

"Daddy, see if I know my La Fontaine fable: *Le corbeau et le renard*."

"Very well, let's hear it," Signor Odoardo assents, taking the open book from the little girl's hands.

Doretta begins:

Maître corbeau, sur un arbre perché,

> Tenait en son bec un fromage;
> Maître . . . maître . . . maître . . .

"Go on."

"Maître . . ."

"Maître renard."

"Oh, yes, now I remember:

> Maître renard, par l'odeur alléché,
> Lui tint à peu près ce langage:
> Hé! bonjour . . ."

At this point Doretta, seeing that her father is not listening to her, breaks off her recitation. Signor Odoardo has, in fact, closed the book upon his forefinger, and is looking elsewhere.

"Well, Doretta," he absently inquires, "why don't you go on?" "I'm not going to say any more of it," she answers sullenly. "Why, you cross-patch! What's the matter?"

The little girl, who had been seated on a low stool, has risen to her feet and now sees why her papa has not been attending to her. The snow is falling less thickly, and the fair head of Signora Evelina has appeared behind the window-panes over the way.

Brave little woman! She has actually opened the window, and is clearing the snow off the sill with a fire-shovel. Her eyes meet Signor Odoardo's; she smiles and shakes her head, as though to say: What hateful weather!

He would be an ill-mannered boor who should not feel impelled to say a word to the dauntless Signor Evelina. Signor Odoardo, who is not an ill-mannered boor, yields to the temptation of opening the window for a moment.

"Bravo, Signora Evelina! I see you are not afraid of the snow."

"Oh, Signor Odoardo, what fiendish weather! . . . But, if I am not mistaken, that is Doretta with you . . . How do you do, Doretta?"

"Doretta, come here and say how do you do to the lady."

"No, no—let her be, let her be! Children catch cold so easily—you had better shut the window. I suppose there is no hope of seeing you to-day?"

"Look at the condition of the streets!"

"Oh, you men . . . you men! . . . The stronger sex . . . but no matter. Au revoir!"

"Au revoir."

The two windows are closed simultaneously, but this time Signora Evelina does not disappear. She is sitting there, close to the window, and it snows so lightly now that her wonderful profile is outlined as clearly as possible against the pane. Good heavens, how beautiful she is!

Signor Odoardo walks up and down the room, in the worst of humors. He feels that it is wrong not to go and see the fascinating widow, and that to go and see her would be still more wrong. The cloud has settled again upon Doretta's forehead, the same cloud that darkened it in the morning.

Not a word is said of La Fontaine's fable. Instead, Signor Odoardo grumbles irritably:

"This blessed room is as cold as ever."

"Why shouldn't it be," Doretta retorts with a touch of asperity, "when you open the window every few minutes?"

"Oho," Signor Odoardo says to himself, "it is time to have this matter out."

And, going up to Doretta, he takes her by the hand, leads her to the sofa, and lifts her on his knee.

"Now, then, Doretta, why is it that you are so disagreeable to Signora Evelina?"

The little girl, not knowing what to answer, grows red and embarrassed. "What has Signora Evelina done to you?" her father continues.

"She hasn't done anything to me."

"And yet you don't like her."

Profound silence.

"And SHE likes you so much!"

"I don't care if she does!"

"You naughty child! . . . And what if, one of these days, you had to live with Signora Evelina?"

"I won't live with her—I won't live with her!" the child bursts out.

"Now you are talking foolishly," Signor Odoardo admonishes her in a severe tone, setting her down from his knee.

She bursts into passionate weeping.

"Come, Doretta, come . . . Is this the way you keep your daddy company? . . . Enough of this, Doretta."

But, say what he pleases, Doretta must have her cry. Her brown eyes are swimming in tears, her little breast heaves, her voice is broken by sobs.

"What ridiculous whims!" Signer Odoardo exclaims, throwing his head back against the sofa cushions.

Signor Odoardo is unjust, and, what is worse, he does not believe what he is saying. He knows that this is no whim of Doretta's. He knows it better than the child herself, who would probably find it difficult to explain what she is undergoing. It is at once the presentiment of a new danger and the renewal of a bygone sorrow. Doretta was barely six years old when her mother died, and yet her remembrance is indelibly impressed upon the child's mind. And now it seems as though her mother were dying again.

"When you have finished crying, Doretta, you may come here," Signor Odoardo says.

Doretta, crouching in a corner of the room, cries less vehemently, but has not yet finished crying. Just like the weather outside,—it snows less heavily, but it still snows.

Signor Odoardo covers his eyes with his hand.

How many thoughts are thronging through his head, how many affections are contending in his heart! If he could but banish the vision of Signora Evelina—but he tries in vain. He is haunted by those blue eyes, by that persuasive smile, that graceful and harmonious presence. He has but to say the word, and he knows that she will be his, to brighten his solitary home, and fill it with life and love. Her presence would take ten years from his age, he would feel as he did when he was betrothed for the first time. And yet—no; it would not be quite like the first time.

He is not the same man that he was then, and she, THE OTHER, ah, how different SHE was from the Signora Evelina! How modest and shy she was! How girlishly reserved, even in the expression of her love! How beautiful were her sudden blushes, how sweet the droop of her long, shyly-lowered lashes! He had known her first in the intimacy of her own home, simple, shy, a good daughter and a good sister, as she was destined to be a good wife and mother. For a while he had loved her in silence, and she had returned his love. One day, walking beside her in the garden, he had seized her hand with sudden impetuosity, and raising it to his lips had said, "I care for you so much!" and she, pale and trembling, had run to her mother's arms, crying out, "Oh, how happy I am!"

Ah, those dear days—those dear days! He was a poet then; with the accent of sincerest passion he whispered in his love's ear:

> I love thee more than all the world beside,
> My only faith and hope thou art,
> My God, my country, and my bride—
> Sole love of this unchanging heart!

Very bad poetry, but deliciously thrilling to his young betrothed. Oh, the dear, dear days! Oh, the long hours that pass like a flash in delightful talk, the secrets that the soul first reveals to itself in revealing them to the beloved, the caresses longed for and yet half feared, the lovers' quarrels, the tears that are kissed away, the shynesses, the simplicity, the abandonment of a pure and passionate love— who may hope to know you twice in a lifetime?

No, Signora Evelina can never restore what he has lost to Signor Odoardo. No, this self-possessed widow, who, after six months of mourning, has already started on the hunt for a second husband, cannot inspire him with the faith that he felt in THE OTHER. Ah, first-loved women, why is it that you must die? For the dead give no kisses, no caresses, and the living long to be caressed and kissed.

Who talks of kisses? Here is one that has alit, all soft and warm, on Signor Odoardo's lips, rousing him with a start.—Ah! ... Is it you, Doretta?—It is Doretta, who says nothing, but who is longing to make it up with her daddy. She lays her cheek against his, he presses her little head close, lest she should escape from him. He too is silent—what can he say to her?

It is growing dark, and the eyes of the cat Melanio begin to glitter in the corner by the stove. The man-servant knocks and asks if he is to bring the lamp.

"Make up the fire first," Signor Odoardo says.

The wood crackles and snaps, and sends up showers of sparks; then it bursts into flame, blazing away with a regular, monotonous sound, like the breath of a sleeping giant. In the dusk the firelight flashes upon the walls, brings out the pattern of the wall-paper, and travels far enough to illuminate a corner of the desk. The shadows lengthen and then shorten again, thicken and then shrink; everything in the room seems to be continually changing its size and shape. Signor Odoardo, giving free rein to his thoughts, evokes the vision of his married life, sees the baby's cradle, recalls her first cries and smiles, feels again his dying wife's last kiss, and hears the last word upon her lips,—DORETTA. No, no, it is impossible that he should ever do anything to make his Doretta unhappy! And yet he is not sure of resisting Signora Evelina's wiles; he is almost afraid that, when he sees his enchantress on the morrow, all his strong resolves may take flight. There is but one way out of it.

"Doretta," says Signor Odoardo.

"Father?"

"Are you going to copy out your letter to your grandmamma this evening?"

"Yes, father."

"Wouldn't you rather go and see your grandmamma yourself?"

"With whom?" the child falters anxiously, her little heart beating a frantic tattoo as she awaits his answer.

"With me, Doretta."

"With YOU, daddy?" she exclaims, hardly daring to believe her ears.

"Yes, with me; with your daddy."

"Oh, daddy, DADDY!" she cries, her little arms about his neck, her kisses covering his face. "Oh, daddy, my own dear daddy! When shall we start?"

"To-morrow morning, if you're not afraid of the snow."

"Why not now? Why not at once?"

"Gently—gently. Good Lord, doesn't the child want her dinner first?"

And Signor Odoardo, gently detaching himself from his daughter's embrace, rises and rings for the lamp. Then, instinctively, he glances once more towards the window. In the opposite house all is dark, and Signora Evelina's profile is no longer outlined against the pane. The weather is still threatening, and now and then a snowflake falls. The servant closes the shutters and draws the curtains, so that no profane gaze may penetrate into the domestic sanctuary.

"We had better dine in here," Signor Odoardo says. "The dining-room must be as cold as Greenland."

Doretta, meanwhile, is convulsing the kitchen with the noisy announcement of the impending journey. At first she is thought to be joking, but when she establishes the fact that she is speaking seriously, it is respectfully pointed out to her that the master of the house must be crazy. To start on a journey in the depth of winter, and in such weather! If at least they were to wait for a fine day!

But what does Doretta care for the comments of the kitchen? She is beside herself with joy. She sings, she dances about the room, and breaks off every moment or two to give her father a kiss. Then she pours out the fulness of her emotion upon the cat Melanio and the doll Nini, promising the latter to bring her back a new frock from Milan.

At dinner she eats little and talks incessantly of the journey, asking again and again what time it is, and at what time they are to start.

"Are you afraid of missing the train?" Signor Odoardo asks with a smile.

And yet, though he dissembles his impatience, it is as great as hers. He longs to go away, far away. Perhaps he may not return until spring. He orders his luggage packed for an absence of two months.

Doretta goes to bed early, but all night long she tosses about under the bed-clothes, waking her nurse twenty times to ask: "Is it time to get up?"

Signor Odoardo, too, is awake when the man-servant comes to call him the next morning at six o'clock.

"What sort of a day is it?"

"Very bad, sir—just such another as yesterday. In fact, if I might make the suggestion, sir, if it's not necessary for you to start to-day—"

"It is, Angelo. Absolutely necessary."

At the station there are only a few sleepy, depressed-looking travellers wrapped in furs. They are all grumbling about the weather, about the cold, about the earliness of the hour, and declaring that nothing but the most urgent business would have got them out of bed at that time of day. There is but one person in the station who is all liveliness and smiles—Doretta.

The first-class compartment in which Signor Odoardo and his daughter find themselves is bitterly cold, in spite of foot-warmers, but Doretta finds the temperature delicious, and, if she dared, would open the windows for the pleasure of looking out.

"Are you happy, Doretta?"

"Oh, SO happy!"

Ten years earlier, on a pleasanter day, but also in winter, Signor Odoardo had started on his wedding-journey. Opposite him had sat a young girl, who looked as much like Doretta as a woman can look like a child; a pretty, sedate young girl, oh, so sweetly, tenderly in love with Signor Odoardo. And as the train started he had asked her the same question:

"Are you happy, Maria?"

And she had answered:

"Oh, so happy!" just like Doretta.

The train races and flies. Farewell, farewell, for ever, Signora Evelina.

And did Signora Evelina die of despair?

Oh, no; Signora Evelina has a perfect disposition and a delightful home. The perfect disposition enables her not to take things too seriously, the delightful home affords her a thousand distractions. Its windows do not all look towards Signor Odoardo's residence. One of them, for example, commands a little garden belonging to a worthy bachelor who smokes his pipe there on pleasant days. Signora Evelina finds the worthy bachelor to her taste, and the worthy bachelor, who is an average-adjuster by profession, admires Signora Evelina's eyes, and considers her handsomely and solidly enough put together to rank A No. 1 on Lloyd's registers.

The result is that the bachelor now and then looks up at the window, and the Signora Evelina now and then looks down at the garden. The weather not being propitious to out-of-door conversation, Signora Evelina at length invites her neighbor to come and pay her a visit. Her neighbor hesitates and she renews the invitation. How can one resist such a charming woman? And what does one visit signify? Nothing at all. The excellent average-adjuster has every reason to be pleased with his reception, the more so as Signora Evelina actually gives him leave to bring his pipe the next time he comes. She adores the smell of a pipe. Signora Evelina is an ideal woman, just the wife for a business man who had not positively made up his mind to remain single. And as to that, muses the average-adjuster, have I ever positively made up my mind to remain single, and if I have, who is to prevent my changing it?

And so it comes to pass that when, after an absence of three months, Signor Odoardo returns home with Doretta, he receives notice of the approaching marriage of Signora Evelina Chiocci, widow Ramboldi, with Signor Archimede Fagiuolo.

"*Fagiuolo*!" shouts Doretta, "*FAGIUOLO*!"[1]

The name seems to excite her unbounded hilarity; but I am under the impression that the real cause of her merriment is not so much Signora Evelina's husband as Signora Evelina's marriage.

---

1 *Fagiuolo*: a simpleton.

L'ARLÉSIENNE

Alphonse Daudet

Translated from the French by Mireille Harmelin and Keith Adams

Alphonse Daudet (1840–1897) was born in Nîmes, to a bourgeois family, and worked briefly as a schoolteacher, a profession he despised, before abandoning it in favour of journalism. He was working at *Le Figaro* when he wrote his first plays, which earned him considerable recognition with Paris literary circles, but it was his collection of stories *Letters from My Windmill* which finally brought him to a wide readership. Daudet's political and social positions were controversial and put him at odds with many of his contemporaries. He was a monarchist who reviled the Republic, and an anti-Semitist who befriended Edouard Drumont, founder of the National Antisemitic League of France. Paradoxically, he was a generous patron to younger writers – including Marcel Proust.

As you go down to the village from the windmill, the road passes a farm situated behind a large courtyard planted with tall Mediterranean nettle trees. It's a typical house of a Provençal tenant farmer with its red tiles, large brown façade, and haphazardly placed doors and windows. It has a weather-cock right on top of the loft, and a pulley to hoist hay, with a few tufts of old hay sticking out. . . .

What was it about this particular house that struck me? Why did the closed gate freeze my blood? I don't know; but I do know that the house gave me the shivers. It was choked by an eerie silence. No dogs barked. Guinea fowl scattered silently. Nothing was heard from inside the grounds, not even the ubiquitous mule's bell. . . . Were it not for white curtains at the windows and smoke rising from the roof, the place could have been deserted.

Yesterday, around midday, I was walking back from the village, by the walls of the farm in the shade of the old nettle trees, when I saw some farm-hands quietly finishing loading a hay wain on the road in front of the farm. The gate had been left open and discovered a tall, white-haired, old man at the back of the yard, with his elbows on a large stone table, and his head in his hands. He was wearing an ill-fitting jacket and tattered trousers. . . . The sight of him stopped me in my tracks. One of the men whispered, almost inaudibly, to me:

—Sush. It's the Master. He's been like that since his son's death.

At that moment a woman and a small boy, both dressed in black and accompanied by fat and sun-tanned villagers, passed near us and went into the farm.

The man went on:

— . . . The lady and the youngest, Cadet, are coming back from the mass. Every day it's the same thing since the eldest killed himself. Oh, monsieur, what a tragedy. The father still goes round in his mourning weeds, nothing will stop him. . . . Gee-up!

The wagon lurched ready to go, but I still wanted to know more, so I asked the driver if I could sit with him, and it was up there in the hay, that I learned all about the tragic story of young Jan.

Jan was an admirable countryman of twenty, as well-behaved as a girl, well-built and open-hearted. He was very handsome and so caught the eye of lots of women, but he had eyes for only one – a petite girl from Arles, velvet and lace vision, whom he had once met in the town's main square. This wasn't well received at first in the farm. The girl was known as a flirt, and her parents weren't local people. But Jan wanted her, whatever the cost. He said:

—I will die if I don't have her. And so, it just had to be. The marriage was duly arranged to take place after the harvest.

One Sunday evening, the family were just finishing dinner in the courtyard. It was almost a wedding feast. The fiancée was not there, but her health and well-being were toasted throughout the meal. . . . A man appeared unexpectedly at the door, and stuttered a request to speak to Estève, the master of the house, alone. Estève got up and went out onto the road.

—Monsieur, the man said, you are about to marry your boy off to a woman who is a bitch, and has been my mistress for two years. I have proof of what I say; here are some of her letters! . . . Her parents know all about it and have promised her to me, but since your son took an interest in her, neither she nor they want anything to do with me. . . . And yet I would have thought that after what has happened, she couldn't in all conscience marry anyone else.

—I see, said Master Estève after scanning the letters; come in; have a glass of Muscat.

The man replied:

—Thanks, but I am too upset for company.

And he went away.

The father went back in, seemingly unaffected, and retook his place at the table where the meal was rounded off quite amiably.

That evening, Master Estève went out into the fields with his son. They stayed outside some time, and when they did return the mother was waiting up for them.

—Wife, said the farmer bringing their son to her, hug him, he's very unhappy. . . .

Jan didn't mention the Arlésienne ever again. He still loved her though, only more so, now he knew that she was in the arms of someone else. The trouble was that he was too proud to say so, and that's what killed the poor boy. Sometimes, he would spend entire days alone, huddled in a corner, motionless. At other times, angry, he would set himself to work on the farm, and, on his own, get through the work of ten men. When evening came, he would set out for Arles, and walk expectantly until he saw the town's few steeples appearing in the sunset. Then he turned round and went home. He never went any closer than that.

The people in the farm didn't know what to do, seeing him always sad and lonely. They feared the worst. Once, during a meal, his mother, her eyes welling with tears, said to him:

—Alright, listen Jan, if you really want her, we will let you take her. . . .

The father, blushing with shame, lowered his head. . . .

Jan shook his head and left. . . .

From that day onwards, Jan changed his ways, affecting cheerfulness all the time to reassure his parents. He was seen again at balls, cabarets, and branding fêtes. At the celebrations at the Fonvieille fête, he actually led the farandole.

His father said: "He's got over it." His mother, however, still had her fears and kept an eye on her boy more than ever. . . . Jan slept in the same room as Cadet, close to the silkworms' building. The poor mother even made up her bed in the next room to theirs. . . explaining by saying that the silkworms would need attention during the night.

Then came the feast day of St. Eli, patron saint of farmers.

There were great celebrations in the farm. . . . There was plenty of Château-Neuf for everybody and the sweet wine flowed in rivers. Then there were crackers, and fireworks, and coloured lanterns all over the nettle trees. Long live St. Eli! They all danced the farandole until they dropped. Cadet scorched his new smock. . . . Even Jan looked content, and actually asked his mother for a dance. She cried with joy.

At midnight they all went to bed; everybody was tired out. But Jan himself didn't sleep. Cadet said later that he had been sobbing the whole night. Oh, I tell you, he was well smitten that one. . . .

The next morning the mother heard someone running across her sons' bedroom. She felt a sort of presentiment:

—Jan, is that you?

Jan didn't reply, he was already on the stairs.

His mother got up at once:

—Jan, where are you going?

He went up into the loft, she followed him:

—In heavens name, son!

He shut and bolted the door:

—Jan, Jan, answer me. What are you doing?

Her old trembling hands felt for the latch. . . . A window opened; there was the sound of a body hitting the courtyard slabs. Then . . . an awful silence.

The poor lad had told himself: "I love her too much. . . . I want to end it all. . . ." Oh, what pitiful things we are! It's all too much; even scorn can't kill love. . . .

That morning, the village people wondered who could be howling like that, down there by Estève's farm.

It was the mother in the courtyard by the stone table which was covered with dew and with blood. She was wailing over her son's lifeless body, limp, in her arms.

THE ATTACK ON THE MILL

Émile Zola

Translated from the French by Edward Vizetelly

Émile Zola (1840–1902). One of the most important figures in nine-teenth- century French literature, Zola was a prolific novelist, playwright and journalist. Born in Paris, Zola spent his early childhood in Aix-en-Provence, where he counted Cézanne among his closest friends. He twice failed the baccalauréat, and unable to attend university, he struggled to find work (and, legend has it, survived by eating sparrows he trapped outside his garret window). In time, he found work as a clerk while writing occasional reviews for newspapers. In 1867, he published his first major novel, *Thérèse Raquin*, which would be the beginning of a cycle called *Les Rougon-Macquart*. As a journalist and commentator, he played a cru-cial role in the liberalization of French politics, and his article *J'accuse* – which publicly excoriated anti-Semitism in the French military – marked a critical turning point in the Dreyfus affair.

I.

Old Merlier's mill was in high feather that fine summer evening. In the court-yard they had set out three tables, end to end, ready for the guests. All the country knew that on that day Merlier's daughter Françoise was to be betrothed to Dominique,— a fellow who had the name of being an idle loafer, but whom the women for eight miles round looked at with glistening eyes, so well-favored was he.

When the court-yard was full, and every one had his glass in his hand, old Merlier raised his very high, saying:—

"This is for the pleasure of announcing to you that Françoise will marry that fellow there in a month, on St. Louis's day."

Then they clinked glasses noisily. Everybody laughed. But old Merlier, raising his voice, went on:—

"Dominique, kiss your intended. That must be done."

And they kissed each other, very red, while the crowd laughed still louder. It was a real jollification. A small cask was emptied. Then when only the intimate friends were left, they chatted quietly. Night had come,—a starlit and very clear night. Dominique and Françoise, sitting side by side on a bench, said nothing. An old peasant spoke of the war the Emperor had declared with Prussia. All the boys in the village were already gone. The day before, troops had passed through. There would be hard knocks going.

"Bah!" said old Merlier, with a happy man's opinion. "Dominique is a foreigner,—he won't go. And if the Prussians come, he will be here to defend his wife."

This notion that the Prussians might come seemed a good joke. They were to be given an A 1 thrashing, and it would be soon over.

"I've seen 'em, I've seen 'em," the old peasant said over and over again.

There was a silence. Then they clinked glasses once more. Françoise and Dominique had heard nothing; they had taken each other softly by the hand, behind the bench, so that no one could see them; and it seemed so good that they stayed there, their eyes lost in the depths of the darkness.

How warm and splendid a night! The village was falling asleep on both sides of the road, tranquil as a child. You only heard from time to time the crowing of some cock, waked too soon. From the great woods hard by came long breaths that passed like caresses over the roofs. The meadows with their black shadows put on a mysterious and secluded majesty, while all the running waters that gushed forth into the darkness seemed to be the cool and rhythmic breathing of the sleeping country. At moments the mill-wheel, fast asleep, seemed to be dreaming, like those old watch-dogs that bark while snoring. It creaked, it talked all by itself, lulled by the falls of the Morelle, whose sheet of water gave forth the sustained and musical note of an organ-pipe. Never had more wide-spread peace fallen over a happier corner of the earth.

Just a month later, day for day, on St. Louis's eve, Rocreuse was in dismay. The Prussians had beaten the Emperor, and were advancing toward the village by forced marches. For a week past, people passing along the road had announced the Prussians,—"They are at Lormière; they are at Novelles:" and hearing that they were approaching so fast, Rocreuse thought every morning to see them come down by the Gagny woods. Still they did not come: this frightened the inhabitants still more. They would surely fall upon the village at night, and cut everybody's throat.

The night before, a little before daybreak, there had been an alarm. The inhabitants had waked up, hearing a great noise of men on the road. The women were just falling on their knees and crossing themselves, when red trousers were recognized through cracks of windows prudently opened. It was a detachment of French. The captain immediately asked for the mayor of the place, and stayed at the mill, after talking with old Merlier.

The sun rose gayly that day. It would be hot at noon. Over the woods floated a yellow light; while in the distance above the meadows rose white vapors. The clean, pretty village awoke in the cool air; and the country, with its river and springs, had the dew-sprinkled loveliness of a nosegay. But this fine weather made no one laugh. They had just seen the captain walk round about the mill, examine the neighboring houses, cross to the other side of the Morelle, and from there study the country through a spyglass; old Merlier, who was with him, seemed to be explaining the country to him. Then the captain stationed soldiers behind walls, behind trees, in holes in the ground. The bulk of the detachment was stationed in the court-yard of the mill. So there was to be a fight? And when old Merlier came back, he was plied with questions. He gave a long nod with his head without speaking. Yes, there was to be a fight.

Françoise and Dominique were in the court-yard looking at him. At last he took his pipe out of his mouth and said simply:—

"Ah! my poor children, there will be no wedding for you to-morrow!"

Dominique, his lips set, a line of anger across his forehead, raised himself up on tiptoe from time to time, with his eyes fixed on the Gagny woods, as if he longed to see the Prussians come. Françoise, very pale, serious, came and went, supplying the soldiers with what they needed. They were making their soup in a corner of the court-yard, and joking while waiting for their meal.

Meanwhile the captain seemed delighted. He had examined the rooms and the great hall of the mill looking out upon the river. Now, sitting by the well, he was talking with old Merlier.

"You have a real fortress here," said he. "We ought to hold till evening. The beggars are late. They should be here by this time."

The miller looked serious. He saw his mill flaming like a torch; but he did not complain, thinking it useless. He only opened his mouth to say:—

"You ought to have some one hide the boat behind the wheel. There is a hole there that will hold her. Perhaps she might be of use."

The captain gave an order. The captain was a handsome man of about forty, tall and with a kindly face. The sight of Françoise and Dominique seemed to please him. He was interested in them, as if he had forgotten the coming struggle. He followed Françoise about with his eyes, and his look told plainly that he found her charming. Then turning to Dominique:—

"So you're not in the army, my boy?" he asked abruptly.

"I'm a foreigner," the young man answered.

The captain seemed only half pleased with this reason. He winked and smiled. Françoise was pleasanter company than cannon. Then, seeing him smile, Dominique added:—

"I'm a foreigner, but I can put a bullet into an apple at five hundred metres.— See, my gun's there, behind you."

"It may be of use to you," the captain said simply.

Françoise had come up, trembling a little. And without minding the people there, Dominique took both the hands she held out to him, and pressed them in his, as if to take her under his protection. The captain smiled again, but added not a word. He remained sitting, his sword between his legs, his eyes looking at vacancy, as if in a dream.

It was already two o'clock. It was growing very hot. There was a dead silence. In the court-yard, under the sheds, the soldiers had fallen to eating their soup. Not a sound came from the village, in which the people had barricaded their houses, doors, and windows. A dog left alone in the road was howling. From the neighboring woods and meadows, motionless in the heat, came a far-off voice, long sustained, made up of every separate breath of air. A cuckoo was singing. Then the silence spread itself over the country also.

And in this slumbering air a shot suddenly burst forth. The captain sprang up quickly; the soldiers dropped their plates of soup, still half full. In a few seconds every man was at his post for the fight; the mill was occupied from top to bottom.

Yet the captain, who had gone out upon the road, could make out nothing: to the right and left the road stretched out, empty and all white. A second shot was heard, and still nothing, not a shadow; but on turning round, he espied, over towards Gagny, between two trees, a light cloudlet of smoke wafted away like gossamer. The wood was still profoundly quiet.

"The rascals have taken to the forest," he muttered. "They know we are here."

Then the firing kept up, harder and harder, between the French soldiers stationed round the mill and the Prussians hidden behind the trees. The bullets whistled across the Morelle, without occasioning any loss on one side or the other. The shots were irregular, coming from every bush; and all you saw was still the little clouds of smoke gently wafted away by the wind. This lasted for nearly two hours. The officer hummed a tune, as if indifferent. Françoise and Dominique, who had stayed in the court-yard, raised themselves up on tiptoe and looked over the wall. They were particularly interested in watching a little soldier, stationed on the brink of the Morelle, behind the hull of an old boat; he was flat on his belly, watched his chance, fired his shot, then let himself slide down into a ditch a little behind him, to reload his rifle; and his movements were so droll, so cunning, so supple, that it made one smile to see him. He must have espied the head of some Prussian, for he got up quickly and brought his piece to his shoulder; but before he fired, he gave a cry, turned over upon himself, and rolled into the ditch, where his legs stiffened out with the momentary convulsive jerk of those of a chicken with its neck wrung. The little soldier had received a bullet full in the breast. He was the first man killed. Instinctively Françoise seized hold of Dominique's hand and squeezed it with a nervous grip.

"Don't stay there," said the captain. "The bullets reach here."

As he spoke a little sharp stroke was heard in the old elm, and a branch fell in zigzags through the air; but the young people did not stir, riveted there by anxiety at the sight. On the outskirts of the wood, a Prussian came out suddenly from behind a tree, as from a side scene, beating the air with his arm, and tumbling over backwards. And then nothing stirred: the two dead men seemed to sleep in the dazzling sunshine; you saw no one in the torpid landscape. Even the crack of the shots stopped. Only the Morelle kept up its silver-toned whispering.

Old Merlier looked at the captain in surprise, as if to ask if it were over.

"Here it comes," the latter muttered. "Look out! Don't stay there."

He had not finished speaking when there came a terrific volley. It was as if the great elm were mowed down; a cloud of leaves whirled about them. Luckily the Prussians had fired too high. Dominique dragged, almost carried Françoise away; while old Merlier followed them, crying out:—

"Go down to the little cellar: the walls are solid."

But they did not mind him; they went into the great hall where ten soldiers or so were waiting in silence, with shutters closed, peeping through the cracks. The captain had stayed alone in the court-yard, crouched down behind the little wall, while the furious volleys continued. The soldiers he had stationed outside yielded ground only foot by foot. Yet they came in, one by one, crawling on their faces, when the enemy had dislodged them from their hiding-places. Their orders were to gain time, not to show themselves; so that the Prussians might not know what numbers they had before them. Another hour went by; and as a sergeant came up, saying that there were only two or three men left outside, the officer looked at his watch, muttering:—

"Half after two. Come, we must hold out four hours."

He had the gate of the court-yard shut, and all preparations were made for an energetic resistance. As the Prussians were on the other side of the Morelle, an immediate assault was not to be feared. To be sure, there was a bridge, a little over a mile off, but they doubtless did not know of its existence; and it was hardly possible that they would try to ford the river. So the officer merely had the road watched. The whole effort was to be made on the side toward the fields.

The firing had once more ceased. The mill seemed dead beneath the hot sun. Not a shutter was opened, not a sound came from the inside. Little by little, meanwhile, the Prussians showed themselves at the outskirts of the Gagny wood. They stretched forth their heads, grew more daring. In the mill, several soldiers had already levelled their rifles, but the captain cried out:—

"No, no, wait. Let them come up."

They were very cautious about it, looking at the mill with evident distrust. This old dwelling, silent and dismal, with its curtains of ivy, made them uneasy. Still they kept advancing. When there were about fifty of them in the meadow opposite, the officer said a single word:—'

"Fire!"

A tearing sound was heard, followed by single shots. Françoise shaken with a fit of trembling, put her hands up to her ears, in spite of herself. Dominique, behind the soldiers, looked on; and when the smoke had blown away a little, he saw three Prussians stretched on their backs in the middle of the field. The rest had thrown themselves down behind the willows and poplars; and the siege began.

For over an hour the mill was riddled with bullets. They whipped its old walls like hail. When they struck stone, you heard them flatten out and fall back into the water. Into wood they penetrated with a hollow sound. Now and then a cracking told that the wheel had been hit. The soldiers inside husbanded their shots,—fired only when they could take aim. From time to time the captain would look at his watch; and as a ball split a shutter and then lodged in the ceiling:—

"Four o'clock," he muttered. "We shall never hold out."

It was true: this terrible firing of musketry was shivering the old mill. A shutter fell into the water, riddled like a piece of lace, and had to be replaced by a mattress. Old Merlier exposed himself every moment, to make sure of the injury done to his poor wheel, whose cracking went to his heart. It was all over with it this time: never would he be able to repair it. Dominique implored Françoise to go, but she would stay with him; she had sat down behind a great oak clothes-press, the sides of which gave out a deep sound. Then Dominique placed himself in front of Françoise. He had not fired yet; he held his gun in his hands, not being able to get up to the windows, whose entire width was taken up by the soldiers. At every discharge the floor shook.

"Look out! look out!" the captain cried of a sudden.

He had just seen a whole black mass come out from the wood. Immediately a formidable platoon fire was opened. It was as if a waterspout had passed over the mill. Another shutter gave way; and by the gaping opening of the window the bullets came in. Two soldiers rolled upon the floor. One did not move; they pushed him up against the wall, because he was in the way. The other squirmed on the ground begging them to make an end of him; but no one minded him: the balls kept coming in; every one shielded himself, and tried to find a loop-hole to fire back through. A third soldier was wounded; he said not a word, he let himself slide down by the edge of a table, with fixed and haggard eyes. Opposite the dead men, Françoise, seized with horror, had pushed her chair aside mechanically, to sit down on the ground next the wall; she felt smaller there, and in less danger. Meanwhile they had gone after all the mattresses in the house, and had half stopped up the window. The hall was getting filled with rubbish, with broken weapons, with gutted furniture.

"Five o'clock," said the captain. "Keep it up. They are going to try to cross the water."

At this instant Françoise gave a shriek. A rebounding ball had just grazed her forehead. A few drops of blood appeared. Dominique looked at her; then stepping up to the window, he fired his first shot, and kept on firing. He loaded, fired, without paying any attention to what was going on near him; only from time to time he would give Françoise a look. For the rest, he did not hurry himself,—took careful aim. The Prussians, creeping along by the poplars, were attempting the passage of the Morelle, as the captain had foreseen; but as soon as one of them risked showing himself, he would fall, hit in the head by a ball from Dominique. The captain who followed this game was astonished. He complimented the young man, saying that he would be glad to have a lot of marksmen like him. Dominique did not hear him. A ball cut his shoulder, another bruised his arm; and he kept on firing.

There were two more men killed. The mattresses, all slashed to bits, no longer stopped up the windows. A last volley seemed as if it would carry away the mill. The position was no longer tenable. Still the officer repeated:—

"Stick to it. Half an hour more."

Now he counted the minutes. He had promised his superior officers to hold the enemy there until evening, and would not draw back a sole's breadth before the time he had set for the retreat. He still had his gracious manner; smiling at Françoise to reassure her. He himself had just picked up a dead soldier's rifle, and was firing.

There were only four soldiers left in the hall. The Prussians showed themselves in a body on the other bank of the Morelle, and it was evident that they might cross the river at any time. A few more minutes elapsed. The captain stuck to it obstinately, and would not give the order to retreat; when a sergeant came running up saying;—

"They are on the road: they are going to take us in the rear."

The Prussians must have found the bridge. The captain pulled out his watch.

"Five minutes more," said he. "They won't be here for five minutes."

Then at the stroke of six, he at last consented to order his men out by a little door opening upon an alley-way. From there they threw themselves into a ditch; they reached the Sauval forest. Before going, the captain saluted old Merlier very politely, excusing himself; and he even added:—

"Make them lose time. We shall be back again."

Meanwhile Dominique stayed on in the hall. He still kept firing, hearing nothing, understanding nothing. He only felt that he must defend Françoise. The soldiers were gone, without his suspecting it the least in the world. He took aim and killed his man at every shot. Suddenly there was a loud noise. The Prussians from the rear, had just overrun the court-yard. He fired his last shot, and they fell upon him as his piece was still smoking.

Four men held him. Others shouted round him in a frightful language. They all but cut his throat off-hand. Françoise threw herself before him in supplication; but an officer came in and took charge of the prisoner. After a few sentences exchanged in German with the soldiers, he turned to Dominique and said roughly, and in very good French:—

"You will be shot in two hours."

II.

It was a rule made by the German staff: every Frenchman not belonging to the regular army, and taken with arms in his hands, should be shot. Even the guerilla companies were not recognized as belligerents. By thus making terrible examples of the peasants who defended their own firesides, the Germans wished to prevent the uprising of the whole country *en masse*, which they dreaded.

The officer, a tall lean man of about fifty, put Dominique through a brief examination. Although he spoke very pure French, he had quite the Prussian stiffness.

"You belong in these parts?"

"No, I am a Belgian."

"Why have you taken up arms? All this can't be any of your business."

Dominique did not answer. At this moment the officer caught sight of Françoise, standing upright and very pale, listening; her slight wound put a red bar across her white forehead. He looked at the young people, one after the other, seemed to understand, and contented himself with adding:—

"You don't deny that you were firing?"

"I fired as long as I was able," Dominique answered quietly.

This confession was needless; for he was black with powder, covered with sweat, spotted with some drops of blood that had run down from the scratch on his shoulder.

"Very well," the officer repeated. "You will be shot in two hours."

Françoise did not cry out. She clasped her hands together, and raised them in a gesture of mute despair. The officer noticed this gesture. Two soldiers had led Dominique away into the next room, where they were to keep him in sight. The young girl had dropped down upon a chair, her legs giving way under her; she could not cry, she was choking. Meanwhile the officer kept looking at her closely. At last he spoke to her.

"That young man is your brother?" he asked.

She shook her head. He stood there stiff, without a smile. Then after a silence:—

"He has lived a long while in these parts?"

She nodded yes, still dumb.

"Then he must know the woods round here very well?"

This time she spoke.

"Yes, sir," she said, looking at him in some surprise.

He said no more, and turned on his heel, asking to have the mayor of the village brought to him. But Françoise had risen, a faint flush on her face, thinking to have caught the drift of his questions, and seeing fresh hope in them. It was she who ran to find her father.

Old Merlier, as soon as the shots had ceased, had run quickly down the wooden steps to look at his wheel. He adored his daughter, he had a stout friendship for Dominique, his intended son-in-law; but his wheel also held a large place in his heart. As the two young ones, as he called them, had come safe and sound out of the scrimmage, he thought of his other love, and this one had suffered grievously. And bending over the huge wooden carcass, he investigated its wounds, the picture of distress. Five paddles were in splinters, the central framework was riddled. He stuck his fingers into the bullet-holes to measure their depth; he thought over how he could repair all this damage. Françoise found him already stopping up cracks with broken bits of wood and moss.

"Father," she said, "you are wanted."

And at last she wept, telling him what she had just heard. Old Merlier shook his head. You didn't shoot people that way. He must see. And he went back into the mill with his silent, pacific air. When the officer asked him for victuals for his men, he answered that the people in Rocreuse were not accustomed to being bullied, and that nothing would be got from them by violence. He took everything upon himself, but on the condition of being allowed to act alone. The officer showed signs, at first, of getting angry at his cool manner; then he gave in to the old man's curt and business-like way of talking. He even called him back to ask him:—

"What do you call these woods there, opposite?"

"The Sauval woods."

"And what is their extent?"

The miller looked at him fixedly.

"I don't know," he answered.

And he walked away. An hour later, the contribution of victuals and money required by the officer were in the court-yard of the mill. Night was approaching; Françoise followed the soldiers' movements anxiously. She did not go far from the room in which Dominique was shut up. At about seven she had a poignant emotion: she saw the officer go into the prisoner's room, and for a quarter of an hour or so she heard their voices raised. One instant the officer reappeared on the threshold, to give an order in German, which she did not understand: but when twelve men came and fell into line in the court-yard with their muskets, she fell a-trembling; she felt ready to die. So it was all over: the execution was to take place. The twelve men waited there ten minutes. Dominique's voice was still raised in a violent refusal. At last the officer came out, slamming the door and saying:—

"Very well; think it over. I give you till to-morrow morning."

And with a motion of his arm, he ordered the twelve men to break ranks. Françoise stayed on in a sort of stupor. Old Merlier, who had not stopped smoking his pipe, while looking at the squad with an air of simple curiosity, came up and took her by the arm with fatherly gentleness. He led her to her room.

"Keep quiet," he said; "try to sleep. To-morrow it will be daylight, and we will see."

When he withdrew he locked her in, for prudence's sake. It was a principle of his that women were no good, and that they made a mess of it whenever they undertook anything serious. But Françoise did not go to bed: she stayed a long time sitting on her bed, listening to the noises in the house. The German soldiers, encamped in the court-yard, were singing and laughing: they must have been eating and drinking up to eleven, for the noise did not stop for an instant. In the mill itself, heavy steps sounded every now and then: no doubt they were relieving sentries. But what interested her above all were noises that she could not make out, in the room under hers. Several times she lay down on the ground; she put her ear to the floor. This room happened to be the one in which Dominique was locked up. He must have been walking from the wall to the window, for she long heard the cadence of his steps: then there was a dead silence; he had doubtless sat down. Besides, the noises stopped; everything was hushed in sleep. When the house seemed to her to slumber, she opened the window as softly as possible, and rested her elbows on the sill.

Outside the night was calm and warm. The slender crescent moon, setting behind the Sauval woods, lighted up the country with the glimmer of a night-taper. The elongated shadows of the great trees barred the meadows with black; while the grass, in the unshaded spots, put on the softness of greenish velvet. But Françoise did not stop to note the mysterious charm of the night. She examined the country, looking for the sentinels that the Germans must have stationed on one side. She plainly saw their shadows, ranged like rungs of a ladder along the Morelle. Only a single one stood opposite the mill, on the other side of the river, near a willow whose branches dipped into the water. Françoise saw him distinctly: he was a big fellow, standing motionless, his face turned towards the sky with the dreamy look of a shepherd.

Then when she had carefully inspected the ground, she went back and sat down upon her bed. She stayed there an hour, deeply absorbed. Then she listened again: in the house not a breath stirred. She went back to the window, and looked out; but no doubt she saw danger in one of the horns of the moon, which still appeared behind the trees, for she went back again to wait. At last the time seemed to have come. The night was quite dark; she no longer saw the sentinel opposite; the country lay spread out like a pool of ink. She listened intently for a moment, and made up her mind. An iron ladder ran near the window,—some bars let into the wall, leading from the wheel up to the loft, down which the millers used to climb to get at certain cog-wheels; then when the machinery had been altered, the ladder had long since disappeared beneath the rank growth of ivy that covered that side of the mill.

Françoise bravely climbed over the balustrade of her window, grasped one of the iron bars, and found herself in empty space. She began to climb down. Her skirts were much in her way. Suddenly a stone broke loose from the masonry, and fell into the Morelle with a resounding splash. She stopped, chilled with a shudder. But she saw that the waterfall, with its continuous roar, drowned out from afar any noise she might make; and she climbed down more boldly, feeling for the ivy with her foot, making sure of the rungs of the ladder. When she had got on a level with the room that was used as Dominique's prison, she stopped. An unforeseen difficulty nearly made her lose all her courage: the window of the room below was not cut regularly, under the window of her chamber; it was some way from the ladder, and when she stretched out her hand she felt only the wall. Would she have to climb up again, without carrying her plan through to the end? Her arms were getting tired; the murmur of the Morelle beneath her began to make her dizzy. Then she tore off little bits of mortar from the wall, barking her fingers. And her strength was giving out: she felt herself falling backwards, when Dominique, at last, softly opened his window.

"It's I," she whispered. "Take me quick,—I'm falling."

It was the first time she had *tutoyé*ed him. He caught her, leaning out, and lifted her into the room. There she had a fit of tears, stifling her sobs so as not to be heard. Then by a supreme effort she calmed herself.

"You are guarded?" she asked in a low voice.

Dominique, still dumbfounded at seeing her thus, made a simple sign, pointing to his door. They heard a snoring on the other side; the sentinel must have given way to drowsiness, and laid him down on the ground across the doorway, thinking that in this way the prisoner could not get out.

"You must run away," she went on rapidly. "I have come to implore you to run away, and to say good-by."

But he did not seem to hear her. He kept repeating:—

"How—it's you, it's you!—how you frightened me! You might have killed yourself."

He took her hands—he kissed them.

"How I love you, Françoise! You are as brave as you are good. I only had one fear,—that of dying without seeing you once more. But you are here, and now they can shoot me. When I have had a quarter of an hour with you, I shall be ready."

Little by little he had drawn her closer to him, and she rested her head upon his shoulder. The danger drew them nearer together. They forgot all in this embrace.

"Ah, Françoise," Dominique went on in a caressing voice, "to-day is St. Louis's day; our wedding day that we have waited for so long. Nothing has been able to separate us, since we are here, all alone, faithful to our tryst. It's our wedding morn now, isn't it?"

"Yes, yes," she repeated, "our wedding morning."

They exchanged a kiss trembling. But of a sudden she broke loose: the terrible reality rose up before her.

"You must run away,—you must run away," she stammered out. "Let us not lose a minute."

And as he stretched out his arms once more to take her in the darkness, she again *tutoyé*ed him:—

"Oh! I beg of you, listen to me. If you die, I shall die. In an hour it will be daylight. I wish you to go at once."

Then rapidly she explained her plan. The iron ladder ran down to the wheel; there he could take the paddles and get into the boat, which was in the recess. After that it would be easy for him to reach the other bank of the river and escape.

"But there must be sentinels there?" he said.

"Only one, opposite, at the foot of the first willow."

"And if he sees me, if he tries calling out?"

Françoise shuddered. She put a knife she had brought with her into his hand. There was a silence.

"And your father, and you?" Dominique continued. "But no, I can't run away. When I am gone, maybe these soldiers will slaughter you. You don't know them. They proposed to show me mercy if I would be their guide through the Sauval forest. When they find me gone, they will stick at nothing."

The young girl did not stop to discuss. She simply answered all the reasons he gave with—

"For the love of me, fly. If you love me, Dominique, don't stay here a minute longer."

Then she promised to climb back to her room. They would not know that she had helped him. She at last took him in her arms, kissed him to convince him, in an extraordinary outburst of passion. He was beaten. He asked not a question further.

"Swear to me that your father knows of what you are doing, and that he advises me to run away."

"It was my father sent me," Françoise answered boldly.

She lied. At this moment she felt nothing but a boundless need of knowing him in safety, of escaping from this abominable thought that the sun would give the signal for his death. When he was gone, all mishaps might rush down upon her; it would seem sweet to her as long as he was alive. The selfishness of her love wished him alive before all else.

"Very well," said Dominique: "I will do as you prefer."

Then they said nothing more. Dominique went to open the window again; but suddenly a noise chilled their blood. The door was shaken, and they thought it was being opened. Evidently a patrol had heard their voices; and both of them, standing pressed against each other, waited in an unspeakable anguish. Each gave a stifled sigh; they saw how it was,—it must have been the soldier lying across the threshold turning over. And really, silence was restored; the snoring began again.

Dominique would have it that Françoise must first climb back to her room. He took her in his arms; he bade her a mute farewell. Then he helped her to seize the ladder, and grappled hold of it in his turn. But he refused to go down a single rung before he knew she was in her room. When Françoise had climbed in, she whispered, in a voice as light as breath:—

"*Au revoir*; I love you!"

She stopped with her elbows resting on the window-sill, and tried to follow Dominique with her eyes. The night was still very dark. She looked for the sentinel, and did not see him; only the willow made a pale spot in the midst of the darkness. For an instant she heard the rustling of Dominique's body along the ivy. Then the wheel creaked, and there was a gentle plashing that told that the young man had found the boat. A minute later, in fact, she made out the dark outline of a boat on the gray sheet of the Morelle. Then anguish stopped her breath. At every moment she thought to hear the sentinel's cry of alarm. The faintest sounds, scattered through the darkness, seemed to be the hurried tread of soldiers, the clatter of arms, the click of hammers of their rifles. Yet seconds elapsed; the country slept in a sovereign peace. Dominique must have been landing on the other bank. Françoise saw nothing more. The stillness was majestic. And she heard a noise of scuffling feet, a hoarse cry, the dull thud of a falling body. Then the silence grew deeper; and as if she had felt death passing by, she waited on, all cold, face to face with the pitch-dark night.

III.

At daybreak, shouting voices shook the mill. Old Merlier had come down to open Françoise's door. She came down into the court-yard, pale and very calm. But there she gave a shudder before the dead body of a Prussian soldier, which was stretched out near the well, on a cloak spread on the ground.

Around the body, soldiers were gesticulating, crying aloud in fury. Many of them shook their fists at the village. Meanwhile the officer had had old Merlier called, as mayor of the township.

"See here," said he, in a voice choking with rage, "here's one of our men who has been murdered by the river-side. We must make a tremendous example, and I trust you will help us to find out the murderer."

"Anything you please," answered the miller in his phlegmatic way. "Only it will not be easy."

The officer had stooped down to throw aside a flap of the cloak that hid the dead man's face. Then a horrible wound appeared. The sentinel had been struck in the throat, and the weapon was left in the wound. It was a kitchen knife with a black handle.

"Look at this knife," said the officer to old Merlier: "perhaps it may help us in our search."

The old man gave a start. But he recovered himself immediately, and answered, without moving a muscle of his face:—

"Everybody in these parts has knives like that. Maybe your man was tired of fighting, and did the job himself. Such things have been known to happen."

"Shut up!" the officer cried furiously. "I don't know what keeps me from setting fire to the four corners of the village."

His anger luckily prevented his noticing the profound change that had come over Françoise's face. She had to sit down on the stone bench near the wall. In spite of herself her eyes never left that dead body, stretched on the ground almost at her feet. He was a big, handsome fellow, who looked like Dominique, with light hair and blue eyes. This resemblance made her heart-sick. She thought of how the dead man had perhaps left some sweetheart behind who would weep for him over there in Germany. And she recognized her knife in the dead man's throat. She had killed him.

Meanwhile the officer talked of taking terrible measures against Rocreuse, when some soldiers came up running. They had only just noticed Dominique's escape. It occasioned an extreme agitation. The officer visited the premises, looked out of the window, which had been left open, understood it all, and came back exasperated.

Old Merlier seemed very much put out at Dominique's flight.

"The idiot!" he muttered: "he spoils it all."

Françoise, who heard him, was seized with anguish. For the rest her father did not suspect her complicity. He shook his head, saying to her in an undertone:—

"Now we are in a fine scrape!"

"It's that rascal! it's that rascal!" cried the officer. "He must have reached the woods. But he must be found for us, or the village shall pay for it."

And addressing the miller:—

"Come, you must know where he is hiding?"

Old Merlier gave a noiseless chuckle, pointing to the wide extent of wooded hillside. "How do you expect to find a man in there?" said he.

"Oh, there must be holes in there that you know of. I will give you ten men. You shall be their guide."

"All right. Only it will take us a week to beat all the woods in the neighborhood."

The old man's coolness infuriated the officer. In fact, he saw the ridiculousness of this *battue*. It was then that he caught sight of Françoise, pale and trembling on the bench. The young girl's anxious attitude struck him. He said nothing for an instant, looking hard at the miller and Françoise by turns.

"Isn't this young man," he at last brutally asked the old man, "your daughter's lover?"

Old Merlier turned livid; one would have thought him on the point of throwing himself upon the officer and strangling him. He drew himself up stiffly; he did not answer. Françoise put her face between her hands.

"Yes, that's it," the Prussian went on: "you or your daughter have helped him to run away. You are his accomplice. For the last time, will you give him up to us?"

The miller did not answer. He had turned away, looking off into the distance, as if the officer had not been speaking to him.

This put the last touch to the latter's anger.

"Very well," he said: "you shall be shot instead."

And he once more ordered out the firing party. Old Merlier still kept cool. He hardly gave a slight shrug of his shoulders: this whole drama seemed to him in rather bad taste. No doubt he did not believe that a man was to be shot with so little ado. Then when the squad had come, he said gravely:—

"You're in earnest, then?—All right. If you absolutely must have some one, I shall do as well as another."

But Françoise sprang up, half crazed, stammering out:—

"Mercy, *monsieur*! don't do any harm to my father. Kill me instead. It's I who helped Dominique to escape. I am the only culprit."

"Be quiet, little girl," cried old Merlier. "What are you lying for? She spent the night locked up in her room, *monsieur*. She lies, I assure you."

"No, I am not lying," the young girl replied ardently. "I climbed down out of the window; I urged Dominique to fly. It's the truth, the only truth."

The old man turned very pale. He saw clearly in her eyes that she was not lying; and the story appalled him. Ah! these children with their hearts, how they spoiled everything! Then he grew angry.

"She's crazy; don't believe her. She is telling you stupid stories. Come, let's have done with it."

She tried to protest again. She knelt down, she clasped her hands. The officer looked quietly on the heart-rending struggle.

"Good God!" he said at last, "I take your father because I haven't got the other one. Try and find the other one, and your father shall go free."

For a moment she looked at him, her eyes staring wide at the atrocity of this proposal.

"It's horrible," she murmured. "Where do you expect me to find Dominique at this time? He's gone; I don't know where he is."

"Well, choose. Him or your father."

"O my God! how can I choose? but even if I knew where Dominique was, I could not choose! It is my heart you are breaking. I had rather die at once. Yes, it would be soonest over so. Kill me, I beg of you, kill me!"

The officer at last grew impatient at this scene of despair and tears. He cried out:—

"I've had enough of this! I'm willing to be good-natured,—I consent to give you two hours. If your sweetheart isn't here in two hours, your father shall pay for him."

And he had old Merlier taken to the room which had been used for Dominique's prison. The old man asked for some tobacco, and fell to smoking. No emotion was detected in his impassive face. Only, when he was alone, two big tears ran slowly down his cheeks. His poor, dear child, how she suffered!

Françoise had stayed in the middle of the court-yard. Some Prussian soldiers passed by, laughing. Some of them called out to her jokes which she did not understand. She stared at the door through which her father had just disappeared. And with a slow movement she raised her hand to her forehead, as if to keep it from bursting. The officer turned on his heel repeating:

"You have two hours. Try to make good use of them."

She had two hours. This sentence kept buzzing in her head. Then, mechanically, she went out of the court-yard, she walked straight before her. Whither should she go? What should she do? She did not even try to decide, because she felt convinced of the uselessness of her efforts. Yet she would have liked to find Dominique. They would have come to an understanding together; they might perhaps have hit upon an expedient. And amid the confusion of her thoughts, she went down to the bank of the Morelle, which she crossed below the dam, at a place where there were some large stones. Her feet led her under the first willow, at the corner of the field. As she bent down she saw a pool of blood that made her turn pale. That was clearly the place. And she followed Dominique's tracks in the trodden grass: he must have run; a long line of strides was to be seen cutting through the field cornerwise. Then, farther on, she lost the tracks; but in a neighboring field she thought she found them again. This brought her to the outskirts of the forest, where all traces were wiped out.

Françoise plunged in under the trees, notwithstanding. It was a relief to be alone. She sat down for a moment; then, remembering her time was running out, she got up again. How long was it since she had left the mill? Five minutes? half an hour? She lost all consciousness of time. Perhaps Dominique had gone and hidden in a copse she knew of, where one afternoon they had eaten filberts together. She went to the copse and searched it. Only a blackbird flew out, whistling its soft, melancholy tune. Then she thought he had taken refuge in a hollow in the rocks, where he sometimes used to lie in ambush for game; but the hollow in the rocks was empty. What was the use of looking for him? she would not find him: and little by little her desire to find him grew furious; she walked on faster. The notion that he might have climbed up a tree suddenly struck her. From that moment she pushed on with up-turned eyes; and that he might know she was near, she called out to him every fifteen or twenty steps. The cuckoos answered her; a breath of air passing through the branches made her think he was there, and was coming down. Once she even thought she saw him; she stopped, choking, having a good mind to run away. What would she say to him? Had she come, then, to lead him away and have him shot? Oh, no, she would not mention these things. She would cry out to him to escape, not to stay in the neighborhood. Then the thought of her father waiting for her gave her a sharp pang. She fell upon the turf, weeping, repeating aloud:—

"My God, my God! why am I here!"

She must have been crazy to come. And as if seized with fright, she ran, she tried to find a way out of the forest. Three times she took the wrong path; and she thought she could not find the mill again, when she came out into a field just opposite Rocreuse. As soon as she caught sight of the village, she stopped. Was she going to return alone?

As she stood there, a voice called to her softly:—

"Françoise! Françoise!"

And she saw Dominique raising his head above the edge of a ditch. Just God, she had found him! So Heaven wished his death? She held back a cry, she let herself slide down into the ditch.

"You were looking for me?" he asked.

"Yes," she answered, her head buzzing, not knowing what she said.

"What's going on?"

She looked down; she stammered out:—

"Why nothing; I was anxious—I wanted to see you."

Then, reassured, he told her that he had not wished to go far. He feared for them. Those rascals of Prussians were just the sort to wreak vengeance upon women and old men. Then all was going well; and he added, laughing:—

"Our wedding will be for this day week, that's all."

Then, as she was still overcome, he grew serious again.

"But what's the matter with you? You are keeping something from me."

"No, I swear to you. I ran to come—"

He kissed her, saying that it was imprudent for either of them to talk any longer; and he wished to get back to the forest. She held him back. She was trembling.

"Listen: perhaps it would be as well for you to stay here, all the same. Nobody is looking for you; you're not afraid of anything."

"Françoise, you are keeping something from me," he repeated.

Again she swore she was keeping nothing from him. Only she had rather know he was near; and she stammered out other reasons besides. She struck him as acting so queerly, that now he himself would not have been willing to leave her. Besides, he believed the French would return. Troops had been sent over Sauval way.

"Ah! let them be in a hurry; let them be here as soon as possible!" he muttered fervently.

At this moment the Rocreuse church clock struck eleven. The strokes came clear and distinct. She sprang up in fright: it was two hours since she had left the mill.

"Listen," she said rapidly: "if we should need you, I will go up to my room and wave my handkerchief."

And she left him, running; while Dominique, very anxious, stretched himself out on the edge of the ditch, to keep his eye on the mill. As she was just running into Rocreuse, Françoise met an old beggar, old Bontemps, who knew the whole country. He bowed to her: he had just seen the miller in the midst of the Prussians; then crossing himself and mumbling some disconnected words, he went his way.

"The two hours are over," said the officer, when Françoise appeared.

Old Merlier was there, sitting on the bench by the well. He was still smoking. The young girl once more implored, wept, fell upon her knees. She wished to gain time. The hope of seeing the French return had grown in her; and while bewailing her fate, she thought she heard the measured tread of an army. Oh! if they had come, if they had delivered them all!

"Listen, *monsieur*, one hour, one hour more! You can surely grant me one hour!"

But the officer was still inflexible. He even ordered two men to take her in charge and lead her away, that they might proceed quietly with the old man's execution. Then a frightful conflict went on in Françoise's heart. She could not let her father be thus murdered. No, no, she would die with Dominique first; and she was bounding toward her room, when Dominique himself walked into the courtyard.

The officer and soldiers gave a shout of triumph. But he, as if no one but Françoise had been there, stepped up to her quietly, a little sternly.

"That was wrong," said he. "Why didn't you bring me back with you? Old Bontemps had to tell me everything. After all, here I am."

IV.

It was three o'clock. Great black clouds had slowly filled the sky, the tail of some not distant thunder-storm. This yellow sky, these copper-colored rags, changed the valley of Rocreuse, so cheerful in the sunshine, to a cut-throat den, full of suspicious shadows. The Prussian officer had been content to have Dominique locked up, without saying anything about what fate he had in store for him. Ever since noon, Françoise had been a prey to infernal anguish. She would not leave the court-yard, in spite of her father's urging. She was waiting for the French. But the hours passed by, night was at hand, and she suffered the more keenly that all this time gained did not seem likely to change the frightful catastrophe.

Nevertheless at about three, the Prussians made preparations to go. A minute before, the officer had closeted himself with Dominique, as on the preceding day. Françoise saw that the young man's life was being decided on. Then she clasped her hands and prayed. Old Merlier, beside her, maintained his mute and rigid attitude of an old peasant who does not struggle with the fatality of facts.

"O my God! O my God!" said Françoise brokenly, "they are going to kill him!"

The miller drew her close to him and took her upon his knee, like a child.

Just then the officer came out; while behind him, two men led Dominique.

"Never, never!" cried the latter. "I am ready to die."

"Think of it well," replied the officer. "This service that you refuse us will be done for us by another. I offer you your life; I am generous. It is only to be our guide to Montredom, through the woods. There must be paths."

Dominique made no answer.

"Then you are still obstinate!"

"Kill me, and let us have done with it," he answered.

Françoise, with hands clasped, implored him from across the yard. She had forgotten all; she would have urged him to some piece of cowardice. But old Merlier grasped her hands, that the Prussians might not see her delirious gesture.

"He is right," he murmured; "it's better to die."

The firing party was there. The officer was waiting for a moment of weakness on Dominique's part. He still counted on winning him over. There was a dead silence. From the distance were heard violent claps of thunder. A sultry heat weighed upon the country; and in the midst of this silence a shriek burst forth:—

"The French! the French!"

It was really they. On the Sauval road, on the outskirts of the wood, you could make out the line of red trousers. Inside the mill there was an extraordinary hubbub. The Prussian soldiers ran about with guttural exclamations. For the rest, not a shot had been fired yet.

"The French! the French!" screamed Françoise, clapping her hands.

She was like mad. She had broken loose from her father's embrace, and she laughed, her arms waving in the air. At last they were coming, and they had come in time, since Dominique was still there, erect!

A terrible firing that burst upon her ears like a thunder-stroke made her turn round. The officer had just muttered:—

"First of all, let us finish this job."

And pushing Dominique up against the wall of a shed with his own hands, he had ordered, "Fire!" When Françoise turned round, Dominique was lying on the ground, his breast pierced with twelve bullets.

She did not weep; she stood there in a stupor. Her eyes were fixed, and she went and sat under the shed, a few steps from the body. She looked at it; at moments she made a vague and childlike movement with her hand. The Prussians had laid hold of old Merlier as a hostage.

It was a fine fight. Rapidly the officer stationed his men, recognizing that he could not beat a retreat without being overpowered. It was as well to sell his life dearly. Now it was the Prussians who defended the mill, and the French that made the attack. The firing began with unheard-of violence. For half an hour it did not stop. Then a dull explosion was heard, and a shot broke off one of the main branches of the hundred-year-old elm. The French had cannon. A battery drawn up just above the ditch in which Dominique had hidden, swept the main street of Rocreuse. From this moment the struggle could not last long.

Ah! the poor mill! Shot pierced it through and through. Half the roofing was carried away. Two walls crumbled. But it was, above all, on the side toward the Morelle that the ruin done was piteous. The ivy, torn from the shattered walls, hung in rags; the river swept away débris of every sort; and through a breach you could see Françoise's room, with her bed, the white curtains of which were carefully drawn. Shot upon shot, the old wheel received two canon-balls, and gave one last groan: the paddles were washed away by the current, the carcass collapsed. The mill had breathed out its soul.

Then the French stormed the place. There was a furious fight with side-arms. Beneath the rust-colored sky, the cut-throat hollow of the valley was filled with slain. The broad meadows looked grim, their rows of poplars streaking them with shadows. To the right and left, the forests were like the walls of a circus, shutting in the combatants; while the springs, the fountains, the running waters, gave forth sounds of sobbing, amid the panic of the country-side.

Under the shed, Françoise had not stirred, crouched down opposite Dominique's body. Old Merlier was killed outright by a spent bullet. Then when the Prussians had been annihilated, and the mill was burning, the French captain was the first man to enter the court-yard. From the beginning of the campaign it was the only success he had won. And all aglow, drawing up his tall figure to its full height, he laughed with his gracious air of a fine cavalier. And seeing Françoise, imbecile, between the dead bodies of her husband and father, amidst the smoking ruins of the mill, he gallantly saluted her with his sword, crying out:—

"Victory! Victory!"

MALARIA

Giovanni Verga

Translated from the Italian by D.H. Lawrence

Giovanni Verga (1840–1922). Born in Sicily to a family of wealthy land-owners, Verga moved to Florence when in his twenties, and later lived in Milan. He began his writing career penning patriotic historical novels, but his fame rests on his later work, which marked him as one of the important novelists of Italian *verismo* (Realism), chronicling the lives of poor peasants and fishermen in Sicily. Verga was little recognised in his lifetime, though some now consider him one of the greatest of all Italian novelists. He was much admired by D.H. Lawrence, who translated a number of his stories, and he had a profound impact on the Italian Neo-realist cinema movement of the 1950s.

And you feel you could touch it with your hand—as if it smoked up from the fat earth, there, everywhere, round about the mountains that shut it in, from Agnone to Mount Etna capped with snow—stagnating in the plain like the sultry heat of June. There the red-hot sun rises and sets, and the livid moon, and the Puddara which seems to float through a sea of exhalations, and the birds and the white marguerites of spring, and the burnt-up summer; and there the wild-duck in long black files fly through the autumn clouds, and the river gleams as if it were of metal, between the wide, lonely banks, that are broken here and there, scattered with pebbles, and in the background the Lake of Lentini, like a mere, with its flat shores, and not a boat, not a tree on its sides, smooth and motionless. By the lake-bed the oxen pasture at will, forlorn, muddied up to the breast, hairy. When the sheep-bell resounds in the great silence, the wag-tails fly away, noiselessly, and the shepherd himself, yellow with fever, and white as well with dust, lifts his swollen lids for a moment, raising his head in the shadow of the dry reeds.

And truly the malaria gets into you with the bread you eat, or if you open your mouth to speak as you walk, suffocating in the dust and sun of the roads, and you feel your knees give way beneath you, or you sink discouraged on the saddle as your mule ambles along, with its head down. In vain the villages of Lentini and Francoforte and Paterno try to clamber up like strayed sheep on to the first hills that rise from the plain, and surround themselves with orange groves, and vineyards, and evergreen gardens and orchards; the malaria seizes the inhabitants in the depopulated streets, and nails them in front of the doors of their houses whose plaster is all falling with the sun, and there they tremble with fever under their brown cloaks, with all the bed-blankets over their shoulders.

Down below, on the plain, the houses are rare and sad-looking, beside the roads wasted by the sun, standing between two heaps of smoking dung, propped up by dilapidated sheds, where the change-horses wait with extinguished eyes, tied to the empty manger. Or by the shore of the lake, with the decrepit bough of the inn sign hung over the doorway, the great bare rooms, and the host dozing squatted on the door-step, with his head tied up in a kerchief, spying round the deserted country every time he wakes up, to see if a thirsty traveller is coming. Or else what looks like little huts of white wood, plumed with four meagre, grey eucalyptus trees, along the railway that cuts the plain in two like a hatchet cleft, where the locomotive flies whistling as the autumn wind, and where at night are coruscations of fiery sparks. Or finally here and there, at the boundaries of the farm-lands marked by a little stone pillar very roughly squared, the farm-places with their roofs shoved up from outside, with their door-frames collapsing, in front of the cracked threshing-floors, in the shade of the tall ricks of straw where the hens sleep with their heads under their wing, and the donkey lets his head hang, with his mouth still full of straw, and the dog rises suspiciously, and barks hoarsely at the stone which falls out from the plaster, at the fire-fly which flickers past, at the leaf which stirs in the inert countryside.

At evening, as soon as the sun sinks, sun-burnt men appear in the doorways, wearing big straw hats and wide canvas drawers, yawning and stretching their arms; and half-naked women, with blackened shoulders, suckling babies that are already pale and limp, so that you can't imagine that they'll ever get big and swarthy and romp on the grass when winter comes again, and the yard-floor will be green once more, and the sky blue, and the country all round laughing in the sun. And you can't imagine where all the people live who go to mass on Sundays, or why they live there, all those who come to the little church surrounded by cactus hedges, from ten miles around, from as far as ever the clanging of the little cracked bell can be heard over the endless plain.

However, wherever there is malaria there is earth blessed by God. In June the ears of wheat hang weighted down, and the furrows smoke as if they had blood in their veins the moment the ploughshare enters them in November. And then those who reap and those who sow must fall like ripe ears as well, for the Lord has said, "In the sweat of thy brow shalt thou eat bread." And when the sweats of fever leave some one of them stiff upon the mattress of maize-sheathes, and there's no need any more of sulphate or of decoction of eucalyptus, they put him on the hay-cart, or across an ass' pack-saddle, or on a ladder, or any way they can, with a sack over his face, and they take him to bury him by the lonely little church, under the thorny cactuses whose fruit no one for that reason eats. The women weep in a cluster, and the men stand looking on, smoking.

So they had carried away the estate-keeper of Valsavoia, who was called Farmer Croce, after he'd been swallowing sulphate and eucalyptus decoction for thirty years. In spring he was better, but at autumn, when the wild-ducks passed again, he put his kerchief on his head and showed himself not oftener than every other day in the doorway; till he was reduced to skin and bone, and had a big belly like a drum, so that they called him the Toad, partly because of his rude, savage manner, and partly because his eyes had become livid and stuck out of his head. He kept on saying before he died, "Don't you bother, the master will see after my children!" And with his wondering eyes he looked them one after another in the face, all those who stood round the bed, the last evening, when they put the candle under his nose. Uncle Menico the goat-herd, who understood those things, said that his liver must be as hard as a stone, and weighed five pounds. But somebody added:

"Well, now he needn't worry about it! He's got fat and rich at his master's expense, and his children don't stand in need of anybody! Do you think he took all that sulphate and put up with all that malaria for thirty years, just to please his master?"

Neighbour Carmine, the host by the lake, had lost all his five children one after the other in the same way, three boys and two girls! Never mind about the girls! But the boys died just when they were getting old enough to earn their bread. So now he was used to it; and as the fever got the last boy under, after having harassed him for two or three years, he didn't spend another farthing, neither for sulphate nor for decoctions, but drew off some good wine and set himself to make all the good fish stews he could think of, to provoke the appetite of the sick youth. He went fishing specially in the mornings, and came back laden with mullet and eels as thick as your arm, and when it was ready he stood before the bed with tears in his eyes and said to his son, "There you are, eat that!" And the rest of the fish Nanni the carter took to town to sell.

"The lake gives, and the lake takes away," said Nanni, seeing Neighbour Carmine weeping in secret. "What's the good, brother?"

The lake had given him good wages. And at Christmas, when eels fetch a good price, they used to have merry suppers before the fire, in the house by the lake, macaroni, sausages, everything you could think of, while the wind howled outside like a wolf that is cold and hungry. And in that way those that were left behind consoled themselves for the ones that were dead. But little by little they were wasting away, so that the mother grew bent like a hook with heart-brokenness, and the father, who was big and fat, was always on the doorstep, so that he needn't see those empty rooms, where his boys used to sing and work. The last one absolutely didn't want to die, and cried and grew desperate when the fever seized him, and even went and threw himself into the lake out of fear of death. But his father could swim, and fished him out again, and shouted at him that that cold bath would bring back the fever worse than ever.

"Ah," sobbed the youth, clutching his hair with his hands, "there's no hope for me, there's no hope for me!" "Just like his sister Agatha, who didn't want to die because she was a bride," observed Neighbour Carmine in private to his wife, sitting on the side of the bed; and she, who for some time now had left off weeping, nodded assent, bent as she was like a hook.

But she, though she was so reduced, and her big fat husband, they both had tough skins, and lived on alone to mind the house. The malaria doesn't finish everybody. Sometimes there's one who will live to be a hundred, like Cirino the simpleton, who had neither king nor kingdom, nor wit nor wish, nor father nor mother, nor house to sleep in, nor bread to eat, and everybody knew him for forty miles around, since he went from farm to farm, helping to tend the oxen, to carry the manure, to skin the dead cattle, and do all the dirty jobs; and got kicks and a bit of bread; he slept in the ditches, on the edges of the fields, under the hedges, or under the sheds for the standing cattle; and lived by charity, straying round like a dog without a master, with two ends of old drawers held together with bits of string on his thin black legs; and he went singing at the top of his voice under the sun which beat down on his bare head, yellow as saffron. He neither took sulphate any more, nor medicines, nor did he catch the fever. A hundred times they had found him stretched out across the road, as if he was dead, and picked him up; but at last the malaria had left him, because it could do no more with him. After it had eaten up his brain and the calves of his legs, and had got into his belly till it was swollen like a water-bag, it had left him as happy as an Easter Day, singing in the sun better than a cricket. The simpleton liked best to stand in front of the stables at Valsavoia, because people passed by, and he ran after them for miles, crying, "Uuh! uuh!" until they threw him a few cents. The host took the cents from him and kept him to sleep under the shed, on the horses' bedding, and when the horses gave him a kick Cirino ran to wake up the master crying, "Uuh!" and then in the morning he currycombed them and groomed them.

Later he had been attracted by the railway which they were building in the neighbourhood. The coach-drivers and wayfarers had become rarer on the road, and the idiot didn't know what to think, watching the swallows in the air for hours, and blinking his eyelids at the sun to make it out. Then the first time he saw all those people stuffed into the big cars that were leaving the station, he seemed to understand. And after that every day he waited for the train, never a minute wrong in his time, as if he had a clock in his head; and while it fled before him, hurling its noise and smoke in his face, he began to run after it, throwing his arms in the air and howling in a tone of anger and menace, "uuh! uuh!" . . . . .

The host too, whenever he saw the train passing in the distance puffing through the malaria, said nothing, but spat after it all he felt, shaking his head before the deserted sheds and the empty jugs. Formerly affairs had gone so well with him that he had had four wives, so that they called him "Killwife," and they said he'd got case-hardened to it, and that he was for taking the fifth, if the daughter of Farmer Turi Oricchiazza hadn't given him answer: "God preserve us! not if he was made of gold, that Christian there! He eats up his fellow-man like a crocodile!"

But it wasn't true that he'd got case-hardened to it, because when Goodwife Santa had died, his third, he had never taken a mouthful of food till midday, nor a drop of water, and he really cried behind the counter of the inn. "This time I want to take one who is used to the malaria," he had said after that event. "I don't want to suffer like this any more."

The malaria killed off his wives, one after the other, but they left him just the same, old and wrinkled, so that it was really hard to imagine that such a man had his own brave homicide on his conscience, intending for all that to take a fourth wife. However, each new time he wanted his wife young and appetizing, for the inn could never prosper without a wife, and for this reason customers had become scarce. Now there was nobody left but Neighbour Mommu, the signalman from the railway just near, a man who never spoke a word, and came to drink his glass between train and train, sitting himself down on the bench by the door with his shoes in his hand, to rest his legs.

"The malaria doesn't get those lot!" thought Killwife, also never opening his mouth, because if the malaria had made them fall like flies there'd have been nobody to keep that railway going. The poor wretch, since the only man who had poisoned his existence had been removed from his sight, had now only two enemies in the world: the railway which took away his customers, and the malaria which carried off his wives. All the other people on the plain, as far as the eye could reach, had their moments of blessedness, even if they had someone in bed sinking bit by bit, or if the fever was beating them down on the doorstep, with their handkerchiefs on their heads and their cloaks over their shoulders. They took pleasure looking round on the young wheat that was rising prosperous and green as velvet, or the wheat-ears waxing like a sea, and they listened to the long singing of the reapers, stretched out in a line like soldiers, and in every little road the bagpipes were heard, behind which swarms of peasants were just arriving from Calabria for the harvest, dusty people bent under their heavy saddle-sacks, the men in front and the women trailing behind, limping and looking with burnt, tired faces at the road which stretched before them. And on the brink of every ditch, behind every clump of aloes, at the hour when evening drops down like a grey veil, the pipes of the watchmen fluted among the ripe ears of grain, which fell silent, motionless, as the wind sank, invaded by the same silence of night.

"There you are!" thought Killwife. "If all that lot of folks can only manage not to leave their bones behind them, and get back home, they'll get back with money in their pockets, they will."

As for him, no! He waited neither for harvest nor anything, and he hadn't the spirit to sing. The evening fell sadly enough, through the empty stables and the dark inn. At that hour the train passed whistling in the distance, and Neighbour Mommu stood beside his signal-box with his flag in his hand; but away up there, when the train had vanished in the shadows, they heard Cirino the simpleton running after it shouting, "Uuh!" And Killwife, in the doorway of the dark, deserted inn, thought to himself that there was no malaria for that lot.

At last, when he could no longer pay the rent for the inn and the stabling, the landlord turned him out after he'd lived there fifty-seven years, and Killwife was reduced to looking for a job on the railway himself, and holding the little flag in his hand when the train passed.

And then, tired with running all day up and down the track, worn out with years and misfortunes, he saw twice a day the long line of carriages crowded with people pass by; the jolly companies of shooters spreading over the plain; sometimes a peasant lad playing the accordion with his head bent, bunched up on the seat of a third-class compartment; the beautiful ladies who looked out of the windows with their heads swathed in a veil; the silver and the tarnished steel of the bags and valises which shone under the polished lamps; the high stuffed seat-backs with their crochet-work covers. Ah, how lovely it must be travelling in there, snatching a wink of sleep! It was as if a piece of a city were sliding past, with the lit-up streets and the glittering shops. Then the train lost itself in the vast mist of the evening, and the poor fellow, taking off his shoes for a moment, and sitting on the bench, muttered, "Ah! for that lot there isn't any malaria."

A LEGEND OF OLD EGYPT

Bolesław Prus

Translated from the Polish by Christopher Kasparek

Bolesław Prus (1847–1912). Born as Aleksander Głowacki to an impoverished family. When he was barely three, his mother died and he spent his childhood being cared for by his grandmother and later his aunt. His difficult early life mean that he struggled to complete his education and, at fifteen, he ran away from school and joined the 1863 Uprising against Imperial Russia, and fought at Białka, where he sustained serious injuries that would lead to a lifelong struggle with agoraphobia. At twenty-five he began working as a newspaper columnist, and a year later was delivering public lectures on subjects of scientific interest. Under nom de plume Bolesław Prus, he began to publish short stories and novels, would become the one of the leading Polish writers of the late nineteenth century. His style was Realist in approach, and his stories and novels offer a complex, sweeping panorama of Warsaw society. He read widely, especially in philosophy, translating John Stuart Mill's "Logic" and eventually embracing Positivism, influenced by the writings of Herbert Spencer and later by Jeremy Bentham. One of his great admirers, Joseph Conrad, considered him "greater than Dickens".

Behold, how vain are human hopes before the order of the world; behold, how vain they are before the decrees that have been written in fiery signs upon the heavens by the Eternal! . . .

Hundred-year-old Ramses, mighty ruler of Egypt, was breathing his last. The chest of the potentate before whose voice millions had quaked half a century, had been invested by a stifling incubus, and it drank the blood from his heart, the strength from his arm, and at times even the consciousness from his brain. The great pharaoh lay like a fallen cedar upon the skin of an Indian tiger, having covered his legs with the triumphal cloak of an Ethiopian king. And stern even with himself, he summoned the wisest physician from the Temple of Karnak and said:

"I know that you have powerful medicines that either kill or cure at once. Prepare me one proper to my illness, and let this end once and for all. . . one way or the other."

The physician hesitated.

"Consider, Ramses," he whispered, "since your descent from the high heavens the Nile has flooded a hundred times; can I give you a medicine that would be uncertain even for the youngest of your warriors?"

Ramses sat up on the bed.

"I must be very ill, priest," he cried, "if you dare give me advice! Be silent and do my bidding. There lives, after all, my thirty-year-old grandson and successor, Horus. And Egypt cannot have a ruler who is unable to mount a chariot and lift a spear."

When the priest, with trembling hand, gave him the terrible potion, Ramses drank it down as a thirsty man drinks a cup of water; then he summoned the most renowned astrologer in Thebes and bade him say frankly what the stars showed.

"Saturn has united with the moon," replied the sage, "which portends the death of a member of your dynasty, Ramses. You did ill to drink the medicine today, for human plans are vain before the decrees that the Eternal writes upon the heavens."

"Naturally, the stars have foretold my death," replied Ramses. "And when might it happen?" he asked the physician.

"Before sunrise, Ramses, either you will be hale as a rhinoceros or your sacred ring will be on Horus' hand."

"Conduct Horus," said Ramses in a voice growing faint, "to the hall of the pharaohs; let him wait there for my last words and for the ring, that there be not a moment's interruption in the exercise of power."

Horus wept (he had a compassionate heart) over his grandfather's approaching death; but as there could be no interruption in the exercise of power, he went to the hall of the pharaohs, surrounded by a large crowd of attendants.

He seated himself on the porch whose marble steps ran down to the river and, full of indefinable sadness, surveyed the countryside.

The Moon, beside which glowed the ominous star Saturn, was just gilding the bronze waters of the Nile, painting the shadows of the gigantic pyramids upon meadows and gardens, and illuminating the entire valley for leagues around. Despite the late hour of the night, lamps burned in huts and buildings, and the populace had come out of their homes and beneath the open heavens. Boats ranged the Nile, thick as on a holiday; in palm forests, along the water's edge, in marketplaces, in streets, and adjacent to Ramses' palace there undulated a countless throng. Notwithstanding this, there was such silence that Horus could hear the rustle of water reeds and the plaintive howls of hyenas seeking prey.

"Why are they gathering like this?" Horus asked a courtier, indicating the immense fields of human heads.

"They wish, lord, to greet you as the new pharaoh and to hear from your lips the benefits that you will bestow upon them."

For the first time the pride of greatness struck the Prince's heart, as the onrushing sea strikes a steep shore.

"And what do those lights mean?" asked Horus.

"The priests have gone to the grave of your mother Sephora to transfer her remains to the pharaohs' catacombs."

Horus' heart was filled anew with grief for his mother, whose remains—due the mercy that she had shown the slaves—the severe Ramses had buried among the slaves.

"I hear horses neighing," said Horus, listening. "Who is riding out at this hour?"

"The chancellor, my lord, has ordered messengers readied to ride to your teacher, Jethro."

Horus gave a sigh at the mention of his beloved friend whom Ramses had banished for instilling, into the soul of his grandson and successor, aversion to war and compassion for the oppressed populace.

"And that little light across the Nile?"

"With that light, O Horus," replied the courtier, "faithful Berenice greets you from her cloister prison. The high priest has sent the pharaoh's barge for her, and when the sacred ring flashes on your hand the heavy cloister door will open and she will return to you, longing and loving."

Having heard these words, Horus asked no more questions; he fell silent and covered his eyes with his hand.

Suddenly he gave a hiss of pain.

"What's the matter, Horus?"

"A bee has stung my leg," replied the Prince, grown pale.

The courtier examined Horus' leg in the greenish moonlight.

"Thank Osiris," he said, "that it wasn't a spider, whose venom can be lethal in this season."

Lo! how vain are human hopes before the irrevocable decrees...

At that moment the commander of the army entered and, bowing, said to Horus:

"Great Ramses, feeling that his body is growing cold, has sent me to you with the order: 'Go to Horus, because I am not long for this world, and do his will as you have done mine. Though he command you to yield Upper Egypt to the Ethiopians and conclude a fraternal alliance with these enemies, do so when you see my ring on his hand, for immortal Osiris speaks through the lips of rulers.'"

"I shall not turn Egypt over to the Ethiopians," said the Prince, "but I will make peace, for I hold dear the blood of my people; write an edict at once and hold mounted messengers at the ready so that, when the first fires light in my honor, they may speed toward the southern sun and carry my favor to the Ethiopians. And write a second edict, that from this hour until the end of time no prisoner of war shall have his tongue torn from his mouth on the field of battle. I have spoken..."

The commander prostrated himself, then withdrew to write the orders; and the Prince asked the courtier to take another look at his wound, which was very painful.

"Your leg has swollen a bit, Horus," said the courtier. "What if, instead of a bee, a spider had stung you!..."

Now the chancellor of the kingdom entered the hall and, bowing to the Prince, said:

"Mighty Ramses, seeing his eyes growing dim, has sent me to you with the order: 'Go to Horus and blindly carry out his will. Though he should order you to release the slaves from their chains and give all the land to the people, you shall do so when you see my sacred ring on his hand, for immortal Osiris speaks through the lips of rulers.'"

"My heart does not reach that far," said Horus. "But write an edict at once, that the people's rents and taxes are lowered by half, and that the slaves shall have three days a week free from labor and shall not have their backs caned without a court judgment. And also write an edict recalling from banishment my teacher, Jethro, who is the wisest and noblest of Egyptians. I have spoken..."

The chancellor prostrated himself, but before he could withdraw to write the edicts, the high priest entered.

"Horus," he said, "any moment now great Ramses will depart to the kingdom of the shades, and his heart will be weighed on the infallible scales by Osiris. And when the sacred ring of the pharaohs flashes on your hand, order and I shall obey you though you were to throw down the wonderful Temple of Amon, for immortal Osiris speaks through the lips of rulers."

"I shall not throw temples down," replied Horus, "but raise up new ones and increase the priests' treasury. I only ask that you write an edict for the solemn transfer of my mother Sephora's remains to the catacombs, and a second edict. . . for the release of beloved Berenice from her cloister prison. I have spoken. . ."

"You do wisely," replied the high priest. "All is in readiness to fulfill these orders, and presently I shall write the edicts; when you touch them with the ring of the pharaohs, I shall light this lamp to announce your favor to the people, and freedom and love to Berenice."

There entered the wisest priest in Karnak.

"Horus," he said, "I do not wonder at your pallor, for your grandfather Ramses is breathing his last. He could not stand the power of the medicine that I was loath to give him, this potentate of potentates. Therefore only the high priest's deputy remains with him in order, when he dies, to remove the sacred ring from his hand and give it to you in token of unlimited power. But you grow still more pale, Horus?" he added.

"Look at my leg," moaned Horus, and he fell into a golden chair whose armrests were carved in the likeness of hawks' heads.

The physician knelt, examined the leg, and backed away, terrified.

"Horus," he whispered, "you have been stung by a very poisonous spider."

"Am I to die? . . . at a moment like this? . . ." asked Horus in a barely audible voice.

And then he added: "How soon will it happen? . . . tell the truth. . ."

"Before the moon hides behind that palm tree. . ."

"Ah, so! . . . And has Ramses long to live? . . ."

"I don't know. . . Maybe they are bringing you his ring right now."

At that moment the ministers entered with ready edicts.

"Chancellor!" cried Horus, grabbing his arm, "if I were to die right now, would you all carry out my orders? . . ."

"Live to your grandfather's age, Horus!" replied the chancellor. "But even were you to step before Osiris' court right after him, your every edict will be carried out, so long as you touch it with the sacred ring of the pharaohs."

"With the ring!" repeated Horus, "but where is it? . . ."

"One of the courtiers was telling me," whispered the commander in chief, "that great Ramses was drawing his last breath."

"I have sent to my deputy," added the high priest, "for him to immediately remove the ring when Ramses' heart stops beating."

"Thank you all! . . ." said Horus. "It's a pity. . . oh, what a pity. . . But, after all, I won't die completely. . . I'll leave blessings, peace, the people's happiness, and. . . my Berenice will regain freedom. . . How long? . . ." he asked the physician.

"Death is a thousand soldier's paces from you," replied the physician sadly.

"Do you hear anybody coming?" said Horus.

No one spoke.

The moon was nearing the palm tree and had just touched its first fronds; the fine sands sifted softly in the clepsydras.

"How far?" whispered Horus.

"Eight hundred paces," replied the physician, "I don't know, Horus, whether you'll have time to touch all the edicts with the sacred ring, even were it brought to you right now. . ."

"Give me the edicts," said the Prince, listening whether anyone was running over from Ramses' apartments. "And you, priest," he turned to the physician, "tell me how much life I have left, so that I may confirm at least the orders dearest to me."

"Six hundred paces," whispered the physician.

The edict reducing the people's rents and the slaves' labor fell from Horus' hands to the floor.

"Five hundred. . ."

The edict on peace with the Ethiopians slipped from the Prince's lap.

"Isn't anyone coming? . . ."

"Four hundred. . ." answered the physician.

Horus became thoughtful, and. . . the order transferring Sephora's remains fell.

"Three hundred. . ."

The same fate met the edict recalling Jethro from banishment.

"Two hundred. . ."

Horus' lips turned livid. With his contracted hand he threw to the floor the edict on not tearing out the tongues of prisoners taken in war, and left only. . . the order to free Berenice.

"One hundred. . ."

Amid the sepulchral silence, a clatter of sandals was heard. Into the hall ran the high priest's deputy. Horus extended his hand.

"A miracle! . . ." cried the arrival. "Great Ramses has recovered. . . He rose briskly from his bed and wants to go on a lion hunt at sunrise. . . And as a sign of favor, Horus, he invites you to accompany him. . ."

Horus looked with failing eye across the Nile, where shone the light in Berenice's prison, and two tears, bloody tears, rolled down his face.

"You do not answer, Horus? . . ." asked Ramses' messenger, in surprise.

"Don't you see he's dead? . . ." whispered the wisest physician in Karnak.

Behold, human hopes are vain before the decrees that the Eternal writes in fiery signs on the heavens.

MOTHER SAUVAGE

Guy de Maupassant

Translated from the French by Linda Cooley and Catarina Ferreira

Guy de Maupassant (1850–1893). Born near Dieppe and educated in Rouen, Maupassant was introduced to Gustav Flaubert while still at school and the master would later be his literary mentor. He worked as a clerk and later in a government ministry while writing short stories. His first success, *Boule de Suif* in 1880, catapulted him to fame in France. Unquestionably the greatest French master of the short story, over the course of his career, Maupassant wrote half a dozen novels and more than 300 stories. A failed suicide attempt in 1892 saw him committed to an asylum where he died a year later. His epitaph, penned by Maupassant himself, reads: "I have coveted everything and taken pleasure in nothing."

Fifteen years had passed since I last visited Virelogne. I returned in the autumn to shoot with my friend Serval, who had finally rebuilt his château, which the Prussians had destroyed.

I loved that district. It is one of those delightful spots which have a sensuous charm for the eyes. You love it with a physical love. Those of us who are enchanted by the countryside, keep tender memories of certain oft-seen springs and woods, certain lakes and hills that have stirred us like joyful events. Sometimes our thoughts turn back to a patch of forest, the edge of a riverbank, or an orchard filled with flowers, seen but once on a bright day, yet they remain in our hearts like the images of certain women in light, gauzy dresses encountered on the street on a spring morning, who leave in soul and body an unquenched desire that is never forgotten, a feeling that one has just passed by happiness.

At Virelogne I loved the whole countryside, dotted as it was with little woods and criss-crossed by glittering brooks like veins carrying blood to the earth. Here, you could fish for crayfish, trout and eels. Divine happiness! Here, there were bathing places and often snipe to be found among the high grass that grew along the banks of these small water courses.

I was stepping along, light as a goat, watching my two dogs running ahead of me. Serval, a hundred metres to my right, was beating a field of lucerne. I turned by the thicket that forms the boundary of the wood of Sandres and I saw a cottage in ruins.

Suddenly I remembered it as I had seen it the last time, in 1869, neat, covered with vines, with chickens before the door. What is sadder than a dead house, with its skeleton standing bare and sinister?

I also recalled that inside its doors, after a very tiring day, the good woman had given me a glass of wine to drink and that Serval had told me the history of its people. The father, an old poacher, had been killed by the gendarmes. The son, whom I had once seen, was a tall, dry fellow who also passed for a fierce slayer of game. People called them "Les Sauvage."

Was it a name or a nickname?

I called to Serval. He came up with his long strides like a crane.

I asked him:

"What's become of those people?"

This was his story:

When war was declared the son Sauvage, who was then thirty-three years old, enlisted, leaving his mother alone in the house. People did not pity the old woman very much because she had money; they knew it.

She remained entirely alone in that isolated dwelling, so far from the village, on the edge of the wood. She was not afraid, however, being of the same strain as the men folk—a hardy old woman, tall and thin, who seldom laughed and with whom one never jested. The women of the fields laugh but little in any case, that is men's business. But they themselves have sad and narrowed hearts, leading a melancholy, gloomy life. The peasants imbibe a little noisy merriment at the tavern, but their helpmates always have grave, stern countenances. The muscles of their faces have never learned the motions of laughter.

Mother Sauvage continued her ordinary existence in her cottage, which was soon covered by the snows. She came to the village once a week to get bread and a little meat. Then she returned to her house. As there was talk of wolves, she went out with a gun upon her shoulder—her son's gun, rusty and with the butt worn by the rubbing of the hand—and she was a strange sight, the tall "Sauvage," a little bent, going with slow strides over the snow, the muzzle of the piece extending beyond the black headdress, which confined her head and imprisoned her white hair, which no one had ever seen.

One day a Prussian force arrived. It was billeted upon the inhabitants, according to the property and resources of each. Four were allotted to the old woman, who was known to be rich.

They were four great fellows with fair complexion, blond beards and blue eyes, who had not grown thin in spite of the fatigue which they had endured already and who also, though in a conquered country, had remained kind and gentle. Alone with this aged woman, they showed themselves full of consideration, sparing her, as much as they could, all expense and fatigue. They could be seen, all four of them, making their toilet at the well in their shirt-sleeves in the gray dawn, splashing with great swishes of water their pink-white northern skin, while La Mère Sauvage went and came, preparing their soup. They would be seen cleaning the kitchen, rubbing the tiles, splitting wood, peeling potatoes, doing up all the housework like four good sons around their mother.

But the old woman thought always of her own son, so tall and thin, with his hooked nose and his brown eyes and his heavy mustache which made a roll of black hair upon his lip. She asked every day of each of the soldiers who were installed beside her hearth: "Do you know where the French marching regiment, No. 23, was sent? My boy is in it."

They invariably answered, "No, we don't know, don't know a thing at all." And, understanding her pain and her uneasiness—they who had mothers, too, there at home—they rendered her a thousand little services. She loved them well, moreover, her four enemies, since the peasantry have no patriotic hatred; that belongs to the upper class alone. The humble, those who pay the most because they are poor and because every new burden crushes them down; those who are killed in masses, who make the true cannon's prey because they are so many; those, in fine, who suffer most cruelly the atrocious miseries of war because they are the feeblest and offer least resistance—they hardly understand at all those bellicose ardors, that excitable sense of honor or those pretended political combinations which in six months exhaust two nations, the conqueror with the conquered.

They said in the district, in speaking of the Germans of La Mère Sauvage:

"There are four who have found a soft place."

Now, one morning, when the old woman was alone in the house, she observed, far off on the plain, a man coming toward her dwelling. Soon she recognized him; it was the postman to distribute the letters. He gave her a folded paper and she drew out of her case the spectacles which she used for sewing. Then she read:

MADAME SAUVAGE: This letter is to tell you sad news. Your boy Victor was killed yesterday by a shell which almost cut him in two. I was near by, as we stood next to each other in the company, and he told me about you and asked me to let you know on the same day if anything happened to him.

I took his watch, which was in his pocket, to bring it back to you when the war is done.

CESAIRE RIVOT,
Soldier of the 2d class, March. Reg. No. 23.

The letter was dated three weeks back.

She did not cry at all. She remained motionless, so overcome and stupefied that she did not even suffer as yet. She thought: "There's Victor killed now." Then little by little the tears came to her eyes and the sorrow filled her heart. Her thoughts came, one by one, dreadful, torturing. She would never kiss him again, her child, her big boy, never again! The gendarmes had killed the father, the Prussians had killed the son. He had been cut in two by a cannon-ball. She seemed to see the thing, the horrible thing: the head falling, the eyes open, while he chewed the corner of his big mustache as he always did in moments of anger.

What had they done with his body afterward? If they had only let her have her boy back as they had brought back her husband—with the bullet in the middle of the forehead!

But she heard a noise of voices. It was the Prussians returning from the village. She hid her letter very quickly in her pocket, and she received them quietly, with her ordinary face, having had time to wipe her eyes.

They were laughing, all four, delighted, for they brought with them a fine rabbit—stolen, doubtless—and they made signs to the old woman that there was to be something good to eat.

She set herself to work at once to prepare breakfast, but when it came to killing the rabbit, her heart failed her. And yet it was not the first. One of the soldiers struck it down with a blow of his fist behind the ears.

The beast once dead, she skinned the red body, but the sight of the blood which she was touching, and which covered her hands, and which she felt cooling and coagulating, made her tremble from head to foot, and she kept seeing her big boy cut in two, bloody, like this still palpitating animal.

She sat down at table with the Prussians, but she could not eat, not even a mouthful. They devoured the rabbit without bothering themselves about her. She looked at them sideways, without speaking, her face so impassive that they perceived nothing.

All of a sudden she said: "I don't even know your names, and here's a whole month that we've been together." They understood, not without difficulty, what she wanted, and told their names.

That was not sufficient; she had them written for her on a paper, with the addresses of their families, and, resting her spectacles on her great nose, she contemplated that strange handwriting, then folded the sheet and put it in her pocket, on top of the letter which told her of the death of her son.

When the meal was ended she said to the men:

"I am going to work for you."

And she began to carry up hay into the loft where they slept.

They were astonished at her taking all this trouble; she explained to them that thus they would not be so cold; and they helped her. They heaped the stacks of hay as high as the straw roof, and in that manner they made a sort of great chamber with four walls of fodder, warm and perfumed, where they should sleep splendidly.

At dinner one of them was worried to see that La Mère Sauvage still ate nothing. She told him that she had pains in her stomach. Then she kindled a good fire to warm herself, and the four Germans ascended to their lodging-place by the ladder which served them every night for this purpose.

As soon as they closed the trapdoor the old woman removed the ladder, then opened the outside door noiselessly and went back to look for more bundles of straw, with which she filled her kitchen. She went barefoot in the snow, so softly that no sound was heard. From time to time she listened to the sonorous and unequal snoring of the four soldiers who were fast asleep.

When she judged her preparations to be sufficient, she threw one of the bundles into the fireplace, and when it was alight she scattered it over all the others. Then she went outside again and looked.

In a few seconds the whole interior of the cottage was illumined with a brilliant light and became a frightful brasier, a gigantic fiery furnace, whose glare streamed out of the narrow window and threw a glittering beam upon the snow.

Then a great cry issued from the top of the house; it was a clamor of men shouting heartrending calls of anguish and of terror. Finally the trapdoor having given way, a whirlwind of fire shot up into the loft, pierced the straw roof, rose to the sky like the immense flame of a torch, and all the cottage flared.

Nothing more was heard therein but the crackling of the fire, the cracking of the walls, the falling of the rafters. Suddenly the roof fell in and the burning carcass of the dwelling hurled a great plume of sparks into the air, amid a cloud of smoke.

The country, all white, lit up by the fire, shone like a cloth of silver tinted with red.

A bell, far off, began to toll.

The old "Sauvage" stood before her ruined dwelling, armed with her gun, her son's gun, for fear one of those men might escape.

When she saw that it was ended, she threw her weapon into the brasier. A loud report followed.

People were coming, the peasants, the Prussians.

They found the woman seated on the trunk of a tree, calm and satisfied.

A German officer, but speaking French like a son of France, demanded:

"Where are your soldiers?"

She reached her bony arm toward the red heap of fire which was almost out and answered with a strong voice:

"There!"

They crowded round her. The Prussian asked:

"How did it take fire?"

"It was I who set it on fire."

They did not believe her, they thought that the sudden disaster had made her crazy. While all pressed round and listened, she told the story from beginning to end, from the arrival of the letter to the last shriek of the men who were burned with her house, and never omitted a detail.

When she had finished, she drew two pieces of paper from her pocket, and, in order to distinguish them by the last gleams of the fire, she again adjusted her spectacles. Then she said, showing one:

"That, that is the death of Victor." Showing the other, she added, indicating the red ruins with a bend of the head: "Here are their names, so that you can write home." She quietly held a sheet of paper out to the officer, who held her by the shoulders, and she continued:

"You must write how it happened, and you must say to their mothers that it was I who did that, Victoire Simon, la Sauvage! Do not forget."

The officer shouted some orders in German. They seized her, they threw her against the walls of her house, still hot. Then twelve men drew quickly up before her, at twenty paces. She did not move. She had understood; she waited.

An order rang out, followed instantly by a long report. A belated shot went off by itself, after the others.

The old woman did not fall. She sank as though they had cut off her legs.

The Prussian officer approached. She was almost cut in two, and in her withered hand she held her letter bathed with blood.

My friend Serval added:

"It was by way of reprisal that the Germans destroyed the chateau of the district, which belonged to me."

I thought of the mothers of those four fine fellows burned in that house and of the horrible heroism of that other mother shot against the wall.

And I picked up a little stone, still blackened by the flames.

SECRET SORROW

Knut Hamsun

Translated from the Norwegian by Robert Ferguson

Knut Hamsun (1859–1952) was a major Norwegian writer, who was awarded the Nobel Prize in Literature in 1920. Hamsun's work spans more than seventy years and shows variation with regard to the subject, perspective and environment. He published more than twenty novels, a collection of poetry, some short stories and plays, a travelogue, and some essays. Because of his support for the Nazis, he was charged with treason and committed to a psychiatric hospital. In 1943, he sent Germany's minister of propaganda Joseph Goebbels his Nobel Prize medal as a gift. Otto Dietrich describes in his memoirs how the meeting between Hamsun and Hitler was the only time that another person was able to get a word in edgeways with the Führer. He attributes the cause to Hamsun's deafness and notes that Hitler remained incensed for several days.

1

I've just met him for the fourth time. He follows me wherever I go, I can never feel safe from him, he appears right in front of me in the most out of the way places. Once I even met him in my room in Kristiania; he had got in before me and was standing there . . .

But let me begin at the beginning.

I met him for the first time in Copenhagen. It was Christmas 1879; I had a place in Klareboderne.

One day as I was sitting alone in my room—I remember very clearly that I was supposed to be copying out some music, and that it was causing me a great deal of trouble, since I was quite unable to read music—there was a knock on my door. Light and subdued, like a woman's knock. I shout: Come in! and a man enters.

A man of about thirty, pale, with a somewhat glowering expression, and narrow in the shoulder, remarkably narrow. He wore a glove on only one of his hands.

He removed his hat as soon as he entered and his large eyes remained fixed on me the entire time as he approached where I sat writing. He apologised for intruding like this; he'd seen me entering and leaving the lodging house a couple of times and it occurred to him that we were old acquaintances. Didn't I remember him from Helsinki, from the police-station in Helsinki?

I had never been to Helsinki, there must be some misunderstanding . . .

No? Then perhaps it was Malmö. The more he thought about it the more certain he was that it was in Malmö he had bumped into me.

But I hadn't been to Malmö either.

He mentioned a couple of other places, and each time I answered he said, 'Just wait now! I'm convinced I've met you before, I just can't recall where.' Finally he mentioned Kristiania, and I grudgingly conceded that we might possibly have come across one another there. He made me feel unsure of myself, and I could not rule out the possibility that I might once have met him in Kristiania.

'I don't have any particular news for you,' he said. 'It just occurred to me to drop in and say hello to a fellow-countryman and old acquaintance.'

We conversed briefly, on matters of no importance, I've completely forgotten what. All I remember is that he formulated himself in a curiously ambiguous way, as if he were really saying something quite different from what he actually said, and that in general he gave the impression of being a secretive man.

When he rose to leave he once again apologised for disturbing me. Among other things he said:

'I get bored. I can't think what to do any more. Sometimes I play a practical joke on the police, just to pass the time. But it's so easy I can hardly be bothered.'

He said this seriously, but I chose to treat it as a joke.

At the door he turned as though suddenly remembering something and invited me to go for a drive with him that evening, 'for old time's sake'. At first I said no—I really can't explain why—but a moment later I accepted his invitation. The last thing he said to me was that I mustn't take any money with me. One could never be too careful. I could leave my money with my landlord, he said. I didn't quite get it, but said yes anyway and promised to be outside The Horse at five o'clock.

Alone again I thought about the man and what he had said. I found it strange that he should have come to visit me. And what was all that about money? To begin with it all seemed very curious, but I soon forgot about it. When you're travelling you soon get to know people, strangers can become friends in less than an hour. I was at The Horse at the appointed time.

The weather was so mild and the streets so muddy that we had to use a carriage. We had the hood up and the windows closed. We drove west through Copenhagen, past Ladegaarden, out along Rolighedsvei and past the waterworks. All that long way we hardly exchanged a word; anyway the carriage rumbled terribly. Once we had crossed Grøndals Bridge and were approaching Utterslev the stranger takes a piece of rope from his pocket and begins playing with it, all the while staring fixedly at me. It's dark in the carriage, but I can see perfectly well what he's doing. We're sitting on the same seat, but turned to face each another, watching each other. Suddenly he says:

'You're not scared, are you?'

At the same time he holds the rope up to my face.

I lied, answering with a quavering voice:

'No, what is there to be scared of?'

But I was shaking with fear and thought of pulling the bell at once and alerting the driver. It annoyed me to have that piece of rope dangling in front of my eyes, so I got up and moved to the front seat.

We drive on like this for a while. Shortly afterwards he turned his gaze away from me and slowly put the rope back in his pocket, as though he had changed his mind about something. Then suddenly he sits bolt upright in his seat, points out of the window as though in great alarm and says:

'Look! Over there!'

Instinctively I turned my head, and at the same moment felt an icy grip around my neck. The scoundrel stood half-upright in front of me with his cold fingers round my throat. I don't know if I screamed, I don't think I did. Suddenly it occurred to me that this person just wanted to scare me, or to tease me, I was convinced that he didn't want to throttle me. It made me angry and I pushed him back as hard as I could. He kept his grip. I felt behind me for the bell-pull, fumbled after it, found it at last and pulled. Still he kept hold of me. He heard clearly that the bell rang, yet he would not let go. We struggled together for some time. He cut me on the throat, just below my right ear, his effrontery knew no bounds, he gave me this wound with a nail or a screwdriver, which he twisted, and it hurt. Then at last I'm able to punch my way free, swinging out and hitting him with solid, brutal blows wherever I could. Then the cabby opens the door, and for the first time I realised that the carriage had stopped.

'Shall we turn back?' asked the driver.

In complete confusion I climbed out of the carriage. My travelling companion remained sitting where he was, calm and collected.

'Yes,' he replied, 'Let's turn back.'

'I'm *walking* back,' I said. 'As far as I'm concerned you can drive this chap to hell.'

'Walking?' repeated the driver. 'On foot?'

The stranger said nothing. Didn't even look at me. Now I got really angry. I shouted to the driver to get going, jumped back into the carriage and slammed the door shut. In my extreme anger I felt remarkably, almost unnaturally, strong.

I pressed myself unnecessarily close to my fellow-passenger, took up as much room as I could, squashed him into a corner. As I twisted and turned in my seat I hit him several times with my elbows. He accepted this, did not react. Not until we were once again in Copenhagen did he say, with a smile:

'Well, I presume you'll report me for this?'

I did not reply.

He put both his feet up on my hat, which I had removed and placed on the seat opposite me so that I could sit upright in the carriage. He brought his heels down hard on the crown and I heard it crack. I became more and more convinced that his sole aim was to frighten me. I felt an intense humiliation.

'But if you are going to report me,' he continued, 'you'd better do it straightaway. I'll be long gone by the time anyone tries to arrest me. I assure you, probably even before daybreak tomorrow I'll be over in Skåne. You'll be wasting your time!' He continued in this vein, about how he'd be gone in a very short while. Then suddenly he said: 'Or maybe I can't be bothered. Maybe I'll have the pleasure of greeting you again tomorrow, on Østergade?'

He didn't say it in a challenging, taunting way. His voice was low, almost melancholy. My hat was gradually being squashed flat under his feet.

I responded that I would have the honour of ignoring him completely, that I would pass by him as though he were thin air if I should meet him again, and walk right over him if he should happen to block my path. I wouldn't waste my words even if they would get you hanged, I said. I despise you and I can't even be bothered to throw you out of the carriage window.

I couldn't have done that anyway, but all the same I said it, the way one says such things. And he accepted it.

Back at The Horse we both got out. I walked off—hatless—while he remained behind to pay the driver.

That was the first time I met him. I still have the mark on my throat he gave me that evening.

2

Some years later, maybe three or four, I was on a short visit to Germany and making the trip from Hamburg to Bremerhafen. The train wasn't due to leave for another ten minutes when I reached the platform, so I had good time. I walked along looking for a good seat and got almost as far as the engine. There a man waves to me from the window of a carriage and to my great surprise I recognise my 'old acquaintance' from the drive through Copenhagen, the man with the dark eyes. I recognised him at once.

I give a start, I feel at once extremely uncomfortable and walk straight past his compartment. But as I did so it occurred to me that I might be giving the impression I was afraid of him, and being now several years older anyway I was not disposed to pass up the chance of another encounter with this interesting person. So I turn round, still as though looking for a seat on the train, and stop in a casual and indifferent sort of way outside his compartment. I open the door and enter.

The compartment was empty, apart from him.

I squeezed past him on the way in and he drew his knees back to let me by. In doing so he looked up as though he hadn't seen me before; and yet I was convinced that he had been waving to me just a few minutes previously. I had even somewhat unwillingly touched my hat and nodded to him, but he made no response.

I sat down in the corner. I was irritated with myself for that little nod and steeled myself to offer him a show of the most sublime indifference. He didn't seem to have aged in the slightest since our last meeting, but his clothes were different. On that first occasion they had been smart, almost elegant; now they were much plainer, a light-coloured, hard-wearing travelling outfit. On the seat directly opposite him was a leather suitcase.

The bell rings and the train sets off.

I made myself comfortable and put my feet up on the seat. About quarter of an hour passed. I acted as though oblivious of my travelling companion. He seemed lost in thought.

Then he reaches into an inside pocket and pulls out an oilcloth bag that looks like some kind of first-aid kit. He opens it and begins examining a number of rusty iron tools which he takes out one by one. They were queer-looking things with hooks on, some flat, some round, some fine, a mixture of large and small. It was obvious to me that this was a collection of jemmies. Nor did he make any attempt to hide what they were. Indeed, he twisted and turned these implements in his hand as if he were already picking locks with them. He even tried to open his suitcase with a couple of them. It was as though he were deliberately trying to show me what the hooks were for. All this time I sat and watched.

Careful! I thought to myself. He's doing this deliberately to taunt you. There's something behind all this. He's leading you on, trying to tempt you in some way.

Ten minutes passed. He takes a small, shiny file from his breast pocket and begins cleaning the jemmies with it. And after he's cleaned each one he places it on the seat beside him. Note how I was sitting: with my legs up on his seat and stretched out towards him. My shoe was almost touching his coat. He sits there, scraping away.

Then, absentmindedly, as though lost in thought, he places one newly sharpened jemmy on my leg and starts on another. The man uses me as a work-surface. I sit there and allow it to happen. I didn't move. Sat waiting for him to do it again. And sure enough, he placed another jemmy on my leg, then another, and another. He treated me as though I were a cushion, as though I were part of the seat. By the time he was finished there was a row of some six of these little hooks ranged along my leg.

I stood up. Not suddenly, but quickly enough to make them all fall to the floor before he could prevent it. I had just one thought in mind: to return some of his profound contempt.

He didn't say anything when the jemmies fell. Just picked them up again in silence, one by one.

At that moment the conductor arrived. To my great surprise I observed that my travelling companion made not the slightest attempt, even now, to hide the hooks. All the time the conductor was present he left them on open display. Not until he had gone did he return the case and its contents to his pocket. It was almost as though he had been waiting for just such an opportunity to show off his dangerous tools.

We journey on for perhaps another half hour, we pass stations, stop, journey on, and still my travelling companion says nothing. Quite deliberately I conducted myself as though I were alone in the compartment. I put my feet up on the seat again, yawned noisily, sang now and then, all just to show him my awesome indifference. Yet none of it seemed to bother him. I lit a cigar and tossed the burning match onto his hand, just threw it away as heedlessly as if there were no one at all sitting there, and I saw it hit his hand. The only reaction was a slight twitching of the mouth as he drew back his lips slightly, almost as though he wanted to smile. Otherwise he sat quietly.

After we had journeyed a little further in this fashion he suddenly looked out of the train window as though he recognised the countryside, got to his feet quickly and picked up his suitcase by one of its straps. He stood like that for a few more minutes until the train came to a halt at a small station. Then he gives me an ironically deep bow, very deep, in complete silence, without looking at me, takes a couple of paces backwards, bows again, and with a broad smile turns and leaves the compartment. He hailed a porter to carry his baggage and walked off.

Throughout the entire journey he had neither spoken to me nor looked me in the face.

3

Years passed, three years, and I met him again in an obscure part of New York, in a gambling den. I was there before him and was sitting at the roulette table when he entered. An attendant offered to relieve him of his hat and coat but he merely shook his head and kept on both. Moments later he removed his hat and carried it in his hand. He turned his attention to the roulette table.

Space was made for him and he began to play. It seemed to me that he followed my bets with more interest than his own. I lost consistently, playing black and a double, black and a double, all the time, always losing. Maybe this was what interested him so much.

Suddenly he says to me straight across the table, in Norwegian:

'Don't you realise that you're being cheated?'

He ran the risk of others besides me understanding his words, and if there were any that did then he would be lucky to get away without spilling his blood. But he said it anyway, in a loud voice, looking directly at me as he spoke.

I pretended I hadn't heard him and carried on backing the same number and colour as before. And I lost just as heavily. I felt a burning and perverse obstinacy: if that person tried once more to involve himself in my affairs then I would speak to the croupier. I was angry and upset. There could no longer be any doubt that I was being cheated, I could see as much myself: the croupier had a key in his hand which he surreptitiously held close to the wheel whenever it was about to stop, and it had already occurred to me several bets ago that there might be a magnet in this key. But I chose to do nothing, just kept on playing and losing my little bets.

Then the stranger says to the croupier:

'Put that key in your pocket!'

His voice was cold and imperious and the croupier obeyed him at once, merely explaining that it was the key to the bank, he kept it in his hand for convenience. But he did as he was told, instantly. I found his obedience insulting and I became angry with him. I pushed my last ten chips onto the black, stood up and left without waiting to see what happened.

After that I did not meet my man again until last winter in Kristiania. I was living up on St Hans' Hill then, I had a fourth-floor room. As I returned from the dining-room after supper one day I found my secretive friend standing in the middle of my room. I had left the key in the keyhole and he had simply let himself in. All he does is hold out his hand and ask for 16 kroner—16 kroner—then he thanks me, thanks me most humbly—twice—then heads for the door. He stops and says:

'My God, how stupid you are!'

He said it turned towards the door, in a tone of utter contempt.

My old bitterness revives and I take a couple of steps towards him. When I see that he is about to open the door and disappear I cannot stop myself from saying:

'Wait! You haven't stolen anything here, have you?'

I say this expressly to hurt him; I did not suspect him of having stolen anything, I merely wished to humiliate him.

He seemed not in the least embarrassed or angered by my words; he simply turned towards me and said, in surprise:

'Stolen?'

And with that he sat down in a chair, opened his coat and from his breast pocket took out a handful of papers, among which I saw a route-map and a small red wallet full of money, absolutely stuffed with notes, several hundred kroner. He held it out to me:

'And what would you have that I might find worth stealing?' he said, smiling.

He had trumped me again. He always trumped me, shamed me, condemned me to ignominy no matter what. He stood up and left and I did nothing, made no attempt to stop him leaving. I let him go. Only when I heard his footsteps on the staircase far below did I think to open the door and then bang it shut again so that it sounded through the whole house. That was all I did.

In his contempt for me he had simply left my 16 kroner behind. I found them on the chair he had been sitting on. And in my shame and anger I left them there for days before picking them up, hoping that he might come back and notice that I had neglected to reclaim them.

Later I heard that he had also visited my landlord and conducted himself in a bizarre fashion. My landlord, who was a police constable, would have nothing to do with him; in his opinion the man was insane. Among other things, the intruder had attempted to buy an antique Dutch coffee pot made of brass that was standing on the stove. He had practically refused to take no for an answer.

Such are the details of my several encounters with this most peculiar person. Recently I have learnt to think of him without rancour. He interests me greatly, and I look forward to meeting him again. I believe I understand now something of his nature and of the reasons for his absurd behaviour. Just a few months ago I met another person, a woman in her thirties, who told me something about herself that put me on the trail. She had once committed a crime which would have earned her several days on bread and water, and the incident continued to disturb her greatly. It was not conscience, nor contrition, but rather an inexplicable longing to be found out. For some time she had positively invited suspicion of herself, but to no avail. Her success in avoiding detection made her heedless and reckless; she wearied of not being unmasked even when she colluded in her own detection. She took steps to make her secret hard to keep. She exposed herself wilfully to arouse people's suspicions. But no matter what she did, no one ever suspected her, no one ever reported her.

The circumstances of her story made me think of my secretive friend, the man with the dark eyes. No doubt he hoped again and again that his behaviour would be enough to drive me to report him to the police. But in this he had failed.

A superior type of person, with a blemished and strangely twisted soul. A human being in psychic pain, suffering, perhaps, because a secret that might bring shame upon him was fated never to be revealed.

ROTHSCHILD'S FIDDLE

Anton Chekhov

Translated from the Russian by Marian Fell

Anton Pavlovich Chekhov (1860–1904) was a Russian playwright and short story writer, who is considered to be among the greatest writers of short fiction in history. His career as a playwright produced four classics and his best short stories are held in high esteem by writers and critics. Along with Henrik Ibsen and August Strindberg, Chekhov is often referred to as one of the three seminal figures in the birth of early modernism in the theatre. Chekhov practised as a medical doctor throughout most of his literary career: "Medicine is my lawful wife," he once said, "and literature is my mistress." A prolific epistoler, his last letter ever sent was to complain about the way German women dressed. Chekhov's body was transported to Moscow in a refrigerated railway car meant for oysters, a detail that offended Gorky.

It was a tiny town, worse than a village, inhabited chiefly by old people who so seldom died that it was really vexatious. Very few coffins were needed for the hospital and the jail; in a word, business was bad. If Yakov Ivanov had been a maker of coffins in the county town, he would probably have owned a house of his own by now, and would have been called Mr. Ivanov, but here in this little place he was simply called Yakov, and for some reason his nickname was Bronze. He lived as poorly as any common peasant in a little old hut of one room, in which he and Martha, and the stove, and a double bed, and the coffins, and his joiner's bench, and all the necessities of housekeeping were stowed away.

The coffins made by Yakov were serviceable and strong. For the peasants and townsfolk he made them to fit himself and never went wrong, for, although he was seventy years old, there was no man, not even in the prison, any taller or stouter than he was. For the gentry and for women he made them to measure, using an iron yardstick for the purpose. He was always very reluctant to take orders for children's coffins, and made them contemptuously without taking any measurements at all, always saying when he was paid for them:

"The fact is, I don't like to be bothered with trifles."

Beside what he received for his work as a joiner, he added a little to his income by playing the violin. There was a Jewish orchestra in the town that played for weddings, led by the tinsmith Moses Shakess, who took more than half of its earnings for himself. As Yakov played the fiddle extremely well, especially Russian songs, Shakess used sometimes to invite him to play in his orchestra for the sum of fifty kopeks a day, not including the presents he might receive from the guests. Whenever Bronze took his seat in the orchestra, the first thing that happened to him was that his face grew red, and the perspiration streamed from it, for the air was always hot, and reeking of garlic to the point of suffocation. Then his fiddle would begin to moan, and a double bass would croak hoarsely into his right ear, and a flute would weep into his left. This flute was played by a gaunt, red-bearded Jew with a network of red and blue veins on his face, who bore the name of a famous rich man, Rothschild. This confounded Jew always contrived to play even the merriest tunes sadly. For no obvious reason Yakov little by little began to conceive a feeling of hatred and contempt for all Jews, and especially for Rothschild. He quarrelled with him and abused him in ugly language, and once even tried to beat him, but Rothschild took offense at this, and cried with a fierce look:

"If I had not always respected you for your music, I should have thrown you out of the window long ago!"

Then he burst into tears. So after that Bronze was not often invited to play in the orchestra, and was only called upon in cases of dire necessity, when one of the Jews was missing.

Yakov was never in a good humor, because he always had to endure the most terrible losses. For instance, it was a sin to work on a Sunday or a holiday, and Monday was always a bad day, so in that way there were about two hundred days a year in which he was compelled to sit with his hands folded in his lap. That was a great loss to him. If any one in town had a wedding without music, or if Shakess did not ask him to play, there was another loss. The police inspector had lain ill with consumption for two years while Yakov impatiently waited for him to die, and then had gone to take a cure in the city and had died there, which of course had meant another loss of at least ten rubles, as the coffin would have been an expensive one lined with brocade.

The thought of his losses worried Yakov at night more than at any other time, so he used to lay his fiddle at his side on the bed, and when those worries came trooping into his brain he would touch the strings, and the fiddle would give out a sound in the darkness, and Yakov's heart would feel lighter.

Last year on the sixth of May, Martha suddenly fell ill. The old woman breathed with difficulty, staggered in her walk, and felt terribly thirsty. Nevertheless, she got up that morning, lit the stove, and even went for the water. When evening came she went to bed. Yakov played his fiddle all day. When it grew quite dark, because he had nothing better to do, he took the book in which he kept an account of his losses, and began adding up the total for the year. They amounted to more than a thousand rubles. He was so shaken by this discovery that he threw the counting board on the floor and trampled it under foot. Then he picked it up again and rattled it once more for a long time, heaving as he did so sighs both deep and long. His face grew purple, and perspiration dripped from his brow. He was thinking that if those thousand rubles he had lost had been in the bank then, he would have had at least forty rubles interest by the end of the year. So those forty rubles were still another loss! In a word, wherever he turned he found losses and nothing but losses.

"Yakov!" cried Martha unexpectedly, "I am dying!"

He looked round at his wife. Her face was flushed with fever and looked unusually joyful and bright. Bronze was troubled, for he had been accustomed to seeing her pale and timid and unhappy. It seemed to him that she was actually dead, and glad to have left this hut, and the coffins, and Yakov at last. She was staring at the ceiling, with her lips moving as if she saw her deliverer Death approaching and were whispering with him.

The dawn was just breaking and the eastern sky was glowing with a faint radiance. As he stared at the old woman it somehow seemed to Yakov that he had never once spoken a tender word to her or pitied her; that he had never thought of buying her a kerchief or of bringing her back some sweets from a wedding. On the contrary, he had shouted at her and abused her for his losses, and had shaken his fist at her. It was true he had never beaten her, but he had frightened her no less, and she had been paralyzed with fear every time he had scolded her. Yes, and he had not allowed her to drink tea because his losses were heavy enough as it was, so she had had to be content with hot water. Now he understood why her face looked so strangely happy, and horror overwhelmed him.

As soon as it was light he borrowed a horse from a neighbor and took Martha to the hospital. As there were not many patients, he had not to wait very long—only about three hours. To his great satisfaction it was not the doctor who was receiving the sick that day, but his assistant, Maxim Nikolaich, an old man of whom it was said that although he quarreled and drank, he knew more than the doctor did.

"Good morning, Your Honor," said Yakov leading his old woman into the office. "Excuse us for intruding upon you with our trifling affairs. As you see, this subject has fallen ill. My life's friend, if you will allow me to use the expression——"

Knitting his gray eyebrows and stroking his whiskers, the doctor's assistant fixed his eyes on the old woman. She was sitting all in a heap on a low stool, and with her thin, long-nosed face and her open mouth, she looked like a thirsty bird.

"Well, well-yes—" said the doctor slowly, heaving a sigh. "This is a case of influenza and possibly fever; there is typhoid in town. What's to be done? The old woman has lived her span of years, thank God. How old is she?"

"She lacks one year of being seventy, Your Honor."

"Well, well, she has lived long. There must come an end to everything."

"You are certainly right, Your Honor," said Yakov, smiling out of politeness. "And we thank you sincerely for your kindness, but allow me to suggest to you that even an insect dislikes to die!"

"Never mind if it does!" answered the doctor, as if the life or death of the old woman lay in his hands. "I'll tell you what you must do, my good man. Put a cold bandage around her head, and give her two of these powders a day. Now then, good-bye! *Bonjour!*"

Yakov saw by the expression on the doctor's face that it was too late now for powders. He realized clearly that Martha must die very soon, if not today, then tomorrow. He touched the doctor's elbow gently, blinked, and whispered:

"She ought to be cupped, doctor!"

"I haven't time, I haven't time, my good man. Take your old woman and go, in God's name. Good-bye."

"Please, please, cup her, doctor!" begged Yakov. "You know yourself that if she had a pain in her stomach, powders and drops would do her good, but she has a cold! The first thing to do when one catches cold is to let some blood, doctor!"

But the doctor had already sent for the next patient, and a woman leading a little boy came into the room.

"Go along, go along!" he cried to Yakov, frowning. "It's no use making a fuss!"

"Then at least put some leeches on her! Let me pray to God for you for the rest of my life!"

The doctor's temper flared up and he shouted:

"Don't say another word to me, blockhead!"

Yakov lost his temper, too, and flushed hotly, but he said nothing and, silently taking Martha's arm, led her out of the office. Only when they were once more seated in their wagon did he look fiercely and mockingly at the hospital and say:

"They're a pretty lot in there, they are! That doctor would have cupped a rich man, but he even begrudged a poor one a leech. The pig!"

When they returned to the hut, Martha stood for nearly ten minutes supporting herself by the stove. She felt that if she lay down Yakov would begin to talk to her about his losses, and would scold her for lying down and not wanting to work. Yakov contemplated her sadly, thinking that tomorrow was St. John the Baptist's day, and the day after tomorrow was St. Nicholas the Wonder-worker's day, and that the following day would be Sunday, and the day after that would be Monday, a bad day for work. So he would not be able to work for four days, and as Martha would probably die on one of these days, the coffin would have to be made at once. He took his iron yardstick in hand, went up to the old woman, and measured her. Then she lay down, and he crossed himself and went to work on the coffin.

When the task was completed Bronze put on his spectacles and wrote in his book:

"For one coffin for Martha Ivanov—2 rubles, 40 kopeks."

He sighed. All day the old woman lay silent with closed eyes, but toward evening, when the daylight began to fade, she suddenly called the old man to her side.

"Do you remember, Yakov?" she asked. "Do you remember how fifty years ago God gave us a little baby with curly golden hair? Do you remember how you and I used to sit on the bank of the river and sing songs under the willow tree?" Then with a bitter smile she added: "The baby died."

Yakov racked his brains, but for the life of him he could not recall the child or the willow tree.

"You are dreaming," he said.

The priest came and administered the Sacrament and Extreme Unction. Then Martha began muttering unintelligibly, and toward morning she died.

The neighboring old women washed her and dressed her, and laid her in her coffin. To avoid paying the deacon, Yakov read the psalms over her himself, and her grave cost him nothing as the watchman of the cemetery was his cousin. Four peasants carried the coffin to the grave, not for money but for love. The old women, the beggars, and two village idiots followed the body, and the people whom they passed on the way crossed themselves devoutly. Yakov was very glad that everything had passed off so nicely and decently and cheaply, without giving offense to any one. As he said farewell to Martha for the last time he touched the coffin with his hand and thought:

"That's a fine job!"

But walking homeward from the cemetery he was seized with great distress. He felt ill, his breath was burning hot, his legs grew weak, and he longed for a drink. Beside this, a thousand thoughts came crowding into his head. He remembered again that he had never once pitied Martha or said a tender word to her. The fifty years of their life together lay stretched far, far behind him, and somehow, during all that time, he had never once thought about her at all or noticed her more than if she had been a dog or a cat. And yet she had lit the stove every day, and had cooked and baked and fetched water and chopped wood, and when he had come home drunk from a wedding she had hung his fiddle reverently on a nail each time, and had silently put him to bed with a timid, anxious look on her face.

But here came Rothschild toward him, bowing and scraping and smiling.

"I have been looking for you, uncle!" he said. "Moses Shakess presents his compliments and wants you to go to him at once."

Yakov did not feel in a mood to do anything. He wanted to cry.

"Leave me alone!" he exclaimed, and walked on.

"Oh, how can you say that?" cried Rothschild, running beside him in alarm. "Moses will be very angry. He wants you to come at once!"

Yakov was disgusted by the panting of the Jew, by his blinking eyes, and by the quantities of reddish freckles on his face. He looked with aversion at his long green coat and at the whole of his frail, delicate figure.

"What do you mean by pestering me, garlic?" he shouted. "Get away!"

The Jew grew angry and shouted back:

"Don't yell at me like that or I'll send you flying over that fence!"

"Get out of my sight!" bellowed Yakov, shaking his fist at him. "There's no living in the same town with mangy curs like you!"

Rothschild was petrified with terror. He sank to the ground and waved his hands over his head as if to protect himself from falling blows; then he jumped up and ran away as fast as his legs could carry him. As he ran he leaped and waved his arms, and his long, gaunt back could be seen quivering. The little boys were delighted at what had happened, and ran after him screaming: "Jew, Jew!" The dogs also joined in the chase barking. Somebody laughed and then whistled, at which the dogs barked louder and more vigorously than ever.

Then one of them must have bitten Rothschild, for a piteous, despairing scream rent the air.

Yakov walked across the common to the edge of the town without knowing where he was going, and the little boys shouted after him. "There goes old man Bronze! There goes old man Bronze!" He found himself by the river where the snipe were darting about with shrill cries, and the ducks were quacking and swimming to and fro. The sun was shining fiercely and the water was sparkling so brightly that it was painful to look at. Yakov struck into a path that led along the riverbank. He came to a stout, red-checked woman just leaving a bath-house. "Aha, you otter, you!" he thought. Not far from the bath-house some little boys were fishing for crabs with pieces of meat. When they saw Yakov they shouted mischievously: "Old man Bronze! Old man Bronze!" But there before him stood an ancient, spreading willow tree with a massive trunk, and a crow's nest among its branches. Suddenly there flashed across Yakov's memory with all the vividness of life a little child with golden curls, and the willow of which Martha had spoken. Yes, this was the same tree, so green and peaceful and sad. How old it had grown, poor thing!

He sat down at its foot and thought of the past. On the opposite shore, where that meadow now was, there had stood in those days a wood of tall birch-trees, and that bare hill on the horizon yonder had been covered with the blue bloom of an ancient pine forest. And sailboats had plied the river then, but now all lay smooth and still, and only one little birch-tree was left on the opposite bank, a graceful young thing, like a girl, while on the river there swam only ducks and geese. It was hard to believe that boats had once sailed there. It even seemed to him that there were fewer geese now than there had been. Yakov shut his eyes, and one by one white geese came flying toward him, an endless flock.

He was puzzled to know why he had never once been down to the river during the last forty or fifty years of his life, or, if he had been there, why he had never paid any attention to it. The stream was fine and large; he might have fished in it and sold the fish to the merchants and the government officials and the restaurant-keeper at the station, and put the money in the bank. He might have rowed in a boat from farm to farm and played on his fiddle. People of every rank would have paid him money to hear him. He might have tried to run a boat on the river, that would have been better than making coffins. Finally, he might have raised geese, and killed them, and sent them to Moscow in the winter. Why, the down alone would have brought him ten rubles a year! But he had missed all these chances and had done nothing. What losses were here! Ah, what terrible losses! And, oh, if he had only done all these things at the same time! If he had only fished, and played the fiddle, and sailed a boat, and raised geese, what capital he would have had by now! But he had not even dreamed of doing all this; his life had gone by without profit or pleasure. It had been lost for nothing, not even a trifle. Nothing was left ahead; behind lay only losses, and such terrible losses that he shuddered to think of them. But why shouldn't men live so as to avoid all this waste and these losses? Why, oh why, should those birch and pine forests have been felled? Why should those meadows be lying so deserted? Why did people always do exactly what they ought not to do? Why had Yakov scolded and growled and clenched his fists and hurt his wife's feelings all his life? Why, oh why, had he frightened and insulted that Jew just now? Why did people in general always interfere with one another? What losses resulted from this! What terrible losses! If it were not for envy and anger they would get great profit from one another.

All that evening and night Yakov dreamed of the child, of the willow tree, of the fish and the geese, of Martha with her profile like a thirsty bird, and of Rothschild's pale, piteous mien. Queer faces seemed to be moving toward him from all sides, muttering to him about his losses. He tossed from side to side, and got up five times during the night to play his fiddle.

He rose with difficulty next morning, and walked to the hospital. The same doctor's assistant ordered him to put cold bandages on his head, and gave him little powders to take; by his expression and the tone of his voice Yakov knew that the state of affairs was bad, and that no powders could save him now. As he walked home he reflected that one good thing would result from his death: he would no longer have to eat and drink and pay taxes, neither would he offend people anymore, and, as a man lies in his grave for hundreds of thousands of years, the sum of his profits would be immense. So, life to a man was a loss—death, a gain. Of course this reasoning was correct, but it was also distressingly sad. Why should the world be so strangely arranged that a man's life, which was only given to him once, must pass without profit?

He was not sorry then that he was going to die, but when he reached home, and saw his fiddle, his heart ached, and he regretted it deeply. He would not be able to take his fiddle with him into the grave, and now it would be left an orphan, and its fate would be that of the birch grove and the pine forest. Everything in the world had been lost, and would always be lost for ever. Yakov went out and sat on the threshold of his hut, clasping his fiddle to his breast. And as he thought of his life so full of waste and losses he began playing without knowing how piteous and touching his music was, and the tears streamed down his cheeks. And the more he thought the more sorrowfully sang his violin.

The latch clicked and Rothschild came in through the garden gate, and walked boldly halfway across the garden. Then he suddenly stopped, crouched down, and, probably from fear, began making signs with his hands as if he were trying to show on his fingers what time it was.

"Come on, don't be afraid!" said Yakov gently, beckoning him to advance. "Come on!"

With many mistrustful and fearful glances Rothschild went slowly up to Yakov, and stopped about two yards away.

"Please don't beat me!" he said with a ducking bow. "Moses Shakess has sent me to you again. 'Don't be afraid,' he said, 'go to Yakov,' says he, 'and say that we can't possibly manage without him.' There is a wedding next Thursday. Ye-es sir. Mr. Shapovalov is marrying his daughter to a very fine man. It will be an expensive wedding, ai, ai!" added the Jew with a wink.

"I can't go" said Yakov breathing hard. "I'm ill, brother."

And he began to play again, and the tears gushed out of his eyes over his fiddle. Rothschild listened intently with his head turned away and his arms folded on his breast. The startled, irresolute look on his face gradually gave way to one of suffering and grief. He cast up his eyes as if in an ecstasy of agony and murmured: "Okh-okh!" And the tears began to trickle slowly down his cheeks, and to drip over his green coat.

All day Yakov lay and suffered. When the priest came in the evening to administer the Sacrament he asked him if he could not think of any particular sin.

Struggling with his fading memories, Yakov recalled once more Martha's sad face, and the despairing cry of the Jew when the dog had bitten him. He murmured almost inaudibly:

"Give my fiddle to Rothschild."

"It shall be done," answered the priest.

So it happened that everyone in the little town began asking:

"Where did Rothschild get that good fiddle? Did he buy it or steal it or get it out of a pawnshop?"

Rothschild has long since abandoned his flute, and now only plays on the violin. The same mournful notes flow from under his bow that used to come from his flute, and when he tries to repeat what Yakov played as he sat on the threshold of his hut, the result is an air so plaintive and sad that everyone who hears him weeps, and he himself at last raises his eyes and murmurs: "Okh-okh!" And this new song has so delighted the town that the merchants and government officials vie with each other in getting Rothschild to come to their houses, and sometimes make him play it ten times in succession.

KABULIWALA

(The Fruit-seller From Kabul)

Rabindranath Tagore

Translated from the Bengali by C. F. Andrews, with the help of the author

Rabindranath Tagore (1861–1941). One of the towering figures in Bengali literature, music and art in the late nineteenth and early twentieth centuries, Tagore wrote both in Bengali and in English. His poetry and prose had a major influence in Europe – though his first trip to London was marred when he mislaid a manuscript of translated poems on the Underground (they were later found at Lost Property). In Europe, he encountered W. B. Yeats, who became a powerful champion of his work. A year later, in 1913, he became the first non-European to win the Nobel Prize for Literature. Tagore's Nobel Prize was stolen from a vault in 2004; the Swedish Academy replaced it with two replicas, one gold, the other bronze.

My five-year-old daughter Mini cannot live without chattering. I really believe that in all her life she has not wasted a minute in silence. Her mother is often vexed at this, and would stop her prattle, but I would not. To see Mini quiet is unnatural, and I cannot bear it long. And so my own talk with her is always lively.

One morning, for instance, when I was in the midst of the seventeenth chapter of my new novel, my little Mini stole into the room, and putting her hand into mine, said: "Father! Ramdayal the door-keeper calls a crow a *krow*! He doesn't know anything, does he?"

Before I could explain to her the differences of language in this world, she was embarked on the full tide of another subject. "What do you think, Father? Bhola says there is an elephant in the clouds, blowing water out of his trunk, and that is why it rains!"

And then, darting off anew, while I sat still making ready some reply to this last saying, "Father! what relation is Mother to you?"

"My dear little sister in the law!" I murmured involuntarily to myself, but with a grave face contrived to answer: "Go and play with Bhola, Mini! I am busy!"

The window of my room overlooks the road. The child had seated herself at my feet near my table, and was playing softly, drumming on her knees. I was hard at work on my seventeenth chapter, where Protrap Singh, the hero, had just caught Kanchanlata, the heroine, in his arms, and was about to escape with her by the third story window of the castle, when all of a sudden Mini left her play, and ran to the window, crying, "A Cabuliwallah! a Cabuliwallah!" Sure enough in the street below was a Cabuliwallah, passing slowly along. He wore the loose soiled clothing of his people, with a tall turban; there was a bag on his back, and he carried boxes of grapes in his hand.

I cannot tell what were my daughter's feelings at the sight of this man, but she began to call him loudly. "Ah!" I thought, "he will come in, and my seventeenth chapter will never be finished!" At which exact moment the Cabuliwallah turned, and looked up at the child. When she saw this, overcome by terror, she fled to her mother's protection, and disappeared. She had a blind belief that inside the bag, which the big man carried, there were perhaps two or three other children like herself. The pedlar meanwhile entered my doorway, and greeted me with a smiling face.

So precarious was the position of my hero and my heroine, that my first impulse was to stop and buy something, since the man had been called. I made some small purchases, and a conversation began about Abdurrahman, the Russians, the English, and the Frontier Policy.

As he was about to leave, he asked: "And where is the little girl, sir?"

And I, thinking that Mini must get rid of her false fear, had her brought out.

She stood by my chair, and looked at the Cabuliwallah and his bag. He offered her nuts and raisins, but she would not be tempted, and only clung the closer to me, with all her doubts increased.

This was their first meeting.

One morning, however, not many days later, as I was leaving the house, I was startled to find Mini, seated on a bench near the door, laughing and talking, with the great Cabuliwallah at her feet. In all her life, it appeared, my small daughter had never found so patient a listener, save her father. And already the corner of her little sari was stuffed with almonds and raisins, the gift of her visitor. "Why did you give her those?" I said, and taking out an eight-anna bit, I handed it to him. The man accepted the money without demur, and slipped it into his pocket.

Alas, on my return an hour later, I found the unfortunate coin had made twice its own worth of trouble! For the Cabuliwallah had given it to Mini, and her mother catching sight of the bright round object, had pounced on the child with: "Where did you get that eight-anna bit?"

"The Cabuliwallah gave it me," said Mini cheerfully.

"The Cabuliwallah gave it you!" cried her mother, much shocked. "Oh, Mini! how could you take it from him?"

I, entering at the moment, saved her from impending disaster, and proceeded to make my own inquiries.

It was not the first or second time, I found, that the two had met. The Cabuliwallah had overcome the child's first terror by a judicious bribery of nuts and almonds, and the two were now great friends.

They had many quaint jokes, which afforded them much amusement. Seated in front of him, looking down on his gigantic frame in all her tiny dignity, Mini would ripple her face with laughter, and begin: "O Cabuliwallah, Cabuliwallah, what have you got in your bag?"

And he would reply, in the nasal accents of the mountaineer: "An elephant!" Not much cause for merriment, perhaps; but how they both enjoyed the witticism! And for me, this child's talk with a grown-up man had always in it something strangely fascinating.

Then the Cabuliwallah, not to be behindhand, would take his turn: "Well, little one, and when are you going to the father-in-law's house?"

Now most small Bengali maidens have heard long ago about the father-in-law's house; but we, being a little new-fangled, had kept these things from our child, and Mini at this question must have been a trifle bewildered. But she would not show it, and with ready tact replied: "Are you going there?"

Amongst men of the Cabuliwallah's class, however, it is well known that the words father-in-law's house have a double meaning. It is a euphemism for jail, the place where we are well cared for, at no expense to ourselves. In this sense would the sturdy pedlar take my daughter's question. "Ah," he would say, shaking his fist at an invisible policeman, "I will thrash my father-in-law!" Hearing this, and picturing the poor discomfited relative, Mini would go off into peals of laughter, in which her formidable friend would join.

These were autumn mornings, the very time of year when kings of old went forth to conquest; and I, never stirring from my little corner in Calcutta, would let my mind wander over the whole world. At the very name of another country, my heart would go out to it, and at the sight of a foreigner in the streets, I would fall to weaving a network of dreams,—the mountains, the glens, and the forests of his distant home, with his cottage in its setting, and the free and independent life of far-away wilds. Perhaps the scenes of travel conjure themselves up before me, and pass and repass in my imagination all the more vividly, because I lead such a vegetable existence, that a call to travel would fall upon me like a thunderbolt. In the presence of this Cabuliwallah, I was immediately transported to the foot of arid mountain peaks, with narrow little defiles twisting in and out amongst their towering heights. I could see the string of camels bearing the merchandise, and the company of turbaned merchants, carrying some of their queer old firearms, and some of their spears, journeying downward towards the plains. I could see—but at some such point Mini's mother would intervene, imploring me to "beware of that man."

Mini's mother is unfortunately a very timid lady. Whenever she hears a noise in the street, or sees people coming towards the house, she always jumps to the conclusion that they are either thieves, or drunkards, or snakes, or tigers, or malaria or cockroaches, or caterpillars, or an English sailor. Even after all these years of experience, she is not able to overcome her terror. So she was full of doubts about the Cabuliwallah, and used to beg me to keep a watchful eye on him.

I tried to laugh her fear gently away, but then she would turn round on me seriously, and ask me solemn questions.

Were children never kidnapped?

Was it, then, not true that there was slavery in Cabul?

Was it so very absurd that this big man should be able to carry off a tiny child?

I urged that, though not impossible, it was highly improbable. But this was not enough, and her dread persisted. As it was indefinite, however, it did not seem right to forbid the man the house, and the intimacy went on unchecked.

Once a year in the middle of January Rahmun, the Cabuliwallah, was in the habit of returning to his country, and as the time approached he would be very busy, going from house to house collecting his debts. This year, however, he could always find time to come and see Mini. It would have seemed to an outsider that there was some conspiracy between the two, for when he could not come in the morning, he would appear in the evening.

Even to me it was a little startling now and then, in the corner of a dark room, suddenly to surprise this tall, loose-garmented, much bebagged man; but when Mini would run in smiling, with her, "O! Cabuliwallah! Cabuliwallah!" and the two friends, so far apart in age, would subside into their old laughter and their old jokes, I felt reassured.

One morning, a few days before he had made up his mind to go, I was correcting my proof sheets in my study. It was chilly weather. Through the window the rays of the sun touched my feet, and the slight warmth was very welcome. It was almost eight o'clock, and the early pedestrians were returning home, with their heads covered. All at once, I heard an uproar in the street, and, looking out, saw Rahmun being led away bound between two policemen, and behind them a crowd of curious boys. There were blood-stains on the clothes of the Cabuli-wallah, and one of the policemen carried a knife. Hurrying out, I stopped them, and enquired what it all meant. Partly from one, partly from another, I gathered that a certain neighbour had owed the pedlar something for a Rampuri shawl, but had falsely denied having bought it, and that in the course of the quarrel, Rahmun had struck him. Now in the heat of his excitement, the prisoner began calling his enemy all sorts of names, when suddenly in a verandah of my house appeared my little Mini, with her usual exclamation: "O Cabuliwallah! Cabuli-wallah!" Rahmun's face lighted up as he turned to her. He had no bag under his arm today, so she could not discuss the elephant with him. She at once therefore proceeded to the next question: "Are you going to the father-in-law's house?" Rahmun laughed and said: "Just where I am going, little one!" Then seeing that the reply did not amuse the child, he held up his fettered hands. "Ali," he said, "I would have thrashed that old father-in-law, but my hands are bound!"

On a charge of murderous assault, Rahmun was sentenced to some years' imprisonment.

Time passed away, and he was not remembered. The accustomed work in the accustomed place was ours, and the thought of the once-free mountaineer spending his years in prison seldom or never occurred to us. Even my light-hearted Mini, I am ashamed to say, forgot her old friend. New companions filled her life. As she grew older, she spent more of her time with girls. So much time indeed did she spend with them that she came no more, as she used to do, to her father's room. I was scarcely on speaking terms with her.

Years had passed away. It was once more autumn and we had made arrange-ments for our Mini's marriage. It was to take place during the Puja Holidays. With Durga returning to Kailas, the light of our home also was to depart to her husband's house, and leave her father's in the shadow.

The morning was bright. After the rains, there was a sense of ablution in the air, and the sun-rays looked like pure gold. So bright were they that they gave a beautiful radiance even to the sordid brick walls of our Calcutta lanes. Since early dawn to-day the wedding-pipes had been sounding, and at each beat my own heart throbbed. The wail of the tune, Bhairavi, seemed to intensify my pain at the approaching separation. My Mini was to be married to-night.

From early morning, noise and bustle had pervaded the house. In the court-yard the canopy had to be slung on its bamboo poles; the chandeliers with their tinkling sound must be hung in each room and verandah. There was no end of hurry and excitement. I was sitting in my study, looking through the accounts, when some one entered, saluting respectfully, and stood before me. It was Rahmun the Cabuliwallah. At first I did not recognise him. He had no bag, nor the long hair, nor the same vigour that he used to have. But he smiled, and I knew him again.

"When did you come, Rahmun?" I asked him.

"Last evening," he said, "I was released from jail."

The words struck harsh upon my ears. I had never before talked with one who had wounded his fellow, and my heart shrank within itself, when I realised this, for I felt that the day would have been better-omened had he not turned up.

"There are ceremonies going on," I said, "and I am busy. Could you perhaps come another day?"

At once he turned to go; but as he reached the door he hesitated, and said: "May I not see the little one, sir, for a moment?" It was his belief that Mini was still the same. He had pictured her running to him as she used, calling "O Cabuliwallah! Cabuliwallah!" He had imagined too that they would laugh and talk together, just as of old. In fact, in memory of former days he had brought, carefully wrapped up in paper, a few almonds and raisins and grapes, obtained somehow from a countryman, for his own little fund was dispersed.

I said again: "There is a ceremony in the house, and you will not be able to see any one to-day."

The man's face fell. He looked wistfully at me for a moment, said "Good morning," and went out. I felt a little sorry, and would have called him back, but I found he was returning of his own accord. He came close up to me holding out his offerings and said: "I brought these few things, sir, for the little one. Will you give them to her?"

I took them and was going to pay him, but he caught my hand and said: "You are very kind, sir! Keep me in your recollection. Do not offer me money!—You have a little girl, I too have one like her in my own home. I think of her, and bring fruits to your child, not to make a profit for myself."

Saying this, he put his hand inside his big loose robe, and brought out a small and dirty piece of paper. With great care he unfolded this, and smoothed it out with both hands on my table. It bore the impression of a little hand. Not a photo-graph. Not a drawing. The impression of an ink-smeared hand laid flat on the paper. This touch of his own little daughter had been always on his heart, as he had come year after year to Calcutta, to sell his wares in the streets.

Tears came to my eyes. I forgot that he was a poor Cabuli fruit-seller, while I was—but no, what was I more than he? He also was a father. That impression of the hand of his little Parbati in her distant mountain home reminded me of my own little Mini.

I sent for Mini immediately from the inner apartment. Many difficulties were raised, but I would not listen. Clad in the red silk of her wedding-day, with the sandal paste on her forehead, and adorned as a young bride, Mini came, and stood bashfully before me.

The Cabuliwallah looked a little staggered at the apparition. He could not revive their old friendship. At last he smiled and said: "Little one, are you going to your father-in-law's house?"

But Mini now understood the meaning of the word "father-in-law," and she could not reply to him as of old. She flushed up at the question, and stood before him with her bride-like face turned down.

I remembered the day when the Cabuliwallah and my Mini had first met, and I felt sad. When she had gone, Rahmun heaved a deep sigh, and sat down on the floor. The idea had suddenly come to him that his daughter too must have grown in this long time, and that he would have to make friends with her anew. Assuredly he would not find her, as he used to know her. And besides, what might not have happened to her in these eight years?

The marriage-pipes sounded, and the mild autumn sun streamed round us. But Rahmun sat in the little Calcutta lane, and saw before him the barren mountains of Afghanistan.

I took out a bank-note, and gave it to him, saying: "Go back to your own daughter, Rahmun, in your own country, and may the happiness of your meeting bring good fortune to my child!"

Having made this present, I had to curtail some of the festivities. I could not have the electric lights I had intended, nor the military band, and the ladies of the house were despondent at it. But to me the wedding feast was all the brighter for the thought that in a distant land a long-lost father met again with his only child.

IN THE LIGHT OF DAY

Constantine P. Cavafy

Translated from the Greek by Victoria Hislop

Constantine P. Cavafy (1863–1933). The foremost Egyptian Greek poet of his generation. Born in Alexandria, Egypt, to Greek parents. After the death of his father, upheaval in Egypt saw his spending much of his childhood in Liverpool and a later period Constantinople. Cavafy permanently returned to Alexandria in 1885. Though one of the major literary figures writing in Greek, Cavafy completed only 150 poems (many others exist as fragments), and refused to have his work published in his lifetime except as broadsheets only for his close friends. He earned his living as a journalist before taking a post at the Egyptian Ministry of Public Works where he worked for thirty years during the British protectorate. The first publication of his work in book form was "Ποιήματα" ("Poems"), published posthumously in Alexandria, 1935.

One evening, after dinner, I was sitting at the Agios Stefanos Casino in Ramleh. My friend Alexander A, who lived nearby, had invited me and another young man from our circle to dine with him. Since there were no musicians that evening, there were few patrons, and my two friends and I had the place virtually to ourselves.

We talked about various topics and, since none of us was particularly rich, conversation naturally turned to money, to the independence and the pleasures that it brings.

One of my friends said that he would like to have three million francs and set about describing what he would do, and, above all, what he would no longer do if he had such a vast sum.

I, being more modest, said I could manage on an income of twenty thousand a year.

"Had I wanted," Alexander A said, "I could have had heaven knows how many millions. But I did not have the courage."

These words seemed strange. We were intimately familiar with the life of our friend Alexander and did not remember him ever being presented with the opportunity to become a millionaire many times over. We assumed he was not talking seriously and that some kind of joke would follow but his face was very serious. We asked him to explain his enigmatic remark.

He hesitated a moment, but then said:

"Were I in different company, amongst those who think themselves 'intellectuals', I would not explain myself for fear of being mocked. But we three are a little above that. Even if we are simpler than them in some ways, it doesn't make us ignorant. In a spiritual sense, perhaps we are more developed than they are."

These words came as no surprise to us. We each held the others in the highest regard.

"Yes," repeated Alexander, "Had I dared, I would be a millionaire many times over, but I was afraid."

"The tale I am about to relate happened some ten years ago. Then, as now, I did not have much money. In fact, I had no money at all. But one way or another I survived and lived tolerably well. I was staying on the Serif Pasa Road in a house that belonged to an Italian widow. I had three well-furnished rooms and a personal servant, in addition to which the landlady's maid was at my disposal.

"One evening I had gone to Rossini's and, having listened to enough nonsense, decided to go home and sleep since I had to rise early the following day, having been invited on an outing to Aboukir.

"I went into my room and, as was my wont, began to pace up and down, brooding over the events of the day. But since nothing interesting had happened, I went to bed.

"I must have been in a dreamless sleep for an hour and a half or two hours. I remember that around an hour after midnight, I was woken by a noise in the road and I did not recall having dreamt.

"I must have fallen asleep again at about one-thirty, at which point it seemed to me that a man had entered my room. He was of average height, some forty years old and was dressed in rather frayed black clothes and a straw hat. On his right hand, there was a ring set with a huge emerald which seemed to me out of keeping with the rest of his attire. He had a black moustache with lots of white hairs and there was something strange in his eyes – a look at once sardonic and melancholy. On the whole, however, he looked unremarkable. The sort of man one might encounter anywhere.

"I asked him what he wanted of me. He did not answer immediately but gazed at me for a few moments as though suspicious or ensuring he had not made a mistake. Then he spoke. His tone was servile.

"You are poor. I know this. I have come to tell you a way to become rich.

"Near where Pompey's pillar stands, I know a place where a vast treasure is hidden. Personally, I want no part of it, but for a small metal box you will find at the bottom. This I will take, all the rest shall be yours.

"And what is this great treasure?" I inquired.

"In part, gold coins," he said, "but in the main, precious stones. There are ten or twelve gold chests full of diamonds and pearls. And I think . . . ," (he paused, as though straining to remember) ". . . sapphires."

I wondered at that moment why he did not simply take what he wanted. Why he needed me? He did not wait for me to ask.

"'I know what you are thinking,' he said. 'Why, you wonder, do I not take what I want myself. There is a reason that prevents me, but one I cannot tell you. There are some things that even I cannot do.'

"As he said 'even I', there came a gleam in his eye that, for a second, transformed him, shrouding him in great nobility. An instant later, however, his humble demeanour returned.

"'So you would do me a great favour if you came with me. I truly need someone and I chose you because I want the best for you. Come and meet me tomorrow. I shall be waiting for you from midday until four on the Petite Place, at the *kafenion* near the blacksmiths' shops.'

"With these words, he vanished.

"The following morning, the dream did not come to my mind when I first woke. But after I had washed and sat down to breakfast, it came back to me and seemed quite strange.

"If only it had been true," I said to myself, then put it from my mind.

"I went on the country outing and enjoyed myself hugely. We were quite a big group, around thirty men and women, and we had an unusually good time. I will not go into detail since it is not really part of this story."

Here, my friend Dimitris remarked:

"You scarcely need to, since I, at least, know them. If I am not mistaken, I was on that excursion."

"Maybe. I don't recall you being there."

"Wasn't this the outing that Markos G. came on before he permanently relocated to England . . . ?"

"Yes, that's right. Then you will remember what a wonderful time we had. So, to get back to this story, I returned from the outing quite tired and rather late. I scarcely had time to change clothes and eat before visiting a friend's family to play cards, where I stayed until two thirty in the morning.

"I won one hundred and fifty francs, returned home extremely pleased with myself, lay down with a light heart and immediately fell asleep, exhausted from my day.

"As soon as sleep overcame me, a strange thing happened. I saw a light in the room and wondered why I had not put it out before going to bed. Then I saw, emerging from the back of the bedroom near the door (it was quite a large room), a man I immediately recognised. He was wearing the same black clothes and the same battered straw hat. He looked displeased and said: 'I waited for you in the *kafenion* from midday until four this afternoon. Why did you not come? I offer you a chance to make your fortune and you do not seize it. I will wait for you again today from midday until four. And you will come, without fail.'"

"Then, as before, he disappeared.

"I woke up in terror. The room was dark and I lit the lamp. The dream had been so real, so vivid that I was both amazed and shocked. I could not resist checking to see whether the door was locked.

"It was locked, as always. I looked at the clock: it was half past three. I had gone to bed at three.

"I will not hide from you, nor am I ashamed to admit, that I was very scared. I was afraid to close my eyes in case I drifted off to sleep again and saw my phantom visitor. I sat in a chair, my nerves on edge.

"At about five o'clock, day broke. I threw open a window and watched as the street slowly came to life. Some doors were open and a few very early milkmen and the first bakers' carts were passing. The light somehow calmed me down and I lay down again and slept until nine.

"When I woke, the memory of the nocturnal horror came to me, but began to lose much of its power. I wondered why I had got myself into such a state. Everyone sees nightmares and I had had many in my life. In any case, this was hardly a nightmare, but rather a dream that I had had before.

"But had I dreamed the same dream twice? Perhaps I had merely dreamed that I had seen that man before. I examined my memory thoroughly and dismissed the idea. I had definitely had the dream two nights earlier. So why then was it strange? The first dream had seemed very vivid and left such a profound impression that I dreamed it again. Here, though, my logic faltered a little, because I did not recall the first dream making an impression. In the course of the following day, I had not thought of it even once. During the excursion and at the party that evening, almost everything else went through my mind, except the dream. So what did that mean?

"Surely it is commonplace that we dream about people whom we have not seen for many years and about whom we have not even thought of for many years? It seems that the memory of them lingers somewhere in the consciousness and they suddenly appear in a dream. So what's so strange about dreaming something twice in the space of only twenty-four hours, even though I hadn't thought of it at all during the entire day?

"Then I wondered whether perhaps I had read somewhere about a hidden treasure and this had worked on my memory. But, though I racked my brain, I didn't think this had happened.

"Finally, tired of thinking about it, I began to dress. I had to attend a wedding and the urgent need to decide what I would wear meant that I almost entirely forgot about the dream.

"I then sat down to breakfast and to pass the time, read a magazine published in Germany. *The Hesperides*, I think it was called.

"I went to the wedding where all of the high society of the city were gathered. At that time I had a large number of acquaintances and so had to repeat countless times that the bride was very beautiful (if a little pale) and that the groom WAS an excellent young man, not to say as rich and blah, blah, blah"

"The wedding finished around eleven thirty and afterwards I went to Voulklis Station to see a big house that had been recommended to me, one I was intending to rent on behalf of a German family from Cairo. They planned to spend the summer in Alexandria. The house was very light and airy and well laid out but not as large as I had been told. Nonetheless, I promised the owner I would recommend the house as suitable. The owner thanked me profusely and, tugging at my heartstrings, told me all her past problems, when and where her late husband had died, how he had travelled to Europe, how she was not the sort of woman to rent out her house, how her father was the doctor to a Pasha (I cannot recall which one). I brought an end to this obligation and returned to the centre of town.

"I arrived home at about one in the afternoon, ate with great appetite and, having sated my hunger and drunk my coffee, I left to visit a friend who was living in a hotel near the Paradiso Kafenion, in order to organise something for the afternoon. It was August, and the sun was sweltering. I was walking slowly down Serif Pasha Road so as not to break out in a sweat and the road, as always at that hour, was deserted. The only person I met was a lawyer with whom I had worked on the documents of sale for a small place in Moharam Bek. It was the last piece of a fairly large plot of land that I had been selling off piecemeal to cover some of my expenses. The lawyer was an honourable man, which was why I had chosen him, but he was garrulous. I would rather he had cheated me of a piece of my land than made my head dizzy with his nonsense. The smallest thing would set him off on a verbal torrent. He rambled on about commercial law, Roman law, brought up Codex Justinianus, previous lawsuits on which he had worked in Smyrna, he sang his own praises, threw in a thousand irrelevancies, and, gripping my lapels (something I hate). I had to put up with his idiot jabbering, because every now and then, when he interrupted his flow, I attempted to learn something about the sale, which for me was of genuine interest.

"These efforts took me off my path, but I went with him. We followed the pavement past the Stock Exchange in the Place des Consuls and turned into the little street leading to the Petite Place. By the time we arrived, I had all the information that I wanted. The lawyer took his leave, remembering that he had to visit a client who lived nearby. I stood for a moment and watched him walk away, cursing the blathering that had taken me far out of my way in the heat of the sun.

"I was about to turn back towards the Paradiso Kafenion when suddenly the fact that I was in the Petite Place seemed strange. I wondered why, and then remembered the dream.

"It's here that the infamous treasure hunter told me to meet him," I said to myself grinning, mechanically turning my head towards the place where the blacksmiths' shops were situated.

"To my horror . . . there was a little coffee shop. And there he sat.

"I felt dizzy and thought I might collapse. I leaned against a small building and looked at him again: the same black clothes, the same straw hat, the same features, the same look in his eyes. He observed me, staring at me hard. I felt absolutely rigid, as though molten iron had been poured inside me. It was mid-day and people were passing by, obliviously, as if nothing out of the ordinary were happening. I alone knew that the most horrifying thing was taking place: that there was a phantom sitting there, possessed of who knew what powers, sprung from what unknown sphere, from which Hell, from which Chaos? All of this paralysed me and I began to tremble. The spectre did not take his gaze from me and I was seized with a dread that he might get up and come towards me, talk to me, take me with him. What human power could help me against him? I threw myself into a carriage and gave the driver a distant address, one I cannot remember.

"When I had recovered somewhat, I saw that I had arrived almost at Sidi Gaber. I was calmer now and began to think about what had happened. I ordered the coachman to return to town. I am mad, I thought. Surely I had made a mistake. It must have been someone who resembled the man in my dream. I must return to make certain. It's possible he has left and that would be proof that he is not the same person, since he told me he would wait for me until four.

"With these thoughts, I had reached the Zizinia Theatre and there, summoning all my courage, I ordered the driver to take me to the Petite Place. My heart was pounding as we approached the *kafenion*. I felt as if it were about to burst. A short distance away, I made the driver stop, grabbing his arm so fiercely that he almost fell from his seat.

"The phantom was still there . . .

"I began to study him, looking for differences between him and the man in the dream. This in itself was evidence that they were one and the same, since anyone else would have demanded that I explain my scrutiny.

"He, on the contrary, simply returned my stare with one filled with anxiety about what I was going to do. It seemed that, as in the dream, he could read my mind, and to dispel any doubt about his identity he turned towards me so that I could clearly see his left hand. He showed me the emerald ring that had made such an impression on me in the first dream, and he did this so deliberately I feared the driver might notice.

"I cried out in terror and asked the driver – who by now was beginning to fear for his passenger's health – to go to Ramleh Avenue. My only aim was to get away. When we arrived there I gave him an address in Agios Stefanos, but seeing him hesitate and muttering to himself, I got down and paid him. I hailed another carriage and ordered it to take me there instead.

"I arrived in a terrible state. I entered the main room in the casino and was horrified when I saw myself in the mirror. I was pale as a corpse. Fortunately the room was empty and I threw myself onto a settee and began to consider what I should do. To return home was impossible for me. To go back to that room where a phantom who appeared by night like a supernatural shadow was the same I had just seen sitting in an ordinary *kafenion* looking like an ordinary man, was unthinkable. I was not thinking logically because, of course, he had the power to find me anywhere. I had not been thinking logically for some time.

"Then I made a decision. I would run to my friend G.V. who lived at that time in Moharam Bek.

"'Who is G.V.?' I asked, 'The eccentric man who was involved in the study of magic?'

"Yes. Him. That was why I made the decision. Of how I took the train, how I reached Moharam Bek, how I anxiously looked left and right like a madman in case the phantom should appear beside me, how I stumbled into G.V.'s place, my memories are scared and confused. All I can clearly remember is that once with him, I began to weep hysterically and to shake all over as I related my horrifying experience.

"G.V. calmed me down and, half serious, half jesting, told me not to be afraid. A phantom would not dare enter his house, and if it did he would banish it immediately. He was familiar with this kind of supernatural presence, he said, and also the means to exorcise it. Moreover, he told me, I had no more reason to fear: the phantom had come to me for a particular reason – to obtain the little iron box which it seemed, he could not get without the aid of a human. The phantom had not succeeded in his aim and must already know from my fear that there was no hope of succeeding. Undoubtedly he would attempt to convince someone else. G.V. was only sorry that I had not informed him earlier so that he might have seen the phantom for himself and talked to it, because, he added, in the History of Phantoms, for spirits and demons to appear in the light of day is extremely rare. None of this calmed me. I spent a turbulent night and awoke the next morning with a fever.

"The ignorance of the doctor and the worsening state of my nervous system brought on a cerebral fever from which I almost died. When I had recovered a little, I asked to know the date. I had fallen ill on August 3 and I thought it must now be seventh or the eighth. It was September 2.

"A short trip to an island in the Aegean speeded my recovery. During my illness, I stayed in the house of my friend V who cared for me with the kind-heartedness you would expect of him. He was annoyed with himself for not having the courage to get rid of the doctor and treat me using magic. I believe this would have cured me just as quickly.

"So you see, my friends, I had the chance to become a millionaire, but I did not dare. I didn't dare – and I didn't regret it."

Here, Alexander fell silent. The utter conviction and the simplicity with which he told the story prevented us from passing comment. In any case, by now it was twenty-seven minutes past midnight. And since the last train for the city departed at twelve thirty, we had to say our goodbyes and part in great haste.

SAN PANTALEONE

Gabriele D'Annunzio

Translated from the Italian by George McLean Harper

Gabriele D'Annunzio (1863–1938) or General Gabriele D'Annunzio, Prince of Montenevoso, Duke of Gallese, to give him his full title, was an Italian writer, poet, journalist and playwright. Born to a family of wealthy landowners in Abruzzo, his precocious talent for poetry led to him publishing his first anthology at the age of sixteen while still at school. The style and the content of his works shocked many contemporary critics; some accused him of corrupting public morals. During the First World War he achieved a different kind of fame as a war hero. In the aftermath of the war, in defiance of the Treaty of Versailles, he occupied the Dalmatian port of Fiume where he ruled as a dictator until December 1920. He became an influential advisor to Mussolini, and is considered one of the architects of Fascism.

I

The great sandy piazza, glittered as if strewn with powdered pumice. Its whitewashed houses held a strange metallic glow, like the walls of an immense furnace cooling off. The glare of the clouds, reflected from the stone pillars of the church at its far end, gave them the appearance of red granite. The church windows blazed as with inward fire. The sacred images had assumed life-like colors and attitudes, and the massive edifice seemed lifted now, in the splendor of the new celestial phenomenon, to a prouder domination than ever, above the houses of Radusa.

Groups of men and women, gesticulating and talking loudly, were pouring from the streets into the square. Superstitious terror grew in leaps and bounds from face to face. A thousand awful images of divine punishment rose out of their rude fancies; and comments, eager disputes, plaintive appeals, wild stories, prayers, and cries were mingled in a deep uproar, as of a hurricane approaching. For some time past this bloody redness of the sky had lasted through the night, disturbing its tranquillity, illumining sullenly the sleeping fields, and making dogs howl.

"Giacobbe! Giacobbe!" shouted some, waving their arms, who till then had stood in a compact band around a pillar of the church portico, talking in low tones, "Giacobbe!"

There came out through the main door, and drew near to those who called him, a long, emaciated man, apparently consumptive, whose head was bald at the top, but had a crown of long reddish hair about the temples and above the nape of the neck. His little sunken eyes, animated with the fire of a deep passion, were set close and had no particular color. The absence of his two upper front teeth gave to his mouth when speaking, and to his sharp chin with its few scattered hairs, the strangeness of a senile faun. The rest of his body was a wretched structure of bones ill-concealed by his clothes. The skin on his hands, his wrists, the back of his arms, and his breast was full of blue punctures made with a pin and india-ink, the souvenirs of sanctuaries visited, pardons obtained, and vows performed.

When the fanatic approached the group at the pillar, a swarm of questions arose from the anxious men. "Well, then? what did Don Console say? Will they send out only the silver arm? Would not the whole bust do better? When would Pallura come back with the candles? Was it one hundred pounds of wax? Only one hundred? And when would the bells begin to ring? Well, then? Well, then?"

The clamor increased around Giacobbe. Those on the outskirts of the crowd pushed toward the church. From all the streets people poured into the square till they filled it. And Giacobbe kept answering his questions, whispering, as if revealing dreadful secrets and bringing prophecies from far. He had seen aloft in the bloody sky a threatening hand, and then a black veil, and then a sword and a trumpet.

"Go ahead! Go ahead!" they urged him, looking in each other's faces, and seized with a strange desire to hear of marvels, while the wonder grew from mouth to mouth in the crowd.

II

The vast crimson zone rose slowly from the horizon to the zenith and bade fair to cover the whole vault of heaven. An undulating vapor of molten metal seemed pouring down on the roofs of the town; and in the descending crepuscule yellow and violet rays flashed through a trembling and iridescent glow. One long streak brighter than the others pointed towards a street which opened on the river-front, and at the end of this street the water flamed away between the tall slim poplar-trunks, and beyond the stream lay a strip of luxuriant country, from which the old Saracen towers stood out confusedly, like stone islets, in the dark. The air was full of the stifling emanations of mown hay, with now and then a whiff from putre-fied silkworms in the bushes. Flights of swallows crossed this space with quick, scolding cries, trafficking between the river sands and the eaves.

An expectant silence had interrupted the murmur of the multitude. The name Pallura ran from lip to lip. Signs of angry impatience broke forth here and there. The wagon was not yet to be seen along the river-road; the candles had not come; Don Consolo therefore was delaying the exposition of the relics and the acts of exorcism; the danger still threatened. Panic fear invaded the hearts of all those people crowded together like a flock of sheep, and no longer venturing to raise their eyes to heaven. The women burst out sobbing, and at the sound of weeping every mind was oppressed and filled with consternation.

Then at last the bells began to ring. As they were hung low, their deep quiv-ering strokes seemed to graze the heads of the people, and a sort of continuous wailing filled the intervals.

"San Pantaleone! San Pantaleone!"

It was an immense, unanimous cry of desperate men imploring aid. Kneeling, with blanched faces and outstretched hands, they supplicated.

"San Pantaleone!"

Then, at the church door, in the midst of the smoke of two censers, Don Consolo appeared, resplendent in a violet chasuble, with gold embroidery. He held aloft the sacred arm of silver, and conjured the air, shouting the Latin words:

"*Ut fidelibus tuis aeris serenitatem concedere digneris. Te rogamus, audi nos.*"

At sight of the relic the multitude went delirious with affectionate joy. Tears ran from all eyes, and through glistening tears these eyes beheld a miraculous gleam emanate from the three fingers held up as if in the act of benediction. The arm appeared larger now, in the enkindled air.

The dim light awoke strange scintillations in the precious stones. The balsamic odor of incense spread quickly to the nostrils of the devotees.

"*Te rogamus, audi nos!*"

But when the arm was carried back and the tolling stopped, in that moment of silence a tinkling of little bells was heard near at hand coming from the river road. Then of a sudden the crowd rushed in that direction and many voices cried:

"It is Pallura with the candles! It is Pallura coming! Here's Pallura!"

The wagon came screeching over the gravel, drawn at a walk by a heavy gray mare, over whose shoulders hung a great shining brass horn, like a half-moon. When Giacobbe and the others made towards her, the pacific animal stopped and breathed hard. Giacobbe, who reached the wagon first, saw stretched out on its floor the bloody body of Pallura, and screamed, waving his arms towards the crowd, "He is dead! He is dead!"

III

The sad news spread like lightning. People crowded around the wagon, and craned their necks to see, thinking no longer of the threats in the sky, because struck by the unexpected happening and filled with that natural ferocious curiosity which the sight of blood awakens.

"He is dead? What killed him?"

Pallura lay on his back upon the boards, with a broad wound in the middle of his forehead, with one ear torn, with gashes on his arms, his sides, and one thigh. A warm stream flowed down to his chin and neck, staining his shirt and forming dark, shining clots on his breast, his leathern belt, and even his breeches. Giacobbe hung over the body; all the rest waited around him; an auroral flush lighted up their perplexed faces; and at that moment of silence, from the river-bank arose the song of the frogs, and bats skimmed back and forth above the heads of the crowd.

Suddenly Giacobbe, straightening up, with one cheek bloody, cried: "He is not dead. He still breathes."

A hollow murmur ran through the crowd, and the nearest strained forward to look. The anxiety of those at a distance commenced to break into clamor. Two women brought a jug of water, another some strips of linen. A youth held out a gourd full of wine.

The wounded man's face was washed; the flow of blood from his forehead was checked; his head was raised. Then voices inquired loudly the cause of this deed. The hundred pounds of wax were missing; only a few fragments of candles remained in the cracks of the wagon-bed.

In the commotion their minds grew more and more inflamed, exasperated, and contentious. And as an old hereditary hatred burned in them against the town of Mascalico, on the opposite bank of the river, Giacobbe said venomously, in a hoarse voice:

"What if the candles have been offered to San Gonselvo?"

It was like the first flash of a conflagration! The spirit of church-rivalry awoke all at once in these people brutalized by many years of blind, savage worship of their own one idol. The fanatic's words flew from mouth to mouth. And beneath the tragic dull-red sky, the raging multitude resembled a tribe of mutinous gypsies.

The name of the saint broke from all throats, like a war-cry. The most excited hurled curses towards the river, and waved their arms and shook their fists. Then all these faces blazing with anger, and reddened also by the unusual light,—all these faces, broad and massive, to which their gold ear-rings and thick overhanging hair gave a wild, barbaric character,—all these faces turned eagerly towards the man lying there, and grew soft with pity. Women, with pious care, tried to bring him back to life. Loving hands changed the cloths on his wounds, sprinkled water in his face, set the gourd of wine to his lips, made a sort of pillow under his head.

"Pallura, poor Pallura, won't you answer?" He lay supine, his eyes closed, his mouth half open, with brown soft hair on his cheeks and chin, the gentle beauty of youth still showing in his features contracted with pain. From beneath the bandage on his forehead a mere thread of blood trickled down over his temples; at the corners of his mouth stood little beads of pale red foam, and from his throat issued a faint broken hiss, like the sound of a sick man gargling. About him attentions, questions, feverish glances multiplied. The mare from time to time shook her head and neighed in the direction of the houses. An atmosphere as of an impending hurricane hung over the whole town.

Then from the square rang out the screams of a woman, of a mother. They seemed all the louder for the sudden hushing of all other voices, and an enormous woman, suffocated in her fat, broke through the crowd and hurried to the wagon, crying aloud. Being heavy and unable to climb into it, she seized her son's feet, with sobbing words of love, with such sharp broken cries and such a terribly comic expression of grief, that all the bystanders shuddered and averted their faces.

"Zaccheo! Zaccheo! My heart, my joy!" screamed the widow unceasingly, kissing the feet of the wounded man and dragging him to her towards the ground.

The wounded man stirred, his mouth was contorted by a spasm, but although he opened his eyes and looked up, they were veiled with damp, so that he could not see. Big tears began to well forth at the corners of his eyelids and roll down over his cheeks and neck. His mouth was still awry. A vain effort to speak was betrayed by the hoarse whistling in his throat. And the crowd pressed closer, saying:

"Speak, Pallura! Who hurt you? Who hurt you? Speak! Speak!"

Beneath this question was a trembling rage, an intensifying fury, a deep tumult of reawakened feelings of vengeance; and the hereditary hatred boiled in every heart.

"Speak! Who hurt you? Tell us! Tell us!"

The dying man opened his eyes again; and as they were holding his hands tightly, perhaps this warm living contact gave him a momentary strength, for his gaze quickened and a vague stammering sound came to his lips. The words were not yet distinguishable. The panting breath of the multitude could be heard through the silence. Their eyes had an inward flame, because all expected one single word.

"Ma—Ma—Mascalico—"

"Mascalico! Mascalico!" shrieked Giacobbe, who was bending over him, with ear intent to snatch the weak syllables from his dying lips.

An immense roar greeted the cry. The multitude swayed at first as if tempest-swept. Then, when a voice, dominating the tumult, gave the order of attack, the mob broke up in haste. A single thought drove these men forward, a thought which seemed to have been stamped by lightning upon all minds at once: to arm themselves with some weapon. Towering above the consciousness of all arose a sort of bloody fatality, beneath the great tawny glare of the heavens, and in the electric odor emanating from the anxious fields.

IV

And the phalanx, armed with scythes, bill-hooks, axes, hoes, and guns, reunited in the square before the church. And all cried: "San Pantaleone!"

Don Consolo, terrified by the din, had taken refuge in a stall behind the altar. A handful of fanatics, led by Giacobbe, made their way into the principal chapel, forced the bronze grille, and went into the underground chamber where the bust of the saint was kept. Three lamps, fed with olive oil, burned softly in the damp air of the sacristy, where in a glass case the Christian idol glittered, with its white head surrounded by a broad gilt halo; and the walls were hidden under the wealth of native offerings.

When the idol, borne on the shoulders of four herculean men, appeared at last between the pillars and shone in the auroral light, a long gasp of passion ran through the waiting crowd, and a quiver of joy passed like a breath of wind over all their faces. And the column moved away, the enormous head of the saint oscillating above, with its empty eye-sockets turned to the front.

Now through the sky, in the deep, diffused glow, brighter meteors ploughed their furrows; groups of thin clouds broke away from the hem of the vapor zone and floated off, dissolving slowly. The whole town of Radusa stood out like a smouldering mountain of ashes. Behind and before, as far as eye could reach, the country lay in an indistinctly lucent mass. A great singing of frogs filled the sonorous solitude.

On the river-road Pallura's wagon blocked the way. It was empty, but still soiled, here and there, with blood. Angry curses broke suddenly from the mob. Giacobbe shouted:

"Let us put the saint in it!"

So the bust was placed in the wagon-bed and drawn by many arms into the ford. The battleline thus crossed the frontier. Metallic gleams ran along the files. The parted water broke in luminous spray, and the current flamed away red between the poplars, in the distance, towards the quadrangular towers. Mascalico showed itself on a little hill, among olive trees, asleep. The dogs were barking here and there, with a persistent fury of reply. The column, issuing from the ford, left the public road and advanced rapidly straight across country. The silver bust was borne again on men's shoulders, and towered above their heads amid the tall, odorous grain, starred with bright fireflies.

Suddenly a shepherd in his straw hut, where he lay to guard the grain, seized with mad panic at sight of so many armed men, started to run up the hill, yelling, "Help! Help!" And his screams echoed in the olive grove.

Then it was that the Radusani charged. Among tree-trunks and dry reeds the silver saint tottered, ringing as he struck low branches, and glittering momentarily at every steep place in the path. Ten, twelve, twenty guns, in a vibrating flash, rattled their shot against the mass of houses. Crashes, then cries, were heard; then a great commotion. Doors were opened; others were slammed shut. Window-panes fell shattered. Vases fell from the church and broke on the street. In the track of the assailants a white smoke rose quietly up through the incandescent air. They all, blinded and in bestial rage, cried, "Kill! kill!"

A group of fanatics remained about San Pantaleone. Atrocious insults for San Gonselvo broke out amid waving scythes and brandished hooks:

"Thief! Thief! Beggar! The candles! The candles!"

Other bands took the houses by assault, breaking down the doors with hatchets. And as they fell, unhinged and shivered, San Pantaleone's followers leaped in, howling, to kill the defenders.

The women, half-naked, took refuge in corners, imploring pity. They warded off the blows, grasping the weapons and cutting their fingers. They rolled at full length on the floor, amid heaps of blankets and sheets.

Giacobbe, long, quick, red as a Turkish scimitar, led the persecution, stopping ever and anon to make sweeping imperious gestures over the heads of the others with a great scythe. Pallid, bare-headed, he held the van, in the name of San Pantaleone. More than thirty men followed him. They all had a dull, confused sense of walking through a conflagration, over quaking ground, and beneath a blazing vault ready to crumble.

But from all sides began to come the defenders, the Mascalicesi, strong and dark as mulattos, sanguinary foes, fighting with long spring-bladed knives, and aiming at the belly and the throat, with guttural cries at every blow.

The mêlée rolled away, step by step, towards the church. From the roofs of two or three houses flames were already bursting. A horde of women and children, wan-eyed and terror-stricken, were fleeing headlong among the olive trees. Then the hand-to-hand struggle between the males, unimpeded by tears and lamentations, became more concentrated and ferocious.

Under the rust-colored sky, the ground was strewn with corpses. Broken imprecations were hissed through the teeth of the wounded; and steadily, through all the clamor, still came the cry of the Radusani:

"The candles! The candles!"

But the enormous church door of oak, studded with nails, remained barred. The Mascalicesi defended it against the pushing crowd and the axes. The white, impassive silver saint oscillated in the thick of the fight, still upheld on the shoulders of the four giants, who refused to fall, though bleeding from head to foot. It was the supreme desire of the assailants to place their idol on the enemy's altar.

Now while the Mascalicesi fought like lions, performing prodigies on the stone steps, Giacobbe suddenly disappeared around the corner of the building, seeking an undefended opening through which to enter the sacristy. And beholding a narrow window not far from the ground, he climbed up to it, wedged himself into its embrasure, doubled up his long body, and succeeded in crawling through. The cordial aroma of incense floated in the solitude of God's house. Feeling his way in the dark, guided by the roar of the fight outside, he crept towards the door, stumbling against chairs and bruising his face and hands.

The furious thunder of the Radusan axes was echoing from the tough oak, when he began to force the lock with an iron bar, panting, suffocated by a violent agonizing palpitation which diminished his strength, blind, giddy, stiffened by the pain of his wounds, and dripping with tepid blood.

"San Pantaleone! San Pantaleone!" bellowed the hoarse voices of his comrades outside, redoubling their blows as they felt the door slowly yield. Through the wood came to his ears the heavy thump of falling bodies, the quick thud of knife-thrusts nailing some one through the back. And a grand sentiment, like the divine uplift of the soul of a hero saving his country, flamed up then in that bestial beggar's heart.

V

By a final effort the door was flung open. The Radusani rushed in, with an immense howl of victory, across the bodies of the dead, to carry the silver saint to the altar. A vivid quivering light was reflected suddenly into the obscure nave, making the golden candlesticks shine, and the organ-pipes above. And in that yellow glow, which now came from the burning houses and now disappeared again, a second battle was fought. Bodies grappled together and rolled over the brick floor, never to rise, but to bound hither and thither in the contortions of rage, to strike the benches, and die under them, or on the chapel steps, or against the taper-spikes about the confessionals. Under the peaceful vault of God's house the chilling sound of iron penetrating men's flesh or sliding along their bones, the single broken groan of men struck in a vital spot, the crushing of skulls, the roar of victims unwilling to die, the atrocious hilarity of those who had succeeded in killing an enemy,—all this re-echoed distinctly. And a sweet, faint odor of incense floated above the strife.

The silver idol had not, however, reached the altar in triumph, for a hostile circle stood between. Giacobbe fought with his scythe, and, though wounded in several places, did not yield a hand's breadth of the stair which he had been the first to gain. Only two men were left to hold up the saint, whose enormous white head heaved and reeled grotesquely like a drunken mask. The men of Mascalico were growing furious.

Then San Pantaleone fell on the pavement, with a sharp, vibrant ring. As Giacobbe dashed forward to pick him up, a big devil of a man dealt him a blow with a bill-hook, which stretched him out on his back. Twice he rose and twice was struck down again. Blood covered his face, his breast, his hands, yet he persisted in getting up. Enraged by this ferocious tenacity of life, three, four, five clumsy peasants together stabbed him furiously in the belly, and the fanatic fell over, with the back of his neck against the silver bust. He turned like a flash and put his face against the metal, with his arms outspread and his legs drawn up. And San Pantaleone was lost.

THE POST BOX

Jalil Mammadguluzadeh

Translated from the Azerbaijani by Vafa Talyshly

Jalil Mammadguluzadeh (1866–1932). Born to Iranian parents in what is now Azerbaijan, Jalil Mammadguluzadeh worked for many years as a teacher in rural schools, before purchasing a publishing house with friends and becoming editor of *Molla Nasraddin*, a satirical magazine whose political positions saw it banned and eventually closed down. He wrote numerous short stories, essays, novels and dramas. He was a champion of his mother tongue, then in danger of disappearing, and is credited as one of those who saved Azeri as a literary language.

It was the 12th day of November. The weather was cold, but it hadn't snowed yet. The doctor examined the Khan's ill wife. He said that she had improved and that it would be possible to start traveling in a week. The Khan was in a hurry to go to Yerevan because he had some very important business matters to attend to there. Also, he was afraid that it would snow and then it would be impossible for his wife to travel in the cold weather. He took up his pen and wrote to his friend Jafar Agha:

"Next week I hope to arrive in Yerevan with my family. Could you please make sure that the rooms where we'll be staying are all warmed up and ready for us? Have the servants lay the rugs, light the stoves and air the rooms. I want to make sure everything will be comfortable for my wife, who is ill. Please reply by telegram. I have taken care of the matter that you asked about. Goodbye!
Sincerely,
VALI KHAN"

The Khan folded the letter into an envelope, addressed and stamped it. He intended to give it to his servant to drop in the post box, but then remembered he had already sent him out on another errand.

Just then he heard someone at the gate. The Khan went out and saw that it was Noruzali [pronounced no-ruz-a-LI] from the village of Itgapan. Noruzali often came to see him and always brought something such as flour, honey or butter. Again this time, Noruzali had not come empty-handed.

As soon as he saw the Khan, he set his walking stick against the wall, started to open the gate and pushed the donkey with the load on its back inside. Then he took three to four chickens from off the donkey's back. He untied the load, placing a few sacks on the ground. Then he raised his eyes to look at the Khan and bowed low in greeting.

"Why do you go to all this trouble, Noruzali?"

"It's no trouble at all, my lord. I am your faithful servant until the day I die," the peasant replied, brushing the dust off his clothes.

As it was nearly one o'clock in the afternoon when the mail would go out, the Khan asked, "Noruzali, do you know where the Post Office is?"

"I'm a villager, how would I know where the Post Office is?"

"Do you know where the Central Courthouse is?"

"Yes, my dear lord, of course I know where it is. I went there last week to complain to the Chief of the Courthouse because the mayor of our village is tormenting us. To tell you the truth, our mayor is originally from another village, and that's why he hates us. Last week two of my calves disappeared. So I went there . . ."

"Hold on. You can tell me the rest of the story later. Listen carefully, there's something I want to tell you. There's a building across the street from the Courthouse, and on the wall there's a box. That's the Postbox. It has a long, narrow lid. Go there, lift the lid, drop the letter inside and come back right away!"

Noruzali carefully took the letter. First he looked at the Khan, then he looked at the letter again with terrified eyes. He went towards the door and bent down to put the letter on the ground.

The Khan shouted, "Don't put it there! It'll get dirty. Go put it in the box right away and come back."

"Khan, my dear Khan, let me hang a bag of oats around the mule's neck. He's come a long way and he's probably tired and hungry."

"No, not now. It can wait a while. You'll miss the mail. You can feed him when you get back.

"All right. Then let me just tie him up. I'm afraid he'll eat all the trees in the yard if I leave him untethered."

"No, no. That's OK. Hurry! Go as fast as you can! Go put the letter in the box and come back!"

Noruzali put the letter inside his jacket.

"My dear Khan, these chickens are still tied up. Poor animals, let me untie them and give them some grain."

Noruzali put his hand in his pocket to get some grain, but the Khan screamed even louder, "No, no! Later, after you've come back!"

Noruzali took his walking stick and started to run like a little child. Then he remembered something else, turned and again pleaded with the Khan, "Khan, there are eggs in one of the sacks. Be careful with them. I'm afraid that the donkey will lie down on them and break them."

The Khan shouted even more loudly, "Stop talking! We're losing time."

Just as Noruzali was about to leave, the Khan called him back.

"Noruzali, don't give the letter to anyone. Don't show it to anyone. Put it in the box and come back right away! Understand?"

"I'm not a child! I'm not as inexperienced as you think. Don't worry, even the mayor wouldn't be able to take this letter away from me."

Noruzali disappeared after saying these words.

The Khan went back into the house and spoke tenderly to his wife, "Well, Light of my Eyes, start getting ready. I wrote a letter to Yerevan so that they'll warm up the rooms. We can go now. You're looking better now, thank God. The doctor says a change of climate will do you good."

As the Khan was speaking to his wife, his servant came in and said, "Khan, whose donkey is in the yard? Who brought those things?"

The Khan replied, "Put those things away! Noruzali brought them from Itgapan village."

The servant took the chickens and eggs to the kitchen and led the donkey off to the stable. Then he opened one of the sacks with flour, took a pinch of it and showed it to the Khan, "This is quality flour."

The Khan looked at the flour and told his servant to start baking the bread.

Two hours later after he had finished eating the bread, the Khan remembered Noruzali and the letter. He summoned his servant, but was told that Noruzali had not come back yet. The Khan was surprised that it was taking him so long. Perhaps Noruzali had put the letter in the postbox and then gone to the bazaar to buy something to eat. Another hour passed, but Noruzali didn't come back.

Finally the Khan called for his servant to go find out what had happened to him. Half an hour later, the servant returned saying that Noruzali was nowhere to be found.

The Khan went out on the balcony and lit a cigarette. He paced up and down the balcony wondering what had happened.

Just then, a policeman dropped by. "Khan, the police chief wants you to come to the police station and bail out your village countryman. If you don't, the chief is going to put him in prison."

The Khan gazed at the man in astonishment. Then he replied, "That villager is such a meek person. What could he possibly have done to get arrested?"

"I don't know exactly what happened. It would be better if you went to the police station yourself."

The Khan got dressed and said nothing to his wife so as not to worry her. Before entering the police station, he looked inside the jail cell and saw Noruzali sitting in a corner along with the other prisoners. He was crying like a child, wiping his tears away with the hem of his chukha.

After the Khan found out what had happened and vouched for Noruzali, the two of them went back to the Khan's place. Noruzali gave some feed to his donkey, sat down against the wall and started crying again.

The Khan went into the house, lit a cigarette, went out on the balcony and called to Noruzali, "Now tell me what happened, Noruzali! Your story sounds very interesting. Someone could write a book about it. Tell me every detail. Start from the beginning when I gave you the letter, and tell me how you ended up in prison."

Noruzali got up and moved closer to the Khan and said, after wiping his tears on his coat, "My dear Khan, forgive me! I am not to blame. I'm just a poor, ignorant peasant from the village. How am I supposed to know about letters, postboxes and post offices? Forgive me, Khan, I beg you. Let me make up for all this trouble. There's no way to undo everything I've done. It must have been God's will. Forgive me, Khan. I'll be your faithful servant until the day I die . . ."

Noruzali came closer and bent down to kiss the Khan's feet.

"Don't make such a big deal out of it, Noruzali. Am I accusing you of anything? Have you done anything wrong to me? So then why should I forgive you?"

"Ah, Khan, you don't know the half of it. That infidel, the son of an infidel took your letter, put it in his pocket and walked off with it.

"Who put the letter in his pocket and went away?"

"That stranger, that Russian guy!"

"Where did he take it?"

"He went into that building you told me about, the one with the box in front. He went inside that building."

The Khan was silent for a moment.

"Didn't you put the letter inside the box?"

"Of course I did! That stranger opened the box somehow and took the letter out as soon as I put it in."

"Were there any other letters inside that box beside ours?"

"Yes, plenty of them. He stole them all."

The Khan started to laugh very loudly. "No, Noruzali, tell the whole story – everything from start to finish exactly as it happened, from start to finish."

"Khan, my dear Khan, I took the letter from you and went to the Central Courthouse building. I found the building you were telling me about and I also found the box. I opened its lid and wanted to put the letter inside it, but then I stopped. I looked at the letter first, then I looked at the box. To be honest, I was afraid that you would get angry with me. I didn't know what to do, whether to put the letter in or not, because I had forgotten to ask you if I should stay near the box after putting the letter in or if I should come back home. I thought, if I put it in and stayed near the box, then I would have to stay until evening.

But as you saw for yourself, my dear Khan, I left the poor donkey hungry and also left the chickens with their legs tied up. I brought some flour as well. And it's still here in the yard. Khan, let your servant and me take the sacks inside the house. I'm afraid that it will rain and the flour will get wet."

"No, Noruzali, don't worry about them . . . Tell me, tell me, what's the rest of the story?"

"So I didn't put the letter in the box. I closed the lid and walked away for a little while. At first I wanted to come and ask you, but then I was scared that you would get angry with me. I was afraid that you'd say that Noruzali was like an animal, like a donkey, that doesn't understand anything. So I leaned against the wall to rest. Then I saw an Armenian boy, about this tall, about 12 or 13. He went up to the box, opened the lid, put a letter inside it exactly like the one you gave me, then closed the lid and went away. I called after him to ask why he put the letter in the box, but he didn't answer. I don't know – maybe he didn't understand me. Anyway he didn't look back.

"A few minutes later, a Russian lady rushed up to the box, put a letter in and left. This time I got brave. I thought to myself that this is probably the way it has to be, that the letters should stay in the box. So I got brave. Having said 'bismillah,' I went and opened the lid of the box, put the letter inside and turned around to come back to your service.

"When I was about this far from the box, that Russian guy went up to it.

At first I thought that he wanted to put a letter inside the box, too. But then I saw that no, he wanted to do something else. He put his hand inside the box. I understood right away that he wanted to steal the letters . . . Khan, I'm speaking too much, forgive me, tell your servant to help me get on my way home, it's getting late."

"No, I won't let you go yet. Tell me what happened after that."

"Well, my dear Khan, may my children be your servants! May I never live another day without your blessing! Well, I saw this guy taking the letters out of the box. He closed the lid and was about to leave. I ran over to him and made him stop. I said, 'Hey you, where are you taking those letters? You think people put their letters in there for you to steal them? Put them back! Noruzali isn't dead yet, and he won't let you steal a letter his Khan gave him. Don't take something that doesn't belong to you. Don't your Russian laws say that stealing is a sin?' Khan, may my children be your servants. Khan, let me go home – it's getting late."

"Don't hurry, you can go later . . . What happened after that?"

"Let me think, where was I . . . Hey, don't let the donkey destroy the grape-vine."

Noruzali wanted to stop the donkey, but the Khan didn't let him. "Noruzali, don't go, don't go yet. Tell me, what happened then?"

"What happened? I begged the guy, telling him that my Khan would kill me if he took the letter away. I told him to give back my Khan's letter. He said no, he wouldn't give it back. Then I saw that he wanted to run away. God knows how furious I was – I took the guy by the shoulders and shoved him to the ground so hard that he started bleeding at the mouth. Then some soldiers came from the Courthouse, beat me up and took me to prison. May I be your servant forever, my Khan! If it weren't for you, they would have sent me to Siberia. There were some other prisoners in there besides me, and they told me that the Russian guy was an official. Well . . . what should I have done? Khan, tell me, I'm not to blame, am I?"

The Khan just laughed and laughed.

It was already dark outside. Noruzali put the empty sacks on the back of his hungry donkey and, beating the donkey with a stick, headed back to his village.

In three days, a telegram came from Yerevan for the Khan. It said, "Received your letter. Rooms are ready." And so the Khan and his wife set out for Yerevan shortly afterwards.

After a month and a half, Noruzali was summoned to court and sentenced to three months in prison for having assaulted a civil servant who was carrying out his duties. Noruzali pleaded innocent. The Khan learned about this latest development three months later. It made him stop to think for a while.

TWENTY-SIX MEN AND A GIRL

Maxim Gorky

Translated from the Russian by J. M. Shirazi

Alexei Maximovich Peshkov (1868–1936) was primarily known as **Maxim (Maksim) Gorky** and was a Russian and Soviet writer, a founder of the socialist realism literary method and a political activist. He was also a five-time nominee for the Nobel Prize in Literature. For a significant part of his life, he was exiled from Russia and later the Soviet Union. In 1932, he returned to USSR on Joseph Stalin's personal invitation and died there in June 1936. A writer born into poverty, his pseudonym, Gorky, literally means "bitter". The largest fixed-wing aircraft in the world in the mid-1930s, the Tupolev ANT-20 was named Maxim Gorky in his honour. Stalin was one of the pallbearers of Gorky's coffin during the funeral.

There were six-and-twenty of us—six-and-twenty living machines in a damp, underground cellar, where from morning till night we kneaded dough and rolled it into kringels. Opposite the underground window of our cellar was a bricked area, green and mouldy with moisture. The window was protected from outside with a closed iron grating, and the light of the sun could not pierce through the window panes, covered as they were with flour dust.

Our employer had bars placed in front of the windows, so that we should not be able to give a bit of his bread to passing beggars, or to any of our fellows who were out of work and hungry. Our employer called us rogues, and gave us half-rotten tripe to eat for our mid-day meal, instead of meat. It was swelteringly close for us cooped up in that stone underground chamber, under the low, heavy, soot-blackened, cobwebby ceiling. Dreary and sickening was our life between its thick, dirty, mouldy walls.

Unrefreshed, and with a feeling of not having had our sleep out, we used to get up at five o'clock in the morning; and before six, we were already seated, worn out and apathetic, at the table, rolling out the dough which our mates had already prepared while we slept.

The whole day, from ten in the early morning until ten at night, some of us sat round that table, working up in our hands the yielding paste, rolling it to and fro so that it should not get stiff; while the others kneaded the swelling mass of dough. And the whole day the simmering water in the kettle, where the kringels were being cooked, sang low and sadly; and the baker's shovel scraped harshly over the oven floor, as he threw the slippery bits of dough out of the kettle on the heated bricks.

From morning till evening wood was burning in the oven, and the red glow of the fire gleamed and flickered over the walls of the bake-shop, as if silently mocking us. The giant oven was like the misshapen head of a monster in a fairy tale; it thrust itself up out of the floor, opened wide jaws, full of glowing fire, and blew hot breath upon us; it seemed to be ever watching out of its black air-holes our interminable work. Those two deep holes were like eyes: the cold, pitiless eyes of a monster. They watched us always with the same darkened glance, as if they were weary of seeing before them such eternal slaves, from whom they could expect nothing human, and therefore scorned them with the cold scorn of wisdom.

In meal dust, in the mud which we brought in from the yard on our boots, in the hot, sticky atmosphere, day in, day out, we rolled the dough into kringels, which we moistened with our own sweat. And we hated our work with a glowing hatred; we never ate what had passed through our hands, and preferred black bread to kringels.

Sitting opposite each other, at a long table—nine facing nine—we moved our hands and fingers mechanically during endlessly long hours, till we were so accustomed to our monotonous work that we ceased to pay any attention to it.

We had all studied each other so constantly, that each of us knew every wrinkle of his mates' faces. It was not long also before we had exhausted almost every topic of conversation; that is why we were most of the time silent, unless we were chaffing each other; but one cannot always find something about which to chaff another man, especially when that man is one's mate. Neither were we much given to finding fault with one another; how, indeed, could one of us poor devils be in a position to find fault with another, when we were all of us half dead and, as it were, turned to stone? For the heavy drudgery seemed to crush all feeling out of us. But silence is only terrible and fearful for those who have said everything and have nothing more to say to each other; for men, on the contrary, who have never begun to communicate with one another, it is easy and simple.

Sometimes, too, we sang; and this is how it happened that we began to sing: one of us would sigh deeply in the midst of our toil, like an overdriven horse, and then we would begin one of those songs whose gentle swaying melody seems always to ease the burden on the singer's heart.

At first one sang by himself, and we others sat in silence listening to his solitary song, which, under the heavy vaulted roof of the cellar, died gradually away, and became extinguished, like a little fire in the steppes, on a wet autumn night, when the gray heaven hangs like a heavy mass over the earth.

Then another would join in with the singer, and now two soft, sad voices would break into song in our narrow, dull hole of a cellar. Suddenly others would join in, and the song would roll forward like a wave, would grow louder and swell upward, till it would seem as if the damp, foul walls of our stone prison were widening out and opening. Then, all six-and-twenty of us would be singing; our loud, harmonious song would fill the whole cellar, our voices would travel outside and beyond, striking, as it were, against the walls in moaning sobs and sighs, moving our hearts with a soft, tantalizing ache, tearing open old wounds, and awakening longings.

The singers would sigh deeply and heavily; suddenly one would become silent and listen to the others singing, then let his voice flow once more in the common tide. Another would exclaim in a stifled voice, "Ah!" and would shut his eyes, while the deep, full sound waves would show him, as it were, a road, in front of him—a sunlit, broad road in the distance, which he himself, in thought wandered along.

But the flame flickers once more in the huge oven, the baker scrapes incessantly with his shovel, the water simmers in the kettle, and the flicker of the fire on the wall dances as before in silent mockery. While in other men's words we sing out our dumb grief, the weary burden of live men robbed of the sunlight, the burden of slaves.

So we lived, we six-and-twenty, in the vault-like cellar of a great stone house, and we suffered each one of us, as if we had to bear on our shoulders the whole three storys of that house.

But we had something else good, besides the singing—something we loved, that perhaps took the place of the sunshine.

In the second story of our house there was established a gold-embroiderer's shop, and there, living among the other embroidery girls, was Tanya, a little maid-servant of sixteen. Every morning there peeped in through the glass door a rosy little face, with merry blue eyes; while a ringing, tender voice called out to us:

"Little prisoners! Have you any kringels, please, for me?"

At that clear sound, we knew so well, we all used to turn round, gazing with simple-hearted joy at the pure girlish face which smiled at us so sweetly. The sight of the small nose pressed against the window-pane, and of the white teeth gleaming between the half-open lips, had become for us a daily pleasure. Tumbling over each other we used to jump up to open the door, and she would step in, bright and cheerful, holding out her apron, with her head thrown on one side, and a smile on her lips. Her thick, long chestnut hair fell over her shoulder and across her breast. But we, ugly, dirty and misshapen as we were, looked up at her—the threshold door was four steps above the floor—looked up at her with heads thrown back, wishing her good-morning, and speaking strange, unaccustomed words, which we kept for her only.

Our voices became softer when we spoke to her, our jests were lighter. For her—everything was different with us. The baker took from his oven a shovel of the best and the brownest kringels, and threw them deftly into Tanya's apron.

"Be off with you now, or the boss will catch you!" we warned her each time. She laughed roguishly, called out cheerfully: "Good-bye, poor prisoners!" and slipped away as quick as a mouse.

That was all. But long after she had gone we talked about her to one another with pleasure. It was always the same thing as we had said yesterday and the day before, because everything about us, including ourselves and her, remained the same—as yesterday—and as always.

Painful and terrible it is when a man goes on living, while nothing changes around him; and when such an existence does not finally kill his soul, then the monotony becomes with time, even more and more painful. Generally we spoke about women in such a way, that sometimes it was loathsome to us ourselves to hear our rude, shameless talk. The women whom we knew deserved perhaps nothing better. But about Tanya we never let fall an evil word; none of us ever ventured so much as to lay a hand on her, even to free a jest she never heard from us. Maybe this was so because she never remained for long with us; she flashed on our eyes like a star falling from the sky, and vanished; and maybe because she was little and very beautiful, and everything beautiful calls forth respect, even in coarse people.

And besides—though our life of penal labor had made us dull beasts, oxen, we were still men, and, like all men, could not live without worshipping something or other. Better than her we had none, and none but her took any notice of us, living in the cellar—no one, though there were dozens of people in the house. And then, to—most likely, this was the chief thing—we all regarded her as something of our own, something existing as it were only by virtue of our kringels. We took on ourselves in turns the duty of providing her with hot kringels, and this became for us like a daily sacrifice to our idol, it became almost a sacred rite, and every day it bound us more closely to her. Besides kringels, we gave Tanya a great deal of advice to wear warmer clothes, not to run upstairs too quickly, not to carry heavy bundles of wood. She listened to all our counsels with a smile, answered them by a laugh, and never took our advice, but we were not offended at that; all we wanted was to show how much care we bestowed upon her.

Often she would apply to us with different requests, she asked us, for instance; to open the heavy door into the store-cellar, and to chop wood: with delight and a sort of pride, we did this for her, and everything else she wanted.

But when one of us asked her to mend his solitary shirt for him, she said, with a laugh of contempt:

"What next! A likely idea!"

We made great fun of the queer fellow who could entertain such an idea, and—never asked her to do anything else. We loved her—all is said in that.

Man always wants to lay his love on someone, though sometimes he crushes, sometimes he sullies, with it; he may poison another life because he loves without respecting the beloved. We were bound to love Tanya, for we had no one else to love.

At times one of us would suddenly begin to reason like this: "And why do we make so much of the wench? What is there in her? eh? What a to-do we make about her!"

The man who dared to utter such words we promptly and coarsely cut short— we wanted something to love: we had found it and loved it, and what we twenty-six loved must be for each of us unalterable, as a holy thing, and anyone who acted against us in this was our enemy. We loved, maybe, not what was really good, but you see there were twenty-six of us, and so we always wanted to see what was precious to us held sacred by the rest.

Our love is not less burdensome than hate, and maybe that is just why some proud souls maintain that our hate is more flattering than our love. But why do they not run away from us, if it is so?

Besides our department, our employer had also a bread-bakery; it was in the same house, separated from our hole only by a wall; but the bakers—there were four of them—held aloof from us, considering their work superior to ours, and therefore themselves better than us; they never used to come into our workroom, and laughed contemptuously at us when they met us in the yard. We, too, did not go to see them; this was forbidden by our employer, from fear that we should steal the fancy bread.

We did not like the bakers, because we envied them; their work was lighter than ours, they were paid more, and were better fed; they had a light, spacious workroom, and they were all so clean and healthy—and that made them hateful to us. We all looked gray and yellow; three of us had syphilis, several suffered from skin diseases, one was completely crippled by rheumatism. On holidays and in their leisure time the bakers wore pea-jackets and creaking boots, two of them had accordions, and they all used to go for strolls in the town garden—we wore filthy rags and leather clogs or plaited shoes on our feet, the police would not let us into the town gardens—could we possibly like the bakers?

And one day we learned that their chief baker had been drunk, the master had sacked him and had already taken on another, and that this other was a soldier, wore a satin waistcoat and a watch and gold chain. We were inquisitive to get a sight of such a dandy, and in the hope of catching a glimpse of him we kept running one after another out into the yard.

But he came of his own accord into our room. Kicking at the door, he pushed it open, and leaving it ajar, stood in the doorway smiling, and said to us:

"God help the work! Good-morning, mates!"

The ice-cold air, which streamed in through the open door, curled in streaks of vapor round his feet. He stood on the threshold, looked us up and down, and under his fair, twisted mustache gleamed big yellow teeth. His waistcoat was really something quite out of the common, blue-flowered, brilliant with shining little buttons of red stones. He also wore a watch chain.

He was a fine fellow, this soldier; tall, healthy, rosy-cheeked, and his big, clear eyes had a friendly, cheerful glance. He wore on his head a white starched cap, and from under his spotlessly clean apron peeped the pointed toes of fashionable, well-blacked boots.

Our baker asked him politely to shut the door. The soldier did so without hurrying himself, and began to question us about the master. We explained to him, all speaking together, that our employer was a thorough-going brute, a rogue, a knave, and a slave-driver; in a word, we repeated to him all that can and must be said about an employer, but cannot be repeated here. The soldier listened to us, twisted his mustache, and watched us with a friendly, open-hearted look.

"But haven't you got a lot of girls here?" he asked suddenly.

Some of us began to laugh deferentially, others put on a meaning expression, and one of us explained to the soldier that there were nine girls here.

"You make the most of them?" asked the soldier, with a wink.

We laughed, but not so loudly, and with some embarrassment. Many of us would have liked to have shown the soldier that we also were tremendous fellows with the girls, but not one of us could do so; and one of our number confessed as much, when he said in a low voice:

"That sort of thing is not in our line."

"Well, no; it wouldn't quite do for you," said the soldier with conviction, after having looked us over.

"There is something wanting about you all you don't look the right sort. You've no sort of appearance; and the women, you see, they like a bold appearance, they will have a well set-up body. Everything has to be tip-top for them. That's why they respect strength. They want an arm like that!"

The soldier drew his right hand, with its turned-up shirt sleeve, out of his pocket, and showed us his bare arm. It was white and strong, and covered with shining yellow hairs.

"Legs and chest, all must be strong. And then a man must be dressed in the latest fashion, so as to show off his looks to advantage. Yes, all the women take to me. Whether I call to them, or whether I beckon them, they with one accord, five at a time, throw themselves at my head."

He sat down on a flour sack, and told at length all about the way women loved him, and how bold he was with them. Then he left, and after the door had creaked to behind him, we sat for a long time silent, and thought about him and his talk. Then we all suddenly broke silence together, and it became apparent that we were all equally pleased with him. He was such a nice, open-hearted fellow; he came to see us without any standoffishness, sat down and chatted. No one else came to us like that, and no one else talked to us in that friendly sort of way. And we continued to talk of him and his coming triumph among the embroidery girls, who passed us by with contemptuous sniffs when they saw us in the yard, or who looked straight through us as if we had been air.

But we admired them always when we met them outside, or when they walked past our windows; in winter, in fur jackets and toques to match; in summer, in hats trimmed with flowers, and with colored parasols in their hands. We talked, however, about these girls in a way that would have made them mad with shame and rage, if they could have heard us.

"If only he does not get hold of little Tanya!" said the baker, suddenly, in an anxious tone of voice.

We were silent, for these words troubled us. Tanya had quite gone out of our minds, supplanted, put on one side by the strong, fine figure of the soldier.

Then began a lively discussion; some of us maintained that Tanya would never lower herself so; others thought she would not be able to resist him, and the third group proposed to give him a thrashing if he should try to annoy Tanya. And, finally, we all decided to watch the soldier and Tanya, and to warn the girl against him. This brought the discussion to an end.

Four weeks had passed by since then; during this time the soldier baked white bread, walked about with the gold-embroidery girls, visited us often, but did not talk any more about his conquests; only twisted his mustache, and licked his lips lasciviously.

Tanya called in as usual every morning for "little kringels," and was as gay and as nice and friendly with us as ever. We certainly tried once or twice to talk to her about the soldier, but she called him a "goggle-eyed calf," and made fun of him all round, and that set our minds at rest. We saw how the gold-embroidery girls carried on with the soldier, and we were proud of our girl; Tanya's behavior reflected honor on us all; we imitated her, and began in our talks to treat the soldier with small consideration.

She became dearer to us, and we greeted her with more friendliness and kindliness every morning.

One day the soldier came to see us, a bit drunk, and sat down and began to laugh. When we asked him what he was laughing about, he explained to us:

"Why two of them—that Lydka girl and Grushka—have been clawing each other on my account. You should have seen the way they went for each other! Ha! ha! One got hold of the other one by the hair, threw her down on the floor of the passage, and sat on her! Ha! ha! ha! They scratched and tore each others' faces. It was enough to make one die with laughter! Why is it women can't fight fair? Why do they always scratch one another, eh?"

He sat on the bench, healthy, fresh and jolly; he sat there and went on laughing. We were silent. This time he made an unpleasant impression on us.

"Well, it's a funny thing what luck I have with the women-folk! Eh? I've laughed till I'm ill! One wink, and it's all over with them! It's the d-devil!"

He raised his white hairy hands, and slapped them down on his knees. And his eyes seemed to reflect such frank astonishment, as if he were himself quite surprised at his good luck with women. His fat, red face glistened with delight and self satisfaction, and he licked his lips more than ever.

Our baker scraped the shovel violently and angrily along the oven floor, and all at once he said sarcastically:

"There's no great strength needed to pull up fir saplings, but try a real pine-tree."

"Why—what do you mean by saying that to me?" asked the soldier.

"Oh, well. . . ."

"What is it?"

"Nothing—it slipped out!"

"No, wait a minute! What's the point? What pinetree?"

Our baker did not answer, working rapidly away with the shovel at the oven; flinging into it the half-cooked kringels, taking out those that were done, and noisily throwing them on the floor to the boys who were stringing them on bast wrappings. He seemed to have forgotten the soldier and his conversation with him. But the soldier had all at once dropped into a sort of uneasiness. He got up on to his feet, and went to the oven, at the risk of knocking against the handle of the shovel, which was waving spasmodically in the air.

"No, tell me, do—who is it? You've insulted me. I? There's not one could withstand me, n-no! And you say such insulting things to me?"

He really seemed genuinely hurt. He must have had nothing else to pride himself on except his gift for seducing women; maybe, except for that, there was nothing living in him, and it was only that by which he could feel himself a living man.

There are men to whom the most precious and best thing in their lives appears to be some disease of their soul or body. They spend their whole life in relation to it, and only living by it, suffering from it, they sustain themselves on it, they complain of it to others, and so draw the attention of their fellows to themselves.

For that they extract sympathy from people, and apart from it they have nothing at all. Take from them that disease, cure them, and they will be miserable, because they have lost their one resource in life—they are left empty then. Sometimes a man's life is so poor, that he is driven instinctively to prize his vice and to live by it; one may say for a fact that often men are vicious from boredom.

The soldier was offended, he went up to our baker and roared:

"No, tell me do-who?"

"Tell you?" the baker turned suddenly to him.

"Well?"

"You know Tanya?"

"Well?"

"Well, there then! Only try."

"You!"

"Her? Why that's nothing to me-pooh!"

"We shall see!"

"You will see! Ha! ha!"

"She'll——"

"Give me a month!"

"What a braggart you are, soldier!"

"A fortnight! I'll prove it! Who is it? Tanya! Pooh!"

"Well, get out. You're in my way!"

"A fortnight—and it's done! Ah, you——"

"Get out, I say!"

Our baker, all at once, flew into a rage and brandished his shovel. The soldier staggered away from him in amazement, looked at us, paused, and softly, malignantly said, "Oh, all right, then!" and went away.

During the dispute we had all sat silent, absorbed in it. But when the soldier had gone, eager, loud talk and noise arose among us.

Some one shouted to the baker: "It's a bad job that you've started, Pavel!"

"Do your work!" answered the baker savagely.

We felt that the soldier had been deeply aggrieved, and that danger threatened Tanya. We felt this, and at the same time we were all possessed by a burning curiosity, most agreeable to us. What would happen? Would Tanya hold out against the soldier? And almost all cried confidently: "Tanya? She'll hold out! You won't catch her with your bare arms!"

We longed terribly to test the strength of our idol; we forcibly proved to each other that our divinity was a strong divinity and would come victorious out of this ordeal. We began at last to fancy that we had not worked enough on the soldier, that he would forget the dispute, and that we ought to pique his vanity more keenly. From that day we began to live a different life, a life of nervous tension, such as we had never known before. We spent whole days in arguing together; we all grew, as it were, sharper; and got to talk more and better. It seemed to us that we were playing some sort of game with the devil, and the stake on our side was Tanya. And when we learned from the bakers that the soldier had begun "running after our Tanya," we felt a sort of delighted terror, and life was so interesting that we did not even notice that our employer had taken advantage of our pre-occupation to increase our work by fourteen pounds of dough a day.

We seemed, indeed, not even tired by our work. Tanya's name was on our lips all day long. And every day we looked for her with a certain special impatience. Sometimes we pictured to ourselves that she would come to us, and it would not be the same Tanya as of old, but somehow different. We said nothing to her, however, of the dispute regarding her. We asked her no questions, and behaved as well and affectionately to her as ever. But even in this a new element crept in, alien to our old feeling for Tanya—and that new element was keen curiosity, keen and cold as a steel knife.

"Mates! To-day the time's up!" our baker said to us one morning, as he set to work.

We were well aware of it without his reminder; but still we were thrilled.

"Look at her. She'll he here directly," suggested the baker.

One of us cried out in a troubled voice, "Why! as though one could notice anything!"

And again an eager, noisy discussion sprang up among us. To-day we were about to prove how pure and spotless was the vessel into which we had poured all that was best in us. This morning, for the first time, it became clear to us, that we really were playing a great game; that we might, indeed, through the exaction of this proof of purity, lose our divinity altogether.

During the whole of the intervening fortnight we had heard that Tanya was persistently followed by the soldier, but not one of us had thought of asking her how she had behaved toward him. And she came every morning to fetch her kringels, and was the same toward us as ever.

This morning, too, we heard her voice outside: "You poor prisoners! Here I am!"

We opened the door, and when she came in we all remained, contrary to our usual custom, silent. Our eyes fixed on her, we did not know how to speak to her, what to ask her. And there we stood in front of her, a gloomy, silent crowd. She seemed to be surprised at this unusual reception; and suddenly we saw her turn white and become uneasy, then she asked, in a choking voice:

"Why are you—like this?"

"And you?" the baker flung at her grimly, never taking his eyes off her.

"What am I?"

"N—nothing."

"Well, then, give me quickly the little kringels."

Never before had she bidden us hurry.

"There's plenty of time," said the baker, not stirring, and not removing his eyes from her face.

Then, suddenly, she turned round and disappeared through the door.

The baker took his shovel and said, calmly turning away toward the oven:

"Well, that settles it! But a soldier! a common beast like that—a low cur!"

Like a flock of sheep we all pressed round the table, sat down silently, and began listlessly to work. Soon, however, one of us remarked:

"Perhaps, after all—"

"Shut up!" shouted the baker.

We were all convinced that he was a man of judgment, a man who knew more than we did about things. And at the sound of his voice we were convinced of the soldier's victory, and our spirits became sad and downcast.

At twelve o'clock—while we were eating our dinners—the soldier came in. He was as clean and as smart as ever, and looked at us—as usual—straight in the eyes. But we were all awkward in looking at him.

"Now then, honored sirs, would you like me to show you a soldier's quality?" he said, chuckling proudly.

"Go out into the passage, and look through the crack—do you understand?"

We went into the passage, and stood all pushing against one another, squeezed up to the cracks of the wooden partition of the passage that looked into the yard. We had not to wait long. Very soon Tanya, with hurried footsteps and a careworn face, walked across the yard, jumping over the puddles of melting snow and mud: she disappeared into the store cellar. Then whistling, and not hurrying himself, the soldier followed in the same direction. His hands were thrust in his pockets; his mustaches were quivering.

Rain was falling, and we saw how its drops fell into the puddles, and the puddles were wrinkled by them. The day was damp and gray—a very dreary day. Snow still lay on the roofs, but on the ground dark patches of mud had begun to appear. And the snow on the roofs too was covered by a layer of brownish dirt. The rain fell slowly with a depressing sound. It was cold and disagreeable for us waiting.

The first to come out of the store cellar was the soldier; he walked slowly across the yard, his mustaches twitching, his hands in his pockets—the same as always.

Then—Tanya, too, came out. Her eyes—her eyes were radiant with joy and happiness, and her lips—were smiling. And she walked as though in a dream, staggering, with unsteady steps.

We could not bear this quietly. All of us at once rushed to the door, dashed out into the yard and—hissed at her, reviled her viciously, loudly, wildly.

She started at seeing us, and stood as though rooted in the mud under her feet. We formed a ring round her! and malignantly, without restraint, abused her with vile words, said shameful things to her.

We did this not loudly, not hurriedly, seeing that she could not get away, that she was hemmed in by us, and we could deride her to our hearts' content. I don't know why, but we did not beat her. She stood in the midst of us, and turned her head this way and that, as she heard our insults. And we—more and more violently flung at her the filth and venom of our words.

The color had left her face. Her blue eyes, so happy a moment before, opened wide, her bosom heaved, and her lips quivered.

We in a ring round her avenged ourselves on her as though she had robbed us. She belonged to us, we had lavished on her our best, and though that best was a beggar's crumb, still we were twenty-six, she was one, and so there was no pain we could give her equal to her guilt!

How we insulted her! She was still mute, still gazed at us with wild eyes, and a shiver ran all over her.

We laughed, roared, yelled. Other people ran up from somewhere and joined us. One of us pulled Tanya by the sleeve of her blouse.

Suddenly her eyes flashed; deliberately she raised her hands to her head and straightening her hair she said loudly but calmly, straight in our faces:

"Ah, you miserable prisoners!"

And she walked straight at us, walked as directly as though we had not been before her, as though we were not blocking her way.

And hence it was that no one did actually prevent her passing.

Walking out of our ring, without turning round, she said loudly and with indescribable contempt:

"Ah, you scum—brutes."

And—was gone.

We were left in the middle of the yard, in the rain, under the gray sky without the sun.

Then we went mutely away to our damp stone cellar. As before—the sun never peeped in at our windows, and Tanya came no more!

CHILD'S PLAY

(Takekurabe, 1895–96)

Ichiyō Higuchi

Translated from the Japanese by Robert Lyons Danly

Ichiyō Higuchi (1872–1896) was the pen name of Japanese author Natsu Higuchi. Specializing in short stories, she was one of the first important writers to appear in the Meiji period (1868–1912) and Japan's first prominent woman writer of modern times. She wrote relatively little as a result of living a brief life – she died at the age of twenty-four – but her stories had a large impact on Japanese literature and she is still appreciated by the Japanese public today. Higuchi's likeness adorns the Japanese 5000-yen banknote as of fall 2004, becoming the third woman to appear on a Japanese banknote, after Empress Jingū in 1881 and Murasaki Shikibu in 2000. Her work is highly regarded for her use of Classical Japanese language, and for that reason people are reluctant to update or translate it into contemporary Japanese, leaving it difficult for the majority of Japanese people to read.

I t's a long way round to the front of the quarter, where the trailing branches of the willow tree bid farewell to the nighttime revellers and the bawdyhouse lights flicker in the moat, dark as the dye that blackens the smiles of the Yoshiwara beauties. From the third-floor rooms of the lofty houses the all but palpable music and laughter spill down into the side street. Who knows how these great establishments prosper? The rickshaws pull up night and day.

They call this part of town beyond the quarter "in front of Daion Temple." The name may sound a little saintly, but those who live in the area will tell you it's a lively place. Turn the corner at Mishima Shrine and you don't find any mansions, just tenements of ten or twenty houses, where eaves have long begun to sag and shutters only close halfway. It is not a spot for trade to flourish.

Outside the tumble-down houses everyone works madly: cutting up paper into queer little pieces, slopping them with paint, spearing them on funny-looking spits. Whole families, the whole neighborhood is wrapped up in the production of these strange, bright paper skewers. They dry the painted scraps in the morning and assemble them at night. And what are these things that have everyone so preoccupied? "You don't know?" a merchant will reply in astonishment. "*Kumade* charms! On Otori day, you ought to see the big-wishers buy them up!"

Year in, year out, the minute the New Year pine bough comes down from the front gate, every self-respecting businessman takes up the same sideline, and by summer hands and feet are splattered with paint. They count on the earnings to buy new clothes for the holidays. If the gods grant prosperity to mere purchasers of these charms, the men who make them figure they stand to reap a windfall. Funny thing, no one hears of any rich men dwelling in these parts.

Most of the people here, in fact, have some connection with the quarter. The menfolk do odd jobs at the less dignified houses. You can hear them in the evenings jiggling their shoe-check tags before they leave for work, and you'll see them putting on their jackets when most men take them off. Wives rub good-luck flints behind them to protect their men from harm. Could this be the final parting? It's a dangerous business. Innocent bystanders get killed when there's a brawl in one of the houses. And look out if you ever foil the double suicide of a courtesan and her lover! Yet off the husbands go to risk their lives each night like schoolboys to a picnic.

Daughters, too, are involved in the quarter: here, a serving girl in one of the great establishments; there, an escort plying back and forth between the teahouse and the brothel. They bustle along with their shop's lantern, an advertisement for all to see. But what will become of these girls once they have graduated from their present course of training? To them, the work is something grand and gala, as if they were performing on a fine wooden stage. Then one day before they know it they have reached the age of thirty, trim and tidy in their cotton coats with matching dresses and their sensible dark blue stockings. They carry their little packages under their arms, and we know what *these* are without asking. Stomp, stomp, they go with the heels of their sandals—they're in an awful hurry—and the flimsy drawbridges flop down across the ditch. "We'll leave it here at the back," they say, setting down their bundles, "it's too far round to the front." So they are needlewomen now, apparently.

Customs here are indeed a little different. You won't find many women who tie their sashes neatly behind their waists. It's one thing to see a woman of a certain age who favors gaudy patterns, or a sash cut immoderately wide. It's quite another to see these barefaced girls of fifteen or sixteen, all decked out in flashy clothes and blowing on bladder cherries, which everybody knows are used as contraceptives. But that's what kind of neighborhood it is. A trollop who yesterday went by the name of some heroine in *The Tale of Genji* at one of the third-rate houses along the ditch today runs off with a thug. They open a lean-to bar, though neither of them knows the first thing about running a business. They soon go broke. The beauty begins to miss her former calling. Her assets are gone with the chopped-up chicken bones left from last night's hors d'oeuvres. Unlike the chicken, however, our charmer can still return to her old nest. People around here, for some reason, find this kind of woman more alluring than your ordinary one.

In such a world, how are the children to escape being influenced? Take the autumn festival. Mother Meng would be scandalized at the speed with which they learn to mimic all the famous clowns; why, there's not a one of them who can't do Rohachi and Eiki. They hear their performances praised, and that night the smart alecks repeat their rounds. It starts at the age of seven or eight, this audacity, and by the time they're fifteen! Towels from the evening bath dangle from their shoulders, and the latest song, in a nasal twang of disrespect, dribbles from the corner of their lips. At school, any moment, a proper music class is apt to lapse into the rhythms of the quarter. Athletic meets ring with the songs of geisha—who needs the school cheer? One sympathizes with their teachers, who toil at the Ikueisha, not far from here. It may be a crowded little schoolhouse—a private school, actually—but the students number close to a thousand, and the teachers who are popular there soon become known. In these parts, the very word *school* is synonymous with the Ikueisha.

Listen to them walking home from school: "Your father sure keeps an eye on the teahouse by the bridge!" they shout at the fireman's boy. It's the wisdom of the street. Children know about the quarter. They scramble over garden walls, imitating firemen. "Hey! You broke the spikes on the fence to keep the thieves away!" A two-bit shyster's son begins his prosecution: "Your old man's a 'horse,' isn't he? Isn't he?" The blood rushes to the defendant's face. The poor boy—he'd sooner die than admit his father collected bills for a brothel. And then there are the favorite sons of the big shots of the quarter, who grow up in lodgings at some remove, free to feign a noble birth. They sport the latest prep-school cap, they have a look of leisure, and they wear their European clothes with style and panache. All the same, it's amusing to watch the others curry favor. "Young master, young master," they call them, when "spoiled brat" would do.

Among the many students at the Ikueisha was Nobuyuki of Ryūge Temple. In time, his thick, black hair would be shorn, and he would don the dark robes of a priest. It may well have been his own choice, and then again perhaps he had resigned himself to fate. His father was a cleric, and already like his father Nobu was a scholar. By nature he was a quiet boy. His classmates considered him a wet blanket and they liked to tease him. "Here—this is your line of work," they would laugh, stringing up a dead cat. "How about offering the last rites?" All that was in the past, however; no one made fun of him now, not even by mistake. He was fifteen and of average height, his dark hair was closely cropped in schoolboy fashion, and yet something about him was different from the others. Although he had the ordinary-sounding name of Fujimoto Nobuyuki, already in his manner were suggestions of the cloth.

The Festival of Senzoku Shrine was set for the twentieth of August, and not a block would there be without a float of its own jostling for glory. Over the ditch and up the side of the embankment they charge: all the young men, pushing, pulling, bent on taking the quarter. The heart beats faster at the mere thought of it. And keep an eye, mind you, on the young ones—once they get wind of what the older boys are up to. Matching kimonos for the whole gang are only the beginning. The saucy things they dream up will give you goose bumps.

The back-street gang, as they preferred to call themselves, had Chōkichi for their leader. He was the fire chief's son—sixteen and full of it. He hadn't walked without his chest puffed out since the day he started policing the fall festival with his father: baton swinging, belt low around the hips, sneering whenever he answered. The firemen's wives all griped among themselves, "If he weren't the chief's boy, he'd never get away with it."

Selfish Chōkichi saw to it that he always got his way. He stretched his side-street influence wider than it really went, until in Shōta, the leader of the main-street gang, Chōkichi knew that he had met his match. Though Shōta was three years younger, he was the son of Tanaka, the pawnbroker; his family had money, he was a likable boy. Chōkichi went to the Ikueisha; Shōta, to a fancy public school. The school songs they sang may have been the same, but Shōta always made a face, as if Chōkichi and his friends at the Ikueisha were poor relations.

With his band of admirers—even some grown-ups numbered among them—for the last two years Shōta's plans for the festival had flowered more luxuriantly than the efforts of Chōkichi's gang. There had been no contest, and, if he lost again this year, all his threats—"Who do you think you're dealing with? Chōkichi from the back streets, that's who!"—would no longer garner even enough members for a swimming team at the Benten Ditch. If it were a matter of strength, he knew he would prevail, but everyone was taken in by Shōta's quiet ways and his good grades. It was mortifying—some of his own gang had gone over on the sly to Shōta's side. Tarokichi and Sangorō, for instance.

Now the festival was only two days away. It looked more and more as if Chōkichi would lose again. He was desperate. If he could just see that Shōta got a little egg on his face, it wouldn't matter if he himself lost an eye or a limb. He wouldn't have to suffer defeat any more if he could recruit the likes of Ushi, the son of the rickshawman, and Ben, whose family made hair ribbons, and Yasuke, the toymaker's boy. Ah, and better still: if he could get Nobu on his side—there was a fellow who'd have a good idea or two.

Near dusk on the evening of the eighteenth, hoping for a chance to persuade Nobu, Chōkichi made his cocky way through the bamboo thicket of the temple. Swatting the mosquitoes that swarmed about his face, he stole up to Nobu's room.

"Nobu? You there? I know people say I'm a roughneck, and maybe I am. But it's no wonder, with the way they goad me. Listen, Nobu, I've had enough of them—ever since last year when that jerk from Shōta's gang picked a fight with my little brother and they all came running and jumped on him and threw him around. I mean, what do you think of something like that? Beating up a little kid and breaking his festival lantern! And then that Donkey from the dumpling shop, who's so big and awkward he thinks he can go around acting like a grown-up! He comes and starts insulting me to my brother behind my back. You know what he said? 'Think Chōkichi's so smart, huh? And your father's fire chief? Well, your big brother isn't head of anything. He's the tail end—a pig's tail end!' That's what he said! All this time I'm off in the parade, pulling our float. When I heard about it later, though, I was ready to get even! But my father found out, and *I'm* the one who got in trouble. And you remember the year before that, don't you? I went over to the paper shop, where a bunch of kids from the main street were putting on their slapstick. You know what snide things they said to me? 'Doesn't the back street have its own games? And all the while they're treating Shōta like king. I don't forget these things, Nobu . . . I don't care how much money he has. Who is he, anyway, but the son of a loan shark? I'd be doing the world a favor to get rid of such a creep. This year, no matter how tough I have to be, I'll see to it that Shōta eats his words. That's why, Nobu—come on—for a friend, you've got to help. I know you don't like this kind of rough stuff. But it's to get our honor back! Don't you want to help me smash that snooty Shōta with his stuck-up school songs? You know when they call me a stupid private-schooler, it goes for you too. So come on. Do me this one favor and help us out. Carry one of the lanterns around at the festival. Listen, I'm eating my heart out, this has been bothering me so much. If we lose this time, it'll be the end of me." Chōkichi's broad shoulders trembled with anger.

"But I'm not very strong."

"I don't care whether you're strong or not."

"I don't think I could carry one of the lanterns."

"You don't have to!"

"You'll lose even with me—you don't care?"

"If we lose, we lose. Look, you don't have to do anything. Just so you're on our side. All we have to do is show you off. It'll attract others. Build up our morale. I know I'm not very smart, but you are. So if they start using big words and making fun of us, you can answer right back in Chinese. I feel better already. You're worth the whole lot of them! Thanks, Nobu." It wasn't often you heard Chōkichi speak so softly.

The one the son of a workman, with his boy's belt and his smart straw sandals; the other like a priest in his somber jacket and his purple band—they were the opposite sides of a coin. More often than not, the two boys disagreed. Yet it was true that Nobu's own parents had a soft spot for Chōkichi. Why, the venerable Head Priest and his wife had heard Chōkichi's first cries as a babe outside the temple gate. And, after all, they did both go to the same school. If people made fun of the Ikueisha to Chōkichi, it reflected on Nobu too. It was a shame that Chōkichi wasn't better liked, but he never had been what you'd call appealing—unlike Shōta, who attracted everyone, even the older boys, for his allies. Nobu wasn't showing any prejudice. If Chōkichi lost, the blame would rest squarely on Shōta. When Chōkichi came to him like this, out of a sense of decency Nobu could hardly refuse.

"All right. I'm on your side. But you'd better keep the fighting down . . . If they start things, we won't have any choice. And if that happens, I'll wrap Shōta around my little finger." Nobu's reticence had already been forgotten. He opened his desk drawer and showed Chōkichi the prized Kokaji dagger his father had brought him from Kyōto.

"Say! That'll really cut!" Chōkichi admired.

Look out—careful how you wave that thing.

Undone, her hair would reach her feet. She wore it swept up and pulled into a heavy-looking roll in the "red bear" style—a frightening name for a maiden's hairdo, but the latest fashion even among girls of good family. Her skin was fair and her nose was nicely shaped. Her mouth, a little large perhaps, was firm and not at all unattractive. If you took her features one by one, it is true, they were not the classic components of ideal beauty. And yet she was a winsome girl, exuberant, soft-spoken. Her eyes radiated warmth whenever she looked at you.

"I'd like to see her three years from now!" young men leaving the quarter would remark when they noticed her returning from the morning bath, her towel in hand and her neck a lovely white above her orange kimono of boldly patterned butterflies and birds, her stylish sash wrapped high at the waist and her lacquered slippers more thickly soled than what one usually saw, even around here.

Her name was Midori and she was from the Daikokuya. She was born in Kishū, though, and her words had the slightest southern lilt. It was charming. There were few who did not enjoy her generous, open nature.

For a child, Midori had a handsome pocketbook, thanks to her sister's success in the quarter. The great lady's satellites knew how to purchase good will: "Here Midori, go buy yourself a doll," the manager would say. "It isn't much, honey," one of the attendant girls would offer, "but it'll buy you a ball, anyway." No one took these gifts very seriously, and the income Midori accepted as her due. It was nothing for her to turn round and treat twenty classmates to matching rubber balls. She had been known to delight her friend the woman at the paper store by buying up every last shopworn trifle. The extravagance day after day was certainly beyond the child's age or station. What would become of her? Her parents looked the other way, never a word of caution.

And wasn't it odd, how the owner of her sister's house would spoil her so? She was hardly his adopted child, or even a relation. Yet ever since he had come to their home in the provinces to appraise her older sister, Midori and her parents had found themselves here at the Daikokuya. They had packed up their belongings, along with her sister, to seek their fortunes in the city.

What lay behind it all would be difficult to say, but today her parents were housekeepers for the gentleman. On the side, her mother took in sewing from the women of the district; her father kept the books at a third-rate house. They saw to it that Midori went to school and that she learned her sewing and her music. The rest of the time she was on her own: lolling around her sister's rooms for half the day, playing in the streets the other half. Her head was full of the sounds of samisen and drum, of the twilight reds and purples of the quarter. New to the city, Midori had bristled when the other girls made fun of her, calling her a country girl for wearing a lavender collar with her lined kimono. She had cried for three days then. Not now, though. It was Midori who would tease when someone seemed uncouth—"What kind of dress is that!"—and no one had quite the nimble wit to return her rebukes.

The festival was to be held on the twentieth, and this year they would have to outdo themselves. Midori's help was needed. "All right. Everyone plan something. We'll take a vote. I'll pay for everything," she responded with her usual generosity. "Don't worry about the cost."

The children were quicker than adults to seize an opportunity. The beneficent ruler seldom comes a second time.

"Let's do a show. We can borrow a shop where everyone can watch us."

"No—that's stupid! Let's build a little shrine to carry around. A good one like they have at Kabata's. Even if it's heavy, it won't matter, once we get it going to a nice beat."

"Yatchoi! Yatchoi!" danced a youth already in the mood, his towel twisted into a festive headband.

"What about us?" "You think Midori's going to have any fun just watching while you're all roughhousing?" "Come on, Midori, have them do something else." The girls, it seemed, would prefer to forgo the celebrations for an afternoon of vaudeville.

Shōta's handsome eyes lit up. "Why don't we do a magic lantern show? I have a few pictures at my house. Midori, you can buy the rest. We can use the paper shop. I'll run the lantern, and Sangorō from the back street can be the narrator. What do you say, Midori? Wouldn't that be good?"

"I like it! If Sangorō does the talking, no one will be able to keep from laughing. Too bad we can't put a picture of him in the show."

Everything was decided. Shōta dashed around to get things ready.

By the next day, word of their plans had reached the back street.

The drums, the samisen! Even in a place never wanting for music, the festival is the liveliest time of year. What could rival it but Otori day? Just watch the shrines try to surpass one another in their celebrations.

The back-street and the main-street gangs each had their own matching outfits, Mōka cotton emblazoned with their street names. "But they're not as nice as last year's," some grumbled. Sleeves were tied up with flaxen cords stained yellow from a jasmine dye. The wider the bright ribbons, everyone agreed, the better. Children under fifteen or so weren't satisfied until they had accumulated all the trinkets they could carry—Daruma dolls, owls, dogs of papier-mâché. Some had eight or nine, even eleven, dangling from their yellow armbands. It was a sight to see them, bells of all sizes jingling from their backs as they ran along gamely in their stockinged feet.

Shōta stood apart from the crowd. Today he looked unusually dapper. His red-striped jacket and his dark-blue vest contrasted handsomely with his boyish complexion. He wore a pale blue sash wrapped tightly round the waist. A second look revealed it to be the most expensive crêpe. The emblems on his collar were exceptional enough to draw attention by themselves. In his headband he had tucked a paper flower. Though his well-heeled feet beat time to the rhythm of the drums, Shōta did not join the ranks of any of the street musicians.

Festival eve had passed without incident. Now at dusk on this once-in-a-year holiday, twelve of the main-street gang were gathered at the paper shop. Only Midori, a long time with her evening toilette, had yet to appear. Shōta was getting impatient.

"What's taking her so long?" He paced in and out the front door. "Sangorō, go and get her. You've never been to the Daikokuya, though, have you? Call her from the garden, and she'll hear you. Hurry up."

"All right. I'll leave my lantern here. Shōta, keep an eye on it; someone might take the candle."

"Don't be such a cheapskate! Stop dawdling."

"I'm off." The boy didn't seem to mind being scolded by his juniors.

"There goes the god of lightning," someone said, and the girls all burst out laughing at the way he ran. He was short and beefy, and, with no neck to speak of, his bulging head suggested one of those wooden mallets. Protruding forehead, pug nose, big front teeth—no wonder he was called Bucktooth-Sangorō. He was decidedly dark-skinned, but what one noticed even more was the expression on his face, dimpled and affable and ready for the clown's role. His eyebrows were so oddly placed as to suggest the final outcome of a game of pin-the-tail-on-the-donkey. He was an amusing child, without a mean streak in him.

To those who did not know how poor he was, Sangorō shrugged off his everyday cotton clothes. "Couldn't get a matching kimono made in time."

He was the eldest of six children. Their father contrived to feed them all by clinging to the handles of a rickshaw. True, he worked the prosperous street in front of the quarter, lined with the teahouses. But somehow the wheels of his cart never turned a real profit. Fast as they spun, they only kept the family going hand-to-mouth.

"*Now* that *you're* thirteen. *I'm* counting on you to help out *boy*," Sangorō's father had told him the year before last. He went to work at the printing shop over in Namiki but, in his lackadaisical way, in ten days he had tired of the job. Seldom did he last more than a month anywhere. From November to January he worked part-time making shuttlecocks for the New Year's games. In summer he helped the iceman near the hospital. Thanks to the comical way he had of soliciting customers, the two of them did a brisk business. A born hawker, the iceman said.

Ever since he had pulled a float last year at the Yoshiwara carnival, his disapproving friends had dubbed him "Mannenchō." He was as bad, they said, as the jesters from that lowliest of slums. But everyone knew Sangorō was a buffoon. No one disliked him; this was his one advantage.

The pawnshop Shōta's people ran was a lifeline for Sangorō and his family, whose gratitude toward the Tanakas was no small thing. True, the daily interest rates they were obliged to pay bordered on the exorbitant; yet without the loans they could scarcely have kept going. How, then, could they begrudge the moneylender his due?

"Sangorō," Shōta and the main-street gang were forever urging him, "come over to our street and play." And how could he refuse Shōta, to whose family they were all indebted? On the other hand, he was born and raised in the back streets, he lived on land belonging to Ryūge Temple, Chōkichi's father owned their house. It wouldn't do to turn his back openly on Chōkichi. When in the end he quietly went over to the main street, the accusing looks were hard for him to bear.

Shōta sat down in the paper shop, tired of waiting for Midori, and began to sing the opening lines of "Secret Love."

"Listen to that!" laughed the shopkeeper's wife. "Singing love songs already—we'll have to keep an eye on this one."

Shōta's ears turned red. "Let's go!" he called to the others in a loud voice he hoped would cover his embarrassment. But as he ran out of the shop, he bumped into his grandmother.

"Shōta—why haven't you come home for dinner? I've been calling and calling, but you're so busy playing you don't even listen. You can all play again after dinner. Thanks," she added in a curt word of parting to the shopkeeper's wife.

Shōta had no choice but to follow her home.

Whenever he left, how lonely it seemed. Only one less person than before, and yet even the grown-ups missed Shōta. It was not that he was boisterous or always cracking jokes, like Sangorō. Such friendliness, though—you don't usually find it in a rich boy.

"But did you see the nasty way his grandmother has?" housewives gossiped on the street corner. "She's sixty-four if she's a day. And her hair done up like a young floozy! At least she doesn't wear all that powder any more."

"You ought to hear her purr and coax to get her loans back. Nothing stops her. You watch—the borrower could die, and she'd be at the funeral to collect. She's the kind who'll try to take her money with her when she goes."

"We can't even hold our heads up to her—that's the power of money."

"Don't you wish you had a little of it?"

"They say she even lends to the big houses in the quarter."

What they wouldn't give to know how much the old crone had.

"How sad it is for one who waits alone by the midnight hearth." The love songs do have a way of putting things.

The breeze felt cool on that summer evening. In the bath Midori had washed the heat of the day away, and now she stood before her full-length mirror getting ready. Her mother took charge of repairing the girl's hairdo. A beauty, even if she did say so, the woman thought, inspecting her daughter from every angle. "You still don't have enough powder on your neck." They had chosen for the occasion a silk kimono in a cool, pale blue. Her straw-colored sash was flecked with gold threads and custom-made to fit her tiny waist. It would be some time, though, before they could begin deciding on the proper sandals.

"Isn't she ready yet?" Sangorō was losing his patience. He had circled the garden wall seven times. How much longer could he go on yawning? The mosquitoes around here were a local specialty, no sooner had he brushed them away than they would buzz back again. A bite on the neck, a bite on the forehead. Just as he had had about all he could take, Midori finally appeared.

"Let's go," she said.

He pulled her sleeve without answering her and began to run.

Midori was soon out of breath. She could feel her heart pounding. "Well, if you're in such a hurry about it, go on ahead."

Sangorō arrived at the paper shop just before her. Shōta, it appeared, had gone home for dinner.

"This isn't going to be any fun. We can't start the lantern show without Shōta," Midori complained, turning to the shopkeeper's wife. "Any checkers? Cut-outs? We'll need *something* to keep us busy till he comes."

"Here we are." The girls immediately began to cut out the paper dolls the shop lady handed them.

The boys, with Sangorō in the lead, replayed entertainments from the Yoshi-wara carnival. Their harmony was odd, but they knew the melodies:

> Come see the thriving quarter—
> The lights, the lanterns under every eave,
> The gaiety of all five streets!

In fact, they remembered perfectly the songs and dances of a year, two years before. They didn't miss a beat; they had every gesture down. A crowd gathered at the gate outside to watch the ten of them, carried away by their own side show.

"Is Sangorō there?" called a voice from among the onlookers. "Come here a minute, quick." It was Bunji, the hairdresser's boy.

"Just a second," yelled Sangorō without a care.

No sooner did he run through the doorway than someone punched him in the face. "You double-crosser! This'll teach you! Who do you think I am? Chōkichi! I'll make you sorry you ever made fun of us!"

Sangorō was dumbfounded. He tried to escape, but they grabbed him by the collar.

"Kill him! Shōta too! Don't let the chicken get away. And Donkey from the dumpling shop—don't think you're going to get off so easy!"

The uproar swelled like the rising tide. Paper lanterns came crashing down from the eaves.

"Mind the lamp. You mustn't fight in front of the shop." The woman's yell was loud enough, but who was listening?

There were fourteen or fifteen of them in the attack, streamers round the heads, their oversize lanterns swinging. Blows were struck in all directions, things trampled underfoot. The outrage of it! But Shōta—the one they were after—was nowhere to be found.

"Hide him, will you? Where is he? If you don't tell us, you'll answer for it." They closed in around Sangorō, hitting and kicking, until Midori couldn't stand to watch. She pushed her way to the front, past the restraining hand of the shop-keeper's wife.

"What are you taking it out on him for? If you want to fight with Shōta, fight with Shōta. He didn't run away and he's not hiding. He's not here, that's all. This is our place. Why do you have to go sticking your noses in? You're such a creep, Chōkichi. Why don't you leave Sangorō alone? There—you've knocked him down. Now stop it! If you want to hit someone, hit me. Don't try to hold me back," she turned to the shopkeeper's wife, shouting abuse at Chōkichi all the while she tried to free herself.

"Yeah? You're nothing but a whore, just like your sister," Chōkichi shot back. He stepped around from behind the others and grabbed his muddy sandal. "This is all you're worth." He threw it at Midori.

With a splatter, it struck her square on the forehead. She turned white, but the shopkeeper's wife held her back. "Don't. You'll get hurt."

"Serves you right," Chōkichi gloated. "By the way, guess who's joined our side. Nobu from Ryūge Temple! So try and get even any time you want." He left Sangorō lying in the shop's front door. "You fools! *Weak*lings! Cowards! We'll be waiting for you. Be careful when you walk through the back streets after dark."

Just then he heard the sound of a policeman's boots. Someone had squealed on them. "Come on!" As fast as they could, Ushimatsu, Bunji, and the ten or so others all scattered in different directions, crouching in hiding places among the alleyways until the coast was clear.

"Damn you, Chōkichi! You bastard. Damn you! Damn you, Bunji! Damn you, Ushimatsu! Why don't you just kill me? Come on. Just try and kill me. I'm Sangorō—and maybe it's not so easy! Even if you did kill me, even if I turned

248

into a ghost, I'd haunt you for the rest of your lives. Remember that, Chōkichi!" Sangorō began to sob. Hot tears rolled down his cheeks. He looked as if he must be aching. His sleeves were torn. His back and hips were covered with dirt.

The force of his anger, beyond his power to control, kept the others back. But the shopkeeper's wife rushed over to him. "It's all right," she soothed him with a pat and helped him to his feet. She brushed the gravel from his clothes. "Don't be upset. There were just too many of them, the rest of us weren't much help, not even a grown-up could do anything. It wasn't a fair match—don't be ashamed. It's lucky you weren't hurt, but you won't be safe going home alone. I'll feel much better if the policeman takes you; it's a good thing he's come. Officer, let me tell you what happened."

As she finished her account, the policeman reached for the boy's hand in his professional way. "I'll take you home."

"No. I'm all right. I can go by myself." He seemed to cringe with shame.

"There's nothing to be afraid of. I'll just take you as far as your house. Don't worry." He smiled at Sangorō and patted him on the head.

But Sangorō shrank back farther. "If my father hears about the fight, I'll get in terrible trouble. Chōkichi's father owns our house."

"How about if I take you as far as the front gate? I won't say anything to get you into trouble." He managed to coax the downcast Sangorō and led him off toward home.

The others felt relieved. But as they watched the two depart, at the corner leading to the back streets, for some reason Sangorō shook loose and broke into a run.

It was as rare as snow falling from a summer sky, but today Midori couldn't brook the thought of school. She wouldn't eat her breakfast. Should they order something special? It couldn't be a cold, she had no fever. Too much excitement yesterday, probably. "Why don't you stay home?" her mother suggested. "I'll go to the shrine for you."

Midori wouldn't hear of it. It was *her* vow to Tarō-sama for her sister's success. "I'll just go and come right back. Give me some money for the offering."

Off she went to the shrine among the paddy fields. She rang the bell, shaped like the great mouth of a crocodile, and clasped her hands in supplication. And what were they for, these prayers of hers? She walked through the fields with her head downcast, to and from the shrine.

Shōta saw her from a distance and called out as he ran toward her. He tugged at her sleeve, "Midori, I'm sorry about last night."

"That's all right. It wasn't your fault."

"But they were after me. If Grandmother hadn't come, I wouldn't have left. And then they wouldn't have beaten up Sangorō the way they did. I went to see him this morning. He was crying and furious. I got angry just listening to him talk about it. Chōkichi threw his sandal at you, didn't he? Damn him, anyway! There are limits to what even he can get away with. But I hope you're not mad at me, Midori. I didn't run away from him. I gulped my food down as fast as I could and was just on my way back when Grandmother said I had to watch the house while she went for her bath. That's when all the commotion must have started. Honest, I didn't know anything about it." He apologized as if the crime were his, not Chōkichi's. "Does it hurt?" Shōta examined Midori's forehead.

"Well, it's nothing that will leave a scar," Midori laughed. "But listen, Shōta, you mustn't tell anyone. If Mother ever found out, I'd get a real scolding. My parents never lay a hand on me. If they hear a dolt like Chōkichi smeared mud on my face with his filthy sandal—." She looked away.

"Please forgive me. It's all my fault. Please. Come on, cheer up. I won't be able to stand it if you're mad at me." Before they knew it, they had reached the back gate of Shōta's house. "Do you want to come in? No one's home. Grandmother's gone to collect the interest. It's lonely by myself. Come on, I'll show you those prints I told you about the other day. There are all kinds of them." Shōta wouldn't let go of her sleeve until Midori had agreed.

Inside the dilapidated gate was a small garden. Dwarf trees were lined up in their pots and from the eaves hung a tiny trellis of fern with a windbell, Shōta's memento from the holiday market. But who would have picked it for the wealthiest house in the neighborhood? Here alone by themselves lived an old woman and a boy. No one had ever broken in: there were cold, metal locks everywhere, and the neighboring tenements kept an eye on the place.

Shōta went in first and found a spot where the breeze blew. "Over here," he called to Midori, handing her a fan. For a thirteen-year-old, he was rather too sophisticated. He took out one color print after another. They had been in his family for generations, and he smiled when Midori admired them. "Shall I show you a battledore? It was my mother's. She got it when she worked for a rich man. Isn't it funny? It's so big. And look how different people's faces were in those days. I wish she were still alive . . . My mother died when I was three, and my father went back to his own family's place in the country. So I've been here with Grandmother ever since. You're lucky, Midori."

"Look out. You'll get the pictures wet. Boys aren't supposed to cry."

"I guess I'm a sissy. Sometimes I get to thinking about things . . . It's all right now, but in the winter, when the moon is out and I have to make the rounds in Tamachi collecting the interest, sometimes when I walk along the ditch, I sit down on the bank and cry. Not from the cold. I don't know why . . . I just think about things. I've been doing the collecting ever since year before last. Grandmother's getting old. It's not safe for her at night. And her eyes aren't so good any more. She can't see what she's doing when she has to put her seal on the receipts. We've had a lot of different men working for us. But Grandmother says they all take us for fools—when it's only an old lady and a boy they have to answer to. She's just waiting for the day when I'm a little older and we can open the pawnshop again. We'll put the family sign out in front, even if things aren't as good as they used to be. Oh, I know people say Grandmother's stingy. But she's only careful about things for my sake. It really bothers me, to hear them talk that way. I guess the people I collect from over in Tōrishinmachi are pretty bad off, all right. I suppose it's no wonder they say things about her. When I think about it, though, sometimes I just can't help it if I cry. I guess I am a weakling. This morning when I went to see Sangorō, he was sore all over, but he still went right on working so his father wouldn't find out about last night. I didn't know what to say. A boy looks pretty silly when he cries, doesn't he? That's why the back street makes fun of Sangorō." He seemed ashamed at his own unmanliness.

Occasionally their eyes would meet.

"You looked so handsome yesterday, Shōta. It made me wish I were a boy. You were the best dressed of them all."

"*I* looked good! *You* were beautiful! Everybody said you were prettier than any of the girls in the quarter, even your sister Ōmaki. Boy, I'd be proud if you were my sister! I'd hold my head up with a girl like you alongside me. But I don't have any brothers or sisters. Hey, Midori, what do you say we have our picture taken? I'll wear what I did yesterday and you can put on one of your best striped kimonos, and we'll have Katō in Suidōjiri take our picture! Won't Nobu be jealous! He'll turn white, he'll be so envious—a milquetoast like him wouldn't know how to turn red. Or maybe he'll just laugh at us. Who cares? If Katō takes a big one, he might use our picture in the window! What's the matter? Don't you like the idea? You don't look very excited." The boy's impatience was disarming.

"What if I look funny? You might not like me any more." Her laugh had a beautiful ring, her spirits had obviously improved.

The cool of the morning had given way to the summer sun. It was time for Midori to be going: "Shōta, why don't you come over this evening? We can float candles on the pond and chase the fish. It'll be easy now that the bridge is fixed."

Shōta beamed as he saw her out. What a beauty Midori was.

Nobu of Ryūge Temple and Midori of the Daikokuya both went to school at the Ikueisha. It had all started at the end of last April, at the spring athletic meet in Mizunoya-no-hara. The cherries had fallen and the wisteria was already in bloom in the shade of the new green leaves. They played their games of tug-of-war and catch and jump rope with such ardor that no one seemed to notice the sun going down. But what had come over Nobu? He had lost his usual composure. He stumbled over the root of a pine by the pond and landed hands-first in the red mud.

Midori, who happened to be going by, took one look at his dirty jacket and proffered her crimson handkerchief. "Here, you can wipe it off with this."

There were those, however, who were jealous of this attention from Midori. "For a priest's son, he sure knows how to flirt. Look at him smile when he thanks her! What's he going to do—take her for his wife? If she goes to live at the temple, then she really will be Miss Daikoku: from Midori of the Daikokuya to Daikoku, goddess of the kitchen! That ought to suit a priest."

Nobu couldn't stomach all the talk. He had never been one to enjoy idle gossip and had always shunned tales about others. How, then, could he tolerate it when he found himself the target of the rumors? He began to dread hearing Midori's name. He was snappish whenever anyone mentioned field day. "You're not going to bring that up again, are you?" It never failed to put him in a bad mood. Yet what reason was there, really, for this loss of temper? He knew he would do better feigning indifference. A stoic face, wait it out, he told himself. He could silence his tormentors with a word or two, but the embarrassment was still there. A cold sweat followed every confrontation.

At first, Midori failed to notice any change. On her way home from school one day she called out with her usual friendliness. Nobu trailed behind amid a cluster of people. The blossoms at the roadside had caught her eye, and she waited for him to catch up. "See the pretty flowers, Nobu? I can't reach them. You're tall enough—won't you pick me some?"

She had singled him out from his younger companions. There was no escaping. He cringed at what he knew the others would be saying. Reaching for the nearest branch, without even choosing, he picked the first flower he saw, a token effort. He flung it at her and was gone.

"Well, if that's how he's going to be! Unsociable thing!"

After several of these incidents, it dawned on Midori: Nobu was being mean to her deliberately. He was never rude to any of the others, only her. When she approached, he fled. If she spoke to him, he became angry. He was sullen and self-conscious. Midori had no idea how to please him, and in the end she gave up trying. Let him be perverse; he was no friend of hers. See if she'd speak to him after he'd cut her to the quick. "Hello's" in the street were a thing of the past. It would take important business indeed before she would deign to talk to him. A great river now stretched between them that all boats were forbidden to cross. Each of them walked alone on separate banks of the stream.

From the day after the festival, Midori came to school no more. She could wash the mud from her face, but the shame could not be scrubbed away so easily.

They sat together side by side at school—Chōkichi's gang and the main-street gang—and one might have expected that they could get along. But there had always been a sharp division.

It was the act of a coward to attack a weak, defenseless girl. Everyone knew Chōkichi was as violent and as stupid as they come. But if he hadn't had Nobu backing him, he could never have behaved so brazenly. And that Nobu! In front of others he pretended to be gentle and wise, but a look behind the scenes would reveal that *he* was the one pulling all the strings. Midori didn't care if he was ahead of her in school, or how good his grades were. So what if he was the young master of Ryūge Temple! She, after all, was Midori of the Daikokuya, and not beholden to him in the slightest. She had never borrowed a single sheet of paper. So who were they to call her a tramp, or those other names Chōkichi had used? She wasn't about to be impressed just because Ryūge Temple had a prominent parishioner or two.

What about the patrons her sister Ōmaki had? The banker Kawa, a steady customer for three years now; Yone, from the stock exchange; and that short one, the member of parliament—why, he'd been all set to buy her sister's contract and marry her, till Ōmaki decided she could do without him. And he was somebody! Just ask the lady who ran Ōmaki's house. Go ahead and ask, if you thought she was making it up. Where would the Daikokuya be without her sister? Why do you think even the owner of the house was never curt with Midori and her parents? Just take that porcelain statue of Daikoku, the one he kept in the alcove. Once when she was playing shuttlecock, she knocked over a vase accidentally and smashed the master's favorite statue to smithereens. He was sitting right in the next room drinking. And all he said was, "Midori, you're turning into a little tomboy." Not one word of reproach. Had it been anyone else, you can be sure, he wouldn't have stopped there. The maids were green with envy. No question about it, the child's privileges derived from her sister's position. Midori knew it, too. Her parents were mere caretakers for the master's house, but her sister was Ōmaki of the Daikokuya. She didn't have to take insults from the likes of Chōkichi. And too bad for him if the little priest wanted to be mean to her. Midori had had enough of school. She was born stubborn and she was not about to suffer anyone's contempt. That day she broke her pencils and threw away her ink; she would spend her time playing with her real friends. She wasn't going to need her abacus or her books.

In the evening they rush into the quarter, at dawn they leave less cheerfully. It's a lonely ride home, with only dreams of the night before to keep a man company. Getaways are under cover. A hat pulled low, a towel around the face. More than one of these gentlemen would rather that you didn't look. To watch will only make you feel uneasy. That smirk of theirs—not half-pleased with themselves as the sting of their lady's farewell slap sinks in. After all, she wouldn't want him to forget her. Careful when you get to Sakamoto. The vegetable carts come barreling back from the early morning market. Watch out when you hit Crazy Street. Until Mishima Shrine, you won't be safe from those who wander home all gaga and enraptured from the night before. Their faces never look so resolute the morning after. It's rude to say it, but don't they all suggest love's fools? The fishwives seldom hesitate to sum them up. Look, there goes a man with money. But that one over there, he couldn't have a penny to his name.

One need hardly cite the Chinese "Song of Everlasting Sorrow" and the heights to which Yang's daughter rose to see that there are times when daughters are more valuable than sons. Many a princess comes into the world among the shanties of the back street. Today she calls herself "Snow" in one of those swank geisha houses over in Tsukiji, a celebrated beauty whose accomplishments in dance have entertained a nobleman or two. But yesterday she was a mere delinquent and she earned her spending money making playing cards, you know. "What kind of tree does rice grow on?" she asks, as if she'd grown up in the lap of luxury. Around here, of course, she is not the celebrity she used to be. Once they leave, they're soon forgotten. Already she has been eclipsed by the dyemaker's second daughter, Kokichi, a home-grown flower of a girl, whose name you'll hear throughout the park. The lanterns are up these days at The New Ivy, in Senzoku, where that one works.

Night and day, it's the daughters that you hear of. A boy is about as useful as a mutt sniffing round the rubbish. Every shopkeeper's son is a wastrel. At seventeen, the age of insolence, the young men band together. Before they go completely gallant—you don't see any flutes tucked into sashes yet—they join up with a leader whose alias is invariably a solemn, grandiose affair. They deck themselves out with matching scarves and matching paper lanterns. It won't be long now before they learn to gamble and to window-shop the quarter. Bantering with the courtesans will begin to come more easily. Even with the serious ones, the family business is only something for the day. Back from the evening bath they come in kimonos of a rakish cut, sandals dragging. "Hey, did you see the new one? At What's-Its-Name? She looks like the girl at the sewing shop, over in Kanasugi. But, with that funny little nose of hers, she's even uglier." It's the only thing remotely on their minds. They bum tobacco, a piece of tissue at every house. The pats and pinches they exchange with each beauty along the way: *these* are the things that bring a lifetime of renown. Even the sons of perfectly upstanding families decide to style themselves as local toughs. They are forever picking fights around the Gate.

Ah, the power of women. One need hardly say more. In the quarter, prosperity makes no distinctions between the autumn and the spring. Escort lanterns are not in vogue these days, and still the men are carried away. All it takes is the echo of a pair of sandals. Here she comes! The little girl from the teahouse who will take them to their ladies. Clip-clop, clip-clop. The sound mingles with the music of the theater. They hear it and they stream into the quarter. If you ask them what they're after, it's a flowing robe, a scarlet collar, a baroque coiffure, a pair of sparkling eyes and lips with painted smiles. The beauties may in fact have little of the beautiful about them. The minute they are courtesans, they climb the pedestal. Those of you from other parts may find it all a little hard to understand.

Needless to say, Midori, who spent her days and nights immersed in such a world, soon took on the color of the quarter. In her eyes, men were not such fearsome things. And her sister's calling was nothing to disparage. When Ōmaki was on the verge of leaving for the city, how Midori had cried. Not in her wildest dreams had she hoped to accompany her sister. And now here they were. Who wouldn't envy a sister like Ōmaki? What with her recent success, it was nothing for her to repay all the debts she had ever owed her parents. Midori had no notion of what price Ōmaki might have paid to reign supreme in her profession. To her it was all a game. She knew about the charms and tricks the girls would use. Simpering to summon men they longed for, like mice grabbing cheese. Tapping on the lattice when they made a wish. She knew the secret signals they would use to give their guests a parting pat. She had mastered the special language of the quarter, and she didn't feel the least embarrassed when she used it.

It was all a little sad. She was fourteen. When she caressed her dolls, she could have been a prince's child. But for her, all lessons in manners and morals and the wifely arts were topics to be left at school. What never ceased to capture her attention were the rumors of her sister's suitors—who was in and who was out of favor—the costumes of the serving girls, the bedding gifts that men would lavish on Ōmaki, the teahouse tips for the introduction of a patron. What was bright and colorful was good, and what was not was bad. The child was still too young to exercise discretion. She was always taken with the flower just before her eyes. A headstrong girl by nature, Midori indulged herself by fluttering about in a world that she had fashioned from the clouds.

Crazy Street, Sleepy Street. The half-witted, groggy gentlemen all pass this way as they head home. At the gate to this village of late risers, the sweepers and the sprinklers have already cleaned the streets. But look down main street. They have roosted for the night among the slums of Mannenchō or Yamabushichō, or perhaps Shintanimachi, and now here they come: what for want of any other word one might as well call "entertainers." The singing candy man. The two-bit player. The puppeteers. The jugglers and the acrobats. The dancers with their parasols. The clowns who do the lion dance. Their dress is as varied as their arts, a gauze of silk, a sash of satin. The clowns prefer the cotton prints from Satsuma, with black bands round the waist. Men, pretty women, troupes of five, seven, even ten, and a lonely old man, all skin and bones, who totters as he clutches his battered samisen. And, look, there's a little girl of five or so they've got to do the Kinokuni dance. Over there, with the red ribbons on her sleeves. But none of them stop here. They know where the business is, and they hurry to the quarter. The guest who has lingered at the teahouse, the beauty in a melancholy mood— these are the ones it pays to entertain. The profits are too good to give it up, or to waste time with benefit performances along the way. Not even the most tattered and suspicious-looking beggar would bother to loiter around here.

A lady minstrel passed before the paper shop. Her hat all but concealed her striking face, yet she sang and played with the bearing of a star. "It's a shame we never get to hear the end of her song," the shopkeeper's wife complained. Midori, bright from her morning bath, was lounging on the shop's front step, watching the parade pass by. She pushed her hair up with her boxwood comb. "Wait here. I'll bring her back!"

The child never mentioned slipping something in the lady's sleeve to coax her to perform but, sure enough, back in tow she came to sing the requested song of thwarted love. "Thank you very much for your patronage," she concluded in her honeyed tone, and even as it echoed they knew that they were not about to hear its likes again.

"To think—a mere child could have arranged it!" bystanders marveled, more impressed with Midori than with the minstrel.

"Wouldn't it be fun to have them all perform?" Midori whispered to Shōta. "The samisen and the flute and the drums! The singers and the dancers! Everything we never get more than just a glimpse of!"

Even for Midori, the proposal was ambitious. "Don't overdo it, girl," Shōta muttered.

"Thus have I heard it spoken," the reverend priest intoned the sutra. As the holy words were carried from the temple by the soft breeze through the pines, they should have blown away all dust within the heart.

But smoke rose from fish broiling in the kitchen. In the cemetery diapers had been seen drying over tombstones. Nothing wrong here in the eyes of the Order, perhaps; those who fancied their clerics above worldly desires, though, found the doings at Ryūge Temple rather too earthly for their tastes.

Here the fortunes of the head priest were as handsome as his stomach. Both had rounded out nicely through the years. The man's glow of well-being beggared description: not the sunny pink of the cherries, not the deep pink of the peach; from the top of his freshly shaven pate to the bottom of his neck, he shone like burnished copper. When he whooped with laughter—bushy, salt-and-pepper eyebrows floating heavenward—the noise of the old man's excess could have toppled Buddha from the altar.

The priest's young wife (she was only in her forties) was not an unattractive woman. Her skin was fair, and she wore her thinning hair in a small, modest bun.

She was always cordial when people came to pray. Even the florist's wife outside the temple gate held her tongue where the reverend's wife was concerned—the fruit, you may be sure, of the temple lady's kindliness: a hand-me-down here, a leftover there. At one time, she herself had been among the parishioners. But her husband died young, and, having nowhere to turn, she came to do the sewing at the temple. In exchange for meals, she took over the washing and the cooking. Before long she was out in the graveyard, sweeping away with the best of the groundsmen. The priest was quick to offer his compassion, and quicker still to calculate the advantages. The woman knew full well that the difference in their ages, some twenty years, might make the arrangement appear a bit unseemly. But she had nowhere else to go, and she came to consider the temple a good place to live out her days and to meet her end. She learned not to lose too much sleep over prying neighbors.

Some in the congregation found the situation shocking. Soon enough, however, they began to acknowledge that in her heart the woman was a good person, and they ceased to censure her. While she was carrying their first child, Ohana, the priest finally made an honest woman of her. A retired oil dealer over in Saka-moto, one of the parishioners who went in for such things, acted as the go-between—if you want to call it that.

Nobu was their second child. Someday he would do his father proud, but at the moment he was a taciturn, moody boy who preferred to pass the day alone in his room. Ohana, on the other hand, was quite the opposite, a lovely girl with fine skin and a soft, plump little chin. To call her a beauty would be going too far, perhaps, but since adolescence she had had her share of admirers. It seemed a shame to waste such a girl, for she might have been a geisha. Who knows? There may be worlds where even Buddha enjoys the music of the samisen. In this world, at any rate, there was the matter of what others said, and talk they would if the daughter of a temple became an entertainer with her skirt hitched up. What the priest did instead was to establish Ohana in a little tea shop in Tamachi. He put her behind the counter, where she could vend her charm. Young men with no idea in their heads how tea was weighed and measured began to gather at the shop. Seldom was Ohana's empty before midnight.

But his holiness was the busy one. Loans to collect, the shop to oversee, funerals to arrange, not to mention all the sermons every month. When he wasn't flipping through accounts, he was going through the sutras. If things didn't let up, he'd wear himself out, he would sigh as he dragged his flowered cushion onto the veranda, where he fanned himself, half-naked, and enjoyed his nightly hooch. He was a fish-eater, and Nobu was the one he sent over to the main street for the broiled eels that he liked. "The big oily ones, if you please." It galled Nobu. His eyes never left his feet as he trudged over to the Musashiya. If he heard voices at the paper shop across the street, he would keep on going. Then, when the coast was clear, he'd dart into the eel shop. The shame he felt! He would never eat the smelly things.

The reverend was nothing if not practical. There were some who might call him greedy, but that never bothered him a whit. He was neither a timid soul nor an idler: give him a spare moment and he'd set about fashioning kumade charms. On Otori day he would have his wife out peddling them. Whatever doubts she may have had about the venture, they were short-lived once his holiness started to bemoan the killing everybody else made, rank amateurs up and down the street. He soon persuaded his reluctant wife, set up a booth not a stone's throw from the temple gate, and installed her there to sell his charms and good-luck hairpins. She tied her hair back with a headband, just like the vendors and all the young men. In the daytime, she knew enough to stay out of sight and mingle with the crowd, leaving the florist's wife to manage things. But when the sun went down—who would have guessed it?—the woman had a field day. At dusk she took over for herself, quite forgetting what a spectacle she made with her sudden itch for profit. "Everything marked down! Prices slashed!" she barked after a customer who backed away. Buffeted and dizzy from the throngs, the victim soon lost his powers of appraisal. They had fled along with memory: two days earlier he had come to this very temple as a pilgrim. "Three for only seventy-five sen." But her price left room to negotiate. "How about five for seventy-three?" "Sold!"

There were, of course, all kinds of sharp practices. Even if no one from the congregation heard, Nobu wondered, what would the neighbors think? And his friends? He could just hear them. Ryūge Temple is selling hairpins now. Nobu's mother is out huckstering like a lunatic. Really, didn't they think they ought to stop?

The reverend priest would hear nothing of it. "Knock it off. You don't know what you're talking about." The mere idea sent the man into paroxysms.

Prayers in the morning, accounts at night. His father's face beamed whenever his fingers touched the abacus. It was enough to turn the boy's stomach. Why on earth had the man become a priest?

There was nothing in his upbringing to make Nobu such a gloomy child. He had the same parents as Ohana. They were part of the same cozy, self-contained family. Yet he was the quiet one. Even when he did speak, his opinions were never taken seriously. His father's schemes, his mother's conduct, his sister's education—to Nobu everything they did was a travesty. He had resigned himself to knowing that they would never listen. How unfair it was. His friends found him contrary and perverse, but in fact he was a weakling. If anyone maligned him in the slightest, he would run for the shelter of his room. He was a coward utterly lacking in the courage to defend himself. At school they called him a brain; his family's station was not lowly. No one knew how weak he really was. More than one of his friends considered Nobu something of a cold fish.

The night of the festival Nobu was sent on an errand to his sister's tea shop in Tamachi, and he was late coming home. Not until the next morning did he learn of the fight at the paper shop. When Ushimatsu and Bunji and the others gave him the details, the full impact of Chōkichi's violent ways startled him anew. What was done was done—but in name he was included in the violence, and it rankled. Now people would be blaming him for the trouble.

It was three days before Chōkichi had the nerve to face Nobu. For once he must have felt a little sheepish about the damage he had done. He did not look forward to Nobu's scolding. "I know you're probably angry," he ventured, having waited for the storm to pass. "I couldn't help it, though. Everything got out of hand. I hadn't meant it to happen. You won't hold it against me, will you, Nobu? How were we to know that you'd be gone and Shōta would fly the coop? It's not as though I planned to beat up Sangorō and pick a fight with that tramp Midori. Things just happened. You don't run away once the lanterns start swinging! All we wanted was to show a little muscle, show 'em who's boss. It's my fault, I know. I should have listened to you. But come on Nobu, if you get mad now, how's it going to look? After I've gone around telling everybody you're on *our* side. You can't leave us in the lurch. Okay, so you don't approve of this one thing. You be the leader, and next time we won't botch things up." Gone was the usual swagger.

Nobu couldn't turn his back on Chōkichi. "All right," he sighed. "But listen— bully the weak ones, and we'll be the ones in disgrace. We're not going to gain anything fighting Sangorō and Midori. If Shōta and his flunkies want to stir up trouble, we can cross that bridge when we come to it. But let's not egg them on." Chōkichi had to promise: no more fights. For a rebuke, it was rather mild.

The innocent one was Sangorō. They had kicked and beaten him to their hearts' content, and he still ached two, three days afterward. He couldn't stand up, he couldn't sit down. Every evening when his father picked up the empty rickshaw and headed for the teahouses, someone would ask him what was wrong with the boy. "Say, your Sangorō looks a little peaked these days," the caterer remarked, almost accusingly. "Somebody give him a pounding?"

Groveling Tetsu they called his father, head always lowered before his betters. It didn't matter who—the landlord or someone with money or the owner of one of the houses in the quarter, where Tetsu pulled his cart—any of them could make the most impossible demands, and the rickshawman would acquiesce. "Indeed, of course, how right you are." Small wonder, then, what his reaction was to the incident with Chōkichi. "He's the landlord's son, isn't he? I don't care if you were right. I won't have you getting into scraps with him. Now go apolo- gize. You ought to know better!" There was no avoiding it. His father made sure that he got down on his knees in front of Chōkichi.

Within a week Sangorō's wounds healed and his temper cooled. He was ready to forget what he'd been angry about. For the price of a carriage ride, he was baby-sitting again for Chōkichi's little brother, walking round with the child on his back and lulling it to sleep with nursery rhymes. Sangorō was sixteen, that age when boys get cocky, but the lumpish figure he cut failed to trouble him. He wandered over to the main street, unconcerned as always. "Hey, Sangorō. Have you forgotten you're a boy?" Midori and Shōta were great ones when it came to teasing. "Some sight you make, with that baby on your back!" It didn't matter, they were still his friends.

In spring the cherry trees blossom in profusion. In summer the lanterns twinkle in memory of the late Tamagiku. In autumn the festival streets overflow with rick- shaws. Count them: seventy-five down the road within the space of ten minutes. Then the autumn holidays are over. Here and there a red dragonfly bobs above the rice fields. Before long, quail will be calling out along the moat. Mornings and evenings, the breeze blows cold. At the sundries shop, pocket warmers now take the place of mosquito incense. It's sad, somehow, that faint sound of the mortar grinding flour at Tamura's, over by the bridge. The clock at Kadoebi's has a melancholy ring. Fires glow through all four seasons from the direction of

Nippori. It's in autumn that one begins to notice them. Smoke rises each time one more soul embarks on the journey to the other shore.

Deftly, a geisha plays on the samisen. The refrain reaches the path along the bank behind the teahouses. A passerby looks up and listens. Not much of a song, really, but moving all the same. "Together we shall spend our night of love." Women who have done time in the quarter will tell you—it's the men who begin visiting in autumn who prove to be the truly faithful ones.

Talk, talk: in this neighborhood, there is always grist for gossip. The details are tedious, but the stories make the rounds. A blind masseuse, she was only twenty, killed herself. With a handicap like hers, love was out of the question. Well she couldn't stand it any more. Drowned herself in Mizunoya Pond. Then there are the incidents too commonplace to rate a rumor. Missing persons: Kichigorō, the greengrocer, and Takichi, the carpenter. How come? "They picked them up for this," a fellow whispers, and pantomimes a gambler dealing out the cards.

A moment ago there were children there, down the street. "Ring-a-ring-a-roses, pocket full of posies." Suddenly it's quiet now, before you notice. Only the sound of rickshaws, loud as ever.

It was a lonely night. Just when it seemed the autumn rains would go on and on falling softly, with a roar a downpour came. At the paper shop they were not expecting anyone. The shopkeeper's wife had closed up for the evening. Inside, playing marbles, were Shōta and Midori, as usual, and two or three of the younger ones. All at once, Midori heard something: "Is that a customer? I hear footsteps."

"I don't hear anything," Shōta said. He stopped counting out the marbles.

"Maybe someone wants to play."

Who could it be? They heard him come as far as the gate, but after that, not a word, not a sound.

"Boo!" Shōta opened the door and stuck his head out. "Hey, who's there?" He could just make out the back of someone walking along beneath the eaves two or three houses up ahead. "Who is it? Do you want to come in?" He had slipped Midori's sandals on and was about to run after him, in spite of the rain. "Oh, it's him." Shōta cupped his hand above his head, mimicking a bald monk. "No use—we can call him all we want, he won't come."

"Nobu?" Midori asked. "That old priest! I'll bet he came to buy a writing brush and scurried off the minute he heard us. Nasty, stupid, toothless, old-maid Nobu! Just let him come in. I'll tell him what I think. Too bad he ran away. Let me have the sandals. I want a look." This time Midori poked her head out. The rain dripped down from the eaves onto her forehead. It gave her a chill. She pulled back, staring at the shadowy figure as he made his way around the puddles. He was four or five houses away by now, and he seemed to cower in the gaslight. His paper umbrella hugged his shoulders. She looked and looked.

Shōta tapped her on the shoulder. "Midori, what is it?"

"Nothing," she said absent-mindedly, returning to the game. "I hate that little altar boy! He can't even conduct his fights in public. He makes that pious, old-maid face of his and goes sneaking round corners. Isn't he awful? My mother says people who are straightforward are the good ones. She's right, don't you think, Shōta? It's a sure thing Nobu has an evil heart, the way he lurks around."

"But at least he knows what's what. Not like Chōkichi, there's a real moron. The boy's a total ignoramus," Shōta said knowingly.

"Cut it out. You and your big words." Midori laughed and pinched him on the cheek. "Such a serious face! Since when are you so grown up?"

Shōta was not amused. "For your information, it won't be long before I *am* grown up. I'll wear a topcoat with square-cut shoulders like the shopkeeper at Kabata's, and the gold watch Grandmother's put away for me. I'll wear a ring. I'll smoke cigarettes. And for shoes—you're not going to see me in any clogs. Oh, no. I'll wear leather sandals, the good kind, with triple-layered heels and fancy satin straps. Won't I look sharp!"

"You in triple heels and a square-cut overcoat?" Midori couldn't help snickering. "Mm, sure, if you want to look like a walking medicine bottle."

"Oh, quiet. You don't think I've stopped growing, do you? I won't be this short forever."

"Seeing is believing. You know, Shōta," Midori said, pointing a sarcastic finger at the rafters, "even the mice laugh when you keep making these promises." Everyone, the shopkeeper's wife included, shook with laughter.

His eyes spun; Shōta was completely serious. "Midori makes a joke of everything. But everyone grows up, you know. Why is what I say so funny? The day will come when I go walking with my pretty wife. I always like things to be pretty. If I had to marry someone like that pock-marked Ofuku at the cracker shop, or the girl at the firewood store with the bulging forehead—no thank you. I'd send her home. No pockmarks for me!"

"How good of you to come, then," the shop wife laughed. "Haven't you noticed my spots?"

"Oh, but you're old. I'm talking about brides. Once you're old, it doesn't matter."

"I shouldn't have said anything," the woman sighed. "Well, let's see now. There's Oroku at the flower shop. She has a pretty face. And Kii at the fruit stand. And who else? Who else, I wonder? Why, the prettiest one is sitting right next to you. Shōta, who will it be? Oroku with those eyes of hers? Kii and her lovely voice? Tell us who."

"What are you talking about? Oroku, Kii—what's so good about them?" Shōta's face turned scarlet, and he backed away from the light, into a corner.

"Does that mean it's Midori, then?"

"How do I know?" He looked away, tapping out a song against the wall. "The water wheel goes round and round."

Midori and the rest had begun another game of marbles. *Her* face was not flushed in the slightest.

There would have been no problem if he hadn't taken the short cut. But every time Nobu went off to Tamachi he took the path along the ditch. And every time he saw it: the lattice gate, the stone lantern, the thatched fence. The summer bamboo blinds were rolled up now along the veranda. He couldn't help remembering things. Behind the glass windows, her mother would be there, like some latter-day widow of Azechi at her rosary; and she would be there too, straight from the ancient tales, a young Murasaki with her hair bobbed. This was the house of the man who owned the Daikokuya.

Yesterday and today the autumn rains had continued. The winter slip Ohana had requested was ready, and Nobu's mother was anxious for her to have it. She didn't like to ask in such weather, but would he mind taking it to the shop in Tamachi on his way to school? The poor girl was waiting for the package. Diffident Nobu could never say no. He took the bundle under his arm, stepped into his clogs, and started out, clinging to his umbrella as the rain lapped at his feet.

He followed the ditch around the quarter, the same path he always took, but today luck was not with him. Just in front of the Daikokuya, the wind came up. He had to tug to keep his umbrella from flying off. He braced his legs against the wind, when the strap on one of his clogs tore clean away. Now what was he to do?

It was almost enough to make him swear. He had no choice but to try repairing the clog himself. He propped his umbrella against the gate and sought shelter underneath its eaves. Yet how was a fledgling cleric to accomplish this sort of handiwork? He was flustered, and no matter how hard he tried, he couldn't fix it. He grew more and more irritated. From his sleeve he took out the draft of his school composition and tore it up, twisting the strips of paper in hopes of somehow fashioning a new strap. But the confounded storm grew worse again, and his umbrella began to roll away in the wind. This was more than he could tolerate! He reached out to grab the umbrella—but it was just his luck—his sister's package fell from his lap into the mud. There, now he had mud on his sleeve, too.

A pathetic sight he made, without an umbrella and stranded barefoot in the downpour. From the window, Midori saw the sad figure beyond the gate. "Look, someone's broken his sandal. Mother, can I give him something to fix it with?" She found a piece of Yūzen crêpe in the sewing drawer and hurried into her clogs. Grabbing an umbrella from the veranda, she dashed out across the stepping stones toward the front gate.

Then she saw who it was. The blood rushed to Midori's head. Her heart pounded as if she had encountered a dreaded fate. She turned to see, was anyone watching? Trembling, she inched her way toward the gate. At that instant Nobu, too, looked around. He was speechless, he felt cold sweat begin to bead. He wanted to kick off the other sandal and run away.

Had Midori been herself, she would have seized on Nobu's predicament to tell him what she thought. She would have sneered at his cowardice and heaped upon him every bit of abuse that he deserved. Didn't he think he owed her an apology? Bossing everyone around from backstage, ruining all the fun at the festival, just because he was angry at Shōta. And letting them beat up helpless Sangorō! He was the one who had incited Chōkichi to call her those names. And what was wrong with being a courtesan, anyway, even if she were one? She didn't owe him anything. With her parents and her sister and the man from the Daikokuya—what did she need to ask favors of a broken-down priest for? He had better stop calling her names. Something to say, was there? Then he could come out in the open, like a man. Any time, any time. She'd meet him. What did he have to say to that? She would have grabbed him by the sleeve and given him a piece of her mind, all right. Nobu would not have had a prayer.

But instead she cringed in the shadows of the gate. She didn't move, her heart throbbed. This was not the old Midori.

Whenever he came near the Daikokuya, timorous Nobu hurried past without so much as looking left or right. But today, the unlucky rain, the unlucky wind, and, to make matters worse, the broken sandal strap! There was nothing for it but to stop and make a new one. He was upset enough already, and then he heard the sound of steps on the flagstones—he felt as if ice water had been poured down his back. Even without looking, he knew who it would be. He shivered and his face changed color. He turned away and pretended to be hard at work. But he was panic-stricken. It didn't look as if the clog would ever be of use again.

From the garden, Midori peered at him. How clumsy he was; he could never do anything right. Who ever heard of trying to make a strap out of anything as flimsy as a piece of paper—or straw, is that what he was using? Old ladies, maybe. It would never hold. Oh, and didn't he know he was getting mud all over the bottom of his jacket? There went the umbrella. Why didn't he close it before he propped it up? How it irritated her to watch his fumbling. "Here's some cloth to fix it with." If only she could have said it. Instead, she stood rooted to the spot, hiding, staring. The girl was oblivious to the rain soaking through her sleeves.

Midori's mother, unaware of what was happening, called out. "Midori, the iron's ready. What are you doing out there? Don't you know better than to play in the rain? You'll catch another cold."

"All right, coming." If only Nobu wouldn't hear. Her heart raced, her head seemed to reel. The last thing she could do was open the gate, but she could not turn her back on him, either. What was she to do? There—she hurled the rag outside the lattice without saying anything. Nobu pretended not to notice. Oh! He was his same old nasty self! It crushed her, the tears welled up. Why did he have to be so mean? Why didn't he just tell her what it was? It made her sick. But her mother kept on calling. It was no use. She started for the house. After all, why should she be sentimental? She wasn't going to let him see Midori eat humble pie.

He heard her walk away; his eyes wandered after her. The scarlet scrap of Yūzen silk lay in the rain, its pattern of red maple leaves near enough to touch. Odd, how her one gesture moved him, and yet he could not bring himself to reach out and take the cloth. He stared at it vacantly, and as he looked at it he felt his heart break.

He bungled everything. Nobu sighed and took the cord from his jacket and wrapped it round the clog. It was unsightly and makeshift, but perhaps it would do, perhaps he could stumble along. But all the way to Ohana's? It was a little late to be wondering that, he thought as he stood up, his sister's package tight under his arm. He had only gone two or three steps when he looked back again at the tatter of silk, bright with autumn maples. It was hard for him to leave it there.

"Nobu, what's the matter? Break your strap? What a sight you are!"

Nobu turned around to see who owned the unexpected voice. It was obnoxious Chōkichi, decked out like a young gallant. He had on his best-dress kimono, and he wore his orange sash profligately low on the hips. His new jacket had a fancy black collar, and the umbrella he carried was festooned with the trademark of one of the houses in the quarter. His high clogs were sporting lacquered rain covers—this was something new. What pride there was in the young man's swagger.

"The strap broke, and I was wondering what to do," Nobu answered helplessly. "I'm not very good at these things."

"No, you wouldn't be. It's all right, wear mine. The straps won't give out."

"But what will you do?"

"Don't worry. I'm used to it. I'll just go like this," he said, tucking up the bottom of his kimono. "Feels much better than wearing sandals, anyway." He kicked off his rain clogs.

"You're going to go barefoot? That won't be fair."

"I don't mind. I'm used to going barefoot. Someone like you has soft feet. You could never walk barefoot on the gravel. Come on, wear these," he urged, arranging his sandals obligingly. What a spectacle: Chōkichi was more detested than the plague god himself, and here he was with soft words on his tongue and bushy eyebrows moving solicitously. "I'll take your sandals and toss them in at the back door. Here, let's switch."

Chōkichi took the broken clogs, and they parted, Nobu bound for his sister's in Tamachi and Chōkichi for home before they met again at school.

The silk shred lay abandoned by the gate. Its red maple leaves shimmered in the rain.

This year there were three Otori fair days. Rain had spoiled the second, but today, like the first, was perfect for a festival. Throngs packed Otori Shrine, young men surged into the quarter through the side gates. They say they've come to pay a visit to the shrine. They are pilgrims, but, ah, the roar of young laughter is loud enough to rend the pillars holding up the heavens, to tear away the very cord from which the earth hangs. Front and back of the main street of the quarter look as if they've been reversed. Today, the side drawbridges are down clear around the moat, and the crowds keep pouring in. "Coming through, coming through." What have we here? Some flat-bottomed boat trying to navigate these waves of people? Who will soon forget the excitement in the air? Peals of laughter, incessant chatter echo from the little shops along the ditch. Strains of the samisen rise from the first-class pleasure houses towering several stories in the sky.

Shōta took a holiday from collecting interest. He dropped in at Sangorō's potato stall, and then he visited his friend Donkey at the dumpling shop. "How are you doing? Making any money?" The sweets looked pretty uninviting.

"Shōta! You're just in time. I've run out of bean jam and don't know what to do. I've already put more on to cook, but they keep coming and I don't want to turn them away. What should I do?"

"Don't be stupid. Look what you've got on the sides of the pot. Add some water and some sugar, and you can feed another ten or twenty people. Everybody does it—you won't be the first. Besides, who's going to notice how it tastes in all this commotion? Start selling, start selling." Shōta was already at the sugar bowl.

Donkey's one-eyed mother was filled with admiration. "You've become a real merchant, Shōta. I'm almost afraid of you."

"This? I saw Clammy do the same thing in the alley. It's not my idea." The woman's praise did not go to his head. "Hey, do you know where Midori is? I've been looking for her since this morning. Where'd she go off to? She hasn't been to the paper shop. I know that. I wonder if she's in the quarter."

"Oh, Midori, she went by a little while ago. I saw her take one of the side bridges into the quarter. Shōta, you should have seen her. She had her hair all done up like this." He made an oafish effort to suggest the splendor of Midori's new grown-up hairdo. "She's really something, that girl!" The boy wiped his nose as he extolled her.

"Yes, she's even prettier than her sister. I hope she won't end up like Ōmaki." Shōta looked down at the ground.

"What do you mean—that would be wonderful! Next year I'm going to open a shop, and after I save some money I'll buy her for a night!" He didn't understand things.

"Don't be such a smart aleck. Even if you tried, she wouldn't have anything to do with you."

"Why? Why should she refuse me?"

"She just would." Shōta flushed as he laughed. "I'm going to walk around for a while. I'll see you later." He went out of the gate.

> Growing up,
>   she plays among the butterflies
>   and flowers.
> But she turns sixteen,
>   and all she knows
>   is work and sorrow.

He sang the popular refrain in a voice that was curiously quavering for him, and repeated it again to himself. His sandals drummed their usual ring against the paving stones, as all at once his little figure vanished into the crowd.

Inside the bustling quarter, Shōta found himself swept along into a corner of the compound. It was there he saw Midori. Why, it certainly was Midori of the Daikokuya; she was talking to an attendant from one of the houses, and, just as he had heard, her hair was done up in the glorious *shimada* style of a young woman. And yet she looked shy today. Colored ribbons cascaded from her hair, tortoise-shell combs and flowered hairpins flickered in the sun. The whole effect was as bright and stately as a Kyōto doll. Shōta was tongue-tied. Any other time, he would have rushed over and taken her arm.

"Shōta!" Midori came running up. "If you have shopping to do, Otsuma, why don't you go on ahead? I'll go home with him." She nodded good-by to the lady.

"Oh, you don't want me around, now that you've found another friend, is that it?" Otsuma smiled as she headed down a narrow street of shops. "I'll be oft to Kyōmachi, then."

"You look nice, Midori." Shōta tugged at her sleeve. "When did you get that new hairdo? This morning? Why didn't you come and show it to me?" He pretended to be angry.

Midori had difficulty speaking. "I had it done this morning at my sister's. I hate it." Her spirits drooped. She kept her head down; she couldn't bear it when a passerby would gawk.

When she felt so awkward and unhappy, flattery only sounded like an insult. People turned to admire her and she thought they were jeering.

"Shōta, I'm going home."

"Why don't you play? Did someone scold you? I bet you had a fight with your sister."

Midori felt her face color. Shōta was still a child, clearly. Where did one begin to explain?

They passed the dumpling shop, and Donkey called out theatrically, "You two sure are friendly." It made her feel like crying.

"Shōta, I don't want to walk with you." She hurried off ahead of him.

She had promised to go with him to the festival, and now here she was, headed in the opposite direction. "Aren't you going to come?" he yelled, running after her. "Why are you going home? You might at least explain!"

Midori walked on without answering, hoping to elude him. Shōta was stunned. He pulled at her sleeve. It was all so strange. Midori's face only turned a deeper red. "It's nothing, Shōta." But he knew that this was not the truth.

He followed her in through the gate at her house and onto the veranda. There was no need to hesitate; he had been coming here to play for years.

"Oh, Shōta," her mother greeted him. "Nice to see you. She's been in a bad mood all day. I don't know what to do with her. See if you can cheer her up."

Shōta became quite the grown-up. "Something the matter, is there?"

"No, no." Her mother gave an odd smile. "She'll get over it in no time. She's just spoiled. I suppose she's been grumpy with her friends, too? I tell you, sometimes I've had it with that girl." Her mother turned to look at her, but Midori had gone into the other room. Her sash and her outer kimono were discarded on the floor and Midori lay face-down underneath a quilt.

Shōta approached her gingerly. "Midori, what is it? Don't you feel well? Please tell me what's the matter." He held back as he spoke to her. What should he do? He folded and unfolded his hands in his lap. Midori said nothing. He could hear her sobbing into her sleeve. Her bangs, too short still for sweeping up into the great hairdo, were matted with tears. Something was terribly wrong, but, child that he was, Shōta had no idea what it could be, or how to console her. He was totally bewildered. "Please tell me what it is. You've never said anything to me, so how can you be angry with me?" He looked at her warily.

"Shōta, it isn't you." Midori wiped her eyes.

But when he asked her what it was, then, she couldn't answer. There were just sad things, vague things. Feelings . . . She couldn't put them into words. They made her cheeks burn. Nothing she could point to—and yet lately everything discouraged her. So many thoughts; none of them would ever have occurred to the Midori of yesterday. This awkwardness all of a sudden! How was she to explain it? If they would just leave her alone . . . she'd be happy to spend night and day in a dark room. No one to talk to her, no one to stare. Even if she felt unhappy, at least she would be spared the embarrassment. If only she could go on playing house forever—with her dolls for companions, then she'd be happy again. Oh! She hated, hated, hated this growing up! Why did things have to change? What she would give to go back a year, ten months, seven months, even.

They were the thoughts of someone already old.

She had forgotten that Shōta was there. But he kept on pestering her until she wanted to drive him away. "For God's sake, go home, Shōta. I feel like dying, with you here. All these questions give me a headache. They make me dizzy. I don't want anybody here! Just go *home!*"

She had never treated him so cruelly; Shōta could make no sense of it. He might as well have been groping through a cloud of smoke. "You sure are acting strange, Midori. I don't know why you talk this way. You must be crazy." The regrets were too much for him. He spoke calmly enough, but now his eyes smarted. This wouldn't help matters.

"Go home! Go home, will you! If you don't get out of here, you're not my friend at all. I hate you, Shōta."

"If that's the way you feel, I'm sorry to have bothered you." He darted off through the garden without so much as a farewell to Midori's mother, who had gone to check the water in the bath.

Shōta made a beeline for the paper shop, ducking, dodging his way through the crowds.

Sangorō was there, his holiday stall sold out and the take jingling in his pocket. Shōta burst in upon them just as Sangorō was playing the part of big brother. "Anything you want—it's yours!" The younger ones jumped up and down with glee. "Hey, Shōta! I was looking for you. I made a lot of money today. I'll treat you."

"You idiot. Since when do you treat me? Don't start talking big." These were rough words for Shōta. "That's not what I came here for." He looked dejected.

"What happened? A fight?" Sangorō shoved a half-eaten doughnut into his pocket. "Who was it? Nobu? Chōkichi? Where? The temple? Was it in the quarter? It won't be like the last time! This time, they won't take us by surprise. There's no way we can lose. I'm ready. Let me lead. We can't chicken out, Shōta."

The call to arms only infuriated him. "Take it easy," Shōta snapped. "There was no fight."

"But you came in here as if something terrible had happened. I thought it was a fight. And besides, if you don't do it tonight, we won't have another chance. Chōkichi's losing his right arm."

"Huh?"

"His accomplice, Nobu. Didn't you hear? I just found out. My father was talking with Nobu's mother. Any day now, he's going off to learn how to be a monk. Once he puts those robes on, they'll cover up his fighting arm. Those long, floppy robes—how can he roll up his sleeves in them? But you know what that means. Next year, you'll have the front and the back street to yourself."

"All right, quiet. For a few coins they'll go over to Chōkichi. I could have a hundred like you, and it wouldn't excite me in the least. They can go where they like for all I care. I'll fight my own battles. It was Nobu I wanted to beat. But if he's running off on me, it can't be helped. I thought he was going next year, after he graduated. What a coward—why is he going so soon?"

But it wasn't Nobu he was worried about. Tonight, there were none of the usual songs from Shōta. Midori was on his mind. The throngs of merrymakers passing in the street only left him feeling lonely. What was there to celebrate?

The lamps went on, and Shōta rolled over on his side. Some festival, everything had ended in a mess!

From that day on Midori was a different person. When she had to, she went to her sister's rooms in the quarter, but she never went to play in town. Her friends missed her and came to invite her to join them in the fun again. "Maybe later. You go on ahead." Empty promises, always. She was cool even to Shōta, once her closest friend. She was forever blushing now. It seemed unlikely that the paper shop would see the old dancing and the games a second time.

People were puzzled. Was the girl sick? "No, no. She'll be her old self again," her mother assured them. "She's just having a rest. One of her little vacations." The woman smiled. And yet there seemed to be more to it.

There was praise for Midori now from some quarters. So ladylike, so well-behaved. Yes, but what a shame, others mourned: she was such a delightful, saucy child.

The front street was quiet suddenly, as if a light had gone out. Seldom did Shōta sing his songs any more. At night you could see him with his lantern making the rounds for the interest payments. The shadow moving along the moat looked chilly, somehow. From time to time, Sangorō would join him, and his voice rang out, comical as ever.

Everyone talked about Nobu, but Midori had not heard any of the rumors. The former spitfire was still closeted away somewhere. With all these changes lately, she hardly knew herself. She was timid now, everything embarrassed her.

One frosty morning, a paper narcissus lay inside the gate. No one knew what it was doing there, but Midori took a fancy to it, for some reason, and she put it in a bud vase. It was perfect, she thought, and yet almost sad in its crisp, solitary shape. That same day—she wasn't sure exactly where—Midori heard of Nobu's plans. Tomorrow he was leaving for the seminary. The color of his robes would never be the same.

THE PATH TO THE CEMETERY

Thomas Mann

Translated from the German by H. T. Lowe-Porter

Thomas Mann (1875–1955) was a German novelist, short story writer, and essayist born into an aristocratic family in Lübeck. He attended the Lübeck Gymnasium before studying for a career in journalism. He began publishing in 1893, but found fame with his epic autobiographical novel, *Buddenbrooks*, published in 1901 to great acclaim. Although he struggled with homosexuality his whole life, Mann married Katia Pringsheim with whom he had six children. When Hitler was elected Chancellor, the family emigrated to Zurich and from there to the United States in 1939 During the Second World War, Mann made a series of addresses to the German people via the BBC condemning Hitler. He was further persecuted in the United States as a suspected communist, and called to testify to the House Un-American Activities Committee, where he was termed "one of the world's foremost apologists for Stalin" He returned to Switzerland in the 1950s, where he lived until his death. He was awarded the Nobel Prize for literature in 1929.

The path to the cemetery ran always parallel to the highway, always side by side, until it had reached its goal; that is to say, the cemetery. On the other side there were human habitations, new structures of the suburbs, part of which were still in the process of completion, and then came fields. As to the highway itself, this was flanked by trees, by knotty beeches of a good old age, and the road was half paved and half bare earth. But the path to the cemetery was thinly strewn with pebbles, which gave it the character of an agreeable footpath. A small, dry ditch, filled with grass and wildflowers, extended between the two.

It was spring, and almost summer already. The whole world smiled. God's blue skies were covered with masses of small, round, compact little clouds, dotted with many snow-white little clumps which had an almost humorous look. The birds twittered in the beeches, and a mild wind swept across the fields.

A wagon from the neighbouring village crept towards the city; it rolled partly upon the paved, partly upon the unpaved part of the highway. The driver let his legs dangle on both sides of the shaft and whistled execrably. In the back part of the wagon there sat a little yellow dog with its back to him, and along its pointed little nose looked back with an unutterably grave and collected mien at the way it had just come. It was an incomparable, a most diverting little dog, worth its weight in gold; but it plays no part in this affair and so we must turn our faces from it.—A detachment of soldiers went marching by. They came from the garrison near by, marched in their own dust, and sang. A second wagon crept from the direction of the city towards the next village. The driver slept, and there was no little dog, for which reason this vehicle is entirely without interest. Two journeymen came striding along, the one hunched-backed, the other a giant in stature. They went barefooted, carrying their boots on their backs, called out cheerily to the sleeping driver, and strode on bravely. The traffic was moderate, regulating itself without complications or accidents. The way to the cemetery was trodden by a solitary man; he walked slowly, with lowered head, and supported himself on a black stick. The man was called Piepsam, Lobgott (Praisegod) Piepsam and nothing else. We proclaim his name with a certain emphasis because subsequently he acted in a most peculiar manner.

He was dressed in black, for he was on the way to the graves of his loved ones. He wore a rough, cylindrical silk hat, a frock-coat shiny with age, trousers which were not only too narrow but also too short, and black kid gloves which were shabby all over. His throat, a long, lean throat with a large Adam's apple, lifted itself from a turnover collar which was frayed and displayed corners which had already become a little rough. But when the man raised his head, which he did at times in order to see how far he still was from the cemetery, then one was treated to a strange sight, a remarkable face, a face which beyond all question one was not likely soon to forget.

This face was smooth-shaven and pale. Between the hollowed-out cheeks there protruded a nose which thickened bulbously at the end, a nose which glowed with an irregular, unnatural red and which, quite superfluously, paraded a mass of little excrescences, unhealthy growths which gave it an unconventional and fantastic look. This nose, the dark rubicundity of which contrasted sharply with the dull pallor of the rest of the face, embodied something unreal and picturesque; it looked as though it were merely affixed like a masquerade nose, like a melancholy joke. But it was not this alone. The man kept his mouth, a broad mouth with sunk corners, tightly closed, and whenever he looked up, he lifted his black eyebrows, which were shot through by little white hairs—lifted them beneath the brim of his hat, so that one might see how inflamed his eyes were and what dark circles surrounded them. In short, it was a face to which one could not permanently refuse the deepest sympathy.

Lobgott Piepsam's appearance was not a joyous one; it fitted in but badly with this charming forenoon, and it was even too dismal for one who was about to pay a visit to the graves of his loved ones. But looking into his heart and soul, one was forced to confess that there were sufficient grounds for all this. He was a trifle depressed?—it is difficult to convey this to people so merry as yourselves—perhaps a bit unhappy;—a trifle badly treated? Well, to tell the truth, he was all of these things not only a trifle, but to a high degree; he was, without any exaggeration, in a bad way.

First of all, he drank. But of this more anon. Furthermore he was a widower, had lost both parents, and stood abandoned by everybody; he had not a single soul to love him in all the world. His wife, whose maiden-name had been Lefeelt, had been reft from his side after she had borne him a child a little less than half a year ago; it was the third child and it had been stillborn. Both of the other children had also died—one of diphtheria, the other of really nothing at all— perhaps out of a general ineptitude. But this had not been enough/for soon after this he had lost his job, had been driven out of his petty position; and that bore a close relation to that passion of his which was mightier than Piepsam.

Formerly he had been able to resist it to some degree, although there were periods when he had been intemperately addicted to it. But after wife and children had been taken from him, after he had lost all his friends and stood alone in the world and without a single support or hold, his vice had mastered him and had broken his spiritual resistance more and more. He had been an official in the service of an insurance society, a kind of higher copyist with a monthly salary of ninety marks. While in his irresponsible condition, he had become guilty of gross negligence, and after having been repeatedly warned, he had been finally discharged as unreliable.

It is clear that this did not by any manner of means lead to a moral revolt on the part of Piepsam, but that he was thenceforth utterly doomed. For you must know that ill fortune slays the dignity of a man—it is just as well to have a little insight into these things. There is a strange and dreadful concatenation of cause and effect here. There is no use in a man's protesting his own innocence; in most cases he will despise himself for his misfortune. But self-contempt and vice have a strange and horrible interrelationship; they feed each other, they play into each other's hands, in a way to make one's blood run cold. And that is the way it was with Piepsam. He drank because he did not respect himself, and he respected himself less and less because the continual shameful defeats of all his good resolutions devoured all his self-confidence. In a wardrobe in his home there usually stood a bottle containing a poisonous yellow fluid, a most pernicious fluid—we must be cautious and not mention its name. Lobgott Piepsam had literally knelt before his wardrobe and almost bitten his tongue in two; and in spite of this he would go down in defeat in the end—We take no pleasure in relating these facts, but they are, after all, instructive.

And here he was walking along the path to the cemetery and prodding the ground with his black cane. A gentle wind played about his nose, but he did not feel it. His eyebrows elevated, he bent a hollow and turbid look upon the world about him—a lorn and miserable creature.—Suddenly he heard a noise behind him and pricked up his ears; a soft rushing sound was approaching with great rapidity from the distance. He turned about and stood still.—It was a bicycle, the tires of which crunched along the pebble-strewn path. It came on in full career, but then slackened its speed, for Piepsam stood in the middle of the way.

A young man sat in the saddle, a youth, a careless youth on a tour. He himself, great heavens, surely made no pretensions to belonging to the great and glorious one of the world! He rode a machine of middling quality—it does not really matter of what make—a wheel costing, say, about two hundred marks. And with this he went pedalling a bit through the country, fresh from the city, riding with flashing pedals into God's green world—hurray! He wore a coloured shirt and a grey jacket, sports leggings, and the jauntiest little cap in the world—a very joke of a cap, with brown checks and a button on the top. And from under this cap a thick mop of blond hair welled forth and stood up above his forehead. His eyes were of a lightning-blue. He came on like Life itself and tinkled his bell, but Piepsam did not move a hair's breadth out of the way. He stood there and looked at Life with a rigid stare.

It looked angrily at him and rode slowly past him, whereupon Piepsam also began to walk on. But when it was ahead of him, he said slowly and with a weighty emphasis: "Number nine thousand seven hundred and seven."

He then pursed up his lips and stared incontinently at the ground, at the same time feeling that Life's eyes were bent upon him in perplexity.

It had turned round, had seized the saddle from behind with one hand, and rode very slowly.

"What?" it asked.

"Number nine thousand seven hundred and seven," repeated Piepsam. "Oh, nothing. I'll report you."

"You will report me?" Life asked, turned still further round, and rode still more slowly so that it was obliged to wobble to and fro with the handlebars.

"Certainly!" replied Piepsam at a distance of five or six steps. "Why?" asked Life, and dismounted. It stood still and seemed full of expectancy.

"You know why well enough."

"No, I don't know why."

"You must know."

"But I do not know why," said Life, "and moreover I am not at all interested why." With this it was about to mount its wheel again. It was not at all at a loss for words.

"I will report you," said Piepsam, "because you ride here, on this path to the cemetery and not out there on the high-road."

"But, my dear sir!" Life said, with an impatient and angry laugh, turned round once more, and stood still. "You see tracks of bicycles along the entire path. Everybody rides here."

"That's all one to me," retorted Piepsam; "I'll report you just the same."

"Well, do whatever you like!" Life cried, and mounted its wheel. It really mounted, it did not disgrace itself by making a mess of this; it gave a single thrust with its foot, sat securely on the saddle, and put forth all efforts to reacquire a speed in accordance with its temperament.

"If you keep on riding here, here on the path to the cemetery, I shall most surely report you!" cried Piepsam in a high and trembling voice. But Life really troubled itself very little about this; it rode off with increasing speed.

Had you seen Lobgott Piepsam's face at this moment, you would have been greatly frightened. He pressed his lips so firmly together that his cheeks and even the rubicund nose were twisted quite out of place, and his eyes, from beneath his unnaturally raised eyebrows, stared with an insane expression after the vehicle as it rolled away. Suddenly he dashed forwards. At a run he traversed the short distance which separated him from the machine, and seized the tool-case beneath the saddle. He held on to it with both hands, literally attached himself to it, and with lips still pressed together in an unnatural manner, dumb, and with wild eyes, he tugged with all his strength at the balancing bicycle as it speeded forwards. Anyone seeing him might well have doubted whether he intended, out of malice, to hinder the young man from riding on, or whether he had been seized by the desire to let himself be taken in tow, to jump on behind and ride along with the young man—to go himself riding a bit through the country, riding with flashing pedals into God's green world—hurray!—The wheel was not able to withstand this desperate drag for any length of time; it stood still, it wobbled, it fell over.

And then Life grew wild. It had lighted upon one foot; then it drew back its right arm and gave Herr Piepsam such a blow on the chest that he staggered back several paces. Then, with a voice which swelled into a threatening tone, it said: "You must be drunk, you fool! You must be off your head! If you dare to hold me up again, I'll give you a smash in the jaw—do you hear? I'll break your neck! And don't you forget it!"

With this it turned its back upon Herr Piepsam, gave an indignant tug to its cap, drawing it tighter upon its head, and once more mounted its wheel. No, it was certainly not at a loss for words. And the business of mounting succeeded as well as before. Again it merely thrust down one foot, sat securely in the saddle, and had the machine once more under full control. Piepsam saw its back diminish more and more rapidly.

He stood there panting and stared after Life. It did not take a header, no accident overtook it, no tire burst, and no stone lay in its path; lightly it sailed on. And then Piepsam began to shout and to scold—one might have called it a bellowing, for it was no longer a human voice.

"You shall not ride there!" he cried. "You shall not! You shall ride out there and not on the path to the cemetery, do you hear? You get off—get off at once! Oh, oh! I'll report you! I'll sue you! God! if you would only take a tumble, if you would only fall off, you windy brute, I would kick you, kick you in the face with my boots, you damned rogue! . . .". Never had the like been seen before! A man calling bad names on the way to the cemetery, a man with a swollen face, bellowing, a man whose scolding renders him hopping mad, who cuts capers, throwing his arms and legs about, and seems unable to control himself. The wheel was really no longer in sight, yet Piepsam still raved and danced in the same spot.

"Hold him! hold him! He is riding on the path to the cemetery! You villain! You impudent clown! You damned ass! If I could only get hold of you, wouldn't I skin you alive, you silly ass, you stupid windbag, you tomfool, you ignorant bounder!—You get off! You get off this very instant! Will nobody kick him into the dirt, the scoundrel?—Riding for pleasure, eh? On the way to the cemetery! Knock him off his wheel, the damned oaf! Oh! Oh! If I only had you, what wouldn't I do? And what else? Eyes blue as lightning, eh? May the devil scratch them out of your face, you ignorant, ignorant, ignorant bounder! . . ."

Piepsam now took to language which is not to be repeated; he foamed, and poured forth in his cracked voice the most shameful terms of reprobation, while the contortions of his body continually increased. A couple of children with a basket and a terrier came over from the high-road; they climbed across the ditch, stood about the screaming man, and looked curiously into his distorted visage. A few labourers, who worked on the new buildings in the vicinity, or had just begun their midday rest, also became attentive, and a number of men as well as some of the women who were mixing mortar came walking towards the group. But Piepsam continued to rave on; he was growing worse and worse. In his blind and insane rage he shook his fists towards heaven and in all directions, shook his legs convulsively, turned himself round and round, bent the knee and leaped into the air again, succumbing to his excessive efforts to shout as loud as possible. He did not pause a single moment in his tirade, he hardly took time to breathe, and it was really astonishing where all his language came from. His face was terribly swollen, his high hat sat far back on his neck, and his false shirt-front, which was not fastened, hung out of his waistcoat. He had long ago arrived at generalities and poured out things which had not the remotest connection with the subject in hand. They dealt with his dissipated life and with religious matters, uttered in a most unsuitable tone and viciously intermingled with curse-words.

"Come on, come on, all of you!" he bellowed. "Not you, not only you, but the rest of you, you with the bicycle caps and eyes blue as lightning! I'll shout truths into your ear so that your blood will run cold for ever, you windy rogues! . . . You grin, do you? Shrug your shoulders? . . .

I drink. . . certainly I drink! I even guzzle, if you care to hear it! What does that mean? It's a long road that knows no turning! The day will come, you good-for-nothing rubbish, when God shall weigh all of us. . . . Oh! oh! The Son of Man will come in the clouds, you innocent *canaille*, and His justice is not of this world! He will cast you into the outermost darkness, you merry wretches, where there is howling and. . . "

He was now surrounded by quite an imposing group of people. A few laughed and a few looked at him with wrinkled brows. More workmen and several more mortar-women had come over from the buildings. A driver had got off his wagon, halting it upon the high-road, and, whip in hand, had also climbed across the ditch. A man took Piepsam by the arm and shook him, but that had no effect. A squad of soldiers marched by and, laughing, craned their neck to look at him. The terrier could no longer hold back, but braced his forelegs against the ground and, with his tail thrust between his legs, howled directly into his face.

Suddenly Lobgott Piepsam cried once more at the top of his voice: "You get off, you get off at once, you ignorant bounder!" described a half-circle with one arm, and then collapsed. He lay there, suddenly struck dumb, a black heap amidst the curious. His cylindrical silk hat flew off, rebounded once from the ground, and also lay there.

Two masons bent over the immovable Piepsam and discussed the case in that wholehearted and sensible tone common to working-men. Then one of them went off at a quick stride. Those who remained behind undertook a few more experiments with the unconscious one. One man dashed water in his face out of a bucket, another poured some brandy out of a bottle into the palm of his hand and rubbed Piepsam's temples with it. But these efforts were crowned with no success.

A short interval thus elapsed. Then wheels were heard, and a wagon came along the high-road. It was an ambulance, drawn by two pretty little horses and with a gigantic red cross painted on each side. It came to a halt, and two men in neat uniforms climbed down from the driver's seat, and while one went to the back part of the wagon to open it and to draw out the stretcher, the other rushed upon the path to the cemetery, pushed the staring crowd aside, and, with the help of one of the men, carried Herr Piepsam to the wagon. He was laid upon the stretcher and shoved into the wagon like a loaf of bread into an oven, whereupon the door snapped shut and the two uniformed men climbed to the driver's seat again. All this was done with great precision, with a few practised turns of the hand, quick and admit, as by trained apes,

And then Lobgott Piepsam was driven away.

MAHESH

Sarat Chandra Chattopadhyay

Translated from the Bengali by Arunava Sinha

Sarat Chandra Chattopadhyay (1876–1938). Born in Debanandapur, in West Bengal, Sarat Chandra was a prominent Bengali novelist and short story writer who chronicled the lives and the plight of lower castes in Bengal. His father had dreamed of being a writer but never completed the stories he began, but Sarat Chandra wrote constantly beginning in his teens. In 1893, he moved to Burma, where he worked in the public works accounts office. Not until her returned to India in 1916 did he publish his first novel. His works have been widely translated and adapted, with more than seventy films based on his novels, including sixteen versions of his novel *Devdas*.

I

The village was named Kashipur. An insignificant village, with an even more insignificant zamindar, but such was his authority that his subjects went in awe of him.

It was the birthday of the zamindar's youngest son. Having performed the holy rituals, Tarkaratna, the priest, was on his way home in the afternoon. The month of Boishakh was drawing to a close, but there was not even a trace of clouds anywhere, the searing sky seemingly pouring fire on everything below. The field stretching to the horizon before him was parched and cracked, with the blood in the veins of the earth escaping constantly through the crevices in the form of vapour. Gazing at it coiling upwards like flames made the head reel with drunkenness.

Gafoor Jolha lived on the edge of this field. The earthen wall surrounding his house had collapsed, merging his yard with the road. The privacy of the inner chambers had all but surrendered itself to the mercy of the passer-by.

Pausing in the shade of a white teak tree, Tarkaratna called out loudly, 'Are you home, Gafra?'

Gafoor's ten-year-old daughter came to the door. 'What do you need Baba for? He's got a fever.'

'Fever! Call the swine! Monster! Godless creature!'

The screaming and shouting brought Gafoor Mian to the door, shivering with fever. An ancient acacia stood next to the broken wall, with a bull tethered to it. Pointing to it, Tarkaratna said, 'What's all this? Have you forgotten this is a Hindu village with a Brahmin zamindar?' Red with rage and the heat, his words were fiery, but Gafoor unable to understand the reason for the outburst could only stare at him.

'When I passed this way in the morning he was tethered there,' said Tarkaratna, 'and now on my way back he's still tethered the same way. Karta will bury you alive if you kill a bull. He's a devout Brahmin.'

'What can I do, Baba Thakur, I have no choice. I've had this fever for several days now. I collapse every time I try to take him to graze.'

'Then turn him loose, he'll find food on his own.'

'Where can I turn him loose, Baba Thakur? The winnowing isn't done, the grain is still lying in the fields. The hay hasn't been sorted, the earth is burning, there's not a blade of grass anywhere. What if he eats someone's grains or hay— how can I turn him loose, Baba Thakur?'

Softening, Tarkaratna said, 'If you can't let him loose at least give him some straw. Hasn't your daughter made any rice? Give him a bowl of starch and water.'

Gafoor did not answer, only looked at Tarkaratna helplessly and sighed.

Tarkaratna said, 'No rice either? What did you do with the hay? Did you sell your entire share without keeping anything for your beast? You butcher!'

Gafoor seemed to lose his power of speech at this cruel accusation. A little later he said haltingly, 'I did get some hay this year, but Karta Moshai took it away to pay for taxes left over from last year. I fell at his feet, I said, "Babu Moshai, you're the supreme authority, where will I go if I leave your kingdom, give me at least a little hay. There's no straw for the roof, we have just the one room for father and daughter, we can still manage with palm leaves this monsoon, but my Mahesh will die of starvation."'

With a mocking smile, Tarkaratna said, 'Really! What a loving name, Mahesh. I'll die laughing.'

Paying no attention to the taunt, Gafoor continued, 'But the lord had no mercy on me. He allowed me some rice to feed us for two months, but all my hay was confiscated and the poor thing got nothing at all.' His voice grew moist with tears. But this evoked no compassion in Tarkaratna, who said, 'What a man you are. You've eaten up everything but don't want to pay your dues. Do you expect the zamindar to feed you? You people live in a perfect kingdom, still you bad-mouth him, you're such wretches.'

An embarrassed Gafoor said, 'Why should we bad-mouth him, Baba Thakur, we don't do that. But how do I pay my taxes? I sharecrop four bighas, but there's been a famine two years in a row—the grains have all dried up. My daughter and I don't even get two meals a day. Look at the house, when it rains we spend the night in a corner, there's not even enough space to stretch our legs. Look at Mahesh, Thakur Moshai, you can count his ribs. Lend me a little hay, Thakur Moshai, let the creature feed to his heart's content for a few days.' Still speaking, he flung himself to the ground near the Brahmin's feet. Leaping backwards hastily, Tarkaratna exclaimed, 'My god, are you going to touch me?'

'No, Baba Thakur, I'm not going to touch you or anything. But give me some hay. I saw your four huge haystacks the other day, you won't even know if a little of it is gone. I don't care if we starve to death, but this poor creature cannot talk, he only stares and weeps.' Tarkaratna said, 'And how do you propose to return the loan?' A hopeful Gafoor said, 'I'll find a way to return it somehow, Baba Thakur, I won't cheat you.'

Snorting, Tarkaratna mimicked Gafoor, 'I won't cheat you! I'll find a way to return it somehow! What a comedian! Get out of my way. I should be getting home, it's late.' Chuckling, he took a step forward only to retreat several steps in fear. Angrily he said, 'Oh god, he's waving his horns, is he going to gore me now?'

Gafoor rose to his feet. Pointing to the bundle of fruit and moistened rice in the priest's hand, he said, 'He's smelt food, he wants to eat. . .'

'Wants to eat? Of course. Both master and bull are well-matched. Can't get hay to eat, and now you want fruits. Get him out of my way. Those horns, some-one will be killed by them.' Tarkaratna hurried away.

Gafoor turned towards Mahesh, gazing at him in silence for a few moments. There was suffering and hunger in the bull's deep black eyes. Gafoor said, 'He wouldn't give you any, would he? They have so much, but still they won't. Never mind.' He choked, and tears began to roll down from his eyes. Going up to the animal, he stroked his back and neck, whispering, 'You are my son, Mahesh, you've grown old looking after us for eight years, I can't even give you enough to eat, but you know how much I love you.'

Mahesh responded by stretching his neck and closing his eyes in pleasure. Wiping his tears off the bull's back, Gafoor murmured, 'The zamindar took away your food, leased out the grazing ground near the crematorium just for money. How will I save your life in this year of starvation? If I turn you loose you'll eat other people's hay, you'll spoil their trees—what do I do with you! You have no strength left, people tell me to sell you off.' No sooner had Gafoor said this in his head than his tears began to roll down again. Wiping them with his hand, he looked around surreptitiously before fetching some discoloured straw from behind his dilapidated house and placing them near Mahesh's mouth, saying, 'Eat up quickly, if not there'll be. . .'

'Baba?'

'Yes, Ma?'

'Come and eat,' said Amina, appearing at the door. After a glance she said, 'You're giving Mahesh straw from the roof again. Baba?'

This was just what he was afraid of. Reddening, he said, 'Old rotten straw, Ma, it was falling off anyway. . .'

'I heard you pulling it out. Baba.'

'No, Ma, not exactly pulling it out. . .'

'But the wall will collapse, Baba. . .'

Gafoor was silent. The house was all they had left, and no one knew better than him that if he continued this way it wouldn't survive the next monsoon. But how long could they go on?

His daughter said, 'Wash your hands and come, Baba, I've served the food.'

Gafoor said, 'Bring the starch out, Ma, let me feed Mahesh first.'

'No starch left today, Baba, it dried in the pot.'

No starch? Gafoor stood in silence. His ten-year-old daughter knew that when the times were bad even this could not be wasted. He washed his hands and went in. His daughter served him rice and vegetables on a brass plate, taking some for herself on an earthen plate. Gafoor said softly, 'I'm feeling cold again, Amina, is it safe to eat with a fever?'

Amina asked anxiously, 'But didn't you say you were hungry?'

'Maybe I didn't have a fever then, Ma.'

'Then let me put it away, you can have it in the evening.'

Shaking his head, Gafoor said, 'Eating cold food will make things worse.'

'What should I do then?' asked Amina.

Gafoor pretended to think before solving the problem. He said, 'Why don't you give it to Mahesh, Ma? You can make me some fresh rice at night, can't you?'

Amina looked at him in silence for a few moments before lowering her eyes, nodding, and saying, 'Yes, Baba, I can.'

Gafoor reddened. Besides the two actors, only someone up there observed this little charade between father and daughter.

II

Five or six days later, Gafoor was seated outside his front door with an anxious expression on his face. Mahesh had not been home since yesterday morning. He himself was too weak to move, so his daughter Amina had searched high and low for the bull. Returning home in the late afternoon, she said, 'Have you heard, Baba, Manik Ghosh's family has taken our Mahesh to the police station?'

'What nonsense,' said Gafoor.

'It's true, Baba. Their servant said, "Tell your father to look for him in the Dariapur pen."'

'What did he do?'

'He got into their garden and destroyed their trees, Baba.'

Gafoor sat in silence. He had imagined all manner of mishaps that might have befallen Mahesh, but had not anticipated this. He was as harmless as he was poor, which was why he had no apprehensions of being punished so severely by any of his neighbours—Manik Ghosh, in particular, for his respect for cows was legendary.

His daughter said, 'It's getting late, Baba, aren't you going to bring Mahesh home?'

'No,' answered Gafoor.

'But they said the police will sell him in the cattle market after three days.'

'Let them sell him,' said Gafoor.

Amina did not know what exactly a cattle market was, but she had noticed her father becoming agitated whenever it was mentioned with reference to Mahesh. She left without another word.

Under cover of the night Gafoor went to Bansi's shop, and said, 'Khuro, I need a rupee,' and deposited his brass plate beneath the raised platform on which Bansi sat. Bansi was familiar with the exact weight and other details of this object. It had been pawned some five times in the past two years, for a rupee each time. So, he did not object this time either.

Mahesh was seen in his usual place the next day. Beneath the same tree, tethered to the same stake with the same rope, the same empty bowl with no food in front of him, the same questioning look in the moist, hungry, black eyes. An elderly Muslim man was examining him closely. Gafoor Mian sat nearby, his knees drawn up to his chin. When the examination was over, the man extracted a ten-rupee note from the knot in his dhoti and, smoothening it repeatedly, went up to Gafoor, saying, 'I don't need change, take the whole thing—here.'

Holding his hand out for the money, Gafoor remained sitting in silence. But just as the old Muslim's companions were about to untie the bull, he suddenly jumped to his feet, saying belligerently, 'Don't you dare touch that rope, I'm warning you.'

They were startled. The old man said in surprise, 'Why not?'

Still furious, Gafoor said, 'What do you mean, why not? It's mine to sell or not. And I'm not selling.' He threw the ten-rupee note on the ground.

They said, 'But you took an advance yesterday.'

'Here's your advance.' Retrieving two rupees from the knot in his dhoti, he flung the coins at them, and they fell with a clatter. Realizing that a quarrel was imminent, the old man said gently with a smile, 'You're putting pressure on us for two rupees more, aren't you? Go on, give his daughter two rupees more. That's what you wanted, isn't it?'

'No.'

'Are you aware that no one will give you a better price?'

'No,' said Gafoor, shaking his head vehemently.

The old man said in annoyance, 'What do you think? Only the skin is worth selling. There's nothing else in there.'

'Tauba! Tauba!' A terrible expletive suddenly escaped Gafoor's lips, and the very next moment he ran into his house threatening to have them thrashed within an inch of their lives by the zamindar's guards unless they left the village at once.

The possibility of trouble made them leave, but soon Gafoor received a summons from the zamindar's court. He realized that word had reached the land-owner.

There were people both refined and unrefined in court. Glaring at Gafoor, Shibu Babu said, 'I don't know how to punish you, Gafra. Do you know where you live?'

Bowing, Gafoor said, 'I do. We're starving, or else I would have paid whatever fine you think fit.'

Everyone present was astonished. They had always considered him an obstinate and bad-tempered man. And here he was on the verge of tears, saying, 'I'll never do it again, Karta.' He proceeded to box his own ears, rubbed his nose into the ground from one end of the court to the other, and then stood up.

Shibu Babu said indulgently, 'All right, enough. Don't do all this again.'

Everyone was shocked when they heard the details. They were certain that only the grace of the zamindar and the fear of punishment had prevented the abject sinner from committing worse trangressions. Tarkaratna was present, and provided the scriptural analysis of the word 'go' for cow, enlightening everyone as to why it was forbidden to allow this godless race of heathens to live within village limits.

Gafoor did not respond to any of this, humbly accepting all the humiliation and vilification and returning home cheerfully. Borrowing the starch from the rice pots of neighbours, he gave it to Mahesh to eat, murmuring many endearments as he stroked the bull's back and horns.

III

The month of Joishtho was drawing to a close. The sun was still harsh and severe in the sky. There was no trace of mercy anywhere. People were afraid to even hope for change, hope that the skies could again be moist and pleasurable with the weight of rain-bearing clouds. It seemed that there would be no cessation to the flames burning constantly across the entire fiery earth—that they would not die down till they had consumed everything.

Gafoor returned home on such an afternoon. He was not used to working as a labourer on someone else's fields, and it had been only four or five days since the fever had subsided. He was as weak as he was exhausted. Still, he had gone out in search of work, but all he had got was the unforgiving heat and sun overhead. He could barely see for hunger and thirst. Standing at the door, he called out, 'Amina, is the food ready?'

His daughter emerged slowly and stood grasping the post without an answer.

Gafoor shouted, 'Not ready? Why not?'

'No rice at home, Baba.'

'No rice? Why didn't you tell me in the morning?'

'But I told you last night.'

Contorting his face and mocking her, Gafoor said, 'Told you last night! How can anyone remember if you tell them at night?' The harsh tone he was using stoked his anger. Contorting his face even further, he said, 'How will there be any rice? Whether the sick father gets any or not, the grown-up daughter will eat five times a day. I'm going to lock up the rice from now on. Give me some water, I'm dying of thirst. Now tell me we have no water either.'

Amina remained standing with her eyes downcast. When Gafoor realized after waiting a few moments that there was not even any water to drink at home, he could control himself no longer. Striding up to his daughter, he slapped her resoundingly, saying, 'Haramjaadi, what do you do all day? Why can't you die?'

Without a word his daughter picked up the empty pitcher and went out in the heat, wiping her eyes. Gafoor felt heartbroken as soon as she was out of sight. He alone knew how he had brought up his daughter after her mother's death. He remembered that it was not the dutiful and affectionate girl's fault. Ever since they had run out of the paltry amount of rice he had received for his work in the fields, they had not had two meals a day. On some days, just one—or not even that. His accusation that Amina was eating five times a day was as impossible as it was untrue. Nor was he unaware of the reasons for the lack of water to drink. The two or three tanks in the village were all dry. The little water there was in the pond behind Shibcharan Babu's house was not available to ordinary people. The water that could be collected by digging a hole or two in the middle of the tanks was fought over by a crowd of people.

Being a Muslim, the young girl was not even allowed near that water. She had to wait for hours, pleading for some water, and only if someone took pity on her, and poured her a little could she bring it home. He knew all this. Perhaps there had been no water that day, or no one had had the time to take pity on his daughter during the battle. Realizing that something like this must have taken place, Gafoor found his own eyes filling with tears. At that moment the zamindar's footman appeared like a messenger of death, screaming, 'Gafra, are you home?'

Gafoor answered bitterly, 'I am. Why?'

'Babu Moshai has sent for you. Come along.'

Gafoor said, 'I haven't eaten yet. I'll come later.'

Unable to tolerate such audacity, the footman swore and said, 'The Babu has ordered me to flog you and force you to come.'

Gafoor forgot himself a second time, uttering an unprintable word in retaliation and said, 'No one is a slave in the kingdom of the empress. I pay my taxes, I won't go.'

But for such a small man to give such a big reason was not just futile but also dangerous. Fortunately, such an insignificant voice would not reach the ears of the important man it was meant for—or else he would have lost both his home and his livelihood. There is no need for an elaborate account of what ensued, but when he returned from the zamindar's court an hour later and lay down in silence, his face and eyes were swollen. The primary cause of such severe punishment was Mahesh. After Gafoor had gone out, Mahesh had broken free from the post, entered the zamindar's yard, eaten his flowers, spoilt the paddy put out in the sun, and, when about to be caught, had made his escape after knocking the zamindar's youngest daughter to the ground. This was not the first time it had happened, but Gafoor had been pardoned earlier on the grounds of being poor. He might have been pardoned this time too had he begged and pleaded as in the past, but what he had said—that he paid his taxes and was no one's servant—was the kind of arrogance from a subject that Shibcharan Babu, being a zamindar, could never tolerate. Gafoor had not protested in the slightest against the thrashing and the humiliation, bearing it all in silence. Back home, too, he sat coiled up in silence. He had no awareness of hunger or thirst, but his heart was burning just like the noonday sky outside. However, when he heard his daughter's stricken cry from the yard, he leapt to his feet and ran outside to find Amina lying on the ground and Mahesh lapping up the water trickling out of the shattered pitcher. Gafoor lost his mind. Picking up the plough-head he had brought home yesterday to repair, he smashed Mahesh's head with it repeatedly.

Mahesh tried to lift his head just once, then his starving, skinny body slumped to the ground. A few tears rolled down his eyes, along with a few drops of blood from his ears. His entire body trembled once or twice, after which, stretching out his front and hind legs, Mahesh died.

Amina sobbed, 'What have you done, Baba, our Mahesh is dead.'

Gafoor had turned to stone, neither moving nor speaking, only staring at a pair of unblinking, bottomless dark eyes.

Within an hour or two, a group of cobblers from one end of the village arrived, and slinging Mahesh up on a pole took him to the dumping ground. Gafoor trembled when he saw their shining knives, but closing his eyes, he didn't say a word.

The neighbours said that the zamindar had sent someone to Tarkaratna to find out what should be done next, 'You may have to sell your house as penance.'

Gafoor did not reply to any of this, burying his face in his knees and not moving.

Late that night he woke his daughter up, saying, 'Amina, we must go.'

She had fallen asleep outside the front door. Rubbing her eyes and sitting up, she said, 'Where will we go, Baba?'

Gafoor said, 'To work at the jute mill in Phulbere.'

His daughter looked at him in astonishment. Despite all their troubles her father had never been willing to work at the jute mill. She had often heard him say that it was impossible to maintain one's faith there, that women had neither honour nor protection.

Gafoor said, 'Hurry up, Ma, we have to walk a long way.'

Amina was about to take the tumbler and the brass plate her father ate from, but Gafoor stopped her. 'Leave them here, Ma, they will pay for my penance for Mahesh.'

He left in the dead of night, holding his daughter's hand. He had no family in this village, no one to inform. Crossing the yard, he stopped abruptly beneath the familiar tree and suddenly burst into tears. Raising his eyes to the star-studded black sky, he said, 'Allah! Punish me as you will, but my Mahesh died with a thirst. There was no land he could graze on. Do not forgive the sin of whoever it was who did not let him eat the grass you gave us, or quench his thirst with the water you gave us.'

THE PURSUED

Horacio Quiroga

Translated from the Spanish by Margaret Sayers Peden

Horacio Silvestre Quiroga Forteza (1878–1937) was a Uruguayan play-wright, poet and short story writer. He wrote stories that, in their jungle settings, use the supernatural and the bizarre to show the struggle of man and animal to survive. He also excelled in portraying mental illness and hallucinatory states, a debt he owed to Edgar Allan Poe, according to some critics. His influence can be seen in the Latin American magical realism of Gabriel García Márquez and the postmodern surrealism of Julio Cortázar. Before Quiroga was two and a half months old, on March 14th 1879, his father accidentally fired a gun he was carrying in his hands and died as a result. His writer friend Ferrando had received bad reviews from a Montevideo journalist, and challenged him to a duel. Quiroga, anxious about his friend's safety, offered to check and clean the gun that was to be used. While inspecting the weapon, he accidentally fired off a shot that hit Ferrando in the mouth, killing him instantly.

One night when I was at Lugones's home, the rain so increased in intensity that we rose to look at it from the windows. The wild pampa wind whistled through the wires and whipped the rain in convulsive gusts that distorted the reddish light from the street lamps. This afternoon, after six days of rain, the heavens had cleared to the south, leaving a limpid cold blue sky. And then, behold, the rain returned to promise us another week of bad weather.

Lugones had a stove, which was extremely comforting to my winter debility. We sat down once again and continued our pleasant chat concerning the insane. Several days before, Lugones had visited an insane asylum, and the bizarre behavior of the inmates, added to behavior I myself had once observed, afforded more than enough material for a comfortable vis-à-vis between two sane men.

Given the circumstance of the weather, then, we were rather surprised when the bell at the street door rang. Moments later Lucas Díaz Vélez entered.

This individual has had quite an ominous influence over a period of my life, and that was the night I met him. As is customary, Lugones introduced us by our last names only, so that for some time I didn't know his given name.

Díaz was much slimmer then than he is now. His black clothes—the color of dark maté tea—his sharp face, and his large black eyes gave him a none too common appearance. The eyes, of surprising steadiness and extreme brilliance, especially demanded one's attention. In those days he parted his straight hair in the middle, and, perfectly smoothed down, it looked like a shining helmet.

Vélez spoke very little at first. He crossed his legs, responding only when strictly necessary. At a moment when I had turned toward Lugones, I happened to see that Vélez was observing me. Doubtless in another I would have found this examination following an introduction very natural, but his unwavering attention shocked me.

Soon our conversation came to a standstill. Our situation was not very pleasant, especially for Vélez, since he must have assumed that we were not practicing this terrible muteness before he arrived. He himself broke the silence. He spoke to Lugones of some honey cakes a friend had sent him from Salta, a sample of which he should have brought that night. They seemed to be of a particularly pleasing variety, and, as Lugones showed sufficient interest in sampling them, Díaz Vélez promised to send him the means to do so.

Once the ice was broken, after about ten minutes we returned to our subject of madmen. Although seeming not to lose a single word of what he heard, Díaz held himself apart from the lively subject; perhaps it was not his predilection. As a result, when Lugones left the room for a moment, I was astonished by his unexpected interest. In one minute he told me a number of anecdotes—his expression animated and his mouth precise with conviction. He certainly had much more love for these things than I had supposed, and his last story, related with great vivacity, made me see that he understood the mad with a subtlety not common in this world.

The story was about a boy from the provinces who, after emerging from the debilitating weakness of typhoid, found the streets peopled with enemies. He underwent two months of persecution, committing, as a result, all kinds of foolish acts. As he was a boy of certain intelligence, he commented on his own case so cleverly that it was impossible to know what to think. It sounded exactly like a farce, and this was the general impression of those who heard him discuss his own case so roguishly—always with the vanity characteristic of the mad.

In this fashion he spent three months displaying his psychological astuteness, until one day his mind was cleansed in the clear water of sanity and his ideas became more temperate.

"He is well now," Vélez concluded, "but several rather symptomatic acts have remained with him. A week ago, for example, I ran into him in a pharmacy; he was leaning against the counter, waiting for what I don't know. We started chatting. Suddenly an individual came in without our seeing him, and, as there was no clerk, he rapped with his fingers on the counter. My friend abruptly turned on the intruder with truly animal quickness, staring into his eyes. Anyone would have similarly turned, but not with that rapidity of a man who is always on his guard. Although he was no longer pursued, he must have retained, unawares, an underlying fear that exploded at the least surprise. After staring for a moment, not moving a muscle, he blinked and averted his disinterested eyes. It was as though he had guarded a dark memory of something terrible that happened to him in another time, something he never wanted to catch him unprepared again. Imagine, then, the effect on him of someone's grabbing his arm on the street. I think it would never leave him."

"Undoubtedly the symptom is typical," I confirmed. "And did the psychological talk come to an end also?"

A strange thing: Díaz became very serious and gave me a cold, hostile look.

"May I know why you ask me that?"

"Because we were speaking precisely *of* that!" I replied, surprised. But obviously the man had seen how ridiculous he had been, because immediately he apologized profusely.

"Forgive me. I don't know what happened to me. I've felt this way at times . . . unexpectedly lost my head. Crazy things," he added, laughing and playing with a ruler.

"Completely crazy," I joked.

"And *so* crazy! It's only by chance I have an ounce of sense left. And now I remember, although I asked your pardon—and I ask it again—that I haven't answered your question. My friend does not talk about psychology any more. And now that he is eminently sane, he does not feel perverse in denouncing his own madness as he did before, forcing that terrible two-edged sword one calls reason, you see? It's very clear. "

"Not very," I allowed myself to doubt.

"Possibly," he laughed, conclusively. "Another really crazy thing." He winked at me and moved away from the table, smiling and shaking his head like someone who is withholding many things he could tell.

Lugones returned, and we dropped the subject—already exhausted. During the remainder of the visit Díaz spoke very little, although it was clear that his own lack of sociability was making him very nervous. Finally, he left. Perhaps he tried to overcome any bad impression he may have made by his extremely friendly farewell, offering his name and the hospitality of his house along with the prolonged clasp of affectionate hands. Lugones went down with him, since the now-dark stairway was so precipitous that no one was ever tempted to try it alone.

"What the devil kind of person is he?" I asked when Lugones returned. He shrugged his shoulders.

"A terrible individual. I don't know how he came to speak ten words to you tonight. He often sits a whole hour without speaking a word, and you can imagine how pleased I am when he's like that. On the other hand, he comes very seldom. And he's very intelligent in his good moments. You must have noticed that, since I heard you talking."

"Yes, he was telling me about a strange case."

"What case?"

"About a friend who is pursued. He knows as much about madness as the devil himself."

"I guess so, since he himself is pursued."

Scarcely had I heard what he said than a flash of explanatory logic illuminated the darkness I had felt in the other. Undoubtedly . . . ! I remembered above all his irritable air when I asked him if he didn't discuss psychology any more. . . . The good madman had thought I had guessed his secret and was insinuating myself into his consciousness. . . .

"Of course!" I laughed. "Now I understand! But your Díaz Vélez is fiendishly subtle!" And I told him about the snare he had thrown out to me to amuse himself at my expense: the fiction of a pursued friend, and his comments. But I had scarcely begun when Lugones interrupted.

"There is no friend; that actually happened. Except that his friend is he himself. He told you the complete truth; he had typhoid, was very ill, and is cured to this degree, and now you see that his very sanity is questionable. It's also very possible that the business of the store counter is true, but that it happened to him. He's an interesting individual, eh?"

"And then some!" I responded, as I toyed with the ashtray.

It was late when I left. The weather had finally settled, and, although one could not see the sky above, he sensed the ceiling had lifted. It was no longer raining. A strong, dry wind rippled the water on the sidewalks and forced one to lean into it at street corners. I reached Santa Fe Street and waited a while for the streetcar, shaking the water from my feet. Bored, I decided to walk; I quickened my pace, dug my hands into my pockets, and then thought in some detail about Díaz Vélez.

The thing I remembered best about him was the look with which he had first observed me. It couldn't be called intelligent, reserving intelligence to be included among those qualities—habitual in persons of certain stature—to be *exchanged* to a greater or lesser degree among persons of similar culture. In such looks there is always an interchange of souls: one delves into the depths of the person he has just met and, at the same time, yields part of his own soul to the stranger.

Díaz didn't look at me that way; he only looked *at* me. He wasn't thinking what I was or what I might be, nor was there in his look the least spark of psychological curiosity. He was simply observing me, as one would unblinkingly observe the equivocal attitude of some feline.

After what Lugones had told me, I was no longer astonished by the objectivity of the madman's stare. After his examination, satisfied surely, he had made fun of me, shaking the scarecrow of his own madness in my face. But his desire to denounce himself, without revealing himself, had less the object of making fun of me than of entertaining himself. I was simply a pretext for his argument and, above all, a point of confrontation; the more I admired the devilish perversity of the madman he was describing to me, the more he must have been furtively rubbing his hands. The only thing that kept him from being completely happy was that I didn't say, "But isn't your friend afraid they'll find him out when he denounces himself that way?" It hadn't occurred to me, because the friend didn't interest me especially. But now that I knew who the pursued one was, I promised myself to provide him with the wild happiness he desired. This is what I was thinking as I walked along.

Nevertheless, two weeks passed without my seeing him. I knew through Lugones that he had been at Lugones's house to bring him the confections—a good gift for him.

"He also brought some for you. Since he didn't know where you live—I don't think you gave him your address—he left them at my house. You must come by and get them."

"Some day. Is he still at the same address?"

"Díaz Vélez?"

"Yes."

"Yes, I suppose so; he didn't say a word about leaving."

The next rainy night I went to Lugones's house, sure of finding Díaz Vélez. Even though I realized, better than anyone, that the logic of thinking I would meet him *precisely* on a rainy night was worthy only of a dog or a madman, the probability of absurd coincidence always rules in such cases where reason no longer operates.

Lugones laughed at my insistence on seeing Díaz Vélez.

"Be careful! The pursued always begin by adoring their future victims. He remembered you very well."

"That doesn't matter. When I see him, it's going to be *my* turn to amuse myself."

I left very late that night.

But I didn't find Díaz Vélez. Not until one noon when, just as I was starting to cross the street, I saw him on Artes Street. He was walking north, looking into all the shop windows, not missing a one, like a person preoccupied. When I caught a glimpse of him, I had one foot off the sidewalk. I tried to stop, but I couldn't, and I stepped into the street, almost stumbling. I turned around and looked at the curb, although I was quite sure there was nothing there. One of the plaza carriages driven by a Negro in a shiny jacket passed so close to me that the hub of the rear wheel left grease on my trousers. I stood still, staring at the horse's hooves, until an automobile forced me to jump out of the way.

All this lasted about ten seconds, as Díaz continued moving away, and I was forced to hurry. When I felt sure of overtaking him, all my hesitation left and was replaced by a great feeling of self-satisfaction. I felt myself in perfect equilibrium. All my nerves were tingling and resilient. I opened and closed my hands, flexing my fingers, happy. Four or five times a minute I put my hand to my watch, forgetting that it was broken.

Díaz Vélez continued walking, and soon I was two steps behind him. One step more and I *could* touch him. But seeing him this way, not even remotely aware of my presence in spite of his delirium about persecution and psychology, I adjusted my step exactly to his. Pursued! Very well . . . ! I noted in detail his head, his elbows, his clenched hands—held a little away from his body—the transverse wrinkles of his trousers at the back of the knee, the heels of his shoes, appearing and disappearing. I had the dizzying sensation that once before, millions of years before, I had done this: met Díaz Vélez in the street, followed him, caught up with him, and, having done so, continued to follow behind him—*behind him*. I glowed with the satisfaction of a dozen lifetimes. Why touch him? Suddenly it occurred to me that he might turn around, and instantly anguish clutched at my throat. I thought that with my larynx throttled like this I wouldn't be able to cry out, and my only fear, my terrifyingly unique fear, was that I would not be able to cry out if he turned around, as if the goal of my existence were suddenly to throw myself upon him, to pry open his jaws, and to shout unrestrainedly into his open mouth—counting every molar as I yelled.

I had such a moment of anguish that I forgot that it was *he* I was seeing: Díaz Vélez's arms, Díaz Vélez's legs, Díaz Vélez's hair, Díaz Vélez's hatband, the woof of Díaz Vélez's hatband, the warp of the warp of Díaz Vélez, Díaz Vélez, Díaz Vélez. . . .

The realization that, in spite of my terror, I hadn't missed one moment of him, Díaz Vélez, assured me completely.

A moment later I was possessed by the mad temptation to touch him without his noticing it, and immediately, filled with the greatest happiness one's own original creative act can hold, softly, exquisitely, I touched his jacket, just on the lower edge—no more, no less. I touched it and plunged my closed fist into my pocket.

I am sure that more than ten people saw me. I was aware of three. One of them, walking in the opposite direction along the sidewalk across the street, kept turning around with amused surprise. In his hand he was carrying a valise that pointed toward me every time he turned.

Another was a streetcar inspector who was standing on the curb, his legs spread wide apart. From his expression I understood that he had been watching us even before I did it. He did not manifest the least surprise or change his stance or move his head, but he certainly did follow us with his eyes. I assumed he was an elderly employee who had learned to see only what suited him.

The third person was a heavy individual with magnificent bearing, a Catalan-style beard, and eyeglasses with gold frames. He must have been a businessman in Spain. He was just passing us, and he saw me do it. I was sure he had stopped. Sure enough, when we reached the corner, I turned around and I saw him, standing still, staring at me with a rich honorable bourgeois look, frowning, with his head thrown back slightly. This individual enchanted me. Two steps later, I turned my head and laughed in his face. I saw that he frowned even more and drew himself up with dignity as if he doubted whether he could be the one intended. I made a vague, nonsensical gesture that disorganized him completely.

I followed Díaz Vélez, once again attentive only to him. Now we had crossed Cuyo, Corrientes, Lavalle, Tucumán, and Viamonte (the affair of the jacket and the three looks had occurred between the latter two). Three minutes later we had reached Charcas, and there Díaz stopped. He looked toward Suipacha, detected a silhouette behind him, and suddenly turned around. I remember this detail perfectly: for a half-second he gazed at one of the buttons on my jacket, a rapid glance, preoccupied and vague at the same time, like someone who suddenly focuses on one object, just at the point of remembering something else. Almost immediately he looked into my eyes.

"Oh, how are you!" he clasped my hand, shaking it rapidly. "I haven't had the pleasure of seeing you since that night at Lugones's. Were you coming down Artes?"

"Yes. I turned in at Viamonte and was hurrying to catch up with you. I've been hoping to see you."

"And I, you. Haven't you been back by Lugones's?"

"Yes, and thank you for the honey cakes; delicious."

We stood silent, looking at each other.

"How are you getting along?" I burst out, smiling, expressing in the question more affection than real desire to know how he was.

"Very well," he replied in a similar tone. And we smiled at each other again.

As soon as we had begun to talk, I had lost the disturbing flashes of gaiety of a few moments before. I was calm again and, certainly, filled with tenderness for Díaz Vélez. I think I had never looked at anyone with more affection than I did at him on that occasion.

"Were you waiting for the streetcar?"

"Yes," he nodded, looking at the time. As he lowered his head to look at his watch, I saw fleetingly that the tip of his nose touched the edge of his upper lip. Warm affection for Díaz swelled from my heart.

"Wouldn't you like to have some coffee? There's a marvelous sun. That is, if you've already eaten and are in no hurry . . ."

"Yes, no, no hurry," he answered distractedly, looking down the tracks into the distance.

We turned back. He didn't seem entirely delighted at the prospect of accompanying me. I wished he were happier and more subtle—especially more subtle. Nevertheless, my effusive tenderness for him so animated my voice that after three blocks Díaz began to change. Until then he had done nothing but pull at his right mustache with his left hand, nodding, but not looking at me. From then on he began to gesticulate with both hands. By the time we reached Corrientes Street—I don't know what damned thing I had said to him—he smiled almost imperceptibly, focusing alternately on the moving toes of my shoes, and gave me a fleeting glance from the corner of his eye.

"Hum . . . now it begins," I thought. And my ideas, in perfect order until that moment, began to shift and crash into each other dizzily. I made an effort to pull myself together, and I suddenly remembered a lead cat sitting on a chair that I had seen when I was five years old. Why that cat? I whistled and quickly stopped. Then I blew my nose and laughed secretly behind my handkerchief. As I had lowered my head, and the handkerchief was large, only my eyes could be seen. And then I peeked at Díaz Vélez, so sure he wouldn't see me that I had the overwhelming temptation to spit hastily into my hand three times and laugh out loud, just to do something crazy.

By now we were in La Brasileña. We sat down across from one another at a tiny little table, our knees almost touching. In the half-dark, the Nile green color of the café gave such a strong impression of damp and sparkling freshness that one felt obliged to examine the walls to see if they were wet.

Díaz shifted in his chair toward the waiter, who was leaning against the counter with his towel over his crossed arms, and settled into a comfortable position.

We sat for a while without speaking, but the flies of excitement were constantly buzzing through my brain. Although I felt serious, a convulsive smile kept rising to my lips. When we had sat down, I had bitten my lips trying to adopt a normal expression, but this overwhelming tic kept breaking through. My ideas rushed headlong in an unending procession, piling onto one another with undreamed-of velocity; each idea represented an uncontrollable impulse to create ridiculous and, especially, unexpected situations; I had a mad desire to undertake each one, then stop suddenly, and begin another: to poke my forked fingers in Díaz Vélez's eyes, to pull my hair and yell just for the hell of it, and all just to do something absurd—especially to Díaz Vélez. Two or three times I glanced at him and then dropped my eyes. My face must have been crimson because I could feel it burning.

All this occurred during the time it took the waiter to come with his little machine, serve the coffee, and go away, first glancing absent-mindedly into the street. Díaz was still out of sorts, which made me think that when I had stopped him on Charcas Street he had been thinking about something quite different from accompanying a madman like me. . . .

That was it! I had just stumbled onto the reason for my uneasiness: Díaz Vélez, a damned and pursued madman, knew perfectly well that he was responsible for my recent behavior. "I'm sure that my friend," he must have said to himself, "will have the puerile notion of wanting to frighten me when next we see each other. If he happens to find me, he'll pretend to have sudden impulses, psychological manifestations, a persecution complex; he'll follow me down the street making faces; he will then take me somewhere to buy me a cup of coffee. . . ."

"You are com-plete-ly wrong," I told him, putting my elbows on the table and resting my chin in my hands. I looked at him—smiling, no doubt—but never taking my eyes off him.

Díaz seemed to be surprised that I had come out with this unexpected remark. "What do you mean?"

"Nothing. Just this: you are com-plete-ly wrong!"

"But what the devil do you mean? It's possible that I'm wrong, I guess. . . . Undoubtedly, it's very probable that I'm wrong!"

"It's not a question of whether you guess, or whether there's any doubt. What I'm saying is this—and I'm going to repeat it carefully so you'll be sure to understand—you-are-com-plete-ly-wrong!"

This time Díaz, jovially attentive, looked at me and then burst out laughing and glanced away.

"All right, let's agree on it!"

"You do well to agree, because that's the way it is," I persisted, my chin still in my hands.

"I think so, too," he laughed again.

But I was very sure the damned fellow knew exactly what I meant. The more I stared at him, the more dizzily the ideas were careening about in my head.

"Dí-az Vé-lez," I articulated slowly, not for an instant removing my eyes from his. Díaz, understanding that I wasn't addressing him, continued to look straight ahead.

"Dí-az Vé-lez," I repeated with the same incurious vagueness, as if a third, invisible person sitting with us had intervened.

Díaz, pensive, seemed not to have heard. And suddenly he turned with a look of frankness; his hands were trembling slightly.

"Look," he said with a decided smile. "It would be good if we terminated this interview for today. You're acting badly and I'll end up doing the same. But first it would be helpful if we spoke to each other frankly, because if we don't we will *never* understand each other. To be brief: you and Lugones and everyone think I'm pursued; is that right or not?"

He continued to stare at me, still with the smile of a sincere friend who wants to eliminate forever any misunderstandings. I had expected many things, anything but this boldness. With these words, Díaz placed all his cards on the table, and we sat face to face, observing each other's every gesture. He knew that I *knew* he wanted to play with me again, as he had the first night at Lugones's, but nevertheless he dared incite me.

Suddenly I became calm; it was no longer a matter of letting the flies of excitement race surreptitiously through my own brain and waiting to see what would happen, but of stilling the swarm in my own mind in order to listen attentively to the buzzing in another's.

"Perhaps," I responded vaguely when he had completed his question.

"*You* thought I was pursued, didn't you?"

"I thought so."

"And that a certain story I told you at Lugones's about a mad friend of mine was to amuse myself at your expense?"

"Yes."

"Forgive me for continuing. Lugones told you something about me?"

"He did."

"That I was pursued?"

"Yes."

"And you believe, more than you did before, that I am, don't you?"

"Exactly."

Both of us burst out laughing, each looking away at the same instant. Díaz lifted his cup to his lips, but in the middle of the gesture noticed that it was empty and set it down. His eyes were even more brilliant than usual, with dark circles beneath them—not like those of a man, but large and purplish like a woman's.

"All right, all right," he shook his head cordially. "It's difficult *not* to believe it. It's possible, just as possible as what I'm going to tell you. Listen carefully: I may or I may not be pursued, but what is certain is that your eagerness that I see that *you* are too will have this result: in your desire to study me, you will make me truly pursued, and then I will occupy myself in making faces at *you* when you're not looking, as you did to me for six blocks only a half-hour ago . . . which certainly is true. And there is another possible consequence: we understand each other very well; you know that I—an *intelligent* and truly pursued person—am capable of feigning a miraculous normality; and I know that you—in the larval stage of persecution—are capable of simulating perfect fear. Do you agree?"

"Yes, it's possible there's something in that."

"Something? No, everything!"

We laughed again, each immediately looking away. I put my elbows on the table and my chin in my hands, as I had a while before.

"And if I truly believe that you are following me?"

I saw those two brilliant eyes fixed on mine.

In the exchange of our glances there was nothing but the perverse question that had betrayed him, the brief suspension of his shrewdness. Did he mean to ask me that? No, but his madness was so far advanced that he could not resist the temptation. He smiled as he asked his subtle question, but the madman, the real madman, had escaped and was peering at me from behind his eyes.

I shrugged my shoulders carelessly, and, like someone who casually places his hand on the table when he is going to shift his position, I surreptitiously picked up the sugar bowl. But the moment I did it, I felt ashamed and put it down. Díaz watched it all without flickering an eyelid.

"Just the same, you were afraid," he smiled.

"No," I replied happily, drawing my chair a little closer. "It was an act, one that any good friend might put on—any friend with whom one has an *understanding*."

I knew that *he* wasn't putting on an act and that behind the intelligent eyes directing the subtle game still crouched the mad assassin, like a dark beast seeking shelter that sends out decoy cubs on reconnaissance. Little by little the beast was withdrawing, and sanity began to shine in his eyes. Once again he became master of himself; he ran his hand over his shining hair, and, laughing for the last time, he stood up.

It was already two o'clock. We walked toward Charcas talking about various things, in mutual tacit agreement to limit the conversation to ordinary things— the sort of brief, casual dialogue a married couple maintains on the streetcar.

As is always true in these circumstances, once we stopped neither of us spoke for a moment, and, also as always, the first thing we said had nothing to do with our farewell.

"This asphalt is in bad shape," I ventured, pointing with my chin.

"Yes, it never is any good," he replied in a similar tone. "When shall we see each other again?"

"Soon. Won't you be going by Lugones's?"

"Who knows. . . . Tell me, where the devil do you live? I don't remember."

I gave him the address. "Do you plan to come by?"

"Some day . . ."

As we shook hands, we couldn't help exchanging a look, and we burst out laughing together for the hundredth time in two hours.

"Good-by, be seeing you."

After a few feet, I walked very deliberately for a few paces and looked over my shoulder. Díaz had turned around, too. We exchanged a last salute, he with his left hand and I with my right, and then we both walked a little faster.

The madman, the damned madman! I could still see his look in the café. I'd seen it clearly. I'd seen the brutish and suspicious madman behind the actor who was arguing with me! So he'd seen me following him in the glass of the shop-windows! Once again I felt a deep need to provoke him, to make him see clearly that *he* was beginning now, he was losing confidence in me, that any day he was going to want to do to me what I was doing to him. . . .

I was alone in my room. It was late and the house was sleeping; in the entire house there was not a sound to be heard. My sensation of isolation was so strong that unconsciously I raised my eyes and looked around. The incandescent gaslight coldly and peacefully illuminated the walls. I looked at the cone and ascertained that it was not burning with the usual small popping. Everything was deathly still.

It is well known that one has only to repeat a word aloud six or seven times for it to lose all meaning and for it to be converted into a new and absolutely incomprehensible utterance. That is what happened to me. I was alone, alone, alone. . . . What does *alone* mean? And as I looked up I saw a man standing in the doorway looking at me.

I stopped breathing for an instant. I was familiar with the sensation, and I knew that immediately the hair would rise at the back of my neck. I lowered my eyes, continuing my letter, but out of the corner of my eye I saw that the man had appeared again. I knew very well that it was nothing. But I couldn't help myself and, suddenly, I looked. That I looked meant I was lost.

And all of this was Díaz's work; he had got me overexcited about his stupid persecutions, and now I was paying for it.

I pretended not to notice and continued writing, but the man was still there. From that instant, in the lighted silence and the empty space behind me surged the annihilating anguish of a man who is alone in an empty house but doesn't feel alone. And it wasn't only this; *things* were standing behind me. I continued my letter, but the eyes were still in the doorway and the things were almost touching me. Gradually the profound terror I was trying to contain made my hair stand on end, and, rising to my feet as naturally as one is capable in such circumstances, I went to the door and opened it wide. But I know what it cost me to do it slowly.

I didn't pretend to return to my writing. Díaz Vélez! There was no other reason why my nerves should be like this. But I was completely certain, too, that—an eye for an eye and a tooth for a tooth—he was going to pay for all this evening's pleasures.

The door to the street was still open, and I listened to the bustle of people leaving the theaters. "He could have attended one of them," I thought. "And since he has to take the Charcas streetcar, it's possible he passed by here.... And if it's his idea to annoy me with his ridiculous games, pretending he already feels himself pursued and knowing that I'm beginning to believe he is . . ."

Someone knocked at the door.

He! I leaped back into my room and extinguished the lamp in a flash. I stood very still, holding my breath. My skin tingled painfully as I awaited a second knock.

He knocked again. And then after a while I heard his steps advancing across the patio. They stopped at my door, and the intruder stood motionless before its darkness. Of course there was no one there. Then suddenly he called me. Damn him! He knew that I had heard him, that I had turned out the light when I heard, and that I was standing, not moving, by the table! He knew *precisely* what I was thinking, and that I was waiting, waiting, as in a nightmare, to hear my name called once again!

He called me a second time. Then, after a long pause, "Ho-racio!"

Damnation! What did my name have to do with all this? What right did he have to call me Horacio, he who in spite of his tormenting wickedness would not come in because he was afraid! "He knows that this is what I am thinking at this instant; he is convinced of it, but the madness is upon him, and he won't come in!"

And he didn't. He stood an instant more before he moved away from the threshold and returned to the entrance hall. Rapidly, I left the table, tiptoed to the door, and stuck out my head. "He knows I'm going to do this." Nevertheless, he continued at a tranquil pace and disappeared.

Considering what had just happened, I appreciated the superhuman effort the pursued one made in not turning around, knowing that behind his back I was devouring him with my eyes.

*

One week later I received this letter:

> My dear X:
> Because of a bad cold, I haven't been out for four days. If you are not afraid
> of the contagion, you would give me great pleasure by coming to chat with
> me for a while.
> Yours very truly,
> Lucas Díaz Vélez

> P.S. If you see Lugones, tell him I have been sent something that will interest
> him very much.

I received the letter at two o'clock in the afternoon. As it was cold and I was
planning to go for a walk, I hurried over to Lugones's.

"What are you doing here at this time of day?" he asked me. I didn't see him
very frequently in the afternoon in those days.

"Nothing. Díaz Vélez sends you his regards."

"So it's still you and Díaz Vélez," he laughed.

"Yes, still. I just received a letter from him. It seems he hasn't been out of the
house for four days."

It was evident to both of us that this was the beginning of the end, and in five
minutes' speculation on the matter we had invented a million absurd things that
could have happened to Díaz. But since I hadn't told Lugones about my hectic
day with Díaz, his interest was soon exhausted and I left.

For the same reason, Lugones understood very little about my visit. It was
unthinkable that I had gone to his house expressly to tell him that Díaz was
offering him more honey cakes; and, since I had left almost immediately, the
man must have been thinking everything except what was really at the heart of
the matter.

At eight o'clock I knocked at Vélez's door. I gave my name to the servant, and
a few moments later an elderly lady, obviously from the provinces, appeared. Her
hair was smooth, and she was wearing a black dressing gown with an interminable row of covered buttons.

"Do you want to see Lucas?" she asked, looking at me suspiciously.

"Yes, ma'am."

"He is somewhat ill; I don't know whether he will be able to receive you."

I objected that nonetheless I had received a note from him. The old lady looked
at me again.

"Please be good enough to wait a moment."

She returned and led me to my friend. Díaz was sitting up in bed with a jacket
over his nightshirt. He introduced us to each other.

"My aunt . . ."

When she withdrew, I said, "I thought you lived alone."

"I used to, but she's been living here with me for the last two months. Bring
up a chair. "

The moment I saw him I was sure that what Lugones and I had conjectured
was true; he absolutely did not have a cold.

"Bronchitis . . . ?"

"Yes, something like that. . . ."

I took a quick look around. The room was like any other room with white-washed walls. He, too, had incandescent gas. I looked with curiosity at the cone, but his whistled, whereas mine popped. As for the rest, a beautiful silence throughout the house.

When I looked back at him, he was watching me. It must have been at least five seconds that he had been watching me. Our glances locked, and a shiver sent its tentacles to the marrow of my bones. But he was completely mad now! The pursued one was living just behind Díaz's eyes. The only thing, absolutely the only thing in his eyes was a murderous fixation.

"He's going to attack me," I agonized to myself. But the obstinacy suddenly disappeared, and after a quick glance at the ceiling Díaz recovered his habitual expression. He looked at me, smiling, and then dropped his eyes.

"Why didn't you answer me the other evening in your room?"

"I don't know."

"Do you think I didn't come in because I was afraid?"

"Something like that."

"But do you think I'm not really ill?"

"No . . . Why?"

He raised his arm and let it fall lazily on the quilt.

"I was looking at you a little bit ago. . . ."

"Let's forget it, shall we!"

"The madman had escaped from me, hadn't he?"

"Forget it, Díaz, forget it!"

I had a knot in my throat. His every word had the effect on me of one more push toward an imminent abyss.

If he continues, he'll explode! He won't be able to hold it back! And then I clearly realized that Lugones and I had been right. Díaz had taken to his bed because he was afraid! I looked at him and shuddered violently. There it was again! The assassin was once more staring through eyes now fixed on me. But, as before, after a glance at the ceiling, the light of normalcy returned to them.

"One thing is certain, it's fiendishly quiet here," I said to myself.

A moment passed.

"Do you like the silence?"

"Absolutely."

"It's funereal. Suddenly you get the sensation that there are things concen-trating too much on you. Let me give you an example."

"What do you mean?"

His eyes were shining with perverse intelligence as they had at other times.

"Well, suppose that you, like me, have been alone, in bed, for four days, and that you—I mean, I—haven't thought about you. Suppose you hear a voice clearly, not yours, not mine, a clear voice, anywhere, behind the wardrobe, in the ceiling—here in this ceiling, for example—calling you, insult—"

He stopped: he was staring at the ceiling, his face completely altered by hatred, and then he shouted, "There are! There are!"

Shaken to my soul, I instantly recalled his former glances; he heard the voice that insulted him from the ceiling, but I was the one who pursued him. No doubt he still possessed discernment enough not to link the two things together.

His face had been suffused with color. Now, by contrast, Díaz had become frightfully pale. Finally, with an effort, he turned away from the ceiling and lay quietly for a moment, his expression vague and his breathing agitated.

I could not remain there any longer. I glanced at the night table and saw the half-open drawer.

"As soon as I stand up," I thought with anguish, "he's going to shoot me dead." But in spite of everything, I rose and approached him to say good-by. Díaz, with a sudden start, turned toward me. In the time it took me to reach his side, his breathing stopped and his fascinated eyes took on the expression of a cornered animal watching the sights of a shotgun drawing near.

"I hope you feel better, Díaz. . . ."

I did not dare hold out my hand, but reason is as violent as madness and is extremely painful to lose. Díaz came to his senses and extended *his* hand.

"Come tomorrow; I'm not well today."

"I'm afraid I . . ."

"No, no, come. Come!" he concluded with imperious anguish.

I left without seeing anyone, feeling, as I found myself free and remembering with horror that extremely intelligent man battling with the ceiling, that I was cured forever of psychological games.

The following day, at eight o'clock in the evening, a boy delivered this note to me:

SIR:
Lucas insists on seeing you. If it wouldn't be a bother I would appreciate your stopping by here today.

Hoping to hear from you, DESOLINDA S. DE ROLDÁN

I had had a disturbing day. I couldn't think about Díaz that I didn't see him shouting again during that horrible loss of conscious reason. His nerves were strung so tight that a sudden blast from a train whistle would have shattered them.

I went, nevertheless, but as I walked along I found I was painfully shaken by the least noise. So when I turned the corner and saw a group in front of Díaz Vélez's door, my legs grew weak—not from any concrete fear, but from coincidences, from things foreseen, from cataclysms of logic.

I heard a murmur of fear.

"He's coming; he's coming!" And everyone scattered into the middle of the street.

"There it is; he's mad," I said to myself, grieved by what might have happened. I ran, and in a moment I stood before the door.

Díaz lived on Arenales Street between Bulnes and Vidt. The house had an extensive interior patio overflowing with plants. As there was no light in the patio, as contrasted with the entryway, the patio beyond lay in deep shadow.

"What's going on?" I asked.

Several persons replied:

"The young man who lives here is crazy."

"He's wandering around the patio. . . ."

"He's naked . . ."

"He keeps running out. . . ."

I was anxious to know about his aunt.

"There she is."

I turned, and there against the window was the poor lady, sobbing. When she saw me she redoubled her weeping.

"Lucas . . . ! He's gone mad!"

"When?"

"Just a while ago. . . . He came running out of his room . . . shortly after I had sent you . . ."

I felt someone was speaking to me.

"Listen, listen!"

From the black depths of the patio we heard a pitiful cry.

"He yells like that every few minutes. . . ."

"Here he comes; here he comes!" everyone shouted, fleeing.

I didn't have time or strength to run away. I felt a muffled, precipitous rush, and Díaz Vélez, livid, completely nude, his eyes bulging out of his head, rushed into the entrance hall, carried me along in front of him, made a ridiculous grimace in the doorway, and ran back into the patio.

"Get out of there; he'll kill you," they yelled at me. "He shot at a chair today."

Everyone had clustered around the door again, peering into the shadows.

"Listen . . . , again."

Now it was a cry of agony that emerged from the depths. "Water . . . ! Water . . . !"

"He's asked for water two times."

The two officers who had just arrived had decided to post themselves on either side of the entrance hall at the rear and seize Díaz the next time he rushed into the hall. The wait was even more agonizing this time. But soon the cry was repeated, and, following it, the scattering of the crowd.

"Here he comes!"

Díaz rushed out, violently hurled an empty vase into the street, and an instant later was subdued. He defended himself fiercely, but, when he saw it was hopeless to resist, he stopped struggling, astonished and panting, and looked from person to person with surprise. He did not recognize me, nor did I delay there any longer.

The following morning I went to have lunch with Lugones and told him the whole story—this time we were very serious.

"What a shame; he was very intelligent."

"Too intelligent," I confirmed, remembering.

All this was June 1903.

"Let's do something," Lugones said to me. "Why don't we go to Misiones? That will give us something to do."

We went, and four months later we returned, Lugones with a full beard and I with a ruined stomach.

Díaz was in an institution. Since the crisis, which had lasted two days, there had been no further incidents. When I went to visit him, he received me effusively.

"I thought I'd never see you again. Have you been away?"

"Yes, for a while. Getting along all right?"

"Just fine. I hope to be completely well before the end of the year."

I couldn't help looking at him.

"Yes," he smiled. "Although I feel fine, I think it's prudent to wait a few months. But deep down, since that night, nothing has happened."

"Do you remember . . . ?"

"No, but they told me about it. I must have been quite a sight, naked."

We entertained ourselves a while longer.

"Look," he said seriously, "I'm going to ask you a favor: come see me often. You don't know how these gentlemen bore me with their innocent questions and their snares. All they succeed in doing is making me bitter, eliciting ideas from me that I don't like to remember. I'm sure that in the company of someone a little more intelligent I will be wholly cured."

I solemnly promised him to do it, and for two months I returned frequently, never denouncing the least fault, sometimes even touching on our old relationship.

One day I found an intern with him. Díaz winked lightly and gravely introduced me to his guardian. The three of us chatted like judicious friends. Nevertheless, I noted in Díaz Vélez—with some pleasure, I admit—a certain fiendish irony in everything he was saying to his doctor. He adroitly directed the conversation to the patients and soon placed his own case before us.

"But you are different," objected the doctor. "You're cured."

"Not really, if you consider that I still have to be here."

"A simple precaution . . . you understand that yourself."

"But what's the reason for it? Don't you think it will be impossible, absolutely impossible, ever to know when I'm sane—with no need for 'precaution,' as you say. I can't be, I believe, more sane than I am now."

"Not as far as I can see," the doctor laughed happily.

Díaz gave me another imperceptible wink.

"It seems to me that one cannot have any greater conscious sanity than this— permit me: You both know, as I do, that I have been pursued, that one night I had a crisis, that I have been here six months, and that *any* amount of time is short for an absolute guarantee that the thing won't return. Fine. This 'precaution' would be sensible if I didn't see all this clearly and discuss it intelligently. . . . I know that at this moment you are recalling cases of lucid madness and are comparing me to that madman in La Plata. The one who in bad moments quite naturally made fun of a broom he thought was his wife but, when completely himself and laughing, still kept his eyes on the broom, so that no one would touch it. . . . I know, too, that this objective perspicacity in following the doctor's opinion while recounting a similar case to one's own is itself madness . . . and the very astuteness of the analysis only confirms it. . . . But . . . even so—in what manner, in what other way, may a sane man defend himself?"

"There is no other way, absolutely none," the intern who was being interrogated burst out laughing. Díaz glanced at me out of the corner of his eye and shrugged his shoulders, smiling.

I had a strong desire to know what the doctor thought about this super-lucidity. At a different time I would have valued such lucidity even at the cost of disordering my nerves. I glanced at the doctor, but the man didn't seem to have felt its influence. A moment later we left.

"Do you think . . . ?" I asked him.

"Hum! I think so . . . ," he replied, looking sideways at the patio. Abruptly, he turned his head.

"Look, look!" he told me, pressing my arm.

Díaz, pale, his eyes dilated with terror and hatred, was cautiously approaching the door, as he had surely done every time I came—*looking at me!*

"Ah! You hoodlum!" he yelled at me, raising his fist. "I've been watching you come for two months now!"

KLEIST IN THUN

Robert Walser

Translated from the German by Christopher Middleton

Robert Walser (1878–1956). Born and raised in Biel in Switzerland, Walser was a precocious writer. By the age of twenty, his early poems and stories began to appear in the pages of the short-lived but highly influential magazine *Die Insel*. In his twenties, he spent five years living in Berlin, where he published three novels, and was much praised by Robert Musil. Despite positive reviews, Walser never managed to live on the meagre income from his writings and worked variously as a servant, a butler and an inventor's assistant. His writings became increasingly radical. Both his mother and brother had suffered from mental illness and, in 1929, Walser too suffered a nervous breakdown, and spent the remainder of his life in asylums and sanatoriums. He died in obscurity and was not "rediscovered" until the 1970s.

Kleist found board and lodging in a villa near Thun, on an island in the river Aare. It can be said today, after more than a hundred years, with no certainty of course, but I think he must have walked across a tiny bridge, ten meters in length, and have pulled a bell rope. Thereupon somebody must have come sliding lizardlike down the stairs inside, to see who was there. "Have you a room to let?" Briefly then Kleist made himself comfortable in the three rooms which, at an astonishingly low price, were assigned to him. "A charming local Bernese girl keeps house for me." A beautiful poem, a child, a heroic deed; these three things occupy his mind. Moreover, he is somewhat unwell. "Lord knows what is wrong. What is the matter with me? It is so beautiful here."

He writes, of course. From time to time he takes the coach to Berne, meets literary friends, and reads to them whatever he has written. Naturally they praise him to the skies, yet find his whole person rather peculiar. He writes *The Broken Jug*. But why all the fuss? Spring has come. Around Thun the fields are thick with flowers, fragrance everywhere, hum of bees, work, sounds fall, one idles about; in the heat of the sun you could go mad. It is as if radiant red stupefying waves rise up in his head whenever he sits at his table and tries to write.

He curses his craft. He had intended to become a farmer when he came to Switzerland. Nice idea, that. Easy to think up, in Potsdam. Poets anyway think up such things easily enough. Often he sits at the window.

Possibly about ten o'clock in the morning. He is so much alone. He wishes there was a voice beside him; what sort of voice? A hand; well, and? A body? But what for? Out there lies the lake, veiled and lost in white fragrance, framed by the bewitching unnatural mountains. How it all dazzles and disturbs. The whole countryside down to the water is sheer garden, it seems to seethe and sag in the bluish air with bridges full of flowers and terraces full of fragrance. Birds sing so faintly under all the sun, all the light. They are blissful, and full of sleep. His elbow on the windowsill, Kleist props his head on his hand, stares and stares and wants to forget himself. The image of his distant northern home enters his mind, his mother's face he can see clearly, old voices, damn it all—he has leapt up and run out into the garden. There he gets into a skiff and rows out over the clear morning lake. The kiss of the sun is indivisible, unabating. Not a breath. Hardly a stir. The mountains are the artifice of a clever scene painter, or look like it; it is as if the whole region were an album, the mountains drawn on a blank page by an adroit dilettante for the lady who owns the album, as a souvenir, with a line of verse. The album has pale green covers. Which is appropriate. The foothills at the lake's edge are so half-and-half green, so high, so fragrant. La la la! He has undressed and plunges into the water. How inexpressibly lovely this is to him. He swims and hears the laughter of women on the shore. The boat shifts sluggishly on the greenish, bluish water. The world around is like one vast embrace. What rapture this is, but what an agony it can also be.

Sometimes, especially on fine evenings, he feels that this place is the end of the world. The Alps seem to him to be the unattainable gates to a paradise high up on the ridges. He walks on his little island, pacing slow, up and down. The girl hangs out washing among the bushes, in which a light gleams, melodious, yellow, morbidly beautiful. The faces of the snow-crested mountains are so wan; dominant in all things is a final, intangible beauty. Swans swimming to and fro among the rushes seem caught in the spell of beauty and of the light of dusk. The air is sickly. Kleist wants a brutal war, to fight in battle; to himself he seems a miserable and superfluous sort of person.

He goes for a walk. Why, he asks himself with a smile, why must it be he who has nothing to do, nothing to strike at, nothing to throw down? He feels the sap and the strength in his body softly complaining. His entire soul thrills for bodily exertion. Between high ancient walls he climbs, down over whose gray stone screes the dark green ivy passionately curls, up to the castle hill. In all the windows up here the evening light is aglow. Up on the edge of the rock face stands a delightful pavilion, he sits here, and lets his soul fly, out and down into the shining holy silent prospect. He would be surprised if he were to feel well now. Read a newspaper? How would that be? Conduct an idiotic political or generally useful debate with some respected official half-wit or other? Yes? He is not unhappy. Secretly he considers happy alone the man who is inconsolable: naturally and powerfully inconsolable. With him the position is one small faint shade worse. He is too sensitive to be happy, too haunted by all his irresolute, cautious, mistrusted feelings. He would like to scream aloud, to weep. God in heaven, what is wrong with me, and he rushes down the darkening hill. Night soothes him. Back in his room he sits down, determined to work till frenzy comes, at his writing table. The light of the lamp eliminates his image of his whereabouts, and clears his brain, and he writes now.

On rainy days it is terribly cold and void. The place shivers at him. The green shrubs whine and whimper and shed rain tears for some sun. Over the heads of the mountains drift monstrous dirty clouds like great impudent murderous hands over foreheads. The countryside seems to want to creep away and hide from this evil weather, to shrivel up. The lake is leaden and bleak, the language of the waves unkind. The storm wind, wailing like a weird admonition, can find no issue, crashes from one scarp to the next. It is dark here, and small, small. Everything is pressed right up against one's nose. One would like to seize a sledge-hammer and beat a way out of it all. Get away there, get away!

The sun shines again, and it is Sunday. Bells are ringing. The people are leaving the hilltop church. The girls and women in tight black laced bodices with silver spangles, the men dressed simply and soberly. They carry prayer books in their hands, and their faces are peaceful, beautiful, as if all anxiety were vanished, all the furrows of worry and contention smoothed away, all trouble forgotten. And the bells. How they peal out, leap out with peals and waves of sound. How it glitters and glows with blue and bell tones over the whole Sunday sunbathed little town. The people scatter. Kleist stands, fanned by strange feelings, on the church steps and his eyes follow the movements of the people going down them. Many a farmer's child he sees, descending the steps like a born princess, majesty and liberty bred in the bone. He sees big-muscled, handsome young men from the country, and what country, not flat land, not young plainsmen, but lads who have erupted out of deep valleys curiously caverned in the mountains, narrow often, like the arm of a tall, somewhat monstrous man. They are the lads from the mountains where cornland and pasture fall steep into the crevasses, where odorous hot grass grows in tiny flat patches on the brinks of horrible ravines, where the houses are stuck like specks on the meadows when you stand far below on the broad country road and look right up, to see if there can still be houses for people up there.

Sundays Kleist likes, and market days also, when everything ripples and swarms with blue smocks and the costumes of the peasant women, on the road, and on the narrow main street. There, on this narrow street, by the pavement, the wares are stacked in stone vaults and on flimsy stalls. Grocers announce their cheap treas-ures with beguiling country cries. And usually on such a market day there shines the most brilliant, the hottest, the silliest sun. Kleist likes to be pushed hither and thither by the bright bland throng of folk. Everywhere there is the smell of cheese. Into the better shops go the serious and sometimes beautiful countrywomen, cau-tiously, to do their shopping. Many of the men have pipes in their mouths. Pigs, calves, and cows are hauled past. There is one man standing there and laughing and forcing his rosy piglet to walk by beating it with a stick. It refuses, so he takes it under his arm and carries it onward. The smells of human bodies filter through their clothes, out of the inns there pour the sounds of carousal, dancing, and eating. All this uproar, all the freedom of the sounds! Sometimes coaches cannot pass. The horses are completely hemmed in by trading and gossiping men. And the sun shines dazzling so exactly upon the objects, faces, cloths, baskets, and goods. Everything is moving and the dazzle of sunlight must of course move nicely along with everything else. Kleist would like to pray. He finds no majestic music so beautiful, no soul so subtle as the music and soul of all this human activity. He would like to sit down on one of the steps which lead into the narrow street. He walks on, past women with skirts lifted high, past girls who carry baskets on their heads, calm, almost noble, like the Italian women carrying jugs he has seen in paintings, past shouting men and drunken men, past policemen, past schoolboys moving with their schoolboy purposes, past shadowy alcoves which smell cool, past ropes, sticks, foodstuffs, imitation jewelry, jaws, noses, hats, horses, veils, blankets, woolen stockings, sausages, balls of butter, and slabs of cheese, out of the tumult to a bridge over the Aare, where he stops, and leans over the rail to look down into the deep blue water flowing wonderfully away. Above him the castle turrets glitter and glow like brownish liquid fire. This might almost be Italy.

At times on ordinary weekdays the whole small town seems to him bewitched by sun and stillness. He stands motionless before the strange old town hall, with the sharp-edged numerals of its date cut in the gleaming white wall. It is all so irretrievable, like the form of a folk song the people have forgotten. Hardly alive, no, not alive at all. He mounts the enclosed wooden stair to the castle where the old earls lived, the wood gives off the odor of age and of vanished human destinies. Up here he sits on a broad, curved, green bench to enjoy the view, but closes his eyes. It all looks so terrible, as if asleep, buried under dust, with the life gone out of it. The nearest thing lies as in a faraway veil-like dreaming distance. Everything is sheathed in a hot cloud. Summer, but what sort of a summer? I am not alive, he cries out, and does not know where to turn with his eyes, hands, legs, and breath. A dream. Nothing there. I do not want dreams. In the end he tells himself he lives too much alone. He shudders, compelled to admit how unfeeling is his relation to the world about him.

Then come the summer evenings. Kleist sits on the high churchyard wall. Everything is damp, yet also sultry. He opens his shirt, to breathe freely. Below him lies the lake, as if it had been hurled down by the great hand of a god, incandescent with shades of yellow and red, its whole incandescence seems to glow up out of the water's depths. It is like a lake of fire. The Alps have come to life and dip with fabulous gestures their foreheads into the water. His swans down there circle his quiet island, and the crests of trees in dark, chanting, fragrant joy float over— over what? Nothing, nothing. Kleist drinks it all in. To him the whole dark sparkling lake is the cluster of diamonds upon a vast, slumbering, unknown woman's body. The lime trees and the pine trees and the flowers give off their perfumes. There is a soft, scarcely perceptible sound down there; he can hear it, but he can also see it. That is something new. He wants the intangible, the incomprehensible. Down on the lake a boat is rocking; Kleist does not see it, but he sees the lanterns which guide it, swaying to and fro. There he sits, his face jutting forward, as if he must be ready for the death leap into the image of that lovely depth. He wants to perish into the image. He wants eyes alone, only to be one single eye. No, something totally different. The air should be a bridge, and the whole image of the landscape a chair back to relax against, sensuous, happy, tired. Night comes, but he does not want to go down, he throws himself on a grave that is hidden under bushes, bats whiz around him, the pointed trees whisper as soft airs pass over them. The grass smells so delicious, blanketing the skeletons of buried men. He is so grievously happy, too happy, whence his suffocation, his aridity, his grief. So alone. Why cannot the dead emerge and talk a half hour with the lonely man?

On a summer night one ought really to have a woman to love. The thought of white lustrous breasts and lips hurls Kleist down the hill to the lakeside and into the water, fully dressed, laughing, weeping.

Weeks pass, Kleist has destroyed one work, two, three works. He wants the highest mastery, good, good. What's that? Not sure? Tear it up. Something new, wilder, more beautiful. He begins *The Battle of Sempach*, in the center of it the figure of Leopold of Austria, whose strange fate attracts him. Meanwhile, he remembers his *Robert Guiscard*. He wants him to be splendid. The good fortune to be a sensibly balanced man with simple feelings he sees burst into fragments, crash and rattle like boulders collapsing down the landslip of his life. He helps him nevertheless, now he is resolute. He wants to abandon himself to the entire catastrophe of being a poet: the best thing is for me to be destroyed as quickly as possible.

What he writes makes him grimace: his creations miscarry. Toward autumn he is taken ill. He is amazed at the gentleness which now comes over him. His sister travels to Thun to bring him home. There are deep furrows in his cheeks. His face has the expression and coloring of a man whose soul has been eaten away. His eyes are more lifeless than the eyebrows over them. His hair hangs clotted in thick pointed hanks over his temples, which are contorted by all the thoughts which he imagines have dragged him into filthy pits and into hells. The verses that resound in his brain seem to him like the croakings of ravens; he would like to eradicate his memory. He would like to shed his life; but first he wants to shatter the shells of life. His fury rages at the pitch of his agony, his scorn at the pitch of his misery. My dear, what is the matter, his sister embraces him. Nothing, nothing. That was the ultimate wrong, that he should have to say what was wrong with him. On the floor of his room lie his manuscripts, like children horribly forsaken by father and mother. He lays his hand in his sister's, and is content to look at her, long, and in silence. Already it is the vacant gaze of a skull, and the girl shudders.

Then they leave. The country girl who has kept house for Kleist says goodbye. It is a bright autumn morning, the coach rolls over bridges, past people, through roughly plastered lanes, people look out of windows, overhead is the sky, under trees lies yellowish foliage, everything is clean, autumnal, what else? And the coachman has his pipe in his mouth. All is as ever it was. Kleist sits dejected in a corner of the coach. The towers of the castle of Thun vanish behind a hill. Later, far in the distance, Kleist's sister can see once more the beautiful lake. It is already quite chilly. Country houses appear. Well, well, such grand estates in such mountainous country? On and on. Everything flies past as you look to the side and drops behind, everything dances, circles, vanishes. Much is already hidden under the autumn's veil, and everything is a little golden in the little sunlight which pierces the clouds. Such gold, how it shimmers there, still to be found only in the dirt. Hills, scarps, valleys, churches, villages, people staring, children, trees, wind, clouds, stuff and nonsense—is all this anything special? Isn't it all rubbish, quotidian stuff? Kleist sees nothing. He is dreaming of clouds and of images and slightly of kind, comforting, caressing human hands. How do you feel? asks his sister. Kleist's mouth puckers, and he would like to give her a little smile. He succeeds, but with an effort. It is as if he has a block of stone to lift from his mouth before he can smile.

His sister cautiously plucks up the courage to speak of his taking on some practical activity soon. He nods, he is himself of the same opinion. Music and radiant shafts of light flicker about his senses. As a matter of fact, if he admits it quite frankly to himself, he feels quite well now; in pain, but well at the same time. Something hurts him, yes, really, quite correct, but not in the chest, not in the lungs either, or in the head, what? Nowhere at all? Well, not quite, a little, somewhere so that one cannot quite precisely tell where it is. Which means: it's nothing to speak of. He says something, and then come moments when he is outright happy as a child, and then of course the girl makes a rather severe, punitive face, just to show him a little how very strangely he does fool around with his life. The girl is a Kleist and has enjoyed an education, exactly what her brother has wanted to throw overboard. At heart she is naturally glad that he is feeling better. On and on, well well, what a journey it is. But finally one has to let it go, this stagecoach, and last of all one can permit oneself the observation that on the front of the villa where Kleist lived there hangs a marble plaque which indicates who lived and worked there. Travelers who intend to tour the Alps can read it, the children of Thun read it and spell it out, letter by letter, and then look questioning into each other's eyes. A Jew can read it, a Christian too, if he has the time and if his train is not leaving that very instant, a Turk, a swallow, insofar as she is interested, I also, I can read it again if I like. Thun stands at the entrance to the Bernese Oberland and is visited every year by thousands of foreigners. I know the region a little perhaps, because I worked as a clerk in a brewery there. The region is considerably more beautiful than I have been able to describe here, the lake is twice as blue, the sky three times as beautiful. Thun had a trade fair, I cannot say exactly but I think four years ago.

[1913]

SEVEN PENNIES

Zsigmond Móricz

Translated from the Hungarian by István Farkas

Zsigmond Móricz (1879–1942). Born in Tiszacsécse, to a poor rural family, the young Móricz proved an able, but unfocused student. At twenty, he briefly studied theology, but within months had given this up to study law, though he did not graduate. At the age of twenty-five, he began working as a journalist in Budapest, and it was here that his interests turned towards literature. He was a war correspondent during the First World War, and his articles focused less on military strategies than on the everyday lives of ordinary soldiers on the front lines. He was appointed vice president of the Vörösmarty Academy by the revolutionary government following the war, only to be imprisoned after the counterrevolution that led to the fall of the Soviet Republic. Móricz published his first story in the review *Nyugat*, which he later went on to edit. This was followed by poems, essays and short stories as well as novels. He was consumed by his writing, saying "Has the Lord created me for this? As long as I can stand it, I will do that which I cannot avoid in any case: write." His stories often depict life in the rural, small-town Hungary he knew intimately as a child. Many of his novels have been adapted for film and television.

The gods in their wisdom have granted the benefit of laughter also to the poor.

The tenants of huts do not wail all the time, often enough a hearty laughter comes ringing from their dwellings. I might even go to the length of saying that the poor often laugh when they have every reason to cry.

I happen to be thoroughly familiar with that kind of world. The generation of the Soós tribe that had brought forth my father went through the direst stages of destitution. At that time, my father worked as a day-labourer in a machine shop. There was nothing for him, nor for anyone else, to brag about in those days. (Yet brag they did.)

And it is a fact that never in my life was I to laugh as much as in those very years of my childhood.

How, indeed, should I ever again have laughed so heartily after I had lost my merry, red-cheeked mother, who used to laugh so sweetly that, in the end, tears came trickling down her cheeks and her laughter ended in a fit of coughing that almost choked her. . .

But she never laughed as merrily as on the afternoon which we spent searching for seven pennies. We searched, and we found them, too. Three were in the drawer of the sewing machine, one in the cupboard. . . the rest were more difficult to find.

My mother found the first three pennies all by herself. She thought there ought to be more coins in the drawer, for she used to turn a penny by sewing and kept whatever she earned in that drawer. To me, the drawer of the sewing machine seemed an inexhaustible gold mine, and whenever you delved into it, all your wishes came true.

Thus I was flabbergasted to see my mother digging into a mess of needles, thimbles, scissors, bits of ribbon, braid and buttons, and, after she had poked around in them a while, to hear her say in astonishment:

"They have gone into hiding."

"Who?"

"The coins," she said with a laugh. She pulled out the drawer.

"Come on, sonny, let us find the wicked things. Naughty, naughty coins."

She squatted on the floor and put down the drawer so cautiously, she seemed to fear its contents might fly away; then she daintily turned it upside down, as though she were catching butterflies under a hat.

You couldn't help laughing over the way she acted.

"Here they are, in here," she giggled, and was in no hurry to lift up the drawer. "If there's but a single one, it must be in here."

I squatted on my heels and watched closely for a shiny coin to creep forth somewhere.

Nothing stirred.

To be quite frank, neither of us really believed that there were any inside. We glanced at each other, laughing over the childish joke.

I touched the drawer as it lay there upside down.

"Ssht!" my mother shushed me. "Keep still, child, or they'll run away. You have no idea how nimble pennies can be. They run so fast, they simply roll away. My, how they roll. . ."

We rocked with laughter. We had seen often enough, how easily the pennies could roll away. When we got over our fit of laughter, I stretched out my hand once more to lift the drawer. "Don't!" mother cried out, and I snatched back my finger as if I had scorched it on a stove.

"Easy, you spendthrift. Why be in such a hurry to send them off? They belong to us only while they are safe here, under the hood. Let them remain there for a little while yet. For, you see, I have to do some washing and for that I need some soap, and for the soap I must have at least seven pennies, they won't give me any for less. I've got three already, I need four more, they must be in this little house. They live here, but they hate to be disturbed, and if they grow angry, they'll vanish and we shan't ever get hold of them again. Easy, then, for money is a delicate thing and must be handled gently. It wants to be respected. It takes offence quickly, like a sensitive lady. . . Don't you know a verse that would lure it from its house?"

Oh, how we laughed while she babbled along! My incantation was odd indeed. It went like this:

"Uncle Coin, I'm no liar, Your house is on fire. . ."

At this I turned the drawer right side up again.

There was every kind of rubbish below it, but coins. . . there were none.

My mother kept rummaging in the heap, making a sour face, but that didn't help.

"What a pity," she said, "that we have no table. It would have been more respectful to turn it over on a table, and then the coins would have stayed put."

I swept up the things and put them back into the drawer. Mother was doing some hard thinking the while. She racked her brains to remember whether she had some time or other put any money elsewhere, but she couldn't recall it.

Of a sudden, I had an idea.

"Mother, I know a place where there is a coin."

"Where is it, sonny? Let us catch it before it melts like snow."

"There used to be one in the drawer of the glass cupboard."

"Oh, my lamb, I'm glad you didn't tell me before, it would surely no longer be there."

We stood up and went to the cupboard that had lost its glass pane ever so long ago; the penny was actually in the drawer I had suspected it to be in. I had been tempted to filch it for the past three days, but I never mustered enough courage to do so. Had I dared, I would have spent it on candy.

"Now we have got four pennies. Don't worry, sonny, that's already the bigger half. All we need is three more. And if it has taken us an hour to find four, we shall find the rest before we have a snack. That will leave me plenty of time to do a batch of washing by nightfall. Come on, let us see, perhaps there are some more in the other drawers."

All would have been well, had each drawer contained one coin. That would have been more than we needed. For, in the prime of its life, the old cupboard had done service in a prosperous dwelling, where it had harboured many treasures. In our home, however, the poor thing contained little enough – weak-chested, worm-eaten, gap-toothed as it was.

Mother chided each drawer as she pulled it open.

"This one used to be rich – once upon a time. This one never had a thing. This one here always lived on tick. As for you, you miserable beggar, you haven't a farthing to your name. This one won't ever have any, we keep our poverty in it. And you there, may you never have a single one: I ask you for a penny just this once, and even so you begrudge it me. This one is sure to be the richest, look!" she burst out laughing, as she jerked open the lowest drawer, which had not a splinter to its bottom.

She hung it around my neck, and we both laughed so hard, we had to sit down on the floor.

"Wait a minute," she started, "I'll get some money in a jiffy. There must be some in your father's suit."

There were some nails in the wall upon which our clothes were hung. My mother delved into the topmost pocket of my father's jacket, and, marvel of marvels, her fingers pulled out a penny.

She could hardly believe her eyes.

"Bless me," she shouted, "here it is. How much does that make? Why, we can hardly manage to count them all up. One – two – three – four – five. . . Five! All we need is two more. Two pennies, that is nothing. Where there are five, there are bound to be two more."

She went about feverishly searching all my father's pockets, but alas, to no avail. She couldn't find another. Even the merriest jokes failed to lure forth two more pennies.

My mother's cheeks burned like two red roses with excitement and exertion. She was not supposed to work, for, whenever she did, she was taken ill. This was, of course, a special kind of work, and you can't forbid people to look for money.

Snack-time came and went. Soon it would be getting dark. My father needed a clean shirt for the morning, and no washing could be done. Well-water alone was not enough to remove the greasy dirt.

Suddenly, mother tapped her forehead:

"How silly of me. I never thought of searching my own pocket! Now that I think of it, I shall have a look."

She did, and sure enough, there was a penny in it. The sixth one.

A veritable fever took hold of us. Just one more penny was lacking. "Let me see your pockets, perhaps there is one in them."

Dear me, it was no good showing them. They were empty.

It was turning dark, and there we were with our six pennies, we might as well have had none for all the use they were. The Jewish grocer granted no credit, and the neighbours were just as penniless as we. Besides, you just couldn't go and ask for one penny!

The best we could do was to have a good laugh over our own misery.

We were in the very throes of it, when a beggar came by, wailing his sing-song prayer for alms.

Mother almost swooned with laughter.

"Stop it, my good man," she said, "I have been idle all afternoon, for I am short of one penny to buy half a pound soap with."

The beggar, a kindly old man, stared at her. "You are short of one penny, you say?"

"One penny, yes."

"I'll give it you."

"A nice thing to take alms from a beggar!"

"Never mind, my child, I can do without it. All I need is a hole in the ground and a shovelful of earth. That will make everything well for me."

He put the penny into my hand and shuffled along amidst our blessings.

"Thank goodness," my mother said. "Now run along. . ."

She stopped short, then burst into ringing laughter.

"I can't wash today in any case, but, just the same, it's none too soon that we scraped together the money: it is getting dark, and I have no kerosene for the lamp."

She laughed so hard, it took her breath away. A fierce murderous fit of coughing shook her body. She swayed on her feet and buried her face in her palms and, as I drew close to support her, I felt something warm trickling down on my hands.

It was blood, her precious, hallowed blood. That of my mother, who could laugh so heartily as few people can, even among the poor.

THE CHESS PLAYERS

Premchand

Translated from the Hindi by David Rubin

Premchand (1880–1936). Born Dhanpat Rai in a village near Varanasi in Uttar Pradesh, 'Munshi' Premchand is regarded as one of the foremost Hindustani writers of the early twentieth century. He was drawn to books at an early age and decided to start working life as a sales boy in a book shop, so he might have access to all the books he could read. His first novels were published under the name Nawab Rai, as were his short stories, *Soz-e-Watan*, which was later banned as seditious by the British government, forcing him to change his name. As "Premchand", he was one of the first Hindi writers to adopt realism in his work, and his stories chronicled the lives of the poor and the urban middle class, tackling national and social issues including corruption and colonialism. His legacy has influenced generations of writers. The scholar David Rubin credits him with creating the genre of the serious short story in Hindi and Urdu and insists that "in both languages, he has remained an unsurpassed master".

It was the era of Wajid Ali Shah[1]. Lucknow was plunged deep in luxurious living. Exalted and humble, rich and poor, all were sunk in luxury. While one might arrange parties for dancing and singing, another would find enjoyment only in the drowsy ecstasy of opium. In every sphere of life pleasure and merry-making ruled supreme. Indulgence in luxury pervaded the government, the literary world, the social order, arts and crafts, industry, cuisine, absolutely every-where. The bureaucrats were steeped in gross sensuality, poets in describing lovers and the sufferings of separation, artisans in creating intricate patterns of gold and silver thread and embroidery, merchants in selling eye shadow, perfumes, unguents and coloring for the teeth. All eyes were dimmed with the intoxication of luxury. No one had any awareness of what was going on in the world. There were quail fights, betting on matches between fighting partridges, here the cloth for *causar*[2] spread out, there shouts of 'What luck, I've made an ace and twelve!' and elsewhere a fierce chess battle getting under way.

From king to beggar all were swept with the same antic spirit, to the point where when beggars were given money they spent it not on bread but on opium

---

1 The last king of Oudh (Avadh); the story takes place in 1856.
2 A game of dice.

or *madak*[3]. By playing chess, cards or *ganjifa*[4] the wits were sharpened, the process of thought was developed, one became accustomed to solving complex problems —arguments of this sort were presented with great vehemence. (The world is not free even today of people of this persuasion!) So if Mirza Sajjad Ali and Mir Raushan Ali spent most of their time sharpening their wits, what reasonable person could object? Both of them were masters of hereditary estates and had no worry about their income, so they could lounge around at home enjoying their idleness. After all, what else was there to do? Early in the morning, after breakfast, they would sit down, set out the board, arrange the chessmen, and warlike stratagems would begin. From then on they were quite unaware of when it was noon or afternoon or evening. Time and time again word would be sent from the kitchen that dinner was ready and the answer would come back: Get on with it, we're coming, set the table, it would reach the point where the cook, desperate, would serve their meal right in their chamber and the two friends would go on with both activities, eating and playing simultaneously.

In Mirza Sajjad Ali's household there was no elder, so the games took place in his drawing room. But this is not to say that the other people of Mirza's household were happy with these goings-on. And not only the members of his household but the neighbours and even the servants were constantly making malicious comments. 'The game's ill-omened! It's destroying the family. Heaven forbid that anybody should become addicted to it, he'd be utterly useless to God or man, at home or in the world! It's a dreadful sickness, that's what.' Even Mirza's wife, the Begam Sahiba, hated it so much that she sought every possible occasion to scold him. But she hardly ever found the chance, for the game would have begun before she woke and in the evening Mirzaji would be likely to appear in the bedroom only after she had gone to sleep. But the servants of course felt the full force of her rage. 'He's asked for *paan*, has he? Well, tell him to come and get it himself! He hasn't got time for his dinner? Then go and dump it on his head, he can eat it or give it to the dogs!' But to his face she could not say anything at all. She was not so angry with him as with Mir Sahib, whom she referred to as 'Mir the Troublemaker.' Possibly it was Mirzaji who laid all the blame on Mir in order to excuse himself.

One day the Begam Sahiba had a headache. She said to the maid, 'Go and call Mirza Sahib and have him get some medicine from the doctor. Be quick about it, run!' When the maid went to him Mirzaji said, 'Get along with you, I'll come in a moment or two.' The Begam Sahiba's temper flared at this. Who could put up with a husband playing chess while she had a headache? Her face turned scarlet. She said to the maid, 'Go and tell him that if he doesn't go at once I'll go out to the doctor myself.'[5] Mirzaji was immersed in a very interesting game, in two more moves he would checkmate Mir Sahib. Irritated, he said, 'She's not on her deathbed, is she? Can't she be just a little patient?'

'Come now,' said Mir, 'go and see what she has to say. Women can be touchy, you know.'

'To be sure,' said Mirza, 'why shouldn't I go? You'll be checkmated in two moves.'

---

3 An intoxicant prepared from opium.
4 A type of card game.
5 For an aristocratic lady in purdah this would be inappropriate.

'My dear fellow, better not count on it. I've thought of a move that will checkmate you with all your pieces still on the board. But go on now, listen to her, why make her feel hurt for no reason at all?'

'I'll go only after I've checkmated you.'

'Then I won't play. Do go and hear her out.'

'I'll have to go to the doctor's, old man. It's not just a mere headache, it's an excuse to bother me.'

'Whatever it is, you really must indulge her.'

'Very well, but let me make just one more move.'

'Absolutely not, until you've gone to her I won't so much as touch a piece.'

When Mirza Sahib felt compelled to go to his wife the Begam Sahiba was frowning, but she said with a moan, 'You love your wretched chess so much that even if somebody were dying you wouldn't think of leaving it! Heaven forbid there should ever be another man like you!'

Mirza said, 'What can I tell you? Mir Sahib simply wouldn't agree. I had a most difficult time of it putting him off so I could come.'

'Does he think everybody is just as worthless as himself? Doesn't he have children too or has he just let them go to the dogs?'

'He's utterly mad about chess,' said Mirza. 'Whenever he comes I'm compelled to play with him.'

'Why don't you tell him off?'

'He's my equal in age and a couple of steps above me in rank, I'm obliged to be courteous with him.'

'In that case, *I'll* tell him off! If he gets angry, let him. Is he supporting us, after all? As they say, "If the queen sulks, she'll only hurt herself." 'Hiriya!' she called her maid, 'Go out and take up the chessboard, and say to Mir Sahib, "The master won't play now, pray be good enough to take your leave."'

'For heaven's sake, don't do anything so outrageous!' said Mirza. 'Do you want to disgrace me? Wait, Hiriya, where are you going?'

'Why don't you let her go? Anybody who stops her will be simply killing me! Very well, then, stop her, but see if you can stop me.'

Saying this, the Begam Sahiba headed for the drawing room in high dudgeon. Poor Mirza turned pale. He began to implore his wife: 'For God's sake, in the name of the holy Prophet Husain! If you go to him it will be like seeing me laid out!' But the Begam did not pay the slightest attention to him. But when she reached the door of the drawing room all of a sudden, finding herself about to appear before a man not of her household, her legs felt as though paralyzed. She peeked inside, and as it happened, the room was empty. Mir Sahib had done a little shifting of the chess pieces and was now strolling outside in order to demonstrate his innocence. The next thing that happened was that the Begam went inside, knocked over the chessboard, flung some of the pieces under the sofa and others outside, then clapped the double doors shut and locked them. Mir Sahib was just outside the door. When he saw the chessmen being tossed out and the jingling of bangles reached his ears he realized that the Begam Sahiba was in a rage. Silently he took his way home.

Mirza said, 'You have committed an outrage!'

She answered, 'If Mir Sahib comes back here I'll have him kicked out straightaway. If you devoted such fervour to God you'd be a saint. You're to play chess while I slave away looking after this household? Are you going to the doctor's or are you still putting it off?'

When he came out of his house Mirza, instead of going to the doctor's, went to Mir Sahib's and told him the whole story. Mir Sahib said, 'So I guessed when I saw the chess pieces sailing outside. I took off at once. She seems to be quick to fly off the handle. But you've spoiled her too much, and that's not at all the way to do things. What concern is it of hers what you do away from her part of the house? Her work is to look after the home. What business does she have with anything else?'

'Well, tell me, where are we going to meet now?'

'No problem, we have this whole big house, so that's settled, we'll meet here.'

'But how am I going to placate the Begam Sahiba? She was furious when I sat down to play at home, so if I play here it could cost me my life.'

'Let her babble, in a few days she'll be all right. But of course you ought to show a little backbone yourself.'

For some unknown reason Mir Sahib's Begam considered it most fitting for her husband to stay far away from home. For this reason she had never before criticized his chess-playing, but on the contrary, if he was late in going she reminded him. For these reasons Mir Sahib had been deluded into thinking his wife was extremely serious and humble. But when they began to set up the chess board in the drawing room and Mir Sahib was at home all day the Begam Sahiba was very distressed. This was a hindrance to her freedom, and all day long she would yearn to be at the door looking out.

Meantime, the servants had begun to gossip. Formerly they had lain around all day in idleness, if someone came to the house, if someone left, it was no business of theirs. Now they were living in fear all twenty-four hours of the day. Orders would come for *paan*, then for sweets. And, like some lover's heart, the *hookah* had to be kept burning constantly. They would go to the mistress and say, 'The master's chess games are giving us a lot of trouble. We're getting blisters on our feet from running all day. What kind of a game is it that starts at dawn and goes on till evening? Diversion for an hour or two, that's enough for any game. Of course we're not complaining, we're your slaves, whatever you command naturally we'll do it; but this game is positively sinister! Whoever plays it never prospers, and surely some disaster will befall his home. It can reach the point where one neighbourhood after another's been known to go to rack and ruin. Everybody in this part of town is gossiping about it. We have eaten your salt, we're grieved to hear bad things about the master, but what can we do?'

Hearing this, the Begam Sahiba would say, 'I don't like it myself, but he won't listen to anybody, so what can be done?'

In their quarter there were also a few people from an earlier generation who began to imagine all sorts of disasters: 'There's no hope now. If our nobles are like this, then God help the country! This chess playing will be the ruin of the kingdom. The omens are bad.'

The entire realm was in an uproar. Subjects were robbed in broad daylight and nobody was there to hear their appeals. All the wealth of the countryside had been drawn into Lucknow to be squandered on whores, clowns and the satisfaction of every kind of vice. The debt to the East India Company kept on growing day by day, and day by day the general misery was getting harder to bear. Throughout the land, because of the wretched conditions, the yearly taxes were no longer collected. Time and again the British resident warned them, but everyone in Lucknow was so drowned in the intoxication of sensual indulgence that not a soul gave any heed.

Well then, the chess games continued in Mir Sahib's drawing room over the course of several months. Newer strategies were devised, new defences organized, and ever new battle formations planned. From time to time quarrels broke out as they played, and they even reached the point of exchanging vulgar insults; but peace was quickly restored between the two friends. At times the game would come to a halt and Mirzaji would return home in a huff and Mir Sahib would go and sit in his own chamber. But with a good night's sleep all the bad feelings would be calmed; early in the morning the two friends would arrive in the drawing room.

One day when they sat engrossed in thorny chess problems an officer of the royal army arrived on horseback and inquired for Mir Sahib. Mir Sahib panicked, wondering what disaster was about to come down on his head. Why had he been summoned? The case appeared desperate. To the servants he said, 'Tell him I'm not at home.'

'If he's not at home where is he?' the horseman demanded. The servant said he didn't know—what was this all about? 'How can I tell *you* what it's about?' said the officer. 'Maybe soldiers are being levied for the army. It's no joke, being the master of rent-free estates. When he has to go to the front lines he'll find out what it's all about.'

'Very well, go along, he'll be informed.'

'It's not just a matter of informing him. I'll come back tomorrow, I have orders to take him back with me.'

The horseman left. Mir Sahib was shaking with terror. He said to Mirzaji, 'Tell me, sir, what's going to happen now?'

'It's a great misfortune! What if I'm summoned too?'

'The bastard said he was coming back tomorrow.'

'It's a calamity, no doubt of it. If we have to go to the front we'll die before our time.'

'Now listen, there's one way out: we won't meet here at the house any more. Starting tomorrow we'll have our game in some deserted place out on the banks of the Gomti. Who could find us there? When that fine fellow comes for me he'll have to go back without us.'

'By Allah, that's a splendid idea! That's certainly the best way.'

In the meantime, Mir Sahib's Begam was saying to that cavalry officer, 'You've got them out of the way very nicely,' and he answered, 'I'm used to making such jackasses dance to my tune. Chess has robbed them of all their common sense and courage. After this they won't stay at home, whatever happens.'

*

From the next day on the two friends would set out from the house at the crack of dawn, carrying with them a rather small carpet and a box of prepared *paan*, and go to the other side of the Gomti river to an old ruined mosque which had probably been built in the time of Nawab Asafuddaula[6]. Along the way they would pick up tobacco, a pipe and some wine, and spread their carpet in the mosque, fill the *hookah* and sit down to play. After that they had no care for this world or the next. Apart from 'check' and 'checkmate,' not another word came out of their mouths. No *yogi* could have been more profoundly plunged in trance. At noon when they felt hungry they would go to some baker's shop and eat something, smoke a pipeful, and then return to engage once more in battle. At times they would even forget all about eating.

Meantime, the political situation in the country was becoming desperate. The East India Company's armies were advancing on Lucknow. There was commotion in the city. People were taking their children and fleeing to the countryside. But our two players were not in the least concerned about it. When they left home they took to the narrow alleyways, fearing lest some government official might catch a glimpse of them and have them forced into military service. They wanted to enjoy the thousands in income from their estates without giving anything in return.

One day the two friends were sitting in the ruined mosque playing chess. Mirza's game was rather weak and Mir Sahib was checking him at every move. At the same time the Company's soldiers could be seen approaching. This was an army of Europeans on their way to impose their rule on Lucknow.

Mir Sahib said, 'The British army's coming. God save us!'

Mirza said, 'Let them come, but now get out of check.'

'Maybe we ought to have a look, let's stand here where we can't be seen.'

'You can look later, what's the rush? Check again.'

'They have artillery too. There must be about five thousand men. What odd-looking soldiers! They've got red faces, just like monkeys, it's really frightening.'

'Don't try to get out of it, sir! Use these tricks on somebody else. Checkmate!'

'What a strange fellow you are! Here we have the city struck with calamity and you can only think of ways to checkmate. Do you have any idea how we're going to get home if the city's surrounded?'

'When it's time to go home we'll see about it then. This is checkmate, your king's finished now.'

The army had marched by. It was now ten in the morning. A new game was set up.

Mirza said, 'What are we going to do about food today?'

'Well, today's a fast day—are you feeling hungrier than usual?'

'Not in the least. But I wonder what's happening in the city.'

'Nothing at all's happening in the city. People are eating their dinner and settling down comfortably for an afternoon nap. The King's in his harem, no doubt.'

By the time they sat down to play again it was three. This time Mirzaji's game was weak. Four o'clock had just struck when the army was heard marching back. Nawab Wajid Ali had been taken prisoner and the army was conducting him to

---

6 Ruler of Oudh, 1775–97; his reign was noted both for debauchery and for the construction of many buildings, especially mosques.

some unknown destination. In the city there was no commotion, no massacre, not a drop of blood was spilled. Until now no king of an independent country could ever have been overthrown so peacefully, without the least bloodshed. This was not that non violence which delights the gods, but rather the sort of cowardice which makes even great cowards shed tears. The king of the vast country of Oudh was leaving it a captive, and Lucknow remained deep in its sensual slumber. This was the final stage of political decadence.

Mirzaji said, 'Those tyrants have imprisoned His Majesty.'

'I suppose so. Look here—check.'

'Just a moment, sir, I don't feel in the mood now. The poor King must be weeping tears of blood at this moment.'

'I'm sure he is—what luxuries will he enjoy as a prisoner? Checkmate!'

'Everybody has to suffer some change in his fortunes,' said Mirza. 'But what a painful situation!'

'True, that's the way things are. Look, checkmate! That does it, you can't get out of it now.'

'God's oath, you're hard-hearted. You can watch a great catastrophe like this and feel no grief. Alas, poor Wajid Ali Shah!'

'First save your own king, then you can mourn for His Majesty. It's checkmate now. Your hand on it!'

The army passed by, taking the King with them. As soon as they were gone Mirza again set up the chess pieces. The sting of defeat is bitter. Mir said, 'Come now, let us compose an elegy for His Majesty.' But Mirza's patriotism had vanished with his defeat. He was eager for vengeance.

It was evening. In the ruins the swallows were returning and settling in their nests, the bats began to chitter. But the players were still at it, like two blood-thirsty warriors doing battle together. Mirzaji had lost three games in a row; the outlook for this fourth game was not good either. He played each move carefully, firmly resolved to win, but one move after the other turned out to be so ill-conceived that his game kept deteriorating. For his part, Mir Sahib was singing a *gazal* and snapping his fingers from sheer high spirits, as though he had come upon some hidden treasure. Listening to him, Mirzaji was furious, but praised him in order to conceal his exasperation. But as his game worsened his patience began to slip out of control until he reached the point of getting angry at everything Mir said.

'Don't change your move, sir,' he would say. 'How can you go back on a move? Whatever move is to be made, make it just once. Why is your hand on that piece? Leave it alone! Until you figure out your move don't so much as touch your piece! You're taking half-an-hour for every move, that's against the rules. Anyone who takes more than five minutes for a move may be understood to be checkmated. You changed your move again! Just be quiet and put that piece back there.'

Mir Sahib's queen was in danger. He said, 'But when did I make my move?'

'You've already made it. Put the piece right there, in that same square.'

'Why should I put it in that square? When did I take my hand off the piece?'

'If you wait till doomsday to make your move, you'll still have to make it.'

'You're the one who's cheating! Victory and defeat depend on fate, you can't win by cheating.'

'Then it's settled, you've lost this game.'

'How have I lost it?'

'Then put the piece back in the same square where it was.'

'Why should I put it there? I won't!'

'Why should you put it there? You *have* to put it there.'

The quarrel was getting worse. Each stuck to his position, neither one would give an inch. Their words began to move to irrelevant matters. Mirza said, 'If anybody in your family had ever played chess then you might be familiar with the rules. But they were just grass-cutters. So how can you be expected to play chess? Real aristocracy is quite another thing. Nobody can become a noble just by having had some rent-free estates given to him.'

'What! Your own lather must have cut grass! My people have been playing chess for generations.'

'Come off it, you spent your whole life working as a cook in Gaziuddin Haidar's house and now you're going around posing as an aristocrat.'

'Why are you defaming your own ancestors?' said Mir. They must all have been cooks. My people have always dined at the King's own table.'

'You grass-cutter you! Stop your bragging.'

'You check your tongue or you'll be sorry! I won't stand for talk like that. I put out the eyes of anybody who frowns at me. Do you have the courage?'

'So you want to find out how brave I am! Come on then, let's have it out, whatever the consequences.'

Said Mir, 'And who do you think is going to let you push them around!'

The two friends drew the swords from their belts. It was a chivalric age when everybody went around carrying swords, daggers, poniards and the like. Both of them were sensualists but not cowards. They were politically debased, so why should they die for king or kingdom? But they did not lack personal courage. They challenged one another formally, the swords flashed, there was a sound of clanging. Both fell wounded, and both writhed and expired on the spot. They had not shed a single tear for their king but gave up their lives to protect a chess queen.

Darkness was coming on. The chess game had been set up. The two kings each on his throne sat there as though lamenting the death of these two heroes.

Silence spread over all. The broken archways of the ruins, the crumbling walls and dusty minarets looked down on the corpses and mourned.

KONG YIJI

Lu Xun

Translated from the Chinese by Yang Xianyi and Gladys Yang

Lu Xun (1881–1936). Born in Shaoxing as Zhou Zhangshou to a wealthy family now in decline, he adopted a penname when he began to publish his work and, as Lu Xun, would become the foremost figure of modern Chinese literature. Writing in vernacular as well as Classical Chinese, Lu Xun was a short story writer, editor, translator, literary critic, essayist and poet. Even after his death, his work was considered an exemplar in the People's Republic of China. Mao Zedong, a fervent admirer, called him "the saint of modern China" (and selectively exploited his work for political gain). On his deathbed, his last words were to his son's future: "On no account let him become a good-for-nothing writer or artist."

The layout of Luzhen's taverns is unique. In each, facing you as you enter, is a bar in the shape of a carpenter's square where hot water is kept ready for warming rice wine. When men come off work at midday and in the evening they spend four coppers on a bowl of wine—or so they did twenty years ago; now it costs ten—and drink this warm, standing by the bar, taking it easy. Another copper will buy a plate of salted bamboo shoots or peas flavored with aniseed to go with the wine, while a dozen will buy a meat dish; but most of the customers here belong to the short-coated class, few of whom can afford this. As for those in long gowns, they go into the inner room to order wine and dishes and sit drinking at their leisure.

At the age of twelve I started work as a pot-boy in Prosperity Tavern at the edge of town. The boss put me to work in the outer room, saying that I looked too much of a fool to serve long-gowned customers. The short-coated customers there were easier to deal with, it is true, but among them were quite a few persnickety ones who insisted on watching for themselves while the yellow wine was ladled from the keg, looked for water at the bottom of the wine pot, and personally inspected the pot's immersion into the hot water. Under such strict surveillance, diluting the wine was very hard indeed. Thus it did not take my boss many days to decide that this job too was beyond me. Luckily I had been recommended by somebody influential, so he could not sack me. Instead I was transferred to the dull task of simply warming wine.

After that I stood all day behind the bar attending to my duties. Although I gave satisfaction at this post, I found it somewhat boring and monotonous. Our boss was a grim-faced man, nor were the customers much more pleasant, which made the atmosphere a gloomy one. The only times when there was any laughter were when Kong Yiji came to the tavern. That is why I remember him.

Kong Yiji was the only long-gowned customer who used to drink his wine standing. A big, pallid man whose wrinkled face often bore scars, he had a large, unkempt, and grizzled beard. And although he wore a long gown it was dirty and tattered. It had not by the look of it been washed or mended for ten years or more, He used so many archaisms in his speech that half of it was barely intelligible. And as his surname was Kong, he was given the nickname Kong Yiji from *kong, yi, ji,* the first three characters in the old-fashioned children's copy book. Whenever he came in, everyone there would look at him and chuckle. And someone was sure to call out:

"Kong Yiji! What are those fresh scars on your face?"

Ignoring this, he would lay nine coppers on the bar and order two bowls of heated wine with a dish of aniseed-peas. Then someone else would bawl:

"You must have been stealing again!"

"Why sully a man's good name for no reason at all?" Kong Yiji would ask, raising his eyebrows.

"Good name? Why, the day before yesterday you were trussed up and beaten for stealing books from the He family. I saw you!"

At that Kong Yiji would flush, the veins on his forehead standing out as he protested, "Taking books can't be counted as stealing. . . . Taking books . . . for a scholar . . . can't be counted as stealing." Then followed such quotations from the classics as "A gentleman keeps his integrity even in poverty," together with a spate of archaisms that soon had everybody roaring with laughter, enlivening the whole tavern.

From the gossip that I heard, it seemed that Kong Yiji had studied the classics but never passed the official examinations and, not knowing any way to make a living, he had grown steadily poorer until he was almost reduced to beggary. Luckily he was a good calligrapher and could find enough copying work to fill his rice bowl. But unfortunately he had his failings too: laziness and a love of tippling. So after a few days he would disappear, taking with him books, paper, brushes, and inkstone. And after this had happened several times, people stopped employing him as a copyist. Then all he could do was resort to occasional pilfering. In our tavern, though, he was a model customer who never failed to pay up. Sometimes, it is true, when he had no ready money, his name would be chalked up on our tally-board; but in less than a month he invariably settled the bill, and the name Kong Yiji would be wiped off the board again.

After Kong Yiji had drunk half a bowl of wine, his flushed cheeks would stop burning. But then someone would ask:

"Kong Yiji, can you really read?"

When he glanced back as if such a question were not worth answering, they would continue, "How is it you never passed even the lowest official examination?"

At once a gray tinge would overspread Kong Yiji's dejected, discomfited face, and he would mumble more of those unintelligible archaisms. Then everyone there would laugh heartily again, enlivening the whole tavern.

At such times I could join in the laughter with no danger of a dressing-down from my boss. In fact he always put such questions to Kong Yiji himself, to raise a laugh. Knowing that it was no use talking to the men, Kong Yiji would chat with us boys. Once he asked me:

"Have you had any schooling?"

When I nodded curtly he said, "Well then, I'll test you. How do you write the *hui*[1] in aniseed-peas?"

Who did this beggar think he was, testing me! I turned away and ignored him. After waiting for some time he said earnestly:

"You can't write it, eh? I'll show you. Mind you remember. You ought to remember such characters, because you'll need them to write up your accounts when you have a shop of your own."

It seemed to me that I was still very far from having a shop of my own; in addition to which, our boss never entered aniseed-peas in his account book. Half amused and half exasperated, I drawled, "I don't need you to show me. Isn't it the *hui* written with the element for grass?"

Kong Yiji's face lit up. Tapping two long fingernails on the bar, he nodded. "Quite correct!" he said. "There are four different ways of writing *hui*. Do you know them?"

But my patience exhausted, I scowled and moved away. Kong Yiji had dipped his finger in wine to trace the characters on the bar. When he saw my utter indifference his face fell and he sighed.

Sometimes children in the neighborhood, hearing laughter, came in to join in the fun and surrounded Kong Yiji. Then he would give them aniseed-peas, one apiece. After eating the peas the children would still hang round, their eyes fixed on the dish. Growing flustered, he would cover it with his hand and, bending forward from the waist, would say, "There aren't many left, not many at all." Straightening up to look at the peas again, he would shake his head and reiterate, "Not many, I do assure you. Not many, nay, not many at all." Then the children would scamper off, shouting with laughter.

That was how Kong Yiji contributed to our enjoyment, but we got along all right without him too.

One day, shortly before the Midautumn Festival, I think it was, my boss, who was slowly making out his accounts, took down the tally-board. "Kong Yiji hasn't shown up for a long time," he remarked suddenly. "He still owes nineteen coppers." That made me realize how long it was since we had seen him.

"How could he?" rejoined one of the customers. "His legs were broken in that last beating up."

"Ah!" said my boss.

"He'd been stealing again. This time he was fool enough to steal from Mr. Ding, the provincial-grade scholar. As if anybody could get away with that!"

"So what happened?"

"What happened? First he wrote a confession, then he was beaten. The beating lasted nearly all night, and they broke both his legs."

"And then?"

"Well, his legs were broken."

"Yes, but after?"

---

1 A Chinese character meaning "aniseed".

"After? . . . Who knows? He may be dead."

My boss asked no further questions but went on slowly making up his accounts.

After the Midautumn Festival the wind grew daily colder as winter approached, and even though I spent all my time by the stove, I had to wear a padded jacket. One afternoon, when the tavern was deserted, as I sat with my eyes closed I heard the words:

"Warm a bowl of wine."

It was said in a low but familiar voice. I opened my eyes. There was no one to be seen. I stood up to look out. There below the bar, facing the door, sat Kong Yiji. His face was thin and grimy—he looked a wreck. He had on a ragged lined jacket and was squatting cross-legged on a mat, which was attached to his shoulders by a straw rope. When he saw me he repeated:

"Warm a bowl of wine."

At this point my boss leaned over the bar to ask, "Is that Kong Yiji? You still owe nineteen coppers."

"That . . . I'll settle next time." He looked up dejectedly. "Here's cash. Give me some good wine."

My boss, just as in the past, chuckled and said:

"Kong Yiji, you've been stealing again!"

But instead of a stout denial, the answer simply was:

"Don't joke with me."

"Joke? How did your legs get broken if you hadn't been stealing?"

"I fell," whispered Kong Yiji. "Broke them in a fall." His eyes pleaded with the boss to let the matter drop. By now several people had gathered round, and they all laughed with the boss. I warmed the wine, carried it over, and set it on the threshold. He produced four coppers from his ragged coat pocket, and as he placed them in my hand I saw that his own hands were covered with mud—he must have crawled there on them. Presently he finished the wine and, to the accompaniment of taunts and laughter, slowly pushed himself off with his hands.

A long time went by after that without seeing Kong Yiji again. At the end of the year, when the boss took down the tally-board, he said, "Kong Yiji still owes nineteen coppers." At the Dragon Boat festival the next year he said the same thing again. But when the Midautumn Festival arrived he was silent on the subject, and another New Year came round without our seeing any more of Kong Yiji.

Nor have I ever seen him since—no doubt Kong Yiji really is dead.

[1919]

THE FREELOADER

Nescio

Translated from the Dutch by Damion Searls

Nescio (1882–1961). Born in Amsterdam, the son of a blacksmith, Jan Hendrik Grönloh worked as an office clerk and later as a businessman. A confirmed idealist and utopian socialist, in 1900, he founded a short-lived commune inspired by the work of Frederik van Eeden. After the failure of the commune, he began to write, adopting the pen name Nescio (Latin for "I know nothing"). He was not a prolific writer – his entire output barely spans 150 pages – and on first publication his stories met with limited success. Not until after the Second World War did critics and readers begin to reappraise his work, and he is now considered one of the foremost Dutch short story writers.

I

Except for the man who thought Sarphatistraat was the most beautiful place in Europe, I've never met anyone more peculiar than the freeloader.

The freeloader you found lying in your bed with his dirty shoes on when you came home late; the freeloader who smoked your cigars and filled his pipe with your tobacco and burned your coal and peered into your cupboards and borrowed your money and wore out your shoes and took your coat when he had to go home in the rain. The freeloader who always ordered in someone else's name, who sat and drank jenever like a prince at the outdoor tables of the Hollandais on other people's tabs, who borrowed umbrellas and never brought them back, who heated Bavink's secondhand stove until it cracked, who wore his brother's double collars and loaned out Appi's books, and took trips abroad whenever he'd hit up his old man for money again, and wore suits he never paid for.

His first name was Japi. I never knew his last name. Bavink showed up with him when he came back from Veere.

All summer long Bavink had been painting in Zeeland and it was in Veere that he saw Japi for the first time. Japi was just sitting there. Bavink wondered once or twice: Now what kind of guy is that? No one knew. He was always sitting by the water somewhere, just sitting, hour after hour, not moving. At noon and at six he went inside for an hour, to eat; the rest of the day he sat. That lasted about three weeks, then Bavink didn't see him anymore.

A couple of days later, Bavink was coming back from Rotterdam. Every now and then Bavink needed to have a lot of people around; he tromped along the Rotterdam harbor for a few days, then he'd had enough. On board the ship from Numansdorp to de Zijpe, there was Japi again, sitting. A stiff, cold wind was blowing pretty hard that morning and there were whitecaps on the water. Every now and then spray splashed up over the railing at the bow of the ship. The glass doors on the foredeck were closed; there was no one at the bow. Just Japi, peering out over the rail and getting completely drenched. "Look at that," Bavink thought, "if it isn't that same guy." He went and stood next to him. The boat pitched and rolled. Japi sat on his little bench, held on tight to his cap, and let himself get soaked. This lasted quite a while, until he noticed that someone was standing next to him. "Nice weather we're having," Bavink said. Japi looked at Bavink with his big blue eyes and kept a tight hold on his cap. Just then a big wave splashed on board. There were drops of water on Japi's face.

"It's all right," Japi said. The front of the ship crashed down onto the water with a jolt. Someone was trying to open the glass door of the salon, but the wind held it shut. "We're making good time," Bavink said, just to have something to say. "Well," Japi said. "Time doesn't mean much to me."

The conversation stalled. Japi looked at the waves. Bavink looked at Japi's gray cap and thought: Who is this guy? Suddenly Japi said, "Look, there's a rainbow in the water." There was part of the arc of a rainbow in the water, but nothing in the sky. Japi looked at Bavink again with his big blue eyes and was talkative all of a sudden.

"Damn pretty here, if you ask me," he said. "It's too bad it can't always be like this." "In an hour we'll be there," Bavink said.

"You going to Zierikzee?" Japi asked.

"Actually, I'm continuing on to Veere tonight," Bavink said. "I see," Japi said. "You're staying there?"

"Yes, I'm staying there and aren't you the gentleman from Amsterdam who always sits by the water?" Then Japi had to laugh and he said, "I do sit by the water a lot, but 'always' is a bit much. At night I lie in bed, I need an hour to get dressed and eat breakfast, I eat lunch for half an hour and at six I have to eat again. But I do sit by the water a lot. That's why I go to Zeeland. I still let the pressure get to me sometimes. Last week I went to Amsterdam. I had to, I was out of money."

"You're from Amsterdam?" Bavink asked. "I am, thank God," Japi said. "Me too," Bavink said. "You don't paint?" Bavink asked. It was a bizarre question to just ask someone, but Bavink was still trying to figure out what kind of guy this was. "No, thank God," said Japi, "and I'm not a poet and I'm not a nature-lover and I'm not an anarchist. I am, thank God, absolutely nothing."

That definitely appealed to Bavink.

The ship pitched, crashed, rolled, and swung from side to side; the water sprayed and poured over the rail; there was no one else to be seen on deck. Up ahead was an endless expanse of water, full of whitecaps; the shadow of a large cloud was a drifting island; far in the distance a black freighter pushed on, pitching wildly. "Look," said Japi, "the *City of Ghent*." You could see in the distance the water spraying up on either side of the bow; water churned and foamed and frothed around the propeller. The waves leapt with sharp crests in the hollow sea, green and blue and yellow and gray and white, depending on the depth and on the reflections of the clouds, nowhere and not for one single moment the same. A little tugboat was towing a barge and two tjalks.

"No," Japi said, "I am nothing and I do nothing. Actually I do much too much. I'm busy overcoming the body. The best thing is to just sit still; going places and thinking are only for stupid people. I don't think either. It's too bad I have to eat and sleep. I'd rather spend all day and all night just sitting."

This, Bavink started to think, was an interesting case. He nodded. Japi was holding his cap on his head with his right hand the whole time, his right arm propped up on the rail. The wind was blowing so hard that Bavink had to cover his nose with his hand to be able to breathe. Japi just sat there like he was sitting at home. Then Japi said that his plan was to stay in Veere for another few weeks, until his cash ran out.

Painting seemed nice enough to him, if you could do it. He couldn't do anything, so he didn't do anything. And after all, you can't express things the way you feel them. He had just one wish: to overcome the body, to no longer feel hunger or exhaustion, cold or rain. Those were the great enemies. You always had to eat and sleep, over and over again, you had to get out of the cold, you got wet and tired or miserable. Now look at that water. It has it good: it just ripples and reflects the clouds, it's always changing and yet always stays the same too. Has no problems at all.

All this time Bavink stood bracing himself with his walking stick, leaning into the wind, and nodding at Japi. He's onto something there, Bavink thought. And he drily asked if Japi was also going on to Veere. So the conversation turned to Zierikzee, Middelburg, Arnemuiden, and all the places where they had both done plenty of walking and standing and sitting around. For Japi had in fact done quite a bit more in his life than just sit by the water in Veere. And Bavink realized before long that Japi could not only walk and stand and sit, he could see too. And talk about it for hours. And when they stepped onto land again at de Zijpe, Japi pointed southwest, at the wide tower of Zierikzee, dimly visible on the horizon, and said, "Fat Jan, patient old Fat Jan, he's still standing. I thought so. Sure, he's still standing." And then Bavink asked if Japi was always in such a good mood and then Japi said "I am," nothing more. And when they got to Zierikzee and stepped off the streetcar Japi flapped the soles of his shoes on the hot cobblestones of some unshaded little street that was just baking in the sun, and stretched, and said that life really was devilishly funny. And then he shook his walking stick threateningly at the sun and said, "Still, this sun! It shines but then it starts to go down, it doesn't go back up again, when it's after noon it has to set. It'll be cool again tonight. Everyone's eyes would pop out of their heads if it didn't go down one day. Nice and warm, huh? My things are sticking to my body. The sea air is steaming out of my collar."

So clearly this "overcoming the body" stuff wasn't meant quite as literally as all that.

At the table, Japi was more than talkative. He talked enough for three, and ate enough for six. "The sea air digs a hole in you," they say in Veere. He drank enough for six more and sang the whole shanty of the *Nancy Brick*. In short, he was bustling and boisterous and Bavink thought a guy like this is worth his weight in gold.

That he was. In the afternoon he took Bavink to the canal ring and walked him three times around Zierikzee. His mouth never stopped moving and his walking stick kept pointing and when the Zierikzeers stopped and stared he walked up to them and called them "young man" and asked after their health and clapped them on the shoulder. Bavink doubled over from laughing so hard. Japi was good at getting even with those well-disposed cultured Dutchmen who have no patience for anyone who doesn't look at least as stupid and tasteless as they do, and who scoff at you and say things about you to your face, in public, as though pastors and priests in even the tiniest villages hadn't been trying to raise people properly for centuries. Japi was a workhorse and he could lay into people, if needed, with such skill and force that even the most brutish lout had to knuckle under. Things didn't go that far in Zierikzee. People in Zeeland are actually pretty nice. Japi liked to say, "The one thing I'm sorry about is that there isn't a brawl in Walcheren every now and then."

II

For two days Bavink and Japi tromped around Veere and already they were thick as thieves. They sat together for hours on the roof of the Hospitaal and looked out over Walcheren and de Kreek and Veergat and the mouth of the Oosterschelde and the dunes on Schouwen. There was Fat Jan again, the Zierikzee tower, now to the north. And there was Goes, and Tall Jan, the Middelburg tower, the spire around which Walcheren turned, the heart of this world. And the tide came in and the tide went out; the water rose and fell. Every night the limping harbormaster came and first he lit the green light on Noorderhoofd, the breakwater, then he came back down and then he had to go around the whole harbor and then you saw him by the tower again and then he opened the wooden gate and climbed the wooden steps and lit the light in that tower too. And then Japi said "Another day, boss," and the limping harbormaster said "Yes, sir, another day." And then when you looked toward Schouwen, you saw the light blinking on and off as it turned. And an hour out to sea the buoy floated and its light shone and went out, shone and went out. And the water sloshed up and down and all through the night the sun that you couldn't see slid past in the north and the last light of day that you could see slid past in the north along with it and turned into the first light of the new morning. One day touched the next, the way they always do in June.

For the earth everything was simple enough. It just turned on its axis and followed its course around the sun and had nothing to worry about. But the people on it fretted out their days with troubles and cares and endless worries, as though without these troubles, these cares, and these worries, the day wouldn't turn into night.

Japi knew better. The sun went down into the ocean by the Walcheren dunes on its own. But Bavink was in a bad way sometimes.

Bavink was someone who usually worked hard. People thought he was pretty good. He had a good laugh about that. He didn't sell anything when he didn't have to; he put aside his best work and never looked at it again, always dissatisfied.

As long as he was working everything went fine, as soon as he stopped he suffered; sometimes he was half dead with fatigue. If people knew how he really saw things, how things gripped him, they would laugh at his bungling, his dismally botched attempts to reproduce that majesty. There were times when Bavink did nothing, just let himself go, neglected everything, looked lazily at everything and thought it was "nice" that things were "so damn beautiful," as he put it. Times when he felt a pain in his skull thinking about all his futile efforts, his "admirable work." Admirable work! It made him want to throw up just thinking about it. "Admirable work," they said. They didn't know the first thing about it. God obviously hadn't kicked them around like Bavink.

He wished he could just give up painting, but that wasn't so simple either: what's inside you wants to come out. And so the torture started up again: work, work, work day and night, paint all day and fret all night, stay with it, work through it, worry about whether you've really got hold of the things this time. He didn't sleep or eat much; at the beginning he would smoke an enormous number of cigars, one after the other, but after the first day he stopped doing that too. He had moments of the greatest bliss, a joy that all his languid submersion in that "delicious beauty" couldn't give him. And then they came to look, this person, that person, they stood behind him in twos and threes and fours and they looked and nodded and pointed. And suddenly it was over. Then he said "Dammit" and went and lay down on his cot and sent someone out for a flask of jenever and he was done. After a few days he put the canvas away with the rest. In the days that followed he was wretched, tired, miserable, numb, and sick, and he started "shuffling around" again, as he put it: doing nothing, loafing, walking around. If he needed money he dragged something out of his "garbage heap," looked for a "scrap" that "somebody would give something for," and sold it. Nobody could change his ways—that's just how he was. His strengths and weaknesses were one. When he sold something, he stuffed the money into his pocket and clinked with guilders and rijksdollars and walked down Kalverstraat whistling a tune. He said a friendly hello and waved happily whenever you ran into him.

Then he came up and stood next to you and slyly showed you all the "coppers" in his pocket, and laughed out loud, and said, "Can you believe those suckers?" He never accepted paper money: you can't clink bills in your pocket. He had to have gold and silver, and when it was too much for him to carry he said he'd "come by to get the rest later."

That was Bavink. Clearly someone in a constant state of overcoming the body would be thoroughly interesting to him. He could learn something from a man like that. Someone who thought it was fine just to let the wind blow through his hair, let the cold, wet wind soak his clothes and his body, who ran his tongue over his lips because the taste of the ocean was so "goddamn delicious," who sniffed his hands at night to smell the sea. Someone who thought it was enough to be alive and in good health, who went on his joyful way between God's heaven and God's earth and thought it was idiotic that people caused themselves so much trouble, and laughed out loud at them, and sat there eternally with his beatific smile, quietly enjoying the water and the sky and the clouds and the fields, and let the rain soak him through without noticing it and then said "I think I'm wet" and laughed. Someone who could eat an expensive meal and drink expensive jenever better than anyone in Holland and then, at other times, on his long walks (because he didn't always sit around, every so often he spent days at a time on his feet), he'd eat dry rolls day in and day out and be moved to tears because out in the open "a piece of bread like this can taste so good."

And when Bavink was working, Japi sat nearby on the grass or back-to-front on a chair inside, smoking. When they were both inside, Japi kept another chair nearby with a little glass of liquor on it, and reached out his hand for it every now and then. And he kept Bavink on track. Bavink had never spoken a word to anyone when he was working but he talked with Japi.

"The hell with it," Japi said, "what does it matter if it's good or not! You do what you can, you're just a poor bastard like everyone else. You have to paint. You can't stop, can you? The things don't care if you don't get them down exactly how you see them. And other people don't understand anything anyway, not the things and not your work and not you. As for me, I could spend my time in a lot more interesting ways than sitting here boozing and eyeballing that mess of paint. You think *I'd* be any worse off?

"No, that's all wrong," he said then, "much too blue—don't you remember what we talked about yesterday? Much too blue. Please. You think it would have grabbed you the way it did if it was that weird blue color?"

Japi was worth his weight in gold to Bavink. Bavink brought him along everywhere. It was Bavink who made Japi what he was when Bavink turned up with him in Amsterdam.

In no time Japi was worse than low on funds. Bavink wouldn't let him go for all the money in the world. Japi's only job was to look through the "garbage heap," and he got the hang of it in no time— never before had "the dump" turned such a profit. Since then, Bavink paid for everything, or almost everything. Now and then Japi got a little money from home. But that didn't make any difference since sometimes they lived it up like tycoons—when they were in the mood they went to Amsterdam for a few days, to Brussels, Paris, Luxembourg, they spent two weeks in Normandy. Japi usually brought along a few things from the scrap heap, "a chip off the old scrap heap" he called it. In France and Belgium he went up to people on the street, rang doorbells. There was no one else in the world Bavink would have let do any of this. But no one else understood the art of keeping Bavink alive, as Bavink said. His conversation was inexhaustible. And he had a memory for landscapes that bordered on the miraculous. He knew everything along the railroad line from Middelburg to Amsterdam: every field, every ditch, every house, every road, every stand of trees, every patch of heather in Brabant, every switch in the tracks. If you had been traveling for hours in the dark and Japi was stretched out asleep on the seats the whole time and you woke him up and asked "Japi, where are we?" you would just have to wait until he fully woke up and all he had to do was listen to the sound of the train on the tracks and then he'd say, "I think we're in Etten-Leur." And he'd be right. He could tell you precisely how, on such-and-such a day, the shadow of such-and-such a tree in Zaltbommel fell on such-and-such a road, and which ships were sailing down Kuilenburg into the Lek at the moment when you and Japi were crossing a given railroad bridge. And then he'd sit attentively at the window: "Now this is coming, now that is coming." For hours. And he'd nod and laugh whenever he saw something he knew especially well. Or else he would say, "Look, the tree is gone," or "Hey, there are new apples on it now, I didn't see any last time." Or: "Two weeks ago the sun was right behind the crown of that tree, now it's a little to the left, and lower, it's because we've gone two more weeks, and we're also running ten minutes late."

III

And so when winter came to Amsterdam they came too, and Japi sat in my room one night and smoked the cigars sitting on my table for the taking, one after another. *My* cigars.

That was the night Hoyer was over. He had just drifted back from Paris again and now he sat there, tall and lanky, wearing a straw hat, in November, and a salmon-colored jacket, and griping about his work, and about girls. He was in the middle of an incomprehensible story about a young lady and a hired coachman and a basket of eels when we heard the stomp of footsteps coming up the stairs. It was in a working-class neighborhood so you could usually just come on up, most of the front doors were left open.

Bavink came in first and said, "How's it going, boys? It's me. Ha, if it isn't Hoyer! How are you, Hoyer? Still griping? Well heartiest greetings to you. To you too, Koekebakker, may you long be with us." Japi stood in the door. They smelled of salt water and grass. "Come in, man, come in!" Bavink invited him in—into *my* apartment.

"For Chrissake," Hoyer said, "would you please be so kind as to shut the door?" "Koekebakker," Bavink said, "this is Japi, a guy who knows how to have a good time. Hoyer's polite as ever, I see. Have a seat, Japi," Bavink said, flopping down into the one free chair, "just pull up that trunk." A gallows-colored sea chest was sitting there, which contained one clean shirt and my sister's letters. "Wait, I'll help," I said. Then we slid the trunk over to the table, Japi and I, and then Japi saw an empty crate of Hoffmann's starch with a picture of a cat on it. I had put soil in it but nothing would grow. "How about that instead," Japi said, "otherwise I'm so low." "I'll take one of these," Bavink said, lighting up one of my cigars. "You too, Japi?" That suited Japi just fine. "What's that you've got there?" Bavink said. *Le Lys dans la vallée* by Balzac was lying on the table. "Ah, good old Balzac. He's no young whippersnapper. Dead, right? Dead a long time. Of course. Where'd you blow in from, Hoyer? What a beautiful coat you have on. Stand up. Too short, man, much too short." Bavink was in an expansive mood. "Geez, I know," Hoyer said. "Why don't you tell us where you've been hiding out, and who's this gentleman?"

Then came the story, accompanied by nods and grins from Japi. And now and then his hand would reach out toward my table, and Hoyer was smoking like a chimney too, I had stopped smoking. "Wait a minute," Bavink said. "Here, I have some special cigars. Kamper Middelburgs, from Bessem & Hoogenkamp by Lange Delft." "I know them," I said.

"My boy," Japi said, taking a look around my attic room, "it looks cozy here. By God, it's cozy here." He stood up and walked over to the wall. "Ah, Breitner.

Very good. And what have we here? It's a bit dark in here. So, good old Anton Mauve. And there we have the city hall, by God." It was a sketch of the Veere city hall. "Bavink," Japi said, "I do believe you're familiar with this. I'll go look for a job *right now* if that isn't a little something of yours."

"You're in luck," Bavink said. "I thought so," Japi said, and he sat back down. "No, really, I'll definitely be coming back here again. I like it here."

Just then the gramophone belonging to the diamond cutter across the street started up. "Clap," Japi said. And we clapped. The four of us stood at the open window and applauded our hearts out. You could hear porch doors opening everywhere, people came outside, some applauded with us, a child started crying, a dog howled as though the whole block would be dead within a month. The diamond cutter never flinched—he was magnificent. A young woman across the street shouted, "Buncha idiots!" A little girl shrieked a few times: "It's Papus! It's Zeppelin!" A kid started playing his harmonica. "It's about time we left," Hoyer said.

So we stomped downstairs. On the fourth and third floors there were loud discussions going on inside. "About us," Japi said. On the second floor there was no one home. "Say, Japi," Bavink said on the street, "you need to get this round." "Sure," Japi said, "let's go." So I got to see what Japi was like that same night. Hoyer's theory was that beer never did any harm, so we drank a very respectable amount of it. Japi didn't have a penny. Hoyer flat-out refused, Bavink was drunk and staring vacantly into space and insisting that "This guy is a damn good fellow and he's getting this round"—he meant Japi— "and the waiter is a damn good fellow too." I had nineteen cents; Hoyer slipped out. I decided to put "the situation" on my tab, the waiter knew me, and at one o'clock the three of us were crossing Frederiksplein, yodeling happily. I got the money back from Bavink later; he absolutely insisted I take it. Japi found it all splendid and three days later he was sitting on the edge of my bed, swinging his legs back and forth; he said it was stupid of Bavink to get so plastered, but "everything worked out." When he left, he had *Le Lys dans la vallée* in his hand.

IV

It was a month later. It had been below freezing for a fortnight but at the beginning of the week there was a sudden change. And now it was night, and raining heavily. All day long it had been raining hard, almost without a break. The water ran in streams down my windowpane. It felt cozy inside. I liked it. I had no stove and my summer coat was still at the pawnshop. I had never owned a winter coat. The frost was a problem; you had to stay in bed out of poverty, it was the only way to keep warm. Usually in these circumstances I would just drop by Bavink's. But just then the man had taken to sleeping all day and walking around all night. I had sat by his stove all night, alone and abandoned—he would have wanted me to but it wasn't exactly fun. And now I sat listening to the rain clatter on the roof and was glad it was thawing, thawing hard. My bread, two thick slices, was directly on the tabletop; my last plate had gotten broken the previous night. Next to the bread was my cash: four blue bills, two rijks-dollar coins, three guilders, and a few cents. And my kerosene burner stood on the floor in the corner, the water was starting to bubble in the little kettle on it. Next to it was my teapot, lid off, ready for the water to boil; there was already tea inside. And I sat with my legs stretched out under the table, barefoot, in a shirt, my hands in my pants pockets, and I looked at my food, at my wonderful money, at the flame of my oil lamp, at the single light of my little burner, and I listened to the rain and I was happy.

It was eight o'clock. I put my watch down on the table next to my money, the watch that was no longer on its way to the pawnshop, and I said, "For now you'll stay right here with Old Man Koekebakker, little watch," and I put my hand back in my pocket. I was used to having conversations with my things since there's so little that's worth saying to most people.

I was out of the woods for now—dear Autumn hadn't let me down. The falling leaves, the southwest wind bending the trees on Veerschenweg even farther to the northeast and blowing snatches of Tall Jan's bells to my ears and making the towers sway and shake in fear beneath the black clouds—I had finally transmuted it to gold at my writing desk and now I could sit and look at it in the form of my own money, money you can count on and that never lets you down and never leaves you in the lurch. I had gotten home an hour before, soaked to the skin, with a loaf of bread, a half pound of butter, six ounces of sausage, a half pound of sugar, three ounces of tea, and a box of twenty-five four-cent cigars—riches I hadn't known since my birthday, and that was months ago. I had already put away the sausage, that was for tomorrow. I had had a little cupboard built next to the window, and that's where I put everything all in a row on the bottom shelf: butter, tea, sugar, sausage, all the things that can taste so good when you haven't had them for a long time. And the rest of the loaf of bread, minus the two slices, was up on a higher shelf.

My clothes were hanging up to dry at the top of the stairs, under the rafters: jacket, sweater, pants, underpants, shirt, and socks. The water started to boil, the lid of the kettle rattled up and down. I looked at the steam and started thinking about how I would get my coat from the pawnshop tomorrow and for once not eat dinner in the kosher restaurant—beef and potatoes for thirty cents, pea soup with meat for thirty-five cents. And I was just thinking that it wouldn't be unreasonable to think about getting a little something to drink in the house when my meditations were interrupted by a heavy footstep outside the door. Someone was fumbling with my door. You couldn't knock because the door was made of wallpaper glued to a couple of screens, if you knocked you would put your hand right through it. People knew that. "It must be Hoyer," I thought, "he can never find the hook." The hook was on the inside but the door never closed properly and you could just get your finger through the crack and open the door from the outside. "Come in," I shouted, too lazy to get up. "Easier said than done," I heard a voice say, "how does it work?" "I don't recognize that voice," I thought, "who can it be?" I stood up and opened the door, and a trickle of water ran over my hand. "It's Japi," the man said. "Come in," I said again. There he stood, water streaming from every fold of his clothes and off his hat too.

"Sure is raining," Japi said. "Can I put my jacket somewhere? Wait a minute, have to put this down first." He took a package wrapped in newspaper out from under his jacket—books, you could tell—and put it on the table. "So, is there somewhere to hang this?" he said, handing me his jacket. He leaned his hat against my little cooking stove.

"One minute, old man," I said, and I took his jacket and hat out to the common area, hung the jacket next to my own wet clothes, and shook out the hat and put it on the floor in the corner.

Japi was already seated, squeezing out his pants legs and looking around. "To what do I owe the pleasure, sir?" "Just call me Japi," he said. He unwrapped the package and put *Le Lys dans la vallée* down on the table. "There you go, friend." "Thanks," I said, "and what are those?" "Oh," Japi said, "some of Appi's books." "Is Appi reading the *Handelsblad* these days?" "No," Japi said, "the paper is from my old man. There's a want ad in there." "A want ad?" "A want ad, look, I just got it from the old man."

"'Seeking assistant clerk for a busy export business'—got that? a *busy* export business—'thorough knowledge of modern languages, steno, typing. Applicants with prior experience in export'—hear that? *prior* experience!—'will enjoy preferential consideration.' *Enjoy* preferential consideration, I like that one. 'Salary: 300–400/yr. Apply at #1296, Handelsblad ofc.' It's like Floris the Fifth. Floris the Stiff more like it. Floris the Stiff jumps over the Overtoom. Never heard that? Why do you think they filled in the Overtoom canal? They got tired of seeing that stiff guy jumping over it all the time. The 300–400 a year sounds nice to me, the rest not so much."

"You think you'll answer the ad?" I asked. "Think?" Japi said. "I *have* to, according to the old man. He says it can't go on like this. I don't see why not. Am I a burden on him? I've slept at home only twice this month, he doesn't give me a cent. Look at this." He stuck out a leg. I saw a brand-new yellow shoe. "What the devil, I know those shoes."—Where had I seen yellow shoes like that?—"They're a bit darker now because of the water," Japi said, and he stuck out his other foot next to the first. "From Appi! And why? Because *I'm* not a burden on my old man, *I* go around in my old shoes till they have more holes than a sieve. Appi's a good guy. Can't paint, and never will, that's for sure, but you can count on him. He didn't have any socks on hand, I'm barefoot in these shoes," Japi said, and good-naturedly pulled up a pants leg to show me his naked leg. "And he has books. I couldn't get through all those books if I read night and day for a year."

Appi's father had a butcher shop that was doing well, he could afford it. And Japi was right when he saw that Appi would never learn how to paint. His father would later get him a job painting houses, signs, and billboards.

I made tea. Squatting next to the burner, I poured the water into the teapot and put it on top of the kettle. Japi sniffed.

"Smells good," he said, and turned all the way around, scooting his chair over so he could sit with his nose right above the teapot. "I had a fight with Bavink," he said. "Really?" I said. I had heard from Hoyer that they were roaming around everywhere together, day and night, that they slept in the same bed—Japi under the covers and Bavink on top—and took turns drinking jenever out of the one beer glass Bavink had left. "I busted his stove Sunday night."

In one night he had heated it so hot that it broke. And still he kept piling more coal in and poking it around and kept looking at the belly and smoking his pipe, with the stove between his knees so to speak. And he didn't say anything, until

Bavink suddenly saw that there was a huge crack in the belly and raised hell. Japi let him thunder on, he stood up and moved his chair away, Bavink opened the grate with the poker and burned a hole in the floor with the glowing coals he dragged out. And when Bavink was still raging, Japi said "You and your stove" and coolly left and went back to his old man's house and put on one of his brother's clean collars and got a piece of pie from his mother that was left over from dessert. He spent one night at home and the next afternoon he ran into Loef on the street, he'd already met him too. Loef, who later drowned swimming, just when he was starting to make something of himself—he took Japi back to Bavink and said, "Here Bavink, I have a stove-buster for you." And Bavink had laughed. And Japi went straight to the shelf and found a new bottle of Bols in the usual place, "next to Dante." And the three of them knocked back most of the bottle and then Japi cut thick slices of Bavink's bread to make sandwiches and then all three of them were off to Amstelveld and they bought a new stove for seventy cents (it was Monday), a prehistoric model, and they got it home in a wheelbarrow, the three of them.

I handed Japi a cup of tea. He drank it out of a mixing bowl, I didn't have a cup for him. He groaned in contentment and banged the bowl down on the table. "What I could really use now is some bread," he said. "Don't mind me, I think I can find it." He'd had his eye on my cupboard for a while. "Hey," he said, "did you know you have meat in the house?" Did I know! He was already putting some sausage on the bread. "Sausage on bread—the people's victuals." My sausage, my treasure, the object of my reveries of luxury: the ham I was saving for tomorrow. Of course Japi went straight for that. I have to admit that he didn't forget about me—he gave me two slices of sausage on every slice of bread. There was enough for that. And Japi ate. How he could eat! The bread was there next to him on the table and he just sliced away. I started to enjoy it. "Don't be shy, Japi, there's enough money." Japi hadn't noticed the money yet. "Damn!" he said. "It's a pot of gold! They must have printed another one of your pieces." I nodded. "As well they should," he said. "What else are those people good for besides paying our expenses. I'd like to know. I've also written a thing or two in my day." He stuffed his mouth full of bread and sausage and wiped his hands on the newspaper before crumpling it up. "I shouldn't be writing anything, though, it's not like I'm any good."

Then out from his inner pocket came an old, moldering, nasty-smelling newspaper with the creases worn through. It was *The Vlagtwedde Sentinel* and he showed me an article with "Letters from Amsterdam" at the top. He'd written six, he said, but his brother had lost the other five. Japi helped himself to another slice of bread. "You don't want any more?" he asked. I declined and Japi took the last quarter pound of my sausage. "The people's victuals" seemed to agree with him. "Did it at night," Japi said with his mouth full, pointing to the paper with his knife. "After hours. I always had to go back to the office in the evening. Sometimes I had to hold my head under the faucet to stay awake. Now I'd say no thank you. What do I care? Nothing. It only tires you out. I'd rather just walk around and look at people and the carriages and the houses. And especially at the pretty girls and the fresh-faced brides. You can always pick out women who have just gotten married, you can tell right away. And then I think about the fun

I don't have with all those dear creatures. I'd rather do that than write about it. What do the numskulls care what I see. They just shuffle down their own streets, staring down at the ground with tedious faces stuck to their heads because it's a lost cause, life is so hard, it makes them miserable. What have they ever done for me? Let 'em keep their couple dollars."

The article was quite well done, but Hoyer said later that he was sure Japi didn't write it.

"Now I could really go for a pint of beer," Japi said, leaning back. "Sorry, man," I said, "none in the house, no beer and no jenever and no clothes to go across the street in, but have a cigar."

The rain clattered on the roof like it was about to break through and the windows were white with water. Japi was not in the mood to go outside, I was sure of that. He lit a cigar, looked at the smoke for a while, then said, "That Hoyer, what kind of a guy is he really?" Hoyer and Japi didn't get along. I'd already realized that. Hoyer was a penny-pincher and spoke his mind too. "He's useless," Japi said, "he should stick to smearing his paints around, he's no good for anything else."

Bavink had left town for the day, "on business" Japi said, and he (Japi) had run into van Houten on the way home from the office. Van Houten, a friend of Bavink's, worked in an office and thought he could write. He had already published a brick of a novel, which had cost the publisher a pretty penny. Japi let himself be invited out to dinner. Hoyer was there too, he was the first one to say, "Hey, freeloader!" Japi thought that was excellent. After all, who among us is not a freeloader? "The bourgeoisie are there to pay our expenses." That same night he had asked Hoyer to loan him a rijksdollar, just to needle him. He knew perfectly well that Hoyer wouldn't happen to have any money on him at the moment. But even big ol' Hoyer got taken eventually, he couldn't help it. Japi borrowed Hoyer's ridiculous salmon-colored coat and never brought it back. Japi didn't get much enjoyment out of it, though. He was always getting into fights about it, and eventually some roughnecks tore a sleeve off, on the bridge in Ouderkerk.

"Look at that," Japi said, "quarter past nine. Time to get going. Listen to that rain." He went and stood by the window. "Pitch black," he said. "Can't see anything through this rain. Phew, I'm shivering, my pants legs are still wet. Too bad you don't have anything to drink in the house." I fetched his jacket. It was still waterlogged.

"Do you have a long way to go in this weather?" I asked. "I could go by the old man's," Japi said, "but that's half an hour away too. That's your nest, is it?" Japi shoved the curtain aside and sat down on my bed and yawned. "I think I'm coming down with something," he said. "You know what you should do, go get a half dram of old jenever, it's on me. I'll pay you back when I get the chance." I was still standing there with his jacket over my arm. "Wear my jacket," he said. I stumbled out to the attic—my sweater was more or less dry. The liquor store wasn't far. I draped Japi's wet jacket over my sweater. The thing felt cold and unpleasant. And I went down the stairs like that and across the street. There was no line and I was back within ten minutes. When I came upstairs I found Japi lying there snoring, in his clothes, with his shoes on. "Hello!" I shouted and shook him by the shoulder. He mumbled something. "Hello, jenever's here."

He looked drowsily up at me and sat up slowly. "Oh," he said, "so I see." He drank a sip. "That'll fix me right up. Say," he said, "can't I spend the night here? I didn't get a wink of sleep last night or today either." What was I supposed to say? He could sleep on the floor, he said, if he could just have something to put under his head. "Thank God," he said, throwing both his shoes across the room at the same time, "Thank God I'm out of those dripping wet monsters!" Then he hung his pants over the back of a chair, "to dry out." He pushed my little burner aside, put Appi's books down in the corner, put his jacket on top, and kept his sweater on. Then he took my best blanket, rolled himself up in it, took another sip of jenever, and lay down with his head on the little pile and said, "Sleep tight."

And I went back to the table and sat down, looked at my money, and dozed off. When I woke up the lamp was out of oil and sputtering. I crept into my bed and slept badly because of the cold. Japi didn't notice a thing.

When day broke and I woke up, for the umpteenth time, I heard him rummaging around. He was busy making tea, had gone downstairs on his own to get water and told my startled neighbor that he was a cousin of mine. He had slept great, was just a bit stiff. He hoped he hadn't woken me up. "I already ate," he said. "I think you're pretty much out of bread." He had to go. He wanted to talk to Bavink who in those days usually went to sleep around ten in the morning. He brought me a mixing bowl of tea in bed and stood by the window slurping his own bowl. He held it tight in both hands and looked out. "Times are tough all over," he said. "Well then, ciao, I can get my jacket from the clothesline myself." At the door he turned around again. "A place like this looks a lot nicer at night."

I thought so too. I stumbled out of bed, cold and miserable. My money was still lying on the table. He had said he didn't need his old man's money, I thought, or the bourgeoisie's money either. *You* try saying that.

V

"Koekebakker," Japi said, "I feel so strange inside." It was one afternoon at Bavink's. I'd stopped by to talk to Bavink but he was out. Japi was sitting at the table with a little dime bottle of ink and a pile of newspapers in front of him. "Koekebakker, I feel so strange inside."

"Well you certainly smell like jenever," I said.

"No," Japi said, "it's not the jenever. I think my soul is too big." Can you believe it? That sponger! "What are the newspapers for, Japi?" I asked. Japi slapped the pile. "*Daily News*, Koekebakker, *Daily News*. Some of them are a month old." "Have to apply for a job again, Japi?" "You guessed it. Can't go on like this. Grab a chair. Look: KH14684, Daily News. Dear Sirs:"—"How many have you done so far?" I asked.—"First one. It's slow going. You people who've never worked in an office, you don't know what it's like. What'll you have to drink, man? You don't mind if I keep going, do you?" and he dipped his pen in the ink and then stared at the blank page. "Koekebakker," Japi said, looking helplessly around and putting down his pen. "It's no good. I'm not the man for this. I worked in an office once, and I'm not cut out for it. I know from experience. I don't understand anything about it. What's the point of it all? I'm perfectly satisfied as I am. Let's just put that all away." And he picked up the stack of newspapers and carefully placed them out of sight beneath the table.

"There, now I can't see them. You don't know what an office job is like, Koekebakker, or you wouldn't laugh. First you go to school till you're eighteen. Do you know how many sheep there are in Australia or how deep the Suez Canal is? My point exactly. But *I* knew all that. Do you know what polarization is? Me neither, but I *used* to. I had to learn the strangest things: 'Credited to the inventory account,' translate that into French. Have a go at that. You have no idea, Koekebakker. And it goes on for years. Then your old man sticks you in an office. And you realize that the reason you learned all those things was so that you could wet slips of paper with a little brush. And it's always the same old routine, be there nine o'clock sharp, sit there quietly for hours and hours. I realized I couldn't do it. I was always late, I really tried to get there on time but it never happened, it had been going on too long. And so boring. They said I did everything wrong and I'm sure they were right about that. I wanted to but I couldn't do it. I'm not the kind of person who is cut out for work. Then they said I was distracting the others. They were probably right about that too. When I complained that this was boring the hell out of me and asked if this was why I had learned all those strange facts at school, the old accountant said, 'Yes, my boy, life's no novel.' I could tell a good joke, and they liked that, but it wasn't enough for them. It didn't take long before the old accountant had no idea what to do with me. When the boss wasn't there I made animal noises or sang funny songs they'd never heard before. The boss's son was a stuck-up little brat who came by the office now and then to get some money. Everything he said was horribly pretentious and he looked down on daddy's employees with an absolutely insufferable, totally unfounded air of superiority. The guys laughed their heads off when I imitated the young gentleman. I ruined a typewriter there too, and misplaced a book. Then they sat me down at a machine they called 'the guillotine.' I had to cut samples. For days and days I sat there and guillotined. All the samples I cut were crooked. They must have known that that was going to happen, what else would they expect? They'd only put me there to prevent anything worse. They threw out the samples—the clients never saw them. But I'd still managed to put a letter in the wrong envelope somehow. It was pretty bad, of course: the man who got the letter wasn't supposed to know that the boss was doing business with the man the letter was written to. The accountant practically had a stroke. That's when I figured it would be better if I left. The boss held out his hand, and I was glad to be on my way too, I shook it heartily up and down. I said I was sorry but that there was nothing I could do about it. I think I meant it too. See, Koekebakker, that's an office job. After that I interned in a stockbroker's office once, looking through newspapers with a book to see if any of the clients' bonds had been selected for redemption. Wouldn't wish it on my worst enemy. They had to get rid of me. I had to copy there too, but I don't think they could ever figure out what I'd copied. I could see it wasn't working out, I couldn't stay focused.

"My old man was at his wit's end. Now he's hoping that things have improved with time. I'm not so sure. Doesn't look that way to me. I'm doing just fine. Did you know Bavink just made a pile of money with his latest painting? *Ditch at*

Kortenhoef with calf and haystack. Look at this." He took out his wallet. "It's bulging with cash, Koekebakker my boy, just bulging with cash. Cold hard cash. I'm going on a trip tomorrow."

"With Bavink?" I asked. "No," Japi said, "not with Bavink. Alone. I'm going to Friesland." "In the middle of winter?" Japi nodded. "To do what?" He shrugged his shoulders. "Do? Nothing. All you people are so pathetically sensible: everything needs a reason and a purpose. I'm going to Friesland, not to do anything, not for anything. No reason. Because I feel like it."

The next day I took him to the station to catch the 7 p.m. express. It was already dark. He was wearing a jacket with the buttons missing, much too big for him, and a hat with a brim that flopped down over his ears, and Appi's new yellow shoes on his feet. In his hand was a paper cigar holder with an advertisement on it. "Wait a second," he said, when we were already downstairs. "I forgot something." He came right back down carrying a fishing pole.

He wasn't very talkative that evening. I couldn't get out of him what he was planning to do with the fishing pole. On the way to the station, he smoked four cigars in half an hour with his paper cigar holder, and when I said goodbye to him at the gate he asked if I happened to have a little tobacco for him.

Six weeks later he came back with six buttons on his jacket and a pair of red velvet slippers on his feet. He refused to give any explanations. Where was his fishing pole? Oh, that, he'd dropped it out of the train. One time he'd fallen in the water himself too, he said. Other than that his lips were sealed. He had obviously not had a shave the whole time, he looked the color of red brick and smelled like cow shit. He brought back two pounds of tobacco that no one else could smoke, he was addicted to it and didn't ask for a cigar for two weeks. Then the two pounds were gone, plus a butt he had brought too. It turned out you couldn't get that kind of tobacco anywhere in Amsterdam. He wrote to Friesland for some more but didn't get an answer. He was inconsolable. After a few days, though, I saw him sitting at Bavink's again with a cigar in his mouth after all, one of Bavink's of course.

VI

The next summer, Japi disappeared again. Then I ran into him on Boulevard du Nord in Brussels. Monsieur Japi was clean-shaven and nattily dressed in a gray hat, a narrow gold-colored silk tie, checkered shirt, belt, white flannel jacket with thin blue pinstripes, white linen pants with impeccable cuffs, brown and white argyle socks, and flat shoes.

How was it going? Dandy. What was he doing here? Strolling back and forth along the boulevards between Gare du Nord and Gare du Midi. Having a good time? Splendid. Residing? In Uccle. Freeloading upon? He laughed but didn't answer. At the Maastricht on Place de Brouckère, we had several glasses of a strong beer Japi had grown fond of. Actually he had all several glasses and I had one, which I didn't finish. He sat majestically straight in his chair and drank with dignity and great pleasure, held forth on the topics of asphalt, the Grote Markt, and the fine weather, then said he had to go and asked where I was staying.

In that case he'd have to come pay me a visit sometime. After saying that, he paid for the beers and left me sitting there in amazement.

He came back to Amsterdam at the beginning of August with a bandaged head. A mine worker in Marchienne-au-Pont had smashed a ceramic pot over his head. He looked more down-and-out than ever. His old man was keeping him on a terribly short leash. He wore his white pants, which hadn't been white for a long time, deep into November. He was not his old self anymore—he talked less, smoked much less. When he came by Bavink's place and Bavink put his cigars on the table, he collapsed into a chair, kept his jacket and hat on, picked up a cigar with difficulty, slowly bit the end off, had trouble finding his matches, hesitated before lighting it, smoked it slowly, and rarely had more than one a night. If he did light a second cigar he would throw most of it away, something he never used to do before. He used to smoke a cigar until the end was too small to hold and then stick a pin in it to smoke the rest. Before long it was burning crooked. One time he let Bavink's stove go out.

We gave up on him.

Then, on a night with a hard frost, between Christmas and New Year's, Hoyer appeared, after we hadn't seen him in months. We chatted about this and that for a while and then he asked about Japi. And started to reminisce. Did we remember how last summer (about six months back at that point) he went rowing with us on the Amstel at night—he was supposed to sit in the bow and keep a lookout because the *Perseverance* was smashing little boats to pieces at the time, it had just sunk a tjalk at the Omval. Japi sat and looked at the reflection of the stars in the water, and held his right hand in the water, and didn't notice any *Perseverance*, so that the *Perseverance* practically had to run aground in the bend to avoid us. They were furious and one of them ran back to the aft deck and chewed us out for being stark raving morons, and threw a stone that plunged into the water in front of our bow. Then Bavink had said he knew something like this would happen and Japi said: "Close one."

"Apropos of which," Hoyer suddenly said—Hoyer liked to throw around fancy phrases—"Apropos of which, I saw Japi in Veere with a French lady, a damned fine looker." All night long the two of them had stood talking together on the stone jetty and looking out over the railing at the lit buoy and the revolving beam of the Schouwen lighthouse, and they'd listened to the waves, and "sucked face," as Hoyer crudely put it. Bavink said again that he always knew something like that would happen, and I said, "What idiots we are, we should have known," and then we couldn't stop talking about Japi and how he wasn't the freeloader we were used to anymore.

It took another month before Japi surfaced. His old man had found him a job and he was supposed to start on March 1. He didn't say that he thought it'd be miserable. He would wait and see what he could make of it. He'd be earning fifty guilders a month. That night there was another severe frost. The stars were bright and terrifyingly high. The stove was cold. The three of us sat with our coats on, collars up, hats on, the way we sat so many times when we were tougher than the capitalist spirit and had nothing to heat the stove with.

Then Japi started talking and talking and wouldn't stop. It was creepy. There you were, he said, hurtling on this earth through the icy blackness of space, where night never ends, the sun had disappeared never to rise again. The earth raced on through the darkness, the icy wind howling behind it. All these heavenly bodies hurtling desolately through space. If one of them hurtles into you then you're lost, lost with all the other fifteen hundred million unlucky people. Japi sat shivering in his coat, it was freezing in the room.

Then he started in again on a different tack. The sun could be so beautiful, shining in the Waal River. He'd seen the sun shining in the Waal near Zaltbommel the last time he'd ridden the train over the bridge. Between the bridge and the city, the sun made a big patch of light on the water. The water flowed by and the sun just shone on it, a hundred, a thousand, a hundred thousand times. Two thousand years ago the sun was already shining on it and the water was flowing by. God knows how long it's been. The sun had risen more than 700,000 times since then, it had set more than 700,000 times, and all that time the water was flowing. The math made him feel sick. How many rainy days had there been in all that time? How many nights had it gotten as cold as tonight, or colder? How many people had seen that water flowing by and seen the sun shining in it and seen all the stars on the nights as cold as this? How many people who are dead now? And how many will still see the water flowing in the future? And two thousand years, that's nothing, the earth has existed for thousands and thousands more years than that and will probably exist for thousands more. The water will probably flow for thousands of years more, without him seeing it. And even if the world did end, that still didn't really mean anything. There would be so much more time after-wards, time would never end. And all that time, he would be dead.

Japi's teeth chattered. There was not a single sip of jenever left in the house and no way to get any on credit.

Then Japi got sentimental. He started to talk about Jeanne, for no particular reason, and as though we already knew everything about her. That her hands were so soft, and so warm, and how her eyes could sparkle. She had dark eyes and black hair. We started getting uncomfortable. He told us the most horribly private things, about a white lace dress, about a lavender silk dress, about her little white feet, about all sorts of body parts you can't write about in a story.

By the end he was talking in French, we heard the words "chert" and "chérie" several dozen times. (He pronounced the final "e" in "chérie.") Then he was speaking Dutch again and got to the point. She was going to divorce her husband, a revolting old prune twenty years older than she was. We found it all rather banal. And on March 1 he had to show up at the office. Then he rubbed his face with his hands and said, "I'm leaving. Shake." He stumbled down the stairs.

He did not show up on March 1. It was April before he was in any shape to go to work again. His freeloading days were over.

One evening a few months later, Bavink saw him sitting on the fourth floor of some office building. He was sitting in the window, working, and the place was brightly lit. Bavink went upstairs. Japi was alone and very busy. Bavink couldn't get anything out of him— he just kept working and hardly said a thing. Bavink nosed around, took a book off the shelf here and there, flipped through it, and put it back, shook his head, said "Whoa" a few times, turned the handle on the mimeograph, looked down at the street, and opened all the windows for some fresh air.

Outside a light snow was falling. Some snowflakes blew in. "Shut the windows, please," Japi said, and kept writing. Then Bavink picked up a copy book, read a bit in it, shook his head again and again, and walked over to Japi, the copy book open in his hand.

"Hey, did you write all this?" Japi barely looked up and just said, "Not all of it." "You're pretty damn smart after all," Bavink said, "this business stuff isn't easy." Then Bavink left.

VII

Japi turned into a hard worker. Not long after Bavink's visit they sent him to Africa. Within two years he was back: sick, half dead. No one heard anything from him until I saw him one November afternoon standing next to the stone wall of the Wijk bij Duurstede harbor. There he stood, staring at the mud. I had trouble recognizing him. He was dressed in a bulky gray coat, much too big for him, with a bulky gray cap down over his eyes and ears. He had on a pair of bulky wide square-toed brown shoes and there were several young men behind him. I thought: That looks like Japi, actually. And yes, it was him, a bit pale and thin and with no beard or mustache and with a strange staring look in his eyes, but definitely Japi.

Japi didn't see anything, didn't hear anything. I tapped him on the shoulder and said, "What are you doing here, how's it going, what's brought you here?" He stuck out his hand and said nothing, and was not surprised. "Just standing here staring," he said.

"I can see that," I said. "Come have a drink?" "Good," Japi said. The louts who were leaning against the stone wall a ways off, amusing themselves for some time with very loud, ill-mannered commentary, now made very respectful greetings, since I had been throwing around quite a bit of money in Wijk bij Duurstede and had even slapped the notary on the back that very Sunday.

After a glass of jenever, some life came back into Japi. He had been working in Africa, tormented by the heat and the mosquitoes, had come down with a fever—spent more time suffering from fever than working or doing anything else. He'd come back that summer practically skin and bones.

His *française* was living in Paris with a young Dutchman who'd been articled to an office for a monstrously long time. Had another boyfriend too, a colonel. Treated him to dinner in Paris and called him a "good beast" in her broken Dutch and laughed in his face. Fastened her garter belt while he was right there so that he'd seen her bare knee. Then sent him away. He had to laugh. He wasn't in love anymore. She'd had a light blue silk slip on. One time he saw her having a drink with the colonel at an outdoor table. The colonel was acting very smug and looked savage and overbearing. She gave Japi the eye behind the colonel's back. She had lung problems and her months were numbered. Still, lively as ever. But had a hard time walking.

And what were Japi's plans? Still a freeloader? He freeloaded on his office, he said; the last day of every month he went and got his money.

Was he going to turn into such a ferocious worker again?

Oh, no. He had driven himself too hard. He'd aged fifteen years in the last three or four.

Then he lit a fresh cigar, one of mine, an expensive one with a band. I was doing well in those days. He took the band off.

He had toiled away, seen his share of misery. It started in Marchienne-au-Pont and Charleroi. He'd gone there for fun, with Jeanne. After three days she had had enough; he stayed. He showed me a little photograph: a grinning death's-head, the daughter of a worker in a glass factory. Seven children, five dead, and the sixth died while he was boarding there, she was the one in the photo. There he had learned to look, had seen what work really is. He'd always known how to have a damned good time spending money while other people earned it. Now he let it get to him and drove himself hard. Thought about becoming a socialist. He'd worked for his bread, been hounded, hounded and oppressed by people and by necessity, just like everyone else. He'd worked nights; in Amsterdam he came home from the office at one or two in the morning, then sat up, brooded, scribbled, written whole novels and burned them.

What could he do? What did they accomplish with all that? He let it get to him, dreamed up fiery speeches and ferocious articles while he sat in the office and worked on his boss's business, worked hard, everyone was amazed at the quantities of work he could put away. The world was still turning, turning exactly the way it always had, and it would keep on turning without him. He let it get to him. Now he was more sensible. He washed his hands of it. There were enough salesmen and writers and talkers and people who let it get to them—more than enough.

And they were always afraid of something and sad about something. Always scared to be late somewhere or get a scolding from someone, or they couldn't make ends meet, or the toilet was stopped up, or they had an ulcer, or their Sunday suit was starting to wear thin, or the rent was due; they couldn't do this because of that and couldn't possibly do that because of this. When *he* was young he was never that stupid. Smoke a couple cigars, chat a little, look around a bit, enjoy the sunshine when it was there and the rain when it wasn't, and not think about tomorrow, not want to become anybody, not want a thing except a little nice weather now and then.

You can't sustain that. He knew that. It couldn't last, it was impossible, you'd need a mountain of money. And he didn't have one. What his old man might leave him wasn't worth the trouble. And he, Japi, thought that was just fine. Now he spent his time staring. It's not like it's possible to accomplish anything anyway. He still hung around the places he used to like and spent his time staring into rivers. He got through several weeks staring in Dordrecht. In Veere he sat up on the roof of the Hospitaal for days. He'd spent September in Nijmegen.

And then, with a few variations, he repeated his old reverie about the water, how it flowed eternally to the west, out toward the sun every night. In Nijmegen there was a doctor who had taken the same walk at the same time every morning for fifty-three years—over the Valkhof hill and down the north side and up the Waalkade to the railroad bridge. That's more than 19,300 times. And always the water flowed to the west. And it didn't mean a thing. It must have flowed like that for a hundred times fifty-three years. Longer. Now there's a bridge over it.

Since just a short time ago, a few years. Which is still a long time. Every year is 365 days; ten years is 3,650 sunrises. Every day is 24 hours, and every hour more goes through the heads of all those constantly worrying people than you could set down in a thousand books. Thousands of worriers who saw that bridge are dead now. And still, it's only been there a short time. The water there has been flowing for much, much longer. And there was a time when the water didn't flow there. That time was even longer, much longer. The worriers have died by the hundreds and hundreds of millions. Who remembers them now? And how many more are going to die after them? They just worry away until God gathers them up. And you'd think God was doing them a favor when he suddenly wiped them away. But God knows better than you or me. All they want to do is fret, and struggle, and keep on struggling. And meanwhile the sun rises, the sun sets, the river there flows to the west and keeps flowing until that too will come to an end.

No, he had no more plans and he wasn't planning to let it get to him anymore either. He would make sure not to do that. He did accept an invitation to dinner that night, and even sang a funny song and gave a crazy speech standing on a chair.

Japi stared for a few months more. He was not in the best of health and the sick benefits from his office had run out. He spent the winter in Amsterdam, where everyone was busy tearing down beautiful houses to replace them with hideous ones, worrying the whole time.

In May he moved to Nijmegen.

He wrote me a postcard from there to say that Jeanne had died of her lung ailment. He had been waiting for that, he wrote.

At half past four one summer morning, during a majestic sunrise, he stepped off the bridge over the Waal. The watchman saw him too late. "Don't worry, old boy," Japi had said, then he stepped off the bridge, his face to the northeast. You couldn't call it a jump, the watchman said, he stepped off.

They found a walking stick in his room that had belonged to Bavink, and six notes on the wall saying "Dammit" and one with "All right then."

The river has kept flowing west since then and people have kept on worrying. The sun still rises too, and Japi's parents still get their *Daily News* every evening.

His trip to Friesland remains a mystery to this day.

[1909–1910]

IN THE PENAL COLONY

Franz Kafka

Translated from the German by Ian Johnston

Franz Kafka (1883–1924). One of the towering figures of twentieth century world literature (you know you'd made it when someone coins the word *Kafkaesque*), Franz Kafka was born to a middle-class, German-speaking Jewish family in Prague, which was then capital of the Kingdom of Bohemia. Only a handful of his stories were published during his lifetime, and on his death, he asked his friend Max Brod to destroy his unpublished manuscripts. It is only because his friend ignored his wishes, that Kafka's masterpieces *The Metamorphosis*, *The Trial*, and *The Castle* were published. His work has been hugely influential on later writers including Philip Roth and J.M. Coetzee. He died in 1924 at the age of forty.

"It's a peculiar apparatus," said the Officer to the Traveler, gazing with a certain admiration at the device, with which he was, of course, thoroughly familiar. It appeared that the Traveler had responded to the invitation of the Commandant only out of politeness, when he had been invited to attend the execution of a soldier condemned for disobeying and insulting his superior. Of course, interest in the execution was not very high, not even in the penal colony itself. At least, here in the small, deep, sandy valley, closed in on all sides by barren slopes, apart from the Officer and the Traveler there were present only the Condemned, a vacant-looking man with a broad mouth and dilapidated hair and face, and the Soldier, who held the heavy chain to which were connected the small chains which bound the Condemned Man by his feet and wrist bones, as well as by his neck, and which were also linked to each other by connecting chains. The Condemned Man had an expression of such dog-like resignation that it looked as if one could set him free to roam around the slopes and would only have to whistle at the start of the execution for him to return.

The Traveler had little interest in the apparatus and walked back and forth behind the Condemned Man, almost visibly indifferent, while the Officer took care of the final preparations. Sometimes he crawled under the apparatus, which was built deep into the earth, and sometimes he climbed up a ladder to inspect the upper parts. These were really jobs which could have been left to a mechanic, but the Officer carried them out with great enthusiasm, maybe because he was particularly fond of this apparatus or maybe because there was some other reason why one could not trust the work to anyone else. "It's all ready now!" he finally cried and climbed back down the ladder. He was unusually tired, breathing with his mouth wide open, and he had pushed two fine lady's handkerchiefs under the collar of his uniform.

"These uniforms are really too heavy for the tropics," the Traveler said, instead of asking some questions about the apparatus, as the Officer had expected. "That's true," said the Officer. He washed the oil and grease from his dirty hands in a bucket of water standing ready, "but they mean home, and we don't want to lose our homeland." "Now, have a look at this apparatus," he added immediately, drying his hands with a towel and pointing to the device. "Up to this point I had to do some work by hand, but from now on the apparatus should work entirely on its own." The Traveler nodded and followed the Officer. The latter tried to protect himself against all eventualities by saying, "Of course, breakdowns do happen. I really hope none will occur today, but we must be prepared for it. The apparatus is supposed to keep going for twelve hours without interruption. But if any breakdowns do occur, they'll only be very minor, and we'll deal with them right away."

"Don't you want to sit down?" he asked finally, as he pulled out a chair from a pile of cane chairs and offered it to the Traveler. The latter could not refuse. He sat on the edge of the pit, into which he cast a fleeting glance. It was not very deep. On one side of the hole the piled earth was heaped up into a wall; on the other side stood the apparatus. "I don't know," the officer said, "whether the Commandant has already explained the apparatus to you." The Traveler made a vague gesture with his hand. That was good enough for the Officer, for now he could explain the apparatus himself.

"This apparatus," he said, grasping a connecting rod and leaning against it, "is our previous Commandant's invention. I also worked with him on the very first tests and took part in all the work right up to its completion. However, the credit for the invention belongs to him alone. Have you heard of our previous Commandant? No? Well, I'm not claiming too much when I say that the organization of the entire penal colony is his work. We, his friends, already knew at the time of his death that the administration of the colony was so self-contained that even if his successor had a thousand new plans in mind, he would not be able to alter anything of the old plan, at least not for several years. And our prediction has held. The New Commandant has had to recognize that. It's a shame that you didn't know the previous Commandant!"

"However," the Officer said, interrupting himself, "I'm chattering, and his apparatus stands here in front of us. As you see, it consists of three parts. With the passage of time certain popular names have been developed for each of these parts. The one underneath is called the bed, the upper one is called the inscriber, and here in the middle, this moving part is called the harrow." "The harrow?" the Traveler asked. He had not been listening with full attention. The sun was excessively strong, trapped in the shadowless valley, and one could hardly collect one's thoughts. So the Officer appeared to him all the more admirable in his tight tunic weighed down with epaulettes and festooned with braid, ready to go on parade, as he explained the matter so eagerly and, while he was talking, adjusted screws here and there with a screwdriver.

The Soldier appeared to be in a state similar to the Traveler. He had wound the Condemned Man's chain around both his wrists and was supporting himself with his hand on his weapon, letting his head hang backward, not bothering about anything. The Traveler was not surprised at that, for the Officer spoke French, and clearly neither the Soldier nor the Condemned Man understood the language. So it was all the more striking that the Condemned Man, in spite of that, did what he could to follow the Officer's explanation. With a sort of sleepy persistence he kept directing his gaze to the place where the Officer had just pointed, and when the question from the Traveler interrupted the Officer, the Condemned Man looked at the Traveler, too, just as the Officer was doing.

"Yes, the harrow," said the Officer. "The name fits. The needles are arranged as in a harrow, and the whole thing is driven like a harrow, although it stays in one place and is, in principle, much more artistic. You'll understand in a moment. The condemned is laid out here on the bed. First, I'll describe the apparatus and only then let the procedure go to work. That way you'll be able to follow it better. Also a sprocket in the inscriber is excessively worn. It really squeaks. When it's in motion one can hardly make oneself understood. Unfortunately replacement parts are difficult to come by in this place. So, here is the bed, as I said. The whole thing is completely covered with a layer of cotton wool, the purpose of which you'll find out in a moment. The condemned man is laid out on his stomach on the cotton wool—naked, of course. There are straps for the hands here, for the feet here, and for the throat here, to tie him in securely. At the head of the bed here, where the man, as I have mentioned, first lies face down, is this small protruding lump of felt, which can easily be adjusted so that it presses right into the man's mouth. Its purpose is to prevent him screaming and biting his tongue to pieces. Of course, the man has to let the felt in his mouth—otherwise the straps around his throat would break his neck." "That's cotton wool?" asked the Traveler and bent down. "Yes, it is," said the Officer smiling, "feel it for yourself."

He took the Traveler's hand and led him over to the bed. "It's a specially prepared cotton wool. That's why it looks so unrecognizable. I'll get around to mentioning its purpose in a moment." The Traveler was already being won over a little to the apparatus. With his hand over his eyes to protect them from the sun, he looked at the apparatus in the hole. It was a massive construction. The bed and the inscriber were the same size and looked like two dark chests. The inscriber was set about two metres above the bed, and the two were joined together at the corners by four brass rods, which almost reflected the sun. The harrow hung between the chests on a band of steel.

The Officer had hardly noticed the earlier indifference of the Traveler, but he did have a sense now of how the latter's interest was being aroused for the first time. So he paused in his explanation in order to allow the Traveler time to observe the apparatus undisturbed. The Condemned Man imitated the Traveler, but since he could not put his hand over his eyes, he blinked upward with his eyes uncovered.

"So now the man is lying down," said the Traveler. He leaned back in his chair and crossed his legs.

"Yes," said the Officer, pushing his cap back a little and running his hand over his hot face. "Now, listen. Both the bed and the inscriber have their own electric batteries. The bed needs them for itself, and the inscriber for the harrow. As soon as the man is strapped in securely, the bed is set in motion. It quivers with tiny, very rapid oscillations from side to side and up and down simultaneously. You will have seen similar devices in mental hospitals. Only with our bed all movements are precisely calibrated, for they must be meticulously coordinated with the movements of the harrow. But it's the harrow which has the job of actually carrying out the sentence."

"What is the sentence?" the Traveler asked. "You don't even know that?" asked the Officer in astonishment and bit his lip. "Forgive me if my explanations are perhaps confused. I really do beg your pardon. Previously it was the Commandant's habit to provide such explanations. But the New Commandant has excused himself from this honourable duty. The fact that with such an eminent visitor"—the Traveler tried to deflect the honour with both hands, but the officer insisted on the expression—"that with such an eminent visitor he didn't even once make him aware of the form of our sentencing is yet again something new, which . . ." He had a curse on his lips, but controlled himself and said merely: "I was not informed about it. It's not my fault. In any case, I am certainly the person best able to explain our style of sentencing, for here I am carrying"—he patted his breast pocket—"the relevant diagrams drawn by the previous Commandant."

"Diagrams made by the Commandant himself?" asked the Traveler. "Then was he in his own person a combination of everything? Was he soldier, judge, engineer, chemist, and draftsman?"

"He was indeed," said the Officer, nodding his head with a fixed and thoughtful expression. Then he looked at his hands, examining them. They didn't seem to him clean enough to handle the diagrams. So he went to the bucket and washed them again. Then he pulled out a small leather folder and said, "Our sentence does not sound severe. The law which a condemned man has violated is inscribed on his body with the harrow. This Condemned Man, for example," and the Officer pointed to the man, "will have inscribed on his body, 'Honour your superiors.'"

The Traveler had a quick look at the man. When the Officer was pointing at him, the man kept his head down and appeared to be directing all his energy into listening in order to learn something. But the movements of his thick pouting lips showed clearly that he was incapable of understanding anything. The Traveler wanted to raise various questions, but after looking at the Condemned Man he merely asked, "Does he know his sentence?" "No," said the Officer. He wished to get on with his explanation right away, but the Traveler interrupted him: "He doesn't know his own sentence?" "No," said the Officer once more. He then paused for a moment, as if he was asking the Traveler for a more detailed reason for his question, and said, "It would be useless to give him that information. He experiences it on his own body." The Traveler really wanted to keep quiet at this point, but he felt how the Condemned Man was gazing at him—he seemed to be asking whether he could approve of the process the Officer had described. So the Traveler, who had up to this point been leaning back, bent forward again and kept up his questions, "But does he nonetheless have some general idea that he's been condemned?" "Not that either," said the Officer, and he smiled at the Traveler, as if he was still waiting for some strange revelations from him. "No?" said the Traveler, wiping his forehead, "then does the man also not yet know how his defence was received?" "He has had no opportunity to defend himself," said the Officer and looked away, as if he was talking to himself and wished not to embarrass the Traveler with an explanation of matters so self-evident to him. "But he must have had a chance to defend himself," said the Traveler and stood up from his chair.

The Officer recognized that he was in danger of having his explanation of the apparatus held up for a long time. So he went to the Traveler, took him by the arm, pointed with his hand at the Condemned Man, who stood there stiffly now that the attention was so clearly directed at him—the Soldier was also pulling on his chain—and said, "The matter stands like this. Here in the penal colony I have been appointed judge. In spite of my youth. For I stood at the side of our Old Commandant in all matters of punishment, and I also know the most about the apparatus. The basic principle I use for my decisions is this: Guilt is always beyond a doubt. Other courts could not follow this principle, for they are made up of many heads and, in addition, have even higher courts above them. But that is not the case here, or at least it was not that way with the previous Commandant. It's true the New Commandant has already shown a desire to get mixed up in my court, but I've succeeded so far in fending him off. And I'll continue to be successful. You want this case explained. It's simple—just like all of them. This morning a captain laid a charge that this man, who is assigned to him as a servant and who sleeps before his door, had been sleeping on duty. For his task is to stand up every time the clock strikes the hour and salute in front of the captain's door. That's certainly not a difficult duty—and it's necessary, since he is supposed to remain fresh both for guarding and for service. Yesterday night the captain wanted to check whether his servant was fulfilling his duty. He opened the door on the stroke of two and found him curled up asleep. He got his horse-whip and hit him across the face. Now, instead of standing up and begging for forgiveness, the man grabbed his master by the legs, shook him, and cried out, 'Throw away that whip or I'll eat you up.' Those are the facts. The captain came to me an hour ago. I wrote up his statement and right after that the sentence. Then I had the man chained up. It was all very simple. If I had first summoned the man and interrogated him, the result would have been confusion. He would have lied, and if I had been successful in refuting his lies, he would have replaced them with new lies, and so forth. But now I have him, and I won't release him again. Now, does that clarify everything? But time is passing. We should be starting the execution, and I haven't finished explaining the apparatus yet."

He urged the Traveler to sit down in his chair, moved to the apparatus again, and started, "As you see, the shape of the harrow corresponds to the shape of a man. This is the harrow for the upper body, and here are the harrows for the legs. This small cutter is the only one designated for the head. Is that clear to you?" He leaned forward to the Traveler in a friendly way, ready to give the most comprehensive explanation.

The Traveler looked at the harrow with a wrinkled frown. The information about the judicial procedures had not satisfied him. However, he had to tell himself that here it was a matter of a penal colony, that in this place special regulations were necessary, and that one had to give precedence to military measures right down to the last detail. Beyond that, however, he had some hopes in the New

Commandant, who obviously, although slowly, was intending to introduce a new procedure which the limited understanding of this Officer could not cope with.

Following this train of thought, the Traveler asked, "Will the Commandant be present at the execution?" "That is not certain," said the Officer, embarrassingly affected by the sudden question, and his friendly expression made a grimace. "That's why we need to hurry up. As much as I regret the fact, I'll have to make my explanation even shorter. But tomorrow, once the apparatus is clean again—the fact that it gets so very dirty is its only fault—I could add a detailed explanation. So now, only the most important things. When the man is lying on the bed and it starts quivering, the harrow sinks onto the body. It positions itself automatically in such a way that it touches the body only lightly with the needle tips. Once the machine is set in this position, this steel cable tightens up into a rod. And now the performance begins. Someone who is not an initiate sees no external difference among the punishments. The harrow seems to do its work uniformly. As it quivers, it sticks the tips of its needles into the body, which is also vibrating from the movement of the bed. Now, to enable someone to check on how the sentence is being carried out, the harrow is made of glass. That gave rise to certain technical difficulties with fastening the needles securely, but after several attempts we were successful. We didn't spare any efforts. And now, as the inscription is made on the body, everyone can see through the glass. Don't you want to come closer and see the needles for yourself."

The Traveler stood slowly, moved up, and bent over the harrow. "You see," the Officer said, "two sorts of needles in a multiple arrangement. Each long needle has a short one next to it. The long one inscribes, and the short one squirts water out to wash away the blood and keep the inscription always clear. The bloody water is then channeled here in small grooves and finally flows into these main gutters, and the outlet pipe takes it to the pit." The officer pointed with his finger to the exact path which the bloody water had to take. As he began to demonstrate with both hands at the mouth of the outlet pipe, in order to make his account as clear as possible, the Traveler raised his head and, feeling behind him with his hand, wanted to return to his chair. Then he saw to his horror that the Condemned Man had also, like him, accepted the Officer's invitation to inspect the arrangement of the harrow up close. He had pulled the sleeping Soldier holding the chain a little forward and was also bending over the glass. One could see how with a confused gaze he also was looking for what the two gentlemen had just observed, but how he didn't succeed because he lacked the explanation. He leaned forward this way and that. He kept running his eyes over the glass again and again. The Traveler wanted to push him back, for what he was doing was probably punishable. But the Officer held the Traveler firmly with one hand, and with the other he took a lump of earth from the wall and threw it at the Soldier. The latter opened his eyes with a start, saw what the Condemned Man had dared to do, let his weapon fall, braced his heels in the earth, and pulled the Condemned Man back, so that he immediately collapsed. The Soldier looked down at him, as he writhed around, making his chain clink. "Stand him up," cried the Officer. Then he noticed that the Condemned Man was distracting the Traveler too much. The latter was even leaning out away from the harrow, without paying any attention to it, wanting to find out what was happening to the Condemned Man. "Handle him carefully," the Officer yelled again. He ran around the apparatus, personally grabbed the Condemned Man under the armpits and, with the help of the Soldier, stood the man, whose feet kept slipping, upright.

"Now I know all about it," said the Traveler, as the Officer turned back to him again. "Except the most important thing," said the latter, grabbing the Traveler by the arm and pointing up high. "There in the inscriber is the mechanism which determines the movement of the harrow, and this mechanism is arranged according to the diagram on which the sentence is set down. I still use the diagrams of the previous Commandant. Here they are." He pulled some pages out of the leather folder. "Unfortunately I can't hand them to you. They are the most cherished thing I possess. Sit down, and I'll show you them from this distance. Then you'll be able to see it all well." He showed the first sheet. The Traveler would have been happy to say something appreciative, but all he saw was a labyrinthine series of lines, criss-crossing each other in all sort of ways. These covered the paper so thickly that only with difficulty could one make out the white spaces in between. "Read it," said the Officer. "I can't," said the Traveler. "But it's clear," said the Officer. "It's very elaborate," said the Traveler evasively, "but I can't decipher it."

"Yes," said the Officer, smiling and putting the folder back again, "it's not calligraphy for school children. One has to read it a long time. You too will finally understand it clearly. Of course, it has to be a script that isn't simple. You see, it's not supposed to kill right away, but on average over a period of twelve hours. The turning point is set for the sixth hour. There must also be many, many embellishments surrounding the basic script. The essential script moves around the body only in a narrow belt. The rest of the body is reserved for decoration. Can you now appreciate the work of the harrow and the whole apparatus? Just look at it!" He jumped up the ladder, turned a wheel, and called down, "Watch out—move to the side!" Everything started moving. If the wheel had not squeaked, it would have been marvelous. The officer threatened the wheel with his fist, as if he was surprised by the disturbance it created. Then he spread his arms, apologizing to the Traveler, and quickly clambered down, in order to observe the operation of the apparatus from below.

Something was still not working properly, something only he noticed. He clambered up again and reached with both hands into the inside of the inscriber. Then, in order to descend more quickly, instead of using the ladder, he slid down on one of the poles and, to make himself understandable through the noise, strained his voice to the limit as he yelled in the Traveler's ear, "Do you understand the process? The harrow is starting to write. When it's finished with the first part of the script on the man's back, the layer of cotton wool rolls and turns the body slowly onto its side to give the harrow a new area. Meanwhile those parts lacerated by the inscription are lying on the cotton wool which, because it has been specially treated, immediately stops the bleeding and prepares the script for a further deepening. Here, as the body continues to rotate, prongs on the edge of the harrow then pull the cotton wool from the wounds, throw it into the pit, and the harrow goes to work again. In this way it keeps making the inscription deeper for twelve hours. For the first six hours the condemned man goes on living almost as before. He suffers nothing but pain. After two hours, the felt is removed, for at that point the man has no more energy for screaming. Here at the head of the bed warm rice pudding is put in this electrically heated bowl. From this the man, if he feels like it, can help himself to what he can lap up with his tongue. No one passes up this opportunity. I don't know of a single one, and I have had a lot of experience. He first loses his pleasure in eating around the sixth hour. I usually kneel down at this point and observe the phenomenon. The man rarely swallows the last bit. He turns it around in his mouth and spits it into the pit. When he does that, I have to lean aside or else he'll get me in the face. But how quiet the man becomes around the sixth hour! The most stupid of them begin to understand. It starts around the eyes and spreads out from there. A look that could tempt one to lie down under the harrow. Nothing else happens. The man simply begins to decipher the inscription. He purses his lips, as if he is listening. You've seen that it's not easy to figure out the inscription with your eyes, but our man deciphers it with his wounds. True, it takes a lot of work. It requires six hours to complete. But then the harrow spits him right out and throws him into the pit, where he splashes down into the bloody water and cotton wool. Then the judgment is over, and we, the Soldier and I, quickly bury him."

The Traveler had leaned his ear towards the Officer and, with his hands in his coat pockets, was observing the machine at work. The Condemned Man was also watching, but without understanding. He bent forward a little and followed the moving needles, as the Soldier, after a signal from the Officer, cut through his shirt and trousers with a knife from the back, so that they fell off the Condemned Man. He wanted to grab the falling garments to cover his bare flesh, but the Soldier held him up and shook the last rags from him. The Officer turned the machine off, and in the silence which then ensued the Condemned Man was laid out under the harrow. The chains were taken off and the straps fastened in their place. For the Condemned Man it seemed at first glance to signify almost a relief. And now the harrow sunk down a stage lower, for the Condemned was a thin man. As the needle tips touched him, a shudder went over his skin. While the Soldier was busy with the right hand, the Condemned Man stretched out his left, with no sense of its direction. But it was pointing to where the Traveler was standing. The Officer kept looking at the Traveler from the side, without taking his eyes off him, as if he was trying to read from his face the impression he was getting of the execution, which he had now explained to him, at least superficially.

The strap meant to hold the wrist ripped off. The Soldier probably had pulled on it too hard. The Soldier showed the Officer the torn-off piece of strap, wanting him to help. So the Officer went over to him and said, with his face turned towards the Traveler, "The machine is very complicated. Now and then something has to tear or break. One shouldn't let that detract from one's overall opinion. Anyway, we have an immediate replacement for the strap. I'll use a chain—even though that will affect the sensitivity of the movements for the right arm." And while he put the chain in place, he kept talking, "Our resources for maintaining the machine are very limited at the moment. Under the previous Commandant, I had free access to a cash box specially set aside for this purpose. There was a store room here in which all possible replacement parts were kept. I admit I made almost extravagant use of it. I mean earlier, not now, as the New

Commandant claims. For him everything serves only as a pretext to fight against the old arrangements. Now he keeps the cash box for machinery under his own control, and if I ask him for a new strap, he demands the torn one as a piece of evidence, the new one doesn't arrive for ten days, and it's an inferior brand, of not much use to me. But how I am supposed to get the machine to work in the meantime without a strap—no one's concerned about that."

The Traveler was thinking: it's always questionable to intervene decisively in strange circumstances. He was neither a citizen of the penal colony nor a citizen of the state to which it belonged. If he wanted to condemn the execution or even hinder it, people could say to him: You're a foreigner—keep quiet. He would have nothing in response to that, but could only add that he did not understand what he was doing on this occasion, for the purpose of his traveling was merely to observe and not to alter other people's judicial systems in any way. True, at this point the way things were turning out it was very tempting. The injustice of the process and the inhumanity of the execution were beyond doubt. No one could assume that the Traveler was acting out of any sense of his own self-interest, for the Condemned Man was a stranger to him, not a countryman and not someone who invited sympathy in any way. The Traveler himself had letters of reference from high officials and had been welcomed here with great courtesy. The fact that he had been invited to this execution even seemed to indicate that people were asking for his judgment of this trial. This was all the more likely since the Commandant, as he had now heard only too clearly, was no supporter of this process and maintained an almost hostile relationship with the Officer.

Then the Traveler heard a cry of rage from the Officer. He had just shoved the stub of felt in the Condemned Man's mouth, not without difficulty, when the Condemned Man, overcome by an irresistible nausea, shut his eyes and threw up. The Officer quickly yanked him up off the stump and wanted to turn his head aside toward the pit. But it was too late. The vomit was already flowing down onto the machine. "This is all the Commandant's fault!" cried the Officer and mindlessly rattled the brass rods at the front. "My machine's as filthy as a pigsty." With trembling hands he showed the Traveler what had happened. "Haven't I spent hours trying to make the Commandant understand that a day before the execution there should be no more food served. But the new lenient administration has a different opinion. Before the man is led away, the Commandant's women cram sugary things down his throat. His whole life he's fed himself on stinking fish, and now he has to eat sweets! But that would be all right—I'd have no objections—but why don't they get a new felt, the way I've been asking him for three months now? How can anyone take this felt into his mouth without feeling disgusted—something that a hundred men have sucked and bitten on as they were dying?"

The Condemned Man had laid his head down and appeared peaceful. The Soldier was busy cleaning up the machine with the Condemned Man's shirt. The Officer went up to the Traveler, who, feeling some premonition, took a step backwards. But the Officer grasped him by the hand and pulled him aside. "I want to speak a few words to you in confidence," he said. "May I do that?" "Of course," said the Traveler and listened with his eyes lowered.

"This process and execution, which you now have an opportunity to admire, have no more open supporters in our colony. I am its only defender, just as I am the single advocate for the legacy of the Old Commandant. I can no longer think about a more extensive organization of the process—I'm using all my powers to maintain what there is at present. When the Old Commandant was alive, the colony was full of his supporters. I have something of the Old Commandant's power of persuasion, but I completely lack his power, and as a result the supporters have gone into hiding. There are still a lot of them, but no one admits to it. If you go into a tea house today—that is to say, on a day of execution—and keep your ears open, perhaps you'll hear nothing but ambiguous remarks. They are all supporters, but under the present Commandant, considering his present views, they are totally useless to me. And now I'm asking you: Should such a life's work," he pointed to the machine, "come to nothing because of this Commandant and the women influencing him? Should people let that happen? Even if one is a foreigner and only on our island for a couple of days? But there's no time to lose. People are already preparing something against my judicial proceedings. Discussions are already taking place in the Commandant's headquarters, to which I am not invited. Even your visit today seems to me typical of the whole situation. People are cowards and send you out—a foreigner. You should have seen the executions in earlier days! The entire valley was overflowing with people, even a day before the execution. They all came merely to watch. Early in the morning the Commandant appeared with his women. Fanfares woke up the entire campsite. I delivered the news that everything was ready. The whole society—and every high official had to attend—arranged itself around the machine. This pile of cane chairs is a sorry left over from that time. The machine was freshly cleaned and glowed. For almost every execution I had new replacement parts. In front of hundreds of eyes—all the spectators stood on tip toe right up to the hills there—the condemned man was laid down under the harrow by the Commandant himself. What nowadays is done by a common soldier was then my work as the senior judge, and it was an honour for me. And then the execution began! No discordant note disturbed the work of the machine. Many people did not look any more at all, but lay down with closed eyes in the sand. They all knew: now justice was being carried out. In silence people listened to nothing but the groans of the condemned man, muffled by the felt. These days the machine no longer manages to squeeze a strong groan out of the condemned man—something the felt is not capable of smothering. But back then the needles which made the inscription dripped a caustic liquid which we are not permitted to use any more today. Well, then came the sixth hour. It was impossible to grant all the requests people made to be allowed to watch from up close. The Commandant, in his wisdom, arranged that the children should be taken care of before all the rest. Naturally, I was always allowed to stand close by, because of my official position. Often I crouched down there with two small children in my arms, on my right and left. How we all took in the expression of transfiguration on the martyred face! How we held our cheeks in the glow of this justice, finally attained and already passing away! What times we had, my friend!"

The Officer had obviously forgotten who was standing in front of him. He had put his arm around the Traveler and laid his head on his shoulder. The Traveler was extremely embarrassed. Impatiently he looked away over the Officer's head. The Soldier had ended his task of cleaning and had just shaken some rice pudding into the bowl from a tin. No sooner had the Condemned Man, who seemed to have fully recovered already, noticed this than his tongue began to lick at the pudding. The Soldier kept pushing him away, for the pudding was probably meant for a later time, but in any case it was not proper for the Soldier to reach in and grab some food with his dirty hands and eat it in front of the famished Condemned Man.

The Officer quickly collected himself. "I didn't want to upset you in any way," he said. "I know it is impossible to make someone understand those days now. Besides, the machine still works and operates on its own. It operates on its own even when it is standing alone in this valley. And at the end, the body still keeps falling in that incredibly soft flight into the pit, even if hundreds of people are not gathered like flies around the hole the way they used to be. Back then we had to erect a strong railing around the pit. It was pulled out long ago."

The Traveler wanted to turn his face away from the Officer and looked aimlessly around him. The Officer thought he was looking at the wasteland of the valley. So he grabbed his hands, turned him around in order to catch his gaze, and asked, "Do you see the shame of it?"

But the Traveler said nothing. The Officer left him alone for a while. With his legs apart and his hands on his hips, the Officer stood still and looked at the ground. Then he smiled at the Traveler cheerfully and said, "Yesterday I was nearby when the Commandant invited you. I heard the invitation. I know the Commandant. I understood right away what he intended with his invitation. Although his power might be sufficiently great to take action against me, he doesn't yet dare to. But my guess is that with you he is exposing me to the judgment of a respected foreigner. He calculates things with care. You are now in your second day on the island. You didn't know the Old Commandant and his way of thinking. You are trapped in a European way of seeing things. Perhaps you are fundamentally opposed to the death penalty in general and to this kind of mechanical style of execution in particular. Moreover, you see how the execution is a sad procedure, without any public participation, using a partially damaged machine. Now, if we take all this together (so the Commandant thinks) surely one could easily imagine that you would not consider my procedure proper? And if you didn't consider it right, you wouldn't keep quiet about it—I'm still speaking the mind of the Commandant—for you no doubt have faith that your tried-and-true convictions are correct. It's true that you have seen many peculiar things among many peoples and have learned to respect them. Thus, you will probably not speak out against the procedure with your full power, as you would perhaps in your own homeland. But the Commandant doesn't really need that. A casual word, merely a careless remark, is enough. It doesn't have to match your convictions at all, so long as it corresponds to his wishes. I'm certain he will use all his shrewdness to interrogate you. And his women will sit around in a circle and perk up their ears. You will say something like, 'Among us the judicial procedures are different,' or 'With us the accused is questioned before the verdict,' or 'We had torture only in the Middle Ages.' For you these observations appear as correct as they are self-evident—innocent remarks which do not impugn my procedure. But how will the Commandant take them? I see him, our excellent Commandant—the way he immediately pushes his stool aside and hurries out to the balcony—I see his women, how they stream after him. I hear his voice—the women call it a thunder voice. And now he's speaking: 'A great Western explorer who has been commissioned to inspect judicial procedures in all countries has just said that our process based on old customs is inhuman. After the verdict of such a personality it is, of course, no longer possible for me to tolerate this procedure. So from this day on I am ordering . . . and so forth.' You want to intervene—you didn't say what he is reporting—you didn't call my procedure inhuman; by contrast, in keeping with your deep insight, you consider it most humane and most worthy of human beings. You also admire this machinery. But it is too late. You don't even go onto the balcony, which is already filled with women. You want to attract attention. You want to cry out. But a lady's hand is covering your mouth, and I and the Old Commandant's work are lost."

The Traveler had to suppress a smile. So the work which he had considered so difficult was easy. He said evasively, "You're exaggerating my influence. The Commandant has read my letters of recommendation. He knows that I am no expert in judicial processes. If I were to express an opinion, it would be that of a lay person, no more significant than the opinion of anyone else, and in any case far less significant than the opinion of the Commandant, who, as I understand it, has very extensive powers in this penal colony. If his views of this procedure are as definite as you think they are, then I'm afraid the time has come for this procedure to end, without any need for my humble opinion."

Did the Officer understand by now? No, he did not yet get it. He shook his head vigorously, briefly looked back at the Condemned Man and the Soldier, who both flinched and stopped eating the rice, went up really close to the Traveler, without looking into his face, but gazing at parts of his jacket, and said more gently than before: "You don't know the Commandant. Where he and all of us are concerned you are—forgive the expression—to a certain extent innocent. Your influence, believe me, cannot be overestimated. In fact, I was blissfully happy when I heard that you were to be present at the execution by yourself. This order of the Commandant was aimed at me, but now I'll turn it to my advantage. Without being distracted by false insinuations and disparaging looks—which could not have been avoided with a greater number of participants at the execution—you have listened to my explanation, looked at the machine, and are now about to view the execution. Your verdict is no doubt already fixed. If some small uncertainties remain, witnessing the execution will remove them. And now I'm asking you—help me with the Commandant!"

The Traveler did not let him go on talking. "How can I do that," he cried. "It's totally impossible. I can help you as little as I can harm you."

"You could do it," said the Officer. With some apprehension the Traveler observed that the Officer was clenching his fists. "You could do it," repeated the Officer, even more emphatically. "I have a plan which must succeed. You think your influence is insufficient. I know it will be enough. But assuming you're right, doesn't saving this whole procedure require one to try even those methods which may be inadequate? So listen to my plan. To carry it out, it's necessary, above all, for you to keep as quiet as possible today in the colony about your verdict on this procedure. Unless someone asks you directly, you should not express any view whatsoever. But what you do say must be short and vague. People should notice that it's difficult for you to speak about the subject, that you feel bitter, that, if you were to speak openly, you'd have to burst out cursing on the spot. I'm not asking you to lie, not at all. You should only give brief answers—something like, 'Yes, I've seen the execution' or 'Yes, I've heard the full explanation.' That's all—nothing further. For that will be enough of an indication for people to observe in you a certain bitterness, even if that's not what the Commandant will think. Naturally, he will completely misunderstand the issue and interpret it in his own way. My plan is based on that. Tomorrow a large meeting of all the higher administrative officials takes place at headquarters under the chairmanship of the Commandant. He, of course, understands how to turn such a meeting into a spectacle. A gallery has been built, which is always full of spectators. I'm compelled to take part in the discussions, though they fill me with disgust. In any case, you will certainly be invited to the meeting. If you follow my plan today and behave accordingly, the invitation will become an emphatic request. But should you for some inexplicable reason still not be invited, you must make sure you request an invitation. Then you'll receive one without question. Now, tomorrow you are sitting with the women in the Commandant's box. With frequent upward glances he reassures himself that you are there. After various trivial and ridiculous agenda items designed for the spectators—mostly harbour construction— always harbour construction—the judicial process comes up for discussion. If it's not raised by the Commandant himself or does not occur soon enough, I'll make sure that it comes up. I'll stand up and report on today's execution. Really briefly—just the report. Such a report is not really customary; however, I'll do it, nonetheless. The Commandant thanks me, as always, with a friendly smile. And now he cannot restrain himself. He seizes this excellent opportunity. 'The report of the execution,' he'll say, or something like that, 'has just been given. I would like to add to this report only the fact that this particular execution was attended by the great explorer whose visit confers such extraordinary honour on our colony, as you all know. Even the significance of our meeting today has been increased by his presence. Should we not now ask this great explorer for his appraisal of the execution based on old customs and of the process which preceded it?' Of course, there is the noise of applause everywhere, universal agreement. And I'm louder than anyone. The Commandant bows before you and says, 'Then in everyone's name, I'm putting the question to you.' And now you step up to the railing. Place your hands where everyone can see them. Otherwise the ladies will grab them and play with your fingers. And now finally come your remarks. I don't know how I'll bear the tension up to then. In your speech you mustn't hold back. Let truth resound. Lean over the railing and shout it out—yes, yes, roar your opinion at the Commandant, your unshakeable opinion. But perhaps you don't want to do that. It doesn't suit your character. Perhaps in your country people behave differently in such situations. That's all right. That's perfectly satisfactory. Don't stand up at all. Just say a couple of words. Whisper them so that only the officials underneath you can just hear them. That's enough. You don't even have to say anything at all about the lack of attendance at the execution or about the squeaky wheel, the torn strap, the disgusting felt. No. I'll take over all further details, and, believe me, if my speech doesn't chase him out of the room, it will force him to his knees, so he'll have to admit it: 'Old Commandant, I bow down before you.' That's my plan. Do you want to help me carry it out? But, of course, you want to. More than that—you have to."

And the Officer gripped the Traveler by both arms and looked at him, breathing heavily into his face. He had yelled the last sentences so loudly that even the Soldier and the Condemned Man were paying attention. Although they couldn't understand a thing, they stopped eating and looked over at the Traveler, still chewing.

From the start the Traveler had had no doubts about the answer he must give. He had experienced too much in his life to be able to waver here. Basically he was honest and unafraid. Still, with the Soldier and the Condemned Man looking at him, he hesitated a moment. But finally he said, as he had to, "No." The Officer's eyes blinked several times, but he did not take his eyes off the Traveler. "Would you like an explanation," asked the Traveler. The Officer nodded dumbly. "I am opposed to this procedure," said the Traveler. "Even before you took me into your confidence—and, of course, I will never abuse your confidence under any circumstances—I was already thinking about whether I was entitled to intervene against this procedure and whether my intervention could have the smallest chance of success. And if that was the case, it was clear to me whom I had to turn to first of all—naturally, to the Commandant. You clarified the issue for me even more, but without reinforcing my decision in any way—quite the reverse. I find your conviction genuinely moving, even if it cannot deter me."

The Officer remained quiet, turned toward the machine, grabbed one of the brass rods, and then, leaning back a little, looked up at the inscriber, as if he was checking that everything was in order. The Soldier and the Condemned Man seemed to have made friends with each other. The Condemned Man was making signs to the Soldier, although, given the tight straps on him, this was difficult for him to do. The Soldier was leaning into him. The Condemned Man whispered something to him, and the Soldier nodded. The Traveler went over to the Officer and said, "You don't yet know what I'll do. Yes, I will tell the Commandant my opinion of the procedure—not in a meeting, but in private. In addition, I won't stay here long enough to be able to get called in to some meeting or other. Early tomorrow morning I leave, or at least I go on board ship." It didn't look as if the Officer had been listening. "So the process has not convinced you," he said to himself, smiling the way an old man smiles over the silliness of a child, concealing his own true thoughts behind that smile.

"Well then, it's time," he said finally and suddenly looked at the Traveler with bright eyes which contained some sort of demand, some appeal for participation. "Time for what?" asked the Traveler uneasily. But there was no answer.

"You are free," the Officer told the Condemned Man in his own language. At first the man did not believe him. "You are free now," said the Officer. For the first time the face of the Condemned Man showed signs of real life. Was it the truth? Was it only the Officer's mood, which could change? Had the foreign Traveler brought him a reprieve? What was it? That's what the man's face seemed to be asking. But not for long. Whatever the case might be, if he could he wanted to be truly free, and he began to shake back and forth, as much as the harrow permitted.

"You're tearing my straps," cried the Officer. "Be still! We'll undo them right away." And, giving a signal to the Soldier, he set to work with him. The Condemned

Man said nothing and smiled slightly to himself. He turned his face to the Officer and then to the Soldier and then back again, without ignoring the Traveler.

"Pull him out," the Officer ordered the Soldier. This process required a certain amount of care because of the harrow. The Condemned Man already had a few small wounds on his back, thanks to his own impatience.

From this point on, however, the Officer paid him hardly any attention. He went up to the Traveler, pulled out the small leather folder once more, leafed through it, finally found the sheet he was looking for, and showed it to the Traveler. "Read that," he said. "I can't," said the Traveler. "I've already told you I can't read these pages." "But take a close look at the page," said the Officer, and moved up right next to the Traveler in order to read with him. When that didn't help, he raised his little finger high up over the paper, as if the page must not be touched under any circumstances, so that using this he might make the task of reading easier for the Traveler. The Traveler also made an effort so that at least he could satisfy the Officer, but it was impossible for him. Then the Officer began to spell out the inscription and then read out once again the joined up letters. "'Be just!' it states," he said. "Now you can read it." The Traveler bent so low over the paper that the Officer, afraid that he might touch it, moved it further away. The Traveler didn't say anything more, but it was clear that he was still unable to read anything. "'Be just!' it says," the Officer remarked once again.

"That could be," said the Traveler. "I do believe that's written there." "Good," said the Officer, at least partially satisfied. He climbed up the ladder, holding the paper. With great care he set the page in the inscriber and appeared to rotate the gear mechanism completely around. This was very tiring work. It must have required him to deal with extremely small wheels. He had to inspect the gears so closely that sometimes his head disappeared completely into the inscriber.

The Traveler followed this work from below without looking away. His neck grew stiff, and his eyes found the sunlight pouring down from the sky painful. The Soldier and the Condemned Man were keeping each other busy. With the tip of his bayonet the Soldier pulled out the Condemned Man's shirt and trousers which were lying in the hole. The shirt was horribly dirty, and the Condemned Man washed it in the bucket of water. When he was putting on his shirt and trousers, the Soldier and the Condemned Man had to laugh out loud, for the pieces of clothing were cut in two up the back. Perhaps the Condemned Man thought that it was his duty to amuse the Soldier. In his ripped-up clothes he circled around the Soldier, who crouched down on the ground, laughed, and slapped his knees. But they restrained themselves out of consideration for the two gentlemen present.

When the Officer was finally finished up on the machine, with a smile he looked over the whole thing and all its parts one more time, and this time closed the cover of the inscriber, which had been open up to this point. He climbed down, looked into the hole and then at the Condemned Man, observed with satisfaction that he had pulled out his clothes, then went to the bucket of water to wash his hands, recognized too late that it was disgustingly dirty, and was upset that now he couldn't wash his hands. Finally he pushed them into the sand. This option didn't satisfy him, but he had to do what he could in the circumstances. Then he stood up and began to unbutton the coat of his uniform. As he did this, the two lady's handkerchiefs, which he had pushed into the back of his collar, fell into his hands. "Here you have your handkerchiefs," he said and threw them over to the Condemned Man. And to the Traveler he said by way of an explanation, "Presents from the ladies."

In spite of the obvious speed with which he took off the coat of his uniform and then undressed himself completely, he handled each piece of clothing very carefully, even running his fingers over the silver braids on his tunic with special care and shaking a tassel into place. But in great contrast to this care, as soon as he was finished handling an article of clothing, he immediately flung it angrily into the hole. The last items he had left were his short sword and its harness. He pulled the sword out of its scabbard, broke it in pieces, gathered up everything—the pieces of the sword, the scabbard, and the harness—and threw them away so forcefully that they rattled against each other down in the pit.

Now he stood there naked. The Traveler bit his lip and said nothing. For he was aware what would happen, but he had no right to hinder the Officer in any way. If the judicial process to which the officer clung was really so close to the point of being cancelled—perhaps as a result of the intervention of the Traveler, something to which he for his part felt duty-bound—then the Officer was now acting in a completely correct manner. In his place, the Traveler would not have acted any differently.

The Soldier and the Condemned Man at first didn't understand a thing. To begin with they didn't look, not even once. The Condemned Man was extremely happy to get the handkerchiefs back, but he couldn't enjoy them very long, for the Soldier snatched them from him with a quick grab, which he had not anticipated. The Condemned Man then tried to pull the handkerchiefs out from the Soldier's belt, where he had put them for safe keeping, but the Soldier was too wary. So they were fighting, half in jest. Only when the Officer was fully naked did they start to pay attention. The Condemned Man especially seemed to be struck by a premonition of some sort of significant transformation. What had happened to him was now taking place with the Officer. Perhaps this time the procedure would play itself out to its conclusion. The foreign Traveler had probably given the order. So that was revenge. Without having suffered all the way to the end himself, nonetheless he would be completely revenged. A wide, silent laugh now appeared on his face and did not go away.

The Officer, however, had turned towards the machine. If earlier on it had already become clear that he understood the machine thoroughly, one might well get alarmed now at the way he handled it and how it obeyed. He only had to bring his hand near the harrow for it to rise and sink several times, until it had reached the correct position to make room for him. He only had to grasp the bed by the edges, and it already began to quiver. The stump of felt moved up to his mouth. One could see how the Officer really didn't want to accept it, but his hesitation was only momentary—he immediately submitted and took it in. Everything was ready, except that the straps still hung down on the sides. But they were clearly unnecessary. The Officer did not have to be strapped down. When the Condemned Man saw the loose straps, he thought the execution would be incomplete unless they were fastened. He waved eagerly to the Soldier, and they ran over to strap in the Officer. The latter had already stuck out his foot to kick the crank designed to set the inscriber in motion. Then he saw the two men coming. So he pulled his foot back and let himself be strapped in. But now he could no longer reach the crank. Neither the Soldier nor the Condemned Man would find it, and the Traveler was determined not to touch it. But that was unnecessary. Hardly were the straps attached when the machine already started working. The bed quivered, the needles danced on his skin, and the harrow swung up and down. The Traveler had already been staring for some time before he remembered that a wheel in the inscriber was supposed to squeak. But everything was quiet, without the slightest audible hum.

Because of its silent working, the machine did not really attract attention. The Traveler looked over at the Soldier and the Condemned Man. The Condemned Man was the livelier of the two. Everything in the machine interested him. At times he bent down—at other times he stretched up, all the time pointing with his forefinger in order to show something to the Soldier. For the Traveler it was embarrassing. He was determined to remain here until the end, but he could no longer endure the sight of the two men. "Go home," he said. The Soldier might have been ready to do that, but the Condemned Man took the order as a direct punishment. With his hands folded he begged and pleaded to be allowed to stay there. And when the Traveler shook his head and was unwilling to give in, he even knelt down. Seeing that orders were of no help here, the Traveler wanted to go over and chase the two away.

Then he heard a noise from up in the inscriber. He looked up. So was the gear wheel going out of alignment? But it was something else. The lid on the inscriber was lifting up slowly. Then it fell completely open. The teeth of a cog wheel were exposed and lifted up. Soon the entire wheel appeared. It was as if some huge force was compressing the inscriber, so that there was no longer sufficient room for this wheel. The wheel rolled all the way to the edge of the inscriber, fell down, rolled upright a bit in the sand, and then fell over and lay still. But already up on the inscriber another gear wheel was moving upwards. Several others followed— large ones, small ones, ones hard to distinguish. With each of them the same thing happened. One kept thinking that now the inscriber must surely be empty, but then a new cluster with lots of parts would move up, fall down, roll in the sand, and lie still. With all this going on, the Condemned Man totally forgot the Traveler's order. The gear wheels completely delighted him. He kept wanting to grab one, and at the same time he was urging the Soldier to help him. But he kept pulling his hand back startled, for immediately another wheel followed, which, at least in its initial rolling, surprised him.

The Traveler, by contrast, was very upset. Obviously the machine was breaking up. Its quiet operation had been an illusion. He felt as if he had to look after the Officer, now that the latter could no longer look after himself. But while the falling gear wheels were claiming all his attention, he had neglected to look at the rest of the machine. However, when he now bent over the harrow, once the last gear wheel had left the inscriber, he had a new, even more unpleasant surprise. The harrow was not writing but only stabbing, and the bed was not rolling the body, but lifting it, quivering, up into the needles. The Traveler wanted to reach in to stop the whole thing, if possible. This was not the torture the Officer wished to attain. It was murder, pure and simple. He stretched out his hands. But at that point the harrow was already moving upwards and to the side, with the skewered body—just as it did in other cases, but only in the twelfth hour. Blood flowed out in hundreds of streams, not mixed with water—the water tubes had also failed to work this time. Then one last thing went wrong: the body would not come loose from the needles. Its blood streamed out, but it hung over the pit without falling. The harrow wanted to move back to its original position, but, as if it realized that it could not free itself of its load, it remained over the hole.

"Help," the Traveler yelled out to the Soldier and the Condemned Man and grabbed the Officer's feet. He wanted to push against the feet himself and have the two others grab the Officer's head from the other side, so he could be slowly taken off the needles. But now the two men could not make up their mind whether to come or not. The Condemned Man turned away at once. The Traveler had to go over to him and drag him to the Officer's head by force. At this point, almost against his will, he looked at the face of the corpse. It was as it had been in his life. He could discover no sign of the promised transfiguration. What all the others had found in the machine, the Officer had not. His lips were pressed firmly together, his eyes were open and looked as they had when he was alive, his gaze was calm and convinced. The tip of a large iron needle had gone through his forehead.

As the Traveler, with the Soldier and the Condemned Man behind him, came to the first houses in the colony, the Soldier pointed to one and said, "That's the tea house."

On the ground floor of one of the houses was a deep, low room, like a cave, with smoke-covered walls and ceiling. On the street side it was open along its full width. Although there was little difference between the tea house and the rest of the houses in the colony, which were all very dilapidated, except for the Commandant's palatial structure, the Traveler was struck by the impression of historical memory, and he felt the power of earlier times. Followed by his companions, he walked closer, going between the unoccupied tables, which stood in the street in front of the tea house, and took a breath of the cool, stuffy air which came from inside. "The old man is buried here," said the Soldier; "a place in the cemetery was denied him by the chaplain. For a long time people were undecided where they should bury him. Finally they buried him here. Of course, the Officer explained none of that to you, for naturally he was the one most ashamed about it. A few times he even tried to dig up the old man at night, but he was always chased off." "Where is the grave?" asked the Traveler, who could not believe the Soldier. Instantly both men, the Soldier and the Condemned Man, ran in front of him and with hands outstretched pointed to the place where the grave was located. They led the Traveler to the back wall, where guests were sitting at a few tables. They were presumably dock workers, strong men with short, shiny, black beards. None of them wore coats, and their shirts were torn. They were poor, oppressed people. As the Traveler came closer, a few got up, leaned against the wall, and looked at him. A whisper went up around the Traveler—"It's a foreigner. He wants to look at the grave." They pushed one of the tables aside, under which there was a real grave stone. It was a simple stone, low enough for it to remain hidden under a table. It bore an inscription in very small letters. In order to read it the Traveler had to kneel down. It read, "Here rests the Old Commandant. His followers, who are now not permitted to have a name, buried him in this grave and erected this stone. There exists a prophecy that the Commandant will rise again after a certain number of years and from this house will lead his followers to a re-conquest of the colony. Have faith and wait!"

When the Traveler had read it and got up, he saw the men standing around him and smiling, as if they had read the inscription with him, found it ridiculous, and were asking him to share their opinion. The Traveler acted as if he hadn't noticed, distributed some coins among them, waited until the table was pushed back over the grave, left the tea house, and went to the harbour.

In the tea house the Soldier and the Condemned Man had come across some people they knew who detained them. However, they must have broken free of them soon, because by the time the Traveler found himself in the middle of a long staircase which led to the boats, they were already running after him. They probably wanted to force the Traveler at the last minute to take them with him. While the Traveler was haggling at the bottom of the stairs with a sailor about his passage out to the steamer, the two men were racing down the steps in silence, for they didn't dare cry out. But as they reached the bottom, the Traveler was already in the boat, and the sailor at once cast off from shore. They could still have jumped into the boat, but the Traveler picked up a heavy knotted rope from the boat bottom, threatened them with it, and thus prevented them from jumping in.

SORROW-ACRE

Isak Dinesen (Karen Blixen)

Translated from the Danish by the author

Karen Blixen (1885–1962). Born to a family of prosperous merchants, Karen Dinesen (later Baroness Karen von Blixen-Finecke), better known by her penname Isak Dinesen, was a Danish author who wrote in both Danish and English. Her first book *Seven Gothic Tales*, written in English, was published in 1934, and the Danish edition appeared later. Criticism of her decision to write and publish in English led her to ensure that later books appeared in Danish first. If she is now most remembered for *Out of Africa*, a memoir of her time living British East Africa (now Kenya), she was also one of the finest short story writers of the twentieth century. Her works are not, strictly speaking, translated – Blixen freely adapted her stories, revising and changing many details between English and Danish versions. On the centenary of her birth, the Asteroid 3318 Blixen was named in her honour.

The low, undulating Danish landscape was silent and serene, mysteriously wide-awake, in the hour before sunrise. There was not a cloud in the pale sky, not a shadow along the dim, pearly fields, hills and woods. The mist was lifting from the valleys and hollows, the air was cool, the grass and the foliage dripping wet with morning dew. Unwatched by the eyes of man, and undisturbed by his activity, the country breathed a timeless life, to which language was inadequate.

All the same a human race had lived on this land for a thousand years, had been formed by its soil and weathers, and had marked it with its thoughts, so that now no one could tell where the existence of the one ceased and that of the other began. The thin grey line of a road, winding across the plain and up and down hills, was the fixed materialization of human longing, and of the human notion that it were better to be in one place than another.

A child of the country would read this open landscape like a book. The irregular mosaic of meadows and cornlands was a picture, in timid green and yellow, of the people's struggle for its daily bread, – the centuries had taught it to plough and sow in this way. On a distant hill the immovable wings of a windmill, in a small blue cross against the sky, delineated a later stage in the career of the bread. The blurred outline of thatched roofs, – a low, brown growth of the earth, – where the huts of the village thronged together, told the history, from his cradle to his grave, of the peasant, the creature nearest to the soil and dependent on it, prospering in a fertile year and dying in years of drought and pests.

A little higher up, with the faint horizontal line of the white cemetery wall round it, and the vertical contour of tall poplars by its side, the red-tiled church bore witness, as far as the eye reached, that this was a Christian country. The child of the land knew it as a strange house, inhabited only for a few hours every seventh day, but with a strong, clear voice in it to give out the joys and sorrows of the land: a plain, square embodiment of the nation's trust in the justice and mercy of heaven. But where, amongst cupular woods and groves, the lordly, pyramidal silhouette of the cut lime avenues rose in the air, there a big country house lay.

The child of the land would read much within these elegant, geometrical ciphers on the hazy blue. They spoke of power; the lime-trees paraded round a stronghold. Up here was decided the destiny of the surrounding land and of the men and beasts upon it, and the peasant lifted his eyes to the green pyramids with awe. They spoke of dignity, decorum and taste. Danish soil grew no finer flower than the mansion to which the long avenue led. In its lofty rooms life and death bore themselves with stately grace. The country house did not gaze upward, like the church, nor down to the ground like the huts: it had a wider earthly horizon than they, and was related to much noble architecture all over Europe. Foreign artisans had been called in to panel and stucco it, and its own inhabitants travelled, and brought back ideas, fashions and things of beauty. Paintings, tapestries, silver and glass from distant countries had been made to feel at home here, and now formed part of Danish country life.

The big house stood as firmly rooted in the soil of Denmark as the peasants' huts, and was as faithfully allied to her four winds and her changing seasons, to her animal life, trees and flowers. Only its interests lay on a higher plane. Within the domain of the lime-trees it was no longer cows, goats and pigs on which the minds and the talk ran, but horses and dogs. The wild fauna, the game of the land, that the peasant shook his fist at, when he saw it on his young green rye or in his ripening wheat-field, to the residents of the country houses was the main pursuit and the joy of existence.

The writing in the sky solemnly proclaimed continuance, a worldly immortality. The great country houses had held their ground through many generations. The families who lived in them revered the past as they honoured themselves, for the history of Denmark was their own history.

A Rosenkrantz had sat at Rosenholm, a Juel at Hverringe, a Skeel at Gammel-Estrup as long as people remembered. They had seen kings and schools of style succeed one another and proudly and humbly had made over their personal existence to that of their land, so that amongst their equals and with the peasants they passed by its name: Rosenholm, Hverringe, Gammel-Estrup. To the King and the country, to his family and to the individual lord of the manor himself it was a matter of minor consequence which particular Rosenkrantz, Juel or Skeel, out of a long row of fathers and sons, at the moment in his person incarnated the fields and woods, the peasants, cattle and game owners: – towards God in Heaven, towards the King, his neighbour and himself, and they were all harmoniously consolidated into the idea of his duties towards his land. Highest amongst these ranked his obligation to uphold the sacred continuance, and to produce a new Rosenkrantz, Juel or Skeel for the service of Rosenholm, Hverringe and Gammel-Estrup.

Female grace was prized in the manors. Together with good hunting and fine wine it was the flower and emblem of the higher existence led there, and in many ways the families prided themselves more on their daughters than on their sons.

The ladies who promenaded in the lime avenues, or drove through them in heavy coaches with four horses, carried the future of the name in their lap, and were, like dignified and debonair caryatides, holding up the houses. They were themselves conscious of their value, kept up their price and moved in a sphere of pretty worship and self-worship. They might even be thought to add to it, on their own, a graceful, arch, paradoxical haughtiness. For how free were they not, how powerful! Their lords might rule the country, and allow themselves many liberties, but when it came to that supreme matter of legitimacy which was the vital principle of their world, the centre of gravitation lay with them.

The lime-trees were in bloom. But in the early morning only a faint fragrance drifted through the garden, an airy message, an aromatic echo of their dreams during the short summer night.

In a long avenue that led from the house all the way to the end of the garden, where, from a small white pavilion in the classic style, there was a great view over the fields, a young man walked. He was plainly dressed in brown, with pretty linen and lace, bareheaded, with his hair tied by a ribbon. He was dark, a strong and sturdy figure with fine eyes and hands, he limped a little on one leg.

The big house at the top of the avenue, the garden and the fields had been his childhood's paradise. But he had travelled and lived out of Denmark, in Rome and Paris, and he was at present appointed to the Danish Legation to the Court of King George, the brother of the late, unfortunate young Danish Queen. He had not seen his ancestral home for nine years. It made him laugh to find, now, everything so much smaller than he remembered it, and at the same time he was strangely moved by meeting it again. Dead people came towards him and smiled at him, a small boy in a ruff ran past him with his hoop and kite, in passing gave him a clear glance and laughingly asked: 'Do you mean to tell me that you are me?' He tried to catch him in the flight, and to answer him: 'Yes, I assure you that I am you,' but the light figure did not wait for a reply.

The young man, whose name was Adam, stood in a particular relation to the house and the land. For six months he had been heir to it all, nominally he was so even at this moment. It was this circumstance which had brought him from England, and on which his mind was dwelling, as he walked along slowly.

The old lord up at the manor, his father's brother, had had much misfortune in his domestic life. His wife had died young, and two of his children in infancy. The one son then left to him, his cousin's playmate, was a sickly and morose boy. For ten years the father travelled with him from one watering-place to another, in Germany and Italy, hardly ever in other company than that of his silent, dying child, sheltering the faint flame of life with both hands, until such time as it could be passed over to a new bearer of the name. At the same time another misfortune had struck him, he fell into disfavour at Court, where till now he had held a fine position. He was about to rehabilitate his family's prestige through the marriage which he had arranged for his son, when before it could take place the bridegroom died, not twenty years old.

Adam learned of his cousin's death, and his own changed fortune, in England, through his ambitious and triumphant mother. He sat with her letter in his hand, and did not know what to think about it.

If this, he reflected, had happened to him while he was still a boy, in Denmark, it would have meant all the world to him. It would be so now with his friends and schoolfellows, if they were in his place, and they would, at this moment, be congratulating or envying him. But he was neither covetous nor vain by nature, he had faith in his own talents and had been content to know that his success in life depended on his ability. His slight infirmity had always set him a little apart from other boys, it had, maybe, given him a keener sensibility of many things in life, and he did not, now, deem it quite right that the head of the family should limp on one leg. He did not even see his prospects in the same light as his people at home. In England he had met with greater wealth and magnificence than they dreamed of, he had been in love with, and made happy by an English lady of such rank and fortune that to her, he felt, the finest estate of Denmark would look but like a child's toy-farm.

And in England, too, he had come in touch with the great new ideas of the age: of nature, of the right and freedom of man, of justice and beauty. The Universe, through them, had become infinitely wider to him, he wanted to find out still more about it and was planning to travel to America, to the New World. For a moment he felt trapped and imprisoned, as if the dead people of his name, from the family vault at home, were stretching out their parched arms for him.

But at the same time he began to dream at night of the old house and garden. He had walked in these avenues in dream, and had smelt the scent of the flowering limes. When at Ranelagh an old gipsy-woman looked in his hand and told him that a son of his was to sit in the seat of his fathers, he felt a sudden, deep satisfaction, queer in a young man who till now had never given his sons a thought.

Then, six months later, his mother again wrote to tell him that his uncle had himself married the girl intended for his dead son. The head of the family was still in his best age, not over sixty, and although Adam remembered him as a small, slight man, he was a vigorous person, it was likely that his young wife would bear him sons.

Adam's mother in her disappointment lay the blame on him. If he had returned to Denmark, she told him, his uncle might have come to look upon him as a son, and would not have married, – nay, he might have handed the bride over to him. Adam knew better. The family estate, in difference from the neighbouring properties, had gone down from father to son ever since a man of their name first sat there. The tradition of direct succession was the pride of the clan and a sacred dogma to his uncle, he would surely call for a son of his own flesh and bone.

But at the news the young man was seized by a strange deep, aching remorse towards his old home in Denmark. It was as if he had been making light of a friendly and generous gesture, and disloyal to someone unfailingly loyal to him. It would be but just, he thought, if from now the place should disown and forget him. Nostalgia, which before he had never known, caught hold of him, for the first time he walked in the streets and parks of London as a stranger.

He wrote to his uncle and asked if he might come and stay with him, begged leave from the Legation and took ship for Denmark. He had come to the house to make his peace with it, he had slept little in the night, and was up so early and walking in the garden, to explain himself, and to be forgiven.

While he walked the still garden slowly took up its day's work. A big snail, of the kind that his grandfather had brought back from France, and which he remembered eating in the house as a child, was already, with dignity, dragging a silver train down the avenue. The birds began to sing, in an old tree under which he stopped a number of them were worrying an owl, the rule of the night was over.

He stood at the end of the avenue and saw the sky lightening. An ecstatic clarity filled the world, in half an hour the sun would rise. A rye-field here ran along the garden, two roe-deer were moving in it, and looked roseate in the dawn. He gazed out over the fields, where as a small boy he had ridden his pony, and towards the wood where he had killed his first stag; he remembered the old servants who had taught him, and their names, some of them were now in their graves.

The ties which bound him to this place, he reflected, were of a mystic nature. He might never again come back to it, and it would make no difference. As long as a man of his own blood and name should sit in the house, hunt in the fields and be obeyed by the people in the huts, wherever he travelled on earth, in England or amongst the Red Indians of America, he himself would still be safe, would still have a home, and would carry weight in the world.

His eyes rested on the church. In old days, before the time of Martin Luther, younger sons of great families, he knew, had entered the Church of Rome, and had given up individual wealth and happiness to serve the greater ideals. They, too, had bestowed honour upon their homes and were remembered in its registers. In the solitude of the morning, half in jest he let his mind run as it listed, it seemed to him that he might speak to the land as to a person, as to the mother of his race. – 'Is it only my body that you want?' he asked her, 'while you reject my imagination, energy and emotions? If the world might be brought to acknowledge that the virtue of our name does not belong to the past only, will it give you no satisfaction?' The landscape was so still that he could not tell whether it answered him yes or no.

After a while he walked on, and came to the new French rose garden laid out for the young mistress of the house. In England he had acquired a freer taste in gardening, and he wondered if he could liberate these blushing captives, and make them thrive outside their cut hedges. Perhaps, he meditated, the elegantly conventional garden would be a floral portrait of his young aunt from Court, whom he had not yet seen.

As once more he came to the pavilion at the end of the avenue his eyes were caught by a bouquet of delicate colours which could not possibly belong to the Danish summer morning. It was in fact his uncle himself, powdered and silk-stockinged, but still in a brocade dressing-gown, and obviously sunk in deep thought. 'And what business, or what meditations,' Adam asked himself, 'drags a connoisseur of the beautiful, but three months married to a wife of seventeen, from his bed into his garden before sunrise?' He walked up to the small slim, straight figure.

His uncle on his side showed no surprise at seeing him, but then he rarely seemed surprised at anything. He greeted him, with a compliment on his early rising, as kindly as he had on his arrival last evening. After a moment he looked to the sky and solemnly proclaimed: 'It will be a hot day.' Adam, as a child, had often been impressed by the grand, ceremonial manner in which the old lord would state the common happenings of existence, – it looked as if here nothing had changed, but all was what it used to be.

The uncle offered the nephew a pinch of snuff.

'No thank you. Uncle,' said Adam, 'it would ruin my nose for the scent of your garden, which is as fresh as the garden of Eden, newly created.'

'From every tree of which,' said his uncle smiling, 'thou, my Adam, mayest freely eat.'

They slowly walked up the avenue together.

The hidden sun was now already gilding the top of the tallest trees. Adam talked of the beauties of nature, and of the greatness of Nordic scenery less marked by the hand of man, than that of Italy. His uncle took the praise of the landscape as a personal compliment, and congratulated him because he had not, in likeness to many young travellers, in foreign countries learnt to despise his native land. No, said Adam, he had lately in England longed for the fields and woods of his Danish home. And he had there become acquainted with a new piece of Danish poetry which had enchanted him more than any English or French work. He named the author, Johannes Ewald, and quoted a few of the mighty, turbulent verses.

'And I have wondered, while I read,' he went on after a pause, still moved by the lines he himself had declaimed', that we have not till now understood how much our Nordic mythology in moral greatness surpasses that of Greece and Rome. If it had not been for the physical beauty of the ancient gods, which has come down to us in marble, no modern mind could hold them worthy of worship. They were mean, capricious and treacherous. The gods of our Danish forefathers are as much more divine than they as the Druid is nobler than the Augur. For the fair gods of Asgaard did possess the sublime human virtues, they were righteous, trustworthy, benevolent and, even within a barbaric age, chivalrous.'

His uncle here for the first time appeared to take any real interest in the conversation, he stopped, his majestic nose a little in the air. 'Ah! – it was easier to them,' he said.

'What do you mean, Uncle?' Adam asked.

'It was a great deal easier,' said his uncle, 'to the northern gods than to those of Greece to be, as you will have it, righteous and benevolent. To my mind it even reveals a weakness in the souls of our ancient Danes that they should consent to adore such divinities.'

'My dear Uncle,' said Adam smiling, 'I have always felt that you would be familiar with the modes of Olympus. Now please give me part in your insight, and tell me why virtue should come easier to our Danish gods than to those of milder climates.'

'They were not so powerful,' said his uncle.

'And does power', Adam again asked, 'stand in the way of virtue?'

'Nay,' said his uncle gravely. 'Nay, power is in itself the supreme virtue. But the gods of which you speak were never all-powerful. They had, at all times, by their side those darker powers which they named the Jotuns, and who worked the suffering, the disasters, the ruin of our world. They might safely give themselves up to temperance and kindness. The omnipotent gods,' he went on, 'have no such recourse. With their omnipotence they take over the woe of the Universe.'

They had walked up the avenue till they were in view of the house. The old lord stopped and ran his eyes over it. The stately building was the same as ever, behind the two tall front windows, Adam knew, was now his young aunt's room. His uncle turned and walked back.

'Chivalry,' he said, 'chivalry, of which you were speaking, is not a virtue of the omnipotent. It will needs imply mighty rival powers for the knight to defy. With a dragon inferior to him in strength what figure will St George cut? The knight who finds no superior forces ready to hand must invent them, and combat windmills, his knighthood itself stipulates dangers, vileness, darkness on all sides of him. Nay, believe me, my nephew, in spite of his moral worth your chivalrous Odin of Asgaard as a Regent must take rank below that Jove who avowed his sovereignty, and accepted the world which he ruled. – But you are young,' he added, 'and the experience of the aged to you will sound pedantic.'

He stood immovable for a moment and then with deep gravity proclaimed: 'The sun is up.'

The sun did indeed rise above the horizon. The wide landscape was suddenly animated by its splendour, and the dewy grass shone in a thousand gleams.

'I have listened to you, Uncle,' said Adam, 'with great interest. But while we have talked, you yourself have seemed to me preoccupied, your eyes have rested in the field outside the garden as if something of great moment, a matter of life and death, were going on there. Now that the sun is up I see the mowers in the rye, and hear them whetting their sickles. It is, I remember you telling me, the first day of the harvest. That is a great day to a landowner and enough to take his mind away from the gods. It is very fine weather, and I wish you a full barn.'

The elder man stood still, his hands on his walking-stick. 'There is indeed', he said at last,' something going on in that field, a matter of life and death. Come, let us sit down here, and I will tell you the whole story.'

They sat down on the seat that ran all along the pavilion, and while he spoke the old lord of the land did not take his eyes off the rye-field.

'A week ago, on Thursday night,' he said, 'someone set fire to my barn at Rødmosegaard, – you know the place, close to the moor, – and burned it all down. For two or three days we could not lay hands on the offender. Then on Monday morning the keeper at Rødmose, with the wheelwright over there, came up to the house, they dragged with them a boy, Goske Piil, a widow's son, and they made their Bible-oath that he had done it, they had themselves seen him sneaking round the barn at nightfall on Thursday. Goske had no good name on the farm, the keeper bore him a grudge upon an old matter of poaching, and the wheelwright did not like him either, for he did, I believe, suspect him with his young wife. The boy, when I talked to him, swore to his innocence, but he could not hold his own against the two old men. So I had him locked up, and meant to send him in to our judge of the district, with a letter.

'The judge is a fool, and would naturally do nothing but what he thought I wished him to do. He might have the boy sent to the convict-prison for arson, or put amongst the soldiers as a bad character and a poacher. Or again, if he thought that that was what I wanted, he could let him off.

'I was out riding in the fields, looking at the corn that was soon ripe to be mowed, when a woman, the widow, Goske's mother, was brought up before me, and begged to speak to me. Anne-Marie is her name, you will remember her, she lives in the small house east of the village. She has not got a good name in the place either. They tell that as a girl she had a child and did away with it.

'From five days' weeping, her voice was so cracked that it was difficult to me to understand what she said. Her son, she told me at last, had indeed been over at Rødmose on Thursday, but for no ill purpose, he had gone to see someone. He was her only son, she called the Lord God to witness on his innocence, and she wrung her hands to me that I should save the boy for her.

'We were in the rye-field that you and I are looking at now. That gave me an idea. I said to the widow: "If in one day, between sunrise and sunset, with your own hands you can mow this field, and it be well done, I will let the case drop and you shall keep your son. But if you cannot do it he must go, and it is not likely that you will then ever see him again."

'She stood up then and gazed over the field. She kissed my riding-boot in gratitude for the favour shown to her.'

The old lord here made a pause, and Adam said: 'Her son meant much to her?'

'He is her only child,' said his uncle. 'He means to her her daily bread and support in old age. It may be said that she holds him as dear as her own life. As,' he added, 'within a higher order of life, a son to his father means the name and the race, and he holds him as dear as life everlasting. Yes, her son means much to her. For the mowing of that field is a day's work to three men, or a three days' work to one man. Today, as the sun rose, she set on to her task. And down there, by the end of the field, you will see her now, in a blue headcloth with the man I have set to follow her and to ascertain that she does the work unassisted, and with two or three friends by her, who are comforting her.'

Adam looked down, and did indeed see a woman in a blue headcloth, and a few other figures in the corn.

They sat for a while in silence.

'Do you yourself', Adam then said, 'believe the boy to be innocent?'

'I cannot tell,' said his uncle, 'there is no proof. The word of the keeper and the wheelwright stand against the boy's word. If indeed I did believe the one thing or the other it would be merely a matter of chance, or maybe of sympathy. The boy', he said after a moment, 'was my son's playmate, the only other child that I ever knew him to like, or to get on with.'

'Do you', Adam again asked, 'hold it possible to her to fulfil your condition?'

'Nay, I cannot tell,' said the old lord, 'to an ordinary person it would not be possible. No ordinary person would ever have taken it on at all. I chose it so. We are not quibbling with the law, Anne-Marie and I.'

Adam for a few minutes followed the movement of the small group in the rye. 'Will you walk back?' he asked.

'No,' said his uncle, 'I think that I shall stay here till I have seen the end of the thing.'

'Until sunset?' Adam asked with surprise.

'Yes,' said the old lord.

Adam said: 'It will be a long day.'

'Yes,' said his uncle, 'a long day. – But,' he added, as Adam rose to walk away, 'if, as you said, you have got that tragedy of which you spoke in your pocket, be so kind as to leave it here, to keep me company.'

Adam handed him the book.

In the avenue he met two footmen who carried the old lord's morning chocolate down to the pavilion on large silver trays.

As now the sun rose in the sky and the day grew hot, the lime-trees gave forth their exuberance of scent, and the garden was filled with unsurpassed, unbelievable sweetness. Towards the still hour of midday the long avenue reverberated like a soundboard with a low, incessant murmur: the humming of a million bees that clung to the pendulous, thronging clusters of blossoms, and were drunk with bliss.

In all the short lifetime of Danish summer there is no richer or more luscious moment than that week wherein the lime-trees flower. The heavenly scent goes to the head and to the heart, it seems to unite the fields of Denmark with those of Elysium, it contains both hay, honey and holy incense, and is half fairyland and half apothecary's locker. The avenue was changed into a mystic edifice, a dryad's cathedral, outward from summit to base lavishly adorned, set with multitudinous ornaments and golden in the sun. But behind the walls the vaults were benignly cool and sombre, like ambrosial sanctuaries in a dazzling and burning world, and in here the ground was still moist.

Up in the house, behind the silk curtains of the two front windows, the young mistress of the estate, from the wide bed, stuck her feet into two little high-heeled slippers. Her lace-trimmed nightgown had slid up above her knee, and down from the shoulder; her hair, done up in curling-pins for the night, was still frosty with the powder of yesterday, her round face flushed with sleep. She stepped out to the midst of the floor and stood there, looking extremely grave and thoughtful, yet she did not think at all. But through her head a long procession of pictures marched, and she was unconsciously endeavouring to put them in order, as the pictures of her existence had used to be.

She had grown up at Court, it was her world, and there was probably not in the whole country a small creature more exquisitely and innocently drilled to the stately measure of a palace. By favour of the old Dowager Queen she bore her name and that of the King's sister, the Queen of Sweden: Sophie Magdalena. It was with a view to these things that her husband, when he wished to restore his status in high places, had chosen her as a bride, first for his son and then for himself. But her own father, who held an office in the Royal Household and belonged to the new Court-Aristocracy, in his day had done the same thing the other way round, and had married a country lady, to get a foothold within the old Nobility of Denmark. The little girl had her mother's blood in her veins. The country to her had been an immense surprise and delight.

To get into her castle court she must drive through the farmyard, through the heavy stone gateway in the barn itself, wherein the rolling of her coach for a few seconds re-echoed like thunder. She must drive past the stables and the timber-mare, from which sometimes a miscreant would follow her with sad eyes, and might here startle a long string of squalling geese, or pass the heavy, scowling bull, led on by a ring in his nose, and kneading the earth in dumb fury. At first this had been to her, every time, a slight shock and a jest. But after a while all these creatures and things, which belonged to her, seemed to become part of herself.

Her mothers, the old Danish country ladies, were robust persons, undismayed by any kind of weather, now she herself had walked in the rain and had laughed and glowed in it, like a green tree.

She had taken her great new home in possession at a time when all the world was unfolding, mating and propagating. Flowers, which she had known only in bouquets and festoons, sprang from the earth round her, birds sang in all the trees. The new-born lambs seemed to her daintier than her dolls had been. From her husband's Hanoverian stud, foals were brought to her to give names, she stood and watched them as they poked their soft noses into their mothers' bellies to drink: of this strange process she had till now only vaguely heard. She had happened to witness, from a path in the park the rearing and screeching stallion on the mare. All this luxuriance, lust and fecundity was displayed before her eyes, as for her pleasure.

And for her own part, in the midst of it, she was given an old husband, who treated her with punctilious respect, because she was to bear him a son. Such was the compact, she had known of it from the beginning. Her husband, she found, was doing his best to fulfil his part of it, and she herself was loyal by nature and strictly brought up, she would not shirk her obligation. Only she was vaguely aware of a discord or an incompatibility within her majestic existence, which prevented her from being as happy as she had expected to be.

After a time her chagrin took a strange form: as the consciousness of an absence. Someone ought to have been with her who was not. She had no experience in analysing her feelings, there had not been time for that at Court. Now, as she was more often left to herself, she vaguely probed her own mind. She tried to set her father in that void place, her sisters, her music-master, an Italian singer whom she had admired, – but none of them would fill it for her. At times she felt lighter at heart, and believed the misfortune to have left her. And then again it would happen, if she were alone, or in her husband's company, and even within his embrace, that everything round her would cry out: Where? Where? so that she let her wild eyes run about the room in search for the being who should have been there, and who had not come.

When, six months ago, she was informed that her first young bridegroom had died, and that she was to marry his father in his place, she had not been sorry. Her youthful suitor, the one time she had seen him, had appeared to her infantile and insipid, the father would make a statelier consort. Now she had sometimes thought of the dead boy, and wondered whether with him life would have been more joyful. But she soon again dismissed the picture, – and that was the sad youth's last recall on to the stage of this world.

Upon one wall of her room there hung a long mirror. As she gazed into it new images came along. The day before, driving with her husband, she had seen, at a distance, a party of village girls bathe in the river, and the sun shining on them. All her life she had moved amongst naked marble deities, but till now it had never occurred to her that the people she knew should themselves be naked under their adriennes and trains, waistcoats and satin breeches, that indeed she herself were naked within her clothes. Now, in front of the looking-glass, she tardively untied the ribbons of her nightgown, and let it drop to the floor.

The room was dim behind the drawn curtains. In the mirror her body was silvery like a white rose, only her cheeks and mouth, and the tips of her fingers and breasts had a faint carmine. Her slender torso was formed by the whale-bones that had clasped it tightly from her girlhood, above the slim, dimpled knee a gentle narrowness marked the place of the garter. Her limbs were rounded as if, at whatever place they were cut through with a sharp knife, a perfectly circular transverse section would be obtained. The side and belly were so smooth that her own gaze slipped and glided, and grasped for a hold. She was not altogether like a statue, she found, and lifted her arms above her head. She turned to get a view of her back, the curves below the waistline were still blushing from the pressure of the bed. She called to mind a few tales about nymphs and goddesses, but they all seemed a long way away, so her mind returned to the peasant-girls in the river. They were, for a few minutes, idealized into playmates, or sisters even, since they belonged to her, as did the meadow and the blue river itself. And within the next moment the sense of forlornness once more came upon her, a *horror vacui* like a physical pain. Surely, surely someone should have been with her now, her other self, like the image in the glass, but nearer, stronger, alive. There was no one, the Universe was empty round her.

A sudden, keen itching under her knee took her out of her reveries and awoke in her the hunting instincts of her breed. She wetted a finger on her tongue, slowly brought it down and quickly slapped it to the spot. She felt the diminu-tive sharp body of the insect against the silky skin, pressed the thumb to it, and triumphantly lifted up the small prisoner between her fingertips. She stood quite still, as if meditating upon the fact that a flea was the only creature risking its life for her smoothness and sweet blood.

Her maid opened the door and came in, loaded with the attire of the day, – shift, stays, hoop and petticoats. She remembered that she had a guest in the house, the new nephew arrived from England. Her husband had instructed her to be kind to their young kinsman, – disinherited, so to say, by her presence in the place. They would ride out on the land together.

In the afternoon the sky was no longer blue as in the morning. Large clouds slowly towered up on it, and the great vault itself was colourless, as if diffused into vapours round the white-hot sun in zenith. A low thunder ran along the western horizon, once or twice the dust of the roads rose in tall spirals. But the fields, the hills and the woods were as still as a painted landscape.

Adam walked down the avenue to the pavilion, and found his uncle there, fully dressed, his hands upon his walking-stick and his eyes on the rye-field. The book that Adam had given him lay by his side. The field now seemed alive with people. Small groups stood here and there in it, and a long row of men and women were slowly advancing towards the garden in the line of the swath.

The old lord nodded to his nephew, but did not speak or change his position. Adam stood by him as still as himself.

The day to him had been strangely disquieting. At the meeting again with old places, the sweet melodies of the past had filled his senses and his mind, and had mingled with new bewitching tunes of the present. He was back in Denmark, no longer a child but a youth, with a keener sense of the beautiful, with tales of other countries to tell, and still a true son of his own land and enchanted by its loveliness as he had never been before.

But through all these harmonies the tragic and cruel tale which the old lord had told him in the morning, and the sad contest which he knew to be going on so near by, in the cornfield, had re-echoed, like the recurrent, hollow throbbing of a muffled drum, a redoubtable sound. It came back time after time, so that he had felt himself to change colour and to answer absently. It brought with it a deeper sense of pity with all that lived than he had ever known. When he had been riding with his young aunt, and their road ran along the scene of the drama, he had taken care to ride between her and the field, so that she should not see what was going on there, or question him about it. He had chosen the way home through the deep, green wood for the same reason.

More dominantly even than the figure of the woman struggling with her sickle for her son's life, the old man's figure, as he had seen it at sunrise, kept him company through the day. He came to ponder on the part which that lonely, determinate form had played in his own life. From the time when his father died it had impersonated to the boy law and order, wisdom of life and kind guardianship. What was he to do, he thought, if after eighteen years these filial feelings must change, and his second father's figure to him take on a horrible aspect, as a symbol of the tyranny and oppression of the world? – what was he to do if ever the two should come to stand in opposition to one another, as adversaries?

At the same time an unaccountable, a sinister alarm and dread on behalf of the old man himself took hold of him. For surely here the goddess Nemesis could not be far away. This man had ruled the world round him for a longer period than Adam's own lifetime and had never been gainsaid by anyone. During the years when he had wandered through Europe with a sick boy of his own blood as his sole companion he had learnt to set himself apart from his surroundings, and to close himself up to all outer life, and he had become insusceptible to the ideas and feelings of other human beings. Strange fancies might there have run in his mind, so that in the end he had seen himself as the only person really existing, and the world as a poor and vain shadow-play, which had no substance to it.

Now, in senile wilfulness, he would take in his hand the life of those simpler and weaker than himself, of a woman, using it to his own ends, and he feared no retributive justice. Did he not know, the young man thought, that there were powers in the world, different from the short-lived might of a despot, and more formidable?

With the sultry heat of the day this foreboding of impending disaster grew upon him, until he felt ruin to threaten not the old lord only, but the house, the name and himself, with him. It seemed to him that he must cry out a warning to the man he had loved, before it was too late.

But as now he was once more in his uncle's company, the green calm of the garden was so deep that he did not find the voice to cry out. Instead a little French air, that his aunt had sung to him up in the house, kept running in his mind. – 'C'est un trop doux effort . . .' He had himself good knowledge of music, he had heard the air before, in Paris, but not so sweetly sung.

After a time he asked: 'Will the woman fulfil her bargain?'

His uncle unfolded his hands. 'It is an extraordinary thing', he said animatedly, 'that it looks as if she might fulfil it. If you count the hours from sunrise till now, and from now till sunset, you will find the time left her to be half of that already gone. And see! – she has now mowed two thirds of the field. But then we will naturally have to reckon with her strength declining as she works on. All in all it is an idle pursuit in you or me to bet on the issue of the matter, we must wait and see. Sit down, and keep me company in my watch.'

In two minds Adam sat down.

'And here,' said his uncle and took up the book from the seat, 'is your book, which has passed me the time finely. It is great poetry, ambrosia to the ear and the heart. And it has, with our discourse on divinity this morning, given me stuff for thought. I have been reflecting upon the law of retributive justice.' He took a pinch of snuff, and went on. 'A new age', he said, 'has made to itself a god in its own image, an emotional god. And now you are already writing a tragedy on your God.'

Adam had no wish to begin a debate on poetry with his uncle, but he also somehow dreaded a silence, and said: 'It may be, then, that we hold tragedy to be, in the scheme of life, a noble, a divine phenomenon.'

'Aye,' said his uncle solemnly, 'a noble phenomenon, the noblest on earth. But of the earth only, and never divine. Tragedy is the privilege of man, his highest privilege. The God of the Christian Church himself, when he wished to experience tragedy, had to assume human form. And even at that,' he added thoughtfully, 'the tragedy was not wholly valid, as it would have become had the hero of it been, in very truth, a man. The divinity of Christ conveyed to it a divine note, the moment of comedy. The real tragic part, by the nature of things there, fell to the executioners, not to the victim. Nay, my nephew, we should not adulterate the pure elements of the cosmos. Tragedy should remain the right of human beings, subject, in their conditions or in their own nature, to the dire law of necessity. To them it is salvation and beatification. But the gods, whom we must believe to be unacquainted with, and incomprehensive of, necessity, can have no knowledge of the tragic. When they are brought face to face with it they will, according to my experience, have the good taste and decorum to keep still, and not interfere.

'No,' he said after a pause, 'the true art of the gods is the comic. The comic is a condescension of the divine to the world of man, it is the sublime vision, which cannot be studied, but must ever be celestially granted. In the comic the gods see their own being reflected as in a mirror, and while the tragic poet is bound by strict laws, they will allow the comic artist a freedom as unlimited as their own. They do not even withhold their own existence from his sports: Jove may favour Lucianos of Samosata. As long as your mockery is in true godly taste you may mock at the gods, and still remain a sound devotee. But in pitying, or condoling with your God, you deny and annihilate him, and such is the most horrible of atheisms.

'And here on earth, too,' he went on, 'we, who stand in lieu of the gods and have emancipated ourselves from the tyranny of necessity, should leave to our vassals their monopoly of tragedy, and for ourselves accept the comic with grace. Only a boorish and cruel master – a parvenu, in fact – will make a jest of his servants' necessity, or force the comic upon them. Only a timid and pedantic ruler, a *petit-maître,* will fear the ludicrous on his own behalf. Indeed,' he finished his long speech, 'the very same fatality which, in striking the burgher or peasant will become tragedy, with the aristocrat is exalted to the comic. By the grace and wit of our acceptance hereof our aristocracy is known.'

Adam could not help smiling a little as he heard the apotheosis of the comic on the lips of the erect, ceremonious prophet. In this ironic smile he was, for the first time, estranging himself from the head of his house.

A shadow fell across the landscape. A cloud had crept over the sun, the country changed colour beneath it, faded and bleached, and even all sounds for a minute seemed to die out of it.

'Ah now,' said the old lord, 'if it is going to rain, and the rye gets wet, Anne-Marie will not be able to finish in time. – And who comes there?' he added, and turned his head a little.

Preceded by a lackey, a man in riding-boots and a striped waistcoat with silver buttons, and with his hat in his hand, came down the avenue. He bowed deeply, first to the old lord and then to Adam.

'My bailiff!' said the old lord.

'Good afternoon, bailiff. What news have you to bring?'

The bailiff made a sad gesture, 'Poor news only, mylord,' he said.

'And how, poor news?' asked his master.

'There is', said the bailiff with weight, 'not a soul at work on the land, and not a sickle going except that of Anne-Marie in this rye-field. The mowing has stopped, they are all at her heels. It is a poor day for a first day of the harvest.'

'Yes, I see,' said the old lord.

The bailiff went on. 'I have spoken kindly to them,' he said, 'and I have sworn at them, it is all one. They might as well all be deaf.'

'Good bailiff,' said the old lord, 'leave them in peace, let them do as they like. This day may, all the same, do them more good than many others. Where is Goske, the boy, Anne-Marie's son?'

'We have set him in the small room by the barn,' said the bailiff.

'Nay, let him be brought down,' said the old lord, 'let him see his mother at work. But what do you say, – will she get the field mowed in time?'

'If you ask me, mylord,' said the bailiff, '1 believe that she will. Who would have thought so? – she is only a small woman. It is as hot a day today, as well, as I do ever remember. I myself, – you yourself, mylord, – could not have done what Anne-Marie has done today.'

'Nay, nay we could not, bailiff,' said the old lord.

The bailiff pulled out a red handkerchief and wiped his brow, somewhat calmed by venting his wrath. 'If', he remarked with bitterness, 'they would all work as the widow works now, we would make a profit on the land.'

'Yes,' said the old lord, and fell into thought, as if calculating the profit it might make. 'Still,' he said, 'as to the question of profit and loss that is more intricate than it looks. I will tell you something that you may not know: the most famous tissue ever woven was ravelled out again every night. But come,' he added, 'she is close by now. We will go and have a look at her work ourselves.' With these words he rose and put his hat on.

The cloud had drawn away again, the rays of the sun once more burned the wide landscape, and as the small party walked out from under the shade of the trees the dead still heat was heavy as lead, the sweat sprang out on their faces and their eyelids smarted. On the narrow path they had to go one by one, the old lord stepping along first, all black, and the footman, in his bright livery, bringing up the rear.

The field was indeed filled with people like a marketplace, there was probably a hundred or more men and women in it. To Adam the scene recalled pictures from his Bible – the meeting between Esau and Jacob in Edom, or the reapers of Boaz in his barley-field near Bethlehem. Some were standing by the side of the field, others pressed in small groups close to the mowing woman, and a few followed in her wake, binding up sheaves where she had cut the corn, as if thereby they thought to help her, or as if at all events they meant to have part in her work. A younger woman with a pail on her head kept close at her side, and with her a number of half-grown children. One of these first caught sight of the lord of the estate and his suite, and pointed to him. The binders let their sheaves drop and, as the old man stood still, many of the onlookers drew close round him.

The woman on whom till now the eyes of the whole field had rested, – a small figure on the large stage, – was advancing slowly and unevenly, bent double as if she were walking on her knees, and stumbling as she walked. Her blue headcloth had slipped back from her head, the grey hair was plastered to the skull, with sweat, dusty and stuck with straw. She was obviously totally unaware of the multitude round her, neither did she now once turn her head or her gaze towards the new arrivals.

Absorbed in her work she again and again stretched out her left hand to grasp a handful of corn, and her right hand with the sickle in it to cut it off close to the soil, in wavering, groping pulls, like a tired swimmer's strokes. Her course took her so close to the feet of the old lord that his shadow fell on her. Just then she staggered and swayed sideways, and the woman who followed her lifted the pail from her head and held it to her lips. Anne-Marie drank without leaving hold of her sickle, and the water ran from the corners of her mouth. A boy, close to her, quickly bent one knee, seized her hands in his own and, steadying and guiding them, cut off a grip of rye.

'No, no,' said the old lord, 'you must not do that, boy. Leave Anne-Marie in peace to her work.'

At the sound of his voice the woman, falteringly, lifted her face in his direction.

The bony and tanned face was streaked with sweat and dust, the eyes were dimmed. But there was not in its expression the slightest trace of fear or pain. Indeed amongst all the grave and concerned faces of the field hers was the only one perfectly calm, peaceful and mild. The mouth was drawn together in a thin line, an eager prim, patient little smile, such as will be seen in the face of an old woman at her spinning-wheel or her knitting, eager on her work, and happy in it. And as the younger woman lifted back the pail, she immediately again fell to her mowing, with an ardent, tender craving like that of a mother who lays a baby to the nipple. Like an insect that bustles along in high grass, or like a small vessel in heavy sea, she butted her way on, her quiet face once more bent upon her task.

The whole throng of onlookers, and with them the small group from the pavilion, advanced as she advanced, slowly and as if drawn by a string. The bailiff, who felt the intense silence of the field heavy on him, said to the old lord: 'The rye will yield better this year than last,' and got no reply. He repeated his remark to Adam, and at last to the footman, who felt himself above a discussion on agriculture, and only cleared his throat in answer.

In a while the bailiff again broke the silence. 'There is the boy,' he said and pointed with his thumb. 'They have brought him down.'

At that moment the woman fell forward on her face, and was lifted up by those nearest to her.

Adam suddenly stopped on the path, and covered his eyes with his hand. The old lord without turning asked him if he felt incommoded by the heat.

'No,' said Adam, 'but stay. Let me speak to you.'

His uncle stopped, with his hand on the stick and looking ahead as if regretful of being held back.

'In the name of God,' cried the young man in French, 'force not this woman to continue.'

There was a short pause. – 'But I force her not, my friend,' said his uncle in the same language, 'and I have never been forcing her. If, three days ago, here within the field, she had rejected my proposition, what harm would have befallen her? None whatever, only her son's case would have proceeded, in accordance with the laws of the country, like any other case of that kind. And she is still free to give up her task at any moment she chooses.'

'Yes,' cried Adam, 'at the cost of her child's life! Do you not see that she is dying? You know not what you are doing, or what it may bring upon you.'

The old lord, perplexed by this unexpected animadversion, after a second turned all round, and his pale, clear eyes sought his nephew's face with stately surprise. His long, waxen face, with two symmetrical curls at the sides, had something of an idealized and ennobled old sheep or ram. He made sign to the bailiff to go on, the footman also withdrew a little, and the uncle and nephew were, so to say, alone on the path. For a minute neither of them spoke.

'In this very place where we now stand,' said the old lord, then, with hauteur, 'I gave Anne-Marie my word.'

'My uncle!' said Adam. 'A life is a greater thing even than a word. Recall that word, I beseech you, which was given in caprice, as a whim. I am praying you more for your sake than for my own, yet I shall be grateful to you all my life if you will grant me my prayer.'

'You will have learnt in school,' said his uncle, 'that in the beginning was the Word. It may have been pronounced in caprice, as a whim, the Scripture tells us nothing about it. It is still the principle of our world, its law of gravitation. My own humble word has been the principle of the land on which we stand, for an age of man. My father's word was the same, before my day.'

'You are mistaken!' cried Adam, 'the Word is creative, it is imagination, daring and passion. By it the world was made. How much greater are not these powers which bring into being, than any restricting or controlling law. You wish the land on which we look to produce and propagate, you should not banish from it the forces which cause, and which keep up life, nor turn it into a desert by dominance of law. And when you look at the people, simpler than we, and nearer to the heart of nature, who do not analyse their feelings, whose life is one with the life of the earth, do they not inspire in you tenderness, respect, reverence even? This woman is ready to die for her son, – will it ever happen to you or me that a woman willingly gives up her life for us? And if it did indeed come to pass, should we make so light of it as not to give up a dogma in return?'

'You are young,' said the old lord. 'A new age will undoubtedly applaud you. I am old-fashioned, I have been quoting to you texts a thousand years old. We do not, perhaps, quite understand one another.

'But if, to your ears, my orthodoxy does now sound antiquated, remember that within a hundred years both mine and your own speech will sound antiquated to the generations then discoursing upon word and life. Have patience, let me explain myself to you.

'Believe me, I have the public welfare as much at heart as you yourself. But should we, in our concern for *le bien commun,* gaze only at those human beings who happen to be about us today, and look neither before or after? When we consider the matter rightly we will find the past generations to be in majority – Well,' he interrupted himself, as Adam made a gesture of impatience, 'let them rest, as they deserve to. But the coming generations, you will agree, must be ever in majority. And when we speak of the welfare of the many we must needs let them have the last word. King Pharaoh, I have been told, made a hundred thousand of his subjects slave for him, and suffer great hardships, in order to build him a pyramid. He might at the same cost, have distributed bread and wine amongst his people, have fed and clothed them, and have been blessed by them. Still even so things would have been with them, today, what they are now: they would all be dead and gone. And a hundred generations have, since the days of King Pharaoh, lifted their eyes to the pyramids with pride and joy, and acclaimed them their own. A great deed, my nephew, – be it even brought forth with tears, aye with blood, – is a fund of resource, a treasure for the coming generations to live on, it is, within hard times and the hour of need, bread to the people.

'But the true insight into these matters,' the old lord went on, 'you will never find, and can never reasonably expect to find, with the common people, to whom the chief concern in life is their daily bread, and who are living, mentally as well as physically, from hand to mouth. Nay, my nephew, it is our affair and our responsibility, we, who have inherited from the past and who know that we are to live on, in name and blood, through the coming centuries. These humble peasants, whose life is one with the life of the earth, and of whom you have spoken with so much fervency, what good are we to them but this: that they may trust us to look after *le bien commun,* not at the moment only, but in the future? And see you now, my good nephew, you and I may find it a little difficult to see eye to eye.

'But with my own people I am, I believe, in good understanding. Anne-Marie might well feel that I were making light of her exploit, if now, at the eleventh hour, I did nullify it by a second word. I myself should feel so in her place. Yes, my nephew, it is possible, did I grant you your prayer and pronounce such an amnesty, that I should find it void against her faithfulness, and that we would still see her at her work, unable to give it up, as a shuttle in the rye-field, until she had it all mowed. But she would then be a shocking, a horrible sight, a figure of unseemly fun, – like a small planet running wild in the sky, when the law of gravitation had been done away with.'

'And if she dies at her task,' Adam exclaimed, 'her death, and its consequences, will come upon your head!'

The old lord took off his hat and gently ran his hand over his powdered head. – 'Upon my head?' he said. 'I have kept up my head in many weathers. Even', he added proudly, 'against the cold wind from high places. In what shape will it come upon my head, my nephew?'

'I cannot tell,' cried Adam in despair, 'I have spoken to warn you. God only knows.'

'Amen,' said the old lord with a little delicate smile. 'Come, we will walk on.'

Adam drew in his breath deeply.

'No,' he said in Danish, 'I cannot come with you. This field is yours, things will happen here as you decide. But I myself must go away. I beg you to let me have, this evening, a coach as far as town. For I could not sleep another night under your roof, – which I have honoured beyond any on earth.'

So many conflicting feelings at his own speech thronged in his breast that it would have been impossible to him to give them words.

The old lord, who had already begun to walk on, stood still, and with him the lackey. He did not speak for a minute, as if to give Adam time to collect his mind. But the young man's mind was in uproar, and would not be collected.

'Must we', the old man asked, in Danish, 'take leave here, in the rye-field? I have held you dear next to my own son. I have followed your career in life from year to year, and have been proud of you. I was happy when you wrote to say that you were coming back. If now you will go away I wish you well.' He shifted his walking-stick from the right hand to the left, and gravely looked his nephew in the face.

Adam did not meet his eyes. He was gazing out over the landscape. In the late mellow afternoon it was resuming its colours, like a painting brought into proper light; in the meadows the little black stacks of peat stood gravely distinct upon the green sward. On this same morning he had greeted it all, like a child running laughingly to its mother's bosom, – now already he must tear himself from it, in discordance, and for ever. And at the moment of parting it seemed infinitely dearer than any time before, so much beautified and solemnized by the coming separation that it looked like the place in a dream, a landscape out of Paradise, and he wondered if it were really the same. But yes – there before him was, once more, the hunting-ground of long ago. And there was the road on which he had ridden today.

'But tell me where you mean to go from here,' said the old lord slowly. 'I myself have travelled a good deal in my days, I know the word of leaving, the wish to go away. But I have learnt by experience that, in reality, the word has a meaning only to the place and the people which one leaves. When you have left my house, – although it will see you go with sadness, – as far as it is concerned the matter is finished and done with. But to the person who goes away it is a different thing, and not so simple. At the moment that he leaves one place he will be already, by the laws of life, on his way to another, upon this earth. Let me know, then, for the sake of our old acquaintance, to which place you are going when you leave here. To England?'

'No,' said Adam. He felt in his heart that he could never again go back to England, or to his easy and carefree life there. It was not far enough away, deeper waters than the North Sea must now be laid between him and Denmark. 'No, not to England,' he said, 'I shall go to America, to the New World.' For a moment he shut his eyes, trying to form to himself a picture of existence in America, with the grey Atlantic Ocean between him and these fields and woods.

'To America?' said his uncle and drew up his eyebrows. 'Yes, I have heard of America. They have got freedom there, a big waterfall, savage red men. They shoot turkeys, I have read, as we shoot partridges. Well, if it be your wish, go to America, Adam, and be happy in the New World.'

He stood for some time, sunk in thought, as if he had already sent off the young man to America, and had done with him. When at last he spoke, his words had the character of a monologue, enunciated by the person who watches things come and go, and himself stays on.

'Take service, there,' he said, 'with the power which will give you an easier bargain than this: that with your own life you may buy the life of your son.'

Adam had not listened to his uncle's remarks about America, but the conclusive, solemn words caught his ear, he looked up. As if for the first time in his life he saw the old man's figure as a whole, and conceived how small it was, so much smaller than himself, pale, a thin black anchorite upon his own land. A thought ran through his head: 'How terrible to be old!' The abhorrence of the tyrant, and the sinister dread on his behalf, which had followed him all day, seemed to die out of him, and his pity for all the creation to extend even to the sombre form before him.

His whole being had cried out for harmony; now, with the possibility of forgiving, of a reconciliation, a sense of relief went through him, confusedly he bethought himself of Anne-Marie drinking the water held to her lips. He took off his hat, as his uncle had done a moment ago, – so that to a beholder at a distance it would seem that the two dark-clad gentlemen on the path were repeatedly and respectfully saluting one another, – and brushed the hair from his forehead. Once more the tune of the garden-room rang in his mind:

> *mourir pour ce qu'on aime*
> *c'est un trop doux effort* ...

He stood for a long time immobile and dumb. He broke off a few ears of rye, kept them on his hand and looked at them.

He saw the ways of life, he thought, as a twined and tangled design, complicated and mazy; it was not given him or any mortal to command or control it. Life and death, happiness and woe, the past and the present, were interlaced within the pattern. Yet to the initiated it might be read as easily as our ciphers, – which to the savage must seem confused and incomprehensible, – will be read by the schoolboy. And out of the contrasting elements concord arose. All that lived must suffer, the old man, whom he had judged hardly, had suffered, as he had watched his son die, and had dreaded the obliteration of his being, – he himself would come to know ache, tears and remorse, and, even through these, the fullness of life. So might now, to the woman in the rye-field, her ordeal be a triumphant procession. For to die for the one you loved was an effort too sweet for words.

As now he thought of it, he knew that all his life he had sought the unity of things, the secret which connects all the phenomena of existence. It was this strife, this dim presage, which had sometimes made him stand still and inert in the midst of the games of his playfellows, or which had, at other moments, – on moonlight nights, or in his little boat on the sea, – lifted the boy to ecstatic happiness. Where other young people, in their pleasures or their amours, had searched for contrast and variety, he himself had yearned only to comprehend in full the oneness of the world. If things had come differently to him, if his young cousin had not died, and the events that followed his death had not brought him to Denmark, his search for understanding and harmony might have taken him to America, and he might have found them there, in the virgin forests of a new world. Now they had been disclosed to him today, in the place where he had played as a child. As the song is one with the voice that sings it, as the road is one with the goal, as lovers are made one in their embrace, so is man one with his destiny, and he shall love it as himself.

He looked up again, towards the horizon. If he wished to, he felt, he might find out what it was which had brought to him, here, the sudden conception of the unity of the Universe. When this same morning he had philosophized, lightly and for his own sake, on his feeling of belonging to this land and soil, it had been the beginning of it. But since then it had grown, it had become a mightier thing, a revelation to his soul. Some time he would look into it, for the law of cause and effect was a wonderful and fascinating study. But not now. This hour was consecrated to greater emotions, to a surrender to fate and to the will of life.

'No,' he said at last. 'If you wish it I shall not go. I shall stay here.'

At that moment a long, loud roll of thunder broke the stillness of the afternoon. It re-echoed for a while amongst the low hills, and it reverberated within the young man's breast as powerfully as if he had been seized and shaken by hands. The landscape had spoken. He remembered that twelve hours ago he had put a question to it, half in jest, and not knowing what he did. Here it gave him its answer.

What it contained he did not know, neither did he inquire. In his promise to his uncle he had given himself over to the mightier powers of the world. Now what must come must come.

'I thank you,' said the old lord, and made a little stiff gesture with his hand. 'I am happy to hear you say so. We should not let the difference in our age, or of our views, separate us. In our family we have been wont to keep peace and faith with one another. You have made my heart lighter.'

Something within his uncle's speech faintly recalled to Adam the misgivings of the afternoon. He rejected them, he would not let them trouble the new, sweet felicity which his resolution to stay had brought him.

'I shall go on now,' said the old lord. 'But there is no need for you to follow me. I will tell you tomorrow how the matter has ended.'

'No,' said Adam, 'I shall come back by sunset, to see the end of it myself.'

All the same he did not come back. He kept the hour in his mind, and all through the evening the consciousness of the drama, and the profound concern and compassion with which, in his thoughts, he followed it, gave to his speech, glance and movements a grave and pathetic substance. But he felt that he was, in the rooms of the manor, and even by the harpsichord on which he accompanied his aunt to her air of Alceste, as much in the centre of things as if he had stood in the rye-field itself, and as near to those human beings whose fate was now decided there. Anne-Marie and he were both in the hands of destiny, and destiny would, by different ways, bring each to the designated end.

Later on he remembered what he had thought that evening.

But the old lord stayed on. Late in the afternoon he even had an idea; he called down his valet to the pavilion and made him shift his clothes, and dress him up in a brocaded suit that he had worn at Court. He let a lace-trimmed shirt be drawn over his head and stuck out his slim legs to have them put into thin silk stockings and buckled shoes. In this majestic attire he dined alone, of a frugal meal, but took a bottle of Rhenish wine with it, to keep up his strength. He sat on for a while, a little sunk in his seat, then, as the sun neared the earth, he straightened himself, and took the way down to the field.

The shadows were now lengthening, azure blue along all the eastern slopes. The lonely trees in the corn marked their site by narrow blue pools running out from their feet, and as the old man walked, a thin, immensely elongated reflection stirred behind him on the path. Once he stood still; he thought that he heard a lark singing over his head, a spring-like sound, his tired head held no clear perception of the season, he seemed to be walking, and standing, in a kind of eternity.

The people in the field were no longer silent, as they had been in the afternoon. Many of them talked loudly between themselves, and a little away a woman was weeping.

When the bailiff saw his master he came up to talk to him. He told him, in great agitation, that the widow would, in all likelihood, finish the mowing of the field within a quarter of an hour.

'Are the keeper and the wheelwright here?' the old lord asked him.

'They have been here,' said the bailiff, 'and have gone away five times. Each time they have said that they would not come back. But they have come back again all the same, and they are here now.'

'And where is the boy?' the old lord asked again.

'He is with her,' said the bailiff. 'I have given him leave to follow her. He has walked close to his mother all the afternoon, and you will see him now by her side, down there.'

Anne-Marie was now working her way up towards them more evenly than before, but with extreme slowness, as if at any moment she might come to a standstill. This excessive tardiness, the old lord reflected, if it had been purposely performed, would have been an inimitable, dignified exhibition of skilled art. One might fancy the Emperor of China advancing in like manner on a divine procession or rite. He shaded his eyes with his hand, for the sun was now just beyond the horizon, and its last rays made light, wild, many-coloured specks dance before his sight. With such splendour did the sunset emblazon the earth and the air, that the landscape was turned into a melting-pot of glorious metals. The meadows and the grasslands became pure gold, the barley-field near by, with its long ears, was a live lake of shining silver.

There was only a small patch of straw standing in the rye-field, when the woman, alarmed by the change in the light, turned her head a little to get a look of the sun. The while she did not stop her work, but grasped one handful of corn and cut it off, then another, and another.

A great stir, and a sound like a manifold, deep sigh, ran through the crowd. The field was now mowed from one end to the other. Only the mower herself did not realize the fact, she stretched out her hand anew, and when she found nothing to it she seemed puzzled or disappointed. Then she let her arms drop, and slowly sank to her knees.

Many of the women burst out weeping, and the swarm drew close round her, leaving only a small open space at the side where the old lord stood. Their sudden nearness frightened Anne-Marie, she made a slight, uneasy movement, as if terrified that they should put their hands to her.

The boy, who had kept by her all day, now fell on his knees beside her. Even he dared not touch her, but held one arm low behind her back and the other before her, level with her collarbone, to catch hold of her if she should fall, and all the time he cried aloud. At that moment the sun went down.

The old lord stepped forward and solemnly took off his hat. The crowd became silent, waiting for him to speak. But for a minute or two he said nothing. Then he addressed her, very slowly.

'Your son is free, Anne-Marie,' he said. He again waited a little, and added: 'You have done a good day's work, which will long be remembered.'

Anne-Marie raised her gaze only as high as his knees, and he understood that she had not heard what he said. He turned to the boy, 'You tell your mother, Goske,' he said, gently, 'what I have told her.'

The boy had been sobbing wildly, in raucous, broken moans; it took him some time to collect and control himself. But when at last he spoke, straight into his mother's face, his voice was low and a little impatient, as if he were conveying an everyday message to her. 'I am free, Mother,' he said. 'You have done a good day's work, that will long be remembered.'

At the sound of his voice she lifted her face to him, a faint, bland shadow of surprise ran over it, but still she gave no sign of having heard what he said, so that the people round them began to wonder if the exhaustion had turned her deaf. But after a moment she slowly and waveringly raised her hand, fumbling in the air as she aimed at his face, and with her fingers touched his cheek. The cheek was wet with tears, so that at the contact her fingertips lightly stuck to it, and she seemed unable to overcome the infinitely slight resistance or to withdraw her hand. For a minute the two looked one another in the face. Then, softly and lingeringly, like a sheaf of corn that falls to the ground, she sank forward on to the boy's shoulder, and he closed his arms round her.

He held her thus, pressed against him, his own face buried in her hair and headcloth, for such a long time that those nearest to them, frightened because her body looked so small in his embrace, drew closer, bent down and loosened his grip. The boy let them do so without a word or a movement. But the woman who held Anne-Marie in her arms to lift her up turned her face to the old lord.

'She is dead,' she said.

The people who had followed Anne-Marie all through the day, kept standing and stirring in the field for many hours, as long as the evening light lasted, and longer. Long after some of them had made a stretcher from branches of the trees, and had carried away the dead woman, others wandered on up and down the stubble, imitating and measuring her course from one end of the rye-field to the other, and binding up the last sheaves, where she had finished her mowing.

The old lord stayed with them for a long time, stepping along a little, and again standing still. As it grew darker he could walk up quite close to them or move amongst them, without being recognized.

In the place where the woman had died the old lord later on had a stone set up, with a sickle engraved on it. The peasants on the land then named the rye-field 'Sorrow-Acre'. By this name it was known a long time after the story of the woman and her son had been forgotten.

THE UPRIGHT REVOLUTION: OR WHY HUMANS WALK UPRIGHT

Ngũgĩ wa Thiong'o

Translated from the Gikuyu by the author

Ngũgĩ wa Thiong'o (1938–). One of the greatest contemporary novelists, James Ngũgĩ was born in Kamiriithu, in Kenya. In the 1950s, during the Mau Mau Uprising against inequalities and injustices in British-controlled Kenya, Ngũgĩ's family were caught up in the insurgency, and his mother was tortured. His early novels were written in English, and he presented them to Chinua Achebe, then advisor on the Heinemann *African Writers* series, which published his first novel *The River Between*. In 1967, he changed his name to Ngũgĩ wa Thiong'o and began to write in his native Gikuyu. He translates his own works into English. In 1976, Ngũgĩ was imprisoned for his writings and when released after a campaign by Amnesty International, he went into exile, living in the United States, where he taught at Yale University. He is perhaps best known for his novel *Wizard of the Crow*, in which he attempts "to sum up Africa of the twentieth century in the context of 2,000 years of world history".

A long time ago humans used to walk on legs and arms, just like all the other four limbed creatures. Humans were faster than hare, leopard or rhino. Legs and arms were closer than any other organs: they had similar corresponding joints: shoulders and hips; elbows and knees; ankles and wrists; feet and hands, each ending with five toes and fingers, with nails on each toe and finger. Hands and feet had similar arrangements of their five toes and fingers from the big toe and thumb to the smallest toes and pinkies. In those days the thumb was close to the other fingers, the same as the big toe. Legs and arms called each other first cousins.

They helped each other carry the body wherever it wanted to go; the market, the shops, up and down trees and mountains, anywhere that called for movement. Even in the water, they worked well together to help the body float, swim or dive. They were democratic and egalitarian in their relationship. They could also borrow the uses of the product of other organs, say sound from mouth, hearing from the ear, smell from the nose, and even sight from the eyes.

Their rhythm and seamless coordination made the other parts green with envy. They resented having to lend their special genius to the cousins. Jealousy blinded them to the fact that legs and hands took them places. They started plotting against the two pairs.

Tongue borrowed a plan from Brain and put it to action immediately. It begun to wonder, loudly, about the relative powers of arms and legs. Who was stronger, it wondered. The two cousin limbs, who had never been bothered by what the other had and could do, now borrowed sound from mouth and begun to claim they were more important to the body than the other. This quickly changed into who was more elegant; arms bragged about the long slim fingers of its hands, at the same time making derisive comments about toes being short and thick. Not to be outdone, toes countered and talked derisively about thin fingers, starving cousins! This went on for days, at times affecting their ability to work together effectively. It finally boiled down to the question of power; they turned to other organs for arbitration.

It was Tongue who suggested a contest. A brilliant idea, all agreed. But what? Some suggested a wrestling match – leg and arm wrestling. Others came up with sword play, juggling, racing, or playing a game like chess or checkers but each was ruled out as hard to bring about or unfair to one or the other limb. It was Tongue once gain, after borrowing thought from Brain, who came with a simple solution. Each set of organs would come up with a challenge, in turns. Arms and legs agreed.

The contest took place in a clearing in the forest, near a river. All organs were on maximum alert for danger or anything that might catch the body by surprise, now that its organs were engaged in internal struggle. Eyes scanned far and wide for the tiniest of dangers from whatever distance; ears primed themselves to hear the slightest sound from whatever distance; nose cleared its nostrils the better to detect scent of any danger that escaped the watchful eyes and the listening ears; and the tongue was ready to shout and scream, danger.

Wind spread news of the contest to the four corners of the forest, water and air. Four legged animals were among the first to gather, many of the big ones holding green branches to show they came in peace. It was a colorful crowd of Leopard, Cheetah, Lion, Rhino, Hyena, Elephant, Giraffe, Camel, long horned Cow and short-horned Buffalo, Antelope, Gazelle, Hare, Mole and Rat. Water-Dwellers, Hippo, Fish, Crocodile, spread their upper part on the banks, leaving the rest in the river. The two leggeds, Ostrich, Guinea-fowl, and Peacock flapped their wings in excitement; birds chirped from the trees; Cricket sang all the time. Spider, Worm, Centipede, Millipede crawled on the ground or trees. Chameleon walked stealthily, carefully, taking its time while Lizard ran about, never settling down on one spot. Monkey, Chimpanzee, Gorilla, jumped from branch to branch. Even the trees and the bush, swayed gently from side to side, bowed, and then stood still in turns.

Mouth opened the contest with a song:

> *We do this to be happy*
> *We do this to be happy*
> *We do this to be happy*

Because we all
Come from one nature.

Arm and Legs swore to accept the outcome gracefully; no tantrums, threats of boycott, strikes or go-slow.

Arms issued the first challenge: they threw a piece of wood on the ground. The leg, left or right, or in combination, was to pick up the piece of wood from the ground and throw it. The two legs could consult each other, at any time in the contest, and deploy their toes, individually or collectively, in any order to effect their mission. They tried to turn it over; push it; they tried all sorts of combinations but they could not pick it up properly: and as for moving it, the best they could do was kick it a few inches away. Seeing this, Fingers borrowed sounds from the mouth and laughed, and laughed. Arms, the challenger, paraded themselves, as in a beauty contest, showing off their slim looks, and then in different combinations picked up the piece of wood. They threw it far into the forest, eliciting a collective sigh of admiration from the contestants and spectators. They displayed other skills: they picked tiny pieces of sand from a bowl of rice; they threaded needles; they made little small pulleys for moving heavier wood; made some spears and threw them quite far, moves and acts that the toes could only dream about. Legs could only sit there and marvel at the display of dexterity and flexibility of their slim cousins. Arms of the spectators clapped thunder in admiration and solidarity with fellow arms, which upset the legs a great deal. But they were not about to concede: even as they sat there looking a little bit glum, their big toes drawing little circles on the sand, they were trying to figure out a winning challenge.

At last, it was the turn of legs and toes to issue a challenge. Theirs, they said, was simple. Hands should carry the whole body from one part of the circle to the other. What a stupid challenge, thought the arrogant fingers. It was a sight to see. Everything about the body was upside down. Hands touched the ground; eyes were close to the ground, their angles of vision severely restricted by their proximity to the ground; dust entered the nose, causing it to sneeze; legs and toes floated in the air: *nyayo juu*, the spectators shouted, and sang playfully.

Nyayo Nyayo juu
Hakuna matata
Fuata Nyayo
Hakuna matata
Turukeni angani

But their attention was fixed on the hands and arms. Organs that only a few minutes before were displaying an incredible array of skills, could hardly move a yard. A few steps, the hands cried out in pain, the arms staggered, wobbled, and let the body fall. They rested and then made another attempt. This time they tried to spread out the fingers the better to hold the ground but only the thumbs were able to stretch. They tried cartwheels but this move was disqualified because for its completion it involved the legs as well. It was the turn of the toes to laugh. They borrowed thick throatal tones from the mouth to contrast their laugh from the squeaky tones the fingers had used. Hearing the scorn, the arms were very angry and they made one desperate attempt to carry the body. They did not manage a step. Exhausted, the hands and fingers gave up. The legs were happy to display their athletic prowess: they marked time, trotted, ran, made a few high jumps, long jumps, without once letting the body fall. All the feet of the spectators stamped the ground in approval and solidarity. Arms raised their hands to protest this unsportslimbship, conveniently forgetting that they had started the game.

But all of them, including the spectators, noted something strange about the arms: the thumbs which had stretched out when the hands were trying to carry the body, remained separated from the other fingers. The rival organs were about to resume their laughter when they noted something else; far from the separated thumb making the hands less efficient, it enhanced their crasping and grasping power. What's this? Deformity transformed into the power of forming!

The debate among the organs to decide the winner went on for five days, the number of fingers and toes on each limb. But try as they could they were not able to declare a clear winner; each set of limbs was best at what they did best; none could do without the other. There begun a session of philosophical speculation: what was the body anyway, they all asked, and they realized the body was them all together; they were into each other. Every organ had to function well for all to function well.

But to prevent such a contest in the future and to prevent their getting in each other's way, it was decided by all the organs, that thenceforth the body would walk upright, feet firmly on the ground and arms up in the air. The body was happy with the decision but it would allow children to walk on all fours so as not to forget their origins. They divided tasks: the legs would carry the body but once they got to the destination, hands would do all the work that needed making or holding tools. While the legs and feet did the heavy duty of carrying, the hands reached out and used their skills to work the environment, and ensure that food reached the mouth. Mouth, or rather, its teeth, would chew it, and send it down the throat to the tummy. Tummy would squeeze all the goodness and then pour it into its system of canals through which the goodness would be distributed to all the nooks and crooks of the body. Then tummy would take the used material into its sewage system, from where the body would deposit it in the open fields or bury it under the soil to enrich it. Plants would grow bear fruit; hands would pluck pick some of it and put in the mouth. Oh, yes, the circle of life.

Even games and entertainments were divided accordingly: singing, laughing and talking were left to the mouth; running and soccer largely left to the legs; while baseball and basketball were reserved for the hands, except that the legs were to do the running. In athletics, the legs had all the field to themselves, largely. The clear division of labor made the human body a formidable bio machine, outwitting even the largest of animals in what it could achieve in quantity and quality.

However the organs of the body realized that the permanent arrangement they had arrived at could still bring conflict. The head being up there might make it feel that it was better than the feet that touched the ground or that it was the master and the organs below it, servants only. They stressed that in terms of power, the head and whatever was below it, were equal. To underline this, the organs made sure that pain and joy of any one of the organs was felt by all. They warned the mouth that when saying my this and that, it was talking as the whole body and not as the sole owner.

They sang:

In our body
There's no servant
In our body
There's no servant
We serve one another
Us for Us
We serve one another
Us for Us
We serve one another
The tongue our voice
Hold me and I hold you
We build healthy body
Hold me and I hold you
We build healthy body
Beauty is unity
Together we work
For a healthy body
Together we work
For a healthy body
Unity is our power

This became the All Body Anthem. The body sings it to this day and this is what tells the difference between humans and animals, or those that rejected the upright revolution.

Despite what they saw, the four-legged animals would have none of this revolution. The singing business was ridiculous. The mouth was made to eat and not to sing. They formed nature's conservative party and stuck to their ways, never changing their habits.

When humans learn from the network of organs, they do well; but when they see the body and the head as parties at war, one being atop of the other, they come close to their animal cousins who rejected the upright revolution.

THE TATTOOER

Jun'ichirō Tanizaki

Translated from the Japanese by Howard Hibbett

Jun'ichirō Tanizaki (1886–1965) was one of the major writers of modern Japanese literature, and perhaps the most popular Japanese novelist after Natsume Sōseki. Some of his works present a shocking world of sexuality and destructive erotic obsessions. Others, less sensational, subtly portray the dynamics of family life in the context of the rapid changes in twentieth-century Japanese society. He was one of six authors on the final shortlist for the Nobel Prize in Literature in 1964, the year before his death. Tanizaki's home in Yokohoma was destroyed in the Great Kanto earthquake. He escaped injury as he was on a bus at the time. His erotic writings were deemed by censors as "injurious to public morals" and banned from publishing during the Second World War. A committed sexual-submissive, Tanizaki would refer formally to his wife as "master".

It was an age when men honored the noble virtue of frivolity, when life was not such a harsh struggle as it is today. It was a leisurely age, an age when professional wits could make an excellent livelihood by keeping rich or wellborn young gentlemen in a cloudless good humor and seeing to it that the laughter of Court ladies and geisha was never stilled. In the illustrated romantic novels of the day, in the Kabuki theater, where rough masculine heroes like Sadakuro and Jiraiya were transformed into women—everywhere beauty and strength were one. People did all they could to beautify themselves, some even having pigments injected into their precious skins. Gaudy patterns of line and color danced over men's bodies.

Visitors to the pleasure quarters of Edo preferred to hire palanquin bearers who were splendidly tattooed; courtesans of the Yoshiwara and the Tatsumi quarter fell in love with tattooed men. Among those so adorned were not only gamblers, firemen, and the like, but members of the merchant class and even samurai. Exhibitions were held from time to time; and the participants, stripped to show off their filigreed bodies, would pat themselves proudly, boast of their own novel designs, and criticize each other's merits.

There was an exceptionally skillful young tattooer named Seikichi. He was praised on all sides as a master the equal of Charibun or Yatsuhei, and the skins of dozens of men had been offered as the silk for his brush. Much of the work admired at the tattoo exhibitions was his. Others might be more noted for their shading, or their use of cinnabar, but Seikichi was famous for the unrivaled boldness and sensual charm of his art.

Seikichi had formerly earned his living as an ukiyoye painter of the school of Toyokuni and Kunisada, a background which, in spite of his decline to the status of a tattooer, was evident from his artistic conscience and sensitivity. No one whose skin or whose physique failed to interest him could buy his services. The clients he did accept had to leave the design and cost entirely to his discretion—and to endure for one or even two months the excruciating pain of his needles.

Deep in his heart the young tattooer concealed a secret pleasure, and a secret desire. His pleasure lay in the agony men felt as he drove his needles into them, torturing their swollen, blood-red flesh; and the louder they groaned, the keener was Seikichi's strange delight. Shading and vermilioning—these are said to be especially painful—were the techniques he most enjoyed.

When a man had been pricked five or six hundred times in the course of an average day's treatment and had then soaked himself in a hot bath to bring out the colors, he would collapse at Seikichi's feet half dead. But Seikichi would look down at him coolly. "I dare say that hurts," he would remark with an air of satisfaction.

Whenever a spineless man howled in torment or clenched his teeth and twisted his mouth as if he were dying, Seikichi told him: "Don't act like a child. Pull yourself together—you have hardly begun to feel my needles!" And he would go on tattooing, as unperturbed as ever, with an occasional sidelong glance at the man's tearful face.

But sometimes a man of immense fortitude set his jaw and bore up stoically, not even allowing himself to frown. Then Seikichi would smile and say: "Ah, you are a stubborn one! But wait. Soon your body will begin to throb with pain. I doubt if you will be able to stand it. . . ."

For a long time Seikichi had cherished the desire to create a masterpiece on the skin of a beautiful woman. Such a woman had to meet various qualifications of character as well as appearance. A lovely face and a fine body were not enough to satisfy him. Though he inspected all the reigning beauties of the Edo gay quarters he found none who met his exacting demands. Several years had passed without success, and yet the face and figure of the perfect woman continued to obsess his thoughts. He refused to abandon hope.

One summer evening during the fourth year of his search Seikichi happened to be passing the Hirasei Restaurant in the Fukagawa district of Edo, not far from his own house, when he noticed a woman's bare milk-white foot peeping out beneath the curtains of a departing palanquin. To his sharp eye, a human foot was as expressive as a face. This one was sheer perfection. Exquisitely chiseled toes, nails like the iridescent shells along the shore at Enoshima, a pearl-like rounded heel, skin so lustrous that it seemed bathed in the limpid waters of a mountain spring—this, indeed, was a foot to be nourished by men's blood, a foot to trample on their bodies. Surely this was the foot of the unique woman who had so long eluded him. Eager to catch a glimpse of her face, Seikichi began to follow the palanquin. But after pursuing it down several lanes and alleys he lost sight of it altogether.

Seikichi's long-held desire turned into passionate love. One morning late the next spring he was standing on the bamboo-floored veranda of his home in

Fukagawa, gazing at a pot of *omoto* lilies, when he heard someone at the garden gate. Around the corner of the inner fence appeared a young girl. She had come on an errand for a friend of his, a geisha of the nearby Tatsumi quarter.

"My mistress asked me to deliver this cloak, and she wondered if you would be so good as to decorate its lining," the girl said. She untied a saffron-colored cloth parcel and took out a woman's silk cloak (wrapped in a sheet of thick paper bearing a portrait of the actor Tojaku) and a letter.

The letter repeated his friend's request and went on to say that its bearer would soon begin a career as a geisha under her protection. She hoped that, while not forgetting old ties, he would also extend his patronage to this girl.

"I thought I had never seen you before," said Seikichi, scrutinizing her intently. She seemed only fifteen or sixteen, but her face had a strangely ripe beauty, a look of experience, as if she had already spent years in the gay quarter and had fascinated innumerable men. Her beauty mirrored the dreams of the generations of glamorous men and women who had lived and died in this vast capital, where the nation's sins and wealth were concentrated.

Seikichi had her sit on the veranda, and he studied her delicate feet, which were bare except for elegant straw sandals. "You left the Hirasei by palanquin one night last July, did you not?" he inquired.

"I suppose so," she replied, smiling at the odd question. "My father was still alive then, and he often took me there."

"I have waited five years for you. This is the first time I have seen your face, but I remember your foot. . . . Come in for a moment, I have something to show you."

She had risen to leave, but he took her by the hand and led her upstairs to his studio overlooking the broad river. Then he brought out two picture scrolls and unrolled one of them before her.

It was a painting of a Chinese princess, the favorite of the cruel Emperor Chou of the Shang Dynasty. She was leaning on a balustrade in a languorous pose, the long skirt of her figured brocade robe trailing halfway down a flight of stairs, her slender body barely able to support the weight of her gold crown studded with coral and lapis lazuli. In her right hand she held a large wine cup, tilting it to her lips as she gazed down at a man who was about to be tortured in the garden below. He was chained hand and foot to a hollow copper pillar in which a fire would be lighted. Both the princess and her victim—his head bowed before her, his eyes closed, ready to meet his fate—were portrayed with terrifying vividness.

As the girl stared at this bizarre picture her lips trembled and her eyes began to sparkle. Gradually her face took on a curious resemblance to that of the princess. In the picture she discovered her secret self.

"Your own feelings are revealed here," Seikichi told her with pleasure as he watched her face.

"Why are you showing me this horrible thing?" the girl asked, looking up at him. She had turned pale.

"The woman is yourself. Her blood flows in your veins." Then he spread out the other scroll.

This was a painting called "The Victims." In the middle of it a young woman stood leaning against the trunk of a cherry tree: she was gloating over a heap of men's corpses lying at her feet. Little birds fluttered about her, singing in triumph;

her eyes radiated pride and joy. Was it a battlefield or a garden in spring? In this picture the girl felt that she had found something long hidden in the darkness of her own heart.

"This painting shows your future," Seikichi said, pointing to the woman under the cherry tree—the very image of the young girl. "All these men will ruin their lives for you."

"Please, I beg of you to put it away!" She turned her back as if to escape its tantalizing lure and prostrated herself before him, trembling. At last she spoke again. "Yes, I admit that you are right about me—I *am* like that woman. . . . So please, please take it away."

"Don't talk like a coward," Seikichi told her, with his malicious smile. "Look at it more closely. You won't be squeamish long."

But the girl refused to lift her head. Still prostrate, her face buried in her sleeves, she repeated over and over that she was afraid and wanted to leave.

"No, you must stay—I will make you a real beauty," he said, moving closer to her. Under his kimono was a vial of anesthetic which he had obtained some time ago from a Dutch physician.

The morning sun glittered on the river, setting the eight-mat studio ablaze with light. Rays reflected from the water sketched rippling golden waves on the paper sliding screens and on the face of the girl, who was fast asleep. Seikichi had closed the doors and taken up his tattooing instruments, but for a while he only sat there entranced, savoring to the full her uncanny beauty. He thought that he would never tire of contemplating her serene masklike face. Just as the ancient Egyptians had embellished their magnificent land with pyramids and sphinxes, he was about to embellish the pure skin of this girl.

Presently he raised the brush which was gripped between the thumb and last two fingers of his left hand, applied its tip to the girl's back, and, with the needle which he held in his right hand, began pricking out a design. He felt his spirit dissolve into the charcoal-black ink that stained her skin. Each drop of Ryukyu cinnabar that he mixed with alcohol and thrust in was a drop of his lifeblood. He saw in his pigments the hues of his own passions.

Soon it was afternoon, and then the tranquil spring day drew toward its close. But Seikichi never paused in his work, nor was the girl's sleep broken. When a servant came from the geisha house to inquire about her, Seikichi turned him away, saying that she had left long ago. And hours later, when the moon hung over the mansion across the river, bathing the houses along the bank in a dream-like radiance, the tattoo was not yet half done. Seikichi worked on by candlelight.

Even to insert a single drop of color was no easy task. At every thrust of his needle Seikichi gave a heavy sigh and felt as if he had stabbed his own heart. Little by little the tattoo marks began to take on the form of a huge black-widow spider; and by the time the night sky was paling into dawn this weird, malevolent creature had stretched its eight legs to embrace the whole of the girl's back.

In the full light of the spring dawn boats were being rowed up and down the river, their oars creaking in the morning quiet; roof tiles glistened in the sun, and the haze began to thin out over white sails swelling in the early breeze. Finally

Seikichi put down his brush and looked at the tattooed spider. This work of art had been the supreme effort of his life. Now that he had finished it his heart was drained of emotion.

The two figures remained still for some time. Then Seikichi's low, hoarse voice echoed quaveringly from the walls of the room:

"To make you truly beautiful I have poured my soul into this tattoo. Today there is no woman in Japan to compare with you. Your old fears are gone. All men will be your victims."

As if in response to these words a faint moan came from the girl's lips. Slowly she began to recover her senses. With each shuddering breath, the spider's legs stirred as if they were alive.

"You must be suffering. The spider has you in its clutches."

At this she opened her eyes slightly, in a dull stare. Her gaze steadily brightened, as the moon brightens in the evening, until it shone dazzlingly into his face.

"Let me see the tattoo," she said, speaking as if in a dream but with an edge of authority to her voice. "Giving me your soul must have made me very beautiful."

"First you must bathe to bring out the colors," whispered Seikichi compassionately. "I am afraid it will hurt, but be brave a little longer."

"I can bear anything for the sake of beauty." Despite the pain that was coursing through her body, she smiled.

"How the water stings! . . . Leave me alone—wait in the other room! I hate to have a man see me suffer like this!"

As she left the tub, too weak to dry herself, the girl pushed aside the sympathetic hand Seikichi offered her, and sank to the floor in agony, moaning as if in a nightmare. Her disheveled hair hung over her face in a wild tangle. The white soles of her feet were reflected in the mirror behind her.

Seikichi was amazed at the change that had come over the timid, yielding girl of yesterday, but he did as he was told and went to wait in his studio. About an hour later she came back, carefully dressed, her damp, sleekly combed hair hanging down over her shoulders. Leaning on the veranda rail, she looked up into the faintly hazy sky. Her eyes were brilliant; there was not a trace of pain in them.

"I wish to give you these pictures too," said Seikichi, placing the scrolls before her. "Take them and go."

"All my old fears have been swept away—and you are my first victim!" She darted a glance at him as bright as a sword. A song of triumph was ringing in her ears.

"Let me see your tattoo once more," Seikichi begged.

Silently the girl nodded and slipped the kimono off her shoulders. Just then her resplendently tattooed back caught a ray of sunlight and the spider was wreathed in flames.

RASHŌMON

Ryūnosuke Akutagawa

Translated from the Japanese by Jay Rubin

Ryūnosuke Akutagawa (1892–1927) was a Japanese writer active in the Taishō period in Japan. Having written over 150 short stories during his brief life, he is regarded as the "Father of the Japanese short story". Japan's premier literary award, the Akutagawa Prize, is named after him. He committed suicide at the age of thirty-five through an overdose of barbital. He was named "Ryūnosuke" ("Son of Dragon") because he was born in the Year of the Dragon, in the Month of the Dragon, on the Day of the Dragon, and at the Hour of the Dragon.

Evening, and a lowly servant sat beneath the Rashōmon, waiting for the rain to end.

Under the broad gate there was no one else, just a single cricket clinging to a huge red pillar from which the lacquer was peeling here and there. Situated on a thoroughfare as important as Suzaku Avenue, the Rashōmon could have been sheltering at least a few others from the rain—perhaps a woman in a lacquered reed hat, or a courtier with a soft black cap. Yet there was no one besides the man.

This was because Kyoto had been struck by one calamity after another in recent years—earthquakes, whirlwinds, fires, famine—leading to the capital's extraordinary decline. Old records tell us that people would smash Buddhist statues and other devotional gear, pile the pieces by the roadside with flecks of paint and gold and silver foil still clinging to them, and sell them as firewood. With the whole city in such turmoil, no one bothered to maintain the Rashōmon. Foxes and badgers came to live in the dilapidated structure, and they were soon joined by thieves. Finally, it became the custom to abandon unclaimed corpses in the upper story of the gate, which made the neighborhood an eerie place everyone avoided after the sun went down.

Crows, on the other hand, flocked here in great numbers. During the day they would always be cawing and circling the roof's high fish-tail ornaments. And when the sky above the gate turned red after sunset, the crows stood out against it like a scattering of sesame seeds. They came to the upper chamber of the gate to peck the flesh of the dead. Today, however, with the late hour, there were no crows to be seen. The only sign of them was their white droppings on the gate's crumbling steps, where long weeds sprouted from cracks between the stones. In his faded blue robe, the man had settled on the topmost of the seven steps and, worrying a large pimple that had formed on his right cheek, fixed his vacant stare on the falling rain.

We noted earlier that the servant was "waiting for the rain to end," but in fact the man had no idea what he was going to do once that happened. Ordinarily, of course, he would have returned to his master's house, but he had been dismissed from service some days before, and (as also noted earlier), Kyoto was in an unusual state of decline. His dismissal by a master he had served for many years was one small consequence of that decline. Rather than say that the servant was "waiting for the rain to end," it would have been more appropriate to write that "a lowly servant trapped by the rain had no place to go and no idea what to do." The weather, too, contributed to the *sentimentalisme* of this Heian Period menial. The rain had been falling since late afternoon and showed no sign of ending. He went on half-listening to the rain as it poured down on Suzaku Avenue. He was determined to find a way to keep himself alive for one more day—that is, a way to do something about a situation for which there was nothing to be done.

The rain carried a host of roaring sounds from afar as it came to envelop the Rashōmon. The evening darkness brought the sky ever lower until the roof of the gate was supporting dark, heavy clouds on the ridge of its jutting tiles.

To do something when there was nothing to be done, he would have to be prepared to do anything at all. If he hesitated, he would end up starving to death against an earthen wall or in the roadside dirt. Then he would simply be carried back to this gate and discarded upstairs like a dog. But if he was ready to do anything at all—

His thoughts wandered the same path again and again, always arriving at the same destination. But no matter how much time passed, the "if" remained an "if." Even as he told himself he was prepared to do anything at all, he could not find the courage for the obvious conclusion of that "if": *All I can do is become a thief.*

The man gave a great sneeze and dragged himself to his feet. The Kyoto evening chill was harsh enough to make him yearn for a brazier full of warm coals. Darkness fell, and the wind blew unmercifully through the pillars of the gate. Now even the cricket was gone from its perch on the red-lacquered pillar.

Beneath his blue robe and yellow undershirt, the man hunched his shoulders and drew his head down as he scanned the area around the gate. *If only there were some place out of the wind and rain, with no fear of prying eyes, where I could have an untroubled sleep, I would stay there until dawn,* he thought. Just then he caught sight of a broad stairway—also lacquered red—leading to the upper story of the gate. *Anybody up there is dead.* Taking care lest his sword, with its bare wooden handle, slip from its scabbard, the man set one straw-sandaled foot on the bottom step.

A few minutes later, halfway up the broad stairway, he crouched, cat-like, holding his breath as he took stock of the gate's upper chamber. Firelight from above cast a dim glow on the man's right cheek—a cheek inflamed with a pus-filled pimple amid the hairs of a short beard. The servant had not considered the possibility that anyone but dead people could be up here, but climbing two or three more steps, he realized that someone was not only burning a light but moving it from place to place. He saw the dull, yellow glow flickering against the underside of the roof, where spider webs hung in the corners. No ordinary person could be burning a light up here in the Rashōmon on a rainy night like this.

With all the stealth of a lizard, the servant crept to the top tread of the steep stairway. Then, hunching down and stretching out his neck as much as possible, he peered fearfully into the upper chamber.

There he saw a number of carelessly discarded corpses, as the rumors had said, but he could not tell how many because the lighted area was far smaller than he had thought it would be. All he could see in the dim light was that some of the corpses were naked while others were clothed. Women and men seemed to be tangled together. It was hard to believe that all of them had once been living human beings, so much did they look like clay dolls, lying there with arms flung out and mouths wide open, eternally mute. Shoulders and chests and other such prominent parts caught the dim light, casting still deeper shadows on the parts lower down.

The stink of the rotting corpses reached him, and his hand flew up to cover his nose. But a moment later the hand seemed to forget its task when a powerful emotion all but obliterated the man's sense of smell.

For now the servant's eyes caught sight of a living person crouched among the corpses. There, dressed in a rusty-black robe, was a scrawny old woman, white-haired and monkey-like. She held a burning pine stick in her right hand as she stared into the face of a corpse. Judging from the long hair, the body was probably a woman's.

Moved by six parts terror and four parts curiosity, the servant forgot to breathe for a moment. To borrow a phrase from a writer of old, he felt as if "the hairs on his head were growing thick." Then the crone thrust her pine torch between two floorboards and placed both hands on the head of the corpse she had been examining. Like a monkey searching for fleas on its child, she began plucking out the corpse's long hairs, one strand at a time. A hair seemed to slip easily from the scalp with every movement of her hand.

Each time a hair gave way, a little of the man's fear disappeared, to be replaced by an increasingly violent loathing for the old woman. No, this could be misleading: he felt not so much a loathing for the old woman as a revulsion for all things evil—an emotion that grew in strength with every passing minute. If now someone were to present this lowly fellow again with the choice he had just been mulling beneath the gate—whether to starve to death or turn to thievery—he would probably have chosen starvation without the least regret, so powerfully had the man's hatred for evil blazed up, like the pine torch the old woman had stood between the floorboards.

The servant had no idea why the crone was pulling out the dead person's hair, and thus could not rationally call the deed either good or evil. But for him, the very act of plucking hair from a corpse on this rainy night up here in the Rashōmon was itself an unpardonable evil. Naturally he no longer recalled that, only moments before, he himself had been planning to become a thief.

So now the servant, with a mighty thrust, leaped from the stairway and, grasping his sword by the bare hilt, he strode forcefully to where the old woman crouched. Terrified at the sight of him, the crone leaped up as if launched by a catapult.

"Where do you think you're going?" he shouted, blocking her way. Panic-stricken, she stumbled over corpses in an effort to flee. She struggled to break past him, but he pushed her back. For a time, the two grappled in silence among the corpses, but the outcome of the struggle was never in doubt. The servant grasped the old woman's arm—sheer skin and bone like the foot of a chicken—and finally twisted her to the floor.

"What were you doing there?" he demanded. "Tell me now, or I'll give you a piece of this."

Shoving her away, he swept his sword from its scabbard and thrust the white steel before her eyes. The old woman said nothing. Arms trembling, shoulders heaving, wide eyes straining from their sockets, she kept her stubborn silence and struggled to catch her breath. Seeing this, the servant realized that this old woman's life or death was governed entirely by his own will. The new awareness instantly cooled the hatred that had been burning so violently inside him. All he felt now was the quiet pride and satisfaction of a job well done. He looked down at her and spoke with a new tone of gentleness.

"Don't worry, I'm not with the Magistrate's Office. I'm just a traveler who happened to be passing beneath the gate. I won't be tying you up or taking you away. I just want you to tell me what you've been doing up here at a time like this."

The old woman stretched her wide eyes still wider and stared hard at the servant. Her red-lidded eyes had the sharpness of a predator-bird's. Then, as if chewing on something, she began to move her lips, which seemed joined with her nose by all her deep wrinkles. He could see the point of her Adam's apple moving on her scrawny neck, and between her gasps the voice that issued from her throat reached the servant's ears like the cawing of a crow.

"I—I was pulling—I was pulling out hair to make a wig."

The servant was startled, and disappointed at how ordinary the woman's answer turned out to be. But along with his disappointment, the earlier hatred and a cold contempt came back to fill his heart. The woman seemed to sense what he was feeling. Still holding in one hand the long hairs she had stolen from the corpse, she mumbled and croaked like a toad as she offered this explanation:

"I know, I know, it may be wrong to pull out dead people's hair. But these people here deserve what they get. Take this woman, the one I was pulling the hair from: she used to cut snakes into four-inch pieces and dry them and sell them as dried fish at the palace guardhouse. If she hadn't died in the epidemic, she'd still be out there selling her wares. The guards loved her 'fish' and they bought it for every meal. I don't think she was wrong to do it. She did it to keep from starving to death. She couldn't help it. And I don't think what I'm doing is wrong, either. It's the same thing: I can't help it. If I don't do it, I'll starve to death. This woman knew what it was to do what you have to do. I think she'd understand what I'm doing to her." The servant returned his sword to its sheath and, resting his left hand on the hilt, listened coolly to her story. Meanwhile, his right hand played with the festering pimple on his cheek. As he listened, a new kind of courage began to germinate in his heart—a courage he had lacked earlier beneath the gate: one that was moving in a direction opposite to the courage that had impelled him to seize the old woman. He was no longer torn between starving to death or becoming a thief. In his current state of mind, the very thought of starving to death was so nearly banished from his consciousness that it became all but unthinkable for him.

"You're sure she would, eh?" the servant pressed her, with mockery in his voice. Then, stepping toward her, he suddenly shot his right hand from his pimple to the scruff of her neck. As he grasped her, his words all but bit into her flesh: "You won't blame me, then, for taking your clothes. That's what *I* have to do to keep from starving to death."

He stripped the old woman of her robe, and when she tried to clutch at his ankles he gave her a kick that sent her sprawling onto the corpses. Five swift steps brought him to the opening at the top of the stairs. Tucking her robe under his arm, he plunged down the steep stairway into the depth of the night.

It did not take long for the crone, who had been lying there as if dead, to raise her naked body from among the corpses. Muttering and groaning, she crawled to the top of the stairway in the still-burning torchlight. Her short white hair hung forward from her head as she peered down toward the bottom of the gate. She saw only the cavernous blackness of the night.

What happened to the lowly servant, no one knows.

[September 1915]

THE STREET
OF CROCODILES

Bruno Schulz

Translated from the Polish by Celina Wieniewska

Bruno Schulz (1892–1942) was a Polish Jewish writer, fine artist, literary critic and art teacher. He is regarded as one of the great Polish-language prose stylists of the twentieth century. In 1938, he was awarded the Polish Academy of Literature's prestigious Golden Laurel award. Several of Schulz's works were lost in the Holocaust, including short stories from the early 1940s and his final, unfinished novel *The Messiah*. Schulz was shot and killed by a German Nazi in 1942 while walking back home toward Drohobycz Ghetto with a loaf of bread. He was obsessed with horses, from his early school days, when an open-ended homework assignment led to him filling a notebook with a story of a horse, to his later paintings as an artist, such as *Stallions and Eunuchs*. Schulz has caused so much intrigue and interest among scholars that a 400-page "Schulz Dictionary" has been compiled.

My father kept in the lower drawer of his large desk an old and beautiful map of our city. It was a whole folio sheaf of parchment pages which, originally fastened with strips of linen, formed an enormous wall map, a bird's-eye panorama.

Hung on the wall, the map covered it almost entirely and opened a wide view on the valley of the River Tysmienica, which wound itself like a wavy ribbon of pale gold, on the maze of widely spreading ponds and marshes, on the high ground rising towards the south, gently at first, then in ever tighter ranges, in a chessboard of rounded hills, smaller and paler as they receded towards the misty yellow fog of the horizon. From that faded distance of the periphery, the city rose and grew towards the centre of the map, an undifferentiated mass at first, a dense complex of blocks and houses, cut by deep canyons of streets, to become on the first plan a group of single houses, etched with the sharp clarity of a landscape seen through binoculars. In that section of the map, the engraver concentrated on the complicated and manifold profusion of streets and alleyways, the sharp lines of cornices, architraves, archivolts, and pilasters, lit by the dark gold of a late and cloudy afternoon which steeped all corners and recesses in the deep sepia of shade. The solids and prisms of that shade darkly honeycombed the ravines of streets, drowning in a warm colour here half a street, there a gap between houses.

They dramatized and orchestrated in a bleak romantic chiaroscuro the complex architectural polyphony.

On that map, made in the style of baroque panoramas, the area of the Street of Crocodiles shone with the empty whiteness that usually marks polar regions or unexplored countries of which almost nothing is known. The lines of only a few streets were marked in black and their names given in simple, unadorned lettering, different from the noble script of the other captions. The cartographer must have been loath to include that district in the city and his reservations found expression in the typographical treatment.

In order to understand these reservations, we must draw attention to the equivocal and doubtful character of that peculiar area, so unlike the rest of the city.

It was an industrial and commercial district, its soberly utilitarian character glaringly underlined. The spirit of the times, the mechanism of economics, had not spared our city and had taken root in a sector of its periphery which then developed into a parasitical quarter.

While in the old city a nightly semi-clandestine trade prevailed, marked by ceremonious solemnity, in the new district modern, sober forms of commercial endeavour had flourished at once. The pseudo-Americanism, grafted on the old, crumbling core of the city, shot up here in a rich but empty and colourless vegetation of pretentious vulgarity. One could see there cheap jerrybuilt houses with grotesque facades, covered with a monstrous stucco of cracked plaster. The old, shaky suburban houses had large hastily constructed portals grafted on to them which only on close inspection revealed themselves as miserable imitations of metropolitan splendour. Dull, dirty and faulty glass panes in which dark pictures of the street were wavily reflected, the badly planed wood of the doors, the grey atmosphere of those sterile interiors where the high shelves were cracked and the crumbling walls were covered with cobwebs and thick dust, gave these shops the stigma of some wild Klondike. In row upon row there spread tailors' shops, general outfitters, china stores, drugstores, and barbers' saloons. Their large grey display windows bore slanting semicircular inscriptions in thick gilt letters: *CONFISERIE, MANUCURE, KING OF ENGLAND*.

The old established inhabitants of the city kept away from that area where the scum, the lowest orders had settled – creatures without character, without background, moral dregs, that inferior species of human being which is born in such ephemeral communities. But on days of defeat, in hours of moral weakness, it would happen that one or another of the city dwellers would venture half by chance into that dubious district. The best among them were not entirely free from the temptation of voluntary degradation, of breaking down the barriers of hierarchy, of immersion in that shallow mud of companionship, of easy intimacy, of dirty intermingling. The district was an El Dorado for such moral deserters. Everything seemed suspect and equivocal there, everything promised with secret winks, cynical stressed gestures, raised eyebrows, the fulfilment of impure hopes, everything helped to release the lowest instincts from their shackles.

Only a few people noticed the peculiar characteristics of that district: the fatal lack of colour, as if that shoddy, quickly growing area could not afford the luxury of it. Everything was grey there, as in black-and-white photographs or in cheap illustrated catalogues. This similarity was real rather than metaphorical because at times, when wandering in those parts, one in fact gained the impression that one was turning the pages of a prospectus, looking at columns of boring commercial advertisements, among which suspect announcements nestled like parasites, together with dubious notices and illustrations with a double meaning. And one's wandering proved as sterile and pointless as the excitement produced by a close study of pornographic albums.

If one entered for example a tailor's shop to order a suit – a suit of cheap elegance characteristic of the district – one found that the premises were large and empty, the rooms high and colourless. Enormous shelves rose in tiers into the undefined height of the room and drew one's eyes towards the ceiling which might be the sky – the shoddy, faded sky of that quarter. On the other hand, the storerooms, which could be seen through the open door, were stacked high with boxes and crates – an enormous filing cabinet rising to the attic to disintegrate into the geometry of emptiness, into the timbers of a void. The large grey windows, ruled like the pages of a ledger, did not admit daylight yet the shop was filled with a watery anonymous grey light which did not throw shadows and did not stress anything. Soon, a slender young man appeared, astonishingly servile, agile, and compliant, to satisfy one's requirements and to drown one in the smooth flow of his cheap sales talk. But when, talking all the time, he unrolled an enormous piece of cloth, fitting folding, and draping the stream of material, forming it into imaginary jackets and trousers, that whole manipulation seemed suddenly unreal, a sham comedy, a screen ironically placed to hide the true meaning of things.

The tall dark salesgirls, each with a flaw in her beauty (appropriately for that district of remaindered goods), came and went, stood in the doorways watching to see whether the business entrusted to the experienced care of the salesman had reached a suitable point. The salesman simpered and pranced around like a transvestite. One wanted to lift up his receding chin or pinch his pale powdered cheek as with a stealthy meaningful look he discreetly pointed to the trademark on the material, a trademark of transparent symbolism.

Slowly the selection of the suit gave place to the second stage of the plan. The effeminate and corrupted youth, receptive to the client's most intimate stirrings, now put before him a selection of the most peculiar trademarks, a whole library of labels, a cabinet displaying the collection of a sophisticated connoisseur. It then appeared that the outfitter's shop was only a facade behind which there was an antique shop with a collection of highly questionable books and private editions. The servile salesman opened further store rooms, filled to the ceiling with books, drawings, and photographs. These engravings and etchings were beyond our boldest expectations: not even in our dreams had we anticipated such depths of corruption, such varieties of licentiousness.

The salesgirls now walked up and down between the rows of books, their faces, like grey parchment, marked with the dark greasy pigment spots of brunettes, their shiny dark eyes shooting out sudden zigzag cockroachy looks. But even their dark blushes, the piquant beauty spots, the traces of down on their upper lips betrayed their thick, black blood. Their overintense colouring, like that of an aromatic coffee, seemed to stain the books which they took into their olive hands, their touch seemed to run on the pages and leave in the air a dark trail of freckles, a smudge of tobacco, as does a truffle with its exciting, animal smell.

In the meantime, lasciviousness had become general. The salesman, exhausted by his eager importuning, slowly withdrew into feminine passivity. He now lay on one of the many sofas which stood between the bookshelves, wearing a pair of deeply-cut silk pyjamas. Some of the girls demonstrated to one another the poses and postures of the drawings on the book jackets, while others settled down to sleep on makeshift beds. The pressure on the client had eased. He was now released from the circle of eager interest and left more or less alone. The salesgirls, busy talking, ceased to pay any attention to him. Turning their backs on him they adopted arrogant poses, shifting their weight from foot to foot, making play with their frivolous footwear, abandoning their slim bodies to the serpentine movements of their limbs and thus laid siege to the excited onlooker whom they pretended to ignore behind a show of assumed indifference. This retreat was calculated to involve the guest more deeply, while appearing to leave him a free hand for his own initiative.

But let us take advantage of that moment of inattention to escape from these unexpected consequences of an innocent call at the tailor's, and slip back into the street.

No one stops us. Through the corridors of books, from between the long shelves filled with magazines and prints, we make our way out of the shop and find ourselves in that part of the Street of Crocodiles where from the higher level one can see almost its whole length down to the distant, as yet unfinished buildings of the railway station. It is, as usual in that district, a grey day, and the whole scene seems at times like a photograph in an illustrated magazine, so grey, so one-dimensional are the houses, the people and the vehicles. Reality is as thin as paper and betrays with all its cracks its imitative character. At times one has the impression that it is only the small section immediately before us that falls into the expected pointillistic picture of a city thoroughfare, while on either side, the improvised masquerade is already disintegrating and, unable to endure, crumbles behind us into plaster and sawdust, into the store room of an enormous empty theatre. The tenseness of an artificial pose, the assumed earnestness of a mask, an ironical pathos tremble on this facade.

But far be it from us to wish to expose this sham. Despite our better judgement we are attracted by the tawdry charm of the district. Besides, that pretence of a city has some of the features of self-parody. Rows of small one-storey suburban houses alternate with many-storeyed buildings which, looking as if made of cardboard, are a mixture of blind office windows, of grey-glassed display windows, of fascia, of advertisements and numbers. Among the houses the crowds stream by. The street is as broad as a city boulevard, but the roadway is made, like village squares, of beaten clay, full of puddles and overgrown with grass. The street traffic of that area is a byword in the city; all its inhabitants speak about it with pride and a knowing look. That grey, impersonal crowd is rather self-conscious of its role, eager to live up to its metropolitan aspirations. All the same, despite the bustle and sense of purpose, one has the impression of a monotonous aimless wandering, of a sleepy procession of puppets. An atmosphere of strange insignificance pervades the scene. The crowd flows lazily by and, strange to say, one can see it only indistinctly; the figures pass in gentle disarray, never reaching complete sharpness of outline. Only at times do we catch among the turmoil of many heads a dark vivacious look, a black bowler hat worn at an angle, half a face split by a smile formed by lips which had just finished speaking, a foot thrust forward to take a step and fixed forever in that position.

A peculiarity of that district are the cabs, without coachmen, driving along unattended. It is not as if there were no cabbies, but mingling with the crowd and busy with a thousand affairs of their own, they do not bother about their carriages. In that area of sham and empty gestures no one pays much attention to the precise purpose of a cab ride and the passengers entrust themselves to these erratic conveyances with the thoughtlessness which characterizes everything here. From time to time one can see them at dangerous corners, leaning far out from under the broken roof of a cab as, with the reins in their hands, they perform with some difficulty the tricky manoeuvre of overtaking.

There are also trams here. In them the ambition of the city councillors has achieved its greatest triumph. The appearance of these trams, though, is pitiful, for they are made of papier-mâché with warped sides dented from the misuse of many years. They often have no fronts, so that in passing one can see the passengers, sitting stiffly and behaving with great decorum. These trams are pushed by the town porters. The strangest thing of all is, however, the railway system in the Street of Crocodiles.

Occasionally, at different times of day towards the end of the week, one can see groups of people waiting at a crossroads for a train. One is never sure whether the train will come at all or where it will stop if it does. It often happens, therefore, that people wait in two different places, unable to agree where the stop is. They wait for a long time standing in a black, silent bunch alongside the barely visible lines of the track, their faces in profile: a row of pale cutout paper figures, fixed in an expression of anxious peering.

At last the train suddenly appears: one can see it coming from the expected side street, low like a snake, a miniature train with a squat puffing locomotive. It enters the black corridor, and the street darkens from the coal dust scattered by the line of carriages. The heavy breathing of the engine and the wave of a strange sad seriousness, the suppressed hurry and excitement transform the street for a moment into the hall of a railway station in tin quickly falling winter dusk.

A black market in railway tickets and bribery in general are the special plagues of our city.

At the last moment, when the train is already in the station, negotiations are conducted in nervous haste with corrupt railway officials. Before these are completed, the train starts, followed slowly by a crowd of disappointed passengers who accompany it a long way down the line before finally dispersing.

The street, reduced for a moment to form an improvised station filled with gloom and the breath of distant travel, widens out again, becomes lighter and again allows the carefree crowds of chattering passers-by to stroll past the shop windows – those dirty grey squares filled with shoddy goods, tall wax dummies, and barber's dolls.

Showily dressed in long lace-trimmed gowns, prostitutes have begun to circulate. They might even be the wives of hairdressers or restaurant bandleaders. They advance with a brisk rapacious step, each with some small flaw in her evil corrupted face; their eyes have a black, crooked squint, or they have harelips, or the tips of their noses are missing.

The inhabitants of the city are quite proud of the odour of corruption emanating from the Street of Crocodiles. 'There is no need for us to go short of anything,' they say proudly to themselves, 'we even have truly metropolitan vices.' They maintain that every woman in that district is a tart. In fact, it is enough to stare at any of them, and at once you meet an insistent clinging look which freezes you with the certainty of fulfilment. Even the schoolgirls wear their hair ribbons in a characteristic way and walk on their slim legs with a peculiar step, an impure expression in their eyes that foreshadows their future corruption.

And yet, and yet – are we to betray the last secret of that district, the carefully concealed secret of the Street of Crocodiles?

Several times during our account we have given warning signals, we have intimated delicately our reservations. An attentive reader will therefore not be unprepared for what is to follow. We spoke of the imitative, illusory character of that area, but these words have too precise and definite a meaning to describe its half-baked and undecided reality.

Our language has no definitions which would weigh, so to speak, the grade of reality, or define its suppleness. Let us say it bluntly: the misfortune of that area is that nothing ever succeeds there, nothing can ever reach a definite conclusion. Gestures hang in the air, movements are prematurely exhausted and cannot overcome a certain point of inertia. We have already noticed the great bravura and prodigality in intentions, projects, and anticipations which are one of the characteristics of the district. It is in fact no more than a fermentation of desires, prematurely aroused and therefore impotent and empty. It is an atmosphere of excessive facility, every whim flies high, a passing excitement swells into an empty parasitic growth; a light grey vegetation of fluffy weeds, of colourless poppies sprouts forth, made from a weightless fabric of nightmares and hashish. Over the whole area there floats the lazy licentious smell of sin, and the houses, the shops, the people seem sometimes no more than a shiver on its feverish body, the gooseflesh of its febrile dreams. Nowhere as much as there do we feel threatened by possibilities, shaken by the nearness of fulfilment, pale and faint with the delightful rigidity of realization. And that is as far as it goes.

Having exceeded a certain point of tension, the tide stops and begins to ebb, the atmosphere becomes unclear and troubled, possibilities fade and decline into a void, the crazy grey poppies of excitement scatter into ashes.

We shall always regret that, at a given moment, we have left the slightly dubious tailor's shop. We shall never be able to find it again. We shall wander from shop sign to shop sign and make a thousand mistakes. We shall enter scores of shops, see many which are similar. We shall wander along shelves upon shelves of books, look through magazines and prints, confer intimately and at length with young women of imperfect beauty, with an excessive pigmentation who yet would not be able to understand our requirements.

We shall get involved in misunderstandings until all our fever and excitement have spent themselves in unnecessary effort, in futile pursuit.

Our hopes were a fallacy, the suspicious appearance of the premises and of the staff were a sham, the clothes were real clothes, and the salesman had no ulterior motives. The women of the Street of Crocodiles are depraved to only a modest extent, stilled by thick layers of moral prejudice and ordinary banality. In that city of cheap human material, no instincts can flourish, no dark and unusual passions can be aroused.

The Street of Crocodiles was a concession of our city to modernity and metropolitan corruption. Obviously, we were unable to afford anything better than a paper imitation, a montage of illustrations cut out from last year's mouldering newspapers.

THE BIRCH GROVE[1]

Jarosław Iwaszkiewicz

Translated from the Polish by Antonia Lloyd-Jones

Jarosław Iwaszkiewicz (1894–1980) also known under his literary pseudonym Eleuter, was a Polish poet, essayist, dramatist and writer. He is mostly recognized for his literary achievements in poetry before the Second World War, but also criticized as a long-term political opportunist in communist Poland, actively participating in the slander of Czesław Miłosz and other expatriates. He was removed from school textbooks soon after the collapse of the Soviet Bloc. He was nominated for the Nobel Prize in Literature four times. As per his wishes, he was buried in a miner's uniform. Some attributed it to an attempt to win communist sympathy, others thought it a metaphor for writer's toil, however a close friend unravelled the mystery by revealing that "Jarosław simply thought he looked good in this type of a uniform".

I

Something in the way Stanisław alighted from the chaise before the porch immediately irritated Bolesław. He flew, or rather fluttered out of the carriage. What struck him most was the bright blue colour of Stanisław's socks, which shone garishly from under his short, baggy trousers, laying siege to his skinny ankles. But apart from that he looked perfectly well. Bolesław looked up to his brother's light blue eyes. They were smiling, and there was a smile on his lips as well, sending fine lines radiating outwards. They kissed in greeting; Bolesław's first kindly thought was, 'Thank God, he's in good health.'

It was a very long time since they had last seen each other. Staś, as Stanisław was nicknamed, had spent the past two years at a sanatorium, but it was several years since they had last met. Bolesław had long since buried himself away at this forestry lodge, and Staś had never been to visit. Quite possibly he wouldn't have recognised him now.

'How are you?' asked Bolesław after a short, silent embrace.

'I'm fine!'

'So you've remembered me at last.'

'What else could I do? The doctors insisted I go to the forest. So where else but here?'

---

1 *Translator's note*: Where the characters' names appear in more than one form (e.g. Malina/Malwina) the translation follows the original Polish text throughout.

As he spoke, he kept interrupting himself to do things. He leaped up the steps into the chaise and drew out a light trunk, put it down on the veranda, and cast off his elegant mackintosh, gloves and travelling cap, just like the ones Bolesław had seen advertised in illustrated magazines. At once they sat down to breakfast, laid out on the veranda.

'I'm awfully tired,' said Staś. 'Two days and two nights' journey.'

Little Ola emerged from inside the house. She had startled blue eyes and was carrying a rather threadbare doll. Silently, she curtsied to her uncle.

'Goodness, what a big girl she is!' cried Staś. Bolesław said nothing. 'What an awful doll! I saw such beautiful dolls abroad, but I forgot to bring her one. What a thoughtless uncle I am!'

Ola went down the porch steps and walked quietly into the forest. The forest began just across the road, which ran between it and the lodge. It was a nasty day, drizzling endlessly. The woods on this side were devoid of undergrowth, and as he was animatedly describing his journey, Staś could see Ola's pale little dress glinting between the tree trunks. He broke off his story.

'You let her run loose like that?' he addressed his older brother. Bolesław just shrugged. 'As I was saying, as soon as I got down into the valley,' he continued, 'I felt awfully tired. What a place Poland is! I thought the journey would never end – the forest goes on and on – God knows where it all comes from.'

'Yes, but it's not very pretty. Just woods.'

'Never mind – I adore pine forests. The doctors were always going on about it – off to the pine forest with you, that's what you need!'

'Over there behind the house there's a very fine birch grove,' said Bolesław, pointing, but without looking that way.

The day was overcast, and from the forest echoed a faint rustle of pine needles brushing against each other.

'You know, two hours of listening to the rustle of pine needles and sand beneath the wheels is awfully dull!' Staś went on, without losing his good humour. 'I find the lack of variety in this region rather boring. So how are you?'

Bolesław shrugged again, and made an indeterminate sound.

'You ought to get someone to take care of the little one, you know.'

'I've been thinking about it . . .'

'Just thinking about it isn't enough.'

Staś pushed back his chair with a wide sweep and took his trunk by the handle. 'Where am I to stay?'

'Left off the hall.'

Bolesław shifted his chair slightly in order to look down the road. The sky between the porch roof and the forest had darkened abruptly and the rain had grown denser. There was an open window right next to the veranda, and he could hear Staś putting his room in order. He plucked at his beard as he listened to his brother rummaging about, unpacking his trunk and washing after his journey, humming all the while. He never stopped humming fashionable European tunes, importing a breath of foreign air. Bolesław frowned and chewed his beard, stuffing it into his mouth.

Staś opened the door from his own room into the next. Bolesław could hear him shuffling about in soft slippers, opening the door into the little hall; he must be peeping into the kitchen. Then he came back down the other side of the house, through Bolesław and Ola's room. Four rooms – that was the entire extent of it.

'I've been right around the house,' said Staś, standing in the doorway. 'I forgot you don't have a piano. I thought you did, and I was looking for it everywhere. It'll be awfully dull here without a piano. Can't we hire one in Sławsk?'

Bolesław didn't answer.

'We'll all be bored to death here.'

Even the word 'death' was not enough to rouse Bolesław from his trance. All he kept thinking was, 'Oh Christ Almighty, what the hell is he doing here?'

Meanwhile Staś had poured himself a glass of hot water from the kettle that stood on the table. He went off to shave, appearing soon after through the window, his face covered in lather. 'Don't you go riding?' he said.

'No, but I've got a saddle.'

'What about a horse?'

'The one on the right,' mumbled Bolesław.

'Does he go?'

'Hm, Janek says he's very good.'

'That's wonderful. I'll do some riding, then,' said Staś and withdrew.

He soon fired another question at Bolesław, asking, 'So how far is it to Sławsk?'

'You came from there, didn't you?'

'But how far is it in miles?'

'About two, two and a half maybe.'

'Do you think it would be possible to bring a piano here?'

'You've seen what the road's like.'

'Of course, but once it dries out?'

'It'll be sandy.'

'But if need be would you let me have the horses?'

'Can't you leave me in peace about your wretched piano?!' said Bolesław impatiently. He stood up and went into the kitchen. Staś went on humming as he shaved. He watched as Ola came slinking up the road, soaked through, but not walking any faster. She stepped carefully across the ruts, shielding her doll with a handkerchief. The sight of her made Stanisław's heart bleed. 'It's going to be tough here,' he said to himself.

Katarzyna, the old servant, was clearing away the breakfast on the veranda. Ola sat down at a little table in a nook and started chatting to her doll.

Staś was inspecting all his knick-knacks, which reminded him of his time abroad. He arranged them on a decrepit, ugly little dressing table standing in the corner. He gazed at the photographs; there he was with Miss Simons and Duparc on the snow at Davos. Smiling faces. The smell of the objects there had been different. Now he was enveloped in the odour of plain pine furniture and freshly washed floors. When he went out onto the porch the sky had brightened.

'Ola, come for a walk. Show me where the birch grove is.'

Ola stood up without a word and took him by the hand. He could feel her cold, skinny little paw in his. Slowly they made their way down the steps. Heavy drops dripped from the roof.

'When it rains early in the morning the weather's always nice later,' said the little girl solemnly.

They walked around the house. And indeed, on the other side there was a lovely birch grove. The trunks stretched skywards like snow-clad pillars, brittle, as if made of sugar or snow. Delicate leaves were trickling down from on high, but all one could see was the vista of white pillars.

'It's pretty here,' said Staś without smiling.

Ola didn't answer. They walked over damp grass, then a well-trodden path. The white tree trunks grew denser, forming a foggy vista; the humidity among the trees had started to vaporise. It was going to be a sunny afternoon.

'It's just a May shower,' said Ola, ever so slowly unwinding the thread of her thoughts.

They were standing in front of a small mound of yellow sand, going black already, but not overgrown with grass. The mound was enclosed by a white birch-wood fence, a very plain structure; sticks had simply been embedded in the ground crosswise. A huge birchwood cross stood over the mound, as white as the trunks of the surrounding trees. Staś was amazed. 'What's this?'

'It's a grave,' replied Ola.

'Whose grave?'

'What do you mean, whose? It's Mummy's.'

'So your mummy's buried here? Why isn't she at the cemetery?'

'It's such a long way,' replied Ola, 'and it's nice and close here.'

'It's nice and close all right, but why wasn't she buried at the cemetery?'

'The flooding after the thaw was terrible. The priest came on horseback.'

'So it was in the spring?'

'On horseback. He heard Mummy's confession and then he just stayed. He was here for two days, he couldn't move – the water had gone everywhere.'

'Did he consecrate this ground?'

'Yes, he did. He said it couldn't be in unconsecrated ground. He kept insisting on taking her to Sławsk.'

'And what did your daddy say?'

'Daddy didn't want to. He said it could be in the birch grove. It's a pretty place.'

'It is pretty!'

'It's very pretty, but I don't like coming here.'

'Don't you?'

'No, I don't. I only come with Daddy. Daddy prays.'

'Your daddy . . .'

'Daddy comes here every day first thing in the morning or towards evening, and on Sundays he and I come and pray here. He reads from the book Mummy used to have.'

'Do you remember your mummy?'

'Of course I do, it's only a year ago.'

'Right. It's a whole year now. And I only found out in the autumn. Your daddy rarely writes.'

'Daddy doesn't like letters.'

'I wrote more often than he did.'

'But Daddy doesn't like your letters, Uncle.'

'Did he ever read them to you?'

'No . . . he did read me one, about how you went sledging. I've got a sledge too, but there aren't any mountains here. Are there big mountains in Switzerland?'

'Huge ones. I'll show you my photographs.'

'Then let's go home now. Show me the photographs, Uncle.'

Back at home he began to show them to her, but she soon got bored. Besides, she didn't really understand what 'hotel', 'sanatorium', or 'Switzerland' meant. As he sat on the oilcloth sofa that stood in his room, the photographs slipped off his knees. He gazed aimlessly out of the window, where rays of sunlight had started to shine through from behind the pine trees. The carpet of pine needles beneath the trees was wreathed in clouds of haze; the spaces between the trunks were filled with mist and vapours. But he wasn't watching the doings of nature; he wasn't even thinking about them. He sat still, wanting to be free of all thought. After a while he repeated, 'Oh, it's going to be tough here.'

He had not yet fully divined the atmosphere, but he already knew it wouldn't be good. He was appalled by his brother's state of mind and tried in vain to imagine what it was like; but as he had never experienced any real loss, it wasn't easy. He had been present at his mother's death, but the actual fact of it had seemed unreal. Afterwards he had been unable to understand it or feel it; it was just as if his mother were always in another room, and finally he got used to the idea that she would never come into the one he was in. But the sandy mound in the birch grove was impossible to ignore. He kept on seeing it, and the network of white tree trunks fading into the distance, creating a white, atomised shade, as if painted with the tip of the brush.

Meanwhile Bolesław was sitting across the hall, on his bed, staring at more or less the same landscape of pine trees, at the smoke among the tree trunks and at the first glimmers reviving on the wet leaves of the brushwood, which those same rays of sunlight were just beginning to reveal amid the desiccated tracery of the forest. Bolesław's thoughts were even less focused than his brother's. Nothing had been able to call him out of the fog that had enveloped him ever since his wife's death; he saw everything through a veil, which greatly impeded his vision, but nothing worse. He did visit the grave regularly, that was true, and on Sundays he said prayers there with Ola, which was all the more upsetting as he wasn't a believer. The mound, the body – to his mind none of it existed, but he really could feel the death of that ugly but dear woman who had been his wife for several years. He could feel her absence. He couldn't forget that she was dead. He remembered her dying, and how she had died. And that was the only thing that was real, everything else was not. That was why his brother's socks were such an awful thing; their colour would haunt Bolesław in his rare dreams. The world that the young man had left behind in order to stir up the mist among the pine trees was truly appalling. Stanisław's arrival was like the advent of a Martian. Yet at the same time it evoked an undeniable sense of reality, of which Bolesław had been deprived for the whole year past.

He thought, for the first time, of the fact that it was a year already, that Basia must have undergone a terrifying change in the coffin, that he would never love anyone ever again, that Ola really was terribly neglected – for he gave no thought at all to the need to engage some sort of teacher for her – in short, that somehow life must go on. Where to and what for he couldn't quite think for the moment, just that it must go on. This line of thought was already a very great change for him, and he owed it to Staś's intolerable presence.

Suddenly on the stairs, then the veranda, the firm tread of strong bare feet resounded. A girl, hot from running, abruptly cast her shadow across Staś's view of the pine trees. 'Where's the master?'

He didn't have time to reply before Bolesław's voice responded from the window on the other side of the veranda doors.

Apparently, the girl's brother Janek, the watchman, who lived in the court-yard, had knocked out a pane of glass in the front door with his hand; he had a deep cut and the wound would need bandaging after a good coating of iodine. Both brothers went to see to the matter, which gave Stanisław the opportunity to get to know the courtyard and its inhabitants.

There weren't many of them – just Janek, his sister and mother, and two teen-age youths, Edek and Olek, who tended the cows and horses; that was it. The courtyard was small and clean, but cheerless. The horses and cows were stabled in a red brick building at ground level, and upstairs there was a small apartment, where the bandaging operation took place, with two rooms for the rifleman and his family, and another little room for the boys. The windows were very small and didn't admit much light. The pine trees began right against the walls of the building, half of which was occupied by the stable. Separately, there was also a shed, a coach house, a henhouse and a small pigsty.

Stanisław went home feeling even sadder and more disheartened. He still wasn't over his tiredness from the long journey; now and then he broke into a sweat. The air after the rain was sultry and the good weather, which had finally settled in the afternoon, did not promise to last for long. He lay down on the oilcloth sofa and waited patiently for lunch. Bolesław kept pacing up and down his room, although there was very little space between his bed and Ola's. She and her doll were sitting in there too, in a corner behind the bed. The moment his mind went blank, Bolesław could hear her teaching the doll to say its prayers.

II

The next few days were exactly alike, with the single difference perhaps that Bolesław spent less time at home. Not only did he have to drive about the forest, supervising one job or another at a clearing or at the sawmill, which were quite far apart, but he also had to drive to town. He hadn't been there for a year; the road was a bit better now, and he had remembered a lot of business left unsettled for ages, so off he went. He preferred to avoid being on his own with his brother, whose clothes, way of life and manner of talking were enough to tear open his almost healed wound. He couldn't bear the pensive joy at life that Staś was so full of; it was there in his every word and gesture, in his smile. Bolesław wouldn't admit it, but in his own brother he saw so much allure, so much winsome charm that he simply couldn't face, not for anything in the world. He couldn't under-stand how exactly, but all that charm and allure cut him off from Basia. So he preferred to stay at the sawmill and listen to the Jews arguing. He would be late for lunch, but Staś would be waiting patiently; he had got into the habit of going for very long walks with Ola, which tired him greatly. Bolesław often found him lying on the oilcloth sofa, and in the evenings he went to bed early and didn't want to go out after sunset.

'It's a habit left over from the sanatorium,' he told his brother.

He was very sweet, but still very tactless – he laughed, he joked, he sang and whistled. Ola had cheered up a bit in her uncle's presence and had learned two German songs which he sang to her. She had hardly ever sung before, but now she would hum to her doll in the evenings, after putting it to bed in a birch-bark cradle. This annoyed and upset Bolesław all the more.

It rained again, and cleared up again, and then the moonlit nights set in. Ola went to bed very late; one evening she sat in her uncle's room on the sofa and watched as the red glow of the rising satellite broke through among the pine trees. She was speechless with wonder, for Staś was telling her how the moon rises in the clear mountain air, and how he had seen a total eclipse emerging from behind a red ridge opposite the sanatorium. It was going to be frosty then, and the air, light and pure, gave a hiss as you breathed it in. The little girl was terrified. But the moon changed from red to white, and brilliant patches of light appeared among the pine trees.

Then they went for a walk among the birches. As they walked to and fro, it all seemed unreal to Staś. It took great strength of will to keep on laughing and joking as he held his little niece by the hand. As they were getting closer to the grave, Ola stopped and wouldn't go further, but he told her gently that she shouldn't be afraid, that there was nothing to be scared of. If and when the time came, he too would wish to lie down in the sand among the marbled tree trunks. They went closer to the fence, and then they saw Bolesław. He was just standing there, but his drooping head and broken figure spoke such volumes that Staś drew back.

'Daddy's there,' said Ola.

They went home in silence. Ola went to bed, and the old cook, Katarzyna, tucked her in, while Stanisław fell to gazing at the pine trees, shining blue in the moonlight.

Suddenly Bolesław burst into his room. He had seen them walking away from him and from the grave, and couldn't resist making some cutting remarks, but Stanisław couldn't understand what was up. Then they went into the dining room and had a cup of tea in silence; finally, Bolesław started telling him the whole story from the very beginning. It was clearly a great relief for him to talk; not only was he casting off a great burden, but at the same time he was breaking the ice between himself and his brother. So, from the very beginning, he told him what Basia had been like, quiet, good and ordinary, but extremely dear; how she had generally been in poor health ever since Ola's birth; what a very snowy winter they had had, and then the awful floodwater, and how the priest had had to come on horseback. It was everything that Ola had summed up in their first conversation, but in far more detail, with references back to themes touched on earlier, with refrains; he spoke very roughly and inarticulately, but Staś listened attentively without once taking his eyes off him. Even if he found his brother's narrative lacking in refinement, through strength of suffering he could feel the full might and tenacity of his whole being, the full strength of his brother's character coming through in his simple words. He realised that Bolesław was a strong person after all, able to suffer terribly and to love deeply. As he listened to this speech, which so perfectly illustrated Bolesław's character, he started comparing himself to his older brother and smiled with compassion. There was nothing deep about him, it was all on the outside, and that was the end of it. And nothing would come of it.

Bolesław wasn't pleased at his own outpouring, and went straight off to bed, but couldn't sleep for ages. To his mind, Staś had taken it all very nonchalantly; he hadn't been at all perturbed – he hadn't shown due concern. He thought this confession of his, by showing Staś what was going on inside him, would bring them closer together. But the next day Staś was even more alien, even more cheerful and unapproachable. Letters had started flooding in for him (the post came twice a week) with foreign stamps, which he carefully cut out and presented to Ola. The days had a fine start now, and they would go for walks. From the veranda or the forest Bolesław would watch Staś's tall, thin figure from afar. Dressed in grey, he almost entirely blended in with the grey glow emanating from the pine forest; he looked almost blue, while Ola's flaxen hair shone like a patch of sunlight trailing after him.

Finally, Stanisław couldn't stand it any longer and decided to have a piano brought from Sławsk.

III

It was a real voyage of the Argonauts. First Staś went to town accompanied by the rifleman who had cut his hand. The journey was long and monotonous in the extreme. It was impossible to sustain one's admiration of the forest and the trees, and for the past few days Staś had been feeling worse: he seemed to have quite a temperature, although since leaving the sanatorium he had promised himself not so much as to look at a thermometer. The sky was grey-blue, like washed-out muslin; pines and birches alternated along the way in a soporific rhythm. Moreover, his attempts at conversation with the rifleman didn't take off, although he was a pleasant enough fellow. Staś wanted to ask him about his sister, but it seemed a bit too forward and intimate. He couldn't think why, but on the way, maybe because of the proximity of her brother, she kept on coming into his mind, common and impetuous, her feet pattering on the veranda floorboards the first time he had seen her. Only now did he remember that in her dark face she had the same limpid grey eyes as her brother. She had watched him closely as he was dressing the rifleman's hand, with the same bandage, apparently, that was now a grey rag, still wound around the palm of his neighbour on the cart. Loose yellow sand shot from the wheels with a faint hum; it was fairly hot and sweat was pouring down Stanisław's neck and body. This gave him a stronger sensation of his own body – the feeling grew more and more ticklish, which was enjoyable but irritating all at once; he gazed aimlessly ahead, as if hearing the humming of the sand inside himself.

The rifleman was simply called Janek, and his sister was Malina. This was the only question which he made up his mind to ask throughout the entire journey. But he was prepared for a lengthy drive, so he didn't notice when the ploughed land began; then on completely flat ground the first rough-cast houses of the town came into sight. They stopped in the market-place; they would have to search about for a piano in working order. Staś started bargaining with the nearest Jew, who consulted another, and soon there were at least a dozen of them crowding around the wagon. They wagged their tongues and waved their arms about, but there was little progress, as first they had to define the problem and weigh up the chances of locating the desired object. Staś listened calmly to all this twittering.

Finally, an obscure alley was identified where there was an apartment with a grand piano for the taking. It was the home of a redundant railway or bank clerk who wanted to rent out the instrument. His wife, still young, lay sick in the same room as it, and as he tried the keys, Staś began to chat with her. The piano was her property – by no means did she wish to sell it, but she would gladly rent it out for a couple of months; they needed the money, they were terribly poor and their child had just died. In a couple of months she would be well again, and she would need the piano back; in the autumn she would start giving music lessons. Staś stared at her closely, but she averted her gaze. From his days in the sanatorium he had grown all too accustomed to the sight of sick people for this woman's face to make any great impression on him, but he didn't doubt for a moment that by autumn she wouldn't be needing the piano. No, she wouldn't, and neither would he, he thought.

The hardest bit was getting it home. The hired wagon dragged along, getting stuck in the sand time and again. Three horses, harnessed to a single shaft, moved crookedly, and the wheels kept grinding into the sand and slipping out of the ruts. The piano was short and not very heavy. Staś had promised the sick woman that he would look after it like his own flesh and blood, so he didn't want to go ahead of the wagon but ordered Janek to follow it at snail's pace. Sitting up in bed, the woman had wept softly as the piano was carried out, which had irritated Staś.

'The old girl will soon have something to moan about,' he had said to himself as he stood in the narrow street supervising the loading. Now, riding behind the piano, as if following a coffin, he could still see the thin woman's tears, large and lucid, streaming down her cheeks.

Evening was setting in fast, but he hardly noticed. It was a May evening, and among the trees a violet haze was already showing; the sky, too, was half lilac, casting blue shadows among the furrows in the sand. The humming of the wheels was almost a sizzle now; the Jew on the coach box above the piano was braying at the horses. Even Staś had lost his good humour.

Only late in the evening did they reach the forestry lodge. With the help of Janek, the Jew from Sławsk, Edek and Olek, and finally Malina, Staś got the piano unloaded and set up in his room. The Jew led the horses off to the courtyard, and total silence fell. Staś sat down at the piano and, placing his hands on the lid, which shone in the gloom, he gazed out of the open window at the night, at the pine trees and the birches – just there began the birch grove – and his heart ached. He never gave it a thought, but life had become very tough indeed now.

He began to play very softly, to avoid waking little Ola. He began to play irrevocably *passé* tunes, which made no sense here at all, such as the tangos and slow foxtrots he used to dance to at the sanatorium, which against the backdrop of this severe landscape were as incongruous as last year's fashions. Especially the Hawaiian tune he had danced to with Miss Simons. It was very pretty, just like his dancing partner, but like her, it made no sense here. Throughout the unloading of the piano Bolesław had not once showed his face. Evidently he had shut himself in his room and wouldn't even come and look at the offensive instrument. The night was very warm, and Staś was no longer thinking about his brother. As he was playing the banal tunes he could sense the pain of this black night, and its terror. For the time being he wanted to remain in ignorance of Bolesław's state of mind.

After a while, Bolesław came in with great commotion, and stormed up and down the room; finally he sat down on the bed, tugging at his beard. Only after a time did he say, 'You know, I find that piano of yours and all your playing very hurtful. You just don't seem to appreciate that you're in a house in mourning.'

'A whole year has gone by,' said Staś, without interrupting his playing. His words sounded florid and theatrical, like the opening of a ballad.

Bolesław shuddered. 'I find that music intensely irritating,' he said.

'So do I,' said Staś and stopped playing. 'It conjures up a world I'll never go back to, and which I never really got to know. I used to gaze at it all from my window. I saw some things through the windowpane that would have been beautiful, if only I could have touched them. But I never did, and I never will. It's like glass, like something made of thin ice . . . Listen, Bolek,' he said, in a serious tone, 'I can tell there's something you haven't realised. You don't know why I've come here.'

'What do you mean?'

'I know my cheerfulness and my music annoy you, but please let me go on just a little longer. You see, I won't be here for very long . . . In my illness, before the final stage there's usually an improvement. It lasts for a few weeks. The doctors take advantage of it to send the patient off, anywhere at all, back home, or to the country, somewhere private, so that he doesn't die at the sanatorium. My remission is already coming to an end. I'm very sorry, my dear fellow, but I really can't help it. I wish I could – at this point he smiled – 'but I can't . . . So please don't give me too much of a fight. I came here to die.'

Bolesław stood still in the darkness, but Staś wasn't looking at him; he was still captivated by the dark night beyond the open window, and was thinking of Miss Simons, regretting that he hadn't fallen in love with her, and humming the Hawaiian tune.

'Why don't you have any nightingales?' he asked after a while.

'There were some . . . but they seem to have stopped singing now.'

Bolesław stood up and paced about the room, but his step was calmer and quieter now, as if he were trying to tread carefully. A couple of times he came towards Staś and stared into his face, pallid in the darkness, his expression fixed, as if on another planet. But Staś took no notice of him; an inner lament was reverberating in his sickly lungs. Only later did he say, 'You see, that's what happens when it passes from the lungs into the intestine . . .'

Bolesław left the room without a word and vanished onto the veranda.

IV

The start of summer was particularly beautiful. The days, not excessively hot, ended in sultry evenings and the nights were silent, peaceful and tender. Bolesław was still getting very little sleep. His brother's confession had failed to build a bridge of conciliation between them. On the contrary, they felt even more ill at ease whenever they sat down to meals together. Bolesław would glance nervously at Staś, but could perceive no symptoms of advancing illness in his brother's face. He had even started to wonder if what Staś had told him had sprung from his morbid imagination. Staś was still playing the piano a lot and was always writing letters; in the afternoons Bolesław usually caught a glimpse of him and Ola wandering among the white trees in the birch grove. In the evenings, when Staś came home, restless and despondent, Bolesław in his turn would roam about between his wife's burial mound, the blackened buildings of the forestry lodge and the courtyard.

Sometimes he would pass by the servants' quarters, whence he could always hear laughter and merry voices. Although the nearest village was a very long way off, Malina was always being visited by one of her male acquaintances. Sometimes, especially on Saturdays and Sundays, there were several of them, and in fleeing from Staś's piano, Bolesław would fall into the orbit of an accordion, which one of these admirers would be playing. After a time Bolesław started to linger in the vicinity, to listen to the laughter and music. Much as he was annoyed by the Hawaiian songs which Staś kept playing so quietly, the loud droning of the accordion began to give him pleasure. The primitive nature of its tunes touched his soul. He couldn't write this music off as a source of hopeless grief. On the contrary, he thought, how good it would be if Basia were still alive, and they were walking about the forest and the courtyard together, holding hands. Basia would certainly have enjoyed such a fine summer, as well as the fact that lads from distant villages were coming to see Malina. Basia always had a soft spot for anyone in love, and always enjoyed romantic stories. Whenever someone told her about a passionate Polish village tragedy she enjoyed it very much, even though there was plenty of talk around there of murder, manslaughter and mutilation. For her, love was all. That was what was going through Bolesław's mind. One day he decided to see which lads came calling at the lodge. He went up to the doorway, where all the inhabitants of the rooms above the stable were sitting around. As he approached the conversation fell silent, and the laughter died away. The assembled company greeted him sincerely, but formally. He noticed that the only outsider was Michał from the neighbouring settlement. He was a solid, resourceful fellow, and Bolesław was very fond of him.

He didn't know if Michał was courting Malina. But he didn't even ask; Michał might simply have been there by chance. He might have dropped in on his way to town to find out what was new in this backwater.

For a while they chatted about the weather, and their forecasts for the hay; Bolesław asked Michał what was new at his settlement, but the conversation didn't develop. Bolesław realised that he made them feel uncomfortable, but he didn't have the strength to tear himself away from them. He wanted contact with people, and the fact that they, were simple people was all the more pleasing.

Finally he had to leave. Maybe something was starting to age or change inside him, he thought to himself, because he felt so fiercely conscious of a need for company and conversation. He passed the birch grove and walked towards his favourite spot, where he could imagine that the forest had ended. In fact there was a ditch there, beyond which stretched tiny plots of land; past these, in a clump of cherry trees, stood old Maryjka's tumbledown cottage, hidden from view, chimney and all, behind the trees. Further on there were more fields, sown with oats, and only after that did the forest begin again. These fields belonged to the forestry lodge and year after year, unfortunately, they were sown with oats, which grew more and more feebly, providing rather poor sustenance for Bolesław's horses.

He had never come here with Basia. Maybe that was why he liked this spot, and as he roamed about each evening (in spite of being tired from working all day) he often came and stood here at the edge of the forest. He gazed into the distance, imagining that the fields went on for ever, that nothing would ever interrupt them, and that there wasn't really a birch grove on the other side of them. But then he came back to reality with the thought that it was just a clearing, with Maryjka's cottage as a little island in the middle.

Other evenings were warm as well. He couldn't stay stuck indoors, where Staś was so often playing on the old, out-of-tune piano. It wasn't good for the instrument to sit in a house surrounded by dense forest. It was getting hoarser and hoarser, and some of the keys had stopped responding. The waltzes and tangos sounded awful on it, but Staś would never stop playing. Sometimes he did nothing else all day, only rising from the piano for meals or to go to bed. He lay down from time to time now; he especially liked to spend the afternoon lying wrapped in a beautiful chequered shawl, a souvenir of Davos.

Bolesław would retreat into the depths of the black pines, but the hoarse voice of the piano pursued him a long way until, turning a vast circle within the forest, he came out beyond the borders of his district. He sat down beneath a pine tree in silence. His thoughts were empty; the wind was faint and only at the very tops a restless whisper ran through the trees. The black branches of the pines gave a hollow rumble, heralding a change in the weather for tomorrow. He sat there for quite a while. As the wind dropped, he heard the thud of footsteps tramping across the carpet of pine needles; someone was walking about nearby, pacing back and forth among the pines. He turned to face that way and heard a muffled voice, but he couldn't make out who was talking. He found it faintly annoying; even here there's no peace, he muttered, and spat.

He stood up and went home. Staś wasn't playing the piano; he wasn't in the dining room or in his bedroom.

Bolesław carried a lamp from his room into the dining room and slowly drank some stewed tea. Katarzyna was already asleep in the kitchen, and there wasn't a sound from the courtyard. Evidently, Michał and his accordion hadn't come by today; maybe it was him out walking in the woods.

Never before had Bolesław thought so clearly how little his life was worth. Never before had it occurred to him that it really wouldn't matter at all if he were to die. And of course it wasn't the fact that the world wouldn't feel a thing, but that even for Bolesław himself his passage from meaningless existence into meaningless non-existence would have no significance at all – it was just an ordinary, but minor step.

He thought of the rituals surrounding his eventual death, and of the funeral, how the old women would lay him out. Katarzyna, of course, and Maryjka, just as for Basia. And would Malina come? Would she too wash his body, as she had his wife's? Maybe not, she was a young girl, after all. How old could she be?

For the first time he started wondering about Malina's presence at the lodge, what she did here, and what she looked like. He couldn't even imagine her properly. When he closed his eyes and tried to conjure up her image in his mind, her features escaped him. All he could see was the oval shape of her head and her plaits, not covered with a headscarf. He couldn't even remember if she was pretty or ugly. 'I must go there tomorrow morning,' he said to himself.

Stanisław didn't come home for ages. Bolesław was surprised, and walked about the house, looking into Staś's room, but no one was there. The grand piano stood with its lid raised, like a bird's wing. Bolesław went up to the keyboard and with one finger tapped out the tune of a song he used to sing as a youth in the army. At the time they were posted in a small town in the south of Russia, and every day he would slip away from the barracks on the sly to see a lovely girl who came out to meet him; she lived nearby. They used to go up to the loft and sleep together in the hay.

He was a bit startled by this tune, which didn't sound very loud beneath his clumsy finger, and he was surprised at his own state of mind. I'm afraid it has happened, he thought, Staś's arrival has completely changed me. Only now could he fully understand Staś's confession of a few days ago. It meant there would be another death in his house, another corpse lying on the bed, another grave in the birch grove or in town; that Staś, always such a stranger to him, with his 'European' smile, would be leaving. And once again the old women would come to wash his corpse, just as they had washed Basia's. Only Malina could not. After all, that's no job for a young girl – it's always done by old women. Nor would she even want to – it was out of the question. Who on earth would come running to wash the wretched body of a consumptive? He was going to die. Maybe it was even for the best; he couldn't imagine what else could become of Staś. A consumptive – that was the only career for him.

Then Staś came back with such a smile on his face, with such a blush in his cheeks, so like a happy person, that the gloomy thoughts took wing from Bolesław's mind.

V

The next day there was an unpleasant row between Bolesław and Staś, for absolutely no reason. At breakfast they began arguing about nothing; Staś didn't like the taste of the butter, so Bolesław called him a 'dandy' and reproached him for coming, and even for the cost of it all. Amazed at his brother's cruelty, Staś left the room as soon as possible. It was early morning and cloudy. The sky was white, the pine trees black. Staś took a roundabout route, tearing up straggly, sorry-looking daisies along the way. He came upon the courtyard from the side overgrown with scrub and nettles, which always grow around rubbish heaps. Just beyond the brick stable block, which looked dark as chocolate, stood a washtub on a small table; Malina was there, doing the laundry. She had her profile turned towards Staś, so he took a good look at her. The line of her brow and nose was very beautiful; she had lovely eyelids which hooded her eyes like flower petals, and fine, classic brows. But the lower half of her face was coarse – her mouth was too big and her teeth too white; in her smile, infrequent in any case, there was something feral, though it didn't put Staś off her. As he was wandering among the trees, he had unconsciously started thinking about her, and felt glad of a way to forget the nasty row with Bolesław. He must think that money has been wasted because I'm going to die anyway, he had said to himself, but only for a moment had this thought concealed other, happier thoughts, like a dark pine tree hiding the bright backdrop of the sky: thoughts of Malina's existence.

Yesterday evening, while out walking in the forest with her, he had discovered that on her birth certificate she was really called Malwina, but her parents had preferred the sound of Malina. Staś had assured her that it was much nicer, and that she really did look like a Malina, not a Malwina. She had laughed a good deal at that.

He watched her every movement as she did the washing and saw her arm muscles, arms which were very white; her breasts were crammed into a small, tight-fitting, faded violet jacket, done up with little buttons. Her hands worked briskly and nimbly, with great competence. She was probably washing her own and Janek's shirts. Or maybe Michał's?

Staś did not approach her, or inquire about her work or health, or the weather; after standing there for a couple of minutes he silently turned and walked away towards the birch grove, so splendid at this time of day. The birches, slanting this way and that, in places formed the nave of a church, and today the bleached pillars had an intense atmosphere. That was usual on these warm, sunless days, presaging rain, but still hot, hanging over the earth as if drawn close to the ground by a low, white sky. His mind was a blank; he was conscious only of being still alive. He wasn't even thinking that soon all this would cease to exist for him. He attached no weight at all to his surroundings. What mattered for him was 'the world', 'Europe' – as he called the gleaming corridors of sanatoria and the cupboards under the stairs where sick people's leather trunks were kept during their temporary storage. He had liked the air there, steeped in the smell of ether and the tunes of Hawaiian songs. He gazed at the sloping white birches with a touch of scorn; they weren't like the *melèzes* that filled the high Alpine valleys. He didn't even know that in his own language they were called larches.

Not for a moment did it occur to Bolesław that Staś was so good-humoured because he had already been through the worst. He had bid farewell to that world, as if it were the real world. Slender Miss Simons and the silky muslin of her dress, the sheer tract of the lake, the clouds over the glaciers, the records from Paris, the trunks from London . . . that was real life. But here there were birch trees and burial mounds, miserable flowers and an abandoned child – this wasn't proper existence. He had arrived here already broken by his farewell to the world; his final link with life was the piano hired in town from his 'sister in sickness'. That was exactly what Bolesław couldn't sense or comprehend at all. He had hurt his brother with his brutal words – when his brother, strictly speaking, was no longer alive.

Through the trees he saw someone coming towards him. It was Janek, Malina's brother. He felt a great liking for him, he even looked like Malina. Bolesław had once told him that Janek had been suspected of murdering someone in the woods; rumour had it he had shot an old woman who was picking berries or mushrooms. Of course, no one knew for sure, but such things are not unheard of. Janek looked nothing like a criminal – he had a round, rosy face and dark, shaggy hair.

He came up to Staś and greeted him, then sat on the ground opposite, casting his rifle aside. He smiled at Stanisław, leaned back and asked, 'So it was you, sir, out walking with Malina yesterday?'

'Yes, it was,' said Staś.

'Because Michał was looking for her all evening – he was so angry. Because Michał's courting her now.'

'Who are you courting, Janek?'

'Michał's very angry. Watch out he doesn't do something to you, sir.'

Stanisław laughed. What on earth could he do to him? Besides, Michał could relax – he wouldn't go out with Malina any more.

'Don't you like her, sir?' said Janek.

'Don't worry. Quite the opposite. I like her too much, and I wouldn't want to get in Michał's way.'

'You can go out with her, sir,' said Janek confidentially, 'as long as Michał doesn't know. Malina likes you, sir, but she's afraid of Michał.'

'So why does she care what he thinks?' said Staś indignantly.

'What do you mean? Michał's going to marry her.'

Then Janek left, as he had to walk his beat. Staś was left alone in the glade and started gazing at the birches again, but something in the landscape had changed. It was no longer so neutral; it had grown sadder, and at the same time happier. Staś smiled at his own delusions. But he was glad – the feeling suddenly swept over him – he was glad that he still had a few days left to live. These days had now grown in his mind to infinite proportions; the hours that were left to him until evening had taken on immense length, and every moment felt like a priceless object, a special gift.

That day for the first time in ages he had taken his temperature. It was 37.9, not so very high yet. His morning weakness passed off towards evening, when a desire for life uplifted him. He asked Bolesław for horses, as he fancied going for a drive. He fetched Ola, and off they went, with Janek driving. As before, sand came pouring from the wheel spokes, but this time the melody didn't sound so sad. Towards evening the sky showed its face for a while, pale and wan, high above their heads and above the tops of the pine trees. The drive was great fun, and stayed in Ola's mind for a long while after, in memory[7] of a particular era in her life. It was the first of the outings which Uncle Staś arranged, and this first had been without Malina. They went to the lake; flat and black, with low shores all round, it was more like a great big puddle, but they liked it very much. Near the shore there was a battered canoe, but in spite of Janek's encouragement, Staś wasn't eager to risk a ride in it. On the way home the sky clouded over again and it began to spit with rain, nothing torrential, just a few warm drops, heralding a long stretch of bad weather. Staś wrapped his little niece in his cloak and gazed at the murky backdrop of trees, warm and green behind a blue veil of rain. The horses were shining wet, and the evening was turning blue and hazy as they drove into the lodge. There was a fragrance of pine needles, and raindrops falling from the leaves and branches onto the decaying veranda roof kept up a gentle tapping, as if holding a conversation. The tapping grew denser and denser, now and then changing into a solid hum, which broke off and then came back again, like a refrain in a soulless piece of music.

Staś sat alone in his room, thinking that he wouldn't see Malina again today. The samovar standing by his window steamed gently in the rain. Michał must be playing his accordion inside the little room, for as soon as the raindrop conversation fell silent, his ear caught faint noises coming from the courtyard.

He was reminded again of all his lost opportunities for love, in Warsaw before his illness, and then in Davos, and it made him feel so sorry that he had never been able to fall in love with anyone.

By the time Miss Simons left, the snow had all gone. On the afternoon of her departure she had worn a black satin dress with sleeves embroidered in silver stars. Leaning over the railing of the wooden staircase she had cast her amorous blue gaze on him, but he was unable to respond. He could feel so much sadness and disappointment in her look that pity welled up inside him. He was so very sorry. He had wanted to tell her something of the kind but he didn't know how to put it. Outside, splendid violet clouds were gathering below the Schiahorn and the Seehorn, and the sky was cold and lilac; Miss Simons's eyes were sad. He really didn't know, nor could he have known, why the feelings that had made her heart sigh had no equivalent in his, neither before nor after. He thought he was a sort of sexless, stupid creature, incapable of summoning up the nerve for even the feeblest of emotions. He may not even have rationalised it like that at the time, but he ascribed these thoughts to himself after the event, sitting here in the dark, listening to the murmur of the rain. He was still forcing them on himself now, when he thought he should do some summing up, to refine and extract the meaning from those days, which had absolutely no meaning at all. Of course, the result of this exercise was futile; he couldn't put it right or interpret it any other way. In the final reckoning, he ascribed this void purely to the fact that he had never been in love.

But not even this idea could keep his attention for long; in mental images his thoughts went racing across the forest and the birch grove to the spot beyond the lodge, behind the blackthorn bushes, where there was a sort of rubbish heap, from where you could see the yellow doors of a brick building and the gateway into the stables, where a short while ago he had seen a young girl washing her brother's and her lover's clothes. Her lover's? He spent a while trying to explain to himself the colloquial expression that Michał was 'courting' Malwina, but he was quite unable to define the range of this word. It could have so many meanings, but it certainly didn't have to mean that Michał was her lover. Perhaps, in passing, he could . . .

The rain kept resuming its roof-top scale-playing more and more often. Finally it began to fall in earnest; fully clothed, Staś lay down on his bed and stared out of the window at the motionless shadows of the trees. After a while it seemed as if the shadows had broadened, and as if someone were shaking the leaves and slender branches of the lime tree that grew under the window.

But no, it was just that the leaves had bowed beneath the weight of accumulated water, then sprung up abruptly as they shook it off. From Bolesław's room light fell on the rain-drenched forest – in its beam the fine threads of raindrops flashed by, but the world beyond remained deep, dark and impenetrable, murmuring mysteriously.

To Staś, life amid this murmur of rain and rustle of wet leaves was pure bliss. Just as outside, there was a gentle pulse in his temples, and his heart was beating stronger. Isolating himself at the forestry lodge, closing the doors to the rest of the world behind him was a unique experience, and he reckoned he had composed an unusual finale for himself. But then it wasn't a finale at all – it was an overture. His life was only just beginning, and it was beautiful, full of harmony.

VI

The next three days, as it poured with rain without the slightest let-up, were the happiest days of Staś's life. The harmony of the world which had revealed itself to him that evening brought him a rare sense of repletion, above which rose the whisper of warm, incessant rain. Everything was beautiful, as if composed like a piece of music or a painting. Leaning its soaking leaves against the roof and almost against the window of his room, the lime tree was as well-constructed as the perfect novel, artfully dividing into branches and topped with a crown of greenery.

As he began to wake up in the morning, the sound of raindrops dripping rhythmically from the roof and the rumbling of water trickling down the gutter into a barrel set below permeated his still sleeping consciousness. Blending with his dreams, this music was like the sounds of an orchestra, the sort that plays at night. He imagined he was in a vast hall, with a great crowd of people, all listening to the murmuring of instruments. Then gradually, without opening his eyes, he became aware of a greenish glow coming from the windows, and then a shudder of deep delight ran through him at the thought of existence. And so the day began, to be completely uneventful throughout, but filled with an inner light. In the radiance of this light even the gloomy Bolesław seemed a being full of joy. Towards evening was best; Staś could feel the heat of his fever, then the weakness would pass and the pulse would start to beat more keenly in his temples. He would wrap a rug around his legs and stretch out on the veranda, where moisture was hanging in the air, and where he only had to reach out an arm to grasp a handful of wet lime leaves, broad and very pleasant to the touch. All the 'European' images, as Staś called them, would recede; it was as if he had never left Poland, as if he had been here since childhood, gazing at the pine trees, the limes and the birches.

Evening would come over the cloudy sky abruptly. The night would deepen along with the rain. No longer able to see, he could hear the rustling sounds even better, which went on vibrating in a range of tones all around him, moving ever closer, until they had taken him entirely into their possession, and he would fall asleep. He would come in to supper frozen through and drink a glass of vodka.

Bolesław would be sitting by the oil lamp, stiff, sad, silent and unapproachable.

Taking no notice, after not speaking all day Staś would start talking about everything under the sun; about Davos, the cafés, the sanatoria, the ladies, of whom there had been so many there, about the music, and the strummings of the symphony orchestras which were like the whisper of the rain here at the lodge. Over these three days he only saw Malina twice, when she came to see Katarzyna on some errand or other and ran past the veranda, pulling her skirt up high, showing her very white bare calves. In a shrill voice she greeted Staś and vanished around the corner of the house without looking up. These moments sent a thrill through his emaciated body like an electric charge. He didn't look round at her either, or stare after her, but he could feel her temporary presence with every nerve in his body. He was shivering more, yet above all, over and above the shivers of cold and the humming of raindrops, one feeling predominated – the feeling of discovery. All his travels and all his acquaintances seemed merely a preparation for these three drizzly nights, when he slept with the feeling in his heart that the greatest possible secret lay hidden there. It all combined into a joy so great as to be too heavy to carry, so it was hard for him to raise himself, to stand up and walk with such a feeling in his heart.

He stood at his bedroom window and gazed at the cloak of grey threads behind which the world lay hidden; he gazed at the uniform ranks of pine trees, as if seeing them for the first time, and suddenly he thought of that girl. 'So this is life,' he kept repeating under his breath, and this phrase, which didn't really mean anything, but was simply a way of offloading all the feelings that had welled up in his heart, became the leitmotif of those memorable days. 'So this is life,' he kept saying at every opportunity.

He felt that at the moment when he had said goodbye to a part of his life, when he had walked away from everything that he imagined to be 'real life', as soon as he had slammed the door shut on it, to die here in peace, only then had life shown him its true face. He didn't stop to wonder why he thought of this life as having been captured or revealed at that particular moment, he was just glad that before leaving this world he had managed to experience all these feelings in one, all-absorbing sensation.

At midday the rain became denser, heavier and more penetrating; one would never have suspected that behind the clouds, sunk so low onto the pine trees, there was a summer sun and a blue sky. But Staś wasn't looking for a blue sky. It might never appear again as far as he was concerned; the rain gladdened him and the cold delighted him, pervading him as he stood gazing out at the grey veils of mist draped over the black branches of the pine trees, washed clean of dust. So I have found it, he kept repeating to himself; he didn't need to ask what exactly he had found. It was a sort of hidden, inexpressible inner meaning, a sort of flip side, the inside lining of everything he could see – trees, houses, buildings and people – it was the background and at the same time the essence of everything, and it filled him with a steady, constant joy. He was afraid it would all change at the first ray of sunlight, and he nervously kept watch in case the sky was clearing over. But the rain kept beating steadily on the roof shingles, simply changing its rhythm from time to time, while the stream flowing down from the gutter into the barrel kept up its hum, loud and strong as ever. So he went about amid this humming sound, as if in a cloud of bliss.

He listened to his own breathing and kept watch on his body, the throbbing in his temples and the pulse in his wrists. Now and then he combed his hair, which fell over his eyes; he looked at himself in the mirror, as if seeking confirmation of his own existence. Then he went into the kitchen and stood by the fire, watching as the water boiled. The blisters forcing their way to the surface, and the steam pushing up the lid gave him a childlike pleasure. He watched the flames leaping from the short dry sticks that Katarzyna had laid beneath the hot plate. The smell of potatoes steamed for the pork tickled his nostrils. After all this warmth and crackling his own room, damp, quiet, grey and murmuring, was an even nicer refuge for his unadulterated bliss.

On the third day, just before evening, blue and green patches of sky appeared in the west and it stopped raining. Staś turned his attention to little Ola, who for all this time had not changed her routine and came in from the rain each day with a dripping wet head and plastered-down hair. Yet the little girl had lost her trust in her uncle and reacted very coldly to his interest in her rag doll, and in the general state of affairs in the nook behind the bed, where she spent all her time when not out walking. For some reason she had developed an aversion towards Staś; it was impossible to tell why. But this aversion soon passed before the patches of sky had changed from green and blue to deep azure, before that azure had coated the entire ceiling of the sky, before a fine, cold evening had set in. Coughing, Staś took Ola by the hand and they went out onto the wet leaves and grass. At first they were in total darkness; only once their eyes had grown fully accustomed to the closing-in of night above the trees did the washed-out expanse of the sky become apparent. All Staś knew was that above the stable there was a little window that should be lit up by now, a very small window, almost square, with four large panes of glass. Through the bushes and leaves, which shook raindrops onto their hair, that was where they went; the window was lit by a small lamp and they could see faint shadows flickering on the walls. There was no one in sight, but from inside the little room came the sounds of an accordion. Ola squeezed Staś's hand more tightly.

'Uncle,' she said, 'can you hear? They're playing music in there.'

Staś had caught the nasal sounds long ago, the chords constantly striking against the seconds, all stamping their mark on his dead heart like a seal on wax. He could clearly hear the tune of a popular song he used to sing in Switzerland, which only now, rearranged in Polish style, had finally got through to this obscure forestry lodge. It sounded completely different now, just as different as his life had become among the birches and pines, his rediscovered life, rediscovered at a moment of utter ruin. So he and little Ola stopped and looked up at the four little squares shining out of the pitch-black wall. He listened keenly to the nasal sevenths and seconds called out of the damp, black nothingness by Michał.

From now on to the very end, he thought, that tune will accompany me, in that same arrangement, transformed from a slow foxtrot into a sort of Cracovienne or fast march, more suited to the performer's Polish temperament. It was quite another tune from the one crooned a couple of years ago by all the street urchins in Zurich, where he had had his first operation. As much as there are any street urchins in Zurich, he thought, and started in a rather rambling way to tell Ola all about the regattas on the beautiful, colonised lake. But his mind wasn't on what he was saying, nor was Ola listening. She tugged at her uncle's hand again. 'Come on,' she said, 'let's go in and listen to Michał.'

For a moment Staś hesitated; Ola's suggestion was the exact expression of his own desires but he was afraid it would be too awkward for the company gathered above the stables. Finally, however, he made up his mind to go in; but no sooner had he entered the cottage than he regretted his step. They were all very embarrassed – the old mother, Janek and Michał. There was a bottle of vodka on the table. Malina alone was not at all confused. She dusted off a little stool with her apron and drew it up for Staś; without so much as looking at her he took Ola on his knee and started up a polite conversation with Michał about the difficulties of playing the accordion. Janek was sitting in the chimney corner before the semi-circular maw of a Russian stove, where wood chips were burning. On the floorboards stood kneaded loaves of bread covered in sackcloth; the fire crackled.

Without looking at the girl Staś could see her every movement, her every glance; she alone existed for him in this company. She poured him a glass of vodka and carried the lamp away to the back of the room, as she had to check that the dough had risen enough. For a while they were left in silence and in shadow; flashes of fire flickered red and gold across the walls. Suddenly Michał leaned back against the wall, stared into the fire and began to play, so languorously and so mournfully that Ola hugged Staś tighter, without taking her eyes from the coarse but expressive face of the performer. They listened to the music in silence.

Stanisław could feel the vodka radiating warmth along his veins, as he ceased to feel the dampness of their walk on his hair, shoes and clothing. He bowed his head and listened to the awful wheezing music, a truly unpleasant sound, stirring up his raw feelings, which until now he had so hastily rushed through the dimly lit recesses of his consciousness. His entire experience seemed a downward slide, and he had so little time left now before the ascent. He had noticed that he was measuring out this time calmly, not thinking about himself or his own death – it was just the world that was going to die.

He noticed that Ola's eyes were wide open, staring at Michał in speechless wonder. He could feel the little girl's heart beating beneath his fingers, and he was afraid his own was beating just as fast. He turned his head and saw Malina standing at the back of the room, in a corner behind the shadow of the stove, leaning against the wall, listening to Michał's music with her head thrown back. Her exquisite, flawless eyelids hooded her eyes; a faint glimmer of light fell on them, on her plaits, and on the wisps of hair protruding from under her headscarf.

Michał played on for some time, until at last he stopped. Staś thanked him, gave him his hand and left, without looking at anyone. Ola wanted to stay longer, so she dragged along after him reluctantly. He scolded her sharply, then at once regretted it.

Out in the night, amid the damp smell of the forest, he picked her up in his arms; light as a bird, he hugged her to him and rained kisses on her brow and hair. She wound her skinny little arms around his neck and pressed her cheek to his, hugging him tightly. He sensed that she was crying, the tears dropping silently from her eyes.

'What's the matter?' he asked.

Choked with sobs, her voice was like the breath of the night in his ear. 'I love Michał so much . . . And Mummy . . . And Mummy . . .'

Staś felt these words send a cold shiver through him. He pressed the fragile figure even tighter to him and covered her mouth with his hand. He was afraid he would start crying too, that beneath the burden of unknown and unadmitted things he would die before his time. He cradled Ola in his arms and walking at a gentle pace towards the house he rocked her to and fro. Now her feet, now her head kept nudging the leaves and bushes and a murmur of raindrops fell on the brushwood. After a while he started talking in a happy, steady voice.

'You're prattling nonsense, Ola, awful nonsense,' he said. 'Just for that I'm going to give you a bath in the raindrops, I'm going to give you a proper bath, a proper bath, I am, I'm going to throw you in the air!'

Ola was laughing now. 'Uncle, Uncle, you'll bash my head against a tree!' she cried. 'No, I'm a cat, I can see in the dark,' said Staś solemnly. And laughing out loud they reached the veranda.

He handed Ola over to Katarzyna, but Bolesław wasn't in. Staś's sense of regret and fear had changed by now into good humour, and at the thought of his brother's loneliness he was overcome with pity. He wanted to go and find him, he wanted to tell him that he wasn't at all upset with him for making a scene, or for the things he had said. He thought he must have gone off into the night again, and would be out among the birches, standing over his wife's little grave. He thought how awful his vigil was, and that it wouldn't do him any good; also that it was wet and that the moisture and rainwater were seeping through the sand covering the coffin where Basia lay, which must be a terrible thought for Bolesław.

Slowly he walked over there, thinking as he went how little focus their life had, how much time they spent escaping from the lichen-blackened lodge, how they were always out and about, how even meal-times were becoming mobile and unfixed, rarely gathering the family of three around the same table.

The damp air had warmed up a bit before nightfall and the ground was steaming. He walked on slowly; as he stretched his legs his heart grew calmer and his shallow breathing deeper. He stopped near the grave and rested his hand on a slanting trunk, feeling its rough and smooth grains beneath his fingers. But Bolesław wasn't there. For a while Staś went on standing there forlornly, trying to feel his way into his brother's thoughts. What went through his head as he stood like this at the spot where a couple of metres away the woman he had loved lay buried beneath the sand? Staś had never loved anyone, so he had never been able to understand fully how Bolesław felt. Only now did he wonder, in this place of decay and new life. And he wasn't even counting how many weeks were left before they would be burying him here. Bolesław was very strong and healthy and would certainly have to go on wandering from the birch grove to the clearing where Maryjka's cottage stood for a long time to come . . .

Michał's music had evaporated from his head; now he was listening to the gentle rustling of the trees, and he was thinking that if one could hear while lying three metres underground, would he be able to hear music played at his grave-side? Maybe not. Earth, solid and heavy, did not let voices in, and deep down a desert-like silence reigns.

He heard a footstep, then a sigh close by. He took his hand from the birch tree and touched the person standing beside him; he felt the same roughnesses and smoothnesses as on the birch bark, the same drops of dew, the same coolness – except that beneath the fabric he was touching a hidden warmth lay slumbering, announcing its presence with a sigh.

Without a word to each other, they moved a few paces away from the grave. To one side a few small bushes grew and the moss on the ground was drier than elsewhere. With gratitude Staś thought how she had come all this way after him. They sat down. Silently he embraced her, his thin arm feeling her broad back, and the ridge of her spine girdled in fleshy muscles. He thought of that other woman, lying in the grave, and then tenderly, gratefully, with a languor he hadn't suspected in himself, he nestled his head against her breast. Just as silently she embraced him, warm and moist with dew, she leaned him back and they lay down together. There they lay for ages, without moving, listening spellbound to the nightlife of the forest, to the murmur of frail birch twigs. Then Staś silently moved his hand to her heart; beneath his palm, beneath the swell of her breast, beneath her ribs he could feel it beating steadily, evenly and earnestly, as if it would never stop.

Then he got up, while she remained lying down, sleepy and serene. He stood up and felt how damp his clothing was; he took out a handkerchief, flicked the earth from his knees, mopped the water from his hair, and dried the scent of love from his face. Then he knelt down and leaned forward, tenderly wiping Malina's face; as he did so, he could feel the perfection of her eyelids, like spring leaves beneath his touch. She lay without moving, saying nothing, just as from the very outset. He thrust his handkerchief into her hand and whispered in her ear: 'Take it as a keepsake.'

Then he got down again and lay on his back; she put her hand beneath his head. He gazed upwards; the sky was pale and distant, and way up high among the branches a star was twinkling.

VII

On days when it drizzled but brightened up later Bolesław was continually on the move about the forest, never taking a break from his work, and it was the same at home where he fretted like a caged animal; he wasn't especially sad, he just felt weighed down. He was physically aware of himself standing up, walking about and eating, as if he were carrying a burden. All these activities and functions seemed drained of colour, and all the more laborious for that. His feeling of desolation had grown so much deeper that he had even stopped going to Basia's grave. On the last few evenings when he had gone there as usual his thoughts had contained such a mixture of elements that for the first time since her death he felt inclined to suspend his visits for the time being.

He grew numb at the thought that there might be another death on the way. Sometimes it felt as if the life they were leading was nothing but a dream, just their imagination, easily dismissed. He thought Staś had told him about his illness for a silly joke or to give him a fright, and he wasn't in any real danger. But the rainy days when his brother had lain at home on the veranda, numb and silent, had filled him with fear that this was the end. So on the evening when the weather cleared and Staś, in a good mood, had gone for a walk with Ola, he was very pleased and even smiled at his own fears. He walked slowly after them; slightly surprised at the direction Staś had chosen, he followed to see where they had gone. When they stopped to look up at the lighted windows above the stables, so did he, and when they went inside he was left alone in the shadow of the rainy night. The accordion music grated on him as he stood and stared up at the lighted window. He saw the lamplight slip away into the depths of the room, and reflections of firelight began to flicker across the walls and window panes. Michał's music struck him as wild and even more piercing than before.

There could be no doubt now that Staś had 'fallen in love' with the rifleman's sister. That was the last straw! What on earth did he see in that simple girl? There were trollops like her by the thousand in these woods, but he had to fall for her, didn't he? All those fine young foreign ladies whose photographs he had set up on the plain wooden table in his room were not enough for him. To put it bluntly, Malina was ugly, though her eyes were pretty and nicely set, with even brows, lids and lashes.

He closed his eyes, though it was almost entirely dark, and tried to imagine the girl's face again. But raindrops were dripping noisily from the roof, bits of debris were rattling in the gutter, and these sounds at close hand prevented him from concentrating. He kept seeing some other pair of eyes, other faces and other eyelids. It felt as if he had only been there for a moment, and hadn't yet managed to do all his thinking, as if Michał's music, muffled from here, though audible, had not yet told him the whole story. The pine forest came almost right up to the building; there were four mature pine trees opposite the small square window, and he was tempted to climb up one to see what was going on inside. But the lowest branches started quite high up, and then he felt ashamed of the idea. 'What's it all coming to?' he said, almost out loud, and drew back against the wall to hear better.

The music stopped, Stanisław and Ola's footsteps rang out, and then came the little girl's smothered whisper, 'I love Michał so much . . . And Mummy . . . And Mummy . . .' He didn't know if Ola had failed to complete her sentence or if the rest of it had blown away on the night breeze. He heard them walk away quietly at first, then making louder and louder rustling noises in the bushes, while he stood still, rooted to the spot, unable to comprehend the words he had just heard, or his own feelings.

At a calm and steady pace he walked a long way into the forest and got home late. There he kept pacing his room again, stopping occasionally at the foot of Ola's bed, where she lay fast asleep. He didn't consider trying to find some hidden meaning in Ola's words; such a very little girl could not possibly know of some awful, vulgar secret, and anyway, it was well over a year now since Basia had died. Michał hadn't gone there at all in those days, he hadn't been courting Malina then; the thought never even crossed his mind. He just wanted to know what the little girl had been saying, but he couldn't ask her that directly. The real meaning of her words would have to remain a mystery, the secret of a dewy night, never to be disturbed. Let silence reign supreme, like the silence in the birch grove, the silence of the grave.

What upset him most was that his dismay at the words he had overheard was almost equal to his rage at Staś's visit to Malina's home. All right, he had only been there for a short time, and only to listen to the music, there were several people in the house, and Ola had gone with him, but all the same it was improper. He decided to have a word with Staś first thing in the morning to point out the inappropriacy of his behaviour. But as soon as he got up, he had to leave at once for a far-off district, where from early morning he had to supervise the job of marking trees for felling.

The weather had not settled; it was rather chilly with a sky full of clouds. He stayed in the forest till evening, overseeing the work, marking the trees with numbers and trying not to think about yesterday evening. In fact, it was like a vision in a dream. And of course he was thinking about Basia a lot and missing her terribly. He remembered her buying berries from an old woman and pouring a mound of wild strawberries from a jug into a dish, he remembered her walking through the forest with Ola in a white dress, and accepting a hare from Michał, which he had brought her as a gift. Yes, so Michał did come by in those days too – but he was a rifleman, wasn't he, a peasant, someone one took no notice of, just as he took no notice of Michał's fiancée, for instance.

He wasn't the hysterical type, and he had too much respect for Basia to think anything bad of her, but the mere mental association of his late wife and carnal thoughts, or the body in general, caused him acute distress. For the first time it occurred to him that Basia could have found someone else attractive. That Michał's perfect build, for instance, could have made an impression on her, could have evoked thoughts he had never suspected her of in the course of their short-lived marriage. That she had realms of sensual existence that had never been any of his business.

He didn't go home for lunch and spent his break at the edge of a clearing, watching the wind dispel the clouds. It was getting ever warmer and finer, and the earth was drying out before one's very eyes. He lay down in a ditch, half-closed his eyes and felt a lassitude come over him which hadn't been able to touch him while he had been blindly occupied with the matter in hand. This lassitude was so very unfamiliar to him that it felt as if some completely alien element were flowing into his veins, like an injection of some magical liquid, changing the very essence of his being.

The afternoon was hot now, crickets were chirruping and there was a scent of June catchfly, blooming pink in the ditch. He scratched at the grass and flowers and felt crumbs of dampish earth beneath his fingernails, and a verse of the Bible came to mind: 'Dust thou art, and unto dust shalt thou return'. Basia had already returned to dust. It was painful for him to think of it; his misfortune was stronger than he was. Moreover he felt his own strength to be a misfortune, his health, the muscularity of his arms, his step, so very confident and resilient, even when he was loping from corner to corner, not knowing what to do with himself, with his life and his distress.

Finally, as he lay there amid the warmth and scent of the flowers, he fell into a fitful sleep, the sort slept on the ground and in grass by people who have slept their whole lives in a bed. When he awoke the workmen had got down to their task without him. They were moving in line along the young forest, scratching marks on the bark of some of the trees; the junior forester from the neighbouring district was walking along marking numbers with a red pencil and a brush soaked in tar.

The birds were singing like mad. The leaves were rich and green. The sense of composure in nature brought him a kind of solace. He sat in the ditch for a while longer, not even wondering if the work were going to plan. Nor was he thinking of his worries; he only had one thing in mind – that if he had still been married, he would never have slept through his lunch hour in a ditch, and that it was better like this, because he could stay here and keep a proper eye on things.

Although the days were long now, it was almost dark by the time he went home. He dismissed the workmen, then stopped to chat for a while with the junior forester, a very genial fellow; then the rifleman came and told him of the damage caused recently by people from the nearest village, about twenty-five kilometres away. Apparently they had sawn into a magnificent old larch but had not managed to bring it down. For a day the tree had stayed standing – the rifleman had seen it – but before he got back the next day with the men, the wind had blown it over, destroying a lot of young trees. Krępski, the junior forester, was annoyed. Bolesław drove him to his lodge, for it was quite a distance and he wasn't in a hurry to get home.

When he got back, he found only Katarzyna at home. She told him that Staś had gone for a walk, and Ola had run off somewhere. In silence he ate his reheated lunch and went out onto the porch. Just as Staś's piano-playing had upset him earlier, now he was maddened by the silence. He would have liked to hear the stupid, hoarse tunes tearing his nerves to shreds. He remembered Michał's accordion and went out into the courtyard. Janek was feeding the horses; upstairs a light was burning. He hesitated for a while, then went up the stairs and opened the door without knocking. He stood in the doorway unnoticed. His daughter was sitting on a bed in the gloom, leaning against Malwina's high pillows. By the bed sat Michał, telling her a complicated fairy tale about some silly people. There was no one else in the room. Ola saw her father, sprang to her feet and ran up to him. 'Daddy, Daddy, Michał's been telling me such wonderful stories.'

Bolesław kissed his daughter. Michał stood up straight and Bolesław took his first careful look at him. He was tall and magnificently well built, with coarse but pleasant features. He had very fair hair and a blond moustache, his eyes were small and very blue. Bolesław smiled at him. Michał gave him a deferential look. He was clearly a good man.

'Don't get up,' said Bolesław, unusually softly, 'let Michał finish the story, then quickly home. It's time for bed!'

He turned and went out, trailed down the stairs and wandered off to one side; he wanted to go into the forest so they couldn't see him, and so he couldn't see anything either. He didn't know how to tell fairy tales, he didn't even know how to talk to Ola, he never knew what he should say to her. But she was all he had left in the world. Staś was right, the little girl was very neglected. But what could he do about it? He was so busy with his work.

Today had been a day of new elements: within surroundings so familiar and so ordinary he had noticed new things. And he didn't regret it; it was as if life had been reawakened in him – it interested him. His midday lassitude had coloured his entire afternoon and evening in an unfamiliar way. He felt as if he were fighting off a dangerous narcotic. For the first time today he had had a good look at Michał, and he could tell he was a fine lad, a likeable sort. For the first time he had felt a pang in his heart at Ola's neglect, a lonely little girl, off to the watchman's room for fairy tales.

Emerging beyond the stable and the pine trees, again as if for the first time, he saw the birch grove where his wife lay buried. The white trunks stood out against the late evening sky, illuminated by the remains of light like pearls set in velvet. Those tree trunks, smooth, white and sculptured, reminded him of women's arms, lots of entangled arms, rising upwards imploringly or exultantly, sometimes bent back downwards in a gesture of submission and resignation. High up, the clusters of arms joined hands, entwining fingers, though some of the trees stood forlorn and single. Moist, steamy air filled the gaps between the birches with condensation, and all together it gave the impression of a sort of temple of the senses. The arms created a glittering colonnade. Never had the forest looked like this before, this forest of anxious whispers, of chill breezes, of wintry nights when the stars were so immense; of autumn days when petals fell like golden rain onto the burial mound, when they hung in the air in a rippling, golden stream. On this June evening there was neither death nor anxiety in the birch grove, but there was life, the forest was breathing it; it had become so powerful and unsettling that Bolesław's own regular breathing suddenly grew troubled. The air caught in his throat and his heart ached. There he stood and gazed; now and then a gentle shudder ran through the forest, the arms slanted and changed formation, then fell back in line; each time the darkness, into which these white limbs were plunging, gave a sweet murmur. Suddenly, like a single point of gold riven into the shadows, the first note of a belated nightingale rang out. It made him choke, still standing there, like a lump of ice. And the lump was melting in his throat, becoming sweet and salty, filling his eyes to overflowing with warmth.

VIII

Neither that evening nor for the next few days did the brothers meet at table. Only over a rapid lunch did they exchange a few banalities. Bolesław had taken to spending the afternoon wherever his work found him, whether at fellings, plantings or land clearances. Staś was free to do as he liked. In the early evening he often took the horses out, driving them himself and taking Ola with him; Malwina would be waiting for them at an agreed spot and they would all go out together. During the drive they hardly exchanged a word. They would travel a stretch of the sandy road, or wander about the forest, and then go home, all in total silence. If Ola was with them she did most of the talking. Staś did not stop to think about what he was doing; Malina just came along for the ride and that was it.

However, he found the girl's silence extremely worrying, as if it must be concealing some sort of ambush or secret that he wouldn't be able to cope with. While driving at her side in the trap, or standing next to her in the forest, he would often take a sidelong look at her calm, pensive profile. There was so much cheerful serenity in it that it had a soothing: effect on his nerves. And his heart needed soothing; his nerves were in tatters, at night he was having hallucinations and he could hardly digest a thing. But whenever he looked at Malwina's low brow, whenever he kissed it, his heart beat steadily.

He had decided not to ask her any questions or to tell her anything. He wouldn't answer any questions about his life, or ask any about her past. He didn't even want to know about Michał. But once he got home, for a long time he would be unable to fall asleep; he kept seeing her face before him and couldn't stop thinking that now it was Michał's turn. Yet Michał seemed to have stopped coming, for in all these days Staś never saw him once.

The whole day was filled with anticipation. In the morning he lay for a long time listening to the sounds of the house – the tapping of Katarzyna's knife as she chopped onions for lunch, or the monotonous crowing of a cockerel shut up in the creaking henhouse. Slowly his body would come to life, drenched in cold sweat from a night full of bad dreams. A shiver, then a shudder would pass through his numb hands and feet, and only then would he have the strength to open his eyes. At once he would notice the windows curtained in green leaves and the light, either sunny or dull as the weather varied. When it was raining he liked to listen to its whisper before looking at the world. But he preferred bright sunlight and fine weather. Then he felt more alive and got up a bit sooner. He would have his breakfast, then sit at the piano, but all the time he would be waiting to hear Malina's firm footsteps and rough voice. During the day she often had something to do in the kitchen and would come running in to see Katarzyna. At one point it did cross his mind that while leading such an idle, inactive life he shouldn't really be listening out for Malina's voice or footsteps. But those other, furtive footsteps seemed to have gone away. He too was starting to think the doctors had made a mistake, and although he didn't feel too strong, he hadn't noticed any changes for the worse. The progress of his illness wasn't making itself apparent. He was hardly eating a thing, but nor was he aware of any particular symptoms. He only felt unwell until midday, but he didn't know whether it was the burden of love or of illness. He knew nothing of either kind of feeling – he was experiencing both love and death for the very first time.

Only by about five did he feel his strength gathering. He was extremely happy with life, although he had a feeling of being obstructed at every turn, as if there were a barrier between himself and reality. At dusk Malwina finished work, smelling of earth and soapsuds. They would meet at a pre-arranged spot and be gripped by a meaningful silence. Sometimes the mere fact that their hands touched as they swayed along gave them pleasure and coloured Staś's entire view of life. Indeed, he was brimful of emotion, he was overflowing with a pure joy he couldn't even talk about, for Malwina wouldn't have understood him.

Gradually he realised that the woman who went walking along the sombre forest paths with him was pure deceit from head to foot. Neither the cause nor the effect were apparent; suffice it to say that the few words Malwina spoke to him were all patent lies, so much so that Staś believed nothing she said, not even things which must have been true by force of nature. At first she denied whatever he asked her. He had soon given up his policy of not asking any questions. On the contrary, the more he could tell that they got him nowhere, the more it annoyed him, and the more inclined he felt to shower the girl with questions.

To every single one she answered in the negative – no, she had never loved anyone; no, she had never had a lover; no, Michał wasn't courting her; no, she didn't know any lad intimately. She went so far as to claim that she had never known any man before Staś, which was patently untrue. He didn't believe it, but eventually such a blur of 'no, no, nos' went running through his head that he stopped believing his own eyes and ears. Miss Simons had confided everything in him; she had been noble and sincere, telling him he wasn't the first man she had loved, that she had had three lovers before him, even that she had stolen money from her father and was a bad daughter. It didn't bother him at the time; he hadn't let any of these confessions upset him. As he looked back at himself during that period of his life, what annoyed and infuriated him most was his own vacuousness. A single day in this wilderness seemed to him fuller than that entire life. He had stopped answering letters with foreign stamps. They had become rarer too; Bolesław no longer had the irritation of finding them in every post.

Malwina's lies were like a cloud of butterflies swarming around her. They were all part of that special aura that both excited and intoxicated Staś. Every day before seeing the girl he promised himself he would keep his mouth shut, but every day he asked her the same questions, which soon became a stereotyped litany, as regular as a ritual. It always ended the same way, with 'I'm boring you, aren't I?', which was met with the final, unfailing and adamant 'No!'

There was only one question that she answered with a wholehearted, sincere 'Yes'. Staś had risked it a couple of days after their first meeting – the question was 'Do you love me?' He realised that this 'yes' was just as false as all the 'nos', but even so it gave him such pleasure that he kept asking the same question, not just daily, but several times a day. What should he say, while she said nothing, as they lay in the bushes together on the damp fabric of the forest, feeling the grass and last year's fallen leaves beneath their toes? As he tightly embraced her warm, ample body in his skinny arms, as he touched her skin, feeling its whiteness at the mere touch? So he kept on mindlessly repeating the same questions in various tones of voice, and she always gave the same answers, without changing her intonation in the slightest. Her answers were like dilatory raindrops falling from leaf to leaf. Only once did she give a different answer.

It was a hot evening. Staś had been feeling reluctant to go out and had put off their meeting until late, at the edge of the forest in view of Maryjka's cottage. That day he was exceptionally weak and could even feel how tired his fingers were from tinkling away at the piano. It was a postal delivery day and he had just received a letter from Miss Simons, who was off to Davos again. With a wry smile he thought of the landscape and houses, and the air smelling of medications, as if made up to a prescription. He rattled out a tune, slowly warbling each note as he hit it – the same old tango that he used to dance to in his former life. The heat was tiring him, but maybe it wasn't tiredness that made him delay his departure for the edge of the forest. The chance of a meeting with Malina was his greatest joy – it was everything, it was his only privilege in life – and he thought of the forest where they met with immense, new-born love. The earth they lay down on was like a loving pet, a tame animal that he could cuddle up to. Malina, the earth, and the forest – it was all as if the good health he would never recover was still cosseting him. Very slowly he descended the veranda steps, looked around at the forestry lodge, dark and sloping, and took in the silence that slumbered in the forest. 'There's sure to be a moon tonight,' he thought.

But there was no moon; as he went by the trees he passed between warmer and cooler streams of air, like a swimmer between currents of water. He found Malina lying stretched out, half asleep beneath a low leaning pine, which had often cloaked their caresses within the canopy of its lower branches. He woke her and passionately repeated his daily questions, and heard the daily answers. The only thing he didn't feel like asking was if she loved him. He hesitated, kissing and embracing her. Only towards the end, when it was time to go home, did he fail to keep his promise to himself. 'Do you love me?' he said; to which came the stifled whisper, 'Do you love me, sir?'

The memory of this unusual inquiry rocked him to sleep faster than usual that night, and woke him earlier, giving him greater strength for the following day. But this strength proved illusory. Towards evening he could hardly lift his feet, but in the light of her gentle question of the night before Malina seemed quite another girl, and all the blatant lies she had told him before took on a ring of truth. He had found her to be capable of feelings he hadn't expected. Strange hopes began to take possession of him. He thought that if all this were to develop into a passionate and impulsive love, his life would end in the clouds, in wonderland. It would be a fabulous finale. But even as he said it he no longer believed such an ending to be possible; he was just pretending to compose a finale for himself, but what he really felt was that he was only just beginning, with a great deal of effort, to construct some meaning for his life – he was only just beginning to live. All his thoughts revolved around the strong, white body which he held in his arms each day; he decided that from this body he was drinking in the juices he needed to conquer his infirmity.

He thought that from then on Malwina would change her replies to his constant questions, that she would answer with something akin to emotion and that maybe she would start to do the asking. But no, she was just as before – meek, quiet, shy and deceitful. She went on saying she had known no men before him and that Michał wasn't courting her. And to the question whether she loved him she answered 'yes' again.

He wanted to change it all, stir it up and get to the heart of this frigid body, but his efforts were all in vain. Only once, a couple of days after that evening, when tired of her passivity, wanting to find out more, he shook her by the shoulders and demanded an answer, she again said something that revealed a darker side.

'What about Michał?' he had asked. 'Do you love him?'

'Yes, I love him too,' she had answered very softly.

IX

That day they had met earlier than usual because it was a Sunday and Malwina didn't have to work that afternoon. It had been unusually hot since early morning and Staś was very tired. He had walked all the way to the lake, a lifeless, black-and-white eye of water, as he had arranged to meet his lover there. At least it was far from home where no one could see them. It was there among the waterside reeds and grasses that Malina had told him she loved Michał too. At first he had taken no notice of this remark, and once he had left the girl, who wanted to stay and bathe, he trailed homewards. The trees stood rigid, perspiring in the hot, static air. All day the sky had been a pure and cloudless sapphire blue. Slender shadows cast a sparse net among the trees. The azure depths of the forest had become strangely crisp and sharply patterned. Bathed in sweat from heat and weakness, Staś could only drag his feet along, stopping now and then for a breath of air. But nothing could refresh him. Breathing was becoming torment. By the time he reached the lodge, it was already fairly late. His brother had gone off somewhere. Inside, the house was cool and pleasant. Ola was lying asleep on her father's bed; flies were buzzing and crawling about her face. In Staś's room the windows were curtained in the green coolness of the lime trees; he sat down at the piano and gazed out of the window at the leaves and trees beyond. Then he began to go over Malina's words in his head.

Altogether it had been a bad day. He and his brother had quarrelled again at table. Bolesław had slammed the door and left his lunch unfinished before rushing out. And now there was Malina's remark. There was something infinitely stupid in those words, as well as the deceit, the simplicity, the utter lack of ability to articulate emotions. For the first time he felt abased by the emotions that had taken such a firm hold on him.

He placed his hands on the keyboard and stared at them mindlessly. Then he noticed that his fingers had grown terribly thin and were extremely bony. From this alone he could tell that the end was getting nearer, but he didn't want to summon up the thought of it. On the contrary, he started imagining a long life.

Later he started to play his favourite Hawaiian song, the one that had played as he danced with Miss Simons. He could remember that occasion perfectly. Now something was starting to happen – a rare event that only occurred when he heard an exotic song. With a deep, cold shudder he was beginning to sense the enormity of all the things he would never, ever see. The great expanse of cold, green oceans, blue seas full of palm trees and islands, ice-cold and blazing hot lands. Women in ports and villages, people, people, people. All the people he might have known, or loved, or simply come across. They weren't here, and he would never get a glimpse of them now. Whenever this feeling had come over him in Switzerland he had immediately obliterated the scenes conjured up by his imagination. 'I shall have far more in life,' he had told himself. But now he knew he would have nothing more in life than the body of a very simple woman, and the flood of unknown, inexpressible worlds engulfed him to the point of choking and gasping for air. How much of it there was in one simple Hawaiian tune, which he had drawn out of the old piano with an easy bit of fingering. The fact that not only would he never know those worlds, but wouldn't even be able to express the thrill they sent running through him was even worse torment. He could feel the omnipotence of nature, the menace of its inexorable rights, its vastness and its indifference. He was staggered by its indifference to his little death – it made his blood run cold, in spite of the heat; it made his hair stand on end to think that death was gradually consuming him, while nature would do nothing, nothing at all to alter the fact – it would just stand by and watch his demise impassively. Billions of people died just as young. He stood up and slammed the piano lid shut with a crash. He was overcome with terror. In the doorway stood Ola, awoken by his music, pale and as if hypnotised.

He took her by the hand, drew her onto the bed and in a tired voice began to tell her once again about the lunar eclipse he had seen in the mountains, how the lifeless red disk hung suspended above the frosty peaks; about the sense of space created by the shadow of the earth as it falls on the moon; how the stars appear larger, more deeply set in the frosty black sky; how the dogs howl with fear in the mountains; and about the eternal murmur of torrents and waterfalls which slowly and relentlessly erode great rocks and sweep them away into the valleys. In the face of this great game of the elements, human life is nothing.

Ola didn't understand any of this, and it frightened her. Staś kept nervously repeating, 'I know you don't understand, but it doesn't matter.'

Then he left her on the bed and walked about the room, bumping into the piano. The little girl sat startled, holding her threadbare doll dangling from her hand.

'It doesn't matter if you don't understand, there's no harm done,' he repeated, 'but I've got no one to tell, and once I'm in the ground you'll remember, when you grow up you'll remember. Just don't remember in the middle of the night or you won't be able to sleep . . . Or maybe you will. People do sleep, in spite of being surrounded by such terrible things – trees, clouds, animals. But none of it means a thing, people do sleep . . .'

He prattled on in this vein, until all of a sudden it grew dark. It took them a moment to realise that it wasn't just nightfall but a storm as well. Now and then Stanisław had a strange but pleasant taste in his mouth, and wiping his tongue on his handkerchief he saw that his spittle was pink. A few drops of blood had trickled from his nose as well. 'That's brought on by the storm,' he thought.

Finally he felt weak from all this chatter. He glanced at Ola, who was sitting on the bed weeping quietly and clutching the doll to her chest in fright. He stopped talking abruptly; moved to emotion, he seized the child in his embrace. And it all ended in tears. They both cried, and along with the tears their fears melted away. They were back on solid ground again, they could no longer see any terrors, just the walls that shielded them from the approaching storm.

They heard the first sough of the wind, and at the same time Bolesław's footsteps on the dark veranda, then in the house, now dark as pitch. 'Shut the windows,' he shouted in a harsh, down-to-earth voice that made them both shudder. They rushed to the windows and shut them quickly. By now it was pouring.

Bolesław lit a lamp, put it in the dining room and stood quietly in the middle. Suddenly a stream of rain dashed against the windowpanes and drops of water lay flattened against the glass. Thunder and lightning came one after another at regular intervals. The sky kept opening, pale blue, revealing the incredible shapes of twisted trees.

'Go to your room,' said Bolesław abruptly to Ola in a menacing tone, his face flashing sternly, doubly illuminated by the lamp and the lightning.

Staś was puzzled by his tone of voice, but before he had worked out the reason for it, Bolesław had explained it.

'Fine things you're up to here,' he said.

Staś was unspeakably alarmed by the start of this scene, not because he feared what Bolesław had to say to him, but because it would be nothing but futile, idle nonsense, which would not only make no difference to his inner state but which could not change his feelings for Malina in the slightest – his final refuge before plunging into the vortex. He just made a wry face in reply. 'Well, what?' he said after a short wait, since Bolesław was still standing there without moving.

Slowly Bolesław turned his own twisted face towards his brother. Staś noticed that the right corner of his mouth kept dropping abruptly of its own accord. In the end he had to hold a hand to his face to get control of it. His teeth flashed between his lips.

'So what am I up to here?' Staś asked again waywardly, though he could feel the blood draining to his legs and had to sit down for a while. He was feeling weaker and weaker, and wanted the conversation over as soon as possible.

'That trollop,' uttered Bolesław throatily.

'Don't be so moralistic, you know perfectly well I haven't taken an oath of chastity.'

'Yes, but in my house.'

Stanisław laughed heartily. 'What an extraordinary thing to say. What on earth do you think? Do you really think a young chap like me can stay celibate? What a daft idea!'

'Well, what about me?'

'What do I care how you manage? Do as you wish – I've had quite enough abstinence in the sanatoria, thank you.'

Bolesław seemed to relent, removed his hand from his face and took a few paces about the room. He stopped at Staś's side. 'It might do you harm.'

'Oh, don't worry. Don't be so concerned – nothing can ever hurt me again.'

The scene appeared to be ending calmly. Staś was smiling almost amicably, but he didn't yet feel strong enough to get up from his chair. He cast his brother an ironical glance. 'You've been spying on us,' he said.

This ironical glance was a mistake. Bolesław scowled again and suddenly started stamping his feet in the middle of the room in a fit of helpless rage. This stamping was answered by a powerful bolt of lightning that struck in the forest somewhere very close by; then an intensive onslaught of sheets of rain laid siege to the windows. Staś stared in helpless amazement at the madman, who was glaring again and had started spouting incoherently.

'You go gadding about, you're always gadding about with her . . . you're everywhere . . . at every turn . . . today . . . always . . . everywhere . . . today . . . by the pond . . .'

Staś was slowly getting a grip on himself, feeling ever greater disgust. He would long since have left the room and fled to his own if it weren't for the strange heaviness he could feel so sharply in his legs, and which was still rising up his body. He looked at his brother with pity almost, quite unable to understand his state of mind. 'There was no need to spy on us. Why should it bother you?' he said.

'Why should it bother me?' exploded Bolesław, more coherently this time. 'How could your behaviour not bother me? One day you tell me you're dying, and next thing you're running after trollops night and day, every single day . . .'

'Once and for all I'm telling you it's none of your business!'

'Yes, but I know more than you do, I know things you don't. I know things you wouldn't even guess.'

Staś felt colder; he was gradually going numb and the thoughts that were flashing through his head were not comforting. Finally, by making a superhuman effort, he stood up and took a few steps towards the door of his own room. But his legs refused to obey him. He stopped and leaned against a small table by the door.

'Wait, wait, I have to tell you what I saw this evening just before the storm. I saw her kissing Michał – more than kissing.'

Staś's view of the world had gone hazy and he could no longer hear the intermittent thunderclaps; it had all fused together into one great crashing in his ears. With the greatest effort of willpower he spoke very calmly, separating each word with long pauses. Even to himself his voice sounded alien. 'What – do – I – care – what – the – girl – gets – up to? She's – not – my – wife – so let – her – kiss – Michał – if – she – wants.'

Bolesław clenched his fists in front of his face and staggered. That was the last thing Staś saw, as the lamp, jolted by his brother's hand, fell suddenly to the floor and went out with a clatter.

'Thank God it didn't catch fire,' said Staś normally. But at that moment a flash of lightning illuminated Bolesław's face as he stood leaning against the wall. In the blaze of light he looked very pale. Staś noticed that he was holding a black object. Suddenly the strength came flooding back to him, and at a single bound he was beside his brother, had seized him by the hands and spread-eagled him against the wall. With all the fingers of his left hand he squeezed Bolesław's wrist. 'Let go,' he hissed, 'let go of it. You'll be the one who's sorry.'

The revolver fell noisily to the floor. Another flash of lightning illuminated both brothers, but by now they had let their muscles slacken and were slumped. Bolesław gripped Staś's arm and whispered in his ear: 'I saw them, you know – there was no one else at home, Janek's in the forest, the old woman's gone to the church fair, and Michał's been waiting all day for her to get back from you, then she came, and it was already dark, so he lit a lamp, I saw them, I did!'

'It's not true,' said Staś, suddenly falling into his brother's tone of voice. 'It's not true, you can't see anything from down below.'

Bolesław's whisper was barely audible. 'I climbed up,' he said, 'I climbed up a pine tree, you know, there are pines there, opposite the windows. I saw everything, clear as day, they didn't put the light out . . .'

Staś pushed his brother away. 'You spy. It really does bother you.'

He set off for his own door, but his legs turned to lead again. Once he had found the chair he sat down in the darkness, but the heaviness had passed higher up his body, to his heart and lungs, obstructing his breathing. He coughed and suddenly felt relieved, too much so, for his head felt light as a vacuum. He pressed his handkerchief to his lips, but it proved a poor defence as the blood poured through his fingers.

X

For the next few days Staś lay semi-conscious in his room with the windows shaded. Katarzyna and Ola looked after him, taking regular turns at feeding him ice-cream and taking his temperature. Meanwhile, in Bolesław something had snapped; he couldn't even turn to face his brother's room. Worse than that, he found it very hard to speak, and in reply to his daughter's questions he emitted noises resembling animal grunts through tightly clenched teeth. On the first day he didn't go to work at all, but sat without moving at a little table in his room. The daylight was reflected in his clear pupils, which had contracted like a cat's eyes; he saw nothing and was aware of nothing. Twice he was sent for to come to the forest, but he didn't go. Only in the afternoon did he drag himself from the hard stool; he didn't touch the lunch left out for him, but went straight to the forest clearance. To the young forester who had been waiting so long for him he simply whispered, 'My brother's very ill,' without further explanation. Nor would he have been able to say more, or maybe it really was the truth for him at that moment. He instinctively felt the seriousness of the illness as an excuse for the rage and impotence which, tangled up inside him, had so completely drained him of strength that he could hardly take a step. He sat on an excavated tree stump, told the forester to do as he wished, and with head hanging waited for evening to set in. He was greatly astonished at the humiliating acts he had so recently performed; he had always regarded himself as a noble sort and it was hard for him to take in the fact that he had actually sat in a pine tree opposite the lighted window of the servants' quarters and with eyes wide open watched Malina and Michał making love.

He had wanted to climb that tree before, but it had seemed a bit inaccessible. However, that evening before the storm he had spotted some knots, which had got him up to the level of the window in a trice. He had been convulsed with fury ever since he had discovered Staś and Malwina's love-making by the lake; in the blazing heat he had crept after them, keeping at a close distance because, confident and carefree as they were, they never looked round once. By squinting a bit, through the network of trees he could clearly see their slowly moving shapes – the tall, thin stooping figure of Staś, and Malwina's yellow headscarf. There they went, hiding among the grey tree trunks, sneaking about among the bushes and low forest undergrowth, while he went after them with a feeling in his heart which he had never felt before. He had gripped the revolver in his pocket, and that was when it first occurred to him that he might make use of it. Anyway, he thought now, it turns out one wouldn't need a revolver to kill Staś.

His feelings when perched in the pine tree had not been so simple. He was watching not only his brother's lover, but also Michał, towards whom he had lately developed some ill-defined feelings and strange suspicions. Of course he couldn't, nor did he want to substantiate these suspicions, but he regarded him with a certain curiosity. In any case he couldn't identify these feelings. They were like the storm, which had suddenly taken hold of the tree he was in and had bent it violently towards the ground.

Now he squeezed his eyes tight shut and kept repeating, 'It's terrible, terrible!' These words, however, referred chiefly to the unlikely capacities that he had discovered in himself.

Three more days of relentless dread lay ahead of him. He couldn't get enough of a grip on himself to issue a single word in a normal voice. The simple instructions he gave Katarzyna were squeezed out through his teeth with the greatest difficulty, and it was just as impossible to speak to the forester or the workmen. He kept his mouth clamped shut all the time, and as much as possible, his eyelids too.

On the third day he ran across Malwina in the forest. She was picking mushrooms, which had sprung up after the storm and were lurking under the bushes in great abundance. He was walking across a spinney, entirely divorced from his surroundings, when suddenly Malwina's purple-and-white striped apron came into view. He stopped and stepped back abruptly, but she smiled placidly and invitingly. Without a word, she drew herself up among the hazel branches and was soon standing tall and slender. Then she showed him her basket full of milk-white mushrooms and said, 'Look how many there are this year, sir.'

Bolesław had never seen her so close up, or on her own before. He kept staring at her straight nose, the perfect arch of her brows and her low forehead. She really was very beautiful. He went on staring at her in silence until finally she blushed and looked down at her basket of mushrooms.

'They'll be for supper tonight,' she said. 'Ola loves them.'

He saw the blush spread to her forehead, covering her entire face; he went on staring, until with an effort she turned her head away, not even looking at the mushrooms now. The simple country girl was embarrassed. She couldn't bear that cold, relentless, cat-like stare.

Suddenly Bolesław spoke, but still with great difficulty, in a strangled voice. 'Master Stanisław is very ill.'

'Yes, I know,' she replied, 'Katarzyna told me. I don't know, should I come and look after him?' she added uncertainly.

At first Bolesław said nothing, then he spluttered out: 'You cannot go on meeting.'

The blush turned a deep purple, she looked away and swung her basket feverishly.

'There's only Michał left now,' Bolesław pitched in.

She bridled and gave him a hard look. 'And what's it to you, sir?'

She leaped up and started to make a run for it, but Bolesław didn't want to let her go. He rushed after her, suddenly feeling the suppleness of his legs. He kept shouting, 'Stop! Stop!', but she was off, and ran headlong into a clearing, in the middle of which stood a single old pine. She leaned against it, breathing heavily and laughing open-mouthed, as far as the heavy breathing would let her.

'Oh, I'm so silly,' she said.

Bolesław, no less exhausted, stopped right beside her. He felt as if he should throw himself on top of her, throttle her and shut that trap of hers. But gradually his fury passed, and his breathing became regular; he stretched out his hand and touched her body. It was warm and silent in the forest. Then he leaned over and kissed her, and turning around suddenly walked off towards the work site at a calm, steady pace.

All his malice was gone; he spoke with ease, imparting some valuable instructions to the young forester, then sat on a stump, lit a cigarette and whistled softly. His eyes didn't close tight, they just blinked a bit.

That same evening he called in at Staś's room. It was the third day since the haemorrhage and Staś had recovered a little strength now, but he could hardly move and his pale white face remained impassive at the sight of his brother. It was already dark and the candles were burning. Bolesław walked about a bit by the piano. Staś took no notice of him. Bolesław wanted to keep moving, but he was arrested by the indifferent, aloof expression on the face lying on the pillows. The only thing apparent in Staś's compressed lips was pain; that alone gave his face a semblance of life. The fact that his brother was suffering and wasn't indifferent drew Bolesław to him with a sudden sense of communion. Neither of them spoke, and it seemed just as difficult for either of them to do so.

At last Staś raised his eyelids and gave his brother a dull stare, in which there was so much perspicacity that Bolesław looked away. It was a terrifying stare, lacklustre and final. Merely raising his deathly heavy eyelids was enough to make speech impossible. But Bolesław did feel capable of speaking; he thought it was the last time he would ever be able to talk to his brother on equal terms, his last chance to ask him some vital questions.

Resolutely he stepped up to the bed and put his hand on Stanisław's prominent collarbone. Meanwhile Staś had looked away, closed his eyes and turned his stare inward; he was back to being lifeless and indifferent.

'Do you know something about Basia? Something I don't know?' asked Bolesław quickly, keeping his hand where it was.

Staś raised his eyes again in pure amazement. 'About Basia?' he just managed to whisper.

'Yes, because you said . . . you don't have a wife, that a wife . . .'

'How could I know anything about Basia?' said Staś more confidently. 'I just said that, because . . . that's what one says, . . . because I don't have a wife.'

For a while Bolesław went on standing over his brother, waiting for him to say more, but nothing happened. He leaned a touch further forward, but Staś was silent; finally he opened his eyes and said quietly: 'Off you go now.'

Confused and distressed, Bolesław retreated to the door. Only from there did he see that under the piano, squeezed in against the wall and hidden behind the lyre-shaped pedal, sat Ola. Her blonde hair was sticking out like ears of corn around her little head, gleaming in the shadow of the instrument. Bolesław called to her, then felt shocked that she had been there all the time. But she calmly scrambled out from under the piano, clutching her inseparable doll. Bolesław took her by the hand and left the room, crossed the hall and went out onto the veranda. The evening was warm, damp and fragrant. Only now did he sense how very stuffy it was in Staś's room, and how pervasive the sickly smell of illness.

They stepped down from the lighted veranda and into the night, into the darkness, which suddenly enveloped them. In the darkness they could sense the trees they were passing, and it also felt as if a gentle, joyful breath of earth were fanning them, cloaked in black but watching over them. They crossed the familiar road and for the first time in many days stood at Basia's grave. Ola noticed that everything had changed greatly since they were last here. She no longer felt afraid, or bored – on the contrary, she enjoyed repeating the words after her father. Ever since Uncle Stanisław had arrived and told her so many important things the world had grown larger, and ever since Michał had been coming to play his accordion the world had grown beautiful.

Indeed, as they stood there among the birches they could hear the sound of his music nearby. Ola felt her father's hand tremble, then he fell to his knees and she heard him weeping with all his heart.

XI

Staś found Bolesław's question about Basia disturbing, though he had no wish, nor was he even able, to let it show. Having fallen into a weakened state of consciousness he just lay still, calm and silent. All he could hear was a loud buzzing, as if a swarm of bees had built their honeycombs in the bedstead. For lack of shutters or curtains the windows were draped in large headscarves, and there he lay in the dark, conscious of nothing but his own pain. His entire intake of life had suddenly been arrested, and everything external had ceased to exist; suddenly left to himself Staś had realised he was nothing but a wretched scrap of humanity, not even fit for death. Everything he had ever done was a pointless hullabaloo, and now only one thing really mattered: how to conceal the pain and reach oblivion. It all reminded him of the piano which he used to play so loud.

On the fourth day of his illness the piano had in fact been taken away; its owner had died, her heirs wanted to realise their property as soon as possible, and without a word of warning, one fine morning they drove up in front of the lodge. Bolesław tried in vain to explain about his brother's illness, but they didn't want to know. He had to agree to give up the instrument. The porters brought the daylight into the sick man's room; the scarves on the windows were lifted and Staś was surprised to see how fine and beautiful it was outside. Then Janek came in too, and all together they encircled the piano, mustered their strength and with a concerted effort lifted it into the air. Slowly they shifted the black box towards the door, tilted it upright and carried it out of Staś's sight, like a large black coffin . . . 'Mine won't be that big,' he thought. He was sorry to lose the piano. He had been feeling the urge to drag himself out of bed one of these days to strike up the Hawaiian song again, which might allow him to feel once again the staggering mass of all the things he would never see. It was easier to evoke that sea of things and to look down into the sweet abyss of the unknown to music. It made him feel a bit drunk, it made his head spin. But now, as he stared at the open door through which the piano had disappeared, he felt a flood of other things – the conclusive ending of everything that was not fear or pain.

So far he had not experienced any particularly onerous physical symptoms, but now sheer torment had set in. His emaciated body ached from lying down, but he couldn't move, for every movement cost him a huge effort and ended in pain, spreading from his back into his limbs. He couldn't eat at all. Katarzyna brought him clear soup or milk, and every other day she mixed ice-cream for him and from early morning he was disturbed by the noise of the machine grating at the ice with a great clatter. Although it disturbed him, this sound from the hall outside was also a source of joy. The clattering of the ice-box was the only sound that could reach him, bearing witness to a great big life still going on beyond his reach. He lay like a tree stump flung onto the riverbank by the current. He was like one of the withered branches he was always noticing on spruces and pines. Now he was just waiting for the final break with life.

He did get up again for a couple of days, with a very great effort indeed, though he managed to move about normally. He went down from the porch, crossed the road and went for a short walk into the forest. The next day he whistled and hummed as he shaved, just as on the day of his arrival at the lodge, and Bolesław even smiled as he listened to him whistling. 'Maybe he'll get better again?' he thought.

But once he had been up for a couple of days, Staś had that stupid sensation of having lost something, which he couldn't shake off. He felt like someone who has worn a ring for years and years and leaves it on the wash-stand; he was dogged by the feeling of having lost some very ordinary, everyday object, and he couldn't think about anything else. It wasn't the lack of the piano, because he had managed to deal with its absence. It was some other, more serious loss, the loss of the element that until now had combined everything he saw and felt into one organic whole.

Now everything around him seemed to have scattered, like the beads of a rosary, like the glass pearls Miss Simoṅs used to wear around her neck. He was still aware of the green light in the windows of his room each morning, but it no longer shone from the inside, it wasn't coming from within him, and on waking he would push it away resentfully; it did nothing to enlighten him, nor did it embody the essence of what he had so joyfully recognised earlier as a new discovery. The pines and lime trees, the rain and fine weather had all disintegrated, they were somewhere else, somewhere separate, tucked away rather nonsensically on another wavelength of his thoughts and senses.

It caused him intense suffering. Neither his illness, nor his lack of strength, nor his incapacity to consume any sort of food at all caused him quite so much pain as losing the entire world, which was turning into chaos and inertia before his very eyes.

He was still whistling and crooning, just as on the first days after his arrival, but even then the whistling had been a way of clouding over reality, from which some new shape for the world was supposed to emerge. But now, as everything went spinning to the rhythm of the song he was humming, he knew that nothing of the kind would ever surface, that it had all collapsed and this was the end – and that made him burn with a worse pain than in his sickly lungs and bowels.

Whenever he stopped humming there was a fearful hush. All of a sudden the house, the forest and the veranda were filled with an emphatic silence. The rustle of pine needles was the only backdrop to his fear and suffering. He got into bed, and each thing that wounded his heart, each thought of loneliness, of the end, of fear, came separately, wildly stabbing him at random – in the head, in the heart, and then at once moved off to make way for another.

This was so terrible that he summoned all his strength just to keep moving, to hum, or to sit on the veranda with the others. Once when he entered the kitchen, the smell of boiled potatoes made him feel violently sick, nor could the murmuring flames catch his attention. He retreated to his bedroom, but he was starting to overcome the fears and weaknesses. Time and again Bolesław noticed a smile on his lips (it really was a smile, not a grimace), but suddenly the smile would vanish, and the expression left on Staś's face was a dreadful mess. Bolesław followed these changes with dismay.

Staś was sitting at lunch with them, but Bolesław could see from his face that he wouldn't get better now. He was horrified by the deadness of his drooping eyes, which didn't even liven up when laughing. They were eating lunch on the porch. Staś was sitting with his back to the light, and Bolesław kept casting short, searching glances at his shaded face. It had slipped away into a vague shadow, it had ceased to represent a person; his brother was dying. Clearly they all sensed it, for even little Ola sat very quietly, making large round eyes at her uncle. But Staś didn't notice their stares; he kept looking around at the forest behind him, and then a gleam would shine in his blue eyes, like a smoky reflection in two dust-caked mirrors. He laughed and, God knows why, started telling them about Miss Simons again. He had had a letter from her that day; she was in Davos again and described everything that was going on at the sanatorium. He remembered a dress she used to wear, and described it in detail to Ola, who listened, staring intently at her uncle and finding it hard to swallow her stale bread; Staś ate nothing and drank only milk. The dress was green, edged in green fur, with a short green velvet jacket to match, with golden stripes. Just like the lake in the forest.

'Just like the lake in the forest,' said Staś, and suddenly glanced at Bolesław, who turned away. This simple comparison reminded them of bitter scenes, and at the same time proved how utterly meaningless they were in view of the change of situation.

When Ola had left the table, Staś asked Bolesław to bury him in the birch grove beside Basia. It might not happen immediately – today he felt fine. He didn't want to mention it to his brother again as there was something rather affected and pompous about it, all very unpleasant; pure showing off. But surely he didn't fancy a twentysomething kilometre trek after all that, for what? Better to bury him right here. 'Won't it be painful for you to have me so near?'

Bolesław said nothing throughout, but after the final question he felt that indeed it would be very painful for him. A new grave beside Basia's would be a great burden for him. He would prefer to take Staś somewhere far away, and then not to have to think about it; he would rather not have those graves constantly in sight. But it occurred to him that he could easily transfer to another job, some-where round Suchedniów, for example, or to Szydłów. Then he would leave the graves here, and it would be hard for him to come and visit them. He would come once a year, or once every two years, perhaps. Yes, Staś could be buried in the birch grove.

Meanwhile Staś was sitting at table opposite him smoking a cigarette; a grey thread of smoke was escaping like breath and dissolving on the heated air, against the backdrop of the trees across the road. For a short while they were silent, then Staś smiled and said, 'And after my death do help yourself to Malina.'

At that Bolesław slammed his fist on the table, but then restrained himself, frowned fiercely, turned away and started stuffing his beard into his mouth, which, recently trimmed by Janek, was too short and he couldn't chew it. This made Staś laugh heartily but he said nothing more. He could feel the afternoon sun warming his back, and the sensation of warmth filling him with bliss.

That day he saw Malina again, and the next day too. A couple of days later he lay down for good and all.

Malwina never came into the room where he lay; it wasn't appropriate. As soon as he took to his bed all contact between them ceased. This did not cause Staś excessive pain; he didn't need Malwina's actual presence – he could imagine her perfectly, and spent days on end thinking about her. Not even thinking, just comparing everything he remembered with everything he had learned from this strong, quiet, loving girl. He knew she was telling lies and that Michał was really her man, that she would marry him and live to a great age, untroubled and robust. He imagined her in old age, common and ordinary, with none of her beauty left. 'Now that's what a life should be,' he said to himself.

Each day now he just lay there getting weaker and weaker, amid the humming of the imaginary hive, in the light of the veiled windows, and he could see it was beautiful sunny July weather. He felt rather abandoned now, as Bolesław was out all day, Katarzyna rarely looked in on him, and Ola preferred to play outside; she was bored with her sickly uncle's smile. One day towards the end of July, when he was already very weak and only felt like looking out of the window as sunset approached, he sat up a bit and propped the pillows higher, which took him a great deal of effort. Sitting up at last, he gazed at the sunlit window frame. The leaves of the nearest trees dangled down the glass and beyond stretched the same never-ending scene: tree trunks, greyness, forest. There wasn't a soul in the entire house or courtyard – everyone had gone off somewhere, and it was very quiet. Yet Staś didn't find the summer silence oppressive; it was full of warmth and benevolence. He was lost in thought, about what he didn't know himself; his bones no longer ached, which brought him a sense of well-being, as amid the dormant silence he melted into the summer afternoon.

Then he heard footsteps crossing the road and coming up to the porch. The steps kept coming nearer and then moving away again; he recognised the tread, which he had so often waited for over this summer: it was Malina. His heart thumped like a hammer, there was a roaring in his temples and cold sweat coated his brow, his back and shoulders. But she didn't come into the house; instead, she withdrew and he could hear her departing footsteps running down the side of the house and off into the forest.

Then a high-pitched voice rang out – Malwina was singing. It was the first time he had ever heard her sing, but he knew at once that it was her. She drew out the long, droning notes with trills. She sang better and finer than is typical of our country folk, but lost none of the pure simplicity of sound. The top five notes came downwards, then rose five tones again and soared on a high note at the top, persistently repeated with the full force of her lungs. From the very first phrase an echo went ringing around the forest, blending in with the singing and acting like an accompaniment with choral undertones, creating a harmony.

The primitive passion of this song sent a shudder through the invalid. His strength gathered as he strained to listen. He knew Malwina was singing for him, and that her song was an alternative for everything she had to say to him. This was what she really wanted to say, not those monotone answers to his meaningless questions.

The first close of day
Is my look that's to say
I don't want to know you no longer . . .

Among the high-pitched, drawn-out notes he recognised these words. His mouth fell open, all at once he could hear and see so many things. His childhood came to mind, and his mother; they were sailing along on a broad silver river, then everything went into a dream. He was kissing his mother, though he knew she was long since dead, and then he was caressing her fingers, soft and plump. The silver of the river mingled with the light coming from the windows opposite his bed, and with the song of his unseen lover.

She repeated the first verse twice, then broke off abruptly, and for a long time there was silence. Staś thought she wouldn't sing any more. He leaned back against the pillows, turning slightly on his side, so he could see the entire world float past his eyes slantwise, a tangle of greyness, coolness and greenery. In vain he sought his mother's eye, just as on his first day at school, but he could see eyes everywhere, half-veiled beneath leaflike lids. No, his mother's eyes were different – these were the dejected pupils of Malwina.

Suddenly the stream of illusions was torn apart as the simple song began again; Malwina had come up closer, she was very near by, and the notes and words of her song were almost tangible, physically entering Staś's room, though he didn't have the strength to get a grip on them.

> *The second close of day*
> *Is the vault far away*
> *About which I ever must wander . . .*

She repeated each verse twice without stopping, shifting into a slightly higher key, but returning towards the end to that persistent, high-pitched note.

The setting sun permeated the woods, flashing among the pine trees and the forest aisles, lining them in rosy vapours. Staś saw his own figure in the forest, tall as in a fairy tale, and knew that his judgement had come. It was a bit like the uprising in which his grandfather took part, and a bit like a dream. The rosy clouds were filling the forest and changing into birds, singing in Malina's voice, '. . . the vault far away, the vault far away', and Staś saw the forest transform itself into a sky-high wooden structure, over which he went leaping, nimble as a squirrel, while Malina was a tiny little figure, as if far off in the mountains, moving along the very bottom of the wooden tower, and it was impossible for them to come together.

Suddenly, from beyond the woods the silver river appeared, and he felt extra-ordinary relief as he gently slid across its steely expanse, glassy tracts of water unyielding to his touch.

Malina fell silent. He became aware of the room again; the empty corner where the piano had stood now weighed on him like a bereavement. On his lips a salty-sweet taste, a sickening odour struck his palate. Another haemorrhage on its way, he thought.

He heard steps right by the front door and someone leaning against the lime tree that grew beneath his window. He was afraid he wouldn't be able to bear the singing so keen and raw, right under his window. Pressing both hands to his pounding heart he cried out, 'Malina, Malina . . .'

But it wasn't a proper shout, just a plaintive, dried-up whisper. Malwina couldn't hear him, and she might have thought Master Stanisław couldn't hear her singing at all. But it was clear she did think he was listening, for she checked her voice and didn't sing as loud. Yet this made her singing even more intense, like a plaintive lullaby.

At the first note Staś went floating out onto the river again, as it ran around a bend. As she went on singing the banks of the river contracted, folding on top of each other, trying to smother him. He struggled to draw breath.

> The third close of day
> Is the stone slab so grey
> Beneath which I ever must slumber . . .

Before she had finished singing the same verse twice, her breathing ever softer and deeper, all the illusions had gone. The longest to linger was the sensation of his mother's presence, but even that passed. He woke up leaning against the pillows with the taste of blood on his lips, his eyes fixed on the carmine spaces between the trees. He was deeply struck by the words, 'the stone slab so grey, beneath which I ever must slumber'. And for the first time with heart and soul he could feel death within him. It was as if his entire essence had clouded around him in the form of a damp, reddish mist and was slowly dissipating, leaving a terrible void.

> . . . and the stone slab so grey
> Beneath which I ever must slumber . . .

With the last of his strength he called back his departing life, and this time it did return. But he knew it wasn't for long; he calmed down a bit as he heard the footsteps retreating. He didn't see Malina. Then, as he repeated the words about the stone slab, he felt childish resentment as he imagined really having to sleep for long, long years in a dark vault beneath a grey stone slab. And he began to weep like a child, until his pillow was wet with tears.

When Bolesław came home that evening, he told him for the first time that he didn't want to die so young. Bolesław was alarmed, but soon got used to it, as Staś kept repeating these words until the very end.

XII

After Staś's death Bolesław realised that finally his own life had sorted itself out. With his brother's absence came peace and quiet, a feeling of harmony with everything around him, which he hadn't had before. All the stopping and starting had finally come to an end, and above all he felt great relief – it was easy to work, and with very little trouble he wrote a letter to the administration asking to be transferred to another forest; he knew he was well regarded and that they wouldn't move him to a worse post. The autumn days were fine, the sun shone relentlessly, the leaves were yellow and the colour itself had a warm and calming effect. The lake, so black in summer, had now changed colour, becoming much more pleasant and alluring ever since it had started to reflect the pale trees, now dying, but destined to regenerate. Now Bolesław was meeting regularly with Malwina by the lake; there was nothing passionate about their meetings, but with every passing day they brought Bolesław greater fondness for life. Not that he was distressed to hear the news she had just given him, namely that Michał wanted to marry her in October. 'That's good,' he said, and bit at his beard, which had grown again. 'That's good. In any case I'm leaving for a new post. I'm to have it from the first of November or from Christmas, and you'll have your wedding before then, so I'll see you married before I go. Are you going to live in Michał's village, or will you both live here?'

She didn't know where she would live; either way, somewhere in the forest, for sure – whether here or there, it was all the same to her. Then she added, 'It's a pity you're leaving, sir, it'll be sad without you and Ola. Only Master Stanisław will be left.'

Staś had in fact been buried in the birch grove, as he had requested, though there had been more than a little difficulty with it. This time there was no excuse of floods – he had died on a fine summer's day after rain, when the road to town was at its most passable. But Bolesław had stuck to his guns. There were no outsiders at the funeral apart from the priest, and the whole thing had passed off with remarkable speed and simplicity. Janek and Michał had carried the coffin on a stretcher, the priest had sprinkled holy water and consecrated the ground alongside Basia's burial mound, then they had buried him, vigorously heaping up the earth; next day, with the help of Olek and Edek, they had made a birchwood fence and a short, stout birchwood cross. No one had wept at the funeral, not even Ola, and everyone had gone straight back to their occupations, because it was high summer and they all had work to do. The priest had harvests on his patch, and Bolesław was busy with autumn fellings. Malina was doing the laundry for her mother, Janek and Michał. Only Ola had nothing to do, and sat all alone in the empty room her uncle had been carried out of, which hadn't yet been cleaned. The little room seemed quite large now that neither the piano nor her uncle's body were in it, and Ola found it rather unnerving. To build up her courage she started talking to her doll. That was how Bolesław found her when he got home; she insisted that from now on she would live in her uncle's room, so the next day Bolesław ordered the floor to be cleaned with lye, the walls to be freshly whitewashed and his daughter's bed to be placed where the piano had been. A new, rather intense but quiet life began to flourish in the dead man's room.

Bolesław didn't go straight home from the lakeside after hearing Malina's news that her wedding to Michał would happen in October. He wanted to make the best of the beautiful evening, to wander about the forest, looking in here and there; or rather what he really wanted to do was to listen to the thoughts and images stirring inside him, leaving a gentle hint of intoxication. It really did feel like intoxication. Love had come out of the blue, and for a short while had changed what was going on inside him, making him quietly cheerful. But it had all started in a dreadful way.

Staś had died in the afternoon, and at once the old women, Janek's mother, Katarzyna and Maryjka, had come and bustled about over washing and dressing the body. Although it was light outside, candles were lit, then the windows were draped in headscarves again. Staś was dressed in two rather tight pairs of pyjamas, one blue and one green, one on top of the other, and it was hard to undress him. Yet the old women managed to unwrap the corpse and laid it out naked on the counterpane. Bolesław was in the room throughout, standing in a corner, mournfully watching the preparations. He was ruminating over what he wanted to say to someone, but there was no one to say it to; nor was he really sure what he should say or what exactly he wanted to say; there probably weren't any words for the things he was thinking. In any case, everything going through his mind was bad – hard, bitter and unruly. He had had enough of it – though he wasn't entirely sure what 'it' was.

Staś lay on the bed, his extreme emaciation pitiful to see: his skin, white and pitted with rough tubercular lesions, was a tight, perfect fit for his narrow chest; his arms lay inert and at ease, the hands much darker than the body. His nipples had gone almost completely black, shrunk by the chill of evening and the chill of death. His face was covered with a handkerchief, while another red peasant kerchief bound up his drooping jaw. But no facial expression was needed: the abandoned body, thin, limp and dry as sticks, was all too expressive. The old women fetched a bowl of warm water and slowly, ceremonially dipped a sponge in it, murmuring prayers as they rubbed down Staś's wretched chest.

At that point Malina came in. Bolesław tensed and took a step forward. Malina stood at the foot of the bed, wanting to stand and gaze at the shameless nakedness of the corpse stretched out before her, but the old women wouldn't let her.

'Fetch some more water and vinegar,' said her mother. But she refused to budge. She looked avidly at Staś, then stepped forward and took the handkerchief from his face; she gave a gentle shriek, or rather sigh, but very quietly. Then she stepped back a pace and started trying to sponge him with the others.

Bolesław took another pace forward and said firmly, 'What's Malina doing here?'

Malina turned around and stared at him. Her eyes were dull, almost white, with narrowed pupils; she stared as if blind, and her large, chiselled features looked almost as dead as Staś's pinched face. She stared around her and turned away, her breasts quivering in her tightly fitting bodice. She was strong and sturdy, expressionless and indifferent.

'Malina, please leave.'

She didn't answer. She picked up the bucket of water and set it down nearer Staś's head, then plunged a long white towel in it.

'Malina, please leave at once,' repeated Bolesław in a hushed, almost desperate tone.

But she went on nonchalantly drawing out the towel, then wrung it out, unwound it and covered Staś's chest with it. The black nipples were hidden beneath the white expanse of the towel.

'Get out!' screamed Bolesław suddenly, and grabbing her by the arm he pushed her forcefully towards the door. She stopped and stared at him again, then she opened the door, went out, and closed it behind her. Throughout it felt as if the terrible words 'Get out!' were still shuddering and swaggering in the room. At once Bolesław came to his senses and bounded after her. Outside he was amazed to find it was already dark. He didn't know which way she had gone, so he softly called out her name a couple of times. He ran down the porch steps and walked briskly over to the courtyard, where he almost tripped over the girl. She was standing impassively beneath a tree, leaning against its white trunk.

Quickly Bolesław said, 'I'm sorry, I don't know what I'm doing, you see, I didn't mean it, Staś is dead, Master Stanisław is dead, he was my only brother, we're going to bury him beside my wife . . .'

There stood Malwina, large as life, impassive, saying nothing. He could sense that she wasn't even looking at him. He touched her: she was warm, her body was hot. He thought of Staś's cold body, of his thin ribcage, lying torpid on the counterpane. He grasped Malwina's arms and suddenly burying his face in her proud, hot bosom, he burst into a fit of weeping. He felt her hands on his head as she pressed him to her. But he didn't weep for long; suddenly he tore away from her and hurried home, where the old women had finished washing Staś and were dressing him in his foreign Sunday-best.

Now, as he walked along the edge of the forest, Bolesław no longer thought of that scene, although for some time he had gone on seeing it vividly. It had often come back to haunt him, thrusting itself into view; meanwhile, his only conscious thoughts were of his new job, the autumn fellings, the impending move and the fact that something needed to be done to care for Ola. The pines had not changed into autumn dress, except that flimsy flakes of reddish bark were floating down from the tree-tops. He ran into Edek and Olek; Maryjka's cows had strayed into the forest and got into the courtyard, so they would have to drive them home. The brown cows were stealing their way through the yellow hazel thickets, with the boys after them, calling out now and then and cracking a short string whip. For a while he followed in their tracks, then stopped at his favourite spot. Maryjka's cottage was drowning in mists and shades of yellow, and it was impossible to see that it was just a clearing. He felt as if he had come out onto broad, open fields. He watched as the large cows, then the boys went down the sandy path. Their silhouettes were blurring as the early autumn evening set in. Peace, peace – almost happiness.

[Zakopane, Atma, 1932]

SALT

Isaac Babel

Translated from the Russian by Peter Constantine

Isaac Emmanuilovich Babel (1894–1940) was a Russian language journalist, playwright, literary translator, and short story writer. He is best
known as the author of *Red Cavalry*, *Story of My Dovecote*, and *Tales
of Odessa*, all of which are considered masterpieces of Russian literature.
Loyal to, but not uncritical of, the Communist Party of the Soviet Union,
Babel fell victim to Joseph Stalin's Great Purge as a result of his long-term
affair with the wife of NKVD chief Nikolai Yezhov. Babel was arrested by
the NKVD at Peredelkino on the night of 15 May 1939. After confessing
under interrogation to being a Trotskyist terrorist and foreign spy, he was
shot on 27 January 1940. Gorky was Babel's greatest supporter and pro-
tector in Soviet Russia. Several of Babel's short stories are dedicated to
him. Legend has it that Babel became famous among the NKVD, fighting
so ferociously at the time of his arrest that he gravely wounded several of
the arresting officers.

Dear Comrade Editor,
I want to tell you of some ignorant women who are harmful to us. I set
my hopes on you, that you who travel around our nation's fronts, have
not overlooked the far-flung station of Fastov, lying afar beyond the mountains
grand, in a distant province of a distant land, where many a jug of home-brewed
beer we drank with merriment and cheer. About this aforementioned station,
there is much you can write about, but as we say back home: you can shovel till
the cows come home, but the master's dung heap never gets no smaller. So I will
only describe what my eyes have seen in person.

It was a quiet, glorious night seven days ago when our well-deserved Red
Cavalry transport train, loaded with fighters, stopped at that station. We were all
burning to promote the Common Cause and were heading to Berdichev. Only,
we notice that our train isn't moving in any way at all, our Gavrilka is not beginning to roll, and the fighters begin mistrusting and asking each other: "Why are
we stopping here?" And truly, the stop turned out to be mighty for the Common
Cause, because the peddlers, those evil fiends among whom there was a countless
force of the female species, were all behaving very impertinently with the railroad
authorities. Recklessly they grabbed the handrails, those evil fiends, they scampered over the steel roofs, frolicked, made trouble, clutching in each hand sacks
of contraband salt, up to five *pood* in a sack. But the triumph of the capitalist
peddlers did not last long. The initiative showed by the fighters who jumped

out of the train made it possible for the struggling railroad authorities to emit sighs from their breasts. Only the female species with their bags of salt stayed around. Taking pity, the soldiers let some of the women come into the railroad cars, but others they didn't. In our own railroad car of the Second Platoon two girls popped up, and after the first bell there comes an imposing woman with a baby in her arms: "Let me in, my dear Cossacks," she says. "I have been suffering through the whole war at train stations with a suckling baby in my arms, and now I want to meet my husband, but the way the railroad is, it is impossible to get through! Don't I deserve some help from you Cossacks?"

"By the way, woman," I tell her, "whichever way the platoon decides will be your fate." And, turning to the platoon, I tell them that here we have a woman who is requesting to travel to her husband at an appointed place and that she does, in fact, have a child with her, so what will your decision be? Let her in or not?

"Let her in," the boys yell. "Once we're done with her, she won't be wanting that husband of hers no more!"

"No," I tell the boys quite politely, "I bow to your words, platoon, but I am astonished to hear such horse talk. Recall, platoon, your lives and how you yourselves were children with your mothers, and therefore, as a result, you should not talk that way!"

And the Cossacks said, "How persuasive he is, this Balmashov!" And they let the woman into the railroad car, and she climbs aboard thankfully. And each of the fighters, saying how right I am, tumble all over each other telling her, "Sit down, woman, there in the corner, rock your child the way mothers do, no one will touch you in the corner, so you can travel untouched to your husband, as you want, and we depend upon your conscience to raise a new change of guard for us, because what is old grows older, and when you need youth, it's never around! We saw our share of sorrow, woman, both when we were drafted and then later in the extra service, we were crushed by hunger, burned by cold. So just sit here, woman, and don't be frightened!"

The third bell rang and the train pulled out of the station. The glorious night pitched its tent. And in that tent hung star lanterns. And the fighters remembered the nights of Kuban and the green star of Kuban. And thoughts flew like birds. And the wheels clattered and clattered. With the passing of time, when night was relieved of its watch and the red drummers drummed in the dawn on their red drums, then the Cossacks came to me, seeing that I am sitting sleepless and am unhappy to the fullest.

"Balmashov," the Cossacks say to me, "why are you so horribly unhappy and sitting sleepless?"

"I bow to you deeply, O fighters, and would like to ask you the small favor of letting me speak a few words with this citizen."

And trembling from head to toe, I rise from my bunk from which sleep had run like a wolf from a pack of depraved dogs, and walk up to her, take the baby from her arms, rip off the rags it's swaddled in and its diaper, and out from the diaper comes a nice fat forty-pound sack of salt.

"What an interesting little baby, Comrades! It does not ask Mommy for titty, doesn't peepee on mommy's skirty, and doesn't wake people from their sleep!"

"Forgive me, my dear Cossacks," the woman cut into our conversation very coolly, "it wasn't me who tricked you, it was my hard life."

"I, Balmashov, forgive your hard life," I tell the woman. "It doesn't cost Balmashov much. What Balmashov pays for something, that is the price he sells it for! But address yourself to the Cossacks, woman, who elevated you as a toiling mother of the republic. Address yourself to these two girls, who are now crying for having suffered under us last night. Address yourself to our women on the wheat fields of Kuban, who are wearing out their womanly strength without husbands, and to their husbands, who are lonely too, and so are forced against their will to rape girls who cross their paths! And you they didn't touch, you improper woman, although you should have been the first to be touched! Address yourself to Russia, crushed by pain!"

And she says to me, "As it is I've lost my salt, so I'm not afraid of calling things by their real name! Don't give me that about saving Russia—all you care about is saving those Yids, Lenin and Trotsky!"

"Right now our topic of conversation is not the Yids, you evil citizen! And by the way, about Lenin I don't really know, but Trotsky is the dashing son of the Governor of Tambov who, turning his back on his high social rank, joined the working classes. Like prisoners sentenced to hard labor, Lenin and Trotsky are dragging us to life's road of freedom, while you, foul citizen, are a worse counter-revolutionary than that White general waving his sharp saber at us from his thousand-ruble horse. You can see him, that general, from every road, and the worker has only one dream—to kill him! While you, you dishonest citizen, with your bogus children who don't ask for bread and don't run out into the wind, you one doesn't see. You're just like a flea, you bite and bite and bite!"

And I truthfully admit that I threw that citizen off the moving train and onto the embankment, but she, being brawny as she was, sat up, shook out her skirts, and went on her deceitful way. Seeing this uninjured woman and Russia all around her, the peasant fields without an ear of corn, the raped girls, and the comrades, many of whom were heading for the front but few of whom would ever return, I wanted to jump from the train and either kill myself or kill her. But the Cossacks took pity on me and said, "Just shoot her with that rifle."

And I took the loyal rifle from the wall and wiped that blot off the face of the working land and the republic.

And we, the fighters of the Second Platoon, swear before you, dear Comrade Editor, and before you, dear Comrades of the editorial office, that we will deal relentlessly with all the traitors who pull us into the pit and want to turn back the stream and cover Russia with corpses and dead grass.

In the name of all the fighters of the Second Platoon,

Nikita Balmashov, Fighter of the Revolution.

A CONVERSATION IN ST. JAMES'S PARK

Josep Pla

Translated from the Catalan by Peter Bush

Josep Pla i Casadevall (1897–1981). A Catalan journalist and author, Josep Pla spent his formative years working as a reporter throughout Europe and Russia. Living under dictatorship for most of his life, he was briefly exiled by Primo de Rivera for a critical article he wrote about the Spanish military policy in Morocco. During the Franco period, a literary prize was established, under his name, for works written and published in Catalan. *La increíble historia del Dr. Floït & Mr. Pla*, a 1997 play, recreates the characters Dr. Jekyll and Mr. Hyde, pitting a Catalan industrialist obsessed with wealth against an educated and indulgent writer, based on Pla.

One afternoon in March when strolling through St. James's Park with my friend Vinyals, I wrestled with the idea of justice. Vinyals was in London to perfect his skills as a dentist, although he'd already qualified and could remove and insert teeth scientifically, with impunity. He was an easy-going, eminently sensible young man who kept abreast of the latest trends and sported a trim mustache.

We were walking leisurely past the wrought-iron gate that closed the fence surrounding the lake. An astonishing sight suddenly halted Vinyals in his tracks. Motionless on the mown grass the other side of the gate, a penguin was opening and closing its long, weary brute of a beak. We stopped opposite the bizarre animal and were shocked to see that the penguin had just stunned and caught a sparrow it was now softening up for consumption. It kept opening and closing the hard, elongated funnel of its beak, and, under the impact, the sparrow gradually assumed a highly flattened disposition. Passersby stopped to watch the bizarre spectacle and were quite upset. The creature toiled perhaps for two minutes. With a greedy look in its bloodshot eyes, it labored away, apparently ignoring its audience. It might possibly have turned around if they'd tried to snatch its prey . . . In any case, when it felt the sparrow was soft enough it stretched its neck and swallowed it without a second thought. A lump appeared beneath its mouth that slowly slipped down its gullet. Then it twitched its head, twisted its neck and the sparrow entered its body. Nothing remained of the bird: beak, toenails, feathers were all thought worthy of digestion. My impression was that the animal had enjoyed every morsel, for it preened itself for a moment before flapping its wings like a gypsy flamenco dancer about to dance a *sevillana*. The penguin finally waddled a few steps over the damp grass and we watched it totter off into the distance with a solemn yet sprightly air.

"My dear Vinyals," I commented as the onlookers drifted disconsolately away, "I believe we have just witnessed a performance that was both instructive and dramatic. The penguin swallowed the sparrow as easily as we swallow a sugar lump before drinking a cup of coffee. The act itself is most regrettable. Sparrows are cheerful, amusing creatures that spend their lives fornicating in full sight of whoever happens to be passing. Sparrows are perhaps the beings on the planet most prone to acts of love and procreation. Not that we humans ever catch a glimpse. Our powers of sight aren't sharp enough to capture certain subtle movements. However, aided by their sophisticated instruments, naturalists and other close observers testify to their existence. Particularly in the morning, sparrows cheep most beautifully. And, you know, the racket made by these tiny birds early on is, it seems, simply a series of spasmodic chirps of voluptuous pleasure. Their erotic acts are extremely swift and their way of pleasuring cannot last for more than a quarter of a second. They do it quickly, and not just once. God made them like that. The penguin, however, ate the sparrow without pursuing any reflections in this vein and not a feather was spared; this is the stark truth."

"You sound quite overjoyed . . . Most weird . . ."

"My dear friend, I have spent a long time in the British Museum Library today meditating on the nature of justice. I skimmed through a pile of grandiloquent tomes and every one stated the idea that justice is extremely important and as natural, say, as my existence or yours. I was soon convinced and marveling. Nonetheless, after leaving the library and taking a short stroll through this tranquil park I have seen a monstrous penguin devour a healthy sparrow that was full of life and full of love for its fellow sparrows. I don't know if you noticed how the strange animal succeeded in catching the sparrow: fascinated by a passing beetle, the sparrow had decided it wanted a nibble and was thus distracted. I'm not in any way rejoicing over what happened. On the other hand, I'm not particularly partial to displaying huge stocks of hypocritical sentimentality. I am simply acknowledging the facts. Sparrows eat beetles, penguins eat sparrows. Why did it all take place? Who knows? Perhaps God merely punished the fixated sparrow . . ."

"There are days when you seem to have a monopoly over the commonplace . . ."

"My dear Vinyals, you are young, you are a dentist and a scientist and it is only natural that sentimentality should blind you to the nature of truth. We converse about a penguin and a sparrow and you find my remarks rather coarse. But the fact is one hears what I just said about these animals said every day about people, and people are shocked but they accept that life is so. You may say it is dangerous to compare like with unlike. I'm not so sure. When cast against the horizons of eternity, humanity's hustle and bustle is as futile as the penguin's stately waddle and its acts are as absurd as the sparrows' voluptuous, morning chirrups. And if God, who is almighty and omniscient, as you are aware, dear Vinyals, condemns and forgives people, why can't he do the same for sparrows? Or do you arrogantly believe, like so many distinguished yet blinkered men, that

God only worries about beings who wear winged collars? You are mistaken. God worries about every living thing and still finds there are too many hours in the day. You are too young to have known Sra Boniquet, Adela, to her friends, now a retired widow living in Sant Feliu de Llobregat. Nevertheless, I will give you a profile of this extraordinary lady who has remained etched on my memory, even after all these years. Adela Boniquet, the wife of Boniquet the architect, was a woman who always longed for more. When I made her acquaintance she wasn't far off forty and was always on the boil. She was a tall, plump woman, honey-natured, soft-skinned, with black tresses, eyes the color of Indian ink with the dreamiest of expressions. She was known to have three official lovers: in the morning a gentleman wearing a white glass-buttoned pique waistcoat paid her a visit – he was a mere South American consul; in the afternoon, from five to six, a fire-raising, radical town councilor called on her; and in the evening, a poet and famous philosopher would drop by, taking advantage of the time her husband spent with friends at his gentlemen's club. It was a harmonious, natural cycle that was never interrupted. You might perhaps conclude that Adela was happy to receive all this attention, that she gave her thanks to heaven and blessed the gift of exuberant promiscuity. If you do, you are sorely mistaken. I can tell you that Adela never spurned approaches in the street or high society and it was relatively easy to win her over with an insistent stare. She led a life obsessed by the pleasures of the flesh and subjected herself to their natural laws with bovine meekness. Boniquet the architect was an absentminded, slightly chaotic man. As long as his supper was on the table at half past eight, he had a change of clothes every two days, and no one touched the papers in his study, he never complained about his lot. Who can doubt he loved his wife? Perhaps he had never told her so. But nor had he ever said as much to the umbrella he took with him when it rained, and how he loved that umbrella! They had the most cordial of relationships, but lived separate lives. I have never met anyone with such a lack of interest in architecture as Adela. Conversely, Sr Boniquet never found the time to inquire how his wife spent her day. His forte was metal and concrete fatigue."

"..."

"In this way Adela enjoyed fifteen glorious years of emotional splendor, and her aggressive overtures towards numerous members of the opposite sex made their minimal contribution to dispelling the dreary, drowsy pall that floats over the big metropolis. Her extravagant behavior was the talk of the town. A friend in the architect's circle hinted vaguely to Sr Boniquet that there was gossip, and, as he was with friends, he made strenuous efforts to pretend that he was annoyed. The moment he left them, however, he forgot all about it. On his way up to his flat he bumped into the philosopher on his way down and bid him a warm farewell. It was only four or five days later that he recalled that he was a cuckold. He summoned Adela and gingerly told her what he'd heard. Adela was livid and retorted that she'd never forget what he'd said or how furious it had made her, however many years went by. It would cost him dear. She forced him to apologize and added that she would *never* forgive him. The architect cursed the bones of the friend who'd made him suffer so. The second he was out in the street, his mind filled with contractors, metals, and reinforced concrete, as if nothing had happened. A few days later, in the midst of all this, when visiting a house he was constructing on the Diagonal, the roof – one he had calculated so carefully – collapsed on top of him. The day before yesterday I went to give my condolences to Adela. She tearfully described the scene her husband had provoked and, as if summing up the depths of her sorrow at his unfortunate, untimely death, she remarked: "God has justly punished him."

"What exactly are you implying?" asked Vinyals the dentist, visibly shaken, after a short pause.

"Oh, nothing very much: that Sra Boniquet had remarked *à propos* of her husband that God had punished him . . ."

"You are a nasty cynic . . ."

"So how would you prefer me, Vinyals, my susceptible friend? You are simply sentimental. You don't like to hear the truth. Whenever I try to take the cotton wool from your ears and help you to understand what reality is like, you retreat indignantly. You look the way I'd expect you to look if I had revealed a vaccination had been discovered that meant people would never suffer from toothache again. You are the victim of the worst possible dysfunction: emotional dysfunction. Obviously you are surprised when you discover that to be the case. That's because the dysfunction is rife and is mistakenly thought to be the natural state of things."

"Are you serious or in jest?"

"What difference does it make?"

"Don't start again! I *am* surprised you say I am sentimental. I rather felt I was an individual shaped by the realism imparted by my particular branch of science. You seem to forget that I am a professional dentist who has made every effort to grasp the philosophical problems his profession raises . . . I see you are laughing . . ."

"No, not at all, I am *not* laughing . . ."

"You must be aware that every technical intervention involves an ethical dilemma."

"Agreed. In your case, the removal and replacement of teeth. Anyway, dear Vinyals, things might have turned out worse for you. Your knowledge is based on the experimental method, a method endorsed by writers and universally praised. Nonetheless it is generally agreed that the results from this method are tentative and unsatisfactory, because man is presumptuous and science proceeds slowly and rarely lifts its head. In fact, my dear Vinyals, you apply the experimental method to toothaches and sore gums while simultaneously loving, dreaming, and even believing in spiritual things. Human beings harbor a confused mixture of the fantastic and the real. Can one separate the two? Fantasy may sow your thoughts with the seeds of madness but that doesn't mean that reality supplies with you rock-hard certainties. Indeed, with every day that goes by you feel your knowledge of teeth becomes less and less secure. You know . . . Not very long ago, in my capacity as a journalist, I was invited to attend one of the largest congresses on physiology to be held in Europe over recent years. Physiology is one of the noblest and most important of sciences because it focuses on the lives of men and animals. I was invited as a journalist, not as a physiologist, through the good offices of friends of mine, daughters of the general secretary of the association. This afforded me the great pleasure of being able to hear in public and in private one of the great scientists of our era, Professor Stevenson from Cambridge, the discoverer, as everyone knows, of a most significant virulent and lethal microbe. The Professor is one of the most civilized men I have ever met. Modest, shrewd, and frugal, hostile to letting the magical or sacred into his life, he spoke of things as they are and was confident enough to tell the truth.

"'Whenever I think of the circumstances in which I made my discovery' – I heard Professor Stevenson remark to a German Nobel Prize winner – 'I can't help but recall the purely random elements that created that chance occurrence. After a terrible spate of very ugly, rude maids my wife took on a beautiful, virginal Scottish girl. I can't find the words to tell you how that changed me and how blissful I felt. I like my peace and comfort but I also like to be surrounded by individuals who are physically attractive. My brain is soon wearied by the spectacle of the monstrous and can never find the strength to abandon the sterile world of moral dilemmas. I was transfigured, as they say, my brain began working overtime, my imagination was aroused and I felt an urgent need to return to my work and research. Only this ingenuous thing we call beauty can plunge us into the states of ingenuousness that are necessary if we are to believe what we are doing is essential. If you don't tell yourself night and day that your puerile scientific activity is really essential, it soon becomes difficult to make any headway. Hope and imagination are vital. I discovered that microbe within a few days. I saw it moving in the preparation under my microscope while I was recalling the dark golden tresses of that Scottish maiden.'"

"You are incorrigibly destructive and have no respect for what is noble in life . . ."

"But that is what Professor Stevenson said in a moment of candor, and I have no reason to doubt it isn't true. I will tell you something else this famous scientist said: 'Sometimes I can't help thinking,' he said to those sitting near him during an official banquet, 'about my scientific publications and professional work. You have probably forgotten how three awards have given the seal of official recognition to my activities. Indeed, the university department in question awarded me three artistic medals. Well, I shall now describe something that will probably shock you. I won the first medal by demonstrating a particular principle, the second by demonstrating the opposite principle, the third and final – the work behind my third medal that was my crowning moment – established irrefutably that the method I had pursued in the two previous pieces of work could only lead us down blind alleys.' My dear Vinyals, as we are all aware, your knowledge as a dentist depends on physiology. And if physiology is what the professor says it is, then it is unlikely that your knowledge of teeth rests on rock-hard certainties."

"I find you somewhat paradoxical and I can't guess what you are really after. You hate everything we might call spiritualism or magic yet at the same time you haven't a single good word to say for science. Do please tell me what you are *really* thinking?"

"Dear Vinyals, the month of March in London is usually cruel and harsh. This afternoon seems an exception: there is a touch of spring in the air. It is a warm afternoon, the park is delightful, and it's a pleasure to converse. I am one of the few people in my country to oppose material progress. I have written against science and against scientists and have even risked cutting a ridiculous figure when stating what I thought was the truth. However, years have gone by and I believe I now see everything in a clearer light. I do regret writing those things not because science, in the meantime, has made any giant steps forward. Science always remains more or less where it was. Its findings are trifling in the extreme. I will go further: science very rarely produces a clear-cut result. Nevertheless I don't wish to imply that one should speak of the poverty of science. Dear Vinyals, I believe it's not the results of a particular science that count, it is the attitude behind them. True, it is hard not to see scientists as self-caricatures. They are typically bad-tempered, aging gentlemen who set out to climb the Alps clutching a box of flea poison. But that is the nature of the beast. Scientists unflinchingly challenge mystery and its lowest sentimental forms, and this is what makes them great. It is in humanity's interest to destroy what is vulgar, magical, and senti- mental. History demonstrates that one of the most uncontrollable sources of human sorrow is mystery and unreality. Men and women kill and torture each other for fantasies that aren't worth a pipeful of tobacco. The most basic form of magic foments tyranny, and sentimentality hallows our rankest ignorance. This is why I like science although I don't think it will ever get anywhere, and why I like scientists themselves, even though they wander miserably in the wilderness. But science never holds anything back, everything is wide-open. And that is what I believe to be essential."

"Do you believe such things are so important? I would never have said . . ."

"Vinyals, dear Vinyals the dentist, these things *are* what is really important and what has always excited me. If you think for a moment with a modicum of insight, you will understand and I won't need to explain further. If you reflect on what has most influenced you in the course of your life, you will soon realize that it is shot through with sentimentality and vulgar errors. The most intelligent men can, with the utmost difficulty, shed that baggage. In my travels through the world, I have met one really outstanding man. I refer to Professor Turull the renowned writer and accomplished humanist. Physically he was yellow as tallow and thin as a rake. You'd often see him in bookshops and if you ever conversed with him he came across as good natured and mild, although he possessed that acid, stubbornly sardonic manner intellectuals often have. He was very studious and worked tirelessly. He wrote very well, in a style that was fluent, elegant, lapidary, and taut. His huge memory seemed to encompass the most vivid recre- ation of the ancient world, one that was not seen through rose-tinted glasses, but a much more complex vision that included the murky areas where anguish and passion rub shoulders. He embellished this knowledge with vast humanist erudition, erudition that enabled him to live a tranquil life and fill his days with scientific order and wise conversation. He was poor, wore a shiny black jacket, threadbare pants, and his knobbly knees and elbows stuck out like lumps of pig iron. He was always short of money and spent his life begging and writing highly obsequious letters to people in high places. He liked to eat well and would turn pale and twitch his fat nose at the bouquet from a glass of vintage wine. He had a traditional kind of maid and when he had the money she cooked him a range of exquisite dishes. I have never ever eaten Catalan-style broad beans with so much relish and insight as in the dining room of that celebrated and erudite professor. Moreover, he always followed up with delicious coffee and, generally speaking, liqueurs and tobacco that showed his excellent taste. He was a civilized man."

" . . ."

"It would be an understatement to say that his ability to cope with everyday life was practically non-existent: he was literally hopeless. By the time I got to know him he'd been living beyond his means for years. He really had no clear idea about what he earned and what he spent. His entire economic activity was devoted to plugging the holes that kept appearing. It was hardly a pleasant way to live. When he started out as a teacher, however, though he had his fair share of headaches and wasted lots of time, he managed to keep up appearances. But as time passed the burden became increasingly onerous and his life became highly disagreeable. His debts started to pile up, innumerable small debts not even he could keep track of, but all together they represented a sum that was too much for the almost impecunious life of that innocent abroad. Scattered around his neighborhood, his debtors were strident and were always trying to pin him down: he owed shopkeepers who were naturally and respectably greedy. The time came when his situation became untenable, and Dr. Turull was pitched into an implacable struggle with his creditors that threatened to choke him. He had to learn all the strategies of the recalcitrant debtor: fake entrances and exits, skill in wriggling out of tight corners, and expertise in formulating the necessary, firm-sounding promises that were devoid of any real substance. Apart from the time one can waste on such wrangles and their intolerable side effects, they have a particularly malign impact in that they embitter the most evenly keeled of temperaments. Heading the professor's queue of creditors was a tall, skinny, hyperactive woman whose skin was the sallow hue of people with jaundice. The professor had put that woman in charge of the upkeep of his underwear – the washing and ironing thereof – and this labor had accrued a debt of three hundred and eighty pesetas. The professor couldn't believe the little she had washed and ironed could have spawned such a large debt. But that was only because Dr. Turull possessed the *vaguest* notion of time: the woman had been washing his underwear for years. According to the professor's housecleaner, the bill was perfectly in order, indeed rather generous, and on the low side. As a bill it simply shared the principal defect of all bills: it had to be paid. The lady became tired of promises and decided she must collect. She spoke to all his creditors and agitated tirelessly. She managed to persuade them to act in concert, and after much coming and going they hired a lively, vociferous young lawyer. Dr. Turull was shortly summonsed to court. The episode had immediate repercussions in academic circles and the world of intellectuals. The professor believed momentarily that the speed at which the situation was deteriorating might lead to a solution in the sense that he lived in hope of a helping hand that would materialize and save him from infamy. But no such hand appeared and he simply confronted sullen, aggressive warnings that constituted *de facto* threats. Professor Turull could see he was done for. Crestfallen, more dead than alive, wiping the sweat from his face – now the color of sodden parchment – he exclaimed in a strained, low-key voice, as if completely sure of himself: 'God will punish this evil woman . . .'"

"That old refrain, that old refrain!" said the dentist, wearily.

"I simply want to demonstrate, my dear Vinyals, that if a man as strong and as knowledgeable as Professor Turull can get it wrong, it is because sentimentality and erroneous habits flow in our blood. Traditions of magic and the supernatural wield such an influence in this world that it is an uphill struggle not to lose one's grip on reality. Individuals who strive to base their lives firmly in reality and eliminate fantastic explanations – which are legion – of why humanity suffers so are dubbed cynical charlatans and denied what people call their daily bread. Our ideas are completely paradoxical on this front. Some people's waywardness enables them to defend contemporary notions of morality only a few days after the end of a war that has led twelve million men to the slaughter, in the flower of their youth, for no point whatsoever. We are possessed by the narcissism of idiots. We discredit an astronomer who is a few seconds out in his calculations of the movements of a quite ordinary star and don't show the slightest contempt for the people who plan a war and cut down men's lives as if they were reaping a field of corn. My dear Vinyals, nobody can say I don't combat the influence of magic and fantasy. I do what I can – which is very little – but you find that tedious."

On that note we reached the end of the park. We heard Big Ben striking four o'clock. The white esplanade of Admiralty Arch in Whitehall stretched before us. We could see the Horse Guards, in their red and white uniforms, against a background of muted chamois-colored stone. On both sides, and in the distance, the characteristic pearl-gray outline of this part of London: the domes, roofs, and large buildings of State. There is nothing grandiose about their jagged profile, but everything is severe and imposing. Dusk was descending. Behind us patches of purple and faded pink in the pristine air of the park stood out against a bluish backdrop. The atmosphere was a subtle blue, and the fine mist cloaked everything in haze. We stood and gaped for a moment, in awe.

"What is that building, Sr Pla?" asked Vinyals the dentist.

"The building with the large radio aerial hoops hanging over its roof is, I believe, the Admiralty."

"And the other building to its right?"

"That palace with the austere, classical lines is the Foreign Office. *El Ministeri de Negocis Estrangers,* if you'd prefer it in low Latin. I see you like the sound of that and even find it slightly exciting. It has the same effect on me, dear Vinyals. The two buildings we see on either side of that murky esplanade are perhaps the two most important in the world. It is one place in the world where people quite naturally doff their hats when they walk past. I don't know if you understand what . . ."

"I understand you perfectly . . . so what do you want to do now?"

"At this time of day the level of noise and bustle in London is deafening, and I must confess I feel rather tired. If you like, we can return to the park and slowly make our way home. You can't imagine how I love to walk through this charming mist and watch reality fade and melt away. Everything is so fragile and the air is like a feather pillow. It is uniquely delightful . . ."

We retraced our steps following the fence around the banks of the lake. Waterfowl were still swimming like shadows over the hazy water. A duck occasionally flew up, its wings beating the weary, twilight air. There were scant passersby. Beyond the trees in the park, car headlights projected a diffuse, gleaming light on the Mall. You could hear the hubbub of the huge, amorphous, distant city. The buzz of big cities has always made me feel deeply depressed. The noise makes me think how futile everything is. I find it oppressive and feel lost there like a speck of mud in the ocean. We suddenly saw a white shadow looming strangely on the other side of the fence. We approached, intrigued, and saw it was a penguin and a bigger specimen than the earlier one. That monster of a bird seemed rooted to the spot and was endlessly opening and closing its long mouth. I thought it was holding a gray, extremely flattened object in its beak. I recalled the battered sparrow from two hours ago. No doubt about it. It was a similar item.

"My dear Vinyals," I said to my companion after contemplating that unpleasant spectacle for a moment. "My dear friend, it is not a mirage: another sparrow has bit the dust. Those monstrous birds aren't stuffed and they never stop . . ."

The penguin was conscientiously going about its business. It slowly opened and closed its mouth and the bones in its beak crunched when they came together like pebbles colliding. You could see its bloodshot, demon eyes in the dark. When the sparrow had turned into soft pulp, the penguin lifted its long neck, twisted, and swallowed. Then, once it was inside its body, the penguin started flapping its short wings as if dancing a *sevillana*. Finally, with its neck hobbling on its slight shoulders, it disappeared into the mist, eyes half-closed, exhausted beak thrust forward, walking at a solemn gait. The dentist was sad. It was almost dark, but the mist charged the air with a luminous spongy texture. I took his arm and we walked on.

"My dear Vinyals," I said after we'd walked in silence for a while, "the penguins and sparrows in St. James's Park have ruined our afternoon. We have witnessed the victory of penguins and the wretched defeat of sparrows. The spectacle, I must confess, was not without interest. Not a feather or toenail of the bird was spared. The poor creature's big brothers and sisters must be feeling fragile. Sparrows are such animated little animals! They spend their lives in full view of the public, inspiring tenderness in lovers and loving non-stop themselves. We can't see how they love one another, but naturalists seem well informed on the subject and report on it in their books. This recent victim was probably a late-riser who wanted to make the most of the final flicker of daylight to enjoy one last fling. The penguin gobbled it down, teeth flashing – to use a zoologically exaggerated image – and that was that. I think the moment has come for us both to repeat what Adela Boniquet and Professor Turull exclaimed in similar circumstances: 'God has justly punished . . . !'"

"That refrain again, dear Pla? You never tire, never give up . . ."

"Vinyals, I'm glad to hear you protest. I put things as best as I can. When I talk about serious matters, I tend to become rather entangled and convoluted. You've just seen me. I won't give up, however. Only a minority of intelligent people has grasped that God does *not* punish sparrows . . ."

THE LIBRARY OF BABEL

Jorge Luis Borges

Translated from the Spanish by Andrew Hurley

Jorge Francisco Isidoro Luis Borges Acevedo (1899–1986) was an Argentine short-story writer, essayist, poet and translator, and a key figure in Spanish-language literature. His best-known books, *Ficciones* (Fictions) and *El Aleph* (The Aleph), published in the 1940s, are compilations of short stories interconnected by common themes, including dreams, labyrinths, libraries, mirrors, fictional writers, philosophy, and religion. Before Borges became one of the famous writers in the world, he had to begin his career by writing advertisements for yogurt. His longest work of fiction is a fourteen-page story, "The Congress". Mick Jagger's 1970 movie *Performance* is inspired by the works of Borges; his name is quoted several times throughout the movie. Irked by the fact he was never awarded the Nobel Prize, some observers speculate that Borges did not receive the award because of his conservative political views, or, more specifically, because he had accepted an honour from Chilean dictator Augusto Pinochet.

> By this art you may contemplate the variation of the 23 letters...
> *Anatomy of Melancholy, Pt. 2, Sec. II, Mem. IV*

The universe (which others call the Library) is composed of an indefinite, perhaps infinite number of hexagonal galleries. In the center of each gallery is a ventilation shaft, bounded by a low railing. From any hexagon one can see the floors above and below—one after another, endlessly. The arrangement of the galleries is always the same: Twenty bookshelves, five to each side, line four of the hexagon's six sides; the height of the bookshelves, floor to ceiling, is hardly greater than the height of a normal librarian. One of the hexagon's free sides opens onto a narrow sort of vestibule, which in turn opens onto another gallery, identical to the first—identical in fact to all. To the left and right of the vestibule are two tiny compartments. One is for sleeping, upright; the other, for satisfying one's physical necessities. Through this space, too, there passes a spiral staircase, which winds upward and downward into the remotest distance. In the vestibule there is a mirror, which faithfully duplicates appearances. Men often infer from this mirror that the Library is not infinite—if it were, what need would there be for that illusory replication? I prefer to dream that burnished surfaces are a figuration and promise of the infinite....Light is provided by certain spherical fruits that bear the name "bulbs." There are two of these bulbs in each hexagon, set crosswise. The light they give is insufficient, and unceasing.

Like all the men of the Library, in my younger days I traveled; I have journeyed in quest of a book, perhaps the catalog of catalogs. Now that my eyes can hardly make out what I myself have written, I am preparing to die, a few leagues from the hexagon where I was born. When I am dead, compassionate hands will throw me over the railing; my tomb will be the unfathomable air, my body will sink for ages, and will decay and dissolve in the wind engendered by my fall, which shall be infinite. I declare that the Library is endless. Idealists argue that the hexagonal rooms are the necessary shape of absolute space, or at least of our *perception* of space. They argue that a triangular or pentagonal chamber is inconceivable. (Mystics claim that their ecstasies reveal to them a circular chamber containing an enormous circular book with a continuous spine that goes completely around the walls. But their testimony is suspect, their words obscure. That cyclical book is God.) Let it suffice for the moment that I repeat the classic dictum: *The Library is a sphere whose exact center is any hexagon and whose circumference is unattainable.*

Each wall of each hexagon is furnished with five bookshelves; each bookshelf holds thirty-two books identical in format; each book contains four hundred ten pages; each page, forty lines; each line, approximately eighty black letters. There are also letters on the front cover of each book; those letters neither indicate nor prefigure what the pages inside will say. I am aware that that lack of correspondence once struck men as mysterious. Before summarizing the solution of the mystery (whose discovery, in spite of its tragic consequences, is perhaps the most important event in all history), I wish to recall a few axioms.

First: *The Library has existed* ab aeternitate. That truth, whose immediate corollary is the future eternity of the world, no rational mind can doubt. Man, the imperfect librarian, may be the work of chance or of malevolent demiurges; the universe, with its elegant appointments—its bookshelves, its enigmatic books, its indefatigable staircases for the traveler, and its water closets for the seated librarian—can only be the handiwork of a god. In order to grasp the distance that separates the human and the divine, one has only to compare these crude trembling symbols which my fallible hand scrawls on the cover of a book with the organic letters inside—neat, delicate, deep black, and inimitably symmetrical.

Second: *There are twenty-five orthographic symbols.*[1] That discovery enabled mankind, three hundred years ago, to formulate a general theory of the Library and thereby satisfactorily solve the riddle that no conjecture had been able to divine—the formless and chaotic nature of virtually all books. One book, which my father once saw in a hexagon in circuit 15–94, consisted of the letters M C V perversely repeated from the first line to the last. Another (much consulted in this zone) is a mere labyrinth of letters whose penultimate page contains the phrase O *Time thy pyramids.* This much is known: For every rational line or forthright statement there are leagues of senseless cacophony, verbal nonsense,

---

1 The original manuscript has neither numbers nor capital letters; punctuation is limited to the comma and the period. Those two marks, the space, and the twenty-two letters of the alphabet are the twenty-five sufficient symbols that our unknown author is referring to. [Ed. note.]

and incoherency. (I know of one semibarbarous zone whose librarians repudiate the "vain and superstitious habit" of trying to find sense in books, equating such a quest with attempting to find meaning in dreams or in the chaotic lines of the palm of one's hand. . . .They will acknowledge that the inventors of writing imitated the twenty-five natural symbols, but contend that that adoption was fortuitous, coincidental, and that books in themselves have no meaning. That argument, as we shall see, is not entirely fallacious.)

For many years it was believed that those impenetrable books were in ancient or far-distant languages. It is true that the most ancient peoples, the first librarians, employed a language quite different from the one we speak today; it is true that a few miles to the right, our language devolves into dialect and that ninety floors above, it becomes incomprehensible. All of that, I repeat, is true— but four hundred ten pages of unvarying M C V's cannot belong to any language, however dialectal or primitive it may be. Some have suggested that each letter influences the next, and that the value of M C V on page 71, line 3, is not the value of the same series on another line of another page, but that vague thesis has not met with any great acceptance. Others have mentioned the possibility of codes; that conjecture has been universally accepted, though not in the sense in which its originators formulated it.

Some five hundred years ago, the chief of one of the upper hexagons[2] came across a book as jumbled as all the others, but containing almost two pages of homogeneous lines. He showed his find to a traveling decipherer, who told him that the lines were written in Portuguese; others said it was Yiddish. Within the century experts had determined what the language actually was: a Samoyed-Lithuanian dialect of Guaraní, with inflections from classical Arabic. The content was also determined: the rudiments of combinatory analysis, illustrated with examples of endlessly repeating variations. Those examples allowed a librarian of genius to discover the fundamental law of the Library. This philosopher observed that all books, however different from one another they might be, consist of identical elements: the space, the period, the comma, and the twenty-two letters of the alphabet. He also posited a fact which all travelers have since confirmed: *In all the Library, there are no two identical books.* From those incontrovertible premises, the librarian deduced that the Library is "total"—perfect, complete, and whole—and that its bookshelves contain all possible combinations of the twenty-two orthographic symbols (a number which, though unimaginably vast, is not infinite)—that is, all that is able to be expressed, in every language. *All*—the detailed history of the future, the autobiographies of the archangels, the faithful catalog of the Library, thousands and thousands of false catalogs, the proof of the falsity of those false catalogs, a proof of the falsity of the *true* catalog, the gnostic gospel of Basilides, the commentary upon that gospel, the commentary on the commentary on that gospel, the true story of your death, the translation of every book into every language, the interpolations of every book into all books,

2 In earlier times, there was one man for every three hexagons. Suicide and diseases of the lung have played havoc with that proportion. An unspeakably melancholy memory: I have sometimes traveled for nights on end, down corridors and polished staircases, without coming across a single librarian.

the treatise Bede could have written (but did not) on the mythology of the Saxon people, the lost books of Tacitus.

When it was announced that the Library contained all books, the first reaction was unbounded joy. All men felt themselves the possessors of an intact and secret treasure. There was no personal problem, no world problem, whose eloquent solution did not exist—somewhere in some hexagon. The universe was justified; the universe suddenly became congruent with the unlimited width and breadth of humankind's hope. At that period there was much talk of The Vindications— books of *apologiæ* and prophecies that would vindicate for all time the actions of every person in the universe and that held wondrous arcana for men's futures. Thousands of greedy individuals abandoned their sweet native hexagons and rushed downstairs, upstairs, spurred by the vain desire to find their Vindication. These pilgrims squabbled in the narrow corridors, muttered dark imprecations, strangled one another on the divine staircases, threw deceiving volumes down ventilation shafts, were themselves hurled to their deaths by men of distant regions. Others went insane. . . .The Vindications do exist (I have seen two of them, which refer to persons in the future, persons perhaps not imaginary), but those who went in quest of them failed to recall that the chance of a man's finding his own Vindication, or some perfidious version of his own, can be calculated to be zero.

At that same period there was also hope that the fundamental mysteries of mankind—the origin of the Library and of time—might be revealed. In all likelihood those profound mysteries can indeed be explained in words; if the language of the philosophers is not sufficient, then the multiform Library must surely have produced the extraordinary language that is required, together with the words and grammar of that language. For four centuries, men have been scouring the hexagons. . . .There are official searchers, the "inquisitors." I have seen them about their tasks: they arrive exhausted at some hexagon, they talk about a staircase that nearly killed them—some steps were missing—they speak with the librarian about galleries and staircases, and, once in a while, they take up the nearest book and leaf through it, searching for disgraceful or dishonorable words. Clearly, no one expects to discover anything.

That unbridled hopefulness was succeeded, naturally enough, by a similarly disproportionate depression. The certainty that some bookshelf in some hexagon contained precious books, yet that those precious books were forever out of reach, was almost unbearable. One blasphemous sect proposed that the searches be discontinued and that all men shuffle letters and symbols until those canonical books, through some improbable stroke of chance, had been constructed. The authorities were forced to issue strict orders. The sect disappeared, but in my childhood I have seen old men who for long periods would hide in the latrines with metal disks and a forbidden dice cup, feebly mimicking the divine disorder.

Others, going about it in the opposite way, thought the first thing to do was eliminate all worthless books. They would invade the hexagons, show credentials that were not always false, leaf disgustedly through a volume, and condemn entire walls of books. It is to their hygienic, ascetic rage that we lay the senseless loss of millions of volumes. Their name is execrated today, but those who grieve over the "treasures" destroyed in that frenzy overlook two widely acknowledged facts: One, that the Library is so huge that any reduction by human hands must be infinitesimal. And two, that each book is unique and irreplaceable, but (since the Library is total) there are always several hundred thousand imperfect facsimiles—books that differ by no more than a single letter, or a comma. Despite general opinion, I daresay that the consequences of the depredations committed by the Purifiers have been exaggerated by the horror those same fanatics inspired. They were spurred on by the holy zeal to reach—someday, through unrelenting effort—the books of the Crimson Hexagon—books smaller than natural books, books omnipotent, illustrated, and magical.

We also have knowledge of another superstition from that period: belief in what was termed the Book-Man. On some shelf in some hexagon, it was argued, there must exist a book that is the cipher and perfect compendium *of all other books,* and some librarian must have examined that book; this librarian is analogous to a god. In the language of this zone there are still vestiges of the sect that worshiped that distant librarian. Many have gone in search of Him. For a hundred years, men beat every possible path—and every path in vain. How was one to locate the idolized secret hexagon that sheltered Him? Someone proposed searching by regression: To locate book A, first consult book B, which tells where book A can be found; to locate book B, first consult book C, and so on, to infinity. . . .It is in ventures such as these that I have squandered and spent my years. I cannot think it unlikely that there is such a total book[3] on some shelf in the universe. I pray to the unknown gods that some man—even a single man, tens of centuries ago—has perused and read that book. If the honor and wisdom and joy of such a reading are not to be my own, then let them be for others. Let heaven exist, though my own place be in hell. Let me be tortured and battered and annihilated, but let there be one instant, one creature, wherein thy enormous Library may find its justification.

Infidels claim that the rule in the Library is not "sense," but "non-sense," and that "rationality" (even humble, pure coherence) is an almost miraculous exception. They speak, I know, of "the feverish Library, whose random volumes constantly threaten to transmogrify into others, so that they affirm all things, deny all things, and confound and confuse all things, like some mad and hallucinating deity." Those words, which not only proclaim disorder but exemplify it as well, prove, as all can see, the infidels' deplorable taste and desperate ignorance. For while the Library contains all verbal structures, all the variations allowed by the twenty-five orthographic symbols, it includes not a single absolute piece of nonsense. It would be pointless to observe that the finest volume of all the many hexagons that I myself administer is titled *Combed Thunder,* while another is titled *The Plaster Cramp,* and another, *Axaxaxas mlö.* Those phrases, at first apparently incoherent, are undoubtedly susceptible to cryptographic or allegorical "reading"; that reading, that justification of the words' order and existence, is itself verbal and, *ex hypothesi,* already contained somewhere in the Library. There is no combination of characters one can make—*dhcmrlchtdj,* for example—that

---

3 I repeat: In order for a book to exist, it is sufficient that it be *possible.* Only the impossible is excluded. For example, no book is also a staircase, though there are no doubt books that discuss and deny and prove that possibility, and others whose structure corresponds to that of a staircase.

the divine Library has not foreseen and that in one or more of its secret tongues does not hide a terrible significance. There is no syllable one can speak that is not filled with tenderness and terror, that is not, in one of those languages, the mighty name of a god. To speak is to commit tautologies. This pointless, verbose epistle already exists in one of the thirty volumes of the five bookshelves in one of the countless hexagons—as does its refutation. (A number *n* of the possible languages employ the same vocabulary; in some of them, the *symbol* "library" possesses the correct definition "everlasting, ubiquitous system of hexagonal galleries," while a library—the thing—is a loaf of bread or a pyramid or something else, and the six words that define it themselves have other definitions. You who read me—are you certain you understand my language?)

Methodical composition distracts me from the present condition of humanity. The certainty that everything has already been written annuls us, or renders us phantasmal. I know districts in which the young people prostrate themselves before books and like savages kiss their pages, though they cannot read a letter. Epidemics, heretical discords, pilgrimages that inevitably degenerate into brigandage have decimated the population. I believe I mentioned the suicides, which are more and more frequent every year. I am perhaps misled by old age and fear, but I suspect that the human species—the *only* species—teeters at the verge of extinction, yet that the Library—enlightened, solitary, infinite, perfectly unmoving, armed with precious volumes, pointless, incorruptible, and secret—will endure.

I have just written the word "infinite." I have not included that adjective out of mere rhetorical habit; I hereby state that it is not illogical to think that the world is infinite. Those who believe it to have limits hypothesize that in some remote place or places the corridors and staircases and hexagons may, inconceivably, end—which is absurd. And yet those who picture the world as unlimited forget that the number of possible books is *not*. I will be bold enough to suggest this solution to the ancient problem: *The Library is unlimited but periodic.* If an eternal traveler should journey in any direction, he would find after untold centuries that the same volumes are repeated in the same disorder—which, repeated, becomes order: the Order. My solitude is cheered by that elegant hope.[4]

---

4 Letizia Alvarez de Toledo has observed that the vast Library is pointless; strictly speaking, all that is required is a *single volume*, of the common size, printed in nine- or ten-point type, that would consist of an infinite number of infinitely thin pages. (In the early seventeenth century, Cavalieri stated that every solid body is the superposition of an infinite number of planes.) Using that silken *vademecum* would not be easy: each apparent page would open into other similar pages; the inconceivable middle page would have no "back."

WHAT REALLY HAPPENED

Banaphul

Translated from the Bengali by Arunava Sinha

Balāi Chānd Mukhopādhyāy (1899–1979) was a Bengali novelist, short story writer, playwright and poet wrote under the pen name Banaphul – meaning "wild flower" in Bengali. In a career spanning more than six decades, he penned thousands of poems, more than five hundred short stories, sixty novels, and a number of plays – and in all that time continued his primary career as a physician. He is most famous for short vignettes, sometimes barely half a page long, which have been compared to the sketches of the Indian artist Nandalal Bose: "He brings a picture to life with a single stroke of the brush."

I was alone in my hostel room in the afternoon. Everyone else was in college, but I wasn't. Tapati had promised to visit. I was waiting for her, the door locked. Vidyapati, Jaydev, Chandidas, Rabindranath—none of them made any sense. Only her face and her eyes did.

. . . Footsteps on the staircase. There was a knock on the door. I opened the door with beating heart. A loutish man with a moustache stood outside.

'Are you the one who wrote this letter to Tapu?'

He pulled out my pink letter from his pocket.

'Yes. Who are you . . . ?'

'I am Tapu's father. Rascal!'

He slapped me. I fell. He left. I stayed on the floor. Do you know what I did as I lay there? I constructed a second Taj Mahal. I made a mausoleum for the love I had never found, would never find. The artwork on this mausoleum was exquisite too. But alas, no one would ever get to see it, for I was not Emperor Shahjahan, I was the impoverished clerk Haran Bose's son Bijon Bose.

DETAILS OF A SUNSET

Vladimir Nabokov

Translated from the Russian by the author and Dmitri Nabokov

Vladimir Vladimirovich Nabokov (1899–1977) was a Russian-American novelist and entomologist. His first nine novels were in Russian, but he achieved international prominence after he began writing English prose. He was a finalist for the National Book Award for Fiction seven times. Nabokov was an expert lepidopterist and composer of chess problems. Nabokov actually discovered and named several species and families of butterfly, and he also assembled a new taxonomy system that is still in use. In 1961 Nabokov's son performed in a production of *La Bohème*. Nabokov arranged for the performance to be recorded. While Dmitri was good as Colline, he couldn't hold a candle to the unknown tenor who was also making his operatic debut in the role of Rodolfo. This is how, thanks to Nabokov's doting fatherhood, the world has documentation of Luciano Pavarotti's very first performance. Nabokov was a self-described synesthete, who at a young age equated the number five with the colour red.

I doubt very much that I was responsible for the odious title ("Katastrofa") inflicted upon this story. It was written in June 1924 in Berlin and sold to the Riga émigré daily Segodnya *where it appeared on July 13 of that year. Still under that label, and no doubt with my indolent blessings, it was included in the collection* Soglyadatay, Slovo, *Berlin, 1930.*

I have now given it a new title, one that has the triple advantage of corresponding to the thematic background of the story, of being sure to puzzle such readers as "skip descriptions," and of infuriating reviewers.

The last streetcar was disappearing in the mirrorlike murk of the street and, along the wire above it, a spark of Bengal light, crackling and quivering, sped into the distance like a blue star.

"Well, might as well just plod along, even though you are pretty drunk, Mark, pretty drunk...."

The spark went out. The roofs glistened in the moonlight, silvery angles broken by oblique black cracks.

Through this mirrory darkness he staggered home: Mark Standfuss, a salesclerk, a demigod, fair-haired Mark, a lucky fellow with a high starched collar.

At the back of his neck, above the white line of that collar, his hair ended in a funny, boyish little tag that had escaped the barber's scissors. That little tag was what made Klara fall in love with him, and she swore that it was true love, that she had quite forgotten the handsome ruined foreigner who last year had rented a room from her mother, Frau Heise.

"And yet, Mark, you're drunk. . . ."

That evening there had been beer and songs with friends in honor of Mark and russet-haired, pale Klara, and in a week they would be married; then there would be a lifetime of bliss and peace, and of nights with her, the red blaze of her hair spreading all over the pillow, and, in the morning, again her quiet laughter, the green dress, the coolness of her bare arms.

In the middle of a square stood a black wigwam: the tram tracks were being repaired. He remembered how today he had got under her short sleeve, and kissed the touching scar from her smallpox vaccination. And now he was walking home, unsteady on his feet from too much happiness and too much drink, swinging his slender cane, and among the dark houses on the opposite side of the empty street a night echo clop-clopped in time with his footfalls; but grew silent when he turned at the corner where the same man as always, in apron and peaked cap, stood by his grill, selling frankfurters, crying out in a tender and sad birdlike whistle: "*Würstchen, würstchen.* . . .

Mark felt a sort of delicious pity for the frankfurters, the moon, the blue spark that had receded along the wire, and, as he tensed his body against a friendly fence, he was overcome with laughter, and, bending, exhaled into a little round hole in the boards the words "Klara, Klara, oh my darling! "

On the other side of the fence, in a gap between the buildings, was a rectangular vacant lot. Several moving vans stood there like enormous coffins. They were bloated from their loads. Heaven knows what was piled inside them. Oakwood trunks, probably, and chandeliers like iron spiders, and the heavy skeleton of a double bed. The moon cast a hard glare on the vans. To the left of the lot, huge black hearts were flattened against a bare rear wall—the shadows, many times magnified, of the leaves of a linden tree that stood next to a streetlamp on the edge of the sidewalk.

Mark was still chuckling as he climbed the dark stairs to his floor. He reached the final step, but mistakenly raised his foot again, and it came down awkwardly with a bang. While he was groping in the dark in search of the keyhole, his bamboo cane slipped out from under his arm and, with a subdued little clatter, slid down the staircase. Mark held his breath. He thought the cane would turn with the stairs and knock its way down to the bottom. But the high-pitched wooden click abruptly ceased. Must have stopped. He grinned with relief and, holding on to the banister (the beer singing in his hollow head), started to descend again. He nearly fell, and sat down heavily on a step, as he groped around with his hands.

Upstairs the door onto the landing opened. Frau Standfuss, with a kerosene lamp in her hand, half-dressed, eyes blinking, the haze of her hair showing from beneath her nightcap, came out and called, "Is that you, Mark?"

A yellow wedge of light encompassed the banisters, the stairs, and his cane, and Mark, panting and pleased, climbed up again to the landing, and his black, hunch-backed shadow followed him up along the wall.

Then, in the dimly lit room, divided by a red screen, the following conversation took place:

"You've had too much to drink, Mark."

"No, no, Mother. . . I'm so happy. . ."

"You've got yourself all dirty, Mark. Your hand is black. . . ."

". . . so very happy. . . . Ah, that feels good . . . water's nice and cold. Pour some on the top of my head. . . more. . . . Everybody congratulated me, and with good reason. . . . Pour some more on."

"But they say she was in love with somebody else such a short time ago—a foreign adventurer of some kind. Left without paying five marks he owed Frau Heise. . . ."

"Oh, stop—you don't understand anything. . . . We did such a lot of singing today. . . Look, I've lost a button. . . . I think they'll double my salary when I get married. . . ."

"Come on, go to bed. . . . You're all dirty, and your new pants, too."

That night Mark had an unpleasant dream. He saw his late father. His father came up to him, with an odd smile on his pale, sweaty face, seized Mark under the arms, and began to tickle him silently, violently, and relentlessly.

He only remembered that dream after he had arrived at the store where he worked, and he remembered it because a friend of his, jolly Adolf, poked him in the ribs. For one instant something flew open in his soul, momentarily froze still in surprise, and slammed shut. Then again everything became easy and limpid, and the neckties he offered his customers smiled brightly, in sympathy with his happiness. He knew he would see Klara that evening—he would only run home for dinner, then go straight to her house. . . . The other day, when he was telling her how cozily and tenderly they would live, she had suddenly burst into tears. Of course Mark had understood that these were tears of joy (as she herself explained); she began whirling about the room, her skirt like a green sail, and then she started rapidly smoothing her glossy hair, the color of apricot jam, in front of the mirror. And her face was pale and bewildered, also from happiness, of course. It was all so natural, after all. . . .

"A striped one? Why certainly."

He knotted the tie on his hand, and turned it this way and that, enticing the customer. Nimbly he opened the flat cardboard boxes. . .

Meanwhile his mother had a visitor: Frau Heise. She had come without warning, and her face was tear-stained. Gingerly, almost as if she were afraid of breaking into pieces, she lowered herself onto a stool in the tiny, spotless kitchen where Frau Standfuss was washing the dishes. A two-dimensional wooden pig hung on the wall, and a half-open matchbox with one burnt match lay on the stove.

"I have come to you with bad news, Frau Standfuss."

The other woman froze, clutching a plate to her chest.

"It's about Klara. Yes. She has lost her senses. That lodger of mine came back today—you know, the one I told you about. And Klara has gone mad. Yes, it all happened this morning. . . . She never wants to see your son again. . . . You gave her the material for a new dress; it will be returned to you. And here is a letter for Mark. Klara's gone mad. I don't know what to think. . . ."

Meanwhile Mark had finished work and was already on his way home. Crew-cut Adolf walked him all the way to his house. They both stopped, shook hands, and Mark gave a shove with his shoulder to the door which opened into cool emptiness.

"Why go home? The heck with it. Let's have a bite somewhere, you and I."

Adolf stood, propping himself on his cane as if it were a tail.

"The heck with it, Mark. . . ."

Mark gave his cheek an irresolute rub, then laughed.

"All right. Only it's my treat."

When, half an hour later, he came out of the pub and said good-bye to his friend, the flush of a fiery sunset filled the vista of the canal, and a rain-streaked bridge in the distance was margined by a narrow rim of gold along which passed tiny black figures.

He glanced at his watch and decided to go straight to his fiancée's without stopping at his mother's. His happiness and the limpidity of the evening air made his head spin a little. An arrow of bright copper struck the lacquered shoe of a fop jumping out of a car. The puddles, which still had not dried, surrounded by the bruise of dark damp (the live eyes of the asphalt), reflected the soft incandescence of the evening. The houses were as gray as ever; yet the roofs, the moldings above the upper floors, the gilt-edged lightning rods, the stone cupolas, the colonnettes—which nobody notices during the day, for day-people seldom look up—were now bathed in rich ochre, the sunset's airy warmth, and thus they seemed unexpected and magical, those upper protrusions, balconies, cornices, pillars, contrasting sharply, because of their tawny brilliance, with the drab façades beneath.

"Oh, how happy I am," Mark kept musing, "how everything around celebrates my happiness."

As he sat in the tram he tenderly, lovingly examined his fellow passengers. He had such a young face, had Mark, with pink pimples on the chin, glad luminous eyes, an untrimmed tag at the hollow of his nape. . . . One would think fate might have spared him.

"In a few moments I'll see Klara," he thought. "She'll meet me at the door. She'll say she barely survived until evening."

He gave a start. He had missed the stop where he should have got off. On the way to the exit he tripped over the feet of a fat gentleman who was reading a medical journal; Mark wanted to tip his hat but nearly fell: the streetcar was turning with a screech. He grabbed an overhead strap and managed to keep his balance. The man slowly retracted his short legs with a phlegmy and cross growl. He had a gray mustache which twisted up pugnaciously. Mark gave him a guilty smile and reached the front end of the car. He grasped the iron handrails with both hands, leaned forward, calculated his jump. Down below, the asphalt streamed past, smooth and glistening. Mark jumped. There was a burn of friction against his soles, and his legs started running by themselves, his feet stamping with involuntary resonance. Several odd things occurred simultaneously: from the front of the car, as it swayed away from Mark, the conductor emitted a furious shout; the shiny asphalt swept upward like the seat of a swing; a roaring mass hit Mark from behind. He felt as if a thick thunderbolt had gone through him from head to toe, and then nothing. He was standing alone on the glossy asphalt.

He looked around. He saw, at a distance, his own figure, the slender back of Mark Standfuss, who was walking diagonally across the street as if nothing had happened. Marveling, he caught up with himself in one easy sweep, and now it was he nearing the sidewalk, his entire frame filled with a gradually diminishing vibration.

"That was stupid. Almost got run over by a bus. . . ."

The street was wide and gay. The colors of the sunset had invaded half of the sky. Upper stories and roofs were bathed in glorious light. Up there, Mark could discern translucent porticoes, friezes and frescoes, trellises covered with orange roses, winged statues that lifted skyward golden, unbearably blazing lyres. In bright undulations, ethereally, festively, these architectonic enchantments were receding into the heavenly distance, and Mark could not understand how he had never noticed before those galleries, those temples suspended on high.

He banged his knee painfully. That black fence again. He could not help laughing as he recognized the vans beyond. There they stood, like gigantic coffins. Whatever might they conceal within? Treasures? The skeletons of giants? Or dusty mountains of sumptuous furniture?

"Oh, I must have a look. Or else Klara will ask, and I shan't know."

He gave a quick nudge to the door of one of the vans and went inside. Empty. Empty, except for one little straw chair in the center, comically poised askew on three legs.

Mark shrugged and went out on the opposite side. Once again the hot evening glow gushed into sight. And now in front of him was the familiar wrought-iron wicket, and further on Klara's window, crossed by a green branch. Klara herself opened the gate, and stood waiting, lifting her bared elbows, adjusting her hair. The russet tufts of her armpits showed through the sunlit openings of her short sleeves.

Mark, laughing noiselessly, ran up to embrace her. He pressed his cheek against the warm, green silk of her dress.

Her hands came to rest on his head.

"I was so lonely all day, Mark. But now you are here."

She opened the door, and Mark immediately found himself in the dining room, which struck him as being inordinately spacious and bright.

"When people are as happy as we are now," she said, "they can do without a hallway," Klara spoke in a passionate whisper, and he felt that her words had some special, wonderful meaning.

And in the dining room, around the snow-white oval of the tablecloth, sat a number of people, none of whom Mark had seen before at his fiancée's house. Among them was Adolf, swarthy, with his square-shaped head; there was also that short-legged, big-bellied old man who had been reading a medical journal in the tram and was still grumbling.

Mark greeted the company with a shy nod and sat down beside Klara, and in that same instant felt, as he had a short time ago, a bolt of atrocious pain pass through his whole frame. He writhed, and Klara's green dress floated away, diminished, and turned into the green shade of a lamp. The lamp was swaying on its cord. Mark was lying beneath it, with that inconceivable pain crushing his body, and nothing could be distinguished save that oscillating lamp, and his ribs were pressing against his heart, making it impossible to breathe, and someone was bending his leg, straining to break it, in a moment it would crack. He freed himself somehow, the lamp glowed green again, and Mark saw himself sitting a little way off, beside Klara, and no sooner had he seen it than he found himself brushing his knee against her warm silk skirt. And Klara was laughing, her head thrown back.

He felt an urge to tell about what had just happened, and, addressing all those present—jolly Adolf, the irritable fat man—uttered with an effort:

"The foreigner is offering the aforementioned prayers on the river. . . ."

It seemed to him that he had made everything clear, and apparently they had all understood. . . . Klara, with a little pout, pinched his cheek:

"My poor darling. It'll be all right. . . .

He began to feel tired and sleepy. He put his arm around Klara's neck, drew her to him, and lay back. And then the pain pounced upon him again, and everything became clear.

Mark was lying supine, mutilated and bandaged, and the lamp was not swinging any longer. The familiar fat man with the mustache, now a doctor in a white gown, made worried growling small noises as he peered into the pupils of Mark's eyes. And what pain! . . . God, in a moment his heart would be impaled on a rib and burst. . ., God, any instant now. . . . This is silly. Why isn't Klara here. . . .

The doctor frowned and clucked his tongue.

Mark no longer breathed, Mark had departed—whither, into what other dreams, none can tell.

THE RESURRECTION
OF MOZART

Nina Berberova

Translated from the Russian by Marian Schwartz

Nina Nikolayevna Berberova (1901–1993) was a Russian-born poet, novelist, playwright, critic and professor of literature whose biography is a classic of the Russian émigré Diaspora. Her fiction has been on best-seller lists in France, and she was named a Chevalier of the Order of Arts and Letters by the French Government in 1989. In 1937, her biography of Tchaikovsky created a sensation because it was the first to deal openly with the composer's homosexuality.

I

In the early days of June 1940, just at the time when the French army was beginning its final and irrevocable retreat after the breach at Sedan, on a quiet warm evening, a group of four women and five men were sitting in a garden under the trees, about thirty miles from Paris. They were in fact talking about Sedan, talking of how the last few days had restored to that name which, like crinoline, had long since gone out of fashion, the ominous connotations it had had before; this town, which none of them had ever seen, and which had died in the time of their grandfathers, seemed to have been resurrected in order to relive the tragic events that were destined for it alone.

The silence was so complete that when they stopped talking and returned to their own private thoughts, they could hear through the open windows the clock ticking in the large old house. The sky was green, clear and lovely, and the stars were just beginning to shine, so few and far-flung that they failed to form any definite pattern. The old trees – acacias, limes – neither breathed nor trembled, as if standing stock-still were a safeguard against something that was invisible to men but somehow immanent in the summer evening. The hosts and their guests had just finished supper; the table had not yet been cleared. Some wine-glasses were still on the table. Slowly, the green light of the darkening sky transformed the faces of the seated company which was now obscured by shadows. They were talking about war and about the omens of war. A young woman, a guest who had driven out from town with her husband and sister, restraining her brassy voice, remarked that she had seen a meteor a fortnight before.

'It was about this time of day. The sky was just as hazy. At first it looked like a falling star, but it was so long and it was so bright.'

'You probably wouldn't even have noticed it a year ago,' said another guest, smiling. This was Chabarov, a bald, robust man with a drooping black moustache and wearing a bright blue shirt. He was a groundsman at a château about eight miles away and had just arrived on his bicycle.

'A year ago,' said Vassily Georgievich Sushkov, the host, a tall man, taller than anyone else at the table, grey-haired but not yet old, with a sharp and furtive look in his eye. 'Yes, it was exactly a year ago today that Nevelsky died. He knew a lot of this was coming. He predicted so much of it.'

'Well, he couldn't have picked a better time to die. At least he doesn't have to see what we see. If he were resurrected he'd either spit in disgust or break down and cry.'

Facing the hostess, at the opposite end of the table, sat a Frenchman brought along by Chabarov but whom no one else really knew. Simply, and without any fussy apology, he asked them to translate what they were all saying.

'Monsieur Daunou, we were talking about the dead, and what they would say if they were resurrected and saw what's going on now,' replied Maria Leonidovna Sushkova.

Daunou took his black pipe out of his mouth, furrowed his brow, and smiled.

'Is it worth waking the dead?' he said, looking his hostess straight in the eye. 'I suppose I might well invite Napoleon to come and have a look at our times, but I'd certainly spare my parents the pleasure.'

Suddenly everyone started talking at once.

'Resurrect them for your sake or for theirs? I don't understand,' Manyura Krein, who had come from Paris, asked with a lively expression, not addressing anyone in particular and no longer trying to conceal her loud voice. She had a full mouth of her very own white teeth, which gave the impression of being false. 'If it were for their sake, then of course you'd resurrect Napoleon and Bismarck and Queen Victoria, and maybe even Julius Caesar. But if I could bring someone from the past back to life for my sake, just for mine, then that's an entirely different thing. That calls for some thought. Such a large choice, so many temptations . . . still, silly as it sounds, I think I'd resurrect Pushkin.'

'A charming, fun-loving, marvellous man,' said Maria Leonidovna Sushkova. 'What a joy it would be to see him alive.'

'Or maybe Taglioni?' continued Manyura Krein. 'I'd lock her up at home so I could look at her whenever I wanted.'

'And then take her to America,' put in Chabarov, 'and let the impresarios tear her to shreds.'

'Come on, if you're going to resurrect anyone, then don't resurrect Taglioni,' said Fyodor Egorovich Krein with barely repressed irritation. He was Manyura's husband, twice her age, and a friend of Sushkov's. 'There's no need to be frivolous. I would make the best of the occasion. I would drag Tolstoy back into God's world. Wasn't it you, dear sir, who denied the role of the individual in history? You who declared that there would be no more wars? And wasn't it you who took a sceptical view of vaccination? No, don't try to wriggle out of it now. Just have a look at the result.' It was evident that Fyodor Egorovich had scores to settle with Tolstoy and that he had an entire text prepared should they happen to meet in the next life.

'*Avec Taglioni on pourrait faire fortune*,' Chabarov repeated his thought in French.

'And I, gentlemen,' piped in Sushkov's mother, who wore heavy violet powder and reeked of some unpleasant perfume, 'and I, gentlemen, would resurrect Uncle Lyosha. Wouldn't he be surprised?'

No one knew who Uncle Lyosha was, so no one said anything for a minute or two. Little by little the conversation had drawn everyone in, taking them far from that evening, that garden and into the past, the recent or the very distant past, as if someone had already made a firm promise to wave a magic wand and fulfil everyone's wish, so that now the only problem was in making a choice, and it was a difficult choice because no one wanted to miscalculate, especially the women.

'No one but Mozart will do for me, though. Yes, it has to be Mozart,' Maria Leonidovna thought to herself. 'There's no one else I want, and it would be useless anyway.'

She had decided not out of any morbid love of music, as can happen with women who have reached a certain age and who are generally thought of as 'cultured', but merely because she connected that name in her mind with her earliest childhood, and because it lived on as something pure, transparent, and eternal that might take the place of happiness. Maria Leonidovna smoked avidly and waited for someone else to say something. She didn't feel like talking herself. It was Magdalena, Manyura Krein's sister, a young woman of thirty, full-figured and pale, with unusually rounded shoulders, who spoke up. The sight of her always brought to mind those undeniable statistics about how in Europe so many millions of young women had been left single because there weren't enough husbands to go round.

'No, I wouldn't resurrect a single famous man,' said Magdalena, with a certain disdain for men of renown. 'I'd much prefer an ordinary mortal. An idealistic youth from the early nineteenth century, a follower of Hegel, a reader of Schiller; or a courtier to one of the French kings.'

She shrugged her heavy shoulders and looked around. But already it was nearly dark, and one could barely make out the faces round the table. But the stars were now quite visible overhead, and the sky seemed familiar again.

Chabarov didn't say anything for a long while. Finally he made a muffled nasal sound, drummed his fingers on the table, opened his mouth, but suddenly hesitated, said nothing, and sank back into his thoughts.

The ninth person present, who had been silent until then, was Kiryusha, Sushkov's nineteen-year-old son and Maria Leonidovna's stepson. In the family he was considered a little backward. Slowly he unglued his thick, wide lips and, gazing trustfully at his stepmother with his blue and very round eyes, asked if it were possible to resurrect two people at the same time.

God alone knows what was going through his dreamy mind at that point. He seemed to think that everything had already been decided by the others and that only the details remained to be settled.

'*Mais c'est un vrai petit jeu*,' noted Daunou with a sad laugh, and immediately everyone seemed to move and smile once more, as if returning from far away. 'Everyone has their own private passion, and everyone is being terribly serious about it.'

Maria Leonidovna just nodded at him. 'Mozart, of course, only Mozart will do,' she repeated to herself. 'And it's a good thing I'm not young any more and don't have any physical interest in seeing him. We could sit up till dawn, and he could play our piano and we'd talk. And everyone would come to see him and listen to him – the neighbours' gardener and his wife, the postman, the shopkeeper and his family, the station master . . . What a joy it would be! And tomorrow there'd be no post, no trains, nothing at all. Everything would be topsy-turvy. And there wouldn't be any war. No, there would be war all the same.'

She lit another cigarette. For a moment the match illuminated her thin, slightly worn face and her delicate, beautiful hands. Everything about her, except her face, was feminine, youthful and sleek, particularly her light and silent walk. Everyone noticed when Maria Leonidovna suddenly got up and walked out under the trees, and then came back to the table, and they could see the lit end of her cigarette in the darkness of the advancing night.

A chill came up about then from the low-lying part of the garden, where two little stone bridges crossed the narrow loops of the flower-banked stream. Old Mrs Sushkova, wrapped in a shawl, was dozing in her chair. Kiryusha was looking up blankly, and it was clear that like the trees and stars he was merely existing and not thinking. And suddenly, somewhere far off, perhaps twenty-five or thirty miles away to the east, where the sun rises in the summer, the sound of gunfire rumbled, burst out, and then disappeared. It was very much like thunder and yet completely different.

'Time we were on our way,' everyone started saying immediately, and Manyura Krein, jangling her bracelets, ran into the house for her coat and bag.

They went through the dining room and big dark hallway and came out into the yard where the car was parked. Sushkov's mother was going back to Paris as well. She put on a hat with a big violet-coloured flower; even her suitcase was a shade of violet. The motor idled a few moments, and then, cautiously spreading its black wings, the car backed up to the gates. Krein, sitting behind the steering wheel, waved once again to those left behind. Manyura, whose porcelain mouth alone was illuminated, smiled behind the glass and said something. The car started up, stopped, shifted into forward, and as if it had hauled itself out, disappeared, leaving behind it a wake of invisible, acrid exhaust.

Chabarov went to find the bicycles.

'We'd be very happy to see you here any time,' Sushkov told the Frenchman. 'We're staying all summer, and on Sundays, as you see, our friends visit. You're always welcome.'

'*Enchanté, monsieur*,' Daunou replied. 'I have spent an unforgettable evening.'

And following behind Chabarov he kissed Maria Leonidovna's hand.

The next day, as usual, Vassily Georgievich took the train into town, leaving Maria Leonidovna and Kiryusha to themselves. That Monday, at one o'clock in the afternoon, several dozen aeroplanes bombed Paris for the first time.

II

News of the bombardment of Paris only came that evening. During the day you could hear the gunfire, but it was so far away that you couldn't tell whether it was in Paris or Pontoise, where it had been a few days before. In the evening the papers arrived, and all the people who lived in the little village, in the centre of which stood a neglected church with a caved-in roof, came spilling out into the modest avenue of sturdy plane trees that led from the café to the *mairie*.

The village consisted almost entirely of old women. Of course they may have only been, as in any French village, about half the population, but they were the ones you saw most often. Seeing them out in the street, talking together or shopping or shaking out a rag or hanging out clothes, they seemed to make up nine-tenths of the inhabitants.

Some of them were no more than fifty, and they were still smart and cheerful, just turning grey, rosy-cheeked and sharp-eyed. Others were wrinkled and toothless, with swollen veins. Others, who could remember the invasion of the Germans in 1870, were hunched up and barely able to put one sore foot in front of the other, and they had darkened hands, long black nails, and lifeless faces. They were all much of a kind, talking to each other in the same way, and using the same words, wherever they met, be it on street corners, beneath the plane trees, or by their front gates. They all wore wide calico aprons that either tied at the back or buttoned in front. Some wore steel glasses on their noses and knitted, rocking in a chair and holding the skein of wool under their left arms. Almost all of them were widows of men killed in the last war, and all without exception had seen either a son or a son-in-law set off for this war.

That evening, in the shady lane that ran alongside the fence to the Sushkovs' garden, the silence was broken. Kiryusha came to tell Maria Leonidovna that Paris had been bombed, buildings destroyed, warehouses burned, and more than a thousand killed or wounded. Maria Leonidovna looked at Kiryusha, who was smiling broadly, and it saddened her that this human being, who was now completely grown, was still the same child she had first met twelve years before. There was a time – and lately she had thought of it often – when he had suddenly decided to learn the alphabet. A brief light had pierced the darkness of that sick brain. He had tried to learn the letters, but nothing ever came of it. It had all ended with Kiryusha's short and relatively happy affair with the girl who worked in the charcuterie. Relatively happy because after that he had started to get gradually worse.

Maria Leonidovna went through Paris in her mind. In that city, above all, was Vassily Georgievich, as well as their pretty, sunny, quiet apartment, which she loved so much. Then there were the Kreins, the Abramovs, the Snezhinskys, Edouard Zontag, Semyon Isaakovich Freiberg, Lenochka Mikhailova, and many many more who could have been wounded or killed. And when she thought about all those people living at various ends of the city, scattered across the old creased map of Paris that she kept in her mind, a flashing light lit up, here and there, and then went out.

'Yes. This had to happen,' she told herself. 'We were talking about it only yesterday. So why did he go? The Kreins could have stayed on, too. Yesterday we said . . . What else were we talking about yesterday? Oh, yes! "You are God, Mozart, and of that fact yourself innocent." One ought to aspire to something that combines everything beautiful, pure and eternal, like those clouds, not all these terrible things, all these murders and lies. Before the ultimate silence closes in on you, shouldn't you listen to what the stars are saying to each other?'

She went over to the little radio, brand new, which Kiryusha was strictly forbidden to go near, and turned the knob. First a French voice spoke, then an English voice, then a German voice. All of it was crammed into that wooden box, separated only by invisible barriers. The voices all said the same thing. And suddenly it switched to music, singing, Spanish or maybe Italian, the voluptuous and carefree strumming of a guitar. But she picked up the word *amore,* and she turned the machine off and walked to the window, from which she could see the village road among the thick fields of oats, green and ash-grey.

On Tuesday, Wednesday and Thursday, soldiers were billeted on the village: heavy green trucks camouflaged with foliage as if decked out for a carnival and bearing numbers written in red lead paint brought in five hundred young, healthy, raucous soldiers and four officers wearing long overcoats and with tired, worried, feverish faces. A billeting officer appeared at Maria Leonidovna's door – the house the Sushkovs rented was by far the best in the village – and she immediately moved Kiryusha into the dining room, giving his room to the captain and the space in the annexe to three sub-lieutenants.

The four officers slept in their clothes. The sentry – sometimes a short, swarthy and yellow-eyed man or else a tall, erect and big-faced one – came to wake them several times during the night. Vassily Georgievich called every day; his call came to the post office at the corner of their side street and the square. A little boy missing his front teeth ran to fetch Maria Leonidovna, and she ran after him in her silent, girlish way, wearing whatever she happened to have on, ran into the tiny single-windowed building, picked up the receiver, and listened to Vassily Georgievich say that everything was fine, that he had received the money, seen Edouard, was eating with the Snezhinskys, would arrive on Saturday.

'I have soldiers staying with me,' she said, still out of breath from running. 'I've given them Kiryusha's room. And the annexe.'

'Maybe I should come? You're not afraid?'

'Why should I be afraid? Goodbye.'

And in fact, at that minute, she thought that she wasn't afraid in the least. In a way, it was even reassuring to have these polite, laconic men close at hand.

But at night she barely slept. She listened. From far away, in the dead of night, she caught the diffuse, persistent sound of a motorcycle. While the sound was on the far side of the woods, it was no more than a whisper, but as it got nearer it became louder and more focused, and then suddenly it was zooming down the lane and stopping at the house next door, where the sentry was posted. The motor was switched off, and then she could hear voices, steps. The gate banged. Someone was walking into the house, into her house, some stranger, and the old blind dog got up from its straw and went to sniff at his tracks in the gravel of the yard, growling. A light went on somewhere, she heard someone running through the house, through the annexe. Something clinked, a door slammed. Kiryusha was asleep close by, in the dining room, whose door she left open. These night sounds didn't frighten her any more. What frightened her was everything that was going on in the world that night.

She wasn't afraid of the quiet strangers either. They left the third night, leaving the doors and the gate wide open, leaving the village in trucks camouflaged with fresh branches. She wasn't afraid of the sentries who came to see them or of the five hundred strong, half-sober soldiers quartered all over the village. She was afraid of the air, the warm June air, through which gunfire rolled across the horizon and submerged her, her house, and her garden, along with the summer clouds. And there was no question that this puff of wind, which was somehow just like time itself, would in the end bring something terrible and ruinous, such as death itself. Just as, looking at the calendar, no one doubted any longer that in five, ten or fifteen days something dreadful was going to happen, so, feeling that faint breeze on her face day and night, she could say with assurance that it would bring to these parts murder, occupation, devastation and darkness.

For the air, over the last few days, had been warm, clear and fragrant. Kiryusha worked in the garden, watering the flowers in front of the house every evening and looking after the neighbours' ducklings. Maria Leonidovna, wearing a bright cotton print dress, and a scarf around her head, went to clean out the annexe, where she found a bag of cartridges which had been left behind and two unsealed letters, which she threw away without reading. There were cigarette butts in the cup by the washstand, and a charred newspaper lay on the floor. She made up Kiryusha's bed in his room and when the woman from next door came over to do the housework, told her to wash all the floors in the house.

On the same day, towards evening, fugitives from Soissons arrived at the neighbours': two fat, pale women, an old man, and some children. A mattress was laid out on the roof of their filthy car, and to the amazed questioning of the villagers the new arrivals explained that this was what everybody was doing now, that this was what would protect you from bullets. The old man was carried into the house by his hands and feet: he was unconscious.

Before night other fugitives arrived to stay in the sky-blue, toy-like house opposite the church. People said that some of the soldiers were still there, and were, spending the night at the other end of the village. There seemed to be a stranger who had come from far away by foot or by car hiding in every house for the night. There were no lights, all was dark, but voices could be heard everywhere from behind the shutters; the café was full of shouting and singing. Under the plane trees the old ladies, who had stayed longer than was normal, spoke in low voices.

Maria Leonidovna locked the front door, hung the curtains over the windows, cleared away the remains of supper, and as she always did, sat in the next room and talked with Kiryusha while he got ready for bed. From time to time he exclaimed happily:

'I cleaned my teeth! I took off my left shoe!'

And if you didn't know it was a nineteen-year-old man in there – who ate enormous meals, snored loudly in his sleep, and couldn't read – you would think it was a ten-year-old boy going to bed and, for a joke, talking in a bass voice.

After she had turned out the light in the dining room and Kiryusha's room and went to her own, she stood for a long time by the open window and looked out at where, in the daytime, she could see the road and the oat-fields. Tomorrow Vassily Georgievich was due to return. The idea was pleasant and consoling. But today Maria Leonidovna had barely given a thought to her husband; in fact she hadn't stopped thinking about Mozart. Or rather, not about Mozart himself. Right now, as a new crescent moon appeared on the edge of this anxious but subdued night, her thoughts took on a special clarity. All day long, or rather, over the last few days and this evening, she had been asking herself the same question, and there was no answer to it: why was it that horror, cruelty, and affliction made themselves felt so easily, became concrete and weighed all the more heavily, whereas everything sublime, gentle, unexpected and full of charm cast a frail shadow across the heart and thoughts, so one couldn't touch it or look at it closely or feel its shape and weight? 'Except for love, of course,' she thought, standing by the window. 'Only love gives that kind of joy. But what about someone who doesn't want to love any more, who can no longer love? I have no one to love; it's too late for me. I have a husband, I don't need anyone else.'

And all of a sudden she thought she heard the latch on the gate click, and she distinctly heard someone come into the yard, take two steps, and stop.

'Who's there?' she asked quietly.

The darkness was not yet total, and the faint, blurred shadow of a man lay on the whitish gravel in the yard. The shadow moved and the gravel crunched. The man must have been able to see Maria Leonidovna clearly as she stood in the open window, to the right of the front door. The door, as Maria Leonidovna recalled, was locked. But the man, who was slowly and purposefully walking across the yard, made no response. She could hardly see him. He walked up the porch stairs, stopped three paces away from Maria Leonidovna, put out his hand, and the door opened. And when he had already walked into the house she wanted to scream. But, as in a dream, she was unable to produce any sound.

He was pale and thin, with a long nose and tangled hair. Everything he had on, from his boots to his hat, seemed to have been borrowed from someone else. His dusty hands were so slender and frail that he couldn't have used them even if he had wanted to. His face was weary, youthful, but it wasn't a boy's face. She could tell that he looked younger than he was, but that in fact he could be over thirty.

'Forgive me for frightening you,' he said in French, but with a slight foreign accent. 'Could I spend the night here somewhere?'

By the light of the lamp illuminating the spacious entryway Maria Leonidovna looked at him, standing silently and barely able to control herself. But the moment he uttered those first words and looked at her with his long, hesitant look, her fear passed, and she asked:

'Who are you?'

But he dropped his eyes.

'Where are you from?'

He shivered slightly, and his fingers clutched the upturned collar of his ample jacket, which might have been covering an otherwise naked body.

'Oh, from far, far away . . . and I'm so tired. I'd like to lie down somewhere, if that's all right.'

'A fugitive,' she decided, 'and maybe he's a Frenchman from some out-of-the-way province. Judging by his age, he could be a soldier; by his clothes, a fugitive? Maybe a spy?'

She led him to the annexe, thinking all the time that he might strike her from behind, but at the same time knowing he wouldn't. By the time they had entered the bedroom, she had lost all fear of him. He didn't even look around, but silently walked over to the bed, sat down on it, and closed his eyes. Between his shoe and trouser-leg she saw a thin, bare ankle.

'Do you want to eat?' she asked, closing the shutters on the low, folding windows from inside. 'It's the war, we're not supposed to show any light on the outside.'

'What did you say?' he asked, shuddering a little.

'I asked whether you'd like to eat something.'

'No, thank you. I had a bite to eat in your local restaurant. They were all full up, though, and couldn't give me a place to stay.'

She realised it was time she went.

'Are you alone?' she spoke again, rearranging something on the table as she passed.

'What do you mean "alone"?'

'I mean, did you come here – to the village – with friends or what?'

He raised his eyes.

'I came alone, just as I am, without any luggage,' he said smiling, but not revealing his teeth. 'And I'm not a soldier, I'm a civilian. A musician.'

She took another look at his hands, said goodnight, and having shown him where to turn off the light, walked out of the room.

That time she gave two turns to the lock in the door and suddenly, feeling a strangely animal weariness, went straight to bed and fell asleep. In the morning, as always, she got up early. Kiryusha was already in the garden bawling out some song, and in the annexe all was quiet.

III

Just before lunch she wondered, anxiously, if something had happened: the shutters and door were still closed. 'Can he still be asleep?' she thought. At four o'clock Vassily Georgievich was due to arrive, and a little before then she went again to see whether her lodger was up. She half-opened the door to the tiny entryway, and then the door of the room. The man was sleeping, breathing evenly. He had not removed any of his clothes, not even his boots. He lay on his back on the wide mattress, the pillow on one side. Maria Leonidovna closed the door again.

Vassily Georgievich was late getting back; the train coming from Paris had stopped for a long time at some bridge. Sushkov had carried a large suitcase from the station to the house, practically a trunk, on his broad, strong shoulder. It was full of things gathered up from their Paris apartment without which Vassily Georgievich could not imagine either his own or his wife's existence. There were his winter coat, Maria's old squirrel coat, warm underwear which he always wore during the winter, an album of photographs of Prague (he had lived in Czechoslovakia for a long time), expensive binoculars in their case, a pound of dried figs, which he liked to keep in reserve, a handsomely bound edition of Montesquieu's *Lettres Persanes*, and Maria Leonidovna's ball gown, sewn for a charity ball the year before at which she had sold champagne. Maria Leonidovna was surprised to see warm underwear and heavy coats in June. But Sushkov assured her that they might be cut off from Paris or could be forced to escape, and then they wouldn't know what was going to happen.

'Escape from here? Yes, of course, we'll have to escape if everyone else does. Those fugitives from Soissons are packing up their things again, and the old man is being carried out of the house to the car.' She took up the newspaper her husband had brought but learned nothing from it. Vassily Georgievich spoke to her sensibly and gently. Sometimes he argued with himself, sometimes he told her what Snezhinsky and Freiberg thought about what was going on. And everything he said was accurate, fair, intelligent.

'So, your officers have gone, have they?' he asked her. 'It must have been worrying for you.'

'They're gone, but since yesterday there's been a' – she wanted to say 'chap' but couldn't – 'man sleeping, staying in the annexe. He's still asleep. He must have come the seventy-five miles on foot.'

'My God, you've been staying here alone with my idiot and you're not afraid to let in strangers,' he exclaimed, never mincing words when it concerned Kiryusha. And catching her hand, scratching himself on her sharp nails, he kissed it several times.

Towards the end of the day Kiryusha told them in his incoherent way that the man staying in the annexe had gone. An hour later Maria Leonidovna heard him return and lock himself in again.

'That man came back. He must be sleeping again. Don't you go bothering him,' she told Kiryusha.

All the next day was the same: the visitor either lay or sat by the window and neither moved nor spoke. It was as if he were waiting for something. Or else he walked to the village for a little while, walked down the lane, across the square, down the avenue of plane trees, bought himself something to eat, and came back quietly.

Strange thoughts occurred to Maria Leonidovna. Sometimes she thought that the man was bound to be arrested. Why hadn't he told her his name? Why was he wearing clothes that didn't belong to him? If he wasn't a spy, then he was a deserter. Maybe he was Russian? In many years of living abroad, Maria Leonidovna had grown used to the fact that there were no half-mad Frenchmen. Did he have a passport or had he thrown everything away, lost it? Had he run out of the house in his underwear and then received clothes from good-hearted people on the way? But perhaps there was nothing wrong and he was just a lonely musician who had been turned out from where he sawed away at his fiddle or gave lessons to young ladies or composed just for himself, dreaming of world acclaim?

But these thoughts came and went, and life went on without interruption. This Sunday was nothing at all like the last, when they had sat in the garden over the samovar with the Kreins. No one came from town. Chabarov and Daunou arrived at five o'clock on bicycles. The three of them sat in Vassily Georgievich's study for a long time and talked, about the war, of course, but in a different way than they had the week before: they were talking about their hopes. Daunou talked about his own hopes, about how they could still put a stop to this insane, iron advance at the Seine and the Marne. Each time Maria Leonidovna looked in on them she had the feeling that the Frenchman wanted to tell her something. He got up and spoke to her in particular, and for some reason she found that unpleasant. He gave her the impression (only her, though) of being an hysteric, and when she left the room she was afraid of running into him later in the dining room, the yard, the garden.

She couldn't have explained her feeling, but Daunou's serious, determined, overly expressive face was before her all the time. She started to make tea, and he came out into the dining room, closing the door behind him as if in despair, and Maria Leonidovna felt that he was about to tell her something she would remember the rest of her life.

'*Nous sommes perdus, madame*,' he said quietly, looking into her face with his small eyes of indeterminate colour. 'Even the Emperor Napoleon himself, whom I wanted to resurrect last Sunday, couldn't do anything now. I'm telling only you this. You make your own decision about where and when you should leave. *Paris est sacrifié*.'

He turned white. His face contorted. But he coughed awkwardly, and everything fell into place again. She was left, frozen, holding the porcelain sugar bowl.

'There will not be a battle on the Loire. The Maginot Line will be taken from the west. Nothing at all is going to happen. It's all over. They'll go all the way to Bordeaux, to the Pyrénées. And then we'll sue for peace.'

At that moment Vassily Georgievich and Chabarov walked out into the dining room, and everyone sat down at the table.

She believed Daunou, but not completely, and for that reason when she and Vassily Georgievich were alone again she was unable to convince him that everything would be as Daunou had said. She said, 'You know, I think it would be best if you didn't go back to Paris again. Let's pack up tomorrow and move to the South, all three of us, Tuesday at the latest. We can spend a month or two in Provence, until things calm down. Like everyone else.'

He listened to her thoughtfully, but couldn't agree.

'What would they say about me at the office? They'd call me a coward. Tomorrow I'm going to Paris, and I give you my word of honour, I'll be back on Wednesday. Even if all's well, I'll be back. Haven't we seen plenty in our time? For them this is terrible, but we've seen a lot worse . . . "Nothing happens at a pace like that, a pace like that,"' he sang brightly.

The next day she was left alone again with Kiryusha. The traveller was still in the annexe.

He continued to get up late, sit by the window, and look out at the yard, at the trees, at the sky. Sitting erect, his hands placed on the windowsill, he looked and listened with a sad and equal attention both to the birds moving about in the lilac bushes and to the distant gunfire and the human talk beyond the gates and in the house. Once or twice he got up, put on his faded, outsize hat, or picked it up, and went out, softly shutting the gate. He walked through the village, taking a good look at what was going on, since every day the people got more and more worried, agitated, and grim. In the evenings he sat for a long time, no longer at the window but on the threshold to the annexe, his eyes half closed, his hand lazily resting on the head of the old dog, who came to sit next to him.

Night fell, the moon glimmered. There was something menacing about the clear sky, the quiet fields, the roads running to and fro, this summer, this world where fate had compelled him to live. When he rested his head on his hand, it seemed he was trying to remember something and that was why he was so quiet, that he couldn't do it. Where was he from? And where should he go, and did he have to go any farther? And what was life, this pulse, this breathing, this waiting, what was this ecstasy, this grief, this war? He was so weak, but he had a powerful harmony in his heart, a melody in his head. Why was he here among all this, among the now incessant noise of the gunfire, among these preparations for departure in village families, where they led out horses, tied up cows, where they sewed up gold into the lining of clothes? He had nothing. Not even a pack. No family, no lover to sew him a shirt, cook him soup, rumple and warm his bed. All he had was music. That's how he had grown up, that's how it had been since he was a child. Feet to carry him, hands to fend off people, and music, and that was it. But there was no point coming, no, no point coming into a world where he would always go unrecognised and unheard, where he was weaker than a shadow, poorer than a bird, as guileless as the simplest flower of the field.

When Kiryusha saw that the dog was sitting beside him and wasn't afraid, he came and sat as well, not daring to sit on the porch, but close by, on a stone. And so all three of them sat for a long time, in silence, until it got dark, and then Kiryusha, taking a deep breath, let out a long, idiotic laugh and went into the house.

IV

On Wednesday morning Vassily Georgievich did not come back. There had been no telephone communication with Paris for two days, and Maria Leonidovna had absolutely no idea what to think. People were saying that there weren't any trains, that the papers hadn't come out, that travel across Paris was impossible, and that people had been deserting Paris for two days. The entire village was packing up and leaving. Those who only the night before had criticised people fleeing from fear were themselves loading things onto carts, cars and perambulators. A swarm of little boys and girls sped around on bicycles. Three rows of small trucks and cars filed down the main road, which passed less than a mile from the village. During the day rumours had been flying around, the gunfire went on constantly, growing ever nearer, and silver aeroplanes sailed high in the sky. Several cars, trying to take a short cut, wound up on the avenue of plane trees and couldn't figure out how to get out, so they looped back and returned to the main road, nosing into the endless chain and continuing southward.

There were artillery, gypsy caravans, trucks loaded with ledgers (and on them sat pale bookkeepers, evacuating the bank, the foundation of the state); people on foot, on bicycles, broken-rank cavalrymen on light horses interspersed with percherons harnessed to long wagons carrying sewing machines, kitchen utensils, furniture, barrels. And high above all the goods and chattels were perched old women, deathly pale and bare-headed; some old women sat in cars, while others went on foot, alone or supported by the arm. Troops hauled decrepit cannons and an empty van surmounted by a magnificent red cross followed behind a sports car out of which leaned a lop-eared dog that looked like a soft toy. Then came the wounded, some of them sitting despondently, holding on to their own leg or arm, a stump that dripped blood on the road. Others vomited air and saliva. People carried hay, unthreshed wheat, factory lathes, tanks of oil. And this odd stream could be seen all the way to the horizon, living and yet already dead.

Up until nightfall Maria Leonidovna cleaned and packed, fully aware that Vassily Georgievich couldn't come by train, just as they couldn't leave by train. From the house she could see the main road, and since morning she had watched the relentless, slowly flowing, sometimes pausing, river of fugitives. The thought that she might be left alone after everyone was gone worried her, and above all the thought that Vassily Georgievich might not return. She was worried as well about Kiryusha, who in the rising panic had suddenly become grotesquely incoherent. In the middle of the day she saw her silent guest a few times, and even greeted him from a distance. She resolved to have a chat with him, find out about him, maybe help him out, and that decision preoccupied her for a few minutes. The evening came, she prepared supper, and just as they were sitting down she heard the sound of a motor, a comforting, familiar sound. Two cars drove into the Sushkovs' yard: in one sat the three Kreins; in the other, Edouard Zontag, Vassily Georgievich, and old Mrs Sushkova. Both cars had left Paris the previous evening. They had been on the road all night and all day.

Manyura Krein broke down in tears when she walked into the house. 'This is too much! Simply too much!' she said with her large mouth. 'This is not to be endured. Children are being led along on foot, old people are hobbling on crutches. I'll never forget this as long as I live.'

But Maria Leonidovna scarcely got to hug her because she had to say hello to Zontag and to Magdalena and follow her husband into the next room and listen to his agitated story about how yesterday afternoon he had realised that she was right, that they should have left on Sunday, that now they might not make it.

'Kiryusha's not too good,' she told him, since even today she considered that that was the most important thing.

Edouard Zontag had longstanding business ties with Vassily Georgievich, and relations between them, for some reason only they understood, were rather strained. He kept aloof, apparently looking on the Kreins as relatives of Maria Leonidovna, and smoked a fat cigar. He was short and used to say that the shorter the man, the fatter the cigar he smoked.

An omelette, cold meat, salad, cheese, an apple tart, just appeared on the table, all at once, and they launched into it haphazardly and greedily, letting the abundance of that house fill them with contentment, fully aware that tomorrow it would all be gone. They drank a lot and talked a lot. They discussed how and when the decision had been made to surrender Paris, the bombing of its northern and western suburbs, and especially how everyone had dropped everything and fled, not only those who had been preparing for it but also those who had had no desire whatsoever to budge; how that night, in total darkness, it took them five hours to get from their apartment to the city limits. How they had been surrounded by thousands upon thousands of others like themselves, how the engine died on them, the radiator boiled over, and they took turns sleeping.

Then they had a conference: what time tomorrow should they go and which road was best? They bent over the map for a long time, sketched something, drew it out, and then drank again and even had another bite to eat, especially the men. In the yard an old lady slaughtered two hens, and Manyura cleaned them on the big kitchen table, lowered her fingers, covered in rings, with varnished nails, down into it, and drew out something slippery. Magdalena and Maria Leonidovna, sitting on their heels by the linen closet, looked for one more pillow-case for Edouard. The men were trying to decide whether or not to drive over to pick up Chabarov, and old Mrs Sushkova wanted to express her opinion too, but no one was listening to her.

She went to her room, that is, to Kiryusha's room, where she was supposed to spend the night, and it immediately began to reek of her perfume in there. Room was found for the Kreins in the house, but Edouard Zontag had to be put in the annexe.

'Wait for me, I'll be back in a minute,' said Maria Leonidovna, and she ran across the yard.

She knocked on the door. He was lying on the bed but not sleeping, and when she came in he raised himself and slowly lowered his long legs in their torn boots and ran his hand over his hair, as if he wanted to smooth it, comb it, give it some semblance of order. She started speaking softly, scarcely glancing in his direction.

'Excuse me, but something's come up. We have a full house. People didn't sleep last night, and there's nowhere to put them. Please, we have a small shed by the garage. Move over there. I feel bad disturbing you, but you understand, there's nothing else I can do. And then, in any case, we'll be leaving early tomorrow morning and you'll have to leave too because we'll be locking up and taking the keys with us. You won't be able to stay.'

He stood up and in the semi-dark (a cold bleak light fell from the entryway where a small lamp was lit) started pacing around the room, evidently at a loss how best to answer her.

'Tomorrow morning? Then why move to the shed? I'll leave tonight.'

She couldn't help feeling glad that he'd said this.

'I feel that I'm chasing you away, practically in the middle of the night. Please stay. There's a folding bed in there. And tomorrow—'

'No, I'll go right now. After all, everyone else seems to be leaving, don't they?'

'Yes, if they haven't already.'

'So I think I'd better go as well. Thank you for letting me spend so many days with you. Really, I'm most grateful to you. There are many people who wouldn't have done it, you know. I'll remember it for a long time, a very long time.'

He turned out to have a thick stick, which he must have cut in the forest the day before. His eyes met Maria Leonidovna's, and his look confused her.

'Wait a moment, I'll bring you something.' She turned around and lightly step-ped out.

'That's not necessary. I don't need anything,' he shouted firmly. 'Don't worry, please. Goodbye.'

In the yard the men were tying something to the roof of the Kreins' car. She ran into the house, pulled fifty francs out of her purse, wrapped the remains of the roast beef and two rolls in a napkin, and went back to the annexe. The little lamp was still burning inside the door, but there was no one there now. He had left quietly, so that no one would notice, and very quickly. In the room it was as if he had never even stayed there; not a single object was out of place.

She looked around, as if he might still be standing somewhere in a corner.

She walked out, went back in again, and then walked to the gate and opened it. Someone was walking alone down the lane – already quite a way away. She watched him for a moment, and suddenly, for no reason, tears came to her eyes, and she couldn't see anything.

'He's leaving, he's leaving,' she said very quietly but distinctly, the way people sometimes utter a meaningless word, and burst into tears. And without understanding what was wrong, or why she had suddenly been overcome by such weakness, she closed the gate gently and went into the house.

In the morning a life began that had nothing to do either with the departed guest or with Maria Leonidovna's secret thoughts. They loaded up the cars so that the spare tyre bumped along behind them on the ground. They locked up the house and sat Kiryusha between his father and grandmother – that day he had exhibited the early signs of rebellion, and they were trying to conceal it. Edouard Zontag, in good form after a night's sleep, was worried that they hadn't taken enough petrol. He took one more long look at the map before setting off. In the first car rode the Kreins and Maria Leonidovna. Manyura rattled on incessantly.

They drove through the deserted village slowly, with difficulty, the spare tyre constantly bumping against the road. When they reached the forest, they started taking country lanes heading in the direction of Blois. They stopped by the château where Chabarov worked as a groundsman. The iron gates were wide open, and horses, still saddled, grazed on the English lawn between young cedars. A French squadron had been stationed there since the previous day. Soldiers were lying on the grass in front of the house and on the ground floor a vast hall, with two rows of windows, and its candelabra, mirrors and bronzes, could be glimpsed through the broken panes.

Chabarov came out wearing corduroy trousers and a matching jacket. The lower half of his face was covered with grey whiskers. Without even saying good morning, he said that he couldn't leave, that he had to stay behind: the night before Daunou (who lived in a nearby hamlet) had been found dead. He had shot himself, and since there was no one left in the area to bury him, Chabarov had decided to bury the body in his garden.

'If these brave lads,' he said gloomily, pointing to the soldiers, 'stay until evening and I manage to dig a suitable hole, then they'll be my witnesses, and that's the best I can hope for. But if they set off before then I'll have to wait for the new authorities to get here. There's no civilian population left.'

Everyone became very quiet as they said goodbye. Krein even got out of the car to embrace him. A minute later both cars drove off downhill, heavy with their loads, following each other closely.

That day, the sound of gunfire came from the other direction, from the northwest. In the sky, with a noise that had not been heard before, like a wail, swooped two German fighter planes.

AN INLAND FISHING TRIP

Halldór Laxness

Translated from the Icelandic by Alan Boucher

Halldór Laxness (1902–1998). Born in Reykjavík, the young Halldór
Gudjónsson spent his early years with his family on Laxnes farm. At the age
of seventeen, he published *Child of Nature*, his first novel, and left Iceland
for Europe. After some years travelling, he converted to Catholicism, living
at Clervaux Abbey in Luxembourg. His religious fervour was short-lived
and, living in the USA, he was drawn to Socialism. His novel *The Great
Weaver from Kashmir* saw him hailed in Iceland as "a literary giant".
His later novels revived the tradition of the Icelandic saga, exemplified
in his trilogy, *Iceland's Bell*. In 1955, he was awarded the Nobel Prize in
Literature, and was praised by the Swedish Academy for having "renewed
the great narrative art of Iceland". He succumbed to Alzheimer's and died
in a nursing home at the age of ninety-five.

D ressed for travelling, his wife had kissed him goodbye and walked away
from the double bed with her suitcase. She opened the door and closed it
behind her. Meanwhile her husband stayed curled up in bed. He listened
intently to her receding steps in the passage and hallway, until the front door
latched sharply shut with a click. As when a catch is released from the spring in
a child's toy, the little man leaps from the box and stands erect with outstretched
arms.

"I am free! Three days and three nights before me! Praise and glory to God
in the highest!"

He sprang out of bed, singing, and executed one or two dance steps on the
floor before brushing his teeth. Then he went to the telephone and dialled the
branch manager's number.

"Is Microbe at home? Still asleep? It doesn't matter. It's me, the cashier, his
friend."

Microbe took a long time to emerge and in the meanwhile his friend waited,
totally emancipated, on the telephone. At last the former came, and the latter,
remembering his position, assumed an attitude.

"Yes, good morning. Sorry to wake you so early, old man. But the wife has
gone. This is the first time she has gone off on holiday on her own for twenty-five
years. You remember I promised to ring as soon as she left. Have you got the
tent and car ready for our fishing trip? If we leave very early tomorrow morning,
camp that evening, and come back the following night, we'll have two good

long days up on the moors. What am I to bring? Hooks, is that all? Whisky, yes of course, that goes without saying. Shall I bring a whole case or half a case? No, a whole case will certainly not be too much. Worms, very well, you look after those. How many hooks shall I get? Seven hundred —as many as that? No, I understand, not worth buying smaller quantities. A few flies? Well, how many? About forty; very well. And food? I see my wife left me a smoked leg of lamb. What's that you're going to call me? Lambkin, indeed, hahaha! You've always been a comic Microbe! Well, my dear fellow, now the soul of Lambkin is really yearning for it! All these years how much I've longed to be where crystal-clear rivers run through long, deep, grassy dales. Grassdale? So you're going to finish the job and give me a surname too! Lambkin Grassdale, eh? Anyway, you're the best friend I have. And we'll meet in good order here in the best room this evening and get everything ready for tomorrow."

Microbe came that evening, as arranged. He was a man of unusual height and enormously fat and therefore had given himself this odd name that signifies something extremely small. He spoke few words at a time and moved little and seldom, but laughed deep inside himself, so that his belly shook. He considered other people funny, especially for being small and thin. Daily he had about him a flock of innocents to amuse him, but from time to time would be entrusted with the care of foreigners on fishing expeditions for his father, the branch manager, who had to do with lakes and salmon rivers. At other times he sat in the inner office with his father and addressed envelopes for the branch, after which he was allowed to stamp them and take them to the post. Privately he avenged himself on people's ordinary names, changing them to accord with the light of a world that he alone inhabited.

Microbe surveyed the best room and saw that all he had commissioned his fellow-fisherman to provide for the journey was there.

"Lambkin Grassdale will not go short on his holiday: seven hundred hooks, forty flies, and a case of whisky. You'll undoubtedly be made branch manager when Father and I are called south to run the head office."

"I am delighted to see you, Microbe. No one has entered this room from time immemorial. The blessed committees on which my wife serves never get beyond the lobby."

"But the paintings—are those supposed to be the rear ends of cows ?" enquired the guest.

"I know you're making fun of them, but it doesn't matter," said his host. "Sit down, I'll mix you a drink."

"Mix what?" said Microbe. "Let me mix my own drink. Where's the soda?"

"I am afraid the soda was simply stolen from me," said Grassdale. "I'm ashamed to admit that I only have water. You know my wife ranks high in the temperance movement."

"Aren't you going to call the girls?" asked Microbe.

Grassdale: "Wouldn't that be going a bit too far, in view of my position as cashier? But if you want to call anyone—womenfolk if you will—then please go ahead."

"My dear fellow, not on my own account," said Microbe. "They bore me. I just sit on them, as one sits on a cat. I meant that if you weren't satisfied with your old woman, there were plenty more. In this day and age the opposite sex is just part of oneself."

Grassdale: "As you know, Microbe, we've been married for twenty-five years. She's the best of wives. She's in child welfare, the Good Templars and the Church-yard Fellowship. But for women like her society would have collapsed long ago.

Microbe: "Has she a hump?"

Grassdale: "No, why should you think that?"

Microbe: "You said she was the best of wives. That's as good as saying she has a hump."

Grassdale: "I meant a fine woman."

Microbe: "Isn't that even worse?"

Grassdale: "It's true, perhaps, that she's a little dry. But she is clean. And she keeps everything dry and clean. She dusts the paintings every day with a feather duster. These things may not be great art, but that's not her fault. No domestic fly has ever thrived here in all these twenty-five years. But now we can have a party, the two of us. What I'm most afraid of is that I may not wake up to my freedom until about the time when she returns."

Microbe: "Let us hope she is tired of you and won't return for a while."

Grassdale: "Tired of me? That never occurred to me before. She is married to me in a correct and moral fashion and no spot has ever fallen upon this house, indoors or out. For twenty-five years I've thought of nothing except how well I was married. I could be promoted from cashier to branch manager any day on that score. Your health!"

Microbe: "I would pinch a woman like that."

Grassdale: "My wife won't be pinched. She's a respectable woman. She would never tolerate a man's hand anywhere near her. She has made me into a respect-able man."

Microbe: "Yes, it's terrible. She must have spiky knees."

Grassdale: "Won't you sit down, my dear fellow, instead of circling round me like that while we talk ? I say, what's this cold feeling I have on the back of my neck? I hope we haven't started a leak anywhere."

Microbe: "Have you never thought of robbing the till?"

Grassdale: "No—in fact that's the only achievement I can claim."

Microbe: "—that you can't claim, you mean."

Grassdale: "I'm sure that if you knew a true woman, Microbe, she would make a respectable man of you, too. She would teach you the difference between good and evil. She would be not only the fulfilment of your life, but the lack of fulfilment also."

Microbe: "Neither applies to me, old man. With me there's neither fulfilment nor lack of fulfilment; never beauty or ugliness, and least of all anything to tell the neighbours about. That's because all is one to me: I am divine. But are you sure your wife hasn't gone to town to meet a man?"

Grassdale: "I know my wife—after twenty-five years."

Microbe: "Their wives are those women whom men never know; least of all after living twenty-five years with them. In fact by then they have become completely incomprehensible."

Grassdale: "I say, Microbe, now I drink without a toast. I'm standing up to scratch my back. Where's that leak?"

Microbe: "Maybe it's the kind of leak that always comes in dry weather."

Grassdale: "Are you trying to tell me that I'm going out of my mind? You're a very bad boy to be saying wicked things about a woman who is the best of women, a fine woman, and a respectable woman. I feel as though something had dripped down my neck in two places. It's branching out and spreading all over my back. And now something cold seems to have got into one of my trouser-legs. Do me a favour and do stop this wandering about. Sit down instead, and drink, and shake your belly over our paintings."

After a while Grassdale returned from a visit to the bathroom with a worm in his hand. "It found its way into my trousers," he said.

"Only one?" said Microbe.

"I think I may have squashed another one in the small of my back. Will you see?"

"I can't stand worms," said Microbe.

"Never mind. Here's to you. Sit down. I want to talk to you a little. I have been thinking about what you said. As always, you were quite right. Nobody knows anyone. The biggest fool of all is one who believes he knows a woman, not to mention his own wife—apart from the man who thinks he knows himself. Now I shall tell you the truth. The year before last my wife became very fond of a certain long-distance coach-driver. She travelled south with him to attend her mother's funeral, and returned with him."

"That's it," said Microbe, "it's always in connexion with funerals or the like that women go astray."

"Listen, now I'll tell you a secret. By the way, what's the time?" said Grassdale.

"The time? Aren't we on a fishing trip, man?"

"Now then, here's one in my hair," said Grassdale. "Do they crawl from you, eh?"

"The man with a worm is drunk. Perhaps you want to go to sleep? It's nearly eleven. I'll call for you in the car at about five in the morning and hoot outside."

"Did you say eleven? and Monday? I say, there's a little something that happens up here in the attic on Mondays at eleven."

Grassdale now took his friend by the hand and led him up the stairs to the attic. Here there was the usual prospect of rafters and a twenty-five-year accumulation of rubbish and junk. By squeezing between broken furniture and rusty iron bedsteads one reached a skylight which could be raised in its frame, opening a gap at the bottom through which one could peep.

"Take care not to show your nose," whispered Grassdale.

A peep revealed the small attic window of the house at the back of the garden. It was now late summer and getting dark at night, and the light was on in the other attic.

"Oh, we're too late," said Grassdale, "she has almost finished."

In the middle of the floor in the other attic a strong-limbed female was standing, engaged in removing her last stitches of clothing. She squeezed a pimple in front of the mirror. Then she put on her nightdress, got into bed, yawned, scratched her hip, and turned out the light. The stage-manager solemnly closed the skylight, the act being over, and looked triumphantly at his audience.

"There, see if I haven't managed to temper the wind to the shorn lamb," he said.

"I don't understand you," said his guest.

"Though my wife may have gone south to have an affair behind my back, I can tell you that I have played this game for years, with all the maidservants of the captain and his wife there in the house across the garden. Every night for the past twenty-five years, when they were not out with their young men, I have undressed them, stitch by stitch, and gone to bed with them. Sometimes I have had two or three in one year. My wife may leave me a smoked leg of lamb, but I have had my share in advance."

But this momentous philandering made little impression on Microbe, who took the opportunity to slip more worms down his host's neck while they were making their way back to resume their drinking.

"Shall I tell you what I have christened this house?" asked Microbe when they were seated. "Peephill. Lambkin Grassdale of Peephill, let's drink to it."

The next morning Lambkin Grassdale of Peephill woke with a headache, nausea, and a general feeling of lassitude. There were worms in the bed. He lay with his collar on, on top of the bedcover, but had taken off his jacket and shoes.

When he had pulled himself together and got up, and especially after he had applied a cold compress to his forehead, he began to recall what had happened. In fact nothing had happened. A good friend had come to visit him. They had chatted together over a drink. But had they bidden each other good night? Suddenly Grassdale remembered that he had planned to go on an inland fishing trip with his friend early that morning. What could the time be? His clock said nine, but was it nine o'clock today or yesterday? He went into the living-room and poured himself a whisky pick-me-up. Then he telephoned to the branch manager's residence and asked for his friend.

He was told that the branch manager's son had left early that morning for the wilderness, to fish for salmon with cabinet ministers and ambassadors.

"So have I really, more or less," said Grassdale, and replaced the receiver. Only he couldn't wake me! But what confounded insect is that on the furniture?

There was no denying it, there was an insect on the chaise-longue. What a state of affairs! he muttered. It was some kind of cross between a blow-fly, a hornet, a tiger-beetle, and a moth. And there was another, and a third. He looked about him and saw that the furniture was covered with them. How had this infernal pest got into the house—not to mention all those worms?—he asked himself. Maybe I have that delirium tremens my wife's pamphlets are always going on about. As he was standing up from his drink, something caught his thigh and held him, tearing his trousers. And there wasn't just the one hook, but wherever he touched the chair he pricked himself. I'm going off my head, said the man, and he drained his glass in horror.

But the pest was not in his mind, it was in a much more serious place: their show drawing-room. On the other hand the case of whisky was gone; only a single bottle left, as a mark of the noble nature of the friend who had passed by. He had wanted to spare my wife the shock of seeing a whole case of whisky, without leaving me totally parched, said the marooned fisherman. But that's just like him, he continued, observing hook after hook in the plush covering of chairs and chaise-longue, and the forty flies to boot. There was also a swarm of the latter in the tablecloth, carpet, and curtains.

He began to try and extract them, but they had been hooked so carefully into the plush that there was no hope of removing them without a tool. But what kind of tool? Scissors? A terrible thought, and surely the last state would be worse than the first! All that he was able to cope with, after a fashion, were the worms, which were genuine; but they were well on the way to drying up, though one or two still showed signs of life about the floor.

After his pick-me-up the spirits of this good man improved and he began to search the telephone directory for the number that might save him. He spoke with the slow delivery of a storyteller nearing the climax of his tale, in a slightly weary, provincial-genteel tone with a touch of some kind of golden age about it.

"Is that the captain's? Yes, how do you do, madam. This is the house at the back of you . . . yes, that one; and this is the branch cashier speaking. Thank you very much indeed, exceptionally well. How very right you are: my wife left the house with her suitcase yesterday morning. Yes, to the south. I hope she has a good time. Yes, she is a remarkable woman. Thank you, no, of course it isn't too late to offer congratulations after twenty-five years. Some people say that a marriage doesn't really begin before the silver wedding. Well now, you amaze me! You've been married to the captain thirty years today, and only just past fifty! May I take the opportunity of offering my heartiest congratulations. I know what an exceptional man the captain is; what a splendid man—a better husband couldn't be found. Eight children. No, there you beat me, madam. Remarkable persons; I knew them by sight when they were small, but never realized there were so many—it's not every day that we compare notes, madam. After all, our front doors face opposite directions and different streets, and one could say that our paths never cross, here or anywhere else, unless we go out by the back door, which is why I have not had the opportunity of taking off my hat to you in all these years. Yet I always nod to your husband, that splendid man, when he comes into the office. But this is not simply a courtesy call, after all these years, I regret to say. Although only a day has passed since my wife went away, there has been a small incident here. There were two anglers in the drawing-room last night, and they dropped something. Sick? Oh no, nothing like that. To tell the truth, a few worms escaped; but that's going to be all right: the worms are beginning to dry up. On the other hand something has got fixed in the furniture. I am afraid that my wife would not be at all pleased if she saw it. Now since I am utterly inex-perienced in the art of putting rooms to rights, whereas you have excellent girls at hand, and I have heard that you have one this summer—'heard', yes, I'm not surprised you say that, hahaha; the fact is that I haven't exactly heard, but seen it and it's natural you should laugh: she often stands at the back in the mornings, beating carpets on the line—I can see she's an excellent girl, as I said before; I mean, excellent where her work is concerned, without being hunchbacked— so it occurred to me that you might be willing to let this girl slip across for a moment and tidy up the drawing-room for me . . ."

Soon after the doorbell rang. He seemed scarcely to know the girl, although he had helped to undress her, squeeze her pimples and all, in a manner not to be gainsaid, once or twice a week for the past year.

"Well, my dear, I am very glad that you are going to help me," he said.

"I've come because the mistress sent me," said the girl.

"I want you to tidy up the drawing-room for me," he said. "There were anglers here last night, and my wife is away. May I offer you a glass of whisky?"

"I'm not in the habit of drinking with married men," said the girl.

"I quite understand," he said. "My wife is an abstainer, too. She only drinks water."

"So do I," said the girl.

"So do the blessed cows. And it's good for them," said the cashier.

"At the outside I drink with my boy-friend, so that he won't drink with other girls," she said.

"So he's like that, is he, the scamp!"

"Of course," said the girl. "Aren't you all like that? What else can one do? One hates it, but it's the only way."

"May I offer you a cigarette, then?" said Grassdale.

"Yes, if you want me to be sick," said the girl. "Please, where's the soap?"

"Maybe a boiled sweet or two?"

"What damned Sodom and Gomorra are you trying to lead me into? Where's the pail? And the scrubber?"

"I'm old enough to be your father, my dear," said Grassdale.

"Old men . . . yes, aren't they perhaps the worst? I've always heard so. What are boys, stupid and with no stomach, beside them? You can be on your guard against a boy, but never an old man. The only time I've been so mad with a man that I could have killed him, it was an old one. Luckily he's in another house."

"Love at a distance," remarked Grassdale.

"I insist on a decent floor-cloth that deserves the name, I say!" cried the girl.

"But my dear, there was never any question of washing all the floors," said the master of the house. "I only want the drawing-room tidied up a bit before my wife comes home; the furniture dusted, and so forth. That's all. In the meanwhile I'm going to play a little."

He showed her into the drawing-room without mentioning the hooks, sat down at the harmonium, and began to sing. But he had not uttered more than a few notes when the door was flung open and the girl stood before him, flabbergasted.

"Who brought those bugs and monsters into the house? Or do they live here? Do the damned things fly, or are they some sort of lice? No one is going to get me to lay a finger on poisonous reptiles!"

"I'll handle the reptiles, if you'll deal with the rest," said the master.

The girl returned to the room, where her eyes now fell upon the hooks. She appeared again in the doorway.

"What have I done to be dragged from the house where I live and am happy, just as we were going to have chicken with wine, and made a fool of in a strange place?" she exclaimed. "What have I done to deserve it?"

"My dear young lady," he replied, "if these can't be removed, what do you suppose my wife is going to say when she comes home?"

"I don't care a damn what your wife says. I haven't been to bed with you," said the girl.

"I'll do my best to help as much as I can," said Grassdale. "What's the best thing to do?"

"Remove the plush and take out the hooks from the inside," said the girl.

He patted her lightly on the behind, like a horse, and strange though it may seem, the girl appeared to calm down a little at this. He tried to demonstrate to her that the venomous reptiles were man-made, and though she believed him no more than was proper, he being a man, she sniffed as an indication that she was no longer angry. However, the hooks continued to be as unextractable from the inside as from the outside of the plush. Of course it would have been possible to cut it all up and rip it off. But what would his wife have said when she came? The furniture had been her contribution to the home; part of her marriage portion. Many of the hooks were triple-barbed and had been inserted with loving care. After two hours' work they had only managed to remove six. By now the girl was hot and red in the face.

"When is your wife coming home?" she asked.

Grassdale said in two days.

Then the girl began to cry. She sobbed, "Dear God, why did I have to get mixed up in this?"

"Don't cry, darling," said Grassdale, and he stroked the girl's hair. "Don't despair. Maybe we'll think of something."

"Don't talk to me," said the girl, and she continued to cry. "I'd never want to be married to you."

"We have worked hard and long, and it's getting late," he said. "How would it be to have a little refreshment before carrying on? I've offered you whisky, a cigarette, and boiled sweets. What do you say to a slice of smoked leg of lamb?"

The girl replied, "Never has a man treated a girl like this before. A married fellow, to hang by his nose at the skylight each night, all the year round, when a respectable girl is going to bed, and then in the end to offer her smoked leg of lamb. I'm off!"

She swept out, slamming three doors behind her: drawing-room, hall, and front door.

And the hooks stayed in the furniture.

What was to be done now? Not only had the girl failed in the role for which she had been cast, but she had made a point of insulting a man old enough to be her father, beside being a branch cashier and maybe destined to higher things in the not-too-distant future. She had humiliated this man without provocation in a most sensitive spot. Was it likely that he would be able to do anything? It occurred to him that for many the only resort in an emergency was to drink their wits away; but what would his wife say about that, on top of everything else?

Although it was summer, he put on a black overcoat, and was about to go out in the hope of meeting a saviour in some form in the street.

The next marvel entered the house by the back door to replace the hope that had sailed out by the front fifteen minutes earlier: a young lady of fashion clad in the latest hobble style on stiletto heels came mincing in across the floor. Lambkin Grassdale removed his coat without a word and gazed in astonishment at this apparition.

She was so swelling with vitality that the bounds of the flesh seemed on the point of bursting away from the soul—with a mountain of up-combed hair so golden that it could have been assisted by chemistry; eyes blue as a colour-photograph; a freshness of cheek beyond nature; a toothbrush smile of the kind that radiates through windscreens in advertisements for the latest car models: the revelation that makes a man turn about in his life and never find his way home again. The dream-woman of the magazine—fairy of modern folklore—she entered the kitchen as if she had always lived there and had just slipped out into the garden to feed the sparrows.

She offered him an oblation on a dish covered with a white cloth. This gift she laid on the low table before the sofa in the hall. She stretched out a strong, well-manicured hand with bronze nails to him, and drew the man into the large, divine triumphal chariot of her soul.

"The maid misunderstood the position, and so I came," said the visitor. "I must make it clear that it was Mama who sent me. We heard you had nothing but smoked leg of lamb. But first of all I want to thank you for all your kindness—when I was little."

"Say nothing of it," he replied. "Please sit down."

"I know you know me," she said. "Oh, can't we drop formality? I've known you, and more than that, from when I slept in a pram out here in the garden. But I've been away for a long time. I've been educating myself, enjoying myself, and working for myself. Now I've returned home I see everything much more clearly than I did before, when it was actually happening. While I was abroad I got to know my old neighbours better in memory than when I saw them every day. That's why at long last I want to thank you for being so good to us girls when we still hadn't much sense, if any. In our eyes you were the man of the world. Papa was often drunk when he was at home."

"Yes, I should say I know the captain's children, who used to put their dolls to sleep on the steps at the back there, while I had no little girl; also those small brothers of yours who, I'm told, are now managers whereas I'm still only a cashier. But it's no wonder you children did well: the captain being such a heroic character; your mother such a fine, strong woman."

"Don't you think Mama is a little too stout?" said the young lady. "And those massive shoulders—but then I'm probably on the way to becoming the same myself!"

"Your mother is a true lady, in both appearance and deed," said the master of the house.

"It's kind of you to say so, but I'm really worried about the ruggedness of her features. Bless me if Mama hasn't turned into a trollwife. It's the truth!"

"She's a woman whom perhaps her neighbour never knew to speak to. But he flees to her in his hour of need. That's why I telephoned this morning."

"We were quite bowled over! We were just about to celebrate her thirtieth wedding anniversary with a chicken, when you, the man of the world, rang in the nick of time! We had been on the point of inviting you over, but didn't like to because Papa was at sea and your wife away in the south. But when we heard about the smoked leg of lamb it was too much for us. It was I who had the idea of bringing you this little something on a dish, and thanking you for this vener-able house that has stood behind us, silent and civilizing."

"Whoever knows the silence of my house need fear no other or greater silence," said the master, smiling. "My wife's committees would sometimes sit, yawning like sylphs, here in the antechamber, of an evening. They were improving the world for both living and dead—instead of putting naughty children to bed. Our drawing-room was too good for committees. The sun stood still in our drawing-room all the summer through. So the years went by."

"There were a few things you didn't know about," said the young lady; and when he just smiled dully, she continued: "for instance, could it have been the hat-raising of our neighbour, the man of the world, that made me begin to suppose I was something? You can just imagine how bright one was in those days! I blush at the thought. Fortunately one learns later that there is only the one sex—and it's just sex."

"As it happens, my wife is away!" he said.

"She's a remarkable woman," replied the girl. "It was quite admirable, the way she looked after this big house: never a speck of dust inside or out, the curtains starched white, pansies and marigolds in the back garden—but for whom? Nobody saw the flowers, apart from us at the captain's. And we could do with them; there was nothing but swedes and potatoes there, and the mud was carried into the house by us children."

"Here there was only one child, young lady: I myself, the child of my wife," said the cashier.

"That's why we were so flabbergasted yesterday morning when we saw her going off with her suitcase," said the young lady. "What happened?"

"One fine day the wife goes away," said the man. "No explanation. Maybe she met someone last year. If so, she may be back in three days. Maybe she met no one and has just vanished into the blue; in which case there's not much likelihood of her returning. The night after she left, the house is in ruins. What has happened can't even be described. I'll consider myself lucky if I survive another night. And as for the third—better not think so far ahead."

She had sat down on the sofa, knees thrust forward and bosom escaping above her neckline. Lifting the cloth from the gift, what should she reveal but a chicken with brown, well-roasted wings, and legs outspread on the dish.

"It must be eaten while it's fresh," said the girl.

The man stared in amazement at this marvel. True enough, he had not tasted food for the past day. On waking that morning his body had ached all over. Now mental suffering had cured him of aching bones, queasy stomach, nausea, headache, hunger, and much else besides. His house, that terrible house, had in fact been razed to the ground and its fall had not only dulled him with sickness, but also robbed him of the presence of mind to praise God in face of a gift from heaven. He expressed himself as follows:

"Up to now nothing has ever happened to me. This is the first time. I am unworthy of it. I don't understand. I have no words; no feelings. Can it be true? Young lady, may I kiss you?"

She stood up and kissed him without hesitation. He continued to stare at the chicken and said, as if talking in his sleep, "A chicken like this has not been served to a man since the priestesses in the Egyptian paintings offered sacrifice to Pharaoh in ancient times. I could follow you to the world's end this very instant."

"My childhood love,' said the girl, and she kissed him again. "Do you suppose it's too good for you? Unzip the back of my dress."

"Unfortunately it is not as simple as all that," he said. "Something terrible has happened. Either my wife has killed herself, or she will kill me when she comes home. Let me show you the drawing-room."

He opened the door and showed the young lady. At first glance there was nothing to see. It was just like any other dreary, sexless provincial reception-room where never a guest is entertained and the abandoned sun continues to fade the colours of the plush all through the long summer day, year in year out.

"Do you see?" he said.

"What?" she asked.

"The flies!"

"What are they for?" she asked.

"Or rather, the hooks. Just look!" he said.

She asked, "Who put them there?"

He answered, "That's my secret. If I told you I would lose my position as cashier. Then all hope of advancement in life would be gone. However, I have calculated that, from the time spent by two in removing six hooks, it would take a full sixty working days to remove them all."

"I've forgotten the rule of three," said the girl.

She glanced at the watch on her wrist and remembered that she had to go; she was expected in town. She said goodbye and walked out by the front door.

The chicken lay on its dish. The master of the house stared in anguish at this well-roasted monstrosity. It was the last straw. Nowhere, either indoors or out, was there a safe refuge from this bird of ill omen. Nothing served with a corpse like this but to bury it; bury it; bury it high up on the mountainside in the middle of the night when all was pitch dark and the town fast asleep. And still the hooks would remain fixed in the furniture.

In the grey twilight of the still evening this worthy man walked into the town. He went to the furniture shop and asked them whether they would buy second-hand furniture. They said they sold new stuff; they didn't buy old. He asked for the head of the establishment and explained that he had to sell his furniture and have it moved away that day, because his wife was bringing home new the next. The proprietor declared that even if the furniture were given him, he would have no room for it in his small shop. On the other hand he said that a young couple living on the corner opposite needed furniture.

The man crossed the street and called on the young couple, who wanted to buy ultra-modern furniture, but had no money.

"Of course mine is classical," said Lambkin Grassdale, though the couple did not understand the word—"still, it's cheap."

"What colour is the covering?" asked the woman.

"Perhaps it needs a new covering," he said.

"Is it worn and ugly?" asked the woman.

Grassdale: "No, it's as good as new. It has hardly ever been sat on. I venture to assure you that this is the most expensive and the highest quality furniture in the town. If you can collect it this evening it is yours. But there are one or two hooks that have got fixed in it."

"No thank you," said the couple, "we're sorry."

After strolling about the town for quite a while in a dignified way, he slipped furtively into the airways office and said that a man had asked him to find out about flights to America.

"When does he want to go?"

"Tonight," he said.

"Has the man a visa?"

But the man had not even a passport. They said that a passport could be obtained in the morning, but a visa was only to be had in the capital, and it could take a week. He said he was sorry but it was out of the question unless it was possible to leave straight away and be in America the following morning.

He wandered out of the town and along the shore, until he came to an ancient jetty where once whales had been flensed and bigger and better guts exposed than anywhere else. This jetty was now used chiefly by people intending to drown themselves. He walked out along the jetty under the wings of the seabirds that circle there with loud cries, night and day, and his every footstep was instinct with a weight of responsibility and moral sense, together with the notion of that norm of Christian conduct that is the keystone in the arch of society. Then the clouds parted, and the sun shone over young men who rowed their boats across the calm water, singing.

He hurried home a little before eleven that evening. It was getting dark. From old habit he crept up to the attic and raised the skylight cautiously from its frame.

The house at the back was dark and silent, except in the maid's attic room, where there was a light as usual. But now, for the first time in twenty-five years, a curtain had been drawn across the window. Misfortunes never come singly. He slunk back down his own attic stairs, an outcast and a ruined man.

The chicken lay on its dish.

I'm quite sure I shan't sleep a wink all night, said the man to himself.

After a while the telephone began to ring. It was the captain's wife. The good woman had somehow got word of their failure to cope with the little misadventure mentioned by him that morning. She said she was going to pop over and see whether she still had the lucky knack she had sometimes had before—wasn't the kitchen door open? After a short interval the captain's wife entered the house, encased in all the corsets that serve to enhance the honour of a plump middle-aged woman. She walked with firm, confident steps and the kind of rustle of silk that went with them, while her shoes squeaked in a distinguished way. After twenty-five years both mother and daughter seemed to be as familiar with the entries to this house as with those of their own.

"How do you do. Thank you so much for your kindness. Please sit down," said the master of the house, and he led her to the settee, which was no more than adequate for her, though designed for two. She affected not to notice the chicken on its dish and enveloped him in the sort of atmosphere that sometimes rises from hot, heather-covered dales on calm summer days.

"I am rather shy by nature," said this big woman; "but I thought there might be something else I could do for you. If nothing more, I could transmit my current to you."

'It would hardly be an exaggeration to say that I'm at my wits' end," he replied, "and more than that. It would take a full sixty working days, at the very least, to put this right. My wife may come home tomorrow; at the latest, the day after. I've tried everything. Beautiful young girls have been here: they could do nothing. I've been to a furniture-maker and offered to sell him the whole suite: no, thank you! I've offered to give it away to a young married couple: no, thank you! I've been to a travel bureau and asked for an immediate flight to America, but of course that was no good, either. Last of all, I went out to the whale jetty to find myself a place there. Tell me the truth, madam, do you think I'm mad?"

"As you can see, I'm a woman in her fifties, the mother of eight and a grandmother many times over. All my days have been spent in the midst of the green valley of life. I have neither the knowledge, the wisdom, nor the looks to solve any man's problems, to say nothing of my own. But I am a little psychic. I have a current. Sit down in my aura and don't be afraid. Women of my age are long past doing any harm. I shall hold your hand; we'll talk quietly together, and I'll give you what I have to give."

"What would you say to your husband if you were to return home and find your best room in ruins?" he enquired.

"I have never had a best room," she replied. "On the other hand my husband often forgot to provide for the home when the children were small; he kept mistresses; sometimes three at once, beside those he had abroad. And he often came home drunk. But I loved him, however often he left the house in ruins. I only needed a night to build it up again. Though there was never any best room; and nothing but potatoes and swedes grew in the garden."

"My wife grew flowers," said the master of the house. "And not only was she a Good Templar and confirmed non-swearer, but also by her efforts the churchyard, with its glory of flowers, became the pride of the community. She dusted the pictures every day—though Microbe laughs at them. And once a quarter she would beat the furniture, which she had brought with her as a wedding portion and which is now done for."

"Heaven knows I look up to this woman also, as a true model of feminine virtue," said the visitor.

"That she was, and will always be, in life or death," said the man. "This is why my misadventure in the drawing-room has completely finished me."

"I hope you will never think of this woman otherwise than with gratitude," said the visitor. "Nor may we forget to thank her for the comfortable churchyard she has prepared for us all."

He said, "Some think this woman has gone south to betray me. Others believe she has gone to do away with herself. What do you think?"

"The worst is yet unspoken," she said.

"But if she comes back, what am I to do?" he asked.

She enclosed one of his hands softly between her palms and answered, "Trust me."

"I think you are a good guest," he said, using the familiar form of speech.

"We must not be familiar," she said. "It would be misunderstood."

"There's no one to hear," he said.

"For that reason, too, it would be a sin," she said. "And beware of leaning your forehead against my eyebrows. Once I found some eyebrow-black on my husband's handkerchief. A man can have no enemy as diabolically cunning as a woman. But you may lay the palm of your hand on the small of my back, where the snake Kundalini sleeps coiled up—that serpent-fire that some call the World-Mother. When woken, it uncoils and climbs up the spine towards the brain, endowing the soul with infinite powers and enabling the human being to perform miracles."

"You are too widely read in esoteric books for me to follow you," said the man. "All I ask is how I am to get the hooks out of the plush."

"You have at your back a house that has been ruined and rebuilt many times; my house," said the woman. "So long as you remember that, nothing you need fear will ever happen. A woman in possession of knees like mine is past sinning; at least in thought, word or deed. If anything goes wrong, it will be enough to call me on the phone. And now that time of night is come when those in the churchyard begin to stir—and we mortals go to our beds and turn out the light."

The venerable matron had risen to her feet.

"You should take me across with you, madam," he said.

"It could be misunderstood," said the woman.

"You won't go without saying goodnight, though," said the man.

"I shall leave the current behind," she said, and was gone.

This great, good woman walked away with firm steps in her squeaking shoes, out through the kitchen, unemotionally and most virtuously closing the back door behind her. All at once the man had quite forgotten about the hooks and was wondering how a woman who had spent so long in the midst of the green valley of life could vanish like smoke the very moment she had redeemed a man.

After he had gone to bed and sunk into a gentle, easy slumber, he suddenly started up at a noise in the outer room, switched on the light and asked, "Who's there?"

"Could it be original sin in felt slippers?" came the answer from outside. "At all events, there's no need to be switching on the light. I began thinking about a little something, all of a sudden, after I had gone to bed: my daughter's good name. I wouldn't want this chicken to foul your wife's dustbin; she might think someone had sneaked in to you from that confounded brothel of a churchyard, where all lie together divinely, in single sex, without morals. I am going to slip that chicken into my dustbin."

Then the woman bade the man goodnight.

GIMPEL THE FOOL

Isaac Bashevis Singer

Translated from the Yiddish by Saul Bellow

Isaac Bashevis Singer (1904–1991) was a Polish-born American writer of novels, short stories, and essays in Yiddish. He was the recipient in 1978 of the Nobel Prize for Literature. His fiction, depicting Jewish life in Poland and the United States, is remarkable for its rich blending of irony, wit, and wisdom, flavoured distinctively with the occult and the grotesque. Singer was a prominent Jewish vegetarian for the last thirty-five years of his life and often included vegetarian themes in his works. Singer's birth date is uncertain; it is widely reported that he presented himself as being younger to authorities to avoid the military draft.

I

I am Gimpel the Fool. I don't think myself a fool. On the contrary. But that's what folks call me. They gave me the name while I was still in school. I had seven names in all: imbecile, donkey, flax-head, dope, glump, ninny, and fool. The last name stuck. What did my foolishness consist of? I was easy to take in. They said, "Gimpel, you know the rabbi's wife has been brought to childbed?" So I skipped school. Well, it turned out to be a lie. How was I supposed to know? She hadn't had a big belly. But I never looked at her belly. Was that really so foolish? The gang laughed and hee-hawed, stomped and danced and chanted a good-night prayer. And instead of the raisins they give when a woman's lying in, they stuffed my hand full of goat turds. I was no weakling. If I slapped someone he'd see all the way to Cracow. But I'm really not a slugger by nature. I think to myself: Let it pass. So they take advantage of me.

I was coming home from school and heard a dog barking. I'm not afraid of dogs, but of course I never want to start up with them. One of them may be mad, and if he bites there's not a Tartar in the world who can help you. So I made tracks. Then I looked around and saw the whole market place wild with laughter. It was no dog at all but Wolf-Leib the Thief. How was I supposed to know it was he? It sounded like a howling bitch.

When the pranksters and leg-pullers found that I was easy to fool, every one of them tried his luck with me. "Gimpel, the Czar is coming to Frampol; Gimpel, the moon fell down in Turbeen; Gimpel, little Hodel Furpiece found a treasure behind the bathhouse." And I like a golem believed everyone. In the first place, everything is possible, as it is written in the Wisdom of the Fathers, I've forgotten just how. Second, I had to believe when the whole town came down on me! If

I ever dared to say, "Ah, you're kidding!" there was trouble. People got angry. "What do you mean! You want to call everyone a liar?" What was I to do? I believed them, and I hope at least that did them some good.

I was an orphan. My grandfather who brought me up was already bent toward the grave. So they turned me over to a baker, and what a time they gave me there! Every woman or girl who came to bake a batch of noodles had to fool me at least once. "Gimpel, there's a fair in heaven; Gimpel, the rabbi gave birth to a calf in the seventh month; Gimpel, a cow flew over the roof and laid brass eggs." A student from the yeshiva came once to buy a roll, and he said, "You, Gimpel, while you stand here scraping with your baker's shovel the Messiah has come. The dead have arisen." "What do you mean?" I said. "I heard no one blowing the ram's horn!" He said, "Are you deaf?" And all began to cry, "We heard it, we heard!" Then in came Rietze the Candle-dipper and called out in her hoarse voice, "Gimpel, your father and mother have stood up from the grave. They're looking for you."

To tell the truth, I knew very well that nothing of the sort had happened, but all the same, as folks were talking, I threw on my wool vest and went out. Maybe something had happened. What did I stand to lose by looking? Well, what a cat music went up! And then I took a vow to believe nothing more. But that was no go either. They confused me so that I didn't know the big end from the small.

I went to the rabbi to get some advice. He said, "It is written, better to be a fool all your days than for one hour to be evil. You are not a fool. They are the fools. For he who causes his neighbor to feel shame loses Paradise himself." Nevertheless the rabbi's daughter took me in. As I left the rabbinical court she said, "Have you kissed the wall yet?" I said, "No; what for?" She answered, "It's the law; you've got to do it after every visit." Well, there didn't seem to be any harm in it. And she burst out laughing. It was a fine trick. She put one over on me, all right.

I wanted to go off to another town, but then everyone got busy matchmaking, and they were after me so they nearly tore my coat tails off. They talked at me and talked until I got water on the ear. She was no chaste maiden, but they told me she was virgin pure. She had a limp, and they said it was deliberate, from coyness. She had a bastard, and they told me the child was her little brother. I cried, "You're wasting your time. I'll never marry that whore." But they said indignantly, "What a way to talk! Aren't you ashamed of yourself? We can take you to the rabbi and have you fined for giving her a bad name." I saw then that I wouldn't escape them so easily and I thought: They're set on making me their butt. But when you're married the husband's the master, and if that's all right with her it's agreeable to me too. Besides, you can't pass through life unscathed, nor expect to.

I went to her clay house, which was built on the sand, and the whole gang, hollering and chorusing, came after me. They acted like bear-baiters. When we came to the well they stopped all the same. They were afraid to start anything with Elka. Her mouth would open as if it were on a hinge, and she had a fierce tongue. I entered the house. Lines were strung from wall to wall and clothes were drying. Barefoot she stood by the tub, doing the wash. She was dressed in a worn hand-me-down gown of plush. She had her hair put up in braids and pinned across her head. It took my breath away, almost, the reek of it all.

Evidently she knew who I was. She took a look at me and said, "Look who's here! He's come, the drip. Grab a seat."

I told her all; I denied nothing. "Tell me the truth," I said, "are you really a virgin, and is that mischievous Yechiel actually your little brother? Don't be deceitful with me, for I'm an orphan."

"I'm an orphan myself," she answered, "and whoever tries to twist you up, may the end of his nose take a twist. But don't let them think they can take advantage of me. I want a dowry of fifty guilders, and let them take up a collection besides. Otherwise they can kiss my you-know-what." She was very plainspoken. I said, "It's the bride and not the groom who gives a dowry." Then she said, "Don't bargain with me. Either a flat 'yes' or a flat 'no'—Go back where you came from."

I thought: No bread will ever be baked from *this* dough. But ours is not a poor town. They consented to everything and proceeded with the wedding. It so happened that there was a dysentery epidemic at the time. The ceremony was held at the cemetery gates, near the little corpse-washing hut. The fellows got drunk. While the marriage contract was being drawn up I heard the most pious high rabbi ask, "Is the bride a widow or a divorced woman?" And the sexton's wife answered for her, "Both a widow and divorced." It was a black moment for me. But what was I to do, run away from under the marriage canopy?

There was singing and dancing. An old granny danced opposite me, hugging a braided white *chalah*. The master of revels made a "God 'a mercy" in memory of the bride's parents. The schoolboys threw burrs, as on Tishe b'Av fast day. There were a lot of gifts after the sermon: a noodle board, a kneading trough, a bucket, brooms, ladles, household articles galore. Then I took a look and saw two strapping young men carrying a crib. "What do we need this for?" I asked. So they said, "Don't rack your brains about it. It's all right, it'll come in handy." I realized I was going to be rooked. Take it another way though, what did I stand to lose? I reflected: I'll see what comes of it. A whole town can't go altogether crazy.

II

At night I came where my wife lay, but she wouldn't let me in. "Say, look here, is this what they married us for?" I said. And she said, "My monthly has come." "But yesterday they took you to the ritual bath, and that's afterward, isn't it supposed to be?" "Today isn't yesterday," said she, "and yesterday's not today. You can beat it if you don't like it." In short, I waited.

Nor four months later she was in childbed. The townsfolk hid their laughter with their knuckles. But what could I do? She suffered intolerable pains and clawed at the walls. "Gimpel," she cried, "I'm going. Forgive me!" The house filled with women. They were boiling pans of water. The screams rose to the welkin.

The thing to do was to go to the House of Prayer to repeat Psalms, and that was what I did.

The townsfolk liked that, all right. I stood in a corner saying Psalms and prayers, and they shook their heads at me. "Pray, pray!" they told me. "Prayer never made any woman pregnant." One of the congregation put a straw to my mouth and said, "Hay for the cows." There was something to that too, by God!

She gave birth to a boy. Friday at the synagogue the sexton stood up before the Ark, pounded on the reading table, and announced, "The wealthy Reb Gimpel invites the congregation to a feast in honor of the birth of a son." The whole House of Prayer rang with laughter. My face was flaming. But there was nothing I could do. After all, I *was* the one responsible for the circumcision honors and rituals.

Half the town came running. You couldn't wedge another soul in. Women brought peppered chick-peas, and there was a keg of beer from the tavern. I ate and drank as much as anyone, and they all congratulated me. Then there was a circumcision, and I named the boy after my father, may he rest in peace. When all were gone and I was left with my wife alone, she thrust her head through the bed-curtain and called me to her.

"Gimpel," said she, "why are you silent? Has your ship gone and sunk?"

"What shall I say?" I answered. "A fine thing you've done to me! If my mother had known of it she'd have died a second time."

She said, "Are you crazy, or what?"

"How can you make such a fool," I said, "of one who should be the lord and master?"

"What's the matter with you?" she said. "What have you taken it into your head to imagine?"

I saw that I must speak bluntly and openly. "Do you think this is the way to use an orphan?" I said, "You have borne a bastard."

She answered, "Drive this foolishness out of your head. The child is yours."

"How can he be mine?" I argued. "He was born seventeen weeks after the wedding."

She told me then that he was premature. I said, "Isn't he a little too premature?" She said, she had had a grandmother who carried just as short a time and she resembled this grandmother of hers as one drop of water does another. She swore to it with such oaths that you would have believed a peasant at the fair if he had used them. To tell the plain truth, I didn't believe her; but when I talked it over next day with the schoolmaster he told me that the very same thing had happened to Adam and Eve. Two they went up to bed, and four they descended.

"There isn't a woman in the world who is not the granddaughter of Eve," he said.

That was how it was; they argued me dumb. But then, who really knows how such things are?

I began to forget my sorrow. I loved the child madly, and he loved me too. As soon as he saw me he'd wave his little hands and want me to pick him up, and when he was colicky I was the only one who could pacify him. I bought him a little bone teething ring and a little gilded cap. He was forever catching the evil-eye from someone, and then I had to run to get one of those abracadabras for him that would get him out of it. I worked like an ox. You know how expenses go up when there's an infant in the house. I don't want to lie about it; I didn't dislike Elka either, for that matter. She swore at me and cursed, and I couldn't get enough of her. What strength she had! One of her looks could rob you of the power of speech. And her orations! Pitch and sulphur, that's what they were full of, and yet somehow also full of charm. I adored her every word. She gave me bloody wounds though.

In the evening I brought her a white loaf as well as a dark one, and also poppyseed rolls I baked myself. I thieved because of her and swiped everything I could lay hands on: macaroons, raisins, almonds, cakes. I hope I may be forgiven for stealing from the Saturday pots the women left to warm in the baker's oven. I would take out scraps of meat, a chunk of pudding, a chicken leg or head, a piece of tripe, whatever I could nip quickly. She ate and became fat and handsome.

I had to sleep away from home all during the week, at the bakery. On Friday nights when I got home she always made an excuse of some sort. Either she had heartburn, or a stitch in the side, or hiccups, or headaches. You know what women's excuses are. I had a bitter time of it. It was rough. To add to it, this little brother of hers, the bastard, was growing bigger. He'd put lumps on me, and when I wanted to hit back she'd open her mouth and curse so powerfully I saw a green haze floating before my eyes. Ten times a day she threatened to divorce me. Another man in my place would have taken French leave and disappeared. But I'm the type that bears it and says nothing. What's one to do? Shoulders are from God, and burdens too.

One night there was a calamity in the bakery; the oven burst, and we almost had a fire. There was nothing to do but go home, so I went home. Let me, I thought, also taste the joy of sleeping in bed in mid-week. I didn't want to wake the sleeping mite and tiptoed into the house. Coming in, it seemed to me that I heard not the snoring of one but, as it were, a double snore, one a thin enough snore and the other like the snoring of a slaughtered ox. Oh, I didn't like that! I didn't like it at all. I went up to the bed, and things suddenly turned black. Next to Elka lay a man's form. Another in my place would have made an uproar, and enough noise to rouse the whole town, but the thought occurred to me that I might wake the child. A little thing like that—why frighten a little swallow, I thought. All right then, I went back to the bakery and stretched out on a sack of flour and till morning I never shut an eye. I shivered as if I had had malaria. "Enough of being a donkey," I said to myself. "Gimpel isn't going to be a sucker all his life. There's a limit even to the foolishness of a fool like Gimpel."

In the morning I went to the rabbi to get advice, and it made a great commotion in the town. They sent the beadle for Elka right away. She came, carrying the child. And what do you think she did? She denied it, denied everything, bone and stone! "He's out of his head," she said. "I know nothing of dreams or divinations." They yelled at her, warned her, hammered on the table, but she stuck to her guns: it was a false accusation, she said.

The butchers and the horse-traders took her part. One of the lads from the slaughterhouse came by and said to me, "We've got our eye on you, you're a marked man." Meanwhile the child started to bear down and soiled itself. In the rabbinical court there was an Ark of the Covenant, and they couldn't allow that, so they sent Elka away.

I said to the rabbi, "What shall I do?"

"You must divorce her at once," said he.

"And what if she refuses?" I asked.

He said, "You must serve the divorce. That's all you'll have to do."

I said, "Well, all right, Rabbi. Let me think about it."

"There's nothing to think about," said he. "You mustn't remain under the same roof with her."

"And if I want to see the child?" I asked.

"Let her go, the harlot," said he, "and her brood of bastards with her."

The verdict he gave was that I mustn't even cross her threshold—never again, as long as I should live.

During the day it didn't bother me so much. I thought: It was bound to happen, the abscess had to burst. But at night when I stretched out upon the sacks I felt it all very bitterly. A longing took me, for her and for the child. I wanted to be angry, but that's my misfortune exactly, I don't have it in me to be really angry. In the first place—this was how my thoughts went— there's bound to be a slip sometimes. You can't live without errors. Probably that lad who was with her led her on and gave her presents and what not, and women are often long on hair and short on sense, and so he got around her. And then since she denies it so, maybe I was only seeing things? Hallucinations do happen. You see a figure or a mannikin or something, but when you come up closer it's nothing, there's not a thing there. And if that's so, I'm doing her an injustice. And when I got so far in my thoughts I started to weep. I sobbed so that I wet the flour where I lay. In the morning I went to the rabbi and told him that I had made a mistake. The rabbi wrote on with his quill, and he said that if that were so he would have to reconsider the whole case. Until he had finished I wasn't to go near my wife, but I might send her bread and money by messenger.

III

Nine months passed before all the rabbis could come to an agreement. Letters went back and forth. I hadn't realized that there could be so much erudition about a matter like this.

Meanwhile Elka gave birth to still another child, a girl this time. On the Sabbath I went to the synagogue and invoked a blessing on her. They called me up to the Torah, and I named the child for my mother-in-law—may she rest in peace. The louts and loudmouths of the town who came into the bakery gave me a going over. All Frampol refreshed its spirits because of my trouble and grief. However, I resolved that I would always believe what I was told. What's the good of *not* believing? Today it's your wife you don't believe; tomorrow it's God Himself you won't take stock in.

By an apprentice who was her neighbor I sent her daily a corn or a wheat loaf, or a piece of pastry, rolls or bagels, or, when I got the chance, a slab of pudding, a slice of honeycake, or wedding strudel—whatever came my way. The apprentice was a goodhearted lad, and more than once he added something on his own. He had formerly annoyed me a lot, plucking my nose and digging me in the ribs, but when he started to be a visitor to my house he became kind and friendly. "Hey, you, Gimpel," he said to me, "you have a very decent little wife and two fine kids. You don't deserve them."

"But the things people say about her," I said. "Well, they have long tongues," he said, "and nothing to do with them but babble. Ignore it as you ignore the cold of last winter."

One day the rabbi sent for me and said, "Are you certain, Gimpel, that you were wrong about your wife?"

I said, "I'm certain."

"Why, but look here! You yourself saw it."

"It must have been a shadow," I said.

"The shadow of what?"

"Just of one of the beams, I think."

"You can go home then. You owe thanks to the Yanover rabbi. He found an obscure reference in Maimonides that favored you."

I seized the rabbi's hand and kissed it.

I wanted to run home immediately. It's no small thing to be separated for so long a time from wife and child. Then I reflected: I'd better go back to work now, and go home in the evening. I said nothing to anyone, although as far as my heart was concerned it was like one of the Holy Days. The women teased and twitted me as they did every day, but my thought was: Go on, with your loose talk. The truth is out, like the oil upon the water. Maimonides says it's right, and therefore it is right!

At night, when I had covered the dough to let it rise, I took my share of bread and a little sack of flour and started homeward. The moon was full and the stars were glistening, something to terrify the soul. I hurried onward, and before me darted a long shadow. It was winter, and a fresh snow had fallen. I had a mind to sing, but it was growing late and I didn't want to wake the householders. Then I felt like whistling, but I remembered that you don't whistle at night because it brings the demons out. So I was silent and walked as fast as I could.

Dogs in the Christian yards barked at me when I passed, but I thought: Bark your teeth out! What are you but mere dogs? Whereas I am a man, the husband of a fine wife, the father of promising children.

As I approached the house my heart started to pound as though it were the heart of a criminal. I felt no fear, but my heart went thump! thump! Well, no drawing back. I quietly lifted the latch and went in. Elka was asleep. I looked at the infant's cradle. The shutter was closed, but the moon forced its way through the cracks. I saw the newborn child's face and loved it as soon as I saw it—immediately—each tiny bone.

Then I came nearer to the bed. And what did I see but the apprentice lying there beside Elka. The moon went out all at once. It was utterly black, and I trembled. My teeth chattered. The bread fell from my hands, and my wife waked and said, "Who is that, ah?"

I muttered, "It's me."

"Gimpel?" she asked. "How come you're here? I thought it was forbidden."

"The rabbi said," I answered and shook as with a fever.

"Listen to me, Gimpel," she said, "go out to the shed and see if the goat's all right. It seems she's been sick." I have forgotten to say that we had a goat. When I heard she was unwell I went into the yard. The nannygoat was a good little creature. I had a nearly human feeling for her.

With hesitant steps I went up to the shed and opened the door. The goat stood there on her four feet. I felt her everywhere, drew her by the horns, examined her udders, and found nothing wrong. She had probably eaten too much bark. "Good night, little goat," I said. "Keep well." And the little beast answered with a "Maa" as though to thank me for the good will.

I went back. The apprentice had vanished.

"Where," I asked, "is the lad?"

"What lad?" my wife answered.

"What do you mean?" I said. "The apprentice. You were sleeping with him."

"The things I have dreamed this night and the night before," she said, "may they come true and lay you low, body and soul! An evil spirit has taken root in you and dazzles your sight." She screamed out, "You hateful creature! You moon calf! You spook! You uncouth man! Get out, or I'll scream all Frampol out of bed!" Before I could move, her brother sprang out from behind the oven and struck me a blow on the back of the head. I thought he had broken my neck. I felt that something about me was deeply wrong, and I said, "Don't make a scandal. All that's needed now is that people should accuse me of raising spooks and *dybbuks*." For that was what she had meant. "No one will touch bread of my baking."

In short, I somehow calmed her.

"Well," she said, "that's enough. Lie down, and be shattered by wheels."

Next morning I called the apprentice aside. "Listen here, brother!" I said. And so on and so forth. "What do you say?" He stared at me as though I had dropped from the roof or something.

"I swear," he said, "you'd better go to an herb doctor or some healer. I'm afraid you have a screw loose, but I'll hush it up for you." And that's how the thing stood.

To make a long story short, I lived twenty years with my wife. She bore me six children, four daughters and two sons. All kinds of things happened, but I neither saw nor heard. I believed, and that's all. The rabbi recently said to me, "Belief in itself is beneficial. It is written that a good man lives by his faith."

Suddenly my wife took sick. It began with a trifle, a little growth upon the breast. But she evidently was not destined to live long; she had no years. I spent a fortune on her. I have forgotten to say that by this time I had a bakery of my own and in Frampol was considered to be something of a rich man. Daily the healer came, and every witch doctor in the neighborhood was brought. They decided to use leeches, and after that to try cupping. They even called a doctor from Lublin, but it was too late. Before she died she called me to her bed and said, "Forgive me, Gimpel."

I said, "What is there to forgive? You have been a good and faithful wife."

"Woe, Gimpel!" she said. "It was ugly how I deceived you all these years. I want to go clean to my Maker, and so I have to tell you that the children are not yours."

If I had been clouted on the head with a piece of wood it couldn't have bewildered me more.

"Whose are they?" I asked.

"I don't know," she said. "There were a lot. . . but they're not yours." And as she spoke she tossed her head to the side, her eyes turned glassy, and it was all up with Elka. On her whitened lips there remained a smile.

I imagined that, dead as she was, she was saying, "I deceived Gimpel. That was the meaning of my brief life."

*

IV

One night, when the period of mourning was done, as I lay dreaming on the flour sacks, there came the Spirit of Evil himself and said to me, "Gimpel, why do you sleep?"

I said, "What should I be doing? Eating *kreplach*?"

"The whole world deceives you," he said, "and you ought to deceive the world in your turn."

"How can I deceive all the world?" I asked him.

He answered, "You might accumulate a bucket of urine every day and at night pour it into the dough. Let the sages of Frampol eat filth."

"What about the judgment in the world to come?" I said.

"There is no world to come," he said. "They've sold you a bill of goods and talked you into believing you carried a cat in your belly. What nonsense!"

"Well then," I said, "and is there a God?"

He answered, 'There is no God either."

"What," I said, "*is* there, then?"

"A thick mire."

He stood before my eyes with a goatish beard and horn, long-toothed, and with a tail. Hearing such words, I wanted to snatch him by the tail, but I tumbled from the flour sacks and nearly broke a rib. Then it happened that I had to answer the call of nature, and, passing, I saw the risen dough, which seemed to say to me, "Do it!" In brief, I let myself be persuaded.

At dawn the apprentice came. We kneaded the bread, scattered caraway seeds on it, and set it to bake. Then the apprentice went away, and I was left sitting in the little trench by the oven, on a pile of rags. Well, Gimpel, I thought, you've revenged yourself on them for all the shame they've put on you. Outside the frost glittered, but it was warm beside the oven. The flames heated my face. I bent my head and fell into a doze.

I saw in a dream, at once, Elka in her shroud. She called to me, "What have you done, Gimpel?"

I said to her, "It's all your fault," and started to cry.

"You fool!" she said. "You fool! Because I was false is everything false too? I never deceived anyone but myself. I'm paying for it all, Gimpel. They spare you nothing here."

I looked at her face. It was black; I was startled and waked, and remained sitting dumb. I sensed that everything hung in the balance. A false step now and I'd lose Eternal Life. But God gave me His help. I seized the long shovel and took out the loaves, carried them into the yard, and started to dig a hole in the frozen earth.

My apprentice came back as I was doing it. "What are you doing, boss?" he said, and grew pale as a corpse.

"I know what I'm doing," I said, and I buried it all before his very eyes.

Then I went home, took my hoard from its hiding place, and divided it among the children. "I saw your mother tonight," I said. "She's turning black, poor thing."

They were so astounded they couldn't speak a word.

"Be well," I said, "and forget that such a one as Gimpel ever existed." I put on my short coat, a pair of boots, took the bag that held my prayer shawl in one hand, my stock in the other, and kissed the *mezzuzah*. When people saw me in the street they were greatly surprised.

"Where are you going?" they said.

I answered, "Into the world." And so I departed from Frampol.

I wandered over the land, and good people did not neglect me. After many years I became old and white; I heard a great deal, many lies and falsehoods, but the longer I lived the more I understood that there were really no lies. Whatever doesn't really happen is dreamed at night. It happens to one if it doesn't happen to another, tomorrow if not today, or a century hence if not next year. What difference can it make? Often I heard tales of which I said, "Now this is a thing that cannot happen." But before a year had elapsed I heard that it actually had come to pass somewhere.

Going from place to place, eating at strange tables, it often happens that I spin yarns—improbable things that could never have happened—about devils, magicians, windmills, and the like. The children run after me, calling, "Grandfather, tell us a story." Sometimes they ask for particular stories, and I try to please them. A fat young boy once said to me, "Grandfather, it's the same story you told us before." The little rogue, he was right.

So it is with dreams too. It is many years since I left Frampol, but as soon as I shut my eyes I am there again. And whom do you think I see? Elka. She is standing by the washtub, as at our first encounter, but her face is shining and her eyes are as radiant as the eyes of a saint, and she speaks outlandish words to me, strange things. When I wake I have forgotten it all. But while the dream lasts I am comforted. She answers all my queries, and what comes out is that all is right. I weep and implore, "Let me be with you." And she consoles me and tells me to be patient. The time is nearer than it is far. Sometimes she strokes and kisses me and weeps upon my face. When I awaken I feel her lips and taste the salt of her tears.

No doubt the world is entirely an imaginary world, but it is only once removed from the true world. At the door of the hovel where I lie, there stands the plank on which the dead are taken away. The gravedigger Jew has his spade ready. The grave waits and the worms are hungry; the shrouds are prepared—I carry them in my beggar's sack. Another *shnorrer* is waiting to inherit my bed of straw. When the time comes I will go joyfully. Whatever may be there, it will be real, without complication, without ridicule, without deception. God be praised: there even Gimpel cannot be deceived.

THE MILK OF DEATH

Marguerite Yourcenar

Translated from the French by Alberto Manguel, in collaboration with the author

Marguerite Yourcenar (1903–1987). Born in Belgium, Marguerite Yourcenar is one of the most important post-war French writers. Her first collection of poetry was published when she was barely nineteen and, in a career that spanned more than sixty years, she wrote novels, short stories, essays, poetry and a three-volume memoir. Her best-known works in English are *Memoirs of Hadrian* and *The Abyss*. Yourcenar spent much of her life in the United States, having moved there in 1939 to live with her partner Grace Frick. Her work earned her many prizes and awards including the Prix Femina and the Erasmus Prize. In 1980, she was the first woman elected to the Académie française.

The long, dappled line of tourists stretched along Ragusa's main street. Braided hats and opulent embroidered jackets swinging in the wind at the entrance of the shops tempted the eyes of travelers in search of inexpensive gifts or costumes for the masked balls held on board ship. It was as hot as only hell can be. The bald Herzegovinian mountains kept Ragusa under the fire of burning mirrors. Philip Mild entered a German alehouse where several fat flies were buzzing in the stifling gloom. Paradoxically, the restaurant's terrace opened onto the Adriatic, which sprang up suddenly in the very heart of the city, there where one would least expect it, and yet that sudden burst of blue did nothing but add yet another color to the motley of the Market Square. A sickening stench rose from a pile of fish leftovers picked clean by almost unbearably white seagulls. There was not a breath of sea air. Philip's friend, the engineer Jules Boutrin, sat at a small zinc table, holding a drink in the shade of a fire-colored parasol that from afar seemed like a large orange floating on the waters.

"Tell me another story, old friend," Philip said, dropping heavily into a chair. "I need both a whiskey and a story told beside the sea—the most beautiful and the least true of all stories imaginable—to make me forget the contradictory and patriotic lies in the papers I just bought on the quay. The Italians insult the Slavs, the Slavs the Greeks, the Germans insult the Russians, the French insult England almost as much as they insult Germany. I imagine they are all in the right. Let's change the subject ... What were you doing yesterday in Scutari, where you insisted on seeing with your very own eyes God knows what engines?"

"Nothing," the engineer replied. "Apart from glancing at a few irrigation works, I spent most of my time in search of a tower. I had heard so many old

Serbian women tell me the story of the Scutari Tower that I felt the need to see its crumbling bricks and to find out whether, as they say, a white trickle really flows from it. But time, wars, and peasants anxious to strengthen their farmhouse walls have demolished it, stone by stone, and the memory of the tower remains only in old wives' tales ... By the way, Philip, are you lucky enough to have what is commonly known as a good mother?"

"I should hope so," the young Englishman replied with irony. "My mother is beautiful, slim, powdered and painted, hard as a shopwindow's reflecting glass. What more can I tell you? When we are out together, I am taken for her older brother."

"There: you are like the rest of us. To think of the fools who argue that our times lack a sense of poetry, as if we had no surrealists, no prophets, no movie stars, no dictators. Believe me, Philip, what we lack is reality. Our silk is artificial, our horribly synthetic food resembles the make-believe dishes with which mummies are stuffed, and our women, who have become immune to unhappiness and old age, are, however, no longer alive. It is only in the legends of semi-barbaric countries that we still find these creatures rich in tears and milk, creatures whose children we would be proud to be. Where have I heard tell of a poet who was incapable of loving any woman because in another life he had met Antigone? A man after my own heart ... A few dozen mothers and women in love, from Andromache to Griselda, have made me wary of these unbreakable dolls whom we take to be real.

"Let Isolde be my mistress, and let the lovely Aude, Roland's beloved, be my sister ... But the one I would have chosen to be my mother is a very young girl from an Albanian legend, the wife of a chieftain from these regions ...

"There were three brothers, and they were building a tower to serve as a lookout against Turkish robbers. They had undertaken the construction themselves, either because it was difficult or too expensive to hire laborers, or because, like true countryfolk, they trusted only their own hands, and their wives took turns bringing them lunch. But each time they managed to reach the point where they were able to place a bunch of herbs on the finished roof, the night wind and the mountain witches would topple their tower as God had once felled Babel. There are many reasons why a tower should not stand, and blame can be laid on the workers' lack of skill, on the unwillingness of the land, or on the insufficient strength of the cement binding the stones. But the Serbian, Albanian, and Bulgarian peasants will admit only one reason for such a disaster: they know that a building will crumble if one has not taken the precaution of walling into the base a man or a woman whose skeleton will support that weighty body of stone until Judgment Day. In Arta, in Greece, you are shown a bridge where a young girl was walled in: a wisp of her hair has sprung through a crack and droops over the water like a blond plant. The three brothers began to look at one another with suspicion, and were careful not to cast a shadow on the rising walls, because it is possible, for want of a better thing, to wall up into an unfinished tower that dark extension of a man which is perhaps his soul, and he whose shadow is so imprisoned dies as one suffering from a broken heart.

"Therefore, in the evening, each of the three brothers would sit as far as possible from the fire, fearing that one of them might approach silently from behind, throw a sack on the shadow, and carry it away, half choking, like a black pigeon. The eagerness which they had put into their work began to wane, and despair instead of weariness bathed their dark foreheads in sweat.

"At last, one day, the eldest brother called the others to him and said: 'Little brothers, brothers with whom I share blood, milk, and baptism; if our tower remains unfinished, the Turks will once again slither up the banks of our lake, hiding behind the reeds. They will rape our farm girls; they will burn in our fields the promise of future bread; they will crucify our peasants on the scarecrows of our orchards, and our orchards will become a fattening ground for crows. Little brothers, we need each other, and a three-leaf clover should not sacrifice one of its three leaves. But each of us has a young, strong wife whose shoulders and fine neck are well accustomed to carrying loads. Let us not decide anything ourselves, my brothers: let us leave the choice to chance, God's figurehead. Tomorrow, at dawn, we shall wall into the foot of the tower whichever one of our wives brings us our food. I ask you but to be silent one night, oh, my brothers, and let us not embrace with too many tears and sighs the one who, after all, has two chances in three of still being alive at sunset.'

"It was easy for him to speak as he did, because he secretly hated his young wife and wanted to be rid of her, so as to replace her with a beautiful Greek girl with fiery hair. The second brother made no complaints, because he had made up his mind to warn his wife upon his return, and the only one to object was the youngest, because he usually kept his promises. Moved by the magnanimity of his brothers, who seemingly renounced what they held dearest in the world in favor of their common task, he ended up allowing himself to be convinced and promised to remain silent throughout the night.

"They returned from the fields at that hour of dusk in which the ghost of the dying light still haunts the countryside. The second brother reached his tent in a foul mood and ordered his wife to help him take off his boots. As she knelt in front of him, he threw his boots in her face and said: 'I've now been wearing this shirt for eight full days, and Sunday will come and I will not have a stitch of white linen to wear. Damn good-for-nothing, tomorrow at the break of day you shall go down to the lake with your basket of washing and you shall stay there till nightfall, with your brushes and your scrubbing board. If you move as much as a hair's breadth away, you shall die.'

"And the young woman promised, trembling, to spend the entire day washing.

"The eldest returned home fully resolved not to say anything to his wife, whose kisses irritated him and whose heavy beauty no longer pleased him. But he had one weakness: he talked in his sleep. That night, the buxom Albanian matron lay awake, wondering what could have displeased her lord and master. Suddenly she heard her husband mutter, as he pulled the blanket over himself: 'Dear heart, my own dear little heart, soon you'll be a widower . . . How peacefully we'll live, cut off from the dark-skinned hag, by the strong stones of the tower . . .'

"But the youngest brother entered his tent, pale and resigned to his fate like a man who has just met Death along the road, its scythe over its shoulder, on its way to reap its harvest. He kissed his child in its wicker cradle, tenderly took his young wife in his arms, and all night long she heard him sobbing against her heart. But the discreet young woman did not ask the cause of such great sadness, because she did not wish to force him to confide in her, and she had no need to know the nature of his sorrows in order to console him.

"The following morning, the three brothers took their pickaxes and hammers and set off toward the tower. The second brother's wife prepared her basketful of linen and knelt down in front of the eldest brother's wife: 'Sister,' she said. 'Sister dear, it is my turn to take the men their food, but my husband has ordered me, under threat of death, to wash his white linen shirts, and my basket is now full.'

"'Sister, sister dear,' said the wife of the eldest brother. 'Willingly would I go take our men their food, but last night a demon crept into one of my teeth . . . Ouch! ouch! All I can do is cry out in pain . . .' And she clapped her hands unceremoniously to summon the wife of the youngest brother.

"'Wife of our youngest brother,' she said, 'dearest little wife of our youngest one, go in our place to feed the men, because the road is long, our feet are tired, and we are not as young or as nimble as you are. Go, little one, and we will fill your basket with delicious things to eat so that the men will greet you with a smile, as a messenger who will make their hunger vanish.'

"And the basket was filled with fish from the lake, preserved in honey and currants, rice wrapped in vine leaves, cheese made from ewe's milk, and salted-almond cakes. The young woman carefully gave her child into the arms of her sisters-in-law and set off along the road, alone, her load upon her head, her fate around her neck like a holy medallion, invisible to all eyes, on which God Himself might have written what death awaited her, and what place in His heaven.

"As soon as the three men glimpsed her from afar, the small figure still indistinct, they ran toward her, the two elder ones uneasy about the success of their plans, and the youngest praying to God. The eldest swallowed an oath as he saw that it was not his dark-skinned wife, and the second thanked the Lord out loud for having spared his washerwoman. But the youngest knelt down, clasped in his arms his young wife's thighs, and, sobbing, begged her forgiveness. Then he dragged himself to his brothers' feet and implored their pity. Finally he stood up, the blade of his knife glittering in the sun. A hammer's blow on his neck sent him gasping for air onto the side of the road. The frightened young woman let her basket fall, scattering the food, to the delight of the shepherd dogs.

"When she realized what was happening, she lifted her hands to heaven. 'Brothers whom I have never failed, brothers by the wedding ring and the priest's blessing, do not put me to death, but rather send word to my father, head of a mountain clan, and he will provide you with a thousand servants for you to sacrifice. Do not kill me: I am so fond of life. Do not place between my loved one and myself a wall of stone.'

"Suddenly she said no more, because she realized that her young husband, lying on the roadside, no longer blinked his eyes, and that his black hair was stained with brains and blood. She let herself be led, neither crying out nor weeping, to the niche cut out of the tower's round wall; seeing that she was going to die, she felt she could save her tears. But when the first brick was laid in front of her sandaled feet, she remembered her child who loved nibbling at her red shoes, like a playful puppy. Hot tears rolled down her cheeks and mingled with the cement that the trowel smoothed down on the stone.

"'Little feet,' she moaned, 'never again will you carry me to the top of the hill to show my body a little sooner to the gaze of my best beloved. Never again will you feel the coolness of running water, until angels wash you on the morning of Resurrection.'

"The wall of bricks and stones rose to the height of her knees covered by a skirt of golden cloth. Erect within her niche, she looked like an image of Mary standing behind her altar.

"'Farewell, dear knees,' said the young woman. 'Never again will you rock my child; never again will I fill my lap with delicious fruit, sitting beneath the lovely orchard tree that gives both nourishment and shade.'

"The wall grew a little higher, and the young woman continued: 'Farewell, dear little hands, hanging down both sides of my body, hands that shall no longer cook the dinner, hands that shall no longer twist the wool, hands that shall no longer lock yourselves around my best beloved. Farewell, my thighs, and you, my belly, you shall never again be great with child or love. Children whom I might have given birth to, little brothers whom I have not had time to give to my only son, you shall keep me company in this prison which shall also be my tomb, and where I shall stand, sleepless, until Judgment Day arrives.'

"The stone wall now reached her bosom, when suddenly a trembling shook the young woman's body and her imploring eyes shone with a look that was like the gesture of two outstretched hands. 'My brothers,' she said. 'Not for my sake, but for the sake of your dead brother, think of my child and do not let him starve. Do not wall up my bosom, my brothers, but allow him access to my breasts beneath the embroidered blouse, and bring my child to me every day, at dawn, at midday, and at dusk. As long as I have a few drops of life in me, they will flow down to the tips of my breasts to feed the child I brought into this world, and when the day comes when all my milk is gone, he shall drink my soul. Allow me this, evil brothers, and if you do, my beloved husband and I shall not cast blame on you when we meet again in God's house.'

"The frightened brothers agreed to grant this last wish and left a space of two bricks at the height of her breasts.

"Then the young woman murmured: 'Dear brothers, place your bricks in front of my mouth, because the kiss of the dead frightens the living, but allow an opening in front of my eyes so that I may see if my milk is doing my child good.'

"They did as she said, and a horizontal gap was left at the height of her eyes. At dusk, at the time when she used to feed her child, he was brought to her down the dusty road lined with low bushes that had been gnawed at by the goats, and the prisoner greeted the infant's arrival with cries of joy and blessings on the heads of the two brothers. Rivers of milk flowed from her hard, warm breasts, and when the child, made of the same stuff as her heart, fell asleep against her bosom, she sang with a voice muffled by the thickness of the brick wall. As soon as her child was plucked from her breast, she ordered he be taken to the campsite to sleep, but all night long the tender chant rose toward the stars, and the lullaby sung from a distance was enough to stop him from crying. The following morning she sang no more, and with a feeble voice she asked how Vania had spent the night. On the next day she fell silent, but she was still breathing, for her breasts, haunted by her respiration, rose and fell imperceptibly inside their cage. A few days later her breath followed her voice, and yet her now motionless breasts lost nothing of their sweet fountain-like abundance, so that the child asleep in the valley of her bosom could still hear her heart. And then the heart that had served her life so well slowed down its pace. Her languishing eyes died out like the reflection of stars in a waterless cistern, and nothing could be seen through the gap except two glassy eyeballs that no longer gazed upon the sky. These, in turn, changed to water and left in their place two empty sockets at the bottom of which Death could be perceived. But the young breasts remained intact and, for two whole years, the miraculous flow continued, until the child himself, weaned, turned his head from the milk.

"Only then did the exhausted breasts crumble to dust and on the brick sill nothing was left but a handful of white ashes. For several centuries, mothers moved by the tale came to trace with their finger the grooves made by the marvelous milk along the red brick; later the tower itself disappeared, and the heavy arches no longer weighed down on the light female skeleton. At last the brittle bones themselves were dispersed, and all that is left here is an old Frenchman roasted by this infernal heat, who tells this story to whoever comes along, a story as worthy of a poet's tears as that of Andromache."

Just then a gypsy woman, horribly covered in golden frippery, came up to the table where the two men were seated. In her arms she held a child, whose sickly eyes were half hidden by a bandage of rags. She bowed deeply, with the insolent servility common only to races of kings and beggars, and her yellow skirts swept the ground. The engineer pushed her away brusquely, deaf to her voice, which rose from a begging tone to a curse.

The Englishman called her back to give her a dinar. "What has come over you, you old dreamer?" he said with impatience. "Her breasts and necklaces are certainly worth those of your Albanian heroine. And the child she carries is blind."

"I know that woman," Jules Boutrin answered. "A doctor from Ragusa told me her story. For months she has been rubbing disgusting ointments on her child's eyes, ointments that swell his eyelids and make passersby pity him. He can still see, but soon he will be as she wishes him to be: blind. That woman will then be certain of her income for the rest of her life, because the care of an invalid is a profitable business. There are mothers . . . and then there are mothers."

WE ONCE WERE HAPPY

Irène Némirovsky

Translated from the French by Sandra Smith

Irène Némirovsky (1903–1942). The daughter of Ukrainian Jewish parents, Némirovsky was born in Kiev under the Russian Empire. At the outbreak of the Russian Revolution, her family fled to Finland and finally settled in France, where she lived for the rest of her life. Even so, she was denied French citizenship. Arrested during the French occupation as a Jew – though she had converted to Catholicism – she was sent to Auschwitz where she died at the age of thirty-nine. Though she published many successful novels during her lifetime, it was the publication of *Suite française* in the late 1990s (her daughter had kept the manuscript for fifty years without reading it), that brought her to a world readership, being translated into thirty-eight languages and selling more than two million copies.

"Your husband . . ."

"No, Mama, *please*, don't talk to me about him . . ."

"Suzanne! Fifteen years of marriage can't be swept aside in an instant," said the elderly Mme. Blanchard, taking her daughter's hand.

Suzanne Lagrange let her hold her hand, but her mother's shows of affection irritated her. Mme. Blanchard was old, stout and placid; white hair framed her fat, flushed face. She was forcing herself to look moved, to show compassion, but Suzanne thought: "She's thinking that the children and I will spend the summer at her house, and that's what she's worried about. Her routine, the servants . . . She hardly cares about me at all . . . She does love me, poor Mama, but how could she understand? No one understands me," she continued thinking, angry and sad, and suddenly feeling weary.

"Suzanne, I know he'd agree to live with you again," said Mme. Blanchard, lowering her voice.

Suzanne sharply shook her head: "No!"

"But you loved each other, you have children, you managed to live together for fifteen years!"

"Fifteen years of fighting! Fifteen years of infidelity! Fifteen years of unhappiness. You know that very well, Mama! I waited because the children were young. But Jeannine is fourteen, and Hubert thirteen! It's over now, over! Don't talk to me about him. As soon as the inventory is complete and the furniture taken to the Drouot Auction House, I'm going to rent out the apartment and leave with the children. If you can put us up, all the better! If not, I'll make other arrangements . . ."

"Really now, Suzanne . . ."

Suzanne frowned and fell silent. She was forty, a tall, thin woman, one of those "long poles" who understood from the time they were adolescents that their physique would not be suitable for cuddling, childish behavior or weeping; such women held back their tears, swallowing them, and looked as if their sorrows gnawed at them from the inside, giving them an irritated, bad-tempered appearance.

"Can I help you with the inventory, Suzanne?"

"No thank you, Mama."

"Do you want to sell everything?"

"Absolutely everything! I hate that furniture!"

"You won't get a quarter of what it's worth."

"I know, Mama, I know . . ."

"Very well,' said Mme. Blanchard, standing up, "Goodbye, my poor dear; I'll expect you home for dinner."

Then she left, and Suzanne was alone.

The children hadn't come home yet. Suzanne was happy to have a few minutes of solitude. She had put off doing the inventory day after day, but it was July: the summer vacation was starting. She had to leave. The children needed to be in the countryside.

She wandered around the armchairs that sat with no slipcovers on them, past the empty tables. She had spent the past three weeks at a friend's place. The house looked abandoned, which made her heart break.

"Come on now, it's time to start the inventory," she said out loud.

Holding a sheet of paper and a pencil, she looked around the room. By selling this furniture, by making arrangements to banish these walls and windows from her sight forever, she felt as if she were taking revenge on her husband. She could not hurt him any other way in his present life: a man who was still young, handsome, and fickle does not fear solitude: he calls it freedom, and takes pleasure in it. But the past belonged to her; she was determined to destroy it with her blind anger.

"How many scenes we had here, how many tears were shed," she thought. "How many nights did I spend on the sofa, alone, waiting for André! And the last time . . ."

She remembered, with extraordinary precision, the slightest word, the most insignificant circumstance of that last time: they had decided to get separated, and it was truly better that way. She shivered: she recognized the sound of her daughter ringing the doorbell.

"Didn't you finish the inventory, Mama?" asked Jeannine when she came into the room.

She took the pencil from her mother's hands.

"Let me help you, Mama! It will be fun."

Jeannine and Hubert only knew that their parents had decided to sell the furniture and move; they would learn about the divorce later on.

"You think it will be fun!" Suzanne murmured. "You think it's fun to see everything you've been looking at since you were born disappear?"

"It's exactly because I've been looking at it for so long, *too* long," said Jeannine, shaking her head.

She was young, with a pink and white complexion; her skin was taut and smooth, her eyes a light grey.

"Let's see. I'm putting down two red armchairs, velvet. One of the legs has been broken and glued back on, Mama."

"Yes, your father . . ."

Suzanne quickly fell silent.

"Five or six years ago, he got angry," she thought, "and so did I. He kicked that poor armchair, even though it had nothing to do with what made him angry . . . Then he was ashamed of how he had behaved . . . We laughed . . . Back then, that's how our arguments ended. What was that argument about? How did it start, anyway? I don't remember. And yet, at the time, it had seemed so serious . . ."

But she immediately remembered other fights, more recent ones, and a wave of disgust and sadness ran through her body.

"One small table made of mahogany . . ."

"You don't know anything, Jeannine; it's not mahogany, it's made of cherry wood. It's a very pretty table, a real 17th century antique . . ."

She suddenly thought: "When the children were little and didn't eat at the dining table yet, André and I sometimes had dinner served to us in the living room, near the fireplace. He would turn off the light and we would talk quietly, in the semi-darkness. That was ten years ago . . . He had the flu all winter long, couldn't shake it off . . . I was so worried. Oh! I would have given anything to be reassured then."

"Two bookcases with glass doors. Books . . ."

"No, leave the books."

She and André had bought some of the books before they got married; they would go around the booksellers' stalls and antique shops, furnishing their future apartment in their minds, in advance, lovingly. That was in 1922. It was impossible to find an apartment. My God! How happy they had been when they found this one, a little dark, a little cold, but enormous and convenient.

"Should I go on, Mama?"

Suzanne tilted her head and stroked the backs of the books. Who would buy these bookcases? Who would use the old settee? Who would switch on the lamp? It was made of Venetian glass; they had bought it in Italy . . . All those trips . . . Arriving at night in an unfamiliar city, the very old hotels, that delightful feeling of disorientation, of freedom, the flower market beneath the windows, the blue arcades in that Spanish town, everything merged together, surging up in her memory, so vivid still . . .

"We once were happy," she suddenly thought. "We had moments of real happiness . . ."

Could such tender moments have happened in fifteen years of fighting, of infidelity, fifteen years of unhappy married life? It seemed inconceivable. Yet here she was rediscovering them all once more; memories rushed around her like children, seeming to quietly call out to her: "It's me . . . Don't you recognize me?... That smile, that kiss, that look . . . The way you burst out laughing when you were young . . . And even those moments of sadness and peace when, after some misunderstanding, he would come back to you, in spite of everything, and you knew that he would always come back to you, if you wanted him to . . ."

"But I don't want him to anymore," she murmured.

Yet she could feel the tears gathering in her eyes. She made a movement to push Jeannine away.

"Leave all this. Go get dressed. As soon as your brother gets home we're going out. We're having dinner at your grandmother's."

"Oh, Mama!" said Jeannine bursting out laughing. "Mama, I'd forgotten about this horrible clock! How lucky that I won't have to look at it anymore! It annoyed me so much!"

"It isn't horrible," replied Suzanne with such vehemence that even she was surprised. "You're a little idiot! You understand nothing! It may be old fashioned, but when your father and I bought it . . ."

She was finding it difficult to speak. Her lips were trembling. André had never liked it: it was she who noticed it one day in a small shop and bought it, she didn't know why. You sometimes feel drawn to something that disappoints you later on. Her sister, her mother and her friends had made fun of her. Only André had said: "No, the clock isn't as ugly as all that . . ."

Jeannine, frightened, looked at the tears running down her mother's face:

"Oh, Mama! What have I done? Please forgive me . . . I didn't mean to upset you . . ."

"You didn't upset me," murmured Suzanne.

She felt so alone! Her children seemed so distant! André was gone, vanished forever from her life. Who else in the world would know the past? Who could she ask: "Do you remember? It was in 1935, in Brittany . . ." or "Do you remember that beautiful summer when we got engaged?"

She was called to the phone. She heard her mother's voice.

"Suzanne, forgive me, I know you're going to be angry with me again, but André is here . . . Wait, don't hang up. He wants to talk to you and . . ."

"What's the point? Really, what is the point?" murmured Suzanne, "You know very well that it's impossible . . ."

"Impossible, impossible!" she said over and over again, but through her tears, the faintest hint of a smile appeared on her lips, the acquiescent smile that only André had ever seen on her face, and she already knew that, once again, she would forgive him.

THE LECTURE

Daniil Kharms

Translated from the Russian by Eugene Ostashevsky

Daniil Kharms (1905–1942) was born in St. Petersburg and grew up amidst the Bolshevik Revolution. As a young man, he became well known as an eccentric poet and performer of the early Soviet literary scene. He died of starvation incarcerated by the state on suspicion of anti-Soviet activities. Kharms was fascinated with Arthur Conan Doyle's Sherlock Holmes, and it is rumoured that his pseudonym "Kharms" was a homophonic tribute to the great detective – Holmes and Kharms sound alike in Russian. He dressed like an English dandy and smoked a calabash pipe. His manuscripts were preserved by his sister and a friend who dragged a suitcase full of Kharms's writings out of his apartment during the blockade of Leningrad and kept it hidden throughout difficult times.

Pushkov said:

"What is woman? An engine of love,"—and immediately got punched in the face.

"What for?" asked Pushkov but, receiving no answer, continued:

"This is what I think: you have to roll up to women from below. Women love that, they only pretend they don't."

Here Pushkov was again socked in the face.

"What's going on, comrades? Fine, if that's the case, I won't even talk!" said Pushkov but, after a quarter of a minute, continued:

"Women are arranged in such a way that they are all soft and moist."

Here Pushkov again got socked in the face. Pushkov tried to look as if he didn't notice anything and continued:

"If you sniff a woman. . ."

But here Pushkov got smashed in the face so hard that he grabbed his cheek and said:

"Comrades, it is absolutely impossible to lecture under such conditions. If this happens again, I won't talk!"

Pushkov waited a quarter of a minute and continued:

"Where were we? Oh—yes! So: Women love to look at themselves. They sit down in front of the mirror totally naked. . ."

As he said that word he was punched in the face again.

"Naked," repeated Pushkov.

"Pow!" they whacked him in the face.

"Naked!" shouted Pushkov.

"Pow!" he got punched in the face.

"Naked! Naked everywhere! Tits and ass!" shouted Pushkov.

"Pow! Pow! Pow!" they kept punching him in the face.

"Tits and ass with a washtub!" Pushkov was shouting.

"Pow! Pow!" the punches rained down.

"Tits and ass with a tail!" shouted Pushkov, spinning to avoid the punches. "Naked nun!"

But then Pushkov was hit with such force that he lost consciousness and fell, as if mowed down, upon the floor.

PING

Samuel Beckett

Translated from the French by the author

Samuel Beckett (1906–1989) was a Nobel prizewinning playwright, novelist, poet and translator. Beckett was born in Dublin and studied at Trinity College Dublin, where he excelled at cricket. (He is the only Nobel Prize winner mentioned in *Wisden*.) He moved to Paris in 1928 and would spend the rest of his life there. In Paris he was introduced to James Joyce, for whom he worked as an amanuensis during the writing of *Finnegans Wake*. He was active in the French resistance during the Second World War. His first novel, *Murphy*, was published in French in 1947, but it was the premiere of *Waiting for Godot* that established his reputation. Beckett wrote the majority of his plays and novels in French and later translated them into English. In 1969, he was awarded the Nobel Prize in Literature. After his death in 1989 he was interred with his wife, Suzanne, in Montparnasse marked by a simple granite gravestone of his own choosing: "any colour, so long as it's grey". Beckett owned a cottage in rural France, which a local labourer helped him to refurbish. In return, Beckett drove the man's son to school (the boy suffered from gigantism and was too big for the school bus). The boy grew up to be WWF superstar, André the Giant.

All known all white bare white body fixed one yard legs joined like sewn. Light heat white floor one square yard never seen. White walls one yard by two white ceiling one square yard never seen. Bare white body fixed only the eyes only just. Traces blurs light grey almost white on white. Hands hanging palms front white feet heels together right angle. Light heat white planes shining white bare white body fixed ping fixed elsewhere. Traces blurs signs no meaning light grey almost white. Bare white body fixed white on white invisible. Only the eyes only just light blue almost white. Head naught eyes light blue almost white silence within. Brief murmurs only just almost never all known. Traces blur signs no meaning light grey almost white. Legs joined like sewn heels together right angle. Traces alone uncover given black light grey almost white on white. Light heat white walls shining white one yard by two. Bare white body fixed one yard ping fixed elsewhere. Traces blurs signs no meaning light grey almost white. White feet toes joined like sewn heels together right angle invisible. Eyes alone uncover given blue light blue almost white. Murmur only just almost never one second perhaps not alone. Given rose only just bare white body fixed one yard white on white invisible. All white all known murmurs only just almost never always the same white invisible. Bare white body fixed ping elsewhere. Only the eyes only just light blue almost white fixed front. Ping murmur only just almost never one second perhaps a way out. Head naught eyes light blue almost white fixed front ping murmur ping silence. Eyes holes light blue almost white mouth white seam like sewn invisible. Ping murmur perhaps a nature one second almost never that much memory almost never. White walls each its trace grey blur signs no meaning light grey almost white. Light heat all known all white planes meeting invisible. Ping murmur only just almost never one second perhaps a meaning that much memory almost never. White feet toes joined like sewn heels together right angle ping elsewhere no sound. Hands hanging palms front legs joined like sewn. Head naught eyes holes light blue almost white fixed front silence within. Ping elsewhere always there but that known not. Eyes holes light blue alone uncover given blue light blue almost white only colour fixed front. All white all known white planes shining white ping murmur only just almost never one second light time that much memory almost never. Bare white body fixed one yard ping fixed elsewhere white on white invisible heart breath no sound. Only the eyes given blue light blue almost white fixed front only colour alone uncover. Planes meeting invisible one only shining white infinite but that known not. Nose ears while holes mouth white seam like sewn invisible. Ping murmurs only just almost never one second always the same all known. Given rose only just bare white body fixed one yard invisible all known without within. Ping perhaps a nature one image same time a little less blue and white in the wind. White ceiling shining white one square yard never seen ping perhaps away out there one second ping silence. Traces alone uncover given black grey blurs signs no meaning grey light almost white always the same. Ping perhaps not alone one second with image always the silence. Given rose only just nails fallen white over. Long hair fallen white invisible over. White scars invisible same white as flesh torn of old given rose only just. Ping image only just almost never one second light time blue and white in the wind. Head naught nose ears white holes mouth white seam like sewn invisible over. Only the eyes given blue fixed front light blue almost white only colour alone uncover. Light heat white planes shining white one only shining white infinite but that known not. Ping a nature only just almost never one second with image same time a little less blue and white in the wind. Traces blues light grey eyes holes light blue almost white fixed front ping a meaning only just almost never ping silence. Bare white one yard fixed ping fixed elsewhere no sound legs joined like sewn heels together right angle hands hanging palms front. Head naught eyes holes light blue almost white fixed front silence within. Ping elsewhere always there but that known not. Ping perhaps not alone one second with image same time a little less dim eye black and white half closed along lashes imploring that much memory almost never. A far flash of time all white all over all of old ping flash white walls shining white no trace eyes holes light blue almost white last colour ping white over. Ping fixed last elsewhere legs joined like sewn heels together right angle hands hanging palms front head naught eyes white invisible fixed front over. Given rose only just one yard invisible bare white all known without within over. White ceiling never seen ping of old only just almost never one second light time white floor never seen ping of old perhaps there. Ping of old only just perhaps a meaning nature one second almost never blue and white in that much memory henceforth never. White planes no traces shining white one only shining white infinite but that known not. Light heat all known all white heart breath no sound. Head naught eyes fixed front old ping last murmur one second perhaps not alone eye unlustrous black and white half closed long lashes imploring ping silence ping over.

THE HARE-LIP

Maírtín Ó Cadhain

Translated from the Irish by Eoghan Ó Tuairisc

Maírtín Ó Cadhain (1906–1970). Born in Connemara, in the west of Ireland, Ó Cadhain is among the most important writers in Irish (*Gaeilge*, as we call it) of modern times. As a young man, he worked as a schoolteacher, but was dismissed for his political affiliations to Irish Nationalism. He wrote numerous short stories, breaking with the oral tradition common in Gaelic literature and embrace modernism. His novel *Cré na Cille* created a sensation when it was first serialised in 1949, and was compared to the works of Beckett and Joyce. A foul-mouth oratorio narrated by more than a dozen voices belonging to the corpses in a graveyard, the densely textured, ambitious novel was long considered "untranslatable" (there is no such thing). It finally appeared in English in 1916, in two separate and very different translations: *The Dirty Dust* (by Alan Titley) and *Graveyard Clay* (by Liam Mac Con Iomaire and Tim Robinson), both published by Yale University Press.

Nora Liam Bhid spent the night as she had spent the previous one making tea for the wedding party. But now the light of an early February morning, fogged and white, was seeping into the half-deserted parlour, and since she had cleared up after yesterday and was now free, again the strangeness of it came nagging at her. The strangeness of being married, the change, the outlandish Plain: that same flicker of unease astir in her ever since the night her father came home from the Galway Fair and began telling her mother in private that he had 'fixed up a strong farmer on the Plain for Nora'. And it had been no cure for that cut-off feeling to see the man himself and his sisters for the first time last week at the matchmaking. Like a female salmon locked in a choked up side-channel and destined never to reach the breeding beds in the clear shallows upriver, Nora had undertaken the marriage bond in the chapel of Ard late last evening. And now, finding no comfort in her mother's mild words, her father's boozy cajolery, her husband's bland imperturbability, or in the chatter of her female in-laws friendly and sly, she went down into the kitchen to the group of her old neighbours who had come from Ard with the wedding party.

The dancing-barn outside had been for some time deserted and the kitchen was now thronged with people who fell silent when she appeared. Wheezing beer-laden breaths, trails of tobacco smoke, specks of sand from the concrete floor floating in a frostfog—all this made the silence a palpable thing confronting her, a phantom, to try and drag from her the words that would express the anguish of her being. It was that time of a wedding morning when a man might go about starting a row and find none to hinder him. The fire had gone out of the drunken voices, the laughter was lifeless. The young folk, it seemed to her, got up without much heart to dance the jig, afraid that the married couples and oldtimers might take advantage of the quiet that was beginning to close in about the house and say it was time to go. Even the young folk from Ard, hardened to revelling and constant labour, every one of them by now was bleary of voice, weary of foot. The only one in the house left with some flinty fire in his footwork and the flush of life in his cheek was Beairtlin, her father's servant-boy.

Nora dropped her head and let that flintspark penetrate her mind, that flush invade her being, till the silence and the unhomely thing receded. She remembered the many spells of innocent courting with him, snatching dulse from him in summer, or in the autumn the two of them on the flags of the dooryard cracking the nuts he had brought her from the hazelgrove of Liss, and nights of fireside chat together when the old couple were gone to bed and she was waiting up for Padraig her brother to come home from a visit. The girls of Ard, who were at the wedding tonight, had often given her a sly dig, suggesting Beairtlin for her. Tonight was the one night none of them would think of him for her, but it was the one night she wouldn't have minded. Beairtlin's witty remarks, that's what used take the bitter edge off her laughter whenever her father and mother were settling a match for her. A pain of regret, dulled not healed. That she had been so slow to speak her mind to him that day, so unwilling to find fault with Providence, when Beairtlin told her that 'the old fellow was making a match for her again, and no one would be given a wisp of consideration except a shopkeeper or a boss-man of the Plain'.

It wasn't because she had been vexed with Beairtlin for what he said that she passed remarks that day about his hare-lip. Instead, she had intended to say that she'd go off warm and willing with him there and then. For when all is said and done, it wasn't his slim and shapely person, his skygrey eye, his cheek red as foxglove, no, it was the hare-lip, that disfigurement he was marked with from the womb—he didn't even try to hide it with a moustache—that attracted her eyes and her passionate lips. It attracted and repelled her, often her disgust got the upper hand, too often, that's what left the web of her young life a heap of grey dust today. Even now it was the hare-lip she saw coming at her like a blood-sucking lamprey through a grey sea-lough. Beairtlin grumbled that 'the Plainers had taken over the house all night with their reel sets', but she couldn't attend to him till the pair of them were out on the middle of the floor dancing the plain set of home.

'So you're spancelled at last?' he said humorously, appearing to hide his vexation.

'God willing,' she answered. She realised fully for the first time what neither match, marriage, nor the wedding itself had given her dearly to understand.

'Have no regrets. You've made a good swap, lashings and leavings and being your own mistress here on the level Plain, in place of the rocks and the slave-labour—and not to mention the vigilant eye of your old fellow—out at Ardbeg. We'll send you an odd cargo of dulse, an odd bottle of poteen, and a bundle of nuts in the autumn.'

Nora's heart missed a beat. She had forgotten until now that there was no dulse, no nuts, no poteen here.

'I spent last night looking for you, Beairtlin, to sing *The Deer's Wood by Casla* for me, but there wasn't a sight of you in the crowd. You'll sing it after this dance. Do. I'm longing to hear it again . . .'

But Beairtlin had hardly cleared his throat for the song when her mother and her husband's sister came and carried her off again to the parlour.

'Time for us to be home,' said the mother. 'Look, it's broad daylight, and your husband Martin here without sleep since the night before last. You two are at home, God bless you, but look at the journey we have before us.'

'Eleven miles to Gaalwaay,' said Martin Ryan, the new husband. He had a slow congealed kind of a voice and the unhomely accent of the Plain. 'And fifteen miles farther west again, isn't that it? That's what he used to tell me, a labouring man I had here one year from Ard.'

Despite their talk of the long miles and the scurry there was for coats and shawls, Nora wouldn't admit that her family and friends were leaving her. She was made to realise it when the Ardbeg girls came kissing her and saying 'not to be homesick, they'd slip over an odd time on a visit'. She recognised every individual shout of the Ardbeg boys going wildly on their bikes back down the Galway road, and that left the Plainsfolk more alien than ever as they took leave of her in the misty morning light. And all with their 'Missus Ryan' so pat on the tongue causing her cold shivers of fears. The cars that had brought the Ardbeg people were humming out on the road, the drivers hooting the horns. As she had done so many times before at the end of a wedding Nora put on her overcoat and walked out to the road. Beairtlin was the last one to crush into the car that held her family.

'It's God's will, Beairtlin,' she said. 'Keep me a handful of dulse.'

Beairtlin had fixed the cape-ends of his raincoat across his mouth. Though her senses swam she caught the meaning in his words which came squeezed out through the hare-lip opening. 'Don't worry. And I'll bring you a bag of nuts too. In the autumn.'

'There's plenty of noots in the cregs hereabouts,' said her husband standing alongside her.

She stood unmoving at the gate, looking after the car until it had passed Crossroads rise, pretending not to have heard her mother's parting words, 'not to be homesick, she'd see them soon again'.

Homesick? That anchor, keeping the spirit though in exile fixed in its native harbour? No, she wasn't homesick. Tossed on a wave's crest at the caprice of God, having cut her life's cable, not a single link left with her natural element since Beairtlin went, she drove on straight ahead like a boat that has lost its bearings to the Crossways rise. She had never been nearer than Galway to this district and it had been dark during the wedding-drive last night, still it wasn't to view the country that she walked to the crest of this hill. Her only idea was to climb the first rise that came her way and get out of this smothering trough between the two waves of past and present. At that moment she couldn't tell whether Martin Ryan was to the left or right of her, she took no interest in the stem of his pipe circling the prominent points while he himself stabbed the queer uncouth names in the face of her illwill and detestation. She didn't notice Ryan leaving her and going back to the house.

The fog was being rolled and thinned out and dragged by a freshening wind in grey diminishing strips to the edge of the Plain. As far as her eye could see, nothing but immense flat fields, no stones, no rock-heaps, and every foot of fencing as straight as a fishing-line except where they were submerged in winter flooding. Here and there a stand of trees, a thicket, down below her a few outcrops of bedrock like knots in a deal table that had been bleached and scoured. The spot where she stood was the most airy hill of all the dull rich expanse. The houses were not strung together here, the nearest wavering thread of smoke seemed to her a mile away. All the houses alike. And the same set of trees sheltering the walls of the haggards. It appeared to her fancy that one immense house had split in the night and all its parts had separated as far as they might out of sheer unneigh- bourliness. She looked back at her husband's house. Not too unlike her father's house in make and appearance, two-storey, slated. But her father's house had looked newer, with a view of the sea, bare hills at the back of it, the house itself seeming a section of granite sliced out of the rock country to be set up as some tall symbolic stone in the middle of the group of thatched houses called Ardbeg. But there was a greater difference still. The two houses were as different as chalk from cheese. Like all the surrounding countryside her new house had a certain stupid arrogance, it reminded her of the smug smile of a shopkeeper examining his bankbook. Boasting to her face that it was no mushroom growth but a part of the everlasting. She knew it was a 'warm' house. She knew her father wouldn't have set her there if it wasn't, in view of her dowry and all the well-heeled upstarts he had refused on her behalf. She shivered to think that from now on she would be simply one of the conveniences among the conveniences of this house.

Here there was no barrier of mountain and sea to restrain a rambling foot or limit a wandering imagination. Nothing but the smooth monotonous Plain to absorb one's yearnings and privacies and weave them into the one drab undiffer- entiated fabric, as each individual drop, whatever its shade, whatever its nature before being engulfed in the womb of it, the ocean transmutes into its own grey phantom face. From now on whatever contact she'd have with home would be only a thin thread in this closeknit stuff.

There was a chilliness in the morning, not a genuine cold—rather like the friendliness of her sisters-in-law. She went in. She noticed there was nothing out of place within. After all the merrymaking the kitchen wasn't disordered enough to be called homely, not to say Irish. Their own kitchen at home had often been more of a shambles after a couple of hours dancing during a neighbourly visit. Apart from the two tables set end to end in the parlour, the attendants had set everything to rights before they went, and there wasn't the slightest thing crooked to mark that an event had taken place, that two lives had been spiritually and bodily woven together in the tie of intercourse under the one roof to ensure the spring of life in that house. The prime events of a man's destiny skimmed across the wide placid surface of this countryside as lightly as a finger-stone is flicked across water.

Sitting she looked about the kitchen, it was the first chance she had got of examining it since she came to the house. There were signs of careful housekeeping, nursing things to last long, on every single item from the saucepans cleaned and scoured to the two tall presses blond and mellow. A burial chamber, the image might have occurred, vessels and furniture set in it never to be moved until time should undo them; but, ignorant of the antiquities, what she did ask herself was how Ryan all on his own had kept the place so spick and span. This house needed no woman's hand. Strangest of all, neither hearth nor fire to be seen. Instead there was a metal range, dull and unwelcoming. The last spark had died somewhere within its womb.

'I wonder where's the turf?' she said to herself, getting up. In order to change this alien cold into a warm intimacy she must heap up a fire that would make the iron range red hot and prove to herself that a warm fire was more than a match for the rigid iron.

'I use nothing but coal,' he said. 'Wouldn't it be better not bother with a fire and take a lie-down on the bed?'

She took fright. Till now she hadn't thought of the bed. That drowsy voice, assured, self-assertive, set up waves of repulsion in her, yet she recognised it as the voice of authority, not to be denied if he felt like bringing the thing to a head.

'I'm not sleepy,' she said at last. But her husband had gone out for the coal. He soon returned and shot a shovelful of it into the maw of the range. His jabs with the poker at the embers got on Nora's nerves. Like a soul gripped by the demon on the edge of desire, the embers were quickly breaking apart and trying to flame. She'd give anything if her husband's father, mother, any of his prating sisters or even a silent one, were here at the hearth.

The smoke of Ryan's pipe was rising up to the loft in measured puffs, unruffled, unconcerned. The smoke of her father's pipe, or Beairtlin's, always made twists and angles as if they were wrestling with something in the air. There was none of the unfenced regions of her homeland in her husband's conversation, none of the wild oats of speech. Prosy and precise, he could hardly be otherwise, for his mind was a smooth plain without the slightest up or down from end to end . . . With his rare attempts at a joke, a smile crinkling the stiff crease of his nose, he reminded her of the god of wisdom trying to be merry a minute. The more she grew accustomed to the local accent the more alien she felt it. She longed for a new twist in the tune—a change of person, change of day, change of time, that it might be night again, or that his voice might be angry, anything but that gentle deadly drone that did nothing now but linger in her ears.

She got up and stood in the doorway in the fresh air. Plump hens just let out were already scrabbling in the flowerbeds on each side of the concrete path that led from the steps at the front gate. What scant flowers had already poked up through the earth had been trampled last night. There was Beairtlin's footprint—how could she mistake it, the many times it had caught her eye, on the bog, in the earth, on the seasand. She was examining the shape of the boot when a heavyfooted man with the soft hat of the region and a cord breeches passed on the road. Nora remembered he was some neighbour of her husband's, he had been given special treatment in the parlour last night. Without slowing his step and with only the slightest turn of his head her way he greeted her briefly. Sparing his words as if every syllable was worth another penny towards the rent. The fog had come down again in a drab shawl over the Plain with only odd slits of visibility. Still she wouldn't have gone back in so quickly if a filthy hen hadn't angered her by scratching away the footprint with a mindless claw from the soft impressionable earth . . .

She sat again in the same chair by the range. With the heat of the fire and the weariness her husband was asleep and snoring—a dull measured snore, peaceful and passionless. The gentle ripple of a languid sea on the shingle in a summer calm. She studied him for the first time as she might some insignificant item of her new life. Long limbs, angular shoulders. Centuries of sun and shower, soil and drudgery, had shaped and marked that robust body, the sinewy neck, the sallow features. A black head of hair edged with grey, sign of strength. Lids shut on those slow dull eyes in which she could imagine neither smile of pleasure nor flash of anger nor the soft haze of desire. Flaring nostrils that wouldn't be too squeamish of smells. A sootblack moustache—she had caught it out of the comer of her eye a few times previously and felt it needed badly to be cut. And now particularly, realising that those thick seal's bristles weren't hiding a hare-lip.

SEVEN FLOORS

Dino Buzzati

Translated from the Italian by Judith Landry and Cynthia Jolly

> **Dino Buzzati** (1906–1972). An Italian author, painter and poet, Dino
> Buzzati was born in San Pellegrino to an aristocratic family. After studying
> law at the University of Milan, he joined the newspaper *Corriere della
> Sera* where he would continue to work throughout his life. He served
> as a war correspondent attached to the Italian navy during the Second
> World War. He published his first novel in 1933, but it was his third
> novel *The Tartar Steppe*, that brought him critical acclaim in Italy and
> fame throughout the world. An acclaimed artist, Buzzati's work was
> often exhibited. In 1971, he was diagnosed with cancer and, as he left
> his hospital room, knowing he would not come back, he took a sheet of
> paper and made a pencil sketch of his armchair. Empty.

One morning in March, after a night's train journey, Giuseppe Corte arrived
in the town where the famous nursing home was. He was a little feverish, but he was still determined to walk from the station to the hospital,
carrying his small bag.

Although his was an extremely slight case, in the very earliest stages, Giuseppe
Corte had been advised to go to the well-known sanatorium, which existed solely
for the care of the particular illness from which he was suffering. This meant that
the doctors were particularly competent and the equipment particularly perti-
nent and efficient.

Catching sight of it from a distance—he recognised it from having seen photos
in some brochure—Giuseppe Corte was most favourably impressed. The building
was white, seven storeys high; its mass was broken up by a series of recesses which
gave it a vague resemblance to a hotel. It was surrounded by tall trees.

Following a brief medical visit, the preliminary to a more accurate and
complete examination, Giuseppe Corte was put in a cheerful room on the seventh
and uppermost floor. The furniture and upholstery were bright and shining like
the wall paper; the armchairs were made of wood, the pillows covered with
multicolored fabrics, and the view from the window swept out over one of the
most beautiful areas of the city. Everything was peaceful, hospitable, and reassuring. Giuseppe Corte put himself right to bed, turned on the over-head light,
and began to read a book he had brought with him. Shortly, the nurse came in to
inquire if there was anything he needed.

Giuseppe Corte didn't need anything, but he began to chat freely with the young woman, asking for information about the clinic. In this way, he learned about the hospital's unique practice of assigning its patients to different floors in accordance with the gravity of their illness. On the seventh floor, the top floor, only the very mildest cases were treated. Those whose forms of the illness weren't grave, but who certainly couldn't be neglected, were assigned to the sixth floor. More serious infections were treated on the fifth floor, and so on and so forth. Gravely ill patients were housed on the second floor; and on the first floor, those for whom all hope had been abandoned.

Not only did this unique system speed up service, it made it unlikely that mildly ill patients would be upset by the unnecessary proximity of other patients who might be suffering agonies, and it guaranteed a homogenous atmosphere on every floor. In addition, treatment could be perfectly graded to offer the best possible results.

Each floor was like a small self-contained world with its own particular rules and special traditions that had no validity on other floors. And since each ward was under the direction of a different doctor, there were precise differences, some absolutely minimal, in methods of treatment: this, despite the fact that the institution's General Director had engraved a single address on the building.

After the nurse left, Giuseppe Corte felt as though his fever had disappeared, and he went to look out the window. He had no interest in the city's panorama, which was completely new to him; instead, he was hoping to catch sight of other patients through the windows on the lower levels. The building's structure of large recesses allowed this type of observation. Giuseppe Corte concentrated most of his attention on the first-floor windows, which seemed very far away and could only be perceived laterally. But he couldn't see anything of interest. Most of the windows were hermetically sealed by gray metal shades, completely lowered.

Corte noticed a man looking out of the window next to his. The two patients eyed each other for a time with growing sympathy, but neither knew how to break the silence. Finally, Giuseppe Corte plucked up his courage and asked, "You too have only just arrived?"

"Oh, no. I've already been here for two months." He was silent for a few moments and then, not knowing how to continue the conversation, he added, "I was looking down at my brother."

"Your brother?"

"Yes," explained the stranger, "we came here together. It's really odd, but he kept getting worse, and, just imagine, now he's already on the fourth."

"The fourth what?"

"On the fourth floor," the man explained, and he pronounced his words with such an expression of commiseration and horror that Giuseppe Corte was almost frightened.

"Are the illnesses so grave on the fourth floor?" he asked cautiously.

"Oh, God," remarked the man, slowly shaking his head. "They're not desperate yet, but there isn't much to be happy about."

With the quizzical ease of people who hear about tragedies that don't concern them, Corte asked, "Well, if they're so grave on the fourth floor, then who gets put on the first?"

"Oh," he said, "the dying are on the first floor. There's nothing for the doctors to do down there. The priest is the only one who works. And of course. . ."

"But there's hardly anyone on the first floor. Almost all the rooms down there are closed up," Giuseppe Corte interrupted, as though expecting confirmation.

"There's hardly anyone, now. But this morning there were many," answered the stranger with a faint smile. "Where you see the shades lowered, it means someone has just died in there. Don't you see that all the shutters are open on the other floors? But, you'll have to excuse me," he added, withdrawing slowly, "I think it's beginning to get cold. I'm going back to bed. Good luck, good luck."

The man disappeared inside and the window was shut with some force. He saw a light switch on inside the room. Giuseppe Corte remained immobile at the window, staring at the lowered shades on the first floor. He stared at them with morbid intensity, trying to imagine the secret funerals of that terrible first floor where patients were interred before their death; and he felt a sense of relief knowing that it was so far away.

Shadows of night descended on the city. One by one, the thousand windows of the sanitorium were illuminated. From the distance, it must have looked as though there were a party underway in a great palace. Only on the first floor, down there at the bottom of the precipice, dozens and dozens of windows remained blind and dark.

Giuseppe Corte was reassured by his general check-up. Usually inclined to expect the worst, he had been prepared for a severe verdict and wouldn't have been surprised if the doctor had recommended that he be put on the floor below. In fact, despite his overall good condition, the fever had shown no sign of abating. Instead, the doctor spoke to him with polite, encouraging words. The illness was lingering, he said, but it was only very mild; everything would probably be over in two or three weeks.

"And then I'll stay on the seventh floor?" Giuseppe Corte had asked him anxiously at this point.

"But, of course!" the doctor answered, amicably patting him on the shoulder. "And where did you think you should have gone? To the fourth, perhaps?" he asked laughing, as if to indicate the absurdity of the idea.

"All the better, all the better," said Corte. "You know, when you're ill, you always imagine the worst."

In fact, Giuseppe Corte stayed in the room that he had originally been assigned. On those rare afternoons when he was allowed to get up, he met some of his fellow patients. He scrupulously followed his treatment and did his best to recover rapidly, although his condition seemed to remain stationary.

About ten days had gone by when the head nurse came in to see Giuseppe Corte. He wanted to ask a kindness, in a purely amicable way: a lady with two children would be arriving at the hospital on the following day; the two rooms right next to his were free, but they needed a third. Would Mr. Corte agree to be transferred to another room, just as comfortable? Giuseppe Corte, of course, didn't cause any difficulty. One room or the other was all the same to him. And, who knows, perhaps a different, more gracious nurse would be assigned to him.

"A heart-felt thank you," said the head nurse with a slight bow. "I confess that

I'm not at all surprised by your kindness and gallantry. If you have no objection, we'll proceed with the transfer in an hour." In a mollifying tone, as though he were mentioning an absolutely negligible detail, he added, "By the way, it'll be necessary to go to the floor below. Unfortunately, there are no other rooms free on this floor. But it's a temporary arrangement," he stipulated, seeing that Corte, suddenly sitting up, had started to open his mouth in protest. "It's an absolutely temporary arrangement. As soon as a room becomes free, and I believe that will be in two or three days, you can come back up."

"I confess," said Giuseppe Corte, smiling to show that he was no baby, "I confess that I don't like this move at all."

"But there's no medical reason for the move. I understand very well what you mean. This is only being done as a courtesy to this woman who prefers not to be separated from her children. For heaven's sake," he added, laughing openly, "don't think that there are other reasons!"

"I'll do it," said Giuseppe Corte, "but it feels like a bad omen."

Thus, Corte moved to the sixth floor. And even though he was convinced that the move had nothing whatsoever to do with the deterioration of his condition, he felt discomfited at the thought that an undeniable obstacle had arisen between him and the normal world of healthy people. On the seventh floor, the port of entry, one still had, in a certain way, contact with the society of people; it could almost be considered an extension of the normal world. But on the sixth floor, one had already entered the real core of the hospital; here, the doctors, nurses, and patients already exhibited a slightly different mentality. It was already understood that those who were indeed ill, although not gravely so, were put on that floor. From the first conversations with his neighbors, the general staff and physicians, Giuseppe Corte became aware that, in that ward, the seventh floor was considered a joke, reserved for dilettante patients who were affected by mere fancy more than anything else. Only on the sixth floor did one, so to speak, begin in earnest.

Nevertheless, Giuseppe Corte understood that in order to return upstairs, to the place where the nature of his illness indicated that he should be, he would certainly encounter some difficulties. In order to return to the seventh floor, he would have to do some complicated maneuvering, even if he made the smallest effort. There was no doubt that if he didn't open his mouth, no one would think to return him to the upper floor of the "pseudo ill."

For this reason, Giuseppe Corte made up his mind not to compromise his rights or allow himself to be enticed by habit. He took great care to assure his fellow patients that he would be visiting them for only a few days, that it had been he who had wanted to come downstairs for a few days as a courtesy to a lady, and as soon as a room became free he would be returning upstairs. The others nodded, hardly persuaded.

Giuseppe Corte's conviction was fully confirmed by the new doctor. Even he admitted that Giuseppe Corte could very well be assigned to the seventh floor. His illness was ab-so-lut-ly ne-gli-gi-ble—and he enunciated this in order to under-score its importance.

But, come to think of it, perhaps Giuseppe Corte might be served just as well on the sixth floor.

"Let's not start that again," the patient interjected at this point. "You told me that I belonged on the seventh floor, and I want to go back there."

"No one has said anything to the contrary," responded the doctor. "I offer you this advice, purely and simply, not as a doc-tor, but as an au-then-tic friend! Your illness, I'll say it again, is extremely mild. It wouldn't be an exaggeration to say that you're not even ill! But, in my opinion, it distinguishes itself from similar forms of illness because of a certain expansion. I'll explain myself: the intensity of the illness is minimal, but its magnitude is considerable; the destructive process of your cells is absolutely just beginning. Perhaps it hasn't even begun, but it tends, I only say tends, to strike vast portions of the organism simultaneously. For this reason alone, it's my professional opinion that you could be cured more efficiently here, on the sixth floor, where the therapeutic methods are more exemplary and intense." For the first time, Giuseppe Corte felt the horror of that sinister expression—the destructive process of his cells.

One day Corte found out that after lengthy consultations with his colleagues, the hospital's General Director had decided to change the way that patients were subdivided. Everyone's level—so to speak—would be downgraded by a half a point. Patients on each floor would be divided into two categories depending on the gravity of their illness. This subdivision would be done essentially by their respective doctors and would be strictly confidential. The inferior of the two groups would be officially transferred to a lower floor. For example, half the patients on the sixth floor—those whose illnesses were slightly more advanced—would pass down to the fifth floor; and the more indisposed residents of the seventh floor would pass to the sixth. The news pleased Giuseppe Corte because such a large number of transfers would make his return to the seventh floor much easier.

When he mentioned his hope to the nurse, however, he was in for a bitter surprise. That is, she knew that he was to be transferred, but not to the seventh floor, rather, to the floor below. For reasons the nurse couldn't explain, Corte had been included in the group of sixth-floor guests whose illness was "grave" and, for this reason, he had to descend to the fifth floor.

As the initial shock wore off, Giuseppe Corte flew into a rage. He screamed that they had swindled him despicably, that he didn't want to hear any talk about other transfers to the floor below, that he was going to go home, that rights were rights, and the hospital administration could not so openly neglect the physicians' diagnoses.

While he was still screaming, the doctor arrived, out of breath, to calm him. He advised Corte to compose himself if he didn't want to see his fever go up. He explained that there had been a misunderstanding, at least, in part. Once again, he admitted that Giuseppe Corte would be in his proper place if they had put him on the seventh floor; but he added that he had a slightly different, if only a very personal, concept of the case.

When one comes to think of it, given the pathological manifestations of his illness, it could—in a certain sense, you understand—also be attended on the sixth level. He himself couldn't begin to explain how Corte had been catalogued with the lower half of the sixth floor. More likely than not, the secretary in management—who had telephoned him only this morning requesting Giuseppe Corte's precise clinical position—made an error in writing. Or perhaps management had slightly "darkened" the prognosis of an expert, but overly concerned, physician. Finally, the doctor advised Corte not to upset himself, to submit to the transfer without protest. After all, the most important thing was the treatment of the illness, not the placement of the patient.

In regard to his treatment, the doctor added that Giuseppe Corte would have nothing to complain about. The physician on the floor below certainly had more experience; he was almost dogmatic in his insistence that the abilities of the doctors continued to increase, at least in the area of management, the lower one descended. The room was just as elegant and comfortable; the panorama was equally grand. It was only from the third floor down was the view cut off by the belt of trees.

Giuseppe Corte, in the grip of a heightening fever, listened and listened with increasing exhaustion to the doctor's meticulous justifications. At last, he realized that he lacked the strength and, above all, the desire to react further to the unjust transfer. And he allowed himself to be taken to the floor below.

Once he was on the fifth floor, Giuseppe Corte's only consolation, although small, was that, in the judgment of the doctors, nurses, and fellow patients, his illness was the least grave in that ward. In short, he could consider himself, for the most part, the most fortunate individual on the fifth floor. But, he was tormented by the thought that two barriers had now arisen between him and the world of normal people.

Spring was advancing, the air becoming warm. But Giuseppe Corte no longer enjoyed leaning from his window as he had during the first days. Even though his fear was pure foolishness, he was stunned by a strange shiver at the sight of the first-floor windows, the majority of which were always shut and whose proximity was much too close.

His illness seemed stationary. Then, after three days on the fifth floor, a discharge appeared on his right leg and showed no sign of abating in the days that followed. It was an infection, the doctor told him, absolutely independent of the principal malady; a disturbance that could happen to the healthiest person in the world. In order to eliminate it as quickly as possible, an intense gamma-ray treatment would be needed.

"And are they able to give me these treatments here?" asked Giuseppe Corte.

"Certainly! Our hospital has everything," responded the doctor, delighted. "There's only one inconvenience."

"What?" asked Corte with a vague presentiment.

"Inconvenient, as a form of expression," the doctor corrected himself. "I meant that the only treatment unit is on the fourth floor, and I wouldn't advise you to make the trek three times a day."

"So, then, nothing?"

"Well, it would be better if you would be so kind as to go down to the fourth floor until the eczema has passed."

"Enough!" screamed Giuseppe Corte. "I've already gone down enough! I would die. I'm not going to the fourth!"

"As you wish," remarked the doctor, conciliatory so as not to irritate him. "But which one of us is in charge here? Mind you, I prohibit you to go downstairs three times a day."

The ugly fact was that the eczema, instead of abating, was slowly spreading.

Giuseppe Corte could find no rest and continually tossed and turned in his bed. He held out, furious, for three days until he had to give in. Of his own accord, he begged the doctor to send him for the treatments and, thus, to be transferred to the lower floor.

Once down there, Corte noted with unexpressed pleasure that he represented an exception. The other patients on the ward were decidedly in very serious condition and couldn't leave their beds even for a minute. Instead, accompanied by the nurses' compliments and expressions of marvel, he had the luxury of going by foot from his room to the treatment room. He spoke to the new doctor, insisting on his very special position: a patient who, in point of fact, had every right to be on the seventh floor had found himself on the fourth. Just as soon as the eczema passed, he intended to return upstairs. He absolutely would not permit any new excuses. He, who should legitimately still be on the seventh floor!

"On the seventh, on the seventh!" exclaimed the doctor smiling. "You patients are always exaggerating! I'm the first to say that you should be happy with your status. From what I see on your medical chart, there have been no great reversals. But all this talk about the seventh floor—excuse my brutal sincerity—there is a certain difference! You're one of the less worrisome cases, I agree, but you're still a patient!"

"So, then, then," remarked Giuseppe Corte, his face lighting up, "which floor would you put me on?"

"Oh, God, it's not easy to say. I've only had a short visit with you. In order to decide. I'd have to follow you for at least a week."

"Okay," insisted Corte, "but roughly, what do you think?"

In order to pacify him, the doctor made believe for a moment that he was pondering the question; then, he nodded to himself and slowly said, "Oh, God, just to make you happy, we could, hmmm, put you on the sixth!" And, as if he were persuading himself, he added, "Yes. Yes, the sixth would do very well."

The doctor thought the patient would be pleased. Instead, an appalled expression spread across Giuseppe Corte's face as he realized that the doctors on the other floors had fooled him. Here was this new doctor, obviously more able and honest, who, in his heart, had assigned him—it was obvious—not to the seventh, but to the sixth floor, and perhaps to the subjacent fifth! That evening his fever rose considerably.

His stay on the fourth floor marked the most tranquil period for Giuseppe Corte since his admission to the hospital. The doctor was a very nice person, solicitous and cordial. He often lingered for hours chatting about a variety of subjects. And Giuseppe Corte conversed willingly, finding many things to talk about concerning his everyday life as a lawyer and man of the world. He tried persuading himself that he still belonged to the society of healthy people, that he was still tied to the business world, that he was interested in public affairs. He tried, but without success, for the conversation invariably fell on his illness.

He became obsessed with the idea of making any improvement whatsoever. Unfortunately, although the treatments had succeeded in arresting the spread of the discharge, there hadn't been enough to eliminate it. Every day, Giuseppe Corte spoke at length about it to the doctor, and he forced himself to appear strong—ironically, without success.

"Tell me, Doctor," he asked one day, "How is the destructive process of my cells?"

"Oh, such ugly words!" the doctor jokingly admonished him. "Where did you ever learn them? It's not good; it's not good especially for a patient! I never want to hear you talk like that again."

"Okay," objected Corte, "but you haven't answered my question."

"Oh, I'll tell you right away," the doctor remarked politely. "The destructive process of the cells, to repeat your horrible expression, is minimal in your case, absolutely minimal. But I would tend to define it as obstinate."

"Obstinate, meaning chronic?"

"Don't make me say what I haven't said. I only mean obstinate. The majority of cases are like that. Infections, even very mild ones, often need aggressive and protracted treatments."

"But, tell me, Doctor, when can I hope to see an improvement?"

"When? Predictions in these cases are rather difficult. But listen," he added after a meditative pause, "I see that you have a sincere and genuine desire to get well. If I weren't afraid of making you angry, I'd give you some advice."

"But tell me, just tell me, Doctor."

"All right. I'll present the problem in very clear terms. If I, struck by this illness, even in its weakest form, were in this sanitorium, which is perhaps the best one in existence, I would have assigned myself of my own accord, and from the first day, from the first day, you understand, to one of the lower floors. I would put myself right on the . . ."

"On the first?" suggested Corte with a forced smile.

"Oh, no! On the first, no," responded the doctor ironically, "this, no! But certainly on the third or even on the second. The treatment is much better on the lower floors, I guarantee. It's a much more complete and robust system; the personnel are more able. Do you know who the soul of this hospital is?"

"Professor Dati, right?"

"Exactly, Professor Dati. He invented the treatment here; he designed this entire establishment. And yet, he, the Master, remains, so to speak, between the first and second floors. His directive effort radiates from there. But, I guarantee, his influence does not go beyond the third floor. Above that point, his very orders are diminished, lose their consistency, deviate. The heart of the hospital is below, and in order to have the best treatment possible, it's necessary to remain below."

"In short," said Giuseppe Corte with a trembling voice, "you're advising me. . ."

"You might add one thing," continued the doctor. "You can add that in your particular case they would be able to look after the eczema. It's nothing of importance, I agree, but it's rather annoying, which after a while could depress your morale; and you know just how important the serenity of the spirit is to one's recovery. The treatments I've given you have only been partially helpful. Why? It could be pure chance, but it could also be that the rays aren't intense enough. The machines are much more potent on the third floor and the likelihood of curing your eczema would be much greater there. You see? Once your recovery is underway, you will have taken the most difficult step. Once you begin to go up, it's difficult to turn back again. When you really feel better, nothing will stop your ascent, either from here or from the floors below, to the fifth, sixth, even, I dare say, to the seventh floor—in accordance with your 'merit'."

"And you believe that this could accelerate the treatment?"

"But there can be no doubt! I already told you what I would do were I in your place."

He and the doctor had these talks every day. Finally the moment came when the patient, tired of suffering from the eczema, and despite his instinctive reluctance to descend to the realm of more serious cases, decided to follow the doctor's counsel and transfer to the floor below.

He noted immediately that a peculiar gaiety reigned over the doctor and the nurses on the third floor; this, despite the fact that the most severe cases were being treated down there. Indeed, he discovered that their happiness increased by the day. His curiosity aroused, having become somewhat friendly with the nurse, he asked why on earth they were so happy.

"Oh, you don't know?" responded the nurse. "We're going on vacation in three days."

"What do you mean, 'we're going on vacation'?"

"Oh, yes. The third floor will be closed and the staff will be gone for two weeks. Every floor has its turn."

"And the patients? What are they supposed to do?"

"Well, since they're relatively few in number, we make one floor out of two floors."

"How? You put the third- and fourth-floor patients together?"

"Oh, no," corrected the nurse, "we put the second- and third-floor patients together. Those of you on this floor will go down below."

"Go to the second?" said Giuseppe Corte, pale as a dead man. "I would have to go down to the second?"

"But of course. What's so strange about it? When we come back to work in two weeks, you'll come back to this room. I don't think that's anything to be afraid of."

Instead, Giuseppe Corte, warned by a mysterious instinct, was overtaken by fear. But, having understood that he couldn't stop the personnel from going on vacation and convinced that the new treatment was helping him (the eczema had almost completely disappeared), he didn't dare oppose the new transfer. Nevertheless, he required—despite the nurses' teasing—that a sign be posted on the door of his new room: "GIUSEPPE CORTE OF THE THIRD FLOOR. PASSING THROUGH." In the entire history of the hospital, there had never been a precedent for this, but the doctors didn't object for they were convinced that even small aversions could provoke a crisis in nervous temperaments such as Corte's.

After all, it was a matter of waiting two weeks, not one day more, not one day less. Giuseppe Corte began to count them with stubborn eagerness, remaining in bed, immobile for hours on end, his eyes fixed on the furniture, which wasn't so modem and bright on the second floor as it was on the upper floors. Instead, it assumed large dimensions and more solemn, severe lines. Once in a while he would listen intently and he seemed to hear vague gasps of agony coming from the floor below, the floor of the dying, the "condemned" ward.

Naturally, all this contributed to his decline. His diminished serenity seemed to encourage the illness, his fever began to rise, and his weakness became more intense. From the window—it was already full summer and the windows were almost always open—he could no longer glimpse the roofs or even the houses of the city, only the green wall of trees encompassing the hospital.

After a week had passed, one afternoon toward two o'clock, the head nurse and three other nurses suddenly entered the room and switched on a little round light. "Are we ready for the transfer?" asked the head nurse in a good-natured, jesting tone.

"What transfer?" asked Giuseppe Corte in a strained voice. "What sort of joke is this now? They aren't returning to the third floor for seven days."

"What third floor?" said the head nurse as though he hadn't understood. "I have orders to bring you to the first. Look here." And he showed him an official form for the passage to the lower floor signed by none other than Professor Dati.

Giuseppe Corte's terror, his consummate anger, exploded in a long scream that echoed throughout the entire ward.

"Quiet. Quiet. For heaven's sake," pleaded the nurses. "There are patients here who aren't well!"

But that wasn't enough to calm him. Finally, the doctor who ran the ward arrived. He was extremely kind and very well-mannered. He asked what had happened, looked at the form, and asked Corte to explain. Then he turned to the head nurse, furious, declaring that there had been a mistake; he hadn't given any such order; for some time there had been an intolerable confusion, and he had been kept in the dark about everything. At last, having said his piece to his subordinate, he turned politely to the patient, excusing himself profoundly.

"Unfortunately, however," the doctor added, "unfortunately, Professor Dati left just an hour ago for a short break; he won't be back for two days. I'm absolutely distressed, but his orders can't be disobeyed. He would be the first one to complain about this sort of error, I guarantee. I don't understand how this could have happened."

By this time a dreadful trembling had seized Giuseppe Corte's body. His ability to take control over himself had abandoned him entirely. Terror overwhelmed him as though he were a child. His sobs resounded through the room.

Thus, because of that accursed error, he had arrived at the final station. He was in the ward of the dying. He, who, after all, considering the gravity of his illness and according to the judgment of much more severe doctors, had the right to be assigned to the sixth, if not the seventh floor! The situation was so grotesque that there were moments when Giuseppe Corte sobbed almost uncontrollably.

Stretched out on the bed as the hot summer afternoon passed slowly over the city, he looked through the window at the green of the trees. He had the impression of having arrived in an unreal world made of preposterous, sterile tiled walls, icy mortuary passages, and white human-like figures without souls. He even began to believe that the trees that he perceived through the window were not real: indeed, he convinced himself of it, noting that the leaves didn't move at all.

The idea so agitated him that Corte rang the bell for the nurse and asked her to bring his eyeglasses. Only then did he calm down a little. With the aid of his glasses, he could reassure himself that they really were green trees and that the leaves did move, if only slightly, with each stirring of the wind.

When the nurse left, he passed a quarter of an hour in complete silence. Six floors, six terrible barriers—even though it was technical error—now hung over Giuseppe Corte with implacable weight. How many years—yes, he had to think in terms of years—how many years would it take for him to rise again to the edge of that precipice?

But, why was the room suddenly so dark? It was still early afternoon. With supreme effort, Giuseppe Corte, who felt himself paralyzed by a strange torpor, looked at his watch on the night stand next to his bed. Three-thirty. He turned his head to the side and saw that the shades, obeying a mysterious command, were slowly lowering, blocking out the passage of light.

THE BOY ON THE TÜNEL

Sait Faik Abasıyanık

Translated from the Turkish by Maureen Freely and Alexander Dawe

Sait Faik Abasıyanık (1906–1954) was one of the greatest Turkish writers
of short stories and poetry and considered an important literary figure
of the 1940s. He brought new life to Turkish short story writing with his
harsh but humanistic portrayals of labourers, fishermen, children, the
unemployed, and the poor. He died on 11 May 1954 in Istanbul. Sait
Faik left his wealth to the Darüşşafaka School for orphans, having taught
in an orphanage as a younger man. He proved to be a better writer than
a businessman: his father persuaded him to run a wheat shop owned by
the family. Abasıyanık bankrupted it within six months.

Nothing is too much for these people

Lately I've been spending my nights in a very strange neighborhood. There's
this black haze that rises from the sea around nine o'clock. It spreads and
spreads, until it has enveloped us all. As the neighborhood sleeps, a cool
breeze wafts through it, seeking human company, but settling down with the
stray dogs and the lonely cats in the dark, quiet streets. Until the new day dawns,
that's all there is.

Once there was a Greek entrepreneur who ran two dynamos on diesel. This
was the only source of electricity; a yellow, morbid *courant continu* that turned
us all into ghostly and indecipherable blurs. Now the municipality and the entrepreneur have had a disagreement and the lights are out. Who knows where these
dark streets might take you after half past eight?

As for the residents – those who are fond of their wives stay at home all night,
smoking at their windowsills, planning the next day's arguments.

In the distance you only see the torches made of rags dipped in any gasoline
they could lay their hands on. The flames slash through the darkness. Staring out
over this haunted landscape, they catch glimpses of the houses along the coast.
They track the lights and the sounds; they drift off into a trance that is not quite
sleep; they see the crabs.

I spoke about these long, dark nights with a Turkish lady who went to a private
lycée (a lady, no less, who speaks both English and French!) and she said:

"Even the people there are too dark!"

Thick mustachioed Greek fishermen, scrawny bare-legged children, Kurdish
porters whose windpipes are bursting from their throats, ninety-year-old Greek

women, the postman and the delivery boy at the corner shop. They can all count themselves among those people, and so can you and I.

So there I was, conversing with this woman. Someone else was standing a little further on. The greengrocer was in his corner, and the delivery boy was halfway up the hill, beautiful and forlorn.

I didn't disagree with her. What would be the point! She is on casual terms with the head of the neighborhood. She gives men ideas, and women advice.

I went into Istanbul that day. And I am writing this description of a boy on the Tünel for the boy on the Tünel, not for this woman – I have long since given up on her.

We entered the Tünel in Beyoğlu. There weren't many people traveling down the hill just then. We were in the second-class car. There were three soldiers in a corner, a woman of a certain age with her daughter-in-law, and further on there was a noisy Armenian group on their way to catch a boat, and the boy, and me.

He had tucked his bare feet beneath the seat as far back as he could. You wouldn't have noticed them unless you had been paying close attention. The train hadn't started moving. The gate dividing the first and second-class cars and the gate to the platform kept opening and closing.

Then they closed with a sigh like the breath of a fish pulled from the sea.

His fingers were curled under his ear lobe and his mouth hung open. His other hand was on his knee; it was filthy and black, but despite the dark olive color of his skin his nails were pure white. His fingers were long and slender. The patterns on his shirt were like oil paint and so pale they were almost white.

He wore a mother-of-pearl hook fastened tightly around his thin, grimy neck. Now for his face . . .

His nose was flat, his mouth wide open and salivating. His large, dark brown eyes were brimming with an innocence that was almost inhuman; they were literally white with astonishment. His hair was a mess, and flecked with cigarette ash.

When the doors closed – I was standing right beside him – he lifted up his head to look at me. I had already assumed my position. I was looking elsewhere, with grave contemplation. First he lowered his eyes, and then his face. Then I started watching him again. The smile on his face was so faint and so true; how it lit up his lips, his eyes, his eyebrows . . .

Oh, to see the joy of this ride in the face of a twelve-year-old boy! Maybe I was that happy my first time, too. We see such joy in children all the time. They clap their hands and cry:

"Look, father! Look how wonderful it is!"

Nothing could stop us showing the joy we felt.

But this boy on the Tünel – he is trying not to show it. Rattling and shaking, we rumble down the hill. Now he is watching the lady standing with her young daughter just across from him. They aren't even looking at him. He seems to relax a bit. Again he looks up at me. I pretend to be deep in my newspaper. He relaxes even more. But then he senses something; he feels my eyes on him, and other eyes, too; and the light and the diabolical slamming of the wheels against the tracks. He can no longer take pleasure in this. There's that little smile again; that tiny, fearful, forlorn burst of innocence. Now from a distance we watch the slow and heavy opening of the hemisphere of the door on the Galata side of the Tünel line; he is watching and so am I. The little smile is still fixed on his face. Now we're on the other side. The little boy's face is glistening like a freshly peeled almond. A bright streak passes across his dark, dark face. It could be a waterfall, it could be a torch. It washes him clean as it bathes him in light. But it passes too quickly for me to see it. The flame flickers, and then there is that sad little smile again. This time he catches me. He catches me watching him. The smile vanishes. I have smothered him with the tired fears of a man who has been on the Tünel a hundred, maybe a thousand times, but still worries it might collapse on him. The doors grind open. As he races away on his long, slender legs, with his pure, white fingernails flashing, I manage to catch up with him. We are out of the Tünel now. Wandering through the evening crowd, his mouth falls open, as he marvels at the speed of his journey, as he watches the next wave of passengers, hurrying up to Beyoğlu. It is almost as if . . . yes. It is almost as if he is taking the scene into his mouth.

Elated, he races away. I watch him go. Even those wide, torn patches on his trousers look pleased. Sewn with large stitches and ripped at the bottom, they speak of the wonders they witnessed, there in that seat on the Tünel.

His black legs plunge into the crowd.

Everything about him tells you that he spends his winters in a tinplate house and his summers in a tent.

We built these funiculars for people, so that they could get to the top of a hill in a single moment. But for a child who doesn't want to show the joy he feels when he rides it for the first time, the Tünel is also a slide.

I won't be so bold as to say that if we can't make our funiculars as slides, it's because we don't appreciate the children who feel such joy on their first ride down. That would be flattering myself. That would be assuming I had the power to build such a slide myself! Let them come to me with their tenders! But what I will say is this:

"Nothing is too much for these people."

Tonight in Edirnekapı a mother will listen to the story of a boy riding the Tünel. "Then this man with these enormous eyes started staring at me," he'll say. "And after that I just couldn't enjoy myself." He'll tell his mother how he just couldn't find it in himself to smile at those strangers. Let alone show them his white teeth. He'll tell her what he heard along the way, and what he couldn't say, and they will be as happy as if they had just taken a ride on the Tünel.

THE SALAMANDER

Mercè Rodoreda

Translated from the Catalan by David Rosenthal

Mercè Rodoreda i Gurguí (1908–1983). Born in Barcelona, Mercè Rodoreda spurned formal schooling at the age of ten and, with the aid of the family library, set about becoming an autodidact. In 1936, at the outbreak of the Spanish Civil War, she went into exile in France. While she had published stories and a novel, *Aloma*, in the 1930s, she was unhappy with her early writing, a dissatisfaction that led to a long hiatus. It was in exile that she wrote the novels *The Time of the Doves* and *Camellia Street* which established her reputation. She did not return to her native Barcelona until 1974, where she completed her novel *A Broken Mirror*. The Mercè Rodoreda prize for short fiction was established in honour of her in 1998.

I walked under the willow tree, came to the patch of watercress, and knelt beside the pond. As usual, there were frogs all around. As soon as I got there they'd come out and bounce up to me. And when I began to comb my hair, the naughtiest ones would start touching my red skirt with the five little plaits on it, or pulling the scalloped border on my petticoats, all full of frills and tucks. And the water'd grow sadder and sadder, and the trees on the hillside slowly darken. But that day the frogs leapt into the water in one jump, and the water's mirror shattered into little pieces. And when the water was all smooth again I saw his face beside mine, like two shadows watching me from the other side. And so he wouldn't think I was frightened, I got up without a word, I began walking through the grass very calmly, and as soon as I heard him following, I looked around and stopped. Everything was quiet, and one edge of the sky was already sprinkled with stars. He'd halted a little ways off, and I didn't know what to do, but suddenly I got scared and started to run. And when I realized he was catching up with me, I stopped underneath the willow with my back against the trunk. He planted himself in front of me, with his arms stretched out on both sides so I couldn't escape. And then, looking into my eyes, he pressed me against the willow and with my hair all dishevelled, between him and the willow tree, I bit my lip so I wouldn't cry out from the pain in my chest and all my bones feeling like they were about to break. He put his mouth on my neck, and it burned where he put it.

The next day the trees on the hill were already black when he came, but the grass was still warm from the sun. He held me again against the willow trunk, and put his hand flat over my eyes. And all at once I felt like I was falling asleep, and the leaves were telling me things which made sense but which I didn't understand, saying them softer and softer and slower and slower. And when I couldn't hear them anymore and my tongue was frozen with terror, I asked him, "And your wife?" And he told me, "You're my wife. Only you." My back was crushing the grass I'd hardly dared walk on when I was going to comb my hair. Just a little, to catch the smell of it breaking. Only you. Afterwards, when I opened my eyes, I saw the blond hair falling and she was bent over, looking at us blankly. And when she realized I'd seen her, she grabbed my hair and said "Witch." Very softly. But she let go of me immediately and grabbed him by his shirt collar. "Go on, go on," she said. And she led him away, pushing him as they went.

We never went back to the pond. We'd meet in stables, under haystacks, in the woods with the roots. But after that day when his wife led him away, the people in the village started looking at me like they didn't see me, and some of them would cross themselves quickly as I went by. After a while, when they saw me coming they'd go into their houses and lock the doors. I started hearing a word which followed me everywhere I went, as if the air whistled it or it came from the light and the darkness. Witch, witch, witch. The doors shut. I walked through the streets of a ghost town, and the eyes I saw between the slits in the curtains were always icy. One morning I had a lot of trouble opening my front door, which was old and cracked by the sun. They'd hung an ox's head in the middle of it, with two little green branches stuck in the eyes. I took it down. It was very heavy, and I left it on the ground since I didn't know what to do with it. The branches began to dry, and while they were drying the head began to stink and there was a swarm of milk-colored worms all around the neck on the side where they'd cut it.

Another day I found a headless pigeon, its breast red with blood, and another a sheep born dead before its time and two rat's ears. And when they stopped hanging dead animals on my door, they started to throw stones. They banged against the window and roof tiles at night, as big as fists ... Then they had a procession. It was the beginning of winter. A windy day with scurrying clouds, and the procession went very slowly, with white and purple paper flowers. I lay on the floor, watching it through the special door I'd made for the cat. And when it was almost in front of the door, with the wind, the saint, and the banners, the cat got frightened by the torches and chants and tried to come in. And when he saw me he let out a great shriek, with his back arched like a bridge. And the procession came to a halt, and the priest gave blessing after blessing, and the altar boys sang and the wind whipped the flames on the torches, and the sexton walked up and down, and everything was a flutter of white and purple petals from the paper flowers. Finally the procession went away. And before the holy water had dried on the walls, I went out looking for him and I couldn't find him anywhere. I searched in the stables, under haystacks, in the woods with the roots – I knew it by heart. I always sat on the oldest root, which was all white and dusty like a bone. And that night, when I sat down, I suddenly realized I had no hope left. I lived facing backwards, with him inside me like a root in the earth. The next day they wrote "witch" on my door with a piece of charcoal. And that night, good and loud so I could hear them, two men said they should have burned me when I was little, along with my mother who used to fly around on eagle's wings when everyone was asleep. That they should have had me burned before they started needing me to pick garlic or tie the grain and alfalfa in sheaves or gather grapes from the poor vines.

One evening I thought I saw him at the entrance to the woods with the roots, but when I got closer he ran away and I couldn't tell if it was him or my desire for him or his shadow searching for me, lost like I was among the trees, pacing to and fro. "Witch," they said, and left me with my pain, which wasn't at all the kind they'd meant to give me. And I thought of the pond and the watercress and the willow's slender branches . . . The winter was dark and flat and leafless. Just ice and frost and the frozen moon. I couldn't move, because to walk around in winter is to walk in front of everybody and I didn't want them to see me. And when spring came, with its joyous little leaves, they built a fire in the middle of the square, using dry wood, carefully cut.

Four men from the village came looking for me: the elders. From inside I told them I wouldn't go with them, and then the young ones came with their big red hands, and broke down the door with an axe. And I screamed, because they were dragging me from my own house, and I bit one and he hit the middle of my head with his fist, and they grabbed my arms and legs and threw me on top of the pile like one more branch, and they bound my arms and feet and left me with my skirt pulled up. I turned my head. The square was full of people, the young in front of the old, and the children off to one side with little olive branches and new Sunday smocks. And while I was looking at the children I caught sight of him. He was standing beside his wife, who was dressed in black with her blond hair, and he had his arm around her shoulder. I turned away and closed my eyes. When I opened them again, two old men came forward with burning torches, and the boys started singing the song of the burning witch. It was a very long song, and when they'd finished it the old men said they couldn't start the fire, that I wouldn't let them light it. And then the priest came up to the boys with his bowl full of holy water, and made them wet the olive branches and throw them on top of me, and soon I was covered with little olive branches, all with tiny shoots. And a little old lady, crooked and toothless, started laughing and went away and after a while she came back with two baskets full of dry heather and told the old men to spread them on the four sides of the bonfire, and she helped them, and then the fire caught. Four columns of smoke rose, and the flames twisted upwards and it seemed like a great sigh of relief went out of the hearts of all those people. The flames rose, chasing after the smoke, and I watched everything through a red downpour. And behind that water every man, woman, and child was like a happy shadow because I was burning.

The bottom of my skirt had turned black. I felt the fire in my kidneys, and from time to time, a flame chewed at my knee. It seemed like the ropes that tied me were already burnt. And then something happened which made me grit my teeth. My arms and legs started getting shorter like the horns on a snail I once touched with my finger, and under my head where my neck and shoulders met, I felt something stretching and piercing me. And the fire howled and the resin bubbled . . . I saw some of the people looking at me raise their arms, and others were running and bumping into the ones who hadn't moved. And one whole side of the fire collapsed in a great shower of sparks, and when the scattered wood began burning again it seemed like someone was saying "She's a salamander." And I started walking over the burning coals, very slowly, because my tail was heavy.

I walked on all fours with my face against the ground. I was going towards the willow tree, rubbing against the wall, but when I got to the corner I turned my head slightly and off in the distance I saw my house, which looked like a flaming torch. There was no one in the street. I went past the stone bench, and then quickly through the house full of flames and glowing coals, towards the willow, towards the watercress, and when I was outside again I turned around because I wanted to see how the roof was burning. While I was staring at it the first drop fell, one of those hot, fat drops that give birth to toads, and then others fell, slowly at first and then faster, and soon all the water in the sky had poured down and the fire went out in a great cloud of smoke. I kept still. I couldn't see a thing, because night had fallen and the night was black and dense. I set out, wading through mud and puddles. My hands enjoyed sinking in the soft mush, but my feet grew weary behind me from getting stuck so often. I would have liked to run, but I couldn't. A clap of thunder stopped me in my tracks. Then came a bolt of lightning, and through the rocks I saw the willow. I was out of breath when I reached the pond. And when, after the mud, which is dirt from the ground, I found the slime, which is dirt from the bottom of the water, I crept into a corner, half-buried between two roots. And then three little eels came along.

At dawn, I don't know if it was the next day or some other, I climbed out slowly and saw the high mountains beneath a sky smudged with clouds. I ran through the watercress and stopped at the trunk of the willow tree. The first leaves were still inside the buds, but the buds were turning green. I didn't know which way to turn. If I didn't watch where I was going, the blades of grass would prick my eyes – and I fell asleep among those blades until the sun was high in the sky. When I woke up I caught a tiny mosquito, and then looked for worms in the grass. Finally I went back to the slime and pretended to be asleep, because the three eels immediately came up, acting very playful.

The night I decided to go to the village there was lots of moonlight. The air was full of smells and the leaves were already fluttering on all the branches. I followed the path with the rocks, very carefully because the smallest things frightened me. When I got to my house, I rested. There was nothing but ruins and nettle bushes, with spiders spinning and spinning. I went around back and stopped in front of his garden. Beside the hollyhocks, the sunflowers hung their round flowers. I followed the bramble hedge without thinking why I was doing it, as if someone were telling me "Do this, do that," and slipped under his door. The ashes in the hearth were still warm. I lay down for a while, and after running around a bit all over I settled down under the bed. So tired that I fell asleep and didn't see the sunrise.

When I woke up there were shadows on the floor, because night was already falling again, and his wife was walking back and forth with a burning candle. I saw her feet and part of her legs, thin at the bottom, swollen higher up, with white stockings. Then I saw his feet, big, with blue socks falling over his ankles. And I saw their clothing fall, and heard them sitting on the bed. Their feet were dangling, his next to hers, and one of his feet went up and a sock fell, and she took off her stockings, pulling them off with both hands, and then I heard the sheets rustling as they pulled them up. They were talking very softly, and after a while, when I'd gotten used to the darkness, the moonlight came in through the window, a window with four panes and two strips of wood that made a cross. And I crawled over to the light and placed myself right under the cross because inside myself, even though I wasn't dead, there was nothing inside me that was totally alive, and I prayed hard because I didn't know if I still was a person or only a little animal, or if I was half person and half animal. And also I prayed to know where I was, because at times I felt like I was underwater, and when I was underwater I felt like I was on the ground, and I never knew where I really was. When the moon went down they woke up, and I went back to my hiding place under the bed, and started to make myself a little nest with bits of fluff. And I spent many nights between the fluff and the cross. Sometimes I'd go outside and go up to the willow tree. When I was under the bed, I'd listen. It was just like before. "Only you," he'd say. And one night when the sheet was hanging on the floor I climbed up the sheet, holding onto the folds, and got into bed beside one of his legs. And he was as quiet as a corpse. He turned a little and his leg pressed down on top of me. I couldn't move. I breathed hard because he was crushing me, and I wiped my cheek against his leg, very carefully so as not to wake him.

But one day she did a housecleaning. I saw the white stockings and the raggedy broom, and just when I least expected it blond hair was dragging on the floor and she shoved the broom under the bed. I had to run because it seemed like the broom was searching for me, and suddenly I heard a scream and saw her feet running towards the door. She came back with a burning torch and jammed half her body under the bed and tried to burn my eyes. And I, clumsy, didn't know which way to run and was dazzled and bumped into everything: the legs on the bed, the walls, the feet on the chairs. I don't know how, I found myself outside and made for the puddle of water under the horses' drinking trough, and the water covered me up but two boys saw me and went to look for reeds and started poking me. I turned and faced them, with my whole head out of the water, and stared right at them. They threw down the reeds and ran away, but immediately they came back with six or seven bigger boys, and they all threw stones and handfuls of dirt at me. A stone hit one of my little hands and broke it, but in the midst of badly aimed stones and in utter terror I was able to get away and run into the stable. And she came looking for me there with the broom, with the children constantly shouting, waiting at the door, and she poked me and tried to make me come out of my corner full of straw and I was dazzled again and bumped into the pails, the baskets, the sacks of carob beans, the horses' hoofs, and a horse reared because I'd bumped into one of his hoofs, and I went up with him. A whack from the broom touched my broken hand and almost pulled it off, and a trickle of black spit oozed from one side of my mouth. But I still was able to get away through a crack, and as I escaped I heard the broom poking and poking.

In the dead of night I went to the woods with the roots. I came out from under some bushes in the light of the rising moon. Everything seemed hopeless. The broken hand didn't hurt, but it was dangling by a sinew, and I had to lift my arm so it wouldn't drag too much. I walked a little crookedly, now over a root, now over a stone, till I got to the root where I used to sit sometimes before they dragged me off to the bonfire in the square, and I couldn't get to the other side because I kept slipping. And on and on and on, towards the willow tree, and towards the watercress and towards my slimy home under the water. The grass rustled in the wind, which whipped up bits of dry leaves and carried off short, bright strands from the flowers beside the path. I rubbed one side of my head against a tree trunk and slowly went towards the pond, and entered it holding my weary arm up, with the broken hand on it.

Under the water streaked with moonlight, I saw the three eels coming. They seemed a little blurred, and intertwined with each other, winding in and out, making slippery knots till the littlest one came up to me and bit my broken hand. A little juice came out of the wrist, looking like a wisp of smoke beneath the water. The eel held onto the hand and slowly pulled it, and while he was pulling, he kept looking at me. And when he thought I wasn't watching he gave one or two hard, stubborn jerks. And the others played at entwining as if they were making a rope, and the one who was biting my hand gave a furious yank and the sinew must have snapped because he carried off the hand and when he had it he looked at me as if to say: "Now I've got it!" I closed my eyes for a while, and when I opened them the eel was still there, between the shadow and the shimmering bits of light, with the little hand in his mouth – a sheaf of bones stuck together, covered by a bit of black skin. And I don't know why, but all of a sudden I saw the path with the stones, the spiders inside my house, the legs hanging over the side of the bed. They were dangling, white and blue, like they were sitting on top of the water, but empty, like spread-out washing, and the rocking water made them sway from side to side. And I saw myself under that cross made of shadows, above that fire full of colors that rose shrieking and didn't burn me . . . And while I was seeing all these things the eels were playing with that piece of me, letting it go and then grabbing it again, and the hand went from one eel to the next, whirling around like a little leaf, with all the fingers separated. And I was in both worlds: in the slime with the eels, and a little in that world of I don't know where . . . till the eels got tired and the slime sucked my hand under . . . a dead shadow, slowly smoothing the dirt in the water, for days and days and days, in that slimy corner, among thirsty grass roots and willow roots that had drunk there since the beginning of time.

THE ANSWER IS NO

Naguib Mahfouz

Translated from the Arabic by Denys Johnson-Davies

Naguib Mahfouz (1911–2006). Born in Cairo, Naguib Mahfouz is one of the finest contemporary writers of Arabic literature. His honest, unsentimental, haunting stories created controversy in his native Egypt, where death threats culminated in an attempted assassination when he was eighty-two. In 1988, Mahfouz became the first (and to date, only) Arabic writer to be awarded the Nobel Prize for Literature. His best known works include *The Cairo Trilogy* and *Children of the Alley*.

The important piece of news that the new headmaster had arrived spread through the school. She heard of it in the women teachers' common room as she was casting a final glance at the day's lessons. There was no getting away from joining the other teachers in congratulating him, and from shaking him by the hand too. A shudder passed through her body, but it was unavoidable.

"They speak highly of his ability," said a colleague of hers. "And they talk too of his strictness."

It had always been a possibility that might occur, and now it had. Her pretty face paled, and a staring look came to her wide black eyes.

When the time came, the teachers went in single file, decorously attired, to his open room. He stood behind his desk as he received the men and women. He was of medium height, with a tendency to portliness, and had a spherical face, hooked nose, and bulging eyes; the first thing that could be seen of him was a thick, puffed-up mustache, arched like a foam-laden wave. She advanced with her eyes fixed on his chest. Avoiding his gaze, she stretched out her hand. What was she to say? Just what the others had said? However, she kept silent, uttered not a word. What, she wondered, did his eyes express? His rough hand shook hers, and he said in a gruff voice, "Thanks." She turned elegantly and moved off.

She forgot her worries through her daily tasks, though she did not look in good shape. Several of the girls remarked, "Miss is in a bad mood." When she returned to her home at the beginning of the Pyramids Road, she changed her clothes and sat down to eat with her mother. "Everything all right?" inquired her mother, looking her in the face.

"Badran, Badran Badawi," she said briefly. "Do you remember him? He's been appointed our headmaster."

"Really!"

Then, after a moment of silence, she said, "It's of no importance at all—it's an old and long-forgotten story."

After eating, she took herself off to her study to rest for a while before correcting some exercise books. She had forgotten him completely. No, not completely. How could he be forgotten completely? When he had first come to give her a private lesson in mathematics, she was fourteen years of age. In fact not quite fourteen. He had been twenty-five years older, the same age as her father. She had said to her mother, "His appearance is a mess, but he explains things well." And her mother had said, "We're not concerned with what he looks like; what's important is how he explains things."

He was an amusing person, and she got on well with him and benefited from his knowledge. How, then, had it happened? In her innocence she had not noticed any change in his behavior to put her on her guard. Then one day he had been left on his own with her, her father having gone to her aunt's clinic. She had not the slightest doubts about a man she regarded as a second father. How, then, had it happened? Without love or desire on her part the thing had happened. She had asked in terror about what had occurred, and he had told her, "Don't be frightened or sad. Keep it to yourself and I'll come and propose to you the day you come of age."

And he had kept his promise and had come to ask for her hand. By then she had attained a degree of maturity that gave her an understanding of the dimensions of her tragic position. She had found that she had no love or respect for him and that he was as far as he could be from her dreams and from the ideas she had formed of what constituted an ideal and moral person. But what was to be done? Her father had passed away two years ago, and her mother had been taken aback by the forwardness of the man. However, she had said to her, "I know your attachment to your personal independence, so I leave the decision to you."

She had been conscious of the critical position she was in. She had either to accept or to close the door forever. It was the sort of situation that could force her into something she detested. She was the rich, beautiful girl, a byword in Abbasiyya for her nobility of character, and now here she was struggling helplessly in a well-sprung trap, while he looked down at her with rapacious eyes. Just as she had hated his strength, so too did she hate her own weakness. To have abused her innocence was one thing, but for him to have the upper hand now that she was fully in possession of her faculties was something else. He had said, "So here I am, making good my promise because I love you." He had also said, "I know of your love of teaching, and you will complete your studies at the College of Science."

She had felt such anger as she had never felt before. She had rejected coercion in the same way as she rejected ugliness. It had meant little to her to sacrifice marriage. She had welcomed being on her own, for solitude accompanied by self-respect was not loneliness. She had also guessed he was after her money. She had told her mother quite straightforwardly, "No," to which her mother had replied, "I am astonished you did not make this decision from the first moment."

The man had blocked her way outside and said, "How can you refuse? Don't you realize the outcome?" And she had replied with an asperity he had not expected, "For me any outcome is preferable to being married to you."

After finishing her studies, she had wanted something to do to fill her spare time, so she had worked as a teacher. Chances to marry had come time after time, but she had turned her back on them all.

"Does no one please you?" her mother asked her.

"I know what I'm doing," she had said gently.

"But time is going by."

"Let it go as it pleases, I am content."

Day by day she becomes older. She avoids love, fears it. With all her strength she hopes that life will pass calmly, peacefully, rather than happily. She goes on persuading herself that happiness is not confined to love and motherhood. Never has she regretted her firm decision. Who knows what the morrow holds? But she was certainly unhappy that he should again make his appearance in her life, that she would be dealing with him day after day, and that he would be making of the past a living and painful present.

Then, the first time he was alone with her in his room, he asked her, "How are you?"

She answered coldly, "I'm fine."

He hesitated slightly before inquiring, "Have you not . . . I mean, did you get married?"

In the tone of someone intent on cutting short a conversation, she said, "I told you, I'm fine."

TOBA TEK SINGH

Saadat Hasan Manto

Translated from the Urdu by Frances W. Pritchett

Saadat Hasan Manto (1912–1955) was an Indo-Pakistani writer, play-wright and author considered among the greatest writers of short stories in South Asian history. He produced twenty-two collections of short stories, one novel and three collections of essays. Manto is best known for his stories about the partition of the subcontinent immediately following independence in 1947. Manto is often compared with D.H. Lawrence, partly because he wrote about taboos of Indo-Pakistani society. He was tried for obscenity six times but never convicted. In his journalism, he predicted the rise of Islamic fundamentalism in Pakistan. Manto was opposed to partition and had refused to go to the newly formed Pakistan, until a Hindu colleague remarked that, were it not for the fact they were friends, he would have killed Manto. The next day Manto packed his bags and took his family to Lahore.

Two or three years after Partition, it occurred to the governments of Pakistan and Hindustan that like criminal offenders, lunatics too ought to be exchanged: that is, those Muslim lunatics who were in Hindustan's insane asylums should be sent to Pakistan, and those Hindus and Sikhs who were in Pakistan's insane asylums should be confided to the care of Hindustan.

There's no telling whether this idea was wise or unwise; in any case, according to the decision of the learned, high-level conferences took place here and there, and finally a day was fixed for the exchange of lunatics. Thorough investigation was made. Those Muslim lunatics whose relatives were all in Hindustan were allowed to remain there. As for the rest, they were sent off to the border. Here in Pakistan, since almost all the Hindus and Sikhs had already left, the question of keeping anyone didn't even arise. As many Hindu and Sikh lunatics as there were, all of them were conveyed, under police protection, to the border.

No telling what was going on that side. But here in the Lahore insane asylum, when word of this exchange arrived, major discussions began to take place. One Muslim lunatic, who every day for twelve years had regularly read the "Zamindar," was asked by a friend, "Molbi Sa'b, what's this 'Pakistan'?"; after much thought and reflection he answered, "It's a kind of place in Hindustan where razors are made."

Having heard this answer, his friend was satisfied.

In the same way, a second Sikh lunatic asked another Sikh lunatic, "Sardarji, why are we being sent to Hindustan?—We don't know the language of that place."

The other smiled: "I know the language of those Hindustaggers—those Hindustanis go strutting around like the devil!"

One day, while bathing, a Muslim lunatic raised the cry of "Long live Pakistan!" with such force that he slipped on the floor and fell, and knocked himself out.

There were also a number of lunatics who were not lunatics. The majority of them were murderers whose relatives had bribed the officers to get them sent to the lunatic asylum, to save them from the coils of the hangman's noose. These understood something of why Hindustan had been partitioned and what Pakistan was. But they too were ignorant of the actual events. Nothing could be learned from the newspapers. The guards were illiterate and crude; nothing could be picked up from their conversation either. They knew only this much: that there's a man, Muhammad Ali Jinnah, whom people call the "Qa'id-e Azam." He has made a separate country for the Muslims, the name of which is Pakistan. Where it is, what its location is—about this they new nothing. This is the reason that in the insane asylum, all the lunatics whose minds were not completely gone were trapped in the dilemma of whether they were in Pakistan or Hindustan. If they were in Hindustan, then where was Pakistan? If they were in Pakistan, then how could this be, since a while ago, while staying right here, they had been in Hindustan?

One lunatic became so caught up in the circle of Pakistan and Hindustan, and Hindustan and Pakistan, that he became even more lunatic. One day he had been sweeping—and then climbed a tree, seated himself on a branch, and gave an unbroken two-hour speech about the subtle problem of Pakistan and Hindustan. When the guards told him to come down, he climbed even higher. When he was warned and threatened, he said, "I don't want to live in either Hindustan or Pakistan. I'll live right here in this tree."

When after great difficulty his ardor was cooled, he came down and began to embrace his Hindu and Sikh friends and weep. His heart overflowed at the thought that they would leave him and go off to Hindustan.

In an M.Sc.-qualified radio engineer, who was Muslim, who used to stroll all day in silence on a special path in the garden entirely apart from the other lunatics, the change that manifested itself was that he removed all his clothing, confided it to the care of a warden, and began to wander all around the garden entirely naked.

A stout Muslim lunatic from Chiniot who had been an enthusiastic worker for the Muslim League, and who bathed fifteen or sixteen times a day, suddenly abandoned this habit. His name was Muhammad Ali. Accordingly, one day in his madness he announced that he was the Qa'id-e Azam Muhammad Ali Jinnah. In imitation of him, a Sikh lunatic became Master Tara Singh. In this madness it almost came to bloodshed, but both were declared 'dangerous lunatics' and shut up in separate rooms.

There was a young Hindu lawyer from Lahore who had been rejected in love and had turned lunatic. When he heard that Amritsar had gone away into India, then he was very sad. He had fallen in love with a Hindu girl from that very city. Although she had rejected the lawyer, even in his madness he hadn't forgotten her. Thus he abused all those Hindu and Muslim leaders who had connived together and made Hindustan into two fragments—his beloved had become Hindustani, and he Pakistani.

When talk of the exchange began, then some of the lunatics comforted the lawyer, saying that he shouldn't mind about it, that he would be sent to Hindu-stan—the Hindustan where his beloved lived. But he didn't want to leave Lahore, because he thought that in Amritsar his practice wouldn't flourish.

In the European ward there were two Anglo-Indian lunatics. When they learned that the English had freed Hindustan and gone away, they were very much shocked. And for hours they privately conferred about the important question of what their status in the lunatic asylum would be now. Would the European Ward remain, or be abolished? Would breakfast be available, or not? Instead of proper bread, would they have to choke down those bloody Indian chapattis?

There was one Sikh who had been in the insane asylum for fifteen years. Strange and remarkable words were always to be heard on his lips: "*Upar di gur gur di annex di be dhyana di mung di daal of the lantern.*" He slept neither by day nor by night. The guards said that in the long duration of fifteen years he hadn't slept even for a moment. He didn't even lie down. Although indeed, he sometimes leaned against a wall.

Because he constantly remained standing, his feet swelled up. His ankles were swollen too. But despite this bodily discomfort, he didn't lie down and rest. When in the insane asylum there was talk about Hindustan-Pakistan and the exchange of lunatics, he listened attentively. If someone asked him what his opinion was, he answered with great seriousness, "*Upar di gur gur di annex di be dhyana di mung di daal of the Pakistan Government.*"

But later, "of the Pakistan Government" was replaced by "of the Toba Tek Singh Government," and he began to ask the other lunatics where Toba Tek Singh was, where he had his home. But no one at all knew whether it was in Pakistan or Hindustan. If they tried to tell him, they themselves were caught up in the perplexity that Sialkot used to be in Hindustan, but now it was said to be in Pakistan. Who knew whether Lahore, which now is in Pakistan, tomorrow might go off to Hindustan? Or all of Hindustan itself might become Pakistan? And who could place his hand on his breast and say whether Hindustan and Pakistan might not both someday vanish entirely?

This Sikh lunatic's hair had grown very thin and sparse. Because he rarely bathed, the hair of his beard and head had clumped together, which gave him a very frightening appearance. But the man was harmless. In fifteen years he'd never quarreled with anybody. The longtime custodians in the insane asylum knew only this much about him: that he had some lands in Toba Tek Singh. He was a pros-perous landlord, when suddenly his mind gave way. His relatives bound him in heavy iron chains, brought him to the insane asylum, got him admitted, and left.

These people came once a month to see him; after checking on his welfare, they left. For a long time these visits took place regularly. But when the confusion over Pakistan-Hindustan began, the visits stopped.

His name was Bishan Singh, but everyone called him "Toba Tek Singh." He had absolutely no idea what day it was, what month it was, or how many years had passed. But every month when his near and dear ones came to visit him, then he himself used to be aware of it. Thus he used to tell the custodian that his visitors were coming. That day he bathed very well, scrubbed his body thoroughly with soap, and put oil on his hair and combed it. He had them bring out clothes that he never wore, and put them on, and in such a state of adornment he went to meet his visitors. If they asked him anything, then he remained silent, or from time to time said, "*Upar di gur gur di annex di be dhyana di mung di dal of the lantern.*"

He had one daughter who, growing a finger-width taller every month, in fifteen years had become a young girl. Bishan Singh didn't even recognize her. When she was a child, she wept when she saw her father; when she'd grown up, tears still flowed from her eyes.

When the story of Pakistan and Hindustan began, he started asking the other lunatics where Toba Tek Singh was. When no reassuring answer was forthcoming, day by day his agitation increased. Now even his visitors didn't come. Formerly, he himself used to be aware that his visitors were coming. But now it was as if even the voice of his heart, which used to tell him of their arrival, had fallen silent.

His great desire was that those people would come who showed sympathy toward him, and brought him fruit, sweets, and clothing. If he asked them where Toba Tek Singh was, they would certainly tell him whether it was in Pakistan or Hindustan. Because his idea was that they came from Toba Tek Singh itself, where his lands were.

In the insane asylum there was also a lunatic who called himself God. When one day Bishan Singh asked him whether Toba Tek Singh was in Pakistan or Hindustan, he burst out laughing, as was his habit, and said, "It's neither in Pakistan nor in Hindustan—because we haven't given the order yet."

A number of times Bishan Singh asked this God, with much pleading and cajoling, to give the order, so that the perplexity would be ended; but he was very busy, because he had countless orders to give. One day, growing irritated, Bishan Singh burst out at him, "*Upar di gur gur di annex di be dhyana di mung di dal of hail to the Guruji and the Khalsa, and victory to the Guruji! Who says this will thrive—the true God is ever alive!*"

Perhaps the meaning of this was, "You're the God of the Muslims! If you were the God of the Sikhs, you'd surely have listened to me!"

Some days before the exchange, a Muslim from Toba Tek Singh who was his friend came to visit him. He had never come before. When Bishan Singh saw him, he moved off to one side and turned to go back, but the guards stopped him.

"He's come to visit you. He's your friend Fazal Din."

Bishan Singh took one look at Fazal Din, and began to mutter something. Fazal Din came forward and put a hand on his shoulder. "I've been thinking for a long time that I'd come see you, but I just didn't get a chance. . . . All your family are well; they've gone off to Hindustan. . . . I helped as much as I could. . . . Your daughter Rup Kaur. . . "

He stopped in the midst of what he was saying. Bishan Singh began to remember something. "Daughter Rup Kaur."

Fazal Din said haltingly, "Yes. . . she. . . she too is fine. . . . She too went off with them."

Bishan Singh remained silent. Fazal Din began saying, "They told me to check on your welfare from time to time. . . . Now I've heard that you're going to Hindustan. . . . Give my greetings to brother Balbesar Singh and brother Vadhava Singh. . . . And sister Amrit Kaur too. . . . Tell brother Balbesar that those brown water buffaloes that he left behind, one of them had a male calf. . . . The other had a female calf, but when it was six days old it died. . . . And . . . and if there's anything I can do for you, tell me; I'm at your service. . . . And I've brought you a little puffed-rice candy."

Bishan Singh confided the bundle of puffed-rice candy to the guard standing nearby, and asked Fazal Din, "Where is Toba Tek Singh?"

Fazal Din said with some astonishment, "Where is it? Right there where it was!"

Bishan Singh asked, "In Pakistan, or in Hindustan?"

"In Hindustan—no, no, in Pakistan." Fazal Din was thrown into confusion.

Bishan Singh went off muttering, "*Upar di gur gur di annex di be dhyana di mung di dal of the Pakistan and Hindustan of the get out, loudmouth!*"

Preparations for the exchange had been completed. Lists of the lunatics coming from here to there, and from there to here, had arrived, and the day of the exchange had also been fixed.

It was extremely cold when the lorries full of Hindu and Sikh lunatics from the Lahore insane asylum set out, with a police guard. The escorting wardens were with them as well. At the Wagah border the two parties' superintendents met each other; and after the initial procedures had been completed, the exchange began, and went on all night.

To extricate the lunatics from the lorries, and confide them to the care of the other wardens, was a very difficult task. Some refused to emerge at all. Those who were willing to come out became difficult to manage, because they suddenly ran here and there. If clothes were put on the naked ones, they tore them off their bodies and flung them away. Someone was babbling abuse, someone was singing. They were fighting among themselves, weeping, muttering. People couldn't make themselves heard at all—and the female lunatics' noise and clamor was something else. And the cold was so fierce that everybody's teeth were chattering.

The majority of the lunatics were not in favor of this exchange. Because they couldn't understand why they were being uprooted from their place and thrown away like this. Those few who were capable of a glimmer of understanding were raising the cries, "Long live Pakistan!" and "Death to Pakistan!" Two or three times a fight was narrowly averted, because a number of Muslims and Sikhs, hearing these slogans, flew into a passion.

When Bishan Singh's turn came, and on that side of the Wagah border the accompanying officer began to enter his name in the register, he asked, "Where is Toba Tek Singh? In Pakistan, or in Hindustan?"

The accompanying officer laughed: "In Pakistan."

On hearing this Bishan Singh leaped up, dodged to one side, and ran to rejoin his remaining companions. The Pakistani guards seized him and began to pull him in the other direction, but he refused to move. "Toba Tek Singh is here!"— and he began to shriek with great force, "*Upar di gur gur di annex di be dhyana di mung di dal of Toba Tek Singh and Pakistan!*"

They tried hard to persuade him: "Look, now Toba Tek Singh has gone off to Hindustan! And if it hasn't gone, then it will be sent there at once." But he didn't believe them. When they tried to drag him to the other side by force, he stopped in the middle and stood there on his swollen legs as if now no power could move him from that place.

Since the man was harmless, no further force was used on him. He was allowed to remain standing there, and the rest of the work of the exchange went on.

In the pre-dawn peace and quiet, from Bishan Singh's throat there came a shriek that pierced the sky. . . . From here and there a number of officers came running, and they saw that the man who for fifteen years, day and night, had constantly stayed on his feet, lay prostrate. There, behind barbed wire, was Hindustan. Here, behind the same kind of wire, was Pakistan. In between, on that piece of ground that had no name, lay Toba Tek Singh.

AXOLOTL

Julio Cortázar

Translated from the Spanish by Paul Blackburn

Julio Cortázar (1914–1984) was an Argentine novelist, short story writer, and essayist. Known as one of the founders of the Latin American Boom, Cortázar influenced an entire generation of Spanish-speaking readers and writers in the Americas and Europe. He died in Paris in 1984 and is interred in the Cimetière de Montparnasse. One night in Buenos Aires, Cortázar was crowded by student fans. The students hurriedly bought up copies of Cortázar's books from nearby bookstores so that he could sign them. A kiosk salesman, apologizing that he had no more of Cortázar's books, optimistically held out a Carlos Fuentes novel for him to sign instead. His most well-known story was the basis of Antonioni's film by the same name, *Blow-Up*. Just before he died, a travel journal was published on which he collaborated with his wife during a voyage from Paris to Marseilles in a camping van. Cortázar signed all author's rights and royalties over to the Sandinista government in Nicaragua; the book has since become a best-seller.

There was a time when I thought a great deal about the axolotls. I went to see them in the aquarium at the Jardin des Plantes and stayed for hours watching them, observing their immobility, their faint movements. Now I am an axolotl.

I got to them by chance one spring morning when Paris was spreading its peacock tail after a wintry Lent. I was heading down the boulevard Port-Royal, then I took Saint-Marcel and L'Hôpital and saw green among all that grey and remembered the lions. I was friend of the lions and panthers, but had never gone into the dark, humid building that was the aquarium. I left my bike against the gratings and went to look at the tulips. The lions were sad and ugly and my panther was asleep. I decided on the aquarium, looked obliquely at banal fish until, unexpectedly, I hit it off with the axolotls. I stayed watching them for an hour and left, unable to think of anything else.

In the library at Sainte-Geneviève, I consulted a dictionary and learned that axolotls are the larval stage (provided with gills) of a species of salamander of the genus Ambystoma. That they were Mexican I knew already by looking at them and their little pink Aztec faces and the placard at the top of the tank. I read that specimens of them had been found in Africa capable of living on dry land during the periods of drought, and continuing their life under water when the rainy season came. I found their Spanish name, *ajolote,* and the mention that they were edible, and that their oil was used (no longer used, it said) like cod-liver oil.

I didn't care to look up any of the specialized works, but the next day I went back to the Jardin des Plantes. I began to go every morning, morning and afternoon some days. The aquarium guard smiled perplexedly taking my ticket. I would lean up against the iron bar in front of the tanks and set to watching them. There's nothing strange in this, because after the first minute I knew that we were linked, that something infinitely lost and distant kept pulling us together. It had been enough to detain me that first morning in front of the sheet of glass where some bubbles rose through the water. The axolotls huddled on the wretched narrow (only I can know how narrow and wretched) floor of moss and stone in the tank. There were nine specimens, and the majority pressed their heads against the glass, looking with their eyes of gold at whoever came near them. Disconcerted, almost ashamed, I felt it a lewdness to be peering at these silent and immobile figures heaped at the bottom of the tank. Mentally I isolated one, situated on the right and somewhat apart from the others, to study it better. I saw a rosy little body, translucent (I thought of those Chinese figurines of milky glass), looking like a small lizard about six inches long, ending in a fish's tail of extraordinary delicacy, the most sensitive part of our body. Along the back ran a transparent fin which joined with the tail, but what obsessed me was the feet, of the slenderest nicety, ending in tiny fingers with minutely human nails. And then I discovered its eyes, its face. Inexpressive features, with no other trait save the eyes, two orifices, like brooches, wholly of transparent gold, lacking any life but looking, letting themselves be penetrated by my look, which seemed to travel past the golden level and lose itself in a diaphanous interior mystery. A very slender black halo ringed the eye and etched it onto the pink flesh, onto the rosy stone of the head, vaguely triangular, but with curved and irregular sides which gave it a total likeness to a statuette corroded by time. The mouth was masked by the triangular plane of the face, its considerable size would be guessed only in profile; in front a delicate crevice barely slit the lifeless stone. On both sides of the head where the ears should have been, there grew three tiny sprigs red as coral, a vegetal outgrowth, the gills, I suppose. And they were the only thing quick about it; every ten or fifteen seconds the sprigs pricked up stiffly and again subsided. Once in a while a foot would barely move, I saw the diminutive toes poise mildly on the moss. It's that we don't enjoy moving a lot, and the tank is so cramped—we barely move in any direction and we're hitting one of the others with our tail or our head—difficulties arise, fights, tiredness. The time feels like it's less if we stay quietly.

It was their quietness that made me lean toward them fascinated the first time I saw the axolotls. Obscurely I seemed to understand their secret will, to abolish space and time with an indifferent immobility. I knew better later; the gill contraction, the tentative reckoning of the delicate feet on the stones, the abrupt swimming (some of them swim with a simple undulation of the body) proved to me that they were capable of escaping that mineral lethargy in which they spent whole hours. Above all else, their eyes obsessed me. In the standing tanks on either side of them, different fishes showed me the simple stupidity of their handsome eyes so similar to our own. The eyes of the axolotls spoke to me of the presence of a different life, of another way of seeing. Glueing my face to the glass (the guard would cough fussily once in a while), I tried to see better those diminutive golden points, that entrance to the infinitely slow and remote world of these rosy creatures. It was useless to tap with one finger on the glass directly in front of their faces; they never gave the least reaction. The golden eyes continued burning with their soft, terrible light; they continued looking at me from an unfathomable depth which made me dizzy.

And nevertheless they were close. I knew it before this, before being an axolotl. I learned it the day I came near them for the first time. The anthropomorphic features of a monkey reveal the reverse of what most people believe, the distance that is traveled from them to us. The absolute lack of similarity between axolotls and human beings proved to me that my recognition was valid, that I was not propping myself up with easy analogies. Only the little hands... But an eft, the common newt, has such hands also, and we are not at all alike. I think it was the axolotls' heads, that triangular pink shape with the tiny eyes of gold. That looked and knew. That laid the claim. They were not *animals*.

It would seem easy, almost obvious, to fall into mythology. I began seeing in the axolotls a metamorphosis which did not succeed in revoking a mysterious humanity. I imagined them aware, slaves of their bodies, condemned infinitely to the silence of the abyss, to a hopeless meditation. Their blind gaze, the diminutive gold disc without expression and nonetheless terribly shining, went through me like a message: "Save us, save us." I caught myself mumbling words of advice, conveying childish hopes. They continued to look at me, immobile; from time to time the rosy branches of the gills stiffened. In that instant I felt a muted pain; perhaps they were seeing me, attracting my strength to penetrate into the impenetrable thing of their lives. They were not human beings, but I had found in no animal such a profound relation with myself. The axolotls were like witnesses of something, and at times like horrible judges. I felt ignoble in front of them; there was such a terrifying purity in those transparent eyes. They were larvas, but larva means disguise and also phantom. Behind those Aztec faces, without expression but of an implacable cruelty, what semblance was awaiting its hour?

I was afraid of them. I think that had it not been for feeling the proximity of other visitors and the guard, I would not have been bold enough to remain alone with them. "You eat them alive with your eyes, hey," the guard said, laughing; he likely thought I was a little cracked. What he didn't notice was that it was they devouring me slowly with their eyes, in a cannibalism of gold. At any distance from the aquarium, I had only to think of them, it was as though I were being affected from a distance. It got to the point that I was going every day, and at night I thought of them immobile in the darkness, slowly putting a hand out which immediately encountered another. Perhaps their eyes could see in the dead of night, and for them the day continued indefinitely. The eyes of axolotls have no lids.

I know now that there was nothing strange, that that had to occur. Leaning over in front of the tank each morning, the recognition was greater. They were suffering, every fiber of my body reached toward that stifled pain, that stiff torment at the bottom of the tank. They were lying in wait for something, a remote dominion destroyed, an age of liberty when the world had been that of the axolotls. Not possible that such a terrible expression which was attaining the overthrow of that forced blankness on their stone faces should carry any message other than one of pain, proof of that eternal sentence, of that liquid hell they were undergoing. Hopelessly, I wanted to prove to myself that my own sensibility was projecting a nonexistent consciousness upon the axolotls. They and I knew. So there was nothing strange in what happened. My face was pressed against the glass of the aquarium, my eyes were attempting once more to penetrate the mystery of those eyes of gold without iris, without pupil. I saw from very close up the face of an axolotl immobile next to the glass. No transition and no surprise, I saw my face against the glass, I saw it on the outside of the tank, I saw it on the other side of the glass. Then my face drew back and I understood.

Only one thing was strange: to go on thinking as usual, to know. To realize that was, for the first moment, like the horror of a man buried alive awaking to his fate. Outside, my face came close to the glass again, I saw my mouth, the lips compressed with the effort of understanding the axolotls. I was an axolotl and now I knew instantly that no understanding was possible. He was outside the aquarium, his thinking was a thinking outside the tank. Recognizing him, being him himself, I was an axolotl and in my world. The horror began—I learned in the same moment—of believing myself prisoner in the body of an axolotl, metamorphosed into him with my human mind intact, buried alive in an axolotl, condemned to move lucidly among unconscious creatures. But that stopped when a foot just grazed my face, when I moved just a little to one side and saw an axolotl next to me who was looking at me, and understood that he knew also, no communication possible, but very clearly. Or I was also in him, or all of us were thinking humanlike, incapable of expression, limited to the golden splendor of our eyes looking at the face of the man pressed against the aquarium.

He returned many times, but he comes less often now. Weeks pass without his showing up. I saw him yesterday, he looked at me for a long time and left briskly. It seemed to me that he was not so much interested in us any more, that he was coming out of habit. Since the only thing I do is think, I could think about him a lot. It occurs to me that at the beginning we continued to communicate, that he felt more than ever one with the mystery which was claiming him. But the bridges were broken between him and me, because what was his obsession is now an axolotl, alien to his human life. I think that at the beginning I was capable of returning to him in a certain way—ah, only in a certain way—and of keeping awake his desire to know us better. I am an axolotl for good now, and if I think like a man it's only because every axolotl thinks like a man inside his rosy stone semblance. I believe that all this succeeded in communicating something to him in those first days, when I was still he. And in this final solitude to which he no longer comes, I console myself by thinking that perhaps he is going to write a story about us, that, believing he's making up a story, he's going to write all this about axolotls.

A DULL AFTERNOON

Bohumil Hrabal

Translated from the Czech by Michael Henry Heim

Bohumil Hrabal (1914–1997). Born in Brno, then part of the Austro-Hungarian Empire, Hrabal studied law at Charles University in Prague, but never practiced the profession, working variously as a travelling salesman, in a theatre, and at a factory. Regarded by many Czechs as one of the finest writers of the twentieth century, Hrabal's best-known novels are *Closely Observed Trains* and *I Served the King of England*, both filmed by acclaimed Czech director Jiří Menzel, who won an Academy Award for Best Foreign Language Film in 1968. After his death, and according to his wishes, he is buried in an oak coffin branded *Pivovar Polná* (Polná Brewery), the brewery where his mother and stepfather met.

Just after noon a young man—no, he was more of a kid—walked into our neighborhood bar. Nobody knew who he was or where he'd come from. Anyway, he sat down at the table under the compressor and ordered three packs of cigarettes and a beer. Then he opened up this book he had with him, and from then on all he did was read, drink, and smoke. His fingers were all yellow, probably from smoking each cigarette down to where it burned him. Now and then he'd feel around on the tablecloth for a cigarette, light it off the old butt, and puff away. But never for a second did he lift his eyes from his book.

For a while nobody paid any attention to him, because it was just before a soccer game, and the place was packed with the pregame regulars, all dressed up and raring to go—full of spirit for whatever team they were rooting for. They kept straightening their backs as if their coats didn't fit, puffing out their chests, and striking poses with their hands in their pockets. And standing there at the counter downing their last beers, they argued over whether their team would win four-one or five-one.

Then out they streamed, laughing and strutting so that you could tell from three blocks off that they were on their way to the game. When they got to the movie theater at the corner they all turned and waved back at the glass doors, where two heads nodded back. One head belonged to old Jupa, whose doctor had made him cut out soccer after he had two heart attacks in the stands, and the other one—it belonged to the bartender, and he couldn't go because he ran the place. The soccer fans held up their hands, gesticulating. By this time they had reached a sign reading *No Burials on Sunday,* the current attraction at our local movie house. But if you looked out the glass doors of our beer place, what you saw was *Burials on Sunday,* because the corner of the building jutted out a little in the direction of the street and covered up the *No.* They were a happy bunch; anyone could tell they had the game all sewed up. Soon they were just tiny specks at the end of our long street.

They missed their streetcar; it rolled past them, its three cars transformed into three red stripes. So they turned around one more time, waved again . . . and then crossed over onto the island in the middle of the street. . . .

At three o'clock the bartender pushed a button, and the compressor motor on the wall above that kid—he was still reading away—the motor started up and a red light came on. The bartender purposely dropped a cracked stein from as high as he could reach, and even though it hit the floor like a cannon ball, that guy just kept on reading. There was even a smile on his face. The bartender waved his hands in front of the kid's eyes but they never left the book. All he did was grin. "He can't hear, he can't see, he's halfway through his second pack of cigarettes, and I'm about to bring him beer number five. I wonder when he's going to take his little trip over to the john? What is this generation coming to?"

Old man Jupa, who was sitting over by the other wall, facing the kid, made a gesture of despair and shook his head as if to say, "What's the use of talking?"

Then in came someone else no one had ever seen before. A slightly hump-backed, gray-haired little guy carrying a pot of sauerkraut. A pot of sauerkraut on a Sunday afternoon! He ordered a beer and put the pot down in front of him—so he wouldn't forget it, I guess. He rubbed his hands together and looked out the door into the street.

Old man Jupa couldn't take it any longer. "What is this generation coming to anyway? I just wonder what that pipsqueak is reading. I bet it's pornography or some kind of thriller. That's what it is—a sleazy detective story. What a dead-head! Everyone else goes to the game, but His Excellency just sits and reads. Disgusting!"

All in all, he wasn't at all bad-looking. He was wearing the kind of sweater only a mother or a girl friend could knit, the kind that weighs a good twenty-five pounds. He had a red bandana around his neck with a well-made knot; it was like those bandanas bricklayers and village musicians used to wear, tied with a knot as small as a jelly bean. And his head, bent over the book, played up a shock of shiny black hair that looked as if it'd just been doused in motor oil.

The bartender squatted on his heels and looked the boy in the face from below. When he'd had his fill, he stood up and said, "I'll be damned if that guy isn't actually crying!" And he pointed to the tears that had begun to fall all over the page—drip, drop, drip—like beer from the tap.

Well, that made old man Jupa furious. "What a bastard! No wonder we don't have any soccer players! Strong as an ox, and he blubbers like a baby! Disgusting!" And he spit on the floor with great gusto.

The little man who'd brought in the pot of sauerkraut opened his hands and said, "It's all on account of the young people having no ideals. When I was his age I was out on the field. Merz, the famous center forward, had taken a bad spill, and the best center forward of all time, Karel Koželuh, had to go in for him. Johnny Dick, our coach, said to me, 'You take over inside left.' So even though I had trained to play outside right, I started my career playing inside left. One time, though, Johnny Dick waved a telegram at me across the field and yelled,

"You're in luck. Our outside right is out.' So I finally did get a chance to play outside right."

The little man looked up at old man Jupa, who had the reputation of being an expert, and Jupa said, "Then you must have known Jimmy too, the back who played with Kuchynka."

"Sure I knew him. But Jimmy was his first name. Do you happen to remember his last name?"

All of a sudden you could've heard a pin drop. Jupa had frozen. Then with a grin the little man started up again. "How could you know, anyway? His name was Jimmy Ottaway, and he was English and a crackerjack player."

"What about Kanhäuser?" snapped Jupa.

But the little guy came back with a gesture that showed in no uncertain terms what he thought of our Jupa. "What are you bringing Kanhäuser into the picture for? He didn't start playing with us until '24!"

By this time the kid was feeling around for another cigarette. He lit it off the old butt and shook his yellow fingers for a few seconds—he must have burned himself—but he never let up reading. And now he was laughing, laughing like a hyena, laughing until he was weak.

Old man Jupa jumped up, banged his fist down hard on the table right next to the book, yelled, "Why, you dirty brat, you! Nobody's going to laugh at me!" and went back to his seat.

The boy was so caught up in what he was reading he had broken out into a sweat, so he wiped off his forehead, loosened the bandana, and rolled up the sleeves of his sweater. He was enjoying the book so much that in a burst of high spirits he banged his fist on the table—and so hard that everything took a leap. The bartender was just bringing him another beer.

"You're not the only one here, pipsqueak," the bartender screamed into his ear. "Keep your little tricks to yourself."

So anyway, the young guy—he was still reading and still chuckling away—felt his way up to the glass of beer, took it out of the bartender's hand, and managed to take a deep drink without moving his eyes off the page.

"Beer number six, cigarette number twenty-one," said the bartender in disgust. "What a generation they're going to make, let me tell you. Christ, if he was my son I'd tear that cigarette out of his mouth, even if his whole chin came with it," he yelled, demonstrating on himself how he'd rip off half the kid's face. "But if I want to teach him a lesson, the smart aleck would have the police on my back in two seconds flat!"

Then, to punctuate his statement, he punched the compressor button. The red light went out.

By now Jupa had regained his composure, and he turned to the little man and said, "People who know something about soccer say that only Bican at the height of his career was up to playing with the Real Club."

The little man pushed his pot of sauerkraut to the middle of the table and said, "Oh no! Bican never had the creativity a center forward needs. The only player who would have been up to the Real Club was Karel Koželuh. Koželuh had a feeling for team play. And why? Because he played outside left to my outside right. That's why." Then he pulled the pot back to the edge of the table, fished out some sauerkraut with the tips of his fingers, raised the limp little sheaf above his head, opened his mouth, and dropped it in. As he munched, he offered some to Jupa. "Help yourself. It's good for you." But all he got for his pains was a face that clearly said, "Anything but sauerkraut. I can never keep it down." Old man Jupa had begun to look awfully small and awfully miserable.

In the meanwhile the kid—his eyes still glued to the book—had stood up. Nobody'd ever have guessed how tall he was. They don't make them much taller. And the way he held that book of his, you'd think he'd never done anything in his life but hold books like that. He pushed back his chair like a count and then stood stock still in the middle of the room. There must have been some magic in what he was reading. Then he made his way over to the door at the other end of the room with *Rest Rooms This Way* painted on it, opened the door as if he'd done it a thousand times before, and disappeared into our old clubroom. (The clubroom used to have a showcase with our pennants and cups, from the time when you could still get a good game of soccer going in our part of Prague, but now it was being used to store crates of beer and soft drinks.)

Anyway, the bartender had just enough time to say, "What a nut," and point to the closing door, when suddenly we heard a loud crash of bottles followed by a soft tinkling of glass. He threw open the door for all to see, and what they saw was that young punk stumbling his way through an ocean of empty bottles, and—get this—his book still planted firmly in front of his face. Finally he got to the next door. He felt around for the doorknob, turned it, and went into the men's room.

The bartender tiptoed up to the door, opened it a crack, and peeked in. Then he closed it again, crossed through the clubroom, came back into the main room, and said mournfully, 'What an awful sight. Picture him—standing there pissing away, and with the other hand he's holding the book—and reading! And that cigarette dangling from his lower lip. No, I've never seen anything like it. I've been serving beer for thirty years now, and never have I seen the likes of it. Maybe I'm wrong, I don't know," and he shook his head, "but this generation will be the death of us."

Jupa asked the little man suspiciously whether he had ever played international ball. "Of course," he answered. "Man, did I have a stroke of hard luck in Stockholm once. I get this beautiful pass, see! So I close my eyes and sidekick it. But the Swedish center half stuck his foot out, and that was the last thing I remembered. Later, in the hospital, Kuchynka told me he heard the bone crack three times and could almost see the stars. I didn't break the leg, though, just tore off the kneecap. You should have seen how it swelled up. It's a good thing we had a real specialist in Prague—our own Johny Madden."

At this point the young guy came back, reading and smoking and making what looked like treble clefs in the air with his cigarette. He leaned against the doorjamb with the toes of one foot resting on the floor and the heel straight up and down. After a while he started back to his seat, but when he got to the center of the room he stopped and wrinkled up his forehead, as if something he'd read had given him a terrible shock. Then he shook his head, and tears as big as hailstones began to fall. Some of them fell on the back of old man Jupa's hand, and Jupa jumped up and shouted, "Nobody's going to cry over me!" Anyway, when the kid finally got back to his place, he practically collapsed into the chair.

Old man Jupa was furious. "Who ever heard of such a thing! Johny Madden a knee specialist. Johny Madden was a coach!" He looked up at the bartender, and the bartender began to laugh.

The guest, who was just about to drop another sheaf of sauerkraut into his mouth, jerked his head forward, threw the sauerkraut back into the pot, and said, "You can't be very up on things if you don't know about the miracles Johny Madden used to perform on sprained ankles. Why, all the ballerinas used to go to him. He had a ballerina in there with him the time they brought me in. 'Don't worry. We'll have you fixed up in no time,' he said to me while he massaged the dancer. Johny Madden . . . he was a great coach too of course. . . ." And he picked up the sauerkraut again, threw his head back, and dropped it into his mouth.

Now old man Jupa had a reputation for being an expert, and he was fit to be tied. He stroked his bald head in self-pity and kept saying, "Impossible, impossible," to himself. He seemed to have begun to shrink as soon as he started talking to the little guy. His neck was gone; his head sat right on his shoulders.

The bartender tried to save the day by pushing the button on the master board. It lit up the red light and started the compressor motor growling. "Sometimes I wonder," he said, "where those punks get their money. When I was a kid, you were a millionaire if you had enough for a few beers!"

"Forget about him," old man Jupa chimed in. "He'll end up in reform school anyway. Just look at him. Four o'clock in the afternoon, this game could knock our team out of first place, and all our noble friend here can do is sit and chain-smoke and get sloshed. Where else is he going to end up but jail? He'll probably go and murder a cigar store lady."

"Hey, waiter!" the kid shouted. And don't think he looked up from his book, either. No, all he did was motion toward himself and rub his thumb and forefinger together to show he was ready to pay.

"Did you see that? Did you hear that? I'm afraid to say anything to him. If only Comenius could see this. . . ." He shook his head and added up the beers. "That'll be seventeen crowns."

The young guy took out a fistful of bills from his pocket the way the little guy picked up the sauerkraut from his pot. Then he separated out two ten-crown bills and put them at the far end of the table, like a pianist reaching for those real low notes. Then he made a "Do what you see fit with the change" gesture with his hand, crumpled up the rest of the money, and stuck it in his pocket like a handkerchief. But the bartender laid down a three-crown note next to the book and said to him, "You can keep your change. I'll have no dealings with a jailbird."

They watched the boy put out his cigarette in the ashtray. He was as careful as if he was ringing a doorbell. Then he felt around on the tablecloth for another cigarette, put it in his mouth, took out his matches, struck one, set fire to the three-crown note, and lit the cigarette with it—all without lifting his eyes from the book. As he inhaled, he waved the flaming bank note in the air, and when it finally began to burn him, he dropped it into the ashtray all twisted and black. It sat there like a piece of carbon paper. Then he leaned his forehead up against his thumb and index finger, looking as much like a monument as a person can.

The bartender spat, bent down, and whispered, "Nothing is holy any more. There was a time when people would climb a fence to catch a feather the wind had blown away, and what does this juvenile delinquent do? He uses money to light his cigarettes! And you can be sure he didn't earn it for himself. How old do you think he is, anyway? Twenty-one? What will he be like when he's thirty? Why, he'll set the whole place on fire."

Then old man Jupa started in again. "What about František Svoboda?"

The little gray-haired guy couldn't have looked more patronizing. "You mean Franci? A great passer and a real tank. But he can't compare with Koželuh. The way Franci passed to Zámora—why, to this very day Zámora jumps out of bed when he dreams of that bomb coming at him. The trouble was, Franci loved picking fights. If you'd ever gone to soccer matches, you'd have remembered his battles with the Hungarians . . . Ferencvárosi Toma Egysilét. Turay, who was known for his brutality, and Toldi, that two-hundred-twenty-five-pound giant, both running wild, and right there in the thick of it—our tank Svoboda. But when it comes to teamwork, Koželuh was impossible to beat. And why? Because he played outside left to my outside right. You follow me?"

Old man Jupa, who couldn't have been more than a few years younger than the little guy, had shrunk so much during the last few minutes that his head was on a level with his stein; all he had to do was tip it a little and he was in business.

The sun beat down. The right-hand side of the street was steeped in bluish shadows, while the roofs on the left-hand side were just barely holding up under the weight of the light. And the *Burials on Sunday* sign—the come-on, in today's lingo—was ablaze with iridescent paint. It was like the light reflecting off hundreds of pocket mirrors. At the end of the street, where you could see right through the trams—there were so few people riding them—paraded a steady stream of walkers in all shapes and sizes, with a baby carriage thrown in here and there for good measure. The kid stood up from under the compressor motor. His face was striped from the light coming in off the street. His eyes were still glued to the book. And taking his coat off the hook, he put one arm through a sleeve and then stood there in that ridiculous-looking pose—one arm in, one arm out—like a scarecrow in a cabbage patch, and kept right on reading.

The little guy added up his own bill, put down the money next to his glass, and picked up the pot of sauerkraut. Old man Jupa stood up, grabbed that pot like it was a life preserver, and shouted, "Are you trying to tell me we play lousy soccer?" And as he shouted, he shook the pot.

But the little guy, who stood opposite him, had held onto it and was shaking it along with Jupa—so hard he almost tore Jupa's arm out of its socket. "Cut the crap now, will you? One day I pivoted twice in a row, and before you knew it the whole team was shouting, 'Play that ball, or you're out of the game on Sunday!' Take Borovička, for example. He's got all the technical know-how but no sense of team play. Or Kučera—a great player, but he hogs the whole show. No, to the best of my knowledge—and I'd swear it on a stack of Bibles—the best soccer ever was played by . . . the best soccer player of all times was Karel Koželuh. And you know why? Because he played outside left to my outside right." And he pulled the pot right out of the hands of a very disgruntled Jupa.

Then he looked out into the street. Over by the coming attractions pictures in front of the movie theater stood this real stacked broad sucking on a hard candy and looking at the pictures. "What a woman!" exclaimed the little man, in a trance. "God, what a woman! Now that's what I call a woman! And you know what she needs. Of course there aren't any real men around nowadays to give it to her. No man today can even begin to understand a woman like that. What a woman!" And shaking his head, he read into that woman just what he had been talking about. Suddenly there she was—twirling her bag and sucking her candy and heading straight for us. When she was all but at the glass door—it even got a little darker inside—she turned again and showed us all her beautiful curves in profile and walked past. "That woman is my ideal," said the little man, and he tucked the pot under his arm and set out after her like a sleepwalker or something.

Anyway, the kid finally pulled on the other sleeve, and—still holding the book in both hands—he spit out the last butt and ground it into the floor with his shoe. Then he put one hand on the glass door, shoved it open, and disappeared. Left the door open and disappeared.

"And not a word the whole time he was here," said the bartender. He just couldn't keep himself from going outside and yelling, "You good-for-nothing pipsqueak!" after the kid, and slamming the door real hard.

The glass gave out a suspicious rattle, and the bartender froze. "Jupa, I'm scared to turn around. Did I break it?" But Jupa shook his head no.

So there they sat, looking out the glass door. A crowd of people buying tickets began to form in front of the movie house. Old man Jupa looked up at the iridescent *No Burials on Sunday* sign and spit. "What an idiotic sign. Let's hope it's not a bad omen for our team." The bartender was nervous by nature, and the kid with the book hadn't exactly helped, so he started brush-cleaning glasses and holding them up to the light to make sure they were clean, just so he wouldn't be the first one to see the soccer crowd turn the corner.

Suddenly old man Jupa cried out, "Here they come!"

The first one to round the corner was Mr. Hurych, followed almost immediately by the others. They were all bedraggled and hunched over; they all looked withered and small, as if they'd gotten drenched and their clothes had shrunk. Right under the *No Burials on Sunday* sign Mr. Hurych tore off his hat, threw it down on the sidewalk, and started jumping on it. The others tried to console him. Then, just to make it absolutely clear how much he was suffering, Mr. Hurych took off his overcoat, threw it down, and started jumping on it too.

"There's something funny going on here," said old man Jupa. "Must have been a tie." And when he saw Mr. Hurych reaching for the doorknob, he opened the door for him himself. Well, Hurych fell in a heap on the first seat he came to and just sat there, looking out into space. The rest of the crowd came in and waited to see what he would do. Finally he picked himself up, took off his jacket, threw it down on the floor, collapsed back onto the bench, and said, "All eleven. No exceptions. Send all eleven to the mines!" And he pointed off in the direction where he figured the nearest mines to be.

Old man Jupa went over to the glass door and looked out. He didn't even notice that the beautiful woman, the one with the twirling handbag, had turned back onto our street, and that the outside right with the pot of sauerkraut was still sleepwalking ten feet behind her. She went into the movie theater, and there he was, right behind her.

So anyway, here was old man Jupa standing in the glass door with his arms stretched out like Christ on the cross. And if anyone had happened to look at him from the side, they would have seen tiny tears making their way down his cheeks. But by then the bartender had begun passing around a tray of fortifying brandy.

THE QUILT

Ismat Chughtai

Translated from the Urdu by Syeda Saiyidain Hameed

Ismat Chughtai (1911–1991) was an eminent Indian writer in Urdu. Considered the grand dame of Urdu fiction, Chughtai was one of the Muslim writers who stayed in India after the subcontinent was partitioned. Along with Rashid Jahan, Wajeda Tabassum and Qurratulain Hyder, Chughtai's work stands for the birth of a revolutionary feminist politics and aesthetics in twentieth-century Urdu literature. Chughtai's most celebrated short story, *Lihaaf* (*The Quilt*), published in 1942, was levelled with charges of obscenity – *Lihaaf* deals with homosexuality in Aligarh. Chughtai chose to contest this charge instead of apologizing and won her case in court.

In the depth of winter whenever I snuggle into my quilt, my shadow on the wall seems to sway like an elephant. My mind begins a mad race into the dark crevasses of the past; memories come flooding in.

Excuse me, but I am not about to relate a romantic incident surrounding my own quilt – I do not believe there is much passion associated with it. The blanket, though considerably less comfortable, is preferable because it does not cast such terrifying shadows, quivering on the wall!

It all began when I was a small girl. All day long I fought tooth and nail with my brothers and their friends. I sometimes wonder why the devil I was so quarrelsome. At my age my older sisters had been busy collecting admirers; all I could think of was fisticuffs with every known and unknown girl or boy I ran into!

For this reason my mother decided to deposit me with an 'adopted' sister of hers when she left for Agra. She was well aware that there was no one in that sister's house, not even a pet animal, with whom I could engage in my favorite occupation! I guess my punishment was well deserved. So Mother left me with Begum Jan, the same Begum Jan whose quilt is imprinted on my memory like a blacksmith's brand.

This was the lady who had been married off to Nawab Sahib for a very good reason, courtesy of her poor but loving parents. Although much past his prime, Nawab Sahib was *noblesse oblige* itself. No one had ever seen a dancing girl or a prostitute in his home. He had the distinction of not only performing the Haj himself, but of being the patron of several poor people who had undertaken the pilgrimage through his good offices.

Nawab Sahib had a strange hobby. Many people are known to have irksome interests like breeding pigeons and arranging cockfights. Nawab Sahib kept himself aloof from these disgusting sports; all he liked to do was keep an open house for students; young, fair and slim-waisted boys, whose expenses were borne entirely by him. After marrying Begum Jan, he deposited her in the house with all his other possessions and promptly forgot about her! The young, delicate Begum began to wilt with loneliness.

Who knows when Begum Jan started living? Did her life begin when she made the mistake of being born, or when she entered the house as the Nawab's new bride, climbed into the elaborate four-poster bed and started counting her days? Or did it begin from the time she realized that the household revolved around the boy-students, and that all the delicacies produced in the kitchen were meant solely for their palates? From the chinks in the drawing-room doors, Begum Jan glimpsed their slim waists, fair ankles, and gossamer shirts and felt she had been raked over the coals!

Perhaps it all started when she gave up on magic, necromancy, séances and whatnot. You cannot draw blood from a stone. Not an inch did the Nawab budge.

Broken-hearted, Begum Jan turned towards education. Not much to be gained here either! Romantic novels and sentimental poetry proved even more depressing. Sleepless nights became a daily routine. Begum Jan slowly let go and consequently became a picture of melancholy and despair.

She felt like stuffing all her fine clothes into the stove. One dresses up to impress people. Now, Nawab Sahib neither found a spare moment from his preoccupation with the gossamer shirts, nor did he allow her to venture outside the home. Her relatives, however, made it a habit to pay her frequent visits which often lasted for months, while she remained a prisoner of the house.

Seeing these relatives disport themselves made her blood boil. They happily indulged themselves with the goodies produced in the kitchen and licked the clarified butter off their greedy fingers. In her household they equipped themselves for their winter needs. But, despite renewing the cotton filling in her quilt each year, Begum Jan continued to shiver, night after night. Each time she turned over, the quilt assumed ferocious shapes which appeared like shadowy monsters on the wall. She lay in terror; not one of the shadows carried any promise of life. What the hell was life worth anyway? Why live? But Begum Jan was destined to live, and once she started living, did she ever!

Rabbo arrived at the house and came to Begum Jan's rescue just as she was starting to go under. Her emaciated body suddenly began to fill out. Her cheeks became rosy; beauty, as it were, glowed through every pore! It was a special oil massage that brought about the change in Begum Jan. Excuse me, but you will not find the recipe for this oil in the most exclusive or expensive magazine!

When I saw Begum Jan she was in her early forties. She sat reclining on the couch, a figure of dignity and grandeur. Rabbo sat against her back, massaging her waist. A purple shawl was thrown over her legs. The very picture of royalty, a real Maharani! How I loved her looks. I wanted to sit by her side for hours, adoring her like a humble devotee. Her complexion was fair, without a trace of ruddiness. Her black hair was always drenched in oil. I had never seen her parting crooked, nor a single hair out of place. Her eyes were black, and carefully plucked eyebrows stretched over them like a couple of perfect bows! Her eyes were slightly taut, eyelids heavy and eyelashes thick. The most amazing and attractive part of her face were her lips. Usually dyed in lipstick, her upper lip had a distinct line of down. Her temples were covered with long hair. Sometimes her face became transformed before my adoring gaze, as if it were the face of a young boy. . . .

Her skin was fair and moist, and looked like it had been stretched over her frame and tightly stitched up. Whenever she exposed her ankles for a massage, I stole a glance at their rounded smoothness. She was tall, and appeared taller because of the ample flesh on her person. Her hands were large and moist, her waist smooth. Rabbo used to sit by her side and scratch her back for hours together – it was almost as if getting scratched was for her the fulfillment of life's essential need, somehow more important than the basic necessities required for staying alive.

Rabbo had no other household duties. Perched on the four-poster bed, she was always massaging Begum Jan's head, feet or some other part of her anatomy. If someone other than Begum Jan received such a quantity of human touching, what would the consequences be? Speaking for myself, I can say that if someone touched me continuously like this, I would certainly rot.

As if this daily massage were not enough, on the days she bathed this ritual lasted a full two hours! The braziers were lit behind closed doors and then the procedure started. Scented oils and unguents were massaged into her shining skin – imagining the friction caused by this prolonged rubbing made me slightly sick. Usually Rabbo was the only one allowed inside the sanctum. Other servants, muttering their disapproval, handed over various necessities at the closed door.

The fact of the matter was that Begum Jan was afflicted with a perpetual itch. Numerous oils and lotions had been tried, but the itch was there to stay. *Hakims* and doctors stated: It is nothing, the skin is clear. But if the disease is located beneath the skin, it's a different matter.

These doctors are mad! Rabbo used to say with a meaningful smile while gazing dreamily at Begum Jan. "May your enemies be afflicted with skin disease! It is your hot blood that causes all the trouble!"

Rabbo! She was as black as Begum Jan was white, like burnt iron ore! Her face was lightly marked with smallpox, her body solidly packed; small, dextrous hands, a tight little paunch and full lips, slightly swollen, which were always moist. A strange and bothersome odor emanated from her body. Those puffy hands were as quick as lightning, now at her waist, now her lips, now kneading her thighs and dashing towards her ankles. Whenever I sat down with Begum Jan, my eyes were riveted to those roving hands.

Winter or summer, Begum Jan always wore kurtas of Hyderabadi *jaali karga*. I recall her dark skirts and billowing white kurtas. With the fan gently rotating on the ceiling, Begum Jan always covered herself with a soft wrap. She was fond of winter. I too liked the winter season at her house. She moved very little. Reclining on the carpet, she spent her days having her back massaged, chewing on dry fruit. Other household servants were envious of Rabbo. The witch! She ate, sat, and even slept with Begum Jan! Rabbo and Begum Jan – the topic inevitably cropped up in every gathering. Whenever anyone mentioned their names, the group burst into loud guffaws. Who knows what jokes were made at their expense? But one thing was certain – the poor lady never met a single soul. All her time was taken up with the treatment of her unfortunate itch.

I have already said that I was very young at that time and quite enamored of Begum Jan. She, too, was fond of me. When mother decided to go to Agra she had to leave me with somebody. She knew that, left alone, I would fight continuously with my brothers, or wander around aimlessly. I was happy to be left with Begum Jan for one week, and Begum Jan was equally pleased to have me. After all, she was Amma's adopted sister!

The question arose of where I was to sleep. The obvious place was Begum Jan's room; accordingly, on the first evening a small bed was placed alongside the huge four-poster. Until ten or eleven that night we played Chance and talked; then I went to bed. When I fell asleep Rabbo was scratching her back. "Filthy wench," I muttered before turning over. In the middle of the night I woke up with a start. It was pitch dark. Begum Jan's quilt was shaking vigorously, as if an elephant was struggling beneath it.

"Begum Jan," my voice was barely audible. The elephant subsided "What is it? Go to sleep." Begum Jan's voice seemed to come from afar.

"I'm scared." I sounded like a petrified mouse.

"Go to sleep. Nothing to be afraid of. Recite the *Ayat-ul-Kursi*."

"Okay!" I quickly began the *Ayat*. But each time I reached "*Yalamu Mabain*" I got stuck. This was strange. I knew the entire *Ayat*!

"May I come to you, Begum Jan?"

"No child, go to sleep." The voice was curt. Then I heard whispers. Oh God! Who was this other person? Now I was terrified.

"Begum Jan, is there a thief here?"

"Go to sleep, child; there is no thief." This was Rabbo's voice. I sank into my quilt and tried to sleep.

In the morning I could not even remember the sinister scene that had been enacted at night. I have always been the superstitious one in my family. Night fears, sleep-talking, sleep-walking were regular occurrences during my childhood. People often said that I seemed to be haunted by evil spirits. Consequently I blotted out the incident from memory as easily as I dealt with all my imaginary fears. Besides, in the daytime the quilt seemed so innocent.

The next night I woke up again, this time a quarrel between Begum Jan and Rabbo was being settled on the bed itself. I could not make out what conclusion was reached, but I heard Rabbo sobbing. Then there were sounds of a cat slobbering in the saucer. To hell with it, I thought and went off to sleep!

In the morning Rabbo had gone off to visit her son. He was a quarrelsome lad. Begum Jan had done a lot to help him settle down in life; she had bought him a shop, arranged a job in the village, but to no avail. She even managed to have him stay with Nawab Sahib. Here he was treated well, a new wardrobe was ordered for him, but ungrateful wretch that he was, he ran away for no good reason and never returned, not even to see Rabbo. She therefore had to arrange to meet him at a relative's house. Begum Jan would never have allowed it, but poor Rabbo was helpless and had to go.

All day Begum Jan was restless. Her joints hurt like hell, but she could not bear anyone's touch. Not a morsel did she eat; all day long she moped in bed.

"Shall I scratch you, Begum Jan?" I asked eagerly while dealing out the deck of cards. Begum Jan looked at me carefully.

"Really, shall I?" I put the cards aside and began scratching, while Begum Jan lay quietly, giving in to my ministrations. Rabbo was due back the next day, but she never turned up. Begum Jan became irritable. She drank so much tea that her head started throbbing.

Once again I started on her back. What a smooth slab of a back! I scratched her softly, happy to be of some assistance.

"Scratch harder, open the straps," Begum Jan spoke. "There, below the shoulder. Ooh, wonderful!" She sighed as if with immense relief.

"This way," Begum Jan indicated, although she could very well scratch that part herself. But she preferred my touch. How proud I was!

"Here, oh, oh, how you tickle," she laughed. I was talking and scratching at the same time.

"Tomorrow I will send you to the market. What do you want? A sleeping-walking doll?"

"Not a doll, Begum Jan! Do you think I am a child? You know I am . . ."

"Yes . . . an old crow. Is that what you are?" She laughed. "Okay then, buy a *babua*. Dress it up yourself, I'll give you as many bits and pieces as you want. Okay?" She turned over.

"Okay," I answered.

"Here." She was guiding my hand wherever she felt the itch. With my mind on the *babua,* I was scratching mechanically, unthinkingly. She continued talking. "Listen, you don't have enough clothes. Tomorrow I will ask the tailor to make you a new frock. Your mother has left some material with me."

"I don't want that cheap red material. It looks tacky." I was talking nonsense while my hand roved the entire territory. I did not realize it but by now Begum Jan was flat on her back! Oh God! I quickly withdrew my hand.

"Silly girl, don't you see where you're scratching? You have dislocated my ribs." Begum Jan was smiling mischievously. I was red with embarrassment.

"Come, lie down with me." She laid me at her side with my head on her arm. "How thin you are . . . and, let's see, your ribs," she started counting.

"No," I protested weakly.

"I won't eat you up! What a tight sweater," she said. "Not even a warm vest?" I began to get very restless.

"How many ribs?" The topic was changed.

"Nine on one side, ten on the other." I thought of my school hygiene. Very confused thinking.

"Let's see," she moved my hand. "One, two, three . . ."

I wanted to run away from her, but she held me closer. I struggled to get away. Begum Jan started laughing.

To this day whenever I think of what she looked like at that moment, I get nervous. Her eyelids had become heavy, her upper lip darkened and, despite the cold, her nose and eyes were covered with tiny beads of perspiration. Her hands were stiff and cold, but soft as if the skin had been peeled. She had thrown off her shawl and in the *karga* kurta, her body shone like a ball of dough. Her heavy gold kurta buttons were open, swinging to one side.

The dusk had plunged her room into a claustrophobic blackness, and I felt gripped by an unknown terror. Begum Jan's deep dark eyes focussed on me! I started crying. She was clutching me like a clay doll. I started feeling nauseated against her warm body. She seemed possessed. What could I do? I was neither able to cry nor scream! In a while she became limp. Her face turned pale and frightening, she started taking deep breaths. I figured she was about to die, so I ran outside.

Thank God Rabbo came back that night. I was scared enough to pull the sheet over my head, but sleep evaded me as usual. I lay awake for hours.

How I wished my Amma would return. Begum Jan had become such a terrifying entity that I spent my days in the company of household servants. I was too scared to step into her bedroom. What could I have said to anyone? That I was afraid of Begum Jan? Begum Jan, who loved me so dearly?

The following day there was another tiff between Begum Jan and Rabbo. I was dead scared of their quarrels, because they signalled the beginning of my misfortunes! Begum Jan immediately thought about me. What was I doing wandering around in the cold? I would surely die of pneumonia!

"Child, you will have my head shaven in public. If something happens to you, how will I face your mother?" – Begum Jan admonished me as she washed up in the water basin. The tea tray was lying on the table.

"Pour some tea and give me a cup." She dried her hands and face. "Let me get out of these clothes."

While she changed, I drank tea. During her body massage, she kept summoning me for small errands. I carried things to her with utmost reluctance, always looking the other way. At the slightest opportunity I ran back to my perch, drinking my tea, my back turned to Begum Jan.

"Amma!" My heart cried in anguish. "How could you punish me so severely for fighting with my brothers?" Mother disliked my mixing with the boys, as if they were man-eaters who would swallow her beloved daughter in one gulp! After all who were these ferocious males? None other than my own brothers and their puny little friends. Mother believed in a strict prison sentence for females; life behind seven padlocks! Begum Jan's "patronage," however, proved more terrifying than the fear of the worlds worst goons! If I had had the courage I would have run out on to the street. But helpless as I was, I continued to sit in that very spot with my heart in my mouth.

After an elaborate ritual of dressing up and scenting her body with warm attars and perfumes. Begum Jan turned her arduous heat on me.

"I want to go home!" I said in response to all her suggestions. More tears.

"Come to me," she waxed. "I will take you shopping."

But I had only one answer. All the toys and sweets in the world kept piling up against my one and only refrain, "I want to go home!"

"Your brothers will beat you up, you witch!" She smacked me affectionately.

"Sure, let them," I said to myself annoyed and exasperated.

"Raw mangoes are sour. Begum Jan," malicious little Rabbo expressed her views.

Then Begum Jan had her famous fit. The gold necklace she was about to place around my neck, was broken to bits. Gossamer net scarf was shredded mercilessly. Hair, which was never out of place, was tousled with loud exclamations of "Oh! Oh! Oh!" She started shouting and convulsing. I ran outside.

After much ado and ministration. Begum Jan regained consciousness. When I tiptoed into the bedroom Rabbo, propped against her body, was kneading her limbs.

"Take off your shoes," she whispered. Mouse-like I crept into my quilt.

Later that night, Begum Jan's quilt was, once again, swinging like an elephant. "Allah," I was barely able to squeak. The elephant-in-the quilt jumped and then sat down. I did not say a word. Once again, the elephant started convulsing. Now I was really confused. I decided, no matter what, tonight I would flip the switch on the bedside lamp. The elephant started fluttering once again, as if about to squat. Smack, gush, slobber – someone was enjoying a feast. Suddenly I understood what was going on!

Begum Jan had not eaten a thing all day and Rabbo, the witch, was a known glutton. They were polishing off some goodies under the quilt, for sure. Flaring my nostrils, I huffed and puffed hoping for a whiff of the feast. But the air was laden with attar, henna, sandalwood; hot fragrances, no food.

Once again the quilt started billowing. I tried to lie still, but it was now assuming such weird shapes that I could not contain myself. It seemed as if a frog was growing inside it and would suddenly spring on me.

"Ammi!" I spoke with courage, but no one heard me. The quilt, meanwhile, had entered my brain and started growing. Quietly creeping to the other side of the bed I swung my legs over and sat up. In the dark I groped for the switch. The elephant somersaulted beneath the quilt and dug in. During the somersault, its corner was lifted one foot above the bed.

Allah! I dove headlong into my sheets!!

What I saw when the quilt was lifted, I will never tell anyone, not even if they give me a lakh of rupees.

ACTION WILL BE TAKEN

Heinrich Böll

Translated from the German by Leila Vennewitz

Heinrich Böll (1917–1985) One of the foremost German writers of the twentieth century, Heinrich Böll was born in Cologne, to a pacifist family that staunchly opposed the rise of Nazism. As a boy, he refused to join the Hitler Youth but was later conscripted into the Wehrmacht. After the war, he worked as a statistician before becoming a writer. His first novel was published in 1949, and he went on to write novels, short stories, radio plays and essays. His writings were controversial in post-war Germany. His novel *The Clown* was scathing in its criticism of the Catholic Church and its support for the Nazi regime He is best known for his novels *Group Portrait with Lady* and *The Lost Honour of Katharina Blum*. He was awarded the Nobel Prize for Literature in 1972.

Probably one of the strangest interludes in my life was the time I spent as an employee in Alfred Wunsiedel's factory. By nature, I am inclined more to pensiveness and inactivity than to work, but now and again prolonged financial difficulties compel me – for pensiveness is no more profitable than inactivity – to take on a so-called job. Finding myself once again at a low ebb of this kind, I put myself in the hands of the employment office and was sent with seven other fellow-sufferers to Wunsiedel's factory, where we were to undergo an aptitude test.

The exterior of the factory was enough to arouse my suspicions: the factory was built entirely of glass brick, and my aversion to well-lit buildings and well-lit rooms is as strong as my aversion to work. I became even more suspicious when we were immediately served breakfast in the well-lit, cheerful coffee shop: pretty waitresses brought us eggs, coffee and toast, orange juice was served in tastefully designed jugs, goldfish pressed their bored faces against the sides of pale-green aquariums. The waitresses were so cheerful that they appeared to be bursting with good cheer. Only a strong effort of will – so it seemed to me – restrained them from singing away all day long. They were as crammed with unsung songs as chickens with unlaid eggs.

Right away I realized something that my fellow-sufferers evidently failed to realize: that this breakfast was already part of the test; so I chewed away reverently, with the full appreciation of a person who knows he is supplying his body with valuable elements. I did something which normally no power on earth can make me do: I drank orange juice on an empty stomach, left the coffee and egg untouched, as well as most of the toast, got up, and paced up and down in the coffee shop, pregnant with action.

As a result I was the first to be ushered into the room where the question-naires were spread out on attractive tables. The walls were done in a shade of green that would have summoned the word "delightful" to the lips of interior decoration enthusiasts. The room appeared to be empty, and yet I was so sure of being observed that I behaved as someone pregnant with action behaves when he believes himself unobserved: I ripped my pen impatiently from my pocket, unscrewed the top, sat down at the nearest table and pulled the questionnaire toward me, the way irritable customers snatch at the bill in a restaurant.

Question No. 1: Do you consider it right for a human being to possess only two arms, two legs, eyes, and ears?
Here for the first lime I reaped the harvest of my pensive nature and wrote with-out hesitation: "Even four arms, legs and ears would not be adequate for my driving energy. Human beings are very poorly equipped."

Question No. 2: How many telephones can you handle at one time?
Here again the answer was as easy as simple arithmetic: "When there are only seven telephones," I wrote, "I get impatient; there have to be nine before I feel I am working to capacity."

Question No. 3: How do you spend your free time?
My answer: "I no longer acknowledge the term free time – on my fifteenth birth-day I eliminated it from my vocabulary, for in the beginning was the act."

I got the job. Even with nine telephones I really didn't feel I was working to capacity. I shouted into the mouth-pieces: "Take immediate action!" or; "Do something! – We must have some action – Action will be taken – Action has been taken – Action should be taken." But as a rule – for I felt this was in keeping with the tone of the place – I used the imperative.

Of considerable interest were the noon-hour breaks, when we consumed nutritious foods in an atmosphere of silent good cheer. Wunsiedel's factory was swarming with people who were obsessed with telling you the story of their lives, as indeed vigorous personalities are fond of doing. The story of their lives is more important to them than their lives, you have only to press a button, and immediately it is covered with spewed-out exploits.

Wunsiedel had a right-hand man called Broschek, who had in turn made a name for himself by supporting seven children and a paralyzed wife by working night-shifts in his student days, and successfully carrying on four business agen-cies, besides which he had passed two examinations with honors in two years. When asked by reporters: "When do you sleep, Mr. Broschek?" he had replied: "It's a crime to sleep!"

Wunsiedel's secretary had supported a paralyzed husband and four children by knitting, at the same time graduating in psychology and German history as well as breeding shepherd dogs, and she had become famous as a night-club singer where she was known as Vamp Number Seven.

Wunsiedel himself was one of those people who every morning, as they open their eyes, make up their minds to act. "I must act," they think as they briskly tie their bathrobe belts around them. "I must act," they think as they shave, triumphantly watching their beard hairs being washed away with the lather: these hirsute vestiges are the first daily sacrifices to their driving energy. The more intimate functions also give these people a sense of satisfaction: water swishes, paper is used. Action has been taken. Bread gets eaten, eggs are decapitated.

With Wunsiedel, the most trivial activity looked like action: the way he put on his hat, the way – quivering with energy – he buttoned up his overcoat, the kiss he gave his wife, everything was action.

When he arrived at his office he greeted his secretary with a cry of "Let's have some action!" And in ringing tones she would call back: "Action will be taken!" Wunsiedel then went from department to department, calling out his cheerful: "Let's have some action!" Everyone would answer: "Action will be taken!" And I would call back to him too, with a radiant smile, when he looked into my office: "Action will be taken!"

Within a week I had increased the number of telephones on my desk to eleven, within two weeks to thirteen, and every morning on the streetcar I enjoyed thinking up new imperatives, or chasing the words take action through various tenses and modulations: for two whole days I kept saying the same sentence over and over again because I thought it sounded so marvelous: "Action ought to have been taken;" for another two days it was: "Such action ought not to have been taken."

So I was really beginning to feel I was working to capacity when there actually was some action. One Tuesday morning – I had hardly settled down at my desk – Wunsiedel rushed into my office crying his "let's have some action!" But an inexplicable something in his face made me hesitate to reply, in a cheerful gay voice as the rules dictated: "Action will be taken!" I must have paused too long, for Wunsiedel, who seldom raised his voice, shouted at me: "Answer! Answer, you know the rules!" And I answered, under my breath, reluctantly, like a child who is forced to say: I am a naughty child. It was only by a great effort that I managed to bring out the sentence: "Action will be taken," and hardly had I uttered it when there really was some action: Wunsiedel dropped to the floor. As he fell he rolled over onto his side and lay right across the open doorway. I knew at once, and I confirmed it when I went slowly around my desk and approached the body on the floor: he was dead.

Shaking my head I stepped over Wunsiedel, walked slowly along the corridor to Broschek's office, and entered without knocking. Broschek was sitting at his desk, a telephone receiver in each hand, between his teeth a ballpoint pen with which he was making notes on a writing pad, while with his bare feet he was operating a knitting machine under the desk. In this way he helps to clothe his family. "We've had some action," I said in a low voice.

Broschek spat out the ballpoint pen, put down the two receivers, reluctantly detached his toes from the knitting machine.

"What action?" he asked.

"Wunsiedel is dead," I said.

"No," said Broschek.

"Yes," I said, "come and have a look!"

"No," said Broschek, "that's impossible," but he put on his slippers and followed me along the corridor.

"No," he said, when we stood beside Wunsiedel's corpse, "no, no!" I did not contradict him. I carefully turned Wunsiedel over onto his back, closed his eyes, and looked at him pensively.

I felt something like tenderness for him, and realized for the first time that I had never hated him. On his face was that expression which one sees on children who obstinately refuse to give up their faith in Santa Claus, even though the arguments of their playmates sound so convincing.

"No," said Broschek, "no."

"We must take action;" I said quietly to Broschek. "Yes," said Broschek, "we must take action."

Action was taken: Wunsiedel was buried; and I was delegated to carry a wreath of artificial roses behind his coffin, for I am equipped with not only a penchant for pensiveness and inactivity but also a face and figure that go extremely well with dark suits. Apparently as I walked along behind Wunsiedel's coffin carrying the wreath of artificial roses I looked superb. I received an offer from a fashionable firm of funeral directors to join their staff as a professional mourner. "You are a born mourner," said the manager, "your outfit would be provided by the firm. Your face – simply superb!"

I handed in my notice to Broschek, explaining that I had never really felt I was working to capacity there; that, in spite of the thirteen telephones, some of my talents were going to waste. As soon as my first professional appearance as a mourner was over I knew: This is where I belong, this is what I am cut out for.

Pensively I stand behind the coffin in the funeral chapel, holding a simple bouquet, while the organ plays Handel's Largo, a piece that does not receive nearly the respect it deserves. The cemetery café is my regular haunt; there I spend the intervals between my professional engagements, although sometimes I walk behind coffins which I have not been engaged to follow, I pay for flowers out of my own pocket and join the welfare worker who walks behind the coffin of some homeless person. From time to time I also visit Wunsiedel's grave, for after all I owe it to him that I discovered my true vocation, a vocation in which pensiveness is essential and inactivity my duty.

It was not till much later that I realized I had never bothered to find out what was being produced in Wunsiedel's factory. I expect it was soap.

HAPPY BIRTHDAY

(Feliz Aniversário)

Clarice Lispector

Translated from the Portuguese by Katrina Dodson

Clarice Lispector (1920–1977) was a Brazilian writer acclaimed internationally for her innovative novels and short stories. Born to a Jewish family in Podolia in Western Ukraine, she was brought to Brazil as an infant, amidst the disasters engulfing her native land following the First World War. She has been the subject of numerous books, and references to her and her work are common in Brazilian literature and music. Several of her works have been turned into films. Clarice had two sons: Pedro and Paulo. Pedro was so precocious that he learned the maid's local dialect in Switzerland in a couple of days. Despite being addicted to sleeping pills, when she couldn't sleep she would call her friends to discuss her personal problems at all times of the day or night. She survived a fire that started when she fell asleep with a lit cigarette in her hand.

The family began arriving in waves the ones from Olaria were all dressed up because the visit also meant an outing in Copacabana. The daughter-in-law from Olaria showed up in navy blue, glittering with "pailletés" and draping that camouflaged her ungirdled belly. Her husband didn't come for obvious reasons: he didn't want to see his siblings. But he'd sent his wife so as not to sever all ties—and she came in her best dress to show that she didn't need any of them, along with her three children: two girls with already budding breasts, infantilized in pink ruffles and starched petticoats, and the boy sheepish in his new suit and tie.

Since Zilda—the daughter with whom the birthday girl lived—had placed chairs side-by-side along the walls, as at a party where there's going to be dancing, the daughter-in-law from Olaria, after greeting the members of the household with a stony expression, plunked herself down in one of the chairs and fell silent, lips pursed, maintaining her offended stance. "I came to avoid not coming," she'd said to Zilda, and then had sat feeling offended. The two little misses in pink and the boy, sallow and with their hair neatly combed, didn't really know how to behave and stood beside their mother, impressed by her navy blue dress and the "pailletés."

Then the daughter-in-law from Ipanema came with two grandsons and the nanny. Her husband would come later. And since Zilda—the only girl among six brothers and the only one who, it had been decided years ago, had the space and time to take in the birthday girl—and since Zilda was in the kitchen with the maid putting the finishing touches on the croquettes and sandwiches, that left: the stuck-up daughter-in-law from Olaria with her anxious-hearted children by her side; the daughter-in-law from Ipanema in the opposite row of chairs pretending to deal with the baby to avoid facing her sister-in-law from Olaria; the idle, uniformed nanny, her mouth hanging open.

And at the head of the large table the birthday girl who was turning eighty-nine today.

Zilda, the lady of the house, had set the table early, covered it with colorful paper napkins and birthday-themed paper cups, scattered balloons drifting along the ceiling on some of which was written "Happy Birthday!", on others "Feliz Aniversario!". At the center she'd placed the enormous frosted cake. To move things along, she'd decorated the table right after lunch, pushed the chairs against the wall, sent the boys out to play at the neighbor's so they wouldn't mess up the table.

And, to move things along, she'd dressed the birthday girl right after lunch. Since then she'd fastened that pendant around her neck and pinned on her brooch, sprayed her with a little perfume to cover that musty smell of hers—seated her at the table. And since two o'clock the birthday girl had been sitting at the head of the long empty table, rigid in the silent room.

Occasionally aware of the colorful napkins. Looking curiously when a passing car made the odd balloon tremble. And occasionally that mute anguish: whenever she watched, fascinated and powerless, the buzzing of a fly around the cake.

Until four o'clock when the daughter-in-law from Olaria arrived followed by the one from Ipanema.

Just when the daughter-in-law from Ipanema thought she couldn't bear another second of being seated directly across from her sister-in-law from Olaria—who brimming with past offenses saw no reason to stop glaring defiantly at the daughter-in-law from Ipanema—at last José and his family arrived. And as soon as they all kissed the room started filling with people greeting each other loudly as if they'd all been waiting down below for the right moment to, in the rush of being late, stride up the three flights of stairs, talking, dragging along startled children, crowding into the room—and kicking off the party.

The birthday girl's facial muscles no longer expressed her, so no one could tell whether she was in a good mood. Placed at the head was what she was. She amounted to a large, thin, powerless and dark-haired old woman. She looked hollow.

"Eighty-nine years old, yes sir!" said José, the eldest now that Jonga had died. "Eighty-nine years old, yes ma'am!" he said rubbing his hands in public admiration and as an imperceptible signal to everyone.

Everyone broke off attentively and looked over at the birthday girl in a more official manner. Some shook their heads in awe as if she'd set a record. Each year conquered by the birthday girl was a vague step forward for the whole family. "Yes sir!" a few said smiling shyly.

"Eighty-nine years old!" echoed Manoel, who was José's business partner. "Just a little bean sprout!" he said joking and nervous, and everyone laughed except his wife.

The old woman showed no expression.

Some hadn't brought her a present. Others brought a soap dish, a cotton slip, a costume jewelry brooch, a little potted cactus—nothing, nothing that the lady of the house could use for herself or her children, nothing that the birthday girl herself could really use and thereby save money for the lady of the house: she put away the presents, bitter, sarcastic.

"Eighty-nine years old!" repeated Manoel nervously, looking at his wife.

The old woman showed no expression.

And so, as if everyone had received the final proof that there was no point making any effort, with a shrug as if they were with a deaf woman, they kept the party going by themselves, eating the first ham sandwiches more as a show of enthusiasm than out of hunger, making as if they were all starving to death. The punch was served, Zilda was sweating, not a single sister-in-law was really helping, the hot grease from the croquettes gave off the smell of a picnic; and with their backs turned to the birthday girl, who couldn't eat fried food, they laughed nervously. And Cordélia? Cordélia, the youngest daughter-in-law, seated, smiling.

"No sir!" José replied with mock severity, "no shop talk today!"

"Right, right!" Manoel quickly backed down, darting a look at his wife whose ears pricked up from a distance.

"No shop talk," José boomed, "today is for Mother!"

At the head of the already messy table, the cups dirtied, only the cake intact—she was the mother. The birthday girl blinked.

And by the time the table was filthy, the mothers irritated at the racket their children were making, while the grandmothers were leaning back complacently in their chairs, that was when they turned off the useless hallway light so as to light the candle on the cake, a big candle with a small piece of paper stuck to it on which was written "89." But no one praised Zilda's idea, and she wondered anxiously if they thought she was trying to save candles—nobody recalling that nobody had contributed so much as a box of matches for the party food that she, Zilda, was serving like a slave, her feet exhausted and her heart in revolt. Then they lit the candle. And then José, the leader, sang with great gusto, galvanizing the most hesitant or surprised ones with an authoritarian stare, "come on! all together now!"—and they all suddenly joined in singing loud as soldiers. Roused by the voices, Cordélia looked on breathlessly. Since they hadn't coordinated ahead of time, some sang in Portuguese and others in English. Then they tried to correct it: and the ones who'd been singing in English switched to Portuguese, and the ones who'd been singing in Portuguese switched to singing very softly in English.

While they were singing, the birthday girl, in the glow of the lit candle, meditated as though by the fireside.

They picked the youngest great-grandchild who, propped in his encouraging mother's lap, blew out the candle in a single breath full of saliva! For an instant they applauded the unexpected power of the boy who, astonished and exultant, looked around at everyone in rapture. The lady of the house was waiting with her finger poised on the hallway switch—and turned on the light.

"Long live Mama!"

"Long live Grandma!"

"Long live Dona Anita," said the neighbor who had shown up.

"Happy Birthday!" shouted the grandchildren who studied English at the Bennett School.

A few hands were still clapping.

The birthday girl was staring at the large, dry, extinguished cake.

"Cut the cake, Grandma!" said the mother of four, "she should be the one to cut it!" she asserted uncertainly to everyone, in an intimate and scheming manner. And, since they all approved happily and curiously, she suddenly became impetuous: "cut the cake, Grandma!"

And suddenly the old woman grabbed the knife. And without hesitation, as if in hesitating for a moment she might fall over, she cut the first slice with a murderer's thrust.

"So strong," the daughter-in-law from Ipanema murmured, and it wasn't clear whether she was shocked or pleasantly surprised. She was a little horrified.

"A year ago she could still climb these stairs better than me," said Zilda bitterly.

With the first slice cut, as though the first shovelful of dirt had been dug, they all closed in with their plates in hand, elbowing each other in feigned excitement, each going after his own little shovelful.

Soon enough the slices were divided among the little plates, in a silence full of commotion. The younger children, their mouths hidden by the table and their eyes at its level, watched the distribution with mute intensity. Raisins rolled out of the cake amid dry crumbs. The anguished children saw the raisins being wasted, intently watching them drop.

And when they went over to see, wouldn't you know the birthday girl was already devouring her last bite?

And so to speak the party was over.

Cordélia looked at everyone absently, smiling.

"I already told you: no shop talk today!" José replied beaming.

"Right, right!" Manoel backed down placatingly without glancing at his wife who didn't take her eyes off him. "You're right," Manoel tried to smile and a convulsion passed rapidly over the muscles of his face.

"Today is for Mother!" José said.

At the head of the table, the tablecloth stained with Coca-Cola, the cake in ruins, she was the mother. The birthday girl blinked.

There they were milling about boisterously, laughing, her family. And she was the mother of them all. And what if she suddenly got up, as a corpse rises slowly and imposes muteness and terror upon the living, the birthday girl stiffened in her chair, sitting up taller. She was the mother of them all. And since her pendant was suffocating her, she was the mother of them all and, powerless in her chair, she despised them all. And looked at them blinking. All those children and grandchildren and great-grandchildren of hers who were no more than the flesh of her knee, she thought suddenly as if spitting. Rodrigo, her seven-year-old grandson, was the only one who was the flesh of her heart, Rodrigo, with that tough little face, virile and tousled. Where's Rodrigo? Rodrigo with the drowsy, conceited gaze in that ardent and confused little head. That one would turn out to be a man. But, blinking, she looked at the others, the birthday girl. Oh how despicable those failed lives. How?! how could someone as strong as she have given birth to those dimwitted beings, with their slack arms and anxious faces? She, the strong one, who had married at the proper hour and time a good man whom, obediently and independently, she respected; whom she respected and who gave her children and repaid her for giving birth and honored her recovery time. The trunk was sound. But it had borne these sour and unfortunate fruits, lacking even the capacity for real joy. How could she have given birth to those frivolous, weak, self-indulgent beings? The resentment rumbled in her empty chest. A bunch of communists, that's what they were; communists. She glared at them with her old woman's ire. They looked like rats jostling each other, her family. Irrepressible, she turned her head and with unsuspected force spit on the ground.

"Mama!" cried the lady of the house, mortified. "What's going on, Mama!" she cried utterly mortified, and didn't even want to look at the others, she knew those good-for-nothings were exchanging triumphant glances as if it was up to her to make the old woman behave, and it wouldn't be long before they were claiming she didn't bathe their mother anymore, they'd never understand the sacrifice she was making. "Mama, what's going on!" she said softly, in anguish, "You've never done this before!" she added loudly so everyone would hear, she wanted to join the others' shock, when the cock crows for the third time you shall renounce your mother. But her enormous humiliation was soothed when she realized they were shaking their heads as if they agreed that the old woman was now no more than a child.

"Lately she's been spitting," she ended up confessing apologetically to everyone.

Everyone looked at the birthday girl, commiserating, respectful, in silence.

They looked like rats jostling each other, her family. The boys, though grown—probably already in their fifties, for all I know!—the boys still retained some of their handsome features. But those wives they had chosen! And the wives her grandchildren—weaker and more sour still—had chosen. All vain with slender legs, and those fake necklaces for women who when it comes down to it can't take the heat, those wimpy women who married off their sons poorly, who didn't know how to put a maid in her place, and all their ears dripping with jewelry—none, none of it real gold! Rage was suffocating her.

"Give me a glass of wine!" she said.

Silence fell suddenly, everyone with a glass frozen in their hand.

"Granny darling, won't it make you sick?" the short, plump little grand-daughter ventured cautiously.

"To hell with Granny darling!" the birthday girl exploded bitterly. "The devil take you, you pack of sissies, cuckolds and whores! give me a glass of wine, Dorothy!" she ordered.

Dorothy didn't know what to do, she looked around at everyone in a comical plea for help. But, like detached and unassailable masks, suddenly not a single face showed any expression. The party interrupted, half-eaten sandwiches in their hands, some dry piece stuck in their mouths, bulging their cheeks with the worst timing. They'd all gone blind, deaf and dumb, croquettes in their hands. And they stared impassively.

Forsaken, amused, Dorothy gave her the wine: slyly just two fingertips' worth in the glass. Expressionless, at the ready, they all awaited the storm.

But not only did the birthday girl not explode at the miserable splash of wine Dorothy had given her but she didn't even touch the glass.

Her gaze was fixed, silent. As if nothing had happened.

Everyone exchanged polite glances, smiling blindly, abstractedly as if a dog had peed in the room. Stoically, the voices and laughter started back up. The daughter-in-law from Olaria, who had experienced her first moment in unison with the others just when the tragedy triumphantly seemed about to be unleashed, had to retreat alone to her severity, without even the solidarity of her three children who were now mingling traitorously with the others. From her reclusive chair, she critically appraised those shapeless dresses, without any draping, their obsession with pairing a black dress with pearls, which was anything but stylish, cheap was all it was. Eyeing from afar those meagerly buttered sandwiches. She hadn't helped herself to a thing, not a thing! She'd only had one of each, just to taste.

And so to speak, once again the party was over.

People graciously remained seated. Some with their attention turned inward, waiting for something to say. Others vacant and expectant, with amiable smiles, stomachs full of that junk that didn't nourish but got rid of hunger. The children, already out of control, shrieked rambunctiously. Some already had filthy faces; the other, younger ones, were already wet; the afternoon was fading rapidly. And Cordélia, Cordélia looked on absently, with a dazed smile, bearing her secret in solitude. What's the matter with her? someone asked with a negligent curiosity, head gesturing at her from afar, but no one answered. They turned on the remaining lights to hasten the tranquility of the night, the children were starting to bicker. But the lights were fainter than the faint tension of the afternoon. And the twilight of Copacabana, unyielding, meanwhile kept expanding and penetrating the windows like a weight.

"I have to go," one of the daughters-in-law said, disturbed, standing and brushing the crumbs off her skirt. Several others rose smiling.

The birthday girl received a cautious kiss from each of them as if her so unfamiliar skin were a trap. And, impassive, blinking, she took in those deliberately incoherent words they said to her attempting to give a final thrust of enthusiasm to something that was no more than the past: night had now fallen almost completely. The light in the room then seemed yellower and richer, the people older. The children were already hysterical.

"Does she think the cake takes the place of dinner," the old woman wondered in the depths of herself.

But no one could have guessed what she was thinking. And for those who looked at her once more from the doorway, the birthday girl was only what she appeared to be: seated at the head of the filthy table, her hand clenched on the tablecloth as though grasping a scepter, and with that muteness that was her last word. Fist clenched on the table, never again would she be only what she was thinking. Her appearance had finally surpassed her and, going beyond her, was serenely becoming gigantic. Cordélia stared at her in alarm. The mute and severe fist on the table was telling the unhappy daughter-in-law she irremediably loved perhaps for the last time: You must know. You must know. That life is short. That life is short.

Yet she didn't repeat it anymore. Because truth was a glimpse. Cordélia stared at her in terror. And, for the very last time, she never repeated it—while Rodrigo, the birthday girl's grandson, tugged at Cordélia's hand, tugged at the hand of that guilty, bewildered and desperate mother who once more looked back imploring old age to give one more sign that a woman should, in a heartrending impulse, finally cling to her last chance and live. Once more Cordélia wanted to look.

But when she looked again—the birthday girl was an old woman at the head of the table.

The glimpse had passed. And dragged onward by Rodrigo's patient and insistent hand the daughter-in-law followed him in alarm.

"Not everyone has the privilege and the honor to gather around their mother," José cleared his throat recalling that Jonga had been the one who gave speeches.

"Their mother, comma!" his niece laughed softly, and the slowest cousin laughed without getting it.

"We have," Manoel said dispiritedly, no longer looking at his wife. "We have this great privilege," he said distractedly wiping his moist palms.

But that wasn't it at all, merely the distress of farewells, never knowing just what to say, José expecting from himself with perseverance and confidence the next line of the speech. Which didn't come. Which didn't come. Which didn't come. The others were waiting. How he missed Jonga at times like this—José wiped his brow with his handkerchief—how he missed Jonga at times like this! He'd also been the only one whom the old woman had always approved of and respected, and this gave Jonga so much self-assurance. And when he died, the old woman never spoke of him again, placing a wall between his death and the others. She'd forgotten him perhaps. But she hadn't forgotten that same firm and piercing gaze she'd always directed at the other children, always causing them to avert their eyes. A mother's love was hard to bear: José wiped his brow, heroic, smiling.

And suddenly the line came:

"See you next year!" José suddenly exclaimed mischievously, finding, thus, just like that, the right turn of phrase: a lucky hint! "See you next year, eh?" he repeated afraid he hadn't been understood.

He looked at her, proud of the cunning old woman who always slyly managed to live another year.

"Next year we'll meet again around the birthday cake!" her son Manoel further clarified, improving on his business partner's wit. "See you next year, Mama! and around the birthday cake!" he said in thorough explanation, right in her ear, while looking obligingly at José. And the old woman suddenly let out a weak cackle, understanding the allusion.

Then she opened her mouth and said:

"Sure."

Excited that it had gone so unexpectedly well, José shouted at her with emotion, grateful, his eyes moist:

"We'll see each other next year, Mama!"

"I'm not deaf!" said the birthday girl gruffly, affectionately.

Her children looked at each other laughing, embarrassed, happy. It had worked out.

The kids went off in good spirits, their appetites ruined. The daughter-in-law from Olaria vengefully cuffed her son, too cheerful and no longer wearing his tie. The stairs were difficult, dark, it was unbelievable to insist on living in such a cramped building that would have to be demolished any day now, and while being evicted Zilda would still cause trouble and want to push the old woman onto the daughters-in-law—reaching the last step, the guests relievedly found themselves in the cool calm of the street. It was nighttime, yes. With its first shiver.

Goodbye, see you soon, we have to get together. Stop by sometime, they said quickly. Some managed to look the others in the eye with unflinching cordiality. Some buttoned up their children's coats, looking at the sky for some hint of the weather. Everyone obscurely feeling that when saying goodbye you could maybe, now without the threat of commitment, be nice and say that extra word—which word? they didn't know exactly, and looked at each other smiling, mute. It was an instant that was begging to come alive. But that was dead. They started going their separate ways, walking with their backs slightly turned, unsure how to break away from their relatives without being abrupt.

"See you next year!" José repeated the lucky hint, waving with effusive vigor, his thinning, white hair fluttering. He really was fat, they thought, he'd better watch his heart. "See you next year!" José boomed, eloquent and grand, and his height seemed it might crumble. But those already a ways off didn't know whether to laugh loudly for him to hear or if it was enough to smile even in the darkness. More than a few thought that luckily the hint contained more than just a joke and that not until next year would they have to gather around the birthday cake; while others, already farther off in the darkness of the street, wondered whether the old woman would hang on for another year of Zilda's nerves and impatience, but honestly there was nothing they could do about it. "Ninety years old at the very least," thought the daughter-in-law from Ipanema melancholically. "To make it to a nice, round age," she thought dreamily.

Meanwhile, up above, atop the stairs and contingencies, the birthday girl was seated at the head of the table, erect, definitive, greater than herself. What if there's no dinner tonight, she mused. Death was her mystery.

TWO MAGICIANS

Satyajit Ray

Translated from the Bengali by Arunava Sinha

> **Satyajit Ray** (1921–1992). Widely regarded as one of the greatest film-makers of the twentieth century, Satyajit Ray was a true polymath. Aside from his career as a film director, he created two of the most popular fictional characters in Bengali children's literature and occasionally worked as a translator (he translated Lewis Carroll's "Jabberwocky" into Bengali). In 1992, less than a month before his death, he was awarded an Honorary Academy Award, making him the first and only Indian yet to receive the honour.

'Five, six, seven, eight, nine, ten, eleven.'

Having counted all the trunks, Surapati turned to his assistant, Anil. 'All right. Send them off to the brake van. Just twenty-five minutes to go.'

'Your compartment is ready too, sir,' Anil said. 'It's a coupe. Both berths are reserved for you. No one will disturb you.' Chuckling, he added, 'The guard's a fan too. He's been to your show at the New Empire. Ah, here he is—this way, sir.'

Biren Bakshi, the guard on the train, extended his right hand towards Surapati with a wide smile.

'If I may, sir, allow me to be honoured by shaking the hand whose tricks have given me so much pleasure.'

A single glance at any of Surapati Mondol's eleven trunks would reveal his identity. The words 'Mondol's Miracles' were stencilled in bold letters on the lids and sides of every trunk. No other explanation was necessary—for, just two months earlier, at the New Empire theatre in Calcutta, the audience had conveyed its appreciation through prolonged applause. The newspapers had been full of praise too. Mondol had been forced to promise the theatre authorities that he would perform again during the Christmas holidays.

'Please do let me know if you need anything, sir.'

The guard escorted Surapati to his compartment. Looking around, Surapati breathed a sigh of relief. It looked comfortable.

'Now if I may take leave, sir. . .'

'Thanks very much.'

When the guard had left, Surapati leaned back against the window and took a packet of cigarettes out of his pocket. This was probably the start of a triumphal journey. Delhi, Agra, Allahabad, Benares, Lucknow. That was all this time around, but there were so many states yet to be covered, numerous cities and towns. And why think of India alone? There was a world beyond—a huge expanse. Being a

Bengali didn't mean being unambitious. Surapati would show everyone. His fame would reach as far as America, home of the magician Houdini, reading about whom used to give him goose pimples once. He would prove to the world how far a boy from Bengal could go. Just let a few years pass. This was just the beginning.

Anil came running. 'All okay, sir. Everything.'

'Have you checked the locks?'

'Yes, sir.'

'Good.'

'I'm just two carriages away.'

'Have they cleared the line?'

'Any moment now. Will you have a cup of tea at Burdwan?'

'Not a bad idea.'

'I'll get you some.'

Anil left. Surapati lit a cigarette and looked out the window. A constant and noisy stream of porters, passengers and vendors streamed past in both directions. As he gazed at them his mind wandered. His eyes clouded over. The hubbub on the platform died down. He went back a long way in time, to a place far away. He was thirty-three now, but then he was only seven or eight years old. A tiny village in Dinajpur district—Panchpukur. It was a quiet autumn afternoon. An old woman was seated in front of Moti the grocer's shop with a gunny bag. People old and young were thronging around her. How old was she? Could be sixty, could be ninety. Her sunken cheeks were criss-crossed with hundreds of creases, which doubled whenever she smiled. She kept up a torrent of words through her missing teeth.

'Bhanumatir khel. Magic!'

The old woman had put on a magic show. For the first and last time. But Surapati never forgot what he saw, and never would. His own grandmother was sixty-five—her entire body shook uncontrollably when she tried to thread a needle. And this old woman had so much magic in her wrinkled hands. She was making things disappear under everyone's noses, and then conjuring them from thin air the next moment—money, marbles, spinning tops, nuts, fruits. Taking a rupee from Kalu Kaka, she made it vanish, sending him into a rage. When she made it materialize again, going off into peals of laughter, Kalu Kaka's eyes turned into saucers.

Surapati had been unable to sleep for several days after this magic show. And even when he eventually did, apparently he would often cry out, 'Magic! magic!' in his sleep.

After this, whenever there was a fair in the village, Surapati would visit it in the hope of watching some more magic. But he hadn't come across anything remarkable.

At sixteen, Surapati moved to his uncle's house on Bipradas Street in Calcutta to study for his intermediate degree. Alongside college textbooks, he read books on magic. Surapati had bought them within a month or two of arriving in the city, and had taught himself all the tricks in the books soon afterwards. He had had to buy several packs of cards. He would stand in front of the mirror for hours on end, practising. Surapati would sometimes perform his magic tricks on Saraswati Puja celebrations in his college or at friends' birthday parties.

He was invited to his friend Gautam's sister's wedding during his second year in college. It was a memorable day in the history of Surapati's magic training, for this was where he met Tripura Babu for the first time. A marquee had been erected in the field behind the enormous house on Swinhoe Street, and Tripura Babu was sitting in one corner, surrounded by guests. He had appeared nondescript at first glance. He was about forty-eight years old, with wavy, parted hair, a jovial expression, and traces of paan juice at the corners of his mouth. You saw countless such people on the streets. But what was happening on the sheet in front of him forced you to change your mind. Surapati couldn't believe his own eyes at first. A silver fifty-paisa coin rolled along to a gold ring placed three feet away, and then escorted the ring back to Tripura Babu. Surapati had been so stupefied that he hadn't even been able to summon up enough strength to clap. And then, the very next moment, another extraordinary piece of magic. Absorbed in the performance, Gautam's uncle had spilled all his matchsticks from the box while trying to light his cigar. As he was about to bend over, Tripura Babu had said, 'Why put yourself to trouble, sir? Allow me.'

Piling the matchsticks in a heap on the floor, Tripura Babu had held out the matchbox in his left hand, calling, 'Come, boys, come along now. . .' And, just like pet dogs or cats, the matchsticks had trooped into the box, one by one.

After the wedding dinner, Surapati had gone up to Tripura Babu who was standing by himself in a corner. Tripura Babu had been astonished by Surapati's interest in magic. 'Bengalis are happy enough just to watch,' he had said, 'I don't find too many people interested in performing. I am genuinely surprised that you're interested.'

Surapati had visited Tripura Babu at home within two days. He lived in a tiny, ramshackle room in a boarding house on Mirzapur Street. Surapati had never seen anyone live in so much poverty and deprivation. Tripura Babu had told Surapati how he made a living. He charged a fee of fifty rupees for a magic show. He barely got two commissions a month. Making more of an effort might have helped, but Surapati had realized that Tripura Babu was not that kind of a man. He couldn't have imagined that such a talented person would be so lacking in ambition. When he said as much, Tripura Babu had answered, 'What's the use? Who's going to value good things in this accursed country? How many people really understand art? How many can tell the original from the counterfeit? You praised my magic so effusively at the wedding the other evening, but no one else did. As soon as they were told dinner was served, they abandoned the magic to line up to worship their bellies.'

Surapati arranged for Tripura Babu to perform on special occasions at a few friends' and relatives' houses. Partly out of gratitude, and mostly out of affection, Tripura Babu had agreed to pass on his magic skills to Surapati. He had objected vehemently when Surapati had mentioned paying him. 'Don't even bring it up,' he had said. 'What is important is that I will have an inheritor. Since you are so interested and so enthusiastic, I will teach you. But don't be in a hurry. You have to dedicate yourself. Haste will achieve nothing. If you learn properly, you will experience the joy of creation. Do not expect too much money or fame. But then you will never share my plight, because you have ambition, which I don't. . .'

'You'll teach me all your tricks, won't you?' Surapati had asked hesitantly. 'Even the one with the coin and the ring?'

Tripura Babu had laughed. 'One step at a time. Don't be impatient. You have to keep at it. It needs dedication. These are ancient arts. This form of magic came about at a time when man had genuine willpower and concentration. Modern man cannot take his mind to that level easily. Have you any idea what an effort I had to make?'

Something happened after about six months of training with Tripura Babu.

On his way to college one day, Surapati noticed colourful posters on every wall in Chowringhee for Chefalo the Great. Going up to a poster to read the details, Surapati learnt that Chefalo was a famous Italian magician who was coming to Calcutta to perform. He would be accompanied by his fellow magician Madame Palermo.

At the New Empire Surapati had watched Chefalo's magic from the one-rupee seats. Incredibly eye-popping and mind-blowing acts, all of them. Surapati had only read about such magic in books. Entire humans disappeared in smoke in front of everyone's eyes, emerging again like Aladdin's genie from coils of smoke. Putting a girl inside a wooden crate, Chefalo sawed the box in half; the girl appeared from a different box within minutes, laughing, without a scratch on her. Surapati's palms had turned red with clapping.

And Chefalo himself was a source of continuous amazement for Surapati. The man was as good an actor as he was a magician. He was dressed in a shiny black suit and a top hat, with a magic wand in his hand. Was there anything Chefalo couldn't conjure out of that hat with his magic skills? On one occasion, he reached into a hat and pulled out a rabbit by its ears. The poor thing had barely finished shaking its ears when pigeons flew out—one, two, three, four. The magic pigeons flew around the hall, their wings rustling. Meanwhile, Chefalo was pulling chocolate bars out of the same hat and tossing them into the audience.

And throughout, Chefalo kept talking. Verbal fireworks. Surapati had read that this was referred to as patter. This patter was the magician's mainstay—while the audience drowned in its currents, the magician performed his sleight of hand unnoticed.

But Madame Palermo was a strange exception. She didn't utter a single word, performing her tricks like a silent robot. When did she perform her sleight of hand, then? Surapati had later found out the answer to this as well. It was possible to perform certain magic tricks on stage that required no sleight of hand. These tricks depended on machines, which were run by people behind the black curtain at the back of the stage. Cutting people into two halves and rejoining them, or making them disappear in smoke, was all a matter of machinery. If you had enough money you could buy these machines—or have them made—to put on these magic tricks. Of course, there was a certain flair and art involved in performing them with showmanship and panache, making them more attractive with glittering clothes and shiny props. Not everyone had mastered this art, which was why wealth was not enough to be a magician. After all, not everyone could. . .

Surapati's web of memories snapped suddenly.

The train had just left the platform with a bone-rattling jerk when the door to the compartment was flung open and the man who entered was. . .what! About to shout in indignation, Surapati held his tongue.

It was Tripura Babu! Tripuracharan Mullick!

Surapati had had similar experiences earlier. Someone he knew well, but hadn't met in a long time, suddenly cropped up in his thoughts or in a discussion and, the next thing you knew, the person was actually in their midst.

But still Surapati felt that Tripura Babu's sudden appearance put all those incidents in the shade. For a few moments he could not even speak. Wiping the perspiration off his forehead with the edge of his dhoti, Tripura Babu set his bundle down on the floor and sat down on the opposite end of the bench. Smiling at Surapati, he said, 'Surprised?'

Gulping, Surapati said, 'Surprised in the sense that—first, I didn't know you were alive.'

'What do you mean?'

'I visited your boarding house shortly after my BA exams. I found the door locked. The manager—I forget his name—said that you'd been run over. . .'

Tripura Babu burst into laughter. 'Something like that would have been wonderful. I'd have been relieved of all my worries.'

'And the second thing is,' added Surapati, 'I was thinking of you just the other day.'

'What's that?' A pall of gloom seemed to settle on Tripura Babu's expression. 'Thinking of me? You still think of me? I'm surprised to hear that.'

Surapati looked contrite. 'What are you saying, Tripura Babu! You think I can forget so easily? You introduced me to magic. I was especially reminded of the old days today. I am travelling for a show. Outside of Bengal for the first time. Did you know I'm a professional magician now?'

Tripura Babu nodded.

'I do. I know everything. And I came here to meet you today because I know everything. Everything that you have done over the past twelve years, how you have established yourself and achieved the fame you have today, is known to me. I was present at New Empire that evening, the first day. In the very last row. I saw how everyone appreciated your craft. I admit to feeling some pride. But. . .'

Tripura Babu paused. Surapati was silent. What could he possibly say? Tripura Babu could not be blamed for feeling disappointed. It was true that Surapati wouldn't be what he was today if Tripura Babu hadn't taught him the fundamentals. And what had Surapati done for him in return? On the contrary, his memory of Tripura Babu had faded over the past twelve years. Even his sense of gratitude had diminished.

Tripura Babu continued, 'I was proud of your success that day. But it was mixed with regret. Do you know why? The path you have chosen is not one of pure magic. A lot of what you're doing is fooling people with smoke and mirrors, tricks using machinery. It's not your own magic. Do you remember mine?'

Surapati had not forgotten. But at the same time he had felt that Tripura Babu had been hesitant about teaching Surapati his best tricks. 'Not yet,' he used to say. The time never came. Chefalo came before that. Surapati began to weave dreams, putting himself in Chefalo's place. He imagined himself travelling around the world performing shows, making a name for himself, giving pleasure to people, earning their approval and applause.

Tripura Babu was gazing out the window absently. Surapati observed him closely. He seemed to be in a bad way. His hair was almost entirely grey, the skin on his face was slack, his eyes were sunken. But had his eyes dimmed at all? It didn't seem so. He had a strangely piercing gaze.

With a sigh, Tripura Babu said, 'Mind you, I understand why you chose this path. I know you believe—and perhaps I am partly responsible for this—that purity is worthless. To perform magic on stage you need a little glitter and show-manship. Isn't that so?'

Surapati didn't deny it. He had concluded as much after watching Chefalo. But was glitter necessarily bad? Times had changed. How much could you earn performing your magic tricks at a wedding, and how many people would come to know of you? He had seen Tripura Babu's plight with his own eyes. What use was magic if performing it in all its purity couldn't even bring you two square meals a day?

Surapati told Tripura Babu about Chefalo. Was something which gave pleasure to thousands, earning their praise, not to be appreciated? Surapati was not dispar-aging pure magic. But there was no future down that route. So he had chosen this one.

Tripura Babu seemed to become agitated suddenly. Hoisting his feet on to the bench they were sitting on, he leaned towards Surapati.

'Look, Surapati, if you had really understood what genuine magic is, you wouldn't have chased the fake kind. Sleight of hand is just one aspect, although there are countless kinds. Like yogic acts, you have to practise them for months and years. But there's so much more. Hypnotism. Bringing people under your control with just a look, turning them into putty in your hands. Then there's clair-voyance, telepathy, thought-reading. You will have unrestricted access to people's thoughts. You can check someone's pulse and tell them what they're thinking. Once you've really mastered the art you won't even have to touch them. Just looking at them for a minute will tell you their innermost secrets, what's in their heart. Is all this magic? These things lie at the root of the finest magic in the world. There are no levers and pulleys here. There is only dedication, devotion, concentration.'

Tripura Babu paused for breath. He had had to talk above the sound of the train, which had probably exhausted him. Now he moved closer to Surapati, saying, 'I wanted to teach you all this, but you didn't care. You couldn't wait. You were taken in by a flashy, foreign charlatan. You abandoned the real path for the one that leads to quick wealth.'

Surapati was silent. He really could not deny any of these allegations.

Placing his hand on Surapati's shoulder, Tripura Babu softened his tone. 'I have come to you with a request, Surapati. I don't know if you can tell from my appearance—but I have really fallen on hard days. I know so much magic, but the magic of making money has eluded me. The lack of ambition has been my undoing—I would hardly have had to worry about how to make a living otherwise. I have come to you out of desperation, Surapati. I have neither the strength nor the youth to establish myself now. But I do have the faith that you will help me during this difficult time, even if it means a little sacrifice. I shan't bother you after that.'

Surapati was perplexed. What did the man want?

Tripura Babu continued, 'The plan may appear somewhat drastic to you, but there is no other way. The trouble is that it isn't just money that I need. I've developed a new desire in my old age, you know. I want to demonstrate my best acts to a large audience. Perhaps, for the first and last time, but I simply cannot suppress this wish.'

Surapati's heart quaked with an unknown fear.

Tripura Babu finally got to the point.

'You're going to Lucknow for a performance. Suppose you were to fall ill at the last moment. And instead of turning back a disappointed audience, what if someone else. . .'

Surapati was flabbergasted. What was Tripura Babu saying! He really must be quite desperate to make such a proposal.

When he didn't speak, Tripura Babu said, 'Because of unavoidable reasons, your guru will perform instead of you—this is what you will inform them. Will people be very disappointed? I don't think so. I am certain that they will enjoy my magic. Still, I propose that you will get half of what you would have been paid for the performance. Whatever's left over will be enough for me. After which you can continue as you are doing now. I won't bother you anymore. But you must give me this one opportunity, Surapati.'

Surapati was furious.

'Impossible! You don't know what you're saying, Tripura Babu. This is my first show outside Bengal. Don't you understand how much depends on the Lucknow performance? Should I begin my career with a lie? How could you even imagine such a thing?'

Tripura Babu looked steadily at Surapati for some time. Then his measured, restrained voice was heard above the clatter of the wheels.

'Are you still interested in the coin-and-ring trick?'

Surapati was startled. But there was no change in Tripura Babu's gaze.

'Why do you ask?'

Smiling, Tripura Babu said, 'I shall teach you the trick if you agree to my proposal. Right now, if you give me your word. And if not. . .'

A train bound for Howrah passed theirs with a grotesque shriek of its whistle. Tripura Babu's eyes glowed repeatedly in the light from the compartments of the other train. When the lights and sound had died down, Surapati said, 'And what if I don't agree?'

'The outcome will not be pleasant, Surapati. There's something you must know. If I'm in the audience, I can disrupt and humiliate any magician—I can even make them completely incapable of performing any magic.'

Taking a pair of cards from his pocket, Tripura Babu extended them to Surapati.

'Show me your sleight of hand. Nothing very difficult. Basic tricks. Bring the jack of clubs from the back to the front with a shake of your wrist.'

It had taken Surapati a mere seven days to perfect this trick in front of the mirror at the age of sixteen.

But today?

Picking up the cards, Surapati discovered his fingers turning numb. Not just his fingers, but also his wrist and elbow. All numb. His vision blurring, Surapati could only see a strange smile on Tripura Babu's lips; he was looking into

Surapati's eyes in an almost inhumanly penetrating way. Surapati's forehead was covered in perspiration, and he felt himself shaking.

'You realize my power now?'

The cards slipped out of Surapati's hand. Gathering them, Tripura Babu said grimly, 'Are you willing?'

Surapati was no longer feeling incapacitated.

In a weak, exhausted voice, he asked, 'You'll teach me the trick, won't you?'

Holding the index finger of his right hand in front of Surapati's nose, Tripura Babu said, 'Because of your indisposition, your guru Tripuracharan Mullick will perform his magic skills instead of you at the first show in Lucknow. Correct?'

'Correct.'

'You will give me half the payment due to you. Correct?'

'Correct.'

'Come, then.'

Fishing a coin out of his pocket, Surapati handed it over, along with the ruby ring on his finger.

Anil arrived at his boss's compartment with some tea when the train stopped at Burdwan, only to find him fast asleep. Surapati sprang up when Anil called out to him softly after some hesitation.

'What. . .what is it?'

'I got you some tea. I disturbed you, please don't mind.'

'But. . . ?' Surapati looked around frenziedly.

'What is it, sir?'

'Tripura Babu?'

'Tripura Babu?' Anil was bewildered.

'No, of course. . . he was killed by a bus. . . in 1951. . . but my ring?'

'Which ring, sir? The ruby's on your finger.'

'Oh yes, of course. And. . .'

Surapati took a coin out of his pocket. Anil noticed that his hand was shaking uncontrollably.

'Come in for a minute, Anil. Quickly. Shut the windows. Yes, watch now.'

Surapati placed the coin at one end of the bench and the ring at the other. Then, praying for all he was worth, he applied the technique acquired in his dream to cast a concentrated gaze on the ring.

Like a dutiful child the coin rolled up to the ring and escorted it back to Surapati.

The cup of tea would have slipped from Anil's hands had Surapati not taken it into his own with a miraculous sleight of hand.

When the curtain rose on the first day of the magic show in Lucknow, Surapati started by expressing his respect for his departed magic teacher Tripuracharan Mullick.

The last trick of the evening—which Surapati termed Pure Indian Magic—was the one with the coin and the ring.

THE LONG CROSSING

Leonardo Sciascia

Translated from the Italian by Avril Bardoni

Leonardo Sciascia (1921–1989). Born in Sicily, and raised in Caltanissetta, Sciascia developed a passion for literature in his teens while studying under the novelist and poet Vitaliano Brancati, who instilled in him a love of French writers. From the early 1950s, he established himself as a controversial commentator on political affairs and his first published writing, *Fables of the Dictatorship*, was a satire on Italian fascism. Sciascia was an outspoken public intellectual, critical of corruption, organised crime and entrenched power in his native Italy. He found fame with the novel *The Day of the Owl*, a fantastical thriller that shed light on the dark side of Sicilian public life. When told that his books in English were shelved in the mystery section, he replied: "At least I hope they will be regarded as metaphysical mysteries."

The night seemed made to order, the darkness so thick that its weight could almost be felt when one moved. And the sound of the sea, like the wild-animal breath of the world itself, frightened them as it gasped and died at their feet.

They were huddled with their cardboard suitcases and their bundles on a stretch of pebbly beach sheltered by hills, between Gela and Licata. They had arrived at dusk, having set out at dawn from their own villages, inland villages far from the sea, clustered on barren stretches of feudal land. For some of them this was their first sight of the sea, and the thought of having to cross the whole of that vast expanse, leaving one deserted beach in Sicily by night and landing on another deserted beach, in America and again by night, filled them with misgivings. But these were the terms to which they had agreed. The man, some sort of traveling salesman to judge from his speech, but with an honest face that made you trust him, had said: "I will take you aboard at night and I will put you off at night, on a beach in New Jersey only a stone's throw from New York. Those of you who have relatives in America can write to them and suggest that they meet you at the station in Trenton twelve days after your departure ... Work it out for yourselves ... Of course, I can't guarantee a precise date ... We may be held up by rough seas or coastguard patrols ... One day more or less won't make any difference: the important thing is to get to America."

To get to America was certainly the important thing; how and when were minor details. If the letters they sent to their relatives arrived, despite the ink-blotched, misspelled addresses scrawled so laboriously on the envelopes, then they would arrive, too. The old saying, "With a tongue in your head you can travel the world," was right. And travel they would, over that great dark ocean to the land of the *stori* (stores) and the *farme* (farms), to the loving brothers, sisters, uncles, aunts, nephews, nieces, cousins, to the opulent, warm, spacious houses, to the motor cars as big as houses, to America.

It was costing them two hundred and fifty thousand lira each, half on departure and the balance on arrival. They kept the money strapped to their bodies under their shirts like a priest's scapular. They had sold all their saleable possessions in order to scrape the sum together: the squat house, the mule, the ass, the year's store of provender, the chest of drawers, the counterpanes. The cunning ones among them had borrowed from the money-lenders with the secret intention of defrauding them, just this once, in return for the hardship they had been made to endure over the years by the usurers' greed, and drew immense satisfaction from imagining the expression on their faces when they heard the news. "Come and see me in America, bloodsucker: I just may return your money—without interest—if you manage to find me." Their dreams of America were awash with dollars. They would no longer keep their money in battered wallets or hidden under their shirts; it would be casually stuffed into trouser pockets to be drawn out in fistfuls as they had seen their relatives do, relatives who had left home as pitiable, half-starved creatures, shriveled by the sun, to return after twenty or thirty years—for a brief holiday—with round, rosy faces that contrasted handsomely with their white hair.

Eleven o'clock came. Someone switched on an electric torch, the signal to those aboard the steamship to come and collect them. When the torch was switched off again, the darkness seemed thicker and more frightening than ever. But only a few minutes later, the obsessively regular breathing of the sea was overlaid with a more human, more domestic sound, almost like buckets being rhythmically filled and emptied. Next came a low murmur of voices, then, before they realized that the boat had touched the shore, the man they knew as Signor Melfa, the organizer of their journey, was standing in front of them.

"Are we all here?" asked Signor Melfa. He counted them by the light of a torch. There were two missing. "They may have changed their minds, or they may be arriving late ... Either way, it's their tough luck. Should we risk our necks by waiting for them?"

They were all agreed that this was unnecessary.

"If anyone's not got his money ready," warned Signor Melfa, "he'd better skip out now and go back home. He'd be making a big mistake if he thought he could spring that one on me when we're aboard; God's truth, I'd put the whole lot of you ashore again. And, as it's hardly fair that everyone should suffer for the sake of one man, the guilty party would get what's coming to him from me and from all of us; he'd be taught a lesson that he'd remember for the rest of his life—if he's that lucky."

They all assured him, with the most solemn oaths, that they had their money ready, down to the last lira.

"All aboard," said Signor Melfa. Immediately each individual became a shapeless mass, a heaving cluster of baggage.

"Jesus Christ! Have you brought the whole house with you?" A torrent of oaths poured out, only ceasing when the entire load, men and baggage, was piled on board— a task accomplished not without considerable risk to life and property. And for Melfa the only difference between the man and the bundle lay in the fact that the man carried on his person the two hundred and fifty thousand lira, sewn into his jacket or strapped to his chest. He knew these men well, did Signor Melfa, these insignificant peasants with their rustic mentality.

The voyage took less time than they expected, lasting eleven nights including that of the departure. They counted the nights rather than the days because it was at night that they suffered so appallingly in the overcrowded, suffocating quarters. The stench of fish, diesel oil and vomit enveloped them as if they had been immersed in a tub of hot, liquid black tar. At dawn they streamed up on deck, exhausted, hungry for light and air. But if their image of the sea had been a vast expanse of green corn rippling in the wind, the reality terrified them: their stomachs heaved and their eyes watered and smarted if they so much as tried to look at it.

But on the eleventh night they were summoned on deck by Signor Melfa. At first they had the impression that dense constellations had descended like flocks onto the sea; then it dawned upon them that these were in fact towns, the towns of America, the land of plenty, shining like jewels in the night. And the night itself was of an enchanting beauty, clear and sweet, with a crescent moon slipping through transparent wisps of cloud and a breeze that was elixir to the lungs.

"That is America," said Signor Melfa.

"Are you sure it isn't some other place?" asked a man who, throughout the voyage, had been musing over the fact that there were neither roads nor even tracks across the sea, and that it was left to the Almighty to steer a ship without error between sky and water to its destination.

Signor Melfa gave the man a pitying look before turning to the others. "Have you ever," he asked, "seen a skyline like this in your part of the world? Can't you feel that the air is different? Can't you see the brilliance of these cities?"

They all agreed with him and shot looks full of pity and scorn at their companion for having ventured such a stupid question.

"Time to settle up," said Signor Melfa.

Fumbling beneath their shirts, they pulled out the money.

"Get your things together," ordered Signor Melfa when he had put the money away.

This took only a few minutes. The provisions that, by agreement, they had brought with them, were all eaten and all that they now had left were a few items of clothing and the presents intended for their relatives in America: a few rounds of goat-cheese, a few bottles of well-aged wine, some embroidered table-centers and antimacassars. They climbed down merrily into the boat, laughing and humming snatches of song. One man even began to sing at the top of his voice as soon as the boat began to move off.

"Don't you ever understand a word I say?" asked Melfa angrily. "Do you want to see me arrested?. . . As soon as I've left you on the shore you can run up to the first copper you see and ask to be repatriated on the spot; I don't give a damn:

everyone's free to bump himself off any way he likes . . . But I've kept my side of the bargain; I said I'd dump you in America, and there it is in front of you . . . But give me time to get back on board, for Crissake!"

They gave him time and enough to spare, for they remained sitting on the cool sand, not knowing what to do next, both blessing and cursing the night whose darkness provided a welcome mantle while they remained huddled on the shore, but seemed so full of menace when they thought of venturing further afield.

Signor Melfa had advised them to disperse, but no one liked the idea of separation from the others. They had no idea how far they were from Trenton nor how long it would take them to reach it.

They heard a distant sound of singing, very far away and unreal. "It could almost be one of our own carters," they thought, and mused upon the way that men the world over expressed the same longings and the same griefs in their songs. But they were in America now, and the lights that twinkled beyond the immediate horizon of sand-dunes and trees were the lights of American cities.

Two of them decided to reconnoiter. They walked in the direction of the nearest town whose lights they could see reflected in the sky. Almost immediately they came to a road. They remarked that it had a good surface, well maintained, so different from the roads back home, but to tell the truth they found it neither as wide nor as straight as they had expected. In order to avoid being seen, they walked beside the road, a few yards away from it, keeping in the trees.

A car passed them. One of them said: "That looked just like a Fiat 600." Another passed that looked like a Fiat 1100, and yet another. "They use our cars for fun, they buy them for their kids like we buy bicycles for ours." Two motorcycles passed with a deafening roar. Police, without a doubt. The two congratulated themselves on having taken the precaution of staying clear of the road.

At last they came to a roadsign. Having checked carefully in both directions, they emerged to read the lettering: SANTA CROCE CAM ARINA—SCOGLITTI.

"Santa Croce Camarina . . . I seem to have heard that name before."

"Right; and I've heard of Scoglitti, too."

"Perhaps one of my family used to live there, it might have been my uncle before he moved to Philadelphia. I seem to remember that he spent some time in another town before going to Philadelphia."

"My brother, too, lived in some other place before he settled in Brooklyn . . . I can't remember exactly what it was called. And, of course, although we may read the name as Santa Croce Camarina or Scoglitti, we don't know how the Americans read it, because they always pronounce words in a different way from how they're spelled."

"You're right; that's why Italian's so easy, you read it exactly how it's written . . . But we can't stay here all night, we'll have to take a chance . . . I shall stop the next car that comes along; all I've got to say is 'Trenton?'. . . The people are more polite here . . . Even if we don't understand what they say, they'll point or make some kind of sign and at least we'll know in what direction we have to go to find this blasted Trenton."

The Fiat 500 came round the bend in the road about twenty yards from where they stood, the driver braking when he saw them with their hands out to stop him. He drew up with an imprecation. There was little danger of a hold-up, he knew, because this was one of the quietest parts of the country, so, expecting to be asked for a lift, he opened the passenger door.

"Trenton?" the man asked.

"*Che?*" said the driver.

"Trenton?"

"*Che trenton della madonna,*" the driver exclaimed, cursing.

The two men looked at each other, seeking the answer to the same unspoken question: Seeing that he speaks Italian, wouldn't it be best to tell him the whole story?

The driver slammed the car door and began to draw away. As he put his foot on the accelerator he shouted at the two men who were standing like statues: "*Ubriaconi, cornuti ubriaconi, cornuti e figli di . . .*" The last words were drowned by the noise of the engine.

Silence descended once more.

After a moment or two, the man to whom the name of Santa Croce had seemed familiar, said: "I've just remembered something. One year when the crops failed around our parts, my father went to Santa Croce Camarina to work during the harvest."

As if they had had a rug jerked out from beneath their feet, they collapsed onto the grass beside the ditch. There was, after all, no need to hurry back to the others with the news that they had landed in Sicily.

THE POISONOUS RABBIT

Italo Calvino

Translated from the Italian by William Weaver

Italo Calvino (1923–1985) was an Italian journalist, short-story writer, and novelist whose whimsical and imaginative fables made him one of the most important Italian fiction writers in the twentieth century. Admired in Britain, Australia and the United States, he was the most-translated contemporary Italian writer at the time of his death. Using the battlename of "Santiago", Calvino joined the Italian Resistance and, for twenty months, endured the fighting in the Maritime Alps until 1945 and the Liberation. His parents were held hostage by the Nazis for an extended period; three times they mock executed his father in front of his mother. After moving to Turin, he often humorously belittled this choice, describing it as a "city that is serious but sad".

When the day comes to leave the hospital, you already know it in the morning and if you're in good shape you move around the wards, practising the way you're going to walk when you're outside; you whistle, act like a well man with those still sick, not to arouse envy but for the pleasure of adopting a tone of encouragement. You see the sun beyond the big panes, or the fog if there's fog; you hear the sounds of the city; and everything is different from before, when every morning you felt them enter – the light and sound of an unattainable world – as you woke behind the bars of that bed. Now, outside, there is your world again. The healed man recognizes it as natural and usual; and suddenly, he notices once more the smell of the hospital.

Marcovaldo, one morning, was sniffing around like that, cured, waiting for them to write certain things in his health insurance book so that he could leave. The doctor took his papers, said to him, "Wait here", and left him alone in the office. Marcovaldo looked at the white-enameled furniture he had so hated, the test-tubes full of grim substances, and tried to cheer himself with the thought that he was about to leave it all. But he couldn't manage to feel the joy he would have expected. Perhaps it was the idea of going back to the warehouse to shift packing cases, or of the mischief his children had surely been up to in his absence, and especially, of the fog outside that made him think of having to step out into the void, to dissolve in a damp nothingness. And so he looked around, with a vague need to feel affection towards something in here; but everything he saw reminded him of torture or discomfort.

Then he saw a rabbit in a cage. It was a white rabbit, with a long, fluffy coat, a pink triangle of a nose, amazed red eyes, ears almost furless flattened against its back. It wasn't all that big, but in the narrow cage its crouching oval body made the wire screen bulge and clumps of fur stuck out, ruffled by a slight trembling. Outside the cage, on the table, there was some grass and the remains of a carrot. Marcovaldo thought of how unhappy the animal must be, shut up in there, seeing that carrot but not being able to eat it. And he opened the door of the cage. The rabbit didn't come out: it stayed there, still, with only a slight twitch of its face, as if it were pretending to chew in order to seem nonchalant. Marcovaldo took the carrot and held it closer, then slowly drew it back, to urge the rabbit to come out. The rabbit followed him, cautiously bit the carrot and began gnawing it diligently, in Marcovaldo's hand. The man stroked it on the back and, meanwhile, squeezed it, to see if it was fat. He felt it was somewhat bony, under its coat. From this fact, and from the way it pulled on the carrot, it was obvious that they kept it on short rations. If it belonged to me, Marcovaldo thought, I would stuff it until it became a ball. And he looked at it with the loving eye of the breeder who manages to allow kindness towards the animal to coexist with anticipation of the roast, all in one emotion. There, after days and days of sordid stay in the hospital, at the moment of leaving, he discovered a friendly presence, which would have sufficed to fill his hours and his thoughts. And he had to leave it, go back into the foggy city, where you don't encounter rabbits.

The carrot was almost finished. Marcovaldo took the animal into his arms while he looked around for something else to feed him. He held its nose to a potted geranium on the doctor's desk, but the animal indicated it didn't like the plant. At that same moment Marcovaldo heard the doctor's step, coming back: how could he explain why he was holding the rabbit in his arms? He was wearing his heavy work coat, tight at the waist. In a hurry, he stuck the rabbit inside, buttoned it all the way up, and to keep the doctor from seeing that wriggling bulge at his stomach, he shifted it around to his back. The rabbit, frightened, behaved itself. Marcovaldo collected his papers and moved the rabbit to his chest, because he had to turn and leave. And so, with the rabbit hidden under his coat, he left the hospital and went to work.

"Ah, you're cured at last?" the foreman Signor Viligelmo said, seeing him arrive. "And what's that growth there?" and he pointed to the bulging chest.

"I'm wearing a hot poultice to prevent cramps," Marcovaldo said.

At that, the rabbit twitched, and Marcovaldo jumped up like an epileptic.

"Now what's come over you?" Viligelmo said.

"Nothing. Hiccups," he answered, and with one hand he shoved the rabbit behind his back.

"You're still a bit seedy, I notice," the boss said.

The rabbit was trying to crawl up his back and Marcovaldo shrugged hard to send it down again.

"You're shivering. Go home for another day. And make sure you're well tomorrow."

Marcovaldo came home, carrying the rabbit by its ears, like a lucky hunter.

"Papà! Papà!" the children hailed him, running to meet him. "Where did you catch it? Can we have it? Is it a present for us?" And they tried to grab it at once.

"You're back?" his wife said and from the look she gave him, Marcovaldo realized that his period of hospitalization had served only to enable her to accumulate new grievances against him. "A live animal? What are you going to do with it? It'll make messes all over the place."

Marcovaldo cleared the table and set the rabbit down in the middle, where it huddled flat, as if trying to vanish. "Don't anybody dare touch it!" he said. "This is our rabbit, and it's going to fatten up peacefully till Christmas."

"Is it a male or a female?" Michelino asked.

Marcovaldo had given no thought to the possibility of its being a female. A new plan immediately occurred to him: if it was a female, he could mate her and start raising rabbits. And already in his imagination the damp walls disappeared and the room was a green farm among the fields.

But it was a male, all right. Still Marcovaldo had now got this idea of raising rabbits into his head. It was a male, but a very handsome male, for whom a bride should be found and the means to raise a family.

"What are we going to feed it, when we don't have enough for ourselves?" his wife asked, sharply.

"Let me give it some thought," Marcovaldo said.

The next day, at work, from some green potted plants in the Management Office, which he was supposed to take out every morning, water, then put back, he removed one leaf each—broad leaves, shiny on one side and opaque on the other—and stuck them into his overalls. Then, when one of the girls came in with a bunch of flowers, he asked her, "Did your boy-friend give them to you? Aren't you going to give me one?" and he pocketed that, too. To a boy peeling a pear, he said, "Leave me the peel." And so, a leaf here, a peeling there, a petal somewhere else, he hoped to feed the animal.

At a certain point, Signor Viligelmo sent for him. Can they have noticed the plants are missing leaves? Marcovaldo wondered, accustomed always to feeling guilty.

In the foreman's office there was the doctor from the hospital, two Red Cross men, and a city policeman. "Listen," the doctor said, "a rabbit has disappeared from my laboratory. If you know anything about it, you'd better not try to act smart. Because we've injected it with the germs of a terrible disease and it can spread it through the whole city. I needn't ask if you've eaten it; if you had, you'd be dead and gone by now."

An ambulance was waiting outside; they rushed and got in it, and with the siren screaming constantly, they went through streets and avenues to Marcovaldo's house, and along the way there remained a wake of leaves and peelings and flowers that Marcovaldo sadly threw out of the window.

Marcovaldo's wife that morning simply didn't know what to put in the pot. She looked at the rabbit her husband had brought home the day before, now in a makeshift cage, filled with shavings. It arrived just at the right moment, she said to herself. There's no money; his wages have already gone for the extra medicines the Public Health doesn't cover; the shops won't give us any more credit. Raise rabbits, indeed! Or wait till Christmas to roast it! We're skipping meals, and we're supposed to fatten a rabbit!

"Isolina," she said to her daughter, "you're a big girl now, you have to learn how to cook a rabbit. You begin by killing it and skinning it, and then I'll tell you what to do next."

Isolina was reading a magazine of sentimental romances. "No," she whined, "you begin by killing it and skinning it, and then I'll watch how you cook it."

"What a help!" her mother said. "I don't have the heart to kill it. But I know it's a very easy matter; you just have to hold it by the ears and hit it hard on the back of the head. As for skinning, we'll see."

"We won't see anything," the daughter said, without raising her nose from the magazine. "I'm not hitting a live rabbit on the head. And I haven't the slightest notion of skinning it, either."

The three little ones had listened to this dialogue with wide eyes.

Their mother pondered for a moment, looked at them, then said, "Children . . ."

The children, as if by agreement, turned their backs on their mother and left the room.

"Wait, children!" their mother said. "I wanted to ask you if you'd like to take the rabbit outside. We'll tie a pretty ribbon around his neck and you can go for a walk with him."

The children stopped and exchanged looks. "A walk where?" Michelino asked.

"Oh, a little stroll. Then go call on Signora Diomira, show her the rabbit, and ask her if she'll please kill it and skin it for us, she's so good at that."

The mother had found the right method: children, as everyone knows, are caught up by the thing they like most, and they prefer not to think of the rest. And so they found a long, lilac-colored ribbon, tied it around the animal's neck, and used it as a leash, fighting over it, and pulling after them the reluctant, half-strangled rabbit.

"Tell Signora Diomira," the mother insisted, "that she can keep a leg for herself! No, better the head. Oh, she can take her pick."

The children had barely gone out when Marcovaldo's room was surrounded and invaded by orderlies, doctors, guards, and policemen. Marcovaldo was in their midst, more dead than alive. "Where is the rabbit that was taken from the hospital? Hurry: show us where it is, but don't touch it; it's infected with the germs of a terrible disease!" Marcovaldo led them to the cage, but it was empty. "Already eaten?" "No, no!" "Where is it then?" "At Signora Diomira's!" And the pursuers resumed their hunt.

They knocked at Signora Diomira's door. "Rabbit? What rabbit? Are you crazy?" Seeing her house invaded by strangers, in white jackets or uniforms, looking for a rabbit, the old woman nearly had a stroke. She knew nothing about Marcovaldo's rabbit.

In fact, the three children, trying to save the rabbit from death, had decided to take it to a safe place, play with it for a while, and then let it go; and instead of stopping at Signora Diomira's landing, they decided to climb up to a terrace over the rooftops. They would tell their mother it had broken the leash and had run off. But no animal seemed so ill-suited to an escape as that rabbit. Making it climb all those steps was a problem: it huddled, frightened, on each step. In the end they picked it up and carried it.

On the terrace they wanted to make it run: it wouldn't run. They tried setting it on the edge of the roof, to see if it would walk the way cats do; but it seemed to suffer vertigo. They tried hoisting it onto a TV antenna, to see if it could keep its balance: no, it fell down. Bored, the children ripped away the leash, turned the animal loose at a place where all the paths of the roofs opened out, an oblique and angular sea, and they left.

When it was alone, the rabbit began moving. It ventured a few steps, looked around, changed direction, turned, then, in little hops and skips, it started over the roofs. It was an animal born prisoner: its yearning for liberty did not have broad horizons. The greatest gift it had known in life was the ability to have a few moments free of fear. Now, now it could move, with nothing around to frighten it, perhaps for the first time in its life. The place was unfamiliar, but a clear concept of familiar and unfamiliar was something it had never been able to formulate. And ever since it had begun to feel an undefined, mysterious ailment gnawing inside itself, the whole world was of less and less interest to it. And so it went onto the roofs; and the cats that saw it hopping didn't understand what it was and they drew back, in awe.

Meanwhile, from skylights, from dormer windows, from flat decks, the rabbit's itinerary had not gone unremarked. Some people began to display basins of salad on their sills, peeking then from behind the curtains, others threw a pear core on the rooftiles and spread a string lasso around it, someone else arranged a row of bits of carrot along the parapet, leading to his own window. And a rallying-cry ran through all the families living in the garrets. "Stewed rabbit today" – or "fricasseed rabbit" – or "roast rabbit".

The animal had noticed these lures, these silent offers of food. And though it was hungry, it didn't trust them. It knew that every time humans tried to attract it with offers of food, something obscure and painful happened: either they stuck a syringe into its flesh, or a scalpel, or they forced it into a buttoned-up jacket, or they dragged it along with a ribbon around its neck . . . And the memory of these misfortunes merged with the pain it felt inside, with the slow change of organs that it sensed, with the prescience of death. And hunger. But as if it knew that, of all these discomforts, only hunger could be allayed, and recognized that these treacherous human beings could provide, in addition to cruel sufferings, a sense – which it also needed – of protection, of domestic warmth, it decided to surrender, to play the humans' game: then whatever had to happen, would happen. So, it began to eat the bits of carrot, following the trail that, as the rabbit well knew, would make it prisoner and martyr again, but savoring once more, and perhaps for the last time, the good earthy flavor of vegetables. Now it was approaching the garret window, now a hand would stretch out to catch it: instead, all of a sudden, the window slammed and closed it out. This was an event alien to its experience: a trap that refused to snap shut. The rabbit turned, looked for other signs of treachery around, to choose the best one to give in to. But meanwhile the leaves of salad had been drawn indoors, the lassos thrown away, the lurking people had vanished, windows and skylights were now barred, terraces were deserted.

It so happened that a police truck had passed through the city, with a loud-speaker shouting: "Attention, attention! A long-haired white rabbit has been lost; it is affected by a serious, contagious disease! Anyone finding it should be informed that it is poisonous to eat; even its touch can transmit harmful germs! Anyone seeing it should alert the nearest police station, hospital, or fire house!"

Terror spread over the rooftops. Everyone was on guard and the moment they sighted the rabbit, which, with a limp flop, moved from one roof to the next, they gave the alarm, and all disappeared as if at the approach of a swarm of locusts. The rabbit proceeded, teetering on the cornices; this sense of solitude, just at the moment when it had discovered the necessity of human nearness, seemed even more menacing to it, unbearable.

Meanwhile Cavalier Ulrico, an old hunter, had loaded his rifle with cartridges for hare, and had gone to take his stand on a terrace, hiding behind a chimney. When he saw the white shadow of the rabbit emerge from the fog, he fired; but his emotion at the thought of the animal's evil bane was so great that the spatter of shot fell a bit off the mark onto the tiles, like hail. The rabbit heard the shot rattle all around, and one pellet pierced its ear. It understood: this was a declaration of war; at this point all relations with mankind were broken off. And in its contempt of humans, at what seemed, to the rabbit, somehow a base ingratitude, it decided to end it all.

A roof covered with corrugated iron sloped down, oblique, and ended at the void, in the opaque nothingness of the fog. The rabbit planted itself there on all four paws, first cautiously, then letting itself go. And so, slipping, surrounded and consumed by its pain, it went towards death. At the edge, the drainpipe delayed it for a second, then it tumbled down . . .

And it landed in the gloved hands of a fireman, perched at the top of a portable ladder. Foiled even in that extreme act of animal dignity, the rabbit was bundled into the ambulance, which set off full-tilt towards the hospital. Also aboard were Marcovaldo, his wife, and his children, to be interned for observation and for a series of vaccine tests.

INCREDIBLE VOYAGE

Shūsaku Endō

Translated from the Japanese by Van C. Gessel

> Shūsaku Endō (1923–1996) was a Japanese author who wrote novels,
> short stories, drama and essays from the rare perspective of a Japanese
> Roman Catholic. Together with Junnosuke Yoshiyuki, Shōtarō Yasuoka,
> Junzo Shono, Hiroyuki Agawa, Ayako Sono (his co-religionist), and
> Shumon Miura, Endō is categorized as one of the "Third Generation",
> the third major group of Japanese writers who appeared after the Second
> World War. He lived most of his life with only one lung, having had the
> other removed after a bout of tuberculosis.

Late autumn in the year 2005. Yamazato Bontarō, a young physician at
the K. University Medical Centre, had just finished making the rounds of
the patients' rooms with Dr Yagyū. When he returned to the deserted laboratory, the head nurse came in to tell him that there was a telephone call for
him, from a woman.

Conscious of the nurse's ears pricked to hear what he had to say, Bontarō picked
up the receiver and said, 'Hello.' He was surprised to hear the voice of Sonomura
Sayuri.

'I'm sorry to bother you. I'm just outside the hospital. Do you think you could
see me?'

'What's the problem?'

'When I was in class today, I coughed suddenly, and some blood came out.'
Sayuri sounded frightened.

'You coughed up blood? Are you sure?'

'Yes. I was frightened and left class early. I came this far, only to find out my
brother isn't there.'

Sayuri was a student in the Literature Department at K. University. Her brother
Gōichi worked with Bontarō under Dr Yagyū's supervision. The two young men
had got to know each another during their first year in medical school; somehow
one strong- and one weak-willed fellow had hit it off smoothly, and they had
become fast friends.

'Please stay where you are. I'll be right there.'

Bontarō quickly hung up the receiver and left the nurses' station. The prospect
of seeing Sayuri made his heart flutter. During his first year at medical school,
she had seemed no more than a budding high-school girl, but recently when he
dropped in at Gōichi's house, she had begun to appear almost dazzlingly beautiful to him. On these occasions he would lament his own unattractiveness, and

would be overcome by the bitter realization that she was like a jewel dangling just beyond his reach. This was the woman who had just summoned him on the telephone.

He raced down the corridor, which was jammed with outpatients. As soon as he reached the main entrance of the hospital he caught sight of her pure white dress. Her tiny face looked as pale as that of a baby bird.

'You said you'd coughed up blood. About how much was there?'

'Around half a cup.'

Tuberculosis, he wondered, or just a simple case of bronchitis? In either case there was no need for concern; with the medical facilities available in the year 2005, treatment of these diseases had become as simple as twisting a baby's arm. At the very worst, she might have lung cancer, but that would be exceptional for someone her age.

'Have you felt like you've had a cold?'

'Yes, now that you mention it. These last couple of days.'

'Then there's nothing to worry about. You've simply got an inflammation of the bronchae,' Bontarō announced with a deliberately cheerful face. 'There's no need to consult your brother. I can fix you up myself. But shall we take some X-rays just to be on the safe side?'

'Where is Gōichi?'

'Probably at the Cancer Centre. It's Dr Inokuchi's day there, and he probably went along with him.'

Sayuri seemed anxious that her brother was not at the hospital, but she did as Bontarō instructed and followed him into No. 3 X-ray Room. He quickly drew up a chart and asked Iwamura, the X-ray technician, to take the pictures. Then he turned around and caught a glimpse of Sayuri's round white shoulder as she quietly began to undress. Flustered, he called, 'Well, thanks,' to Iwamura and headed down the corridor.

The sun shone warmly through the windows as an outpatient asked him directions to the examination room. Eventually Sayuri finished with the X-rays and came to see him, running her fingers through her tousled hair.

'Will I be all right?'

'What are you talking about? Of course you'll be all right. Even if it's TB, we're no longer living in the days when it took a year or two of treatment. They were grateful back then to have streptomycin to use. Now we don't even bother with drugs; we just burn up the afflicted area with electrical radiation. Recovery takes a mere two weeks.'

How happy he would be if a charming young woman like this were to love him, he thought. But that could never be. Sayuri would doubtless marry some wealthy young man.

The X-rays were ready in twenty minutes. Bontarō decided to show them to Dr Fukanuma, a chest specialist in Internal Medicine. His own eye could detect no abnormalities in the X-rays, but he wanted to get a second opinion.

'To me, your chest looks like that of a baby. But I'd like a distinguished physician to have a look at the pictures. Please wait here.'

Glancing at the X-rays that exposed her ribs and lungs for all to see, Sayuri blushed and nodded her head.

Dr Fukanuma was in Internal Medicine Laboratory No. 1, peering into a microscope. When he saw Bontarō he called, 'Hi!' Though they worked in different departments, Bontarō was fond of this burly doctor.

'Fine. I'll have a look at them.'

'From what I've seen, there aren't any cavities in the lung area. And there don't appear to be any shadows in the bronchial passages.'

'Ah-hah. Then it's probably a simple case of bronchitis.' As he peered at the lighted screen, Dr Fukanuma poked a cigarette into his mouth and lit it with his cigarette lighter. Then suddenly he put out the lighter and said softly, 'Wait a minute! What's this? This spot here near the heart . . . I don't like this. I don't like it at all.'

'Where, Doctor?'

Fukanuma looked searchingly at Bontarō's anxious face, then pointed to a spot on the X-ray with his stubby finger. It was smaller than a bean, a spot that on casual examination might be mistaken for a blood vessel.

'Doctor, is it cancer?'

'I think so. We'll need to do some more thorough tests, but . . .'

Fukanuma's diagnosis proved correct. The detailed examinations were performed by Bontarō and Sayuri's brother Gōichi, who came hurrying back to the hospital when he heard the news. The Eccleman Reaction was positive; the electronic brain scan came back positive – everything supported the diagnosis that the mucosa between the heart and lungs had been attacked by cancer. Unfortunately, since it lay in the region between the heart and lungs, the cancer was in the most precarious position, surgically speaking. I regret to have to inform you that, even in the year 2005, the only way to cure cancer was through surgery; I do, however, have an obligation to report the facts as they exist. I cannot tell a lie.

'Does Sayuri know about this?' Bontarō asked, a dismal expression on his face. He had never dreamed that his offhand diagnosis would be refuted by such grave findings.

'We've told her that it's tuberculosis. She doesn't know anything about medical science,' said Gōichi, his face stiff. 'At the moment she's resting peacefully in her room.'

'It's a dangerous operation. Do you want to go through with it?'

'What choice have we got? Father's agreed to it.'

Bontarō knew how hazardous this operation could be. To date, at K. University they had seen only two cases of lung cancer in this part of the body; in both instances surgery had failed. The patients had died on the operating table. Knowing this history, Bontarō could understand how Gōichi felt as he pondered his sister's chances for survival.

I must point out here that surgery in the year 2005 was nothing like the procedures you are familiar with today. In 1998, at the University of California, microgamma rays that could shrink objects to a fraction of their normal size were discovered; this led to a sweeping revolution in surgical technique. Dr Friedman was conducting research at the University on cancer-destroying rays, when one day he accidentally turned the No. 606 light-rays on his laboratory mice and went out for lunch. When he returned to his laboratory, he was astounded to find that the mice had shrunk to the size of fleas, and that the wire cage which contained them had been reduced to the size of a soya bean. This discovery had as profound an effect on the medical world as the discovery of penicillin and streptomycin, which began the antibiotic revolution of the 1940s.

For instance, surgeons no longer anaesthetized their patients and cut into their bodies and internal organs as they do today. When such antiquated methods are used, unsightly scars are left on the patient's body, even when extensive plastic surgery is done. Furthermore, it is a very serious matter to cut open the human body. How much more desirable to shrink the doctor to one-thousandth the size of a body – precisely half the size of a flea – have him slip inside the patient's body, cut out the infected areas from within, and then slip back out again. Not a single scar would remain. The patient could leave the hospital with a body as pristine as the one he had brought in before the operation.

The American film *Fantastic Voyage* was based upon this imaginary premise, but in Bontarō's day the procedure was no longer a fantasy. Dr Friedman's micro-gamma rays were being used far and wide throughout the Japanese medical world. Surgeons reduced to one-thousandth the size of the human body rode in proportionately-diminished submarines, and it was a routine chore for them to travel through the human body and do their operations from within.

Sayuri's surgery was scheduled for 3 October. Four doctors were set to perform the procedure: the operating surgeon would be Dr Inokuchi, said to be without peer among cancer specialists. His first assistant was to be Dr Hirano, his second assistants Bontarō and the patient's brother, Gōichi. In Bontarō's case, he had stepped forward and requested that he be allowed to participate. Naturally he was motivated by his undisclosed love for Sayuri.

'So you'll join us, will you?' After Dr Inokuchi gave his premission, Gōichi clutched Bontarō's hand and thanked him in a voice brimming with emotion.

It was a funny feeling, climbing inside the body of one's beloved. Consider for a moment how fascinating it would be to enter into the body of the woman you love and examine her stomach or her heart or her large intestines. As an assistant surgeon Bontarō had already entered the bodies of some twenty women patients, but this time he awoke each day with a tingly sort of feeling inside, and he could not force himself to remain dispassionately detached.

'I wonder if a woman as beautiful as Sayuri really does have a stomach? And intestines too?' Logic clearly dictated the answer, but to a man in Bontarō's state of mind it seemed remarkable that she could have such commonplace organs.

29 September: SS Reaction Tests; Cardiological Tests.

30 September: PTA Test.

One might think these are tests for the patient, but that is not so. They are tests for the doctors who will be performing the operation, to determine whether they have the strength to endure changes in atmospheric pressure within the patient's body. Bontarō and Gōichi naturally underwent these tests, and were given passing marks in the examination room.

On 2 October, Bontarō found time between his chores and his research to drop into Sayuri's room. Her aunt was just in the process of peeling some fruit for her.

'Well, tomorrow's the day!'

Sayuri, unaware that she was suffering from cancer and under the impression that she had tuberculosis, was not in particularly low spirits.

'I'm so embarrassed.'

'Why?'

'Well, after all, you and my brother will be going inside my body.'

'There's nothing to be embarrassed about. All you have to do is fall asleep for three hours, and we'll be inside you and finished off before you know what's happened.'

'How rude!'

Still, as he saw Sayuri blinking her eyes to ward off the sunlight that poured through the window, he thought how beautiful she was. Her aunt was the glamorous actress Yoshinaga Sayuri, who had enjoyed great popularity in the Japanese film world some fifty years earlier, and it was said that Sayuri was the very image of her.

'In any case, you set your mind at rest about tomorrow,' he said, leaving the room. With the gentle autumn sun stroking his shoulders, he felt happy.

3 October, 10 a.m. In Operating Theatre No. 27 at K. University, doctors and nurses wearing large white face-masks and gowns – and looking very much like astronauts – gazed gravely down at the body of Sayuri stretched out on the operating table. She had already been anaesthetized, and was as motionless as a wax doll.

'It's 10.05, isn't it?' The surgical team, led by Dr Inokuchi, nodded goodbye to the anaesthetist, the cardiologist and the nurses, and entered a separate chamber. This room was in fact an elevator. After thick doors had closed with a dull clatter, the entire chamber was filled with a purple radiating light. The micro-gamma rays were beginning to pour in from all directions.

With each passing second their bodies grew smaller, but they were unaware of the change, since they were all shrinking together.

The elevator began its descent underground. Down below a submarine twice the size of a flea was awaiting them.

The vessel was supplied with aqualungs and all the necessary surgical equipment. Gōichi, the patient's brother, had been selected to pilot the craft.

Once the four doctors had boarded the submarine, it was automatically sucked into a gigantic glass tube by a pneumatic inhalator. The glass tube was in reality the hypodermic syringe being used by the doctors up above.

In the United States microscopic-sized doctors were introduced into the patient's body through the eye duct, but in Japanese hospitals at Tokyo University, Keiō, and here at the K. University Medical Centre, they were sent along with the injection fluid into the patient's bloodstream, employing a technique discovered by Doctor Okazaki, a member of the Japan Academy. The injection fluid was scheduled to be shot into the patient's body at 10.30 a.m.; beside Dr Inokuchi, Bontarō started the countdown.

'Ten, nine, eight, seven . . .'

Soon they felt a minor shock, then a landscape like the surface of the moon opened up before their eyes. But it was not the surface of the moon; it was Sayuri's epidermis. They had arrived at the spot where they would be injected into her body. As far as they could see the area was thickly overgrown with what appeared to be reeds withered by the cold of winter; this was in fact the downy growth of hair on the surface of her skin.

Although he had already participated in twenty intravenous operations, on this occasion Bontarō was deeply moved. *Ah, so this is Sayuri's skin!* Careful that Inokuchi and Hirano did not observe him, Bontarō studied her epidermis with excitement in his eyes. A second shockwave. Churning bubbles of water thrashed about both sides of the vessel. At last they were being injected into the patient's body.

How can one describe the insider's view of the bloodstream that appeared momentarily outside the window of their submarine?

Lord Bagen-Saylor, who observed the very bottom of the ocean depths, wrote the following description in his book *The Mystery of the Sea*:

> I have never witnessed a realm as splendid, as sumptuous and dazzling as the bottom of the ocean. I had never known that a palace so magnificent could exist upon the face of this planet.

These words of Lord Bagen-Saylor can be applied to the view of the human body afforded to physicians in the year 2005. Inside the bloodstream, dancing about randomly overhead, were swarms of white and red corpuscles. It is true that here one cannot see the many colours of the fish that populate the depths of the ocean, but those who have once witnessed the ballet performed by these corpuscles can never forget the sight.

The sound they heard, like the intermittent beating of a drum, was the pounding of the heart. As they drew closer to the sound, the surgeons knew they were approaching the diseased area.

Objects like brown strands of seaweed floated by. These were human fatigue toxins, which are normally expelled from the body in the urine. The greater the number of these brown threads present, the stronger the indication that the subject was tired or that something was amiss in the body.

'There are a great many fatigue toxins, aren't there?' Dr Hirano said to Dr Inokuchi. Bontarō held his ear to the communicator which kept them in contact with the outside. The team of doctors in the operating theatre remained in constant touch with the submarine.

'Pulse – normal. Blood pressure – unchanged.' Bontarō announced the report to Dr Inokuchi in a loud voice. The doctor nodded vigorously and muttered, 'It's time to determine whether the cancer has spread beyond this region.'

The drum-like pounding of the heart grew still louder. They were at last nearing the afflicted zone.

'What's our velocity?' Gōichi reported their speed to Dr Hirano, who then pressed a button on top of the control panel. A screen set up inside the submarine displayed vividly enlarged X-ray photographs of the patient's lesions.

'Let's get ready.'

The four men removed their white gowns. Underneath their gowns they wore wet-suits and aqualungs. From a large box they removed a variety of instruments that looked like fire extinguishers. Among these instruments were several razor-sharp electronic scalpels that would cut away at the diseased area while spraying it with a mist of disinfectant.

For several minutes now their craft had been drifting alongside Sayuri's lungs, which looked like clusters of large pink balloons. Blood vessels criss-crossed the surface of these balloons like meshwork.

'Look at that!' Dr Inokuchi raised his hand and pointed. 'Already there's been a discoloration caused by the cancer cells.'

In one area the pink region had begun to fade, to be replaced by a disagreeably leaden coloration. As the X-rays had shown, cancer had spread from this point onto the mucilaginous zone extending to the heart.

'Stopping engines!' Gōichi shouted and pushed a button.

After consultation with Dr Inokuchi, Hirano gave instructions to the two younger assistants. 'We'll be cutting out a large portion starting at the B segment of the lower lung lobe. Is that clear?'

'I'll go first,' Dr Inokuchi announced, and with him at the head, the four left their craft. Their aqualungs swaying in the currents, and their oxygen inhalators clutched between their teeth, they swam through the bloodstream towards the infected area. Bontarō stayed in constant contact with the team of doctors above.

'How is the patient's condition?' He started to ask, 'How is Sayuri?' but caught himself.

'Satisfactory. Patient is sleeping soundly. No changes in pulse, blood pressure, or electrocardiogram,' came the reply from the operating theatre. It was time to begin the internal surgery.

'I shall start making the incision.' Thus began the doctors' difficult, painstaking task.

Two hours later, the fearsome cancer cells had all been cut away. To insure that there would be no reoccurrence in the scar tissue, a healthy dose of the powerful antibiotic ACM – discovered by Dr Umezawa at Tokyo University – was applied liberally to the wound with a giant atomizer.

'A clean cut!' Dr Hirano signalled triumphantly to Dr Inokuchi with his hand. The operation had gone without a hitch, and according to the information from above, the patient displayed virtually no dangerous after-effects.

'The way this looks, there seems very little chance of a relapse.'

'This will provide invaluable data for our medical department.'

When they returned to the submarine, the four surgeons removed their wet-suits and aqualungs, and sat down for a leisurely glass of whisky. The post-operative drink was especially delectable. The most appetizing whisky was that consumed after an operation had gone smoothly.

'Don't drink too much and get us into an accident,' Dr Hirano said jokingly to Gōichi, who responded, 'I'm really very grateful to all of you. Thanks to you my sister will get her health back.'

'She will indeed. Once she's back on her feet, you've got to find her a good husband.'

'When that time comes, I'll have to rely on you gentlemen for help once again.'

Bontarō listened to the casual banter between his three colleagues with a touch of melancholy. After today's success, Sayuri would be restored to normal health within two months. She would go back to the university. That beautiful, vibrant face would be walking down the streets of the city once more. But then she will have nothing more to do with me. The very thought grieved him.

'Well, let's head back.' Gōichi, unaware of the disposition of his friend's heart, slid into the driver's seat.

Inside the blood vessels visibility was poor. The quantity of blood cells had increased with the flow of blood from the surgical wound. The entire region was as blue as a sea of ink (as you may know, blood is not red; within the body, untouched by oxygen, it shone a vivid blue). Somewhat apprehensively, Dr Hirano asked Gōichi. 'Is everything all right?'

'Yes. Just fine, I think.'

They had travelled far enough that the density of the blood within the vessels should have been thinning a bit, but their field of vision still had not cleared. It was peculiar.

'Are you sure you didn't take a wrong turn somewhere?'

'I . . . don't think I did.'

But when the surrounding corpuscles began to decrease in number, they realized that their craft was nowhere near the pink-coloured pulmonary region, but was in fact advancing down some sort of passage with brownish, multi-pleated walls.

'Hey! Where are we?' Bontarō was first to notice the incongruity. The brown walls were contracting slightly, like some living thing, and emitting a great many objects that resembled thread ravellings. Before Bontarō realized what these were, Gōichi grasped the entire situation, and with a pale face, shouted, 'Hello! We're in the large intestine! Damnation! I never could hold my liquor, and with all the celebration over the success of Sayuri's operation, I've drunk too much whisky. Damn it!'

Just as drunken driving in an automobile was a misdemeanour in the 1980s, so was it unlawful in 2005 for a surgeon piloting through the human bloodstream to be under the influence.

'Can't we go back the way we came?' asked Dr Hirano, rising from his chair. But Gōichi shook his head.

'It's impossible. I'm sorry. As you know, there is no way to go against the current, given the air pressure that surges into the intestinal tract from the stomach.'

'All too true.'

'Doctor, I don't know how to apologize.'

'Don't worry about that; think of a way to get us out of here.'

'We can charge ahead through the intestine and get out by way of my sister's anus.'

'Good. We'll do it!'

Bontarō had participated in many internal operations, but this was the first time he had been inside the intestines. And to have to exit through the rectal opening . . .

So this . . .

A brownish liquid surrounded the craft. The rubbery mountains that were the inner walls of the intestine stretched ahead as far as the eye could see. It was like feeling one's way in the dark through a long tunnel.

So this is Sayuri's intestine!

He was moved beyond words. What a strange sensation to find himself inside the intestines of a woman he thought incomparably beautiful! Within the body of this lovely woman were the same intestines and stomach that any ordinary person possessed. Although rationally he had always known this, until now he had not sensed the tangible reality of it all. But here it was right before his very eyes.

The long tunnel of intestines wound its way endlessly forward.

'Wait!' Something suddenly dawned on Dr Hirano, and he bounded from his chair. 'Before the operation, your sister did evacuate her bowels, didn't she?'

'Pardon?'

Realizing how Gōichi must feel, Hirano rephrased his question. 'What I mean to say is, the patient was cleaned out with an enema before surgery, wasn't she?'

'I . . . think so.' Gōichi was at pains to answer this question. But Dr Hirano's concern was not to be taken lightly. If in fact the intestines had not been irrigated, eventually their submarine would collide with the stool that blocked the end of Sayuri's alimentary canal. They had no way of knowing whether their miniscule vessel could penetrate such a mass.

'I'll check with the head nurses in the operating theatre.' Bontarō hurriedly picked up the communicator and brought it to his ear. Strangely, there was no response. The problem was not mechanical failure; just as radio waves grow indistinct high up in the mountains, the vital electric waves that flowed through the bloodstream could not reach the outside world from within the intestinal tract.

'Hello? Hello! Doctor, I can't get through!'

'You can't? Well, keep trying!'

Before long the fluid that enveloped the submarine began to be tinged with a markedly yellow colour. Apparently Dr Hirano's fears were being confirmed. The patient's bowels had not been evacuated before surgery.

'Do you think we could smash through a stool of ordinary consistency in this craft?'

'If it's on the diarrhetic side, there should be no problem. But if it's solid, there is no way we'll get through it.' Gōichi's head drooped. 'Doctor, please let me go outside the craft.'

'What would you do out there?'

'I'm embarrassed to have to say this, but my sister has always been plagued by constipation. I would imagine that up ahead we will find a remarkably solid stool.'

'Hmmm.'

'I shall therefore cut a hole in my sister's stool with the surgical scalpel. A hole just big enough for our ship to pass through.'

Bontarō could not stand by and let his friend undertake this formidable task alone. 'You can't do it by yourself. I'll go with you.'

'You will? Thank you! But you must be sure to wear your gas mask.'

Gas masks were kept on hand in the submarine in case unusually foul odours should sweep through the body. And they had to be prepared for the presence of noxious methane gas within the intestines. Bontarō and Gōichi donned their aqualungs once again and put on their gas masks; then, strapping oxygen cylinders to their backs, they left the submarine.

They swam through the cloudy yellow liquid. On and on they swam. Were this not Sayuri, even Bontarō would have turned back. Soon they rounded the second bend.

Ahead of them, an enormous grey object began sluggishly to move. Without warning, the grey figure detached itself from the intestinal wall and darted at the two men, twisting its body as if to attack them and swallow them up.

'Look out! A threadworm!'

'What? A threadworm?'

'Yes! A threadworm that's sucking all the nourishment out of your sister's intestines. Why didn't you give her some worm medicine?'

'We don't have time to argue about it. We'll kill it with our scalpels!'

They stabbed at the approaching threadworm with their surgical knives. A white fluid squirted out around them. Showing its sharp teeth, the worm writhed in agony. Two more thrusts, then three. It was a fight to the death between man and threadworm.

The battle was over in five minutes. Bontarō's arms were heavy with weariness, and for a few moments he was dazed. He thought of the summer two years before, when he and Sayuri had gone to Gōichi's summer cottage in Hayama and put on aqualungs to go spear-fishing. He couldn't understand why such a memory should surface at a time like this.

A solid black precipice loomed before them. They swam back and forth, jabbing at the obstruction with their scalpels. It had the consistency of clay, but seemed to be quite thick.

'Listen, at this rate it will take us more than a day to dig a hole large enough for the submarine. There's no alternative. I'll ask Dr Inokuchi and Dr Hirano to abandon ship.'

'Are you just going to leave the craft here in the intestines?'

'I'll give my sister a diarrhetic tomorrow and get her to excrete it.'

While Gōichi returned to the submarine, Bontarō plied his scalpel with all his might. After ten minutes all the feeling had gone out of his arms. 'Why didn't they give her an enema?' He cursed the careless nurses. He wanted to give them a good piece of his mind.

Suddenly a hole broke open in front of him. Fortunately his scalpel had been gouging away at the thinnest portion of the mass.

'I've done it!' Encouraged by his success, Bontarō dug in with increased vigour. At the same time, the figures of the two chief doctors – safely equipped with gas marks – could just be distinguished in the distance through the muddy liquid.

After passing through the large clay-like formation, the doctors at long last reached the tip of the alimentary canal. Yet here, too, an impasse they had not considered was awaiting them. Bontarō was the first to realize it. He looked around at the three masked men and said, 'Doctors, the anus isn't necessarily open all the time. In fact, speaking in strictly clinical terms, under ordinary circumstances it remains in a closed position. With our flagging energy, we will not be able to force our way through that orifice. We cannot make contact with the team outside. What shall we do?'

After struggling this far, they had no idea what to do next.

'We're almost out of oxygen.'

'How much is left?'

'We'll only last another ten minutes or less.'

The four men no longer had the energy to go back the way they had come. Unless something were done, however, Dr Inokuchi – the pride of the K. University Medical Centre – Dr Hirano, Gōichi and Bontarō would all die a miserable death in the faecal matter inside the intestines. A miserable shitty death.

To what end have I studied so diligently? Even if they did belong to Sayuri, how miserable to breathe his last here inside her intestines, thought Bontarō. It would grieve his mother back home to find out that her son had studied so hard only to meet with such an end. The face of his aged mother in the provinces darted across his mind.

'I have just one idea,' Dr Inokuchi, who had been silent up till now, said gravely.

'What is it, Doctor?'

'We'll make the patient fart.'

'Fart?'

'That is correct. If we cause the patient to pass wind, the anus will open. And we will be blown out by the rush of wind. This will of course place our bodies under considerable stress, but we'll just have to accept that. It's the only way.'

'Are you sure we won't get whiplash?'

'Listen, this is no time to be worrying about whiplash!'

'But, Doctor, how are we going to make her break wind?'

'We must all stimulate the inner wall of the intestine here. Use both hands and tickle it as hard as you can. I don't know whether it will work or not, but let's give it a try.'

The four doctors began to stroke the brown wall with their hands. They did their best to make it budge. But the wall, like a huge rocky cliff, did not even flinch.

'One more time!'

The second attempt also ended in failure. A third try fared no better.

'It's no good.'

'Just once more. If that doesn't work, we'll all join hands and die singing "At Sea Be My Body Water-soaked".'

As they tried a fourth time, their eyes began to swim. They had exhausted every resource of mind and body. Then, far in the distance, they heard Gōichi calling, 'Doctor, the intestine has started to move!' At that instant, Bontarō was swept up by ninety-mile-an-hour winds like those at the centre of a typhoon. As he lost consciousness, he knew he had been saved.

Five days later Bontarō was able to walk again, and that morning he summoned up the courage to visit Sayuri's room.

He was uneasy. He wondered whether he could still feel love for Sayuri after the experience he had gone through.

When he knocked on the door, he heard her charming voice. Dressed in a pale blue gown, she was eating some gelatin with the help of a nurse.

'How are you?' .

'I'm fine. Thank you so much.'

Sayuri had no inkling of the route the doctors had used to exit from her body. That was a medical secret, something that could not be divulged to the patient.

'My, what's happened to you? Look at your face!'

Bontarō's face was covered with dark red bruises, souvenirs of the hurricane-strength winds that had struck him squarely in the face as he was whisked from her intestines.

'Oh, nothing. I got drunk and fell down the stairs.' Bontarō mustered a pained grin. Blissfully ignorant, Sayuri flashed her pearly-white teeth in surprise and said, 'What a stinker you are!'

Her face was stunning. One by one Bontarō recalled the experiences he had endured inside her intestines five days earlier – swimming out of the submarine with a gas mask on his face; the combat with the threadworm; breaking through the wall of clay. Despite it all, he thought she was beautiful. He knew he loved her. In the end love had won out over physiology.

'You're right. I'll be more careful from now on.'

He went out into the hallway, drinking deeply of the euphoria that rightfully belonged to a doctor in the year 2005. But then, seeing a patient restored to health is a great joy for a doctor in any day and age.

ALL THAT IS GONE

Pramoedya Ananta Toer

Translated from the Indonesian by Willem Samuels

Pramoedya Ananta Toer (1925–2006). Born in Blora, Java, in the former Dutch East Indies, Pramoedya Ananta Toer's work chronicles Indonesia's struggle for independence, the Japanese occupation, and the post-colonial dictatorships of Sukarno and Suharto. His writings saw him imprisoned both by the Dutch Government and later by the Suharto regime. While incarcerated on the Island of Buru, he wrote his most famous work, *The Buru Quartet*. Since he was not permitted access to writing materials, he recited the text to other prisoners who had it written down and smuggled out.

The Lusi River skirts the southern edge of the city of Blora. In the dry season, its bed of stone, gravel, mud, and sand heaves upward to expose itself to the sky, leaving scattered shallow pools. But when the rainy season comes and the forested hills are covered by clouds and the sun refuses to shine for forty to fifty hours, the river's greenish water changes to a mud-clotted yellow and rises to a level of twenty meters or even higher. The peaceful current becomes a crazed torrent. The river, swirling through its course, clutches at and then rips out clumps of bamboo from the banks like a child pulling weeds. It fells the levees and sucks into itself the bordering fields. So suddenly, the Lusi transforms itself.

From my home one can see groves of bamboo, blackish green in color, the tops of which weave and twist gently when the wind blows. When I was a boy, the dance of the tips and the whistle of the staves as the wind rushed through them never failed to frighten me. I can recall running in terror to my mother, burying my head in her lap, and starting to cry. Even now I can still hear her chiding me, "Whatever are you whining for?"

Her hands, no longer the soft hands of a girl, stroke my thin cheeks. Between my sobs, I gasp, "The bamboo is crying, Mama!"

Taking my head in her hands, she pulls me to her lap and tries to reassure me, "No, my baby, it's not crying. It's singing to you."

And then she starts to sing, something soothing and sweet, a folk song perhaps that rocks me, sways me, and then finally drowns my fears. Often it is her gentle voice that lulls me to sleep. Sometimes, as she sings, I run my fingers through her wind-tousled hair. I play with the lobes of her ears and the diamond-studded earrings that adorn them until finally, I hear her calm, sweet voice: "Come now, you're sleepy. I'll put you to bed." Hearing that, I open my eyes as wide as possible, hoping to persuade her to continue the song, but more often than not I find myself unable to keep my eyelids raised. But all that is gone now, vanished, along with the riverbanks and the clumps of bamboo that the high waters of the Lusi drag away.

Once, during an afternoon nap, I dreamt I found a one-cent piece, and when I awoke I clenched my fist for fear of losing the money I had found in my dream. I jumped out of bed and ran to find my mother. "Mama, Mama!" I called to her in joy, "I found a one-cent coin!"

She smiled at me, taking pleasure in my delight. "Wherever did you find it?" she asked. "Where is it now?"

I stuck out my fist and yelled, "Here it is! Right here in my hand!" But upon opening my fist I found my hand completely empty.

"Where did you say it was?" my mother asked me softly.

I stood there, dumbfounded by shock and disappointment. I wept as a great feeling of emptiness entered my chest.

My mother laughed and coaxed me gently: "You were only dreaming. You're awake now. Don't cry . . ." But I continued to sob.

My mother lifted the edge of her blouse to dry my tears. "Hush, be quiet now . . ." From the fold in her waistcloth, she took out a half-cent coin and handed it to me. I played with the coin in silence, as I tried to repress my lingering disappointment.

"It's late," my mother told me. "It's time for your bath. Nyi Kin will help you."

I removed myself from Mother's lap, but when I didn't immediately make my way toward the bath, her features darkened and her voice—no gentleness there now—grew stern: "Go on, off with you!"

Her tone, harboring no room for protest, made me reconsider an appeal. Slowly I walked away to look for the servant.

I can still see Nyi Kin quite clearly. Like so many women in this world, she had been forced to marry a man she didn't even know. And all that the marriage gave to her was syphilis, an illness that left her with an intense dislike of men. The disease destroyed her relationship with her husband and caused them to divorce. It robbed her of one of her eyes, wasted her beauty, and caused deterioration in one of her hip joints. When she walked she dragged her leg.

During the day Nyi Kin had little time to bemoan her fate; chores took up most of her attention. But when night came and her painful weariness made it difficult for her to sleep, it was then she mourned her loss.

Nyi Kin's arranged marriage, illness, and divorce had taken place before she came to work at our house. Perhaps it was because she had no children of her own—the syphilis had eaten her womb—that she showered so much attention on me. Even now, whenever I think of her, no matter where I am, I can feel her love and affection.

Sometimes Nyi Kin would stroke my cheeks as if I were her own child. When carrying me, she'd hide her face behind the long scarf she always wore around her neck, but then suddenly pull it away and pucker her lips. "Boo!" she'd say.

No matter how many times she did this, I'd always break out in giggles. Such pleasure that little game gave me. And she too would laugh with delight, but then just as suddenly stop the game and refuse to show her face. When I finally succeeded in pulling the scarf away, I'd find her staring vacantly. The precarious nature of her existence seemed to emanate from her reddened eyes. Hastily she'd pull my face against her own and hold it there for a long time; I imagine now that she was dreaming of the children she longed for but would never bear.

Nyi Kin always set aside part of her wages to buy snacks, most of them going to me. It wasn't until later that I learned my mother paid her just 80 Dutch cents a month.

Like my mother, Nyi Kin was always telling me stories, but they were different from the ones that Mother told, which were about Asian war heroes. Nyi Kin's stories were about talking animals who had created for themselves kingdoms in the jungle. I can't recall how old I was when she told me these tales, but I do remember that she would remark how good the people of yore must have been to be able to understand the speech of animals. People these days, she said, are too sinful. They're cruel and unkind to one another, which is why, she also told me, they can't understand what animals say.

She talked about her own experiences as a girl and about an incident that had taken place when she was only a few years older than I was at the time. That particular story I would ask her to repeat again and again. She never refused, and each time I listened with surprise and awe. This is how the tale went:

> "I was just a girl at the time and the bupati who governed the Blora regency was Ndoro Kanjeng Said. One year, for some reason, our area experienced a double rainy season. The Lusi River rose over its banks, and our safe and peaceful city was soon buried beneath the muddy floodwaters. Because the city square lies on high ground, that bit of land became an island in the midst of a large sea. All the people in the area were herded by the rising waters to the square. They brought their children, their buffalo, and their cattle with them. Those who didn't leave their homes quickly enough risked being swept away to the river's mouth.
>
> "Down and down the rains came, and soon even the regent's home was jammed with people. So then what he did was he went out of his house with a whip in his hand, and walked to the water's edge, which was already lapping at the city square. He lashed the water with his whip and said a prayer. And slowly, very slowly but just as surely, the waters began to recede and finally retreated to the banks of the Lusi."

I remember that story very clearly. Nyi Kin had about twenty-five tales that she would tell me again and again, but to me they always seemed new and I never failed to listen with rapt attention. She told me about babies crying in the rain and how courageous the regent had been, how willingly the people served him, and how they had bowed to him when he came out of the house to save them from the flood.

Her story put me in awe of the regent. By the time I was born, he was long dead and buried. Even so, the mere mention of his name, Ndoro Kanjeng Said, evokes a kinder world that still lingers in the memory of the people of Blora.

Other stories that Nyi Kin told were about the gods and cacodemons that roam the world by day and night in search of people who are not on guard. Or, when looking at the clouds, she would recant fantastic tales from the *Rama-yana*—how Dasamuka had hidden behind the clouds in wait for Sita and about his struggle with the great *garuda* bird Jatayu, who tried to stop him.

She told me about the heroes of the *Mahabharata,* too. She told them in a simple yet beautiful way. I was able to understand some of what she told me and stood in awe of the greatness of people of olden days. Looking back now, I see that I was like many people, both now and then, who would rather think about the past than deal with the present.

Important moments in life are not easily erased from memory, even that of a child. Such moments remain until the end of one's life. I remember one time when it was dark in the house and I was crying. My home was far from the closest power line and when night fell, the house grew gloomy inside. I remember Mother taking me outside that night. The dew made my body damp and shiverish, but it also helped to assuage the emptiness I was feeling inside. Maybe I had just been hot, I don't know, but Mother kissed my chin and whispered softly to me, "Oh, my little darling, why do you cry so much? Don't you know your mother is tired from working all day? Go to sleep, my baby. Tomorrow the sun will bring a new day and with it a new sky and new air. Then you can play to your heart's content."

The timbre of my mother's voice helped to soothe my feelings. I embraced her and gave her breasts my tears. She held my head against her chest, and I listened to the beating of her heart. As she began to sing, my fidgeting eased. The night's cool air and the dew seemed to make her song all the more poignant. After that, I don't remember what happened; when I next opened my eyes the sun was high in the sky and outside was the new day my mother had promised. I had a new day, a new sky, new air, and a new song, too. But all that is gone now, vanished from sensory perception to live forever in memory.

I remember the time when Nyi Kin suddenly disappeared. "She's sick," the other kids told me, but even so, I couldn't understand why she had left without say-ing goodbye. I looked for her everywhere but couldn't find her. I started to cry. I must have cried for at least two hours. Mother tried to calm me by offering me a banana, but that did nothing to check my tears. I felt an incredible emptiness inside me. Mother kept telling me: "Nyi Kin's gone home, honey. She's not feeling well, and when a person's sick you can't be near her or you'll get sick, too."

Mother's words did little to fill the vacuum inside me either. I kept on crying until exhaustion finally forced my body to sleep. When I awoke, the emptiness was still there and I started to cry again. Tears fell from my eyes like the drops of liquid that used to seep from Nyi Kin's hollow socket, the one she would wipe with the tip of her scarf.

Gradually, the emptiness abated and finally disappeared. Other things came to occupy my mind. Even so, at times, when I suddenly remembered Nyi Kin, I would ask again, "When is Nyi Kin coming back?" But Mother's answer was always, "She's still ill."

At that age I didn't know that Nyi Kin's house was not far from ours, only six or seven houses away. It wasn't until years later that Mother revealed the real reason Nyi Kin had gone: Nyi Kin liked to take spices from the kitchen, she said, and my mother would not allow thievery of any kind.

Nyi Kin was replaced by a younger woman. I was three years old at the time and had a baby sister who was one year old. Because I slept with the servant, I always woke up at five in the morning. She had to rise early to cook the fried rice for my parents' foster children—who weren't really foster children, but children whose parents had placed them with us—before they left for school. The two of us would squat together beside the hearth while frying the rice. When any crisp rice stuck to the bottom of the wok, I'd ask her for it and eat it right there.

I can't remember the servant's name, but I do remember that she, like Nyi Kin, was very fond of me. She had been raised on a farm and had once been married to a farmer, but after their crops failed they had separated.

An incident involving that servant took place when I was three or four years old and is still remarkably vivid in my mind. One morning I asked her for the crackled rice, which I then proceeded to nibble on while sitting on my haunches in front of the hearth. Our kitchen was not in the house but in an attached structure, the roof of which was made of corrugated zinc with upturned edges that had been fixed to a set of stakes. Seen from the inside, the roof had a triangular-shaped hole at each end, and it was through one of those holes I saw the most amazing thing. At 5 a.m., the sky looked completely dark from inside the kitchen, especially when one was facing the fire. But that morning, while I was sitting there, I looked up at one of the holes and saw a big head peering inside. I could make out a beard, eyebrows, and a big white moustache, but the face of the creature looking at me was black, even blacker than the sky outside. I didn't do anything. I just sat there in the predawn light, looking at that big face as I nibbled on my crackled rice. I didn't say anything either and, in the days that followed, the face began to appear regularly.

Finally, one day, when seeing the face, I pointed at the window and said to the servant, "Look! There it is! I told you! There's a big black head peeking at us again!"

The servant raised her head to look at the hole beneath the roof and started to laugh at me. "Of course there is," she said dryly, "but *I* can't see anything."

"But I saw it," I told her. "I saw a head, a really big head."

"Well I didn't," she said with just as much certainty. "What did it look like?"

"It was black. I saw a black face."

"You're fibbing. There's nothing out there."

I was unable to make her believe me; and our little conversation died right there.

Once I told Mother about what I had seen, but she didn't take me seriously either. As a matter of fact, she frowned and looked at me as if she were angry. "Has someone been telling you stories about devils? Who's been telling you about devils?"

At that age I already knew about devils, and I asked her: "Do you think it was really a devil I saw?"

"Who's been telling you those stories?" she asked suspiciously.

"Nobody. I saw him myself, Mama."

"You mustn't lie. Who taught you to lie? Nyi Kin, or is it that new servant? Tell me."

"Nobody, Mama, I saw him myself."

When Mother went off to question the servant, she responded with what I told her: "Every morning he tells me he sees the devil out there, but whenever I look up at the hole, I never see anything."

"Well, you must not tell him stories," Mother warned her.

"Oh no, ma'am, I'd never do that."

"There's no need to scare him."

"Oh no, ma'am. I wouldn't do that.

After that I stopped telling people about the face I saw through the hole beneath the roof every morning. But then one morning something happened even more out of the ordinary: That day, I was in the kitchen and I saw the head peek inside and then, a moment later, a monkey almost as large as myself jumped down from the hole. It leaped at the servant, who took off running around the central hearth. In the firelight I could see fear distorting the servant's features, but for whatever reason she neither screamed nor called for help. As the monkey tore around the kitchen, it grazed against me but didn't stop to bother me. It seemed intent on catching the servant. The two of them ran around and around in circles, one playing the hunter, the other the prey. But then, all of a sudden, the monkey vanished—I don't know where it went—and the servant collapsed on her haunches completely out of breath. I stared at her in silence. When she finally stood, I saw that there was a plate-size puddle of water on the ground where she had been squatting.

"You wet yourself," I commented.

The servant looked down at the puddle shimmering with the reflections of the firelight. She tossed some ashes on the pool of urine and walked away.

This experience was so overwhelming for me, I felt that I had to tell someone about it. It made me excited just to think about retelling it. When the other kids awoke, I ran in to tell them, but seeing that my mother was also awake, the desire to do so suddenly vanished. I didn't have the nerve. I knew my mother would say I was lying.

Later, after my father and the other kids had gone to school, the house was quiet. It was then that the servant approached my mother. "Ma'am, I would like to quit today," she said.

"But why? Aren't you happy here?"

"It's fine here, ma'am, but . . ." She didn't continue.

Mother didn't try to make her change her mind, and that very same day the servant left, never to return. I wanted to tell Mother what had happened, but I didn't. So, for the rest of the household, the servant's departure left little impression at all.

A few years later, when I finally did tell my mother about the incident, she cleared up—or at least thought that she cleared up—the mystery: "That would have been the Suryos' monkey," she told me. "They used to let it run loose in the morning." Memories differ, it seems. Our neighbor, Mr. Suryo, did indeed once own a monkey, but as I recall, that was not until a few years later.

Wherever that monkey had come from, it no longer mattered. The monkey—the one with the big head, white eyebrows, beard, and moustache—that had chased the servant was gone. It vanished like the banks of the river and the groves of bamboo dragged away by the floodwaters of the Lusi.

My father was the principal of a private school, and in the morning, when I'd see him getting ready to leave, I'd ask him to take me along. He'd almost always say no and I would start to cry. I don't know why, but there was an emptiness inside me that always made me want to cry.

"When you're big, you can go to school too," my parents would tell me, in an attempt to get me to stop. That usually helped to cheer me up.

"Can I really, Mama? Can I, Papa?"

"Why of course. And you can go to college in Surabaya, or to Batavia, or maybe even to Europe!"

After I had calmed down, my father would kiss me on both cheeks and get ready to leave. Only then could he safely walk away. Even so, I'd sometimes run after him, forcing Mother to follow me out to the road to try to make me stop. When this happened, I would start to cry again. But if Mother again said no, and absolutely forbade me to go, I dared not protest.

I remember well the feeling of what it was like when my father was not at home. I had a paint can to which my mother had fastened wheels and a string, and I'd pull it behind me wherever I went. There must have been something inside the can, because it clattered and clanked as I pulled it behind me, but the sound it made seemed to soothe my fears and encourage delight. But that, too, is gone now, just like the riverbanks and the clumps of bamboo that are dragged away by the floodwaters of the Lusi.

Usually when Father returned from school he would be laughing and in a good mood. Coming into the house, he'd always call out my name first and then that of my one-year-old sister. Then and only then, after kissing me and seeing that I was well, would he change his clothes and sit down to eat with Mother at the dining table. I'd join them but I ate on my feet, standing beside Mother. She would take a spoon of food from off her plate and put it in my open mouth. Then I'd run around the room and not return to my place until the mouthful of rice or whatever it was had been chewed and swallowed.

"Tastes good, does it?" my father would usually ask. And I'd answer with a laugh, "Gr-e-ea-a-t!"

My father never ate very much, not more than half a plate. Very rarely did he eat all the rice that my mother served him. But before my father had finished and left the dinner table, my full stomach would have already made me start to yawn. That's when my father would say to me: "You're falling asleep on your feet. Off with you; it's time for bed!"

Only when he said that would I realize that I was drowsy, but that didn't make me want to go to sleep. Mother always had to trundle me off to bed and stay with me, patting me on the thigh, until I fell asleep. I could see her hazy shape through my half-closed eyes. A smile revealed her small but evenly shaped teeth; a glow of love and affection radiated from her almond-shaped eyes.

But that too is gone now, carried away long ago, leaving with me only memories and feelings of wonder.

My mother, whose father was a Muslim cleric, was quite devout. I have no memory of my grandfather or what he looked like, but I remember Mother praying each and every day, except for the times she was pregnant. With her body almost completely enclosed in a pure white robe, only her face and fingers were visible when she prayed. Sometimes she held a rosary in her hand. When she was praying, I wouldn't dare approach her. I always waited outside the room where she prayed until she finished.

"Why do people pray, Mama?" I once asked her.

"To obtain God's blessings," she told me. "You pray for those who have sinned, that they return to the good and proper way. You pray for safety and peace. When you're bigger you'll understand why. You're still little. It's better for you to play than pray."

As to why this was, I never enquired further.

On nights when my father wasn't home, I'd often be awoken by the sound of my mother reciting her prayers. With Mother's clear and lilting voice, her prayers were like songs for me that kept the dark and silent night at a safe distance. Whether she was singing or praying, her voice was a pleasure to hear. And in the morning, when I woke up, if my father wasn't home yet, she would still be in her room praying.

One time, in the middle of the night, when I was awakened by her prayers, I went to her room. "It's late, Mama," I said to her. "Why are you still praying?"

Taking my chin in her thumb and forefinger, she pulled my head to her lap. Not saying anything, she kissed me instead. I could feel the warmth of her breath as she pressed her nose against my cheek.

She then began to pray again, but now her voice was hoarse and shaky.

"How come you're still praying?" I asked again.

"To make sure your father is safe. To keep him away from temptation." She looked at me quizzically. "Shouldn't you be in bed?"

I answered her question with one of my own: "How come Papa isn't home?"

Once again, she answered my question with a kiss that she pressed firmly on my cheeks.

"Where is Papa?" I asked again.

"Working," she finally said.

"But why is he working so late?" I asked.

"Because he has lots of work to do."

"When is he coming home?"

"When you wake up, your father will be home. Come now; it's time to go back to sleep."

She took me back to my bed and sang me a lullaby. When I woke up she was still praying, but her voice had now regained its clarity. To my ears, her voice didn't seem to be human at all; it was the sound of purity itself. I wanted to ask her whether my father had come home, but I didn't have the energy to get up, and I fell asleep again. I dreamt of my parents and my little sister.

In the morning when I awoke again I ran to find Mother. "Where's Papa?" I asked her.

"Your father has gone to school."

"Did he come home?"

"Yes, he did and before he left he looked in on you. He kissed you and then went off to school."

"Why doesn't he stay home and play with me?"

"Because he has to make a living so that he can buy clothing for you and food for the family."

I stopped pestering her, but late that day, when my father came home, I ran up to him and asked him, "Why didn't you come home last night? When I woke up last night, you weren't here."

My father laughed, but his laughter seemed hollow to my ears. On his face was a look of false cheer. My mother sat motionless in her chair, her head bowed.

"Mama stayed up all night praying!"

My father's laughter died immediately.

"Why don't you stay at home and play with me?"

Father laughed again. This time his laugh didn't sound false, but he still wouldn't answer me. We went to the dining table, and while we were eating I asked him, "Papa, can I go out with you at night?"

My question caused him to chuckle. "You're still too young," he said. "When you're big you won't have to go out with anyone at all. You can go anywhere you want, all by yourself."

I suddenly marveled at the miracle of age. His promise made me jump with joy.

"And can I go to Grandma's alone?"

"Of course you can. But not just yet. You're still too small."

"That's enough," my mother said in reprimand. "Stop asking your father so many questions. He's tired and wants to take a nap. And you should take one too."

That conversation, that incident, that too is gone, carried away and not likely ever to return.

In my mind's eye I can see clearly a day when I was afraid to approach my mother. It was a Sunday morning, and my parents' foster children had all gone off to a picnic site where the young people in our small town liked to gather. The house was quiet. Father was gone; only my mother, my sister, and the servant were at home. Feeling lonely, I went to find my mother and found her lying beside my sister on the bed. My sister was asleep, but my mother was staring up at the mosquito net that hung over the bed.

"Mama!" I called to her.

She didn't answer me; she didn't even move. With a great deal of effort I managed to climb up and onto the bed, and then I saw that my mother's eyes were red. Now and again she would wipe them with the flannel of my sister's blanket. I didn't know what to say. I sat there, silent for quite a while. I was frightened. Finally, with my voice trembling, I asked, "Why are you crying. Mama?"

It was only then that she looked at me. She pulled me to her side and hugged me.

"Why?" I asked again.

"It's nothing, my baby."

For some reason, right at that moment, I remembered a time, a beautiful time, when we'd gone to Rembang by train. There, looking out to the sea's horizon, we watched the ever restless and ever pounding sea whose every wave roared as it rushed to the shore. The horizon's base was a deep blue, almost black in color; closer to the shore it was a lighter blue; and at our feet, where the water tickled and rippled as it licked our skin, it was yellowish with churning sand.

"When can we take the train again?" I asked her. "When can we go to Rembang and look at the sea?"

My mother said nothing. It was as if she too were suddenly feeling the rush of the wind singing through the pines that line the Rembang shore.

My grandparents, my mother's parents, lived in Rembang, and upon hearing the name of her hometown Mother started to cry. Not knowing why, I asked her yet again: "Why are you crying?"

She sat up and kissed me repeatedly. Her tears felt cool on my cheeks. She spoke slowly as if attempting to control her voice: "We're going to leave Blora, my darling, and stay in Rembang forever."

"Why forever, Mama?"

"Don't you like the sea?"

"I do, Mama. Sure, I'd like to live by the sea," I consented happily. "When do we move?"

My happiness seemed to make my mother cry even harder.

"Soon," she said.

"When, Mama?"

"I don't know, I just don't know, but you'll be happy there, won't you?" My mother wiped her tears with my sister's blanket.

"Sure I will. Papa's coming too, isn't he?"

My question startled her. I saw that she was staring straight ahead, not even blinking or looking at me. I don't know why, but the look on her face suddenly made me afraid, and I started to bawl. My mother kissed me again and said softly: "Hush, don't cry . . ." Then my sister, startled by my shriek, also began to cry. Mother immediately put her to her breast. For a time, as she nursed my sister, she said nothing more, but her eyelids trembled and her gaze flitted from one place to another.

Finally, she told me, "Your father will be going to Rembang too."

"That's good," I told her, "because if Papa doesn't go, I don't want to go either. I'd rather stay here. Where is he, anyway?"

"Papa's at work."

I then repeated the question I had once asked her: "Why doesn't Papa ever stay home and play with me?"

"Because he has a great deal of work to do."

"But he's always working, Mama."

"Yes, he is," she said flatly.

When hearing her say that, I felt something grab me inside but could not quite figure out what that something was.

By this time I had stopped crying, and I asked, "Why were you crying, Mama?"

Not answering my question, she instead asked me listlessly, "Have you eaten?"

"Yes, but when Papa comes home I'll eat again. I like eating with you and Papa. It's so late and he's still not home . . . He'll come home tonight, won't he? Won't he?"

"Probably. He'll probably be home tonight."

"Did he come home last night, Mama?" I asked her.

"Yes, he came home last night, but you were already asleep. You didn't hear him, that's all. He even went to your bed and kissed you four times."

I laughed with pleasure.

"You were praying last night, weren't you, Mama?" As I asked that question, I heard, somewhere in my memory, Mother's prayers from the night before.

"No," she said, contradicting me. "I spent last night darning. You were asleep and Papa was reading. The other kids were asleep, too. And now it's time for you to sleep."

"If Papa comes home, wake me, Mama. You'll wake me, won't you?"

My mother coughed. I asked no more questions. I watched her finish nursing my sister, after which she stretched out silently and stared upward toward the top of the mosquito net. I still didn't say anything. I saw that her eyes were red, but I didn't say anything more. Then I too fell asleep.

When I awoke, Mother was still beside me, silently staring at the mosquito net. Her eyes had lost their redness. Before getting out of bed, I asked her, "Is Papa home?"

My mother's body twitched slightly. She turned over to look at me.

"No, he's not, honey. But you slept for a long time, didn't you? That means you must be in good health. Now get out of bed and ask the servant to give you a bath, okay?"

I wanted to see my father and would not put off seeing him any longer. I refused and began to whine. "No! I want Papa. Where's Papa, Mama?"

"He'll be home soon, honey. Take your bath. When you're clean, he'll come home."

When I still didn't budge, my mother spoke more firmly: "I said call the servant to give you your bath."

This time I didn't care about the harshness of her voice.

"I want Papa!" I demanded. "Where's Papa?"

"He's working," she said stiffly. "Now take a bath!"

When I ignored her, her resoluteness suddenly disappeared. Kissing me affectionately, she got up and lifted me from the bed. She placed my feet on the floor, and after kissing me on my chin, spoke to me lovingly. "Papa will be home soon.

But you have to take your bath. When you've had your bath, Papa will play with you. It's getting late. When Papa comes, I'll call you. Now go and take your bath."

The affection in her voice softened my rebelliousness, and slowly I stumbled off to find the servant.

After my bath, when I found that my father still wasn't home, I felt that familiar emptiness and began to cry again. This time I brushed off my mother's promises and bribes of food. I refused her coaxing and pleading.

The night grew later and later and still my father didn't come. With that feeling of emptiness welling inside me, I cried and would not stop. I screamed and felt as if I could go on screaming forever. My mother took me outside, but even the cool night air had no effect on the emptiness I felt. I knew that my crying upset my mother, but I wasn't going to be assuaged by her display of patience and care. She spoke softly and lovingly, but I continued to call out for my father. Even when her voice grew angrier in tone, I still continued to wail. The night deepened.

Between my outpourings of tears and screams I heard my mother invoke the name of the Most Powerful and beg for His forgiveness. But I continued to cry and to call for my father. It was pitch-black outside. When I cried, Mother never tried to threaten or frighten me; she attempted to ease my heartache with kind words and swaddle me in her affection. But this time it was of no use.

Finally, in desperation, my mother called for Dipo, one of my foster brothers, and told him to find my father and bring him home.

"Where should I look for him?" Dipo asked.

"I don't know. Just keep on looking until you find him. Tell him to come home, that his son is having a fit."

My mother, with the weight of my body in her arms, went back into the house. My tears began to subside, but after a time, when my father still hadn't returned, I began to scream and wail again. Then, I remember—it's like seeing through a fog now—my mother carrying me into the front room. She also carried a lantern, which she held up to the clock on the wall.

"It's three o'clock in the morning," she said, perturbed.

With the lamp still in her hand, she went to the back room.

"Papa! Papa!" I screamed again.

"He'll be home shortly, my baby. Now go to sleep!"

But my father still didn't come and I cried again, sometimes sobbing, at other times screaming.

Finally my father did return, with Dipo trailing behind.

"Papa, Papa!" I screamed. I don't know how many times I called for him.

My mother went to my father and without saying a word handed me to him. She then walked silently off toward her bedroom.

"Papa . . ." I sobbed again.

My father held me to his chest. His clothes, cool from the night air, felt damp to the touch. Slowly but surely, my tears subsided and then, finally, were gone, leaving small shudders that racked my chest. Walking with me in his arms, my father said to me: "My boy, my boy. Don't cry. Papa's here, isn't he? Now go to sleep. Sleep. It's late. Listen. Isn't that a rooster?"

I listened carefully and, sure enough, I could hear the crowing of a rooster.

"It's almost dawn," he said slowly.

The morning felt so silent. The heaving of my chest subsided and finally stopped. My father carried me to Mother's bed. I heard her crying faintly, her head buried beneath the pillow. Even as my father stroked her hair, she continued to cry. My father said nothing; my mother was speechless too. The only sound was my mother's sobs, which caused my own heart to tremble. Moving silently and with great care, my father left the room, carrying me outside and into the cool early morning light.

"Why must you cry so much?" he asked me.

"I waited for you and you didn't come home," I said half in tears. "Mama said that when it got dark you would come home, but you didn't come."

"But I'm home now, aren't I?" he said softly. "So now it's time for you to sleep. Come on . . ."

My father sang slowly. His deep voice was both soft and soothing. After that I don't remember what happened, but when I awoke I found my father asleep beside me. A short while later, sleep robbed me of consciousness again.

When I next awoke, the sun was high. Because it was a holiday, my father hadn't gone to work. I found him and my mother sitting, facing each other, in the front room. After the servant had given me my bath, I ran back into the front room. "You're not going away again, are you, Papa?" I screamed at my father.

My mother looked at my father, who laughed and chucked me under the chin. "No," he said, "I don't have to work today. You're not going to cry again, are you?"

"Mama was crying again yesterday," I told him.

My father looked at my mother, but she didn't say anything. He said nothing either. I began to shout and scream happily as if nothing had happened between them and nothing were happening around me.

"Mama said we're going to Rembang," I announced.

My father looked at my mother again but still said nothing.

"I'm going, and the baby, too. We're going to see the sea. You'll come with us, won't you, Papa?"

Once more my father turned toward my mother but then turned back to me. "Of course I will. When do we leave?"

I looked at my mother and asked her coyly, "When are we going to Rembang, Mama?"

She didn't say anything. She seemed incapable of answering. Her almond eyes reddened and glazed. A moment later they were pools of water, but just as a teardrop began to fall, she quickly wiped it away with the hem of her blouse. Not understanding what was happening, I began to scream and cry again. Something felt wrong inside, and when my mother rose from her seat and left the room, I began to scream louder. I ran after her and pulled on her sarong.

"Why are you crying, Mama?"

My mother picked me up, rocked me slowly in her arms, and then carried me away. But still she said nothing. She carried me to my bed and there laid her face on my chest. My father stayed where he was.

Yes, that incident too stands out clearly in my mind. But that part of my life—

like the riverbanks and clumps of bamboo swept away by the Lusi River—is now gone.

Every year at Lebaran, at the end of the fasting month, Father would buy a load of firecrackers. He'd also give me and my sister and my mother and the foster kids a set of new clothes and some spending money. We'd set off the firecrackers on the ground in front of the house and all the neighbor kids would come running over to watch them explode.

Such an immeasurable sense of delight those holidays gave me, but that same sense of delight was not always evident in the look on my mother's face. The holidays seemed to be a sad time for her, especially after my father began to spend less and less time at home.

Gradually, I grew used to my father's absences and no longer threw a fit every time he left. Mother no longer was forced to send one of the boarders out to call him home. For a very long time I didn't know where my father went when he was not at school. My mother never asked him where he went. She never said anything at all when he left and never greeted him when he returned. It seemed like whenever my father left the house Mother was off somewhere working, in the kitchen, the back room, or the garden.

I, too, rarely asked my father where he went. When I did ask him, his answer was always, "Work." And if I followed that question with another, such as, "Can I come along?" he wouldn't even turn to look at me as he answered me: "No, you may not. When you're older, you can go out by yourself. Now go and play with the others." Then he walked quickly away.

On the Lebaran holidays my mother would watch us kids setting off firecrackers from her chair in the front room. She never said anything, but her lips moved constantly as a rosary passed through her fingers. Once when I did approach her she told me: "You should not play with firecrackers on Lebaran. Our religion forbids it. Firecrackers are used for Chinese celebrations and have no place in Muslim ceremonies."

Regardless of my mother's opinion, my father continued to buy us firecrackers for Lebaran, that is until one of the kids got hurt. After that, he never bought them again.

Then, one day, something really important happened. My grandfather, my mother's father, died and my father rented an automobile to take the family to Rembang. I don't really remember what happened there, but after our return to Blora, my mother was different. She seemed to droop, to lose all her strength. She mourned the loss of her father, I knew, but I also sensed there was something more. In the week after her father died my mother cried continuously.

"Everybody has to die sometime," I heard my father say in an attempt to calm her. "That's what life is about."

But Mother wasn't ready to receive that kind of solace, and her bouts of crying grew worse. I see now my mother must have felt that she had lost her last refuge, the only real place she had to run to outside of her religion.

A week went by, and if at that time I could have better expressed myself, I'm sure I would have said that Mother had finally surrendered herself to some greater force. When Father left the house at night, she never said a word. She acted as if nothing were wrong. At the same time, she seemed to grow even closer to us children. In the end we had become her refuge.

In moments of solitude—not when the world outside was quiet but when her own heart was still—my mother would take us for a walk. We'd hike one or two kilometers from the house, and she'd tell us stories about the things she saw in the world outside. She'd tell us about the birds, and their habits and food; about the waters of the Lusi as we crossed the bridge above it; about the fields and rice, and the insects that devoured both the farmers' crops and their hopes; about the wind and clouds and the sun and the stars; and almost always about the lives of the poor. The knowledge I found as a child was increased greatly on these walks.

In the evenings my mother would gather us together around the bench in the garden and tell us about plants, the clumps of bamboo swaying in the wind, about fruit trees and ships and trains and automobiles and bicycles. My mother was a good storyteller, and sometimes she'd tell us about cities she had visited and about her own family or her studies and teachers in school. And even though we were just kids, she'd tell us about politics and Indonesia's colonization by the Dutch. I can still remember her stories about people who had been active in the political struggle for independence and had been jailed or exiled as a result. But like all the other things, those times too have been carried away to disappear from the realm of our senses.

My mother's real mother—not her stepmother in Rembang—lived near my home-town of Blora. She had moved there after remarrying, and sometimes she'd come to the house with fruit. She sold vegetables to make a living. Early in the morning she'd stop the farmers who were on the way to the market with vegetables and she'd buy their produce to sell to the city's *priayi,* the "gentry" as it were, or those people who liked to think of themselves as *priayi.*

My grandmother's husband made his living by selling roasted skewers of chicken at the market. About the only time he came to our house was to borrow money. He had once been a farmer, but for some reason his crops always failed. The people of my hometown believed that a man who fathers a child out of wedlock will forever experience misfortune. I didn't hear about this until I was older, but when I did, I began to wonder if that is what had happened to my step-grandfather. Whatever the case, I never had the nerve to ask whether it was true.

Sometimes, when my mother's stepfather came to the house, she'd get a look of intense irritation on her face. Once she spoke to me about him, though some-what indirectly: "You must never do what is forbidden," she advised. "Just look at your grandfather and you'll see the consequence! Everything he does fails. It's pitiful. His prayers and hopes are wasted."

With my limited mental grasp, I didn't understand what she meant, and I asked her more directly, "What about Grandpa, Mama?"

"When you're older, you'll understand," was all she had to say. I never asked again.

My mother liked to work in the garden and, if I weren't off playing, I would follow her there. As she worked, stories flowed from her mouth—instructive tales mostly, stories with morals to teach us to respect nature, to be proud of what we do, and to work hard. In my young boy's mind I wasn't always able to grasp what she was trying to tell me, and in numerous instances it was not until years later that I came to understand what she had been saying.

"People live from their own sweat, and when you're an adult, that's how it will be for you too. And anything you obtain, if it doesn't come from your own hard work, will not be right. Even the things that people give to you."

But like everything else, that is gone now, never to return, forever to reside in memory and the mind.

The waters of the Lusi flood and ebb; they rise and fall, become shallow and deep. So too with everything that took place in my childhood days.

"You can do whatever you want with the things you justly earn, even your own life and your own body. Everything," my father once told me, "everything you justly earn."

How long does it take to speak a sentence? The sound of his voice was but for a few moments. A momentary tremble of sound waves, and then it was gone, not to be repeated. Yet, like the Lusi that constantly skirts the city of Blora, like the waters of that river, the remembered sound of that voice, coursing through memory, will continue to flow—forever, toward its estuary and the boundless sea. And not one person knows when the sea will be dry and lose its tide.

But all that is gone, gone from the grasp of the senses.

PATRIOTISM

Yukio Mishima

Translated from the Japanese by Geoffrey W. Sargent

Yukio Mishima (1925–1970) is the pen name of Kimitake Hiraoka, a Japanese author, poet, playwright, actor, film director, founder of the Tatenokai, and nationalist. Mishima is considered one of the most important Japanese authors of the twentieth century. After failing to stage a *coup d'état* to restore the Emperor's pre-war powers, Mishima committed ritual suicide by *seppuku*. His father, a man with a taste for military discipline, employed parenting tactics such as holding the young boy up to the side of a speeding train. Mishima was featured as a photo model in *Young Samurai: Bodybuilders of Japan*.

1.

On the twenty-eighth of February, 1936 (on the third day, that is, of the February 26 Incident), Lieutenant Shinji Takeyama of the Konoe Transport Battalion— profoundly disturbed by the knowledge that his closest colleagues had been with the mutineers from the beginning, and indignant at the imminent prospect of Imperial troops attacking Imperial troops—took his officer's sword and ceremonially disemboweled himself in the eight-mat room of his private residence in the sixth block of Aoba-chō, in Yotsuya Ward. His wife, Reiko, followed him, stabbing herself to death. The lieutenant's farewell note consisted of one sentence: "Long live the Imperial Forces." His wife's, after apologies for her unfilial conduct in thus preceding her parents to the grave, concluded: "The day which, for a soldier's wife, had to come, has come...." The last moments of this heroic and dedicated couple were such as to make the gods themselves weep. The lieutenant's age, it should be noted, was thirty-one, his wife's twenty-three; and it was not half a year since the celebration of their marriage.

2.

Those who saw the bride and bridegroom in the commemorative photograph— perhaps no less than those actually present at the lieutenant's wedding—had exclaimed in wonder at the bearing of this handsome couple. The lieutenant, majestic in military uniform, stood protectively beside his bride, his right hand resting upon his sword, his officer's cap held at his left side. His expression was severe, and his dark brows and wide-gazing eyes well conveyed the clear integrity of youth. For the beauty of the bride in her white over-robe no comparisons were adequate. In the eyes, round beneath soft brows, in the slender, finely shaped nose, and in the full lips, there was both sensuousness and refinement. One hand, emerging shyly from a sleeve of the overrobe, held a fan, and the tips of the fingers, clustering delicately, were like the bud of a moonflower.

After the suicide, people would take out this photograph and examine it, and sadly reflect that too often there was a curse on those seemingly flawless unions. Perhaps it was no more than imagination, but looking at the picture after the tragedy it almost seemed as if the two young people before the gold-lacquered screen were gazing, each with equal clarity, at the deaths which lay before them.

Thanks to the good offices of their go-between, Lieutenant General Ozeki, they had been able to set themselves up in a new home at Aoba-chō in Yotsuya. "New home" is perhaps misleading. It was an old three-room rented house backing onto a small garden. As neither the six- nor the four-and-a-half-mat room downstairs was favored by the sun, they used the upstairs eight-mat room as both bedroom and guest room. There was no maid, so Reiko was left alone to guard the house in her husband's absence.

The honeymoon trip was dispensed with on the grounds that these were times of national emergency. The two of them had spent the first night of their marriage at this house. Before going to bed, Shinji, sitting erect on the floor with the sword laid before him, had bestowed upon his wife a soldierly lecture. A woman who had become the wife of a soldier should know and resolutely accept that her husband's death might come at any moment. It could be tomorrow. It could be the day after. But, no matter when it came—he asked—was she steadfast in her resolve to accept it? Reiko rose to her feet, pulled open a drawer of the cabinet, and took out what was the most prized of her new possessions, the dagger her mother had given her. Returning to her place, she laid the dagger without a word on the mat before her, just as her husband had laid his sword. A silent understanding was achieved at once, and lieutenant never again sought to test his wife's resolve.

In the first few months of her marriage Reiko's beauty grew daily more radiant, shining serene like the moon after rain.

As both were possessed of young, vigorous bodies, their relationship was passionate. Nor was this merely a matter of the night. On more than one occasion, returning home straight from maneuvers, and begrudging even the time it took to remove his mud-splashed uniform, the lieutenant had pushed his wife to the floor almost as soon as he had entered the house. Reiko was equally ardent in her response. For a little more or a little less than a month, from the first night of their marriage, Reiko knew happiness, and the lieutenant, seeing this, was happy too.

Reiko's body was white and pure, and her swelling breasts conveyed a firm and chaste refusal; but, upon consent, those breasts were lavish with their intimate, welcoming warmth. Even in bed these two were frighteningly and awesomely serious. In the very midst of wild, intoxicating passions, their hearts were sober and serious.

By day the lieutenant would think of his wife in the brief rest periods between training; and all day long, at home, Reiko would recall the image of her husband. Even when apart, however, they had only to look at the wedding photograph for their happiness to be once more confirmed. Reiko felt not the slightest surprise that a man who had been a complete stranger until a few months ago should now have become the sun about which her whole world revolved.

All these things had a moral basis, and were in accordance with the Education Rescript's injunction that "husband and wife should be harmonious." Not once did Reiko contradict her husband, nor did the lieutenant ever find reason to scold his wife. On the god shelf below the stairway, alongside the tablet from the Great Ise Shrine, were set photographs of their Imperial Majesties, and regularly every morning, before leaving for duty, the lieutenant would stand with his wife at this hallowed place and together they would bow their heads low. The offering water was renewed each morning, and the sacred sprig of *sasaki* was always green and fresh. Their lives were lived beneath the solemn protection of the gods and were filled with an intense happiness which set every fiber in their bodies trembling

3.

Although Lord Privy Seal Saitō's house was in their neighborhood, neither of them heard any noise of gunfire on the morning of February 26. It was a bugle, sounding muster in the dim, snowy dawn, when the ten-minute tragedy had already ended, which first disrupted the lieutenant's slumbers. Leaping at once from his bed, and without speaking a word, the lieutenant donned his uniform, buckled on the sword held ready for him by his wife, and hurried swiftly out into the snow-covered streets of the still darkened morning. He did not return until the evening of the twenty-eighth.

Later, from the radio news, Reiko learned the full extent of this sudden eruption of violence. Her life throughout the subsequent two days was lived alone, in complete tranquility, and behind locked doors.

In the lieutenant's face, as he hurried silently out into the snowy morning, Reiko had read the determination to die. If her husband did not return, her decision was made: she too would die. Quietly she attended to the disposition of her personal possessions. She chose her sets of visiting kimonos as keepsakes for friends of her schooldays, and she wrote a name and address on the stiff paper wrapping in which each was folded. Constantly admonished by her husband never to think of the morrow, Reiko had not even kept a diary and was now denied the pleasure of assiduously rereading her record of the happiness of the past few months and consigning each page to the fire as she did so. Ranged across the top of the radio were a small china dog, a rabbit, a squirrel, a bear, and a fox. There were also a small vase and a water pitcher. These comprised Reiko's one and only collection. But it would hardly do, she imagined, to give such things as keepsakes. Nor again would it be quite proper to ask specifically for them to be included in the coffin. It seemed to Reiko, as these thoughts passed through her mind, that the expressions on the small animals' faces grew even more lost and forlorn.

Reiko took the squirrel in her hand and looked at it. And then, her thoughts turning to a realm far beyond these childlike affections, she gazed up into the distance at the great sunlike principle which her husband embodied. She was ready, and happy, to be hurtled along to her destruction in that gleaming sun chariot—but now, for these moments of solitude, she allowed herself to luxuriate in this innocent attachment to trifles. The time when she had genuinely loved these things, however, was long past. Now she merely loved the memory of having once loved them, and their place in her heart had been filled by more intense passions, by a more frenzied happiness. . . . For Reiko had never, even to herself, thought of those soaring joys of the flesh as a mere pleasure. The February cold, and the icy touch of the china squirrel, had numbed Reiko's slender fingers; yet, even so, in her lower limbs, beneath the ordered repetition of the pattern which crossed the skirt of her trim *meisen* kimono, she could feel now, as she thought of the lieutenant's powerful arms reaching out toward her, a hot moistness of the flesh which defied the snows.

She was not in the least afraid of the death hovering in her mind. Waiting alone at home, Reiko firmly believed that everything her husband was feeling or thinking now, his anguish and distress, was leading her—just as surely as the power in his flesh—to a welcome death. She felt as if her body could melt away to the merest fraction of her husband's thought.

Listening to the frequent announcements on the radio, she heard the names of several of her husband's colleagues mentioned among those of the insurgents. This was news of death. She followed the developments closely, wondering anxiously, as the situation became daily more irrevocable, why no Imperial ordinance was sent down, and watching what had at first been taken as a movement to restore the nation's honor come gradually to be branded with the infamous name of mutiny. There was no communication from the regiment. At any moment, it seemed, fighting might commence in the city streets, where the remains of the snow still lay.

Toward sundown on the twenty-eighth Reiko was startled by a furious pounding on the front door. She hurried downstairs. As she pulled with fumbling fingers at the bolt, the shape dimly outlined beyond the frosted-glass panel made no sound, but she knew it was her husband. Reiko had never known the bolt on the sliding door to be so stiff. Still it resisted. The door just would not open.

In a moment, almost before she knew she had succeeded, the lieutenant was standing before her on the cement floor inside the porch, muffled in a khaki greatcoat, his top boots heavy with slush from the street. Closing the door behind him, he returned the bolt once more to its socket. With what significance, Reiko did not understand.

"Welcome home."

Reiko bowed deeply, but her husband made no response. As he had already unfastened his sword and was about to remove his greatcoat, Reiko moved around behind to assist. The coat, which was cold and damp and had lost the odor of horse dung it normally exuded when exposed to the sun, weighed heavily upon her arm. Draping it across a hanger, and cradling the sword and leather belt in her sleeves, she waited while her husband removed his top boots and then followed behind him into the "living room." This was the six-mat room downstairs.

Seen in the clear light from the lamp, her husband's face, covered with a heavy growth of bristle, was almost unrecognizably wasted and thin. The cheeks were hollow, their luster and resilience gone. In his normal good spirits he would have changed into old clothes as soon as he was home and have pressed her to get supper at once, but now he sat before the table still in his uniform, his head drooping dejectedly. Reiko refrained from asking whether she should prepare the supper.

After an interval the lieutenant spoke.

"I knew nothing. They hadn't asked me to join. Perhaps out of consideration, because I was newly married. Kanō, and Homma too, and Yamaguchi."

Reiko recalled momentarily the faces of high-spirited young officers, friends of her husband, who had come to the house occasionally as guests.

"There may be an Imperial ordinance sent down tomorrow. They'll be posted as rebels, I imagine. I shall be in command of a unit with orders to attack them. . . . I can't do it. It's impossible to do a thing like that."

He spoke again.

"They've taken me off guard duty, and I have permission to return home for one night. Tomorrow morning, without question, I must leave to join the attack. I can't do it, Reiko."

Reiko sat erect with lowered eyes. She understood clearly that her husband had spoken of his death. The lieutenant was resolved. Each word, being rooted in death, emerged sharply and with powerful significance against this dark, unmovable background. Although the lieutenant was speaking of his dilemma, already there was no room in his mind for vacillation.

However, there was a clarity, like the clarity of a stream fed from melting snows, in the silence which rested between them. Sitting in his own home after the long two-day ordeal, and looking across at the face of his beautiful wife, the lieutenant was for the first time experiencing true peace of mind. For he had at once known, though she said nothing, that his wife divined the resolve which lay beneath his words.

"Well, then . . ." The lieutenant's eyes opened wide. Despite his exhaustion they were strong and clear, and now for the first time they looked straight into the eyes of his wife. "Tonight I shall cut my stomach."

Reiko did not flinch.

Her round eyes showed tension, as taut as the clang of a bell.

"I am ready," she said. "I ask permission to accompany you."

The lieutenant felt almost mesmerized by the strength in those eyes. His words flowed swiftly and easily, like the utterances of a man in delirium, and it was beyond his understanding how permission in a matter of such weight could be expressed so casually.

"Good. We'll go together. But I want you as a witness, first, for my own suicide. Agreed?"

When this was said a sudden release of abundant happiness welled up in both their hearts. Reiko was deeply affected by the greatness of her husband's trust in her. It was vital for the lieutenant, whatever else might happen, that there should be no irregularity in his death. For that reason there had to be a witness. The fact that he had chosen his wife for this was the first mark of his trust. The second, and even greater mark, was that though he had pledged that they should die together he did not intend to kill his wife first—he had deferred her death to a time when he would no longer be there to verify it. If the lieutenant had been a suspicious husband, he would doubtless, as in the usual suicide pact, have chosen to kill his wife first.

When Reiko said, "I ask permission to accompany you," the lieutenant felt these words to be the final fruit of the education which he had himself given his wife, starting on the first night of their marriage, and which had schooled her, when the moment came, to say what had to be said without a shadow of hesitation. This flattered the lieutenant's opinion of himself as a self-reliant man. He was not so romantic or conceited as to imagine that the words were spoken spontaneously, out of love for her husband.

With happiness welling almost too abundantly in their hearts, they could not help smiling at each other. Reiko felt as if she had returned to her wedding night.

Before her eyes was neither pain nor death. She seemed to see only a free and limitless expanse opening out into vast distances.

"The water is hot. Will you take your bath now?"

"Ah yes, of course."

"And supper. . . ?"

The words were delivered in such level, domestic tones that the lieutenant came near to thinking, for the fraction of a second, that everything had been a hallucination.

"I don't think we'll need supper. But perhaps you could warm some sake?"

"As you wish."

As Reiko rose and took a *tanzen* gown from the cabinet for after the bath, she purposely directed her husband's attention to the opened drawer. The lieutenant rose, crossed to the cabinet, and looked inside. From the ordered array of paper wrappings he read, one by one, the addresses of the keepsakes. There was no grief in the lieutenant's response to this demonstration of heroic resolve. His heart was filled with tenderness. Like a husband who is proudly shown the childish purchases of a young wife, the lieutenant, overwhelmed by affection, lovingly embraced his wife from behind and implanted a kiss upon her neck.

Reiko felt the roughness of the lieutenant's unshaven skin against her neck. This sensation, more than being just a thing of this world, was for Reiko almost the world itself, but now—with the feeling that it was soon to be lost forever—it had freshness beyond all her experience. Each moment had its own vital strength, and the senses in every corner of her body were reawakened. Accepting her husband's caresses from behind, Reiko raised herself on the tips of her toes, letting the vitality seep through her entire body.

"First the bath, and then, after some sake . . . lay out the bedding upstairs, will you?"

The lieutenant whispered the words into his wife's ear. Reiko silently nodded.

Flinging off his uniform, the lieutenant went to the bath. To faint background noises of slopping water Reiko tended the charcoal brazier in the living room and began the preparations for warming the sake.

Taking the *tanzen*, a sash, and some underclothes, she went to the bathroom to ask how the water was. In the midst of a coiling cloud of steam the lieutenant was sitting cross-legged on the floor, shaving, and she could dimly discern the rippling movements of the muscles on his damp, powerful back as they responded to the movement of his arms.

There was nothing to suggest a time of any special significance. Reiko, going busily about her tasks, was preparing side dishes from odds and ends in stock. Her hands did not tremble. If anything, she managed even more efficiently and smoothly than usual. From time to time, it is true, there was a strange throbbing deep within her breast. Like distant lightning, it had a moment of sharp intensity and then vanished without trace. Apart from that, nothing was in any way out of the ordinary.

The lieutenant, shaving in the bathroom, felt his warmed body miraculously healed at last of the desperate tiredness of the days of indecision and filled—in spite of the death which lay ahead—with pleasurable anticipation. The sound of his wife going about her work came to him faintly. A healthy physical craving, submerged for two days, reasserted itself.

The lieutenant was confident there had been no impurity in that joy they had experienced when resolving upon death. They had both sensed at that moment—though not, of course, in any clear and conscious way—that those permissible pleasures which they shared in private were once more beneath the protection of Righteousness and Divine Power, and of a complete and unassailable morality. On looking into each other's eyes and discovering there an honorable death, they had felt themselves safe once more behind steel walls which none could destroy, encased in an impenetrable armor of Beauty and Truth. Thus, so far from seeing any inconsistency or conflict between the urges of his flesh and the sincerity of his patriotism, the lieutenant was even able to regard the two as parts of the same thing.

Thrusting his face close to the dark, cracked, misted wall mirror, the lieutenant shaved himself with great care. This would be his death face. There must be no unsightly blemishes. The clean-shaven face gleamed once more with a youthful luster, seeming to brighten the darkness of the mirror. There was a certain elegance, he even felt, in the association of death with this radiantly healthy face.

Just as it looked now, this would become his death face! Already, in fact, it had half departed from the lieutenant's personal possession and had become the bust above a dead soldier's memorial. As an experiment he closed his eyes tight. Everything was wrapped in blackness, and he was no longer a living, seeing creature.

Returning from the bath, the traces of the shave glowing faintly blue beneath his smooth cheeks, he seated himself beside the now well-kindled charcoal brazier. Busy though Reiko was, he noticed, she had found time lightly to touch up her face. Her cheeks were gray and her lips moist. There was no shadow of sadness to be seen. Truly, the lieutenant felt, as he saw this mark of his young wife's passionate nature, he had chosen the wife he ought to have chosen.

As soon as the lieutenant had drained his sake cup he offered it to Reiko. Reiko had never before tasted sake, but she accepted without hesitation and sipped timidly.

"Come here," the lieutenant said.

Reiko moved to her husband's side and was embraced as she leaned backward across his lap. Her breast was in violent commotion, as if sadness, joy, and the potent sake were mingling and reacting within her. The lieutenant looked down into his wife's face. It was the last face he would see in this world, the last face he would see of his wife. The lieutenant scrutinized the face minutely, with the eyes of a traveler bidding farewell to splendid vistas which he will never revisit. It was a face he could not tire of looking at—the features regular yet not cold, the lips lightly closed with a soft strength. The lieutenant kissed those lips, unthinkingly. And suddenly, though there was not the slightest distortion of the face into the unsightliness of sobbing, he noticed that tears were welling slowly from beneath the long lashes of the closed eyes and brimming over into a glistening stream.

When, a little later, the lieutenant urged that they should move to the upstairs bedroom, his wife replied that she would follow after taking a bath. Climbing the stairs alone to the bedroom, where the air was already warmed by the gas heater, the lieutenant lay down on the bedding with arms outstretched and legs apart. Even the time at which he lay waiting for his wife to join him was no later and no earlier than usual.

He folded his hands beneath his head and gazed at the dark boards of the ceiling in the dimness beyond the range of the standard lamp. Was it death he was now waiting for? Or a wild ecstasy of the senses? The two seemed to overlap, almost as if the object of this bodily desire was death itself. But, however that might be, it was certain that never before had the lieutenant tasted such total freedom.

There was the sound of a car outside the window. He could hear the screech of its tires skidding in the snow piled at the side of the street. The sound of its horn re-echoed from nearby walls. . . . Listening to these noises he had the feeling that this house rose like a solitary island in the ocean of a society going as restlessly about its business as ever. All around, vastly and untidily, stretched the country for which he grieved. He was to give his life for it. But would that great country, with which he was prepared to remonstrate to the extent of destroying himself, take the slightest heed of his death? He did not know; and it did not matter. His was a battlefield without glory, a battlefield where none could display deeds of valor: it was the front line of the spirit.

Reiko's footsteps sounded on the stairway. The steep stairs in this old house creaked badly. There were fond memories in that creaking, and many a time, while waiting in bed, the lieutenant had listened to its welcome sound. At the thought that he would hear it no more he listened with intense concentration, striving for every corner of every moment of this precious time to be filled with the sound of those soft footfalls on the creaking stairway. The moments seemed transformed to jewels, sparkling with inner light.

Reiko wore a Nagoya sash about the waist of her *yukata,* but as the lieutenant reached toward it, its redness sobered by the dimness of the light, Reiko's hand moved to his assistance and the sash fell away, slithering swiftly to the floor. As she stood before him, still in her *yukata,* the lieutenant inserted his hands through the side slits beneath each sleeve, intending to embrace her as she was; but at the touch of his finger tips upon the warm naked flesh, and as the armpits closed gently about his hands, his whole body was suddenly aflame.

In a few moments the two lay naked before the glowing gas heater.

Neither spoke the thought, but their hearts, their bodies, and their pounding breasts blazed with the knowledge that this was the very last time. It was as if the words "The Last Time" were spelled out, in invisible brushstrokes, across every inch of their bodies.

The lieutenant drew his wife close and kissed her vehemently. As their tongues explored each other's mouths, reaching out into the smooth, moist interior, they felt as if the still-unknown agonies of death had tempered their senses to the keenness of red-hot steel. The agonies they could not yet feel, the distant pains of death, had refined their awareness of pleasure.

"This is the last time I shall see your body," said the lieutenant. "Let me look at it closely." And, tilting the shade on the lampstand to one side, he directed the rays along the full length of Reiko's outstretched form.

Reiko lay still with her eyes closed. The light from the low lamp clearly revealed the majestic sweep of her white flesh. The lieutenant, not without a touch of egocentricity, rejoiced that he would never see this beauty crumble in death.

At his leisure, the lieutenant allowed the unforgettable spectacle to engrave itself upon his mind. With one hand he fondled the hair, with the other he softly stroked the magnificent face, implanting kisses here and there where his eyes lingered. The quiet coldness of the high, tapering forehead, the closed eyes with their long lashes beneath faintly etched brows, the set of the finely shaped nose, the gleam of teeth glimpsed between full, regular lips, the soft cheeks and the small, wise chin . . . these things conjured up in the lieutenant's mind the vision of a truly radiant death face, and again and again he pressed his lips tight against the white throat—where Reiko's own hand was soon to strike—and the throat reddened faintly beneath his kisses. Returning to the mouth he laid his lips against it with the gentlest of pressures, and moved them rhythmically over Reiko's with the light rolling motion of a small boat. If he closed his eyes, the world became a rocking cradle.

Wherever the lieutenant's eyes moved his lips faithfully followed. The high, swelling breasts, surmounted by nipples like the buds of a wild cherry, hardened as the lieutenant's lips closed about them. The arms flowed smoothly downward from each side of the breast, tapering toward the wrists, yet losing nothing of their roundness or symmetry, and at their tips were those delicate fingers which had held the fan at the wedding ceremony. One by one, as the lieutenant kissed them, the fingers withdrew behind their neighbor as if in shame. . . . The natural hollow curving between the bosom and the stomach carried in its lines a suggestion not only of softness but of resilient strength, and while it gave forewarning of the rich curves spreading outward from here to the hips it had, in itself, an appearance only of restraint and proper discipline. The whiteness and richness of the stomach and hips was like milk brimming in a great bowl, and the sharply shadowed dip of the navel could have been the fresh impress of a raindrop, fallen there that very moment. Where the shadows gathered more thickly, hair clustered, gentle and sensitive, and as the agitation mounted in the now no longer passive body there hung over this region a scent like the smoldering of fragrant blossoms, growing steadily more pervasive.

At length, in a tremulous voice, Reiko spoke.

"Show me. . . . Let me look too, for the last time."

Never before had he heard from his wife's lips so strong and unequivocal a request. It was as if something which her modesty had wished to keep hidden to the end had suddenly burst its bonds of constraint. The lieutenant obediently lay back and surrendered himself to his wife. Lithely she raised her white, trembling body, and—burning with an innocent desire to return to her husband what he had done for her—placed two white fingers on the lieutenant's eyes, which gazed fixedly up at her, and gently stroked them shut.

Suddenly overwhelmed by tenderness, her cheeks flushed by a dizzying uprush of emotion, Reiko threw her arms about the lieutenant's close-cropped head. The bristly hairs rubbed painfully against her breast, the prominent nose was cold as it dug into her flesh, and his breath was hot. Relaxing her embrace, she gazed down at her husband's masculine face. The severe brows, the closed eyes, the splendid bridge of the nose, the shapely lips drawn firmly together . . . the blue, clean-shaven cheeks reflecting the light and gleaming smoothly, Reiko kissed each of these. She kissed the broad nape of the neck, the strong, erect shoulders, the powerful chest with its twin circles like shields and its russet nipples. In the armpits, deeply shadowed by the ample flesh of the shoulders and chest, a sweet and melancholy odor emanated from the growth of hair, and in the sweetness of this odor was contained, somehow, the essence of young death. The lieutenant's naked skin glowed like a field of barley, and everywhere the muscles showed in sharp relief, converging on the lower abdomen about the small, unassuming navel. Gazing at the youthful, firm stomach, modestly covered by a vigorous growth of hair, Reiko thought of it as it was soon to be, cruelly cut by the sword, and she laid her head upon it, sobbing in pity, and bathed it with kisses.

At the touch of his wife's tears upon his stomach the lieutenant felt ready to endure with courage the crudest agonies of his suicide.

What ecstasies they experienced after these tender exchanges may well be imagined. The lieutenant raised himself and enfolded his wife in a powerful embrace, her body now limp with exhaustion after her grief and tears. Passionately they held their faces close, rubbing cheek against cheek. Reiko's body was trembling. Their breasts, moist with sweat, were tightly joined, and every inch of the young and beautiful bodies had become so much one with the other that it seemed impossible there should ever again be a separation. Reiko cried out. From the heights they plunged into the abyss, and from the abyss they took wing and soared once more to dizzying heights. The lieutenant panted like the regimental standard-bearer on a route march. . . . As one cycle ended, almost immediately a new wave of passion would be generated, and together—with no trace of fatigue—they would climb again in a single breathless movement to the very summit.

4.

When the lieutenant at last turned away, it was not from weariness. For one thing, he was anxious not to undermine the considerable strength he would need in carrying out his suicide. For another, he would have been sorry to mar the sweetness of these last memories by overindulgence.

Since the lieutenant had clearly desisted, Reiko too, with her usual compliance, followed his example. The two lay naked on their backs, with fingers interlaced, staring fixedly at the dark ceiling. The room was warm from the heater, and even when the sweat had ceased to pour from their bodies they felt no cold. Outside, in the hushed night, the sounds of passing traffic had ceased. Even the noises of the trains and streetcars around Yotsuya station did not penetrate this far. After echoing through the region bounded by the moat, they were lost in the heavily wooded park fronting the broad driveway before Akasaka Palace. It was hard to believe in the tension gripping this whole quarter, where the two factions of the bitterly divided Imperial Army now confronted each other, poised for battle.

Savoring the warmth glowing within themselves, they lay still and recalled the ecstasies they had just known. Each moment of the experience was relived. They remembered the taste of kisses which had never wearied, the touch of naked flesh, episode after episode of dizzying bliss. But already, from the dark boards of the ceiling, the face of death was peering down. These joys had been final, and their bodies would never know them again. Not that joy of this intensity—and the same thought had occurred to them both—was ever likely to be re-experienced, even if they should live on to old age.

The feel of their fingers intertwined—this too would soon be lost. Even the wood-grain patterns they now gazed at on the dark ceiling boards would be taken from them. They could feel death edging in, nearer and nearer. There could be no hesitation now. They must have the courage to reach out to death themselves, and to seize it.

"Well, let's make our preparations," said the lieutenant. The note of determination in the words was unmistakable, but at the same time Reiko had never heard her husband's voice so warm and tender.

After they had risen, a variety of tasks awaited them.

The lieutenant, who had never once before helped with the bedding, now cheerfully slid back the door of the closet, lifted the mattress across the room by himself, and stowed it away inside.

Reiko turned off the gas heater and put away the lamp standard. During the lieutenant's absence she had arranged this room carefully, sweeping and dusting it to a fresh cleanness, and now—if one overlooked the rosewood table drawn into one corner—the eight-mat room gave all the appearance of a reception room ready to welcome an important guest.

"We've seen some drinking here, haven't we? With Kanō and Homma and Noguchi. . ."

"Yes, they were great drinkers, all of them."

"We'll be meeting them before long, in the other world. They'll tease us, I imagine, when they find I've brought you with me."

Descending the stairs, the lieutenant turned to look back into this calm, clean room, now brightly illuminated by the ceiling lamp. There floated across his mind the faces of the young officers who had drunk there, and laughed, and innocently bragged. He had never dreamed then that he would one day cut open his stomach in this room.

In the two rooms downstairs husband and wife busied themselves smoothly and serenely with their respective preparations. The lieutenant went to the toilet, and then to the bathroom to wash. Meanwhile Reiko folded away her husband's padded robe, placed his uniform tunic, his trousers, and newly cut bleached loin-cloth in the bathroom, and set out sheets of paper on the living-room table for the farewell notes. Then she removed the lid from the writing box and began rubbing ink from the ink tablet. She had already decided upon the wording of her own note.

Reiko's fingers pressed hard upon the cold gilt letters of the ink tablet, and the water in the shallow well at once darkened, as if a black cloud had spread across it. She stopped thinking that this repeated action, this pressure from her fingers, this rise and fall of faint sound, was all and solely for death. It was a routine domestic task, a simple paring away of time until death should finally stand before her. But somehow, in the increasingly smooth motion of the tablet rubbing on the stone, and in the scent from the thickening ink, there as unspeakable darkness.

Neat in his uniform, which he now wore next to his skin, the lieutenant emerged from the bathroom. Without a word he seated himself at the table, bolt upright, took a brush in his hand, and stared undecidedly at the paper before him.

Reiko took a white silk kimono with her and entered the bathroom. When she reappeared in the living room, clad in the white kimono and with her face lightly made up, the farewell note lay completed on the table beneath the lamp. The thick black brushstrokes said simply: "Long Live the Imperial Forces—Army Lieutenant Takeyama Shinji."

While Reiko sat opposite him writing her own note, the lieutenant gazed in silence, intensely serious, at the controlled movement of his wife's pale fingers as they manipulated the brush.

With their respective notes in their hands — the lieutenant's sword strapped to his side, Reiko's small dagger thrust into the sash of her white kimono—the two of them stood before the god shelf and silently prayed. Then they put out all the downstairs lights. As he mounted the stairs the lieutenant turned his head and gazed back at the striking, white-clad figure of his wife, climbing behind him, with lowered eyes, from the darkness beneath.

The farewell notes were laid side by side in the alcove of the upstairs room. They wondered whether they ought not to remove the hanging scroll, but since it had been written by their go-between, Lieutenant General Ozeki, and consisted, moreover, of two Chinese characters signifying "Sincerity," they left it where it was. Even if it were to become stained with splashes of blood, they felt that the lieutenant general would understand.

The lieutenant, sitting erect with his back to the alcove, laid his sword on the floor before him.

Reiko sat facing him, a mat's width away. With the rest of her so severely white the touch of rouge on her lips seemed remarkably seductive.

Across the dividing mat they gazed intently into each other's eyes. The lieutenant's sword lay before his knees. Seeing it, Reiko recalled their first night and was overwhelmed with sadness. The lieutenant spoke, in a hoarse voice:

"As I have no second to help me I shall cut deep. It may look unpleasant, but please do not panic. Death of any sort is a fearful thing to watch. You must not be discouraged by what you see. Is that all right?"

"Yes."

Reiko nodded deeply.

Looking at the slender white figure of his wife the lieutenant experienced a bizarre excitement. What he was about to perform was an act in his public capacity as a soldier, something he had never previously shown his wife. It called for a resolution equal to the courage to enter battle; it was a death of no less degree and quality than death in the front line. It was his conduct on the battlefield that he was now to display.

Momentarily the thought led the lieutenant to a strange fantasy. A lonely death on the battlefield, a death beneath the eyes of his beautiful wife. . . in the sensation that he was now to die in these two dimensions, realizing an impossible union of them both, there was sweetness beyond words. This must be the very pinnacle of good fortune, he thought. To have every moment of his death observed by those beautiful eyes — it was like being borne to death on a gentle, fragrant breeze. There was some special favor here. He did not understand precisely what it was, but it was a domain unknown to others: a dispensation granted to no one else had been permitted to himself. In the radiant, bridelike figure of his white-robed wife the lieutenant seemed to see a vision of all those things he had loved and for which he was to lay down his life—the Imperial Household, the Nation, the Army Flag. All these, no less than the wife who sat before him, were presences observing him closely with clear and never-faltering eyes.

Reiko too was gazing intently at her husband, so soon to die, and she thought that never in this world had she seen anything so beautiful. The lieutenant always looked well in uniform, but now, as he contemplated death with severe brows and firmly closed lips, he revealed what was perhaps masculine beauty at its most superb.

"It's time to go," the lieutenant said at last.

Reiko bent her body low to the mat in a deep bow. She could not raise her face. She did not wish to spoil her make-up with tears, but the tears could not be held back.

When at length she looked up she saw hazily through the tears that her husband had wound a white bandage around the blade of his now unsheathed sword, leaving five or six inches of naked steel showing at the point.

Resting the sword in its cloth wrapping on the mat before him, the lieutenant rose from his knees, resettled himself cross-legged, and unfastened the hooks of his uniform collar. His eyes no longer saw his wife. Slowly, one by one, he undid the flat brass buttons. The dusky brown chest was revealed, and then the stomach. He unclasped his belt and undid the buttons of his trousers. The pure whiteness of the thickly coiled loincloth showed itself. The lieutenant pushed the cloth down with both hands, further to ease his stomach, and then reached for the white-bandaged blade of his sword. With his left hand he massaged his abdomen, glancing downward as he did so.

To reassure himself on the sharpness of his sword's cutting edge the lieutenant folded back the left trouser flap, exposing a little of his thigh, and lightly drew the blade across the skin. Blood welled up in the wound at once, and several streaks of red trickled downward, glistening in the strong light.

It was the first time Reiko had ever seen her husband's blood, and she felt a violent throbbing in her chest. She looked at her husband's face. The lieutenant was looking at the blood with calm appraisal. For a moment—though thinking at the same time that it was hollow comfort—Reiko experienced a sense of relief.

The lieutenant's eyes fixed his wife with an intense, hawk-like stare. Moving the sword around to his front, he raised himself slightly on his hips and let the upper half of his body lean over the sword point. That he was mustering his whole strength was apparent from the angry tension of the uniform at his shoulders. The lieutenant aimed to strike deep into the left of his stomach. His sharp cry pierced the silence of the room.

Despite the effort he had himself put into the blow, the lieutenant had the impression that someone else had struck the side of his stomach agonizingly with a thick rod of iron. For a second or so his head reeled and he had no idea what had happened. The five or six inches of naked point had vanished completely into his flesh, and the white bandage, gripped in his clenched fist, pressed directly against his stomach.

He returned to consciousness. The blade had certainly pierced the wall of the stomach, he thought. His breathing was difficult, his chest thumped violently, and in some far deep region, which he could hardly believe was a part of himself, a fearful and excruciating pain came welling up as if the ground had split open to disgorge a boiling stream of molten rock. The pain came suddenly nearer, with terrifying speed. The lieutenant bit his lower lip and stilled an instinctive moan.

Was this *seppuku*?—he was thinking. It was a sensation of utter chaos, as if the sky had fallen on his head and the world was reeling drunkenly. His will power and courage, which had seemed so robust before he made the incision, had now dwindled to something like a single hairlike thread of steel, and he was assailed by the uneasy feeling that he must advance along this thread, clinging to it with desperation. His clenched fist had grown moist. Looking down, he saw that both his hand and the cloth about the blade were drenched in blood. His loincloth too was dyed a deep red. It struck him as incredible that, amidst this terrible agony, things which could be seen could still be seen, and existing things existed still.

The moment the lieutenant thrust the sword into his left side and she saw the deathly pallor fall across his face, like an abruptly lowered curtain, Reiko had to struggle to prevent herself from rushing to his side. Whatever happened, she must watch. She must be a witness. That was the duty her husband had laid upon her. Opposite her, a mat's space away, she could clearly see her husband biting his lip to stifle the pain. The pain was there, with absolute certainty, before her eyes. And Reiko had no means of rescuing him from it.

The sweat glistened on her husband's forehead. The lieutenant closed his eyes, and then opened them again, as if experimenting. The eyes had lost their luster, and seemed innocent and empty like the eyes of a small animal.

The agony before Reiko's eyes burned as strong as the summer sun, utterly remote from the grief which seemed to be tearing herself apart within. The pain grew steadily in stature, stretching upward. Reiko felt that her husband had already become a man in a separate world, a man whose whole being had been resolved into pain, a prisoner in a cage of pain where no hand could reach out to him. But Reiko felt no pain at all. Her grief was not pain. As she thought about this, Reiko began to feel as if someone had raised a cruel wall of glass high between herself and her husband.

Ever since her marriage her husband's existence had been her own existence, and every breath of his had been a breath drawn by herself. But now, while her husband's existence in pain was a vivid reality, Reiko could find in this grief of hers no certain proof at all of her own existence.

With only his right hand on the sword the lieutenant began to cut sideways across his stomach. But as the blade became entangled with the entrails it was pushed constantly outward by their soft resilience; and the lieutenant realized that it would be necessary, as he cut, to use both hands to keep the point pressed deep into his stomach. He pulled the blade across. It did not cut as easily as he had expected. He directed the strength of his whole body into his right hand and pulled again. There was a cut of three or four inches.

The pain spread slowly outward from the inner depths until the whole stomach reverberated. It was like the wild clanging of a bell. Or like a thousand bells which jangled simultaneously at every breath he breathed and every throb of his pulse, rocking his whole being. The lieutenant could no longer stop himself from moaning. But by now the blade had cut its way through to below the navel, and when he noticed this he felt a sense of satisfaction, and a renewal of courage.

The volume of blood had steadily increased, and now it spurted from the wound as if propelled by the beat of the pulse. The mat before the lieutenant was drenched red with splattered blood, and more blood overflowed onto it from pools which gathered in the folds of the lieutenant's khaki trousers. A spot, like a bird, came flying across to Reiko and settled on the lap of her white silk kimono.

By the time the lieutenant had at last drawn the sword across to the right side of his stomach, the blade was already cutting shallow and had revealed its naked tip, slippery with blood and grease. But, suddenly stricken by a fit of vomiting, the lieutenant cried out hoarsely. The vomiting made the fierce pain fiercer still, and the stomach, which had thus far remained firm and compact, now abruptly heaved, opening wide its wound, and the entrails burst through, as if the wound too were vomiting. Seemingly ignorant of their master's suffering, the entrails gave an impression of robust health and almost disagreeable vitality as they slipped smoothly out and spilled over into the crotch. The lieutenant's head drooped, his shoulders heaved, his eyes opened to narrow slits, and a thin trickle of saliva dribbled from his mouth. The gold markings on his epaulettes caught the light and glinted.

Blood was scattered everywhere. The lieutenant was soaked in it to his knees, and he sat now in a crumpled and listless posture, one hand on the floor. A raw smell filled the room. The lieutenant, his head drooping, retched repeatedly, and the movement showed vividly in his shoulders. The blade of the sword, now pushed back by the entrails and exposed to its tip, was still in the lieutenant's right hand.

It would be difficult to imagine a more heroic sight than that of the lieutenant at this moment, as he mustered his strength and flung back his head. The movement was performed with sudden violence, and the back of his head struck with a sharp crack against the alcove pillar. Reiko had been sitting until now with her face lowered, gazing in fascination at the tide of blood advancing toward her knees, but the sound took her by surprise and she looked up.

The lieutenant's face was not the face of a living man. The eyes were hollow, the skin parched, the once so lustrous cheeks and lips the color of dried mud. The right hand alone was moving. Laboriously gripping the sword, it hovered shakily in the air like the hand of a marionette and strove to direct the point at the base of the lieutenant's throat. Reiko watched her husband make this last, most heart-rending, futile exertion. Glistening with blood and grease, the point was thrust at the throat again and again. And each time it missed its aim. The strength to guide it was no longer there. The straying point struck the collar and the collar badges. Although its hooks had been unfastened, the stiff military collar had closed together again and was protecting the throat.

Reiko could bear the sight no longer. She tried to go to her husband's help, but she could not stand. She moved through the blood on her knees, and her white skirts grew deep red. Moving to the rear of her husband, she helped no more than by loosening the collar. The quivering blade at last contacted the naked flesh of the throat. At that moment Reiko's impression was that she herself had propelled her husband forward; but that was not the case. It was a movement planned by the lieutenant himself, his last exertion of strength. Abruptly he threw his body at the blade, and the blade pierced his neck, emerging at the nape. There was a tremendous spurt of blood and the lieutenant lay still, cold blue-tinged steel protruding from his neck at the back.

5.

Slowly, her socks slippery with blood, Reiko descended the stairway. The upstairs room was now completely still.

Switching on the ground-floor lights, she checked the gas jet and the main gas plug and poured water over the smoldering, half-buried charcoal in the brazier. She stood before the upright mirror in the four-and-a-half-mat room and held up her skirts. The bloodstains made it seem as if a bold, vivid pattern was printed across the lower half of her white kimono. When she sat down before the mirror, she was conscious of the dampness and coldness of her husband's blood in the region of her thighs, and she shivered. Then, for a long while, she lingered over her toilet preparations. She applied the rouge generously to her cheeks, and her lips too she painted heavily. This was no longer make-up to please her husband. It was make-up for the world which she would leave behind, and there was a touch of the magnificent and the spectacular in her brushwork. When she rose, the mat before the mirror was wet with blood. Reiko was not concerned about this.

Returning from the toilet, Reiko stood finally on the cement floor of the porchway. When her husband had bolted the door here last night it had been in preparation for death. For a while she stood immersed in the consideration of a simple problem. Should she leave the bolt drawn? If she were to lock the door, it could be that the neighbors might not notice their suicide for several days. Reiko did not relish the thought of their two corpses putrefying before discovery. After all, it seemed, it would be best to leave it open. . . . She released the bolt, and also drew open the frosted-glass door a fraction. . . . At once a chill wind blew in. There was no sign of anyone in the midnight streets, and stars glittered ice-cold through the trees in the large house opposite.

Leaving the door as it was, Reiko mounted the stairs. She had walked here and there for some time and her socks were no longer slippery. About halfway up, her nostrils were already assailed by a peculiar smell.

The lieutenant was lying on his face in a sea of blood. The point protruding from his neck seemed to have grown even more prominent than before. Reiko walked heedlessly across the blood. Sitting beside the lieutenant's corpse, she stared intently at the face, which lay on one cheek on the mat. The eyes were opened wide, as if the lieutenant's attention had been attracted by something. She raised the head, folding it in her sleeve, wiped the blood from the lips, and bestowed a last kiss.

Then she rose and took from the closet a new white blanket and a waist cord. To prevent any derangement of her skirts, she wrapped the blanket about her waist and bound it there firmly with the cord.

Reiko sat herself on a spot about one foot distant from the lieutenant's body. Drawing the dagger from her sash, she examined its dully gleaming blade intently, and held it to her tongue. The taste of the polished steel was slightly sweet.

Reiko did not linger. When she thought how the pain which had previously opened such a gulf between herself and her dying husband was now to become a part of her own experience, she saw before her only the joy of herself entering a realm her husband had already made his own. In her husband's agonized face there had been something inexplicable which she was seeing for the first time. Now she would solve that riddle. Reiko sensed that at last she too would be able to taste the true bitterness and sweetness of that great moral principle in which her husband believed. What had until now been tasted only faintly through her husband's example she was about to savor directly with her own tongue.

Reiko rested the point of the blade against the base of her throat. She thrust hard. The wound was only shallow. Her head blazed, and her hands shook uncontrollably. She gave the blade a strong pull sideways. A warm substance flooded into her mouth, and everything before her eyes reddened, in a vision of spouting blood. She gathered her strength and plunged the point of the blade deep into her throat.

FULL TIDE

Kōno Taeko

Translated from the Japanese by Lucy North

Kōno Taeko (1926–2015) was one of the most important Japanese women writers of the second half of the twentieth century. She established a reputation for herself as an acerbic essayist, a playwright and a literary critic. By the end of her life she was a leading presence in Japan's literary establishment, and one of the first women writers to serve on the Akutagawa Literary Prize committee. Alternative sexual practices is a popular theme that permeates Kōno's writing, such as sadomasochism and spouse-swapping.

Michi-shio, 1964

The children had gotten their mother to help them change into travel outfits: their hats on, they were all ready to go. But their mother was now busy getting herself dressed, and told them as she tied on her sash: "Now, all of you go and say goodbye to Grandma Hotta."

A merchant family, they had always lived in the section of the city that was traditionally home to the wholesale trade. From now on, however, they were going to live in a new place in the suburbs, away from the family business. For a long time the girl had been hearing from her parents how nice it would be to live in their own house, on the city outskirts where the air was clean. And now, finally, it was happening: it was summer, and the girl was just ten years old.

The house they were moving to had been built on a plot of land an hour away from their business—her father intended to commute every day. With her younger sister, she would switch schools, and her brother, who wasn't in school yet, would start kindergarten in their new neighborhood in the spring.

A few days before, after attending her primary school's final assembly and closing ceremony before summer vacation, the girl had felt strange as she walked out the gate and realized that she wouldn't be back next fall. But she didn't feel too sad—the family shop would stay where it was. She was bound to come this way occasionally. Her friends seemed to take that for granted. "When will we see you again?" they asked when she said goodbye. "Can you come visit over the holidays?"

She was, in fact, longing to start her new life in the suburbs. She'd already visited the area a few times with her family—it was right on the sea, with mountains close by, and in between the sea and the mountains was a river with sandbars and beautiful grassy banks lined with rows of pine trees. At the foot of the mountains was a park with a slide said to be the highest in Japan. "Just one more time," the girl remembered begging her parents, as they tried to persuade her to leave. She had scampered back to the slide which rose steeply above her in the late-afternoon spring sunshine—and, thinking back on it, the girl felt a fresh stab of nostalgia. The strap of her rubber swimming cap smelled of the sea, and she recalled her mounting excitement as she walked along the grassy bank, smelled the salt air, and listened to the pounding of the surf get louder and louder.

But the girl had not seen her new house yet.

"What's it like?" she couldn't help asking her parents. Apparently, it wasn't creaky and dark like their old house—and it was only a stone's throw from the sea.

"You'll be able to go to the beach in your swimsuit and robe!" her father told her.

The girl's eyes opened wide: "Really?"

It didn't matter one bit that they would leave the streets where the girl had lived all her life. She felt a little anxious about going to a new school in the fall, but that was still more than a month away. Her whole heart had been longing for the day of their departure and the idea that they would have to go say goodbye to Grandma Hotta hadn't even crossed her mind.

But when her mother told them to go, the girl stood up immediately, took off the hat she had been trying on in front of the mirror to see if the elastic strap belonged in front of her ears or behind them, and flung it aside.

"Remember to tell Grandma that you'll write. And that you'll come back and visit from time to time," her mother added, glancing at her back in the mirror, her hands busy with the knot of her sash. "And don't forget to say, 'We hope that you stay well!'"

The girl nodded obediently, and beckoned her brother and sister.

"Go through the front today," their mother called.

Grandma Hotta was an old lady who lived all alone, just three doors down the street from them. She had suffered a series of terrible misfortunes, the girl had heard. She and her husband had once run a wholesale paper business, but had gone bankrupt, soon after which her husband and her only child, a daughter, had died. Now she lived at the end of a small alleyway, in a tiny place, consisting of the kitchen and one two-mat room of her former residence. The rest had been sold off and made into the accounting office of a copper-ware dealer. Despite her poverty, however, the neighbors still acknowledged the old lady's previous status as the wife of a prosperous shopkeeper: they called her "O-ie," "O-ie-san," or, in the local dialect, "O-e-han." * In the girl's family, too, the grown-ups always referred to the old lady as "Hotta no O-e-han."

It was possible to enter the old lady's house from the back of their own. At the end of the garden, by the little cottage where the children often played, was a wooden warehouse built up against the family storehouse: at its far end was a sliding door, and opening that, they would find themselves right inside Grandma Hotta's house. The door was usually kept closed and locked, however, with a bolt on the old lady's side.

That day, the girl escorted her brother and sister out to the street, where trucks,

---

* The "ie" of "O-ie-san" means "household/family." The name means something like "Mistress," and was traditionally used by the merchant class in Osaka.

carts, and bicycles were busily passing, and turned down the little alley to the old lady's front entrance. They pounded on the heavy wooden door, which had a smaller one set within it, and shouted all together, "Grandma!"

"Yes, yes. I'm coming," they heard her say in the same way she did when they went via the warehouse. They heard her wooden clogs cross the earthen floor, then a pause, and the bolt rattled back.

"We've come to say goodbye," the girl announced as soon as the door opened.

"Really? Thank you, dear. It's very nice of you to remember me."

The old lady looked at the children in their travel clothes. "Are you leaving right away? I suppose you don't have time to come in for a little while. . . ."

The kitchen was spacious, large enough to have catered to the needs of an entire family. Now it served as the old lady's living space and entryway as well. There were two skylights in the ceiling, and directly below them, several detachable planks gleamed darkly, covering a small cellar. A rough mat had been laid alongside these.

O-ie-san stepped back to fetch three cushions stacked neatly at the far end of the mat. She set them on the edge of the raised floor for the children, and settled herself opposite them, in front of the simple unlit charcoal brazier.

"Thank you for coming," she said, formally. She was slight of stature and very pale, and her hair was nearly all white.

"When we get there, I'm going to swim every day!" the girl's sister announced.

"Me too!" her brother said. "Mummy bought me a float!"

Grandma Hotta gave her usual response: she had a habit of opening her eyes, which were very wide to begin with, wider still, so they almost met her eyebrows.

"I see," she nodded.

Now would be a good time to carry out her duty, the girl thought, taking a deep breath.

"But we'll come back and visit you, Grandma!" she said. "And we'll write you letters. And we hope that you stay well!"

"Thank you, my dear," the old lady replied. She nodded several times, dabbing her eyes with her sleeve.

The girl was only saying what her mother had told her she should, but she realized that Grandma Hotta was genuinely touched. It occurred to her that Grandma Hotta must be terribly lonely, and that she would be even lonelier when they went away. Remembering that she might have left without saying goodbye, the girl felt ashamed.

Her mother always took very good care of poor old O-ie-san. Two years ago, a fierce typhoon had blown up across their part of the country, with gale-force winds and floods. As soon as her mother saw signs of the coming storm, she sent a clerk from the store over to bring O-ie-san back to their house. Their mother took O-ie-san to the theater, and was always visiting her, almost every day. Whenever the old lady wasn't feeling well, her mother would report her health to her father, even though he usually disliked being bothered by anything unrelated to his work.

"She's no longer running a fever," her mother would say. "But she's still a little dizzy. I'll go over after dinner and see how she is."

On summer nights, the children would play with fireworks and sparklers in the back garden. They would go out into the dark with their mother, taking fireworks, matches, and a bucket of water. Glimpsing a pale shape in the gloom, they might suddenly hear O-ie-san's voice say, quietly: "I'm out here enjoying the cool. I hope you don't mind."

"No, not at all," the girl's mother would reply, quickly disappearing into the cottage, and a light would come on, throwing wan rays out the small round window. The girl would see O-ie-san sitting in the small rattan child's chair that she always brought out with her, fanning herself with a round paper fan.

"What a lovely cool breeze," her mother would remark, coming out and sitting on the edge of the veranda.

The children set about lighting their sparklers. Each time she brought a flame to the tip of one, the girl's fingers would tremble slightly. She had to be careful: she could never tell exactly where the first sparks would shoot out. Then the darkness suddenly would be ablaze, and transfixed, she would be in another world. The sparkler would make fiery, spitting sounds, fizzling away before her eyes. In those few seconds, though, she knew the sparkler was living for all it was worth—fiercely, keenly, in a beautiful world of color and light. Even when everything became dark and still once more, the girl would be sure that she still saw something there, glowing and fizzling away.

"This one next," her brother would say.

Sometimes, the girl would be aware of her mother and the old lady gazing at the sparklers, their faces reflecting the light, but they mostly just chatted. The children would light firecrackers, which shot out at unexpected angles with a loud bang. "Oh!" the women would exclaim: "That made me jump!"

Some nights when they went into the garden to play with sparklers, though, O-ie-san wouldn't be out there enjoying the cool night air. Then, their mother would urge them to go and invite her to join them. But no one would want to go alone to fetch her—it was too scary to go all that way through the dark warehouse. Even the girl was afraid, and she was the eldest.

Through the open door of O-ie-san's house, the girl caught sight of her mother walking up the alley.

"Did everybody say goodbye nicely?" she asked, entering the house.

"They're all such good children," O-ie-san said. "Thank you so much for your kindness this morning," she said to their mother. "You're always so very kind."

So her mother, the girl realized, must have come by herself to see the old lady earlier in the day.

O-ie-san came out to the end of the alley to see them all off. "Good luck!" she said to the children. "Grow up healthy and strong."

Though the girl was going to switch to a new school once summer vacation was over, that didn't mean she got out of holiday homework. At the closing ceremony, their teacher gave all the girls in her class a copy of *Summer Holiday Companion*. She'd been told that she must be sure to complete all its exercises and hand it in to her teacher at her new school at the beginning of the next term.

After breakfast every morning the girl filled in that day's homework in her study book. Then she went straight out with her brother and sister, accompanied by the maid, to swim in the sea. After that, they all had a snack and took a midday nap, and then the children went out by themselves to play in the parks along the grassy river banks lined by pine trees.

In the old house it had been the rule that their father took his bath first, before anyone else. But after they moved to the new house in the suburbs, he told them to have their baths over and done with before he returned. So every day the children were fresh and clean by 5:30. Sometimes their mother would bring them when she went to meet their father on his way home from work.

Away in the distance, astride the river at its source, the mountain peaks bathed in the warm glow of the setting sun. The evening air around them would be pleasantly cool. Even the rush of the water sounded much less noisy and hurried than during the day. The lights in the windows would have just been turned on, and the houses flashing into view between the pine trees all looked very safe and secure behind their hedges. Far away, they would hear the clang of the railway crossing bell.

One evening, as they all went out together to meet him, the girl's brother and sister headed diagonally across the road, a little in front, and up on to the grassy bank.

"Don't go up there," her mother called. "Stay on the road. That's right."

Then she turned to the girl, who was walking beside her.

"You know," she said, "I often think about all of your futures. Of course, I can't say for sure what kind of husbands you and your sister will marry, or what sort of lives you'll lead, but don't think you're always going to be this happy, dear. We're almost too happy. Life isn't always like this."

The girl didn't know it then, but a time would come in her life when she would recall her mother's words over and over again. That evening, she assumed her mother referred to Grandma Hotta and her terrible misfortunes—it had already been some time since she'd last thought of her.

Several evenings later, a fireworks display was held at the beach. Their parents took them to watch it, and for the first time the children saw real fireworks shooting up high into the sky.

It was a few days after that when swarms of plump moth-like insects with dark brown wings came flying through the garden and along the rows of pine trees. According to her father, the swarms came in even greater numbers to the city—so many that they blotted out the sun. There was a long article about them in the newspaper: the insects were known as "one-stroke skippers."

The girl sent off two postcards to Grandma Hotta. The first one was about the fireworks display, and the second one about the one-stroke skippers. She began to feel a little bored now with the seaside and the river. Addressing the postcards, she found out that Grandma Hotta's given name was Tsuné.

Fall came, and the children had their father take them to the park with the tallest slide in Japan. It was their first visit since moving to their new house. In the summer, he'd told them, the slide would be burning hot, impossible to touch.

On November 3rd, a national holiday, crowds of people started gathering on the shore in the morning. They'd all heard about a naval parade with over a dozen ships. The ships were due to go by at around two o'clock, but just in case, the children urged their mother to take them there a good hour early.

The scheduled hour for the ships' arrival passed, and still nothing appeared on the horizon. In the meantime, the clear blue skies became sullen and gray. A mist seemed to have gathered out at sea. By now, quite a crowd had collected, and a row of stalls selling roasted chestnuts, paper balloons and other festive things had been set up, but with nothing else to entertain them except the heavy waves rolling in and crashing on the shore, the enthusiasm soon dampened. Some people started shivering in the cold sea spray.

It was three o'clock.

"When are the ships coming?" the girl's brother asked.

"Can't we go home?" her sister asked. "We can come back later."

"But what if we miss them?" the girl scolded her. "I'm not going with you." Bored, the children started to quarrel.

"There they are!" somebody shouted. "Now I can see them!"

The girl looked out to sea.

"Where?" she asked. "Where are they?"

"There," her mother pointed to the distance. "Way over to the left. See?" She lifted the girl's brother up in her arms.

All of them stood staring out to the left of the river mouth, where, far away, in the mist joining the low sky with the murky sea, they saw a slightly darker blur.

"*That's* a warship?" The girl's sister turned back and looked up at her mother.

"Keep your eye on it," her mother said. "It's getting bigger." The blur did seem to be getting longer. But it was just a vague shape slowly extending to the right, not taking on the outline of a warship at all.

The dark gray blur, flat and long like a sash, had reached the midpoint of the bay. Then, suddenly, near the head of the line, far out to sea, a single black silhouette of a ship came a bit more sharply into view. From the shore rose a shout of admiration. But the next minute, like a ghost, it faded back into the gray.

The day had grown quite dark. A dull drone, like an airplane engine, could be heard in the distance. The gray line was still there, but now it stretched from one side of the bay to the other, so they could no longer tell if it was even moving. At one moment, the girl realized no ships were appearing on the left any more. And then it began to rain.

She didn't write O-ie-san about watching the naval parade, nor their visit to the park with the very tall slide. The truth was, her city days were fast fading from her memory. She was preoccupied with the new friends she'd made at her new school. She invited them to her house to play, and was invited to theirs.

Sometimes, back when they'd been living in the city, she would come home from school in the afternoon, and her mother would say, after giving her a snack: "It's *sekki* today." *Sekki* was the last day of the month, the day for settling accounts. That all of the houses in their neighborhood were especially busy with their own affairs meant that she shouldn't go over to her friends' homes, and they couldn't come over to hers.

But in her new neighborhood, nobody seemed to bother with *sekki*. A few of her friends came from families with shops in the city like hers, but most of their fathers worked in an office or a company, so it didn't matter if she visited on the last day of the month. As they played at being grown-ups, she learned new words like "department manager," "company director," "bonus," and "transfer."

At her new school, fathers didn't come on parents' day to observe classes. Only mothers did. She found two of them particularly amazing: one was a lady who wore Western clothes and a hat with a fluffy crimson feather; the other hummed along with the children during their singing class. The girl had never seen such eccentric mothers in her old school.

A year passed. Soon the girl no longer noticed anything surprising about her new environment. Then, suddenly, yet another change came over her way of life—a change that didn't just affect her and her family, however. It was the beginning of outright war with China.

The army was starting its advance on enemy territory, winning victory after victory. The children were told by their teacher that they should study as hard as they could, so they wouldn't put their soldiers to shame. They should copy the example of the children of Japan's ally, Germany, who were not only robust and healthy, but obedient and industrious too. They were told the same thing again during the opening lecture of summer-school classes.

One evening, playing with sparklers in the garden, the children placed on the ground a spiral-shaped firecracker with something like a candle wick at one end. Holding a match up to this, the girl lit it carefully, and then jumped back. The firework started spitting out blue sparks, somersaulting madly about and bathing the garden in a dazzling white light.

The light turned yellow.

"It's changed color!" her sister cried.

Next it turned red. Her brother put his hands to his ears. The fiery husk leaped into the air, made a terrifically loud bang, and then lay still.

Her sister let her breath out, "That was my favorite."

Just then came a man's voice from the other side of the fence: "Are you the people playing with fireworks?"

"Yes," the girl answered, remembering the loud bang.

"Japan is at war!" the voice shouted, as if he'd been waiting to pounce on her reply. "What'll you do if Japan loses because you've wasted gunpowder on your games? Don't you dare play with fireworks ever again, do you hear? Children who do are not Japanese children! I'll be back to check."

The deep voice was replaced by the sound of wooden clogs on the road, retreating into the night.

The children were crestfallen. Even her brother—who had been excitedly pointing into the box of fireworks and saying, "This one next!"—was silent.

"What's the matter?" Their mother came out to the edge of the veranda. The children went up to her and explained.

Their father, who was in the sitting-room, commented, "What a jerk!" and went back to reading his newspaper.

"Well, but...," their mother said dubiously. "Are there any fireworks left?" she asked the children. "Or have you used them up?"

"We still have some," the girl replied.

"Well, let's put them away till the war's over. Mommy'll put them in a tin and store them very carefully."

The girl went to fetch the box of fireworks that she'd left on a rock in the garden. Only a few remained, but she could see two fat sticks and a spiral-shaped one her sister had said was her favorite kind. She felt very sad and disappointed as she handed the box over to her mother. The fireworks weren't the source of her sadness: even if she were encouraged to play with them, she knew she would never feel that same joy again.

That summer, the beach fireworks were canceled. When the fall term started, it was clear that the war would already affect the girl's life at school.

Once a week they had a lesson in national ethics: their teacher would lead a party of them to a nearby Shinto shrine and have them pray to the gods for victory in the war. And once a month, during composition class, they were all made to write letters of comfort and encouragement to soldiers at the front.

The girls set about avidly collecting foil—the silver paper, they were told, could be used to manufacture ammunition and military supplies. On the seventh of every month, in commemoration of the declaration of war on China, they would all bring their silver balls of foil in to school to hand them in. It wasn't only the size that counted: the balls had to be packed solid, or they weren't worth anything. The girls could never get enough foil from candy wrappers, so they also looked out for the silver linings of cigarette packs. She and her sister reminded their father over and over to bring home from the shop as many empty packs as he could, and to collect the clerks' too. But often he forgot, and on the night before the seventh, he would find his brand new packs torn open for their spoils and ransacked.

In the fall of that same year, the girl's class made a school trip to the city to view a Great Exhibition on Japan's Holy War. A large relief map showed the enemy territory, with the rising-sun flag sticking out of each place Japan occupied. They saw photographs of soldiers trudging through mud, followed by lines of horses, tanks, and cannon; more photographs taken in the thick of battle; and still more of the army marching in formation and entering a city that had capitulated at last. Grenades and bayonets, weapons of war, were laid out in neat rows for the children to see. Occupying the center of the room was a huge concrete bust of the enemy's supreme commander, his face a grotesque caricature and his head riddled with bullet holes.

A banner went up on the gatepost of a house in the neighborhood to mark a departure to the battlefront. Others soon followed. Every day on her way to school the girl would catch sight of yet another house that had given a family member to the war. Sometimes in the evenings, she heard cheers and shouts coming from two different places in the same neighborhood, celebrations for soldiers going off to fight.

One day at morning assembly her teacher appeared before them in military uniform, his head closely shaven. Her class walked with him all the way to the main train station, and saw him off to war.

In the spring two years later, the girl graduated from her grammar school and started going to girls' secondary school. Her new school was in the city near the family shop. By now the war was in full swing. She and her sister and her brother (who was in grammar school by this time) weren't collecting silver foil anymore. There was no more foil to be had.

The girl, who now wore a wristwatch, began commuting to school by bus and tram, but she still had to wear her primary-school uniform. Finally, in May, the secondary-school uniforms, sailor tops and skirts, were distributed. Though they seemed at first sight like the real thing, the proper navy blue serge, they were actually made of rayon, a cheap synthetic material with a brown tinge, which soon grew fuzzy and developed a nasty shine. Her mother taught her to place the skirt under her mattress every night with layers of newspaper between the sixteen pleats. Sharp in the morning, by midday the pleats would be gone.

All the students in the grades above her wore sailor suits made of proper navy blue wool. The girl felt so envious—of the deep blue of their material, of the way their blouses' collars and cuffs crisply folded back and their skirts' pleats opened and closed like a fan with each step. If only she'd been born a year earlier! Compared to theirs her version was miserable—and some girls in the next grade were her age by traditional count. If she had been born just one month earlier, in March, it would have been all right!

Again and again, the girl bemoaned her fate, weeping, to her parents. After a few weeks, some of her classmates came to school wearing uniforms made of the real material. They were hand-me-downs adjusted to fit, but they looked just like the ones the older girls wore. The girl couldn't help begging her parents to let her have a uniform like these.

Her father at last asked a tailor who was a friend of his whether he would make his daughter a uniform. The man said that he would. Her father had her drop by the family business one day after school, so that he could take her to the tailor to have her measurements taken.

The family had moved to the suburbs three years ago. The girl had been coming into the city to go to school, of course, and she'd also accompanied her mother sometimes on shopping trips. But she hadn't actually visited the family store, and she hadn't visited O-ie-san, either, not even once, since they had all gone to say goodbye.

Seeing her father busy with a customer, the girl told him she'd be over at Grandma Hotta's, and went back out to the street.

"Hey, wait." Her father came out after her. "I'm ready now. Let's go."

"But I want to visit Grandma Hotta."

"We don't have time."

She hurried to collect her satchel, which she'd left inside the store.

The girl could not take her eyes off the cloth that the tailor produced for her school uniform. She looked at it from far away, then peering at it closely, stroked its smooth edge. The more she looked at it, the more difficult it was to tear her eyes away.

"It is a fine piece of cloth," the tailor agreed. "And I'm afraid it's my last." As he occupied himself with taking the girl's measurements over her shabby uniform, he remarked: "I see what you mean. No wonder you hate to wear this."

When they left the tailor's, her father announced that he was taking her out to dinner. The two of them walked to a nearby traditional restaurant. To her surprise, however, when they went into one of the private rooms, somebody was already waiting there: Grandma Hotta.

"Sorry we're late," her father said to the old lady, after greeting her.

O-ie-san brushed this politely aside and turned to the girl, and gazed at her. "Oh, how you've grown. . . ." she said.

The girl found it very strange that her father hadn't said anything about inviting O-ie-san to dinner—and anyway, it had always been her mother who took care of the old lady. Her father hadn't objected, but she had never seen him talk to O-ie-san, let alone do anything kind for her.

But the girl knew better than to question him now.

The waitress placed a brocade scroll of gold and purple in front of her father. The girl wondered what it could be. He took hold of it without any signs of surprise.

"This place is still as nice as ever," O-ie-san remarked to the girl's father.

"What shall we order?" he said, unrolling the menu and studying it.

So O-ie-san must have come to this restaurant before, the girl realized. Quite a while ago, and more than once—when could that have been? Probably before the war began, maybe before she was old enough to go to school—perhaps even been before she was born.

When the dishes came to the table, the girl's father pressed O-ie-san to eat.

"Well then," the old lady said, bowing her head. "I will accompany you, if I may."

"Of course," he said.

"Of course!" echoed the little girl.

"What do you mean?" her father laughed at her. "*You're* the one accompanying *us.*"

That day, the girl's father, who was fond of saké, didn't drink a drop. The three of them first talked together about how the girl had been since the family moved to the suburbs. Soon, however, she found herself silently listening to the two adults. The names of people she'd never heard of cropped up, and some of them, it seemed, weren't even living any more.

Dinner came to an end, and it was time to say goodbye. They let O-ie-san take the first taxi and waited for a second, but none ever came.

"It doesn't matter," her father said, beckoning to her as he stepped out of the restaurant. "We can walk. We'll go for a stroll."

It was an evening in May, and only a little past eight o'clock, but even so, the streets and shops were almost totally deserted.

"Everything's gotten so dark and gloomy, Father," the girl remarked, carrying her satchel, as she walked with him.

"Hasn't it. Are you surprised?"

"I didn't think it would be this gloomy."

Since the area was once a thriving entertainment district, its lack of excitement was stark. Neon signs were against the law these days, so nothing lit up the night sky in bright colors any more. Very few of the shop windows had lights on. The whole district looked about to fall asleep, as if it were making a futile effort to keep awake only because it was supposed to be a place people spent money and enjoyed themselves. The restaurant owners had all closed up for the night. And everybody out in the dark streets was walking at a strangely brisk pace—not hurrying to reach any destination, the girl realized, but only because the streets were so empty that nobody got in their way. The sight made the girl feel even sadder about all the changes that had taken place.

"We should have telephoned Mother before we left," the girl said, suddenly remembering.

"It's all right," her father replied. "Mother knows we're together. But listen. I don't want you to go telling anyone at home that I invited Grandma Hotta out to dinner today."

"Why not?"

"Just don't."

"Not even Mother?"

"Not even Mother."

"Well, was it a secret from me, as well, really?"

"Don't be silly."

"But you didn't tell me anything before we got there."

"You found out when we arrived. Now listen: today we went to Suehiro restaurant and had steak, just the two of us. Understand?"

The girl nodded.

They walked along for a while, when she suddenly asked: "But why aren't I allowed to tell them anything about it at home?"

"You really don't understand, do you?" her father said, softly.

Many years later, the girl learned that O-ie-san's daughter had, in fact, killed herself. She had thrown herself into the sea, soon after finding out that Father was engaged to the woman who would become the girl's mother. O-ie-san, who had already lost her husband and all her possessions, was left quite alone in the world. But even though he was the cause of this final blow, O-ie-san loved the girl's father as if he were her own son.

By the time she heard the true story, the girl was nearly thirty years old. The person who told her couldn't say for sure if her mother knew of all that had happened. Of course, by that time, O-ie-san was long since dead. The girl's father, too, had passed away. Only her mother was still alive, but the girl never dared to ask her.

Walking through the deserted streets with her father, though, she still knew nothing.

"You see," her father explained to her. "I wanted to treat Grandma, just once, to something really nice, while she can still appreciate it. Everything is getting so scarce, now, with the war going on. Soon there won't be anything nice to eat. It doesn't matter for us. We'll be able to buy anything we want once Japan has won the war. But that's not the case for Grandma—that's why I thought I'd like to treat her to something special, now, while it's still possible. . . ."

That didn't explain why she should not tell her mother—after all, her mother had always lavished the old lady with kindness.

But all at once, the girl was strangely moved by her father's words.

"All right," she promised, as if she no longer cared about the reason. "I won't tell anybody! Not even Mother!"

Had she been moved by the intensity her father's words seemed to contain? No, more likely it was the intensity of her own feelings about "war."

The girl and her father walked on until they reached a bridge, where they stopped for a while. The river, once full of shimmering reflections from the shining neon night sky, now lay in complete darkness. Only the faint rippling of the water could be heard as the river flowing out to sea rose slowly with the incoming tide.

THE TRAIL OF YOUR BLOOD IN THE SNOW

Gabriel García Márquez

Translated from the Spanish by Edith Grossman

Gabriel José de la Concordia García Márquez (1927–2014) was a Colombian novelist, short-story writer, screenwriter and journalist. Considered one of the most significant authors of the twentieth century and one of the best in the Spanish language, he was awarded the 1982 Nobel Prize for Literature. Upon García Márquez's death in April 2014, Juan Manuel Santos, the President of Colombia, declared him "the greatest Colombian who ever lived". As a young man, he lived in a brothel known as "The Skyscraper". He was famously punched in the face by Mario Vargas Llosa at a theater in Mexico, beginning one of the most famous feuds in literary history. He has always refused to let *One Hundred Years of Solitude* be turned into a movie, claiming "they would cast someone like Robert Redford and most of us do not have relatives who look like Robert Redford". He smoked sixty cigarettes a day until he was almost fifty. He saw his eighty-seventh birthday.

At nightfall, when they reached the frontier, Nena Daconte realized that her finger with the wedding band on it was still bleeding. The Civil Guardsman, a rough wool blanket covering his patent-leather tricorn hat, examined their passports in the light of a carbide lantern as he struggled to keep his footing in the fierce wind blowing out of the Pyrenees. Although the two diplomatic passports were in perfect order, the guard raised the lantern to make certain that the photographs resembled their faces. Nena Daconte was almost a child, with the eyes of a happy bird, and molasses skin still radiant with the bright Caribbean sun in the mournful January gloom, and she was wrapped up to her chin in a mink coat that could not have been bought with the year's wages of the entire frontier garrison. Her husband, Billy Sánchez de Ávila, who drove the car, was a year younger and almost as beautiful, and he wore a plaid jacket and a baseball hat. Unlike his wife, he was tall and athletic and had the iron jaw of a timid thug. But what best revealed the status of them both was the silver automobile whose interior exhaled a breath of living animal; nothing like it had ever been seen along that impoverished border. The rear seat overflowed with suitcases that were too new and many gift boxes that were still unopened. It also held the tenor saxophone that had been the overriding passion of Nena

Daconte's life before she succumbed to the disquieting love of her tender beach hoodlum.

When the guard returned the stamped passports, Billy Sánchez asked him where they could find a pharmacy to treat his wife's finger, and the guard shouted into the wind that they should ask in Hendaye, on the French side. But the guards at Hendaye were inside a warm, well-lit glass sentry box, sitting at a table in their shirtsleeves and playing cards while they ate bread dipped in large glasses of wine, and all they had to see was the size and make of the car to wave them on into France. Billy Sánchez leaned on the horn several times, but the guards did not understand that he was calling them, and one of them opened the window and shouted with more fury than the wind:

"*Merde! Allez-vous-en!*"

Then Nena Daconte, wrapped in her coat up to her ears, got out of the car and asked the guard in perfect French where there was a pharmacy. As was his habit, the guard, his mouth full of bread, answered that it was no affair of his, least of all in a storm like this, and closed the window. But then he looked with more attention at the girl wrapped in the glimmer of natural mink and sucking her hurt finger, and he must have taken her for a magic vision on that fearful night, because his mood changed on the spot. He explained that the closest city was Biarritz, but in the middle of winter, and in that wind howling like wolves, they might not find a pharmacy open until Bayonne, a little farther on.

"Is it serious?" he asked.

"It's nothing," Nena Daconte said, smiling and showing him the finger with the diamond ring and the almost invisible scratch of the rose on the tip. "It was just a thorn."

Before they reached Bayonne, it began to snow again. It was no later than seven, but they found the streets deserted and the houses closed to the fury of the storm, and after turning many corners and not finding a pharmacy, they decided to drive on. The decision made Billy Sánchez happy. He had an insatiable passion for rare automobiles and a papa with too many feelings of guilt and more than enough resources to satisfy his whims, and he had never driven anything like the Bentley convertible that had been given to him as a wedding gift. His rapture at the wheel was so intense that the more he drove the less tired he felt. He wanted to reach Bordeaux that night. They had reserved the bridal suite at the Hotel Splendid, and not all the contrary winds or snow in the sky could hold him back. Nena Daconte, on the other hand, was exhausted, in particular by the last stretch of highway from Madrid, which was the edge of a cliff fit for mountain goats and lashed by hailstorms. And so after Bayonne she wrapped a handkerchief around her ring finger, squeezing it tightly to stop the blood that was still flowing, and fell into a deep sleep. Billy Sánchez did not notice until close to midnight, when the snow had ended and the wind in the pines stopped all at once and the sky over the pastureland filled with glacial stars. He had passed the sleeping lights of Bordeaux but stopped only to fill the tank at a station along the highway, for he still had the energy to drive to Paris without a break. He was so delighted with his big, £25,000 toy that he did not even ask himself if the radiant creature asleep at his side—the bandage on her ring finger soaked with blood and her adolescent dream pierced for the first time by lightning flashes of uncertainty—felt the same way too.

They had been married three days before and ten thousand kilometers away, in Cartagena de Indias, to the astonishment of his parents and the disillusionment of hers, and with the personal blessing of the archbishop. No one except the two of them understood the real basis or knew the origins of that unforeseeable love. It had begun three months before the wedding, on a Sunday by the sea, when Billy Sánchez's gang had stormed the women's dressing rooms at the Marbella beaches. Nena had just turned eighteen; she had come home from the Châtellenie school in Saint-Blaise, Switzerland, speaking four languages without an accent, and with a masterful knowledge of the tenor saxophone, and this was her first Sunday at the beach since her return. She had stripped to the skin and was about to put on her bathing suit when the panicked stampede and pirate yells broke out in the nearby cabanas, but she did not understand what was going on until the latch on her door splintered and she saw the most beautiful bandit imaginable standing in front of her. He wore nothing but a pair of fake leopard-skin string briefs, and he had the peaceful, elastic body and golden color of those who live by the ocean. Around his right wrist he wore the metal bracelet of a Roman gladiator, and around his right fist he had coiled an iron chain that he used as a lethal weapon, and around his neck hung a medal with no saint, which throbbed in silence to the pounding of his heart. They had attended the same elementary school and broken many piñatas at the same birthday parties, for they both came from the provincial families that had ruled the city's destiny at will since colonial days, but they had not seen each other for so many years that at first they did not recognize one another. Nena Daconte remained standing, motionless, doing nothing to hide her intense nakedness. Then Billy Sánchez carried out his puerile ritual: He lowered his leopard-skin briefs and showed her his respectable erected manhood. She looked straight at it, with no sign of surprise.

"I've seen them bigger and harder," she said, controlling her terror. "So think again about what you're doing, because with me you'll have to perform better than a black man."

In reality not only was Nena Daconte a virgin, but until that moment she had never seen a naked man, yet her challenge was effective. All that Billy Sánchez could think to do was to smash the fist rolled in chain against the wall and break his hand. She drove him to the hospital in her car and helped him endure his convalescence, and in the end they learned together how to make love the correct way. They spent the difficult June afternoons on the interior terrace of the house where six generations of Nena Daconte's illustrious ancestors had died; she played popular songs on the saxophone, and he, with his hand in a cast, contemplated her from the hammock in unrelieved stupefaction. The house had countless floor-to-ceiling windows that faced the fetid stillwater of the bay, and it was one of the largest and oldest in the district of La Manga, and beyond any doubt the ugliest. But the terrace with the checkered tiles where Nena Daconte played the saxophone was an oasis in the four-o'clock heat, and it opened onto a courtyard with generous shade and mango trees and banana plants, under which there was a grave and a nameless tombstone older than the house and the family's memory. Even those who knew nothing about music thought the saxophone was an anachronism in so noble a house. "It sounds like a ship," Nena Daconte's grandmother had said when she heard it for the first time. Nena Daconte's mother had tried in vain to have her play it another way and not, for the sake of comfort, with her skirt up around her thighs and her knees apart, and with a sensuality that did not seem essential to the music. "I don't care what instrument you play," she would say, "as long as you play it with your legs together."

But those ship's farewell songs and that feasting on love were what allowed Nena Daconte to break the bitter shell around Billy Sánchez. Beneath his sad reputation as an ignorant brute, which he had upheld with great success because of the confluence of two illustrious family names, she discovered a frightened, tender orphan. While the bones in his hand were knitting, she and Billy Sánchez learned to know each other so well that even he was amazed at the fluidity with which love occurred when she took him to her virgin's bed one rainy afternoon when they were alone in the house. Every day at the same time, for almost two weeks, they caroused, passionate and naked, beneath the astonished gaze of the portraits of civil warriors and insatiable grandmothers who had preceded them in the paradise of that historic bed. Even in the pauses between love they remained naked and kept the windows open, breathing the air of ships' garbage wafting in from the bay, its smell of shit, and listening in the silence of the saxophone to the daily sounds from the courtyard, the single note of the frog beneath the banana plants, the drop of water falling on nobody's grave, the natural movements of life that they had not had the opportunity to learn before.

When her parents returned home, Nena Daconte and Billy Sánchez had progressed so far in love that the world was not big enough for anything else, and they made love anytime, anyplace, trying to reinvent it each time they did. At first they struggled in the sports cars with which Billy Sánchez's papa tried to quiet his own feelings of guilt. Then, when the cars became too easy for them, they would go at night into the deserted cabanas of Marbella where destiny had first brought them together, and during the November carnival they even went in costume to the rooms for hire in the old slave district of Getsemaní, under the protection of the matrons who until a few months before had been obliged to endure Billy Sánchez and his chain-wielding gang. Nena Daconte gave herself over to furtive love with the same frenetic devotion that she had once wasted on the saxophone, until her tamed bandit at last understood what she had meant when she said he would have to perform like a black man. Billy Sánchez always returned her love, with skill and the same enthusiasm. When they were married, they fulfilled their vow to love each other over the Atlantic, while the stewardesses slept and they were crammed into the airplane lavatory, overcome more by laughter than by pleasure. Only they knew then, twenty-four hours after the wedding, that Nena Daconte had been pregnant for two months.

And so when they reached Madrid they were far from being two sated lovers, but they had enough discretion to behave like pure newlyweds. Their parents had arranged everything. Before they left the plane, a protocol officer came to the first-class cabin to give Nena Daconte the white mink coat with gleaming black trim that was her wedding present from her parents. He gave Billy Sánchez the kind of shearling jacket that was all the rage that winter, and the unmarked keys to a surprise car waiting for him at the airport.

Their country's diplomatic mission welcomed them in the official reception room. Not only were the ambassador and his wife old friends of both families, but he was the doctor who had delivered Nena Daconte, and he was waiting for her with a bouquet of roses so radiant and fresh that even the dewdrops seemed artificial. She greeted them both with false kisses, uncomfortable with her somewhat premature status as bride, and then accepted the roses. As she took them she pricked her finger on a thorn, but she handled the mishap with a charming ruse.

"I did it on purpose," she said, "so you'd notice my ring."

In fact, the entire diplomatic mission marveled at the splendor of the ring, which must have cost a fortune, not so much because of the quality of the diamonds as for its well-preserved antiquity. But no one noticed that her finger had begun to bleed. They all turned their attention to the new car. The ambassador's amusing idea had been to bring it to the airport and have it wrapped in cellophane and tied with an enormous gold ribbon. Billy Sánchez did not even notice his ingenuity. He was so eager to see the car that he tore away the wrapping all at once and stood there breathless. It was that year's Bentley convertible, with genuine leather upholstery. The sky looked like a blanket of ashes, a cutting, icy wind blew out of the Guadarrama, and it was not a good time to be outside, but Billy Sánchez still had no notion of the cold. He kept the diplomatic mission in the outdoor parking lot, unaware that they were freezing for the sake of courtesy, until he finished looking over the smallest details of the car. Then the ambassador sat beside him to direct him to the official residence, where a luncheon had been prepared. En route he pointed out the most famous sights in the city, but Billy Sánchez seemed attentive only to the magic of the car.

It was the first time he had traveled outside his country. He had gone through all the private and public schools, repeating courses over and over again, until he was left adrift in a limbo of indifference. The initial sight of a city other than his own, the blocks of ashen houses with their lights on in the middle of the day, the bare trees, the distant ocean, everything increased a feeling of desolation that he struggled to keep in a corner of his heart. But soon he fell, without being aware of it, into the first trap of forgetting. A sudden, silent storm, the earliest of the season, had broken overhead, and when they left the ambassador's residence after lunch to begin their drive to France, they found the city covered with radiant snow. Then Billy Sánchez forgot the car, and with everyone watching he shouted with joy, threw fistfuls of snow over his head, and wearing his new coat, rolled on the ground in the middle of the street.

Nena Daconte did not realize that her finger was bleeding until they left Madrid on an afternoon that had turned transparent after the storm. It surprised her, because when she had accompanied the ambassador's wife, who liked to sing Italian arias after official luncheons, on the saxophone, her ring finger had hardly bothered her. Later, while she was telling her husband the shortest routes to the border, she sucked her finger in an unconscious way each time it bled, and only when they reached the Pyrenees did she think of looking for a pharmacy. Then she succumbed to the overdue dreams of the past few days, and when she awoke with a start to the nightmarish impression that the car was going through water, it was a long while before she remembered the handkerchief wrapped around her finger. She saw on the illuminated clock on the dashboard that it was after three, made her mental calculations, and only then realized that they had passed Bordeaux, as well as Angoulême and Poitiers, and were driving along the flooded dike of the Loire. Moonlight filtered through the mist, and the silhouettes of castles through the pines seemed to come from fairy tales. Nena Daconte, who knew the region by heart, estimated that they were about three hours from Paris, and Billy Sánchez, undaunted, was still at the wheel.

"You're a wild man," she said. "You've been driving for more than eleven hours and you haven't eaten a thing."

The intoxication of the new car kept him going. He had not slept very much on the plane, but he felt wide awake and energetic enough to be in Paris by dawn.

"I'm still full from the embassy lunch," he said. And he added, with no apparent logic, "After all, in Cartagena they're just leaving the movies. It must be about ten o'clock."

Even so, Nena Daconte was afraid he would fall asleep at the wheel. She opened one of the many presents they had received in Madrid and tried to put a piece of candied orange in his mouth. But he turned away.

"Real men don't eat sweets," he said.

A little before Orléans the fog cleared, and a very large moon lit the snow-covered fields, but traffic became more difficult because enormous produce trucks and wine tankers merged onto the highway, all heading for Paris. Nena Daconte would have liked to help her husband with the driving, but she did not dare even to suggest it: He had informed her the first time they went out together that nothing is more humiliating for a man than to be driven by his wife. She felt clearheaded after almost five hours of sound sleep, and she was happy too that they had not stopped at a hotel in the French provinces, which she had known since she was a little girl making countless trips there with her parents. "There's no more beautiful countryside in the world," she said, "but you can die of thirst and not find anyone who'll give you a free glass of water." She was so convinced of this that at the last minute she had put a cake of soap and a roll of toilet paper in her overnight bag, because in French hotels there was never any soap, and the paper in the bathrooms was last week's newspapers cut into little squares and hung from a nail. The only thing she regretted at that moment was having wasted an entire night without making love. Her husband's reply was immediate.

"I was just thinking it must be fantastic to fuck in the snow," he said. "Right here, if you want."

Nena Daconte gave it serious thought. The moonlit snow at the edge of the highway looked fluffy and warm, but as they approached the suburbs of Paris the traffic grew heavier, and there were clusters of lit factories and numerous workers on bicycles. If it had not been winter, it would have been broad daylight by now.

"We'd better wait until Paris," said Nena Daconte. "All nice and warm in a bed with clean sheets, like married people."

"It's the first time you've turned me down," he said.

"Of course," she replied. "It's the first time we've been married."

A little before dawn they washed their faces and urinated at a roadside restaurant and had coffee with warm croissants at the counter, where truck drivers drank red wine with breakfast. In the bathroom Nena Daconte saw that she had bloodstains on her blouse and skirt, but she did not try to wash them out. She tossed her blood-soaked handkerchief into the trash, moved her wedding ring to her left hand, and washed the wounded finger with soap and water. The scratch was almost invisible. Yet as soon as they were back in the car it began to bleed again, and Nena Daconte hung her arm out the window, certain that the icy air from the fields had cauterizing properties. This tactic proved useless too, but she was still unconcerned. "If anyone wants to find us it'll be very easy," she said with her natural charm. "All they have to do is follow the trail of my blood in the snow." Then she thought more about what she had said, and her face bloomed in the first light of dawn.

"Imagine," she said. "A trail of blood in the snow all the way from Madrid to Paris. Wouldn't that make a good song?"

She did not have time to think again. In the suburbs of Paris her finger bled in an uncontrollable flood, and she felt as if her soul were escaping through the scratch. She had tried to stop the flow with the toilet paper she carried in her bag, but it took longer to wrap her finger than to throw the strips of bloody paper out the window. The clothes she was wearing, her coat, the car seats were all becoming soaked, in a gradual but irreparable process. Billy Sánchez became really frightened and insisted on looking for a pharmacy, but by then she knew this was no matter for pharmacists.

"We're almost at the Porte d'Orléans," she said. "Go straight ahead, along Avenue du Général Leclerc, the big one with all the trees, and then I'll tell you what to do."

This was the most difficult part of the trip. The Avenue du Général Leclerc was jammed in both directions, an infernal knot of small cars and motorcycles and the enormous trucks that were trying to reach the central markets. The useless clamor of the horns made Billy Sánchez so agitated that he shouted insults in chain-wielding language at several drivers and even tried to get out of the car to hit one of them, but Nena Daconte managed to convince him that although the French were the rudest people in the world, they never had fistfights. It was one more proof of her good judgment, because at that moment Nena Daconte was struggling not to lose consciousness.

It took them more than an hour just to get around the Léon de Belfort traffic circle. Cafés and stores were lit as if it were midnight, for it was a typical Tuesday in an overcast, filthy Parisian January, with a persistent rain that never solidified into snow. But there was less traffic on the Avenue Denfert-Rochereau, and after a few blocks Nena Daconte told her husband to turn right, and he parked outside the emergency entrance of a huge, gloomy hospital.

She had to be helped out of the car, yet she did not lose her calm or her lucidity. As she lay on the gurney waiting for the doctor on duty, she answered the nurse's routine questions regarding her identity and medical history. Billy Sánchez carried her bag and gripped her left hand, where she was wearing her wedding ring; it felt languid and cold, and her lips had lost their color. He stayed at her side, holding her hand, until the doctor arrived and made a brief examination of her wounded finger. He was a very young man with a shaved head and skin the color of old copper. Nena Daconte paid no attention to him, but turned a livid smile on her husband.

"Don't be afraid," she said, with her invincible humor. "The only thing that can happen is that this cannibal will cut off my hand and eat it."

The doctor completed his examination, then surprised them by speaking very correct Spanish with a strange Asian accent.

"No, children," he said. "This cannibal would rather die of hunger than cut off so beautiful a hand."

They were embarrassed, but the doctor calmed them with a good-natured gesture. Then he ordered the cot wheeled away, and Billy Sánchez tried to follow, clutching his wife's hand. The doctor took his arm and stopped him.

"Not you," he said. "She's going to intensive care."

Nena Daconte smiled again at her husband, and continued waving good-bye until she disappeared from sight at the end of the corridor. The doctor stayed behind, studying the information that the nurse had written on a clipboard. Billy Sánchez called to him.

"Doctor," he said. "She's pregnant."

"How far along?"

"Two months."

The doctor did not give this fact as much importance as Billy Sánchez had expected. "You were right to tell me," he said, and walked after the cot. Billy Sánchez was left standing in the mournful room that smelled of sick people's sweat, was left not knowing what to do as he looked down the empty corridor where they had taken Nena Daconte, and then he sat down on the wooden bench where other people were waiting. He did not know how long he sat there, but when he decided to leave the hospital it was night again and still raining, and oppressed by the weight of the world, he still did not know what to do.

Nena Daconte was admitted at nine-thirty on Tuesday, January 7, as I learned years later from the hospital records. That first night, Billy Sánchez slept in the car, which was parked outside the emergency entrance, and very early the next day he ate six boiled eggs and drank two cups of café au lait in the closest cafeteria he could find, for he had not had a full meal since Madrid. Then he went back to the emergency room to see Nena Daconte, but they managed to make him understand that he had to use the main entrance. There, at last, an Asturian maintenance man helped him communicate with the receptionist, who in fact confirmed that Nena Daconte had been admitted to the hospital, but that visitors were allowed only on Tuesdays, from nine to four. That is, not for another six days. He tried to see the doctor who spoke Spanish, whom he described as a black man with a shaved head, but nobody could tell him anything on the basis of two such simple details.

Reassured by the news that Nena Daconte was in the registry, he returned to the car. A traffic officer made him park two blocks away, in a very narrow street, on the even-numbered side. Across the street was a renovated building with a sign: "Hôtel Nicole." It had only one star, and the reception area was very small, with just a sofa and an old upright piano, but the owner, whose voice was high and fluty, could understand clients in any language as long as they had money. Billy Sánchez with his eleven suitcases and nine gift boxes took the only free room, a triangular garret on the ninth floor, which he came to after a breathless climb up a circular staircase that smelled of boiled cauliflower. The walls were covered with a sad paper, and there was no room at the one window for anything but the dim light from an interior courtyard. There was a double bed, a large armoire, a straight-backed chair, a portable bidet, and a washstand with a bowl and pitcher, so that the only way to be in the room was to lie on the bed. Worse than old, everything was forlorn, but very clean, and with a salutary odor of recent medicine.

If he had spent the rest of his life in the attempt, Billy Sánchez could not have deciphered the enigmas of that world founded on a talent for miserliness. He never solved the mystery of the stairway light that went out before he reached his floor, and he never discovered how to turn it on again. He needed half a morning to learn that on the landing of each floor there was a little room with a toilet that one flushed by pulling a chain, and he already had decided to use it in the dark, when he discovered by accident that the light went on when the lock was bolted on the inside, so that no one would forget to turn it off again. The shower, which was at the end of the hall, and which he insisted on using twice a day as he did in his own country, one paid for separately, and in cash, and the hot water, controlled from the office, ran out in three minutes. Yet Billy Sánchez was thinking with sufficient clarity to realize that this way of doing things, so different from his own, was in any case better than being outdoors in January, and he felt so confused and alone that he could not understand how he ever had lived without the help and protection of Nena Daconte.

When he went up to his room on Wednesday morning, he threw himself face-down on the bed with his coat on, thinking about the miraculous creature who was still bleeding two blocks away, and he soon fell into so natural a sleep that when he awoke his watch said five o'clock, but he could not tell whether it was afternoon or morning, or what day of the week it was, or what city, with windows lashed by wind and rain. He waited, awake in the bed, always thinking about Nena Daconte, until he confirmed that in fact day was breaking. Then he went to have breakfast in the same cafeteria as the day before, and there he learned it was Thursday. The lights in the hospital were on and it had stopped raining, and so he leaned against the trunk of a chestnut tree outside the main entrance, where doctors and nurses in white coats walked in and out, hoping he would see the Asian physician who had admitted Nena Daconte. He did not see him then, or that afternoon after lunch, when he had to end his vigil because he was freezing. At seven he had another café au lait and two hard-boiled eggs that he chose from the display counter himself after two days of eating the same thing in the same place. When he went back to the hotel to sleep, he found his car alone on one side of the street, with a parking ticket on the windshield, while all the others were parked on the opposite side. It was a difficult task for the porter at the Hôtel Nicole to explain to him that on odd-numbered days one could park on the odd-numbered side of the street, and on even-numbered days on the other side. Such rationalist stratagems proved incomprehensible to a purebred Sánchez de Ávila, who almost two years before had driven the mayor's official car into a neighborhood movie theater and wreaked absolute havoc while the intrepid police stood by. He under-stood even less when the porter advised him to pay the fine but not to move his car at that hour, because he only would have to move it again at midnight. As he tossed and turned on the bed and could not sleep, he thought for the first time not only about Nena Daconte, but about his own grievous nights in the gay bars at the public market in Cartagena of the Caribbean. He remembered the taste of fried fish and coconut rice in the restaurants along the dock, where the schooners from Aruba moored. He remembered his house, the walls covered with heartsease, where it would be just seven o'clock the night before, and he saw his papa in silk pajamas reading the newspaper in the coolness of the terrace.

He remembered his mother—no one ever seemed to know where she was, regardless of the hour—his desirable, talkative mother, who wore a Sunday dress and a rose behind her ear when night fell, stifling with heat in the encumbrance of splendid fabric. One afternoon when he was seven years old, he had gone into her room without knocking and found her naked in bed with one of her casual lovers. That mishap, which they had never mentioned, established a complicitous relationship between them that proved more useful than love. But he was not conscious of that, or of so many other terrible things in his only child's loneliness, until the night he found himself tossing in the bed of a sad Parisian garret, with no one to tell his sorrows to, and in a fierce rage with himself because he could not bear his desire to cry.

It was a beneficial insomnia. He got out of bed on Friday wounded by the evil night he had spent, but determined to give definition to his life. He decided at last to break the lock on his suitcase and change his clothes, since all the keys were in Nena Daconte's bag, along with most of their money and the address book where, perhaps, he might have found the number of someone they knew in Paris. At his usual cafeteria he realized that he had learned to say hello in French, and to ask for ham sandwiches and café au lait. He knew it never would be possible to order butter or any kind of eggs because he never would learn to pronounce the words, but butter was always served with the bread, and the hard-boiled eggs were displayed on the counter, where he could take them without having to ask for them. Moreover, by the third day, the waiters recognized him and helped when he tried to make himself understood. And so at lunch on Friday, as he was trying to set his head to rights, he ordered a veal fillet with fried potatoes and a bottle of wine. He felt so good then that he ordered another bottle, drank almost half of it, and crossed the street with the firm resolve to force his way into the hospital. He did not know where to find Nena Daconte, but the providential image of the Asian doctor was fixed in his mind, and he was sure he would find him. He did not go in through the main door but used the emergency entrance, which had seemed less well guarded to him, but he could not get past the corridor where Nena Daconte had waved good-bye. A guard with a blood-spattered smock asked him something as he walked by, and he paid no attention. The man followed him, repeating the same question over and over in French, and at last grabbed him by the arm with so much force that he stopped him short. Billy Sánchez tried to shake him off with a chain-wielder's trick, and then the guard shit on his mother in French, twisted his arm at the shoulder into a hammerlock, and without forgetting to shit a thousand times on his whore of a mother almost carried him to the door, raging with pain, and tossed him out into the middle of the street like a sack of potatoes.

That afternoon, aching with the punishment he had received, Billy Sánchez began to be an adult. He decided, as Nena Daconte would have done, to turn to his ambassador. The hotel porter, who despite his unsociable appearance was very helpful and very patient with languages, found the number and address of the embassy in the telephone book and wrote them down on a card. A very amiable woman answered the phone, and in no time Billy Sánchez recognized the diction of the Andes in her slow, colorless voice. He started by identifying himself, using his full name, certain the two great families would impress the woman, but the voice on the telephone did not change. He heard her recite her lesson by heart: His Excellency the Ambassador was not in his office at the moment and was not expected until the next day, but in any event he could be seen only by appointment, and then only under extraordinary circumstances. Billy Sánchez knew he would not find Nena Daconte by this route either, and he thanked the woman for the information with as much amiability as she had used in giving it. Then he took a taxi and went to the embassy.

It was at 22 Rue des Champs-Élysées, in one of the quietest districts in Paris, but the only thing that impressed Billy Sánchez, as he himself told me in Cartagena de Indias many years later, was that for the first time since his arrival the sunshine was as bright as in the Caribbean, and the Eiffel Tower loomed over the city against a radiant sky. The functionary who received him in the name of the ambassador looked as if he had just recovered from a fatal disease, not only because of his black suit, oppressive collar, and mourning tie, but also because of his judicious gestures and hushed voice. He understood Billy Sánchez's concern but reminded him, without losing any of his discretion, that they were in a civilized country whose strict norms were founded on the most ancient and learned criteria, in contrast to the barbaric Americas, where all one had to do to go into a hospital was bribe the porter. "No, dear boy," he said. His only recourse was to submit to the rule of reason and wait until Tuesday.

"After all, there are only four days left," he concluded. "In the meantime, go to the Louvre. It is worth seeing."

When he went out, Billy Sánchez found himself on the Place de la Concorde without knowing what to do. He saw the Eiffel Tower above the rooftops, and it seemed so close that he tried to walk there along the quays. But he soon realized it was farther than it appeared and kept changing position as he looked for it. And so he began to think about Nena Daconte as he sat on a bench along the Seine. He watched the tugs pass under the bridges, and to him they did not look like boats but itinerant houses, with red roofs and flower pots on the windowsills and clotheslines stretched across the deck. For a long while he watched a motionless fisherman, with a motionless rod and a motionless line in the current, and he tired of waiting for something to move, until it started growing dark and he decided to take a taxi back to the hotel. That was when he realized he did not know its name or address and had no idea where in Paris the hospital was located.

Stupefied by panic, he went into the first café he came to, asked for a cognac, and tried to put his thoughts in order. While he was thinking he saw himself repeated over and over and from many different angles in the numerous mirrors on the walls, saw that he was frightened and alone, and for the first time since the day of his birth he thought about the reality of death. But with the second glass of cognac he felt better, and had the providential idea of returning to the embassy. He looked in his pocket for the card with its address, and discovered that the name and street number of the hotel were printed on the other side. He was so shaken by the experience that he did not leave his room again for the entire weekend except to eat and move the car from one side of the street to the other. For three days the same filthy rain that had been falling the morning they had arrived continued to fall. Billy Sánchez, who had never read an entire book, wished he had one to fend off his boredom as he lay on the bed, but the only books he found in his wife's suitcases were in languages other than Spanish. And so he kept waiting for Tuesday, contemplating the peacocks repeated across the wallpaper and always thinking about Nena Daconte. On Monday he straightened the room, wondering what she would say if she found it in that state, and only then did he discover that the mink coat was stained with dried blood. He spent the afternoon washing it with the perfumed soap he found in her overnight bag, until he succeeded in restoring it to what it had been when it was carried onto the airplane in Madrid.

Tuesday dawned overcast and icy, but without the rain. Billy Sánchez was up at six and waited at the hospital entrance with a throng of relatives bringing gifts and bouquets of flowers to the patients. He went in with the crowd, carrying the mink coat over his arm, asking no questions and with no idea where Nena Daconte could be, but sustained by the certainty that he would meet the Asian doctor. He walked through a very large interior courtyard, with flowers and wild birds, and on each side were the wards: women to the right and men to the left. Following the other visitors, he entered the women's ward. He saw a long line of female patients in hospital gowns sitting on their beds, illuminated by the great light of the windows, and he even thought it was all much more cheerful than one could imagine from the outside. He reached the end of the corridor and then walked back, until he was certain that none of the patients was Nena Daconte. Then he walked around the exterior gallery again, peering through the windows at the men's ward, until he thought he recognized the doctor he was looking for.

And in fact he had. The doctor was examining a patient with some other doctors and several nurses. Billy Sánchez went into the ward, moved one of the nurses away from the group, and stood facing the Asian doctor, who was bent over the patient. He spoke to him. The doctor raised his sorrowful eyes, thought a moment, then recognized him.

"But where the hell have you been?" he asked.

Billy Sánchez was perplexed.

"In the hotel," he said. "Right here, around the corner."

Then he found out. Nena Daconte had bled to death at ten minutes past seven on the evening of Thursday, January 9, after sixty hours of failed efforts by the most qualified specialists in France. She had been lucid and serene to the end, instructing them to look for her husband at the Plaza-Athénée, where she and Billy Sánchez had a reservation, and giving them the necessary information for reaching her parents. The embassy had been informed by an urgent cable from the Foreign Office on Friday, when Nena Daconte's parents were already flying to Paris. The ambassador himself took care of the formalities for the embalming and the funeral, and stayed in touch with the police prefecture in Paris during the efforts to locate Billy Sánchez. An emergency bulletin with his description was broadcast from Friday night to Sunday afternoon over radio and television, and during those forty hours he was the most wanted man in France. His photograph, found in Nena Daconte's handbag, was displayed everywhere. Three Bentley convertibles of the same model had been located, but none of them was his.

Nena Daconte's parents had arrived at noon on Saturday and sat with the body in the hospital chapel, hoping until the last minute that Billy Sánchez would be found. His parents also had been informed and were ready to fly to Paris, but in the end they did not because of some confusion in the telegrams. The funeral took place on Sunday at two in the afternoon, only two hundred meters from the sordid hotel room where Billy Sánchez lay in agonies of loneliness for the love of Nena Daconte. The functionary who had received him at the embassy told me years later that he himself received the telegram from the Foreign Office an hour after Billy Sánchez left his office, and went to look for him in the discreet bars along the Rue du Faubourg-Saint-Honoré. He confessed to me that he had not paid much attention to Billy Sánchez when he saw him, because he never imagined that the boy from the coast, dazzled by the novelty of Paris and wearing such an unbecoming shearling coat, could have so illustrious an origin in his favor.

On the same night when he endured his desire to cry with rage, Nena Daconte's parents called off the search and took away the embalmed body in the metal coffin, and those who saw it repeated over and over again for many years that they never had seen a more beautiful woman, dead or alive. And therefore when Billy Sánchez at last entered the hospital on Tuesday morning, the burial had already taken place in the mournful cemetery of La Manga, a few meters from the house where they had deciphered the first keys to their happiness. The Asian doctor who told Billy Sánchez about the tragedy wanted to give him some tranquilizers in the hospital waiting room, but he refused. Billy Sánchez left without saying good-bye, without anything to say thank you for, thinking that the only thing he needed with great urgency was to find somebody and beat his brains out with a chain in revenge for his own misfortune. When he walked out of the hospital, he did not even realize that snow with no trace of blood was falling from the sky, in tender, bright flakes that looked like the downy feathers of doves, or that there was a festive air on the streets of Paris, because it was the first big snowfall in ten years.

TEARS FOR SALE

Samira 'Azzam

Translated from the Arabic by Lena Jayyusi and Elizabeth Fernea

Samira 'Azzam (1927–1967). Born in Mandatory Palestine, the daughter of a Christian Orthodox goldsmith, Samira 'Azzam left her homeland during the Palestinian exodus in 1948. In Iraq, she worked as headmistress of an all-girls school. Her first collection of short stories, *Small Things* (1954), examines women's role in Palestinian society. She published two further collections of short stories *The Big Shadow* and *The Clock and the Man.*

I never knew how Khazna could manage to be, at the same time, both a professional mourner for the dead and a professional beautician for brides. I had heard a lot about Khazna from my mother and her friends, but actually saw her for the first time when a neighbor of ours died. He was a man wasted by illness long before the age of fifty. So we were not surprised one day when a neighbor called out to my mother and announced without sadness, "Ah, Um Hassan! Around us and not upon us . . . so-and-so has passed away . . ."

The wake for this man was a chance for me to sneak off unobserved with the boys and girls of the neighborhood. I felt I was going to spend an exciting day. I was not against that at all. We would all be able to stare at the waxen face of the dead man, to watch how his wife and daughters wept for him, and to see how the hired mourners clapped rhythmically while they chanted their well-worn phrases of lamentations and mourning.

Hand in hand, my girlfriend and I were able to squeeze between the legs of the people crowding in front of the dead man's house, to a place not far from the door. Here were numerous children who had come, like us, to taste the excitement that accompanies death. We did not move from our places until a big fist, Khazna's fist, pushed us all aside as she stood, filling the door with her great, broad frame. In a matter of seconds she had assumed an emotional face, unraveled her two braids of hair, extracted from her pocket a black headband that she tied around her forehead, and let out a cry so terrible that I could feel my heart contract. Khazna pushed her way through the women crowded into the room to a corner where a jug of liquid indigo stood. She daubed her hands and face with the indigo till her face was so streaked with blue it looked like one of the masks salesmen hung up in their shops during feast days. Then she took her place at the dead man's head, let out another piercing cry, and began to beat her breast violently. From her tongue rolled out rhythmic phrases that the women repeated after her, and tears began to flow from their eyes. It seemed as though

Khazna was not just lamenting that one dead man, our neighbor, but, rather, was weeping for all of the town's dead, arousing in one woman anguish over a lost husband and in another sorrow over a dead son or departed brother.

Soon one could no longer tell which of the women was the dead man's wife or sister. If the keening women paused a moment in fatigue, Khazna would revive their sorrow with a special mournful chant, following it with another terrible cry. The tears would gush forth once more, the sobbing would become more intense, the sounds of anguish greater. And in this room of grief, Khazna was the center, with a tongue that did not tire and a voice like an owl, a large woman with an uncanny ability to affect sorrow. If one could say that reward is given in exchange for the amount of effort expended, then only a sum so large as to move in Khazna this seemingly inexhaustible store of anguish could compensate her for this tremendous performance of sorrow.

I still remember Khazna when the men came to carry the dead body to its wooden coffin. She stood beside the deceased, begging the pallbearers to be gentle with the dear one, to have mercy on him and not be too quick to cut his ties with this world. One of the men, fed up with Khazna's chatter, finally pushed her away so that he and his companions could lift the body. Black scarves were waved in farewell, and the women's exhortations poured forth, this one charging the dead man to greet her husband in the other world, that one asking him to speak to her mother there. Khazna proceeded to fill the neighborhood with shrieks so loud they could be heard above all the other cries.

Once the men had left the house, the procession of mourners made its way slowly down our street, bearing the coffin upon which the fez of the departed one bounced up and down. Then it was time for the women to rest a little from the grief they had imposed on themselves, and they were invited to eat at a table set in one of the inside rooms. Khazna was the first to wash her face, roll up her sleeves, and stuff her big mouth with as much food as her hand could reach. But I also noticed that she was careful to secrete some extra food in her bosom. If she felt that someone noticed her doing this, she would smile wearily and say, "It's just a bit for my daughter, Mas'ouda . . . I got the news of death before I had time to fix her something to eat. And, of course, eating the food of the wake is an act pleasing to God."

That day I realized that Khazna was not a woman like other women and that she was almost more necessary for the ritual of death than the deceased. I never forgot her big mouth, her dreadful grip, her wild flowing hair. Whenever I heard of a death, I would head for the house of the deceased with my girlfriend, propelled by my curiosity, my desire for sensation, my search for something I could tell my mother about if she herself were not there. The sight of Khazna herself would divert me from the face of the deceased. I would find my eyes riveted on her person, watching her hands as they moved from her breast to her face to her head. Those blows, together with the dirges and chants, seemed to have a special rhythm, a rhythm designed to intensify the pain of the family's loss and instill anguish in the visitors at the wake.

Some time passed before I had the opportunity to see the other face of Khazna —as she appeared in her role as *mashta*, or beautician for the brides. There at the wedding she was—the same black hair but now combed back and adorned with flowers, the same ugly face but made up so it scarcely resembled that mourning face streaked with indigo. Outlined with kohl, her eyes seemed much larger. Her wrists wore heavy bracelets (who said the trade of death was not profitable?), and her mouth would open in loud laughter and only half close again, while she chewed a huge piece of gum between her yellow teeth.

That day I began to understand that Khazna had as special a place with brides as she had with the dead. Her task began the morning of the wedding day when she would appear in order to remove the bride's unwanted hair with a thick sugar syrup. She would pencil the bride's eyebrows while conveying in whispers (or what she thought were whispers) the sexual obligations to come. If the girl's face reddened in embarrassment, Khazna would first laugh mockingly and then reassure her that two or three nights would be enough to make an expert of any bride. She, Khazna, would guarantee this, she insisted, provided the bride used a perfumed soap and a cream hair lotion (which she could, of course, buy from Khazna herself).

In the evening the women would come dressed up and perfumed, wearing flowers in their hair or on their shoulders, to hover round the bride on her dais. Then Khazna's ululations would rip the sky over our town.

Khazna performed memorably on the dance floor, circling constantly while she joked with the women, using words so rude they provoked laughter. And when, amidst the winks of the guests, the bridegroom would come to take his bride, Khazna would conduct the couple ceremoniously to the door of the bridal chamber, for she had the right to watch over them. At that time I did not really understand why Khazna took such care to stand at the door of the bridal chamber, waiting for something, in curiosity and nervousness. But as soon as a sign was given, a knock at the door and the showing of a bloodied handkerchief, would let out a memorable ululation for which the bridegroom's family had apparently been waiting.

When the men heard that ululation of Khazna's, they would twirl their moustaches. The women would rise together. In a single movement and from every direction or corner would emerge a ululation of pride and exultation. Khazna would then depart, content, her pocket full, followed by expressions of good wishes on all sides that she would see a happy wedding day for her daughter.

Mas'ouda's happy wedding day was something to which Khazna looked forward and for which she put away bracelets and other treasures. For she had no one else to inherit all she had collected from the town's wakes and weddings.

But heaven decreed that Khazna should not have her happiness. That summer the germs of typhoid fever took it upon themselves to create a season of death for Khazna unlike any other season in memory. I will not forget that summer. The sun would not rise without another death in the town. It was said that in one day alone Khazna lamented three clients.

The typhoid fever did not miss Mas'ouda, and death had no pity; it chose her despite Khazna's pleas.

One morning the town woke up to the news of the death of Khazna's little one, and people's curiosity was aroused almost at the same moment the wretched child's life ended.

How would Khazna grieve for her daughter ... would it be in a manner unknown to ordinary mourning occasions? What chants and dirges would she recite in her own bereavement? Would it be a wake that would turn the whole neighborhood upside down?

I could not overcome my own curiosity and my pity for Khazna's loss, so I went to her, I sought her, as did crowds of other women who went to repay some of their own debt to her over the years.

Her single room was small. About twenty people sat, and the rest hovered near the door. I did not hear Khazna's voice and searched for her, looking across the tops of peoples' heads. To my surprise, she was not crying. She sat on the floor in a corner of the room, grim and silent. She had not bound her head with a black scarf nor smeared her face with indigo. She did not beat her breast nor tear her dress. She sat there not moving, not making a sound.

For the first time I found myself seeing a Khazna who was not affecting emotion. I was looking at the face of a women in such pain she seemed about to die from that pain. Her sorrow was mute, her suffering that of those who feel deep loss, who experience total bereavement.

A few of the women tried to weep, to cry out, but she looked at them in such a stunned way, as though rejecting their demonstrations of grief, that they gradually fell silent, astonished and indignant.

When the men came to take away the only creature who had ever given her the opportunity to express her emotions honestly, Khazna did not cry out or tear her dress. She simply looked at the pallbearers with dazed eyes and, like one lost, followed them down the street toward the mosque. At the cemetery she laid her head down on the fresh earth that housed the little body of Mas'ouda, and she rested on the grave for many hours. Only God knows exactly how long she stayed there.

People returned from the wake saying many things about Khazna. Some said she had become so mad she appeared to be rational; some said she had no tears left after a lifetime of wakes; and of course someone said that Khazna did not cry because she was not given any money.

A few, a very few chose to say nothing, letting Khazna in her silence say everything.

THE EYES OF THE STATUE

Camara Laye

Translated from the French by Una MacLean

Camara Laye (1928–1980). An African writer born in French Guinea (now the République de Guinée). He studied in Conakry, the colonial capital, and moved to France at the age of nineteen to study engineering. Here he penned two of the earliest and most influential works in Franco-phone African literature, *The African Child* and *The Radiance of the King*. He returned to Guinea after its independence and held various posts in government, but conflicts with President Ahmed Sékou Touré and a brief incarceration forced him into exile. From 1964 until his death, Laye lived in Senegal, where he worked as a research fellow in Islamic studies at the University of Dakar.

She stopped walking for a moment – ever since she had set out, she had been feeling as though she had earned a moment's rest – and she took stock of her surroundings. From the top of the hill on which she stood, she saw spread out before her a great expanse of country.

Far away in the distance was a town, or rather the remains of a town, for there was no trace of movement to be seen near it, none of the signs of activity that would suggest the presence of a town. Perhaps it was merely distance that hid from her sight all the comings and goings, and possibly once within the town, she would be borne along on the urgent flood of activity. Perhaps . . .

'From this distance anything is possible,' she was surprised to hear herself say aloud.

She mused on how, from such a vast distance, it seemed still as though anything could happen, and she fervently believed that if any changes were to take place, they would occur in the intervals when the town was hidden by the trees and undergrowth.

There had been many of these intervals and they were nearly always such very long intervals, so long that it was now by no means certain that she was approaching the town by the most direct route, for there was absolutely nothing to guide her and she had to struggle continually against the intertwining branches and tangled thorns and pick her way around a maze of swamps. She had tried very hard to cross the swamps, but all she had succeeded in doing was getting her shoes and the hem of her skirt soaking wet and she had been obliged to retrace her steps hurriedly, so treacherous was the surface of the ground.

She couldn't really see the town and she wasn't going straight towards it except for the rare moments when she topped a rise. There the ground was sparsely planted with broom and heath and she was far above the thickly wooded depths of the valleys. But no sooner had she finished scrambling up the hills than she had to plunge once more into the bushes and try to force her way through the impenetrable undergrowth where everything was in her way, cutting off her view and making her walk painful and dangerous again.

Perhaps I really ought to go back, she said to herself, and certainly that would have been the most sensible thing to do. But in fact she didn't slacken her pace in the least, as though something away over there was calling to her, as though the distant town were calling. But how could an empty town summon her? A silent, deserted town!

For the closer she came to it, the more she felt that it must really be a deserted city, a ruined city in fact. The height of the bushes and the dense tangled undergrowth about her feet convinced her. If the town had still been inhabited, even by a few people, its surroundings would never have fallen into the confusion through which she had been wandering for hours; surely she would have found, instead of this tangled jungle, the orderly outskirts of which other towns could boast. But here there were neither roads nor paths; everything betokened disorder and decay.

Yet once more she wondered whatever forced her to continue her walk, but she could find no reply. She was following an irresistible urge. She would have been hard put to it to say how this impulse had arisen or indeed to decide just how long she had been obeying it. And perhaps it was the case that if only she followed the impulse for long enough, she would no longer be capable of defying it, although there was no denying that it was grossly irrational. At any rate the urge must have been there for a very long time, as she could tell from the tiredness of her limbs and moreover it was still very dose. Couldn't she feel it brimming up within her, pressing on her breast with each eager breath she drew? Then all of a sudden she realized that she was face to face with it.

'The urge is me,' she cried.

She proclaimed it defiantly, but without knowing what she was defying, and triumphantly, although unaware of her opponent. Whom had she defied, and what could she be triumphing over? It was not simply that she was identifying herself with the strange compulsion in order to get to know more of it and of herself. She was obliged to admit that the urge was indefinable, as her own being for ever escaped definition.

After one final struggle with the branches and obstacles, and after skirting one more morass, she suddenly emerged in front of the city, or what remained of it. It was really only the traces of a town, no more than the traces, and in fact just what she had feared to find ever since she set out, but so sad, so desolate, she could never have imagined such desolation. Scarcely anything but rough heaps of walls remained. The porticoes were crumbling and most of the roofs had collapsed; only a column here or a fragment of a wall there proclaimed the former splendour of the peristyles. As for the remaining buildings, they seemed to waver uncertainly, as though on the very point of tumbling. Trees had thrust their branches through broken windows; great tufts of weeds pushed the blocks and the marble slabs upwards; the statues had fallen from their niches; all was ruined and burst asunder.

I wonder why these remains seem so different from the forests and bush I have come through already? she said to herself. There was no difference except for the desolation and loss, rendered all the more poignant by the contrast with what had once been. What am I searching for here? she asked herself once more. I ought never to have come.

'Many people used to come here once,' said an old man who appeared out of the ruins.

'Many people?' she said. 'I have not seen a single soul.'

'Nobody has been here for a very long time,' said the old man. 'But there was a time when crowds of people visited the ruins. Is that what you have come for?'

'I was coming towards the city.'

'It certainly was a great city once, but you have arrived too late. Surely you must have been delayed on the road.'

'I should not have been so late but for my battles with the trees and undergrowth and all my detours around the swamps. If only they hadn't held me back . . .'

'You should have come by the direct route.'

'The direct route?' she exclaimed. 'You cannot have any idea of the wilderness round this place.'

'All right, all right,' he said. 'I do have some idea of it. As a matter of fact when I saw that people had stopped coming, I guessed how it was. Perhaps there isn't any road left?'

'There isn't even a bush path!'

'What a pity,' he said. 'It was such a fine town, the most beautiful city in all the continent.'

'And now what is it?' she said.

'What is it?' he replied dismally.

With his stick he began to mow down the nettles that rose thick and menacing about them.

'Look at this,' he said.

She saw, in the midst of the nettles, a fallen statue, green with moss, a humiliated statue. It cast upon her a dead, grey glance. Presently she became aware that the look was not really dead, only blind, as the eyes were without pupils, and it was in fact a living gaze, as alive as a look could be. A cry came from it, an appealing cry. Was the statue bewailing its loneliness and neglect? The lips drooped pitiably.

'Who is it?' she asked.

'He was the ruler who lived in this place. His rooms can still be seen.'

'Why don't you set up the statue over there?' she said. 'It would be better there than among all these nettles.'

'That is what I wanted to do. As soon as the statue fell from its alcove I wanted to put it back, but I simply hadn't the strength. These stone sculptures are terribly heavy.'

'I know,' she replied, 'and after all it is merely a stone sculpture.'

But was it merely carved stone? Could sculptured stone have cast upon her such a piercing glance? Perhaps, then, it wasn't mere stone. And even if it were nothing more than mere stone, the fact remained that for all the nettles and moss and the vagaries of fortune that it had endured, this stone would still outlast man's life. No, it could not be mere stone. And with this sort of distress in its look, this cry of distress . . .

'Would you care to visit his rooms?' asked the old man.

'Yes, take me there,' she answered.

'Pay particular attention to the columns,' he told her. 'No doubt there is only one hall left here now, but when you consider the number of broken and fallen columns it does look as though there used to be at least ten halls.'

With the end of his stick he pointed out the marble stumps and debris of broken slabs buried in the grass.

'This gateway must have been exceedingly high,' he said, gazing upwards.

'It can't have been higher than the palace, surely,' she said.

'How can we tell? I haven't seen it any more than you have. By the time I arrived here it had already fallen into the grass; but those who were here before my time declared that it was an astonishing entrance. If you could put all this debris together again, I dare say you would get a surprise. But who could tackle such a task?'

He shrugged his shoulders and continued, 'You would need to be a giant, to have the hands and the strength of a giant.'

'Do you really believe that a giant . . . ?'

'No,' he replied. 'Only the ruler himself, who had it erected, could do it. He could certainly manage it.'

She gazed at the niches where great tufts of grass had been bold enough to replace the statues. There was one space, larger than all the rest, where the weeds grew particularly ostentatiously, like a flaming torch.

'That is the niche, over there, where he used to stand before his fall among the nettles,' he remarked.

'I see,' she said. 'But now there is nothing left but wild grass and the memory of his agony.'

'He used to find this city and his palace trying enough. He personally super-vised the building of the entire place. He intended his town to be the biggest and this palace the highest. He wanted them built to his own scale. Now he is dead, his heart utterly broken.'

'But could he have died any other way?'

'No, I suppose he carried his own death within him, like us all. But he had to carry the fate of a felled Goliath.'

By this time they had reached the foot of a staircase and he pointed out a little door at the end of the corridor on the left.

'That is where I live,' he told her. 'It is the old porter's lodge. I suppose I could have found somewhere a little more spacious and less damp, but after all, I am not much more than a caretaker. In fact, a guide is only a caretaker.'

So saying, he began to make his way painfully up the steps. He was a decrepit old man.

'You are looking at me? I know I'm not much better than the palace! All this will crumble down one day. Soon all this will crumble down on my head and it won't be a great loss! But perhaps I shall crumble before the palace.'

'The palace is older,' she said.

'Yes, but it is more robust. They don't build like that nowadays.'

'What have you been saying?' she demanded. 'You are not stone! Why compare your body to a palace?'

'Did I compare myself to a palace? I don't think so. My body is certainly no palace, not even a ruined one. Perhaps it is like the porter's lodge where I live, and perhaps I was wrong to call it damp and dark, perhaps I should have said nothing about it. But I must pause for breath. These stairs. At my age no one likes climbing stairs.'

And he wheezed noisily, pressing his hand over his heart as though to subdue its frantic beating.

'Let us go,' he said at last, 'up the few remaining steps.'

They climbed a little higher and reached a landing with a great door opening off it, a door half wrenched from its hinges.

'Here are the rooms,' he said.

She saw an immense apartment, frightfully dilapidated. The roof had partly collapsed, leaving the rafters open to the sky. Daylight streamed in upon the debris of tiles and rubbish strewn upon the floor. But nothing could take from the chamber its harmonious proportions, with its marble panel, its tapestry and paint-ings, the bold surge of its columns, and the deep alcoves between them. It was still beautiful, in spite of being three-quarters ruined. The torn and rotten tapestries and the peeling paintings were still beautiful; so were the cracked stained-glass windows. And although the panelling was practically torn away, the grandeur of the original conception remained.

'Why have you let everything deteriorate so far?' she asked.

'Why indeed? But now it is too late to do anything about it.'

'Is it really too late?'

'Now that the master is no longer here . . .' He tapped the panels with his stick.

'I don't know how the walls are still standing,' he said. 'They may last a fair time yet. But the rain floods through the roof and windows and loosens the stones. And then when the winter storms come! It is those violent storms that destroy everything.'

He dislodged a scrap of mortar.

'Just look, it's no more than a bit of grey dust. I can't think why the blocks don't fall apart. The damp has destroyed everything.'

'Was this the only room the master had?' she asked.

'He had hundreds of them and all of them richly furnished. I've pushed the movable stuff into one of the smaller rooms, which was less damaged.'

He opened a door concealed in the panelling.

'Here is some of it,' he said.

She beheld a jumble of carved furniture, ornaments, carpets and crockery.

'Gold dishes, please note. The master would eat off nothing but gold. And look at this. Here he is in his robes of state.' He pointed to a canvas where the face of the statue was portrayed.

The eyes were marvellously expressive. They were so even in the statue, although the sculptor had given them no pupils, but here they were infinitely more expressive and the look that they gave was one of anguish. 'Is no one left near me?' they seemed to ask. And the droop of the mouth replied, 'No one.' The man had known they would all forsake him; he had long foreseen it. Neverthe-less she, she had come! She had fought through the bush and she had wandered around the swamps, she had felt fatigue and despair overwhelming her, but she had triumphed over all these obstacles and she had come, she had come at last. Had he not guessed she would come? Yet possibly this very foresight had but accentuated the bitter line of his set lips. 'Yes,' said those lips, 'someone will come, when all the world has ceased to call. But someone who will be unable to soothe my distress.'

She swung round. This reproach was becoming unbearable, and not only this reproach, which made all her goodwill seem useless, but the cry of abandonment, the wild lonely appeal in his look.

'We can do nothing, nothing at all for him,' the old man declared.

And she replied, 'Is there ever anything we can do?' She sighed. In her innermost being she felt the anguish of this look; one might have thought it was she who cried, that the cry of loneliness welled up from her own lonely heart.

'Perhaps you can do something,' he said. 'You are still young. Although you may not be able to do anything for yourself, you might perhaps help others.'

'You know very well that I cannot even do that,' she said.

She seemed overwhelmed, as though she bore the ruins on her own shoulders.

'Are there still more rooms?' she asked him.

'Lots of them, but it is getting late; the sun is sinking.'

Daylight was fading fast. The light had become a soft, rosy glow, a light that was kinder to details, and in it the great room took on a new aspect. The paintings and panels regained a freshness that was far from theirs by right. This sudden glow was the gentlest of lights. But not even this light could calm a tormented heart.

'Come along,' called the old man.

'Yes,' she answered.

She imagined that once she went out of this hall and its adjoining storeroom, her heart would perhaps calm down. She thought that perhaps she might forget the great cry coming from the storeroom. Yes, if only she could get away from this palace, leave these ruins, surely she could forget it. But was not the cry inside herself?

'The cry is within me,' she exclaimed.

'Stop thinking about it,' advised the old man. 'If you hear anything, it's because the silence has got on your nerves. Tomorrow you will hear nothing.'

'But it is a terrible cry.'

'The swans have an awful cry too,' he remarked.

'Swans?'

'Yes, the swans. To look at them gliding over the water you might never believe it. Have you ever happened to hear them cry? But of course not; you are scarcely more than a child, and, with less sense than one, you probably imagine that they sing. Listen, formerly there were lots of swans here; they were at the very gate of the palace. Sometimes the lake was covered with them like white blossoms. Visitors used to throw scraps to them. Once the tourists stopped coming, the swans died. No doubt they had lost the habit of searching for food themselves and so they died. Very well, never, do you hear me, never, did I hear a single song coming from the pond.'

'Why do you have to tell me all this? Have I ever told you that I believe swans sing? You didn't need to speak to me like that.'

'No, maybe I shouldn't have said it, or I should have said it less suddenly at least. I'm sorry. I even believed that swans sing myself once. You know how it is – I am old and lonely and I have got into the habit of talking to myself. I was talking to myself then. I once believed that the lord of this palace, before he died, sang a swan-song. But no, he cried out. He cried so loudly that—'

'Please tell me no more,' she begged.

'All right. I suppose we shouldn't think about all that. But let's go.'

He carefully closed the storeroom door and they made their way towards the exit.

'Did you mean to leave the door of the big room open?' she asked once they had reached the landing.

'It hasn't been shut for a long time,' he replied. 'Besides, there is nothing to fear. No one comes here now.'

'But I came.'

He glanced at her.

'I keep wondering why you came,' he said. 'Why did you?'

'How can I tell?' she said.

Her visit was futile. She had crossed a desert of trees, and bush and swamps. And why? Had she come at the summoning of that anguished cry from the depth of the statue's and the picture's eyes? What way was there of finding out? And moreover it was an appeal to which she could not respond, an appeal beyond her power to satisfy. No, this impulse that had moved her to hasten towards the town had been mad from the start.

'I don't know why I came,' she repeated.

'You shouldn't take things to heart like that. These painters and carvers are so crafty, you know, they can make you work out the portrait, for instance. Have you noticed the look in the eyes? We begin by wondering where they found such a look and eventually we realize they have taken it from ourselves, and these are the paradoxes they would be the first to laugh at. You should laugh too.'

'But these paradoxes, as you call them, which come from the depth of our being, what if we cannot find them there?'

'What do you find within yourself?' he answered her.

'I have already told you: unbearable loneliness.'

'Yes,' he said, 'there is something of that in each one of us.'

'But in me . . .'

'No, not more than in anyone else,' he insisted. 'Don't imagine that others are any less alone. But who wants to admit that? All the same, it is not an unendurable state of affairs. It is quite bearable in fact. Solitude! Listen, solitude isn't what you imagine. I don't want to run away from my solitude. It is the last desirable thing left me; it is my only wealth, a great treasure, an ultimate good.'

Is he just saying that to comfort me? she wondered. But it is not consolation, a shared solitude can be no consolation. The sharing only makes the solitude doubly lonely.

Aloud she said, 'That doesn't console me in the least.'

'I didn't think it would,' he replied. They had by now reached the foot of the staircase and the old man showed her the little corridor leading to his room.

'My lodge is here.'

'Yes, I know,' she said. 'You've told me already.'

'But I haven't told you everything: I didn't say that my room is right beneath the staircase. When visitors used to climb up there in throngs, they were walking over my lodge. Do you understand?'

'Yes.'

'No, you don't understand at all; you don't realize that they were marching on my head, wiping their feet on my hair. I had plenty of hair in those days.'

'But they weren't really wiping their feet,' she said. 'They—'

'Don't you think it was humiliating enough anyway?'

She did not know how to reply. The old man seemed slightly crazy: some of what he said was very sensible, but a lot of it was sheer nonsense. That solitude has gone to his head, she told herself, and she looked at him afresh. He was certainly very old. There must be times when age and loneliness together . . . Aloud she remarked, 'I don't know,' and then, all of a sudden, 'What made you say that solitude is an ultimate good?'

'How very young you are,' was his only reply. 'You should never have come here.' He made off towards his lodge, saying, 'I'm going to prepare a meal.'

'I shall rest here awhile,' she said as she climbed the steps.

'Yes, do have a rest. You've certainly earned one. I shall call you when the food is ready.'

She sat down and gazed at the evil weeds. The nettles were by far the most numerous and reminded her of the ocean. They were like a great green sea that surged around the palace trying to drown it, and ultimately they would completely engulf it. What could mere stones do against such a powerful wave? A wave with the deceptive smoothness of velvety leaves, a wave that hid its poisons and its sorcery beneath a velvet touch. It seemed to her fevered imagination that the wave was already rising. Or was it simply the darkness? Was it night, which was burying the lowest steps? No, it was really the wave of nettles, imperceptibly advancing in its assault upon the palace. A transient attack, no doubt. Probably this sea of nettles had tides like the ocean. And perhaps it wasn't merely a simple tide. Perhaps . . .

She leaped to her feet. The tide was about her ankles. She climbed several steps and the tide rose as quickly.

'Caretaker!' she screamed.

But she could no longer see the porter's lodge. Perhaps the sea had already entered the room while she was sitting down. She couldn't be certain now whether it had a door that shut. Even suppose it did have, how could a door stop such a wave?

What is to become of me? she asked herself. She climbed a few more steps, but the tide continued to pursue her; it really was following her. She paused; perhaps if she stopped, the tide in its turn might stop rising. But instead it flowed right up to her, covering her shoes. Feverishly she resumed her upward flight and gained the landing opposite the doorway of the main hall. But to her horror she realized that the wave was there almost as soon. It was inches away. Must she drown in those horrible weeds?

She rushed to open the storeroom door, only to find that the sea had beaten her and had borne everything away, literally washed off the face of the earth.

There was no longer any storeroom left! It had been engulfed beneath the flood of nettles, with its furniture and tapestries and dishes, and the portrait as well. Only the cry, the great cry of anguish remained, and it had become vaster and louder, more piercing and heart-rending than ever. It swelled to fill the whole earth! It seemed to her as though nothing could silence it any more and that whatever she did she could never escape. Her heart could never escape again. Yet at the same time she tried to bolt the door upon it as though in spite of all she knew she might evade it yet. But what could she escape to? There was no way of escape left open; it was either the cry or the flood. She was a prey to this cry and in no time she would be the victim of the flood. She was trapped between two floods, the one that swallowed up the storeroom and was lying in wait menacingly on its threshold, and the other one, which had pursued her step by step up the stairs and across the great hall. She had no choice but to cast herself into one of these two floods which were soon to merge. Placed as she was, she could neither advance nor retreat.

'Caretaker!' she cried.

But did she actually shriek? No sound came from her lips. Terror was throttling her. It had her by the throat. She only imagined she had shouted.

At the second attempt she could not even pretend to herself that she had shouted. She no longer even had the will to cry out. She realized that her terror was so extreme that she could never shout again. Nevertheless she continued to struggle hopelessly; she fought and struggled silently and in vain.

And meanwhile the flood was steadily rising beyond her ankles and up her legs. Confident of its power, it rose more rapidly than ever.

Then, while she was struggling and trying desperately to regain her voice, she suddenly caught sight of the statue. The sea of weeds had lifted it and was tossing it on its waves.

She stopped struggling to watch it and at once she could see that its eyes were looking at her just as they had done when the old man had first thrust aside the nettles. It was the same look, the same cry of distress and bitter loneliness.

She longed to awake from her nightmare and she tried once more to call for help, but in vain. Must she really die alone beneath the flood of weeds, all alone? She hid her face in her arms.

A little later she felt a blow on her forehead and she felt as if her skull were bursting.

THE VOICE OF
THE TURTLE

Guillermo Cabrera Infante

Translated from the Spanish by Peter Bush

Guillermo Cabrera Infante (1929–2005) was a novelist, short-story writer, film critic, and essayist who was the most prominent Cuban writer living in exile and the best-known spokesman against Fidel Castro's regime. In 1998 he was awarded Spain's Cervantes Prize. He died on February 21, 2005, in London. His parents were founding members of the Cuban Communist Party. He co-wrote the script for Richard C. Sarafian's 1971 cult film *Vanishing Point* under the pseudonym Guillermo Caín. His great-uncle Pepe was a vegetarian, a nudist and an unsuccessful inventor who was so violently opposed to tobacco that when he heard that Hitler disliked smoking, he became a Nazi.

A story my mother-in-law told me

caguama: the biggest known species of marine turtle, weighing in at up to forty stones, though its meat is inedible.

Cuba on Hand, 1936

When I first met my mother-in-law she was called Carmela, but she hadn't been born to that name. At the age of four she went missing for several days and her mother made a vow to the virgin of the Carmen: if she were found alive, Carmen would be her name. On the third day they found her on an island the other side of the river, where crocodiles still swam. As a child I had seen manatees in the same river and it was as wild as ever. Carmela now swears she was carried across the river by a lanky, long-haired man who walked on water. The whole family thought it was no lesser a person than Jesus who had put her safely on the island. Ever since my mother-in-law's been Carmen, Carmela.

She told me another story that was no less incredible. It happened before her tenth birthday. A village boy had fallen in love with a local beauty and his love did not go unrequited. They wanted to marry but he was very poor. And so was she. Everybody in the village was poor. But he didn't even have a job. Despite their hopelessness, they lived on hope. Not knowing what to expect, they had their expectations. One day he realized there was no future in a village which lived in the past and decided, with his best friend, to go in search of fame and fortune. Ironies of fate, he found one but not the other, although for a moment he believed he had really found both. The only source of life the village knew was the sea – and off to the sea he went.

But he didn't take to the sea. He suggested to his friend that they should explore the coast and together they headed for Los Caletones, in the opposite direction to the bay and the river. On the then deserted beach of Los Caletones an enormous whale had appeared one day, become beached and had died. When discovered it was already putrefying (people learned of its existence from the large gathering of vultures, a strange sight, because scavengers don't usually venture seawards) and the village entrepreneurs braved the stench and managed to extract from the carcass a great quantity of spermaceti which fetched a good price in the capital. Los Caletones seemed full of promise.

But they scoured the whole beach and found only flotsam and jetsam. Despondently they decided to go back to the village, the boy who wanted to marry more downcast than his friend who didn't want to get married. (Or, at any rate, not immediately.) On their way back to the village, scrambling out between two sand dunes, they saw a caguama. They already knew something you don't know about caguama.

> The caguama is a reptile and like the crocodile moves well in water (rivers, seas) but poorly on land. It is in its element in the sea, where it can spend hours underwater, coming up for air very occasionally. Once a caguama, the Indian name for a giant turtle, reaches the sea, after making an ungainly exit from its shell, only the female returns to dry land, to lay her eggs. The male – it is known – never returns. The caguama moves slowly on land because her feet have turned into flippers for swimming and because she can tip the scales at two thousand pounds. Others measure two yards by three. A zoologist once said, 'carrying her shell as armour', the caguama has no need to be as swift as Achilles, or to furrow the waves like Ulysses. But the caguama continues swimming even when she is out of the sea and flaps her way over the few metres of beach to her nest. That is how she makes the return journey from and to the sea. Like all reptiles, the caguama practises internal fertilization and detecting her sex is no easy matter. In many species, on the other hand, it is possible to make out the sex of an adult animal. When the caguama has laid her eggs, her sex assumes a strangely human aspect. The belief has always been that the caguama sees little and hears less, though some species do have a voice, particularly when on heat. Those who have been in close contact with a caguama say it possesses an intelligence that is only possible in a mammal.

Both saw her at the same time and thought the same thoughts at the same time. The two boys bore some comparison, except one was good-looking and the other wasn't. But both were equally strong and often did identical press-ups, wrestled and executed other trials of strength for their own enjoyment. They were, in fact, the strongest boys in the village, only one was clever and the other wasn't. Now the cleverer of the two conceived an idea which he didn't have to tell his friend (they often had the same thoughts at the same time) but just resolved to put it into practice and his friend was only seconds behind in coming forward. He tried to get hold of the huge animal who was heading laboriously seawards. They would make a fortune from selling her meat (that was all but inedible), its tortoiseshell (though it wasn't a hawksbill) and the fat stored underneath her carapace, well known to be (only they knew this) better than chicken grease. 'Caguama fat, can cure all,' went the refrain which they knew and took to be truly axiomatic – although they didn't know what an axiom was.

The frightened caguama stopped in her tracks, not because she could make out one of the boys but because her feet had felt the vibration of the shoes running towards her. As often on her journey, the caguama sighed, not because she sensed the end was nigh (a caguama lives to be a hundred), but because she is a marine animal who always sighs on land. (Some people believe it is the release of breath left over from the energy needed to move over the sand, when she finally comes to a halt.) Be that as it may, in their excitement not one of the boys heard this land-locked siren's muted song. (Or perhaps one of them did.) They closed in on the caguama, shouting excitedly, enthusiastically, and at once got to work turning over a turtle paralysed by the hullabaloo. We know that a caguama on its back becomes helpless and requires help to recover its quadruped state. An upturned caguama is a dead caguama. Better than dead for the two boys: she is worth a fortune. Shouting each other on, with much heaving, more misspent heaving than ever before, they managed to turn over the animal, which flapped its legs in the air, as if air were water. The caguamas, they thought, aren't as intelligent as we are. Although only one of the pair was intelligent.

One of the boys or perhaps the other (they were indistinguishable) suggested going to borrow the travois from his uncle who lived in the nearby hillocks. Now you know what a hillock is when it's not being a hill, but perhaps few of you know what a travois is. It is a vehicle used by the Plains Indians and takes the place of the wheel they never knew. Though simple, it is a great invention. You need only to find three long poles, two act as converging axles where force is applied, and the third pole becomes a crossbar which can also carry a frame. The travois is pulled from the other end and can take a considerable weight. The uncle owning the travois apparently lived nearby. The other youth walked off through the sand dunes.

Meanwhile, the first boy watched over the caguama. He knew she was immobilized for ever and wasn't afraid she would roll over, though he wasn't sure she mightn't be stolen in that state of stasis. While he watched, the lad was thinking of the endless quantity of combs, clasps, jewel boxes and other luxury items to be made from such a specimen. The caguama would be a source of untold wealth in the village. If getting her there was a matter of muscle, selling the caguama required grey matter. His friend could drag it along by himself but only he could sell it, get rich and get married.

With these thoughts running through his head and feeling bored, he decided to take a close look at the caguama. The skin on her chest and belly seemed hard but was pale, almost white, and gave the already vulnerable animal a soft, silky aspect that belied its dark carapace. The lower covering ended in the flippers that were very strong and still plying the air, as if the animal didn't realize it was immobile in its armoured shell. Caguamas are stupid, thought the boy. Then the caguama stopped pawing to puff out air in an even louder sigh. The boy was alarmed by this almost human sound, this mixture of despair and resignation. But curiosity is stronger than alarm and he carried on inspecting. You stupid, stupid bitch. Then he made what he thought was a wonderful discovery.

The caguama's sex had suddenly come into sight. After her egg-laying, according to one naturalist, it is common – the result of the effort of laying dozens of eggs very, very quickly or perhaps down to a natural reaction – the caguama's vagina is left exposed. In this case to prying eyes. The caguama was now showing her sex that appeared virgin (turtles, unlike manatees, have hairless pubes) and the lad felt curiosity giving way to dour desire. He decided (or intuited) that he had to penetrate the caguama, a female for the taking. There and then. He took one shamefaced look round. Saw nobody. Los Caletones were always deserted and it would take his friend some time to drag the travois that distance. The youth walked once more around the caguama and the animal stirred a little as she sensed him, but then quietened down again. The boy returned to her pudenda that now moved in what he took to be a strong sucking movement. The softest areas of the depilated (or girlish) sex trembled. Driven by his own sex, the boy opened his rustic flies (no need to drop underwear poor people don't wear) and took out a big, fat penis whose darkness contrasted with the female whiteness (though next to the animal, his penis seemed puny.) He got close in, lay almost horizontal atop the caguama. With one hand (his left, being a left-hander) he clung to the carapace and, with the help of his right, inserted an anxious penis into the vast vagina, which swallowed it whole. He felt a pleasure that seemed extraordinary, perhaps because till then he had known only masturbation, but also because it was an animal pleasure: he was committing bestialism but he didn't know it. Ecstasy occurred a second before he in turn was penetrated, apparently, on all sides at the same time.

When a caguama is on heat (and the combination of egg-laying followed by sudden penetration had now created within her conditions similar to being on heat) she is subject to opposing but equally peremptory forces. One force is paralysis: the passivity of the female before her male attacker. The other is action to secure a coitus that is underway. Fornication always occurs out to sea, where the couple is weightless yet at the same time under tons of sea-pressure per square metre. Sometimes caguamas couple out in the Gulf Stream and are visible from the beach. Copulation is, then, often threatened by adverse elements. But nature, evolution or whatever has endowed the caguama with mechanical aids to union. The female of the species is equipped with an appendix of the same material as her shell, a sharp, curved point that she uses to hold on tight to the macho during coitus. This hook remains hidden as the male mounts the female and tries to maintain a penetrating position on the slippery, wave-tossed carapace, a precarious state the female immediately makes secure. The hook (or rather harpoon) is launched from its secret place within the female to catch its prey. The female literally nails the male from below and behind. Only the roughness of its carapace prevents the caguama, like the male praying mantis, from being killed by the female during coitus.

The other boy, meanwhile, was returning to the beach cheerfully pulling his heavy travois behind him, proving how strong he was. He was almost singing. When he left the hills and cleared his way through the overgrown coast, he saw in the distance what became an increasingly intimate couple as he drew near. He stopped suddenly not out of prudery but fear. He will never forget what he then saw. He moved nearer. He knew a caguama is a passive animal (tame was the preferred word) and although he didn't know what you know, he did see what he did see. The other boy, his friend, was rigid on top of the turtle and bleeding on all sides from under and over his trousers: from buttocks, legs, feet and calfskin shoes. A summary inspection revealed that the other boy had fainted (he wasn't dead yet though he had reason enough to die several times) and when he got as close to the other boy as fear, horror and the flow of blood making a puddle on the sand allowed him, he finally saw the unheard of weapon (or fragment thereof) with which the caguama had hoisted his friend. Had there been an autopsy, it would have shown how the animal's shaft had penetrated the intruding fornicator just above the coccyx, how the harpoon's curved action had transfixed the anus from top to bottom, twisted its hook into his rectum and drilled through it crossways, before shredding the prostate and obliterating both testicles (or just the one) until the end came to rest like another duct within a penis which was doubly rigid.

The other youth realized his friend was badly injured and certain to die if he stayed on the beach. He didn't try to extricate him or even to move him. Not from any intelligent inhibition or sense of pity, but because he was increasingly terrified. Now he wasn't sure whether to fear the inevitable death of his only friend or the dangers of the caguama, which now seemed an awesome apparition. He had an idea that in other circumstances would have been his salvation: the travois would do the job it was intended for and drag his friend and the caguama to the village. With more strength than skill he pushed the two axles of the travois over the loose, soft sand and inserted them under the sides of the beast. When the artefact was in place, he secured it with the ropes he had brought with him. He tied down the caguama and his friend, who was now livid, a deathly pale. The pallor emphasized the perfect features that now seemed etched on his rustic face. Unhappily he began to pull his happy burden.

How the other boy managed to drag the couple the eight leagues to the village is as extraordinary as the tragedy inspiring his feat. He finally reached the village after midday and was met by the usual indifference. But as ever in villages, the extraordinary presence immediately assembled a public that was too shocked to react to the horror confronting them. It was like a fairground. But among the last to arrive was the would-be fiancée, on a day whose horror had its limits. Obviously she immediately recognized her boyfriend. What she didn't see was him half-opening his eyes at the hue and cry.

Nobody saw that because right then the caguama, immortal like all turtles, let out a kind of scream that seemed to emerge not from the beast's mouth but from the open lips of the fiancée before her betrothed. Still atop the turtle, the boy closed his eyes and for a moment imagined he was dreaming his wedding night.

THE CRIME OF AN INNSBRUCK SHOPKEEPER'S SON

Thomas Bernhard

Translated from the German by Martin Chalmers

Thomas Bernhard (1931–1989). An Austrian novelist, playwright and poet, Bernhard is considered one of the most important post-war authors writing in German. His novels and plays offer a bleak view of human folly compared by some to Strindberg. His unsparing portrait of his native Austria as "a country that is rotting away, falling apart, run by the political parties in an unholy alliance with the Catholic Church" earned him little appreciation in his home country, and his last play, *Heldenplatz*, led to public demonstrations and a dispute about censorship. Bernhard suffered from ill health throughout his life, requiring constant medication as a result of childhood tuberculosis, and his continuing ill health caused him to seek assisted suicide at the age of fifty-eight. In his will, Bernhard forbade any new stagings of his works or publication of unpublished writings in Austria, though his decision was later overturned by his heir in 1999.

Even after a brief acquaintance with him I had extremely revealing insights into his development, into his childhood above all: sounds, smells in his parents' home, now many years behind him, he described to me again and again, the eeriness of a shopkeeper's gloomy house; his mother and the grocery-stillness and the birds trapped in the darkness in the high vaulting; the behaviour of his father, who in the shopkeeper's house in Anichstrasse constantly gave the orders of a ruthless master of properties and people. Georg always talked of his sisters' lies and slanders, of the devilish tricks with which siblings can often proceed against siblings; sisters have a criminal craving to destroy brothers, brothers to destroy sisters, brothers to destroy brothers and sisters to destroy sisters. His parents' house had never been a house of children, as are most of the other houses, parents' houses, especially in better areas, better atmospheric conditions, but a terrible adults' house, furthermore a huge and damp one, in which children have never come to the world, but right away dreadful arithmeticians, big-mouth infants with a nose for business and for the suppression of altruism.

Georg was an exception. He was the centre of attention, but thanks to his worthlessness, thanks to the scandal which he represented for the whole family, always frightened and embittered by him, not least where they tried to cover it up, a horribly crooked and crippled centre of attention, which they wanted out of the house at all costs. He was so greatly and in the most dreadful way deformed by nature that they always had to hide him. After they had been disappointed down to the depths of their faecal and victual detestableness by the doctors' skills and by medical science altogether, they implored in mutual perfidiousness a fatal illness for Georg, which would remove him from the world as swiftly as possible; they had been prepared to do anything, if he would just die; but he didn't die and, although all of them together have done everything to make him fall fatally ill, he did not once fall *dangerously* ill (neither in Innsbruck, where, separated by the River Inn, he had grown up a couple of hundred yards away from me— neither knew of the other—nor later, during our Viennese studies in a room on the third floor of a house in Zirkusgasse); among them he had only grown larger and larger and ever more ugly and frail, ever more worthless and in need of help, but without his organs being affected, which functioned better than their own ... This development on Georg's part embittered them, above all, because at the very moment at which he had been thrown by his screaming mother onto a cornerstone of the washhouse floor, they had come to the decision to revenge themselves in their way for the horrible surprise of the birth of an initially huge, damp and fat, but then, even if ever larger, then ever more delicate and healthy unsightly 'cripple son' (as his father called him), and to compensate themselves for an injustice that cried to heaven; like conspirators, they had decided to get rid of him, of Georg, and without coming into conflict with the law, even before he, as they ruminated, could deal them a possibly fatal injury through his mere existence; for years they believed that the point in time at which they would no longer have to put up with him was close, but they were deceived, had deceived themselves, his health, his lack of illness—as far as Georg's lungs, Georg's heart, all the other important organs were concerned—were stronger than their will and their shrewdness.

In part dismayed, in part megalomaniac, they noted, as he rapidly grew larger and healthier and more delicate and more intelligent and more ugly, that he, they really believed so, had not come out of their centuries' old merchants' substance and had remained stuck at home with them; after several still-births, they had presumably deserved one of their own, a straight—not crooked—piece of timber of merchant stock, who should support them one and all right from the very first moment, then later carry, raise even higher one and all, raise parents and sisters even higher *up,* than they already were; and what they got, where from seemed strange to them, because ultimately nevertheless by the father out of the mother, was a creature that, as they saw it, had been such a useless, ever deeper and deeper thinking beast, that even had a claim to clothing and to entertainment, and that one was supposed to support it instead of being supported, feed instead of being fed, pamper instead of being pampered; on the contrary, in his complete uselessness Georg was and perpetually remained a lump of flesh that was constantly in their way and lay heavily in their stomachs and who even wrote poems. Everything about him was different; they felt him to be the greatest disgrace in their family otherwise composed solely of reality and not in the least out of imagination. In the room in the Zirkusgasse in Vienna which we had rented after meeting in an inn in the Leopoldstadt district and joining forces, he talked again and again of his 'child's dungeon at Innsbruck', and he flinched in front of his listener, in front of me, who for years, for eight semesters, was his only listener, when he thought he had to utter the always, for him, difficult word, 'horsewhipping'. Cellars and hallway and attic stores far too big, far too huge for him, stone steps far too high for him, trapdoors that were too heavy, jackets and trousers and shirts (his father's worn-out jackets and trousers and shirts) far too wide for him, whistles from his father, screams from his mother that were too shrill, the sniggering of his sisters, leaps by rats, the barking of dogs, cold and hunger, narrow-minded loneliness, schoolbags that were far too heavy for him, loaves of bread, sacks of Indian corn, sacks of flour, sacks of sugar, sacks of potatoes, shovels and steel wheelbarrows, incomprehensible instructions, tasks, threats and orders, punishments and chastisements, strokes and blows made up his childhood. Years after he had left home, he was still tormented by the cured sides of pork lugged by him down to the cellar and again lugged up out of the cellar (and lugged by him with what terrible pain). Even years later and four hundred and fifty miles away, in Vienna, he still anxiously crossed, head down, the parental Innsbruck shopkeeper's yard, descended, shaken by fever, to the parental Innsbruck shopkeeper's cellar. When, cuffed day in day out into the parental commercial arithmetic, he made a mistake, he was (not yet six the first time) locked into the cellar vault by his father or by his mother or by one of his sisters, and then for a while called only 'criminal'; at first, only his father had called him a criminal, but later, as he remembered, his sisters, too, then even his mother had joined in. Completely 'incapable of bringing up a child', she, whom he now imagined, after years, in his time as a student in Vienna, he saw in a mellower light, because he was separated from her by many mountains, always completely yielded, when it came to Georg, to the stronger side of the family, that is, to his father and his sisters. With shocking regularity, father and mother had beaten him several times a week with the whip.

In his childhood, the sons screamed in the houses of the Innsbruck shopkeepers, as did the pigs in the houses of the Innsbruck butchers. In his home, everything had no doubt been worse. His birth, so they assured him at every opportunity, had led to their ruin. His father had constantly described him as 'unconstitutional', his father incessantly needled him with the word 'unconstitutional'. His sisters took advantage of him for their plots, using their sharpening minds with ever greater perfection. He was everyone's victim. When I saw into his childhood and into his Innsbruck, I saw into my childhood and my Innsbruck, with how much dismay simultaneously into my own, which had been dominated not by the same dreadfulness but by an even greater infamy, for my parents did not act out of bestial violence, as his did, but out of a radical philosophical violence coming from the head and from nowhere but the head and from heads.

Every day, early in the morning, an embitterment, saddening, deeper than by nature admissible, thrust our painful, incompetent heads together into one whole, hopeless, dull state of conjecture: everything in us and on us and about us suggested that we were lost, I just as much as he, whatever we had to look at and whatever we had to work out, whatever we had to walk and stand and sleep and dream, whatever it had to do with. For days Georg was often in the most remote

Higher Imagination, as he called it, and at the same time he always walked, as I was continually forced to observe, back and forth in his desperations, which also overshadowed me, from a certain point in time we, both the laws and their makers, and the day-in-day-out coarse annihilators of every law, all at once went together and as if together forever through the whole great pathological schema of colours, in which nature had to express itself in each one of us as the most painful of all human pains. For years we lodged, even if on the surface of the capital, then nevertheless in a system of protective conduits created by us for us and only visible to us; but in these conduits we also uninterruptedly breathed in a deadly air; we walked and we crawled almost entirely only in these conduits of our youthful despair and youthful philosophy and youthful science always towards ourselves ... these conduits led us out of our Zirkusgasse room, in which we sat in our chairs at the table, usually stricken by the power of judgement and by the monstrous excess of history, stricken by ourselves, over our books, dreadful bunglings, adulations and mockeries of our own and the whole geological genealogy, into the old, ancient body of the city and back out of it again to our room ... Georg and I spent eight dreadful semesters together, had to spend them together, in this way that I've only hinted at, in the Zirkusgasse room; no pause of any kind had been permitted us; in all the eight semesters, in which I had sickened myself of jurisprudence, Georg no less of his pharmacy, we had not been capable of raising ourselves from our stooped posture, from both our deformities (I, too, had already been deformed), because, of course, as already indicated, we had always, in everything and everyone, to move in our conduits and hence stooped low, not capable of raising ourselves from this necessity into a less bent one, no matter by how little; in all the eight semesters we had not once had the strength to get up and leave ... We had not even had the strength, because we didn't feel like it, to open the window of our Zirkusgasse room and let in fresh air ... still less had we had just one of the *invisible powers* ... Our disposition, like our mind, had been so firmly sealed up that by human standards we should one day have suffocated in ourselves, we were not so far away from it, had not something that did not come from us, could not come *from one of us,* such a metaphysical intervention from outside in us or from deep inside us, produced an alteration in our condition out of two like conditions, Georg's and mine ... In the course of tremendously complicated proceedings against us, in the atmosphere of the capital, which to us remained atonic, our souls also shrunk together. As so many of our age we were without backing, had been deeply dug and deeply buried into the idea that says that there is nowhere, neither inside nor out, a possibility of fresh air and what it can produce, *unleash* or *efface*, and, indeed, for us in the Zirkusgasse room there was no fresh air; eight semesters long no fresh air.

We each of us had a name, one of many, which had come into existence in the mountains, many generations ago, one left of the Inn, one right of the Inn, countless generations in his case, had grown ever larger, but which now, as a destroyer of ourselves, at the end of parental curses and feats of arithmetical skill, had been transplanted to the shamelessly, as we were forced to see, self-pityingly decaying capital. Each of us was enclosed in his significant name and could not get out again. Neither knew the dungeon of the other, the guilt, the crime of the other, but each *suspected* that the other's dungeon and the other's guilt and crime were his own. Our mistrust for each other and of each other had over time increased in the same measure as we more and more belonged together, did not want to leave each other. Yet we hated each other, and we were the most opposite creatures one can imagine; everything of one shone from the other, indeed *out of the other,* but the two of us did not resemble each other in any way or any thing, in no sentiment at all, in nothing. And yet either of us could have been the other, everything of one could have come from the other . . . I often told myself, that I *could* be Georg, everything that Georg was, that meant, however, that nothing of Georg was *from* me . . . How other students, when they have been sent to the capital, enthusiastically find pleasure and refreshment in its possibilities of distraction, remained a mystery to us, nothing aroused our enthusiasm, nothing found favour with us, the spirit of the capital was a dead one, its entertainment apparatus too primitive for us.

From the beginning, we, he and I, operated with keen perception, in almost every case we subjected everything to our deadly criticism; finally, our attempts to break out failed, everything weighed on us, we fell ill, we constructed our conduit system. Already in our first weeks we had withdrawn from the silent megalomania of Vienna, from the city in which there was no longer any history, any art and any scholarship, in which there was no longer anything. But even before my arrival in Vienna, still on the train, I (as he also), we had both, independently of each other, been attacked by an illness, by a fever gradually making us sad, I by a *distraction to the point of fatal over-sensitivity*, moving logically from everything external into myself, in my subconscious just as in full consciousness and, sitting in one of our many dark express train compartments, which are drawn through the land at high speed, in awareness of myself and in awareness of what went with me always, was surprised by the first thoughts of suicide, the signs of suicide, for a long time. With what a grey and extraordinarily severe gloominess did I all at once have to cope with between the Melk Hills! On this journey, which I had been forced to make against my will, I had several times wished for my death, swift, sudden, painless, of which only a picture of peace is left behind; especially on the dangerous curves, as close by the Danube at Ybbs. The journey of young people from the provinces to the capital in order to begin a feared course of studies, for a course of studies which most of them don't want, almost always proceeds to the accompaniment of the most dreadful state in the brain and mind and emotions of the person concerned and deceived and hence tortured. The thought of suicide in one apprehensively, and in all cases always less boldly than expected, approaching at twilight by train a secondary school or college or university in the capital, is most natural. How many and not a few whom I knew and with whom I grew up and who have been mentioned to me by name have already thrown themselves from the moving train shortly after taking leave of their parents at their local station . . . As far as Georg and I are concerned, we never revealed our suicide perspectives to each other, we only knew of each other that we were at home in them. We were enclosed in our thoughts of suicide as in our room and in our conduit system, as in a complicated game, comparable to advanced mathematics. In this advanced suicide game we often left each other completely in peace for weeks. We studied and thought about suicide; we read and thought about suicide; we hid away and slept and dreamed and thought about suicide. We felt abandoned in our thoughts of suicide, undisturbed; no one bothered about us. We were at liberty to kill ourselves at any time, but we did not. As much as we had always been strangers to each other, there were never any of the many hundreds of thousands of odourless human secrets between us, only the secret of nature *as such,* which we knew about. Days and nights were like verses of an infinitely harmonious dark song to us.

On the one hand, his family had already known from the start that he was unsuitable for his father's business profession and so for taking over the shop on Anichstrasse which demanded someone like them, on the other hand they were far from giving up hope that Georg, the cripple, could become, almost overnight, possibly from one blow of the whip to the next, what they from the start wanted him to be: the successor to the grocer who was now already in his sixties! Finally, however, they had decided, as if by agreement, behind his, Georg's back, overnight, for always, in favour of his older sister, and from that moment on they stuffed, whatever way they could, everything that they could, all their shopkeepers' powers and all their shopkeepers' knowledge into fat, ruddy, rustic Irma, a person who on her fat legs walked all day long through the shopkeeper's house like a heavy cow; summer as winter in puffed sleeves, she, who was just twenty and engaged to a butcher's assistant from Natters, her calves constantly discharging pus, grew into a pillar of the shop. At the same moment at which they had decided on the sister as successor (no doubt also in view of her fiancé!), they consented to Georg going to university. They had been afraid of losing face. But they didn't permit him, as he had wished, to study pharmacy in Innsbruck, where, in addition to the commercial apprenticeship, he had completed the grammar school with a good record, or in nearby Munich, but only in distant Vienna far to the east, which he and all of them had always hated. They wanted him as far away from themselves as possible, to know him far away, and the capital really was at the end of the world. Every young person today knows what an exile there means! It had made no difference that he had tried to make clear to them that Vienna, the capital, had for decades been the most backward of all European university towns; there was no course of study in Vienna that could be recommended; he had to go to Vienna and, if he did not want to make do with the lowest of all allowances known to me, he had to remain in Vienna, the most dreadful of all old cities of Europe. Vienna is such an old and lifeless city, is such a cemetery, left alone and abandoned by all of Europe and all of the world, we thought, what a vast cemetery of crumbling and premodern curiosities!

As if he had been me, that's what I always felt in the last period when we were together, and with especial intensity towards the end of the year when, before falling asleep, he hinted at everything of which we knew nothing at all. . . His inability, just once in his life to make himself intelligible, was also mine . . . His childhood, which had appeared to him endless, not a thousand years long, like that of the author of *Moby Dick*: the uninterruptedly vain attempt to win the confidence of his parents and of the other people around him, at least of those closest to him. He had never had a real friend—but who knows what that is—only people who made fun of him, secretly feared him; he was always someone, who disturbed the harmony of another or several others in his way, through his deformity, he was continually disturbing . . . Wherever he went, wherever he stayed, he was an ugly spot of colour on the beautiful calm background . . . People were only there (he thought) to set traps for him, no matter who or what they were, what they represented, there was nothing that did not set a trap for him, not even religion. Finally, he was darkened by his own feeling . . . His awakening had no doubt also been one into the madness of hopelessness . . . He had all at once, and I had already felt safe, torn open the door to my childhood with the brutality of the sick, oppressed, despairing . . . Every morning, he woke up in the firmly locked cell of a new age-old day.

Whereas for me, figures which are easily recognized as comic, indeed even as playful, again and again appeared in front of the gloomy backdrop of my childhood, something like that never happened to my friend; when he looked into the past, only terrifying occurrences were visible to him, and what had been put on there and was still being put on there was even more terrifying; he wanted, therefore, he said repeatedly, to look as little as ever he could, not look at all into the past, which was like the present and the future, which *was* present and future, not look at all; but that wasn't possible; his childhood, his youth, his whole life had been a vast ice-cold stage, only there to terrify him, and the leading roles on this stage were always only taken by his parents and his sisters; again and again, they invented something new to upset him. Sometimes he wept, and when I asked him why, he replied: because he couldn't draw the stage curtain; he was too weak to do it; less and less often was he able to draw the stage curtain, he was afraid that one day he would be unable to draw it all; wherever he went, wherever he found himself, in whatever condition he was, he was forced to watch his play; the most terrible scenes took place again and again in his parents' house in Innsbruck, in the shopkeeper's house; father and mother as driving forces of its deadly scenery, he always saw and heard them. Often, in his sleep, he said the words 'father' and 'mother' and the words 'whip' and 'cellar' or a 'No no!' finally hunted to death by one of his persecutors, which was to do with his many chastisements. In the early morning, his body, crippled, yet refined to the point of a chastity forbidden to nature (he had the skin of mortally ill girls), was wet, a fever, which couldn't be measured, already weakened him before he had even got up. We usually did not eat breakfast, because eating and drinking disgusted us. The lectures disgusted us. The books disgusted us. The world to us was a perverse bestial and perverse philosophical plague and repulsive operetta. During the last February, Georg had been constantly sad and, in his sadness, always alone. He, who was one year younger, was forced to be afraid in the evenings under the conditions known to both of us, supported by hand movements, movements of his head, among all the names of deceased or of still living creatures and objects feared by him. The letters addressed to him, the few, contained, like those to me, only admonitions to recovery, nothing good-natured. Once he had pronounced the word 'tactless', he had meant the world was at least tactless. How different we both would have had to be, to turn our backs on this cemetery, which the capital had been, which the capital *is*. We were too weak to do it. In the capital, everyone is too weak. 'This city is a cemetery which is dying out!' is the last thing he had said; after this statement, which did not give me pause for thought, at first, which had the same standing as all the rest by him recently, I had, it was the fourteenth, half past ten in the evening, gone to bed. When I was woken, just before two by a noise, because Georg had been completely still, probably not least for the one reason, that under no circumstances did he want to wake me up (and now I know how agonizing that must have been for him), I made the dreadful discovery, which Georg's parents now describe as their son's crime against himself and against his family. Georg's father had already arrived in Vienna from Innsbruck at ten the next morning and requested that I throw light on the matter. When I had returned from the hospital to which Georg had been taken, Georg's father was already in our room, and I knew, even though it had still been dark because of the bad weather, there was no further change that day, that the man packing Georg's things was his father. Although also from Innsbruck, I had never seen him before. Once, however, my eyes had got used to the darkness and were also able to take advantage of the darkness, and I shall never forget this keenness of my eyes, I saw that this man, who was wearing a black coat with a sheepskin lining, that this man, who gave the impression of being in a hurry and was throwing everything of Georg's onto a heap, in order to remove it, that this man and that everything connected to him bore the blame for Georg's misfortune, for the catastrophe.

COLD SPRING

Aharon Appelfeld

Translated from the Hebrew by J. Sloane

Aharon Appelfeld (1932–2018). One of the greatest Israeli writers of his generation, Appelfeld was born in the village of Jadova, in what is now Ukraine. During the capture of the village by the Romanian army, when he was nine years old, he witnessed the murder of his mother. He and his father were deported to a Nazi concentration camp, from which Aharon escaped and spent three years in hiding. After the war, he immigrated to Palestine two years before the declaration of Israel's independence. He studied Hebrew and Yiddish literature at university, and although his first language was German, he chose to write in Hebrew. He wrote his first collection of short stories in 1960. He first gained international attention with his novel *Badenheim 1939*. His short stories earned him considerable praise, especially the collection *Blooms of Darkness*. Philip Roth described his stories as "small, intimate and quietly narrated, and yet are transfused into searing works of art by Appelfeld's profound understanding of loss, pain, cruelty and grief".

Seven days late, we learned that the war was over. We heard that the day after the war ended everyone was very happy. The fact is, sounds reminiscent of the war's beginning did filter into our bunker, but we did not know that these were after-war pangs, so we listened in silence.

When we removed the cover of our hiding place and daylight suddenly descended into the bunker, we did not know what to do. Our faces took on an expression of naïve amazement, like the face of a stutterer.

Zeitel said, 'Don't rush out into the cold.'

Berel and Hershel curled up, not wanting to move.

The first to leave, rushing out with a powerful burst and thrusting his beard ahead of him, was old Reb Isaac.

'Sonya!' he called, as though she were waiting for him at the doorway.

Outside lay a lucid winter. Great lights glittered in the distance, too strong for the naked eye. The horizon was a firm, solid blue. In the evening we returned and covered the bunker.

'What did you see?' asked Zeitel in the middle of the night, but we were tired and said, 'Nothing.' Then we fell asleep again.

In the morning we were in no hurry to remove the cover again. The army band beat out thunderous rhythms above our heads, the music spiralled happily, and peasants yelled: 'Hurray, the war is over!' In the afternoon a company of Russian soldiers wandered over. 'Do you know the war is over?'

'Yes,' answered Berel, 'only we're tired.'

We did not know where to go now that the war was over, so we sat at the entrance of the bunker, and when we grew thirsty we sucked the white snow that melted nicely between our fingers. Company after company of soldiers passed singing and whooping; their victory yells echoed and passed over us. The snow did not melt. In the evenings sparkling clouds of smoke piled up in the sky. Nights we no longer went out to the fields to search for potatoes, but slept huddled together in a circle. As we lay in hibernation, a heavy shudder ran through our limbs. We posted no watchmen to listen for strange noises, but Zeitel would rouse us at midnight. 'Do you hear?'

Old Reb Isaac could not just sit and wait. The second day, he suddenly fled the bunker, going off into the snowy fields. I remember his hands flapping in the distance like wings.

'Sonya,' he called through the clear air. 'Sonya.' He did not return to the bunker. We were fast asleep and did not notice his absence. Only Zeitel said from time to time, 'Reb Isaac went out without his coat.'

After we had got used to the light, we would go out and watch the Russian soldiers march past singing. We did not go very far, just around the bunker. The idea occurred to none of us that the time had come to take to the road. We had food. The soldiers abandoned piles of bread and sausages and vodka, but we were not hungry. The bunker was full of food but none of us went near it. Zeitel would spread out her hands and say, 'Maybe you'll eat something.' Berel grew fat, so heavy he could barely stand. Hershel, on the other hand, shot up tall, like a plant springing in the shade. Zeitel could not help saying, 'Look at Hershel.' And Berel said, 'You have no appetite. Good. I'll eat all the more.'

Hershel sat apart from us, and fell into a brown study. Nobody went near him; it was clear that he was not one of us any more. He was sailing off somewhere and there was no stopping him, for he could see what we could not.

At times a company of soldiers stopped to eat and rest with us. They were flushed with victory and did not ask any questions. But they let us forage after them, and sometimes were amazed. 'Jews.'

The battlefront moved away, the railroad tracks were repaired, and the snow began to soften—not all at once, but in layers, from the surface down. There were no human voices. You could hear the sound of saws in the forest, and the sound of axes, and the sound of wood being piled up and loaded.

Zeitel said, 'I shiver whenever I hear these sounds. Why haven't I become used to them?'

Max smiled. 'Winter is passing.'

The snow began to thaw, baring the earth. Steel helmets that had been discarded were scattered in the fields. A burned-out jeep lay on its side wearing a helpless expression, one tail-light gleaming red.

Zeitel said, 'It's a good thing we stayed in the bunker and were not so foolish as to follow the refugees.'

We did not bother to repair the leaks in the bunker, as we had done every year toward spring. The water began seeping in, and we had to curl up in the corners of the bunker.

Max and I used to go out and watch the army cars speeding down the road, their wheels throwing up clods of mud behind them.

Zeitel said, 'Children, why are you standing outside?'

One morning we awoke to find the bunker full of water. Now we knew we could not remain. We took our bundles out of the bunker, and Berel grumbled, 'Just when you want to sleep, it fills up with water.'

Max glanced inside and said, 'Our bunker.'

Then we left.

Where were we to go?

Zeitel said, 'Let's go to the village.'

Hershel said, 'Let's go to the road where the cars pass.'

In the distance moved long lines of refugees; their feet seemed to sink in the thawing snow. Huddled together in the bunker we used to talk and talk. Now we five walked in silence.

Zeitel remembered something and said, 'I forgot the wooden spoon in the bunker. Maybe I ought to go back and get it.'

Carts loaded with trees moved very slow, leaving a trail of dripping resin. Cows were taken to pasture.

A peasant woman stood at the door of her house with a little girl, and the woman said, 'Look, Jews! You see, they are going to look for their families.'

'Those are Jews?' wondered the little girl.

After a time we turned off the main road into a narrower one. Facing us was a green hill with a monastery looking down from the peak. Holiday bells were pealing and Hershel said, 'Christian holiday.'

The sun stood in the middle of the sky, it was hot and a mouldy smell rose from our clothes. 'We might go down to the river and wash,' said Max.

'God forbid, God forbid,' said Zeitel. 'Not in this cold weather.'

We sat down to rest in the sun. 'The sun is good,' said Hershel.

And Max remembered the bunker and said, 'Our bunker is full of water.'

We took out the bread and the bottle of vodka. 'I have a bad taste in my mouth,' said Hershel. But smelling the vodka, he said, 'Seeing vodka makes me happy.'

We sat and stared at the red monastery, and saw the sun going down by degrees, and heard the bells hurriedly calling.

At last, Berel stood up and said, 'What are we sitting here for? It's late, it will soon be night.'

Hershel said, 'We should walk along the main road.'

Berel thought it would be better to start off toward the monastery.

Max said, 'It's good to walk.'

Berel grew angry and said, 'If you people don't want to go to the monastery, I'll go alone. I'm not afraid of going alone. As a matter of fact. . .'

Zeitel interfered and said, 'Sh . . . sh . . . Are you quarrelling now? All the years we sat in the bunker we never quarrelled—should we quarrel now?'

We moved slowly in silence. At first we all kept together. Then, gradually, the knot loosened. An angry cloud hung over our heads. Berel lengthened his stride. Hershel dawdled behind. Toward evening we reached the monastery. The walls that had looked low and narrow from a distance now loomed high and forbidding. They were enclosed by rigid iron gates.

'Who is there?' asked the monk.

We told him.

'We have too many refugees already,' said the monk's voice.

'But only for one night,' Zeitel raised her voice.

'Every inch is taken,' he replied.

Berel climbed up the wall, stood on the top, and said, 'I'm a Christian.'

'Look at the Jew pretending he's a Christian,' laughed the monk.

His face smarting, Berel crawled down, and Zeitel said, 'What's all the fuss? We'll sleep here, next to the wall. The winter is over, we can spread straw on the ground.'

When we got up in the morning, the angry cloud of contention had not lifted. We continued to walk. The morning was large and clear and bright. Behind us trailed the monastery prayers.

Zeitel said, 'So hot.' She remembered Reb Isaac. 'I wonder what Reb Isaac is doing now.'

'You're always complaining.' Berel grew angry.

'I don't mean anyone is to blame, God forbid. But why did we let him go? All the years we looked after him—then, on the happy day, we let him go,' said Zeitel.

Berel walked faster. We sensed the anger that was driving him. It forced him to keep going, never to look behind. He ran with his head lowered. By afternoon he was far away.

Max said, 'Maybe we ought to run after him.'

'Even if we ran, we couldn't catch him,' sighed Zeitel.

The footprints Berel left in the earth were deep and we were able to follow them. Max shouted, 'Berel, Berel! We don't have the strength to run after you. Wait, wait.' Toward evening, Berel was swallowed up in the dusk.

'That would not have happened if Reb Isaac were here,' said Zeitel. 'But what are we standing around for?' She hurried us. We knew we would do whatever Zeitel said.

It grew very dark, but Zeitel said, 'We won't rest till we find him.'

At midnight we found Berel, by his groans. He was sitting with his back propped up against a tree.

'Let me alone, let me alone, let me rest,' he said.

Zeitel went over to him and said, 'I'm going to take care of you.' She made him sip some water.

Hershel and Max carried Berel, Zeitel and I trailed behind. We were in good spirits, the way we had been in the bunker. Max hummed Russian marching songs, and even Berel's heavy breathing was part of the celebration. Reconciliation was in the air.

Max said, 'Let go, Hershel. I want to carry him by myself.'

'Look at the hero,' said Zeitel.

We came across a lean dog and Max said, 'Look at the dog,' and ran over to stroke it.

We decided to ask the peasants for a place to lodge.

'You want to sleep at my place?' asked the peasant woman. 'I can tell from your looks you've just come out of a bunker. Now you're trying to locate your relatives, aren't you?'

'We're looking for a place to sleep,' said Berel.

'Ah,' smiled the peasant woman. She seemed to like what Berel had said.

In the ante-room she spread out straw, lit the oven, and said, 'You poor people, lie down and sleep.'

I do not remember that night. But I do remember the tongues of flame that licked my back. The wounds all over my body gaped painfully. A sweet languor dissolved through my limbs. The hayseed crackled in the oven, shooting sparks. I sensed my voice returning. Tomorrow I would be able to speak again. The moment we lifted the cover of the bunker when we learned the war was over, a stream of cold air had numbed my throat, and I had not been able to talk ever since.

The next morning our bodies ached and we could not rise. It was Max who got up at last and said, 'Where's Berel?'

'Woe is me!' screamed Zeitel.

'Where is Berel?' we asked the peasant woman.

'Don't worry, he's in my room.'

'Give us a chance to speak to him,' pleaded Zeitel.

'The nerve of these people! You think he's badly off with me?' asked the peasant woman.

'Berel!' shouted Max, but Berel did not answer.

Zeitel covered her face with a kerchief and said, 'The son of Nachman Katz and the grandson of Rappoport. What have we done to deserve this?'

I had not regained the power of speech. I tried to say something but could not. I felt that if only I could speak I would be able to suggest a solution. A vast loneliness descended on us, the sun's rays seemed to sink, heavy and rough, and Zeitel said, 'If Reb Isaac were with us, such a thing would never have happened. A tragedy.'

Hershel walked behind us. His face was silent. We saw that his eyes were clouded, he was deep in inner meditation. We did not know what visions were being shown him.

We had been walking for an hour or so when Zeitel stopped and said, 'Children, perhaps we ought to go back. He must be sitting alone feeling sorry now. How could we have allowed that filthy peasant woman to steal him from us? What if we meet his father? Could we tell him that we left Berel with a filthy peasant woman? Let us go back, children.'

But even as she spoke. Zeitel knew we could not go back. We felt heavy and weary.

In the distance moved long lines of refugees. Tall peasants stood in the field mowing grass. 'Hey you,' a peasant yelled to us. 'Over there go the refugees looking for their relatives. Don't you have any relatives? Is that why you're in no hurry?'

Hershel was depressed, his face yellow with sadness. Max and I walked at Zeitel's side. Hershel plodded heavily behind, his every step a sigh.

'You remember the night we went into the bunker?' Max broke the silence. 'You didn't want to go in, Zeitel. Now the bunker is full of water. It held up all those years, and on the last day it filled with water. The dampness must have been too much for it.'

We took out the last of our bread and sausage and sat down to eat. 'Hershel, if you don't eat, neither will we. A person can't walk if he doesn't eat. You've got to keep up your strength, it's a long trip,' Zeitel reprimanded Hershel.

We came to a cross-road, and Max said, 'I'll walk over and ask where the roads go.'

'Well, I found out,' he said when he returned. 'One road goes to Tulz, the other to Raditz.'

'Raditz,' said Hershel. 'No Raditz for me. They'll never see my face there again.'

'Well, where shall we go?'

We were standing there in a quandary when an old peasant approached us, his cheeks wrinkled in a smile, and began talking to us in our language.

'You're Jews,' he said. 'I like your food. I did a lot of business with Jews. You want to take my advice? It's good advice. Down there, on the slope of that hill, lives a man who is very famous in these parts, there's no one like him when it comes to dealing with spirits. He'll tell you who is still alive and worth searching for, and who has been killed. Why tire yourselves walking the roads? Go over to his hut and he'll tell you. Take my advice.'

'What do you think?' said Max, the blue vein throbbing in his forehead.

Zeitel's face grew very serious. She took off her kerchief.

Hershel raised his head and said, 'I don't believe in magic.'

The straw-roofed hut was low, with a narrow door.

'Do our people believe in magic?' asked Hershel.

'It can't do us any harm,' said Zeitel, taking hold of his sleeve. 'Let's go in, children.'

'Quiet, quiet,' a man greeted us at the door. 'Take your shoes off, take your shoes off. It's forbidden to wear shoes in a holy place.'

Barefoot, we stood outside the room. Zeitel held on to the three of us.

'People have come,' said the doorkeeper. 'They've taken their shoes off. Shall I let them in?'

'In a while,' answered a muffled voice from the large room.

After that we heard, 'It is permitted now.'

The doorkeeper placed himself at the head of our group, and said, 'Follow me.' We walked close together, like links in a taut chain, the way we used to walk on those nights when we left the bunker to hunt for potatoes. We heard the sound of bells, and of wheels, and of a great rushing back and forth. We sensed the darkness growing deeper; in a moment we would be in its dumb heart.

Two candlesticks stood in a comer, the candles flickering.

'Now cover your faces,' said the magician, 'and repeat after me.'

I do not remember what he told us to say, but I remember that we repeated the words loudly and the room was full of trembling and sound.

'Now,' said the old man, 'I have sanctified you and you may see visions from the other worlds.'

One by one they ascended the stage, shrouded in blue, and we recognized them by their rustling and the way they lifted their necks.

Zeitel broke away from us, shouting, 'We are orphaned, children, we are orphaned.' We could not hold her.

'I cannot show you anything with all this noise,' said the magician.

Hershel took off his caftan and said, 'Here's the pay of your magic.'

'This is not magic,' the sorcerer called after him.

We pulled Zeitel outside. Hershel stood bare-armed, the bones of his body sticking out. We did not see Zeitel's face. She covered it with her fists and shouted, 'Children, we are orphans, children, we are orphans.'

Outside, the winter lay cold. Clouds rent the huge silence, the trees were hung with a gleaming red that stained the premature blossoms. When Zeitel caught sight of Hershel's bare body, she started up and said, 'Where's your caftan? Put it on quick, you'll catch your death of cold.'

That night Zeitel awoke and said, 'Did you see, did you see?' She was having a bad dream.

Max took off his coat and said, 'Hershel, let's share this.'

The night deepened, the dogs in the village were awake and howling, Zeitel kept raising her head and covering Hershel. The darkness pressed down on us.

Zeitel said, 'If anybody sees Reb Isaac—my heart tells me he will come—don't let him go to that place, God forbid.'

In the morning we saw a man ploughing in the distance, and a woman walking behind him. Zeitel said, 'I see Berel.'

'No, it's a peasant you see,' said Hershel.

The spring sun passed through the clouds. Max's face shone white. Zeitel became herself again, and said, 'If only we were all together once more, the way we used to be in the bunker, and Reb Isaac and Berel were with us . . . if only . . . I could walk to the end of the world.'

BEFORE THE BATH

Ismail Kadaré

Translated from the Albanian by Peter Constantine

Ismail Kadaré (1936–) is an Albanian novelist, poet, essayist and play-wright. He has been a leading literary figure in Albania since the 1960s. He focused on poetry until the publication of his first novel, *The General of the Dead Army*, which made him famous inside and outside of Albania. His works have been published in about forty-five languages. In 2005 he became the first winner of the Man Booker International Prize. After offending the authorities with a politically satirical poem in 1975, he was forbidden to publish for three years. During the 1990s and 2000s he was offered multiple times to become President of Albania, but declined.

He approached the tub of hot water, his eyes clouding with pleasure (how many times had he dreamt of this tub in his cold tent on the plains!), and just as he dipped one foot in the water he turned and looked at his wife, who was walking a few steps behind him. Her face still wore the flickering smile, but, even more than by the smile, his attention was caught by the metallic sheen of the object twinkling beneath the fabric his wife was carrying in her hands. Although his whole body was moving towards the bath, climbing into the tub, his curiosity still made him turn his head to see what the metallic object might be. (Perhaps during his long absence new utensils had been invented — even for bathing.) At that very moment he saw his wife almost above him, ready to cast the unfurled fabric over him ("What is this crazed woman doing?" he thought. "Who has ever heard of a man drying himself before a bath instead of after?"), and an instant later, before he was even seized by the terror of the thought that the fabric looked more like a net, he felt his arms entangled, and in the same instant saw the short axe in his wife's hands. The pain on the right side of his neck and the first spray of blood seemed to coincide with the shout of "Murder!" which he heard as if from the mouth of another.

He found himself outside the tub again, as if to amend an error, and, as before, he dipped one foot in the water, then saw his wife who was walking a few steps behind him, saw the flash of the axe beneath the fabric and, unable to make out what was happening, before he was even seized by the terror of the fabric turning into a net that bound his arms, he heard the first slash, and the blood reddened the water.

He found himself outside the tub again, as if to amend something, but this time slowly, as if he were coolly trying to resolve a misunderstanding. He approached the tub—the hot steam made everything seem more distant—his eyes clouding with pleasure (how many times had he dreamt of this tub in his cold army tent, when frantically, covered in grime, he had made love to a captive!), and just as he dipped one foot in the water he turned and looked at his wife, as if to assure himself that happiness was very near. Her face still wore that flickering smile, like a flickering, shifting mask, but, even more than by the smile, his attention was caught by the metallic sheen of the object twinkling coldly beneath the fabric his wife was carrying in her hands. And yet he thought as intensely of the love he would be making to her very soon as he thought that this metal—or rather hoped that this metal—had something to do with one of her surprises, those sudden and pleasurable surprises when he returned after long separations . . . At that very moment he saw his wife above him and the fabric turning into a net, his arms caught, the axe, the slash, the spray of blood, the cry of "Murder!" all happening in such quick succession that they intermingled and became one, until he found himself again outside the tub, moving towards her, found his wife walking a few steps behind him with the fabric in her hands, and this time the memory of the tent on the plains, his wife's mask-like smile, the flashing of the axe as it hit the water, all intermingled with lightning speed, making way for the slowness that was to follow. Before he saw his wife, he saw her shadow on the water, and then, when he saw her holding the unfurled fabric, he wanted to say to her "Darling, what is this new little trick of yours?" But it was just at this moment when the fabric took on a new guise, with nodes and nerves like those on the wings of bats, and the fabric slowly flew over his head, and the closer it came, the more clearly he saw that it was a net, and before he even felt his arms grow numb as it touched them, before the axe hit him in the neck, he said to himself "This is the end," and from the moment of this thought to the moment the blood reddened the water it seemed as if an interminable time had passed.

He found himself outside the tub again, moving towards her, as he had a million times before, experiencing with different rhythms this final fragment, these last twenty-two seconds of his life. This was the hell of Agamemnon of the House of Atreus, murdered by his wife on the first day of his return from the Plains of Troy, at thirteen hundred hours and twenty minutes, March 31, in the year eleven hundred and ninety-nine before our era.

THE BREADNUT AND THE BREADFRUIT

Maryse Condé

Translated from the French by Richard Philcox

Maryse Condé (1937–). Born and raised in Guadeloupe, Condé studied English at the Sorbonne and at the age of twenty-two, taught variously in Guinea, Senegal and Ghana. Her first novel was published in 1976, and since then she has written many novels and plays. She is a scholar of Francophone literature and Professor Emerita of French at Columbia University and now divides her time between New York and Guadeloupe. She is best known for her novel *Segu* which was awarded the Prix de l'Académie française in 1988.

I met my father when I was ten years old.

My mother had never uttered his name in my presence, and I had ended up thinking that I owed my life to her unbending will-power alone. My mother walked staunchly along life's straight and narrow path. Apparently she only strayed once to follow the unknown face of my father, who managed to seduce her before handing her back to a life of duty and religion. She was a tall woman and so severe she seemed to me to be devoid of beauty. Her forehead disappeared under a white and violet headtie. Her breasts vanished in a shapeless black dress. On her feet were a pair of plimsolls carefully whitened with blanc d'Espagne. She was laundress at the hospital in Capesterre, Marie-Galante, and every morning she used to get up at four o'clock to clean the house, cook, wash, iron, and goodness knows what else. At twenty to seven she would open the heavy doors after shouting:

'Sandra! I'm off!'

Twenty minutes later, our neighbor Sandra hammered on the dividing wall and yelled: 'Etiennise! Time to get up!'

Without further ado I would sit up on the mattress that I laid out each evening beside my mother's mahogany bed and reflect on the sullen day that lay ahead. Monday, Tuesday, Wednesday, Friday, and Saturday were as alike as two pins. Things were different on Thursdays and Sundays because of catechism and Sunday school.

So when I was ten my mother bent her tall figure in two and came and sat down opposite me.

'Your father's a dog who'll die like a dog in the trash heap of his life. The fact is

I have to send you to the lycée in Pointe-à-Pitre. I haven't got enough money to put you in lodgings. Who would lodge you, come to that? So I shall have to ask him.'

In one go I learned that I had passed my entrance exams, that I was going to leave my island backwater, and that I was going to live far from my mother. My happiness was so overwhelming that, at first, words failed me. Then I stammered out in a feigned sorrowful tone of voice: 'You'll be all by yourself here.'

My mother gave me a look that implied she didn't believe a word. I know now why I thought I hated my mother. Because she was alone. Never the weight of a man in her bed between the sheets drawn tight like those of a first communicant. Never the raucous laughter of a man to enlighten her evenings. Never a good fight in the early hours of the dawn! Our neighbors in tears would walk around with bruises, bumps, and split lips that spoke of pain and voluptuousness. But my mother, she modelled herself along the lines of Saint Thérèse de Lisieux and Bernadette Soubirou.

At that time—I'm talking about the end of the fifties—the town of Capesterre numbered a good many souls, how many I don't know exactly. Everything seemed drowsy. The teachers who had us recite 'the River Loire has its source in the Mont Gerbier-de-Jonc', the priests who had us stumble through 'One God in three distinct persons', and the town crier beating his drum 'Oyez, oyez!'

Only the sea, a crazed woman with eyes of amethyst, leapt in places over the rocks and tried to take men and animals alike by the throat.

Three times a week a boat left Grand Bourg, Marie-Galante, for the actual island of Guadeloupe. It was loaded with black piglets, poultry, goats, jerricans of 55% rum, matrons with huge buttocks and children in tears. One late September morning my mother made the sign of the cross on my forehead, kissed me sparingly, and entrusted me and my few belongings to the captain. Hardly had we left the jetty on which the crowd grew smaller and smaller than my joy gave way to a feeling of panic. The sea opened up like the jaws of a monster bent on swallowing us. We were sucked into the abyss, then vomited out in disgust before being dragged back again. This merry-go-round lasted an hour and a half. Women with rosaries in hand prayed to the Virgin Mary. Finally we entered the mauve waters of the harbor with Pointe-à-Pitre shining as a backdrop.

I spent three days without seeing my father, who was away 'on business' in Martinique. In his absence I got to know my stepmother, a small woman draped with jewelry and as rigid as my mother, as well as my half-sister, who was almost blonde in a pleated skirt. She ignored me disdainfully.

When he leaned against the door of the cubby hole I had been allotted in the attic, it seemed to me that the day began to dawn on my life. He was a fairly dark-skinned mulatto whose curly hair had begun to grey. A web of wrinkles surrounded his dark grey eyes. 'What a damned Negress your mother is, even so!' he laughed in a sparkle of teeth. 'She didn't even tell me you were born and now point blank she writes to make me "face up to my responsibilities". But I have to admit you're the spitting image of your father!'

I was terribly flattered I resembled such a handsome gentleman! Etienne Bellot, my father, came from an excellent family. His father had been a public notary. His elder brother had taken over his father's practice and his sister had married a magistrate. When at the age of twenty he had failed part one of the baccalauréat for the fourth time he had the brilliant idea of getting Larissa Valère, the only daughter of the big ironmonger on Market Square, with child. He was married off therefore in great pomp at the Cathedral of Saint Pierre and Saint Paul, four months before his daughter was due to be born, then appointed to replace his father-in-law who was getting on in years. Not for long! It was soon discovered that the daily takings of the ironmongery, substantial as they were, vanished into thin air among the men with whom he lost at cards in the bars of the Carenage district, the women he bedded just about everywhere, and the professional cadgers. Larissa therefore took her seat at the till and stayed there from that day on.

I was not the only illegitimate child of Etienne's, even though I was the only resident one. Oh no! After Sunday school there was a stream of boys and girls of every age and every color who came to greet their begetter and receive from the hand of Larissa a brand new ten franc note that she took out of a box specially reserved for this purpose. The stream dried up for lunch and siesta only to resume in greater force from four o'clock in the afternoon until night fall. My father, who never moved from his bed on Sunday, the Lord's Day, kept his bedroom door firmly closed, never letting a smile or a caress filter through.

In fact nobody found grace in his heart except for Jessica, my almost blonde half-sister whose grey eyes, the very image of her father's, seldom looked up from her twopenny novels. I soon learned that one of Etienne's mistresses had maliciously struck Larissa down with a mysterious illness that had laid to rest two other legitimate children—both boys—and that Jessica was the couple's greatest treasure.

Larissa must have been very lovely. Now gone to seed, there remained the fern-colored eyes behind her glasses and teeth of pearl that her smile sometimes revealed. The only times she left the house were to sit straight-back at the till or to go to confession or mass. Up at four like my mother, Larissa, who had three domestics, would let no one iron her husband's drill suits, shirts, underwear, and socks. She polished his shoes herself. She prepared his coffee and served him his breakfast, the only meal he took at a fixed time. All day long he came and went, and his place remained set for hours on end while the ice turned to water in the little bucket next to his glass where the flies drowned themselves in despair. When he was at home, somebody would be waiting for him in the sitting room, on the pavement, at the wheel of a car, and he would hurry off to some mysterious rendezvous from which he returned late at night, always stumbling on the fifth stair that led to the first floor. I don't quite know how he became interested in me. For weeks he scarcely gave me a look and found it quite natural for me to be treated hardly better than a domestic, clad in Jessica's old dresses, wearing a worn-out pair of sandals and studying from her old books that were literally falling to pieces. On Sundays when Larissa was doing the distribution she used to give me two ten franc notes and I went to the 'Renaissance' to watch the American films in technicolor.

One day I was sitting in the yard studying for a poetry recitation. I remember it was a poem by Emile Verhaeren:

> Le bois brûlé se fendillait en braises rouges
> Et deux par deux, du bout d'une planche, les gouges
> Dans le ventre des fours engouffraient les pains mous.

He loomed up beside me amidst a warm smell of rum, cigarettes, and Jean-Marie Farina eau de Cologne and tore the book from my hands.

'For God's sake! The rubbish those people teach you! Do you understand anything?'

I shook my head.

'Wait there. I've got just what you need.'

He plunged inside the house, stopping Larissa who was already busy laying the table: 'No, honey dear, I've no time to eat.' Then he came back brandishing a little thin book: 'Now read that instead!' Larissa intervened and firmly took it out of his hands: 'Etienne! Don't fill that child's head with rubbish!'

I never did know what book my father wanted me to read, but strangely enough, from that day on the ice was broken. He got into the habit of stopping in the dining room near the corner of the table where I did my homework and leafing through my books, commenting: 'The Alps! What's got into them to teach you about the Alps? I bet you don't even know the names of the mountains in this country of ours?'

'There's the Soufrière!'

'All right, next Thursday I'll take you to the Soufrière. We'll leave as soon as it's light. I'll take Jessica along too. It will do her good to get away from the twopenny romances by Delly and Max du Veuzit! Larissa, you'll prepare a picnic hamper for us.'

Larissa did not even bother to reply and went on checking the cook's accounts. 'A bunch of mixed vegetables for the soup. A bunch of chives. A box of cloves.'

I did not hold it against my father for not keeping his promises or for not turning up for his appointments. He was usually fast asleep when we were to leave at dawn. Or else he did not come home until midnight when we were supposed to go out in the evening.

No, I did not hold it against him.

If it had not been for him I would never have dreamed, imagined, hoped, or expected anything.

If it had not been for him I would never have known that mangoes grow on mango trees, that ackees grow on ackee trees, and that tamarinds grow on tamarind trees for the delight of our palates. I would never have seen that the sky is sometimes pale blue like the eyes of a baby from Europe, sometimes dark green like the back of an iguana, and sometimes black as midnight, or realized that the sea makes love to it. I would never have tasted the rose apples after a swim down by the river.

He actually only took me out once. One Saturday afternoon Larissa and Jessica had gone to pay a visit to the family and I was languishing away with one of the girl domestics who was as scared as I was in this old wooden house where the spirits were simply waiting for nightfall to haunt our sleep. My father burst in and stared at me in surprise.

'You're all alone?'

'Yes, Larissa and Jessica have gone to Saint-Claude.'

'Come with me.'

A woman was waiting for him on the other side of the Place de la Victoire: jet black with her lips daubed bright red and loops dancing in her ears.

'Whose child is that?' she asked in surprise.

'It's mine.'

'Larissa is really going too far. It wouldn't kill her to buy two yards of cotton! Look how the child's got up!'

My father looked at me and perhaps saw me for the first time in my Cinderella rags. 'You're right,' he said, puzzled. 'How about buying her a dress at Samyde's?'

They bought me a salmon taffeta dress trimmed with three flounces that clashed with my plimsolls which nobody thought of changing. While we walked along, the woman undid my four plaits greased with palma-christi oil that were knotted so tightly they pulled back the skin on my forehead, and rearranged them in 'vanilla beans'. Thus transfigured, I took my seat in the motor coach, *Mary, Mother of All the Saints,* that rumbled off to Saint Rose.

Sabrina, who was heavy with child through the doings of Dieudonné, master sail-maker, was being married off. The priest, who was a good old devil, had closed his eyes to the bride's 'hummock of truth' and agreed to give the nuptial blessing.

The wedding ceremony was being held in a spacious house circled by a veranda and built somewhat negligently amidst a tangle of bougainvillea and allamanda a few feet from the sea that gave a daily show under the sun. A table several feet long had been set up under an awning of woven coconut palms stuck here and there with little bouquets of red and yellow flowers. In each plate the women were arranging piles of black pudding, as big as two fingers, together with slices of avocado pear. A band was already playing under a tree and the flute of the hills answered the call of the *ti-bwa* and the *gwo-ka*. I did not mix with the group of children as I thought their games quite insipid. I preferred to listen in on the conversation of the grown-ups whose coarse jokes I guessed without understanding them. That's how I found myself beside my father whose tongue had been loosened by too much rum:

'We don't get two lives Etiennise. Down there under the ground there are no wooden horses and the merry-go-round has stopped turning. We're all alone, cramped in our coffins, and the worms are having a feast day. So as long as your heart keeps beating make the most of it. Don't take any notice of people who say: "Ah, what a bitch life is! A crazed woman who knows neither rhyme nor reason. She hits out right, she hits out left, and pain is the only reality." Let me tell you, that woman. . . .' Unfortunately somebody intervened and I never knew the end of the story. When my father returned his mind had turned to other things.

'My parents used to tell me: "We are mulattoes. We do not frequent niggers." I never understood why. My best friends are niggers you know. The first woman I made love to was a negress. What a woman! Ah, what a woman! When she opened her legs she swallowed me up! Your mother was the same. What a woman!

Mme Delpine recommended her to Larissa for the ironing as she did wonders with her instruments. And not only with them, believe me! Unfortunately, she had a serious frame of mind. Father Lebris had filled her head with all sorts of tomfoolery about Mary and virginity. She used to sleep in the attic. The afternoon I set upon her like poverty laying hands on the pauper she was reading "The Imitation of Our Lord Jesus Christ." You should have heard her beg me: "Let me be, Monsieur Etienne, God will punish you. Let me be!" You bet if I let her be. . . .'

And instead of rebelling against the calvary of my poor ravished albeit raped mother, I uttered a raucous laugh. I laughed chickenheartedly.

'Each time it was one hell of a job. I'm sure it was all pretense and she enjoyed it as much as I did. And then one morning she disappeared. Without a word of explanation. Without even asking for her wages. Larissa was furious. . . .'

Another crime to add to my list: I showed no signs of pity for my mother; neither for the terror of her discovery and her flight to her native island nor for the family lamentations, the neighbors' malicious gossip, and that pathetic gesture to cover my illegitimacy, the name of Etiennise, daughter of Etienne.

When we got home on Sunday around three o'clock in the afternoon, Larissa, who had never raised a hand against me, gave me a thorough beating, claiming that I had lost my best school dress. I know what infuriated her, it was this growing intimacy with my father.

My mother saw it immediately. Hardly had I set foot on the jetty where she was waiting than she ran her eyes over me significantly and said: 'You're very much his daughter now!'

I didn't answer. I spent the Christmas holidays barricaded behind the hostile silence that I had raised between us, the unjust cruelty of which I only understood too late, much too late.

I didn't realize to what extent she was suffering. I didn't see the taut features of her face droop and slacken. The wheeze in her respiration, keeping back the grief, escaped my attention. Her nights were wracked with nightmares. In the mornings she would plunge into prayer.

The intimacy with my father soon took an unexpected turn from which I obviously did not dare shy away. He entrusted me with little notes to hand to all the girls at the lycée who had caught his eye.

'Give this from me to that little yellow girl in the fourth form.'

'And this one to the tall girl in the second form.'

It soon became a genuine commerce of billets-doux. You would never imagine how ready they were, these young girls from a reputable family seen at church on Sundays, closely chaperoned by father, brothers, and mother and stumbling with beatitude on their return from the altar, how ready they were to listen to the improper propositions of a married man with a reputation.

I devised a daring technique. I would approach the coveted prey while she was chatting with her classmates in the school yard. I would stand squarely in front of her and hand her the note folded in four without saying a word. Somewhat surprised, but unsuspecting, she would take it from me, open it, start to read and then blush deeply as far as the color of her skin would let her. My father did not exactly treat the matter lightly:

MY LITTLE DARLING,
Ever since I saw you on the Place de la Victoire I have been madly in love with you. If you do not want to have a death on your conscience meet me tomorrow at 5 p.m. on the second bench in the allée des Veuves. I'll be waiting for you with a red dahlia in my buttonhole. . . .
Waiting for an answer in which I hope you will accept.

The effect of such an epistle was radical. Before class was over the victim would hand me a folded sheet accepting the rendezvous.

While I was in form three a new pupil arrived, Marie-Madeleine Savigny. She had just arrived from Dakar where her father had been a magistrate and her African childhood had given her an aristocratic languor. She called her sandals 'samaras' and her mother's domestics 'boyesses'. Every able-bodied man in Pointe-à-Pitre was eaten up with desire for her, and my father more than the rest.

When I brought her the traditional billet-doux she cast her hazel eyes over it and without a moment's hesitation tore it up, scattering the pieces of paper at the foot of a hundred-year old sandbox tree. My father did not consider himself beaten. With me as the go-between he returned to the attack the next day and the next. By the end of the third week Marie-Madeleine had not given an inch while my father was an absolute wreck. Back home on time he would be watching for me from the balcony and then rush down the stairs as impetuous as a teenager.

'Well?'

I shook my head. 'She won't even take the letter from me.'

His face dropped and he became the outrageously spoiled little boy he had once been. He had been his mother's favorite, his grandmother's; his father's sisters and his mother's sisters, who showered him with kisses, turned a blind eye to his caprices and called him voluptuously 'Ti-mal'. In June Marie-Madeleine caused a stir by not entering for part one of the baccalauréat. A few weeks later we learned she was to marry Jean Burin des Rosiers, the fourth son of a rich white creole factory owner. Great was the stupor! What! A white creole to marry a colored girl? And not even a mulatto into the bargain! For although he was a magistrate, Mr Savigny was but a common copper-colored nigger! As for the mother, she was halfcoolie! Such an event had not occurred since 1928, the year of the terrible hurricane, when a Martin Saint Aurèle had married a Negress. But the family had turned their backs on him and the couple had lived in poverty. Whereas the Burin des Rosiers were welcoming their daughter-in-law with open arms. The world was completely upside down!

Everyone had just regained their calm when Marie-Madeleine, who no longer needed to lace herself up in corsets, exhibited at least a six-month-old belly in her flowing flowery silk dresses.

My father joined in the rush for the spoils. In the middle of a circle of lecherous listeners I heard him recount, without ever trying to deny the fact, how he had tasted Marie-Madeleine's secret delights but unlike Jean had not let himself be caught red-handed.

I spent an awful summer holiday on Marie-Galante. Since I was soon to enter the lycée in the rue Achille René-Boisneuf and take physics and chemistry with the boys, my mother got it into her head to make me a set of clothes. She went down to the Grand Bourg where she bought yards and yards of material, patterns, marking crayon, and a pair of tailor's scissors. . . . Every day when she came back from the hospital there were the unending fitting sessions. I could not bear the touch of her fidgety hands and her grumbling: 'This side hangs all right. Why doesn't the other side do the same?'

On Sunday, August 15, I refused to accompany her in the flared dress she was so proud of. She looked me straight in the eyes: 'If you think he worships you why doesn't he pay for your dresses?'

It was true that for the three years or so I had been living with my father I had never seen the color of his money, except for Larissa's two little brand-new notes. I was doomed to gaze from afar at the books in the bookshops, the perfume in the perfume shops, and the ice creams at the ice-cream parlor.

Whenever she had the opportunity, my mother sent me two or three dirty banknotes with a note that always read: 'I hope you are keeping well. Your affectionate maman, Nisida.'

I was thus able to buy my exercise books and pens and fill my inkpot with blue ink from the seas of China.

When school started again in October my father stopped his traffic of billets-doux. I felt so frustrated, deprived as I was of my mean little mission as a go-between, that I would have gladly drawn his attention to the pretty chicks (that's how he used to call them) who scratched around untouched in the school yard. I soon discovered the key to the mystery. He had fallen head over heels in love with the very pretty wife of a Puerto-Rican tailor by the name of Artemio who had opened his small shop on the rue Frébault. Lydia was a righteous woman. Or perhaps quite simply she did not like my father. She talked freely to her husband of these constant advances that troubled her, and the husband, hotheaded as Latins are wont to be, resolved to give the brazen fellow a lesson he would not forget. He hired the services of three or four bullies, one of whom was a former boxer nicknamed 'Doudou Sugar Robinson'. They lay in wait one evening for my father while he was striding across the Place de la Victoire and left him lifeless at the foot of a flame tree. Around midnight Larissa was presented with an inert, blood-stained body. Transfigured, she swooped down on her husband, who was finally at her mercy. For weeks it was a constant traffic of herb teas, poultices, frictions with arnica and pond leeches destined to suck out the bad blood. Once the doctor had turned his back carrying off his sulfanilamides, in came the *obeah* man with his roots. Every Sunday after the high mass the priest popped in to describe the flames of hell to the notorious sinner.

My father never recovered from this misadventure. In his enthusiasm, Doudou Sugar Robinson had fractured his eyebrow, crushed his nasal bone and broken his jaw in three places. All this knitted together again very badly and the good souls of Pointe-à-Pitre shook their heads: 'God works in mysterious ways! And he used to be such a handsome man!'

But above all, it was his pride and his morale that took a beating. My father realized he had become a laughingstock. He became easily offended and susceptible. He quarrelled with his best friends. He lost that vitality that had made him so popular with the ladies. He became sad, vindictive, and whimpering.

As for me, with the typical cruelty of teenagers, I hastened to keep my distance from the hero who was no longer a hero and who shuffled around harking back to his former conquests. I began to look at him in a new light. What exactly was he worth?

I was pondering upon this when I learned that my mother had been taken to the hospital.

Less than one year later she died of cancer, having hidden the first symptoms from everyone.

A WOMAN LIKE ME

Xi Xi

Translated from the Chinese by Howard Goldblatt

Xi Xi (1938–). Zhang Yan was born in Shanghai and moved with her family to Hong Kong at the age of twelve. She worked for many years as a primary school teacher, and was an outspoken advocated for teachers' rights. She edited a number of literary magazines, including "Plain Leaf Literature". Under the penname Xi Xi, she is an accomplished poet, novelist, and essayist, but is perhaps most famous in her native country as a screenwriter, and one of the pioneers of experimental film in Hong Kong. Xi Xi is an ardent soccer fan – in part because her father is a ticket checker at a bus station, who also worked as a team coach and referee.

A woman like me is actually unsuitable for any man's love. So the fact that the emotional involvement between Xia and me has reached this point fills even me with wonder. I feel that the blame for my having fallen into this trap, from which there is no escape, rests solely with Fate, which has played a cruel trick on me. I am totally powerless to resist Fate. I've heard others say that when you truly like someone, what may be nothing more than an innocent smile directed your way as you sit quietly in a corner can cause your very soul to take wing. That's exactly how I feel about Xia. So when he asked me: Do you like me? I expressed my feelings toward him without holding back a thing. I'm a person who has no concept of self-protection, and my words and deeds will always conspire to make me a laughingstock in the eyes of others. Sitting in a coffee shop with Xia, I had the appearance of a happy person, but my heart was filled with a hidden sorrow; I was so terribly unhappy because I knew where Fate was about to take me, and now the fault would be mine alone. I made a mistake at the very beginning by agreeing to accompany Xia on a trip to visit a schoolmate he hadn't seen for a long time, then later on, by not declining any of his invitations to go to the movies. It's too late for regret now, and, besides, the difference between regretting and not regretting is too slight to be important, since at this very moment I am sitting in the corner of a coffee shop waiting for him. I agreed to show him where I work, and that will be the final chapter. I had already been out of school for a long time when I first met Xia, so when he asked me if I had a job, I told him that I had been working for several years.

What sort of job do you have?

He asked.

I'm a cosmetician.

I said.

Oh, a cosmetician.

He remarked.

But your face is so natural.

He said.

He said that he didn't like women who used cosmetics and preferred the natural look. I think that the reason his attention had been drawn to my face, on which I never use makeup, was not my response to his question but because my face is paler than most people's. My hands too. Both my hands and my face are paler than most people's because of my job. I knew that as soon as I divulged my occupation to him, he would jump to the same erroneous conclusion that all my former friends had. He has already assumed that my job is to beautify the appearance of girls in general, such as adding just the right touch of color to the face of a bride-to-be on her wedding day. And so when I told him that there were no days off in my job, that I was often busy Sundays, he was more convinced than ever that his assumption was correct. There were always so many brides on Sundays and holidays. But making brides-to-be beautiful is not what I do; my job is to apply the final cosmetic touches to people whose lives have already come to an end, to make them appear gentle and at peace during their final moments before leaving the world of man. In days past I had brought up the subject of my occupation to friends, and I always immediately corrected their momentary misconception, so that they would know exactly what sort of person I am. But all my honesty ever brought me was the loss of virtually all my friends. I frightened them all off; it was as though the me who was sitting across from them drinking coffee was actually the ghost of their own inner fears. And I never blamed them, for we all have an inborn, primitive timidity where the unknown mysteries of life are concerned. The main reason I didn't give a fuller answer to Xia's question was my concern that the truth would frighten him; I could no longer allow my unusual occupation to unsettle the friends around me, something for which I could never forgive myself. The other reason was my natural inability to express what I think and feel, which, over a long period of time, has led to my habit of being uncommunicative.

But your face is so natural.

He said.

When Xia said that, I knew that it was a bad omen for the emotional road he and I were taking; but at that moment he was so happy—happy because I was a woman who didn't use makeup on herself. Yet my heart was filled with sadness.

I don't know who will someday be applying makeup to my face—will it be Aunt Yifen? Aunt Yifen and I have one hope in common: that in our lifetimes we will never have to make up the face of a loved one. I don't know why, after the appearance of this unlucky omen, I continued going on the pleasure excursions with Xia, but maybe, since I'm only human, I lack self-control and merely go where Fate takes me, one ordained step after another. I have no logical explanation for my behavior, and I think that this might just be what humans are all about: much of our behavior is inexplicable, even to ourselves.

Can I come and see you work?

Xia asked.

That shouldn't be a problem.

I said.

Will they mind?

He asked.

I don't imagine any of them will.

I said.

The reason Xia asked if he could see how I worked was that every Sunday morning I have to go to my workplace, and on those days he never has anything else to do. He offered to walk me to work, and since he'd be there already, he might as well hang around and take a look. He said he wanted to look at the brides-to-be and their maids of honor and all the hustle and bustle; he also wanted to watch me as I made the pretty ones prettier or the unattractive ones plain. I agreed without a second's thought. I knew that Fate had already led me up to the starting line and what was about to happen was a foregone conclusion. So here I am, sitting in a small coffee shop waiting for Xia, and from here we'll go together to my workplace. As soon as we get there he'll understand everything. Xia will know then that the perfume he thought I was wearing for him actually serves to mask the smell of formaldehyde on my body. He'll also know then that the reason I wear white so often is not a conscious effort to produce an appearance of purity but merely as a convenience in going to and coming from work. The strange medicinal odor that clings to my body has already penetrated my bones, and all of my attempts to wash it off have failed. Eventually, I gave up trying and even got to the point where I no longer even notice the smell. Xia knows nothing of all this, and he even once commented to me: That's a very unusual perfume you wear. But everything will soon become crystal clear. I've always been a technician who can fashion elegant hairdos and tie a bow tie with the very best. But so what? Look at these hands of mine; how many haircuts and trims have they completed on people who could no longer speak, and how many bow ties have they tied around the necks of totally solemn people? Would Xia allow me to cut his hair with them? Would he allow me to tie his tie carefully for him? In the eyes of others, these soft, warm hands have become cold; in the eyes of others, these hands, which were made to cradle a newborn infant, have already become the hands for touching the white bones of skeletons.

There may have been many reasons why Aunt Yifen passed her skills on to me and they can be clearly perceived through her normal daily remarks. Sure, with these skills, no one would ever have to worry about being out of work and would be assured of a good living. So how can a woman like me, with little schooling and not much knowledge, compete with others in this greed-consumed, dog-eat-dog world? Aunt Yifen was willing to pass the consummate knowledge of this life work on to me solely because I was her niece. She had never let anyone watch her when she was working until the day she took me on as her apprentice, when she kept me by her side instructing me in every detail, until I lost my fear of being alone with the cold, naked corpses. I even learned how to sew up the sundered bodies and split skulls as though they were nothing more than theatrical costumes. I lost my parents when I was very young and was reared by Aunt Yifen. The strange thing is that I began to resemble her more and more, even becoming as taciturn as she, as pale of hand and face as she, and as slow in my movements as she. There were times when I couldn't shake my doubts that instead of being me, I had become another Aunt Yifen; the two of us were, in fact, one person—I had become a continuation of Aunt Yifen.

From today on, you'll not have to worry about your livelihood.

Aunt Yifen had said.

And you'll never have to rely upon anyone else to get through life, like other women do.

She had said.

I really didn't understand what she had meant by that. I couldn't figure out why I wouldn't have to worry about my livelihood if I learned what she had to teach me, or why I wouldn't have to rely upon anyone else to get through life, like other women do. Was it possible that no other profession in the world could free me from worrying about my livelihood or let me avoid having to rely upon others to get through life? But I was only a woman with little knowledge, so of course I would not be able to compete with other women. Therefore, it was strictly for my own good that Aunt Yifen had taken such pains to pass her special skills on to me. Actually, there is not a single person in this city who doesn't need help from someone in our profession. No matter who they are—rich or poor, high or low—once Fate has brought them to us, we are their final consolation; it is we who will give them a calm, good-natured appearance and make them seem incomparably gentle. Both Aunt Yifen and I have our individual hopes, but in addition to these, we share the common hope that in our lifetimes we will never have to make up the face of a loved one. That's why I was so sorrowful last week: I had a nagging feeling that something terrible had happened, and that it had happened to my own younger brother. From what I heard, my younger brother had met a young woman whose appearance and temperament made her the envy of all, a woman of talent and beauty. They were so happy together, and to me it was a stroke of joyous good fortune. But the happiness was all too short-lived, for I soon learned that—for no apparent reason—that delightful young woman had married a man she didn't love. Why is it that two people who are in love cannot marry but wind up spending the rest of their lives as the bitter victims of unrequited love? My younger brother changed into a different person; he even said to me: I don't want to live anymore. I didn't know what to do. Would I someday be making up the face of my own younger brother?

I don't want to live anymore.

My younger brother had said.

I couldn't understand how things could have reached that stage. Neither could my younger brother. If she had merely said: I don't like you anymore. He would have had nothing more to say. But the two of them were clearly in love. It was not to pay a debt of gratitude, nor was it due to economic hardships, so could it be that in this modern, civilized society of ours there are still parents who arrange their daughters' marriages? A lifetime covers many long years; why must one bow to Fate? Ai, I only hope that during my lifetime I will never have to make up the face of a loved one. But who can say for sure? When Aunt Yifen formally took me on as an apprentice and began passing her consummate skills on to me, she said: You must follow my wishes in one respect before I will take you on as my apprentice. I didn't know why she was being so solemn about it. But she continued with extreme seriousness: When it is my turn to lie down, you must personally make up my face; you are not to permit any stranger to so much as touch my body. I didn't feel that this would present any problems, but I was surprised by her inflexibility in the matter. Take me, for example: when it is my turn to lie down, what will the body I leave behind have to do with me? But that was Aunt Yifen's one and only personal wish, and it is up to me to help her fulfill it, if I am still around when that day comes. On this long road of life, Aunt Yifen and I are alike in that we harbor no grandiose wishes; Aunt Yifen hopes that I will be her cosmetician, and I only hope to use my talents to create the "most perfectly serene cadaver," one that will be gentler and calmer than all others, just as though death were truly the most beautiful sleep of all. Actually, even if I am successful, it will be nothing more than a game to kill a little time amid the boredom of life; isn't the entirety of human existence meaningless anyway? All my efforts constitute nothing more than an exercise in futility; if I someday manage to create the "most perfectly serene cadaver," will I gain any rewards from it? The dead know nothing, and my efforts will surely go unnoticed by the family of the deceased. Clearly, I will not hold an exhibition to display to the public my cosmetic skills and innovations. Even less likely is the prospect that anyone will debate, compare, analyze, or hold a forum to discuss my cosmetic job on the deceased; and even if they did, so what? It would cause as much of a stir as the buzzing of insects. My work is purely and simply a game played for the benefit of myself in my workroom. Why then have I bothered to form this hope in the first place? More than likely to provide a stimulus for me to go on working, because mine is a lonely profession: no peers, no audience, and, naturally, no applause. When I'm working, I can only hear the faint sound of my own breathing; in a room filled with supine bodies—male and female— I alone am breathing softly. It's gotten to the point where I imagine I can hear the sounds of my own heart grieving and sighing, and when the hearts of others cease producing sounds of lament, the sounds of my own heart intensify.

Yesterday I decided to do the cosmetic work on a young couple who had died in a love-inspired suicide pact, and as I gazed into the sleeping face of the young man, I realized that this was my chance to create the "most perfectly serene cadaver." His eyes were closed, his lips were pressed lightly together, and there was a pale scar on his left temple. He truly looked as though he were only sleeping very peacefully. In all my years of working on thousands of faces, many of which had fretful, distressed looks on them, the majority appearing quite hideous, I had done what I felt was most appropriate to improve their looks, using needle and thread or makeup to give them an appearance of unlimited gentleness. But words cannot describe the peaceful look on the face of the boy I saw yesterday, and I wondered if his suicide should be viewed as an act of joy. But then I felt that I was being deceived by appearances, and I believed instead that his had been an act of extreme weakness; I knew that, considering my position, I should have nothing to do with anyone who lacked the courage to resist the forces of Fate. So not only did I abandon all thoughts of using him to create the "most perfectly serene cadaver," I refused to even work on him, turning both him and the girl who had joined him in stupidly resigning themselves to Fate's whims over to Aunt Yifen to let her carefully repair the cheeks that had been scalded by the force of the powerful poison they had ingested.

Everyone is familiar with Aunt Yifen's past, because there are some around who personally witnessed it. Aunt Yifen was still young at the time, and she not only liked to sing as she worked but she talked to the cadavers who lay in front of her, as though they were her friends. It wasn't until later that she became so uncommunicative. Aunt Yifen was in the habit of telling her sleeping friends everything that was in her head—she never kept a diary—letting her monologues stand as a daily record of her life. The people who slept in her presence were mankind's finest audience: they listened to her voluble outpourings for the longest time, yet her secrets were always completely safe with them. She told them how she had met a young man and how they had shared the happiness of all young lovers whenever they were together, even though there were times when they had occasional ups and downs. In those days Aunt Yifen went to a school of cosmetics once a week, rain or shine, fifty weeks a year, to learn new techniques, until she had mastered all that the instructors could teach her. But even when the school informed her that there was nothing left for her to study, she persisted in asking if there weren't some new techniques that they could pass on to her. Her interest in cosmetology was that keen, almost as though it were inborn, and her friends were sure that someday she would open a grand salon somewhere. But no, she merely applied this knowledge of hers to the bodies of the people who slept in front of her. Her young lover knew nothing of any of this, for he was convinced that physical beauty was a natural desire of all girls, and that this particular one was simply fonder of cosmetics than most. That is, until that fateful day when she brought him along and showed him where she worked, pointing out the bodies that lay in the room and telling him that although hers was a lonely profession, in a place like this, one encountered no worldly bickerings, and that no petty jealousies, hatreds, or disputes over personal fame or gain existed; when these people entered the world of darkness, peace and gentleness settled over each and every one of them. He was shocked beyond belief; never in his wildest dreams had he thought that she could be a woman like this, one engaged in this sort of occupation. He had loved her, had been willing to do anything for her, vowing that he would never leave her, no matter what, and that they would grow old together, their mutual love enduring until death. But his courage failed him, his nerve abandoned him there among the bodies of people who could no longer speak and who had lost the ability to breathe. He let out a loud yell, turned on his heel and ran, flinging open every door that stood in his way. Many people saw him in a state of complete shock as he fled down the street. Aunt Yifen never saw him again. People sometimes overheard her talking to her silent friends in her workroom: Didn't he say he loved me? Didn't he say he would never leave me? What was it that suddenly frightened him so? Later on, Aunt Yifen grew more and more uncommunicative. Maybe she had already said everything she wanted to say, or maybe since her silent friends already knew all about her, there was no need to say anything more—there truly are many things that never need to be spoken. When Aunt Yifen was teaching me her consummate skills, she told me what had happened. It was I whom she had chosen as her apprentice, not my younger brother, and although there were other factors involved, the major reason had been that I was not a timid person.

Are you afraid?

She asked.

Not at all.

I said.

Are you timid?

She asked.

Not at all.

I said.

Aunt Yifen selected me as her successor because I was not afraid. She had a premonition that my fate would be the same as hers, and neither of us could explain how we grew to be so much alike, although it may have had its origins in the fact that neither of us was afraid. There was no fear in either one of us. When Aunt Yifen was telling me about what had happened to her, she said: I will always believe that there have to be others somewhere who are like us, people who are unafraid. This was before she had become so uncommunicative; she told me to stand by her side and watch how she reddened lips that had already become rigid, and how she worked gently on a pair of long-staring eyes until she had coaxed them into restful sleep. At that time she still talked now and then to her sleeping friends: And you, why were you afraid? Why do people who are falling in love have so little faith in love? Why do they not have courage in their love? Among Aunt Yifen's sleeping friends were many who had been timid and cowardly, and they were even quieter than the others. She knew certain things about her sleeping friends, and sometimes, as she powdered the face of a girl with bangs on her forehead, she would say to me: Ai! Ai! What a weak girl she was. She gave up the man she loved just so she could be considered a filial daughter. Aunt Yifen knew that this girl over here had placed herself into Fate's hands, of her own accord, out of a sense of gratitude, while that one over there had done the same by meekly accepting her lot. She talked about them not as though they had been living, feeling, thinking human beings, but merely pieces of merchandise.

What a horrible job!

My friends said.

Making up the faces of dead people! My God!

My friends said.

I wasn't the least bit afraid, but my friends were. They disliked my eyes because I often used them to look into the eyes of the dead, and they disliked my hands because I often used them to touch the hands of the dead. At first it was just dislike, but it gradually evolved into fear, pure and simple; not only that, the dislike and fear that at first involved only my eyes and hands later on included everything about me. I watched every one of them drift away from me, like wild animals before a forest fire or farmers before a swarm of locusts. Why are you afraid? I asked them. It's a job that someone has to do. Is it that I'm not good enough at what I do, or that I'm not professional enough? But I gradually grew to accept my situation—I got used to being lonely. So many people search for jobs that promise sweetness and warmth, wanting their lives to be filled with flowers and stars. But how does a life of flowers and stars give one the chance to take firm strides in life? I have virtually no friends left today; a touch of my hands reminds them of a deep and distant land of ice and cold, while a look into my eyes produces innumerable images of silent floating spirits, and so they have become afraid. There is nothing that can make them look back, not even the possibility that there is warmth in my hands, that my eyes can shed tears, or that I am warmhearted. And so I began to be more and more like Aunt Yifen, my only remaining friends being the bodies of the deceased lying in front of me. I surprised myself by breaking the silence around me as I said to them: Have I told you that tomorrow I'm going to bring someone named Xia here to meet you? He asked me if you would object, and I told him you wouldn't. Was I right in saying that? So tomorrow Xia will be here, and I think I know how it's all going to end, because my fate and Aunt Yifen's are one and the same. I expect to see Xia as his very soul will take wing the moment he steps foot in here. Ai! We cause each other's souls to take wing, but in different ways. I will not be startled by what happens, because the outcome has already been made clear to me by a variety of omens. Xia once said to me: Your face is so natural. Yes, my face is natural, and a natural face lacks the power to remove someone else's fear of things.

I once entertained the thought of changing my occupation; is it possible that I am incapable of doing the kinds of work that other women do? Granted that I'm not qualified to be a teacher, a nurse, or a secretary or clerk in an office building, but does that mean I can't work as a saleswoman in a shop, or sell bakery products, or even be a maid in someone's home? A woman like me needs only a roof over her head and three square meals a day, so there must be some place I could fit in. Honestly speaking, with my skills I could easily find work as a cosmetician for brides-to-be, but the very thought that lips I was applying color to could open to reveal a smile stops me cold. What would be going through my mind at a time like that? Too many memories keep me from working at that occupation, which is so similar to the one I have now. I wonder, if I did change jobs, would the color return to my pale face and hands? Would the smell of formaldehyde that has penetrated to my very bones completely disappear? And what about the job I have now, should I keep Xia completely in the dark about it? Hiding the past from a loved one is dishonest, even though there are countless girls in the world who will do anything to cover up their loss of chastity and the authentic number of years they have lived. But I find people like that despicable. I would have to tell Xia that for a long time I had done cosmetic work on the sleeping bodies of the deceased. Then he would know and would have to acknowledge what sort of woman I am. He'd know that the unusual odor on my body is not perfume but formaldehyde, and that the reason I wear white so often is not symbolic of purity but a means of making it more convenient for going to and coming from work. But all of this is as significant as a few drops of water in a vast ocean. Once Xia learns that my hands often touch the bodies of the deceased, will he still be willing to hold my hand as we cross a fast-flowing stream? Will he let me cut his hair for him, or tie his tie? Will he be able to bear my gazing intently at him? Will he be able to lie down in my presence without fear? I think he will be afraid, extremely afraid, and like all my friends, his initial shock will turn into dislike and then fear, and he will turn away from me. Aunt Yifen once said: There can be no fear where love is concerned. But I know that although what many people call love is unyielding and indomitable on the surface, it is actually extraordinarily fragile and pliable; puffed-up courage is really nothing but a layer of sugar-coating. Aunt Yifen said to me: Maybe Xia is not a timid person. That's one of the reasons why I never went into detail with him about my occupation. Naturally, another reason was that I'm not very good at expressing myself, and maybe I'd botch what I wanted to say, or I'd distort what I hoped to express to him by choosing the wrong place or time or mood. My not making it clear to Xia that it is not brides-to-be whom I make up is, in actuality, a sort of test: I want to observe his reaction when he sees the subjects I work on. If he is afraid, then he'll just have to be afraid. If he turns and flees, then I'll just tell my sleeping friends: Nothing really ever happened at all.

Can I see how you work?

He asked.

That shouldn't be a problem.

I said.

So here I am, sitting in the corner of a coffee shop waiting for Xia to arrive.

I spent some of this time carefully thinking things over: Maybe I'm not being fair to Xia by doing it this way. If he feels frightened by the work I do, is that his fault? Why should he be more courageous than the others? Why does there have to be any relationship between a fear of the dead and timidity where love is concerned? The two may be totally unrelated. My parents died while I was still young, and I was reared by Aunt Yifen. Both my younger brother and I were orphans. I don't know very much about my parents, and the few things I have learned were told to me later by Aunt Yifen. I remember her telling me that my father was a cosmetician for the deceased before he married my mother. When they were making their plans to get married, he asked her: Are you afraid? No, I'm not, she said. I believe that the reason I'm not afraid is that I take after my mother—her blood flows in my veins. Aunt Yifen said to me that my mother lives on in her memory because of what she had once said: I'm not afraid, and love is the reason. Perhaps that's why my mother lives on in my memory too, however faintly, even though I can no longer recall what she looked or sounded like. But I believe that just because she was my mother and that she said that love had kept her from being afraid does not mean that I have the right to demand the same attitude of everyone else. Maybe I ought to be hardest on myself for accepting my fate from the time I was a child and for making this occupation that others find so hard to accept my life's work. Men everywhere like women who are gentle, warm, and sweet, and such women are expected to work at jobs that are intimate, graceful, and elegant. But my job is cold and ghostly dark, and I'm sure that my entire body has long been tainted by that sort of shadowy cast. Why would a man who exists in a world of brightness want to be friendly with a woman surrounded by darkness? When he lies down beside her, could he avoid thinking that this is a person who regularly comes into contact with cadavers, and that when her hands brush up against his skin, would that remind him that these are hands that for a long time have rubbed the hands of the dead? Ai! Ai! A woman like me is actually unsuitable for any man's love. I think that I myself am to blame for all that has happened, so why don't I just get up and leave and return to my workplace; I have never known anyone by the name of Xia, and he will forget that he once had such a woman for a friend, a cosmetician who made up the faces of brides-to-be. But it's probably too late for that now.

I see him there through the window, crossing the street and walking this way. What's that in his hand? What a large bouquet of flowers! What's the occasion? Is it someone's birthday? I see him enter the coffee shop; he spots me sitting in this shadowy corner. The sun is shining brightly outside, and he has brought some of it in with him, for the sun's rays are reflected off of his white shirt. He is just like his name, Xia—eternal summer.

Hey, happy Sunday!

He says.

These flowers are for you.

He says.

He is so happy. He sits down and has a cup of coffee. We have had so many happy days together. But what is happiness, after all? Happiness is fleeting. There is such sadness in my heart. From here it is only a walk of three hundred paces before we arrive at my workplace. After that the same thing will happen that happened years ago. A man will come flying through that door as though his very soul had taken leave of him, and he will be followed by the eyes of the curious until he disappears from view. Aunt Yifen said: Maybe somewhere there is a man of true courage who is unafraid. But I know that this is just an assumption, and when I saw Xia crossing the street heading this way, a huge bouquet of flowers in his hand, I already knew, for this was truly a bad omen. Ai! Ai! A woman like me is actually unsuitable for any man's love; perhaps I should say to my sleeping friends: Aren't we all the same, you and I? The decades fly by in the blink of an eye, and no matter what the reason, there's no need for anyone to shock anyone else out of their senses. The bouquet of flowers Xia brought into the coffee shop with him is so very, very beautiful; he is happy, but I am laden with grief. He doesn't know that in our profession flowers symbolize eternal parting.

DEAD LETTER

Khalida Husain

Translated from the Urdu by Amina Azfar

Khalida Husain (1938–). Born and educated in Lahore, Khalida Asghar studied Urdu at the Punjab University Oriental College. Her first short story, "The Wagon," was published in 1963. Having published a number of highly-praised short stories, she vanished from the Urdu literary world after her marriage. In 1967, she and her husband moved to Karachi. It was only twelve years later, in 1977 that she once again began to publish, under her married name Khalida Husain. She has since published several anthologies of short stories, some of which have been translated into English and Hindi. Husain has taught in several Pakistani universities and now lives in Islamabad.

1

How should I address you? I thought hard about this, and finally put down the image of you that I carry in my mind at the head of this letter. What else can one mean to another human being with whom one has spent just a few days? No doubt, when you think of me you too can see nothing but a short blank line. Anyway, it is my duty to inform you that I have arrived, and am looking for a house here. As soon as I have found a suitable place I will send for you; rather, I'll come and fetch you.

This is a strange city. You could call it an unfeeling city. Everybody is busy with his own affairs. I find this a trait common to all cities; but though they are all busy in their own world, city dwellers also block one another's path. What are those paths, you would want to know, and you are right to ask that. I have not understood to this day what those paths are on which we move forward, and how others block our destination. No doubt we too blight the destination of others in the same way. Perhaps I too have barred your path—like a black cat. Who knows?

We could learn nothing about one another in the few days we were together. A few days are quite insignificant; people spend a lifetime together and still don't understand each other's language. This is what happened with my parents: they lived together for fifty years, yet they spoke different tongues. The thought makes me feel better, for it shows that a few days together may be no different than many years spent in one another's company: both become just a moment in a lifeless acknowledgement of another's presence.

And then, we hardly know what to expect from one another. You probably know nothing about my preferences in food, in dress, or my favourite authors.

And I? What do I know of your. . . But let's forget all that. I'll inform you when I've found a house.

2

I am going to stop getting into this rigmarole of how to address you. Even the short blank line is beginning to fade. It's my old weakness, perhaps an innate shortcoming, that if I try hard to hold something in my mind it becomes slippery, fades, and eludes my grasp. And anyway, what use would it be for me to try to keep you in my mind when I am hundreds of miles away?

In my last letter I mentioned that looking for a house was a strange experience. Most probably you have never had the experience, because house hunting is a man's job, not a woman's. The houses that one sees! Empty houses to which the odour of former occupants still clings, and their shades hang like cobwebs from the doors and windows; the rustle of departed souls obstructs at every step. Who knows who the people were that lived in these houses, how they lived there and why they left; how many breathed their last there and how many drew their first breath within these walls? Those are my thoughts as I look at the dirty or clean walls, at the empty cupboards and at the gaping ventilators.

Either I don't look like a reliable person, or house rents have soared for no particular reason. But the outcome is that when I hear the sum that is being demanded, I am silenced. I have seen dozens of houses by now. All I do every day I am off from work is to read the house ads in the newspapers and then ply the streets of the city on my scooter. Now it has come to this that I often forget where I am going and for what purpose, and I am left with the feeling that I've been wandering on those streets for centuries. And then, somewhere at the back of my mind a faded short blank line comes floating in, and then I think of you. Who are you, I think, and what links you to me? Have you ever thought about our relationship? Your letters don't reach me because I don't have a permanent address, I move from one hotel to another. Sometimes, judging me to be a homeless outsider, friends take me to their house and keep me there for a couple of days. Anyway, you probably get my letters regularly since *your* address will never change.

I think women have permanent addresses which change no more than once in a lifetime. Even if they do change people don't accept them and keep writing to the same address as before. No doubt all those letters reach the dead letter office. Have you ever thought about the dead letter office? It is a strange department indeed. All those letters which are not addressed to anyone, or whose addressees do not exist, probably lie there rotting. You can think of it as a kind of graveyard for letters.

Anyhow, I was supposed to be talking about the house I am looking for. How far I have drifted from the point! But that is how I've become in my daily life as well—I drift far away from my starting point and forget why I am where I have got to.

Sometimes I wonder what I will do on my days off if I succeed in finding a house. Then, I think that if that happened, of course I would send for you. But then what kind of routine would my life have afterward? The truth is that I have never shared my time, activities, my room or my bathroom with anyone, and now I find it very strange to do so. When I spent those few days with you I realized with amazement that one has to share everything with another person. The experience was partly pleasant but mostly sickening. Forgive me, you probably hate what I am saying. But I think you must have felt the same way. We all have our own way of doing things—of falling asleep, waking up, breathing. Those few days I spent reflecting how different your way of breathing was from mine. And the dreams you were dreaming while you lay beside me were inaccessible to me. Nor could you knock and come into the dreams that I was dreaming. But despite this we continued to share our sleep. The fact is that it is impossible to do away with boundaries; because it is boundaries that separate one being from another and allow each to be a distinct entity. Without these dividing lines the whole world would be a mush, a strange runny mush in which you and I, all humanity, beasts, birds and plants, rocks and stones would float around uselessly.

So that is what sharing life is like, and what it amounts to.

3

What shall I write? For a long time I have been twirling the pen between my fingers. Its nib is old and worn out. Yes, so I was telling you that I am looking for a house—a house I can rent, a house in which I can live with you. It seems I've been house hunting for a long time because now I forget the purpose for which I keep wandering on the streets. When people in the office ask me, 'Why do you keep wandering about all day? Haven't you had enough of sightseeing in all these years?' I remember that of course it is for a serious purpose that I am out on the streets; I am house hunting. And yes, I haven't told anyone here about you. No particular reason; I just didn't feel like telling them. I think that if they knew, the people at the office would ask me all kinds of questions about you, and they would speculate how you and I had lived together. It would be sickening! (Yes, I do tend to use this word a lot these days.) You had said you would send me the photographs when they were developed. But of course since I have no permanent address where can you send them? And then sending photographs is risky, for often they do not arrive at their destination, and do not reach the person (in this case me) they are meant for. And listen, if those people knew about us they might ask me your name. I believe people have fine names. What name can I give you? Often I fall asleep thinking about this. I wonder what your family thinks of me? They probably wonder what kind of a man I am since I have not even been able to find a house to live in. But listen, the truth is that after all these years I have finally found a house.

I am sure you must be happy to hear this, very happy indeed. But I am not happy. As a matter of fact I am in a strange quandary. The way I found this house was quite bizarre. Yesterday was a holiday and as usual I looked up the papers for advertisements of houses to let and rode off on my scooter to look for them. These days I've been living in a small room on the eleventh floor of a hotel. When I come back from office in the evening, dusk has already fallen. I look down from the window at toy people, toy cars. All those toy things seem to be running this way and that, and I am amazed at how busy they are. Then the street lights come on, the streets sparkle, and I feel as though I am dreaming. So you see, one way of spending one's life is to spend it watching others. What do you think? But I know nothing of your views.

Anyway, so I found a house. It happened this way: Yesterday being a holiday, I set out on my house hunt and arrived at this house. When I rang the doorbell a woman looked down from the upper floor. Before I could tell her why I was there she smiled and said, 'Come in, the door is open.' I pushed the door slightly and it opened. It was dark inside and I could just see a staircase leading up. I climbed up, groping at the walls on the two sides of the stairway. Suddenly there were no more stairs, and she stood before me.

'The bulb here has gone out. This room, up here, is vacant. It has a small balcony, a kitchen, a bathroom, and also a storeroom. I occupy the two rooms downstairs. Don't worry about the rent. You can give me whatever you can afford.'

When I looked at her in astonishment she laughed. She looked strange when she laughed, like someone in a dark, anguished dream.

'But I can pay very little,' I said, stroking my hair out of habit.

'I said the rent is not a problem. All I want is someone who will look after these rooms permanently.' And then she asked me an unseemly question, 'How come your hair has turned gray so early?'

'Hair?' I had never thought about my hair. So that's how long the house hunting had taken.

I laughed. 'Yes, hunting for a house did it.'

'I thought so,' and she laughed again. Suddenly I felt my heart go heavy. A strange sleep was enfolding me.

'Are you alone?' she enquired.

'Alone? No.' I looked for something to sit on, and pulling up a stool that stood near by, I sat down. 'No, I am not alone'.

'Then bring her. But first satisfy yourself. In a few months you will get used to the house'. She handed me the keys to the house without bringing up the subject of rent.

So now I have a house. It has one rather large room, a gallery and a balcony. But I can't understand how I have got the house for so little rent. I think she lives alone downstairs. I haven't seen her for the last few days. For the present I have brought a bed, two chairs, and a table. Then there is my trunk and two sacks fdled with books which I have still not opened. You can arrange everything as you want when you arrive.

4

I have not asked you to come yet, nor have I come to fetch you. The reason is I want to satisfy myself about the house first. The surprising thing is that everything works in this house. The water supply and electricity are reliable, the meters work, the bills are accurate. Yet there is a strange sense of restlessness in this room. Whenever I enter the place everything seems to stare at me. Wherever I turn I feel I am under observation. My own chair, table, bed, even my toothbrush, stare at me. You are not laughing, are you? No? It is not loneliness that makes me feel this way, for I have always been alone, though never under scrutiny.

Ever since I have moved into these rooms I feel myself imprisoned, every-where—on the open road, in the office, the hotel. I am not a free man anywhere. It is as though somebody is writing down every move that I make. A whole record is being kept on me.

I would have sent for you straightaway but the situation here is very strange. Yesterday, for the first time in the last four months the landlady came up. She was dressed in a shining black dress and was probably going out. She said, 'If you don't mind I'll leave these in the gallery. There are too many cats these days.'

She left a basket full of dazzling white pigeons in my gallery. The birds had probably lived in the house for many years. Straightaway they began to strut about, perfectly at ease. As soon as she had left them she descended the stairs.

I have never had the chance to tell you that I have no interest in birds and animals. As a child I never kept pets. So, I was offended by her leaving the pigeons with me, and when she had left I began to think that it was just as well that I hadn't sent for you. It's four months now since she left those pigeons and she has still not come back to take them away. Nor do they show any inclination to leave their new roosting place. They stroll about in a leisurely fashion, and some-times they go on a short flight after which they sit on the parapet or settle on the ventilators. It is an astonishing fact that in the last four months their number has doubled. They frequently land on my writing table, and mess up the gallery. I used to feel suffocated in the beginning, so one day I went and knocked at her door.

She came out. 'What is it?' she asked me. Her face showed great exhaustion and there were black circles round her eyes.

'Excuse me, all those pigeons you. . .'

'Oh, the pigeons? You needn't worry. They are so happy with you, they never once returned to me. In any case they are birds of sacred descent. How can you be angry with them?' and she banged the door shut.

I am certain you will not like this house. It is a house where I am surrounded by pigeons, like a man in a throng of humans. Sometimes they perch on my shoul-ders and sometimes they settle themselves in my lap. Even when I am reading or writing I have to put up with their cooing all around me. I would like to leave this house but where would I find another for so little rent? That is my dilemma. Do think of a solution. You did not answer my last letter. I ask her every day if there is mail for me (we share a letterbox), but she shakes her head. Have you really not written to me?

5

So many months, or perhaps years, have gone by. I kept thinking I should inform you of the situation, but now it has become impossible for me to write. In my last letter I wrote to you that she told me they were sacred birds and I should not be angry with them. Many days later when I returned from office, she arrived with a tray full of grain. As soon as the pigeons saw her, they flew to her and gathered round her. The sight had a peculiar effect on me. I was pained when I saw the empty roosting places of the pigeons among the ventilators and was reminded of the deserted and echoing houses I had seen. A strange anxiety and sadness turned into a lump in my throat and my eyes filled with tears. She laughed when she saw that. 'No I won't take them away,' she said, 'Their home is now this house.' Then she left, leaving a large empty basket in one corner of my gallery, saying, 'Your things have not arrived yet, so this can stay here. Don't worry, I'll take it away when she arrives.'

And then the white pigeons resumed their cooing and their sauntering around me. Once again some of them flew up to the ventilators and perched there, and it seemed to me that everything was back to normal. The world which had been suddenly abandoned was inhabited once more, the roads were galvanized, the lights had come on. It was a strange feeling. Suddenly I remembered that I had had the same feeling once before, when waking up from a deep sleep I had gone to the bathroom. There on the washbasin were your scented, coloured soap and your toothbrush, and not far from them lay your red glass bangles. So, today I had the same feeling and I thought that I will let these harmless birds stay here, if you permit me.

But then something extraordinary happened, something that really upset me. In fact I am still worried about it. The people at the office enquire everyday, but I don't know what to tell them.

What happened was this: One day I came home from work and was climbing the stairs when I saw a strange scene. A row of fat, well-fed brown rats was charging up the stairs and scuttling towards my room. I held my stomach with revulsion and almost trampled on one of the rats. When I arrived upstairs they had scattered and were out of sight.

I could not touch food the whole of that day and simply rolled on the bed as though with fever. Over and over again I trembled with horror, the tremors running through my whole body. All through the following night I sat as though numbed. Finally I rose and went downstairs. I knocked at her door and as usual she opened it slightly.

'Listen! Rats! Hordes of them! A whole row of them just went into my room. Is this a house? What kind of a house is this?' My temples were throbbing with rage and my words came out muddled.

'Rats? Maybe there are, but they are harmless. They come out in this weather. They'll go away. Get a mousetrap.'

There weren't one or two of them! I was amazed at her pigheadedness. But she had banged the door shut.

Now tell me, how can I bring you here? Birds swarm this place all day. Nights, it is the reign of the rats. They make a dreadful clatter. What happened one night was so horrible that I hesitate to tell you about it. That night I felt something jumping on my quilt. I threw off the quilt and turned on the light. Would you believe it, countless brown rats with red muzzles were scuttling all over my bed! That night they scampered away and disappeared as soon as the light was turned on. I retched and vomited all night, revolted by my own body, which had shared the bed with rodents. The vomiting left my throat a huge sore and I made up my mind that I would leave the house that very morning. But when morning came I reflected that nowhere in the city could I find a house for so little rent.

So now how should I address you? Listen, now they are not afraid of coming out even in the light. Frequently they are my bedfellows. Tell me, why are they drawn to my body? Isn't it the same body that was with you for a few days? Or was that all fantasy? At least answer my letters! What am I to think of myself? If I leave this house where do I bring you? And if I keep it—it is hardly a suitable place for you. But as for that, now even I am perhaps. . . well anyway.

6

I knocked at her door again and again. I pleaded with her, begged her to tell me how all those creatures have become my cohabitants. I know it was all plotted by her, why else would she ask for such little rent? She no longer asks me for the rent by the first of every month; I go and toss it into her doorway. All my books have turned to dust inside the sacks; each word in them is a speck of dust and has blown away. Those sacks that I had not even opened! What kind of a situation is this? It seems as though centuries have gone by. I am ashamed to send for you now, to address you. I could not even support a burden as pleasant as you! I wish I had brought you with me right in the beginning, and not fallen a prey to doubts about the meaning of sharing one's life. I wish I had not detached myself from you and you from me. But it's all done now.

Nowadays she comes upstairs frequently, stops by the door and asks me with her usual dark, haunted smile, 'When are you bringing her?'

I feel like picking up something and flinging it at her head, but then my whole body becomes numb like a somnambulist's. Even my mind is often inactive these days, like an old, worn-out, useless clock.

There is not a bit of space on the floor here, neither in this room nor in the gallery. Everywhere it's either the rodents prancing about, or the birds fluttering their wings and their eggs rolling about. I am amazed at the fertility of these creatures. Is life so fertile? So, would I also. . . ? Could it ever happen? You can hardly tell me.

I don't even feel like asking you anymore. I have lost count of days, weeks, and months. An uninterrupted, nameless, time; inhaling and exhaling; the company of heterogeneous beings. . . I think I am due for retirement in a few days. Once that happens I doubt if I'll feel the need to even leave this room. She says she will bring me my three meals a day. All for a minimal rent! I think she said it because when I returned from work yesterday, the empty basket she had placed in a corner of the gallery contained some puppies. I am not affected by anything anymore, so this time I didn't query her about it. Of her own she arrived with a dish of biryani, and placing it on the table before me she said, 'Eat. You must be hungry.' Then, she pointed to the basket and continued, 'They're of very good stock. They'll be useful when they are grown. Incidentally, they are quite harmless, but they have to be inoculated for rabies. One of these days I'll take them to have it done. For the present there's no danger of their catching the disease.' Then she asked me with a smile, 'When are you bringing her?'

I made no answer and she left. After she had gone I overturned the plate of biryani. In no time the biryani was gone and the plate licked clean.

It is astonishing how so many assorted creatures, of categories hostile to each other, are busy procreating and live peacefully together.

Now I would like to ask you one last question: Have you read the story of the female innkeeper who used to place a lamp on a cat's head and in its light play dice with her guests? She always won. At the critical moment the cat would shake her head and put out the lamp. Without the light it would be pitch dark and the guest would lose the game no matter how close to winning he had been before that.

The occupants of the basket in the gallery, those puppies with the shining coats, have now grown, and resemble wolves. There is a spark of pure wildness in their eyes. Their black coats dazzle the eye, and the pointed teeth growing out of their dark pink jaws and encircling their red tongues, glow in the dark. They don't bother me nor am I responsible for them. Now I have given up all intentions of moving to another place, for where could I find better accommodation? She brings me a plate of biryani covered with a flower-patterned handkerchief every day, and is happy to see me. As soon as she leaves I overturn the plate. The following day she takes away the plate without a word.

But a strange thing happened yesterday. After a long time she asked me, 'When are you bringing her?' After a long time too, a savage emotion rumbled inside me. It was an extraordinary rumbling. Controlling myself with difficulty I answered her question. But as soon as they heard my reply, those creatures with the shining black coats, sharp, pointed teeth, and red tongues gathered around me lovingly, and became engrossed in conversation with me. What more can I write?

BEFORE DARKNESS FALLS

António Lobo Antunes

Translated from the Portuguese by Margaret Jull Costa

António Lobo Antunes (1942–) is a Portuguese novelist and medical doctor. He was forced to serve with the Portuguese Army in the Portuguese Colonial War (1961–1974). He published his first two novels in 1979 and, since then, there have been twenty-one others, earning him a succession of European prizes. He has been named as a contender for the Nobel Prize in Literature. After a long rivalry with José Saramago, when the *New York Times* called for a comment on Saramago's Nobel Prize victory, he grumbled that the phone was out of order and abruptly hung up. In 2007, he underwent surgery for intestinal cancer, and, knowing how his body would look cut open, recorded the experience in a series of articles.

For reasons I won't go into right now, the last few difficult weeks have forced me to think about the past and the present and to forget about the future. Especially the past: I have rediscovered the smell and the echo of hospitals, the atmosphere like soft white felt through which the nurses glide like swans and that so thrilled me when I was an intern, the silence of rubber, the gleam of metal, people speaking in hushed tones as if in church, the sad solidarity of waiting rooms, the interminable corridors, the terrifyingly solemn ritual that I watch wearing a tremulous smile that serves as my walking stick, a fake courage barely disguising my fear. Especially the past because the future is getting narrower and narrower and I say especially the past because the present has become the past too, memories that I thought were lost and that return without my realizing they were lost, the Sunday markets at Nelas, the squeals of the suckling pigs

(I remember the squeals of the suckling pigs so vividly now)

a ring bearing the emblem of Benfica that when I was five I thought was beautiful and that my parents thought hideous, and that at fifty I still think is beautiful even though I also think it's hideous and feel that now is the right moment to start wearing it again given that I don't have that much time left for large pleasures. I want the ring with the Benfica emblem, I want my grandmother alive, I want the house in Beira, I want everything that I allowed to slip away and that I need, I want Gija to scratch my back before I go to bed, I want Zé Rebelo's pine woods, I want to play Ping-Pong with my brother João, I want to read Jules Verne, I want to go to the fair and ride on the figure-eight roller coaster, I want to see Costa Pereira save a penalty from Didi, I want to eat sweet eggy desserts. I want codfish cakes with tomato rice, I want to go to the school library and get a thrill from reading Fialho de Almeida's racy *The Redhead* in secret, I want to fall in love all over again with the wife of the Pharaoh in *The Ten Commandments* as I did when I was twelve and to whom I remained staunchly faithful for one whole summer, I want my mother, I want my little brother Pedro, I want to buy ruled paper with thirty-five lines a page from the grocery store so that I can write poetry counting out the stresses on my fingers, I want to play ice hockey again, I want to be the tallest in the class, I want to blow on my marbles for luck

ox-blood cat's eye rainbow and coral

I want Frias at Senhor André's school to tell us about the films he's seen, to talk about the Boy, the Girl and the Boy's Friend, in films I only ever saw through Frias's descriptions of them

(Manuel Maria Camarate Frias, where are you now?)

and his descriptions were much better than the films, Frias imitated the sound track, the noise of the horses, the gunfire, the brawl in the saloon, he imitated this so well it was as if we could see it all, and Norberto Noroeste Cavaleiro, the man who thought I was trying to break into his car and who boomed at me

—Dr. Cavaleiro to you, you young devil

the first time a grown-up had called me names and I felt like telling him that my father was a doctor too, and that when I first went into the locker room at Futebol Benfica, Ferra-O-Bico explained to the others

—Blondie's dad is a doctor

and a circle of respectful silence formed around me, Blondie's dad is a doctor, I want to get a cab at the door of my house and hear the driver ask

—Is this where a guy called João lives, the hockey player?

and I want to feel the same amazement that he should talk about my dad like that, I want to break one of my arms and have a plaster cast on it, or, better still, my leg, and have to use crutches and amaze the girls the same age as me, a small boy on crutches

I thought then and I think now

there isn't a girl who doesn't want to fall in love with him, what's more the cars stop to let you cross the road, I want my grandfather to draw me a horse, then get on that horse and ride away, I want to bounce up and down on the bed, I want to eat goose barnacles, I want to smoke a furtive cigarette, I want to read the *World of Adventures,* I want to be the Cisco Kid and Mozart at the same time, I want to eat Santini's ice cream, I want a flashlight with batteries for Christmas, I want chocolate umbrellas, I want my Aunt Gogó to give me my lunch

—Open your mouth now, Toino

I want a plate of lupine seeds, I want to be Sandokan, the Tiger of Malaysia, I want to wear long pants, I want to jump off trams while they're still moving, I want to be a ticket collector, I want to play all the plastic trumpets in the world, I want a shoebox full of silkworms, I want my soccer cigarette cards, I want there to be no hospitals, no patients, no operations, I want to have time to get up the courage to tell my parents that I love them very much

(I don't know if I can)

to tell my parents that I love them very much before darkness falls, ladies and gentlemen, before the final darkness falls.

WAITING FOR WINTER

Antonio Tabucchi

Translated from the Italian by Frances Frenaye

Antonio Tabucchi (1943–2012). The young Tabucchi discovered a love for literature, languages and translation when, as a university student travelling through Europe, he stumbled upon a poem by Fernando Pessoa on a Paris bookstall. He was so captivated that when he returned to Italy, he studied Portuguese and, in time, would become one of the foremost experts on Pessoa, and a translator of his poems. From his early thirties, he wrote novels and short stories, and first gained recognition with his novel *Indian Nocturne*, and international fame with his novel *Pereira Maintains*. With his wife, María José de Lancastre, he translated many works by Pessoa into Italian.

Then the smell of all those flowers . . . positively nauseating. The house, too, the rain veiling the trees, the objects in glass cases—Spanish fans, a pregnant Madonna of Cuzco, baroque angels, seventeenth-century pistols—all of them nauseating. This, too, was sorrow, one of its signs of pain—the sheer unbearableness of the things around us, their stolid, peremptory presence, impervious to change, living in unassailable immanence, unassailable because of its flagrant and innocent physical presence. I shan't make it, she said to herself; I know I shan't make it. As she spoke, she touched her warm forehead and braced herself against the back of the chair. She felt a knot of grief in her throat, and she looked in the mirror. She saw a noble, austere, almost haughty figure and thought: That's me, it's not possible. But it *was* she and there, too, lay her pain. Part of the sorrow of an old woman, wounded by death, was the pain already inherent in that figure of a pale, well-dressed old lady, her head covered by a black lace mantilla, a mantilla made with weary skill, as she well remembered, in a dark room, by taciturn and unhappy Spanish women. And she thought of Seville, many years before, the Giralda Tower, the Virgin of the Macarena, the solemn commemoration, in a hall with sober dark furniture, of a long-dead poet.

At this moment there was a knock at the door, and Françoise appeared. "Madame, the Minister is asking if you will see him." What a treasure, Françoise! She seemed so tiny, so frail, with her mouselike face and the round glasses which made her look like an ageless child; she was so totally and obtusely intelligent. "Tell him to wait in the small drawing room," she answered. "I'll be there in a few moments." She liked to talk this way. "A few moments," "a second," "let him wait a moment"—these gave her an urbane way of being proud and detached from herself, like an actor who wants to be a different person on stage in order to forget the emptiness he feels within. She looked again into the mirror and adjusted the mantilla. You mustn't cry, she said to the beautiful old woman looking out at her. Remember, you mustn't cry.

But she couldn't have cried. Because the Minister was pink-cheeked, pudgy and dressed in black; he bowed and kissed her hand; he was a man who was equal to the situation; he was cultivated, unlike most of his kind, and sincerely admired the dead writer. These things didn't call for tears. If he had been a mediocre, indifferent governmental type, carrying out his official duty, uttering appropriate set phrases and ceremonial commonplaces, then she might have given way to her diffuse and ambiguous sorrow. But not with the man who stood before her, genuinely regretful for the loss to the nation. "Our culture," he said, "has lost its greatest voice." This was incontrovertibly true, but it left no room for tears. She thanked him with a clear, honest sentence. This, too, belonged to the man-made conventional code of mourning, which has no connection with the dark shapes of sorrow. How she would have liked to cry! Then he struck a note of gratitude, a feeling less intense than sorrow, one which, for the moment, lay at the outer edge of her soul, together with nostalgia. And, with that gratitude, he spoke of plans and projects, of a debt of appreciation, which the government wanted to repay with a museum or a foundation, giving grants and fellowships and official celebrations. Recurrent celebrations, he specified. This brightened her, brought her a comfortless relief, causing her to think of a future that had already arrived, of a conventional monument. She reflected, also, how the nation had grown, matured and turned intelligent, in its fashion, something that he had hoped for all his life. Yes, she said, yes, certainly the nation deserved this inheritance. She thanked the Minister for the proposal and the offer, but she was still living in this house and here, for a short time, she would stay. Life can last only so long, and she didn't want to share hers with a nation's feelings, however noble.

Meanwhile the sun had risen higher, and a crowd had gathered in the garden. The Minister took his leave, and she went to stand at the window. The rain had given way to watery mist, which seemed to rise out of the ground. Cars drew up silently, and out of them got solemn-faced men whom the master-of ceremonies met with an umbrella and led to the door. The functional and efficient formality of a state funeral afforded her subtle relief because it appealed to her pragmatic sense of ritual. She realized that she could not linger in her solitude, and so she drew the curtains and started down the stairs, without holding on to the banister, slowly, her head held proudly high, her eyes dry, looking people in the eye as if she saw nobody, as if her look were trained elsewhere, perhaps towards the past or into herself, but certainly not there, among the objects of the tastefully arranged vigil room. She took her place at the head of the coffin, as if she were watching over a living man rather than a dead one, waiting for people to bow, kiss her hand and murmur words of sympathy and farewell. And while she stood there, removed from herself as well as from others, her heart beat calmly and regularly, remaining apart from the absolute devastation that was like a physical weight on her shoulders, from the terrible, incontrovertible evidence of the facts.

She let Françoise break in on the line, greeting her with serene detachment as if she were another visitor. Submissively, almost with relief, she let herself be led down what seemed an endlessly long hall and drank a hot broth, which was like yet another obligation imposed upon her. "No, I don't want to rest," she said in response to the girl's affectionate solicitude. "I'm not tired, and you needn't worry about me. I'll bear up." The words came from far away, as if someone else were pronouncing them, and she let Françoise oblige her to lie down, unlacing her shoes and passing a handkerchief dipped in eau de cologne across her forehead. He was running on the beach; behind the beach were the ruins of a Greek temple, and he was stark naked, nude like a Greek god with a laurel crown on his head. His testicles danced in a comical way as he ran, and she couldn't help laughing. She laughed so hard that she thought she was choking, and then she woke up.

She woke up abruptly, with a feeling of anxiety because she must have slept too long and everything must be over; visits, speeches, ceremonies, the funeral, perhaps even the day. Now it must be evening; Françoise was surely waiting in the hall, with reddened eyes and the air of a stoic sparrow, waiting to tell her: "I had to let you sleep. You couldn't hold out any longer." She went to the door, where she could hear the murmur of the guests below. From the anteroom she heard the Chinese clock strike two frivolous strokes. All of a sudden and for the first time, she hated that tiny, precious, monstrous timepiece. And yet she had bought it herself, imagining that she'd always treasure it. No, she said to herself forcefully, I won't think of Macao. For today I don't want to remember anything. In fact, she had slept for only ten minutes. She went into the bathroom and redid her make-up. The short sleep had disarranged her hair and left two deep furrows in the powder on her cheeks. She thought of masking their pallor with some rouge, then decided against it. She brushed her teeth in order to dull the taste of camphor in her mouth. Strange that the nausea brought on by so many flowers in the house should take on the taste of camphor.

She went out, knowing that Françoise would be waiting in the small drawing room. She had made an appointment with the German publisher for two o'clock and didn't want to keep him waiting. When she came in, the solemn gentleman stood up and made a brief bow. He was stout, obese in fact, and somehow this cheered her. Françoise was sitting down with a notebook on her lap. "If you prefer to speak in your own language, my secretary will serve as interpreter." The corpulent gentleman nodded. He spared her banal outpourings and came straight to the point, in honest, businesslike fashion, a procedure that had its advantages. "I'm buying the diary," he said in French. "Your husband lived in my country during crucial years; he knew important political and literary people, and his memoirs are valuable to us." He gave a slight cough and fell silent, in anticipation of a response that was not forthcoming. This seemed to perplex him because he stiffened and advanced, boldly, into the area of money. "I'll pay in marks," he said, "right away, before there's a contract; all I need is an option." He spoke in German, and Françoise promptly translated. The interposition of a translation made the proposal less vulgar, and she was grateful to him for this subtlety. Also it facilitated her reply; her words, passed on by Françoise in other words that were to her incomprehensible, took on a life of their own, which did not belong to her or concern her, which no longer had a meaning. She would have her secretary write to him, she said, but surely he understood that this was no time for decisions. Of course she would take into account that this was the first offer, but for the moment, if he would excuse her, she must fulfil other obligations . . .

She looked to Françoise. Other obligations . . . she didn't quite know which, and didn't care. Françoise was looking at her notebook and taking care of everything. As she followed Françoise, she gave in to this childish feeling. The sensation of being an abandoned child rose from the buried depths of her weary old body and broke through the ruins of the intervening years, giving her, once more, an overwhelming urge to sob and weep without restraint, and, at the same time, an almost feverish lightheartedness. For a moment she felt that the child reawakened within her might jump and dance or sing a nonsense song. Whatever had given her the urge to cry also took the urge away. And then a harsh light was coming out of the library, the floor was covered with wires, and someone was talking overloudly. "They're after an interview for the TV evening news," said Françoise. "The agency president called in person. I set a limit of three minutes, but if you don't feel up to it. I'll send them away. *Ils sont des bêtes,*" she added scornfully.

It wasn't actually so. The TV reporter was an emaciated, intelligent-looking young man, tormenting the microphone with his bony hands. He seemed to be very well acquainted with the dead writer's work, and began by quoting from one of his youthful books. Beneath his acute but casual manner she felt a touch of embarrassment. He asked her to interpret a sentence which had become proverbial, symbolic of a whole generation, a sentence which even schoolbooks had picked up, in a positive sense, of course, because schoolbooks go for the positive. And here he was, asking her whether, in that definition of man, there wasn't a grain of irony, a perfidiously disguised negative hint. The insinuation made her feel happy. It allowed her to make an evasive reply, disguised as inexperience, to take refuge in the role of the great man's widow, who can reveal his taste in neckties. And so her answer was disarmingly banal, so inadequate that it lived up to exactly what the reporter expected. It confirmed, in the highest degree, that she was a subtly intelligent woman, the perfect helpmeet, who could provide precious first-hand information. All of which led, inevitably, to a biographical indiscretion, a subtle indiscretion, because the reporter was well-mannered and hoped, for the benefit of the TV audience, that she would tell him an episode of their life story. Which meant *his* life story. And she obliged—why not?—with a moralistic tale, one tinged with nobility, because that is what the public relishes, especially the everyday public. As she spoke, she had a feeling of bitterness towards herself. She would rather have told a quite different story, but not to this well-mannered young man, under the dazzling lights. She fell silent and smiled, in an exhausted but dignified manner.

Of the drive to the cathedral she registered nothing except for such confused fleeting images as the senses take in but do not retain. She was driven in a black car, upholstered in grey, with a muffled engine and a silent driver. At the service, too, she was there and not there, present with her body alone while she allowed her mind to range at random through the geography of memory: Paris, Capri, Taormina, and then, suddenly, a picturesque humble cottage which—it was almost funny— she couldn't place. She concentrated her efforts on a room whose insignificant details she vividly remembered, on a plain brass bed with a simple picture of the Holy Family hanging above it. Incredible that she couldn't recall the location. Where *was* it? Meanwhile the archbishop had pronounced a long homily, doubtless of a very high calibre. She felt cold. This, she thought, was the only sensation, indeed the only feeling that could hold her attention. Her stomach was cold, as if a huge block of ice were pressing against its walls, so that during the rest of the service she kept her hands tightly folded on her lap. Then the cold spread to her limbs, not into her hands, which were burning, but into her arms and shoulders, her legs and feet, which were without feeling, as if frozen, although she spasmodically wriggled her toes. Shivers ran through her body, and she couldn't hide them. She clenched her teeth so that they would not chatter, until she felt pain in the muscles of her face and neck. Françoise became aware that she was ill at ease; she took her hands into her own and whispered into her ear something which she did not catch, perhaps that she should leave. It didn't matter, because the ceremony was over, the coffin was being borne down the central aisle, and she found herself back in the same car with the same driver, who was taking her home, while Françoise had thrown her coat over her and put an arm around her shoulders in an attempt to warm her. It wasn't easy to part company graciously, to convey to Françoise, tactfully but firmly, that she didn't want her to stay overnight, that she wanted to enter and remain in the big, empty house unaccompanied, that the maid could attend to any need, that this was the first evening of her solitude and she wanted to enter into her solitude alone. Finally she drew herself away, Françoise kissed her, her eyes shining with tears, and she went into the silent front hall. Immediately she rang the bell for the maid and told her to withdraw because there was nothing to be done, except, please, to disconnect the telephone. As she went up the stairs she heard the odious Chinese clock strike seven times. She stopped on the landing and opened, almost greedily, its glass case, then deliberately advanced the minute hand to eight, nine, ten, eleven, twelve o'clock. When it reached there, she said to herself: It's already tomorrow. After that she went through another full cycle and said: It's already the day after tomorrow. Then she turned the hand the other way, and the clock obediently struck decreasing numbers. She went back down the stairs and into the library, where there was a vague smell of stale cigarettes. In order to drive it away, she lit a stick of incense and threw open a window. It was pouring rain. In the fireplace the maid had laid a little pyramid of logs, with pine cones for kindling. At the touch of a match flames shot up so brightly that there was no need for the hanging lamp. She turned it off. Then she opened the safe and took out a mahogany box. The manuscripts were piled up in perfect order, like banknotes, with rubber bands around them. On every bundle there was a date, and the writer's signature. She pulled them all out and looked them over. It was difficult to choose. She thought of the novel, but decided against it. The novel should come last, perhaps in February. And it was too soon for the play. She paused over the other bundles. The poems would be a good choice, but perhaps the diary would be better still. She weighed it in her hand and looked at the length. Three hundred was the number on the last page. Good God! She sat down on the armchair in front of the fireplace and crumpled the first page into a ball, so as to be able to throw it into the fire without having to lean too far forward. It turned a tobacco colour before turning to ashes. Poor fool, she said, poor dear fool. She leaned back in the chair and looked up at the ceiling. The winter would be long; it had scarcely begun. She felt tears flood her eyes and let them run down her cheeks, abundant, uncontrollable.

GARDEN OF MY CHILDHOOD

Oh Jung-hee

Translated from the Korean by Ha-yun Jung

Oh Jung-hee (1947–) is a South Korean writer. Oh has won both the Yi Sang Literary Award and the Dongin Literary Award, Korea's most prestigious prizes for short fiction, and her works have been translated into multiple foreign languages in Southeast Asia, Latin America and Europe.

Note: *The narrator and her family have fled the Korean War and arrived at a small village where they are renting a room from a one-eyed carpenter whose daughter Bu-ne is rumored to have gone mad and died. The narrator's father was taken away while they were fleeing, and the family has not heard from him since. Her mother has taken up a job working nights at a restaurant in town.*

Mother slept late. Older Sister and Second Brother had long ago left for school. When sunlight landed on her make-up-smeared face, puffy and swollen from a hangover, Mother turned over, blocking it with the back of her hand.

Older Brother turned his back to us and as always, began to read the English textbook in a loud voice. I walked around Mother's head and got out of the room.

The corner store was at the entrance of the village, on the other side of the road that led into town. The young woman would be fanning herself with her skirt hiked above her knees, or catching flies with a flyswatter when I got to the door and looked around inside, and without saying anything, she would open the flower-shaped tin lid of the wide-mouthed glass jar and take out two pieces of candy. Sometimes she would scoop up an extra handful of coarse sugar from the bottom of the jar and hand it to me with a blank face. There were also times when she just glanced out the tiny window on her door and yawned lazily, apparently not wanting to bother coming out, as she told me to leave the money and take the candy myself. She knew that I always had money for exactly two pieces, never more, for I always stole the same amount from Mother's purse, and I never bought anything else but candy.

On such days, after taking out the two pieces, I would linger before closing the lid. If she didn't seem to be watching, I quickly grabbed another piece and ran out, yelling, Here's the money. When I put the candy, as big as a cow's eye, inside my mouth, my cheek stuck out as if it were about to burst. I knew how to make the two pieces of candy last until way after lunch time. I could not go home anyway, until they were all melted and gone.

I walked aimlessly along the newly paved road. Along the side of the road, the leaves on the corn stalks hung low, covered with dust, and the silk holding the full, ripe ears was turning yellow.

As I walked down the dusty road, I sucked the candy as slowly as I could, to make the sweetness last longer. *Boom, boom.* I heard cannons in the distance. People said the sound came from beyond many layers of faraway mountain ridges. I stopped many times to remove the candy from my mouth and hold it up to see how small it got, then put it in my pocket. After taking about ten steps, only after the sweetness in my mouth was completely gone, I put the candy back in my mouth. The sticky sweetness of the candy made my fingers glue together like a duck foot.

At the end of the paved road was Older Sister's school. It was a squat single-story wooden building. Next to the gate, right outside the fence of hardy orange trees along the edge of the school yard, a vendor spun cloud-like blossoms of cotton candy. He poured a fistful of white powder into a large funnel-shaped tin container and stuck a thin wooden stick inside, then stepped on the foot pedal. Layer by layer, the cotton candy wrapped around the stick and bloomed into a shiny white flower, just like a cotton blossom. I never got tired of watching. As I stood staring at the sticks of cotton candy, multiplying into five, then ten, the vendor said, You want one, then go get some money, and put down the eleventh cotton candy with a boastful clang. I could hear clear, shrill singing from the open windows of the old wooden building, painted black with tar.

Halfway up the hill behind the school was an orphanage, fenced with barbed wire. On the other side of the barbed wire stood a shack with high windows that looked like a warehouse and a couple of military tents. There were piles of square wooden bars and bricks here and there, probably for construction. The sun was so bright but there was no shade, so the girls sat head to head in the sliver of space under the wooden bars leaning against the wall, taking turns catching lice for one another, while the shirtless boys fetched water in pails.

Second Brother always envied these kids. He said they made sharp knives out of nails, could lick off the blood from their wounds with their tongues, ran away in groups of three or four every night, and every time, the same number of children would be caught and brought in from somewhere. This kind of talk made Older Sister shudder with fear. Second Brother said there was no one in his class who did not get scared when one of these kids spit out between his teeth, I'll see you after school. And without fail, the gang would be waiting in one of the dark back alleys on the way home. Picking you up and throwing you upside down into a toilet was as easy for them as eating porridge.

A girl who was licking milk powder off her hand approached the barbed wire fence.

"You want some?"

I stuck out my hand. She held up her hand then blew the tiny pinch of remaining powder into my eye.

"Get lost, you fatso."

Someone banged the oxygen tank outside the shack, *clang, clang, clang, clang*.
"We're hungry," *clang, clang, clang*.
"Come and eat," *clang, clang, clang*.
The children all got up and ran, their hair bouncing, and disappeared inside.

I put the remaining candy in my mouth and walked back the way I came, then past the village and into town.

There was no market today so the mid-day streets were quiet, only the hammering from the blacksmith's shop echoing clear and loud.

I walked slowly to the end of the street, chasing the local bus that had just dropped off two passengers, peering inside the dead quiet alleys, the hair salon, the pub, the inn.

Whenever I passed these streets, I always thought of Father. How far was it from here, the spot where Father was pulled off the truck by men in military uniforms. Even in my faint memory, I somehow felt that we were not too far from where Father got off the truck.

The blacksmith heated a piece of metal on sizzling oak charcoal and forged the blade with heavy hammering. Every time he pounded with the hammer, the flesh under his arm swelled up, bubbling and trembling. As I walked past the farmers who had come to get their tools repaired lying asleep in front of the shop with ruddy faces, I came to a sudden stop. There among the men was the one-eyed carpenter, curled up on his side with the familiar tool sack tucked under his head.

I returned home long after sunset. It was time for Mother to leave for work.

Older Sister was pacing around the vegetable patch with Little Brother on her back. She tried hard to hide a smile as she pouted at me. It was a sign that there was good news.

"You wretched little girl, where have you been?"

Grandmother snapped at me as she washed the stone mortar at the well. Older Brother was reading his book in the room, but rushed to carry the mortar into the kitchen as soon as Grandmother was done, as if he had been watching intently all along.

Inside the kitchen, it was hot and dark like the inside of a steamer, with the cooking stove already lit and water boiling. Now I knew exactly what was going on. Grandmother thumped her knuckles on my head when I kept going back and forth from the kitchen to the backyard, wearing a huge grin on my face. Then she spoke suggestively to Mother who was leaving, her face all made up.

"Make sure you come home for dinner tonight."

Grandmother had brought home a lost chicken again. Grandmother's laundry basin was huge compared to the amount of laundry we usually had. Sometimes inside that basin was a big old chicken sitting with its legs folded as if it were dead, glaring at us. Grandmother found them poking around the vegetable patches outside the village. She always insisted that they did not belong to anyone.

When Grandmother shoved the chicken's head under its wing, placed it inside the mortar and pounded down with a pestle, the chicken died instantly, without a squawk.

The weather was so hot that our clothes stuck to our skin, but Grandmother shut the kitchen door and pulled out the feathers, blinking her eyes as sweat rolled down her face.

We closed our door tight and gulped down the hot chicken stock, dripping sweat.

Grandmother placed the drumstick and intestines on Older Brother's bowl of rice before we could get our hands on them.

The clean-up was handled just as quickly and efficiently. Older Brother mixed the feathers with ashes so that they would not fly away, and buried them deep in a corner of our garden. The black clots of blood on the kitchen floor disappeared without a trace when we swept it with a sprinkle of soil.

Grandmother placed the bones, stripped of any trace of meat, behind the kitchen cupboard where no one could see. She was going to use them to lure centipedes, to use as medicine.

We opened the door and sat out on the wooden verandah, wiping our oily lips with the backs of our hands.

When we first moved here, there were rumors in the village that chickens were disappearing and the owners would come around our place, looking for their missing chicken. People whispered that it must the refugees from outside the village who were doing it. But it was only after a year had passed that Grandmother actually started to go out with the huge laundry basin on her head. No matter what the circumstances, the truth was that we were wandering refugees, no better than beggars.

At first Older Brother would not even touch the chicken. We were aghast when he trashed his share of the soup into the rice rinsing bowl, as if he had something to prove. But he could not deny his vigorous adolescent appetite for long.

Grandmother fed me a fistful of coarse salt, and baking soda to Little Brother. She said we might get our stomachs horribly upset from food that we weren't used to eating. The salt was bitter and strong, stinging and burning my throat as it went down.

In the middle of the night, I woke up with a bad thirst. I felt my way across the sleeping bodies and opened the door.

You eat salt, you need water.

Mother was still awake and she let out a laugh, smelling of alcohol, and Grandmother threatened, "If you pee in your sleep, I'm going to send you all around the village with a straw basket on your head."

The well was deep. Inside, the sky sat dark and round, endlessly sucking in the rope on the well-bucket, then in one unguarded second, it cracked with a splash and scattered into a thousand pieces.

Mist was falling, wet and shiny like fine shards of glass. I pulled up the bucket and drank, then poured the rest of the water on my feet and released the rope on the bucket again, endlessly, gazing into the well. There, it was silent and at the same time full of unknowable sounds. It seemed like I could hear someone's breathing, much like a sigh of lament, mixed in with those sounds.

A mouse scurried out from under the verandah of Bu-ne's room. Moonlight penetrated deep into the cracks on the wooden flooring. I got closer and looked under the verandah. There was a pair of shoes, one standing up and one fallen on its side, as if the mouse had just been playing with them. I pulled them out. They were a pair of high heels, the toe and heel sharp as blades, filled with dust and dirt inside. I shook out the dirt and rubbed the shoes to give them a shine, then gently pushed in my wet feet. I swung forward, feeling like my ankles were about to give. I took the shoes off neatly on the terrace stone and put my eye on the door. It was dark inside so I could not see anything between the dense wooden frames. But strangely, I did not feel afraid like before.

The persimmons had just started to turn red and one by one they fell, sporadically, as if they had just been reminded.

Sitting outside in the middle of the night and staring at Bu-ne's room like this, everything so quiet, the events that went on during the day felt as hazy and distant as a dream. Mother coming home drunk every night, the times I spent sucking my thumb like a mouse under the dirty blankets, all seemed like a long, weary dream. Could it be possible that the real me had been left behind as bits and pieces of sensations in the folds of faraway memories, revisited with longing. Just as it was with Father. Father was very tall. Or maybe this was something I simply associated with Father, because of Grandmother's remarks that Older Brother, who was well-built, looked just like Father.

After dinner when the winds cooled down, Father used to carry me outside on his shoulders. It was so high up there on Father's shoulders that I felt dizzy and shaky, as if I were about to float into the air like a balloon.

A little one will be born soon. Father spoke as if he were singing, squeezing my thighs tightly. There is a baby inside Mommy's tummy.

Hold on tight. And when I held on to his hair, as he told me to, I got his sticky and greasy hair tonic all over my hands.

Father stayed with me as the grip on my frail thighs and ankles, as something vaguely warm and soft, as something large, as a back drenched in sweat. But could it be that all these memories were merely a distant dream, a fabrication of my imagination.

Father will return when the war is over. We hadn't heard from him in two years but Grandmother was persistent. But despite the affectionate memories and the hopeless waiting, Father's possible return also worried and scared us. Even Older Brother seemed to feel this way, coldly threatening Mother upon her late return, What will Father say when he comes back.

Just as we grew accustomed to the taste of lost chicken, just as my hands reaching for Mother's wallet got bolder and the amount they grabbed got larger, just as Grandmother got more skilled in the art of secret and silent butchering, just as the chickens eventually learned to yield at a mere glance, burying their heads under their wings and surrendering, Father would also have changed. This vague, fog-like unfamiliarity that now filled every fold of the time that Father spent away from us would likely come back to us as a new war. Could it be that perhaps this hopeless waiting and affectionate reminiscing was our way of trying to cover up and to ask for forgiveness, for not wanting Father to ever come back, for choosing to believe that Father was never coming back.

The sound of cannons that traveled from the other side of the mountain ridge would suddenly remind this quiet, sunken village of the war, and the refugees that arrived every now and then brought word that outside, there was still a war going on.

A HOT DOG IN A WARM BUN

Dubravka Ugrešić

Translated from the Croatian by Michael Henry Heim

Dubravka Ugrešić (1949–). A novelist and essayist whose work has been translated into more than twenty languages, Dubravka Ugrešić has taught at many American and European universities, including Harvard, UCLA and the Free University of Berlin. During the Balkan conflict, Ugrešić maintained a staunch anti-war stance (on her application form for a Croatian passport, under "ethnicity" she wrote "none") which led to her being branded a "public enemy", and prompted her to leave Croatia and settle in Amsterdam, where she now lives.

1.

On the twenty-fifth of March a truly unbelievable thing took place in Zagreb. Nada Matić, a young doctor specializing in plastic surgery, awoke in her room and looked at the clock. It was 6:15. Nada jumped out of bed, jumped into the shower, squatted under the stream of water, then, lighting a cigarette, jumped into a terry cloth robe. It was 6:25. She pulled on her gray spring suit, daubed some rouge on her cheeks, and grabbed her bag. It was 6:30. She locked the door, finished the cigarette in the elevator, and hurried off to catch her tram.

By the time Nada Matić stepped off the tram, it was 6:50. And just then, right in the middle of the square, Nada Matić was overcome by a sudden, unusually intense hunger. She rushed over to the Skyscraper Cafeteria, which served hot dogs in warm buns, nervously called out to the waitress, "More mustard, please!" greedily grabbed the hot dog, and impatiently threw away the napkin. (That is what Nada Matić did. That is what I do too: I always dispose of those unnecessary and shamefully tiny scraps of paper waitresses use for wrapping hot dogs.)

Then she set off across the square. She was about to bring the hot dog to her lips, when—was it some dark sense of foreboding or a ray of the March morning sun alighting on the object in question, illuminating it with its own special radiance? In either case and to make a long story short, she glanced down at the fresh pink hot dog and her face convulsed in horror. For what did she see peering through the longish bun and ocherish mustard foam but a genuine, bona fide . . . ! Nada came to a complete and utter halt. No, there could be no doubt. "Glans, corpus, radix, corpora cavernosa, corpora spongiosa, praeputium, frenulum, scrotum," our heroine, Nada Matić, thought, running through her totally useless anatomy class knowledge and still not believing her eyes. No, that thing in the bun was most definitely not a hot dog!

Utterly shaken, Nada resumed her journey to the Municipal Hospital at a much slower pace. It had all come together in a single moment: the anatomy lesson, plastic surgery, the desire to specialize in aesthetic prosthetics—it had all flashed before her eyes like a mystical sign, a warning, the finger of fate, a finger which, if we may be forgiven the crudeness of our metaphor, peered out of the bun in so tangible, firm, fresh, and pink a state as to be anything but an illusion.

Nada Matić decided to give the "hot dog" issue top priority. Taking the "hot dog" to the laboratory and dropping it in a bottle of Formalin would have been the simplest solution, of course, but what would her colleagues have said? Nada looked here and there for a litter basket; there were none in sight. As she'd thrown the napkin away and had no paper tissues, she tried to hide the "hot dog" by coaxing it into the bun with her finger, but smooth, slippery, and springy as it was, it kept sliding out, the head gleaming almost maliciously in Nada's direction.

It then occurred to Nada that she might stop off at a cafe and just happen to leave the "hot dog" on the lower shelf of one of the tables she often stood beside— she had said goodbye to three umbrellas that way—but in the end she lost her nerve. For the first time in her life Nada felt what it was like to be a criminal . . .

Oh, before I forget, I ought to tell you a few things about our heroine. Nada Matić is the kind of shortish, plumpish blonde that men find attractive. But her generous, amicable, amorous character kept getting in her way, and men disappeared from her life, poor thing, without her ever quite understanding why. Abandoned by no fault of her own, she naturally and periodically found herself involved in hot and heavy escapades with married medical personnel of the male sex.

Suddenly Nada felt terribly sorry for herself: her whole life seemed to have shrunk into that grotesque symbol of bun-cum-relay-race-baton. No, she'd better take care of it at once. She gave the bun an unconscious squeeze and the hot dog peeked out at her again, turning her self-pity to despair. And just as she noticed a broken basement window and was about to toss it away, bun and all, who should pass by with a cold nod but one of the surgeons, Otto Waldinger. Quick as lightning, Nada stuffed the "hot dog" into her pocket, smearing gooey mustard all over her fingers . . . The bastard! Scarcely even acknowledging her, while not so long ago . . . !

And then she spied a mercifully open drain. She removed the "hot dog" from her pocket with great care and flung it into the orifice. It got stuck in the grating. She nudged it with her foot, but it refused to budge. It was too fat.

At that point up sauntered a good-looking, young policeman.

"Identity papers, please."

"What for?" Nada mumbled.

"Jaywalking."

"Oh," said Nada, rummaging frenetically through her bag.

"What's the matter?" asked the policeman, looking down at the grating. "Lost your appetite?" A good inch and a half of the "hot dog" was sticking out of the bun. Nada Matić went pale . . .

But at this point everything becomes so enveloped in mist that we cannot tell what happened next.

2.

Mato Kovalić, a writer (or, to be more specific, a novelist and short story writer), awoke rather early and smacked his lips, which he always did when he awoke though he could not for the life of him explain why. Kovalić stretched, moved his hand along the floor next to the bed until it found his cigarettes, lit one, inhaled, and settled back. There was a full-length mirror on the opposite wall, and Kovalić could see his bloated gray face in it.

During his habitual morning wallow in bed he was wont to run through the events of the previous day. The thought of the evening's activities and Maja, that she-devil of an invoice clerk, called forth a blissful smile on his face, and his hand willy-nilly slid under the covers . . . Unbelievable! No, absolutely impossible!

Kovalić flung back the blanket and leaped up as if scalded. There he felt only a perfectly smooth surface. Kovalić rushed over to the mirror. He was right. There he saw only an empty, smooth space. He looked like one of those naked, plastic dummies in the shop windows. He pinched and pulled at himself several times, he slapped his face to see whether he was awake, he jumped in place once or twice; and again he placed his hand on the spot where only the night before there had been a bulge . . . No, it was gone!

But here we must say a few words about Kovalić and show the reader what sort of man our hero is. We shall not go into his character, because the moment one says something about a writer all other writers take offence. And to point out that Kovalić was a writer who divided all prose into two categories, prose with balls and prose without (he was for the former), would be quite out of place in these circumstances and might even prompt the reader to give a completely erroneous and vulgar interpretation to the whole incident. Let us therefore say instead that Kovalić greatly valued—and wished to write—novels that were true to life, down to earth. What he despised more than anything was symbols, metaphors, allusions, ambiguities, literary frills; what he admired was authenticity, a razor-edged quality where every word meant what it meant and not God knows what else! He was especially put off by intellectualizing, attitudinizing, high-blown flights of fancy, genres of all kinds (life is too varied and unpredictable to be forced into prefabricated molds, damn it!) and—naturally—critics! Who but critics, force-fed on the pap of theory, turned works of literature into paper monsters teeming with hidden meanings?

Kovalić happened to be working on a book of stories called *Meat*, the kingpin of which was going to be about his neighbor, a retired butcher positively in love with his trade. Kovalić went on frequent drinking bouts with the man for the purpose of gathering material: nouns (brisket, chuck, flank, knuckle, round, rump, saddle, shank, loin, wienerwurst, weisswurst, liverwurst, bratwurst, blood pudding, etc.), verbs (pound, hack, gash, slash, gut, etc.), and whole sentences. "You shoulda seen me go through them—the slaughterhouse ain't got nothing on me!"; "A beautiful way to live a life—and earn a pile!"; "My knives go with me to the grave." Kovalić intended to use the latter, which the old man would say with great pathos, to end the story with a wallop.

We might add that Kovalić was a good-looking man and much loved by the women, a situation he took completely for granted.

Well, dear readers, now you can judge for yourselves the state our hero was in when instead of his far from ugly bulge he found a smooth, even space.

Looking in the mirror, Kovalić saw a broken man. God, he thought, why me? And why not my arms or legs? Why not my ears or nose, unbearable as it would have been.

What good am I now? . . . Good for the dump, that's what! If somebody had chopped it off, I wouldn't have made a peep. But to up and disappear on me, vanish into thin air . . . ?! No, it's impossible! I must be dreaming, hallucinating. And in his despair he started pinching the empty space again.

Suddenly, as if recalling something important, Kovalić pulled on his shoes and ran out into the street. It was a sunny day, and he soon slowed his pace and began to stroll. In the street he saw a child peeling a banana, in a bar he saw a man pouring beer from a bottle down his gullet, in a doorway he saw a boy with a plastic pistol in his hand come running straight at him; he saw a jet cross the sky, a fountain in a park start to spurt, a blue tram come round a bend, some workers block traffic dragging long rubber pipes across the road, two men walking towards him, one of whom was saying to the other, "But for that you really need balls . . ."

God! thought Kovalić, compulsively eyeing the man's trousers. Can't life be cruel!

Queer! the cocky trousers sneered, brushing past him.

I must, I really must do something, thought Kovalić, sinking even deeper into despair. And then he had a lifesaver of a thought . . . Lidija! Of course! He'd go and see Lidija.

3.

You never know what's going to happen next, thought Vinko K., the good-looking young policeman, as he jaywalked across the square. Pausing in front of a shop window, he saw the outline of his lean figure and the shadow of his stick dangling at his side. Through the glass he saw a young woman with dark, shining eyes making hot dogs. First she pierced one half of a long roll with a heated metal stake and twisted it several times; then she poured some mustard into the hollow and stuffed a pink hot dog into it. Vinko K. was much taken with her dexterity. He went in and pretended to be waiting his turn, while in fact he was watching the girl's pudgy hands and absentmindedly twirling his stick.

"Next!" her voice rang out.

"Me?! Oh, then I might as well have one," said a flustered Vinko K., "as long as . . ."

"Twenty!" her voice rang out like a cash register.

Vinko K. moved over to the side. He subjected the bun to a close inspection: it contained a fresh hot dog. Meanwhile, two more girls had come out of a small door, and soon all three were busy piercing rolls and filling them with mustard and hot dogs.

Vinko K. polished off his hot dog with obvious relish and then walked over to the girls.

"Care to take a break, girls?" he said in a low voice. "Can we move over here?" he added, even more softly.

Squeezed together between cases of beverages and boxes of hot dogs, a sink, a bin, and a broom, Vinko K. and the waitresses could scarcely breathe.

"I want you to show me all the hot dogs you have on the premises," said a calm Vinko K.

The girl opened all the hot dog boxes without a murmur. The hot dogs were neatly packed in cellophane wrappers.

"Hm!" said Vinko K. "Tell me, are they all vacuum-packed?"

"Oh, yes!" all three voices rang out as a team. "They're all vacuum-packed!"

A long, uncomfortable silence ensued. Vinko K. was thinking. You never knew what would happen next in his line. You could never tell what human nature had in store.

Meanwhile the girls just stood there, huddled together like hot dogs in a cellophane wrapper. All at once Vinko K.'s fingers broke into a resolute riff on one of the cardboard boxes and, taking a deep breath, he said, as if giving a password, "Fellatio?"

"Aaaaah?!" the girls replied, shaking their heads, and though they did not seem to have understood the question they kept up a soft titter.

"Never heard of it?" asked Vinko K.

"Teehee! Teehee! Teehee!" they tittered on.

"Slurp, slurp?" Vinko K. tried, sounding them out as best he could.

"Teehee! Teehee! Teehee!" they laughed, pleasantly, like the Chinese.

Vinko K. was momentarily nonplussed. He thought of using another word with the same meaning, but it was so rude he decided against it.

"Hm!" he said instead.

"Hm!" said the girls, rolling their eyes and bobbing their heads.

Vinko K. realized his case was lost. He sighed. The girls sighed back compassionately.

By this time there was quite a crowd waiting for hot dogs. Vinko K. went outside. He stole one last glance at the first girl. She glanced back, tittered, and licked her lips. Vinko K. smiled and unconsciously bobbed his stick. She too smiled and vaguely nodded. Then she took a roll and resolutely rammed it onto the metal stake.

But at this point everything becomes so enveloped in mist again that we cannot tell what happened next.

4.

"Entrez!" Lidija called out unaffectedly, and Kovalić collapsed in her enormous, commodious armchair with a sigh of relief.

Lidija was Kovalić's best friend: she was completely, unhesitatingly devoted to him. Oh, he went to bed with her all right, but out of friendship: she went to bed with him out of friendship too. They didn't do it often, but they had stuck with it for ages—ten years by now. Kovalić knew everything there was to know about Lidija; Lidija knew everything there was to know about Kovalić. And they were never jealous. But Kovalić the writer—much as he valued sincerity in life and prose—refused to admit to himself that he had once seen their kind of relationship in a film and found it highly appealing, an example (or so he thought) of a new, more humane type of rapport between a man and a woman. It was in the name of this ideal that he gave his all to her in bed even when he was not particularly up to it.

They had not seen each other for quite some time, and Lidija started in blithely about all the things that had happened since their last meeting. She had a tendency to end each sentence with a puff, as if what she had just produced was less a sentence than a hot potato.

Lidija had soon trotted out the relevant items from the pantry of her daily life, and following a short silence—and a silent signal they had hit upon long before—the two of them began to undress.

"Christ!" cried Lidija, who in other circumstances was a translator to and from the French.

"Yesterday . . ." said Kovalić, crestfallen, apologetic. "Completely disappeared . . ."

For a while Lidija simply stood there, staring wide-eyed at Kovalić's empty space; then she assumed a serious and energetic expression, went over to her bookcase, and took down the encyclopedia.

"Why bother?" asked Kovalić as she riffled the pages. "Castration, castration complex, coital trophy—it's all beside the point! It's just disappeared, understand? Dis-ap-peared!"

"Bon Dieu de Bon Dieu . . . !" Lidija muttered. "And what are you going to do now?"

"I don't know," Kovalić whimpered.

"Who were you with last?"

"Girl named Maja . . . But that's beside the point."

"Just wondering," said Lidija, and said no more.

As a literary person in her own right, Lidija had often cheered Kovalić up with her gift for the apt image. But now her sugar-sweet sugarbeet, her pickle in the middle, her poor withered mushroom, her very own Tom Thumb, her fig behind the leaf, her tingaling dingaling, her Jack-in-the-box had given way to—a blank space!

All of a sudden Lidija had a divine inspiration. She threw herself on Kovalić and for all the insulted, humiliated, oppressed, for all the ugly, impotent, and sterile, for all the poor in body, hunched in back, and ill in health—for every last one she gave him her tenderest treatment, polishing, honing him like a recalcitrant translation, fondling, caressing, her tongue as adroit as a keypunch, kneading his skin with her long, skilful fingers, moving lower and lower, seeking out her Jack's mislaid cudgel, picking and pecking at the empty space, fully expecting the firm little rod to pop out and give her cheek a love tap. Kovalić was a bit stunned by Lidija's abrupt show of passion, and even after he began to feel signs of arousal he remained prostrate, keeping close tabs on the pulsations within as they proceeded from pitapat to rat-tat-tat to boomety-boom, waiting for his Jack to jump, his Tom to thump, he didn't care who, as long as he came out into the open . . . !

Kovalić held his breath. He felt the blank space ticking off the seconds like an infernal machine; felt it about to erupt like a geyser, a volcano, an oil well; felt himself swelling like soaked peas, like a tulip bulb, like a cocoon; felt it coming, any time now, any second now, any—pow! boo-oo-oom! cra-a-a-sh-sh-sh!

Moaning with pleasure, Kovalić climaxed, climaxed to his great surprise—in the big toe of his left foot!

Utterly shaken, Kovalić gave Lidija a slight shove and peered down at his foot. Then, still refusing to believe that what happened had happened, he fingered the toe. It gave him a combination of pleasure and mild pain—and just sat there, potato-like, indifferent. Kovalić stared at it, mildly offended by its lack of response.

"Idiot!" said Lidija bilingually, and stood up, stalked out, and slammed the door.

Kovalić stretched. The smooth space was still hideously smooth. He wiggled his left toe, then his right . . . The left one struck him as perceptibly fatter and longer.

It did happen, thought Kovalić. There's no doubt about it. It actually happened. Suddenly he felt grateful to Lidija. The only thing was, did he really climax in his toe or was his mind playing tricks on him? Kovalić leaned over and felt the toe again, then went back to the smooth space, and finally, heaving a worried sigh, lit a cigarette.

"Anyone for a nice homemade sausage?" asked a conciliatory Lidija, peeking in from the kitchen.

Kovalić felt all the air go out of him: Lidija's proposition was like a blow to the solar plexus; it turned him into the butt of a dirty joke.

Kovalić was especially sensitive to cliches; he avoided them in both literature and life. And now he was terribly upset. By some absurd concatenation of events his life had assumed the contours of a well-established genre (a joke of which he was the punch line). How could life, which he had always thought of as vast—no, boundless—how could life give in to the laws of a genre? And with nary a deviation! Kovalić was so distressed he felt tears welling in his eyes. How he loved— literature! It was so much better, more humane, less predictable, more fanciful . . . In a well-written story Lidija would have offered him nothing less than a veal cutlet; in the low genre of life, Lidija, she gives him—a sausage!

But suddenly Kovalić felt hungry . . .

5.

On Saturday, the seventh of April, Nada Matić awoke from a nightmare she had had for many nights. She would dream she was working in her office at Plastic Surgery. It was crammed with anatomical sketches, plaster molds, and plastic models—all of "hot dogs" of the most varied dimensions. Suddenly in trooped a band of students who tore them all to pieces, laughing and pointing at her all the while. Nada thought she would die of shame, and to make matters worse she felt something sprouting on her nose—an honest to goodness sausage! At that point the scene would shift to the operating room, where she—Nada—and Dr. Waldinger were performing a complex procedure. But there was a round hole in the white sheet covering the patient, and she couldn't stop staring through it at his hideous smooth space. Then the scene would shift again, and she and Otto Waldinger were in a field pulling out a gigantic beet. She was holding Otto around the waist when suddenly she was attacked by a gigantic mouse! She could feel its claws on her thighs.

Nada Matić was drinking her morning coffee, smoking a cigarette, and leafing through the evening paper. She would seem to have acquired the fine habit of perusing the Saturday classifieds. Suddenly an item in the "Lost and Found" column caught her eye. She did a double take, stunned by a wild but logical thought: if someone were to lose something like that, it would only be natural for him to try to find it!

> On the twenty-fifth of March, I left a collapsable umbrella in the Skyscraper Cafeteria. Would the finder please return it. No questions asked. Phone xyz and ask for Milan.

Nada jumped out of her seat. The ad was perfectly clear! The umbrella was obviously a respectable substitution for that. The fact that it was collapsible made the whole thing absolutely unambiguous!

Nada grabbed the telephone and dialed the number. The conversation was to the point: That's right. Five o'clock. See you there. Good-bye.

At five o'clock that afternoon Nada Matić rang the doorbell of a Dalmatinska Street apartment. A dark man of about thirty opened the door.

He could well be the one, thought Nada and said, "Hello, my name is Nada Matić."

"And mine is Milan Miško. Come in."

"Are you the one who lost his umbrella?"

"That's right."

"At the cafeteria?"

"The Skyscraper."

"Collapsable?"

"Yes, yes," said Milan Miško, the owner of the lost umbrella, in an amiable voice. "Do come in." Nada went in.

They sat down. The owner of the collapsable umbrella brought out a bottle of wine and two glasses.

"So, you're the one who lost it," Nada said tellingly and took a sip of the wine.

"That's right."

"God, how thick can he be?" thought Nada, beginning to feel annoyed. She took a long look at that place, but could make nothing out. She had to put it into words! But how?

"It must have been hard for you," she said, trying a more direct approach.

"With all the spring showers, you mean? I'd have picked up another one, but you do get attached to your own . . ."

"What was it like? Your umbrella, I mean," she asked its owner nonchalantly.

"Oh, nothing special . . . You mean, what color, how long?"

"Yes," said Nada, swallowing hard, "how long . . . ?"

"Oh, standard size," he said, as calm as could be. "You know—collapsible." And he looked over at Nada serenely. "The kind that goes in and out."

Now there could be no doubt. Nada resolved to take the plunge and call a spade a spade, even if it meant humiliating herself. After all, she had played her own bitter part in the affair. So she took the sort of deep breath she would have taken before a dive, half-shut her eyes, stretched out her arms in a sleepwalker's pose, and—jumped! I'm wrong, she thought as she flew mentally through the air, terribly, shamefully wrong. But it was too late to retreat.

And though at this point everything becomes enveloped in mist again, we can guess exactly what happened.

6.

The waitress switched off the light and shut the door after the other girls. For some reason she didn't feel like going with them. She sat down for a short rest and looked through the window at the passersby and the brand names atop the buildings. As she bent over to take off the slippers she wore at work, her hand happened to graze her knee. She let her hand rest on the knee and froze in that position as if listening for something. Then, heaven knows why, she thought of the dark handsome guy who'd left his umbrella in the cafeteria a week or so before and that good-looking young policeman with the funny, kinky questions—both of them so attractive and somehow connected . . . Or had she noticed them and had they registered with her mainly because they had—of that she was sure—noticed her?

Sheltered by the darkness, the cartons, and the glass, the girl sat with her legs slightly parted, relaxed, peering out of the window at the passersby, when suddenly her hands reached by themselves for one of the cardboard boxes, pulled out a few packages of hot dogs, and started tugging feverishly at the cellophane wrappers. God, what was she doing? What was she doing? What if somebody saw her . . . ? Nobody saw her.

She slowly brought a raw hot dog to her lips and quickly stuffed it into her mouth. The hot dog slid down her throat, leaving practically no taste behind. She grabbed a second and quickly chewed it up. Then a third, a fourth, a fifth . . .

There in the heart of the city, enslaved by the darkness, the cartons and the glass, sat a waitress with her legs slightly parted and her dark, shining eyes peering out at the passersby while she gobbled hot dog after hot dog. At one point the image of a gigantic, ravenous female mouse flashed through her mind, but she immediately forgot it. She was following the movements of her jaws and listening in on her gullet.

7.

In the afternoon of the seventh of April there was a nervous ring at Kovalić's door. Kovalić was a bit taken aback to see a good-looking young policeman carrying an unusual-looking bundle.

"Are you Mato Kovalić the writer? Or, rather, the novelist and short story writer?"

"I am," said Kovalić with a tremor in his voice.

"Well, this is yours. Sign here."

"But. . ." Kovalić muttered.

"Good-bye," said the policeman and, with a knowing wink, added, "and good luck!"

"But officer . . . !" Kovalić cried out. It was too late. The policeman had disappeared into the lift.

Kovalić unwrapped the bundle with trembling hands. Out of the paper fell a bottle filled with a clear liquid, and floating in that liquid was his very own . . . ! Unbelievable! Kovalić was beside himself. For several moments he stood stock still; then he went back and cautiously removed the object from the bottle and started inspecting it.

That's it, all right—the real thing! Kovalić thought aloud. He'd have recognized it anywhere! And he jumped for joy—though carefully clutching it in his hands.

Since, however, it is a well-known fact that nothing on this earth lasts for very long, our hero suddenly frowned. He had had a terrifying thought. What if it wouldn't go back on?

With indescribable terror in his heart Kovalić walked over to the mirror. His hands were trembling. He carefully returned the object to its former place. Panic! It refused to stick! He brought it up to his lips, warmed it with his breath, and tried again. No luck!

"Come on, damn you!" Kovalić grumbled. "Stick! Stick, you stupid fool!" But the object fell to the floor with a strange, dull, cork-like thud. "Why won't it take?" Kovalić wondered nervously. And though he tried again and again, his efforts were in vain.

Crushed, Kovalić was left holding his own, his very own and now, very useless part. And much as Kovalić stared at it, it clearly remained indifferent to his despair and lay there in his hand like a dead fish.

"Ba-a-a-a-astard!" Kovalić screamed in a bloodcurdling voice and flung the object into a corner and himself onto his bed. "No, I'm not dreaming," Kovalić whispered into his pillow. "This can't be a dream. This is madness, lunacy . . ." And with that he fell asleep.

8.

Lidija typed out the word malady and paused. She was still on page one. The translation of the report was due on Monday morning at the Department of Veterinary Medicine.

She stood up, stretched, and switched on the light. She glanced out of the window. It was still day, but the street was gray and empty and smooth from the rain.

She went into the kitchen and opened the refrigerator door out of habit. She peered in without interest and slammed it shut.

Then she went into the bathroom, turned on the tap, and put her wrist under a jet of cold water. It felt good. She glanced up at the mirror. All at once she felt like licking it. She moved in close to its smooth surface. Her face with tongue hanging out flashed into sight. She drew back slowly. A smooth and empty gesture. Like her life. "Smooth, empty, empty, smooth," she murmured on her way back to the kitchen.

On the kitchen table Lidija noticed a few dried-out bits of bread. She touched them. She liked the way dry crumbs pricked the pulp of her fingers. She moistened her finger with saliva, gathered up the crumbs, and went into the combined bedroom and living room. Again she looked out at the street, preoccupied, nibbling on the crumbs from her finger and on the finger itself. The street was empty.

And then she noticed a good-looking young policeman. He had a limber way about him and was crossing the smooth street, or so it seemed to Lidija, as if it were water. Suddenly she opened the window, breathed deeply, pursed her lips for a whistle, and stopped . . . What was she doing, for Heaven's sake? What had got into her . . . ?

The policeman looked up. In a well-lit window he saw an unusual-looking young woman standing stock still and staring at him. His glance came to rest on her full, slightly parted lips. He noticed a crumb on the lower one . . . Or was he just imagining it? Suddenly he had a desire to remove that real or imagined crumb with his own lips.

"What if she really . . ." flashed through his mind as he noiselessly slipped into the main door. But what happened next we really have no idea.

9.

Kovalić awoke with a vague premonition. His head felt fuzzy, his body leaden. He lay completely motionless for a while when all at once he felt an odd throbbing sensation. He tore off the blanket, and lo and behold!—it was back in place.

Kovalić couldn't believe his eyes. He reached down and fingered it—yes, it was his, all right! He gave it a tug just to make sure—yes, it popped out of his hand, straight, taut, elastic. Kovalić jumped for joy and leaped out of bed, rushing over to the mirror for a look. No doubt about it: there it stood, rosy, shiny, and erect— and just where it had been before. Kovalić cast a worried glance at the bottle. He saw a little black catfish swimming about as merrily as you please. Intent on engineering clever turns within its narrow confines, it paid him no heed.

"Oh!" Kovalić cried out in amazement.

Then he looked back down below. Situation normal: stiff and erect! Trembling with excitement, Kovalić raced to the phone.

At this point, however, the events are temporarily misted over by censorship, and the reader will have to deduce what happened from the following lines.

Exhausted and depressed, her eyes circled in black, her mouth dry, Maja the invoice clerk lay on her back apathetically staring at that horrid black fish. It was making its two-thousand-one-hundred-and-fifty-first turn in the bottle. At last she picked herself up slowly and started gathering her clothes the way an animal licks its wounds. Suddenly her eyes lit on a slip of paper lying next to her left shoe.

The paper contained a list of names in Kovalić's handwriting. Vesna, Branka,

Iris, Goga, Ljerka, Višnja, Maja, Lidija. All the names but Lidija's (hers too!) had lines through them.

"Monster!" she said in a hoarse, weary voice, and slammed the door.

Kovalić stared apathetically at the lower half of his body. It was in place, sprightly and erect as ever. He flew into a rage, bounded out of bed, bolted to the bottle, and smashed it to the floor. The catfish flipped and flopped for a while, then calmed down. Kovalić gleefully watched the gill contractions subside. But it was still erect.

"Down, monster!" Kovalić shouted and gave it a mean thwack. It swayed and reddened, but then spryly, with a rubber-like elasticity, sprang back into place and raised its head at Kovalić almost sheepishly.

"Off with you, beast!" Kovalić screamed. The object refused to budge.

"I'll strangle you!" Kovalić bellowed. The object stared straight ahead, curtly indifferent.

"I wish you'd never been found," Kovalić whimpered, and flung himself onto the bed in despair. "You bastard, you! I'll get you yet . . . !" And he burst into sobs, mumbling incoherent threats into the pillow. Then, wiping his tears, he raised his fist into the air, Heaven knows why, and muttered, "I'll put you through the meat grinder!" And all of a sudden the old butcher's saying went off like an alarm in his brain: My knives go with me to the grave!

And the fear and trembling caused by this new piece of data sent Kovalić reeling—and into a dead faint.

10.

Well, dear readers, now you see the sort of thing that happens in our city! And only now, after much reflection, do I realize how much in it is unbelievable—starting from the alienation of the object in question from its rightful owner. Nor is it believable that authors should choose such things to write stories about. First, they are of no use either to literature or to the population, the reading population, and secondly, they are of no use . . . well, either. And yet, when all is said and done, there is hardly a place you won't find similar incongruities. No, say what you will, these things do happen—rarely, but they do.

For my part, I have a clear conscience. I have stuck to the plot. Had I given myself free rein, well, I don't know where things would have ended! And even so, what happened to Nada Matić? Who is Milan Miško? What became of Vinko K.? And Lidija and the waitress and the butcher? To say nothing of our hero Mato Kovalić? Is he doomed to spend his life getting it—down?!

But I repeat: I have stuck to the plot. Though if the truth be told, I did insert two nightmares from my own childhood, to wit: 1) the sausage dream ("Watch out or a sausage will sprout on your nose," my grandfather used to say when he got angry with me), and 2) the beet dream (I can recall no more terrifying story from my childhood than the one in which a whole family gathered to pull out a big, beautiful, and completely innocent beet!).

In connection with said plot may I suggest the following points as worthy of further consideration:

1. How did the object alienated from its owner, Mato Kovalić, find its way into the bun?

2. How did Vinko K. discover its owner?

3. Miscellaneous.

All that is merely by the by, of course, in passing. I myself have no intention of taking things any further . . . But if you, honored readers, decide to do so, I wish you a merry time of it and a hearty appetite!

FAMILY LIFE

Quim Monzó

Translated from the Catalan by Peter Bush

Joaquim Monzó i Gómez (1952–). Quim Monzó, as he is widely known,
cut his teeth as a war correspondent in the 1970s, reporting from Vietnam,
Northern Ireland and East Africa. His first collection of short stories was
published in 1978, and he has since published three collections of stories
and several novels. In an interview in *El Punt* Monzó says "... the air is
full of stories. You walk along the street and they're everywhere. However,
to find where the story is, you have to go sculpting it, removing everything
that is accessory." Monzó has also translated authors as diverse as J.D.
Salinger, Thomas Hardy, Ernest Hemingway and Roald Dahl.

Armand ran into the workshop, making an engine noise with his mouth
and stamping on the wood shavings on the floor so they crackled underfoot: the louder the better. He walked twice around the carpenter's
bench; looked at all the tools perfectly aligned on the wall, the saws, gouges,
clamps and planes, each in their rightful place (marked by a suitable outline,
roughly penciled in); and went up the passageway at the rear of which the house,
properly speaking, began. Uncle Reguard had put his workshop in the back of
his house, and although the grown-ups always entered through the front door,
Armand preferred to go in via the workshop. He was fascinated by the fact
that his uncle's workplace was right at the back of his house. In contrast, he
lived in an apartment, and his father's carpentry workshop occupied a ground-
floor space four blocks from where they lived. His cousins had a similar set up.
Uncle Reguard was the only member of the family to have his workshop and
home together; separated by a small bedroom, that now acted as a junk room.
If you came from the workshop, you then reached the parlor with the big table,
chandelier, armchairs, passages, and bedroom doors.

By the time Armand reached the parlor everyone was already there kissing,
laughing, chatting, raising their voices to make themselves heard: his father, uncles
and aunts, and more distant uncles, aunts, and cousins, who weren't cousins at all
and were only described as such because they belonged to branches of the family
so remote they didn't know what precise labels to give them.

They ate lunch, a meal that lasted hours, and then the post-lunch conversations started, when the smoke from the cigars began to curl around everything.
Empty champagne bottles piled up in the room between the house and workshop,
the aunts kept slicing cake, and the older cousins put records on the turntable.
The atmosphere was heavy with the aroma of hot chocolate. The young cousins

(Armand, Guinovarda, Gisela, Guitart, and Llopart . . .) asked permission to leave the table and ran to Eginard's bedroom to play with wooden houses that had roofs, doors, and windows painted in a range of colors. When the bedroom door was half open, Armand could see the harp in the corner of the passage. It was a harp Uncle Reguard had built thirty years ago, and it was one of the family's prized possessions, because (so Armand's father would say) he had combined carpentry with the art of crafting string instruments. For as long as he could remember, Armand had seen the harp at Uncle Reguard's and always in the same place: in the corner made by the bend in the passage. He thought it was more beautiful than all the harps in the photographs and drawings that he'd cut out from magazines (and kept in a blue folder at home): a harp in the hands of a mythological god, a Sumerian harp topped by the head of an animal he couldn't identify, the Irish coat-of-arms, two Norwegian harps (one topped by a dragon's head and the other by the head of a blind-folded woman), and a harp made from a tree branch that Harpo Marx was plucking.

Cousin Reguard came into the bedroom, crying and smiling, in the midst of cheering adults. His right hand was holding a chocolate and peppermint ice cream, and his left hand was bandaged. It was a scene Armand had often seen in these family get-togethers, whether they were held in their home, their cousins', or the homes of other more distant cousins, some of who even lived in other cities. A boy would appear with a bandaged left hand. The bandage was always wrapped around his ring finger. Armand knew there was no longer a finger under the bandage, and that the bandage would eventually fall away, revealing a tiny, perfectly healed stump. Armand surveyed the hands of his family. As he'd registered some time ago, everyone over nine was missing the ring finger of their left hand.

Armand was seven when he first realized it was no accident that one of the boys would always leave the party with his ring finger cut off. He'd not really paid much attention till now. It was true he'd noticed the older kids were missing that finger, but it was a completely normal state of affairs for him. It had never been any different. He thought the absence must be synonymous with adult life. Every adult in the family lost that finger for a reason that eluded him and that didn't concern him one little bit. So many things eluded him—he knew he wouldn't understand them until he became an adult, and he didn't worry about a trifle that was quite unimportant when compared to the other issues that preoccupied him at the time: the spirit of sacrifice displayed by St. Bernard dogs, the origins of existence, or the offside trap in football. As he saw it, in order to hit adolescence and abandon the world of little kids, he too would have to lose his ring finger. He thought it was understandable, normal, and desirable, like losing his milk teeth.

When he started to go to school, he was surprised to see how many adults had four fingers and a thumb on each hand, as if *that* were completely normal. He thought theirs was a surprising, eccentric, and rather unpleasant circumstance, and he was proud to belong to such a consistent family. As the months passed, and he spent more time in the company of other kids, he started to think that perhaps the members of his family experienced random accidents and that these accidents always led to the loss of the ring finger. The boy he shared a desk with at school told him it was quite common for carpenters to lose fingers. The carpenter near his house (he went on) was missing three. His mother had told him it happened to lots of carpenters, because one day or another the blade of the circular saw would slice a finger off. Armand knew that wasn't the case in his family. They were carpenters, but it wasn't the circular saw that sliced off their fingers, or any other accident. At the age of nine, the kids weren't yet carpenters and didn't even know that's what they wanted to be when they grew up; even though from time immemorial all the members of his family had showed an undeniable inclination towards that trade, and apart from a few exceptional cases, they invariably ended up as carpenters.

Armand spent his nights ruminating about this mystery. Perhaps there was a guild rule that obliged them to chop off that finger? He reached a conclusion he wasn't sure how to verify; they chopped that first finger off to get them used to the idea. Losing that first finger meant they lost their fear of the possible loss of others. They realized it wasn't such a big deal; it gave them courage and helped them tackle their trade with true valor. One thing sent his head into a whirl: he'd met the father of a school friend, from another class, who also happened to be a carpenter, and none of his fingers were missing (he used to take a look whenever he picked up his son at the end of the school day).

As the adults didn't consider it a tragedy, and seemed particularly happy at the exact moment when the finger disappeared (especially the parents of the boy whose finger was amputated), Armand didn't find it tragic either. Until that afternoon two years ago, when he became conscious for the first time that, on whatever day of the year a member of the family celebrated a ninth birthday, they lost that finger, and it would be his fate too; he felt frightened that afternoon. He was with his cousins in the bedroom, playing with those wooden houses. Eginard, Gisela, and Gimfreu had all had that finger chopped off. Llopart and he still retained all four fingers, and that meant they were still kids. When Eginard got up from their game, Armand went over to him, swallowed, and asked him what the finger business was all about. Llopart, Gisela, and Gimfreu all looked around for a moment, then went back to the game they were playing, going in and out of the houses. Eginard asked him to repeat the question, perhaps to get more time to think up his reply. Armand expanded his question: What was the finger thing all about? They'd cut off little Reguard's today; they cut a finger off from everyone, one day or another, when they reached the age of nine. Llopart looked at them all, clueless. Eginard got up, stroked Armand's head, and dragged him gently out of the bedroom. Armand wouldn't relent: Why was everyone in their family missing the same finger on their left hand, a finger people outside their family kept? Armand scrutinized Eginard's finger; it had been chopped off at the metacarpus— a clean scar from a perfect strike.

And why the ring finger on the left hand and not the little finger on the right, or an index finger? Was it some hygienic measure, the reason for which had been forgotten with the passage of time? He just couldn't understand. It was evident it was an ancestral custom, but how had it originated? Had they practiced it for centuries? Or simply decades? On his ninth birthday, his father found him crying in bed.

"I don't want my finger chopped off."

"What an odd thing to say!"

"I want to be normal, like the other kids at school."

"Being normal has nothing to do with having one finger more or one less."

His father wiped away his tears and told him that normal is a cultural value and consequently completely relative; some people like crew-cuts, others like long hair, some prefer a beard and mustache, some only a mustache and others only a beard, and some even shave the whole lot off; there are nations where both men and women depilate themselves and others where only the women do. We cut our toenails, and that's precisely what makes us different from animals and primitive peoples who prefer to keep them very long. Armand disagreed with these comparisons. Hair and nails grow again, fingers don't. The sun was shining through the window; father and son looked at the warm lines the beams were tracing on the ground.

"You don't have to make your mind up immediately."

"I've already made it up, and I don't want to do it."

"Why not?"

"You can't play the harp if you're a finger short."

He surprised even himself. He'd said that quite spontaneously. Nevertheless, although he'd not realized that or thought about it before, it was out in the open, his father was in the know, and it could very well be true that he wanted to be a harpist, so he kept to his story. Months ago he'd seen a television report about Nicanor Zabaleta playing the harp, and it was quite obvious he needed all his fingers. A harpist needed every single one. His father was looking at him solemnly. He'd never seen him so solemn.

"If you like music, there are lots of different instruments. It doesn't have to be a harp."

"But I like the harp."

"You're just obsessed with the harp at your uncle's. But the world of musical instruments doesn't stop at the harp. Just think how many others there are: the kettledrum, the bass drum, the tambourine, the bongo, the triangle . . ." Armand stared at him, betraying no sign of excitement at these possibilities. "Perhaps you think the maracas are small potatoes, but what about the drums? Drums give lots of scope: the bass drum, the ordinary drum, the tom-tom, the cymbals and the snare. And never forget the xylophone!"

Armand spent the next few months in a very jumpy state. The belief had always circulated in the family (always mentioned jokingly) that they'd cut a kid's finger off one day, but it would grow back with time. Some said it would be a sign that something was about to happen, but they never got around to saying exactly what. Others said that, in effect, the finger would grow back but that this would mean nothing in particular. That story sowed fresh doubts in Armand's mind: What if he refused to let them chop his finger off and he was the chosen one whose finger would grow back after it had been removed? What an absurd situation! His refusal would prevent that miracle from ever happening.

He was obsessed by fingers. He noticed how some people wore a ring on the ring finger of their left hand. In his family, nobody had a ring finger, so they always wore it on the little finger, and when it came to the marriage ceremony, the priest always looked on impassively when the time came for the bride and bridegroom to put their rings on. Armand once saw a complete stranger in the street who was missing the ring finger of his left hand, and he spent days investigating whether he was a distant relative, so distant he didn't even know him. Perhaps other families shared the same tradition. Or similar ones? Perhaps they amputated other fingers, or other parts of the body . . . but why? What sense did it make? And what did they do with the fingers they'd chopped off? Did they bury them? Armand imagined them buried vertically, like asparagus shoots, in small graveyards for fingers. Perhaps they cremated them.

He gradually started to see his parents and the rest of his relatives through different eyes. What kind of macabre tradition were they cherishing; how could they go along with it so pitilessly? As he didn't trust them, he slept with his left hand under the pillow where he rested his head. He'd calculated that it would be quite impossible for them to lift up his head, remove the pillow, take his hand out, and slice his finger off without waking him up. He would sometimes dream that, despite all these precautions, his parents (their faces glowing sanctimoniously) managed to lift up his head and pillow, extract his hand, and chop off his finger with a single deft slice of the carving knife.

He had a panic attack when he discovered there would be a family reunion the following Sunday. For the first time he was a candidate to lose a finger. He and Guitard were the two most likely cousins. Both were now nine years old. He had been nine for three months, Guitard for seven. If seniority was an issue, it was Guitard's turn. But amputations weren't always carried out according to the principle of seniority, and that meant it could very well be his turn this time.

Sunday came, and they didn't chop off his finger, or Guitard's, but Teodard's, a cousin who had a month to go before his ninth birthday; theoretically, they should have left him intact. Guitard was furious. He was up for the chop and *not* that cousin. They told him why they'd moved Teodard forward: his mother was pregnant, so they'd wanted to get the whole business over and done with—when the new baby arrived, there'd be no need to worry about the big brother's finger. Armand was intrigued by Guitard's attitude. He asked him if he wasn't shocked by the idea of having his finger chopped off. Why should he be? On the contrary, he couldn't see what the problem was and was shocked Armand even asked the question.

"They aren't chopping your neck off. It's only a finger, and not even the most important one at that."

Guitard was crazy about becoming a grown up. Consequently, at the next family reunion, he ran into the room where the other kids were playing with toy trains, proudly waving his bandaged finger.

*

When the new cousin was born (they called him Abelard), there was a big fuss, whispered exchanges, and sudden silences whenever a youngster entered a bedroom. All the secrecy aroused Armand's curiosity. But he found out only three days later that Abelard had been born with five fingers and a thumb on his left hand.

The whole family was alarmed. What would they do when Abelard made it to nine? If they chopped one finger off, he would have eight, not seven like everybody else. According to some, this might be seen as an offensive point of comparison, and two should be chopped off so he was like the rest of the family. Conversely, others thought it would be excessive to cut two off, if they cut off only one from everybody else. Only one should be amputated. This is what they'd always done, and there was no reason to start changing their tradition. The debates followed various tangents, got very involved, and always came back to square one. Finally, they reached the obvious conclusion: this was an exceptional case and, as such, merited an exceptional solution. Besides, there was no need to rush things. Abelard wouldn't be nine for years, and that's when the decision should be taken.

This reconciliatory conclusion fell flat, however, a few weeks later when cousin Gerarda was born: she also had an extra finger, and it was also on her left hand. So Abelard's case was no longer exceptional, and the first serious doubts began to appear. It made no sense to delay a decision until Abelard and Gerarda were nine. A stenotypist uncle, a jazz fan, dared to ask what the point was in continuing with the whole tradition. It was the provocation they were all waiting for. The family reacted as one. An immemorial legacy couldn't be questioned simply because of the random occurrence of two babies being born with five-fingered left hands. The dissident was told his question was out of order, and with a great sense of purpose, a date was fixed for their next reunion: a month later, at the beginning of December.

Within the week, however, news came from Barbastre of a third cousin's birth (quite a distant one): five fingers. It suddenly became clear that speaking of random occurrences was inappropriate and that delaying a decision for nine years resolved nothing. Some family members argued there was no cause for alarm; the fact that children in the family were being born with five fingers on one hand was the consequence of a logical process of evolution. Even Uncle Reguard speculated that so many centuries (some spoke of millennia) of cutting off ring fingers had finally led to a mutation: babies in the family were being born with an extra finger in order to compensate for the one they'd lose at the age of nine. Other family members thought that his opinion was absurd and refused to accept there could be such a significant mutation after a few centuries, or even a few millennia. In fact, it didn't matter who was right. For the first time, there was a deep schism in the family that threatened their harmony. On the one side, there were those who believed two fingers should be chopped off of children with five-fingered left hands (the ring finger, as usual, and this new intermediate finger between the ring finger and middle finger that doesn't have a special name) and there was no need to wait until they were nine: it should be done immediately, in a show of strength, to stamp out any dissent. On the other, there were those who believed that, if the tradition was to cut off one finger, however many anatomical variants there might be, they should continue being loyal to tradition and only chop one finger off. A third opinion appeared in the heat of the debate, initially a minority view, defended by the stenotypist uncle and two sisters-in-law: they denounced the custom itself as barbaric.

It was particularly significant that the sisters-in-law had denounced the practice—after becoming convinced during their courtship, people who married into the family had always turned into the most enthusiastic champions of the rite. In fact, one of the culminating moments in the festivities (and the source of perennial leg-pulling in family reunions) was when, if relationships looked rock-solid, a member of the family would address their future partner, saying he must tell her something before their betrothal could be ratified. It was an act that would initially seem strange, though it wasn't at all, and their joint future as a married couple depended on a proper understanding of the tradition. And then they would go on to say, "When our children turn nine, we chop the ring finger off their left hand."

The idea would always meet with reticence (as if it were a kind of joke) and immediately after (when it was realized it was no joke) with horror. The objections were always the same: "How can you do something so barbaric in this day and age?", "What's the point?", "You're not going to do that to *our* children!" Then the persuasion process began, hours of conversation and arguments. Day after day refining, clarifying, stressing until the future spouse finally understood. From that point on they became the most ardent champions of the act, and (although, in principle, nobody asked them to do this) they surrendered their own ring fingers, so they could fully enter into the spirit of the family. They were also the first to demand the rite be carried out when the child was nine, with no holds barred, and volunteered to keep the child's hand still.

That was why revisionism from that quarter of the family, from the converts who seemingly clung to the custom most, was so serious. But this consideration gradually ceased to be important; soon there were no distinctions, and everyone joined the initial caucus formed by the stenotypist and the two sisters-in-law. A fourth cousin was born with five fingers. Everything now escalated to a crisis-point: people began to distance themselves, and the reunion arranged for the beginning of December was postponed *sine die*. "Until a final decision is reached." But many assumed this was simply a way to get them out of the fix and intuited that there never would be a final decision, apart from that declaration, which apparently wasn't one.

They bought a harp for Armand and signed him up for music and harp lessons on Tuesdays and Thursdays after school. He practiced conscientiously and assiduously on the weekends, but it didn't always show in performance. As it became clear the family custom of chopping off fingers was now a thing of the past, Armand's desire to play the harp gradually waned, and the next year, the harp stayed in a corner accumulating dust, until years later when Elisard, one of his five-fingered cousins, took an interest. Whenever there was a family lunch at Armand's (now they were lucky to have seven or eight relatives when before twenty or more always came), Elisard would go into Armand's bedroom and play the harp. Every get-together he played better. Until in the end he was playing compositions by Halffter, Milhaud, and Ginastera, and (a family special request) songs from Paraguay, and a Mexican tune he kept encoring ever more zestfully. Armand's parents suggested giving him the harp as a gift. Armand interpreted that as a hint (as a reproach, after he'd defended his vocation as a harpist so energetically and then shown so little interest). He saw no point in pandering to them and said he couldn't care less what they did with it. His parents decided to present it to Elisard the next time he visited.

But Elisard never returned to Armand's. Without the cohesive element of the ceremony, family reunions became more and more infrequent; less people went to the few that were held, and soon everyone found an excuse not to go: in winter, people had to go skiing; in the summer, to the beach; and in any season of the year there was always some commitment that couldn't be cancelled. Within a few years, family reunions were ancient history, and even the closest relatives became strangers they spoke to once a year at most, and then on the phone.

Elisard was the only one everyone still had news of, because over time (some say it had to do with his small anatomical extra) he turned into an exceptional harpist, who restored to the instrument the prestige and high standing it had lost as a result of being little played for many years. Armand thought differently. He thought Elisard was a child prodigy who'd enjoyed a few years as a star but, as he got older, he cut a pathetic figure: he, his harp, and his mannered melodies. Now, as he leaned on the bar, Armand saw Elisard yet again on the TV next to the shelves of bottles. He looked around, swore at the top of his voice and advocated the need to reinstate the old custom of chopping off ring fingers, starting with that famous harpist's. The others propping up the bar don't even look at him. As they don't listen to him, he recounts the story of his family. Two patrons who do finally pay him some attention decide he's either mad or drunk, or both things at once. Only one girl seems to take a positive interest, and she sidles over when he stops talking. She is pretty and has a lovely smile and a lock of brown hair that hides half of her face, the way some women hide a glass eye.

LAST EVENINGS ON EARTH

Roberto Bolaño

Translated from the Spanish by Chris Andrews

Roberto Bolaño Ávalos (1953–2003) was a Chilean novelist, short-story writer, poet and essayist. In 1999, Bolaño won the Rómulo Gallegos Prize for his novel *Los detectives salvajes* (*The Savage Detectives*), and in 2008 he was posthumously awarded the National Book Critics Circle Award for Fiction for his novel *2666*. He died at the age of fifty after a long period of declining health. Bolaño was arrested by the Pinochet regime on suspicion of being a "terrorist" and spent eight days in custody. He was rescued by two former classmates who had become prison guards. After moving to Spain in 1977, he supported himself with work as a dishwasher, campground custodian, bellhop, and garbage collector. Bolaño was expelled from school because, among other crimes, he kept correcting the teachers.

This is the situation: B and his father are going to Acapulco on holiday. They are planning to leave very early, at six in the morning. B sleeps the previous night at his father's house. He doesn't dream or if he does he forgets his dreams as soon as he opens his eyes. He hears his father in the bathroom. He looks out of the window; it is still dark. He gets dressed without switching on the light. When he comes out of his room, his father is sitting at the table, reading the sports news from the day before, and breakfast is ready. Coffee and ranch-style eggs. B says hello to his father and goes into the bathroom.

His father's car is a 1970 Ford Mustang. At six-thirty in the morning they get into the car and head out of the city. The city is Mexico City, and the year in which B and his father leave Mexico City for a short holiday is 1975.

Overall, the trip goes smoothly. Leaving the city both father and son feel cold, but as they leave the high valley behind and begin to descend into the state of Guerrero, the temperature rises and they have to take off their sweaters and open the windows. B, who is inclined to melancholy (or so he likes to think), is at first completely absorbed in contemplating the landscape, but after a few hours the mountains and forests become monotonous and he starts reading a book instead.

Before they get to Acapulco, B's father pulls up in front of a roadside café. The café serves iguana. Shall we try it? he suggests. The iguanas are alive and they hardly move when B's father goes over to look at them. B leans against the mudguard of the Mustang, watching him. Without waiting for an answer, B's father orders a portion of iguana for himself and one for his son. Only then does B move away from the car. He approaches the open-air eating area – four tables under a canvas shade that is swaying slightly in the gentle breeze – and sits down at the table furthest from the highway. B's father orders two beers. Father and son have rolled up their sleeves and unbuttoned their shirts. Both are wearing light-coloured shirts. The waiter, by contrast, is wearing a black, long-sleeved shirt and doesn't seem bothered by the heat.

Going to Acapulco? asks the waiter. B's father nods. They are the only customers at the café. Cars whiz past on the bright highway. B's father gets up and goes out the back. For a moment B thinks his father is going to the toilet, but then he realises he has gone to the kitchen to see how they cook the iguanas. The waiter follows him without a word. Then B hears them talking. First his father, then the man's voice, and finally the voice of a woman B can't see. B's forehead is beaded with sweat. His glasses are misted and dirty. He takes them off and cleans them with the corner of his shirt. When he puts them back on he notices his father watching him from the kitchen. He can see only his father's face and part of his shoulder, the rest is hidden by a red curtain with black dots, and B has the intermittent impression that this curtain separates not only the kitchen from the eating area but also one time from another.

Then B looks away and his gaze returns to the book lying on the table. It is a book of poetry. An anthology of French surrealist poets translated into Spanish by the Argentine surrealist Aldo Pellegrini. B has been reading this book for two days. He likes it. He likes the photos of the poets. The photo of Unik, the one of Desnos, the photos of Artaud and Crevel. The book is thick and covered with transparent plastic. It wasn't covered by B (who never covers his books), but by a particularly fastidious friend. So B looks away from his father, opens the book at random and comes face to face with Gui Rosey, the photo of Gui Rosey and his poems, and when he looks up again his father's head has disappeared.

The heat is stifling. B would be more than happy to go back to Mexico City, but he isn't going back, at least not yet, he knows that. Soon his father is sitting next to him and they are both eating iguana with chilli sauce and drinking more beer. The waiter in the black shirt has turned on a transistor radio, and now some vaguely tropical music is blending with the noises of the jungle and the noise of the cars passing on the highway. The iguana tastes like chicken. It's tougher than chicken, says B, not entirely convinced. It's tasty, says his father, and orders another portion. They have cinnamon coffee. The man in the black shirt serves the iguana, but the woman from the kitchen brings out the coffee. She is young, almost as young as B; she is wearing white shorts and a yellow blouse with white flowers printed on it, flowers B doesn't recognise, perhaps because they don't exist. As they drink their coffee, B feels nauseous, but he says nothing. He smokes and looks at the canvas shade, barely moving, as if weighed down by a narrow puddle of rainwater from the last storm. But it can't be that, thinks B. What are you looking at? asks his father. The shade, says B. It's like a vein. But he doesn't say the bit about the vein, he only thinks it.

They arrive in Acapulco as night is falling. For a while they drive up and down the avenues by the sea with the windows wide open and the breeze ruffling their hair. They stop at a bar and go in for a drink. This time B's father orders tequila. B thinks for a moment. Then he orders tequila too. The bar is modern and has air-conditioning. B's father talks to the waiter and asks him about hotels near the beach. By the time they get back to the Mustang a few stars are visible and for the first time that day B's father looks tired. Even so, they visit a couple of hotels, which for one reason or another are unsatisfactory, before finding one that will do. The hotel is called La Brisa: it's small, a stone's throw from the beach, and has a swimming-pool. B's father likes the hotel. So does B. It's the off season, so the hotel is almost empty and the prices are reasonable. The room they are given has two single beds and a small bathroom with a shower. The only window looks on to the terrace, where the swimming-pool is. B's father would have preferred a sea view. The air-conditioning, they soon discover, is out of order. But the room is fairly cool, so they don't complain. They make themselves at home: each opens up his suitcase and puts his clothes in the wardrobe. B leaves his books on the bedside table. They change their shirts. B's father takes a cold shower while B just washes his face, and when they are ready they go out to dinner.

The reception desk is manned by a short guy with teeth like a rabbit. He's young and seems friendly. He recommends a restaurant near the hotel. B's father asks if there's somewhere lively nearby. B understands what his father means. The receptionist doesn't. A place with a bit of action, says B's father. A place where you can find girls, says B. Ah, says the receptionist. For a moment B and his father stand there, without speaking. The receptionist crouches down, disappearing behind the counter, and reappears with a card, which he holds out. B's father looks at the card, asks if the establishment is reliable, then extracts a note from his wallet, which the receptionist is quick to intercept.

But after dinner, they go straight back to the hotel.

The next day, B wakes up very early. As quietly as possible he takes a shower, brushes his teeth, puts on his bathing suit, and leaves the room. There is no one in the hotel dining room, so B decides to go out for breakfast. The hotel is on a street that runs straight down to the beach, which is empty except for a boy hiring out paddle boards. B asks him how much it costs for an hour. The boy quotes a price that sounds acceptable, so B hires a board and pushes off into the sea. Opposite the beach is a little island, towards which he steers his craft. At first he has some trouble, but soon he gets the hang of it. At this time of day the sea is crystal clear and B thinks he can see red fishes under the board, about a foot and a half long, swimming towards the beach as he paddles towards the island.

It takes exactly fifteen minutes for him to get from the beach to the island. B doesn't know this, because he is not wearing a watch, and for him time slows down. The crossing seems to last an eternity. At the last minute, waves rear unexpectedly, impeding his approach. The sand is noticeably different from that of the hotel beach; back there it was a golden, tawny colour, perhaps because of the time of day (though B doesn't think so), while here it is a dazzling white, so bright it hurts your eyes to look at it.

B stops paddling and just sits there, at the mercy of the waves, which begin to carry him slowly away from the island. By the time he finally reacts, the board has drifted halfway back. Having ascertained this, B decides to turn around. The return is calm and uneventful. When he gets to the beach, the boy who hires out the boards comes up and asks if he had a problem. Not at all, says B. An hour later B returns to the hotel without having had breakfast and finds his father sitting in the dining room with a cup of coffee and a plate in front of him on which are scattered the remains of toast and eggs.

The following hours are hazy. They drive around aimlessly, watching people from the car. Sometimes they get out to have a cold drink or an ice cream. In the afternoon, on the beach, while his father is stretched out asleep in a deck chair, B rereads Gui Rosey's poems and the brief story of his life or his death.

One day a group of surrealists arrives in the south of France. They try to get visas for the United States. The north and the west of the country are occupied by the Germans. The south is under the aegis of Pétain. Day after day, the US Consulate delays its decision. Among the members of the group are Breton, Tristan Tzara, and Péret, but there are also less famous figures. Gui Rosey is one of them. In the photo he has the look of a minor poet, thinks B. He is ugly, he is impeccably dressed, he looks like an unimportant public servant or a bank clerk. Up to this point, a few disagreements, but nothing out of the ordinary, thinks B. The surrealists gather every afternoon at a café by the port. They make plans and chat; Rosey is always there. But one day (one afternoon, B imagines), he fails to appear. At first, he isn't missed. He is a minor poet and no one pays much attention to minor poets. After a few days, however, the others start to worry. At the *pension* where he is staying, no one knows what has happened; his suitcases and books are there, undisturbed, so he clearly hasn't tried to leave without paying (as guests at certain *pensions* on the Côte d'Azur are prone to do). His friends try to find him. They visit all the hospitals and police stations in the area. No one can tell them anything. One morning the visas arrive. Most of them board a ship and set off for the United States. Those who remain, who will never get visas, soon forget about Rosey and his disappearance; people are disappearing all the time, in large numbers, and they have to look out for themselves.

That night, after dinner at the hotel, B's father suggests they go and find a bit of action. B looks at his father. He is blond (B is dark), his eyes are grey, and he is still in good shape. He looks happy and ready to have a good time. What sort of action? asks B, who knows perfectly well what his father is referring to. The usual kind, says B's father. Drinking and women. For a while B says nothing, as if he were pondering a reply. His father looks at him. The look might seem inquisitive, but in fact it is only affectionate. Finally B says he's not in the mood for sex. It's not just about getting laid, says his father, we'll go and see, have a few drinks, and enjoy ourselves with some friends. What friends, says B, we don't know anyone here. You always make friends when you're out for a ride. The expression 'out for a ride' makes B think of horses. When he was seven his father bought him a horse. Where did my horse come from? asks B. This takes his father completely by surprise. What horse? he asks. The one you bought me when I was a kid, says B, in Chile. Ah, Hullabaloo, says his father, smiling. He was from the island of Chiloé, he says, then after a moment's reflection he starts talking about brothels again. The way he talks about them, they could be dance halls, thinks B. Then they both fall silent.

That night they don't go anywhere.

While his father is sleeping, B goes out on to the terrace to read by the swimming-pool. There is no one there apart from him. The terrace is clean and empty. From his table B can see part of the reception area, where the receptionist from the night before is standing at the counter reading something or doing the accounts. B reads the French surrealists, he reads Gui Rosey. To tell the truth, Gui Rosey doesn't interest him much. He is far more interested in Desnos and Éluard, and yet he always ends up coming back to Rosey's poems and looking at his photo, a studio portrait, in which he has the air of a solitary, wretched soul, with his large, glassy eyes and a dark tie that seems to be strangling him.

He must have committed suicide, thinks B. He knew he was never going to get a visa for the States or Mexico, so he decided to end his days there and then. B imagines or tries to imagine a town on the Mediterranean coast of France. He still hasn't been to Europe. He has been all over Latin America, or almost, but he still hasn't set foot in Europe. So his image of a Mediterranean town is derived from his image of Acapulco. Heat, a small, cheap hotel, beaches of golden sand and beaches of white sand. And the distant sound of music. B doesn't realise that there is a crucial element missing from the soundtrack of this scene: the rigging of the small boats that throng the ports of all the towns on the Mediterranean coast, especially the smaller ones. The sound of the rigging at night, when the sea is as still as a mill pond.

Suddenly someone comes on to the terrace. The silhouette of a woman. She sits down at the farthest table, in a corner, near two large urns. A moment later the receptionist appears, bringing her a drink. Then, instead of going back to the counter, he comes over to B, who is sitting by the edge of the pool, and asks if he and his father are having a good time. Very good, says B. Do you like Acapulco? asks the receptionist. Very much, says B. How was the San Diego? asks the receptionist. B doesn't understand the question. The San Diego? For a moment he thinks the receptionist is referring to the hotel, but then he remembers that the hotel is called something else. Which San Diego? asks B. The receptionist smiles. The club with the hookers. Then B remembers the card the receptionist gave his father. We still haven't been, he says. It's a reliable place, says the receptionist. B moves his head in a way that could mean almost anything. It's on Constituyentes, says the receptionist. There's another club on the avenue, the Ramada, but I wouldn't recommend it. The Ramada, says B, watching the woman's motionless figure in the corner of the terrace and the apparently untouched glass in front of her, between the enormous urns, whose shadows stretch and taper off under the neighbouring tables. Best to steer clear of the Ramada, says the receptionist. Why? asks B, for something to say, although he has no intention of visiting either club. It's not reliable, says the receptionist, and his bright little rabbit-like teeth shine in the semi-darkness that has suddenly submerged the terrace, as if someone at reception had switched off half the lights.

When the receptionist goes away, B opens his book of poetry again, but the words are illegible now, so he leaves the book open on the table, shuts his eyes and, instead of the faint chimes of rigging, he hears an atmospheric sound, the sound of enormous layers of hot air descending on the hotel and the surrounding trees. He feels like getting into the pool. For a moment he thinks he might.

Then the woman in the corner stands up and begins to walk towards the stairs that lead from the terrace to the reception area, but she stops midway, as if she felt ill, resting one hand on the edge of a raised bed in which there are no longer flowers, only weeds.

B watches her. The woman is wearing a loose, light-coloured summer dress, cut low, leaving her shoulders bare. He expects her to start walking again, but she stands still, her hand still gripping the edge of the raised bed, looking down, so B gets up with the book in his hand and goes over to her. The first thing that surprises him is her face. She must be about sixty years old, B guesses, although from a distance, he wouldn't have said she was more than thirty. She is North American, and when B approaches she looks up and smiles at him. Good night, she says, rather incongruously, in Spanish. Are you all right? asks B. The woman doesn't understand and B has to ask again, in English. I'm just thinking, says the woman, smiling at him fixedly. For a few seconds B considers what she has said to him. Thinking, thinking, thinking. And suddenly it seems to him that this declaration conceals a threat. Something approaching over the sea. Something advancing in the wake of the dark clouds invisibly crossing the Bay of Acapulco. But he doesn't move or make any attempt to break the spell that seems to be holding him captive. Then the woman looks at the book in B's left hand and asks him what he is reading, and B says: poetry. I'm reading poems. The woman looks him in the eye, with the same smile on her face (a smile at once bright and faded, thinks B, feeling more uneasy by the moment), and says that she used to like poetry, once. Which poets? asks B, keeping absolutely still. I can't remember them now, says the woman, and again she seems to lose herself in the contemplation of something visible only to her. B assumes she is making an effort to remember and waits in silence. After a while she looks at him again and says: Longfellow. And straight away she starts reciting lines with a monotonous rhythm that sound to B like a nursery rhyme, a far cry, in any case, from the poets he is reading. Do you know Longfellow? asks the woman. B shakes his head, although in fact he has read some Longfellow. We did it at school, says the woman, with her immutable smile. And then she adds: It's too hot, don't you think? It is very hot, whispers B. There could be a storm coming, says the woman. There is something very definite about her tone. At this point B looks up: he can't see a single star. But he can see lights in the hotel. And, at the window of his room, a silhouette watching them, which makes him start, as if struck by the first, sudden drops of a tropical downpour.

For a moment he is bewildered.

It's his father, on the other side of the glass, wrapped in a blue dressing-gown that he must have brought with him (B hasn't seen it before and it certainly doesn't belong to the hotel), staring at them, although when B notices him, he steps back, recoiling as if bitten by a snake, lifts his hand in a shy wave, and disappears behind the curtains.

The Song of Hiawatha, says the woman. B looks at her. The Song of Hiawatha, the poem by Longfellow. Ah, yes, says B.

Then the woman says good night and makes a gradual exit: first she goes up the stairs to reception, where she spends a few moments chatting with someone B can't see, then, in silence, she sets off across the hotel lobby, her slim figure framed by successive windows, until she turns into the corridor that leads to the inside stairs.

Half an hour later, B goes back to the room and finds his father asleep. For a few seconds, before going to the bathroom to brush his teeth, B stands very straight at the foot of the bed, gazing at him, as if steeling himself for a fight. Good night, dad, he says. His father gives not the slightest indication that he has heard.

On the second day of their stay in Acapulco, B and his father go to see the cliff divers. They have two options: they can watch the show from an open-air plat-form or go to the bar-restaurant of the hotel overlooking the precipice. B's father asks about the prices. The first person he asks doesn't know. He persists. Finally an old ex-diver who is hanging around doing nothing tells him what it costs: six times more to watch from the hotel bar. Let's go to the bar, says B's father without hesitating. We'll be more comfortable. B follows him. The other people in the bar are North American or Mexican tourists wearing what are obviously holiday clothes; B and his father stand out. They are dressed as people dress in Mexico City, in clothes that seem to belong to some endless dream. The waiters notice. They know the sort, no chance of a big tip, so they make no effort to serve them promptly. To top it off, B and his father can hardly see the show from where they are sitting. We would have been better off on the platform, says B's father. Although it's not bad here either, he adds. B nods. When the diving is over, having drunk two highballs each, they go outside and start making plans for the rest of the day. Hardly anyone is left on the platform, but B's father recognises the old ex-diver sitting on a buttress and goes over to him.

The ex-diver is short and has a very broad back. He is reading a cowboy novel and doesn't look up until B and his father are at his side. He recognises them and asks what they thought of the show. Not bad, says B's father, although in preci-sion sports you need experience to be able to judge properly. Would I be right in guessing you were a sportsman yourself? asks the ex-diver. B's father looks at him for a few moments and then says, You could say that. The ex-diver gets to his feet with an energetic movement as if he were back on the edge of the cliff. He must be about fifty, thinks B, so he's not much older than my father, but the wrinkles on his face, like scars, make him look much older. Are you gentlemen on holiday? asks the ex-diver. B's father nods and smiles. And what was your sport, sir, if I might ask? Boxing, says B's father. How about that, says the ex-diver, so you must have been a heavyweight? B's father smiles broadly and says yes.

Before he knows what is going on, B finds himself walking with his father and the ex-diver towards the Mustang, and then all three get into the car and B hears the directions the ex-diver is giving his father as if they were coming from the radio. For a while the car glides along the Avenida Miguel Alemán, but then it turns and heads inland and soon the tourist hotels and restaurants give way to an ordinary cityscape with tropical touches. The car keeps climbing, heading away from the golden horseshoe of Acapulco, along badly paved or unpaved roads, until it pulls up beside the dusty pavement in front of a cheap restaurant, a fixed-menu place (although, thinks B, it's really too big for that). The ex-diver and B's father get out of the car immediately. They have been talking all the way and while they wait for him on the pavement, they continue their conversation gesturing incomprehensibly. B takes his time getting out of the car. We're going to eat, says his father. So it seems, says B.

The place is dark inside and only a quarter of the space is occupied by tables.

The rest looks like a dance floor, with a stage for the band, surrounded by a long balustrade made of rough wood. At first, B can't see a thing, until his eyes adjust to the darkness. Then he sees a man coming over to the ex-diver. They look alike. The stranger listens attentively to an introduction that B doesn't catch, shakes hands with his father and a few seconds later turns to B. B reaches out to shake his hand. The stranger says a name and his handshake, which is no doubt meant to be friendly, is not so much firm as violent. He does not smile. B decides not to smile either. B's father and the ex-diver are already sitting at a table. B sits down next to them. The stranger, who looks like the ex-diver and turns out to be his younger brother, stands beside them, waiting for instructions. The gentleman here, says the ex-diver, was heavyweight champion of his country. So you're foreigners? asks his brother. Chileans, says B's father. Do you have red snapper? asks the ex-diver. We do, says his brother. Bring us one, then, a red snapper Guerrero-style, says the ex-diver. And beers all round, says B's father, for you too. Thank you, murmurs the brother, taking a notebook from his pocket and painstakingly writing down an order that, in B's opinion, a child could easily remember.

Along with the beers, the ex-diver's brother brings them some savoury crackers to nibble and three rather small plates of oysters. They're fresh, says the ex-diver, putting chilli sauce on all three. Funny, isn't it. This stuff's called chilli and so's your country, says the ex-diver, pointing to the bottle full of bright red chilli sauce. Yes, intriguing, isn't it, admits B's father. Like the way the sauce is the opposite of chilly, he adds. B looks at his father with barely veiled incredulity. The conversation revolves around boxing and diving until the red snapper arrives.

Later, B and his father leave the premises. The hours have flown without them noticing and by the time they climb into the Mustang, it is already seven in the evening. The ex-diver comes with them. For a moment, B thinks they'll never get rid of him, but when they reach the centre of Acapulco the ex-diver gets out in front of a billiard hall. When he has gone, B's father comments favourably on the service at the restaurant and the price they paid for the red snapper. If we'd had it here, he says, pointing to the hotels along the beachfront boulevard, it would have cost an arm and a leg. When they get back to their room, B puts on his bathing suit and goes to the beach. He swims for a while and then tries to read in the fading light. He reads the surrealist poets and is completely bewildered. A peaceful, solitary man, on the brink of death. Images, wounds. That is all he can see. And the images are dissolving little by little, like the setting sun, leaving only the wounds. A minor poet disappears while waiting for a visa to admit him to the New World. A minor poet disappears without leaving a trace, hopelessly stranded in some town on the Mediterranean coast of France. There is no investigation. There is no corpse. By the time B turns to Daumal, night has already fallen on the beach; he shuts the book and slowly makes his way back to the hotel.

After dinner, his father proposes they go out and have some fun. B declines this invitation. He suggests to his father that he go on his own, says he's not in the mood for having fun, he'd prefer to stay in the room and watch a film on TV. I can't believe it, says his father, you're behaving like an old man, at your age! B looks at his father, who is putting on clean clothes after a shower, and laughs.

Before his father goes out, B tells him to take care. His father looks at him from the doorway and says he's only going to have a couple of drinks. You take care yourself, he says, and gently shuts the door.

Once he's on his own, B takes off his shoes, looks for his cigarettes, switches on the TV, and collapses on to the bed again. Without intending to, he falls asleep. He dreams that he is living in (or visiting) the city of the Titans. All there is in the dream is an endless wandering through vast dark streets that recall other dreams. And in the dream his attitude is one that he knows he doesn't have in waking life. Faced with buildings whose voluminous shadows seem to be knocking against each other, he is, if not exactly courageous, unworried or indifferent.

A while later, just after the end of the programme, B wakes up with a jolt, and, as if responding to a summons, switches off the TV and goes to the window. On the terrace, half-hidden in the same corner as the night before, the North American woman is sitting with a cocktail or a glass of fruit juice in front of her. B observes her indifferently, then walks away from the window, sits on the bed, opens his book of surrealist poets, and tries to read. But he can't. So he tries to think, and to that end he lies down on the bed again, with his arms outstretched, and shuts his eyes. For a moment he thinks he is on the point of falling asleep. He even catches an oblique glimpse of a street from the dream city. But soon he realises that he is only remembering the dream, opens his eyes and lies there for a while contemplating the ceiling. Then he switches off the bedside lamp and goes back over to the window.

The North American woman is still there, motionless. The shadows of the urns stretch out and touch the shadows of the neighbouring tables. The reception area, fully lit, unlike the terrace, is reflected in the swimming-pool. Suddenly a car pulls up a few yards from the entrance of the hotel. His father's Mustang, thinks B. But no one appears at the hotel gate for a very long time and B begins to think he must have been mistaken. Then he makes out his father's silhouette climbing the stairs. First his head, then his broad shoulders, then the rest of his body, and finally the shoes, a pair of white moccasins that B, as a rule, finds profoundly disgusting, but the feeling they provoke in him now is something like tenderness. The way he came into the hotel, he thinks, it was like he was dancing. The way he made his entrance, it was as if he had come back from a wake, unconsciously glad to be alive. But the strangest thing is that, after appearing briefly in the reception area, his father turns around and heads towards the terrace: he goes down the stairs, walks around the pool and sits at a table near the North American woman. And when the guy from reception finally appears with a glass, his father pays and, without even waiting for him to be gone, gets up, glass in hand, goes over to the table where the North American woman is sitting and stands there for a while, gesticulating and drinking, until, at the woman's invitation, he takes a seat beside her.

She's too old for him, thinks B. Then he goes back to the bed, lies down, and soon realises that all the sleepiness weighing him down earlier has evaporated. But he doesn't want to turn on the light (although he feels like reading); he doesn't want his father to think (even for a moment) that he is spying on him. He thinks about women; he thinks about travel. Finally he goes to sleep.

Twice during the night he wakes up with a start and his father's bed is empty. The third time, day is already dawning and he sees his father's back: he is sleeping deeply. B switches on the light and stays in bed for a while, smoking and reading.

Later that morning B goes to the beach and hires a paddle board. This time he has no trouble reaching the island opposite. There he has a mango juice and swims for a while in the sea, alone. Then he goes back to the hotel beach, returns the board to the boy, who smiles at him, and takes a roundabout way back to the hotel. He finds his father in the restaurant drinking coffee. He sits down beside him. His father has just shaved and is giving off an odour of cheap aftershave that B finds pleasant. On his right cheek there is a scratch from ear to chin. B considers asking him what happened last night, but in the end decides not to.

The rest of the day goes by in a blur. At some point B and his father walk along a beach near the airport. The beach is vast, and it is lined with numerous wattle-roofed shacks where the fishermen keep their gear. The sea is choppy; for a while B and his father watch the waves breaking in the bay of Puerto Marqués. A fisherman tells them it's not a good day for swimming. You're right, says B. His father goes in for a swim anyway. B sits down on the sand, with his knees up, and watches him advance to meet the waves. The fisherman shades his eyes and says something that B doesn't catch. For a moment the head and arms of his father swimming out to sea vanish from his visual field. Now there are two children with the fisherman. They are all standing, looking out to sea, except for B, who is still sitting down. A passenger plane appears in the sky, curiously inaudible. B stops looking at the sea and watches the plane until it disappears behind a rounded hill covered with vegetation. He remembers waking up, exactly a year ago, in Acapulco airport. He was returning from Chile, on his own, and the plane stopped in Acapulco. He remembers opening his eyes and seeing an orange light with blue and pink overtones, like the fading colours of an old film, and knowing then that he was back in Mexico and safe at last, in a sense. That was in 1974 and B had not yet turned twenty-one. Now he is twenty-two and his father must be about forty-nine. B closes his eyes. Because of the wind, the fisherman's and the boys' cries of alarm are almost unintelligible. The sand is cold. When he opens his eyes he sees his father coming out of the sea. He shuts his eyes and doesn't open them again until he feels a large wet hand grip his shoulder and hears his father's voice proposing they go and eat turtle eggs.

There are things you can tell people and things you just can't, thinks B disconsolately. From this moment on he knows the disaster is approaching.

In spite of which the next forty-eight hours go by in a placid sort of daze that B's father associates with 'The Idea of the Holiday' (B can't tell whether his father is serious or pulling his leg). They go to the beach, they eat at the hotel or at a reasonably priced restaurant on the Avenida López Mateos. One afternoon they hire a boat, a tiny plastic rowing-boat, and follow the coastline near their hotel, along with the trinket vendors who peddle their wares from beach to beach, upright on paddle boards or in very shallow-bottomed boats, like tightrope walkers or the ghosts of drowned sailors. On the way back they even have an accident.

B's father takes the boat too close to the rocks and it overturns. In itself, this is not dramatic. Both of them can swim quite well and the boat is built to float when overturned; it isn't hard to right it and climb in again. And that is what B and his father do. Not the slightest danger at any point, thinks B. But then, when both of them have climbed back into the boat, B's father realises that he has lost his wallet. Tapping his chest, he says: My wallet, and without a moment's hesitation he dives back into the water. B can't help laughing, but then, stretched out in the boat, he looks down, sees no sign of his father, and for a moment imagines him diving, or worse, sinking like a stone, but with his eyes open, into a deep trench, over which, on the surface, in a rocking boat, his son has stopped laughing and begun to worry. Then B sits up and, having looked over the other side of the boat and seen no sign of his father there either, jumps into the water, and this is what happens: as B goes down with his eyes open, his father, open-eyed too, is coming up (they almost touch), holding his wallet in his right hand. They look at each other as they pass, but can't alter their trajectories, or at least not straight away, so B's father keeps ascending silently while B continues his silent descent.

For sharks, for most fish in fact (flying fish excepted), hell is the surface of the sea. For B (and many, perhaps most, young men of his age) it sometimes takes the form of the sea bed. As he follows in his father's wake, but heading in the opposite direction, the situation strikes him as particularly ridiculous. On the bottom there is no sand, as he had for some reason imagined there would be, only rocks, piled on top of each other, as if this part of the coast were a submerged mountain range and he were near the top, having hardly begun the descent. Then he starts to rise again, and looks up at the boat, which seems to be levitating one moment and about to sink the next, and in it he finds his father sitting right in the middle, attempting to smoke a wet cigarette.

Then the lull comes to an end, the forty-eight hours of grace in the course of which B and his father have visited various bars in Acapulco, lain on the beach and slept, eaten, even laughed, and an icy phase begins, a phase which appears to be normal but is ruled by deities of ice (who do not, however, offer any relief from the heat that reigns in Acapulco), hours of what, in former days, when he was an adolescent perhaps, B would have called *boredom*, although he would certainly not use that word now, *disaster* he would say, a private disaster whose main effect is to drive a wedge between B and his father: part of the price they must pay for existing.

It all begins with the appearance of the ex-diver, who, as B realises straight away, has come looking for his father, and not the family unit, so to speak, constituted by father and son. B's father invites the ex-diver to have a drink on the hotel terrace. The ex-diver says he knows a better place. B's father looks at him, smiles, and says OK. As they go out into the street, the light is beginning to fade. B feels an inexplicable stab of pain and thinks that perhaps it would have been better to stay at the hotel and leave his father to his own devices. But it's already too late. The Mustang is heading up the Avenida Constituyentes and from his pocket B's father takes the card that the receptionist gave him days ago. The nightspot is called the San Diego, he says. In the ex-diver's opinion, it's too expensive. I've got money, says B's father; I've been living in Mexico since 1968, and this is the first time I've taken a holiday. B, who is sitting next to his father, tries to see the ex-diver's face in the rear-view mirror, but can't. So first they go to the San Diego and for a while they drink and dance with the girls. For each dance they have to give the girl a ticket bought beforehand from the bar. To begin with, B's father buys only three tickets. There's something unreal about this system, he says to the ex-diver. But then he starts enjoying himself and buys a whole bundle. B dances too. His first dance partner is a slim girl with Indian features. The second is a woman with big breasts who, for a reason that B will never discover, seems to be preoccupied or cross. The third is fat and happy, and after dancing for a little while, she whispers into B's ear that she's high. What did you take? asks B. Magic mushrooms, says the woman, and B laughs. Meanwhile B's father is dancing with a girl who looks like an Indian and B is glancing across at him from time to time. Actually, all the girls look like Indians. The one dancing with his father has a pretty smile. They are talking (they haven't stopped talking, in fact) although B can't hear what they are saying. Then his father disappears and B goes to the bar with the ex-diver. They start talking too. About the old days. About courage. About the narrow coves where the ocean waves break. About women. Subjects that don't interest B, or at least not at the moment. But they talk anyway.

Half an hour later his father comes back to the bar. His blond hair is wet and freshly combed (B's father combs his hair back) and his face is red. He smiles and says nothing; B observes him and says nothing. Time for dinner, says B's father. B and the ex-diver follow him to the Mustang. They eat an assortment of shellfish in a place that's long and narrow, like a coffin. As they eat, B's father watches B as if he were searching for an answer. B looks back at him. He is sending a telepathic message: There is no answer because it's not a valid question. It's an idiotic question. Then, before he knows what is going on, B is back in the car with his father and the ex-diver, who talk about boxing all the way to a place in the suburbs of Acapulco. It's a brick and wood building with no windows and inside there's a juke-box with songs by Lucha Villa and Lola Beltrán. Suddenly B feels nauseous. He leaves his father and the ex-diver and looks for the toilet or the back yard, or the door to the street, belatedly realising that he has had too much to drink. He also realises that apparently well-meaning hands have prevented him from going out into the street. They don't want me to get away, thinks B. Then he vomits several times in the yard, among piles of beer boxes, under the eye of a chained dog, and having relieved himself, gazes up at the stars. A woman soon appears beside him. Her shadow is darker than the darkness of the night. Were it not for her white dress, B could hardly make her out. You want a blow-job? she asks. Her voice is young and husky. B looks at her, uncomprehending. The whore kneels down beside him and undoes his fly. Then B understands and lets her proceed. When it's over he feels cold. The whore stands up and B hugs her. Together they gaze at the night sky. When B says he's going back to his father's table, the woman doesn't follow him. Let's go, says B, but she resists. Then B realises that he has hardly seen her face. It's better that way. I hugged her, he thinks, but I don't even know what she looks like. Before he goes in he turns around and sees her walking over to pat the dog.

Inside, his father is sitting at a table with the ex-diver and two other guys. B comes up to him from behind and whispers in his ear: Let's go. His father is playing cards. I'm winning, he says, I can't leave now. They're going to steal all our money, thinks B. Then he looks at the women, who are looking at him and his father with pity in their eyes. They know what's going to happen to us, thinks B. Are you drunk? his father asks him, taking a card. No, says B, not any more. Have you taken any drugs? asks his father. No, says B. Then his father smiles and orders a tequila. B gets up and goes to the bar, and from there he surveys the scene of the crime with manic eyes. It is clear to B now that he will never travel with his father again. He shuts his eyes; he opens his eyes. The whores watch him curiously; one offers him a drink, which B declines with a gesture. When he shuts his eyes, he keeps seeing his father with a pistol in each hand, entering through an impossibly situated door. In he comes, impossibly, urgently, with his grey eyes shining and his hair ruffled. This is the last time we're travelling together, thinks B. That's all there is to it. The juke-box is playing a Lucha Villa song and B thinks of Gui Rosey, a minor poet who disappeared in the south of France. His father deals the cards, laughs, tells stories, and listens to those of his companions, each more sordid than the last. B remembers going to his father's house when he returned from Chile in 1974. His father had broken his foot and was in bed reading a sports magazine. What was it like? he asked, and B recounted his adventures. An episode from the chronicle of Latin America's doomed revolutions. I almost got killed, he said. His father looked at him and smiled. How many times? he asked. Twice, at least, B replied. Now B's father is roaring with laughter and B is trying to think clearly. Gui Rosey committed suicide, he thinks, or got killed. His corpse is at the bottom of the sea.

A tequila, says B. A woman hands him a half-full glass. Don't get drunk again, kid, she says. No, I'm all right now, says B, feeling perfectly lucid. Then two other women approach him. What would you like to drink? asks B. Your father's really nice, says the younger one, who has long, black hair. Maybe she's the one who gave me the blow-job, thinks B. And he remembers (or tries to remember) apparently disconnected scenes: the first time he smoked in front of his father; he was fourteen, it was a Viceroy cigarette, they were sitting in his father's truck waiting for a goods train to arrive, and it was a very cold morning. Guns and knives, family stories. The whores are drinking tequila with Coca-Cola. How long was I outside vomiting? wonders B. You were kind of jumpy before, says one of the whores. You want some? Some what? says B. He is shaking and his skin is cold as ice. Some weed, says the woman, who is about thirty years old and has long hair like the other one, but dyed blonde. Acapulco Gold? asks B, taking a gulp of tequila, while the two women come a little closer and start stroking his back and his legs. Yep, calms you down, says the blonde. B nods and the next thing he knows there is a cloud of smoke between him and his father. You really love your dad, don't you, says one of the women. Well, I wouldn't go that far, says B. What do you mean? says the dark woman. The woman serving at the bar laughs. Through the smoke B sees his father turn his head and look at him for a moment. A deadly serious look, he thinks. Do you like Acapulco? asks the blonde. Only at this point does he realise that the bar is almost empty. At one table there are two men drinking in silence, at another, his father, the ex-diver, and the two strangers playing cards. All the other tables are empty.

The door to the patio opens and a woman in a white dress appears. She's the one who gave me the blow-job, thinks B. She looks about twenty-five, but is probably much younger, maybe sixteen or seventeen. Like almost all the others, she has long hair, and is wearing shoes with very high heels. As she walks across the bar (towards the bathroom) B looks carefully at her shoes: they are white and smeared with mud on the sides. His father also looks up and examines her for a moment. B watches the whore opening the bathroom door, then he looks at his father. He shuts his eyes and when he opens them again the whore is gone and his father has turned his attention back to the game. The best thing for you to do would be to get your father out of this place, one of the women whispers in his ear. B orders another tequila. I can't, he says. The woman slides her hand up under his loose-fitting Hawaiian shirt. She's checking to see if I have a weapon, thinks B. The woman's fingers climb up his chest and close on his left nipple. She squeezes it. Hey, says B. Don't you believe me? asks the woman. What's going to happen? asks B. Something bad, says the woman. How bad? I don't know, but if I was you, I'd get out of here. B smiles and looks into her eyes for the first time: Come with us, he says, taking a gulp of tequila. Not in a million years, says the woman. Then B remembers his father saying to him, before he left for Chile: 'You're an artist and I'm a worker.' What did he mean by that? he wonders. The bathroom door opens and the whore in the white dress comes out again, her shoes immaculate now, goes across to the table where the card game is happening, and stands there next to one of the strangers. Why do we have to go? asks B. The woman looks at him out of the corner of her eye and says nothing. There are things you can tell people, thinks B, and things you just can't. He shuts his eyes.

As if in a dream, he goes back out to the patio. The woman with the dyed-blonde hair leads him by the hand. I have already done this, thinks B, I'm drunk, I'll never get out of here. Certain gestures are repeated: the woman sits on a rickety chair and opens his fly, the night seems to float like a lethal gas among the empty beer boxes. But some things are missing: the dog has gone, for one, and in the sky, to the east, where the moon hung before, a few filaments of light herald dawn. When they finish, the dog appears, perhaps attracted by B's groans. He doesn't bite, says the woman, while the dog stands a few yards away, baring its teeth. The woman gets up and smoothes her dress. The fur on the dog's back is standing up and a string of translucent saliva hangs from his muzzle. Stay, Fang, stay, says the woman. He's going to bite us, thinks B as they retreat towards the door. What happens next is confused: at his father's table, all the card players are standing up. One of the strangers is shouting at the top of his voice. B soon realises that he is insulting his father. As a precaution he orders a bottle of beer at the bar, which he drinks in long gulps, almost choking, before going over to the table. His father seems calm. In front of him are a considerable number of banknotes, which he is picking up one by one and putting into his pocket. You're not leaving here with that money, shouts the stranger. B looks at the ex-diver, trying to tell from his face which side he will take. The stranger's probably, thinks B. The beer runs down his neck and only then does he realise he is burning hot.

B's father finishes counting his money and looks at the three men standing in front of him and the woman in white. Well, gentlemen, we're leaving, he says. Come over here, son, he says. B pours what is left of his beer on to the floor and grips the bottle by the neck. What are you doing, son? says B's father. B can hear the tone of reproach in his voice. We're going to leave calmly, says B's father, then he turns around and asks the women how much they owe. The woman at the bar looks at a piece of paper and reads out a sizeable sum. The blonde woman, who is standing halfway between the table and bar, says another figure. B's father adds them up, takes out the money and hands it to the blonde: What we owe you and the drinks. Then he gives her a couple more bills: the tip. Now we're going to leave, thinks B. The two strangers block their exit. B doesn't want to look at her, but he does: the woman in white has sat down on one of the vacant chairs and is examining the cards scattered on the table, touching them with her fingertips. Don't get in my way, whispers his father, and it takes a while for B to realise that he is speaking to him. The ex-diver puts his hands in his pockets. The one who was shouting before starts insulting B's father again, telling him to come back to the table and keep playing. The game's over, says B's father. For a moment, looking at the woman in white (who strikes him now, for the first time, as very beautiful), B thinks of Gui Rosey, who disappeared off the face of the earth, quiet as a lamb, without a trace, while the Nazi hymns rose into a blood-red sky, and he sees himself as Gui Rosey, a Gui Rosey buried in some vacant lot in Acapulco, vanished for ever, but then he hears his father, who is accusing the ex-diver of something, and he realises that unlike Gui Rosey he is not alone.

Then his father walks towards the door, stooping slightly, and B stands aside to give him room to move. Tomorrow we'll leave, tomorrow well go back to Mexico City, thinks B joyfully. And then the fight begins.

OPPRESSIVE TANGO

Herta Müller

Translated from the German by Donal McLaughlin

Herta Müller (1953–) is a Romanian-born German novelist, poet and essayist. Her work offers an unflinching account of violence, cruelty and terror, often set against the backdrop of Ceauşescu's repressive Communist regime in Romania. In 1982, her first novel was published in Romania – though in a state-censored version; her second *The Land of Green Plums* was published in Germany. Having been previously refused permission to emigrate to Germany, she was finally allowed to move to Berlin in 1987, where she still lives. Many consider her greatest work to be *The Hunger Angel*, a prose poem depicting the persecution of Romania's German minority during the Stalinist occupation. In 2009, Müller was awarded the Nobel Prize for Literature. In its citation the Swedish Academy praised her as a writer who "with the concentration of poetry and the frankness of prose, depicts the landscape of the dispossessed".

Mother's suspender belt cuts deep into her hips, pushes her stomach over her laced corset. Mother's suspender is a light-blue damask with pale tulips, has two rubber studs and two rustproof fasteners.

Mother lays her black silk stockings on the table. The stockings have fat see-through legs. Black glass, they are. The stockings have opaque round heels and opaque pointed toes. Black stone, they are.

Mother pulls the silk stockings up over her legs. The pale tulips float from her hips over her tummy. The white studs turn black, the fasteners close.

Mother slips her stone toes, presses her stone heels, into the black shoes. Her ankles are two black stone necks.

The bell sounds a single word, hard and dull. The bell sounds from the graveyard. The bell tolls.

Mother is carrying the dark wreath of fir and white chrysanthemums. Grandmother is carrying the wreath that rattles, with its little white stones, the round picture of Mary, smiling, and Szüz Mária Köszönöm in the faded script of the old monarchy. The wreath shakes between Grandmother's forefinger and her thin wrist that is rubbed-raw.

I am carrying a bundle of the untidy delicate fern and a handful of candles as white and cold as my fingers.

Mother's dress falls in black folds. Mother's shoes take short clattering steps. Mother's tulips float round Mother's tummy.

The bell tolls, and in its toll is one word. There is an echo before it, and after it, that never fades. With her glass legs and stone ankles, Mother toddles into the echo of the word, into the toll. Ahead of the steps Mother takes, walks little Sepp with a wreath of evergreen and white chrysanthemums.

I walk between the dark wreath of fir and the wreath of rattling stones. I walk behind the untidy fern.

I walk through the graveyard gate, the bell before my eyes. I can feel the toll of the bell beneath my hair. I can feel its toll in the pulse next to my eyes, and in my wrists, weary beneath the fern. I can feel the knot at the end of the swinging bell-rope in my throat.

Grandmother's forefinger is bruised at the bottom of her nail. Grandmother's forefinger is dead. She hangs the rattling wreath with the little white stones over Father's face on the gravestone. Where Father's deep eyes are, is now the smiling Mary and her exposed-red heart. Where Father's firm lips are, is now the Hungarian script of the old monarchy.

Mother stands, bowed over the dark wreath of fir. Her stomach presses over her tummy. The white chrysanthemums roll onto Mother's cheeks. Mother's black dress billows in the wind blowing round the graves. Mother's black glass foot has a slight white crack running up her leg to the stud, to where the tulips float on her tummy.

Grandmother plucks at the untidy fern round the edge of the grave with her dead finger. I place the white candles between the fern's fine fibres, bore my cold fingers into the earth.

The match flickers blue in Mother's hand. Mother's fingers tremble, and the flame trembles. The earth devours my finger-joints. Mother carries the flame round the grave. Don't bore into the grave, she says, it's just not done. Grandmother sticks out her dead finger, points to the smiling Mary, her exposed-red heart.

The priest is standing on the chapel steps. Black folds lie over his shoes. The folds crawl up over his stomach to beneath his chin. Behind his head swings the bell-rope, its thick knot. The priest says: Let us pray for the living and the dead souls, and joins his bony hands across his stomach.

The fir bends its needles; the fern, its crumpled fibres. There is the smell of snow from the chrysanthemums, the smell of ice from the candles. The air above the graves turns black and hums a prayer: and Thou, O Prince of the Heavenly Host, deliver us from exile. Above the chapel tower, the night is as black as Mother's glass feet.

The candles ooze a tangle of trickling roots from their fingers. The trickles hit the air, turn as stiff as my ribs. The charred wicks have crumbled and won't light. A clod of earth falls beneath the fern between the spent candles.

The chrysanthemums are now on Mother's forehead. Don't sit on the grave, she says, it's just not done. Grandmother extends her dead finger. The crack on Mother's glass leg is the breadth of Grandmother's finger.

The priest says: Today, my dear faithful, is All Saints' Day, today our dearly departed, our dead souls, rejoice. Today is their feast day.

Little Sepp stands with his hands joined over the wreath of evergreen at the next grave: Deliver us, Lord, from this exile. In the quivering light his grey hair quivers.

On his red accordion, little Sepp accompanies the white brides who waft through the village; accompanies the paired-off wedding guests, with their bows of white wax, round the altar to below the smiling Mary, her exposed-red heart; accompanies the cake, a Vanille Torte with two wax doves on top, to before the bride. On his red accordion, he plays the oppressive tango for the arms and legs of the men and women.

Little Sepp has short fingers and tiny shoes. He spreads his short fingers to press the keys. The broad keys are snow, the narrow keys earth. He seldom presses the narrow keys. When he does, the music is cold.

Father's thighs press against Mother's tummy, where the pale tulips are floating.

The bride who wafts past is our neighbour. She beckons me with her forefinger. She cuts me a rib of cake and, with a weak smile, places the doves in my hand.

I close my hand. The doves warm against my skin, begin to sweat. I poke the wax doves into a meat dumpling and into the bread I then bite from. I swallow bread and hear the oppressive tango.

Mother dances past the end of the table with the floating tulips and Uncle's thighs. The chrysanthemums are round her mouth now. Don't play with your food, she says, it's just not done.

The priest raises his bony hands in the name of the Lord: Deliver us from exile. From his hands, a shifting tangle – smoke, this time – rises and floats around the knot in the bell-rope, then climbs into the tower.

The grave has sunk, Mother says. It needs two loads of clay and a load of fresh manure if the flowers are to grow. Mother's black shoe crunches the sand. Your uncle can do that for his dead brother, Mother says.

Grandmother hooks the wreath with the small white stones on her dead finger.

Father's deep eyes look at Mother's black glass foot with the white crack. Mother's black shoes walk over the molehills between the graves of strangers.

We go through the graveyard gate. The village turns in on itself, smells of fir and fern, chrysanthemums and trickling tangles.

Ahead of the steps I take, walks little Sepp.

The village is black. The clouds are black damask.

Grandmother rattles the wreath with the small white stones. Mother crushes my fingers in her hand.

Father is our dead soul. Today is Father's feast day and so he dances past the village.

Mother's suspender belt cuts deep into her hips. In the oppressive tango, Father presses his thighs against a cloud of black damask.

THE STONE GUEST

Hamid Ismailov

Translated from the Uzbek by Shelley Fairweather-Vega

Hamid Ismailov (1954–) was born in 1954 in Kyrgyzstan. Ismailov moved to Uzbekistan as a young man. He writes both in Russian and Uzbek and his novels and poetry have been translated into many European languages, including German, French and Spanish. In 1994 he was forced to flee to the UK because of his "unacceptable democratic tendencies". He now works for the BBC World Service. *The Railway* was his first novel to be published in English in 2006, followed by *A Poet and Bin-Laden* in 2012. His work is still banned in Uzbekistan today. The Uzbek secret service, on reading a lightly fictionalised account of a savage police beating in one of Ismailov's novels, contacted him through an intermediary and, concerned about accuracy but not about reputation, corrected some of the bloody details.

Suhrob Surataliyev's friends used to tease him by calling him Zurab Tsereteli. Suhrob was a sculptor by trade, but he was somewhat less of a household name than the popular Tsereteli, whose oversized monuments loomed over so many Moscow squares. Our sculptor Suhrob, instead, was a serious artist, and quite well-respected among the elite of Moscow's art community. It had been forty or more years since Suhrob had come to Moscow, so he often imagined he was a child of this metropolis, forgetting that he had in fact been born on the banks of Andijan's fetid Kutan canal in provincial Uzbekistan. He felt as if the clay of his own statue, so to speak, had been gathered from *this* land, not that one.

Virtually all fine art is premised on building and adding on, but the art of sculpture, as the great sculptor Michelangelo taught, consists of nothing but carving out and discarding. He once famously said that his *David* had always been there in the marble, and his job was solely to chip away everything unnecessary. Step by step, I think, that kind of habit works its way into you: this carving-out and discarding seems to seep into your very life, and you start to look at everything from this point of view, with a critical eye. What is empty or incidental or useless has no place in your heart, and you find yourself always striving to reach the essence of things, the stone at the center, the very core of things. Well, some people are just built that way, aren't they?

Our Suhrob took that approach, and because of that, some of his acquaintances would have characterized him as an arrogant, crude man, while only those very few close to him knew that was only true superficially.

But come with me, please, and let's take a closer look ourselves, remaining faithful to Michelangelo's rule within this story of ours. We will shun the useless side roads and delve straight to the heart of the matter.

Recently, aside from all the other immigrants here, poverty-stricken Uzbeks and Tajiks, Kyrgyz and Azeris, have been leaving their hopelessly poor homelands and converging in hordes on Moscow. Back in Soviet times you would have found them only out at Kazan Station or the big exhibition grounds on the outskirts of the city. But one time back then, during intermission at the Kremlin ballet, Suhrob spotted a collective farm worker, a real hick-from-the-sticks, conspicuous among the crowd, and the sight of him cast Suhrob the sculptor, far into that night, deep into a state of shock. He was so overwhelmed by feeling that he was moved to create his masterpiece, the *Gir'ya*, his very own Uzbek *Pietà*. In that sculpture, over a Jesus just taken down from the cross, there hovered his mother the Virgin Mary and his beloved Mary Magdalene, weeping, and both of them were now the very image of Uzbek village women, crafted as if from the purest white bread dough; and there, just a bit removed from the mourning women, that same collective farm worker stood sentinel.

But now people straight from villages in the old country were crowding in everywhere in heaps, they squeezed into corners and swarmed like ants, they peeped out of every small house and apartment building in Moscow, and Suhrob the sculptor felt lost for a time. Perhaps an uncommon sort of jealousy stirred awake in his heart, but Suhrob, who once took pride in being one of those rare people who claimed both Genghis Khan and Tamerlane as their ancestors, now started to feel like a worthless, worn-out old penny. Now he was a little embarrassed to call himself an Uzbek or to put on his golden *duppi* to go to a party or a banquet.

What's more, Suhrob's enlightened and refined friends, as they complained of their daily troubles, naturally would turn to Suhrob when they whined about all these people flooding through the city's open gates, as they put it, as if to say, "You're one of us, after all," expecting Suhrob to sympathize. That kind of thing tended to make Suhrob a bit hot under the collar. At home he used to take all his bitterness and anger out on his gentle Russian wife, his Mashenka.

"Look," Suhrob would say, raging, "It's not as if they came here for a laugh! If life was so great in their homeland they would never have thrown out their families and left their warm homes, tossed out the fruit and come to this freezing weather, to live like filthy dogs! The other day I read in the newspaper that the apartment-block basements are lined with cardboard boxes, it said they're living there in the hundreds. In another place a Russian sold his house, and he sold along with it four hens, two geese, and all sorts of old household junk, plus an Uzbek servant. Can you imagine? It's the twenty-first century, you know?!"

Poor Masha could only shake her head, but the truth was that when the sculptor was angry no blood flowed to his brain, only his fist; so into that fist he would take a chunk of plaster, or failing that a pulp of raw bread dough, and set to work passionately kneading it, putting out all kinds of shapes known only to himself and his wrath.

Suhrob the sculptor simply got down to work. But I feel obliged to remind you, now, of this rule of Michelangelo's. Please do not use your imagination to put the pieces together and deduce that Suhrob was some sort of patriot, thinking only of his homeland and the people in it. His Uzbekness, I must say, did not go much deeper than the way he wore his golden *duppi* on his head once each year, and the way he placed before each guest who visited his studio a ceramic dish of raisins atop a tablecloth of embroidered silk. If you need more proof than that, consider, please, a letter he once wrote me in what you might generously call Uzbek, an excerpt of which I humbly submit here.

"Salamalaykum my friend! Those things about Toir, the artistes that I know they have the same problem. Maybe to combine them with Rashidov regimen. Just now the words of the deceased Konchalovsky, they are hitting my memory: the artistes, they can not to take part in big lyings. Otherways, how great may they be?"

God knows I do not bring this up to mock him—I only want to show you what I mean. In any case, Suhrob's Uzbekness had been shrinking and shrinking in his almost half a century of Moscow life, even to the point, as I mentioned before, that he had practically been renamed Zurab Tsereteli.

But now let's extricate ourselves from this short preface, and get to the story itself.

One winter day, Suhrob was working at his studio on Kievskaya Naberezhnaya when the telephone rang. Fortune had it that it was his wife Masha.

"Is everything all right?" she asked. "Just now somebody called from your old village and asked for you. I told him you'd be back this evening, and he asked whether you had a cell phone, because he had something important to discuss with you," she reported. "He's going to call again in five minutes, so I'm calling to ask you what I should say."

To tell the truth, Suhrob wasn't actually working on anything very important at the time, but he still didn't like being distracted at work, usually.

"Who was it who called? Did you ask his name?" he asked.

Masha replied with her usual kindness. "No, it didn't occur to me. But he's just about to call again, so I'll ask then. Is everything all right there?" she asked her husband again.

"Well, if you really want to know, you're the one who talked with him, not me, so would I know if everything was all right there, or would you?" demanded Suhrob.

"No, just asking, I'm worried," Masha answered, to which Suhrob replied,

"If he calls, you can give him the number at the studio. But don't tell him it's the number at the studio. Say I'm out somewhere and give him the number," he told her.

After that conversation, all the bits and pieces of things he had been working on seemed to have slipped from his fingers. Suhrob, lost in thought, took a few black raisins from the ceramic dish on the embroidered tablecloth. Who was he, the man who had called? Who was even left in that village? His mother had died when he was a child, and after his father was released from prison, he took a new wife, and they had two or three children together. Suhrob had grown up and served his time in the military, then left for good for Moscow to study and live there. He learned from his stepmother's letters that his father was later arrested again and disappeared somewhere in the system. But at one point he stopped receiving news from his stepmother about herself or his younger stepbrother and stepsisters. Just like water dries up from the canals in the summertime, the letters also broke off, and Suhrob never did return to his old village, and nobody from there ever appeared to inquire about him.

But now there had been this phone call . . .

These shapeless thoughts had his heart beating full and heavy, and then the telephone rang, once, a local call.

"Hello!" Suhrob's voice was a bit gruffer than usual.

"Get me Suhrob-aka!" There was nothing Russian in the pronunciation of the voice barking out the order.

Suhrob kept silent for a moment, and not because he was pretending somebody was calling him to the telephone; that unrefined voice had thrown him a bit off balance. But finally, he answered, "Yes, this is he," and then forged ahead. "And who is this?" he asked, answering rudeness with rudeness.

The voice on the telephone instantly grew warmer. "Salamalaykum, Uncle! This is your nephew Sangin. Your sister Farrah's youngest son."

"Mine sister Farrah's?" interrupted Suhrob, in his awkward Uzbek. "Who . . ."

"Well when you were kids you called her Faya. Her son."

"Ah, yes, Faya . . . Yes, I know. Where you are?"

"OK, so we came to Moscow to work, right, and the FMS grabbed us, the cops are after us, saying we don't have any papers. You gotta tell them, you have to prove, right, that I'm your nephew."

"Where you are right now?"

"Hold on, this jerkoff here wants to talk to you."

Suhrob was relieved to hear some sort of captain's voice come on the line, in Russian.

After a bit of questioning he learned that this nephew of his, Sangin, along with another friend from back home, had been stopped by Federal Migration Service officers in an outdoor market without the proper identification documents. Since they had no money to pay the fine, they were being subjected to administrative detention and were then to be sent home. Sangin had apparently announced he had come to see a highly respectable relative, and offered up Suhrob's name from a scrap of paper he had kept tucked safely away. The officer wanted to check, just in case.

"If you accept full responsibility for these kids, we are prepared to let them go. But you will have to come to the station to fetch them," the officer finished up. And whether obeying this order or out of some other sort of enthusiasm, ten seconds later Suhrob was rushing to the Kievskaya metro station, to ride out to Altufyevo on the very outskirts of the city, to pluck from jail a nephew he had never met.

Ordinarily Suhrob avoided taking the Metro to the Moscow city limits. The subway system was none too safe, lately, for Uzbeks. No, with his gray hair, Suhrob had never had any serious problems with the riff-raff and skinheads, but he was sometimes taken for a Georgian or a Chechen, and people would casually swear at him, or the younger ones would call him Bin Laden.

This time, maybe due to the bitter Moscow cold that night, he rode the train all the way to Altufyevo without incident. The handful of young drunks fooling around didn't even give him a glance. Up he went and came out at ground level, where snow was falling softly down and down, as if the very greatest sculptor of all had been heedlessly flinging white plaster dust over all the bits and pieces of creation.

Suhrob asked the way from a snow-covered old woman walking by, and when he entered the FMS room at the police station, he saw two skinny young men sitting there, wearing cotton knit tracksuits here in the depths of winter, squeezed into a corner in front of a police officer. In a single glance with his discerning eyes, Suhrob recognized the form and figure of his own father in the one on the left. The boy's face suddenly brightened, and up he leapt into Suhrob's embrace.

"Uncle, Uncle, look what this asshole tried to do! You've rescued us, Uncle!!"

One hour later, after all the bits and pieces had been entered into the computer and a statement had been signed, those two young men, Suhrob's kin and countrymen, were in his own home. His Mashenka was flummoxed by the sight of them wearing only their tracksuits against the harsh winter cold. She was a mother, after all, so she gave them warm coats and bustled about making tea; but as the cold started to melt off their bodies, unwashed for months, a putrid smell began to spread, and poor Masha's sensitive sentiments were overwhelmed. Suhrob quickly felt the same. What I mean is that Suhrob shared Masha's kind feelings, but he also could not ignore the terrible stink of the young men's horse-like sweat.

Perhaps the sculptor's heart had been hardened by too much stonework, or perhaps it simply had no room for silly sentimentalities, and so finally Suhrob spoke up, in his clumsy Uzbek again.

"Your tea, are you all done? Here, put on these coats, we will go," he told the boys, hoping to hurry them along. "I take you somewhere for the night. We discuss everything in the morning."

That same evening, Suhrob took his nephew and his friend to his studio, and put two benches together for a bed, and a wool rug from off the ground over them for a quilt, and then he took the very last metro home at one o'clock in the morning. Masha wasn't asleep yet, having waited up for his arrival.

Another time I might have told you in great detail about the bitter conversation that took place between them, and how Suhrob's troublesome thoughts kept him tossing to and fro all night long, but there is this law hanging around my neck like a noose: the sculptor's method demands that I not let the small bits and pieces distract me on my bumpy-thumpy road.

The next morning, groggy from lack of sleep, Suhrob finally woke up in the wintry weather, and once he made his way to his studio he entered it with a clear mind. He entered, and that clarity vanished completely: those two good-for-nothings had turned the whole place upside down! Maybe they had been looking for another quilt last night or for a samovar for this morning's tea—but no matter. Books had been tossed into the outstretched arms of some statues, and other statues' heads were crammed onto bookshelves, and as if that weren't enough, the ceramic dish lay on the embroidered tablecloth broken in four pieces, mixed with a scattering of black raisins. And this is only what I can see through Suhrob's eyes, leaving aside the hellish smell, and the sound of their shameless snoring.

And then an insult that was left over from his adolescence sprang to Suhrob's mind and tongue, and he had a strange, irrepressible urge to say something like "Mother*fuckers*!" But when he stormed over to the corner where those two soundly sleeping small bodies lay he mixed up his Uzbek insults, and instead of "motherfuckers" he ended up with, "Hey, you whoresluts, get up!"

It came out quite pitifully. His voice was hoarse and tight with excitement, and he was screaming like some sort of madman. "You still lie there in your shits!?" he shouted, another mixed-up echo from his childhood.

The two boneheads turned over unwillingly, slowly. "The fuck you yelling for, asshole? What?" said one, and rolled over to go back to sleep.

At that Suhrob grabbed the coats covering the two of them with both hands and pulled them away. "Get up, motherfuckers!" he finally yelled.

Shuddering from the cold, the two tried to wipe the sleep from their eyes. "Damn, what's with you, old man, talking like that?" they asked, standing up.

"Here is two thousand for you. Go to Kazan Station and go home!"

The two of them seemed to relax at the sight of the money. "OK, old man. Hey, got any clothes?"

"Go! Get out!"

And so Suhrob, having offered them not a drop of tea, and after finding two good Scottish sweaters to thrust upon them on top of the money in their hands, and seeing them straight to the door, and shutting the door behind them, found himself alone. And right away he got to thinking. Had he done the right thing? Who knows? What was done was done. Maybe he should have kept in touch with his friends back home, or sent them presents once in a while . . .

The day was already ruined. And what remained of it did not look too promising. Suhrob busied himself cleaning up the mess they had left behind, trying to put his studio back in order, filing the books neatly back on their shelves, wiping up plaster dust, and gluing the four ceramic pieces back together—and as a result ending up with five where once there had been four. But wasn't his heart broken in teeny-tiny pieces, too?

He was secretly blaming his own meanness; it was eating him up inside. The telephone rang. He picked it up, and it was his nephew Sangin.

"You're gonna be pissed, Uncle," he said, "But there's no fucking train tickets. These guys here say there's a plane. They say they can set us up, OK? But we need some more cash. So now what, Uncle?"

A sculptor's hands and wits are always sharp and decisive, as we know. Suhrob spoke with no hesitation. "You know clock tower at Kiev Station? I bring you the money."

The money could come or go, but he wanted his peace of mind. From the one thousand dollars he had saved up here and there, and stowed away from his wife for emergencies, Suhrob took four hundred, and set out into the snow once again.

He waited under the clock tower at Kiev Station for half an hour, then gave the two young men the four hundred dollars ("three hundred for tickets, one hundred to buy something for village," he said), and then he went back to his studio. Interestingly enough, everyone he met on the street looked like an Uzbek to him. Or maybe they *were* all actually Uzbeks.

Back at his studio, Suhrob kept thinking of that awkward watch he had kept under the clock, and those two innocent boys kept appearing before his eyes.

Suhrob suddenly bit his lip. Though his nephew had been wearing the Scottish sweater he had given him that morning, his buddy had been wearing some sort of worn-out old suit and the same flimsy old tracksuit.

To distract himself from them, Suhrob kneaded some clay, wanting to salvage just one thing from the day's misfortunes. But no matter the circumstances, a hand cannot shape a form on its own—so the clay only dried in his hands, and he could only let it crumble back into teeny-tiny pieces.

When you peel an onion, and you try to dig too deep into the core, past the first layer, and tears come to your eyes—that was the kind of mood Suhrob was in. Had he done the right thing? Or should he have found the boys some little job to do, like all the others, instead of sending them back to where they had come from? He had friends, after all, and he might have found the right kind of place for them, even if it was just as night watchmen or doing this-or-that at the Center for the Arts. There were plenty of Uzbek night watchmen in Moscow. Surely there was room for one or two more.

I wonder if sculptors, as a class, generally maintain a greater distance from their doubts and regrets. When you chip a piece off a rock, it can never go back into place. There's no use wishing that shape back together again. But why, at his age, was he now, contrary to custom, still tottering back and forth like this? After all, he hadn't sent his nephew to his death or damnation—he had sent him back to his own motherland, his fatherland! But still Suhrob's heart felt forged in clay, still his heart, just like that ceramic dish, would not be glued back together . . .

"Well, now I'm a poet!" he muttered, having a chuckle at what had happened, and in that instant he realized what he should fashion out of the chunk-and-hunk of clay he had been kneading.

The early winter darkness had already started to descend. He was just setting out to add a fresh piece of clay onto the old one when the telephone rang once again.

"Salamalaykum, Uncle, I'm at the airport. This asshole here says that for this kinda money we can't get a fucking ticket for two more days. He says if we wanna go today he needs another two hundred, and then he can get us tickets, OK? So what do you wanna do, Uncle? Should I send this guy to the clock tower? You gotta help me out, OK?"

Suhrob put down the receiver without answering. His hands were dirty. He'd have to wash them. And it wasn't just his hands. He had smeared clay onto the phone, too, and the telephone was still beeping nervously. He picked up the receiver again, and now he slammed it down angrily, clay shooting out in all directions, and the receiver, cracked down the middle, finally quieted down.

Suhrob gave his hands a rub and a scrub, then went back to his store of money, took out two hundred dollars, quickly added two hundred more, threw his coat in on top, and again went out into the snow. Curiously enough, this time there was no waiting—an Uzbek man stood lurking under the clock. Suhrob didn't like the looks of this one too much, either. When he came closer, he caught a whiff of cheap beer coming off of him, winter weather aside. And under the man's leather jacket, Suhrob thought he could see one of that morning's Scottish sweaters.

"Who you are?" Suhrob demanded, skipping all the formalities.

"Salamalaykum, Uncle, your nephew sent me. Said you'd give me the cash."

But Suhrob wasn't listening. "Hey, kid! Where you get that?"

He poked at the sweater hidden under the man's jacket, and when the young man slipped away, Suhrob's thumbs caught on his leather jacket.

"Whoa, fuck off, old man! This is real leather! You trying to wreck it? The fuck you doing? This cost some serious money!"

In an instant Suhrob, just like peeling away a rind, was doing his best to rip off the jacket, as if, following the habits of his craft, he meant to peel away layer upon layer to reach the true core of this young man. But just at that moment a police officer appeared out of nowhere, and his thunderous voice joined in the fray. "Starting trouble here, motherfuckers? I've had it up to here with you black-asses!" he roared in Russian.

Never in Suhrob's life had he had a personal run-in with the police, and for that reason, he set about defeating himself. "I'm just here, Comrade Sergeant, Sir, to pass on some money to my relatives," he said.

"Comrade Senior Sergeant!" the policeman corrected him. "Money, huh? What money?"

"Right here. My friend is flying to Tashkent, so I wanted to—" started Suhrob, taking out his four hundred dollars.

"So you're planning a little smuggling, too, motherfucker? Paying for your hashish?" asked the officer, his voice full of menace, and Suhrob finally appreciated the state of affairs. Now this worthless Uzbek here would probably have some grass in his pocket, and the thought made Suhrob sick to his stomach.

"Uncle. Don't be an idiot. Give him a hundred," hinted the foul-smelling man, switching back to Uzbek.

Never in his life had Suhrob bribed anyone, but it only took him a single instant, in a fog of fear, to take a hundred dollars from the pile of money and offer it to the policeman.

"What's this now, motherfucker? Trying to bribe a law enforcement official? In the course of his official duties? You know what that'll get you?" raged the senior sergeant, until the other Uzbek man took the money that was in Suhrob's hand, and took the policeman by the elbow.

"All right, boss, let's have a friendly conversation, just between us," he said, and led him off to one side.

The police officer grumbled and growled, but he slipped back behind the wall from which he had emerged.

This left Suhrob in an interesting position. Some part of him was begging him to go, but he was too ashamed to try to escape. Would that take care of the money situation? If so, the whole filthy mess would be finished. But what if that Uzbek was working with the police, too? Then disappearing would be a good option. At that thought, Suhrob started to move away from the clock. Slowly but surely he began to take heart. The streetlamps had not yet been lit. Twenty or thirty steps more and he would disappear into the crowd. At the thought, his pace quickened—and then all of a sudden there came a shout in Uzbek.

"Whoa, old man, where you off to?"

Suhrob stopped in his tracks, thinking he would now have to face not just the police, but all the myriad Uzbeks huddling around Kiev Station. But no, it was only that same half-drunk young man approaching him again.

"Uncle, hold up, you need to tell them I gave that jerk-off bastard two hundred. You tell your nephew so he doesn't blame me."

Suhrob just nodded, and with no farewell, set off into the blue-black snow, into the snow falling on snow.

Once he returned to his studio, his hands and his heart trembled for quite some time, and he took a half-empty bottle of vodka out of the refrigerator, and a tin cup, and drank it down in two gulps, no chaser. The fire started inside him. At that moment, another ring rang out, and Suhrob jumped, startled. It wasn't the telephone. It was worse: the doorbell. At first Suhrob feared it must be the police, but he quickly realized that the police don't usually ring the bell—they pound on the door. Then he wondered if they'd come back for more money. But there was a second ring, not so much demanding as apologetic. "What will be, will be!" he said, and gripping his tin cup and half bottle of vodka, he headed for the door.

He opened it—and there stood two unfamiliar people. One man, one woman.

"Mr. Soo-rab?" asked the man, in English, and Suhrob's addled memory recalled that at that very hour an honored guest was supposed to be arriving from the Metropolitan Museum in New York City.

He remembered, and with that tin cup and half bottle of vodka in his hand, Suhrob had no idea how to welcome this respectable pair of people, and he could neither offer a hello nor extend his hand in greeting. He was completely at a loss. But those two were Americans, and they each laughed loudly with a grimace, then patted him on the shoulder and said something in English about how he was taking his inspiration Russian-style. And they entered his studio without any excess formalities.

But here I've digressed again on another literary tangent. Didn't I tell you that, like a good sculptor, we will not be distracted by the skin and shell of events, but will go straight to the core? So I won't go through the pageantry of Suhrob's long discussion with this esteemed pair, whom he had been expecting for quite some time, except to mention that Suhrob's studio smelled so strongly of vodka and those two filthy migrants that there was nothing he could do to cover it up. The more he tried, the more sympathetic the Americans acted, but they must have thought that Russian habits had infected even him, and with their Western arrogance they were keen to excuse him for that. Instead let's go straight to the point when, at eleven o'clock that night, Suhrob showed them out and went home, wanting nothing more than to return to his faithful Mashenka.

Masha had not heard a thing about the day's events since that morning. "Did you send off your nephew?" was all she asked.

"I sent him off," he replied, and he gave a fuller report about his American visitors. They talked over the pageantry of their long discussion, and suddenly Suhrob felt that to those Americans he was just like *them*: some sort of migrant laborer, a beggar. Hadn't he tried to ingratiate himself to them, in order to sell his work to them at a higher price? When they said there was no money for art nowadays, didn't he offer up his uniqueness? With his secret beggary, how was he any better from all those other Uzbeks? Did it make it any better that his customers were Americans instead of Russians??

Thinking those thoughts, Suhrob again could not fall asleep until late at night, and he lay tossing and turning under his blankets. But there's an element of literature here, too.

The next day . . . The next day, nothing happened. The telephone did not ring, and the police did not come looking for him. The Americans also chose to stay away. The day after that, too, passed uneventfully. When the third day came, the studio had been tidied up, the broken ceramic pieces and empty vodka bottles had been thrown in the garbage, and a handful of black raisins nestled inside the golden *duppi*, which sat upside down to serve as a bowl atop the embroidered silk tablecloth. Suhrob took the last two hundred dollars that remained in his stash, meaning to present it to his Mashenka that very evening. And just now, as he paused to listen to his own heart, finally calm, a new sculpture project was taking shape in his imagination. Maybe he'd call it the *Guestworker*. Something like that.

That evening, returning home, Suhrob gave Masha the two hundred dollars, and the two of them relaxed with an expensive bottle of French wine while they sat watching television. The news showed a story about sixty-eight illegal immigrants from Central Asia being forced by the police out of an old building, scheduled to be torn down, that they had turned into a campsite and guest house. No—and Suhrob looked very closely—his nephew Sangin was not among them, but the sight of those sixty-eight human beings living like dogs set Suhrob's heart pounding again.

That night, once again, Suhrob could not sleep. He blamed his insomnia on the wine he had drunk, the news he had watched, and also the duplicity with which he had treated his Mashenka; his thoughts raced in all directions and gave him no rest.

Once upon a time in his youth, when he had just come to Moscow, Suhrob too had been forced to spend the night in places unfit for a dog. And he remembered diving into his studies during the day, first human anatomy, then the study of form, then the arts of stone cutting and clay working. He knew that all that suffering had been for the sake of the respected position he enjoyed today. Yet could that position save him, now, from burning in fire and flames like a stone statue? Not a bit! In all his indecision, the fire and flames were consuming him! Was Suhrob, who had measured his life since a very young age in terms of work upon great work, now falling victim to the petty bits and pieces of meaningless, everyday life? Or was he simply consoling himself with those bits and pieces?

You can talk and talk, but isn't the point to avoid breaking other people's hearts, fragile as glass? Suhrob thought first of his angelic Mashenka. And Suhrob thought of his sister Farrah, whom he never knew, and her scoundrel of a son, Sangin. What could he do to make them all happy?

He thought and thought, and an idea came to him. He imagined a contraption like a cannon, sitting on the seashore. His younger sister had been placed inside it, and then as if shot from a slingshot she flew off, far over the ocean. She soared in free flight out to sea, and she emerged from the sea foam as a perfect statue, the goddess Aphrodite. Maybe he could sell that contraption to the Americans! It would make him piles of money . . .

In the morning, when he awoke in the undispersed semi-darkness of winter, he realized that the idea of the catapult machine still haunted him from out of the grogginess of night. Perhaps it had been a dream, but a strong desire to build the thing still lingered. Suhrob didn't know whether to laugh or to cry when dawn came. By the time he reached his studio, the gloom of that dream still had not dissipated, and he felt unable to apply hand or mind to any sort of work. Again Suhrob was plagued by thoughts about himself and his life. Yet we will not be distracted. We will not go back on our promise: we have agreed to be loyal to the art of sculpture, and we will proceed according to its rules.

It was around noon when the phone rang. An unfamiliar, official-sounding Russian voice asked his name.

"This is Suhrob Surataliyev," answered Suhrob.

"Are you responsible for the individual known as Sangin Surataliyev?" the voice asked.

"Sorry, I'm just . . . could you repeat that?" Suhrob was playing for time, out of craftiness or denial. The voice at the other end sounded as if it were buried in paperwork.

Suhrob instantly thought to put down the receiver. That good-for-nothing was subjecting him to one more disaster! But he was unable to keep silent.

"Excuse me, is everything all right?" he asked.

"No, that's the problem. Nothing is all right!" the voice snapped at him, and then went on aggressively. "What's all this about? Didn't you promise my colleagues you'd look after him? Didn't you tell them you'd watch him and take care of him?"

"Excuse me, but what exactly happened?" interrupted Suhrob impatiently.

"Did you give him money to spend at the casino at the airport? He lost it all, started a fight, and in the middle of the ruckus he named you—"

"What? What money?"

"Are you asking the questions now? I, Sir, am supposed to be interrogating *you*!"

At that, Suhrob's spirits began to sink. His knees shook. Feeling weak, he took a seat on the alabaster lap of a statue, and the statue cracked under him. There was no point hiding now.

"I apologize, Comrade—what did you say your name was? Yes, it's true, I gave Sangin some money to send him back home. He . . . he's a scoundrel, a fool . . ." And all the pain and animosity of Suhrob's last few days came pouring out. This unfamiliar voice had penetrated right to his boiling-roiling heart. He told him about his visit to Altufyevo, about his studio being turned upside down, about how the expensive Scottish sweaters he had given them were gone, along with every last bit of money he had kept from his wife—and they weren't even really related at all! Suhrob bundled all of this up and released his anger into the phone.

"I have no such relative. Do whatever you like with him!" he declared, concluding his angry lament.

Funny, usually officials demonstrate less patience, but this one maintained complete silence until Suhrob was done speaking. Once Suhrob's bitter complaining was done, the man held to this respectful silence for a time, and then he continued.

"I apologize, but we have nothing left to do with him," he said. "A skinhead went mad and stabbed him in his jail cell. I was calling to tell you that you may come and collect his body."

That December night was a snowless one, so far, as if the great sculptor in the sky was just about to tear a statue apart by hand and plaster dust would soon be settling everywhere. Suhrob and Masha were on the road to Domodedovo Airport, and I, too, am ready to depart now from what I agreed to on a whim. That's enough, I think. Literature is my art. That other profession is a merciless one, hacking at stone, peeling layer upon layer of wood away from the core; and whether he ever reached the heart, the pit, or not, I don't want to watch Suhrob Surataliyev the sculptor, on a harsh Moscow winter's night, carrying the corpse of his frozen rascal of a nephew, like a stone statue, from the jail to a waiting hearse. Was this his life's work, his most heartrendingly perfect statue? Was this the very elemental core of all his searching and striving? The naked, sharp truth is what it was, I say. I want to be done with this type of art, so foreign to me, in which I've been nothing but migrant laborer myself. Much better to wrap up in a warm, soft layer of conjecture and invention, don't you think?

Come, let us start down our own path again. Suhrob Surataliyev's friends used to tease him by calling him Zurab Tsereteli . . .

BANKERS

László Krasznahorkai

Translated from the Hungarian by Ottilie Mulzet

László Krasznahorkai (1954–). Born in Gyula, László Krasznahorkai spent five years studying for a degree in law, before going on to take a degree in Hungarian language and literature at Eötvös Loránd University where his thesis focused on the work of Sándor Márai As a student, Krasznahorkai worked for the publishing company Gondolat Könyvkiadó as an editor, a post he continued until becoming a freelance writer in 1984, A year later, he published his first novel, *Sátántangó*, a dazzling, experimental, challenging work that catapulted him to the forefront of literary life in Hungary. The poet and translator George Szirtes spent eight to ten years working on the "slow lava flow of narrative, a vast black river of type" that became his equally dazzling translation of the novel, and widely acclaimed in English as a masterpiece, is still his best known. Krasznahorkai first left communist Hungary in 1987, travelling to West Berlin for a fellowship, and in the 1990s, he travelled widely in Mongolia, China, and later Japan – immersing himself in cultures which would ultimately result in stylistic changes his writing. His work has earned him numerous prizes, including the 2015 Man Booker International Prize, and the 2013 Best Translated Book Award in Fiction. He has adapted a number of his novels for the screen with director Béla Tarr. According to his literary agent, he now "lives in reclusiveness in the hills of Szentlászló".

Paul Werchowenski
Mürsel Ertas
Ixi Fortinbras
Any resemblance to persons living or dead is coincidental.

Your name is pretty odd you know—he turned his head toward the back seat to the man who, when they met, had only said: I am Paul's friend, Paul had said nothing in reply, and Paul didn't even help, didn't even explain what this person was doing there in the car, and even later on he didn't even find out, and when this man said: I'm Paul's friend, this man didn't even look at him, like someone who didn't consider this introduction to be important, when he came out from the doors of the terminal to the car with Paul, this man extended his hand and said something unintelligible: he held his hand, and said something in the English that they all took up immediately as their common language, but all the while he didn't even look at him, instead he cast his gaze somewhere beyond his shoulder, namely off in a completely different direction, toward the sliding doors of the tiny provincial airport, as if he were still waiting for someone else, and whoever had just arrived—that is to say, him—was not the person he was waiting for, he had been preparing for something more than this, some more significant personality: they shook hands, this clearly meant nothing to him, thought Ixi Fortinbras, clearly he must have come just now with Paul from the bank, and Paul obviously didn't know what to do with him, so you brought him out here to the airport; Ixi? Paul's friend asked with a kind of sarcasm in his voice: Ixi, with an x?—yes—you say it with an i in front and an i in back?—no, both those letters should be pronounced like the letter e in English—fine, but Fortinbras, really? like in that, um, whatchamacallit, right?—yes, that's it, he answered and as far as he was concerned the discussion was closed; he turned his head away toward the window, beyond the row of sparsely placed alternating factory build-ings, tenements, and battered meadows that ran alongside the airport runways, there was nothing out of the ordinary, already in the first minutes he began to try to determine when he would recognize that he had not arrived in just any old place, but there was nothing, there were exactly the same factory buildings and tenements and fields as anywhere else, well, fine, of course it was just Kiev, he thought, but he said to Paul that he really didn't notice anything at all here that would serve to indicate that . . . and you won't either, answered Paul, winking conspiratorially at his friend, if this really were his friend here sitting beside him, this tense man clothed from head to toe in a discrete plum-colored Pierre Cardin-like getup and no other distinguishing features, who then added, oh, you didn't come here for that old chewed-up piece of shit, did you?—because no one is interested in that anymore, everyone is beyond that, reeeeally . . . well, of course, he continued, the catastrophe tourists still come, they're interested, but even if they go there to get their little dose of horror, they still find nothing, and especially not there, because there's nothing there anymore supposedly, I myself never went, but everyone says the whole thing is just so embarrassing; this man grimaced and looked at Paul, and then, because there was no reaction whatsoever, he turned his head back toward the windshield and gestured with his left hand, with an undu-lating movement that was hard for Fortinbras in the back seat to understand, maybe it meant: well enough about that already, in any event, he said to Paul—clearly continuing their earlier conversation that had been interrupted only due to Fortinbras' arrival and his getting into the car—originally, he said, she had been here at Deutsche Bank, then she left for a few months to go to Bucharest, and then she left again—and this is the main thing—to Tirana, and in Tirana she became the manager of Internal Audits and she spent two years there, the honest truth was that she wanted to get away from there as well, but the lady CEO, hired by the previous owner, didn't really . . . didn't really like her either, older ladies never really like young women, especially if the woman, the young woman in question, Teresa, is in a position to oppose her in certain matters, and an intern . . . an internal audits manager can do just that, and officially Teresa wasn't even under the CEO's supervision, but under that of the supervisory board, because the job of Internal Audits is of course to supervise the bank with the owner's interests in mind, whereas the CEO, in a managerial function, falls under the purview of

Internal Audits—well, now given all this, Teresa just had to get out of there . . .
meaning she wanted to get out of Tirana? Paul interrupted, yes, that's right, out
of Tirana, that's it exactly, the friend answered, and then whatshisnameagain, the
Director of Internal Audits for Felicitas, I mean Banca Fortas in Genoa, who was
responsible for the supervision and oversight of Internal Audits for all the subsidiary banks, he convinced her to go to Genoa, to work for him, this happened
one and a half years ago, and they were getting on well in that situation, but then
there was this distance, and there was this other position, because then Heinz was
in Genoa, and sometimes he went to Tirana, well, and Teresa was really good at
fulfilling her responsibilities, she did everything just as they wanted, um, the connection between Tirana and Genoa was ideal, and in Teresa's opinion this Heinz
was much more professional and capable than the guy before, and after that she
went to Genoa, and no doubt after a very short time, Teresa realized that she
found the Italian mentality extremely difficult to bear, they are incapable of making decisions, they take their sweeeecct time, it takes them at least two or three
months to decide on something, and they always they take their sweeeeeet time,
and Paul's friend made that same undulating motion again, to show just how they
were taking their sweeeeeet time, Paul was quiet, he gazed ahead, his hands on the
steering wheel, listening attentively to the account which—at the beginning—was
not so bothersome to Fortinbras there in the back seat, because he thought: why
not, obviously there was some little problem going on here and he had just
dropped into the middle of things, maybe that's what Paul was thinking when he
ignored him and simply let him be immediately exposed in media res to the daily
life of Kiev, Fortinbras looked out the window, already they were crossing one of
the concrete bridges above the Dnieper in the heavy traffic, he looked out of the
window and he saw Imexbank, then he saw Pravex Bank, and then Privatbank,
and Ukreximbank, Oshchadbank, UkrSibbank, Ukrsocbank, Rodovid Bank,
Megabank, Bank Kiew, Brokbiznyesbank, Astrabank, Khresatikbank, Universal-
bank, Diamantbank, then he saw Nadra Bank, Delta Bank, Energobank, Fortuna-
bank, Renesans Kapitol, and so on—good heavens, thought Fortin-bras, what is
going on here, every other building is a bank, what in the world could this be, why
are there so many banks here, but there was no way for him to pose any questions, because the conversation in the front seat had remained very intense, it was
impossible to interrupt or stop it, and Paul, yielding to his own forgiving character,
was just letting his interlocutor speak, and he spoke and spoke, he just kept talking and talking: in my opinion, Italy is the only European country where it isn't
customary for the top leadership of the bank to have university degrees; the larger
part, i.e. most of them, attend vocational schools after their high-school exams,
umm, and on top of that there are innumerable employees who are from completely different fields, for example humanities graduates, so in consequence she
considered this Heinz to be good on a professional level, but as for the entire team
working there—wait a second, Paul interrupted, what exactly was this Heinz to
Teresa? Heinz?—he was the boss who lured her over there, fine, Paul asked again,
but who did he lure over there, Teresa?—yes, Teresa, that's who I'm talking about,
and, well, as Heinz was the lowest-level Internal Audit manager to whom people
had to report, the one responsible for the subsidiary banks, so—Paul picked up
the thread of conversation again: this Heinz wasn't at the highest supervisory

level that the subsidiary banks had to report to?—no, no, no, the other nodded—
he was the lowest-level manager, above him there were still two others, do you
understand?—and these two others, who do they supervise? Paul interrupted
once again with a question—they supervise the people one level below them,
came the answer—so in other words, the ones who are always one level below?—
yes, that's exactly right, and then there is the highest level of management, responsible for supervising the entire bank—and thus they supervise the Italian part
as well, but only the subsidiary banks?—yes, only the subsidiary banks, the
primary bank doesn't lie within their scope of authority, yes, only those subsidiary
banks that are located in Europe, well now—Paul's friend pulled his index finger
along his forehead—so what happened here was that she didn't like the Italian
work ethic too much, that's one thing, the other was that—and this was something
she hadn't noticed before—there was nothing to reproach Heinz with from a
professional standpoint, but she just couldn't stand his style, his ways, in other
words he was like, I don't know, she says that he was like—I would say this
myself—a woman between fifty and sixty, with her cycles, when ooooh, she can
be very sweet and everything, then she flies into a rage, and there's no way to tell
when it is going to be one or the other, so they never know in the morning when
he comes into the office if he will be one way or the other, it's impossible to know
if his wife is the reason for this, or him, his wife sits at home all day, they're
Genoese, but they live in Milan, and it could be that he was always like this, or
he just got that way, but whatever, the main thing is that she couldn't stand this
kind of style, or this kind of behavior that he was displaying with her, there were
stomachaches, and so on and so on, and now after all this, with two years to go
with this division in her contract, she sits down to chat with him and tells him that
she can't stand it anymore, and so then he told her, this was last year in August,
not to get so worked up, because if she could go to Moscow in the autumn for
two months, mainly to clear up the conflicts and set things straight in their
Moscow office, by the time she got back he wouldn't be there, of course this had
to be taken on faith, and of course two months later, when Teresa came back he
was still there: he was there, he is there, and with all certainty he will be there—
who are you talking about now? asked Paul—Heinz, answered his friend, and she
said that she certainly couldn't bear it, she sat down with Heinz more than once,
and they weren't able to work things out, sometimes he's more normal and he's
inclined to understand, and when he isn't more normal, then he just argues—tell
me about another time when Teresa was upset, Paul interrupted—fine, I'll tell you
about a very specific incident, he raised his left palm for Paul to be silent, he knew
what he wanted, he already had a concrete example: here you have it, there's an
internal audit, well, now you need to know that she had already been in Moscow
for two months, and in Moscow the chairman was the kind of person who'd been
chairman there for thirty years already, the Italian Communist Party had sent him
to Moscow, I think it's clear that he had other duties, he's senile already, but
supposedly on good terms with Putin, to such a degree that he visits him socially,
no one dares touch him, but he isn't normal; now you have to really understand
that literally he really isn't normal, well, and then this happened: Teresa was there,
and after advertising several times, they hired a lady as head of Internal Audits—
Ludmila, or whatever her name was—Teresa said that she had been hired from

somewhere else, she was capable, this was some time . . . in October or November, in the middle of the month, well, then it happened when Teresa came back and it turned out that this lady, as the head of Internal Audits, had the responsibility of inspecting the various divisions of the bank, they had a work plan, she was the one who created it, it had been approved in Genoa, and the work plan determined which divisions would be inspected by the employees, and it was decided that procurements had to be audited as well, and they were audited, well, now it turned out that in procurements some guy purchased something from a vendor without getting other offers, I don't know if it was hardware or software, in other words some kind of info . . . information technology, or some kind of service for the bank, something the bank uses for its own needs, and the main thing was that it turned out there was some scandal, in other words they had never opened tender, and in that case you're supposed to accept the most advantageous proposal, right? well, that's not what happened this time, this woman wrote a report about it, and the report first got to the CEO, and the CEO sent it on—because he had to—to the chairman, well, and now the chairman began to rage that this was absurd, and the main thing was that he wanted to kick out this woman who wrote the report, well now it was an impossible situation, it was impossible to argue with him, because it was perfectly clear that he wanted to protect the person who had arranged this purchase, well, after all this—but, Paul asked again, who arranged the purchase?—we don't know, answered the other—well, but what's his position?—maybe department head or something like that, his friend spread his hands apart, well, now after all this Teresa goes to Genoa to the department of Internal Audits, to say what happened, and discuss what to do now, and they talk, and they say that as a matter of fact this woman can't be saved, because nobody is going to confront this chairman in Moscow, because this Moscow chairman is under the protection of the first or the second most important person in Genoa who's also an old prick, who, if they call him, he hands down an order, and the result is always what they want, but Fortinbras didn't react to this, it was impossible to connect to or follow what the two people in the front seat were talking about, and they showed no sign of interest in how much their guest was able to follow their conversation—if he understood nothing at all, that was fine too, indeed maybe it was even better if he was getting nothing from this story, or account; not only was the content and meaning of this conversation unclear to Fortinbras, but the reason for it escaped him as well—why was Paul's friend putting on this performance, and why for Paul, and what did he expect from Paul—apart from listening to this account, nothing was clear, was he seeking advice, or did Paul have anything to do with anyone in this story? it was all perfectly obscure, Fortinbras determined, and in addition he could barely hope that later on he might begin to catch the drift of what they were talking about, that then it would become more clear, it was obvious that the entire story—if this was indeed a story—was just a cloud of obscurity in the best of cases and nothing else, so Fortinbras tuned out, he didn't pay attention, the words reached him from the seats in front, but he just heard them, and he no longer bothered with their meaning, they drove across a few wide intersections, then they reached a luxury residential complex surrounded by fences, with guards standing in the gates, they turned in, they parked, and they went up an elevator to the ninth floor to a large apartment—it was not at all clear to Fortinbras whose it was—and when he tried to ask, Paul smilingly choked the words in him, signaling to him that well, that's not interesting, the main thing is that you'll feel good here, you can relax, take a shower, he put his hand on his back with a friendly gesture, look, and he lifted his watch to check, in four minutes it will be twelve o'clock, let's say that we'll come back for you at two, is that enough time? of course, answered Fortinbras, I'm not tired, well, that's fantastic, fantastic and fantastic, Paul smiled at him, then they left him alone, he showered, he wrapped himself up in the towel, and he stood next to the large plate-glass window in the spacious room, comprised for some unknown reason of completely irregular angles; he stared outside, but he only saw the apartment blocks of the housing complex forming a semicircle, then through a gap between the buildings a small section of the Dnieper, he had no idea what district of the city he was in, so what are your plans, Paul asked him afterward, when he came back for him a little before three, my plans, Fortinbras looked at him confusedly, I don't have any plans in particular, but if I could choose something, then more than anything else I'd like to get to, well you know, the Zone—we won't be able to go in there, Paul explained, just maybe up to the border, if you insist on it, because supposedly the radiation over there is too much, I don't believe it, but I guess it changes from time to time, he concluded, and put a cigarette into his mouth, but he didn't light it, he sat leaning back against one of the windowsills, and explained to Fortinbras that he didn't think a trip to the Zone was at all worth it, and he didn't deny that it was possible to get into the Zone's inner section for one hundred fifty dollars or something like that, but he made a dismissive movement with his hand, indicating that was nothing, it wasn't a question of money, but that there was nothing to see there, and then suddenly he began talking about how Kiev was really beautiful, Fortinbras should believe him: it was much more worthwhile to look around Kiev a little bit; yes, answered Fortinbras, but right now as it happens I'm really interested in the Zone, because I understand, he continued more quietly, that it's not really interesting for you here in Kiev, but you know I was never here, and it's hair-raising—I know it isn't for you—how the radiation spreads out here for up to one hundred kilometers, it's just . . . I understand, I understand, Paul nodded from the window sill, so we'll go see it tomorrow, no problem, that's fine, he said, but at least let me show you something of the city today, then we'll go have dinner tonight, all right? a wide smile, Fortinbras nodded, quickly threw on some clothes, and already they were downstairs in the car, luckily that friend or business associate was no longer sitting there so they could go just the two of them, and Fortinbras was very happy about this, he even expressed his joy, and Paul in a calm voice answered that this Mürsel wasn't a bad fellow, believe me, I've known him for a while, it's just that well, he always has something to say and it can get a little tiring, but he's a fine fellow, there's no problem with him, they cut across streets, and then they drove on through the wide boulevards, there were more unusually wide intersections, clearly they were getting closer to the city center, how much longer until the center, Fortinbras asked, that's it already, you're there, answered Paul, here's a market, and sometimes on the weekend I come here to get vegetables and things like that, vegetables?! Fortinbras looked at him, and things like that?! while his host, shaking his head, just smiled, but he didn't answer, he just nodded, yes, of course—but you eat vegetables, here?! he repeated, aha, Paul turned towards him for a moment and there was a kind of paternal forbearance in his regard, how could we not when the finest vegetables in all of Kiev are right here—well, but—there's no but, Paul swept Fortinbras's objections away, then suddenly Saint Sophia appeared before them, and the visitor was definitively struck dumb, they parked nearby, but before visiting the church they sat down in a Serbian restaurant, where they had some cold cocktails and something to eat, then they went into the silent courtyard of Saint Sophia, there were no crowds at all as Fortin-bras had imagined that there would be, at least here, but there weren't any, he even asked about it: where are they, Paul, where are the tourists? at which point Paul looked at him seriously, he waited, and then finally he said: they're all in the Zone; and they stopped in the courtyard, Paul gazed fixedly into his eyes, and he looked at Paul, trying to discern if he was joking now or what, but then Paul laughed, slapped his friend on the back, and said you really are far gone, Ixi, try not to take things so seriously, but well, what was he supposed to do, Fortinbras thought to himself, if things were serious, it didn't make any difference if one looked away from how serious they are, they remained just as serious, and he almost even said this immediately to Paul, but then he didn't speak, he was a little crushed by the strange arrogance of his friend's reply, and so a little crushed, he stepped into the interior spaces of St. Sophia, and it wasn't only because of this arrogance, but because generally—he had to admit to himself—his friend had really changed quite a lot since last time they had met, it wasn't only obvious from his external appearance—because over the past couple of years Paul had clearly lost weight and had been working out—you could almost see the contours of his muscles beneath the jacket shoulders—but there were inner changes too, there in the interior part of Paul, in his character, in his nature some great change had taken place, there was, in Paul, a quality that he had never experienced before, a cynicism, Fortinbras had discovered in him a kind of impudence and he was really not too happy about that, he really wasn't, because by now Paul was his only friend, and he knew that at their age there would be no others, but then what should he do, he kept thinking, with this cynical impudence, what, he asked himself as he looked at the glorious church interior, and his brain worked over this again and again, he thought about this in front of the frescoes too, and he thought about it in front of the mosaics, all the while realizing that what he was seeing was dazzling, but without Paul it wasn't worth anything, and in general without Paul, his true friend, nothing was worth anything, he walked back and forth through the soft gold, from which, it seemed to him, the entire building had been constructed, he crept here and there in the small labyrinths of the columns and the walls, and he could hardly give himself over to this unparalleled space, in addition to which Paul became visibly restless after just a few minutes, he—who in the old days would have been capable of remaining in an architectural miracle like this for hours—was impatiently waiting for when they would finish here practically as soon as they stepped inside, yes, this was Paul now, more than anything else now he wanted to get things done, in place of the old tranquility some kind of general, restive impatience vibrated inside him, yes, this was what the world meant to Paul now, a succession of things following one after the other, in which he, Paul, had to take care of each individual thing, to take care of things on his own behalf, one after the other in succession, and then came the next one, for example him and the fact that he was here, the fact that Paul had invited him as a guest to Ukraine, and now he, Fortinbras, was the thing that had to be taken care of, and he would take care of it; just a quick telephone call to see if he was in the mood to come to Kiev, that was enough, and the plane ticket was already there in his laptop, everything happened so quickly that there was no time to prepare, my God, where am I going, he had thought about just what kind of dangerous situation was he getting himself into, and in general: anywhere, because he couldn't even bear the thought of danger, let alone a real danger, danger had been, for the last ten years of his life, a major category: it was in other words what he could not tolerate, he had excluded it from his life, freeing himself from the smallest, the very tiniest dangers, he sniffed them out and avoided them by wide margins, he never undertook anything in which even the very minutest chance of danger could be hypothesized, he wasn't paranoid, no, he was only someone who sensed the dangers that were already there, if possible, in even the most minuscule of events, so that he wasn't just imagining they were there, but he sensed—if it was at all possible to sense them—the dangers that were present already; and now it was exactly he, who had this kind of relation to dangerous events, who had come here at Paul's bidding, he, whose excessive sensitivity was well known among his friends, and first and foremost among them Paul as he knew him the best, and here he was in close proximity to the infamous Zone, not much further than one hundred kilometers, he had looked at the map on the plane, I've gone mad, where am I going, Paul says something and I jump, fine, it was always like that, but one day I'm really going to pay for this, and maybe that one day is today, that's what he was thinking about up there in the atmosphere, but then after he had gotten off the plane these thoughts disappeared, because he was absorbed by what was around him, and if only that friend or business associate hadn't been in Paul's car, and if only he and Paul hadn't had to spend the first hours after his arrival crushed by the incoherent stories of this Pierre Cardin-suit guy, instead of both of them spending at least the first day together and having a chance to speak, because it had been almost two years since they had last seen each other, but what does that matter now, Fortinbras thought to himself among the dense curvilinear columns of the Sophia with their dark golden glimmering, here I am with him now among these dense curvilinear columns with their dark golden glimmering, and the saints gazed down on him from the mosaics and the frescoes from the opulent gold, very soulfully, they looked down on him, and for him, perhaps, because of these gazes, he had no desire to quickly be done with it, as Paul had clearly indicated with his body language, you stay here, he whispered into his ear, I'll wait for you outside, and already Paul was outside in the courtyard, but this is impossible, he thought, is this Paul? and he just looked back at the saints in the mosaics and the frescoes, as if they would know, but they didn't know anything, nothing in the whole world, they just looked at him soulfully and they just asked him: what happened to the past, they stared at him, and they asked him: where is it?—where is that place where their soulful nature would mean something, but that place wasn't anywhere anymore, what could have happened with Paul, Fortinbras asked himself worriedly, what is this whole thing with this athlete's pumped-up exterior, this frivolous cynicism, and his heart was aching, and the Sophia was so beautiful, but he couldn't put it off anymore, he had to leave these soulful saints in their golden light prematurely, because Paul's mute urging from outside made his staying there completely sense-less, and once again he sat in the car, and the car glided along, and for a while Paul didn't say anything, then finally he spoke, and Paul suggested he show him the city; he thanked him, but in the meantime he had been thinking the best thing would be to sit down somewhere and discuss this matter in a tranquil setting, but of course there was no tranquil setting anywhere, and after a drive through the city, they sat down in a café, you'll like it, Paul noted as they went by foot for the last two hundred meters, and they passed in front of a house and the plaque on the house informed them that Bulgakov had lived here, and when he noticed this, he immediately wanted to take a look at the inside of the house, but Paul impa-tiently waved him down, saying oh, that's not interesting, leave it, there's nothing to see in there, cafés are much more interesting, let's go already, so on they went, passing among a row of repugnant street artists, you'll see, Paul kept saying, encouraging him, this place is the greatest, but it wasn't, just four walls painted in four different colors, a gussied-up stucco ceiling, Austro-Hungarian Art Deco tables and chairs, with a few better dressed figures by the tables, but he, Ixi, had absolutely no idea why Paul liked this place so much, and he understood even less what why Paul thought that he, Ixi, would like it, why would he like it, with its cheap kitsch for tourists, that's the kind of place it was, in any event he didn't want to dampen his friend's enthusiasm, so he noted in a restrained manner that it was pleasant, but immediately afterward he mentioned the Bulgakov house again, and he was asking something about Bulgakov and Kiev, but Paul just looked at him with a surprised or rather a blank gaze, he gulped down his coffee, he didn't know anything about Bulgakov, and in general Paul didn't know any-thing about anything, he was obviously interested only in local political and busi-ness gossip, and why—Fortinbras broke his inner silence—why don't we talk about the Sophia or about Bulgakov, he asked Paul that question, and Paul did not conceal his resentment, we already talked about Bulgakov and we were in the Sophia, Paul said harshly and a little angrily, what do you want already, but well what had come over Paul? Fortinbras asked himself ever more sorrowfully, what the hell has happened, he looked at him, he looked into his eyes, and they were Paul's old eyes, but everything else had changed, this Paul Werchowenski is not the same person who used to be my friend, Fortinbras said to himself that evening at dusk, and he was dejected, you're tired, Paul noted kindly, as they were headed toward the restaurant chosen for their evening meal, it's nothing, nothing, he brushed off the remark dispiritedly, and just sank down into the soft hum of the Audi A4, he wasn't even interested so much anymore in the Dnieper, or the city, and especially not in the restaurant that had been chosen with all the special dishes, this is the best that you can get here, said Paul loudly, and he ordered one dish after another, you're tired, he repeated again later on, but you know when you're tired you mustn't lie down, listen, and he leaned in closer towards him, I'll take you somewhere, okay? and there was a roguish look in his eyes, somewhere? Fortinbras asked, yes, Paul smiled at him, and we'll get rid of that tiredness, and they were already driving along the streets of Kiev toward the outskirts, the housing estates disappeared, and only ever larger buildings could be seen, con-cealed by enormous fences, inasmuch as anything could be seen in the darkness, then they stopped at one gate, Paul said something, and he showed something like a pass to the guard, they turned into a huge park, then they were inside a building that was something like a castle gone mad, there was a huge crowd, and noise, smoke, thumping canned music, but Paul just gestured for him to wait a minute, we're not there yet, Fortinbras followed him, they went upward somewhere in an elevator, and they stepped out into a corridor where there was complete silence, and it was so empty that he really thought they weren't in the same building, their steps were swallowed up by thick carpets, then Paul pressed a buzzer, and he tapped out a code onto a pad next to a door, he showed some kind of card to a camera, the door opened, they stepped in, but then there was another door, as if they had walked into an elevator, but behind their backs the first door closed with a loud bang, something had happened but it was impossible to tell what, there was a small quiver or something, that's all they could feel, then the second door opened, and then they were inside some kind of little hole and across from them was another door, then something happened again, and finally this third door opened as well, and Fortinbras took one step toward a huge open room, but he felt too much gravity in his step, yes, that was the first thing that he noticed, that movement here had become heavy, as if in this room gravity had increased, Paul gently pushed him ahead, he took another step, and he realized that they were in an aquarium, Fortinbras was rooted to the spot, he wasn't seeing an aquarium from the outside, but they were, in the most decisive sense of the word, inside an aquarium, there was no doubt, but there was not a drop of water upon them, around them there were a few naked women swimming around, their long blonde hair undulating behind them, Fortinbras just looked, then he looked at Paul, but Paul was so happy to see Fortinbras so surprised that he didn't say anything, whatever will be will be, later on he would find out what kind of trick this was, he took a few steps forward, with Paul urging him on, go on, go on, let's go, and the women floated beside them and above them with their cascading blonde hair, it was an incredible sight, around them the walls burned with gold, as did the ceiling and the floor, it seemed like it was all made of gold, the whole thing was blinding, because the light was shining so brightly from somewhere, Paul just stood half a step behind him, enjoying the effect, and the effect was huge, as even after one minute Fortinbras was incapable of speaking, then a naked woman floated over to him in the water, which could hardly be water, she stroked his chest, then her hand slid down his stomach to his sexual organs, it was very beautiful and very lovely, it was so beautiful and so pretty that in the first moment Fortinbras thought this was also some kind of trickery, just as everything here was a kind of trickery, and it might have been true, Paul gently took his arm and led him toward an almond-shaped opening leading into a kind of cave, but there he already felt the presence of water down by his legs, it splashed around his shoes, and yet nothing got wet, on the other hand real-looking women came forward, and there they were, and they greeted the two men, do you hear their English? it's flawless! Paul exclaimed enthusiastically, come on, he pulled him along, let's sit down there, and he led him over to a scarlet couch, they were served champagne and fruits, but the champagne wasn't champagne, the fruit wasn't fruit, only the women were real, they sat next to them, they wore lustrous, satiny, bluish glimmering bathing suits which emphasized their figures with unbelievable precision, so much so that Fortinbras blushed, not only because of their breasts and the nipples of their breasts, but the curve of their bottoms, and the secretive components of their vaginas were sharply and enticingly delineated; and there were only bodies here, bodies and enticement and offers and nightmares, which caused him to realize more or less where they were, yes, Paul said to him, this is what a brothel is like here, what do you think, but the women are so beautiful and pretty, Fortinbras answered faintly, there's no way they can be prostitutes, but they are, very much so, try it out, pick one, whichever one you want is yours, said Paul not bothering to lower his voice, and at his further prompting he had to choose one, all the while hearing Paul's ever more enthusiastic voice: so, what do you say, Ixi, well, what do you say to this, my old man? and the woman unbuttoned his fly, and climbed into his lap, while at the same time another woman leant over his shoulder, touching his face with a breath-light touch, caressing his mouth, prying it open with playful strength, and she pressed some kind of pill into his mouth, then he remembered that the pill was blue, the woman thrust her tongue into his mouth, and this tongue played inside his mouth spreading the pill all over his palate, but immediately after that his brain felt like it was exploding, and it was horrifically good, and then he was outside in the cosmos, for one hundred years, and, in the cosmos, there was a mild breeze blowing, and everywhere there were thousands and thousands of billions of radiant stars, and everything was ascending somewhere with insane speed, and in the meantime he ended up underneath a huge rainbow made up of a billion colors, really this rainbow was composed of a billion different colors, he was filled with unspeakable happiness, he was in an immeasurably deep space and endless darkness which nonetheless shone, and then falling, some kind of sickly giddiness, and finally just an incandescent beam of light, an unbearable thundering, every sound hurt, and a million sounds were attacking him, Paul leaned above him, then sat down beside him on the bed, please, turn it off, turn it off, he begged Paul, at which Paul, laughing, stood beside him, turned off the music, and his head was splitting with unbearable pain, close the curtains, I beg you, Paul, he begged, but I closed all the curtains already, Paul laughed, but at least he was there in the apartment that was known to him, where they had arrived before, at least Paul was there next to him, that was good, but what wasn't good was that Paul was laughing in a completely different way than the way Paul used to laugh, there was something in his laughter that was painful to Fortinbras, so he asked him: please don't laugh, fine, said Paul, then I won't laugh, and he laughed some more, but in exchange you start pulling yourself together, because it will be nine-thirty in a second, and if you really want to go we've got to set off now, he said go?! where?! Fortinbras leaned up on his elbows, well, didn't you want to go to the Zone? and it was hard taking a shower, although both of them thought that would help, it didn't help, every single drop of water coming from the shower head struck him with massive force, look, Paul opened the door from time to time, maybe instead we should just put it off if you're like this, no, no way, I'll be fine in a second, he answered, and he forced himself to let the drops of water fall on him from the shower head, and already he had dried off by himself, and he got dressed by himself, just when he went down to the elevator he needed a bit of support in case he lost his balance, because sometimes he would still lose his balance, that's the last symptom, Paul reassured him, your balance will still be looking for itself for a moment, and they were already headed off toward the nearby highway, this time on the inner side of the Dnieper, we'll pick up Mürsel here, Paul said suddenly at a traffic light, like someone who makes all the decisions in these matters, and he turned off, but at first Fortinbras had no idea what was going on: who was this Mürsel, and why did they have to turn off for him, in place of his brain there was an enormous ice-cold chunk of stone, so that he only began to realize where this was headed when he got a glimpse of Mürsel, oh, the guy from yesterday, oh no, anything but that, this flashed through the ice-cold stone, but he mumbled something to him as a way of greeting, I thought—Paul turned back to Fortinbras—it would be more pleasant to make the trip in company, no? and already in the front of the car they were launching into yesterday's theme, Paul wasn't interested in the Zone at all, Fortinbras realized, he lives one hundred kilometers from it, and it's not interesting to him, he looked at the sparse alternation of buildings next to the highway: pubs, apartment houses, farms, shops, tin-roofed churches—they had set off to the north, toward the Zone; and Mürsel, who was not wearing Pierre Cardin this time, but Cerruti, was already in the thick of things, namely that in his view, joint stock companies in shared ownership functioned exactly like those massive enterprises in the old socialist era with no supervision on the part of the owners, in which the management functions as a kind of quasi-owner, and the real owners, who are after all the distributed shareholders, have no idea of what's going on, they have zero representation at the general meetings, they tell them whatever they want, resulting in an inner structure, which, I tell you, is built upon the logic of buddies and friends, there's no role anywhere for expertise, absolutely no question of who is appropriate for a given job, and as a matter of fact this was the case with us too—don't be mad, you Pavel Morozov, Paul said to him, but the parallel wasn't completely clear—still, said Mürsel, who this time was in Cerruti, and with the strong gestures familiar from yesterday: he half turned around so he could speak to Paul, who was behind the steering wheel: but here, you see, the situation is once again personal, because this Italian, this Ficino ended up here in Kiev, because among all the countries where Banco Fortas has subsidiary banks, Kiev is the only place where they will hire someone as a chairman without a university degree, everywhere else a university degree is required, this is determined by the local authorities, so it's up to Kiev, that's the rule here, that's how it is by law for credit institutions, and that's how it should be, nothing will change in this regard, the law concerning credit institutions formulates the rules for banks, including the human rules of the game, well, what's interesting about this is—just imagine, Mürsel shook his head—Albania is the country with the strictest credit-bank regulations, and I know this because once a long time ago I was the chairman of a local supervisory board there, because over there in Albania everything is delegated from Genoa, and I was the only one with the piece of parchment qualifying me to be chair of the supervisory board, well, of course it didn't happen that way, but the joke is that I was the only one with the parchment, do you get it, the whole thing is a joke, just a joke, but that's not the interesting part, well, and so he came here to Kiev, and he lured me over here as well—who's this now? Paul interrupted—well, who am I talking about, you're not paying attention, Paul, I'm talking about that Ficino, who else would I be talking about, well, to cut a long story short, first he was in Tirana, but then he came here to Kiev, because no parchment is needed here, and then he brought me over here, I accepted the offer, I came—but this Ficino, Paul interrupted again, what is he at the bank, he's the chairman, answered Mürsel a little impatiently, because as I was telling you, even somebody without a parchment can be chairman, and he can come here . . . well, now you have to know that this subsidiary had been sold half a year before we came here, previously it was in the ownership of the mayor of Kiev, it was his and only his, and for sure they paid off the Italian trade delegation and the inspectors, and they bought just one big pile of shit, because the quality of the outstanding debts was shit, how should I put it, you know what that means, and in this case the owning family had a financial interest in most of the extended credit, there's no doubt—Mürsel spread his hands apart, well, as he had gotten out of it he must have known that the whole thing was just one big pile of shit, namely that the chance that the credit would be repaid was small, if not nonexistent, the prospect, namely, of repayment, was not going to happen, or at least not any time soon, and a lot of this debt had to be appraised, on the basis of which certain provisions had to be made for liabilities which in all likelihood would not be repaid, you understand, it's clear, well, but there are regulations here, right? and the outstanding liabilities and the investments have to be classified—this is how it is all over the world—they're assessed on a quarterly basis, but here, you know, there are several degrees of assessment, and for each degree of classification there are four or five other classifications, and for each of these, with the exception of the highest one—with which accordingly there is no problem—for each degree, local legislation determines a percentage for the liability reserves, these are basic things, what can I say, but so that your friend can understand, the main thing is—Mürsel now turned around to Fortinbras—the main thing is that the provision for liabilities is taken from earnings and placed in a particular account which is not included in those earnings, well, now you should know—he turned back to Paul—that the family—that is the former owner, or mainly his son—definitely—although of course it can't be proved definitively—paid off this guy, this Ficino, for a song, namely he was invited to go sailing on their personal yacht on the Dnieper, he was invited to parties at their home, to receptions and the like, and it's possible that they gave him something, the result of which was that Ficino began to prefer this family, particularly the son of this family, and this preference meant that the family had the money here in deposits, and it was earning much higher than the usual interest rates, well you understand, and now the relationship between myself and this chairman began to quickly deteriorate—he turned back again to Fortinbras—in as much as I'm kind of like a manager in this situation, but just to make things clear, in principle the CEO, and not the chairman, should be the one running the bank, because he's the one who's running the place, and the chairman shouldn't even be interfering with the functioning of the bank, but this guy Ficino interfered and he interfered because he's Italian and the bank is Italian, and the CEO is a Ukrainian who's afraid of Italians, but not of me of course; but my own position is kind of special, because normally I wouldn't be reporting to a manager but directly to the CEO, I'm responsible for the treasury, as you know, in other words resource allocation, and I always ask for—or, to put it more bluntly, order—written documentation for every verbal request, which comes to me from the Italians

—well, Ficino did a whole bunch of things which chiefly favored the family members of the former owner, umm, and there were other things too, and in every instance I asked to get it as a written request, well, his tactic was that he always did what he wanted to do, and then somebody else would take the blame, and then he would scream that this idiot had screwed up, well, now, however, there was a paper trail for everything, and so he couldn't do that anymore, well, and as a matter of fact I was the one who got it in the neck when I followed this procedure every single time, which I could make light of, but he didn't, instead he was enraged continually, and he turned more and more against me, and as he turned against me, I also was compelled to react, and his position became more and more entrenched . . . who's this now, Fortinbras put forth the question, but only to himself, because he was even less interested in this story, if that was possible, of which he didn't even understand half, because he only paid attention occasionally, sometimes just picking up a word here and there, so that it was difficult, he wasn't interested, the story bored him, indeed, after a while, in the heavy traffic, by the time they left Kiev, he already felt an aversion for this story, and he tried to prevent Mürsel's words from reaching his consciousness, he watched the road in front of them, which was lined with either birch trees or beech trees, he didn't know which, he didn't know trees, maybe they were birch trees, and he looked at the buildings, appearing infrequently now alongside the road, and the roadside vendors: there were many of them for a while after they left Kiev, then they too became ever more infrequent, they were selling cucumbers, lettuce, potatoes, and tomatoes on carpets spread out on the ground, my God, cucumbers, lettuce, potatoes, tomatoes?!—do you have a Geiger counter? he suddenly asked Paul in Danish, interrupting Mürsel, a what? Paul jerked his head back, a Geiger counter, repeated Fortinbras with emphasis, still in the language they shared, why would I need one, Paul frowned, and then quickly turned back to the direction they were going, because he felt that he had held Fortinbras' gaze too long, they were going to crash into something, and all the while Mürsel understood nothing, he looked at Paul, and he looked at Fortinbras, to try to see what was going on, but it didn't last too long, he couldn't bear the pause which was far too long for him, and already he launched into the story again, but Fortinbras decided that from this point on he wasn't going to listen to him at all, not even a word, he felt hurt by Paul's reaction, and by the fact that it didn't even occur to Paul that what obviously seemed to him to be a superfluous precaution, to someone else, for example to him, Fortinbras, was hardly superfluous at all, and that nothing was clearer than the fact that if somebody were headed toward some kind of danger—even if voluntarily, as they were now—then at the very least the most minimal of precautions should be taken, because they were headed toward danger now, on this highway with vegetable sellers sparsely scattered along its edge, more threatening than the most lethal of danger, and Fortinbras at this moment in Paul's car didn't want to explain why he insisted on approaching this menace, he didn't want to, because he knew he desired it, and while he was repulsed by his own desire in vain, he wanted to be there, because what he was feeling was something that was stronger in him than nature, or maybe it was an exaggerated fear of everything that was scary, and this was his desire, his wish: to somehow come into the proximity of that strength of which there never had been and never would be anything more formidable, because this was the one thing that man had started and had been unable to stop—so, you want a Geiger counter, Paul interrupted Mürsel, and he turned to the back seat once again, really, why didn't you say so, why are you so interested in the Zone, what the hell do you want there, Paul turned to the front again, and he seemed a little agitated, but really, tell us already, he continued, what the hell is so interesting for you that you want to go where nobody else wants to go, where nobody ever wanted to go, to wallow in catastrophe like that, it's really not how I knew you, Ixi, Paul lowered his voice, and he grimaced as if he were sorry, Fortinbras saw his eyes glancing back in the mirror, and then he realized that he was sorry, he said to himself, for certain he was sorry, and that's why he was quiet, Fortinbras was quiet, and for a while no one said anything, even Mürsel needed some time to realize that it would be best for him to start speaking and break the silence, because this silence didn't bode anything good, it had all promised to be so much fun, to take this strange character to the Zone, to take this person with a more than strange name, Mürsel noted to himself and finding his voice again, he said: he tripped me up, he simply didn't give me a bonus, claiming that there were losses in the treasury but that wasn't true because the whole bank had been having losses last year, Mürsel raised his voice, well, and then this thing happened in December—and here Mürsel held a slight pause for the sake of effect, but Paul just gazed fixedly at the road, in the back their guest was gazing at the road just as fixedly, just as people in a car usually do, everyone looks at the road, and he too was looking at the road, Mürsel thought to himself that if someone is sitting in a moving vehicle, there's nothing else to do than look at the road in front, although you could also look, for example, at the landscape on the side, if the landscape is interesting, but here it isn't, still, though, you could look at it, Mürsel continued his monologue—yes, when this thing happened in December—but actually it all began six months before that, with the liquidity problems at the bank, and that was caused, among other things, by the fact that the founding capital was too small, the parent branch was supposed to raise it, and the Italians didn't like this idea, no one liked it, and they had no intention of raising the founding capital, especially at a subsidiary, and now here comes Ficino, who—I don't know exactly what the transaction was—transferred the family's money over there through some bank, but with additional interest, it's likely that Ficino had promised the son this additional interest earlier, 10 percent on the dollar to be exact, which is pretty high, right, and now I come into the picture, because I wasn't willing to pay out this extra high interest, namely I asked Ficino to put it in writing that the interest for this transaction would be this high, and this happened six months before, and it was executed with a termination date of one year, so that the money would be with us for one year, and in the meantime in December the Italians in Genoa decided that nonetheless they would raise the founding capital, and of course Ficino was shitting bricks for something like that to happen, something critical like that, because then there could be huge problems if it emerged that here was this 10 percent extra interest on this money, so he wanted to get out of it, but still—Mr. Ertas, said Paul, what kind of sums are we talking about here, could you give me a sense of that so I can have an idea, well, Mürsel shook his head slowly, and he began to pout a little, well, imagine it to be about ten … Paul glanced sharply at him—or rather, Mürsel pulled his index finger along his forehead—something like, umm, a sum of a hundred million dollars, well something like that, it doesn't matter now, the main thing is that in December Ficino was told to terminate the family's extra interest, but it still wasn't decided if this would be a tactical move, and they they would reinstate it on December 31, and the money would be called in once again, or was it final, nobody knew, and so Ficino and his people were maneuvering, and that was the problem, because according to the law the obligatory reserves which a given bank has to make on the basis of foreign sources, in other words for the central bank it's a question of the deposit as a guarantee for the given amount, well, now you also know very well, if you're familiar at all with macroeconomics and theory, that for every deposit the percentage will be different, and now no one could decide if it should be valid for a half-year or a whole year, and Ficino and his crew were counting on it being a transitional thing, accordingly one half year, but in the meantime it emerged that this wasn't possible, because it could only be for one year—no, I'm wrong, they were counting on one year, and it could only be for half a year, and because of that they had fewer reserves than they should have had; in cases like that usually the central bank imposes a fine, and now Ficino began to get frantic, saying that there had been a mistake, it was bungled, the calculations were wrong and so on, namely he was talking about the treasury, well, I asserted that this wasn't true: I didn't make any mistakes, and we didn't make any mistakes, because I said to him, to Ficino: you said, right here in this room what the information was, this was the conversation that I heard, and of course Ficino wasn't satisfied, they began to investigate who was responsible, the wrangling began, internal audits, and Ficino tried in every way he could to smear it on me, but I was right there with all the written orders as well as the regulation stating that this wasn't my responsibility but the responsibility of the back office, but the back office themselves could hardly be completely responsible, because if they had no information, which they didn't, then the back office couldn't decide what to do or what not to do, in any event things were looking pretty bad for Ficino, and so he decided that as the whole affair was not clean he would split the part of the bank that deals with these deposits off from Treasury, and move it to the back office so that nothing like this could happen in the future, which is absurd, because this division would have no idea what the info was, so that the problem wasn't solved, because the right solution would be for the treasury to function in two parts in coordination with each other, in other words there was a lot of tension and that's the way it is even now, and now I want to get out of there, as a matter of fact it's an open secret that I want out, but I don't know what you have to say about this, and Mürsel turned to Paul, and he was quiet, and he waited for Paul to say something, but Paul didn't say anything, and Fortinbras was convinced that it was because he also wasn't paying any attention and didn't even care that Mürsel was waiting for his reply and that this was because he was thinking about him, Fortinbras, and the situation was becoming uncomfortable, I would be so happy to jump out of this car, thought Fortinbras, I'd jump out, and I would undo the fact that I am here, he felt that Paul comprehended that something had changed between them, and that's what he was thinking about, and not about Mürsel's story, which was likely no more interesting to him that it was to his guest here in the back seat, Mürsel continued to be silent, and maybe now he just realized that his story hadn't really thrown anyone into a fever here, Mürsel cast a glance back, and this glance was clearly full of rage, and he cast a glance to the side as well, at Paul, and this glance was clearly full of hurt, the Audi A4 hummed along softly, you can't go faster than the speed limit here, said Paul in the friendliest possible voice, there are so many policemen, they're lying in wait, we can't take any risks, is that okay? and Paul turned around again, and looked at Fortinbras, and smiled at him; and that's all it took for Paul to pull himself together, Paul always needed only twenty seconds to regain his composure, and that dear smile appeared on his face again, that smile Fortinbras loved so much, and now too he was grateful for it even if it wasn't sincere, he was grateful to Paul that there hadn't been a rupture, he didn't want that, and he smiled back, and with that a very important accord was created between them, and that was exactly how their friendship had started too, when they were both still in Hungary, when they both went to pester a deputy department head at the Ministry: Fortinbras was seeking financial support for a Danish-Hungarian exhibit in his gallery, and Paul also needed funding for something at his bank from this deputy department head, and they warmed up to each other, two foreigners among the wild herdsmen, then it turned out that there was only one sum of money allocated for cultural events like this, and among the two projects only one could be awarded the sum, and then Paul came over to him, and that smile was on his face, as he allowed the money to go to the gallery project, and that's how they arranged it, and of course he, Fortinbras, returned the favor as soon as he could, so that they met up with each other ever more frequently, and they parted company as inseparable good friends, and then over the years they visited each other, and Paul said that he never would have believed that at his age he would still be able to find a true friend, and Fortinbras also admitted that the situation with him was exactly the same, he found it inconceivable that he would be able to find such a deep and true friend in anyone, and it had all started to be torn apart yesterday and today up until this moment, but now it was resolved, that is once again Paul had resolved it, he was so grateful to him there in the back seat that he didn't even know what to do, and so as not to bother Mürsel again, who had regained his presence of mind, and had explicated a few of the finer points from the story—almost imperceptibly he reached out towards the seat in front, and he gently patted Paul on the shoulder, just so lightly, like a breath, and Paul didn't turn his head back to him, but for a second he did a little bit, and Fortinbras felt that he had received this reconciliation gratefully, indeed he received this subtle indication of apology, and nothing would ever separate them now, it was only these strange circumstances that troubled them sometimes, and maybe the only reason for the trouble was his own excessive sensitivity, thought Fortinbras, and he gazed penitently at the road in front of them, through the windshield in between the heads of Paul and Mürsel, the road in front of them leading toward the Zone, the road on which not one single vegetable seller could be seen anymore, the road was lined by birch or beech trees—I think, thought Fortinbras, that they're birch.

SILVER RAIN

Paweł Huelle

Translated from the Polish by Antonia Lloyd-Jones

> **Paweł Huelle** (1957–) is a novelist and author of a volume of verse. He has also worked as an employee of the "Solidarity" press office, university lecturer, journalist, director of the Gdańsk Polish Television Center and, most recently, as a columnist for *Gazeta Wyborcza*. Huelle has found enormous success as a writer and been honored with many prestigious awards. As a young boy, he and his friends would scavenge for unexploded German bombs and take them apart to turn into fireworks.

To Zbigniew Żakiewicz

Anusewicz was no great believer in prophetic dreams, Sibylline oracles or palmistry. And yet, when he woke up that day bathed in sweat and gasping for breath he felt that something must be going to happen. Nina, aged twenty, beautiful and alluring, had been dancing in a meadow, as if specially for him. He walked towards her slowly, feeling the soft blades of grass tickling his feet. They embraced passionately, suddenly naked like Adam and Eve under the apple tree. He felt an intense spasm of pleasure as he pressed his lips to her full breasts. Straight after that, God knows why or what for, Father Wołkonowicz had appeared in the meadow. In a patched cassock and shabby shoes, with drops of sweat on his brow, he was roaring and thundering the words of Isaiah about the Earth and its immoral inhabitants being burned to ashes. But why a moment later had all three of them ended up in a palatial ballroom? And what was the military band in German uniform that was playing to them from the courtyard supposed to mean? Now wearing a starched shirt front and an impeccably cut tail-coat Father Wołkonowicz was waltzing with Nina, dressed like a bride, while he, Anusewicz, went after them, also to the rhythm of a waltz, through deserted halls and galleries, down corridors and staircases.

The dream had no clear end. For some time Anusewicz gazed at the ceiling, and he wasn't sure if it was his flat, or that strangely empty, unfamiliar palace. As soon as he got up and caught sight of himself in the mirror, he felt profound disappointment. In the meadow his body had been supple and agile. In the real world to which he had returned, it offered a rather discouraging sight. His sagging pot belly, the grey tufts of sparse hair on his head and his drooping shoulders were a pitiless reminder of the years gone by. The magical, rejuvenating power of the dream appealed to him very much. Over breakfast it occurred to him that he hadn't felt desire for several years at least. But why Nina? And why Father Wołkonowicz?

The Russians had deported her right at the start, in 1939. The Germans had shot Father Wołkonowicz as a hostage three years later. In fact, all trace of Nina had been lost. Had she died in a camp? Had she left Siberia with Anders' Army and ended her days many years later in London, or in sunny California? What could it matter nowadays... Where were they now?

As he left the house, Anusewicz kept repeating this question over and over, and it caused him pain. He did in fact believe deeply in the immortality of the soul, but did that automatically entail the resurrection of the body? Was it really quite so certain? If a body that had crumbled to dust could return to its former shape, he might not only see Nina again one day, but that entire long-dead world. Vistas through the pine trees at dawn, sheets spread to dry in the meadows, the larch-wood beams of the house at Rudzieńszczyzna, his father in riding boots, or a snowflake on his mother's fur collar. But does God bother with such trivia? There was plenty to imply that He had a hundred times more serious troubles, from hurtling, disintegrating galaxies, via endless wars, to volcanoes and common floods.

Anusewicz passed the brewery, and in the passage under the electric railway tracks he bought three purple roses. As he boarded the tram he felt sure his dream hadn't appeared by accident. The presence of Father Wołkonowicz was proof of that. A cleric, no matter what his denomination, always means some sort of change. Perhaps when he got home from the theatre he'd find a letter from Nina in the post box? That would be a surprise. 'I'm coming in a month and I must see your grandchildren.' Some miraculous escapes, years of hunger and hoping against hope; yes, they'd have something to talk about over a carafe of dogberry vodka. But as he got off the tram not far from the Uphagen mansion, he came to the conclusion that he wouldn't want to see Nina old and wrinkled, not even with an American set of false teeth. The Nina he had seen in his dream was immortal and happy. The one he would greet on the threshold of his flat would only be a poor copy, an imitation of that one. But he had no time for further reflections. As ever, he presented the flowers to Miss Andruszkiewicz, and as ever, she gave him the key to the storeroom.

In pitch darkness Anusewicz felt for the spotlight switch, and a focused stream of light shifted along the shelves and pegs, picking the puppets' immobile heads and bodies out of the darkness. Sindbad the Sailor had his glassy eye on Alice, Dratewka the Cobbler was curled up next to Big Ears, a sad Ali Baba was leaning his chin on Grandpa Utopek the lighthouse-keeper, and a Little Owl with floppy wings was perching on Pinocchio's nose like a roosting hen. Anusewicz had brought their gestures, their trials and tribulations and their funny little catch-phrases to life many times, lending them his voice and hand movements. Now that he was retired, he came here once a month, and in the total silence he acted out his own improvised scenes with them. Sometimes the Wicked Stepmother spoke the words of Lady Macbeth, or Johnny Dunderhead waved his arms about and spouted the same twaddle as the old and new politicians.

Without a second thought, Anusewicz took a white-armed, sheet-wearing Grim Reaper from the rack. He untangled the strings, adjusted the fastening of the silver scythe and made him patter to and fro, as if on stage. He snapped his great big teeth just as he should, and rattled his scythe like mad. But Anusewicz wasn't happy with something. Only when the Grim Reaper started tap dancing to the rhythm of the swing he was softly whistling, did he smile at him and say:

'Now I can see it, old man, you've got a great future ahead of you.'

The Grim Reaper spread his arms and bowed politely to the invisible audience. But that was all. No new idea, no improvisation or funny sketch occurred to Anusewicz. He usually spent an hour here, sometimes more, without looking at his watch, but this time every minute was dragging on unbearably. On top of that he had an unpleasant feeling, as though in the darkness beyond the bright shaft of the spotlight, four eyes were watching him: those of Nina and Father Wołkonowicz. When he put on the overhead lamp, he didn't feel any better, because there was another thought that wouldn't stop pestering him – that someone connected with this morning's dream was waiting for him at home, while he was wasting his time here to no purpose.

'Better cut it short,' he said out loud. 'The worst thing is uncertainty.'

Somewhat surprised, Miss Andruszkiewicz packed the Grim Reaper in a plastic bag for him and, without the usual chat, he set off for the tram stop. What was he going home for? A dream was just a dream, nothing but a stupid nightmare. He could easily stay at the theatre. The inspiration would come at the right moment, yes, it was sure to.

And indeed, the letterbox was quite empty, there was no scrap of paper shoved in the door, and without his wife bustling about or his grandchildren's hullabaloo the flat seemed unnaturally quiet. Anusewicz shambled into the kitchen, and then, as he drank a cold Elbląg beer he stood the Grim Reaper on his desk. Among the family photographs, books and notes, without any scenery or spotlights he looked quite harmless. Anusewicz's fingers took hold of the strings again, and sounding suitably strident, he recited:

O my noble ancient Sire,
The world makes noise 'til it doth tire,
The young man can, the old must try
To bolt, or else he'll choke and die.

The Grim Reaper made his robe rustle, rapped his scythe and sang the next couplet in a different, maybe slightly Belarussian accent:

My crown and sceptre I'd concede
If from death's dance I could be freed.
What bitter tears an old man weeps
As death's grim ballet jumps and leaps.

The big wooden boots tapped on the desktop. Anusewicz purred in satisfied agreement, but the next couplet remained unspoken. This was because of Mr Winterhaus, who just at that moment knocked at the front door. With the Grim Reaper resting on his arm, Anusewicz rather reluctantly opened it, and for a while both gentlemen stood looking at each other in silence.

'I am Vinterhaus,' said Winterhaus. 'May I please talk vith you?'

'Naturally,' replied Anusewicz, and led his guest into the dining room.

But there was nothing natural about it.

'There's a bit of a problem, as there alvays is with this sort of conversation,' sighed Winterhaus, 'but I couldn't put it off any longer. You know? I've been up these stairs three times before und run avay. I vas afraid.'

'Of me?' asked Anusewicz in amazement.

'Of the situation. You know? I used to live here. Until the end of the var.'

'Oh, I see,' said Anusewicz. 'That's interesting.'

The man didn't look like the typical German, though his well-groomed grey hair combined with his gold-rimmed spectacles, not to mention his accent, spoke for themselves.

'Do you want to take some pictures?' asked Anusewicz, after an awkward silence. 'Look round the rooms? There aren't many of the old things left. The mirror in the bathroom, the shoe cupboard, nothing else. You must know,' he went on, a little irritated, 'I wasn't the first tenant. There was a clerk from the Poznań area here before me, and before him there was a tailor, a Jew. The tailor moved out in 1947, to some suburb of Wrzeszcz, the clerk got a promotion to Warsaw, and then I moved in. It was, just a moment, let me think. . . yes, it was in 1949, in May. What else do you want to know?'

'This is no ordinary matter,' said Winterhaus hesitantly. 'I don't vant any photographs or souvenirs, nothing. I came here because of my father. I kept having the same incredible dream. You know? He left treasure in the kitchen dresser that stood next to the stove. All his life he kept saying: "Helmut, it must be there." But I did not believe him. Und ven he died, every night I dreamed about the dresser und the coins. Every night. Und then I suffered from *Schlaflosigkeit,* und the doctor told me: "Vhy don't you go there, Herr Vinterhaus, and make sure there's no dresser, no treasure, nothing there."'

Anusewicz wiped the sweat from his brow. He couldn't remember a kitchen dresser. The stove, of course, with the metal hotplate, stood in the kitchen for many years until the gas was connected. But a dresser? The only dresser had been in the dining room, here, where the storage unit now stood and the television. He had sold it for a song, in 1971 or 2. It had cloudy glass doors and scratched veneer in an awful cherry colour. But the question of the coins interested him greatly.

'So was there a lot of it?' he asked. 'Gold, I guess?'

'Oh, I don't know,' said Winterhaus. 'You know, he collected those coins that vere minted in Danzig — that is, in Gdansk,' he corrected himself, 'vithout letting my mother, me or my brother know about it. He vas alvays increasing his collection. The more of them he had, the greater his fear that she vould find out he kept spending money on them. Und he vas so afraid that ven the time came to escape, he couldn't get them out, because she vould have seen vhat he'd been spending money on for so many years. You understand?'

'I do. But did you ever see the coins?'

'Never.'

'What about your mother? Or your brother?'

'They never did either. Und aftervards no one vould believe him. It was only this dream of mine, und then the doctor, as I told you.'

'There are all sorts of dreams,' said Anuscwicz. 'Today for instance I dreamed I was in the meadow at our Rudzieńszczyzna. I'm sure you don't know where that is.'

'No.'

'In the East,' sighed Anusewicz. 'It's in Belarus now.'

Winterhaus nodded sympathetically. But he didn't look upset, at least not for that reason. He followed his host into the kitchen and was happy to accept a beer. He showed where the dresser had stood and described exactly what it had been like.

'Oh!' cried Anusewicz. 'You said the dresser, the dresser, but it was a kitchen cupboard – in three parts, right?'

'Right.'

'And which one were the coins hidden in?'

'In the middle bit, the biggest. That's vhat my father said. Und that's vhat I dreamed.'

'Benek!' exclaimed Anusewicz. 'Oh yes, Benek! But has he still got it?'

And before Winterhaus had had time to say another word, Anusewicz had put on his shoes, thrown his jacket over his shoulders and commanded:

'Let's go, Mr Winterhaus, quickly.'

At this point there was a slight controversy. Winterhaus suggested they take a taxi, and that he would pay. But Anusewicz refused to agree to that, and doggedly insisted on taking the tram, which – as always in such cases – didn't come for ages.

'Who is Benek?' asked Winterhaus at last.

'He's Bernard, my brother-in-law, my wife's brother,' explained Anusewicz.

Then he added that the cupboard in question, or to be precise, its biggest, middle bit, had long since been given to Bernard, who had got married to Barbara and needed furniture.

'He's either thrown it out, or he's got it somewhere in the cellar,' Anusewicz pondered aloud. 'But what if he found it?'

At this point Anusewicz remembered how Bernard had surprised everyone a few years ago by suddenly buying a car. Where had he got so much money from out of the blue? But he didn't mention it to Winterhaus. In the crowded tram the conversation flagged, and when they boarded a bus near the Upland Gate and headed towards Orunia, Winterhaus said in a hushed tone:

'You know vhat? I'm not concerned about the money, the property. I just vanted to check if my father vas telling the truth or not. Und that dream, if you please. Do you believe in dreams? Und then the *Schlaflosigkeit* – er, insomnia.'

'Hmm,' mumbled Anusewicz, 'some dreams portend something, they tell us something. Others are meaningless, just idiotic. And who'd know the difference?'

The bus stopped by the Radunia Canal, in the shade of some old trees. As they got out, to their right the old Jesuit church rose from the hills, while to their left the gently sloping upland declined more and more slowly into a completely flat depression, cut across by canals and a patchwork of fields. They headed left, passing some poor, rented apartment blocks, some small factories, warehouses and railway tracks, until finally, under the shade of some chestnut trees, the cobblestones came to an end, and they went into a field road.

'My father,' said Winterhaus, 'vas an official at the Danziger Strassenbahn, that is the electric trams. Tovards the end of the var they made him the director.'

'And mine,' said Anusewicz, 'had Rudzieńszczyzna. Not much land, but a lot of forests, sawmills, a watermill, lakes. . .'

'He didn't go to the var,' Winterhaus continued, 'because he vas lame, in the right leg.'

'Neither did mine,' explained Anusewicz, 'because he was too old. But the Soviets took him and he never came back. Never. Then, when the Germans came, they shot Uncle Witold, and I was left alone with my mother.'

'Und my older brother,' added Winterhaus, 'vas killed at Kursk. The Führer sent a letter und a posthumous *kreuz*.'

'I was an only child,' said Anusewicz.

Both gentlemen walked the last stretch of road across the weir in silence. Bernard's cottage was by the canal, among mouldering willows, burdock leaves and grass that no one had mown. In the yard lay the wreck of an old truck, some rusty sheets of metal, some bricks from a demolished building, and some rolls of wire. The nose of a punt was poking out of a dense clump of nettles; full of holes, it had been taken over by the hens.

'Don't say anything,' Anusewicz warned. 'I'll do the talking.'

Barbara was making soup. The children were on holiday, near Kościerzyna, and Benek, so she said, was out driving the taxi. Anusewicz came straight to the point. Did Barbara remember that white cupboard they'd brought them from Wrzeszcz by horse and cart? It was two days after the wedding, when they moved into this ruin and started renovating it.

'How could I fail to remember?' laughed Barbara. 'You boys drank for three days on end – you, Benek and that carter, Bieszke – and I had to feed his old nag and patch the roof because it was pouring. Men,' she snorted. 'You lot are never any use.'

Anusewicz waved his hands. Why remind him of those things? The point was the cupboard from the flat on Gołębia Street. This gentleman, Mr Winterhaus, had come from Germany looking for some family documents and photographs. They had to help him, because they were probably hidden in that cupboard...

'*Was ist verloren?*' said Barbara to Mr Winterhaus.

'Oh, I can speak Polish,' he replied, bowing and kissing her hand. 'My grandmother taught me Polish, because she vas a Pole, though her surname vas Kosterke.'

'Where is that cupboard? Have you still got it somewhere?' pressed Anusewicz. 'We'll take a look and be on our way, it's no great bother. You see, Barbara, Mr Winterhaus used to live in our flat, what I meant to say is, we live where he used to, and when the Ruskies came he didn't have time to take everything with him. In that cupboard there were...'

'...some Tsarist roubles,' laughed Barbara, 'a pile of gold. Will you take it with you? There'll be a bit less mould in the junk heap. It's there, in the shed by the canal. I'm making dinner – will you have some soup afterwards?'

Anusewicz cleared his throat affirmatively and, leading Winterhaus across the yard, headed for the tin box of a garage that Barbara so generously called the shed. Indeed, it was chock-full of junk. Apart from carpenter's tools, empty crates, withered boat ribs, car parts, hoes, spades, canvas sacks, bottles and jam jars there were also several broken stools, a chair full of holes, a ripped sofa, a clapped-out moped, a children's wicker pushchair, some skis, a small cast-iron stove, hooks and lines for catching eels, a radio in an ebonite box, as well as a chipped bidet and an easel.

'Oh!' said Winterhaus. 'This is something!'

'But where's the cupboard?' said Anusewicz, flapping his arms about helplessly. 'I can't see it anywhere.'

It took them a while to notice it: a piece of cloth of a sky-blue colour, with a white dove and the inscription 'PEACE-MIR'. The dove was holding a twig in its beak, though it was hard to tell if it was an olive one, and the whole drawing was ringed by a symbolic laurel wreath.

'Well,' said Anusewicz, tearing the banner off the cupboard, 'we've got you at last! Where should it be?'

'Here, at the bottom,' said Winterhaus, pointing. 'Ve've got to remove the first layer of the floor. That's vhat I dreamed. Und that's vhat my father said.'

They found a chisel and some hammers and rapidly got down to work. Under the first layer of plywood there was a second, then yet another one, and finally to the amazed Anusewicz, and the no less amazed Winterhaus, several rows of narrow compartments appeared, in which the coins lay wrapped in bandages, like the beads on an abacus. Every crack had been stuffed with cotton wool and then filled with putty.

'Your dad was a pretty good conspirator,' said Anusewicz, digging out one bundle after another. 'You could have turned this box upside down and even then nothing would have rattled. Look, look, here are some bigger ones. . .'

They made space on a carpentry table and laid out the little round parcels one after another. Once they had extracted the last one, Anusewicz patted Winterhaus on the back and added:

'You start.'

With trembling fingers, Winterhaus unwound the first rag. A silver coin the size of a dollar fell onto the table.

'Well I never, well I never,' whispered Anusewicz. The reverse showed Christ in a long robe, holding a royal orb; around him ran the imprecation, "DEFENDE NOS CHRISTE SALVATOR." On the obverse there were two lions rampant, holding up the emblem of the city, entwined with the inscription, "MONETA NOVA CIVI GEDANENSIS." Above the animals' manes there was also a date: 1577.

'It's from a time of var,' stated Winterhaus. 'Instead of the Polish king they minted it vith the image of Jesus.'

'War, yes, yes, war,' said Anusewicz, unwinding the next bit of rag, from which he extracted a small coin, clearly considerably older, because it had a very worn-out face. 'And what might this one be?'

Winterhaus took off his glasses, used the left lens as a magnifying glass, and said:

'This is the coin of a Pomeranian duke. You see the griffin? Oh, it says here: "DANCEKE DOMINI ZWANTOPELK." Take a look.'

Once he had positioned the lens at the right distance, Anusewicz positively whistled in admiration. With his proudly unfurled standard and shield of the House of Griffins, the Kashubian Duke Świętopełk was spurring on his horse.

'In those days,' he muttered, 'my ancestors still worshipped sacred serpents.'

But Winterhaus hadn't heard him. As he undid the next few bundles, onto the table fell jingling groshy, thalers, half thalers, three-groshy coins and ducats, and it looked like silver rain, with a chance piece of gold glittering here and there among them. The Jagiellonians, the Saxons, the Waza Kings and the Griffins, Prussian Commanders and Electors all lay beside each other amicably now, as if they had never been divided by drawn swords, battlefields, customs duties, intrigue, treacherous murders and battleships sunk at the bottom of the bay. There were no duplicates. Only a five-ducat piece with the head of King Władysław and a panorama of the city on the reverse featured in three, non-identical specimens.

'*Schlaflosigkeit*' sighed Winterhaus contentedly, 'I don't think I'm going to suffer from it any more.'

'Oh no, surely not.' Anusewicz was restoring the cupboard to its former appearance. 'But how will you export it all? You have to have special permission. Are there any documents confirming ownership? Because if not, you might have a problem.'

'Oh, I hadn't thought about that at all. You know? The main thing is, I've checked up on my dream. Now I know my father vasn't a madman.'

'You're not going to give them to a museum, are you?'

'A museum? Vhy not? The Tramdriver Vinterhaus Collection – it could be very famous.'

This gentle dispute would probably have rambled on, if the agitated Bernard hadn't come crashing into the tin hut as if pursued by fire.

'Oh, wow.' He let out a long whistle. 'What fine documents you've found in *my* cupboard. And she believed you were looking for some photographs, the stupid woman.' He tapped his forehead. 'I knew you were up to something in here, so I dash down, and there you have it – there's something going on behind my back. I'm Benek,' he offered Winterhaus his hand. 'Taxicab at your service.'

'Vinterhaus,' said Winterhaus.

'Now don't go over the top,' said Anusewicz, trying to appease his brother-in-law. 'That cupboard wasn't mine or yours.'

Bernard couldn't tear his eyes from the coins. He picked them up, inspected them and moved them from place to place.

'Really? In that case, whose was it? As Mr Winterhaus didn't take it with him, first it belonged to the Jew, then that chap from Poznań, and then you. And you gave it to me. Simple, eh? Clear as day. There should be a finder's reward, surely. I don't want anyone to lose. What do you think, *her* Winterhaus?'

'Veil, qvite, qvite, I do not know your law. I think Mister Bernard should receive something. Mister Anusevicz too. Though on the other hand I think this is a complete collection. Do you understand me, gentlemen? I think here there are *alles* the coins minted in Danzig – in Gdansk,' he corrected himself, 'from Duke Świętopełk to the Free City. I propose offering you three thousand marks to share, *gut?*'

'Three thousand marks? In the commie era that was real money,' said Bernard, turning a Saxon Elector's ducat in his hand, 'but nowadays? Nowadays you couldn't buy a new car for that.'

'What is it that makes you Kashubians even more rapacious than vultures?' Anusewicz let loose. 'Come on, Benek, where's our sense of honour? Where's our sense of honour?'

'You lay off the Kashubians! Just look at him, barefoot Antek from beyond the River Bug. A noble gesture, eh? The nobles drained Poland dry long ago, and now the sun shines out of their arses. Fancied themselves as "brothers and gentlemen", ha ha ha!'

'Yes? Yes?' Anusewicz jumped up, gobbling like a turkeycock. 'And who sided with the Germans? Who murdered Leszek the White?'

'Someone vas murdered?' asked Winterhaus, shifting nervously from foot to foot. 'That is politics, do not qvarrel, do not qvarrel.'

But the brothers-in-law weren't listening to their guest any more, just to their own hot blood. Bernard could put up with a lot aimed at himself and his compatriots, but never the idea of ascribing the murder of the Polish Prince Leszek to the Kashubian Duke Świętopełk. Whereas Anusewicz could turn a deaf ear to the remarks about barefoot Antek and a noble gesture, but never to such a base insinuation that the nobles, the brothers and gentlemen, had drunk away the old Poland. And so it began. First with a shove, which led to an exchange of blows.

When Barbara came into the shed, she saw her husband and Anusewicz on the floor, locked together in a wrestling clinch. Clutching his head in both hands, Winterhaus was running around the brothers-in-law repeating:

'*Alles in Ordnung! Alles in Ordnung!* Vhy this *Lärm*. Vhy this *Krawall*? I vill give four thousand marks. Four und a half thousand!'

But that didn't help at all, nor did Barbara's shouts and pushes. The fight was no longer about the money, but about which would come out on top – the Kashubian hotheadedness or the Borderlands quick temper? Which heraldic emblem – the winged Griffin of Pomerania or the mounted Chaser of Pahonia? And it's impossible to say where it would have ended if not for Barbara. Her practical, female reason prompted a simple, effective solution. She ran out of the shed for a moment and came back armed with a rubber garden hose. A jet of cold water soon made the brothers-in-law stop fighting. They spluttered as they wiped their faces, where there wasn't a trace of satisfaction to be seen.

'In five minutes I'm going to serve the dinner, and I don't want to hear a word about this,' said the arbitrator, pointing at the coins.

And so the first spoonfuls of beetroot soup went down their throats in total silence. The only sound to creep onto the veranda and interrupt the clatter of cutlery and discreet slurping was the whistling of swallows, as they flitted between the eaves of the house and the canal. Mr Winterhaus glanced at Anusewicz's black eye and Bernard's torn shirt, then again at the spreading maple, in whose shade a swaggering cockerel was preening his magnificent feathers.

'*Ja,*' he said at last, downing a glass of plain vodka, 'my father vas a strange man. That tram,' he mused, 'the night tram that vas blown up by a bomb. . .'

'Was it a barricade tram?' asked Anusewicz. 'I saw some of those the year after the war, buried in rubble.'

The eel fricassee served before the main course delayed Mr Winterhaus' answer a bit, though in fact it wasn't an answer, but a story that he only interrupted to dig out bones, clink glasses and make lip-smacking noises.

That night before the attack, when the Russian artillery were cleaning the barrels of their cannon and calculating their trajectories, Direktor Winterhaus made his way to the tram depot and roamed around the empty halls, immobile points and switched-off lamps; and when he came upon the last tramcar that had not been militarised, he hopped aboard, raised the bow collector and set off for the city, remembering the old days when he was still an ordinary tram driver. First he travelled the No 3 route, then the No 5, and next the 7, halting at all the stops and calling out their names; and he drove like that from Friedenschloss to Weichselbahnhof, from Broesen to Ohra and Emaus, changing the points himself at the sidings and punching the tickets; and the Schupo and SS night patrols saluted him, because the prudent Direktor Winterhaus had put a picture of the Führer in the front window of the tram between two oil lamps, like in a Catholic church, so they thought it was a propaganda run to keep up the fighting spirit, which was highly recommended, which was sorely needed, as there were already deserters and defeatists hanging from the hundred-year-old boughs along Grosse Allee, with signs on their chests reading: 'I refused to die for the Führer and the Fatherland', and their shoes rapped against the tramcar windows like drops of March rain or sleet; and like this Direktor Winterhaus's tram flashed down the defiles between buildings, past parks and along the city avenues, right up to the moment when the ground shook and the first shells hit the Lower Town and Granary Island, right up to the moment when great tongues of flame began to consume the red Gothic of the Hanseatic League; and that was when Direktor Winterhaus threw the picture of the Führer in the mud, blew out the oil lamps and hung a white sheet on the tramcar, but it wasn't much help, because the tramlines had already been torn up, ripped apart by grenades, and he couldn't go any further, so he jumped off the tram and ran for home; and just then a shell exploded behind him, and the last civilian tram in the city of Danzig flew into thousands of tiny pieces of glass, metal and wood, and Direktor Winterhaus stopped, shocked by this sudden transformation, and realised that this was the absolute end of his tramcar career, which he had started as an assistant mechanic, and the absolute end of this city, which would never be what it had been again.

'Beautiful,' sighed Anusewicz. 'The shoes of the hanged defeatists peeking in the windows, and that white sheet.'

'I can't see anything beautiful in that,' cut in Bernard, getting down to some chops, like everyone else. 'They got it up the arse because they deserved it. But that was too little. Too little. They should have all been sent to Siberia as Stalin wanted.'

'It is very cold there,' said Winterhaus.

This matter-of-fact comment prompted general merriment at the table. They joked about the Russians and Siberia for a good while, and once the vodka and puddings were finished, Bernard tapped the homemade wine, and amid the buzzing of flies and the chirping of cicadas, the warm afternoon by the canal took on its full bucolic splendour.

To this day no one knows who hit upon the idea of the boating escapade. Was it Anusewicz, who was thinking back to the boats on Saint John's Eve at Rudzieńszczyzna? Or Bernard, who had fished in Kashubia since childhood? Or maybe Mr Winterhaus, whose memory prompted some rather vague images of stone sluices, drawbridges and canals as the landscape of this part of the city? In any case, it came out of nowhere. As she bustled around the table, Barbara suddenly noticed that the three gentlemen, who shortly before were dozing in their cane armchairs, had disappeared from the veranda. Their voices, loud and cheerful, were now coming from the water's edge. She ran over there and saw Bernard and Anusewicz dragging a rubber dinghy out of the shed.

'You must be mad!' she cried. 'Going fishing in that state? There's no question of it.'

But her female spirit, wanting to curb the spirit of the restless men once again that day, had to give way, because a boyish spirit craving variety and adventure had jointly entered the three gentlemen.

'What fishing?' growled Bernard. 'We just want a bit of a ride, to cool off.'

'Yes, yes,' added Anusewicz. 'The view of the city from this side is unusual.'

Finally, once the army dinghy had been inflated and Bernard had fixed an outboard motor to the stern, the gentlemen got on board. Barbara managed to hand them a thermos of coffee and some shortbread from the jetty, just in case. For a while the engine refused to fire up, and the dinghy spun around its own axis.

'What a bloody load of crap,' Bernard ranted. 'I haven't used it since last year.'

But this obstacle gave way too. After the umpteenth tug at the rope, the air was rent apart by a dreadful roar, and then amid a cloud of petrol fumes and a whirring noise the dinghy moved forward majestically, cutting across a green curtain of duckweed. Leaning out over the semicircular prow, Anusewicz commanded:

'Go right, Bernard, right I say, there are some bits of old stakes in the middle.'

Bernard nodded agreeably, but his brother-in-law's warnings didn't unduly bother him. He knew every bit of sunken scrap metal and every dangerous tree root on these waters. It wasn't for nothing that he'd fished for eels here, in every legitimate and illegitimate way. Finally, once they had sailed along the river to the sluice, as he gazed at the bastions covered in reeds, grass and burdock, Mr Winterhaus said:

'I vas here on a picnic vith my father. But it looked completely different then.'

'Yes,' explained Bernard. 'Nowadays you can't sail into the city this way. The sluice isn't navigable. But we can carry the dinghy to the other side – in fact why don't we?'

Not without some mild puffing and panting, the three gentlemen carried the rubber boat across a bank of earth, over the stone rim surrounding the sluice, and dropped it back into the water beside the bindweed-choked ruins of a building that looked like an old granary. The view they now had in sight delighted Winterhaus in particular. In a dense tunnel of greenery, there before them lay the brown thread of the Motława river, reflecting the Gothic brickwork of church and town hall towers among the clouds.

'I have made a decision – I brought ze treasure,' said Winterhaus, and to Anusewicz and Bernard's amazement, from his inside jacket pocket he brought out a little canvas sack, with the old coins jingling inside it like a heavily laden swarm of bees getting ready for flight. Anusewicz and Bernard exchanged glances, but there was no time to investigate why Winterhaus had brought the money with him, or when and in what imperceptible way he had done it.

As the motorised dinghy sailed under the bridge at Elbąska Street and passed the ugly tower blocks on Kamienna Grobla, the landing stage and the old granaries on Chmielna Street, Mr Winterhaus took his father's coins out of the grey bag at random, and sorted them into three piles, monotonously chanting:

'This is for me, this is for Mr Benek, this is for Anusevicz. This is for me, this is for Mr Benek, this is for Anusevicz.'

Unseen, they slipped past Ołowianka, and at the level of the Polish Hook, where instead of embankments, granaries and buildings, huge ships' hulls began to surround them, Anusewicz felt worried that they may have gone too far, and may not be allowed to sail here in such a cockleshell, especially one made of rubber. Bernard was of a different opinion: they'd go and see the walls of the fortress and then turn back level with the monument, because if you want an outing, that's an outing, and as for navigation, he used to sail here ten years ago on the pusher-tug 'Buhaj' and knew every buoy here, as well as all the customs men and the port police. As they reached Westerplatte, Mr Winterhaus finished dividing the coins and handed the brothers-in-law their shares of the treasure.

'We must celebrate this,' said Benek, extracting a hip flask from his inside pocket. 'Well, here's to reconciliation. Look over there, Mr Winterhaus – that's the monument to our heroes, they were the first people in Europe, Mr Winterhaus, to tell Hitler: *No pasaran.*'

'Oh yes, I know it vasn't like Czechoslovakia here – ve could even hear those shots at our house.'

'And that's where the battleship Schleswig-Holstein was moored,' said Anusewicz, pointing.

'On a nice, friendly visit, *herzlich willkommen!*' added Bernard, turning the rudder so that the dinghy described a wide semicircle and was now sailing towards the city.

The little tin cup from the hip flask did the rounds smoothly from hand to hand, and soon the harbour smell of grease, rather dirty water and fish was mixed with the aroma of the coffee that Anusewicz poured into a mug from Barbara's thermos.

'A beautiful day, a beautiful day,' repeated Winterhaus. 'I never dreamed about anything like this.'

'Life is more beautiful than dreams,' said Anusewicz confidently, 'as you can see for yourself.'

He was going to add something else, but the dreamy Winterhaus began to chant in a pure, strong voice:

> Das Wandern ist des Müllers Lust,
> das Wandern, das Wandern

and tossed his head to encourage the brothers-in-law to join in with him, at which Anusewicz and Bernard chorused:

> das Wandern, das Wandern

at which Winterhaus even more joyfully jumped to the first line of the second verse:

> Vom Wasser haben wir's gelernt

and in a now perfectly harmonised trio all the sailors chorused:

> Vom Wasser haben wir's gelernt,
> vom Wasser, vom Wasser.

And although it wasn't a rushing stream, beside which there should have been a mill and a half-timbered house, but a port canal, where from the banks instead of fir trees steel cranes shot into the sky, at that moment all three really did feel like wanderers descending from the mountains and coming across an enchanting, isolated farmhouse, and there inside. . .

However, the song was never finished. At the words about the master and the mistress, something grated on the port side, hissed and puffed, and seconds later the dinghy began to sink surprisingly quickly in the dark-green swirl of the

Motława. Bernard didn't even have time to unhitch the motor, which with a hiss and a gurgle dragged the floppy sheet of rubber to the bottom.

'Jesus Christ, Mr Winterhaus! Can you swim?' cried Anusewicz.

But doggy-paddling in hectic circles, Winterhaus hadn't heard the question, though he kept repeating:

'*Mein Gott, mein Gott,* all is lost, *alles.*'

And indeed, there was nothing to save. The little sack containing Winterhaus' coins and the plastic bag filled with Bernard's share had gone to the bottom just as rapidly as the dinghy burdened with its motor. Only Anusewicz, who had parcelled out his portion among all his jacket pockets, had not lost anything, but when they started swimming towards the quay, all this ballast weighed him down dreadfully. He kicked off his shoes, and once he had recovered a bit of vigour after the initial shock, he tried using one hand to empty his brim-full pockets. But it wasn't easy. His jacket had gone as stiff as armour, and Anusewicz found that he was having more and more difficulty keeping above the surface. Finally, with immense effort, he pulled first his left, then his right arm out of the sleeves, and now, very much lighter, he was the last to swim to shore.

Struggling and striving, they finally overcame the slimy ledge protruding from the quay. They lay on the grass and stared at the sky in silence.

'It has all drownded,' said Winterhaus at last.

'When I get hold of the Ruski who sold me that army surplus boat, I'll smash his face in,' threatened Bernard.

They got up and went on their way, Winterhaus holding one salvaged shoe, Bernard barefoot, and Anusewicz in grey socks. While the shade of the chestnut trees and the walls of the warehouses on Wiosna Ludów Street, where they had landed, were still protecting them, they didn't yet feel the worst, but once they crossed the small bridge over the Radunia Canal, and in the light of the setting sun walked into the Fish Market, full of tourists and traders, they couldn't help feeling that everyone's gaze was aimed directly at them. Fortunately it wasn't far to the small hotel on Straganiarska Street where Mr Winterhaus was staying, and in a few minutes they were there. Once they were in his room, with a view onto the leaning tower of Saint John's, Anusewicz found that he still had one coin left in his shirt pocket.

'It should be for you,' he said, handing the golden disc to Winterhaus, 'as a souvenir.'

'No, no, please keep it,' said Winterhaus, who was changing his trousers. 'I'll call a taxi for you, und this evening I am inviting you out for supper.'

'For supper?' said the brothers-in-law in amazement.

'I vill ask you to write a short statement for my vife. Saying that the money vas found, und then sank, *gut*? So she does not think I am not normal. It's enough that she thinks about my father like that.'

'May he rest in peace,' muttered Bernard, as they got into the taxi.

Anusewicz was quiet; his heart was beating irregularly, he felt breathless and wanted to be at home as soon as possible. He didn't listen to the taxi driver and Bernard's prattle when they got stuck in a traffic jam near the shipyard and the three crosses. Just as on waking that morning, some strange thoughts were bothering him again. Was Nina trying to tell him something important? Did Father

Wołkonowicz appearing beside her in the meadow portend some change in his life? It was true that the day had been a mad one in every respect, but could that really have been the reason why after so many years those two had crossed deep, gloomy rivers of oblivion to appear in his dream? And what on earth could it mean – the coins of a German who had a Polish grandmother, falling into the muddy ooze at the bottom of the port river?

Under drooping eyelids, Anusewicz saw the meadows of Rudzieńszczyzna spread out along the meandering Rudejka River, peasants raking hay, and Mr Żubrowicz, who had driven down by wagonette from Kniaziowska Góra, humming:

> It's Anusewicz, there he sprawls,
> The lazy old idler, scratching his balls.

It was an old, neighbourly squabble, and Anusewicz's father would customarily reply:

> It's Żubrowicz, that silly old chump,
> Drank away his farm and bought up a swamp.

What had originally happened and why the Anusewiczes didn't like the Żubrowiczes, he had no idea, and he knew he would never find out.

Locked away in his own thoughts, he said goodbye to Bernard and went inside the pleasantly cool flat. He drank a few sips of beer and lay down on the sofa. The Grim Reaper, left standing on his desk, gazed at Anusewicz with his immobile, glassy expression.

'Hey, old man,' he said affectionately, 'I got away from you today, you know. By a whisker, or I'd have drowned.'

And then he felt something strange. First the sofa began to spin, and with it the entire room. Once again the military band began to boom, invisible this time. The Grim Reaper jumped down to the floor, began whirling in triple time and started to grow, getting bigger by the second, and once he had reached human dimensions, he threw off his sheet-like habit. It was no longer the Grim Reaper, but Nina, aged twenty, beautiful and alluring, dancing on the carpet, as if specially for him. He wanted to go up to her, and just as in his dream, which he remembered perfectly, to touch her body. Nina began to laugh and made off into the dining room. Anusewicz went after her, but behind the wall the dining room was no longer there, just the meandering river and the meadow, the same one he remembered from his dream. On it he saw the Żubrowiczes, the Anusewiczes and all the others – those he remembered and those he had long since forgotten. Nina gave him her hand and led him towards them, but Father Wołkonowicz barred their way and told Anusewicz to look behind him. He saw his own body, which no longer belonged to him, and his wife Zofia leaning over him. She sat down on the sofa, and removed a gold coin from her husband's clenched fingers. The royal portrait did not attract her attention, but the view of the city on the reverse seemed strangely familiar. Above earthworks, forts and canals, above the tower of the Holy Virgin Mary, Saint Nicholas', Saint Catherine's and the Town Hall, above the port, the suburb and the Long Market she saw three Hebrew letters, illuminating it all from a cloud of laurel branches, blessing the city and the world. She couldn't decipher them, but guessing what they meant, she whispered that ineffable name and, holding back her tears, closed her husband's eyelids.

'Do you want to go back there?' Anusewicz heard a powerful voice, that didn't belong to Father Wołkonowicz.

'No,' he replied, 'of course not.'

And off he went, across the soft, damp meadow of Rudzieńszczyzna.

ON THE ROAD AT EIGHTEEN

Yu Hua

Translated from the Chinese by Andrew F. Jones

Yu Hua (1960–). Born in Hangzhou, Yu Hua worked as a government dentist for several years before escaping to become a writer in the 1980s, because he did not enjoy "looking into people's mouths the whole day". He was marked by the fact that he grew up during the Cultural Revolution, a theme that recurs in his writing – particularly his two-volume novel *Brothers*, which was a huge bestseller when first published in 2005–6, though it drew harsh criticism in China for its crude humour. Yu Hua has written four novels, six collections of stories, and three collections of essays.

The asphalt road rolls up and down like it's pasted on top of ocean waves. Walking down this little highway in the mountains, I'm like a boat. This year, I turned eighteen. The few brownish whiskers that have sprouted on my chin flutter in the breeze. They've only just taken up residence on my chin, so I really treasure them. I've spent the whole day walking down the road, and I've already seen lots of mountains and lots of clouds. Every one of the mountains and every one of the clouds made me think of people I know. I shouted out each of their nicknames as I walked by. So even though I've walked all day, I'm not tired, not at all. I walked through the morning, now it's the tail end of the afternoon, and it won't be long until I see the tip of dusk. But I haven't found an inn.

I've encountered quite a few people along the road, but none of them has known where the road goes or whether there's an inn there. They all tell me: "Keep walking. You'll see when you get there." I think what everyone said was just terrific. I really am just seeing when I get there. But I haven't found an inn. I feel like I should be worried about that.

I think it's weird that I've walked all day and only seen one car. That was around noon, when I'd just begun to think about hitchhiking. But all I was doing was thinking about hitchhiking. I hadn't started to worry about finding an inn – I was only thinking about how amazing it would be to get a lift from someone. I stood by the side of the road waving at the car, trying my best to look casual. But the driver hardly even looked at me. The car or the driver. They hardly even looked at me. All they fucking did was drive right by. So I ran, chasing the car as fast as I could, just for fun, because I still hadn't started to worry about finding an inn. I ran until the car had disappeared, and then I laughed at myself, but I discovered that laughing too hard made it difficult to breathe, so I stopped. After that I kept walking, happy and excited, except that I started to regret that I hadn't picked up a rock before I started waving at the car.

Now I really want a lift, because dusk is about to fall and I can't get that inn out of my goddamned head. But there haven't been any cars all afternoon. If a car came now, I think I could make it stop. I'd lie down in the middle of the road, and I'm willing to bet that any car would come to a screeching halt before it got to my head. But I don't even hear the rumble of an engine, let alone see a car. Now I'm just going to have to keep walking and see when I get there. Not bad at all: keep walking and see when you get there.

The road rolls up and down from hill to valley, and the hills tempt me every time, because before I charge up to the top, I think I'll see an inn on the other side. But each time I charge up the slope, all I see is another hill in the distance, with a depressing trough in between. And still I charge up each hill as if my life depended on it. And now I'm charging up another one, but this time I see it. Not an inn, but a truck. The truck is pointed toward me, stalled in the middle of the highway in a gully between two hills. I can see the driver's ass pointing skyward and, behind it, all the colors of the approaching sunset. I can't see the driver's head because it's stuffed under the hood. The truck's hood slants up into the air like an upside-down lip. The back of the truck is piled full of big wicker baskets. I'm thinking that they definitely must be packed with some kind of fruit. Of course, bananas would be best of all. There are probably some in the cab, too, so when I hop in, I can eat a few. And I don't really care if the truck's going in the opposite direction as me. I need to find an inn, and if there's no inn, I need a truck. And the truck's right here in front of me.

Elated, I run down to the truck and say, "Hi!"

The driver doesn't seem to have heard me. He's still fiddling with something under the hood.

"Want a smoke?"

Only now does he pull his head out from under the hood, stretch out a black, grimy hand, and take the cigarette between his fingers. I rush to give him a light, and he sucks several mouthfuls of smoke into his mouth before stuffing his head back under the hood.

I'm satisfied. Since he accepted the smoke, that means he has to give me a lift. So I wander around to the back of the truck to investigate what's in the wicker baskets. But they're covered, and I can't see, so I sniff. I smell the fragrance of apples. And I think: Apples aren't too bad either.

In just a little bit, he's done repairing the truck, and he jumps down from the hood. I rush over and say, "Hey, I need a ride." What I don't expect is that he gives me a hard shove with those grimy hands and barks, "Go away!"

I'm so angry I'm speechless, but he just swings on over to the driver's side, opens the door, slides into the cab, and starts the engine. I know that if I blow this opportunity, I'll never get another one. I know I should just give up. So I run over to the other side, open the door, and hop in. I'm ready to fight if necessary. I turn to him and yell: "Then give me back my cigarette!" The truck's already started to move by now.

He turns to look at me with a big, friendly smile and asks, "Where you headed?"

I'm bewildered by this turnaround. I say, "Doesn't matter. Wherever."

He asks me very nicely, "Want an apple?" He's still glancing over at me.

"That goes without saying."

"Go get one from the back."

How am I supposed to climb out of the cab to the back of the truck when he's driving so fast? So I say, "Forget it."

He says, "Go get one." He's still looking at me.

I say, "Stop staring at me. There's no road on my face."

With this, he twists his eyes back onto the highway.

The truck's driving back in the direction I just came from; I'm sitting comfortably in the cab, looking out the window and chatting with the driver. By now, we're already the best of friends. I've found out that he's a private entrepreneur. It's his own truck. The apples are his, too. I hear change jingling in his pockets. I ask him, "Where are you going?"

He says, "I just keep driving and see when I get there."

It sounds just like what everyone else said. That's so nice. I feel closer to him. I want everything I see outside the window to be just as close, just as familiar, and soon all those hills and clouds start to bring more friends to mind, so I shout out their nicknames as we drive by.

Now I'm not crying out for an inn anymore. What with the truck, the driver, the seat in the cab, I'm completely at peace. I don't know where the truck's going, and neither does he. Anyway, it doesn't matter, because all we have to do is keep driving, and we'll see when we get there.

But the truck broke down. By that time, we were as close as friends can be. My arm was draped over his shoulder and his over mine. He was telling me about his love life, and right when he'd got to the part about how it felt the first time he held a woman's body in his arms, the truck broke down. The truck was climbing up a hill when it broke down. All of a sudden the squeal of the engine went quiet like a pig right after it's been slaughtered. So he jumped out of the truck, climbed onto the hood, opened up that upside-down lip, and stuffed his head back under it. I couldn't see his ass. But I could hear the sound of him fiddling with the engine.

After a while, he pulled his head out from under the hood and slammed it shut. His hands were even blacker than before. He wiped them on his pants, wiped again, jumped down, and walked back to the cab.

"Is it fixed?" I asked.

"It's shot. There's no way to fix it."

I thought that over and finally asked, "Now what do we do?"

"Wait and see," he said, nonchalantly.

I was sitting in the cab wondering what to do. Then I started to think about finding an inn again. The sun was just falling behind the mountains, and the hazy dusk clouds looked like billows of steam. The notion of an inn stole back into my head and began to swell until my mind was stuffed full of it. By then, I didn't even have a mind. An inn was growing where my mind used to be.

At that point, the driver started doing the official morning calisthenics that they always play on the radio right there in the middle of the highway. He went from the first exercise to the last without missing a beat. When he was finished, he started to jog circles around the truck. Maybe he had been sitting too long in the driver's seat and needed some exercise. Watching him moving from my vantage point inside the truck, I couldn't sit still either, so I opened the door and jumped out. But I didn't do calisthenics or jog in place. I was thinking about an inn and an inn and an inn.

Just then, I noticed five people rolling down the hill on bicycles. Each bike had a carrying pole fastened to the back with two big baskets on either end. I thought they were probably local peasants on their way back from selling vegetables at market. I was delighted to see people riding by, so I welcomed them with a big "Hi!" They rode up beside me and dismounted. Excited, I greeted them and asked, "Is there an inn around here?"

Instead of responding they asked me, "What's in the truck?"

I said, "Apples."

All five of them pushed their bikes over to the side of the truck. Two of them climbed onto the back, picked up about ten baskets full of apples, and passed them upside down to the ones below, who proceeded to tear open the plastic covering the top of the wicker and pour the apples into their own baskets. I was dumbstruck. When I finally realized exactly what was going on, I made for them and asked, "Just what do you think you're doing?"

None of them paid the slightest bit of attention to me. They continued to pour the apples. I tried to grab hold of someone's arm and screamed, "They're stealing all the apples!" A fist came crashing into my nose, and I landed several feet away. I staggered up, rubbed my nose. It felt soft and sticky, like it wasn't stuck to my face anymore but only dangling from it. Blood was flowing like tears from a broken heart. When I looked up to see which of them had hit me, they were already astride their bikes, riding away.

The driver was taking a walk, lips curling out as he sucked in deep draughts of air. He had probably lost his breath running. He didn't seem to be at all aware of what had just happened. I yelled toward him, "They stole your apples!" But he kept on walking without paying any attention to what I had yelled. I really wanted to run over and punch him so hard that his nose would be left dangling, too. I ran over and screamed into his ear, "They stole your apples." Only then did he turn to look at me, and I realized that his face was getting happier and happier the longer he looked at my nose.

At that point, yet another group of bicycles descended down the slope. Each bike had two big baskets fastened to the back. There were even a few children among the riders. They swarmed by me and surrounded the truck. A lot of people climbed onto the back, and the wicker baskets flew faster than I could count them. Apples poured out of broken baskets like blood out of my nose. They stuffed apples into their own baskets as if they were possessed. In just a few seconds, all the apples in the truck had been lowered to the ground. Then a few motorized tractor carts chugged down the hill and stopped next to the truck. A few big men dismounted and started to stuff apples into the carts. One by one, the empty wicker baskets were tossed to the side. The ground was covered with rolling apples, and the peasants scrabbled on their hands and knees like ants to pick them all up.

It was at that point that I rushed into their midst, risking life and limb, and cursed them, "Thieves!" I started swinging. My attack was met with countless fists and feet. It seemed like every part of my body got hit at the same time. I climbed back up off the ground. A few children began to hurl apples at me. The apples broke apart on my head, but my head didn't break. Just as I was about to rush the kids, a foot came crashing into my waist. I wanted to cry, but when I opened my mouth, nothing came out. There was nothing to do but fall to the ground and watch them steal the apples. I started to look around for the driver. He was standing a good distance away, looking right at me, and laughing as hard as he could. Just so I knew that I looked even better now than I had with a bloody nose.

I didn't even have the strength for anger. All I could do was gaze out at everything that was making me so angry. And what made me the angriest of all was the driver.

Another wave of bicycles and tractors rolled down the hill and threw themselves into the disaster area. There were fewer and fewer apples rolling on the ground. A few people left. A few more arrived. The ones who had arrived too late for apples began to busy themselves with the truck. I saw them remove the window glass, strip the tires, pry away the planks that covered the truck bed. Without its tires, the truck obviously felt really low, because it sank to the ground. A few children began to gather the wicker baskets that had been tossed to the side a moment before. As the road got cleaner and cleaner, there were fewer and fewer people. But all I could do was watch, because I didn't even have the strength for anger. I sat on the ground without moving, letting my eyes wander back and forth between the driver and the thieves.

Now, there's nothing left but a single tractor parked beside the sunken truck. Someone's looking around to see if there's anything left to take. He looks for a while and then hops on his tractor and starts the engine.

The truck driver hops onto the back of the tractor and looks back toward me, laughing. He's holding my red backpack in his hand. He's stealing my backpack. My clothes and my money are in the backpack. And food and books. But he's stealing my backpack.

I'm watching the tractor climb back up the slope. It disappears over the crest. I can still hear the rumble of its engine, but soon I can't even hear that. All of a sudden, everything's quiet, and the sky starts to get really dark. I'm still sitting on the ground. I'm hungry, and I'm cold, but there's nothing left.

I sit there for a long time before I slowly stand up. It isn't easy because my whole body aches like crazy every time I move, but still I stand up and limp over to the truck. The truck looks miserable, battered. I know I've been battered too.

The sky's black now. There's nothing here. Just a battered truck and battered me. I'm looking at the truck, immeasurably sad, and the truck's looking at me, immeasurably sad. I reach out to stroke it. It's cold all over. The wind starts to blow, a strong wind, and the sound of the wind rustling the trees in the mountains is like ocean waves. The sound terrifies me so much that my body gets as cold as the truck's.

I open the door and hop in. I'm comforted by the fact that they didn't pry away the seat. I lie down in the cab. I smell leaking gas and think of the smell of the blood that leaked out of me. The wind's getting stronger and stronger, but I feel a little warmer lying on the seat. I think that even though the truck's been battered, its heart is still intact, still warm. I know that my heart's warm, too. I was looking for an inn, and I never thought I'd find you here.

I lie inside the heart of the truck, remembering that clear warm afternoon. The sunlight was so pretty. I remember that I was outside enjoying myself in the sunshine for a long time, and when I got home I saw my dad through the window packing things into a red backpack. I leaned against the window frame and asked, "Dad, are you going on a trip?"

He turned and very gently said, "No, I'm letting you go on a trip."

"Letting me go on a trip?"

"That's right. You're eighteen now, and it's time you saw a little of the outside world."

Later I slipped that pretty red backpack onto my back. Dad patted my head from behind, just like you would pat a horse's rump. Then I gladly made for the door and excitedly galloped out of the house, as happy as a horse.

THE MAN WITH
THE LIGHT

José Eduardo Agualusa

Translated from the Portuguese by Daniel Hahn

José Eduardo Agualusa (1960–). Considered one of Africa's most important writers, Agualusa was born in Huambo, in modern-day Angola. He studied agronomy and silviculture in Lisbon. Both as a novelist and a reporter Agualusa has become an important voice of his country. He has a weekly column in the Brazilian newspaper *O Globo*. In 2007, Agualusa and his translator won the Independent Foreign Fiction Prize for *The Book of Chameleons*. His novel *A General Theory of Oblivion* was shortlisted for the Man Booker International Prize 2016 and won the International Dublin Literary Award 2017. His books have been published in almost thirty countries and he now lives on the Island of Mozambique, where he works as a writer and journalist. He also has been working to establish a public library on the island.

For Miguel Petchkovsky and Paula Tavares

Nicolau Alicerces Peshkov had an enormous head, or maybe it had simply caused the rest of him to shrivel away, but either way, it definitely looked as though it had been attached to the wrong body by mistake. His hair, what was left of it, was weedy and red, his face covered in freckles. His unlikely name, his even more extraordinary physiognomy, the whole lot was due to the travels through the Huambo highlands of an itinerant Russian, who in his alcoholic ravings boasted of having served as an officer in Nicholas II's cavalry. Besides the name and the freckles, Nicolau Alicerces Peshkov had inherited his father's passion for cinema and his old projector. It was precisely that name, those freckles, and that projector, which is to say, his Russian heritage, that nearly landed him in front of a firing squad.

He had just spent two days and a night hiding in a crate of dried fish. He'd been woken with a start by a crackle of gunfire. He didn't know where he was. This was always happening to him. He sat up in his bed and tried to remember, as the gunfire outside grew: he had arrived at dusk, pedalling his old bicycle, he'd rented a room in the boarding house run by a Portuguese man, he'd said goodbye to little James, who had family in the village, and gone to bed. It was a small room. The bedstead was iron, with a wooden board across the top and no mattress.

A sheet, which was clean but threadbare, flimsy, covering the board. An enamel chamber-pot. On the walls, somebody had painted a blue angel. A good picture. The angel looked straight at him, looked at something that wasn't there, with the same luminous and hopeless aloofness as Marlene Dietrich.

Nicolau Alicerces Peshkov, whom the Mucubal people called The Man with the Light, opened the window of his room, hoping to discover the reasons for the war. He peered out and saw that all along the road an armed mob was moving, some of them soldiers, mostly young civilians with red ribbons round their heads. One of the young men pointed, shouting, and another opened fire in his direction. Nicolau still didn't know what war this was, but he did know that, regardless, he was on the wrong side – he was the Indian here, and he had nothing better than a little tomahawk with which to defend himself. He left the bedroom, in his underpants, went into the kitchen, opened a door and discovered a long and narrow back yard, blocked at the far end by a high adobe wall. He managed to jump the wall, by climbing a pathetic-looking mango tree that grew alongside it, and found himself in another yard, this one broader, more run-down, next to a wattle-and-daub hut that looked like it was used as a storeroom. He thought about James Dean. What would the kid do in this situation? He'd definitely know what to do, James was an expert in getting away. He saw a laundry tank, filled to the top with water, covered by a tarp. James Dean would climb inside the tank, and stay there for as long as necessary, waiting to grow scales. He, however, would not fit into this prison. His body might, actually, but not his head. It was in this state of despair that, hearing the mob getting closer, he noticed the crate of fish. The smell was appalling, a strong stench of rotting seas, but there was just enough space for a crouching man. And so he climbed into the crate and waited.

Looking through a gap in the crate, he saw the mob with the ribbons arrive. They were dragging by the neck five poor guys whose only crime, it seemed, was speaking Umbundu, urging them on with kicks and blows from their rifle-butts. They lay the men down on their backs and resumed their beating, with their weapons, their belts, heavy sticks, shouting that this was just for starters. Soon after this, a woman with a pistol appeared and, with a glance, forced the aggressors aside, pressed the gun to the neck of one of the poor wretches and fired. Then did the same to the other four. Next, they brought forward two young boys and four older women, one carrying a small child on her back, all crying and wailing. When they saw the bodies, their screaming grew louder. One of the soldiers cocked his rifle: 'Anyone who mourns the dead dies too.'

The others began raining down blows on the group, not even sparing the child, while a guy with a video camera danced around them.

Nicolau Alicerces Peshkov turned away from the gap, and squeezed his eyes shut. It was no good: even with his eyes closed, he saw two of the beribboned young men rape one of the women; he saw them kill the child, with blows from their rifle butts, and the rest of the group with bullets and kicks.

He emerged from the box on the evening of the following day. He was so exhausted, and such was the torment in his puny breast, that he didn't notice the soldier who was sitting right next to the crate, watching over the corpses. The man looked at him with surprise, as happy as a little boy who'd just found the lucky charm in the fruitcake, and led him by the hand to the police station. At the door, a very tall, thin man with a full beard seemed to be waiting for them. They took him to a windowless room, sat him on a chair. The tall man asked his name.

'Peshkov? Nicolau Peshkov?! You're Russian, comrade? That's very convenient – I studied in Moscow, at the Lubyanka, I speak Russian better than Portuguese.'

And he unleashed a stream of impenetrable gibberish that seemed to amuse everybody. Seeing the others laugh, Nicolau Peshkov laughed, too, but only out of politeness, because what he really needed to do was cry.

The tall man abruptly turned serious. He pointed to a leather case on his desk. 'Do you know what this is?' Nicolau Peshkov recognised it as the case in which he kept his projector and his movies. He explained who he was. For forty years, he had been travelling the country with this contraption. He was proud to have brought the seventh art to the most remote and hidden corners of Angola – places forgotten by the rest of the world. In colonial times, he'd travelled by train. Benguela, Ganda, Chianga, Lépi, Catchiungo, Chinguar, Cutato, Catabola, Camacupa, Munhango, Luena. Wherever the train happened to stop, he would get out. He would unfurl the screen, put the projector on the tripod, set out half a dozen canvas chairs for the dignitaries of the town. People would come from far away, from the surrounding bush-country, from places with secret names, even places with no names at all. They would offer him goats, chickens, eggs, game. They would sit on the other side of the screen, facing into the projector's light, and watch the movie back to front.

The war that followed independence destroyed the railroad and he was restricted to the outskirts of the big cities. He soon lost everything he had managed to earn in the twenty previous years. He concentrated on the south. He travelled by bicycle, with his assistant, the young James Dean, between Lubango and Humpata, between Huíla and Chibia. Sometimes he ventured as far south as Mossâmedes. Maybe Porto Alexandre. Baía dos Tigres. Never anywhere else. He would bring a white sheet, pin it to the wall of a hut, any wall would do, set up the projector and run the movie. James Dean would pedal the whole time to generate the electricity. On a tranquil, moonless night, there was no cinema better.

The tall man listened with interest. He took some notes.

'And you can prove you really are the individual you claim to be?'

Prove it? Nicolau Peshkov took a yellowing piece of paper from his shirt pocket and carefully unfolded it. It was a cutting from the *Jornal de Angola*. An interview published five years earlier: 'The Last Cinema Hero'. In the photo, which was black and white, Nicolau Alicerces Peshkov was posing next to his bicycle, hands on the handlebars, his enormous head slightly out of focus.

The tall man snatched the cutting, turned it over and started to read some article or other about the importance of manioc flour. 'Not that one, *chefe*,' groaned Nicolau Peshkov, 'please, read the story on the other side. Look at the photo. That's me.' The tall man looked at him with contempt:

'Comrade Peshkov, a man like you, who can't even speak his father's language, you'd tell me what I should and shouldn't read?!'

He read the article to the end. No, not right to the end, because it was cut off halfway.

'Where's the rest of this article?'

Nicolau Alicerces Peshkov spoke slowly.

'Please, *chefe* – that's not the right article. The relevant article, the one that means I can prove that I am my own person, that article is on the other side.'

The tall man lost his patience.

'Fuck! You think we're all stupid here?! I'm asking where the rest of this article is. If you don't answer I'll have you shot for withholding information. I'm going to count to ten.'

Maybe he doesn't know how to count to ten, thought Nicolau Peshkov. But unfortunately, he did. The man counted to ten, slowly, then turned his chair around and sat for a few long moments facing the wall. Then he turned back, opened the case on his desk and took out the projector.

'Right, you little stooge – show us this movie, then. I want to see what it is you've been filming. Military targets, I'll bet.'

Nicolau Peshkov asked for a clean sheet, a hammer and some nails. He stretched the sheet taut and nailed it to the wall. He set the projector up on a chair. He didn't say a word. He had learned a lot in these past few hours. The movie was, in its way, his own work. The work of a lifetime. He had pieced it together, almost frame by frame, using what remained of his father's movies. He asked for the light to be turned out. One of the soldiers climbed onto a stool and carefully unscrewed the bulb from the ceiling.

Peshkov plugged the machine into the electricity and an utterly pure light fell onto the sheet. The first scene showed a family being attacked by birds inside their own home. This episode had a real impact on the audience (it always did). The tall man spoke for all of them: 'Did you see that?! Like wild dogs, those birdies are.' Then they saw an old man perched on a roof playing a violin. 'It's to drive away the birds,' concluded one of the guards. 'The guy's a sorcerer.' There was also a cowboy kissing his girlfriend in front of a waterfall. Finally, a man with sad eyes, hat on his head, saying goodbye to a couple at an airport. When the couple boarded their plane, another guy appeared with a gun, but the one in the hat was quicker and shot him. Most likely the couple were running away from those birds. *The End.*

The projector light trembled, went out, and there was a great silence. Finally, the tall man stood up, climbed onto the stool and screwed the ceiling bulb back in. He sighed.

'You can go, Peshkov. Get out of here. The movie stays.'

Nicolau Alicerces Peshkov went out into the street. An enormous moon shone over the sea. He drew a comb from the back pocket of his trousers, and with it smoothed down the last of his red hair.

He straightened up and went in search of James Dean. The kid would know what to do.

DESIRE

Manon Uphoff

Translated from the Dutch by Sam Garrett

Manon Uphoff (1962–). Born in Utrecht in the Netherlands, Uphoff was the ninth of a family of thirteen children living in a modest apartment. As a young woman, she had a fractious relationship with formal education, and misbehaviour and truancy led to her being sent away to school. She dropped out at sixteen, though some years later, in 1987, she enrolled in university to study literature. Her childhood and adolescence are an important influence on her early writings. Her first collection of short stories, *Desire*, published in 1995, was nominated for prestigious the AKO Literature Prize. Since then, she has published a number of collections of stories and several novels. In 2002 she received the first C.C.S. Crone Award for her literary work.

The winter was cold, with frost on the pane. The chill forced its way in through cracked window frames. The girl, quiet by nature, had just turned fifteen. A lot was happening to her that winter. Sometimes she sat in the bus and picked at her cuticles till the skin tore. Then she stared at the slowly welling, thickening drop of blood as it trickled down at an angle.

She liked fairy tales, but not the ones with happy endings. The Little Mermaid dissolving into foam amid the waves, the Snow Queen who kissed a child's heart to ice, and the Red Shoes, which forced Karen to dance upon her mother's grave—these interested her.

But that winter she read no fairy tales. In her older brother's room—where it was warmer than anywhere else in the house—she pored over a book called *The Geisha*. The cover had a charcoal drawing of two young women: Lucille and Amaryllis. The writer wanted to make love to both of them, preferably at the same time. Lucille and Amaryllis weren't upset by this. The girl was sure she'd think that was terrible—you can only surrender yourself to one person.

On a Saturday night in January, at the club where they only let her in because she'd made herself look years older, an Oriental-looking man bought her a drink. She'd been standing under the disco ball for hours, in a white blouse and tight jeans, but he had just come in. He was much older than she was. His hair shone, and the girl thought his narrow eyes were mysterious. The way he gave her the drink, his hand momentarily brushing the back of hers, frightened her. She couldn't take her eyes off him.

A little later, when she saw his nails, gleaming dimly like the inside of a shell, she knew she would go with him.

At two o'clock they left the club. Cars drove off honking and girls collapsed giggling into their boyfriends' arms. The doorman tapped his gold-braided hat and watched as they turned the corner.

The strange man and the girl walked through the center of town without a word. With each step her curiosity grew: not so much about this man, but about herself.

They crossed a bridge and walked out onto a lawn. The air was cold. It's not true that someone else can burn you with their heat, but the touch of his soft palm against hers burned anyway. In the grass, wet from melted patches of snow, they lay down. Up close, her nose buried in the worsted of his coat, she tried to find her way past all his strange smells to a smell she knew. Water was soaking through her clothes. Her teeth started chattering and the blood drained out of her face. She worried that her lipstick would dry and her mascara would run, and he'd think she was a child.

"It's too cold here," the man said. He helped her to her feet. Her hair was wet. There was grass on her coat and jeans.

He asked her to go home with him, and she said "yes," following the same urge that drove her to tug at the translucent skin around her nails in the bus and watch the lines of welling blood. The excitement grew in her. She felt she was swelling and drawing the darkness of night up into her, like a flower does sweet water. On the town square she imagined she was no longer in any normal city—she was in a world of glass and stone, where she and the man were the only two warm animals. The thrum of distant cars sounded like bumblebees. Drops of rain began rolling slowly over her cheeks, down her neck, and the walk went on and on and on.

"Have you been in Holland long?" the girl asked at last.

"No," the man said. "Only two years. And I don't know if I'm going to stay."

They turned down a side street. The girl thought about her parents' house, her brother's room with the book about the geisha lying on the bed. How there, in that room, you could hear her mother's breathing. About her little sister, who would be asleep now, thumb moistly in her mouth—and the Barbies and the horse on the floor.

"Do you live by yourself?" she asked.

"No." A smile crossed the man's face. "Here we are." They stopped in front of a blue door and he pulled a key ring out of his pocket. There were colored cords of silk hanging on it.

"I don't live by myself. There are a lot of people upstairs—we'll have to be quiet."

She followed him cautiously up the dark stairs.

The cloth of coats scraped against her cold cheeks. The man put a key in the lock.

The girl stood behind him. Over his shoulder she looked into the room and the light. Rows of metal beds stood left and right, with men sitting on all of them, except one. There was laughter and mumbling, and faces turned toward her. With narrow eyes they looked at her.

"Welcome!" one of them said. His skin was yellowish and dry. He had a magazine in one hand. On the glossy cover lay a naked woman, legs spread, eyes closed in ecstasy.

He read from right to left and slapped the page teasingly as she walked past.

The man held her hand and led her into the far corner of the room. In front of his bed was a black curtain attached to metal rails—like in a hospital.

"Don't be afraid," he said, pushing the curtain aside carefully. Little tufts of grass fell from her coat onto the gray blanket. He closed the curtains and fastened them with a safety pin. The laughter from the room grew louder.

"They won't do anything," the man said as she sat on the bed and counted the beats of her heart. He played calmly with her fingers.

"Before long they'll sleep and leave us alone. Women almost never come here."

They waited until it was quiet and they could hear the soft snoring of people in peaceful sleep. A little lamp was burning. It was so low that the shadows it cast on the wall were large and wide.

"How old are you?" he asked. "Fourteen? Fifteen?"

She didn't answer.

"You've made yourself look older than you are."

She felt his lips approach her throat, and then a sudden hard bite that made her list sideways, like a boat after a hard gust.

"Girl," he said. His hand was a fish gliding up under the cloth, across her skin. He pulled the blouse up over her head, his nails ticking against her nipples. His mouth searched for hers and his tongue slid in like an oyster. The saliva in his mouth tasted sweet and warm.

He pushed her under the blankets and pulled on the zipper of her pants, which jammed until he broke it.

"I'll do it," the girl whispered. In a panic, she pulled the stiff material down as fast as she could.

"Soft," he whispered. He held a little fold of her belly in his mouth, rolling it between his sharp teeth.

"I don't know him," the girl thought. "He's a stranger. I don't know him."

A few times that winter, in the warm city bus to school, she had pushed the stop button too early, on purpose. One time she'd been with her father. When the doors opened with a hiss, he made her get out—because the driver would expect her to.

That's just how it would be with this man.

"You're soft, still. A real girl." He petted her breasts, almost in surprise. "I think it's lovely that you're white."

She *was* white. When she looked down, his head was like a black stone between her legs. His lips were pressing against her pubic hair and his tongue slid in slowly. She wanted to stop him. A stranger . . . but a warm and dark glow made her belly heavy, her legs heavy, and she closed her eyes—following the path of the heat.

"Don't stop," she said, startled at her sudden desire, her craving to hold onto this heat. "Just keep doing that." Her pelvis pushed up and she ran her hands through his stiff dark hair, forcing his head down harder, as if she were a nut with a hard shell, and now that the shell was cracked, power and rage came pouring out, and a wanting, a wanting that frightened her.

The heavy strands of his hair fell across her fingers.

"Keep doing that," she said again, but he stopped. She heard the crackling of paper, a rustling. His elbow jabbed her suddenly and sharply in the side.

"I'm going in you," he said, bending over her, enveloping her. "Don't be afraid. Don't yell or scream."

She saw his shoulders where the muscles bunched together, and the pounding of the vein in his neck. The mouth with the full red lips. She tensed her own muscles, but he was faster than she'd thought. A flaming white pain and a sharpness between her legs. With all her might she tried to pull back, but his mouth bore down on hers and his back and limber hips arched over her like a net.

"Don't fight," he said. "Don't fight."

But the pain, which stabbed harder now that she had tensed all her muscles in panic and pushed up her pelvis to force him off, made her stronger. She bucked so hard that he shot out of her. Hipbone cracked against hipbone.

"Don't!" he said. "What are you doing? It's going to happen *anyway*!"

"No!" the girl said, feeling a sudden powerful rage. "You have to fight too!"

He grabbed her by the waist and pushed her back on the sheet.

"You're scared," he said. "But don't be scared." With a hard lunge he went back in her and grabbed her buttocks hard with his fingertips.

"It hurts!"

She dug her nails into his back and pulled down hard. The skin began swelling under her fingers right away, and she saw his eyes pinch shut in pain. She pushed her mouth against his and bit into his lower lip. Lukewarm blood dripped into her mouth. He looked at her with dark gleaming eyes. There were beads of sweat on his forehead.

"You have to fight too."

There was squeezing, growling and thrusting. His hands and hers were everywhere, and everywhere her nails left clawing stripes that filled with red, but he didn't remove himself from her, and the flaming feeling between her legs remained. Even though she bucked her hips and hissed words she'd never used before.

Slowly the burning ebbed away and the heaviness disappeared. He was still in her. She had braced herself for new pain, but he moved only slightly, or not at all. Very calmly. Obliquely. Suddenly she heard her own moaning, and she gushed out like water on a stone floor. He went on, moving in her like a young animal.

"Woman," he whispered in her ear. "Now you're a woman."

The girl took her hands off his back and looked. The man's blood was deep under her nails and he was swathed in an odor she'd never smelled before. There was sweat on his shoulders and his stomach moved up and down. His lower lip was thick and swollen where she'd bitten it.

To her own surprise, she wasn't tired. The pain was gone and she didn't know whether she was happy or frightened, furious or proud.

He lay down beside her, sighing.

"I'm not tired," the girl thought, pulling the white sheet up over herself. "I'm not tired."

The stripes on his back were white and his hand reached for hers across the sheet, but she pulled her hand back and looked. At his shiny hair. The darkness of night. The rips in the curtain fastened with a safety pin. At the little lines of clotted blood. His cock lying limp across his thigh, which she dared look at only now. The condom leaking out slowly on the sheet.

And when he was rested and went into her again, her fingertips pushed hard against his ass, setting the rhythm for him to go in. She bit his throat, sniffing up his smells, and cupped his neck in her hand, as though she was holding a kitten.

The next morning they hardly spoke. He woke up, kissed her, went to sit on the edge of the bed, and quickly and silently put his clothes on. The light from outside was struggling through the window.

"Where are you going?" she asked, feeling around between the sheets for her underwear.

"Work," he said. "I have to go to work. What are you going to do? Will I see you again tonight? Will you come to me tonight?"

"No," the girl said. "I won't come back here anymore."

"You're a woman now," he said. "I'd like it if you came here tonight."

But she shook her head.

Ten minutes after he went away, she left the room. The men were sleeping in their beds, breathing quietly, their backs hunched under the gray blankets. The magazines were lying open on the floor.

Outside it was chilly, but the sun was already shining weakly. She searched her coat for a bus ticket. She found one and waited for the bus that would take her home.

At the house, her mother was sitting at the table with a cup of coffee. The lady from next door across from her.

"Well? Did you have fun at your girlfriend's?" she asked. "Did the two of you go out dancing?"

"Oh, no," she said. "It was kind of late. We didn't really feel like it."

She left the room and climbed the stairs. The door to her brother's room was open a crack. He hadn't come home. The book about the geisha, with the picture of Amaryllis and Lucille on the cover, was still lying on his bed. Their firm breasts with nipples touching. The girl closed the door and turned the key in the lock. She pulled her torn jeans and panties down carefully over her shaking legs. There wasn't much blood, just a little dark spot. The sheet in his room had been worse. She looked at the spot on the cotton and at her pubic hair curling up. She thought about the Little Mermaid, who had traded her beautiful singing voice for real human legs. The pain that had cut into her at every step—and how she had turned to foam on the sea.

She thought about the Ice Queen in the solitude of her cold palace, where every human heart froze at once. She thought about the angel Gabriel, standing before the doors of the church with a flaming sword, waiting—for the little girl who danced and danced, her feet in red shoes, across her mother's grave, and on and on and on. Until her feet were cut off, and she found rest. But didn't get the shoes back.

"At least I fought," the girl said out loud to herself, pulling up her panties and jeans. The zipper's copper-colored teeth stuck out crookedly.

THE SON IN LAW

Teresa Solana

Translated from the Spanish by Peter Bush

Teresa Solana (1962–) was born in Barcelona in 1962, where she currently lives. A philosopher by training, she tried her hand at various lines of employment before embracing literary translation. She directed the National Translation Centre in Spain for seven years and now devotes her time to writing her own novels and translating them into Spanish. *A Not So Perfect Crime*, her first novel, won the 2007 Brigada 21 Prize for best noir in Catalan and *A Shortcut to Paradise*, her second, was short-listed for the 2008 Salambó Prize for best novel in Catalan. She is translated into several languages. Solana herself is often a character in her fiction – in one novel the character of Solana, a writer, hires private detectives to do some research for her next novel; the real-life Solana then wrote her next novel based on the fictional research uncovered by her fictional detectives in the last novel.

The *mossos* came this morning. I'd been expecting them for days.

When I opened the door, they were still panting. That's nothing unusual. Visitors all get to my attic flat on the seventh on their last legs: there's no lift. The stairs have high steps and they're an effort to climb, and instead of taking it calmly, like Carmeta and me, they must have pelted up like lunatics. I reckon their uniforms will have set the neighbours' tongues wagging as there are a number of pensioners with nothing better to do than look through their spy-holes at my staircase. I only hope the *mossos* don't decide to question them, because my neighbours love to stir things. In any case, I don't think they suspect any funny business.

There was a man and a woman, nice and polite they were, and she was much younger. My hair was in a tangle, I wasn't made up and was wearing the horrible sky-blue polyester bathrobe and granny slippers I'd taken the precaution of buying a few days ago at one of the stalls in the Ninot market. The bathrobe is very similar to the one worn by Conxita the eighty-year old on the second floor, but it looked too new so I put it through the washing-machine several times the day before yesterday so it was more like an old rag, which is how I wanted it to look. Now the bathrobe was frayed and flecked with little bobbles of fluff, and, to round off the effect, I spilt a cup of coffee I was drinking on my bust. The woman tactfully scrutinized me from head to toe, dwelling on the stains and dishevelled hair, and I was really lucky one of the police belonged to the female sex since we ladies take much more notice of the small details than the men folk do. She seemed very on the ball and I trust she drew her own conclusions from my shabby appearance.

Her colleague, fortyish and with Paul Newman's eyes, was the one in charge. He introduced himself very nicely, asked me if I was who I am and said he just had a few questions he wanted to ask. A routine enquiry, he added smiling soothingly. I'd nothing to worry about. I adopted the astonished expression I'd been rehearsing for days in front of the mirror and invited them into the dining room.

As they followed me down the passage, I made sure I gave them the impression I was a frail, sickly old dear struggling to walk and draw breath. I exaggerated, because I'm pretty sprightly for my age and, thank God, I'm not in bad health, although I tried to imitate the way Carmeta walks, dragging my feet at the speed of a turtle, as if every bone in my body was aching. Both homed in on the sacks of cement, the tins of paint and workmen's tools that are still in the passage, and asked me if I was having building work done. I told them the truth: that after all that rain, the kitchen ceiling collapsed and it had been a real mess.

"If only you'd seen it. . . ! You'd have thought a bomb had dropped!" I told them with a sigh. "And it was so lucky I was watching the telly in the dining room. . . !"

The young policewoman nodded sympathetically and said that's the drawback with top flats, though an attic has lots of advantages because you get terraces and plenty of light. "What's more," she added shyly, "with all the traffic there is in the Eixample, you don't hear the noise from the cars or breathe in so many fumes." I agreed and told her a bit about what the Eixample was like almost fifty years ago when Andreu and I came to live here.

Visibly on edge, her colleague immediately interjected and asked me if I'd had any news of my son-in-law. I adopted my slightly senile expression again and said I hadn't.

The policeman persisted. He wanted to know the last time I saw Marçal and if I'd spoken to him by phone. I told him as ingenuously as I could that I'd not heard from him for some time and politely enquired why he was asking.

"He disappeared a week ago and his family think something untoward may have happened. That's why we're talking to everyone who knows him," he replied softly. "I suppose you don't know where he's got to, do you?"

"Who?" I said pretending to be in the early stages of Alzheimer's.

"Your son-in-law."

"Marçal?"

"Yes, Marçal."

"Sorry. . . What was it you just asked me?"

Like old people who really don't cotton on, I changed the subject and asked them if they'd like a drink, a coffee, an infusion, or something stronger. When they asked me if I knew he and my little girl were negotiating a divorce and if I was aware my son-in-law had a restraining order in force because she'd reported him for physical abuse, I simply looked at the floor and shrugged my shoulders. Reluctantly, I confessed I suspected things weren't going too well.

"But all married couples have problems. . . I didn't want to harp on about theirs." And added, shaking my head, "Nowadays women don't have the patience. . . In my time. . ."

I didn't finish my sentence. There was no need. The young policewoman looked at me affectionately and gave one of those condescending smiles liberated young females of today reserve for us old grey-heads with antiquated ideas. Out of the corner of one eye, I registered she'd had a French manicure and wore a wedding ring. To judge by her pink cheeks and smiley expression that young woman must still be in her honeymoon phase.

Before they could start grilling me about Marçal and his relationship with Marta again, I quickly began to gabble on about stuff that was totally unrelated. An old dear who lives by herself, has nobody to talk to and spends her day sitting on her sofa in front of the telly watching programs she doesn't understand. My grouses made them uneasy and the man finally glanced at his watch and said they must be leaving. Their visit (because you couldn't really call it an interrogation) had lasted under ten minutes. When they were saying goodbye, they repeated I shouldn't worry. That it was probably just a misunderstanding.

Marta, my little daughter, will soon be thirty-six. I'm seventy-four, and it's no secret Andreu and I were getting on when I got pregnant with Marta. Now it's quite normal to have your first baby at forty but it wasn't in my day. If you didn't have a bun in the oven before you were thirty, people scowled at you, as if it was a sin not to have children. The kindest comment they'd make was that you weren't up to it. If you were married and childless, you suddenly became defective.

Marta is an only child. As she was such a latecomer, the poor dear didn't have a brother or sister. Apart from Carmeta and Ramon, who are kind of pretend aunt and uncle, my little girl doesn't have any real ones or cousins. From the day we buried her father, may he rest in peace, Marta's only had Carmeta and me, as you can hardly count Ramon, Carmeta's husband, after he had his stroke. Carmeta has to feed him with some sort of puree she buys at the chemists that she administers with a syringe through a rubber tube that goes in through his nose and down to his stomach, a torture that's simply prolonging his agony because his doctors say he'll never recover. They insisted to Carmeta that Ramon isn't suffering, though we spend the whole blessed day with him and are not so sure about that.

Carmeta's the same age as me, and, though I can't complain about my health, she's rather the worse for wear. A cancer she can't see the back of. She and Ramon didn't have children, and both doted on Marta like an aunt and uncle from the day she was born. My daughter loves them and they love her. If it hadn't been for his stroke, I'd cross my heart and swear Ramon would have given my son-in-law a face lift and things would have turned out differently.

A pity none of us was in the know a year ago.

We were completely in the dark.

Even though we sometimes said our little girl seemed to be behaving a bit strangely. Sluggishly. As if she were unhappy. But we all have our off moments, don't we?

Our little girl put on a brave front. Partly because she didn't want us to worry, and partly because she was embarrassed to acknowledge her husband beat her. If I'd never decided to buy some pastries and pay her a visit one day, after accompanying Carmeta to her chemo session, I expect we'd still be none the wiser and it would be life as usual. That morning, when Marta opened the door barricaded behind a pair of huge sunglasses, our alarm bells immediately started ringing. Something was amiss. She pretended she had conjunctivitis and that's why she was wearing dark glasses at home, but Carmeta, who's a suspicious sort, didn't swallow that and snatched them from her face. Our hearts missed several beats when we saw that black eye lurking under layers of makeup.

At first she denied it. Carmeta and I are no fools and applied the third degree and she finally caved in. In floods of tears she confessed her husband drank too much and beat her now and then. A punch, a slap, a shove. . . He'd put it down to stress at work, when he calmed down. He'd also say he would kill her, if she ever told anyone.

I saw a bruise on my little girl's left arm and told her to strip off. The poor thing couldn't bring herself to say no and agreed, reluctantly. Then Carmeta and I burst into tears. Our darling Marta was black and blue all over her body. From that day on we never referred to him by his name again. My son-in-law became the Animal, the Son of a Bitch, or the Bastard. We got weaving. We persuaded Marta to report him and the three of us went to see a lawyer. Marta was afraid nobody would believe her and that the judge would take her child away, but the lawyer did a good job reassuring her and, in the end, made a start on the paperwork. And it was true, with his executive suits and silk ties, the Bastard seemed like a normal person.

A cunt of a normal person who beat his wife and threatened to kill her.

And our little girl, quite naturally, was scared.

But now she had us on her side.

The Bastard went to live with his sister and disappeared from our lives for months on end. Marta, who'd been reduced to skin and bones by all the unpleasantness, even began to put on weight. Until one evening he appeared out of the blue at her place and said he was going to kill her.

It was only a matter of time.

Depending on his patience.

And Carmeta suddenly saw the light.

No well-intentioned law could protect Marta. If he put his mind to it, the Bastard would sooner or later do the evil deed. As he said, it was only a matter of time. A matter of waiting until one of us lowered her guard or the judge decided there were more serious cases to see to and that our little girl no longer needed protection. That she could manage on her own.

It's not hard to intimidate someone. Or kill them.

And, in the meantime, the Bastard would sour her life.

Her and everybody else's.

It's a piece of luck I have an attic flat and that's it got a terrace. The woman *mosso* was right. Attics can be very inconvenient but they have lots of advantages. And if you don't agree, just ask the Bastard.

Andreu and I rented this flat on the Eixample just before we got married, and the only item my husband insisted on when we were courting and looking for a flat was that the flat should have a small terrace. My parents didn't have a terrace because we lived on the third floor, but when the weather was good we'd go up to the flat roof and enjoy the cool of evening and gossip with the neighbours. I'd go there with my friends in the summer. We put our swimsuits on, lay our beach towels on the red tiles and imitated the film stars in our magazines and listened to the radio and drank fizzy lemonade or tepid Coca Cola pretending it was Martini. Then we'd have to fight off sunstroke with aspirins, water packs and vinegar, but it was worth it. When you're young, there's a solution to everything.

It's not that my little terrace is any great shakes. All the same, twenty-two square meters are enough for a pine, lemon, and orange tree, a magnolia, a decent size jasmine and a bougainvillea, not to mention the dozens of pots of roses, petunias, daisies and chrysanthemums I've put in every cranny. When Andreu and I set foot there for the first time, I could hardly imagine how this little terrace would turn out to be so providential.

Because, I don't know how I could have helped my little girl without the terrace.

And I reckon that's what a mother's for: to be around to give a helping hand to her children when they've got problems. Whether they like it or not.

It was Carmeta who came up with the solution. She's always been very imaginative. The terrace and the kitchen the downpour ruined gave her the idea, and it was no sooner said than done. Neither of us was prepared to wait with arms folded while the little girl was left at the mercy of an obsolete legal system and a lunatic who wanted to bump her off. We had to do something and do it quick, before we rued the day. As Carmeta said, a stitch in time saves nine.

I called the Bastard on his mobile a couple of weeks ago from a phone-box and told him we should have a chat. I persuaded him by saying I had to tell him about a new development that was going to make Marta slow up on the divorce, and, as I knew he was short of cash because he drank over the odds and had got the sack, I added I wanted to give him a present of a weekend away with Marta. Three or four days in a good hotel with a swimming pool, all expenses paid, would help them make the peace, I told him. My call and sudden interest in saving their marriage took him by surprise, but, as Carmeta had anticipated, the financial bait hooked him.

Early the next morning, Carmeta came to my flat carrying a sports-bag. Her face looked rough and she confessed she'd had a bad night. I told her I could ring the Bastard and give him an excuse if she'd rather leave it for another day, but she'd hear none of it nothing. The tranquillizers she'd taken were beginning to impact and she already felt slightly better, or so she said.

"What do you reckon? Should we have a little drop of something to put us in the mood?" I suggested hesitantly.

"No alcohol!" replied Carmeta most professionally. "What we need are anti-stress pills. We're far too nervy."

Carmeta took the anti-depressants out of her bag the doctor had prescribed after telling her she had cancer and offered me one. As Carmeta is the expert when it comes to pills, I meekly swallowed it and said nothing. Out of the corner of an eye I noted that she took two. I went to the kitchen and made two cups of tea while Carmeta changed her clothes in the bedroom. Carmeta had brought an old tracksuit top and slippers. I was also wearing old clothes that would have to be thrown away.

The Bastard arrived at around eleven. Grudgingly, I pecked him on both cheeks and led him into the dining room. With a studiedly senile smile, I offered him a cognac that the idiot accepted in a flash while he sprawled on the sofa. I took my opportunity to go into the kitchen.

"Marçal!" I shouted, trying to ensure my voice didn't sound rude. "Could you help me get the bottle of cognac from the top shelf. I can't reach it. . ."

I'd left the knife under a tea cloth on the kitchen top, and Carmeta was skulking behind the door, holding her breath. As soon as I heard his footsteps, I shut the window and switched on the radio.

The second Marçal stepped into the kitchen, Carmeta stuck the carving knife into the small of his back. The attack took him by surprise and he started howling. Before he had time to react I grabbed the knife from under the tea cloth and stuck it in violently. Blood spurted from his neck and through the air like a liquid streamer splashing everywhere.

Still screaming, the Animal lifted his hands to his neck in an attempt to stop the haemorrhaging, but from the way the blood was bubbling out, I knew he had no chance. I'd stuck it right in his carotid artery, and that thrust, driven by a mother's fury, was a death sentence.

He collapsed in under a minute. Carmeta and I left him agonizing on the kitchen floor and went into the bathroom. We washed our hands and faces, changed our blood-soaked tops and went into the dining room. We wanted the Bastard to die alone, like a dog. And he did. A Beatles song on the radio drowned out his cries.

By the time we went back to the kitchen, my son-in-law was dead. The floor had turned into a red puddle, was awash with blood. The son of a bitch had left one hell of a mess. We pulled on washing up gloves, grabbed the bucket and cloth and started cleaning up. The two of us were at it for a good hour but even so it still wasn't spotless. After checking his body had stopped bleeding, we stripped him and put his clothes in the washer on a cold-water program, added a squirt of one of those stain removers advertised on the telly. We wiped him a bit with the cloth. Then I took some rolls of bandage from a drawer and Carmeta and I bound him like a mummy. As we were intending to cut him into small chunks, we thought it would be less stressful if he were bandaged. I started on his head and Carmeta on his feet.

It took us ages because the Bastard weighed more than ninety kilos and wasn't easy to lift. When we'd finished bandaging, we left him and went back to the dining room. The effort had left us exhausted. We saw it was lunchtime and though neither Carmeta nor I were hungry, we behaved ourselves, ate a banana and drank a glass of sugared water to re-energize ourselves. We also took another anti-depressant each. Carmeta, who was worn out, dozed off straightaway, and I decided to let her sleep and take a nap myself. When she woke up, she swallowed another batch of tranquillizers and we both returned to our task. Our day wasn't over yet.

Carmeta went to fetch the electric saw and brought it into the kitchen. Luckily one of her neighbours is still into do-it-yourself and the store-room in her building isn't locked. We pulled our rubber gloves back on and plugged in the saw that worked perfectly. We sawed his head off first and placed it whole inside a rubbish bag, and, then, his arms and legs, all in small chunks. We distributed the pieces in different sacks and left his torso till last. As that's where the entrails are, Carmeta and I thought it would be best to empty them out before starting to reduce the eventual mess.

I took my courage into my own hands and very carefully made an incision from the top to the bottom of his mutilated corpse trying to tear only the skin. I must have burst his gut, because all of a sudden, a horrific stink filled the kitchen and I had to open the window and squirt air-freshener around. Each of us pulled on one side of his torso and succeeded in separating his ribs and wrenching out his heart and lungs. His heart slipped out of Carmeta's grasp and the moment it sloshed on the ground I started to retch and vomit. As I'd practically been fasting I only brought up yellow bile, but I felt queasy and my stomach was churning.

Carmeta rushed me into the dining room and forced me to stretch out on the floor with my legs in the air. When she saw that I was showing signs of life, she went back to the kitchen.

"Don't move. I'll gut the Son of a Bitch," she said.

There was still some sun on the terrace. The pale rays of spring barely gave out any heat but were a pleasant reminder of other happier evenings when with Andreu, may he rest in peace, Carmeta and Ramon we'd rustle up a bread, tomato and mountain ham snack on the terrace and stay there late into the night chatting about this and that, never imagining that one day this small terrace of mine, with its views of Montjuïc and its flowerpots, would be an improvised cemetery. Necessity is the mother of invention, or so they say.

We buried the head next to the lemon-tree, the one with the biggest pot, and stuffed his hands and feet into the ceramic pot with the pine tree. We stuck his entrails in with the magnolia, his heart with the bougainvillea and his liver with the orange tree, and divided the rest up among the remaining pots, taking care not to damage the flowers. We'd scarcely finished when we realized there were still seven or eight pieces of meat in a bag and we had no receptacles left, but at that time of night after toiling the whole day, we were fit to drop, so I suggested to Carmeta that we should wrap them in foil and put them in the freezer.

"We'll think of something tomorrow after we've had a rest."

Carmeta looked in a bad way again. Although she wasn't complaining, her grimaces showed the pain she was in. I helped her shower and wash her hair, and switched on a wash-load of tops, towels and cloths we'd used to clean up the kitchen. The foam in the washing machine turned pink.

Ignoring her protests, I accompanied her home, and on the way, threw the Bastard's clothes in a rubbish container. Carmeta could hardly stand straight, so I made her a glass of hot milk and forced her to eat biscuits before going to bed. I waited until she fell asleep and, while Carmeta snored, I changed Ramon's nappies and gave him his supper. Just before I left, as I was giving him a kiss on the forehead, I thought how sooner or later we'd have to do something to help him too. Good people don't deserve to end like that.

The minute I opened the door to my flat, I realized that, if I continued on an empty stomach, without any food input, my blood pressure would take a dive and I'd faint. In the morning, before the Bastard arrived, I'd taken the precaution of leaving some sandwiches in the dining room so as not to have to go back into the kitchen. As my stomach was slightly queasy, I had a couple of spoons of anti-gut-ache syrup and ate a ham sandwich and apple while watching the news. The sandwich and apple went down well, and I was soon asleep on the sofa in front of the telly that was still on. That night, unlike others, I didn't have a nightmare.

The next morning I got up early and spent it giving the rest of the flat a thorough clean. Although they say bleach doesn't remove traces of blood, I'd bet anything you like that if the police decided to investigate they wouldn't find a scrap of evidence. I took a mid-morning break and first phoned Marta, who was at work, and then Carmeta, who'd got up and was feeling better. I continued cleaning. When I finished, it was past four and my back was aching.

I took the tops, cleaning cloths and towels out of the drier, put everything in plastic sacks and went out. I threw the sacks into four different containers on my way to Ramon and Carmeta's. Carmeta was in much better spirits and was waiting for me with a bottle of *cava* in the fridge which we drank while we kept Ramon company.

The building-workers came the following day and gutted the kitchen with their hammers. They also chipped out the wall and floor tiles. They worked a good two weeks in my kitchen, and now I have a new ceiling, designer tiles and a built-in kitchen. The tiles and cupboards are nothing out of the ordinary because they were bought in a sale, but altogether it looks really good.

I know I must keep my lips sealed and can't tell my little girl not to worry, that the Bastard won't ever lay his hand on her again. Marta knows nothing. Nothing at all. She's still very young and God knows how she'd react if she knew what Carmeta and I had done. Besides, what with her kid and her work, Marta has enough headaches, and it would be the last straw if she had to cope with moral dilemmas or stupid remorse. So mum's definitely the word! As Carmeta says, if what we did is wrong, we'll settle our account in the world beyond, with whoever.

Some girls from our yoga group are coming to supper tomorrow. We'll take advantage of the good weather and dine on the terrace. Just in case, I've bought a good supply of incense sticks, I mean, just in case the Bastard starts to get smelly and sour our supper. As Carmeta has got to start another round of chemo and is leaving the class, it will be a kind of farewell party. I've also scrubbed myself from the class, because I'm going to live in her place for a while from tomorrow. When she starts being sick and feeling like a wet rag, Carmeta will need someone to accompany her to hospital and lend her a helping hand with Ramon.

We both know she's not got much time left. She knows and I know, so no need to mention it. Nonetheless, tomorrow's farewell will be a whale of party: we'll eat and drink until our livers give up on us. Our style has never been to turn tragic, and even less so when we've both got one foot on the other side. What's coming our way is coming.

I live very near the Ninot market where I shop every day. I like to look around the stalls and gossip with the saleswomen and locals from the neighbourhood. As I buy there daily and never use the freezer, I'd completely forgotten the packets that were still there. That morning, the visit by the police made me remember I must do something with all that and I rang Carmeta. I told her I was thinking of going to the florists and buying some earth and a couple of big pots.

"Forget about the pots. . . !" Carmeta retorted. "Go to the Ninot and see if you can buy some spongy mushrooms and fairy rings. And buy garlic and onions as well." "Tomorrow," she added in an authoritarian tone, "we shall eat roast pork and spring mushrooms!"

Initially I objected, mostly on behalf of the other girls. But, by the cold light of day, I have to agree it's not a bad solution.

YOU'RE THE ANGEL

Miljenko Jergović

Translated from the Croatian by David Williams

Miljenko Jergović (1966–) was born in Sarajevo, in former Yugoslavia. Jergović began contributing to literary magazines in his teens. His factual novel *Volga, Volga*, about a car and its driver, is a chronicle of the Bosnian war and internal conflicts that marked the breakup of Yugoslavia. His stories and novels have been translated into more than twenty languages.

When I was born a dog started barking in the hall of the maternity ward. Dr. Srećko ripped the mask from his face, tore out of the delivery suite, and said *to hell with the country where kids are born at the pound!* I still didn't understand at that point, so I filled my lungs with a deep breath and for the first time in my life confronted a paradox: though I didn't have others to compare it to, the world where I'd appeared was terrifying, but something forced me to breathe, to bind myself to it in a way I never managed to bind myself to any woman. Recounting the event later, first to my mother, and then my father, and as soon as I grew up, to friends, they brushed me off, said I was making stuff up, that I couldn't have remembered anything, that there was no way I could've started drawing ontological conclusions the first time I cried. At first I was pissed they thought me a liar, and I wasn't above spilling a few bitter tears, hitting myself in the head, and yelling *you'll be sorry when I'm dead!* With the passing of years I calmed down, having figured that this world, of which I already knew a little and could compare with my experience and my dreams, was predicated on mistrust and the peculiar human tendency to think you a total idiot whenever you told the truth and take you seriously the second you started lying. This aside, relatively early on, when I was about five or six, I came to the conclusion that everything connected with death was a downer and so decided to shelve my threats of dying, at least until I solved the problem of God's existence. God was important as a possible witness; he'd be there to confirm my final mortal experience and he could vouch for me that I hadn't lied about the one in the delivery suite.

Does God exist? I asked my grandma Olga Rejc, because of anyone I met in those first six years of my life, she seemed most trustworthy. *For some people he does, for others he doesn't,* she replied calmly, like it was no big deal, like it was something you only talked about all casual and indifferent. *Does he exist for us?* It was most diplomatic formulation I could manage. The thing was, I'd already noticed how my family placed exceptional value on my socialization efforts and loved me talking about stuff in the first-person plural: *when are we having lunch, when are we going out, when are we coming down with the flu* . . . at least at the outset I thought questions of faith would be best set in this context. *For me, God doesn't exist,* she said, *I can't speak for you though.* It was then I learned about truths you only spoke for yourself and in your own name. I was pretty okay with all this, though less than thrilled I hadn't been able to resolve the God question off the bat.

Ten years later I still wasn't straight with God, but I'd figured the moment Grandma decided he didn't exist. It was early spring, everyone was out somewhere and I'd stayed back at home alone. As usual I started rummaging through their wardrobes. I never knew what I was looking for but always found something, something linked to the family, Mom and Dad, Grandma and Grandpa, something they'd tried to hide from me for some reason. Their private histories were so dark, or at least they thought them so, and my investigative spirit so very much alive, that after a few months' work on their biographies I knew way more from my secret sources than they ever told or admitted to me in the rest of my life put together. My starter's curiosity soon turned into an obsession, and then into a mania. I'd be disappointed if I didn't turn up something juicy or dirty. I wanted proof my father was a homosexual, my mother an ex-tram driver, Grandpa a spy or at least a gambler who'd lost half of Sarajevo in a game of Preference. I loved them all, you have to believe me, but even more I loved the little testimonies of things they'd wanted to hush up so they'd make it into heaven – if only in the eyes of their son and grandson.

But that was the day I discovered the false bottom in the big bedroom wardrobe. I lifted up the base and found a carved wooden box, a round glass container, and a green folder full of documents. I laid everything out on the rug, heaved a sigh, and opened the box. It was full of dirt. Regular brown dirt with little stones and blades of long-dried grass that disintegrated to the touch. *They won't be planting flowers in this dirt,* I thought, and then, not without some trepidation, sunk my fingers into the box to explore. But there was nothing there, just pebbles, grass, and all this dirt. You wouldn't believe the amount of dirt that can fit in a wooden box. Much more than you'd think. You want to picture what I'm talking about, then tomorrow grab a cardboard box – I mean, I doubt you've a wooden one at hand – go to the park, and fill it up with dirt. You won't believe your eyes!

I moved on to the glass container. It held a pocket watch, a ring (it was too big for my ring finger, I tried it on), this miniature metal figurine of some saint, a tie pin, and a little booklet by Anton Aškerc, printed in Slovenian, the pages the thinnest I've ever seen. The only other things were these two green army buttons with spread-winged eagles, which gave me the heebie-jeebies because I had the feeling I'd seen them somewhere before.

Before opening the folder I stopped to think of all the stuff you're not supposed to know about in life. I wondered about the secrets that have to stay secret so the world makes some kind of sense, but since I couldn't remember any, I decided to push on. The folder contained three bits of paper. A birth certificate in the name of M.R., a baptism certificate in the name of M.R., and a telegram that read: "We hereby inform you that private M.R. perished in battle against a Partisan band on September 10."

M.R. was my uncle. I knew he died in the war, and I knew he wasn't a Partisan, but I'd never dreamed that he was the enemy.

I put everything back in its place and closed the wardrobe. Closing it, I knew nothing in my life would ever be the same as before I discovered the false bottom. I also knew my investigations into the family were over. Now it was time for asking questions, but only of those who questions wouldn't hurt and who could answer them without leaving a bloody trail in their wake.

I waited for days for my chance, but it never came. Grandma almost never left the house, and when she did Mom wasn't there, and Mom was the only one I could ask. She didn't know her brother. She was born four months before he died, and although he never saw her, he gave her her name. Grandpa had wanted to call her Regina, but M. wanted his sister named after a tree native to Bosnia. The tree's native to other countries too, but we didn't care about other countries because they were just places Grandpa, Uncle, my father, and everyone else went to war.

I went to see Mom at work. *Can we have half an hour alone?* She frowned, and I could already tell what she was thinking: *he's going to admit he's a druggie, he's got some girl pregnant, he got his fourteenth F in math, he's a homosexual . . .* I wagged my index finger left-right, though we hadn't yet said a word. I sat down. *Everything's fine, just give me a second.* But Mom just got more wound up. I had to get it out before she jumped out the window and broke her leg. Me: *I opened the wardrobe.* Mom: *It had to happen sometime.* Me: *I found something.* Mom: *What?* Me: *Everything.* Mom: *Even the dirt?* Me: *From the grave, right?* Mom: *Please, just one thing. Don't ever tell her.* Me: *I know. I came to you.*

The part of the story that follows I learned back then, from my mom, and it goes something like this. When he finished high school, the same one I'd attend fifty years later, my uncle got the draft. Because he spoke perfect German and had a German grandfather, they put him in a unit formally part of the Wehrmacht but made up of our people. They sent them to Slavonia in Croatia. My grandpa combed the city in a blind panic, badgering one acquaintance after another in one office after another, just trying to get his son out of the army. But of all his connections, only a Communist one proved any good. A friend, a manager in the railways and member of the resistance, told him how it could be arranged for M. to desert his unit and be taken in by Bosnian Partisans a couple of kilometers from his base. Grandpa was all for the idea, but when he relayed it to Grandma, she got scared. For a start she thought in his German uniform the Partisans would shoot her son on sight, and even if they didn't, he'd be sure to lose his head in a Partisan one. More to the point, she was of the view that he was safer being the enemy. Grandpa tried to persuade her, but it did no good. He hollered so loud the whole apartment shook, desperate because he himself wasn't sure what was best, but also because he was certain how it all might end, who had justice on their side, and who would win the war. Mom of course had no idea what all Grandpa's hollering was about, but I'm sure he hollered the exact same thing when I was just a boy and he told me the story of the Second World War: *Hitler's an idiot. That's what I said right back in 1939. Idiots lose wars, but they kill more people than you could ever imagine. And then that trash Pavelić came along. He sent our kids to Stalingrad and turned them into criminals. He created a shitty little state dangling out a big Kraut ass. That was Pavelić for you, and I knew that from the get-go, but that knowledge doesn't help you any, because it won't save your neck.* I think that was also about the gist of what he yelled at Grandma in the fall of 1971, when he again made the house shake and went as red in the face as the Party flag, and his lips went blue and Mom went up to him and shook him by the shoulders and said *Dad, calm down, calm down . . .* But he wouldn't calm down, he just went on, hollering about Maks Luburić, who cooked people in boiling water and in March 1945 skinned Grandpa's rail-wayman friend alive in the house of horror in Skenderija. Then Mom started crying, imploring *Daddy, sweetheart, please stop, for God's sake, I beg of you . . .* Suddenly he calmed down, not for God's sake, but because of her tears. He put a funny face on and said *let us alone you silly woman, can't you see we're talking about men's stuff.* Then he turned to me and whispered *politics isn't for women. They just start bawling. Golda Meir is the exception.* Back then I didn't know Grandpa had tricked me, that he'd actually told me another story, not the one I thought he was telling me. Mom didn't bawl like other women when politics came up. That I know from when I found the box.

Anyway, when Grandpa was done yelling at Grandma, having failed to convince her to go along with the Partisan plan, which she steadfastly rejected, Grandpa started living months of his own private hell. He'd wake at night, bathed in sweat, with a single recurring thought: that M. wasn't coming home, and that if he did, the sum of Pavelić's and Hitler's crimes would be on his conscience. Grandma was only worried about one thing: that her son stayed alive, the how was no matter. It was in those months she started praying to God.

How they took the news of Uncle's death, whether they cried, yelled, screamed, or just absorbed it in silence, I'll never know. A few months after the liberation of Sarajevo four young guys in Partisan uniforms showed up on their doorstep. Grandma cried, Grandpa held his face in his hands to keep it from crumbling like a ceramic mask. One of the young guys put his hand on Grandma's shoulder and said *don't cry, madam. You've got another child. Look at your little girl. M. talked about his baby sister every day.* My mom, a blond baroque angel, sat on her potty in the corner.

Seven days after my uncle's death, the unit in which he'd been stationed deserted in its entirety and went over to the Partisans. To that point M. had been their only casualty. At war's end three more lay dead. But they were no longer the enemy.

Grandpa and Grandma lived together for a full thirty years after the death of their son, never speaking of him. They held their silence in front of others and probably held it between themselves. Don't expect me to be so banal as to say I know Grandma blamed herself for her son's death. She never once set foot in a church again, she forgot Christmas and Easter, and only once a year did Grandpa put on his best suit and head to Sarajevo Cathedral for midnight mass. He didn't have much of an ear, but he liked singing the songs heralding the birth of the eternal child.

Grandma didn't decide that God doesn't exist, more that he just had nothing to do with her. She stopped believing in him even if he did exist. Grandpa died in 1972, and Grandma began her dying in the early spring of 1986. She had throat cancer and it got harder and harder for her to breathe. Sometimes she'd call me by M.'s name. They were little slips and I didn't call her on them. Or maybe they weren't little slips at all. By that time I was her only surviving son.

At the beginning of June, an ambulance came and took her to the hospital to die. They cut her throat open, but she still couldn't breathe. She fixed her gaze straight ahead and set her hands together. I smiled like it was all no big thing and that she'd be better tomorrow. But I knew exactly what was going down. Death came slyly and unfairly. It grabbed my grandma by the throat and shook everything left out of her. What was left was the memory of her son. She died during the night of the fifth of June.

Like all old folk, she'd talked about her funeral while still in good health. Under no circumstances whatsoever did she want her photograph to appear in her obituary, over her dead body. But she didn't mention anything about a priest. No one had asked of course. That would have been stupid.

Over her dead body, we got a priest and paid for a memorial service. I can't explain why to you. Maybe so that God, if he exists, smartens up his act. That's how a friend of Grandma's put it.

I never even visited her grave come All Saints' Day. I can't tell you why. I just didn't ever feel like it. I was sorry she'd died, particularly in such a terrible way; I guess I thought visiting the grave would be to honor such a death. A few days before this most recent war, my friend Ahmed's father died. On my way back from the janazah, instead of heading for the exit gate I decided to take a walk over to the Catholic plots. On the tombstone under which my grandpa and grandma were buried, a huge black dog lay sprawled out in the sun. I sat down beside him, and he lifted his head lazily, looking at me with half-closed eyes. I'd long since stopped caring that no one had believed my first insight and first memory, the one of a dog barking in the hall of the maternity ward the moment before I let out my first scream. *You're the angel, aren't you?* He wagged his tail on the marble a couple of times and sunk back into sleep. My hand followed him.

THE NIMROD FLIPOUT

Etgar Keret

Translated from the Hebrew by Miriam Shlesinger and Sondra Silverston

Etgar Keret (1967–). Born in Tel Aviv, Etgar Keret is the author of six bestselling story collections. His writing has been published in *Harper's Magazine*, *The New York Times*, *The Paris Review*, and *Zoetrope*. *Jellyfish*, his first film as a director along with his wife, Shira Geffen, won the Caméra d'Or prize for best first feature at Cannes in 2007. In 2010 he was named a Chevalier of France's Order of Arts and Letters. Keret's father was arrested for peeing on a wall when drunk. It was the wall of the French Embassy, and the arresting police assumed it was an obscure act of political protest. His brother heads up the movement for the legalization of marijuana in Israel.

MIRON FREAKS OUT

When it comes to Miron's problem, there are, as they say, several schools of thought. The doctors think it's some trauma he suffered when he was in the army that resurfaced all of a sudden in his brain, like a turd that comes floating back at you in the toilet long after you've flushed. His parents are convinced it's all because of the mushrooms he ate in the East, which turned his brain to quiche. The guy who found him there and brought him back to Israel says it's because of this Dutch girl he met in Dharamsala, who broke his heart. And Miron himself says it's God who's messing with his mind. Tapping into his brain like a bat, telling it one thing, then the opposite, anything, just to pick a fight. According to Miron, after He created the world, God pretty much rested on His laurels for a couple of million years. Until Miron came along all of a sudden, and started asking questions, and God broke out in a sweat. Because God could tell straight off that unlike the rest of humanity, Miron was nobody's chump. As soon as you gave him the smallest opening, he'd slam right through it, and God—as everyone knows—is really big on dishing it out, but not on taking it, and the last thing He feels like putting up with is a rebuttal, especially from a guy like Miron, and from the minute He realized what was going on, He just kept driving Miron around the bend, hassling him whenever He could, with everything from bad dreams to girls who wouldn't put out. Anything to make him fall apart.

The doctors asked Uzi and me to help them a little with Miron's case history, because the three of us have known each other all our lives. They asked us all kinds of questions about the army, about what had happened with Nimrod. But most of it we couldn't remember, and even the little bit that we did remember we didn't tell them because the truth was that they didn't exactly look like nice guys, and Miron had told us a couple of things that bordered on something you'd see on *60 Minutes*. After that, during visiting hours, Miron begged us to bring him some hummus from the hunchback, because more than anything else, it was the food here that was doing him in. "It's been three weeks since I got here," he figured, "and if you add that to the four months in the East, that's almost six months without hummus. I wouldn't wish that on my worst enemy, I really wouldn't." So we went to get him some. The hunchback said he didn't do takeout. "Only sit-down," he snarled, half-menacing, half-indifferent, the way he does. "I'm not running a snack bar here." So we ordered a plate of hummus, and stuck it in the pita ourselves. When we got back, Miron's mother was there. She said hi to Uzi, but not to me. She hasn't spoken to me for years, on account of me influencing her son to experiment with drugs. We didn't give him the hummus while she was still there, because we were afraid she'd tell the doctors. So we waited for her to leave. Meanwhile, the *ful* was getting cold, but that didn't matter to Miron, who wolfed it down. Three days later they discharged him. The doctors said his reaction to the medications was remarkable. Miron still insists it was on account of the hummus.

UZI LOSES IT

In June, Miron and I went down to Sinai. Uzi was supposed to come too, but he stood us up at the last second for an appointment with some dot-com German from Düsseldorf who could put up millions for a project with Uzi's company. It was supposed to be a kind of celebration, in honor of the fact that Miron wasn't considered crazy anymore, and Uzi felt kind of embarrassed about his childish attraction to money, so he promised that as soon as his appointment was over he'd join us there. "I'll bet you anything he doesn't show," Miron said. "A double bet: First off, he won't show, and second, give him three more months and he'll marry the Turnip." I didn't want to bet Miron about either, because what he said sounded depressing but basically true. Turnip was our code name for Uzi's obnoxious girlfriend who was also deep into all those virtual hi-tech deals that Uzi loved to manage. I remember him asking us once why we called her Turnip, and Miron told him something about how it was because turnips are underrated: some people don't realize how good they can be. Uzi didn't really buy it, but he never asked about it again.

If life is one big party, Sinai is definitely the chill-out room. And even Miron and I, who hardly did anything in regular life anyway, could appreciate the ultimate nothingness of the place. Everywhere you looked on our beach, you saw dozens of spaced-out hippie chicks, and Miron kept hitting on them, going on about all the time he'd spent in the East. It even worked, sometimes. Me, I didn't have the energy, or the coordination either. So I just smoked lots of weed, stared at the sea, and kept debating whether to order a pineapple pancake for lunch or take my chances with the fish. I also kept an eye on Miron from a distance, checking to see if he'd really straightened out. He still came up with some pretty weird stuff, like for instance when he insisted on taking a shit right near our hut because he was too lazy to walk all the way to the restaurant. But the truth is that he used to do stuff like that before he went crazy too.

"I have a good feeling about that short one with the navel stud," he told me at night after we came back from the restaurant on the beach. "You have to admit, she's cute, isn't she?" The two of us were sitting around, out of it, just staring out at the sea. "Listen," I told him, "about that whole thing when they put you away, I know Uzi and me acted like it was no big thing, but you scared the shit out of us." Miron just shrugged. "It was pretty freaky, like suddenly I started hearing voices—talking, singing. Like some broken radio that you can't figure out how to turn off. It drives you up the wall. You can't think straight even for a second. I'm telling you, I felt as if someone was trying to flip me out. And then it just stopped." Miron took one more drag on the cigarette, and put it out in the sand. "And I'll tell you something else," he said. "I know this sounds wacked, but I think it was Nimrod."

The next day, contrary to all our predictions, Uzi arrived. Too bad I didn't take Miron up on his bet. As soon as Uzi put his bag down in the hut he dragged us straight to the restaurant, chewed some squid, and told us all about how the German guy had turned out to be even more of a pushover than he'd expected, and how happy he was to be with us, with his best friends, in Sinai, his favorite place in the whole world. After that, he went charging up and down the beach, calling "Yo Bro" at anything that moved, and hugging every Bedouin or Egyptian who wasn't fast enough to get away. When he got tired of that too, Uzi made us play backgammon with him, and after he beat both of us, he clobbered one of the Bedouins too, and then he made the Bedouin traipse up and down the beach behind his bald opponent yelling, "Watch out, girls, Abu-Gara's big." Miron tried to chill him out with a joint, but that only made Uzi crazier. He started coming on strong to a forty-year-old American tourist, gave up in no time, ate three pancakes, told Miron and me that he couldn't get over the peace and quiet of the place, ordered kebab, and suggested that maybe the three of us and his new Bedouin friend, who turned out to be a taxi driver, could go down to play the casino at Taba. Miron was dead set against it, because he figured he was just about to get lucky with navel stud, but Uzi was so worked up that he didn't stand a chance. "No shit," Miron said as soon as we got into the taxi. "The guy's completely lost it."

Abu-Gara and the Bedouin made a killing at Taba, swooping down on one table after the next, leaving nothing behind them but shattered croupiers and scorched earth. Between killings, Uzi wolfed down enormous slabs of apple pie and chocolate mousse cake. Miron and me just sat there, watching patiently, waiting for him to wear himself out. But the thing was, he just kept getting stronger and stronger. Once Uzi and the Bedouin had finished humiliating the casino and divvying up their winnings, we took the taxi to the border station. Miron and me reminded Uzi that we were supposed to be heading back, but he said it was out of the question. As far as he was concerned, the day was still young, and there was no reason not to cash in at a couple of clubs in Eilat before heading back. He made sure to give the Bedouin his business card, and they kissed about eighty times. Miron made one more try to persuade the Bedouin to take us back to the beach, leaving Uzi to continue his escapades on his own, but the Bedouin told us off and insisted that for us to leave a wonderful friend like Abu-Gara right in the middle of a celebration would be a disgrace, and he'd have loved to come with us himself except he wasn't allowed to cross the border. After that he kissed us too, got into the taxi, and disappeared. When Uzi got tired of the Spiral, we went to the Yacht Pub and then to some hotel called the Blue Something, and only then, after Miron and I had refused two different times to let him get some call girls sent up to our room, Uzi turned over on his stomach and started to snore.

Ever since that time in Sinai, Uzi's company's been on a roll. After the German pushover, Uzi found two other suckers, one an American and the other from India, and it looked like he was about to knock the whole world on its ass. Miron said it only went to show how crazy all those businesspeople were. Because the fact was that ever since Uzi'd gone off the deep end, he'd been getting bigger and bigger. Sometimes we'd still try to drag him with us to the beach or the pool hall, but even when he did come, he was so busy the whole time telling everyone how much he was enjoying it and what a great time we were having together, and checking the voice mail on his cell phone, that after an hour with him you'd simply lose the desire to live. "Don't worry. He'll outgrow it," I'd try to tell Miron, as Uzi got caught up in another transatlantic call just when it was his turn to shoot. "Sure," Miron would say in the tone of an ex-wacko who's got it all figured out, "and if it's doing the rounds, you're next."

NEXT IN LINE TO LOSE HIS SHIT

The next morning, I woke up in an utter panic. I had no idea what was causing it. I lay there, pressing my back to the mattress, trying not to move till I could figure out what had me so scared. But the more time went by, the less I could figure out what brought it on, and the more scared I got. I lie there in bed frozen, and keep telling myself, in the second person, as calmly as I can, "Take it easy, man, take it easy. This isn't really happening, it's all in your head." But the thought that this thing, whatever it is, is inside my head makes it a thousand times more horrifying. I decide to tell myself who I am, to say my name a few times in a row. That's bound to help me get a grip on myself. Except that all of a sudden even my name is gone. At least that gets me out of bed. I crawl around the house, searching for bills, mail, anything with my name written on it. I open the front door and look at the other side of it, where there's an orange sticker with the inscription: "Have a hell of a life!" In the hallway there's the loud laughter of kids and the sound of footsteps approaching. I close the door and lean against it. Stay cool. In a minute I'll remember, or not—maybe I never had a name. Whatever happens, that isn't why I'm sweating so hard that my pulse is about to blow my brains out, that's not it, it's something else. "Take it easy," I whisper to myself again. "Take it easy, whatever your name is. This can't go on much longer, it'll be over soon."

As soon as it eased up, I phoned Uzi and Miron, and arranged to meet them both at the beach. It was just a few hundred yards from my place, and I had no problem remembering how to get there, except that all the streets suddenly looked different, and I had to keep stopping to check the signs to make sure they were really the right ones. Not just the streets, everything looked different, even the sky was kind of squashed, and low.

"I told you your turn would come," Miron says, and sucks at the red tip of his Wave-on-a-Stick Popsicle. "First I lost it, then Uzi." "I didn't lose it," Uzi protested. "I was just a little high, that's all." "Whatever," Miron went on. "It's your turn now." "Ron isn't losing it either," Uzi said, beginning to get worked up. "Why do you keep putting those ideas in his head?" "Ron?" I ask. "Is that my name?" "Know what?" Uzi concedes. "Maybe he has lost it a little. Can I get a bite?" Miron hands him the Popsicle, knowing perfectly well he'll never see it again. "Tell me," he asks. "When it started, didn't you feel there was someone in your head?" "I don't know." I hesitated. "Maybe I did." "I'm telling you," Miron whispered, as if it was a secret. "I could feel him. He was saying things that only he could know. I'm sure it was Nimrod."

NIMROD'S FLIPOUT

Until he turned twelve, Nimrod was a shitty person. The kind of whiner that, if he wasn't your best friend, you'd have kicked his ass a long time ago. And then one day, just before his bar mitzvah, they put insoles in his shoes, and suddenly the guy was a whole new human being. Yes, Miron, Uzi, and I had been friends with Nimrod even before that, but now, when he became nice too, it actually started to be fun to be around him.

Later, in high school, Uzi and me were in the honors program and Miron and Nimrod went to vocational school and mostly the beach. Then came the army. Miron was drafted six months before us, and by the time our turn came he'd sucked up to enough people to make sure we'd all be in the same unit with a cushy office job. Nimrod used to call it the padded pad.

Most of the time, we didn't do anything except sit around in the canteen, threatening to file complaints against our commanders, and go home every day at five. Other than that, Uzi would surf at the Sheraton, I was forever jerking off, Miron took courses at the Open University, and Nimrod had a girlfriend. Nimrod's girlfriend was as good as they get, and because all of us except him were virgins, that made her even better. I remember I once asked Miron what he would do—hypothetically, I mean—if she came to his house, say, and asked him to fuck her. And Miron said he didn't know, but whatever he did, he'd regret it the rest of his life. Which is a nice answer but knowing him, he'd be sure to take the fucking option first and the regretting option second.

But with Nimrod it wasn't even that he was horny; he was simply in love with her. Her name was Netta, which is a name that I still love to this day, and she was a paramedic at the infirmary. Nimrod told me once that he could lie next to her in bed for hours without getting bored, and that the place he liked her to touch the most was the spot on his foot where everyone had an arch but his was flat.

At the base we would do guard duty twice a month, and once every two months we had to stay the weekend, which Nimrod always managed to arrange for days when Netta had infirmary duty so that even on guard duty they were together. A year and a half later, she left him. It was a strange kind of split, even she couldn't really explain why it happened, and after that Nimrod didn't care when his guard duty came out. One Saturday, Miron, Nimrod, and I were on duty together. Uzi had just managed to forge some kind of a medical pass for himself. We were all on the same patrol—Miron first, Nimrod second, and me third. And even before I had a chance to replace him, this officer rushed in and said that the guy on duty had put a bullet in his head.

ROUND TWO

The second time Miron lost it, it was much more unpleasant. We didn't say a word about it to his parents, and I just moved in with him till it passed. Most of the time he kept quiet, sitting in the corner and writing a kind of book to himself, which was supposed to eventually replace the Bible. Sometimes, when we'd run out of beer or cigarettes, he would swear at me a little, with conviction, and say that I was really a demon disguised as a friend, and I'd been sent to torment him. Other than that, he was almost bearable. Uzi, on the other hand, took his extended period of sanity very hard. He didn't admit it, but it seemed like he'd really had it with that skyrocketing international company of his. Somehow, whenever he flipped, he had a lot more energy to write all these grim prospectuses and things and go to boring meetings. Now that he was a little more sane, the whole businessman thing was that much harder to handle. Even though it seemed as if his company was about to go public and he'd be sitting back, raking in a couple of million. Me, I'd been fired from another job, and Miron, in a lucid moment when he was off beer and cheap cigarettes, said that he was the one who'd gotten me fired with his unearthly spiritual powers. I don't know, maybe all those jobs just aren't for me, and all I should really do is sit it out till Uzi strikes it rich and tosses me a little.

The second time Uzi started going batshit proved once and for all that there was definitely a rotation thing going on, and I started to worry because I knew I was next. Miron, who'd chilled out by then, kept insisting it had something to do with Nimrod. "I don't know what he wants exactly. Maybe he wants us to even the score or something. But one thing's for sure, so long as we don't do it—whatever it is—I don't think it's going to stop." "Even what score?" I countered. "Nimrod killed himself." "How do you know?" Miron wouldn't let it go that easily. "Maybe he was murdered. Besides, maybe it isn't exactly vengeance. Maybe it's just something he wants us to do so he can rest in peace. Like in those horror films, you know, where they open a bar on an ancient burial ground, and as long as it stays there, the ghosts can't rest in peace." In the end, we decided that Miron and I would go to the Kiryat Shaul cemetery to make sure nobody had set up a Coke-and-mineral-water stand on Nimrod's grave by mistake. The only reason I agreed to go there with him was that I was freaking out about it being my turn soon. The truth was that of the three of us, my crack-up was the worst.

Nimrod's grave had stayed exactly the same. We hadn't been there in six years. At first, on Memorial Day for the fallen soldiers, his mother still used to call us. But with all those military rabbis and those aunts who'd faint away again every year, we weren't exactly eager to go. We kept telling ourselves that we'd go some other day, on our own special memorial day, except we always put it off. Last time we talked about it, Uzi said that actually every time we went to shoot pool together or took in a movie or a pub or whatever, it was a commemoration of Nimrod too, because when the three of us are together, then even if we're not exactly thinking about him, he's there.

It took Miron and me maybe an hour to find the grave, which actually seemed to be well tended and clean, with a couple of stones on top as proof that someone had been there not too long before. I looked at the dates on the grave and thought about how I was just about to turn thirty, and Nimrod wasn't even nineteen yet. It was kind of weird, because somehow, whenever I thought about him he was sort of my age, when in fact I hardly had any hair left and he was not much more than a kid. On our way out, we returned the cardboard yarmulkes to the box by the gate, and Miron said he didn't have any more ideas, but we could always have a séance. Outside the cemetery, on the other side of the fence, there was a fat, shaggy cat chewing a piece of meat. I looked at him, and as if he felt it, he looked up from the chunk of meat and smiled at me. It was a mean and ruthless smile, and he went back to chewing the meat without lowering his gaze. I felt the fear running through my body, from the hard part of my brain to the soft part of my bones. Miron didn't notice there was something wrong with me, and kept on talking. "Relax, Ron," I told myself. The fact that I remembered my name made me so happy tears came to my eyes. "Take a deep breath, don't fall apart. Whatever it is, it'll pass." At that very moment, in the smelly office of some attorney in Petah Tikva, Uzi was chickening out of signing a deal that would transfer thirty-three percent of his company's shares to an anonymous group of Polish investors for a million and a half bucks. Think about it, if only he'd stayed flipped out for another fifteen minutes, he could have taken us and the Turnip on a Caribbean cruise, and instead he was on his way home in a number-54 bus from Petah Tikva with an asshole driver who wouldn't even turn on the AC.

TRI-LI-LI-LI-LA

When Uzi announced he was going to marry the Turnip, we hardly even put up an argument. Somehow we'd known it would happen. Uzi lied and said it was his idea, and that it was mainly so he could take out a mortgage from the bank for an apartment that he'd planned to buy anyway someplace near Netanyah. 'How can you marry her?" Miron tried to reason with him, without much conviction. "You don't even love her." "How can you say I don't love her?" Uzi protested. "We've been together for three years. D'you know I've never cheated on her?" "That's not because you love her," Miron said. "It's just because you're uncoordinated." We were just shooting pool, and Uzi had clobbered both of us with the bull's-eye shots of someone who'd made up his mind to squeeze every drop out of the little bit of luck he still had left, quickly, before it had a chance to run out. There was only the eight ball left, and it was Uzi's turn. "Let's make a bet," I said, in an act of desperation. "If you pocket the eight ball, Miron and I will never call her Turnip again, ever. And if you miss, then you drop the whole wedding thing for a year." "When it comes to feelings, I never make bets," Uzi said, and pocketed the eight effortlessly. "Besides," he said, smiling, "it's too late. We've already printed up the invitations." "What were you thinking, betting him like that?" Miron told me off later. "That shot was a sure thing."

By the time the date rolled around, Uzi had managed to lose it two more times, and on both occasions he said he would call it all off, but changed his mind right away. As for me, I just crashed in Miron's apartment while it was going on. Now that we were wigged out most of the time, it was much nicer living together. And besides, I couldn't really afford my own place. Miron had stolen a big pile of wedding invitations from Uzi, and we would use them to make filters for joints. "How can you go and marry someone whose mother's name is Yentl?" he would ask Uzi whenever we'd smoke a joint together, and Uzi would just stare at the ceiling and give that spaced-out laugh of his. The truth was that even though I was on Miron's side on this, I could see it wasn't much of an argument.

Three days before the wedding we held a séance. We bought a piece of blue construction paper, I drew all the letters on it with a black marker, and Miron got a glass from the kitchen, one of those cheap ones. He said he'd had it for ages, from his parents' house, and that Nimrod must have used it. We turned out all the lights and placed the glass in the middle of the board. Each of us put a finger on it, and we waited. After five minutes, Uzi got tired of sitting there, and said he had to take a shit. He turned on the lights in the living room, found a week-old sports section, and locked himself in the bathroom. Miron and me rolled a joint meanwhile. I asked Miron—if it had worked, and if the glass had moved, what did he expect to happen. That pissed Miron off, and he said it was too early to say it hadn't succeeded and that just because Uzi gets bored with everything so quickly, it didn't mean that it wasn't going to work. After Uzi finally came out of the bathroom, Miron switched the lights back off and asked us both to concentrate. We put our fingers on the glass again, and waited. Nothing happened. Miron insisted that we try again, and neither of us could work up the energy to argue with him. A few minutes later, the glass began to move. Slowly at first, but within seconds it was racing all over the board. Miron left his finger on it the whole time and kept writing down with his other hand each of the letters that it stopped on. T-r-i-l-i-l-i-l-i-l-a the glass hummed, and came to a smooth stop on the exclamation mark in the right-hand corner of the board. We waited a while longer, and nothing happened. Uzi turned on the light. "Tri-li-li-li-la?" he said, annoyed. "What are we, in kindergarten or something? You moved it, Miron, so don't give me any Agent Mulder shit. Tri-li-li-li-la? Fuck it. I'm beat. I've been up since seven. I'm going to sleep at Liraz's." Liraz was the Turnip's name, and she lived close by. Miron kept staring at the board with the letters he'd drawn even after Uzi left, and for a while I read the sports supplement that Uzi had taken to the bathroom, and when I'd read it all, I told Miron I was going to crash. Miron said OK, but that first he just wanted us to give one more chance to the thing with the glass, because no matter how much he thought about it, that Tri-li-li-li-la thing didn't mean a thing to him. So we turned out the light again, and put the glass in place. This time it started moving right away, and Miron took down the letters.

D-O-N'-T-L-E-A-V-E-M-E-A-L-O-N-E the glass said, and then it stopped again.

MAZEL TOV

The wedding itself was awful, with a rabbi who thought he was a comedian and a DJ who played Enrique Iglesias and Ricky Martin. Still, Miron met this girl there with a squeaky voice but an amazing body. Plus, after the ceremony, he freaked Uzi out when he told him that the glass he'd stepped on was the one we'd used for Nimrod's séance. While this was going on, I got another of my anxiety attacks and puked about four pounds of chopped liver in the toilet.

That same night, Uzi and the Turnip flew off on their honeymoon in the Seychelles. Me and Miron sat on the balcony drinking coffee. Miron had a new thing going now. Whenever he'd make us coffee, he'd always make one instant for Nimrod too in the séance glass, and he'd put it on the table, the way you leave out a glass for Elijah on Passover, and after we were through drinking, he'd pour it down the sink. Miron did his version of the DJ, and I laughed. The truth was we were incredibly sad. You could call it chauvinist, possessive, egocentric, lots of names, but the whole wedding thing weighed us down. I asked Miron to read me a chapter from that book of his, the one he writes whenever he flips, and is supposed to replace the Bible. Actually, I'd asked him a million times, and he'd never do it. When he's flipped he's scared someone will steal his ideas, and when he's sane he's just embarrassed. "Come on," I said. "Just a chapter, like a kind of bedtime story." And Miron was so depressed that he agreed. He pulled a bunch of his scribbled pages out of his shoe drawer. Before he started reading, he looked at me and said, "You realize it's just the two of us left now, don't you? I mean, Uzi will still be one of us and all, but he won't be on Nimrod's rounds." "How can you tell?" I said, even though in my heart I'd thought of this even before he said it. "Listen," Miron said. "Even Nimrod knows it isn't right to pick on someone who's already married. The way he flips us out isn't always the best idea either, but the truth is that he wouldn't be doing it to us if he didn't feel deep inside that we agree. There's nothing we can do about it. We're screwed, Ron. There's just me and you, one week each, like kitchen duty."

Miron picked up the pile of pages and cleared his throat, like a radio announcer who chokes in the middle of reading the news.

"And if one of us suddenly goes?" I asked.

"Goes?" Miron looked up from his pages, confused. "Goes where?"

"I don't know," I said, smiling. "Just goes. Imagine what if tomorrow the woman of my dreams comes on to me in the street, and we fall in love, and I marry her. Then you'd be the only one left to flip with Nimrod, full-time, alone."

"Right." Miron gulped down the last drops of his coffee. "Good thing you're so ugly."

LIZARD

Kim Yŏng-ha

Translated from the Korean by Dafna Zur

Kim Yŏng-ha (1968–) began writing career with his first novel *I have the right to destroy myself*, which won him the much-coveted Munhakdongne Prize in 1995. Since then, he has gained a reputation as the most talented and prolific Korean writer of his generation, publishing five novels and three collections of short stories. In autumn 2008, he resigned all his jobs to devote himself exclusively to writing. Kim also translates novels written in English, most recently a Korean adaptation of F. Scott Fitzgerald's *The Great Gatsby*. As a child, he suffered poisoning from coal gas and lost all of his memories from before the age of ten.

1

> *Kiss the snake on the tongue. If it senses fear it'll devour you instantly. But if you kiss it without fear it'll take you through the garden, through the gate to the other side. Ride the snake to the end of time.*
> —JIM MORRISON, from the movie *The Doors*

Want to hear the one about the smoke woman? he asks me.

Sure, go ahead.

He's smoking a cigarette. Watching the smoke seep out of his mouth, twist, coil, and drift off.

Okay. One day a man's body turns up. The officer at the scene finds the place littered with cigarette butts. The place reeks of cigarette smoke—it's so strong it covers up the smell of decomposition.

So? . . . I look at him wide-eyed, urging him on.

So how'd he die? Good question. The officer investigates different possibilities. First, he schedules an autopsy. Which is more involved than the usual exam—in an autopsy, you actually cut into the body as well as looking around it for clues. And then the officer discovers something very interesting.

What's that?

The man was naked from the waist down. And there was a large quantity of semen.

I've heard that men ejaculate when they die, I say with a shiver.

He shakes his head.

That's if you're strangled. But there were no signs of strangulation on this guy. If you're strangled, your neck is all black and blue. None of that on him, though.

So? . . .

So the officer starts to suspect there's a woman involved.

He could have been masturbating, you know.

No he couldn't. First of all, nobody dies masturbating. Second, the semen was too spread out. Strange as it all seems.

I know nothing about how men masturbate, but he was so confident in his answer that I had to give in. He's always like that. No doubts about anything. Language seems to come so easy to him. No hesitating, no beating around the bush. Talking to him is like watching a movie or reading a novel. All of a sudden he feels like a stranger. How long has it been since he started coming into my room? How long since he spread himself so naturally over the far corner of my bed? Oh, well. It's all because of the *lizard*. I turned to look at my white walls. They're bare, except for the looming *lizard*.

What are you thinking about? He's noticed I've turned my head.

I look away from the *lizard*.

Nothing.

Men are always asking women what they're thinking. But women don't think the way men do. Men think with their heads, but women think with their bodies. That's why they can't be as articulate as men. Really, it's something that just can't be explained. All I can do is feel the traces of the man and the *lizard*. That's why "Nothing" is the only answer I can come up with.

Go on with the story, I tell him.

But he just offers me a weak smile and shakes his head.

Later.

He dresses and steps out. And off he goes, leaving me with a *lizard,* a dead man, and a large quantity of semen. I have no idea where he's going. He asks no questions, gives no answers.

I first met him in the fall of 1995. It was cold for that time of year, and extremely windy—a street sign blew over on someone's head that day. I was teaching English to junior high kids at a cram school in Kangnam at the time. I was about to photocopy some handouts and in he walked.

Are you still looking for teachers? he asked.

The funny thing was, I'd seen him get out of the elevator and plod up to the door, and still he took me by surprise. Maybe because he didn't look like he had any intention of working at a cram school. What was it about him? He was, after all, wearing the cram-school outfit—navy blue shirt and black pants—so what was it that threw me off?

I guess you could say there was something otherworldly about him. There are people like that. People you bump into on the street and come away feeling like you've bumped into a ghost. People you walk right up to prepared to pass straight through. People who will turn into a heap of ash if you give them a little nudge. You can see them in the subways, too. They look like they've been sitting there for centuries and aren't about to go anywhere. People who make it seem that the subways will run forever, just for them. There are people like that. And he was one of them.

What do you teach?

Korean.

The way he said it was so awkward it made me doubt for a moment that we even taught it there. Korean . . . Korean . . . I mumbled it over and over on our way to the principal's office. And from that day on he taught Korean.

2

The Indians say the first shaman invented sex. They call him "the one who makes you crazy."

—JIM MORRISON, *The Doors*

You have to transform yourself, he mumbled to me the second time we went drinking. With that, he produced an object wrapped in white paper and placed it on the table.

A present, he said.

I tore the wrapping off, and what I saw made me flinch. A *lizard*. A black metal *lizard*. It was so elaborate that if I hadn't touched it I'd have thought it was real.

Hang it so it looks like it's crawling down your wall. You'll get a rise out of your friends the first time they see it.

I felt a bit leery about all this but put the *lizard* in my handbag nonetheless.

Where'd you buy it?

In the tropics. *Lizards* are as common as ants down there. From the time you're a kid you get used to *lizards* crawling over your belly and your legs. They're everywhere. There's even a *lizard*-worshiping tribe.

Really?

Did you know that a *lizard*'s tail grows back if you cut it off? That's why *lizards* symbolize regeneration and rebirth. People in Europe in the Middle Ages prayed to the salamander. They thought it was a fire-breathing *lizard*; they believed salamanders lived in fire. Chameleons are *lizards* too. *Lizards* have no past. That's what makes them gods. For them there's nothing but the present, an eternal present.

I gave him a long, hard look. I just couldn't figure him out. I'd only been out with him twice, and yet not a word about his past. I couldn't tell you where he'd gone to school, where he was from, or where he'd worked.

We said goodbye and I went home and dutifully studied the walls of my room, which were bare except for a single coat hanger. My friends tell me it doesn't look like a girl's room. Which makes me realize I've never bought anything to decorate it. Not even the standard picture frame. A boring education will do that to you.

I hammered a nail into the wall opposite my bed and hung the *lizard* by the loop in its twisty tail. He was right—it really did look like it was crawling down the wall. And suddenly the wall buzzed with tension.

I saw the *lizard* in my dreams that night. I knew it was supposed to be hanging motionless but there it was crawling down the wall, slow and sinuous, expanding and contracting. The strange thing was, none of this struck me as the least bit extraordinary. It actually made me impatient to see it moving so slowly. I bolted awake and looked at the wall. The *lizard* was hanging there, just where it's supposed to be.

3

The world is a monster of energy, without beginning and without end. This world is a will to power and nothing besides.

—JIM MORRISON, *The Doors*

The *lizard* started coming to me right around the third time he and I went out drinking. I arrived at home that night to discover that the boiler was off and my room was cold. The room looked exactly as it had when I left. When that happens and you live by yourself you lose heart. You come home and open your door hoping for a miracle—but nothing has changed. Then again, it's supposed to be bad luck if you clean your room at night. So I jumped into bed. The alcohol I'd drunk was leaving an uncomfortable path as it spread through my blood vessels. I turned off the lights and stared at the *lizard* hanging on my wall. I played with the idea of giving it a name. But I couldn't come up with anything and in the meantime I drifted off to sleep.

The lizard is creeping down the wall. I can't move. I feel like I'm tied down. I can't make a squeak. There's music. The slow solemn beat of a drum. The rhythm is familiar but I can't place it. The beat is punctuated by a hiss. Is that what it sounds like when the *lizard*'s tongue flickers? I keep my eye on the *lizard*. It's the only thing I can do. The *lizard* is creeping toward my bed. And then he's out of sight. He's entered my blind spot. Now I'm twice as scared. Scared, but excited. The hissing grows louder than the drumbeat. There, the *lizard*'s head, at the foot of my bed. Suddenly I'm in a rain forest, still in my bed. There's bright sunlight all around, and birdsong and the distant beating of drums. The lizard has mounted my leg. I feel something I've never felt before, like an electric shock. And then a voice, my father's voice. I can barely hear it. He's speaking very fast. I'm frightened. I've been bad, I tell him. I don't know what I've done but I beg his forgiveness. He's naked and his face is angry as it approaches my bed in the rain forest.

The *lizard* has slithered up my thighs. It's embarrassing having my father there. His face is red with anger. He's going to beat me, I know it. I'm scared. The *lizard* has stopped. Out comes the tongue and it starts licking my thighs. Feels like ice water running down my thighs. Uncomfortably cold, but gently ticklish. In spite of my best intentions the *lizard*'s tongue awakens sensations long dormant. Father comes closer, looking back and forth from me to the *lizard*. I can hear my mother's laughter in the distance. She's telling him, See, I told you. I told you she's got spunk. Father doesn't answer.

The *lizard* is moving up. It's reached my vagina. I want to scream. But my father and mother are looking on. Dirty whore. This *lizard* is yours? My father scolds me. I want to defend myself, but the words don't come out. Pleasure overwhelms me.

It's all so strange. Never have I been satisfied by a man. They're either in too much of a hurry or awkward. So sex is always a drag for me. I don't understand how men can be so horny and yet so incapable in bed.

I'm twenty-five and I've slept with three men. The first one was just a boy. He'd kiss like he was trying to suck my tongue out, then tear my clothes off and penetrate me as fast as he could. I guess I should feel grateful he took the time to kiss me. The second one would make a dash for the bathroom to wash himself as soon as he ejaculated. He made me feel as if I had soiled him. And then he'd conk out for the night while the foreign substance was still wiggling inside me. The third one was just plain scared of sex. He'd go through with it, but he obviously wanted to get it over with as soon as possible. He kept asking, did he come too soon, was his penis too small, was I really satisfied? It was so tiresome. No, he never gave me an orgasm, but it would have been worse to disappoint him so I just lied. Oh yes, it was lovely—absolutely wonderful. And then he'd go to sleep. I don't think he really believed me.

But this is different. A sharp wave of pleasure spreads through me. I can't bear it! I don't hear the drumbeat anymore. Can't see Mom or Dad, either. And then I see the face of the man who gave me the *lizard*. He stands there in the dark, a faint shadow, smiling. And then I'm awake. But I still can't move. The sun is coming out. I desperately force my eyes open and stare at the wall. The *lizard* is nowhere in sight. I shake my head violently, I trying to clear my head. I feel along the wall for the switch and my eyes return to where the *lizard* should be hanging.

And there it is, exactly where it's supposed to be.

4

I'm a fake hero. A joke that God's played on me.
                    —JIM MORRISON, *The Doors*

I lost contact with most of my friends the year I taught at the cram school. Most cram school teachers go to work in the afternoon and don't head home until well past midnight. My friends worked different schedules that made it impossible for us to meet. But I was used to odd hours. Father was a minister in a small church, one he had established himself. It was on the third floor in an apartment complex, and none too big—maybe a thousand square feet or so. Mother was busy from sunup to sundown doing the things you would expect a minister's wife to do—keeping in touch with the parishioners, cleaning the sanctuary, helping Father with his sermons, and keeping up with the housework. She was even busier the days there were early-morning and late-night prayer meetings. Father was always somber, Mother was always obedient, I was always bored. We lived in a small room off the sanctuary; I felt like we were surrounded by hymns. Very rarely I'd catch a glimpse of Mother and Father having sex. Father's heavy breathing would wake me and I could hear Mother moaning from somewhere inside the blankets. Her moans sounded like the inarticulate recitations of the parishioners. I never could understand what she was trying to say. Sometimes she'd cry out. When she did that, Father scolded her.

And once in a while he beat her. The house was dirty; or where had she put the sermon? Mother took her beatings silently, the big wooden cross looming over his head.

A large sign hung at the entrance to the sanctuary: *Faith, Hope, Love.* But neither Mother nor Father seemed to have any hope for me, or faith or love for that matter. I spent my days playing on the swing in the neighborhood playground or poking around the shops nearby. I hated church.

Years went by but Father's church failed to grow. And then Mom disappeared. She left no word, just up and vanished. The parishioners talked about her whenever they could, their gossip revolving about Satan, snakes, and running away. At the time I was in the habit of drawing snakes in my diary. I'd be staring off into space and then realize I'd filled the page with coils of snakes. I'd write *Mommy, I miss you* and decorate the words with writhing reptiles.

Father remarried a churchgoer some ten years his junior and moved the church. I transferred to a university in Seoul, able finally to leave home. I lied to my father when I spoke with him on the phone: Yes, I go to church every day; the minister's sermons are great, they're really inspiring; and I'm in the choir. At school I majored in mathematics. I spent four years struggling with differential calculus and integral calculus. The innocent and straightforward world of mathematics appealed to me. The first midterm I ever took in differential and integral calculus asked me to "prove that 1 is larger than 0." I did it using epsilon and delta. I even managed to produce a complex drawing of a flower as part of a calculus problem. That's how I spent my early twenties, hovering between 1 and 0.

Even now I draw the occasional snake. I was never afraid of them, maybe because I never actually saw one in the flesh. I remember the adults whispering into my young ears that a snake had wrapped itself around my mother. What a joke. I knew what they said was all a lie. I think I was jealous of my mother. I wanted to run away from that church and its oppressive hymns, too. To a place where I wouldn't have a cross looking down on me all the time.

5

The first time I did it, I saw God.

—PAMELA, *The Doors*

The *lizard* entered me a few days after I had that dream. I think it was late in the afternoon and I was sitting in front of the VCR with a cold beer, watching a Hollywood action flick, when I dropped off to sleep.

The dream begins with the *lizard*'s familiar movement. It's darting down the wall. Doesn't scare me one bit. The *lizard* is coming toward the bed. I remember that if you cut off a *lizard*'s tail, it starts to grow back right away. I'd like to talk to the *lizard*. The *lizard* climbs onto the bed. Mom is going somewhere. I'm sorry, Mom. I beg her forgiveness, not really knowing what I've done wrong. The *lizard* has climbed up on my foot and it's coming closer. Its tongue is caressing my every curve. Oh, please. I can't move, I bite down hard on my lip, I cry out.

I'm younger now. I'm lying down. I'm wearing a short skirt and there's a ribbon in my hair. The *lizard* is presenting me with an image. I'm a little girl and I'm playing with myself as I gaze at the naked images of Adam and Eve. Excitement rushes over me. The scene changes. I'm in Sunday school, the minister's daughter, touching the penis of one of the boys in my class. I slowly lower his trousers, staring, wanting to put his penis in my mouth. It's suddenly bigger. And the boy is taller—he's an adult. A lush forest of hair rings his penis, and I delight in running my fingers through it. I put his penis in my mouth and feel it harden.

My mouth starts to hurt. His penis has turned into a block of wood and I can barely extract it from my mouth. But now it's a neon cross. I kneel piously before this red, glistening cross. My saliva is dribbling from it. I wonder who he is. I raise my head and look into his face. I've never seen him before.

The *lizard* closes this image and proceeds to prowl my crotch, its tongue and tail teasing my vagina and inner thighs. I'm sweating all over. The *lizard*'s head is coming closer and closer. Suddenly my legs are wide open. The *lizard* is gazing at my sex. I'm embarrassed—it's inspecting a part of me that I myself have never examined. He draws his tongue in and starts to enter me. I thought it would hurt but it doesn't. I am wet enough and this knowledge both shames and excites me. I can feel the *lizard* wiggling into me. My head feels like it's going to explode. Now only its tail is visible. Something inside me is trembling violently. It could be the *lizard,* but I'm not really sure.

What are you up to? Mom asks. Suspicious, she examines my bed from the corner of her eye. I pray that she won't see the *lizard*. Deeper, I beg it. She mustn't see its tail. I urge it all the way inside me, but its tail is still showing. Mother hasn't discovered the *lizard* yet. Even with her looking on, my excitement slowly reaches a climax. The ice-cold *lizard* is making its way deeper inside me. I grimace and try to contain my excitement. Mother looks on, dispassionate. Mother. I hurt terribly. She looks like she doesn't believe me.

Mother wants to take the *lizard* away from me, I know she does. I tense my muscles to keep the *lizard* in. The *lizard* crawls deep inside me, so deep that its tail isn't showing anymore. Mom can't see the *lizard* now. The *lizard* is mine, all mine. I grin at my mother as that ice-cold *lizard* wiggles and turns inside me. Mother is grinning back at me. Her grin grows wider. The head of a snake appears at her mouth, and the body slithers out. She bends over to help it out. It looks like she's vomiting. Mommy, I ask her, where's the baby? It died, you know that. I mean, we killed it, don't you remember? Mommy, no. I didn't kill it. I never saw it. The snake that crawled out of my mother has vanished. I awake from my dream and look at the wall. The *lizard* is gone. I shut my eyes again. The dream resumes. The *lizard* starts wiggling inside my belly again. My anus throbs with pain. Please, no. The *lizard* starts to slither out my backside. I want to have a baby. Mother. I'll have your baby for you, Mother. I entreat her, fighting back my pain, but she leaves without listening. The *lizard* exits me. I am overcome with pain and exhaustion. I slowly wake and look at the wall. The *lizard* is nowhere to be seen. Of course not. Because it's still with me, asleep. The phone rings, clearing my head a bit more. Wrong number. I look up again at the wall.

The *lizard* is there, exactly where it's supposed to be.

6

Lizards *have no past. That's what makes them gods. For them there's nothing but the present, an eternal present.*

—KIM YŎNG-HA, *"Lizard"*

Since the *lizard* entered me that first time I've had sex a few times; an old boyfriend got back in touch. But it was business as usual when I slept with him. Which is to say I felt nothing. The whole time we were having sex I kept thinking about the *lizard*. I wish your penis was colder, I told him. He sat up and said, You've really changed. He had a very solemn expression on his face.

That was the end of that. He never came back. Maybe I really had changed, like he said. I snorted. And what if I had? The man who gave me the *lizard* told me I had to transform myself. Well, isn't that what you'd call changing? I remembered his words when I looked at the *lizard*. It was showing up regularly in my dreams. It would enter my anus and exit from my mouth, or enter through my vagina and exit through my eyes. Either way the sensation was almost the same. The days after I had the dream I was too tired to talk. I did feel refreshed and energized, though.

Once in a while at the cram school I'd see the man who had given me the *lizard*. He'd pass by with a mysterious smile. I wondered sometimes if he was there in my dreams, watching. I felt like his eyes could see right through me. Maybe that was why I felt myself blush whenever I spotted the nape of his neck. Why it was the nape of his neck I can't say. But once I saw him in the cram-school cafeteria in the basement. He was all by himself, spooning hot soup and rice to his mouth. I stood at the door, my eyes fixed on his back. He ate silently, his head lowered, while I focused on the nape of his neck. There was a stubborn tenacity in those clenched neck muscles. They made him seem lonely. Something about that neck, I don't know what, reminded me of the *lizard*. I wanted to embrace him. It wasn't even about sex. I just wanted to rush up to him, put my arms around him, and press my lips to the nape of his neck. I couldn't eat at the cafeteria that day.

I often saw him after that. He'd come over to my place once a month or so. We listened to music, shared a drink. He didn't want to have sex. I wasn't interested, either. And so we'd sit together talking quietly and refreshing each other's drink. He said he enjoyed traveling. Working at the cram school was for him an ideal arrangement—no relationships to commit to, and the freedom to leave at any moment.

And here we are. I'm waiting for him to come back and finish the story about the smoke lady. Then again he may never come back. Maybe I'll have to finish the story myself. I even started to imagine that he was back.

Come on, finish the story.

The detective discovers the dead man's diary at the scene.

He starts talking. I light a cigarette for him. The smoke seeps deep into my lungs.

The diary tells of a most captivating woman: Will I see her tonight? She overpowers my senses. I spend the whole day just waiting for this woman.

He goes on with the story.

The detective does some detecting and learns that the man graduated from college but was unemployed and spent his days doing god-knows-what in his room—he was a vagrant, friendless in Seoul. His few acquaintances said they never saw him with a woman. A prostitute, perhaps? He didn't exactly have the means to buy a woman. So who was she?

Didn't you say he scheduled an autopsy? I ask.

He answers: He did, and the result was that the victim had had a fatal heart attack. The detective then resumes his search for evidence, but finds nothing he can connect to the woman. So he gets to thinking. He goes back to the scene, does yet another search, and a second diary turns up. This diary contains the following entry: My one pleasure is making creations out of smoke. Yesterday I made a car and I made an alcoholic beverage. I drank my smoky drink and drove my sporty car. I shut the windows tight to keep the smoke inside my room and to keep the air still. And yet it lasts only a moment. I need a woman. The detective closes the diary and concludes his report. Direct cause of death: heart attack. He rules out homicide and suicide. This was a case of death by natural causes.

I understand now, I say. The man created a woman out of smoke. He was caressed by her, and they had sex. But he's not allowed to touch her. She'll disappear if he does. She slowly drifts down and embraces him. His every sense is overwhelmed.

He nods in agreement. That's right. But the detective keeps that part of the story to himself. Who will believe him? And it makes little difference if no one does.

Cigarette smoke can be very comforting, I say, smoking a cigarette myself. I look up at the *lizard*. It looks bigger than usual today. I crawl into bed, craving sleep. The man keeps his distance as usual. I turn off the lights and drift off to sleep.

As I sleep, I sense someone opening the window to my room and climbing in. I think it's him, but my head is heavy. I hear him taking his clothes off. We've never slept together, and yet he calmly climbs into my bed as if he were my husband. His hands move gently from my feet up my knees and thighs. His hands are cold. I feel goose bumps all over. He climbs on top of me. His cold hard penis pushes inside me. Mustn't shout. I steady myself. And I mustn't touch him. If I do he'll vanish. His penis moves slowly. Violent pleasure explodes inside me. I tremble with a satisfaction I've never felt with a man. A neon cross flashes in the distance. He's thrusting more strongly now. His cold penis slides all over my body. I'm soaked through. I'm afraid his cold penis will pierce me. You must transform yourself, I remember him telling me. His words reverberate. Ahhh, I'm going away—go past the tropical sunshine, through the forest of crosses, and you'll arrive at the playground. I want to scream but nothing comes out. My ears ring with the rhythmical beating of the tribal drums. It feels like his penis is coming out my ears. My eardrums are about to explode.

I'm languishing. He gets up and dresses. And then he's gone, like smoke. Carefully I open my eyes and look toward the wall. The *lizard* is gone. I don't bother to turn the lights on to make sure. I simply close my eyes again. And fall asleep. A most tranquil sleep. I never want to wake up.

SHE FREQUENTED CEMETERIES

Dorthe Nors

Translated from the Danish by Martin Aitken

Dorthe Nors (1970–). A novelist and short story writer and translator, Nors studied at Aarhus University and worked as a teacher for some years before publishing her first novel *Soul* in 2001. She was first introduced to an Anglo-American readership in 2009 when several American magazines published stories by her, leading *The New Yorker* – for the first time – to publish a Danish writer. Since then, a collection of her short stories, *Karate Chop* has been published in English, together with her novel *Mirror, Shoulder, Signal*, which was a finalist for the Man Booker International Prize 2017.

She started frequenting cemeteries that summer, preferring the ones others rarely visited. She could go straight from social events with white wine, canapés, and peripheral acquaintances, cycle to the nearest cemetery, and find the corner where no one ever really went. At the far end of Vestre Cemetery, by the Inuit and the Faeroese and the war graves, down by the disused chapel was a quiet spot. Well away from the plots where brewers, publishers, and prime ministers lay shoulder to shoulder and were dead. There was no edged grass, no small ponds with specially purchased ducks. Most of all, it resembled the hinterland of Jutland, depopulated and with plywood boards across the windows, and through it all a diagonal tunnel of willow trees. No one ever went there, so that was where she liked to go. In the same way, she was fond of the Jewish cemetery and the Catholic cemetery, and, provided she chose the right times and the right spots, Assistens Cemetery could be quiet, too.

Her favorite, though, was just between Frederiksberg and Valby. It was best in the twilight. In late July the evenings were still long and the place was like an overgrown park. Walking along the paths in the cemetery she found the unkempt graves of long-forgotten painters and poets, and at the northern end she came across a section where roses grew everywhere. The bushes had grown over the stones, weeds had tangled up in them, and they were the same roses her mother had at home. Pink, with small flowers, and no one bothered to cut them back. When she got to this part of the cemetery she would stroll peacefully around the paths as if she was drawing arabesques with her feet.

She was thirty-five years old and that summer she was avoiding her girlfriends. Now and then they would call her and ask about meeting up, but she would decline whenever possible. She knew they would be troubled by her situation, and that her way of dealing with what she claimed had happened would excite them and cause them to speculate impulsively. On a few occasions she tried to explain the situation to them, but it had not been pleasant. A few of them had tried to talk her out of it, suggesting her condition was the result of loneliness or biology. One had interrogated her. Was she quite sure, was it wise, wouldn't it be better if . . . All of them wanted to give her advice, even if she didn't need any. She knew why she was going to the cemeteries, why she continued to walk back and forth, and around and about, eating ice cream and rolling rose petals between her fingers. She was waiting, and while she was waiting she was putting something behind her and trying to find a new way of looking at the future. She walked slowly and if not devoutly then at least pensively and with a sense for the little things she didn't feel she'd noticed for years. She saw the wild cats that lived in the bushes. She saw how they drank water from the pond in the middle of the cemetery. She saw the magpie's young and the graves that had fallen in and the gravestones that had tipped over so it looked like the dead and their monuments were about to change places. As summer passed she saw the plants grow and fade, and some evenings she would pick a few of the pink roses and take them home with her to put in a vase on the bedside table. She thought mostly about how hard it was to be allowed to believe that good would arrive and how things would be when in spite of everything it did.

What had happened wasn't exactly spectacular. She had met a man. That was all. She loved him, and the way she loved him had made her settle into a place inside her where intangible things took on natural substance. She felt at home there and she knew that at some point she would look back on this summer as the one when she stopped holding back. Her feelings were strong and reciprocated. She sensed it, yet she knew also it would take time before they could be together. He was in mourning for things he'd lost, and his mourning was unhurried. She could see that when he looked up at her from the table. But she was all right with it, because when he looked at her she was in no doubt and could abandon herself to the hope that he would bring all the good with him when he came.

But there was no way she could explain this to her girlfriends. They demanded evidence. They wanted to know who had died, why he kept crying, and if it really wasn't just his own fault. They wanted to know if she'd looked into him and if she knew what laying down arms involved. She mustn't get her heart broken, they said. That was the important thing. Not to get her heart broken. And all the time they jumped from floe to floe with their dreams of disappearing into the current, losing control, abandoning themselves. Always trying to fill in the empty spaces and keep things moving in the meantime. Doing their best to avoid going home too early to their little apartments that reminded them of coffee bars and bus shelters every time they stepped through the door. Love, nothing less. That was what they wanted. That was what they craved, unconditionally. It was what they talked about when they put their arms under hers and dragged her through the parks, as though the parks were eyes in a storm that had to be sat out, and now she had found it. But she couldn't tell them. There was no way she could share it with them, so that summer she frequented cemeteries.

She would focus on her job, including her hospitality duties, but when it was done she would get on her bike and be gone. In the early evening she would pass through the iron gates into Park Cemetery, stroll past the dead painters, the poets, and head for the place where the pink roses were. When she got there she would walk between the graves, and as she went she closed her eyes to the parts of reality the others were keeping a watch on and imagined the man, who could only be with her in spirit, lacing his fingers in hers. They would walk there in various scenarios, sometimes silently, but together. They would be walking there when he said he loved her. Things like that would be said as they walked side by side through the cemeteries in the various stages of their as-yet-uninitiated time together. She had no trouble picturing the man zigzagging in between the small plots with a child on his shoulders. She could see the man and the child leap out from among the bushes where the wild cats lived. She could feel him kiss her behind the cemetery toilets, see the child fall and hurt itself, hear the wheels of the buggy squeak. Often he would sit down on one of the benches a little farther on and pat the space beside him so she would sit there with him, and that was what she did.

There was nothing secretive about it. She was in love with someone, and while it was going on she thought about the good that had happened and the good that was going to happen. The noise of traffic on Søndre Fasanvej and Roskildevej remained a distant hum as she stole names for the child from the gravestones, and it felt nice, the same way it felt nice to let her thoughts sink into the earth where one day they themselves would lie, white through to the bone and tangled up in each other while the world carried on above them. That was okay, she thought. That kind of death was a good thing, and she would tell him that when he came, and she would tell the child when it was old enough, and perhaps a particularly distraught girlfriend one day. Until then she would keep it to herself, frequent the cemeteries, waiting and occasionally squatting down to see the cats stretch their necks toward the water.

ORANGES

Mirja Unge

Translated from the Swedish by Kari Dickson

Mirja Unge (1973–) is a Swedish novelist and short story writer acclaimed as one of the leading writers of her generation. She published her first novel *Det var ur munnarna orden kom* (*Out of Your Mouth the Words Come*) in 1998, which won the Katapult Prize for best debut novel. This was followed by *Järnnätter* (*Anticlockwise*) and a second novel *Motsols* (*Tide*) which was shortlisted for the Swedish Radio Award. Her stories and novel, focussing on the the confusing experiences of young girls growing up, have earned her a devoted fanbase among young readers in her native Sweden. *It Was Just, Yesterday* was published in English in 2011.

It was nice of them to come and, like, bother about the fact you're turning eighteen and that. I hadn't really thought about it, just stood there in the door and they sang happy birthday and Anita got all soppy and was running around now, in her dressing gown, putting on the coffee and making breakfast. And they'd got Linus with them too, stood there in the hallway in his snow-covered trainers with ten bloody roses that he'd bought, and he held them out and he hugged me and I hadn't showered or washed my hair so it just hung lank and looked greasy, I thought, but it didn't seem to bother him because he nuzzled in, even though I kind of froze a bit. And Sara took Vicke out of the cage where he was dozing, because she liked having him on her lap and he liked it too and sat there grinding his teeth when she scratched him between the ears and he was bloody overweight even though Anita had had him on a diet for ages now.

Mum hadn't met Linus, though I'd told her I hung out with him, so she knew about him and all that, and now he was sitting there, on the bench in the kitchen where we usually sat, Anita and me, now he was sitting there, and he smuggled the *snus* out of his mouth and back into the tin. And Sara and Magda had presents and things that they piled up on the table and Anita had got some clothes on and was sitting, smoking under the fan, and offered her yellow Blend cigarettes to everyone but no one wanted one. Magda rolled her John Silver and sat down with Anita by the fan and Linus drank his coffee and looked at me and gave me a knowing smile and Sara sat there, feeding Vicke crispbread, so he was happy as a pig in shit because no one bothered about him otherwise. Linus stretched his hand out under the table and stroked my knee and Anita said she thought it was really nice to meet Linus as well because I've heard so much about you, she said, and Linus gave a lopsided smile and stroked my knee. Aren't you going to open them then, Magda said, and I played with my fringe and it was really nice of them to get presents and all that, so I picked the smallest one and unwrapped some really cool earrings with the peace sign on, and then I realised what was in the other one when I gave it a shake, and Magda grinned and Linus packed some *snus* and put it in and wiped his fingers on his jeans. I started to unwrap the second present and Anita shuffled around barefoot in her Scholls and put some buns in the oven to defrost. I pulled the paper off and there was a tape inside, and how Magda'd got me a tape of Eddie Medusa I don't know, but it was a brand new tape and she grinned and said that it was a fucking good recording, much better than the one I've got, she said, and Anita wondered what it was and said that I should put it on the cassette player, there in the kitchen, but no fucking way, I thought. Anita put the buns down on the table and Linus and Sara started to eat. Jesus, thanks, I said, and nice of you to come and all that, and I held Linus' hand under the table, kind of warm and sweaty it was, and he sneaked a smile and slurped his coffee and flicked his blond fringe, his eyes brown below. Really nice of you to come, I said, because I realised that they must've got up early to take the bus out here and sacrificed a lie-in and all that. And Magda grinned and blew smoke up into the fan because it had probably been her idea to come here and to drag Linus along too, and he hadn't been here yet, even though we'd been together since the beginning of December. Magda had some wool with her and was going to plait me a friendship bracelet because she made really fucking cool ones. She got out her wool and I had to choose the colours and it was going to be a totally cool black and white one. Magda tied the wool to a safety pin and fixed it to her jeans and started to twist the wool and she was so fucking good at getting the pattern and all that. And Linus was comfortable on the kitchen bench and looked like he sat there all the time, drinking Anita's coffee. They all seemed to be getting on fine so I nipped out to the toilet and sprayed my hair and put on some mascara and when I came back again Anita was sitting, leaning forwards so she could see down the road, and I leant forwards as well and saw someone cycling down the road and it was wonky, I mean the bike was wonky as hell, and it was still icy right out to the main road. Look, there's someone coming down here on a bicycle, Anita said, and stubbed out her cigarette and leant forwards. Wow, your dad's coming too now, Anita said, and pulled another fag out of the packet. Could be anyone, that, I said. I mean, we had neighbours, didn't we. We didn't live in total fucking isolation. It is him, Anita said, so Lennart's got the bike out, obviously, and has come all the way over here, she said, and I saw that it was him cycling towards us, slowly slipping down the icy road, and the new kid was on the back, the new kid was sitting on the back, glaring out from under a sheepskin hat. And he's got the new kid with him, Anita said. No doubt he wants to say happy birthday to you. That's probably why he's cycled over here, because he's never had a driving licence and he obviously can't afford to take the bus, Anita said, and I knew only too well and so did everyone else in the town, for that matter, that Lennart cycles, and he's almost always hanging around in town with his bike. Ah, there's Linda's dad coming now, Anita said, and I said to her to sit by the fan and smoke and not wander around all over the place, because it stinks of cigarettes in here now, I said. And Magda and Sara looked out of the window at Lennart and saw him slipping on the ice. Is that your dad, Magda said, and leant forward and stared.

I didn't know that he was your dad, she said, and I mean she'd obviously seen him before, though they hadn't actually met, but they'd seen him around town with his bike. Standing there all the time, he was, with his bike, outside the supermarket, staring and saying hello to the people who went in. Linus spread another piece of bread and sat there and chewed and was always bloody hungry, he was, and Vicke sat grinding his teeth on Sara's lap, and I saw Lennart brake and slide on his bike on the icy road outside, and then he lifted the new kid off and locked up the bike and he had this bloody great basket on the handlebars. You won't have met Linda's dad, Anita said, and I said that she should cut more bread because Linus wanted more, didn't he, I said, and Linus grinned and said if there was any, well. The doorbell rang and there was a knock on the door and I skidded out into the hall in my woolly socks and opened the door and Lennart was standing there, smiley and bright, and the new kid was behind him all snotty in her waterproofs. Well, Lennart said, and nodded down at the new kid, now we can say happy birthday to Linda, he said, talking down to the new kid. Really nice of you to come, I said, and he barged into the hall with his basket and I peeked in and he'd obviously gone to town, Lennart, and packed it full of presents. Yes, he was smiling away, and the new kid was holding on to his trouser leg. Come on in then, I said, and he wiped away the new kid's snot with his hand. Should we go in, he asked the new kid, bending down, and I said of course they should come in. Is he coming in, Anita called from the kitchen, and Lennart bent down slowly and pulled the new kid's boots off. Well, they've asked us in now, Lennart said to the kid, and he didn't have a jacket on, I noticed, just several sweaters that he started to peel off. The layered method, I said, and he bent down over the kid and said well, we'd better go in now, and he obviously didn't have any money, Dad didn't have money, but he had layers of sweaters instead and he was standing there peeling them off, and underneath it all he was really sinewy and skinny as he walked across the floor with the kid hanging onto his trouser leg. Well, let's go into the kitchen then, he said to the kid, and I followed behind. Lennart lifted the new kid up onto the sofa, so there sat the kid, staring at Vicke who was perched crunching crispbread on Sara's lap. Lennart had holes under the arms of his innermost t-shirt, I noticed, and Linus sat and chewed on his sandwich and Magda sat by the fan smoking and plaiting the wool bracelet and Lennart looked at them for a while but he didn't say anything, even though they said hello to him, and Lennart stared back and Linus started to fidget with his *snus* and Madga lit another. There's other people here, Lennart said to the new kid. It's Linda's friends who're sitting here, you see, he said, and the kid sat there and squirmed in her waterproofs and was too bloody hot, I reckon. Oh, we've forgotten the basket, Lennart said, and went out to get it. Anita sat on the worktop with a cigarette and I said that she should hold it under the fan because it stinks of fags in here now, I said, and Lennart came in with the basket and cleared a space on the table for it, and Linda's eighteen now, you see, Lennart said to the new kid. You've got a lot with you there, Linus said, and Lennart smiled and stretched over and buttered a piece of bread, and he found some old mugs on the draining board and emptied one and filled it with coffee and stood there drinking. And it was quiet, just the whir of the fan and Vicke grinding his teeth when Sara pulled his ears and scratched them, and the basket stood there, big and full on the table, and he'd cycled out here with it. Really nice of you to come, I said, and he smiled and sort of raised his eyebrows and he got sick pay, only he didn't have any money, to come here with such a big basket, I said, and he smiled. But we'd like the basket back later, wouldn't we, he said to the new kid, and well of course he'd get it back, I understood that, I said, and I mean what would I do with it anyway? The new kid squirmed in her waterproofs and Linus searched for my hand under the table, a sweaty and warm hand he had, and he held mine. Anita said why don't we put on that tape, even though there was no fucking way we were going to. Oh well, said Anita, and sat there on the worktop tipping her shoe. And Magda eyed up the basket and said well, go on then, are you not going to open them, she said, and of course I would, wouldn't I. Couldn't it wait a while, or was there a rush, I said, and I didn't know how much time they had or how long they could stay and, I mean, hang out. Sara leant over towards the new kid and undid the zip on her rain jacket and the new kid started to take it off and Lennart smiled and said so you're getting help to take off your waterproofs. And should we help Linda to open her presents, he said to the kid, and stretched over and took one out of the basket and the kid pulled at the string and paper and suddenly an orange rolled out onto the table and Linus and Magda started to laugh their heads off and the kid stared at them and Anita sat on the worktop and tapped the ash from her cigarette and tipped her shoe on her toe. Give Linda a present, Lennart said to the kid, and the kid reached over and got hold of a present and gave it to me and that's nice, I said to the kid, and pulled at the string around the present and unwrapped another orange, and Madga and Linus laughed like before. Bloody good idea that, the oranges, Magda said, and Sara giggled and Anita lit up another cigarette and ran her thumb over her lower lip. And the kid handed me another present and I could feel that it was, well, round, I don't know, and I unwrapped an orange and Magda giggled and Sara asked if she could get one and of course she could. I went and got the coffee pot and asked if anyone wanted any, and Lennart held out his mug and I said to him that he could take a clean mug, because Anita had been drinking buttermilk from that one, I said, but Lennart smiled and winked and Magda said aren't you going to unwrap them all, then, and of course I am, but there isn't any rush, is there, and no need to bloody stress, I said, and Magda shrugged and rolled another John Silver and Anita took a drag and blew the smoke at the window and I said that she might as well open the window now, if she was going to blow smoke in that direction, otherwise it won't get out, I said. Okay, okay, Anita said, and opened the window and I sat down at the table again and took out another present and pulled at the string and unwrapped an orange that rolled out and over to the others, and Sara was sitting there giggling and peeling now, and Linus grinned and Magda thought it was a really cool idea, she said, and lit up her John Silver and I unwrapped another one that rolled away and the paper fell onto the floor and the string, and the new kid just stared and Lennart nodded and smiled and said to the kid that Linda's eighteen now, you see, Lennart said, and I unwrapped the presents and the oranges rolled all over the table and then lay still and Linus stopped grinning and packed in some *snus* and Anita sat balancing her Scholl shoe on her toe and I unwrapped oranges, one after the other, I unwrapped them and they rolled out of the paper and lay there shiny and orange on the table. Sara asked if she could peel one for the kid as well, and of course she can have one, and you too, I said, you can have one too. And there were only a few parcels left at the bottom now, and I picked them out and unwrapped them. Linus sat with his lip stretched over the *snus* and Sara chewed her orange while she peeled another and Mum dropped her slipper and fished it up again with her toe. I took the last present out of the basket and unwrapped it and is that the last one, Sara said, and I nodded and Linus sat with his mouth open and stared as I unwrapped it. I pulled off the string and unwrapped the last orange and it rolled out onto the table and lay there with the rest. There was silence and Magda got up and looked in the basket and then sat down again. The fan whirred and I reached for the last orange and started to peel it. Really nice of you to come, I said, and Lennart smiled. Magda sat and plaited the wool bracelet and kept her eyes on it and Linus had obviously taken a large pinch of *snus* and was numbed by it.

IN THE AISLES

Clemens Meyer

Translated from the German by Katy Derbyshire

Clemens Meyer (1977–) is a German novelist and short story writer. He studied German Literature Institute in Leipzig, though his studies were briefly interrupted by a spell in a youth detention centre. He worked as a security guard, forklift truck driver and labourer before publishing his first novel *Als wir träumten* in 2006. A collection of short stories, *All the Lights*, was published in English translation in 2011. His second novel was published in English as *Bricks and Mortar* in 2016. The novel won the prestigious Bremer Literaturpreis in 2014, and was shortlisted for the Deutsche Buchpreis in 2013.

Before I became a shelf-stacker and spent my evenings and nights in the aisles of the cash-and-carry market, filling shelves, fetching pallets from high on the storage shelves with the forklift, now and then helping one of the last customers of the evening and getting to know all kinds of food, I'd been working on building sites for a couple of years.

I hadn't given up of my own accord but I wouldn't have kept it up all that long, even if the boss hadn't fired me. I was a builder's mate, lugging sacks of cement and plasterboard, gutting flats – that meant I knocked the plaster off the walls, tore out fireplaces and chimneys with a big sledgehammer we used to call 'Rover', until I was covered in soot and dirt and spent hours getting the soot and dust out of my nose at home. The firm didn't even pay well and the boss was a bastard. The guy came from Bavaria; I've met people from Bavaria who were actually OK though.

I can't remember exactly when all the fuss with the boss started, but I do know we were demolishing an old roof that day. We found a big pigeon's graveyard, two pigeons still alive and perfectly still in among all the bones, piles of feathers and pigeon shit and decomposing and mummified corpses, and we could only tell by their eyes and their heads, moving slightly every now and then, that they were waiting. We fetched the Portuguese guys and they killed them with a blow of a spade. Then we tipped lime over the pigeon graveyard and shovelled it all into buckets and tipped them down the rubbish chute fastened to the scaffolding outside.

And after that we didn't feel much like hard work any more; the pigeons had got to us. We took the tiles off another section of the roof, not exactly motivated, removed the roof battens with wrecking bars, and then we took a lunch break.

We usually had our lunch break at eleven thirty, and when the bells of the church just round the corner rang at twelve we went back to work.

But when the bells rang that day we were still sitting with the Portuguese guys.

They were drinking red wine out of cartons, passing them around. The Portuguese guys spoke very bad German and earned even less than we did and lived in tiny basement flats in one of the buildings owned by the boss. They drank red wine at work because they knew the boss wouldn't fire them – they worked too well for too little money. They did bricklaying and plastering, and sometimes they were builder's mates like us, lugging sacks of cement, gutting flats until they were covered in soot and dust.

And then when the fuss with the boss started and I'd slapped him round the face on both sides with my cement-encrusted glove, they all came to me one after another and shook my hand, pressed it and pumped it, said, 'You did good thing' in broken German, laughed and said, 'You find new job, you good worker,' and patted me on the back.

'Lazy bastard,' the boss had called me, and I hadn't even been holding a wine carton any more, I was just sitting on an upturned bucket and leaning on the wall and trying to think of nothing at all.

And I wasn't a lazy bastard, even if I had overdone it a bit with my lunch break.

And when I started the job as a shelf-stacker in the cash and carry they noticed straight away that I wasn't a lazy bastard. I'd got the job through someone I knew, a guy who'd been working there for four years.

I'd got him a job seven or eight years ago and he knew I'd been out of work since the fuss at the building site, so when a job came up in the 'Shelf-filling/ Night' department he'd put my name down for it. I made a real effort, stacking the stock on the shelves where they showed me, pulling a large barred cart along behind me to put empty cartons and packaging into. They explained how to use the little manual pallet jacks for lifting and moving pallets of stock around. They had electric pallet jacks too, called 'ants', for transporting several pallets stacked up, but I wasn't allowed to use those ones yet.

It wasn't one of those cash-and-carries that anyone could shop at. The customers had to have a special card; they had to run a company, self-employed people and that kind of thing who were buying for their businesses. We had a food section and a non-food section, but I was only ever on food and beverages. It was a huge market, on two floors with clothing and electronics upstairs. The food section was on the lower floor, and made up of different departments like Processed Food, Confectionery, Frozen Food, Delicatessen, Fruit and Vegetables and a couple of other ones I can't remember now.

The aisles between the shelves were very wide so there was space for the forklifts. The forklifts operated all day long, even when the market was open for customers. The forklift drivers fetched large pallets out of the storage shelves, which went right up to the ceiling on top of the normal shelves where the customers took the stock from and put it in their trolleys.

To start with I was always wondering why there weren't any terrible accidents, why no pallets tipped off the forks and crushed ten customers to death, why no feet got squashed under the large iron wheels of the forklifts. But later, when I had a forklift licence of my own and whizzed along the aisles in my yellow forklift, fetching pallets of beer or milk or sacks of flour down from the shelves, I knew it was all a matter of relaxing, taking care and judging distances right – and routine. But the most important thing, I thought, was that you had to be absolutely convinced while you were transporting pallets up or down that you were in the very centre of the market.

It took me a while to learn how to drive a forklift. They let me do my practice after opening hours, when the only people in the aisles were from 'Shelf-filling/ Night'. One of the long-term staff was a registered examiner, but another long-term guy gave me practice lessons until I'd managed to learn all the secrets of driving and operating a forklift. Actually it was just the half-hour before the end of our shift at one a.m. Under his supervision, I drove his forklift – which I shared with him later – slowly along the aisles, stopped in the right position parallel to the shelf, positioned the fork and moved it upwards. Then when the fork was at the level of the pallet I steered the truck until the ends of the fork were just above the openings in the pallet. Then I pressed a lever on the control panel in front of me, and the fork lowered and slipped into the openings in the pallet. Then I pressed the other lever and the pallet rose slowly.

'You're doing well,' said Bruno, his big hand next to me on the control panel, 'just don't raise it too quickly or you'll bump it at the top.'

Bruno was a pretty tall, stocky man, actually more stocky than tall, probably in his mid-fifties with white hair, but when you saw him from a distance he looked like a wrestler or a heavyweight boxer. He had a big block of a head that perched directly on his shoulders, almost no neck at all between the lapels of his white overall, and his hands, one of which was now resting on the forklift control panel next to me, were the size of plates. He wore a broad leather cuff around his right wrist to protect his tendons. He worked in the beverages department, where they fetched the largest pallets down from the shelves – crates of beer and juice and other drinks, which were roped together but still swayed ominously to and fro on the pallet as we lowered them out of the shelves.

Bruno had been working in the cash and carry for over ten years, always on beverages, and even though he wasn't the department manager it was him who kept the place running.

'You're doing well, Lofty,' he said. 'You'll soon have your licence.' He called me Lofty, like most of my workmates did, because I was nearly six foot three.

'Forget it,' I said. 'I know I'm making a mess of it.'

He laughed. 'Oh, don't worry. The longer it takes, the better for me. I have a nice quiet time with you. Better than all that hard graft.' He pointed a thumb over at the beverages section. I heard bottles clinking through the shelves. Another workmate was lugging the last crates of the day.

'There was one time,' said Bruno, watching me attempt to get a pallet of salt boxes back onto the shelf, 'one time I dropped a load of beer. Couple of years ago now. The rope tore. Shit happens.' He reached into the pocket of his overall and took out a couple of ropes. He never threw them away when we cut them off the big beer pallets with our Stanley knives once we'd got them down in one piece. 'Always come in handy.' He had a little farmyard outside of town, with a stable and a few animals. He lived there with his wife; she took care of the animals and everything else while he was at work. Bruno always had this special smell to him, of animals and manure, but it wasn't as if he stank; he just smelt faintly, and there was something else in the mixture that he brought along from his farm, something strangely sweet, more like bitter-sweet, but I never worked out what it might be.

'Bring her down now,' said Bruno, checking his watch, 'time to clock off.'

'OK,' I said. I'd finally managed to get the salt pallet in the right gap. I extracted the fork, moved the truck back slightly, then pressed one of the levers and the fork came down very slowly from the very top, with a hissing and whooshing sound from the air expelled from the hydraulics. I waited until the fork touched the tiled floor and then positioned it so that the forks weren't parallel to the ground. 'Only drive with the forks tipped, never with the fork raised except when you're stacking.'

I'd had to watch a couple of instruction films where they listed all these terrible accidents as a deterrent and then showed some of the consequences. Lopped-off limbs, flattened feet, people skewered on the fork, and the more I saw of this forklift inferno, the more often I wondered if I'd chosen the right job. But the other staff at the cash and carry were nice enough, and I didn't intend to skewer them on the fork or drive over their feet.

'Are you coming, Bruno?'

'No, you drive it on your own, you know how to do it now.' Sometimes Bruno stood on the tipped forks, even though that wasn't allowed, and rode back to the recharging station with me. I drove off and saw him walking down the aisle in the other direction. He walked slightly hunched, his arms splayed a little way from his body as if he expected a surprise attack from one of the shelves at any moment. I tried to imagine him working on the building site with me, me explaining everything to him and showing him how to do the job, but I just couldn't imagine the man demolishing a roof. Maybe it was his white hair, and that smell of his animals didn't go with the dust.

I drove to the recharging station, right at the back of the warehouse by the delivery bay. I drove along the empty, brightly lit aisles, past the freezers and the long rows of refrigerated shelves against the walls. Ours was the last shift and I only saw a workmate now and then. They were standing in the aisles, doing their last chores, standing at the blue wheeled desks and writing lists of the damaged or torn-open stock we always found on the shelves; others were getting their forklifts ready for the night at the recharging station. I didn't know all of their names yet, and even later, once I'd been working at the warehouse for a while and had scraped through the forklift test ('It'll end in tears, Lofty'), I took a shifty look at the name tags on their overalls when I talked to them or needed help.

'Thanks, Ms Koch,' I said, and she smiled and said, 'No problem.'

I saw her looking at my overall, but I'd lost my name tag and hadn't got a new one yet.

'Christian,' I said and gave her my hand. 'Marion,' she said. She'd lent me her forklift because a customer had asked for a bottle of Wild Turkey just before closing time. I'd fetched the whisky pallet down from the shelf, given him the bottle and then filled up the empty compartment. Bruno was using our forklift over in the beer section. It was a Friday, it was summer, and people were buying beer by the crateload.

'Shall we have a coffee? It's on me.'

'OK,' she said, and then we went to the vending machine. There were two coffee machines in the warehouse, one at the delivery bay and one in front of the cold storage room, and that one was closer.

I'd come across her in the aisles a couple of times before and we'd nodded hello, and seeing as she was quite pretty I'd smiled every time.

She wasn't there every night, she worked days as well; only me and five other guys were always on nights.

'You did your test quite quickly.' She sipped at her coffee, and then she blew into the little clouds of steam. She smiled; she'd probably heard about how much trouble I'd had with it.

'Bruno was a good teacher,' I said and looked at the name tag on her chest again. 'M. Koch, Confectionery'.

'Bruno's a good guy,' she said. 'You can always go to him when you need help, or when you're fed up and you fancy a coffee and a chat.' She smiled and blew into her coffee, then she drank a few mouthfuls.

'Get fed up often, do you?'

'Don't be so cheeky, rookie.' She held her coffee in front of her name tag and tapped me on the shoulder with the index finger of her free hand. Then she laughed, and I couldn't help joining in. There was something about her and the way she talked to me that I liked a lot. When I'd sat down in her forklift ('But don't make a tour of it, I need it back again') I'd felt the warmth on the seat where she'd just been sitting.

She seemed to be a couple of years older than me, maybe in her mid-thirties. She had quite short hair that was always kind of messy. We drank our coffee and talked about this and that.

We stood at the vending machine for a long time, and I kept putting more money in and refilling our cups. We were standing behind the piles of crates and stock so the only people who could see us were people who wanted to take a coffee break of their own. 'Be right back.' I went to the shopping trolley containing food just coming up to the best-before date. Sometimes there were three or four trolleys, and sometimes it was my job to take the trolleys to the ramp by the delivery bay where the rubbish bins were. Bread, chocolate, meat, milk, all still good for a few more days, and if I was hungry I tried to sneakily stuff myself with as much as possible of the best things before I threw them in the bins. Chocolate truffles, ciabatta with Serrano ham, Kinder chocolate. If one of the bosses caught me I could take off my overalls and leave, but I just couldn't resist it. The stuff was being chucked out anyway, and I think most of us took the odd sneaky helping.

I tore open the packaging of a chocolate cake, cut two large slices with my Stanley knife, put them in the pockets of my overalls and went back over to Marion.

'I thought you'd had enough of me.'

'No,' I said, 'not at all. Hold out your hand.' She gave me a questioning look but then held her hand out flat, and I took a piece of cake out of my pocket and placed it on her hand. 'Hey, rookie,' she said, 'you're a bit of a daredevil, aren't you?'

It wasn't until later that I thought I'd actually put her at risk. If they'd caught us . . . but we were safe behind the crates, and anyway the big bosses had left ages ago and the boss of 'Shelf-filling/Night' was pretty relaxed and often disappeared to the toilets for a quick smoke, even though it wasn't allowed, and I'd seen him with his mouth full and a big salami in his hand before. And Marion seemed to have gauged the risk; she smiled at me and said thanks and ate the cake.

'Got a bit of a thing about her, Lofty, have you?'

'No, rubbish! I'm just asking, that's all.' It was after eleven and we were stacking large cartons of juice packs on the juice shelf. Bruno leaned against the forklift and said, 'She's married. He's a bastard though. Met him a couple of times, at work parties and the Christmas do. He used to be a nice guy, I heard, but he's been a right bastard since he lost his job. There's your chance, Lofty.'

'Hey, leave it out,' I pushed two cartons onto the shelf. 'I just think she's nice, that's all.'

'Oh yeah, she's nice all right, Marion is.' He nodded. We carried on working in silence until twelve, then I had to go over to Processed Foods; there was only one woman there, Irina Palmer, and the twenty-kilo flour sacks were too heavy for her. Irina was very nice and she showed me around the processed food aisles once we were done. She smelled quite strongly of cold smoke and she coughed quite a lot, and while I was lifting the flour sacks off the pallet and lugging them to the shelves she'd disappeared in the direction of the toilets.

'Right,' she said and led me along the pasta aisle, 'it's all a question of practice, you'll see for yourself after a while. It's important if a customer asks you.' She coughed and stroked the lapels of her overall. She was about the same age as Bruno and just about as stocky too, and I'd seen them heading for the toilets together a few times; Bruno liked a quick smoke now and then, but not as often as Irina, and he didn't cough like she did either.

'Right, here's the normal spaghetti, then comes chitarra, that's kind of straight pasta, we only have one brand though and hardly anyone ever asks for it.' She was moving quite quickly to and fro in front of the shelf, touching the packets and cartons with both hands. 'Here's the fusilli, they're like spirals, penne lisce, penne rigate, tortellini, tortelloni, macaroni, macaroncini, pappardelle, wide fettucine, then here's the trenette, the same only thinner, rotelle for soups, orecchiette, they look like little ears, and if someone asks for vermicelli they want spaghetti and they're from Sicily.' She pronounced the names of the pasta like a real Italian, moving faster and faster in front of the shelf and showing me all kinds of pasta varieties that I'd never eaten and never even heard of. And then, when she showed me the 'farfalle' and the 'rigatoni', she suddenly said in the same tone of voice, with the same roll of the R: 'You like Marion from Confectionery, don't you?'

I couldn't help laughing. 'All I did was get her a coffee.' And when she nodded and rocked her head like an Italian mama and opened her mouth to reply, I said, 'Yeah, she's really nice.'

'Listen, Christian,' she took a step closer to me, and because she hadn't called me 'Lofty' like most of the others – funnily enough they'd often called me that on the building site as well, even though there were a few guys there even taller than me – well, anyway I knew right away there was something important coming now. 'Listen, Marion's very fragile, I know she doesn't look like it, I mean, she's, how can I put it, she's never at a loss for words, but you mustn't hurt her, do you get me . . . ?'

'No,' I said, not laughing any more. 'I don't want to.'

She nodded and said, 'It's none of my business, but I like young Marion a lot.'

Then the boss's voice came over the loudspeakers, telling us we could clock off now; actually he was only the boss when the other bosses weren't there. I walked over to the staff exit with Irina Palmer, coughing even as she held her cigarettes in her hand ready for the next one, and then we went to get changed.

A couple of weeks passed until I next saw Marion from Confectionery. She'd been working days for a while, but when I didn't meet her in the aisles or at the vending machine after that Bruno told me she was off sick. 'Anything serious?' I asked.

'Don't know,' he said, but I could tell that wasn't true.

'Come on, tell me.'

'Forget it,' he said. 'If you like her, don't ask.'

And then we stacked six-packs of alcohol-free beer on the shelves.

Twenty minutes before the end of our shift – we were on our last round of the beverages aisles – he said to me, 'Come on, I want to show you something.'

I followed him. We heard Irina coughing in the pasta aisle but Bruno carried on until we came to the fish and shellfish and then he stopped.

We called this section 'The Sea'. There was a large sales counter behind a roller door. Next to it and behind it and all around it were tanks and small pools of live fish, live crabs and prawns, and crates filled with ice and cooled with the dead fish and shellfish in them. The roller door was already halfway down and we ducked underneath it. Inside, the lights were dimmed, only a few strip lights glowing yellow on the ceiling. He took me over to a large tank with a couple of tubes running in and out of it. 'The water has exactly the same salt content as the ocean they come from,' he said. 'Just a tiny bit more or less and they'd die sooner or later.'

They were large crabs, lobsters or something, lying next to each other and on top of each other in the tank, packed so tightly they could hardly move. I went closer up and saw that their pincers were held together with rubber bands.

'They stay in here,' said Bruno, 'until somebody buys them.'

'But their pincers,' I said, and I saw a particularly large crab moving its arms with the tied-up pincers and touching the glass.

'So they don't hurt each other, you see, and so they don't hurt anyone who wants to take them out.'

I squatted down in front of the tank, my face directly in front of the glass. They had strange long eyes, dark telescopic eyes that came out of their little heads like tiny fingers. The lobsters moved around in the water that flowed in and out again through the tubes, but they didn't have much space and some of them looked as if they were dead already or just about to die, lying still between the others. Their long, thin eyes; I don't know why, but their eyes really did my head in. 'Jesus,' I said, standing up again.

'Yeah,' said Bruno. We stood in silence by the tank for a good while then, looking at the water bubbling and the big pile of lobsters.

'Look at that one,' I said. 'The one right at the back, the big bugger. He's got one arm loose.'

'Where?' asked Bruno, and I went round the glass tank and showed him the lobster, which kept opening and closing the one pincer it had managed to get free from the rubber band, opening and closing. It wasn't moving anything else, as if only its one arm was still alive. 'If he's clever . . .' I said.

'You mean he could cut the others . . .'

'Imagine it though,' I said. 'They'd have their work cut out tomorrow morning . . .'

Bruno laughed, then he shook his head. 'I told you, Lofty, they'd just hurt each other.'

We heard the boss's voice over the tannoy – the end of our shift. We ducked out again under the half-closed roller door, Bruno took the forklift to the recharging station, then we went to the staff exit and the changing room. 'Shall I give you a lift?'

'OK,' I said, 'if you don't mind the detour.' I usually took the last bus but Bruno gave me a lift home now and then, even though he actually had to go in the other direction. We hung up our overalls in our lockers, put away a couple of other things, had a bit of a chat with the others, most of them looking tired, we swiped our cards through the machine, and then we walked past the boss, who shook everyone's hand goodbye, down to the staff car park.

'About Marion,' he said in the car.

'No,' I said. 'You don't have to tell me.'

'She has it pretty tough sometimes,' he said, but I just nodded and looked out into the night.

We were standing outside my house. We'd already said goodbye and as he started to get back in the car I said, 'How about a beer – you've got a quarter of an hour, haven't you?'

'Yeah,' he smiled, locking his car and coming back over to me. 'My wife's asleep anyway.' We went inside and sat down in my little kitchen. I took two beers out of the fridge and opened them. 'Lugging beer around all night,' he said and clinked his bottle against mine, 'makes you thirsty, doesn't it?'

'I get hungry as well sometimes with all that lovely stuff we carry around at work.'

'You were pretty daring, that thing with the cake. That impressed her, that did.'

'How do you know that then?'

'It does her good, Lofty, someone treating her nice like that.'

The kitchen window was open slightly and I heard a train crossing the bridge. 'Help yourself to an ashtray if you want to smoke.'

'I will, thanks,' he said. I went over to the fridge and put the ashtray on the table, and he lit up. 'When you get home from work, can you go to sleep right away?'

'No,' I said, 'not usually.'

'Me neither. I've got this bench, out the front, and that's where I sit then, even if it's cold out. I have a wee drink there and I can look at the fields. I like looking at the fields. It's never quite dark, all the lights from the city, you know?'

'Have you got kids?'

'No, we haven't.'

'Sorry. It's none of my business.'

'It's OK.' We fell silent, drinking and both looking out of the slightly open window into the night. He stubbed out his cigarette in the ashtray and drank up his beer. 'I'd better go.'

'I'll see you to the door.'

We said goodbye out the front. 'We could do this again, eh?'

'Yeah, let's,' I said. 'That'd be good.'

He nodded and walked to his car. 'See you tomorrow, Lofty.'

'See you.'

He was very quiet the next day and the days after; we worked in silence and he disappeared straight away after our shift, and I took the bus home. I was usually the only passenger; the bus drivers knew me by now and said hello or 'Home time at last, eh?' And if I wasn't tired already I got tired on the way, leaning my head against the window, and sometimes I even fell asleep but the drivers woke me; they knew where I had to get off. Then at home I perked up again and spent a long time sitting on my own in the kitchen, drinking beer and looking out into the night and waiting to get tired again.

'So you're doing OK are you, rookie?' She stood in front of me, hands planted on her hips, and gave me an angry stare, two small creases above her nose. Her hair seemed to be even shorter now, and her face had somehow got slightly less angular, but perhaps it only seemed that way to me; I hadn't seen her for three weeks.

'How long do I have to work here until I stop being a rookie?'

'If you help me for a minute I'll think about it.'

'Marion . . .' I said.

'So are you coming or not? I asked Bruno but he's busy.'

'I've got things to do as well, but . . .'

'I can ask someone else.'

She turned away and went to leave, but I was standing behind her and said, 'Don't run away, Marion, I'm coming, this crap can wait. I'll always help you if you want, you know that.'

'Rookie,' she said, turning to face me. She pressed her lips together, so firmly that her mouth was a thin line. 'Marion,' I said. 'You talk too much,' she said. 'There's work waiting for us. Well, come on then.' She looked around but the aisle was empty, then she took my hand and set off. She held my hand quite tightly pressed, and I felt her warmth, remembered the warmth on the seat of her forklift, then she suddenly let go and I walked along next to her.

'Bruno says you're doing well.'

'Oh, does he?'

'If he says so it must be true. Irina was singing your praises too.' I wanted to turn off into the confectionery aisle but she took my hand again for a brief moment and pulled me further along. 'I'm standing in on Delicatessen and Frozen Food today.' We went through the open roller door to the cold storage room. I saw her looking over at the vending machine. But when she saw me looking at her she turned her head aside. 'We've got to go to Siberia,' she said. 'We'd better wrap up warm.' She went to one of the lockers and came back with two thick padded jackets and two hats. I helped her into her jacket, then put one on myself. She handed me one of the hats and I put it on her head carefully, pulling it over her short hair. 'Hey,' she said, and I tugged the hat down over her ears. 'I need to see, you know. I've got a list, we have to get loads of stuff for the freezers.' She tugged at her hat, then pointed at a couple of trolleys. 'You go and get two trolleys, or better three, we've got quite a lot to fill up outside.' We put gloves on too, and once we were wrapped up as warm as Eskimos we couldn't help laughing.

And then we were in Siberia, twenty degrees below freezing, our breath came in clouds, and we took large hunks of frozen pork and beef and threw them in the trolleys; it sounded as if we were throwing stones.

'Imagine if they locked us in here, by accident I mean.' I was standing on the little ladder, handing down a large venison loin to her. I could feel the cold even through my gloves.

'You wish.'

'Hey, now you're the cheeky one.' I climbed down from the ladder, folded it closed and leant it against the wall. 'Hmm,' she said, 'I guess we'd have to lug meat around all night to keep ourselves from freezing.'

'I guess we would.' We pushed the three trolleys over to another spot. We'd already filled two of them. Our faces were red, our skin felt really tight, as if it were about to tear. 'Brass monkeys in here,' I said.

'Don't be so soft, we're nearly finished.' We were standing close together, the tiny clouds of steam mingling between our faces, and as we were piling crates of frozen pizza in the trolley she suddenly turned to me and looked at me, her hat down to her eyebrows. I didn't say anything, just looked at her. It seemed as if I could feel her breath through the thick padded jacket. 'Nice,' she said, 'it's nice of you to help me.' We stood there like that for a while in silence, then I said, 'Do you know how Eskimos say hello?' And I was surprised how quiet my voice sounded in the big cold storage room, as if the cold was swallowing it up. She looked at me, and I bent my head down to her and rubbed my nose against hers. She stayed still and quiet, not moving, and after a few seconds I felt her nose moving too.

At some point we turned back to the shelves. 'Now I know,' she said. Then we put the last of the pizza cartons in the trolley.

When I got to work the next day I went straight to the beverages aisles. Bruno always came a bit earlier to fetch the forklift from the recharging station, but I couldn't find either him or the forklift.

There were more customers in the aisles than usual for the time of day. Perhaps there were a couple of good special offers on, and sometimes there are just days when people want to go shopping; I've never understood why that is. And I walked along the aisles; perhaps Bruno had something to do in another section, lending a hand, but actually they always gave me that kind of job, and then I saw the boss of 'Shelf-filling/Night'. He was leaning against the whisky shelf, the customers passing right by him, but he seemed not to notice them at all as he stared at the tiled floor. I went up to him.

'Hi boss,' I said, 'I'm looking for Bruno.'

He looked up and stared at me in surprise. 'Bruno?'

'Yes,' I said. 'I'm on Beverages today, aren't I?'

'You'll have plenty to do on Beverages for a while – Bruno's not coming back.' He gazed past me and I suddenly knew Bruno was dead. I felt like I had to vomit, and I leant against the shelf next to the boss. 'He just went and hanged himself. That stupid bastard went and hanged himself.' I felt a fist in my stomach; it wouldn't let me go.

'No one knows anything. I've known him for more than ten years. No one knows anything. Get your forklift and take care of the beverages.'

'OK, Dieter,' I said. I had trouble walking straight, and I kept thinking, 'Bruno's dead. Bruno's hanged himself.'

I met all sorts of workmates as I wandered down the aisles and then realised I had to go to the recharging station. They seemed to know already and we just nodded at each other, some of them looking at me as if they wanted to talk about it with me, but I kept walking until I was at his forklift. I pulled the big charging cable out of the socket. I'd forgotten to switch the power off first; that was pretty dangerous, all it took was a touch of the contacts. I held onto the forklift and gave a quiet laugh: 'One down's enough for now!' I got in, put the key in the ignition, and then I drove back to the aisles.

There was that smell, of animals and stables. His smell was still in the little cab, and I wouldn't have been surprised if the seat had still been warm. I drove the forklift to Beverages and worked with his smell in my nostrils all night long.

And that smell again, country air, it was fertilising time. I stood on the narrow road leading to the graveyard – I could see it ahead, a little gate, the roof of the chapel – then I turned around and walked back down the road. The funeral would be starting any minute; there were a few workmates there and the bosses, and I'd brought flowers especially, but I walked back through the little village a couple of bus stops outside of town.

I stopped outside his house. It wasn't far from the bus stop; he'd described it to me a few times. It was a perfectly normal two-storey detached house, like you'd find in lots of villages, not one of those old half-timbered ones or anything. The road was empty and I climbed over the fence. Maybe the gate wasn't even locked, that's probably normal in the kind of villages where everybody knows everybody, but I kind of felt inhibited about going into his place through the gate. I walked around the house. A stable, a couple of sheds, chickens pecking away at the ground, further back I saw two cows in a fenced-in field. At first I wanted to go in the stable, but then I saw the bench. It was against the back wall of one of the sheds. I went over to it. I sat down and looked out at the fields. There was a tractor with a trailer in one of them. It seemed not to be moving, and I could only tell by the couple of trees at the edge of the field that someone was driving it. A couple of birds flapped up around it. Why should I go into the stable? I didn't know which beam it was anyway. I watched the tractor.

'Raise the fork right to the top,' said Marion.

'Why?'

'Hey come on, just do it. Bruno showed me it. I don't know, I like it.' I raised the empty fork as high as it would go. The forklift made its usual sounds, a humming and a metallic pling, then I let go of the lever. I tipped my head back and looked up at the fork, still swaying slightly. 'And now?'

'Let it down again, but really slowly. And then keep quiet.'

I moved the lever a tiny bit, and the carriage with the fork lowered itself down again slowly. 'And now? I don't understand.'

'You have to be quiet. Really quiet. That sound, can you hear it, it's like the sea.'

And she was right; I heard it now too and I was surprised I'd never noticed it before. The fork lowered with a hissing and whooshing sound from the air expelled from the hydraulics, and it really did sound like the wash of waves in the sea. The fork came lower; I sat in the forklift, my head slightly inclined. She stood right next to me, one hand on the control panel. 'Can you hear it?' she whispered, and I nodded. Then we listened in silence.

ACKNOWLEDGEMENTS

I owe a great debt to many people who helped in the creation of this anthology.

I would like to thank my dear friend and agent, the late David Miller, who, with the connivance of Anthony Cheetham, gave me the gift of compiling this anthology. Thanks to my editor Helen Francis, for her encouragement, her support and her exemplary patience and to Emma Brady, for her tireless and invaluable work.

Thanks to James Roxburgh, Sam Wells and Anna Rebecca for their assistance in my research.

Above all I would like to thank translators everywhere, without whom – self-evidently – this book would not have been possible. In addition to all those who brought life to the words of the authors contained in these pages, I would like to thank those who, in person, in conversation, by email, by messenger offered advice and suggestions and frequently led me to discoveries I would never have made. Some are friends, others I know only through the translation hive mind made possible by social media. The following list is woefully incomplete; it is certainly an inadequate expression of my gratitude:

Daniel Hahn, Anne McLean, Shaun Whiteside, Peter Bush, Ros Schwartz, Lulu Norman, Louise Rogers Lalaurie, Deborah Smith, Jeffrey Zuckerman, Sarah Ardizzone, Antonia Lloyd Jones, David Colmer, Maureen Freely, Ruth Ahmedzai Kemp, Susan Bernofsky, Sandra Smith, Nick Caistor, Victoria Hislop, Lisa Rose Bradford, Lucy North, Jennifer Feeley, Rachel Hildebrandt, Mary Ann Newman, Alex Zucker, Sophie Voillot, Ellen Elias-Bursac, Tony Chambers, Ezra E. Fitz, Anna Gunin, Shelley Fairweather-Vega, Sam Schnee, Martin Cassell, Ani Jackson, Meg Matich, James Kates, M. René Bradshaw, Jamie Richards, Laurel Ann Taylor, Katherine Adams, Camilla Lu Chen and Mattho Mandersloot.

ACKNOWLEDGMENTS

EXTENDED COPYRIGHT